SHORT FICTION:
AN INTRODUCTORY
ANTHOLOGY

EDITED BY
DAVID RAMPTON
AND
GERALD LYNCH

University of Ottawa

HARCOURT BRACE JOVANOVICH, CANADA
Toronto Montreal Orlando San Diego
London Sydney Tokyo

Canadian Cataloguing in Publication Data

Main entry under title:

Short fiction: an introductory anthology

ISBN 0-7747-3148-6

1. Short stories. 2. Short stories, Canadian (English).* 3. Short stories, English—Translations from foreign languages.   I. Rampton, David, 1950–   . II. Lynch, Gerald, 1953–   .

PN6120.2.S48 1992   808.83'1   C90-095626-7

Acquisitions Editor: *Heather McWhinney*
Developmental Editor: *Deborah Adamczyk*
Editorial Co-ordinator: *Marcel Chiera*
Editorial Assistant: *Kerry Gibson*
Copy Editor: *Judith Turnbull*
Cover and Interior Design: *Landgraff Design Associates*
Typesetting and Assembly: *Q Composition Inc.*
Printing and Binding: *Webcom Limited*

Cover Art: Philip Surrey, *La promenade à Verdun*, oil on canvas
Collection: Musée du Québec, 51.168
Photographer: Patrick Altman
Reproduced with the permission of Nicolas Edward Simpson.

∞   This book was printed in Canada on acid-free paper.

1 2 3 4 5   96 95 94 93 92

PREFACE

T his anthology is intended for courses in short fiction. Its purpose is to
offer a chronological survey of the short story from the early nineteenth century to the present, including classic stories that have worked
well in the classroom and stories by both older and newer writers that deserve
to be better known. The anthology also features various kinds of fiction:
gothic tales, fables, comic anecdotes, magic realism, metafiction, as well as
all those stories that realistically portray the lives of men and women in the
context of their time and place. Approximately one-third of the stories are
by Canadians, and these constitute within the anthology as a whole a chronological survey of the short story in Canada. We have also included a generous sampling of stories in translation to give the student an idea of how
the short story has developed in other languages. In addition to the usual
information, the biographical headnote to each selection offers critical commentary on the author's work. In its sections on plot, character, setting,
point of view, and theme, the Introduction illustrates for students some
ways in which these aspects of short stories might be discussed in essays;
and it concludes with a series of questions that should prove useful in the
classroom. Like any anthology, this one offers a selection of short stories that
reflects the tastes and preferences of the editors and a number of other
people who contributed to its creation.

We are grateful to our colleagues in the Department of English at
the University of Ottawa for their many valuable suggestions.

We are also grateful to the following reviewers for their insights
and constructive criticisms: Diane Austin, University of New Brunswick; George Casey, Memorial University; John R. Doheny, University
of British Columbia; Stan Dragland, University of Western Ontario;
Mary Ann Gillies, University of Calgary; Greig Henderson, University
of Toronto; Ronald C. Johnson, University of British Columbia; Terry
Matheson, University of Saskatchewan; Murry McGillivray, University
of Calgary; Elizabeth Miller, Memorial University; Tony Steele, University of Manitoba; Warren Stevenson, University of British Columbia;
William H. New, University of British Columbia; Herbert Weil, University of Manitoba; and Joe Zezulka, University of Western Ontario.

Thank you to Heather McWhinney and Deborah Adamczyk at
Harcourt Brace Jovanovich for their encouragement and support since
the inception of this project. And thank you to our families for their
support and patience.

Acknowledgements

Nikolay Gogol. "The Nose" reprinted from *Russian Stories*, translated and edited by Gleb Struve.

Leo Tolstoy. "The Three Hermits" reprinted from *Russian Stories*, translated and edited by Gleb Struve.

Guy de Maupassant. "The Return" copyright 1924 and renewed 1952 by Alfred A. Knopf, Inc. Reprinted from *The Collected Novels and Stories of Guy de Maupassant*, translated by Ernest Boyd. Reprinted by permission of the publisher.

Kate Chopin. "The Storm" reprinted by permission of Louisiana State University Press from *The Complete Works of Kate Chopin*, edited by Per Seyersted. Copyright © 1969 by Louisiana State University Press.

Joseph Conrad. "Heart of Darkness" reprinted from *Youth and Two Other Stories* by Joseph Conrad with the permission of Doubleday & Company.

Anton Chekhov. "A Lady with a Dog" and "In the Hollow" copyright © Ronald Hingley 1975. Reprinted from *The Oxford Chekhov* vol 9 *Stories 1898–1904* (1975) by permission of Oxford University Press.

Edith Wharton. "Roman Fever." Reprinted with permission of Charles Scribner's Sons, an imprint of Macmillan Publishing Company, from *Roman Fever and Other Stories* by Edith Wharton. Copyright 1934 by *Liberty Magazine*, renewed 1962 by William R. Tyler.

Duncan Campbell Scott. "The Little Milliner" from *In the Village of Viger* by Duncan Campbell Scott. Copyright © 1973 and reprinted with the permission of John G. Aylen, Ottawa, Canada.

Stephen Leacock. "The Hostelry of Mr. Smith" from *Sunshine Sketches of a Little Town* by Stephen Leacock. Used by permission of the Canadian Publishers, McClelland & Stewart, Toronto.

Sherwood Anderson. "Death in the Woods" reprinted by permission of Harold Ober Associates Incorporated. Copyright 1926 by The American Mercury, Inc. Copyright renewed 1953 by Eleanor Copenhaven Anderson.

E.M. Forster. "The Road from Colonus." From *The Collected Tales of E.M. Forster* published by Sidgwick & Jackson, London. Reprinted by permission of the publisher.

James Joyce. "Araby" and "The Boarding House" from *Dubliners* by James Joyce. Originally published by B.W. Huebsch in 1916. Definitive text copyright © 1967 by The

Estate of James Joyce. Reprinted by permission of the publisher, Viking Penguin, a division of Penguin Books USA Inc.

Virginia Woolf. "Kew Gardens" from *The Complete Shorter Fiction of Virginia Woolf* by Virginia Woolf. Reprinted by permission of the Estate of Virginia Woolf and The Hogarth Press.

Franz Kafka. "The Metamorphosis" from *The Metamorphosis, The Penal Colony, and Other Stories* by Franz Kafka, translated by Edwin and Willa Muir. Copyright 1948 by Schocken Books Inc. Copyright renewed 1975 by Schocken Books Inc. Reprinted by permission of Schocken Books, published by Pantheon Books, a division of Random House, Inc.

D.H. Lawrence. "The Horse Dealer's Daughter" and "Odour of Chrysanthemums" from *Complete Short Stories* by D.H. Lawrence. Copyright 1922 by Thomas Seltzer. Renewed copyright 1950 by Frieda Lawrence. Reprinted by permission of the publisher, Viking Penguin, a division of Penguin Books USA Inc.

Isak Dinesen. "Babette's Feast" from *Anecdotes of Destiny* by Isak Dinesen (Penguin Books, 1986), copyright © Isak Dinesen, 1958.

Katherine Mansfield. "The Daughters of the Late Colonel." Copyright 1922 by Alfred A. Knopf, Inc. and renewed 1950 by John Middleton Murry. Reprinted from *The Short Stories of Katherine Mansfield*, by permission of the publisher.

Ethel Wilson. "A Visit to the Frontier" by Ethel Wilson. Reprinted by permission of Macmillan of Canada, A Division of Canada Publishing Corporation.

Katherine Anne Porter. "That Tree" from *Flowering Judas and Other Stories*, copyright 1935 and renewed 1963 by Katherine Anne Porter, reprinted by permission of Harcourt Brace Jovanovich, Inc.

Isaac Babel. "The Story of My Dovecot" by Isaac Babel. Reprinted by permission of S.G. Phillips, Inc. from *The Collected Stories of Isaac Babel*. Copyright © 1955 by S.G. Phillips, Inc.

F. Scott Fitzgerald. "Babylon Revisited." Reprinted with permission of Charles Scribner's Sons, an imprint of Macmillan Publishing Company, from *Taps at Reveille* by F. Scott Fitzgerald. Copyright 1931 by Curtis Publishing Company, renewed 1959 by Frances Scott Fitzgerald Lanahan.

William Faulkner. "Dry September." Copyright 1930 and renewed 1958 by William Faulkner. Reprinted from *Selected Short Stories of William Faulkner*, by permission of Random House, Inc.

Ernest Hemingway. "Soldier's Home." Reprinted with permission of Charles Scribner's Sons, an imprint of Macmillan Publishing Company, from *In Our Time* by Ernest Hemingway. Copyright 1925 by Charles Scribner's Sons, renewed 1953 by Ernest Hemingway.

Vladimir Nabokov. "Spring in Fialta." From *Nine Stories* by Vladimir Nabokov. Reprinted by permission of Vintage Books, a Division of Random House, Inc.

Jorge Luis Borges. "The Garden of the Forking Paths" from Jorge Luis Borges: *Labyrinths*. Copyright © 1962, 1964 by New Directions Publishing Corporation. Reprinted by permission of New Directions Publishing Corporation. Canadian rights only.

Seán O'Faoláin. "Admiring the Scenery." From *The Collected Stories of Seán O'Faoláin*. Copyright 1937 by Séan O'Faoláin. By permission of Little, Brown and Company.

John Steinbeck. "The Chrysanthemums." From *The Long Valley* by John Steinbeck. Copyright 1937, copyright © renewed 1965 by John Steinbeck. Reprinted by permission of the publisher, Viking Penguin, a division of Penguin Books USA Inc.

Frank O'Connor. "Guests of the Nation" and "First Confession." From *Collected Stories* by Frank O'Connor. Copyright © 1981 by Frank O'Connor. Reprinted by permission of Joan Daves Agency.

Morley Callaghan. "Ancient Lineage" from *Morley Callaghan's Stories* by Morley Callaghan. Reprinted by permission of Macmillan of Canada, A Division of Canada Publishing Corporation.

Graham Greene. "Across the Bridge" from *Collected Short Stories* by Graham Greene. Copyright 1949, renewed copyright © 1977 by Graham Greene. Reprinted by permission of the publisher, Viking Penguin, a division of Penguin Books USA Inc.

Isaac Bashevis Singer. "The Spinoza of Market Street" from *The Spinoza of Market Street* by Isaac Bashevis Singer. Copyright © 1961 by Isaac Bashevis Singer. Renewal copyright © 1989 by Isaac Bashevis Singer. Reprinted by permission of Farrar, Straus and Giroux, Inc.

Sinclair Ross. "One's a Heifer" from *The Lamp at Noon* by Sinclair Ross. Used by permission of the Canadian Publishers, McClelland & Stewart, Toronto.

Gabrielle Roy. "Hoodoo Valley." From *Garden in the Wind* by Gabrielle Roy. Translated by Alan Brown, © 1975, 1977. Reprinted with permission of Fonds Gabrielle Roy and McClelland & Stewart Publishers.

Sheila Watson. "Antigone" reprinted from *Four Stories* by permission of the author.

Eudora Welty. "No Place for You, My Love" from *The Bride of the Innisfallen*, copyright 1952 and renewed 1980 by Eudora Welty, reprinted by permission of Harcourt Brace Jovanovich, Inc.

John Cheever. "Goodbye, My Brother." Copyright 1951 by John Cheever. Reprinted from *The Stories of John Cheever*, by permission of Alfred A. Knopf, Inc.

Julio Cortázar. "End of the Game." From *End of the Game and Other Stories* by Julio Cortázar, translated by Paul Blackburn. Copyright © 1967 by Random House, Inc. Reprinted by permission of Pantheon Books, a Division of Random House, Inc.

Bernard Malamud. "The Magic Barrel" from *The Magic Barrel* by Bernard Malamud. Copyright © 1950, 1951, 1952, 1953, 1954, 1955, 1956, 1958 by Bernard Malamud. Renewal copyright © 1986 by Bernard Malamud. Reprinted by permission of Farrar, Straus and Giroux, Inc.

Carson McCullers. "A Tree. A Rock. A Cloud" from *The Ballad of the Sad Café and Collected Short Stories* by Carson McCullers. Copyright 1936, 1941, 1942, © 1955 by Carson McCullers. Copyright © renewed 1979 by Floria V. Lasky. Reprinted by permission of Houghton Mifflin Company.

Shirley Jackson. "The Lottery" from *The Lottery* by Shirley Jackson. Copyright © 1948, 1949 by Shirley Jackson. Renewal copyright © 1976, 1977 by Lawrence Hyman, Barry Hyman, Mrs. Sarah Webster and Mrs. Joanne Schnurer. Reprinted by permission of Farrar, Straus and Giroux, Inc.

Doris Lessing. "The Old Chief Mshlanga" from *This Was the Old Chief's Country* by Doris Lessing. Copyright 1951 by Doris Lessing. Reprinted by permission of Jonathan Clowes Limited, London, on behalf of Doris Lessing.

Jacques Ferron. "The Jailer's Son" from *Selected Tales of Jacques Ferron*. Copyright © 1984 House of Anansi Press. Reprinted with the permission of Stoddart Publishing Co. Limited, 34 Lesmill Road, Don Mills, Ontario, Canada.

Mavis Gallant. "The Ice Wagon Going Down the Street." From *Home Truths* by Mavis Gallant © 1981. Reprinted by permission of Macmillan of Canada, A Division of Canada Publishing Corporation.

Italo Calvino. "Crystals" from *Tzero* by Italo Calvino, translated by William Weaver, copyright © 1967 by Giulio Einaudi editore s.p.a., Torino, English translation copyright © 1969 by Harcourt Brace Jovanovich, Inc. and Jonathan Cape Ltd., reprinted by permission of Harcourt Brace Jovanovich, Inc.

Nadine Gordimer. "Some Monday for Sure" from *Selected Stories* by Nadine Gordimer. Reprinted by permission of Penguin Books USA Inc.

Norman Levine. "We All Begin in a Little Magazine" reprinted by permission of the author.

James Baldwin. "Previous Condition." Excerpt from *Going to Meet the Man* by James Baldwin, copyright 1948, 1951, 1957, 1958, 1960, 1965 by James Baldwin. Used by permission of Doubleday, a division of Bantam Doubleday Dell Publishing Group, Inc.

Flannery O'Connor. "Revelation" from *Everything That Rises Must Converge* by Flannery O'Connor. Copyright © 1964, 1965 by the Estate of Mary Flannery O'Connor. Reprinted by permission of Farrar, Straus and Giroux, Inc.

Margaret Laurence. "The Mask of the Bear" from *A Bird in the House* by Margaret Laurence. Used by permission of the Canadian Publishers, McClelland & Stewart, Toronto.

Gabriel García Márquez. "Death Constant Beyond Love" from *Collected Stories* by Gabriel García Márquez. Copyright © 1984 by Gabriel García Márquez. Reprinted by permission of HarperCollins Publishers.

John Barth. "Lost in the Funhouse" copyright © 1967 by The Atlantic Monthly Company. From *Lost in the Funhouse* by John Barth. Used by permission of Doubleday, a division of Bantam Doubleday Dell Publishing Group, Inc.

Jack Hodgins. "The Concert Stages of Europe." From *The Barclay Family Theatre* by Jack Hodgins © 1981. Reprinted by permission of Macmillan of Canada, A Division of Canada Publishing Corporation.

Eric McCormack. "Eckhardt at a Window." From *Inspecting the Vaults* by Eric McCormack. Copyright © Eric McCormack, 1987. Reprinted by permission of Penguin Books Canada Limited.

Joyce Carol Oates. "Dying" from *Upon the Sweeping Flood* by Joyce Carol Oates. Copyright © 1966 by Joyce Carol Oates. Reprinted by permission of John Hawkins & Associates, Inc.

Raymond Carver. "Menudo." From *Where I'm Calling From* by Raymond Carver, copyright © 1986, 1987, 1988 by Raymond Carver. Reprinted with permission of Atlantic Monthly Press.

Margaret Atwood. "The Grave of the Famous Poet" from *Dancing Girls* by Margaret Atwood. Used by permission of the Canadian Publishers, McClelland & Stewart, Toronto.

Patrick O'Flaherty. "A Small Place in the Sun" reprinted from *A Small Place in the Sun* by permission of Breakwater Books.

Sandra Birdsell. "The Bride Doll" from *Ladies of the House*, © Sandra Birdsell (Turnstone Press, 1984). Reprinted by permission.

Edna Alford. "The Bid." Reprinted from *The Garden of Eloise Loon* by Edna Alford by permission of the publisher, Oolichan Books.

Ann Beattie. "Shifting" copyright © 1976, 1977, 1978 by Ann Beattie. Reprinted from *Secrets and Surprises* by Ann Beattie by permission of Random House, Inc.

Katherine Govier. "The Immaculate Conception Photography Gallery" by Katherine Govier. Copyright © 1990 by Katherine Govier. Reprinted by permission of the author.

Ian McEwan. "First Love, Last Rites" reprinted from *First Love, Last Rights* by Ian McEwan by permission of the publisher, Jonathan Cape Ltd.

Jane Urquhart. "The Death of Robert Browning" reprinted by permission of The Porcupine's Quill, Incorporated and the Canadian Publishers, McClelland & Stewart, Toronto.

Guy Vanderhaeghe. "Man Descending." From *Man Descending* by Guy Vanderhaeghe © 1982. Reprinted by permission of Macmillan of Canada, A Division of Canada Publishing Corporation.

Tatyana Tolstaya. "Peters." From *On the Golden Porch* by Tatyana Tolstaya, translated by Antonina Bouis. Copyright © 1989 by Tatyana Tolstaya. reprinted by permission of Alfred A. Knopf, Inc.

CONTENTS

INTRODUCTION   1
Honoré de Balzac (1799–1850) *Sarrasine* 15
Nathaniel Hawthorne (1804–1864) *The Birthmark* 42
                 My Kinsman, Major Molineux 55
Edgar Allan Poe (1809–1849) *The Fall of the House of Usher* 72
              Ligeia 87
Nikolay Gogol (1809–1852) *The Nose* 101
Herman Melville (1819–1891) *Bartleby the Scrivener* 122
Leo Tolstoy (1828–1910) *The Death of Iván Ilých* 153
          The Three Hermits 198
Mark Twain (1835–1910) *The Notorious Jumping Frog of*
              Calaveras County 205
Henry James (1843–1916) *The Jolly Corner* 210
Guy de Maupassant (1850–1893) *The Return* 239
Kate Chopin (1851–1904) *The Storm* 246
Joseph Conrad (1857–1924) *Heart of Darkness* 252
Anton Chekhov (1860–1904) *A Lady with a Dog* 322
            In the Hollow . . . . : 335
Sara Jeannette Duncan (1861–1922) *A Mother in India* 368
Edith Wharton (1862–1937) *Roman Fever* 397
Duncan Campbell Scott (1862–1947) *The Little Milliner* 409
Stephen Leacock (1869–1944) *The Hostelry of Mr. Smith* 418
Stephen Crane (1871–1900) *The Open Boat* 435
Sherwood Anderson (1876–1941) *Death in the Woods* 456
E.M. Forster (1879–1970) *The Road from Colonus* 467
James Joyce (1882–1941) *Araby* 477
           The Boarding House 481
Virginia Woolf (1882–1941) *Kew Gardens* 488
Franz Kafka (1883–1924) *The Metamorphosis* 494
D.H. Lawrence (1885–1930) *The Horse Dealer's Daughter* 534
           Odour of Chrysanthemums 547

Isak Dinesen (1885–1962) *Babette's Feast* 565

Katherine Mansfield (1888–1923) *The Daughters of the Late Colonel* . . 592

Ethel Wilson (1888–1980) *A Visit to the Frontier* 609

Katherine Anne Porter (1890–1980) *That Tree* 619

Isaac Babel (1894–1941) *The Story of My Dovecot* 632

F. Scott Fitzgerald (1896–1940) *Babylon Revisited* 641

William Faulkner (1897–1962) *Dry September* . . . . 660 ✓

Ernest Hemingway (1899–1961) *Soldier's Home* 671

Vladimir Nabokov (1899–1977) *Spring in Fialta* 678

Jorge Luis Borges (1899–1986) *The Garden of Forking Paths* 695

Elizabeth Bowen (1899–1973) *The Demon Lover* 703

Seán O'Faoláin (b. 1900) *Admiring the Scenery* 710

John Steinbeck (1902–1968) *The Chrysanthemums* 718

Frank O'Connor (1903–1966) *Guests of the Nation* 727

 First Confession 737

Morley Callaghan (1903–1990) *Ancient Lineage* 746

Graham Greene (1904–1991) *Across the Bridge* 751

Isaac Bashevis Singer (b. 1904) *The Spinoza of Market Street* 760

Sinclair Ross (b. 1908) *One's a Heifer* 775

Gabrielle Roy (1909–1983) *Hoodoo Valley* 789

Sheila Watson (b. 1909) *Antigone* 798

Eudora Welty (b. 1909) *No Place for You, My Love* 806

John Cheever (1912–1982) *Goodbye, My Brother* 823

Julio Cortázar (1914–1984) *End of the Game* 841

Bernard Malamud (1914–1986) *The Magic Barrel* 852

Carson McCullers (1917–1967) *A Tree. A Rock. A Cloud* 867

Shirley Jackson (1919–1965) *The Lottery* 874

Doris Lessing (b. 1919) *The Old Chief Mshlanga* 883

Jacques Ferron (1921–1985) *The Jailer's Son* 894

Mavis Gallant (b. 1922) *The Ice Wagon Going Down the Street* 899

Italo Calvino (1923–1985) *Crystals* 919

Nadine Gordimer (b. 1923) *Some Monday for Sure* 926

Norman Levine (b. 1923) *We All Begin in a Little Magazine* 940

James Baldwin (1924–1987) *Previous Condition* 948

Flannery O'Connor (1925–1964) *Revelation* 962

Margaret Laurence (1926–1987) *The Mask of the Bear* 981

Gabriel García Márquez (b. 1928) *Death Constant Beyond Love* 998

John Barth (b. 1930) *Lost in the Funhouse* 1006
Donald Barthelme (1931–1989) *Captain Blood* 1025
Alice Munro (b. 1931) *Who Do You Think You Are?* 1030
                   Friend of My Youth 1045
Mordecai Richler (b. 1931) *Mervyn Kaplansky, Wordsmith* 1063
Robert Coover (b. 1932) *The Brother* 1082
Elizabeth McGrath (b. 1932) *Fogbound in Avalon* 1088
Edna O'Brien (b. 1932) *My Mother's Mother* 1104
John Updike (b. 1932) *A & P* 1117
                  The Happiest I've Been 1123
Philip Roth (b. 1933) *The Conversion of the Jews* 1135
Austin C. Clarke (b. 1934) *When He Was Free and Young and He
                 Used To Wear Silks* 1149
Rudy Wiebe (b. 1934) *Where Is the Voice Coming From?* 1158
Carol Shields (b. 1935) *Sailors Lost at Sea* 1166
Audrey Thomas (b. 1935) *Initram* 1176
Alistair MacLeod (b. 1936) *Island* 1190
Jack Hodgins (b. 1938) *The Concert Stages of Europe* 1217
Eric McCormack (b. 1938) *Eckhardt at a Window* 1233
Joyce Carol Oates (b. 1938) *Dying* 1243
Raymond Carver (1939–1988) *Menudo* 1259
Margaret Atwood (b. 1939) *The Grave of the Famous Poet* 1272
Patrick O'Flaherty (b. 1939) *A Small Place in the Sun* 1281
Sandra Birdsell (b. 1942) *The Bride Doll* 1287
Edna Alford (b. 1947) *The Bid* 1298
Ann Beattie (b. 1947) *Shifting* 1312
Katherine Govier (b. 1948) *The Immaculate Conception
                Photography Gallery* 1323
Ian McEwan (b. 1948) *First Love, Last Rites* 1332
Jane Urquhart (b. 1949) *The Death of Robert Browning* 1342
Guy Vanderhaeghe (b. 1951) *Man Descending* 1352
Tatyana Tolstaya (b. 1951) *Peters* 1363
GLOSSARY OF CRITICAL TERMS 1375
INDEX OF AUTHORS AND STORIES......................... 1380

INTRODUCTION

W e read stories because they instruct and delight us, and we analyze them to understand more about what we have learned and enjoyed. Such analysis often takes the form of dividing a story into its component parts—plot, character, setting, point of view, theme—the traditional categories critics have used to comment on fiction. Of course, in a well-crafted story, these elements function together. Still, those interested in discussing the reading experience, and in becoming better readers, can benefit from some consideration of these components in isolation.

Plot

Plot is the unfolding of an action over time—any action, from a series of happenings in the external world to the most subtle shift in a character's inner emotional world, to the movement of an image or symbol toward crystallization. For most readers, plot and character remain the primary attractions of stories and novels, and it is unfair to dismiss such interests with the criticism "She reads only for plot" or "He likes to identify with the hero." These aspects of fiction remain as essential to an engaging story as rhythm is to memorable poetry. All forms of literature enact the working out of a plot of some sort, and all contain a "narrative," the order in which the chronological events of a plot are related.

There are many kinds of plots: surprise-ending plots, plots with a twist, plots with parallel or multiple story lines, mystery plots, and so forth. Thinking of stories in terms of plot inevitably leads to an awareness of their structural similarities. For example, perhaps the oldest of plots is the one that describes a journey or a quest: there are journeys to new places, such as those in E.M. Forster's "The Road from Colonus" or Joseph Conrad's "Heart of Darkness"; journeys into the past, such as that embarked upon by Alice Munro's narrator in "Friend of My Youth"; circular journeys, such as those described in Sinclair Ross's "One's a Heifer" and Eric McCormack's "Eckhardt at a Window";

and journeys downwards, such as that begun by Ed in Guy Vander-haeghe's "Man Descending." Pondering such similarities enriches our literary experience.

In the short story, the development of a plot most often follows a pattern wherein expository writing provides essential information regarding setting, background, character, and whatever else the reader needs to know. A typical plot involves a conflict, and this conflict can be of many kinds: a struggle between characters, a struggle within a character, a conflict between a character and her environment, a problem related to the telling of the story, and so forth. In Stephen Leacock's "The Hostelry of Mr. Smith," for example, the conflict is between Mr. Smith and the town he lives in, Mariposa. Leacock introduces it this way: "But on this particular afternoon, in spite of the sunshine and deep peace, there was something as near to profound concern and anxiety as the features of Mr. Smith were ever known to express."

Conflict gives rise to tension within the story, and to a concomitant pleasurable tension in the reader, a curiosity to see the outcome. In Leacock's story, Smith, threatened with having his hotel shut down, devises a plan to win the Mariposans' support, but the fate of his hotel's liquor licence must hang in the balance throughout the various machinations of Smith and the plot. In the traditional plot, the tension mounts as the action rises—the plot thickens—to a climax. In our example, the fateful news regarding the revocation of Smith's liquor licence arrives by messenger: "And it was just at the moment when Mr. Smith said this that Billy, the desk-clerk, entered the room with the telegram in his hand." Finally the problem of Smith's status in Mariposa achieves a resolution: "Then Nivens, the lawyer, and Mr. Gingham (as a provincial official) took it [the petition favouring Smith] down to the county town, and by three o'clock that afternoon the news had gone out from the long distance telephone office that Smith's licence was renewed for three years."

The resolution is followed by a dénouement, the aftermath of the resolved climactic action. In "The Hostelry of Mr. Smith," the concluding paragraphs reveal that the newly licensed Smith has no intention of maintaining the expensive frills in his hotel that have helped him beguile the Mariposans—that, in effect, the powerful individual has manipulated the gullible community.

The plot of most stories, then, follows this pattern: a situation, a conflict, rising action and accompanying tension, a climax, a resolution, and a dénouement. Needless to say, not many stories follow the pattern so neatly, and many contemporary stories follow it not at all, or they play with the traditional order through irony and parody. (See, for example, the discussion of plot in John Barth's "Lost in the Funhouse.")

If plot describes an action that unfolds over time, then the handling of time within a story is the essence of plot. In this regard, two techniques of the storyteller's art deserve attention: flashback and fore- shadowing. The first interrupts the chronological presentation of the action to provide information from a time before the action of the story begins, or at least something outside the expected sequence of the plot. For example, at the climactic moment when Mr. Smith is handed the telegram informing him of the fate of his sojourn in Mariposa, Leacock's narrator interrupts: "But stop—it is impossible for you to understand the anxiety with which Mr. Smith and his associates awaited the news from the Commissioners, without first realizing the astounding progress of Mr. Smith in the three past years, and the pinnacle of public eminence to which he had attained." This flashback begins with a brief justification of itself ("it is impossible for you to understand . . . without first realizing . . ."), then establishes the precise period it will cover ("the three past years"). The lengthy section that follows provides, as should all flashbacks, information that is necessary to the resolution of the plot: from this particular flashback, Leacock's readers come to see that Mr. Smith will shrewdly overcome any opposition.

A counterpoint to the flashback, the foreshadowing technique does not so much interrupt the action as anticipate its resolution. An obvi- ous example might be the appearance of a gun in Act One of a play which, according to the old saw, must always go off in the Third. But foreshadowing can be achieved much more subtly: an earlier action, seemingly insignificant, is repeated later in the story; a foreboding description, such as that which opens Poe's "The Fall of the House of Usher," contains in microcosm the story's final effect; an image of symbolic significance recurs intermittently; a word or gesture is echoed; a seemingly inconsequential action or attitude is seen upon reflection to foreshadow the resolution of the story itself. In Margaret Laurence's "The Mask of the Bear," the reference in the first sentence to Grandfa- ther Connor's bearskin coat anticipates Vanessa's discovery at the end of the story of a bear mask in a museum. In Alice Munro's "Who Do You Think You Are?" Ralph Gillespie's talent for imitating Milton Homer foreshadows—in a strangely retroactive manner— not only the limitations of Rose's future career as an actress but also Ralph's doom in the small town of Hanratty. In Guy Vanderhaeghe's "Man Descending," the opening scene depicting the protagonist sneaking a drink bodes ill for the fate of his marriage. It might even be said that if every word of a story should tend toward its total effect, as Edgar Allan Poe contended, then ideally every word is a foreshadowing. Foreshadowing is the essence of literary art, but it is also a means for the literary artist to weave into the verbal tapestry of his story clue- like threads for the careful reader.

Character

Plot and character are closely linked, not only as primary sources of readers' pleasure but also as elements in the short story itself. As Henry James once remarked, "What is character but the determination of incident? What is incident but the illustration of character?" Let us consider some examples that illustrate how this interdependence works. In "Odour of Chrysanthemums," D.H. Lawrence introduces Elizabeth Bates this way: "She was a tall woman of imperious mien, handsome, with definite black eyebrows. Her smooth black hair was parted exactly. For a few moments she stood steadily watching the miners as they passed along the railway: then she turned towards the brook course. Her face was calm and set, her mouth was closed with disillusionment." Not every author feels obliged to provide readers with this catalogue of physical traits; others offer similar information but more casually or subtly. Why is it important for Lawrence to delineate thus his principal character? The answer lies in the connection James alludes to. An "imperious mien" might belong to someone who likes to give orders, and Elizabeth Bates is a woman who issues a number of orders in the short space of the story. She will feel "counter-manded" at a crucial point, a somewhat unusual word to use for a human being, but a word that takes its logical place in the matrix of associations that Lawrence builds up around her by using the word "imperious." "Handsome" is another epithet over which readers might pause. It is usually associated with men, and this is a story about traditional assumptions concerning men and women, their roles, their interactions. Elizabeth is a woman who has in some sense assumed the role of head of the household: the references to her appearance, her determination, and her disillusionment should prepare us for the emotional conflicts that follow. Note also how words like "definite," "steadily," and "exactly" add to the overall effect of clarity and purpose, complementing the list of physical attributes that imply certain character traits. In this description of his character, then, Lawrence does much more than provide readers with the details from which they can put together their own mental picture. Rather he uses carefully chosen words to sketch the outlines of a personality that will play a determining role in the events that ensue.

Here is part of an introductory section from another story, Raymond Carver's "Menudo":

Two days ago, in the afternoon, Amanda said to me, "I can't read books any more. Who has the time?" It was the day after Oliver had left, and we were in this little café in the industrial part of the city. "Who can concentrate anymore?" she said, stirring her coffee. "Who reads? Do you read?" (I shook my head.) "Somebody must read, I guess. You see all these books around in store windows, and there are those clubs. Somebody's reading," she said. "Who? I don't know anybody who reads."

That's what she said, apropos of nothing—that is, we weren't talking about books, we were talking about our *lives*. Books had nothing to do with it.

"What did Oliver say when you told him?"

Then it struck me that what we were saying—the tense, watchful expressions we wore—belonged to the people on afternoon TV programs that I'd never done more than switch on and then off.

Note how Carver uses dialogue to characterize his protagonist. (In a story told in the first person, an introductory catalogue of features would be distinctly odd.) Carver's narrator, in reporting his own conversations, teaches us as much about what he feels as we learn from a different viewpoint about Lawrence's Elizabeth Bates. Having an extra-marital affair obviously creates a trauma for both characters, and the details of the conversation help convey this tension, as does the narrator's own commentary on these details. It is a self-conscious trauma, since he sees his own actions in the double mirror provided by retrospection and the artistic forms that convey experience—hence the references to books and soap operas, with the suggestion that behaviour can be learned from and conventionalized by the forms in which people are most often exposed to it. Faithful to the vocabulary and rhythms of the tense exchange between the lovers, Carver also conveys the extent to which that speech, those expressions, "belong" to a mode of culture that pre-empts any attempt at a "genuine" exchange.

Here is how Franz Kafka presents a rather different sort of character in "The Metamorphosis":

As Gregor Samsa awoke one morning from uneasy dreams he found himself transformed in his bed into a gigantic insect. He was lying on his hard, as it were armor-plated, back and when he lifted his head a little he could see his domelike brown belly divided into stiff arched segments on top of which the bed quilt could hardly keep in position and was about to slide off completely. His numerous legs, which were pitifully thin compared to the rest of his bulk, waved helplessly before his eyes.

A man wakes up as a dung beetle: "absurd," "grotesque," "preposterous" might be our first reactions. And certainly such news in the more sensationalistic but equally imaginative *National Enquirer* would detain us no longer. In the *Enquirer*, the shocking metamorphosis would be itself the point, and a short article replete with exclamation marks would say all that needed to be said. But because Kafka is interested in characterizing his pathetic protagonist, he proceeds rather differently. We notice, for instance, that Gregor Samsa's thoughts and feelings remain human, even while his body is transformed, and Kafka's story proceeds to explore the implications of this split. The reader becomes involved in the process because Gregor's responses mimic the reader's own: perhaps it's just a dream, Gregor thinks, but the narrator notes laconically, "It was no dream." Perhaps it is a hallucination? "What about sleeping a little longer and forgetting all this nonsense?" muses Gregor, but he is accustomed to sleeping on his right side and cannot turn over. The quiet, rational, earnest, hopeless exploration for a "solution" to his "problem" constitutes the whole of this strange story.

Kafka characterizes Gregor in other ways. We learn about his artistic tastes in the description of the picture above his bed or in the scene in which he listens to his sister playing the violin. We also learn about his stormy relations with his father in the account of their confrontations. The scrupulous attention to such details marks the story as "realistic." Yet the story also shows us that realism in character portrayal is a literary convention whose limits Kafka tests. As the story proceeds, we may be tempted to conclude that this beetle is Kafka's portrayal of modernity's alienating effects, surroundings, the outsider who is loathsome to the materialistic, insensitive defenders of the status quo. By violating one of the conventions of realism and turning his character into a beetle, Kafka invites us to consider the symbolic implications of man as a beetle, but the question might as easily involve an examination of the conventions of storytelling as a survey of symbolic implications. In a story that turns on a situation to which any response is ultimately absurd, we have to ponder how appropriate such a symbolic reading might actually be. Critics have also advanced political and psychological explanations for Gregor's "metamorphosis," yet the great achievement of the characterization in this story is Kafka's skill in suggesting myriad explanations even while he makes us aware of how arbitrary any single choice would be.

Setting

Setting denotes the spatial and temporal location of a story. In F. Scott Fitzgerald's "Babylon Revisited," for example, the story is set in Paris in the 1930s:

> Outside, the fire-red, gas-blue, ghost-green signs shone smokily through the tranquil rain. It was late afternoon and the streets were in movement; the *bistros* gleamed. At the corner of the

Boulevard des Capucines he took a taxi. The Place de la
Concorde moved by in pink majesty; they crossed the logical
Seine, and Charlie felt the sudden provincial quality of the
left bank.

In this and similar passages, Fitzgerald selects those details that lead
readers to see Paris as a city of sin, a "Babylon Revisited," in which
American expatriates led a riotous life in the 1920s, but a city that now
looks and feels different as the reality of middle age, its responsibilities and demands, asserts itself. Details can be chosen for a variety of
purposes, and those Charlie's eye selects as he wanders the streets provide Fitzgerald with the appropriate setting for the contrast between
past and present that he wants to evoke.

When we speak about the setting of a story, then, we often mean
more than the physical or geographical location where the events
take place. In this paragraph from William Faulkner's "Dry September,"
we see again the range of effects available to a writer interested in
creating a setting that is not just a backdrop for the action:

Through the bloody September twilight, aftermath of sixty-two
rainless days, it had gone like a fire in dry grass—the rumor,
the story, whatever it was. Something about Miss Minnie Cooper and a Negro. Attacked, insulted, frightened: none of them,
gathered in the barbershop on that Saturday evening where
the ceiling fan stirred, without freshening it, the vitiated air,
sending back upon them, in recurrent surges of stale pomade
and lotion, their own stale breath and odors, knew exactly
what had happened.

Faulkner's description has both naturalistic accuracy and important
thematic implications. The twilight is "bloody" because of the dust-
filled clouds still illuminated by the sun that has disappeared, and the
word hints at the violence to come, a violence that is occasioned in
part by the weather that has turned the twilight this colour. Faulkner
uses a simile to describe how the rumour spreads—"like a fire in dry
grass"—making the figurative language of the story itself a product of
the setting. The paragraph then shifts to a second, related setting, one
that is man-made as opposed to natural. As the rest of the story makes
clear, the people who inhabit this world are in moral terms as stale
and vitiated as the air they breathe. (Note, too, how the sentence that
describes this fetid atmosphere is made up of heavy, balanced clauses
that mimic the movement of the ineffectual fan and the weight it
attempts to displace.)

It is interesting to compare Faulkner's autumn evening with one
described by Edgar Allan Poe in "The Fall of the House of Usher,"
noting how Poe creates a mood that reflects the emotions of the character who sees and reproduces the scene:

During the whole of a dull, dark, and soundless day in the autumn of the year, when the clouds hung oppressively low in the heavens, I had been passing alone, on horseback, through a singularly dreary tract of country; and at length found myself, as the shades of the evening drew on, within view of the melancholy House of Usher. I know not how it was—but, with the first glimpse of the building, a sense of insufferable gloom pervaded my spirit. I say insufferable; for the feeling was unrelieved by any of that half-pleasurable, because poetic, sentiment, with which the mind usually receives even the sternest natural images of the desolate or terrible. I looked upon the scene before me—upon the mere house, and the simple landscape features of the domain—upon the bleak walls—upon the vacant eye-like windows—upon a few rank sedges—and upon a few white trunks of decayed trees—with an utter depression of soul which I can compare to no earthly sensation more properly than to the after-dream of the reveller upon opium—the bitter lapse into everyday life—the hideous dropping off of the veil. There was an iciness, a sinking, a sickening of the heart—an unredeemed dreariness of thought which no goading of the imagination could torture into aught of the sublime.

The reader is likely to be struck initially by the sheer extravagance of the detail. If all Poe wanted to convey was that his narrator felt profoundly depressed on first seeing the house, he could have said that in as many words, yet the excess of such a passage is part of its point. The repetitive drumbeat of the *d*-sound in the first sentence lends a funereal cadence to the narrator's journey, and the house makes its appearance on the promontory erected by the last three words of the sentence. Notice how sparing Poe is with actual detail: two phrases allude to walls and windows, two more to the vegetation around the house; the rest is emotional and mental reaction, "internal" detail that places the emphasis squarely on the relationship between the observer and the setting. In the concluding sentence, Poe suggests that there is such a thing as an aesthetic faculty that normally enables the observer to see the landscape as a work of art and to distance herself from its emotional effect. Without this ability to maintain distance, the passage tells us, the landscape *is* the observer, and distinctions between subject and object become blurred. Notice, too, how the images the narrator uses to explain the internal effects of the scene—opium withdrawal, dream worlds, phantasmagoria—are the details appropriate to the external scene and to the events it portends. The events of the story do unfold in a world comparable to a nightmare.

Point of View

Point of view, the particular angle from which the story is told, determines how readers feel about the various elements of a story, controlling as it does complex emotional responses while mediating the story's content and the author's intentions. As such, point of view is arguably the most difficult aspect of fiction to discuss clearly in a short space, partly because it is as much a function of such complex elements as the writer's style, his use of figurative language, and the overall tone of the story as it is a function of the decision to tell the story in the first or third person.

What the terms "first person" and "third person" actually describe is whether the tale is related from within or without, whether by an "I" or an anonymous narrator (the fictitious observer who tells the story). Beyond this basic distinction, the writer makes choices as to the extent of the narrator's involvement in the story: some first-person narrators are the protagonists of their stories, while others are only peripherally involved in the events; some third-person narrators are omniscient, all-knowing, moving freely among the minds of their characters, while others limit themselves to the mind of one character in a manner that has come to be called third-person subjective.

When reading first-person stories, students should carefully assess the accuracy of what is reported; that is, they should be alert to the question of the narrator's reliability. In Sinclair Ross's "One's a Heifer," an adolescent boy goes alone on horseback in search of some missing cattle. At a key moment in the story, the boy reports that he has spotted them: "And then at last I really saw them. It was nearly dusk, and along with fifteen or twenty other cattle they were making their way towards some buildings that lay huddled at the foot of the sandhills. They passed in single file less than fifty yards away, but when I pricked Tim forward to turn them back he floundered in a snowed-in water-cut." What, readers might wonder, is the status of the "really saw them" when the discovery is made at "nearly dusk," with the boy's cattle picked out from "fifteen or twenty" others from a distance of some "fifty yards." Add to this the boy's bone-weariness after a long, cold day on horseback and we begin to understand why in courts of law and in fiction the evidence of eye/"I"-witnesses is often considered the most unreliable. The narrator's doubtful testimony gains in importance when we learn that his belief that he has "really" found his missing cattle leads him to the climactic confrontation with a maddened bachelor and initiates him into a frustrated rite of passage.

In contrast to the limitations of any first-person narrator, a third-person omniscient narrator moves freely across time and space, in and out of the minds of her characters. The omniscient narrator is, in fact, godlike in relation to the story, seeing all, knowing all—omniscient. In Kate Chopin's "The Storm," the omniscient narrator gives a convincing picture of the thoughts and feelings of a woman attracted to her former lover, as well as conveying the thoughts of other characters. The third-person omniscient point of view is still employed in the stories of modern writers, as for example in James Joyce's "The Boarding House," where Mrs. Mooney rides roughshod over her wayward daughter Polly in a restrictive Irish rooming house:

> Polly knew that she was being watched, but still her mother's
> persistent silence could not be misunderstood. There had
> been no open complicity between mother and daughter, no
> open understanding but, though people in the house began
> to talk of the affair, still Mrs. Mooney did not intervene. Polly
> began to grow a little strange in her manner and the young
> man was evidently perturbed. At last, when she judged it to be
> the right moment, Mrs. Mooney intervened. She dealt with
> moral problems as a cleaver deals with meat: and in this case
> she had made up her mind.

Here evidently is a narrator who knows what Polly knows before she knows it, what her mother knows before she reveals it, what the boarders are talking about, and how the "young man" felt—and who manages to balance all of that knowledge with the skill that the third-person omnisicient point of view demands. This viewpoint has become, however, somewhat less popular with contemporary writers because it implies the existence of a universal truth that they find implausible.

Another kind of third-person narration aims less intrusively for an ideal of objectivity, though one that remains, because of the associations of images and connotations of words, impossible to achieve. In Morley Callaghan's "Ancient Lineage," we see this aesthetic of letting the story tell itself executed with a skill to rival that of Ernest Hemingway (who influenced Callaghan in matters of prose style), with a rhetorically denuded narrative voice directing a camera eye across the scene:

> The young man from the Historical Club with a green magazine
> under his arm got off the train at Clintonville. It was getting
> dark but the station lights were not lit. He hurried along the
> platform and jumped down on the sloping cinder path to the
> sidewalk.
>
> Trees were on the lawns alongside the walk, branches
> drooping low, leaves scraping occasionally against the young
> man's straw hat. He saw a cluster of lights, bluish-white in the

dusk across a river, many lights for a small town. He crossed the
lift-lock bridge and turned on to the main street. A hotel was
at the corner.

That, readers should conclude, is a straightforward, unbiased, third-
person narration of a story's beginning, an objective presentation of
setting and event. Readers might still wonder about such elements as
the juxtaposition of a "young man" and a "Historical Club," or the
possible associations of entrapment, even of malevolent entanglement,
in the lush vegetation, but they have no reason to question the narrator's
reliability (though they should continue to be wary of his designs
upon them).

The following passage from Alice Munro's "Who Do You Think
You Are?" illustrates the third-person subjective point of view:

Rose went on talking like this, though she wished she could
stop. She was talking in what elsewhere might have been
considered an amusing, confidential, recognizably and meaninglessly flirtatious style. She did not get much response from
Ralph Gillespie, though he seemed attentive, even welcoming.
All the time she talked, she was wondering what he wanted
her to say. He did want something. But he would not make
any move to get it. Her first impression of him, as boyishly
shy and ingratiating, had to change. That was his surface.
Underneath he was self-sufficient, resigned to living in bafflement, perhaps proud. She wished that he would speak to
her from that level, and she thought he wished it, too, but
they were prevented.

In this passage we are listening to a third-person narrator, but one who
has limited herself to the consciousness of one character, the protagonist Rose: we see only what Rose sees, experience her sensations only,
hear her thoughts. We are told from Rose's viewpoint that Ralph
Gillespie "seemed attentive," whereas a less subjective third-person
narrator would take liberties in transcribing Ralph's responses. In an
intriguing way, we can also see how this passage enacts the writer's
dilemma. Just as Rose proceeds to wonder about the impossibility of
making contact with Ralph at a deeper level, so Munro's narrator feels
limited by her inability to convey complexities of personality that,
because of the limited nature of language, cannot be transcribed, but
can only be spoken of, as she says, "in translation."

Nor is the author limited by his choice of point of view at the outset.
For example, in a scene from D.H. Lawrence's "Odour of Chrysanthemums," following an accident at a mine, some men arrive at Elizabeth
Bates's house with her husband's body, and one of her children is awakened by the noise. When Elizabeth goes upstairs to calm her daughter,
the narrator, who has to this point been describing events from her point

of view, stays downstairs with the men and reports the scene as they would have experienced it. "Then she must have bent down and kissed the children," runs the sentence that marks the conclusion of the incident. The implication of "must have" is "I don't know for sure. I can only go by the sound I heard." By choosing to limit his narrator here, who at other times reports Elizabeth's inmost thoughts and feelings, Lawrence marks off an area of intimacy between parent and child where no trespass is allowed. In a story concerning intimate human relations, this kind of narrative detail can be seen to illustrate the extent to which point of view is a part of the whole literary/artistic fabric.

Theme

Theme is the central idea that a short story illustrates. The answer to the question "What is this story about?" would be a statement of its theme. For example, Joseph Conrad's "Heart of Darkness" explores the theme that the mission to extend European civilization may be a rationale for conquest that simply satisfies base desires. Near the beginning of the story, a group of men is gathered on a small boat at the mouth of the Thames watching the sun go down. One of them, a seaman named Marlow, begins a story about a journey to Africa, but just before he does, Conrad's narrator says this:

> The yarns of seamen have a direct simplicity, the whole meaning of which lies within the shell of a cracked nut. But Marlow was not typical (if his propensity to spin yarns be excepted), and to him the meaning of an episode was not inside like a kernel but outside, enveloping the tale which brought it out only as a glow brings out a haze, in the likeness of one of these misty halos that sometimes are made visible by the spectral illumination of moonshine.

Conrad provides us here with a useful distinction between two types of stories. Stories of the first type reveal their theme in the same straightforward and eminently satisfying way that a nutshell disgorges a nut. Readers of Guy de Maupassant's "The Return" or Sara Jeannette Duncan's "A Mother in India" should identify those stories as examples of this type. Most detective stories (and popular fiction generally), which depend on sudden revelations at the end, also belong in this category. Conrad's story is one of the second type. This does not mean that it simply leaves the reader with a series of vague impressions, Conrad's "haze" or "misty halos." The writer may narrate an inconclusive series of events that, like the events of life itself, refuse to yield up a "kernel" of meaning. Or she may proceed, as Conrad does in "Heart of Darkness," to entertain propositions about human nature like "Imperialism has acted as a force for progress and has at the same time been responsible for monstrous cruelty" or "Civilized man's capacity for disgust when confronted by meaningless suffering is an index of his moral progress and, at the same time, the means by which that progress can be undone." Marlow begins by asking his civilized listeners to recall a time when Britons were themselves the beneficiaries and victims of imperialism, in this case Roman imperialism; in other words, he seeks to establish some sort of common ground between his story and his listeners. Every writer must of course do the same; the vision conveyed is uniquely the writer's, but common experiences and assumptions make it comprehensible to the reader. We do not have to be planning a river journey to the heart of the African continent to feel that Marlow's experience has important links with our own.

These are "kernels" of truth we arrive at after analyzing various episodes in the narrative, but as the passage above suggests, there are subtleties and implications that are ultimately as important as these. Indeed, the auto-commentary in Conrad's story implies that, just as there are experiences that are difficult to convey in language, there are narratives that stubbornly resist being reduced to any kind of para-phrasable meaning at all. This last point is important, for it reminds us of the dangers of reducing stories to a given theme, to a set of generaliza-tions or meanings that the experience of careful reading and, indeed, literary art itself refutes.

Suggestions for Classroom Discussion
A Student Checklist

1. Questions about Form
   a) How is the story told? Which events are omitted from the actual telling and which events are dramatized? How does the order in which events are narrated (chronological, flashback) influence our response to them?
   b) Who tells the story? The main character, a minor character, an observer, an impersonal voice?
   c) If the story is told in the third person, from whose point of view is it told?
   d) How reliable is the point of view? How self-conscious is the narrator?
   e) What is the significance of the imagery, diction, or tone?
   f) What shift or variation occurs in the imagery, setting, diction, tone?
   g) What is the significance of the title, the introduction, the conclusion?

2. Questions about Character

   a) Describe a given character, explaining his or her personal characteristics, motives, and actions.

   b) How do we respond to a given character? Does the author try to manipulate our response?

   c) Compare him or her to other characters. How do other characters relate to a given character?

   d) How do we learn about the character: physical description, reported dialogue, thoughts and feelings?

   e) What are the implications of a character's actions? What system of values do they suggest?

   f) Which traits make a character individual or unique? Which traits tend to make him or her typical or universal?

   g) How does a given character change in the course of a story? How do our perceptions of the character change?

   h) Does the character control his or her own destiny? How do the acts and decisions of others, material conditions, social circumstances, or simply chance influence his or her life?

3. Questions about Theme

   a) What does the story tell us about the social, moral, economic, and political values of the society it depicts?

   b) What is the writer's view of human nature? Of the characters' potential for happiness? Of their capacity for freedom?

   c) What is the symbolic significance or value of a given object, idea, or event in the context of the story? How does the author imply what the symbol stands for and its range of additional meanings?

   d) What ambiguities does the writer explore? Are issues easily resolved or is the story open-ended?

   e) What thematic purpose is served by the metafictional aspects of the story, those passages that draw our attention to the process of writing itself? What techniques does the writer use to comment on the problems involved in representing any action or event in fiction?

Students should keep in mind that they can best answer these questions by commenting on specific passages. While not all of the questions are relevant to every story, students will discover that the application of some to stories by writers as different as Stephen Leacock, Vladimir Nabokov, and Edna O'Brien will eventually reveal the genuine unity of the seemingly amorphous genre that is the short story.

HONORÉ DE BALZAC

(1799–1850)

H *onoré de Balzac was born in Tours, the son of the Deputy Mayor*
and his young wife. He studied law at Paris, but he had decided
from an early age to become a writer, and with his parents' support set out
to prove that he could. A two-year stint produced a tragedy, Cromwell
(1819), that was pronounced a flop by all who read it, and a professor
advised Balzac to take up any profession but literature. His other strug-
gles in Paris with his reluctant genius are the stuff of legend: a love
affair with a woman whose money was promptly lost in a business
venture ruined by Balzac's mismanagement; hack work to stave off
starvation; debts of 100,000 francs; stunning successes and abysmal
failures in Parisian society; a boundless ambition that minimized all
setbacks and craved ever-increasing adulation. As one critic has rightly
said of Balzac, "Life was always littler than his vision of it." In a love
letter to a duchess, Balzac said of himself, "In my five feet three inches
I contain every possible inconsistency and contrast," concluding that he
was "astonished by nothing more than myself." A Polish countess, Mme
Hanska, became his patroness at a crucial point, and her love and support
(and money) provided Balzac with the stability necessary to realize at
least part of his grand dreams. In 1841 he decided to make a great number
of his novels into a vast "comédie humaine." Having driven himself at
a superhuman pace to achieve this goal, he died of a heart and lung
ailment in Paris. Balzac can be crude, conventional, journalistic, senti-
mental, melodramatic, but the sheer fecundity of his genius, the mon-
strous meticulousness of his documentation, and the extraordinary
energy of the presentation give his novels an epic grandeur that has
never been equalled. His best-known novels include The Chouans
(1829), Louis Lambert *(1832),* Eugénie Grandet *(1833),* Old Goriot
(1834–35), The Lily in the Valley *(1835–36), and* Lost Illusions
(1837–43).

Sarrasine

I was deep in one of those daydreams which overtake even the shal-
lowest of men, in the midst of the most tumultuous parties. Midnight
had just sounded from the clock of the Elysée-Bourbon. Seated in a
window recess and hidden behind the sinuous folds of a silk curtain, I
could contemplate at my leisure the garden of the mansion where I was
spending the evening. The trees, partially covered with snow, stood out

dimly against the grayish background of a cloudy sky, barely whitened by the moon. Seen amid these fantastic surroundings, they vaguely resembled ghosts half out of their shrouds, a gigantic representation of the famous Dance of the Dead. Then, turning in the other direction, I could admire the Dance of the Living! a splendid salon decorated in silver and gold, with glittering chandeliers, sparkling with candles. There, milling about, whirling around, flitting here and there, were the most beautiful women of Paris, the richest, the noblest, dazzling, stately, resplendent with diamonds, flowers in their hair, on their bosoms, on their heads, strewn over dresses or in garlands at their feet. Light, rustling movements, voluptuous steps, made the laces, the silk brocades, the gauzes, float around their delicate forms. Here and there, some overly animated glances darted forth, eclipsing the lights, the fire of the diamonds, and stimulated anew some too-ardent hearts. One might also catch movements of the head meaningful to lovers, and negative gestures for husbands. The sudden outbursts of the gamblers' voices at each unexpected turn of the dice, the clink of gold, mingled with the music and the murmur of conversation, and to complete the giddiness of this mass of people intoxicated by everything seductive the world can hold, a haze of perfume and general inebriation played upon the fevered mind. Thus, on my right, the dark and silent image of death; on my left, the seemly bacchanalias of life: here, cold nature, dull, in mourning; there, human beings enjoying themselves. On the borderline between these two so different scenes, which, a thousand times repeated in various guises, make Paris the world's most amusing and most philosophical city, I was making for myself a moral macédoine, half pleasant, half funereal. With my left foot I beat time, and I felt as though the other were in the grave. My leg was in fact chilled by one of those insidious drafts which freeze half our bodies while the other half feels the humid heat of rooms, an occurrence rather frequent at balls.

"Monsieur de Lanty hasn't owned this house for very long, has he?"

"Oh yes. Maréchal Carigliano sold it to him nearly ten years ago."

"Ah!"

"These people must have a huge fortune."

"They must have."

"What a party! It's shockingly elegant."

"Do you think they're as rich as M. de Nucingen or M. de Gondreville?"

"You mean you don't know?" . . .

I stuck my head out and recognized the two speakers as members of that strange race which, in Paris, deals exclusively with "whys" and "hows," with "Where did they come from?" "What's happening?" "What has she done?" They lowered their voices and walked off to talk in greater comfort on some isolated sofa. Never had a richer vein been offered to seekers after mystery. Nobody knew what country the Lanty family came from, or from what business, what plunder, what piratical activity, or what inheritance derived a fortune estimated at several millions. All the members of the family spoke Italian, French, Spanish, English, and German perfectly enough to create the belief that they must have spent a long time among these various peoples. Were they gypsies? Were they freebooters?

"Even if it's the devil," some young politicians said, "they give a marvelous party."

"Even if the Count de Lanty had robbed a bank, I'd marry his daughter any time!" cried a philosopher.

Who wouldn't have married Marianina, a girl of sixteen whose beauty embodied the fabled imaginings of the Eastern poets! Like the sultan's daughter, in the story of the Magic Lamp, she should have been kept veiled. Her singing put into the shade the partial talents of Malibran, Sontag, and Fodor, in whom one dominant quality has always excluded over-all perfection; whereas Marianina was able to bring to the same level purity of sound, sensibility, rightness of movement and pitch, soul and science, correctness and feeling. This girl was the embodiment of that secret poetry, the common bond among all the arts, which always eludes those who search for it. Sweet and modest, educated and witty, no one could eclipse Marianina, save her mother.

Have you ever encountered one of those women whose striking beauty defies the inroads of age and who seem at thirty-six more desirable than they could have been fifteen years earlier? Their visage is a vibrant soul, it glows; each feature sparkles with intelligence; each pore has a special brilliance, especially in artificial light. Their seductive eyes refuse, attract, speak or remain silent; their walk is innocently knowledgeable; their voices employ the melodious wealth of the most coquettishly soft and tender notes. Based on comparisons, their praises flatter the self-love of the most sentient. A movement of their eyebrows, the least glance, their pursed lips, fill with a kind of terror those whose life and happiness depend upon them. Inexperienced in love and influenced by words, a young girl can be seduced; for this kind of woman, however, a man must know, like M. de Jaucourt, not to cry out when he is hiding in a closet and the maid breaks two of his fingers as she shuts the door on them. In loving these powerful sirens, one gambles with one's life. And this, perhaps, is why we love them so passionately. Such was the Countess de Lanty.

Filippo, Marianina's brother, shared with his sister in the Countess's marvelous beauty. To be brief, this young man was a living image of Antinous, even more slender. Yet how well these thin, delicate proportions are suited to young people when an olive complexion, strongly defined eyebrows, and the fire of velvet eyes give promise of future male passion, of brave thoughts! If Filippo resided in every girl's heart as an ideal, he also resided in the memory of every mother as the best catch in France.

The beauty, the fortune, the wit, the charms of these two children, came solely from their mother. The Count de Lanty was small, ugly, and pock-marked; dark as a Spaniard, dull as a banker. However, he was taken to be a deep politician, perhaps because he rarely laughed, and was always quoting Metternich or Wellington.

This mysterious family had all the appeal of one of Lord Byron's poems, whose difficulties each person in the fashionable world interpreted in a different way: an obscure and sublime song in every strophe. The reserve maintained by M. and Mme de Lanty about their origin, their past life, and their relationship with the four corners of the globe had not lasted long as a subject of astonishment in Paris. Nowhere perhaps is Vespasian's axiom better understood. There, even bloodstained or filthy money betrays nothing and stands for everything. So long as high society knows the amount of your fortune, you are classed among those having an equal amount, and no one asks to see your family tree, because everyone knows how much it cost. In a city where social problems are solved like algebraic equations, adventurers have every opportunity in their favor. Even supposing this family were of gypsy origin, it was so wealthy, so attractive, that society had no trouble in forgiving its little secrets. Unfortunately, however, the mystery of the Lantys presented a continuing source of curiosity, rather like that contained in the novels of Ann Radcliffe.

Observers, people who make it a point to know in what shop you buy your candlesticks, or who ask the amount of your rent when they find your apartment attractive, had noticed, now and then, in the midst of the Countess's parties, concerts, balls, and routs, the appearance of a strange personage. It was a man. The first time he had appeared in the mansion was during a concert, when he seemed to have been drawn to the salon by Marianina's enchanting voice.

"All of a sudden, I'm cold," a lady had said who was standing with a friend by the door.

The stranger, who was standing next to the women, went away.

"That's odd! I'm warm now," she said, after the stranger had gone. "And you'll say I'm mad, but I can't help thinking that my neighbor, the man dressed in black who just left, was the cause of my chill."

Before long, the exaggeration native to those in high society gave birth to and accumulated the most amusing ideas, the most outrageous expressions, the most ridiculous anecdotes about this mysterious personage. Although not a vampire, a ghoul, or an artificial man, a kind of Faust or Robin Goodfellow, people fond of fantasy said he had something of all these anthropomorphic natures about him. Here and there, one came across some Germans who accepted as fact these clever witticisms of Parisian scandal-mongering. The stranger was merely an old man. Many of the young men who were in the habit of settling the future of Europe every morning in a few elegant phrases would have liked to see in this stranger some great criminal, the possessor of vast wealth. Some storytellers recounted the life of this old man and provided really curious details about the atrocities he had committed while in the service of the Maharaja of Mysore. Some bankers, more positive by nature, invented a fable about money. "Bah," they said, shrugging their shoulders in pity, "this poor old man is a *tête génoise!*"

"Sir, without being indiscreet, could you please tell me what you mean by a *tête génoise?*"

"A man, sir, with an enormous lifetime capital and whose family's income doubtless depends on his good health."

I remember having heard at Mme d'Espard's a hypnotist proving on highly suspect historical data that this old man, preserved under glass, was the famous Balsamo, known as Cagliostro. According to this contemporary alchemist, the Sicilian adventurer had escaped death and passed his time fabricating gold for his grandchildren. Last, the bailiff of Ferette maintained that he had recognized this odd personage as the Count of Saint-Germain. These stupidities, spoken in witty accents, with the mocking air characteristic of atheistic society in our day, kept alive vague suspicions about the Lanty family. Finally, through a strange combination of circumstances, the members of this family justified everyone's conjectures by behaving somewhat mysteriously toward this old man, whose life was somehow hidden from all investigation.

Whenever this person crossed the threshold of the room he was supposed to inhabit in the Lanty mansion, his appearance always created a great sensation among the family. One might have called it an event of great importance. Filippo, Marianina, Mme de Lanty, and an old servant were the only persons privileged to assist the old man in walking, arising, sitting down. Each of them watched over his slightest movement. It seemed that he was an enchanted being upon whom depended the happiness, the life, or the fortune of them all. Was it affection or fear? Those in society were unable to discover any clue to help them solve this problem. Hidden for whole months in the depths of a secret sanctuary, this family genie would suddenly come forth, unexpectedly, and would appear in the midst of the salons like those fairies of bygone days who descended from flying dragons to interrupt the rites to which they had not been invited. Only the most avid onlookers were then able to perceive the uneasiness of the heads of the house, who could conceal their feelings with unusual skill. Sometimes, however, while dancing a quadrille, Marianina, naïve as she was, would cast a terrified glance at the old man when she spied him among the crowd. Or else Filippo would slip quickly through the throng to his side and would stay near him, tender and attentive, as though contact with others or the slightest breath would destroy this strange creature. The Countess would make a point of drawing near, without seeming to have any intention of joining them; then, assuming a manner and expression of servitude mixed with tenderness, submission, and power, she would say a few words, to which the old man nearly always deferred, and he would disappear, led off, or, more precisely, carried off, by her. If Mme de Lanty were not present, the Count used a thousand stratagems to reach his side; however, he seemed to have difficulty making himself heard, and treated him like a spoiled child whose mother gives in to his whims in order to avoid a scene. Some bolder persons having thoughtlessly ventured to question the Count de Lanty, this cold, reserved man had appeared never to understand them. And so, after many tries, all futile because of the circumspection of the entire family, everyone stopped trying to fathom such a well-kept secret. Weary of trying, the companionable spies, the idly curious, and the politic all gave up bothering about this mystery.

However, even now perhaps in these glittering salons there were some philosophers who, while eating an ice or a sherbet, or placing their empty punch glass on a side table, were saying to each other: "It wouldn't surprise me to learn that those people are crooks. The old man who hides and only makes his appearance on the first day of spring or winter, or at the solstices, looks to me like a killer . . ."

"Or a confidence man . . ."

"It's almost the same thing. Killing a man's fortune is sometimes worse than killing the man."

"Sir, I have bet twenty louis, I should get back forty."

"But, sir, there are only thirty on the table."

"Ah, well, you see how mixed the crowd is, here. It's impossible to play."

"True . . . But it's now nearly six months since we've seen the Spirit. Do you think he's really alive?"

"Hah! at best . . ."

These last words were spoken near me by people I did not know, as they were moving off, and as I was resuming, in an afterthought, my mixed thoughts of white and black, life and death. My vivid imagination as well as my eyes looked back and forth from the party, which had reached the height of its splendor, and the somber scene in the gardens. I do not know how long I meditated on these two faces of the human coin; but all at once I was awakened by the stifled laugh of a young woman. I was stunned by the appearance of the image which arose before me. By one of those tricks of nature, the half-mournful thought turning in my mind had emerged, and it appeared living before me, it had sprung like Minerva from the head of Jove, tall and strong, it was at once a hundred years old and twenty-two years old; it was alive and dead. Escaped from his room like a lunatic from his cell, the little old man had obviously slipped behind a hedge of people who were listening to Marianina's voice, finishing the cavatina from *Tancredi*. He seemed to have come out from underground, impelled by some piece of stage machinery. Motionless and somber, he stood for a moment gazing at the party, the noises of which had perhaps reached his ears. His almost somnambulatory preoccupation was so concentrated on things that he was in the world without seeing it. He had unceremoniously sprung up next to one of the most ravishing women in Paris, a young and elegant dancer, delicately formed, with one of those faces as fresh as that of a child, pink and white, so frail and transparent that a man's glance seems to penetrate it like a ray of sunlight going through ice. They were both there before me, together, united, and so close that the stranger brushed against her, her gauzy dress, her garlands of flowers, her softly curled hair, her floating sash.

I had brought this young woman to Mme de Lanty's ball. Since this was her first visit to the house, I forgave her her stifled laugh, but I quickly gave her a signal which completely silenced her and filled her with awe for her neighbor. She sat down next to me. The old man did not want to leave this lovely creature, to whom he had attached himself with that silent and seemingly baseless stubborness to which the extremely old are prone, and which makes them appear childish. In order to sit near her, he had to take a folding chair. His slightest movements were full of that cold heaviness, the stupid indecision, characteristic of the gestures of a paralytic. He sat slowly down on his seat, with circumspection, muttering some unintelligible words. His worn-out voice was like the sound made by a stone falling down a well. The young woman held my hand tightly, as if seeking protection on some precipice, and she shivered when this man at whom she was looking turned upon her two eyes without warmth, glaucous eyes which could only be compared to dull mother-of-pearl.

"I'm afraid," she said, leaning toward my ear.

"You can talk," I answered, "He is very hard of hearing."

"Do you know him?"

"Yes."

Thereupon, she gathered up enough courage to look for a moment at this creature for which the human language had no name, a form without substance, a being without life, or a life without action. She was under the spell of that timorous curiosity which leads women to seek out dangerous emotions, to go see chained tigers, to look at boa constrictors, frightening themselves because they are separated from them only by weak fences. Although the little old man's back was stooped like a laborer's, one could easily tell that he must have had at one time a normal shape. His excessive thinness, the delicacy of his limbs, proved that he had always been slender. He was dressed in black silk trousers which fell about his bony thighs in folds, like an empty sail. An anatomist would have promptly recognized the symptoms of galloping consumption by looking at the skinny legs supporting this strange body. You would have said they were two bones crossed on a tombstone.

A feeling of profound horror for mankind gripped the heart when one saw the marks that decrepitude had left on this fragile machine. The stranger was wearing an old-fashioned gold-embroidered white waist-coat, and his linen was dazzlingly white. A frill of somewhat yellowed lace, rich enough for a queen's envy, fell into ruffles on his breast. On him, however, this lace seemed more like a rag than like an ornament. Centered on it was a fabulous diamond which glittered like the sun. This outmoded luxury, this particular and tasteless jewel, made the strange creature's face even more striking. The setting was worthy of the portrait. This dark face was angular and all sunk in. The chin was sunken, the temples were sunken; the eyes were lost in yellowish sockets. The jaw-bones stood out because of his indescribable thinness, creating cavities in the center of each cheek. These deformations, more or less illuminated by the candles, produced shadows and strange reflections which suc-ceeded in erasing any human characteristics from his face. And the years had glued the thin, yellow skin of his face so closely to his skull that it was covered all over with a multitude of circular wrinkles, like the ripples on a pond into which a child has thrown a pebble, or star-shaped, like a cracked windowpane, but everywhere deep and close-set as the edges of pages in a closed book. Some old people have presented more hideous portraits; what contributed the most, however, in lending the appearance of an artificial creature to the specter which had risen up before us was the red and white with which he glistened. The eyebrows of his mask took from the light a luster which revealed that they were painted on. Fortunately for the eye depressed by the sight of such ruin, his cadaverous skull was covered by a blond wig whose innumerable curls were evidence of an extraordinary pretension. For the rest, the feminine coquetry of this phantasmagorical personage was rather strongly emphasized by the gold ornaments hanging from his ears, by the rings whose fine stones glittered on his bony fingers, and by a watch chain which shimmered like the brilliants of a choker around a woman's neck. Finally, this sort of Japanese idol had on his bluish lips a fixed and frozen smile, implacable and mocking, like a skull. Silent and motionless as a statue, it exuded the musty odor of old clothes which the heirs of some duchess take out for inventory. Although the old man turned his eyes toward the crowd, it seemed that the movements of those orbs, incapable of sight, were accomplished only by means of some inperceptible artifice; and when the eyes came to rest on something, anyone looking at them would have concluded that they had not moved at all. To see, next to this human wreckage, a young woman whose neck, bosom, and arms were bare and white, whose figure was in the full bloom of its beauty, whose hair rose from her alabaster forehead and inspired love, whose eyes did not receive but gave off light, who was soft, fresh, and whose floating curls and sweet breath seemed too heavy, too hard, too powerful for this shadow, for this man of dust: ah! here were death and life indeed, I thought, in a fantastic arabesque, half hideous chimera, divinely feminine from the waist up.

"Yet there are marriages like that often enough in the world," I said to myself.

"He smells like a graveyard," cried the terrified young woman, pressing against me for protection, and whose uneasy movements told me she was frightened. "What a horrible sight," she went on. "I can't stay here any longer. If I look at him again, I shall believe that death itself has come looking for me. Is he alive?"

She reached out to the phenomenon with that boldness women can summon up out of the strength of their desires; but she broke into a cold sweat, for no sooner had she touched the old man than she heard a cry like a rattle. This sharp voice, if voice it was, issued from a nearly dried up throat. Then the sound was quickly followed by a little, convulsive, childish cough of a peculiar sonorousness. At this sound, Marianina, Filippo, and Mme de Lanty looked in our direction, and their glances were like bolts of lightning. The young woman wished she were at the bottom of the Seine. She took my arm and led me into a side room. Men, women, everyone made way for us. At the end of the public rooms, we came into a small, semicircular chamber. My companion threw herself onto a divan, trembling with fright, oblivious to her surroundings.

"Madame, you are mad," I said to her.

"But," she replied, after a moment's silence, during which I gazed at her in admiration, "is it my fault? Why does Mme de Lanty allow ghosts to wander about in her house?"

"Come," I replied, "you are being ridiculous, taking a little old man for a ghost."

"Be still," she said, with that forceful and mocking air all women so easily assume when they want to be in the right. "What a pretty room!" she cried, looking around. "Blue satin always makes such wonderful wall hangings. How refreshing it is! Oh! what a beautiful painting!" she went on, getting up and going to stand before a painting in a magnificent frame.

We stood for a moment in contemplation of this marvel, which seemed to have been painted by some supernatural brush. The picture was of Adonis lying on a lion's skin. The lamp hanging from the ceiling of the room in an alabaster globe illuminated this canvas with a soft glow which enabled us to make out all the beauties of the painting.

"Does such a perfect creature exist?" she asked me, after having, with a soft smile of contentment, examined the exquisite grace of the contours, the pose, the color, the hair; in short, the entire picture.

"He is too beautiful for a man," she added, after an examination such as she might have made of some rival.

Oh! how jealous I then felt: something in which a poet had vainly tried to make me believe, the jealousy of engravings, of pictures, wherein artists exaggerate human beauty according to the doctrine which leads them to idealize everything.

"It's a portrait," I replied, "the product of the talent of Vien. But that great painter never saw the original and maybe you'd admire it less if you knew that this daub was copied from the statue of a woman."

"But who is it?"

I hesitated.

"I want to know," she added, impetuously.

"I believe," I replied, "that this Adonis is a . . . a relative of Mme de Lanty."

I had the pain of seeing her rapt in the contemplation of this figure. She sat in silence; I sat down next to her and took her hand without her being aware of it! Forgotten for a painting! At this moment, the light footsteps of a woman in a rustling dress broke the silence. Young Marianina came in, and her innocent expression made her even more alluring than did her grace and her lovely dress; she was walking slowly and escorting with maternal care, with filial solicitude, the costumed specter who had made us flee from the music room and whom she was leading, watching with what seemed to be concern as he slowly advanced on his feeble feet. They went together with some difficulty to a door hidden behind a tapestry. There, Marianina knocked softly. At once, as if by magic, a tall, stern man, a kind of family genie, appeared. Before entrusting the old man to the care of his mysterious guardian, the child respectfully kissed the walking corpse, and her chaste caress was not devoid of that graceful cajolery of which some privileged women possess the secret.

"Addio, addio," she said, with the prettiest inflection in her youthful voice.

She added to the final syllable a marvelously well-executed trill, but in a soft voice, as if to give poetic expression to the emotions in her heart. Suddenly struck by some memory, the old man stood on the threshold of this secret hideaway. Then, through the silence, we heard the heavy sigh that came from his chest: he took the most beautiful of the rings which adorned his skeletal fingers, and placed it in Marianina's bosom. The young girl broke into laugher, took the ring, and slipped it onto her finger over her glove; then she walked quickly toward the salon, from which there could be heard the opening measures of a quadrille. She saw us:

"Ah, you were here," she said, blushing.

After having seemed as if about to question us, she ran to her partner with the careless petulance of youth.

"What did that mean?" my young companion asked me. "Is he her husband? I must be dreaming. Where am I?"

"You," I replied, "you, madame, superior as you are, you who understand so well the most hidden feelings, who know how to inspire in a man's heart the most delicate of feelings without blighting it, without breaking it at the outset, you who pity heartache and who combine the wit of a Parisienne with a passionate soul worthy of Italy or Spain—"

She perceived the bitter irony in my speech; then, without seeming to have heard, she interrupted me: "Oh, you fashion me to your own taste. What tyranny! You don't want me for myself!"

"Ah, I want nothing," I cried, taken aback by her severity. "Is it true, at least, that you enjoy hearing stories of those vivid passions that ravishing Southern women inspire in our hearts?"

"Yes, so?"

"So, I'll call tomorrow around nine and reveal this mystery to you."

"No," she replied, "I want to know now."

"You haven't yet given me the right to obey you when you say: I want to."

"At this moment," she replied with maddening coquetry, "I have the most burning desire to know the secret. Tomorrow, I might not even listen to you . . ."

She smiled and we parted; she just as proud, just as forbidding, and I just as ridiculous as ever. She had the audacity to waltz with a young aide-de-camp; and I was left in turn angry, pouting, admiring, loving, jealous.

"Till tomorrow," she said, around two in the morning, as she left the ball.

"I won't go," I thought to myself. "I'll give you up. You are more capricious, perhaps a thousand times more fanciful . . . than my imagination."

The next evening, we were both seated before a good fire in a small, elegant salon, she on a low sofa, I on cushions almost at her feet, and my eyes below hers. The street was quiet. The lamp shed a soft light. It was one of those evenings pleasing to the soul, one of those never-to-be-forgotten moments, one of those hours spent in peace and desire whose charm, later on, is a matter for constant regret, even when we may be happier. Who can erase the vivid imprint of the first feelings of love?

"Well," she said, "I'm listening."

"I don't dare begin. The story has some dangerous passages for its teller. If I become too moved, you must stop me."

"Tell."

"I will obey."

Ernest-Jean Sarrasine was the only son of a lawyer in the Franche-Comté, I went on, after a pause. His father had amassed six or eight thousand livres of income honestly enough, a professional's fortune which at that time in the provinces, was considered to be colossal. The elder Sarrasine, having but one child and anxious to overlook nothing where his education was concerned, hoped to make a magistrate of him, and to live long enough to see, in his old age, the grandson of Matthieu Sarrasine, farmer of Saint-Dié, seated beneath the lilies and napping through some trial for the greater glory of the law; however, heaven did not hold this pleasure in store for the lawyer.

The younger Sarrasine, entrusted to the Jesuits at an early age, evidenced an unusual turbulence. He had the childhood of a man of talent. He would study only what pleased him, frequently rebelled, and sometimes spent hours on end plunged in confused thought, occupied at times in watching his comrades at play, at times dreaming of Homeric heroes. Then, if he made up his mind to amuse himself, he threw himself into games with an extraordinary ardor. When a fight broke out between him and a friend, the battle rarely ended without bloodshed. If he was the weaker of the two, he would bite. Both active and passive by turns, without aptitude and not overly intelligent, his bizarre character made his teachers as wary of him as were his classmates. Instead of learning the elements of Greek, he drew the Reverend Father as he explained a passage in Thucydides to them, sketched the mathematics teacher, the tutors, the Father in charge of discipline, and he scribbled shapeless designs on the walls. Instead of singing the Lord's praises in church, he distracted himself during services by whittling on a pew; or when he had stolen a piece of wood, he carved some holy figure. If he had no wood, paper, or pencil, he reproduced his ideas with bread crumbs. Whether copying the characters in the pictures that decorated the choir, or improvising, he always left behind him some gross sketches whose licentiousness shocked the youngest Fathers; evil tongues maintained that the older Jesuits were amused by them. Finally, if we are to believe school gossip, he was expelled for having, while awaiting his turn at the confessional on Good Friday, shaped a big stick of wood into the form of Christ. The impiety with which this statue was endowed was too blatant not to have merited punishment of the artist. Had he not had the audacity to place this somewhat cynical figure on top of the tabernacle!

Sarrasine sought in Paris a refuge from the effects of a father's curse. Having one of those strong wills that brook no obstacle, he obeyed the commands of his genius and entered Bouchardon's studio. He worked all day, and in the evening went out to beg for his living. Astonished at the young artist's progress and intelligence, Bouchardon soon became aware of his pupil's poverty; he helped him, grew fond of him, and treated him like his own son. Then, when Sarrasine's genius was revealed

in one of those works in which future talent struggles with the efferves-
cence of youth, the warmhearted Bouchardon endeavored to restore him
to the old lawyer's good graces. Before the authority of the famous
sculptor, the parental anger subsided. All Besançon rejoiced at having
given birth to a great man of the future. In the first throes of the ecstasy
produced by his flattered vanity, the miserly lawyer gave his son the
means to cut a good figure in society. For a long time, the lengthy and
laborious studies demanded by sculpture tamed Sarrasine's impetuous
nature and wild genius. Bouchardon, foreseeing the violence with which
the passions would erupt in this young soul, which was perhaps as
predisposed to them as Michelangelo's had been, channeled his energy
into constant labor. He succeeded in keeping Sarrasine's extraordinary
impetuosity within limits by forbidding him to work; by suggesting distractions when he saw him being carried away by the fury of some idea,
or by entrusting him with important work when he seemed on the point
of abandoning himself to dissipation. However, gentleness was always
the most powerful of weapons where this passionate soul was concerned,
and the master had no greater control over his student than when he
inspired his gratitude through paternal kindness.

At twenty-two, Sarrasine was necessarily removed from the salutary
influence Bouchardon had exercised over his morals and his habits. He
reaped the fruits of his genius by winning the sculpture prize established
by the Marquis de Marigny, the brother of Mme de Pompadour, who did
so much for the arts. Diderot hailed the statue by Bouchardon's pupil as
a masterpiece. The King's sculptor, not without great sorrow, saw off to
Italy a young man whom he had kept, as a matter of principle, in total
ignorance of the facts of life.

For six years, Sarrasine had boarded with Bouchardon. As fanatic in
his art as Canova was later to be, he arose at dawn, went to the studio,
did not emerge until nightfall, and lived only with his Muse. If he went
to the Comédie-Française, he was taken by his master. He felt so out of
place at Mme Geoffrin's and in high society, into which Bouchardon tried
to introduce him, that he preferred to be alone, and shunned the pleasures
of that licentious era. He had no other mistress but sculpture and Clotilde,
one of the luminaries of the Opéra. And even this affair did not last.
Sarrasine was rather ugly, always badly dressed, and so free in his nature,
so irregular in his private life, that the celebrated nymph, fearing some
catastrophe, soon relinquished the sculptor to his love of the Arts. Sophie
Arnould made one of her witticisms on this subject. She confessed her
surprise, I believe, that her friend had managed to triumph over statuary.

Sarrasine left for Italy in 1758. During the journey, his vivid imagination caught fire beneath a brilliant sky and at the sight of the wonderful
monuments which are to be found in the birthplace of the Arts. He
admired the statues, the frescoes, the painting, and thus inspired, he came

to Rome, filled with desire to carve his name between Michelangelo's and
M. Bouchardon's. Accordingly, at the beginning, he divided his time
between studio tasks and examining the works of art in which Rome
abounds. He had already spent two weeks in the ecstatic state which
overwhelms young minds at the sight of the queen of ruins, when he
went one evening to the Teatro Argentina, before which a huge crowd
was assembled. He inquired as to the causes of this gathering and everyone answered with two names: Zambinella! Jomelli! He entered and took
a seat in the orchestra, squeezed between two notably fat *abbati*; however,
he was lucky enough to be fairly close to the stage. The curtain rose. For
the first time in his life, he heard that music whose delights M. Jean-
Jacques Rousseau had so eloquently praised to him at one of Baron
d'Holbach's evenings. The young sculptor's senses were, so to speak,
lubricated by the accents of Jomelli's sublime harmony. The languorous
novelties of these skillfully mingled Italian voices plunged him into a
delicious ecstasy. He remained speechless, motionless, not even feeling
crowded by the two priests. His soul passed into his ears and eyes. He
seemed to hear through every pore. Suddenly a burst of applause which
shook the house greeted the prima donna's entrance. She came coquettishly to the front of the stage and greeted the audience with infinite grace.
The lights, the general enthusiasm, the theatrical illusion, the glamour of
a style of dress which in those days was quite attractive, all conspired in
favor of this woman. Sarrasine cried out with pleasure.

At that instant he marveled at the ideal beauty he had hitherto sought
in life, seeking in one often unworthy model the roundness of a perfect
leg; in another, the curve of a breast; in another, white shoulders; finally
taking some girl's neck, some woman's hands, and some child's smooth
knees, without ever having encountered under the cold Parisian sky the
rich, sweet creations of ancient Greece. La Zambinella displayed to him,
united, living, and delicate, those exquisite female forms he so ardently
desired, of which a sculptor is at once the severest and the most passionate
judge. Her mouth was expressive, her eyes loving, her complexion dazzlingly white. And along with these details, which would have enraptured
a painter, were all the wonders of those images of Venus revered and
rendered by the chisels of the Greeks. The artist never wearied of admiring
the inimitable grace with which the arms were attached to the torso, the
marvelous roundness of the neck, the harmonious lines drawn by the
eyebrows, the nose, and the perfect oval of the face, the purity of its vivid
contours and the effect of the thick, curved lashes which lined her heavy
and voluptuous eyelids. This was more than a woman, this was a masterpiece! In this unhoped-for creation could be found a love to enrapture any
man, and beauties worthy of satisfying a critic. With his eyes, Sarrasine
devoured Pygmalion's statue, come down from its pedestal. When La
Zambinella sang, the effect was delirium. The artist felt cold; then he felt

a heat which suddenly began to prickle in the innermost depth of his being, in what we call the heart, for lack of any other word! He did not applaud, he said nothing, he experienced an impulse of madness, a kind of frenzy which overcomes us only when we are at the age when desire has something frightening and infernal about it. Sarrasine wanted to leap onto the stage and take possession of this woman: his strength, increased a hundredfold by a moral depression impossible to explain, since these phenomena occur in an area hidden from human observation, seemed to manifest itself with painful violence. Looking at him, one would have thought him a cold and senseless man. Fame, knowledge, future, existence, laurels, everything collapsed.

"To be loved by her, or die!" Such was the decree Sarrasine passed upon himself. He was so utterly intoxicated that he no longer saw the theater, the spectators, the actors, or heard the music. Moreover, the distance between himself and La Zambinella had ceased to exist, he possessed her, his eyes were riveted upon her, he took her for his own. An almost diabolical power enabled him to feel the breath of this voice, to smell the scented powder covering her hair, to see the planes of her face, to count the blue veins shadowing her satin skin. Last, this agile voice, fresh and silvery in timbre, supple as a thread shaped by the slightest breath of air, rolling and unrolling, cascading and scattering, this voice attacked his soul so vividly that several times he gave vent to involuntary cries torn from him by convulsive feelings of pleasure which are all too rarely vouchsafed by human passions. He was presently obliged to leave the theater. His trembling legs almost refused to support him. He was limp, weak as a sensitive man who has given way to overwhelming anger. He had experienced such pleasure, or perhaps he had suffered so keenly, that his life had drained away like water from a broken vase. He felt empty inside, a prostration similar to the debilitation that overcomes those convalescing from serious illness.

Overcome by an inexplicable sadness, he sat down on the steps of a church. There, leaning back against a pillar, he fell into a confused meditation, as in a dream. He had been smitten by passion. Upon returning to his lodgings, he fell into one of those frenzies of activity which disclose to us the presence of new elements in our lives. A prey to this first fever of love derived equally from both pleasure and pain, he tried to appease his impatience and his delirium by drawing La Zambinella from memory. It was a kind of embodied meditation. On one page, La Zambinella appeared in that apparently calm and cool pose favored by Raphael, Giorgione, and every great painter. On another, she was delicately turning her head after having finished a trill, and appeared to be listening to herself. Sarrasine sketched his mistress in every pose: he drew her unveiled, seated, standing, lying down, chaste or amorous, embodying through the delirium of his pencils every capricious notion that can enter our heads when we think intently about a mistress. However, his fevered thoughts went beyond drawing. He saw La Zambinella, spoke to her, beseeched her, he passed a thousand years of life and happiness with her by placing her in every imaginable position; in short, by sampling the future with her. On the following day, he sent his valet to rent a box next to the stage for the entire season. Then, like all young people with lusty souls, he exaggerated to himself the difficulties of his undertaking and first fed his passion with the pleasure of being able to admire his mistress without obstruction. This golden age of love, during which we take pleasure in our own feeling and in which we are happy almost by ourselves, was not destined to last long in Sarrasine's case. Nevertheless, events took him by surprise while he was still under the spell of this vernal hallucination, as naïve as it was voluptuous. In a week he lived a lifetime, spending the mornings kneading the clay by which he would copy La Zambinella, despite the veils, skirts, corsets, and ribbons which concealed her from him. In the evenings, installed in his box early, alone, lying on a sofa like a Turk under the influence of opium, he created for himself a pleasure as rich and varied as he wished it to be. First, he gradually familiarized himself with the overly vivid emotions his mistress's singing afforded him; he then trained his eyes to see her, and finally he could contemplate her without fearing an outburst of the wild frenzy which had seized him on the first day. As his passion became calmer, it grew deeper. For the rest, the unsociable sculptor did not allow his friends to intrude upon his solitude, which was peopled with images, adorned with fantasies of hope, and filled with happiness. His love was so strong, so naïve, that he experienced all the innocent scruples that assail us when we love for the first time. As he began to realize that he would soon have to act, to plot, to inquire where La Zambinella lived, whether she had a mother, uncle, teacher, family, to ponder, in short, on ways to see her, speak to her, these great, ambitious thoughts made his heart swell so painfully that he put them off until later, deriving as much satisfaction from his physical suffering as he did from his intellectual pleasures.

"But," Mme de Rochefide interrupted me, "I still don't see anything about either Marianina or her little old man."

"You are seeing nothing but him!" I cried impatiently, like an author who is being forced to spoil a theatrical effect.

For several days, I resumed after a pause, Sarrasine had reappeared so faithfully in his box and his eyes had expressed such love that his passion for La Zambinella's voice would have been common knowledge throughout Paris, had this adventure happened there; however, in Italy, madame, everyone goes to the theater for himself, with his own passions, and with a heartfelt interest which precludes spying through opera glasses. Nevertheless, the sculptor's enthusiasm did not escape the attention of the singers for long. One evening, the Frenchman saw that they were laughing at him in the wings. It is hard to know what extreme actions he might not have taken had La Zambinella not come onto the stage. She gave Sarrasine one of those eloquent glances which often reveal much more than women intend them to. This glance was a total revelation. Sarrasine was loved!

"If it's only a caprice," he thought, already accusing his mistress of excessive ardor, "she doesn't know what she is subjecting herself to. I am hoping her caprice will last my whole life."

At that moment, the artist's attention was distracted by three soft knocks on the door of his box. He opened it. An old woman entered with an air of mystery.

"Young man," she said, "if you want to be happy, be prudent. Put on a cape, wear a hat drawn down over your eyes; then, around ten in the evening, be in the Via del Corso in front of the Hotel di Spagna."

"I'll be there," he replied, placing two louis in the duenna's wrinkled hand.

He left his box after having given a signal to La Zambinella, who timidly lowered her heavy eyelids, like a woman pleased to be understood at last. Then he ran home to dress himself as seductively as he could. As he was leaving the theater, a strange man took his arm.

"Be on your guard, Frenchman," he whispered in his ear. "This is a matter of life and death. Cardinal Cicognara is her protector and doesn't trifle."

At that moment, had some demon set the pit of hell between Sarrasine and La Zambinella, he would have crossed it with one leap. Like the horses of the gods described by Homer, the sculptor's love had traversed vast distances in the twinkling of an eye.

"If death itself were waiting for me outside the house, I would go even faster," he replied.

"*Poverino!*" the stranger cried as he disappeared.

Speaking of danger to a lover is tantamount to selling him pleasures, is it not? Sarrasine's valet had never seen his master take so much care over his toilette. His finest sword, a gift from Bouchardon, the sash Clotilde had given him, his embroidered coat, his silver-brocade waistcoat, his gold snuffbox, his jeweled watches, were all taken from their coffers, and he adorned himself like a girl about to appear before her first love. At the appointed hour, drunk with love and seething with hope, Sarrasine, concealed in his cape, sped to the rendezvous the old woman had given him. The duenna was waiting for him.

"You took a long time," she said. "Come."

She led the Frenchman along several back streets and stopped before a rather handsome mansion. She knocked. The door opened. She led Sarrasine along a labyrinth of stairways, galleries, and rooms which were lit only by the feeble light of the moon, and soon came to a door through whose cracks gleamed bright lights and from behind which came the joyful sounds of several voices. When at a word from the old woman he was admitted to this mysterious room, Sarrasine was suddenly dazzled at finding himself in a salon as brilliantly lighted as it was sumptuously furnished, in the center of which stood a table laden with venerable bottles and flashing flagons sparkling with ruby facets. He recognized the singers from the theater, along with some charming women, all ready to begin an artists' orgy as soon as he was among them. Sarrasine suppressed a feeling of disappointment and put on a good face. He had expected a dim room, his mistress seated by the fire, some jealous person nearby, death and love, an exchange of confidences in low voices, heart to heart, dangerous kisses and faces so close that La Zambinella's hair would have caressed his forehead throbbing with desire, feverish with happiness.

"*Vive la folie!*" he cried. "*Signori e belle donne*, you will allow me to take my revenge later and to show you my gratitude for the way you have welcomed a poor sculptor."

Having been greeted warmly enough by most of those present, whom he knew by sight, he sought to approach the armchair on which La Zambinella was casually reclining. Ah! how his heart beat when he spied a delicate foot shod in one of those slippers which in those days, may I say, madame, gave women's feet such a coquettish and voluptuous look that I don't know how men were able to resist them. The well-fitting white stockings with green clocks, the short skirts, the slippers with pointed toes, and the high heels of Louis XV's reign may have contributed something to the demoralization of Europe and the clergy.

"Something?" the Marquise replied. "Have you read nothing?"

La Zambinella, I continued, smiling, had impudently crossed her legs and was gently swinging the upper one with a certain attractive indolence which suited her capricious sort of beauty. She had removed her costume and was wearing a bodice that accentuated her narrow waist and set off the satin panniers of her dress, which was embroidered with blue flowers. Her bosom, the treasures of which were concealed, in an excess of coquetry, by a covering of lace, was dazzlingly white. Her hair arranged something like that of Mme du Barry, her face, though it was partially hidden under a full bonnet, appeared only the more delicate, and powder suited her. To see her thus was to adore her. She gave the sculptor a graceful smile. Unhappy at not being able to speak to her without witnesses present, Sarrasine politely sat down next to her and talked about music, praising her extraordinary talent; but his voice trembled with love, with fear and hope.

"What are you afraid of?" asked Vitagliani, the company's most famous singer. "Go ahead; you need fear no rivals here." Having said this, the tenor smiled without another word. This smile was repeated on the lips of all the guests, whose attention contained a hidden malice a lover would not have noticed. Such openness was like a dagger thrust in Sarrasine's heart. Although endowed with a certain strength of character, and although nothing could change his love, it had perhaps not yet occurred to him that La Zambinella was virtually a courtesan, and that he could not have both the pure pleasures that make a young girl's love so delicious and the tempestuous transports by which the hazardous possession of an actress must be purchased. He reflected and resigned himself. Supper was served. Sarrasine and La Zambinella sat down informally side by side. For the first half of the meal, the artists preserved some decorum, and the sculptor was able to chat with the singer. He found her witty, acute, but astonishingly ignorant, and she revealed herself to be weak and superstitious. The delicacy of her organs was reflected in her understanding. When Vitagliani uncorked the first bottle of champagne, Sarrasine read in his companion's eyes a start of terror at the tiny explosion caused by the escaping gas. The love-stricken artist interpreted the involuntary shudder of this feminine constitution as the sign of an excessive sensitivity. The Frenchman was charmed by this weakness. How much is protective in a man's love!

"My strength your shield!" Is this not written at the heart of all declarations of love? Too excited to shower the beautiful Italian with compliments, Sarrasine, like all lovers, was by turns serious, laughing, or reflective. Although he seemed to be listening to the other guests, he did not hear a word they were saying, so absorbed was he in the pleasure of finding himself beside her, touching her hand as he served her. He bathed in a secret joy. Despite the eloquence of a few mutual glances, he was astonished at the reserve La Zambinella maintained toward him. Indeed, she had begun by pressing his foot and teasing him with the flirtatiousness of a woman in love and free to show it; but she suddenly wrapped herself in the modesty of a young girl, after hearing Sarrasine describe a trait which revealed the excessive violence of his character. When the supper became an orgy, the guests broke into song under the influence of the Peralta and the Pedro-Ximenes. There were ravishing duets, songs from Calabria, Spanish seguidillas, Neapolitan canzonettas. Intoxication was in every eye, in the music, in hearts and voices alike. Suddenly an enchanting vivacity welled up, a gay abandon, an Italian warmth of feeling inconceivable to those acquainted only with Parisian gatherings, London routs, or Viennese circles. Jokes and words of love flew like bullets in a battle through laughter, profanities, and invocations to the Holy Virgin or *il Bambino*. Someone lay down on a sofa and fell asleep. A girl was listening to a declaration of love unaware that she was spilling sherry on the tablecloth. In the midst of this disorder, La Zambinella remained thoughtful, as though terrorstruck. She refused to drink, perhaps she ate a bit too much; however, it is said that greediness in a woman is a charming quality. Admiring his mistress's modesty, Sarrasine thought seriously about the future.

"She probably wants to be married," he thought. He then turned his thoughts to the delights of this marriage. His whole life seemed too short to exhaust the springs of happiness he found in the depths of his soul. Vitagliani, who was sitting next to him, refilled his glass so often that, toward three in the morning, without being totally drunk, Sarrasine could no longer control his delirium. Impetuously, he picked up the woman, escaping into a kind of boudoir next to the salon, toward the door of which he had glanced more than once. The Italian woman was armed with a dagger.

"If you come any closer," she said, "I will be forced to plunge this weapon into your heart. Let me go! You would despise me. I have conceived too much respect for your character to surrender in this fashion. I don't want to betray the feeling you have for me."

"Oh no!" cried Sarrasine. "You cannot stifle a passion by stimulating it! Are you already so corrupt that, old in heart, you would act like a young courtesan who whets the emotions by which she plies her trade?"

"But today is Friday," she replied, frightened at the Frenchman's violence.

Sarrasine, who was not devout, broke into laughter. La Zambinella jumped up like a young deer and ran toward the salon. When Sarrasine appeared in her pursuit, he was greeted by an infernal burst of laughter.

He saw La Zambinella lying in a swoon upon a sofa. She was pale and drained by the extraordinary effort she had just made. Although Sarrasine knew little Italian, he heard his mistress saying in a low voice to Vitagliani: "But he will kill me!"

The sculptor was utterly confounded by this strange scene. He regained his senses. At first he stood motionless; then he found his voice, sat down next to his mistress, and assured her of his respect. He was able to divert his passion by addressing the most high-minded phrases to this woman; and in depicting his love, he used all the resources of that magical eloquence, that inspired intermediary which women rarely refuse to believe. When the guests were surprised by the first gleams of morning light, a woman suggested they go to Frascati. Everyone enthusiastically fell in with the idea of spending the day at the Villa Ludovisi. Vitagliani went down to hire some carriages. Sarrasine had the pleasure of leading La Zambinella to a phaeton. Once outside Rome, the gaiety which had been momentarily repressed by each person's battle with sleepiness suddenly revived. Men and women alike seemed used to this strange life, these ceaseless pleasures, this artist's impulsiveness which turns life into a perpetual party at which one laughed unreservedly. The sculptor's companion was the only one who seemed downcast.

"Are you ill?" Sarrasine asked her. "Would you rather go home?"

"I'm not strong enough to stand all these excesses," she replied. "I must be very careful; but with you I feel so well! Had it not been for you, I would never have stayed for supper; a sleepless night and I lose whatever bloom I have."

"You are so delicate," Sarrasine said, looking at the charming creature's pretty face.

"Orgies ruin the voice."

"Now that we're alone," the artist cried, "and you no longer need fear the outbursts of my passion, tell me that you love me."

"Why?" she replied. "What would be the use? I seemed pretty to you. But you are French and your feelings will pass. Ah, you would not love me as I long to be loved."

"How can you say that?"

"Not to satisfy any vulgar passion; purely. I abhor men perhaps even more than I hate women. I need to seek refuge in friendship. For me, the world is a desert. I am an accursed creature, condemned to understand happiness, to feel it, to desire it, and, like many others, forced to see it flee from me continually. Remember, sir, that I will not have deceived you. I forbid you to love me. I can be your devoted friend, for I admire your strength and your character. I need a brother, a protector. Be all that for me, but no more."

"Not love you!" Sarrasine cried. "But my dearest angel, you are my life, my happiness!"

"If I were to say one word, you would repulse me with horror."

"Coquette! Nothing can frighten me. Tell me you will cost my future, that I will die in two months, that I will be damned merely for having kissed you."

He kissed her, despite La Zambinella's efforts to resist this passionate embrace.

"Tell me you are a devil, that you want my money, my name, all my fame! Do you want me to give up being a sculptor? Tell me."

"And if I were not a woman?" La Zambinella asked in a soft silvery voice.

"What a joke!" Sarrasine cried. "Do you think you can deceive an artist's eye? Haven't I spent ten days devouring, scrutinizing, admiring your perfection? Only a woman could have this round, soft arm, these elegant curves. Oh, you want compliments."

She smiled at him sadly, and raising her eyes heavenward, she murmured: "Fatal beauty!"

At that moment her gaze had an indescribable expression of horror, so powerful and vivid that Sarrasine shuddered.

"Frenchman," she went on, "forget this moment of madness forever. I respect you, but as for love, do not ask it of me; that feeling is smothered in my heart. I have no heart!" she cried, weeping. "The stage where you saw me, that applause, that music, that fame I am condemned to, such is my life, I have no other. In a few hours you will not see me in the same way, the woman you love will be dead."

The sculptor made no reply. He was overcome with a dumb rage which oppressed his heart. He could only gaze with enflamed, burning eyes at this extraordinary woman. La Zambinella's weak voice, her manner, her movements and gestures marked with sorrow, melancholy, and discouragement, awakened all the wealth of passion in his soul. Each word was a goad. At that moment they reached Frascati. As the artist offered his mistress his arm to assist her in alighting, he felt her shiver.

"What is wrong? You would kill me," he cried, seeing her grow pale, "if I were even an innocent cause of your slightest unhappiness."

"A snake," she said, pointing to a grass snake which was sliding along a ditch. "I am afraid of those horrid creatures." Sarrasine crushed the snake's head with his heel.

"How can you be so brave?" La Zambinella continued, looking with visible horror at the dead reptile.

"Ah," the artist replied, smiling, "now do you dare deny you are a woman?"

They rejoined their companions and strolled through the woods of the Villa Ludovisi, which in those days belonged to Cardinal Cicognara. That morning fled too quickly for the enamored sculptor, but it was filled with a host of incidents which revealed to him the coquetry, the weakness, and the delicacy of this soft and enervated being. This was woman herself, with her sudden fears, her irrational whims, her instinctive worries, her impetuous boldness, her fussings, and her delicious sensibility. It happened that as they were wandering in the open countryside, the little group of merry singers saw in the distance some heavily armed men whose manner of dress was far from reassuring. Someone said, "They must be highwaymen," and everyone quickened his pace toward the refuge of the Cardinal's grounds. At this critical moment, Sarrasine saw from La Zambinella's pallor that she no longer had the strength to walk; he took her up in his arms and carried her for a while, running. When he came to a nearby arbor, he put her down.

"Explain to me," he said, "how this extreme weakness, which I would find hideous in any other woman, which would displease me and whose slightest indication would be almost enough to choke my love, pleases and charms me in you? Ah, how I love you," he went on. "All your faults, your terrors, your resentments, add an indefinable grace to your soul. I think I would detest a strong woman, a Sappho, a courageous creature, full of energy and passion. Oh, soft, frail creature, how could you be otherwise? That angelic voice, that delicate voice would be an anomaly coming from any body but yours."

"I cannot give you any hope," she said. "Stop speaking to me in this way, because they will make a fool of you. I cannot stop you from coming to the theater; but if you love me or if you are wise, you will come there no more. Listen, monsieur," she said in a low voice.

"Oh, be still," the impassioned artist said. "Obstacles make my love more ardent."

La Zambinella's graceful and modest attitude did not change, but she fell silent as though a terrible thought had revealed some misfortune to her. When it came time to return to Rome, she got into the four-seated coach, ordering the sculptor with imperious cruelty to return to Rome alone in the carriage. During the journey, Sarrasine resolved to kidnap La Zambinella. He spent the entire day making plans, each more outrageous than the other. At nightfall, as he was going out to inquire where his mistress's palazzo was located, he met one of his friends on the threshold.

"My dear fellow," he said, "our ambassador has asked me to invite you to his house tonight. He is giving a magnificent concert, and when I tell you that Zambinella will be there . . ."

"Zambinella," cried Sarrasine, intoxicated by the name, "I'm mad about her!"

"You're like everyone else," his friend replied.

"If you are my friends, you, Vien, Lauterbourg, and Allegrain, will you help me do something after the party?" Sarrasine asked.

"It's not some cardinal to be killed? . . . not . . .?"

"No, no," Sarrasine said, "I'm not asking you to do anything an honest person couldn't do."

In a short time, the sculptor had arranged everything for the success of his undertaking. He was one of the last to arrive at the ambassador's but he had come in a traveling carriage drawn by powerful horses and driven by one of the most enterprising *vetturini* of Rome. The ambassador's palazzo was crowded; not without some difficulty, the sculptor, who was a stranger to everyone present, made his way to the salon where Zambinella was singing at that very moment.

"Is it out of consideration for the cardinals, bishops, and abbés present," Sarrasine asked, "that she is dressed like a man, that she is wearing a snood, kinky hair, and a sword?"

"She? What she?" asked the old nobleman to whom Sarrasine had been speaking. "La Zambinella." "La Zambinella!" the Roman prince replied. "Are you joking? Where are you from? Has there ever been a woman on the Roman stage? And don't you know about the creatures who sing female roles in the Papal States? I am the one, monsieur, who gave Zambinella his voice. I paid for everything that scamp ever had, even his singing teacher. Well, he has so little gratitude for the service I rendered him that he has never consented to set foot in my house. And yet, if he makes a fortune, he will owe it all to me."

Prince Chigi may well have gone on talking for some time; Sarrasine was not listening to him. A horrid truth had crept into his soul. It was as though he had been struck by lightning. He stood motionless, his eyes fixed on the false singer. His fiery gaze exerted a sort of magnetic influence on Zambinella, for the *musico* finally turned to look at Sarrasine, and at that moment his heavenly voice faltered. He trembled! An involuntary murmur escaping from the audience he had kept hanging on his lips completed his discomfiture; he sat down and cut short his aria. Cardinal Cicognara, who had glanced out the corner of his eye to see what had attracted his protégé's attention, then saw the Frenchman: he leaned over to one of his ecclesiastical aides-de-camp and appeared to be asking the sculptor's name. Having obtained the answer he sought, he regarded the artist with great attention and gave an order to an abbé, who quickly disappeared.

During this time, Zambinella, having recovered himself, once more began the piece he had so capriciously interrupted; but he sang it badly, and despite all the requests made to him, he refused to sing anything else. This was the first time he displayed that capricious tyranny for which he would later be as celebrated as for his talent and his vast fortune, due, as they said, no less to his voice than to his beauty.

"It is a woman," Sarrasine said, believing himself alone. "There is some hidden intrigue here. Cardinal Cicognara is deceiving the Pope and the whole city of Rome!"

The sculptor thereupon left the salon, gathered his friends together, and posted them out of sight in the courtyard of the palazzo. When Zambinella was confident that Sarrasine had departed, he appeared to regain his composure. Around midnight, having wandered through the rooms like a man seeking some enemy, the *musico* departed. As soon as he crossed the threshold of the palazzo, he was adroitly seized by men who gagged him with a handkerchief and drew him into the carriage Sarrasine had hired. Frozen with horror, Zambinella remained in a corner, not daring to move. He saw before him the terrible face of the artist, who was silent as death.

The journey was brief. Carried in Sarrasine's arms, Zambinella soon found himself in a dark, empty studio. Half dead, the singer remained in a chair, without daring to examine the statue of a woman in which he recognized his own features. He made no attempt to speak, but his teeth chattered. Sarrasine paced up and down the room. Suddenly he stopped in front of Zambinella.

"Tell me the truth," he pleaded in a low, altered voice. "You are a woman? Cardinal Cicognara . . ."

Zambinella fell to his knees, and in reply lowered his head.

"Ah, you are a woman," the artist cried in a delirium, "for even a . . ." He broke off. "No," he continued, "he would not be so cowardly."

"Ah, do not kill me," cried Zambinella, bursting into tears. "I only agreed to trick you to please my friends, who wanted to laugh."

"Laugh!" the sculptor replied in an infernal tone. "Laugh! Laugh! You dared play with a man's feelings, you?"

"Oh, have mercy!" Zambinella replied.

"I ought to kill you," Sarrasine cried, drawing his sword with a violent gesture. "However," he went on, in cold disdain, "were I to scour your body with this blade, would I find there one feeling to stifle, one vengeance to satisfy? You are nothing. If you were a man or a woman, I would kill you, but . . ."

Sarrasine made a gesture of disgust which forced him to turn away, whereupon he saw the statue.

"And it's an illusion," he cried. Then, turning to Zambinella: "A woman's heart was a refuge for me, a home. Have you any sisters who resemble you? Then die! But no, you shall live. Isn't leaving you alive condemning you to something worse than death? It is neither my blood nor my existence that I regret, but the future and my heart's fortune. Your feeble hand has destroyed my happiness. What hope can I strip from you for all those you have blighted? You have dragged me down to your level. *To love, to be loved!* are henceforth meaningless words for me, as they are for you. I shall forever think of this imaginary woman when I see a real woman." He indicated the statue with a gesture of despair. "I shall always have the memory of a celestial harpy who thrusts its talons into all my manly feelings, and who will stamp all other women with a seal of imperfection! Monster! You who can give life to nothing. For me, you have wiped women from the earth."

Sarrasine sat down before the terrified singer. Two huge tears welled from his dry eyes, rolled down his manly cheeks, and fell to the ground: two tears of rage, two bitter and burning tears.

"No more love! I am dead to all pleasure, to every human emotion."

So saying, he seized a hammer and hurled it at the statue with such extraordinary force that he missed it. He thought he had destroyed this monument to his folly, and then took up his sword and brandished it to kill the singer. Zambinella uttered piercing screams. At that moment, three men entered and at once the sculptor fell, stabbed by three stiletto thrusts.

"On behalf of Cardinal Cicognara," one of them said.

"It is a good deed worthy of a Christian," replied the Frenchman as he died. These sinister messengers informed Zambinella of the concern of his protector, who was waiting at the door in a closed carriage, to take him away as soon as he had been rescued.

"But," Mme de Rochefide asked me, "what connection is there between this story and the little old man we saw at the Lantys'?"

"Madame, Cardinal Cicognara took possession of Zambinella's statue and had it executed in marble; today it is in the Albani Museum. There, in 1791, the Lanty family found it and asked Vien to copy it. The portrait in which you saw Zambinella at twenty, a second after having seen him at one hundred, later served for Girodet's *Endymion*; you will have recognized its type in the Adonis."

"But this Zambinella—he or she?"

"He, madame, is none other than Marianina's great-uncle. Now you can readily see what interest Mme de Lanty has in hiding the source of a fortune which comes from—"

"Enough!" she said, gesturing to me imperiously. We sat for a moment plunged in the deepest silence.

"Well?" I said to her.

"Ah," she exclaimed, standing up and pacing up and down the room. She looked at me and spoke in an altered voice. "You have given me a disgust for life and for passions that will last a long time. Excepting for monsters, don't all human feelings come down to the same thing, to horrible disappointments? Mothers, our children kill us either by their bad behavior or by their lack of affection. Wives, we are deceived. Mistresses, we are forsaken, abandoned. Does friendship even exist? I would become a nun tomorrow did I not know that I can remain unmoved as a rock amid the storms of life. If the Christian's future is also an illusion, at least it is not destroyed until after death. Leave me."

"Ah," I said, "you know how to punish."

"Am I wrong?

"Yes," I replied, with a kind of courage. "In telling this story, which is fairly well known in Italy, I have been able to give you a fine example of the progress made by civilization today. They no longer create these unfortunate creatures."

"Paris is a very hospitable place," she said. "It accepts everything, shameful fortunes and bloodstained fortunes. Crime and infamy can find asylum here; only virtue has no altars here. Yes, pure souls have their home in heaven! No one will have known me. I am proud of that!"

And the Marquise remained pensive.

NATHANIEL HAWTHORNE

(1804–1864)

*N*athaniel Hawthorne was born on July 4 in Salem, Massachusetts, a town inhabited by his Puritan ancestors since early colonial times. He was an indifferent student at Bowdoin College, but he made a number of friends (future president Franklin Pierce, Longfellow) and read widely in eighteenth-century fiction. He returned to Salem in 1825, where he lived in semi-seclusion with his mother and sisters for twelve years. Though Hawthorne liked to emphasize the hermit-like aspects of this period of his life, we know now that he socialized with a number of people and travelled extensively. But the years did serve as an important apprenticeship, and he produced some of his most memorable fiction during this early stage of his career. He had great trouble finding a publisher willing to take a chance on a collection of his stories, but with the help of a friend from college Twice-Told Tales was published in 1836. A happy marriage distracted him from writing for a time, but when he suddenly lost his government job, he settled down to write The Scarlet Letter (1850), which became an American classic, with The House of the Seven Gables following in 1851. In 1853, President Pierce appointed him American consul in Liverpool. His duties and his travels prevented him from writing much fiction. The Marble Faun (1860) won him general acclaim again, but his attempts at other romances were left unfinished, partly because of his failing creative energies, partly because the Civil War had changed the public's taste in literature. The psychological insights in Hawthorne's fiction reveal his fascination with the secrets people try to keep hidden: sin and its corrupting effects, guilt and the way it colours one's view of the world, and the possibility of redemption. His fiction takes readers into that border region where, as in a room lit by moonlight, all the details "seem to lose their actual substance, and are so spiritualized by the universal light, that they become things of intellect. . . . Thus, therefore, the floor of our familiar room has become a neutral territory, somewhere between the real world and fairy-land, where the Actual and the Imaginary may meet, and each imbue itself with the nature of the other."

The Birthmark

I n the latter part of the last century there lived a man of science, an eminent proficient in every branch of natural philosophy, who not long before our story opens had made experience of a spiritual affinity more attractive than any chemical one. He had left his laboratory to the care of an assistant, cleared his fine countenance from the furnace smoke, washed the stain of acids from his fingers, and persuaded a beautiful woman to become his wife. In those days, when the comparatively recent discovery of electricity and other kindred mysteries of Nature seemed to open paths into the region of miracle, it was not unusual for the love of science to rival the love of woman in its depth and absorbing energy. The higher intellect, the imagination, the spirit, and even the heart might all find their congenial aliment in pursuits which, as some of their ardent votaries believed, would ascend from one step of powerful intelligence to another, until the philosopher should lay his hand on the secret of creative force and perhaps make new worlds for himself. We know not whether Aylmer possessed this degree of faith in man's ultimate control over Nature. He had devoted himself, however, too unreservedly to scientific studies ever to be weaned from them by any second passion. His love for his young wife might prove the stronger of the two; but it could only be by intertwining itself with his love of science and uniting the strength of the latter to his own.

Such a union accordingly took place, and was attended with truly remarkable consequences and a deeply impressive moral. One day, very soon after their marriage, Aylmer sat gazing at his wife with a trouble in his countenance that grew stronger until he spoke.

"Georgiana," said he, "has it never occurred to you that the mark upon your cheek might be removed?"

"No, indeed," said she, smiling; but, perceiving the seriousness of his manner, she blushed deeply. "To tell you the truth, it has been so often called a charm that I was simple enough to imagine it might be so."

"Ah, upon another face perhaps it might," replied her husband; "but never on yours. No, dearest Georgiana, you came so nearly perfect from the hand of Nature that this slightest possible defect, which we hesitate whether to term a defect or a beauty, shocks me, as being the visible mark of earthly imperfection."

"Shocks you, my husband!" cried Georgiana, deeply hurt, at first reddening with momentary anger, but then bursting into tears. "Then why did you take me from my mother's side? You cannot love what shocks you!"

To explain this conversation, it must be mentioned that in the centre of Georgiana's left cheek there was a singular mark, deeply interwoven, as it were, with the texture and substance of her face. In the usual state of her complexion—a healthy though delicate bloom—the mark wore a tint of deeper crimson, which imperfectly defined its shape amid the surrounding rosiness. When she blushed it gradually became more indistinct, and finally vanished amid the triumphant rush of blood that bathed the whole cheek with its brilliant glow. But if any shifting motion caused her to turn pale there was the mark again, a crimson stain upon the snow, in what Aylmer sometimes deemed an almost fearful distinctness. Its shape bore not a little similarity to the human hand, though of the smallest pygmy size. Georgiana's lovers were wont to say that some fairy at her birth hour had laid her tiny hand upon the infant's cheek, and left this impress there in token of the magic endowments that were to give her such sway over all hearts. Many a desperate swain would have risked life for the privilege of pressing his lips to the mysterious hand. It must not be concealed, however, that the impression wrought by this fairy sign manual varied exceedingly according to the difference of temperament in the beholders. Some fastidious persons—but they were exclusively of her own sex—affirmed that the bloody hand, as they chose to call it, quite destroyed the effect of Georgiana's beauty and rendered her countenance even hideous. But it would be as reasonable to say that one of those small blue stains which sometimes occur in the purest statuary marble would convert the Eve of Powers to a monster. Masculine observers, if the birthmark did not heighten their admiration, contented themselves with wishing it away, that the world might possess one living specimen of ideal loveliness without the semblance of a flaw. After his marriage,—for he thought little or nothing of the matter before,—Aylmer discovered that this was the case with himself.

Had she been less beautiful,—if Envy's self could have found aught else to sneer at,—he might have felt his affection heightened by the prettiness of this mimic hand, now vaguely portrayed, now lost, now stealing forth again and glimmering to and fro with every pulse of emotion that throbbed within her heart; but, seeing her otherwise so perfect, he found this one defect grow more and more intolerable with every moment of their united lives. It was the fatal flaw of humanity which Nature, in one shape or another, stamps ineffaceably on all her productions, either to imply that they are temporary and finite, or that their perfection must be wrought by toil and pain. The crimson hand expressed the ineludible gripe in which mortality clutches the highest and purest of earthly mould, degrading them into kindred with the lowest, and even with the very brutes, like whom their visible frames return to dust. In this manner, selecting it as the symbol of his wife's liability to sin, sorrow, decay, and death, Aylmer's sombre imagination was not long in rendering the birthmark a frightful object, causing him more trouble and horror than ever Georgiana's beauty, whether of soul or sense, had given him delight.

At all the seasons which should have been their happiest he invariably, and without intending it, nay, in spite of a purpose to the contrary, reverted to this one disastrous topic. Trifling as it at first appeared, it so connected itself with innumerable trains of thought and modes of feeling that it became the central point of all. With the morning twilight Aylmer opened his eyes upon his wife's face and recognized the symbol of imperfection; and when they sat together at the evening hearth his eyes wandered stealthily to her cheek, and beheld, flickering with the blaze of the wood fire, the spectral hand that wrote mortality where he would fain have worshipped. Georgiana soon learned to shudder at his gaze. It needed but a glance with the peculiar expression that his face often wore to change the roses of her cheek into a deathlike paleness, amid which the crimson hand was brought strongly out, like a bas-relief of ruby on the whitest marble.

Late one night, when the lights were growing dim so as hardly to betray the stain on the poor wife's cheek, she herself, for the first time, voluntarily took up the subject.

"Do you remember, my dear Aylmer," said she, with a feeble attempt at a smile, "have you any recollection, of a dream last night about this odious hand?"

"None! none whatever!" replied Aylmer, starting, but then he added, in a dry, cold tone, affected for the sake of concealing the real depth of his emotion, "I might well dream of it; for, before I fell asleep, it had taken a pretty firm hold of my fancy."

"And you did dream of it?" continued Georgiana, hastily; for she dreaded lest a gush of tears should interrupt what she had to say. "A terrible dream! I wonder that you can forget it. Is it possible to forget this one expression?—'It is in her heart now; we must have it out!' Reflect, my husband; for by all means I would have you recall that dream."

The mind is in a sad state when Sleep, the all-involving, cannot confine her spectres within the dim region of her sway, but suffers them to break forth, affrighting this actual life with secrets that perchance belong to a deeper one. Aylmer now remembered his dream. He had fancied himself with his servant Aminadab, attempting an operation for the removal of the birthmark; but the deeper went the knife, the deeper sank the hand, until at length its tiny grasp appeared to have caught hold of Georgiana's heart; whence, however, her husband was inexorably resolved to cut or wrench it away.

When the dream had shaped itself perfectly in his memory Aylmer sat in his wife's presence with a guilty feeling. Truth often finds its way to the mind close muffled in robes of sleep, and then speaks with uncompromising directness of matters in regard to which we practise an unconscious self-deception during our waking moments. Until now he had not been aware of the tyrannizing influence acquired by one idea over his mind, and of the lengths which he might find in his heart to go for the sake of giving himself peace.

"Aylmer," resumed Georgiana, solemnly, "I know not what may be the cost to both of us to rid me of this fatal birthmark. Perhaps its removal may cause cureless deformity; or it may be the stain goes as deep as life itself. Again: do we know that there is a possibility, on any terms, of unclasping the firm gripe of this little hand which was laid upon me before I came into the world?"

"Dearest Georgiana, I have spent much thought upon the subject," hastily interrupted Aylmer. "I am convinced of the perfect practicability of its removal."

"If there be the remotest possibility of it," continued Georgiana, "let the attempt be made, at whatever risk. Danger is nothing to me; for life, while this hateful mark makes me the object of your horror and disgust,— life is a burden which I would fling down with joy. Either remove this dreadful hand, or take my wretched life! You have deep science. All the world bears witness of it. You have achieved great wonders. Cannot you remove this little, little mark, which I cover with the tips of two small fingers? Is this beyond your power, for the sake of your own peace, and to save your poor wife from madness?"

"Noblest, dearest, tenderest wife," cried Aylmer, rapturously, "doubt not my power. I have already given this matter the deepest thought— thought which might almost have enlightened me to create a being less perfect than yourself. Georgiana, you have led me deeper than ever into the heart of science. I feel myself fully competent to render this dear cheek as faultless as its fellow; and then, most beloved, what will be my triumph when I shall have corrected what Nature left imperfect in her fairest work! Even Pygmalion, when his sculptured woman assumed life, felt not greater ecstasy than mine will be."

"It is resolved, then," said Georgiana, faintly smiling. "And, Aylmer, spare me not, though you should find the birthmark take refuge in my heart at last."

Her husband tenderly kissed her cheek—her right cheek—not that which bore the impress of the crimson hand.

The next day Aylmer apprised his wife of a plan that he had formed whereby he might have opportunity for the intense thought and constant watchfulness which the proposed operation would require; while Georgiana, likewise, would enjoy the perfect repose essential to its success. They were to seclude themselves in the extensive apartments occupied by Aylmer as a laboratory, and where, during his toilsome youth, he had made discoveries in the elemental powers of Nature that had roused the admiration of all the learned societies in Europe. Seated calmly in this laboratory, the pale philosopher had investigated the secrets of the highest cloud region and of the profoundest mines; he had satisfied himself of the causes that kindled and kept alive the fires of the volcano; and had explained the mystery of fountains, and how it is that they gush forth, some so bright and pure, and others with such rich medicinal virtues, from the dark bosom of the earth. Here, too, at an earlier period, he had studied the wonders of the human frame, and attempted to fathom the very process by which Nature assimilates all her precious influences from earth and air, and from the spiritual world, to create and foster man, her masterpiece. The latter pursuit, however, Aylmer had long laid aside in unwilling recognition of the truth—against which all seekers sooner or later stumble—that our great creative Mother, while she amuses us with apparently working in the broadest sunshine, is yet severely careful to keep her own secrets, and, in spite of her pretended openness, shows us nothing but results. She permits us, indeed, to mar, but seldom to mend, and, like a jealous patentee, on no account to make. Now, however, Aylmer resumed these half-forgotten investigations; not, of course, with such hopes or wishes as first suggested them; but because they involved much physiological truth and lay in the path of his proposed scheme for the treatment of Georgiana.

As he led her over the threshold of the laboratory, Georgiana was cold and tremulous. Aylmer looked cheerfully into her face, with intent to reassure her, but was so startled with the intense glow of the birthmark upon the whiteness of her cheek that he could not restrain a strong convulsive shudder. His wife fainted.

"Aminadab! Aminadab!" shouted Aylmer, stamping violently on the floor.

Forthwith there issued from an inner apartment a man of low stature, but bulky frame, with shaggy hair hanging about his visage, which was grimed with the vapors of the furnace. This personage had been Aylmer's underworker during his whole scientific career, and was admirably fitted for that office by his great mechanical readiness, and the skill with which, while incapable of comprehending a single principle, he executed all the details of his master's experiments. With his vast strength, his shaggy hair, his smoky aspect, and the indescribable earthiness that incrusted him, he seemed to represent man's physical nature; while Aylmer's slender figure, and pale, intellectual face, were no less apt a type of the spiritual element.

"Throw open the door of the boudoir, Aminadab," said Aylmer, "and burn a pastil."

"Yes, master," answered Aminadab, looking intently at the lifeless form of Georgiana; and then he muttered to himself, "If she were my wife, I'd never part with that birthmark."

When Georgiana recovered consciousness she found herself breathing an atmosphere of penetrating fragrance, the gentle potency of which had recalled her from her deathlike faintness. The scene around her looked like enchantment. Aylmer had converted those smoky, dingy, sombre rooms, where he had spent his brightest years in recondite pursuits, into a series of beautiful apartments not unfit to be the secluded abode of a lovely woman. The walls were hung with gorgeous curtains, which imparted the combination of grandeur and grace that no other species of adornment can achieve; and, as they fell from the ceiling to the floor, their rich and ponderous folds, concealing all angles and straight lines, appeared to shut in the scene from infinite space. For aught Georgiana knew, it might be a pavilion among the clouds. And Aylmer, excluding the sunshine, which would have interfered with his chemical processes, had supplied its place with perfumed lamps, emitting flames of various hue, but all uniting in a soft, impurpled radiance. He now knelt by his wife's side, watching her earnestly, but without alarm, for he was confident in his science, and felt that he could draw a magic circle round her within which no evil might intrude.

"Where am I? Ah, I remember," said Georgiana, faintly; and she placed her hand over her cheek to hide the terrible mark from her husband's eyes.

"Fear not, dearest!" exclaimed he. "Do not shrink from me! Believe me, Georgiana, I even rejoice in this single imperfection, since it will be such a rapture to remove it."

"O, spare me!" sadly replied his wife. "Pray do not look at it again. I never can forget that convulsive shudder."

In order to soothe Georgiana, and, as it were, to release her mind from the burden of actual things, Aylmer now put in practice some of the light and playful secrets which science had taught him among its profounder lore. Airy figures, absolutely bodiless ideas, and forms of unsubstantial beauty came and danced before her, imprinting their momentary footsteps on beams of light. Though she had some indistinct idea of the method of these optical phenomena, still the illusion was almost perfect enough to warrant the belief that her husband possessed sway over the spiritual world. Then again, when she felt a wish to look forth from her seclusion, immediately, as if her thoughts were answered, the procession of external existence flitted across a screen. The scenery and the figures of actual life were perfectly represented, but with that bewitching, yet indescribable difference which always makes a picture, an image, or a shadow so much more attractive than the original. When wearied of this, Aylmer bade her cast her eyes upon a vessel containing a quantity of earth. She did so, with little interest at first; but was soon startled to perceive the germ of a plant shooting upward from the soil. Then came the slender stalk; the leaves gradually unfolded themselves; and amid them was a perfect and lovely flower.

"It is magical!" cried Georgiana. "I dare not touch it."

"Nay, pluck it," answered Aylmer,—"pluck it, and inhale its brief perfume while you may. The flower will wither in a few moments and leave nothing save its brown seed vessels; but thence may be perpetuated a race as ephemeral as itself."

But Georgiana had no sooner touched the flower than the whole plant suffered a blight, its leaves turning coal-black as if by the agency of fire.

"There was too powerful a stimulus," said Aylmer, thoughtfully.

To make up for this abortive experiment, he proposed to take her portrait by a scientific process of his own invention. It was to be effected by rays of light striking upon a polished plate of metal. Georgiana assented; but, on looking at the result, was affrighted to find the features of the portrait blurred and indefinable; while the minute figure of a hand appeared where the cheek should have been. Aylmer snatched the metallic plate and threw it into a jar of corrosive acid.

Soon, however, he forgot these mortifying failures. In the intervals of study and chemical experiment he came to her flushed and exhausted, but seemed invigorated by her presence, and spoke in glowing language of the resources of his art. He gave a history of the long dynasty of the alchemists, who spent so many ages in quest of the universal solvent by which the golden principle might be elicited from all things vile and base. Aylmer appeared to believe that, by the plainest scientific logic, it was altogether within the limits of possibility to discover this long-sought medium; "but," he added, "a philosopher who should go deep enough to acquire the power would attain too lofty a wisdom to stoop to the exercise of it." Not less singular were his opinions in regard to the elixir vitae. He more than intimated that it was at his option to concoct a liquid that should prolong life for years, perhaps interminably; but that it would produce a discord in Nature which all the world, and chiefly the quaffer of the immortal nostrum, would find cause to curse.

"Aylmer, are you in earnest?" asked Georgiana, looking at him with amazement and fear. "It is terrible to possess such power, or even to dream of possessing it."

"O, do not tremble, my love," said her husband. "I would not wrong either you or myself by working such inharmonious effects upon our lives; but I would have you consider how trifling, in comparison, is the skill requisite to remove this little hand."

At the mention of the birthmark, Georgiana, as usual, shrank as if a redhot iron had touched her cheek.

Again Aylmer applied himself to his labors. She could hear his voice in the distant furnace room giving directions to Aminadab, whose harsh, uncouth, misshapen tones were audible in response, more like the grunt or growl of a brute than human speech. After hours of absence, Aylmer reappeared and proposed that she should now examine his cabinet of chemical products and natural treasures of the earth. Among the former he showed her a small vial, in which, he remarked, was contained a gentle yet most powerful fragrance, capable of impregnating all the breezes that blow across a kingdom. They were of inestimable value, the contents of that little vial; and, as he said so, he threw some of the perfume into the air and filled the room with piercing and invigorating delight.

"And what is this?" asked Georgiana, pointing to a small crystal globe containing a gold-colored liquid, "It is so beautiful to the eye that I could imagine it the elixir of life."

"In one sense it is," replied Aylmer; "or rather, the elixir of immortality. It is the most precious poison that ever was concocted in this world. By its aid I could apportion the lifetime of any mortal at whom you might point your finger. The strength of the dose would determine whether he were to linger out years, or drop dead in the midst of a breath. No king on his guarded throne could keep his life if I, in my private station, should deem that the welfare of millions justified me in depriving him of it."

"Why do you keep such a terrific drug?" inquired Georgiana in horror.

"Do not mistrust me, dearest," said her husband, smiling; "its virtuous potency is yet greater than its harmful one. But see! here is a powerful cosmetic. With a few drops of this in a vase of water, freckles may be washed away as easily as the hands are cleansed. A stronger infusion would take the blood out of the cheek, and leave the rosiest beauty a pale ghost."

"Is it with this lotion that you intend to bathe my cheek?" asked Georgiana, anxiously.

"O, no," hastily replied her husband; "this is merely superficial. Your case demands a remedy that shall go deeper."

In his interviews with Georgiana, Aylmer generally made minute inquiries as to her sensations, and whether the confinement of the rooms and the temperature of the atmosphere agreed with her. These questions had such a particular drift that Georgiana began to conjecture that she was already subjected to certain physical influences, either breathed in with the fragrant air or taken with her food. She fancied likewise, but it might be altogether fancy, that there was a stirring up of her system—a strange, indefinite sensation creeping through her veins, and tingling, half painfully, half pleasurably, at her heart. Still, whenever she dared to look into the mirror, there she beheld herself pale as a white rose and with the crimson birthmark stamped upon her cheek. Not even Aylmer now hated it so much as she.

To dispel the tedium of the hours which her husband found it necessary to devote to the processes of combination and analysis, Georgiana turned over the volumes of his scientific library. In many dark old tomes she met with chapters full of romance and poetry. They were the works of the philosophers of the middle ages, such as Albertus Magnus, Cornelius Agrippa, Paracelsus, and the famous friar who created the prophetic Brazen Head. All these antique naturalists stood in advance of their centuries, yet were imbued with some of their credulity, and therefore were believed, and perhaps imagined themselves to have acquired from the investigation of Nature a power above Nature, and from physics a sway over the spiritual world. Hardly less curious and imaginative were the early volumes of the Transactions of the Royal Society, in which the members, knowing little of the limits of natural possibility, were continually recording wonders or proposing methods whereby wonders might be wrought.

But, to Georgiana, the most engrossing volume was a large folio from her husband's own hand, in which he had recorded every experiment of his scientific career, its original aim, the methods adopted for its development, and its final success or failure, with the circumstances to which either event was attributable. The book, in truth, was both the history and emblem of his ardent, ambitious, imaginative, yet practical and laborious life. He handled physical details as if there were nothing beyond them; yet spiritualized them all and redeemed himself from materialism by his strong and eager aspiration towards the infinite. In his grasp the veriest clod of earth assumed a soul. Georgiana, as she read, reverenced Aylmer and loved him more profoundly than ever, but with a less entire dependence on his judgment than heretofore. Much as he had accomplished, she could not but observe that his most splendid successes were almost invariably failures, if compared with the ideal at which he aimed. His brightest diamonds were the merest pebbles, and felt to be so by himself, in comparison with the inestimable gems which lay hidden beyond his reach. The volume, rich with achievements that had won renown for its author, was yet as melancholy a record as ever mortal hand had penned. It was the sad confession and continual exemplification of the shortcomings of the composite man, the spirit burdened with clay and working in matter, and of the despair that assails the higher nature at finding itself so miserably thwarted by the earthly part. Perhaps every man of genius, in whatever sphere, might recognize the image of his own experience in Aylmer's journal.

So deeply did these reflections affect Georgiana that she laid her face upon the open volume and burst into tears. In this situation she was found by her husband.

"It is dangerous to read in a sorcerer's books," said he with a smile, though his countenance was uneasy and displeased. "Georgiana, there are pages in that volume which I can scarcely glance over and keep my senses. Take heed lest it prove as detrimental to you."

"It has made me worship you more than ever," said she.

"Ah, wait for this one success," rejoined he, "then worship me if you will. I shall deem myself hardly unworthy of it. But come, I have sought you for the luxury of your voice. Sing to me, dearest."

So she poured out the liquid music of her voice to quench the thirst of his spirit. He then took his leave with a boyish exuberance of gayety, assuring her that her seclusion would endure but a little longer, and that the result was already certain. Scarcely had he departed when Georgiana felt irresistibly impelled to follow him. She had forgotten to inform Aylmer of a symptom which for two or three hours past had begun to excite her attention. It was a sensation in the fatal birthmark, not painful, but which induced a restlessness throughout her system. Hastening after her husband, she intruded for the first time into the laboratory.

The first thing that struck her eye was the furnace, that hot and feverish worker, with the intense glow of its fire, which by the quantities of soot clustered above it seemed to have been burning for ages. There was a distilling apparatus in full operation. Around the room were retorts, tubes, cylinders, crucibles, and other apparatus of chemical research. An electrical machine stood ready for immediate use. The atmosphere felt oppressively close, and was tainted with gaseous odors which had been tormented forth by the processes of science. The severe and homely simplicity of the apartment, with its naked walls and brick pavement, looked strange, accustomed as Georgiana had become to the fantastic elegance of her boudoir. But what chiefly, indeed almost solely, drew her attention, was the aspect of Aylmer himself.

He was pale as death, anxious and absorbed, and hung over the furnace as if it depended upon his utmost watchfulness whether the liquid which it was distilling should be the draught of immortal happiness or misery. How different from the sanguine and joyous mien that he had assumed for Georgiana's encouragement!

"Carefully now, Aminadab; carefully, thou human machine; carefully, thou man of clay," muttered Aylmer, more to himself than his assistant. "Now, if there be a thought too much or too little, it is all over."

"Ho! ho!" mumbled Aminadab. "Look, master! look!"

Aylmer raised his eyes hastily, and at first reddened, then grew paler than ever, on beholding Georgiana. He rushed towards her and seized her arm with a gripe that left the print of his fingers upon it.

"Why do you come hither? Have you no trust in your husband?" cried he, impetuously. "Would you throw the blight of that fatal birthmark over my labors? It is not well done. Go, prying woman! go!"

"Nay, Aylmer," said Georgiana with the firmness of which she possessed no stinted endowment, "it is not you that have a right to complain. You mistrust your wife; you have concealed the anxiety with which you watch the development of this experiment. Think not so unworthily of me, my husband. Tell me all the risk we run, and fear not that I shall shrink; for my share in it is far less than your own."

"No, no, Georgiana!" said Aylmer, impatiently; "it must not be."

"I submit," replied she, calmly. "And, Aylmer, I shall quaff whatever draught you bring me; but it will be on the same principle that would induce me to take a dose of poison if offered by your hand."

"My noble wife," said Aylmer, deeply moved, "I knew not the height and depth of your nature until now. Nothing shall be concealed. Know, then, that this crimson hand, superficial as it seems, has clutched its grasp into your being with a strength of which I had no previous conception. I have already administered agents powerful enough to do aught except to change your entire physical system. Only one thing remains to be tried. If that fail us we are ruined."

"Why did you hesitate to tell me this?" asked she.

"Because, Georgiana," said Aylmer, in a low voice, "there is danger."

"Danger? There is but one danger—that this horrible stigma shall be left upon my cheek!" cried Georgiana. "Remove it, remove it, whatever be the cost, or we shall both go mad!"

"Heaven knows your words are too true," said Aylmer, sadly. "And now, dearest, return to your boudoir. In a little while all will be tested."

He conducted her back and took leave of her with a solemn tenderness which spoke far more than his words how much was now at stake. After his departure Georgiana became rapt in musings. She considered the character of Aylmer and did it completer justice than at any previous moment. Her heart exulted, while it trembled, at his honorable love—so pure and lofty that it would accept nothing less than perfection nor miserably make itself contented with an earthlier nature than he had dreamed of. She felt how much more precious was such a sentiment than that meaner kind which would have borne with the imperfection for her sake, and have been guilty of treason to holy love by degrading its perfect idea to the level of the actual; and with her whole spirit she prayed that, for a single moment, she might satisfy his highest and deepest conception. Longer than one moment she well knew it could not be; for his spirit was ever on the march, ever ascending, and each instant required something that was beyond the scope of the instant before.

The sound of her husband's footsteps aroused her. He bore a crystal goblet containing a liquor colorless as water, but bright enough to be the draught of immortality. Aylmer was pale; but it seemed rather the consequence of a highly-wrought state of mind and tension of spirit than of fear or doubt.

"The concoction of the draught has been perfect," said he, in answer to Georgiana's look. "Unless all my science have deceived me, it cannot fail."

"Save on your account, my dearest Aylmer," observed his wife, "I might wish to put off this birthmark of mortality by relinquishing mortality itself in preference to any other mode. Life is but a sad possession to those who have attained precisely the degree of moral advancement at which I stand. Were I weaker and blinder, it might be happiness. Were I stronger, it might be endured hopefully. But, being what I find myself, methinks I am of all mortals the most fit to die."

"You are fit for heaven without tasting death!" replied her husband. "But why do we speak of dying? The draught cannot fail. Behold its effect upon this plant."

On the window seat there stood a geranium diseased with yellow blotches which had overspread all its leaves. Aylmer poured a small quantity of the liquid upon the soil in which it grew. In a little time, when the roots of the plant had taken up the moisture, the unsightly blotches began to be extinguished in a living verdure.

"There needed no proof," said Georgiana, quietly. "Give me the goblet. I joyfully stake all upon your word."

"Drink, then, thou lofty creature!" exclaimed Aylmer, with fervid admiration. "There is no taint of imperfection on thy spirit. Thy sensible frame, too, shall soon be all perfect."

She quaffed the liquid and returned the goblet to his hand.

"It is grateful," said she, with a placid smile. "Methinks it is like water from a heavenly fountain; for it contains I know not what of unobtrusive fragrance and deliciousness. It allays a feverish thirst that had parched me for many days. Now, dearest, let me sleep. My earthly senses are closing over my spirit like the leaves around the heart of a rose at sunset."

She spoke the last words with a gentle reluctance, as if it required almost more energy than she could command to pronounce the faint and lingering syllables. Scarcely had they loitered through her lips ere she was lost in slumber. Aylmer sat by her side, watching her aspect with the emotions proper to a man the whole value of whose existence was involved in the process now to be tested. Mingled with this mood, however, was the philosophic investigation characteristic of the man of science. Not the minutest symptom escaped him. A heightened flush of the cheek, a slight irregularity of breath, a quiver of the eyelid, a hardly perceptible tremor through the frame,—such were the details which, as the moments passed, he wrote down in his folio volume. Intense thought had set its stamp upon every previous page of that volume; but the thoughts of years were all concentrated upon the last.

While thus employed, he failed not to gaze often at the fatal hand, and not without a shudder. Yet once, by a strange and unaccountable impulse, he pressed it with his lips. His spirit recoiled, however, in the very act; and Georgiana, out of the midst of her deep sleep, moved uneasily and murmured as if in remonstrance. Again Aylmer resumed his watch. Nor was it without avail. The crimson hand, which at first had been strongly visible upon the marble paleness of Georgiana's cheek, now grew more faintly outlined. She remained not less pale than ever; but the birthmark, with every breath that came and went, lost somewhat of its former distinctness. Its presence had been awful; its departure was more awful still. Watch the stain of the rainbow fading out of the sky, and you will know how that mysterious symbol passed away.

"By Heaven! it is well nigh gone!" said Aylmer to himself, in almost irrepressible ecstasy. "I can scarcely trace it now. Success! success! And now it is like the faintest rose color. The slightest flush of blood across her cheek would overcome it. But she is so pale!"

He drew aside the window curtain and suffered the light of natural day to fall into the room and rest upon her cheek. At the same time he heard a gross, hoarse chuckle, which he had long known as his servant Aminadab's expression of delight.

"Ah, clod! ah, earthly mass!" cried Aylmer, laughing in a sort of frenzy, "you have served me well! Matter and spirit—earth and heaven—have both done their part in this! Laugh, thing of the senses! You have earned the right to laugh."

These exclamations broke Georgiana's sleep. She slowly unclosed her eyes and gazed into the mirror which her husband had arranged for that purpose. A faint smile flitted over her lips when she recognized how barely perceptible was now that crimson hand which had once blazed forth with such disastrous brilliancy as to scare away all their happiness. But then her eyes sought Aylmer's face with a trouble and anxiety that he could by no means account for.

"My poor Aylmer!" murmured she.

"Poor? Nay, richest, happiest, most favored!" exclaimed he. "My peerless bride, it is successful! You are perfect!"

"My poor Aylmer," she repeated, with a more than human tenderness, "you have aimed loftily; you have done nobly. Do not repent that, with so high and pure a feeling, you have rejected the best that earth could offer. Aylmer, dearest Aylmer, I am dying!"

Alas! it was too true! The fatal hand had grappled with the mystery of life, and was the bond by which an angelic spirit kept itself in union with a mortal frame. As the last crimson tint of the birth-mark—that sole token of human imperfection—faded from her cheek, the parting breath of the now perfect woman passed into the atmosphere, and her soul, lingering a moment near her husband, took its heavenward flight. Then a hoarse, chuckling laugh was heard again! Thus ever does the gross fatality of earth exult in its invariable triumph over the immortal essence which, in this dim sphere of half development, demands the completeness of a higher state. Yet, had Aylmer reached a profounder wisdom, he need not thus have flung away the happiness which would have woven his mortal life of the selfsame texture with the celestial. The momentary circumstance was too strong for him; he failed to look beyond the shadowy scope of time, and, living once for all in eternity, to find the perfect future in the present.

My Kinsman, Major Molineux

A fter the kings of Great Britain had assumed the right of appointing the colonial governors, the measures of the latter seldom met with the ready and general approbation, which had been paid to those of their predecessors, under the original charters. The people looked with most jealous scrutiny to the exercise of power, which did not emanate from themselves, and they usually rewarded the rulers with slender gratitude, for the compliances, by which, in softening their instructions from beyond the sea, they had incurred the reprehension of those who gave them. The annals of Massachusetts Bay will inform us, that of six governors, in the space of about forty years from the surrender of the old charter, under James II, two were imprisoned by a popular insurrection; a third, as Hutchinson inclines to believe, was driven from the province by the whizzing of a musket ball; a fourth, in the opinion of the same historian, was hastened to his grave by continual bickerings with the house of representatives; and the remaining two, as well as their successors, till the Revolution, were favored with few and brief intervals of peaceful sway. The inferior members of the court party, in times of high political excitement, led scarcely a more desirable life. These remarks may serve as preface to the following adventures, which chanced upon a summer night, not far from a hundred years ago. The reader, in order to avoid a long and dry detail of colonial affairs, is requested to dispense with an account of the train of circumstances, that had caused much temporary inflammation of the popular mind.

It was near nine o'clock of a moonlight evening, when a boat crossed the ferry with a single passenger, who had obtained his conveyance, at that unusual hour, by the promise of an extra fare. While he stood on the landing-place, searching in either pocket for the means of fulfilling his agreement, the ferryman lifted a lantern, by the aid of which, and the newly risen moon, he took a very accurate survey of the stranger's figure. He was a youth of barely eighteen years, evidently country-bred, and now, as it should seem, upon his first visit to town. He was clad in a coarse grey coat, well worn, but in excellent repair; his under garments were durably constructed of leather, and sat tight to a pair of serviceable and well-shaped limbs; his stockings of blue yarn, were the incontrovertible handiwork of a mother or a sister; and on his head was a three-cornered hat, which in its better days had perhaps sheltered the graver brow of the lad's father. Under his left arm was a heavy cudgel, formed of an oak sapling, and retaining a part of the hardened root; and his equipment was completed by a wallet, not so abundantly stocked as to incommode the vigorous shoulders on which it hung. Brown, curly hair, well-shaped features, and bright, cheerful eyes, were nature's gifts, and worth all that art could have done for his adornment.

The youth, one of whose names was Robin, finally drew from his pocket the half of a little province-bill of five shillings, which, in the depreciation of that sort of currency, did but satisfy the ferryman's demand, with the surplus of a sexangular piece of parchment valued at three pence. He then walked forward into the town, with as light a step, as if his day's journey had not already exceeded thirty miles, and with as eager an eye, as if he were entering London city, instead of the little metropolis of a New England colony. Before Robin had proceeded far, however, it occurred to him, that he knew not whither to direct his steps; so he paused, and looked up and down the narrow street, scrutinizing the small and mean wooden buildings, that were scattered on either side.

"This low hovel cannot be my kinsman's dwelling," thought he, "nor yonder old house, where the moonlight enters at the broken casement; and truly I see none hereabouts that might be worthy of him. It would have been wise to inquire my way of the ferryman, and doubtless he would have gone with me, and earned a shilling from the Major for his pains. But the next man I meet will do as well."

He resumed his walk, and was glad to perceive that the street now became wider, and the houses more respectable in their appearance. He soon discerned a figure moving on moderately in advance, and hastened his steps to overtake it. As Robin drew nigh, he saw that the passenger was a man in years, with a full periwig of grey hair, a wide-skirted coat of dark cloth, and silk stockings rolled about his knees. He carried a long and polished cane, which he struck down perpendicularly before him, at every step; and at regular intervals he uttered two successive hems, of a peculiarly solemn and sepulchral intonation. Having made these observations, Robin laid hold of the skirt of the old man's coat, just when the light from the open door and windows of a barber's shop, fell upon both their figures.

"Good evening to you, honored Sir," said he, making a low bow, and still retaining his hold of the skirt. "I pray you to tell me whereabouts is the dwelling of my kinsman, Major Molineux?"

The youth's question was uttered very loudly; and one of the barbers, whose razor was descending on a well-soaped chin, and another who was dressing a Ramillies wig, left their occupations, and came to the door. The citizen, in the meantime, turned a long favored countenance upon

Robin, and answered him in a tone of excessive anger and annoyance. His two sepulchral hems, however, broke into the very centre of his rebuke, with most singular effect, like a thought of the cold grave obtruding among wrathful passions.

"Let go my garment, fellow! I tell you. I know not the man you speak of. What! I have authority, I have—hem, hem—authority; and if this be the respect you show your betters, your feet shall be brought acquainted with the stocks, by daylight, tomorrow morning!"

Robin released the old man's skirt, and hastened away, pursued by an ill-mannered roar of laughter from the barber's shop. He was at first considerably surprised by the result of his question, but, being a shrewd youth, soon thought himself able to account for the mystery.

"This is some country representative," was his conclusion, "who has never seen the inside of my kinsman's door, and lacks the breeding to answer a stranger civilly. The man is old, or verily—I might be tempted to turn back and smite him on the nose. Ah, Robin, Robin! even the barber's boys laugh at you, for choosing such a guide! You will be wiser in time, friend Robin."

He now became entangled in a succession of crooked and narrow streets, which crossed each other, and meandered at no great distance from the water-side. The smell of tar was obvious to his nostrils, the masts of vessels pierced the moonlight above the tops of the buildings, and the numerous signs, which Robin paused to read, informed him that he was near the centre of business. But the streets were empty, the shops were closed, and lights were visible only in the second stories of a few dwelling-houses. At length, on the corner of a narrow lane, through which he was passing, he beheld the broad countenance of a British hero swinging before the door of an inn, whence proceeded the voices of many guests. The casement of one of the lower windows was thrown back, and a very thin curtain permitted Robin to distinguish a party at supper, round a well-furnished table. The fragrance of the good cheer steamed forth into the outer air, and the youth could not fail to recollect, that the last remnant of his travelling stock of provision had yielded to his morning appetite, and that noon had found, and left him, dinnerless.

"Oh, that a parchment three-penny might give me a right to sit down at yonder table," said Robin, with a sigh. "But the Major will make me welcome to the best of his victuals; so I will even step boldly in, and inquire my way to his dwelling."

He entered the tavern, and was guided by the murmur of voices, and fumes of tobacco, to the public room. It was a long and low apartment, with oaken walls, grown dark in the continual smoke, and a floor, which was thickly sanded, but of no immaculate purity. A number of persons, the larger part of whom appeared to be mariners, or in some way connected with the sea, occupied the wooden benches, or leather-bottomed chairs, conversing on various matters, and occasionally lending their attention to some topic of general interest. Three or four little groups were draining as many bowls of punch, which the great West India trade had long since made a familiar drink in the colony. Others, who had the aspect of men who lived by regular and laborious handicraft, preferred the insulated bliss of an unshared potation, and became more taciturn under its influence: Nearly all, in short, evinced a predilection for the Good Creature in some of its various shapes, for this is a vice, to which, as the Fast-day sermons of a hundred years ago will testify, we have a long hereditary claim. The only guests to whom Robin's sympathies inclined him, were two or three sheepish countrymen, who were using the inn somewhat after the fashion of a Turkish Caravansary; they had gotten themselves into the darkest corner of the room, and, heedless of the Nicotian atmosphere, were supping on the bread of their own ovens, and the bacon cured in their own chimney-smoke. But though Robin felt a sort of brotherhood with these strangers, his eyes were attracted from them, to a person who stood near the door, holding whispered conversation with a group of ill-dressed associates. His features were separately striking almost to grotesqueness, and the whole face left a deep impression in the memory. The forehead bulged out into a double prominence, with a vale between; the nose came boldly forth in an irregular curve, and its bridge was of more than a finger's breadth; the eyebrows were deep and shaggy, and the eyes glowed beneath them like fire in a cave.

While Robin deliberated of whom to inquire respecting his kinsman's dwelling, he was accosted by the innkeeper, a little man in a stained white apron, who had come to pay his professional welcome to the stranger. Being in the second generation from a French protestant, he seemed to have inherited the courtesy of his parent nation; but no variety of circumstance was ever known to change his voice from the one shrill note in which he now addressed Robin.

"From the country, I presume, Sir?" said he, with a profound bow. "Beg to congratulate you on your arrival, and trust you intend a long stay with us. Fine town here, Sir, beautiful buildings, and much that may interest a stranger. May I hope for the honor of your commands in respect to supper?"

"The man sees a family likeness! The rogue has guessed that I am related to the Major!" thought Robin, who had hitherto experienced little superfluous civility.

All eyes were now turned on the country lad, standing at the door, in his worn three-cornered hat, grey coat, leather breeches, and blue yarn stockings, leaning on an oaken cudgel, and bearing a wallet on his back. Robin replied to the courteous innkeeper, with such an assumption of consequence, as befitted the Major's relative.

"My honest friend," he said, "I shall make it a point to patronize your house on some occasion when—" here he could not help lowering his voice—"I may have more than a parchment three-pence in my pocket. My present business," continued he, speaking with lofty confidence, "is merely to inquire the way to the dwelling of my kinsman, Major Molineux."

There was a sudden and general movement in the room, which Robin interpreted as expressing the eagerness of each individual to become his guide. But the innkeeper turned his eyes to a written paper on the wall, which he read, or seemed to read, with occasional recurrences to the young man's figure.

"What have we here?" said he, breaking his speech into little dry fragments. " 'Left the house of the subscriber, bounden servant, Hezekiah Mudge—had on when he went away, grey coat, leather breeches, master's third best hat. One pound currency reward to whoever shall lodge him in any jail in the province.' Better trudge, boy, better trudge."

Robin had begun to draw his hand toward the lighter end of the oak cudgel, but a strange hostility in every countenance, induced him to relinquish his purpose of breaking the courteous innkeeper's head. As he turned to leave the room, he encountered a sneering glance from the bold-featured personage whom he had before noticed; and no sooner was he beyond the door, than he heard a general laugh, in which the innkeeper's voice might be distinguished, like the dropping of small stones into a kettle.

"Now is it not strange," thought Robin, with his usual shrewdness, "is it not strange, that the confession of an empty pocket, should outweigh the name of my kinsman, Major Molineux? Oh, if I had one of these grinning rascals in the woods, where I and my oak sapling grew up together, I would teach him that my arm is heavy, though my purse be light!"

On turning the corner of the narrow lane, Robin found himself in a spacious street, with an unbroken line of lofty houses on each side, and a steepled building at the upper end, whence the ringing of a bell announced the hour of nine. The light of the moon, and the lamps from numerous shop windows, discovered people promenading on the pavement, and amongst them, Robin hoped to recognise his hitherto inscrutable relative. The result of his former inquiries made him unwilling to hazard another, in a scene of such publicity, and he determined to walk slowly and silently up the street, thrusting his face close to that of every elderly gentleman, in search of the Major's lineaments. In his progress, Robin encountered many gay and gallant figures. Embroidered garments, of showy colors, enormous periwigs, gold-laced hats, and silver hilted swords, glided past him and dazzled his optics. Travelled youths, imitators of the European fine gentlemen of the period, trod jauntily along, half-dancing to the fashionable tunes which they hummed, and making poor Robin ashamed of his quiet and natural gait. At length, after many pauses to examine the gorgeous display of goods in the shop windows, and after suffering some rebukes for the impertinence of his scrutiny into people's faces, the Major's kinsman found himself near the steepled building, still unsuccessful in his search. As yet, however, he had seen only one side of the thronged street; so Robin crossed, and continued the same sort of inquisition down the opposite pavement, with stronger hopes than the philosopher seeking an honest man, but with no better fortune. He had arrived about midway towards the lower end, from which his course began, when he overheard the approach of some one, who struck down a cane on the flag-stones at every step, uttering, at regular intervals, two sepulchral hems.

"Mercy on us!" quoth Robin, recognising the sound.

Turning a corner, which chanced to be close at his right hand, he hastened to pursue his researches, in some other part of the town. His patience was now wearing low, and he seemed to feel more fatigue from his rambles since he crossed the ferry, than from his journey of several days on the other side. Hunger also pleaded loudly within him, and Robin began to balance the propriety of demanding, violently and with lifted cudgel, the necessary guidance from the first solitary passenger, whom he should meet. While a resolution to this effect was gaining strength, he entered a street of mean appearance, on either side of which, a row of ill-built houses was straggling towards the harbor. The moonlight fell upon no passenger along the whole extent, but in the third domicile which Robin passed, there was a half-opened door, and his keen glance detected a woman's garment within.

"My luck may be better here," said he to himself.

Accordingly, he approached the door, and beheld it shut closer as he did so; yet an open space remained, sufficing for the fair occupant to observe the stranger, without a corresponding display on her part. All that Robin could discern was a strip of scarlet petticoat, and the occasional sparkle of an eye, as if the moonbeams were trembling on some bright thing.

"Pretty mistress,"—for I may call her so with a good conscience, thought the shrewd youth, since I know nothing to the contrary—"my sweet pretty mistress, will you be kind enough to tell me whereabouts I must seek the dwelling of my kinsman, Major Molineux?"

Robin's voice was plaintive and winning, and the female, seeing nothing to be shunned in the handsome country youth, thrust open the door, and came forth into the moonlight. She was a dainty little figure, with a white neck, round arms, and a slender waist, at the extremity of which her scarlet petticoat jutted out over a hoop, as if she were standing in a balloon. Moreover, her face was oval and pretty, her hair dark beneath the little cap, and her bright eyes possessed a sly freedom, which triumphed over those of Robin.

"Major Molineux dwells here," said this fair woman.

Now her voice was the sweetest Robin had heard that night, the airy counterpart of a stream of melted silver; yet he could not help doubting whether that sweet voice spoke gospel truth. He looked up and down the mean street, and then surveyed the house before which they stood. It was a small, dark edifice of two stories, the second of which projected over the lower floor; and the front apartment had the aspect of a shop for petty commodities.

"Now truly I am in luck," replied Robin, cunningly, "and so indeed is my kinsman, the Major, in having so pretty a housekeeper. But I prithee trouble him to step to the door; I will deliver him a message from his friends in the country, and then go back to my lodgings at the inn."

"Nay, the Major has been a-bed this hour or more," said the lady of the scarlett petticoat; "and it would be to little purpose to disturb him tonight, seeing his evening draught was of the strongest. But he is a kind-hearted man, and it would be as much as my life's worth, to let a kinsman of his turn away from the door. You are the good old gentleman's very picture, and I could swear that was his rainy-weather hat. Also, he has garments very much resembling those leather—But come in, I pray, for I bid you hearty welcome in his name."

So saying, the fair and hospitable dame took our hero by the hand; and though the touch was light, and the force was gentleness, and though Robin read in her eyes what he did not hear in her words, yet the slender waisted woman, in the scarlet petticoat, proved stronger than the athletic country youth. She had drawn his half-willing footsteps nearly to the threshold, when the opening of a door in the neighborhood, startled the Major's housekeeper, and, leaving the Major's kinsman, she vanished speedily into her own domicile. A heavy yawn preceded the appearance of a man, who, like the Moonshine of Pyramus and Thisbe, carried a lantern, needlessly aiding his sister luminary in the heavens. As he walked sleepily up the street, he turned his broad, dull face on Robin, and displayed a long staff, spiked at the end.

"Home, vagabond, home!" said the watchman, in accents that seemed to fall asleep as soon as they were uttered. "Home, or we'll set you in the stocks by peep of day!"

"This is the second hint of the kind," thought Robin. "I wish they would end my difficulties, by setting me there to-night."

Nevertheless, the youth felt an instinctive antipathy towards the guardian of midnight order, which at first prevented him from asking his usual question. But just when the man was about to vanish behind the corner, Robin resolved not to lose the opportunity, and shouted lustily after him—

"I say, friend! will you guide me to the house of my kinsman, Major Molineux?"

The watchman made no reply, but turned the corner and was gone;

yet Robin seemed to hear the sound of drowsy laughter stealing along the solitary street. At that moment, also, a pleasant titter saluted him from the open window above his head; he looked up, and caught the sparkle of a saucy eye; a round arm beckoned to him, next he heard light footsteps descending the staircase within. But Robin, being of the household of a New England clergyman, was a good youth, as well as a shrewd one; so he resisted temptation, and fled away.

He now roamed desperately, and at random, through the town, almost ready to believe that a spell was on him, like that, by which a wizard of his country, had once kept three pursuers wandering, a whole winter night, within twenty paces of the cottage which they sought. The streets lay before him, strange and desolate, and the lights were extinguished in almost every house. Twice, however, little parties of men, among whom Robin distinguished individuals in outlandish attire, came hurrying along, but though on both occasions they paused to address him, such intercourse did not at all enlighten his perplexity. They did but utter a few words in some language of which Robin knew nothing, and perceiving his inability to answer, bestowed a curse upon him in plain English, and hastened away. Finally, the lad determined to knock at the door of every mansion that might appear worthy to be occupied by his kinsman, trusting that perseverance would overcome the fatality which had hitherto thwarted him. Firm in this resolve, he was passing beneath the walls of a church, which formed the corner of two streets, when, as he turned into the shade of its steeple, he encountered a bulky stranger, muffled in a cloak. The man was proceeding with the speed of earnest business, but Robin planted himself full before him, holding the oak cudgel with both hands across his body, as a bar to further passage.

"Halt, honest man, and answer me a question," said he, very resolutely. "Tell me, this instant, whereabouts is the dwelling of my kinsman, Major Molineux?"

"Keep your tongue between your teeth, fool, and let me pass," said a deep, gruff voice, which Robin partly remembered. "Let me pass, I say, or I'll strike you to the earth!"

"No, no, neighbor!" cried Robin, flourishing his cudgel, and then thrusting its larger end close to the man's muffled face. "No, no, I'm not the fool you take me for, nor do you pass, till I have an answer to my question. Whereabouts is the dwelling of my kinsman, Major Molineux?"

The stranger, instead of attempting to force his passage, stept back into the moonlight, unmuffled his own face and stared full into that of Robin.

"Watch here an hour, and Major Molineux will pass by," said he.

Robin gazed with dismay and astonishment, on the unprecedented physiognomy of the speaker. The forehead with its double prominence, the broad-hooked nose, the shaggy eyebrows, and fiery eyes, were those which he had noticed at the inn, but the man's complexion had undergone a singular, or more properly, a two-fold change. One side of the face blazed of an intense red, while the other was black as midnight, the division line being in the broad bridge of the nose; and a mouth, which seemed to extend from ear to ear, was black or red, in contrast to the color of the cheek. The effect was as if two individual devils, a fiend of fire and a fiend of darkness, had united themselves to form this infernal visage. The stranger grinned in Robin's face, muffled his party-colored features, and was out of sight in a moment.

"Strange things we travellers see!" ejaculated Robin.

He seated himself, however, upon the steps of the church-door, resolving to wait the appointed time for his kinsman's appearance. A few moments were consumed in philosophical speculations, upon the species of the *genus homo*, who had just left him, but having settled this point shrewdly, rationally, and satisfactorily, he was compelled to look elsewhere for amusement. And first he threw his eyes along the street; it was of more respectable appearance than most of those into which he had wandered, and the moon, "creating, like the imaginative power, a beautiful strangeness in familiar objects," gave something of romance to a scene, that might not have possessed it in the light of day. The irregular, and often quaint architecture of the houses, some of whose roofs were broken into numerous little peaks; while others ascended, steep and narrow, into a single point; and others again were square; the pure milk-white of some of their complexions, the aged darkness of others, and the thousand sparklings, reflected from bright substances in the plastered walls of many; these matters engaged Robin's attention for awhile, and then began to grow wearisome. Next he endeavored to define the forms of distant objects, starting away with almost ghostly indistinctness, just as his eye appeared to grasp them; and finally he took a minute survey of an edifice, which stood on the opposite side of the street, directly in front of the church-door, where he was stationed. It was a large square mansion, distinguished from its neighbors by a balcony, which rested on tall pillars, and by an elaborate Gothic window, communicating therewith.

"Perhaps this is the very house I have been seeking," thought Robin.

Then he strove to speed away the time, by listening to a murmur, which swept continually along the street, yet was scarcely audible, except to an unaccustomed ear like his; it was a low, dull dreamy sound, compounded of many noises, each of which was at too great a distance to be separately heard. Robin marvelled at this snore of a sleeping town, and marvelled more, whenever its continuity was broken, by now and then a distant shout, apparently loud where it originated. But altogether it was a sleep-inspiring sound, and to shake off its drowsy influence, Robin arose, and climbed a window-frame, that he might view the interior of the church. There the moonbeams came trembling in, and fell down upon the deserted pews, and extended along the quiet aisles. A fainter, yet more awful radiance, was hovering round the pulpit, and one solitary ray had dared to rest upon the opened page of the great bible. Had Nature, in that deep hour, become a worshipper in the house, which man had builded? Or was that heavenly light the visible sanctity of the place, visible because no earthly and impure feet were within the walls? The scene made Robin's heart shiver with a sensation of loneliness, stronger than he had ever felt in the remotest depths of his native woods; so he turned away, and sat down again before the door. There were graves around the church, and now an uneasy thought obtruded into Robin's breast. What if the object of his search, which had been so often and so strangely thwarted, were all the time mouldering in his shroud? What if his kinsman should glide through yonder gate, and nod and smile to him in passing dimly by?

"Oh, that any breathing thing were here with me!" said Robin.

Recalling his thoughts from this uncomfortable track, he sent them over forest, hill, and stream, and attempted to imagine how that evening of ambiguity and weariness, had been spent by his father's household. He pictured them assembled at the door, beneath the tree, the great old tree, which had been spared for its huge twisted trunk, and venerable shade, when a thousand leafy brethren fell. There, at the going down of the summer sun, it was his father's custom to perform domestic worship, that the neighbors might come and join with him like brothers of the family, and that the wayfaring man might pause to drink at that fountain, and keep his heart pure by freshening the memory of home. Robin distinguished the seat of every individual of the little audience; he saw the good man in the midst, holding the scriptures in the golden light that shone from the western clouds; he beheld him close the book, and all rise up to pray. He heard the old thanksgivings for daily mercies, the old supplications for their continuance, to which he had so often listened in weariness, but which were now among his dear remembrances. He perceived the slight inequality of his father's voice when he came to speak of the Absent One; he noted how his mother turned her face to the broad and knotted trunk; how his elder brother scorned, because the beard was rough upon his upper lip, to permit his features to be moved; how his younger sister drew down a low hanging branch before her eyes; and how the little one of all, whose sports had hitherto broken the decorum of the scene, understood the prayer for her playmate, and burst into clamorous grief. Then he saw them go in at the door; and when Robin would have entered also, the latch tinkled into its place, and he was excluded from his home.

"Am I here, or there?" cried Robin, starting; for all at once, when his thoughts had become visible and audible in a dream, the long, wide, solitary street shone out before him.

He aroused himself, and endeavored to fix his attention steadily upon the large edifice which he had surveyed before. But still his mind kept vibrating between fancy and reality; by turns, the pillars of the balcony lengthened into the tall, bare stems of pines, dwindled down to human figures, settled again in their true shape and size, and then commenced a new succession of changes. For a single moment, when he deemed himself awake, he could have sworn that a visage, one which he seemed to remember, yet could not absolutely name as his kinsman's, was looking towards him from the Gothic window. A deeper sleep wrestled with, and nearly overcame him, but fled at the sound of footsteps along the opposite pavement. Robin rubbed his eyes, discerned a man passing at the foot of the balcony, and addressed him in a loud, peevish, and lamentable cry.

"Halloo, friend! must I wait here all night for my kinsman, Major Molineux?"

The sleeping echoes awoke, and answered the voice; and the passenger, barely able to discern a figure sitting in the oblique shade of the steeple, traversed the street to obtain a nearer view. He was himself a gentleman in his prime, of open, intelligent, cheerful, and altogether prepossessing countenance. Perceiving a country youth, apparently homeless and without friends, he accosted him in a tone of real kindness, which had become strange to Robin's ears.

"Well, my good lad, why are you sitting here?" inquired he. "Can I be of service to you in any way?"

"I am afraid not, Sir," replied Robin, despondingly; "yet I shall take it kindly, if you'll answer me a single question. I've been searching half the night for one Major Molineux; now, sir, is there really such a person in these parts, or am I dreaming?"

"Major Molineux! The name is not altogether strange to me," said the gentleman, smiling. "Have you any objection to telling me the nature of your business with him?"

Then Robin briefly related that his father was a clergyman, settled on a small salary, at a long distance back in the country, and that he and Major Molineux were brothers' children. The Major, having inherited riches, and acquired civil and military rank, had visited his cousin in great pomp a year or two before; had manifested much interest in Robin and an elder brother, and, being childless himself, had thrown out hints respecting the future establishment of one of them in life. The elder brother was destined to succeed to the farm, which his father cultivated, in the interval of sacred duties; it was therefore determined that Robin should profit by his kinsman's generous intentions, especially as he had seemed to be rather the favorite, and was thought to possess other necessary endowments.

"For I have the name of being a shrewd youth," observed Robin, in this part of his story.

"I doubt not you deserve it," replied his new friend, good naturedly; "but pray proceed."

"Well, Sir, being nearly eighteen years old, and well grown, as you see," continued Robin, raising himself to his full height, "I thought it high time to begin the world. So my mother and sister put me in handsome trim, and my father gave me half the remnant of his last year's salary, and five days ago I started for this place, to pay the Major a visit. But would you believe it, Sir? I crossed the ferry a little after dusk, and have yet found nobody that would show me the way to his dwelling; only an hour or two since, I was told to wait here, and Major Molineux would pass by."

"Can you describe the man who told you this?" inquired the gentleman.

"Oh, he was a very ill-favored fellow, Sir," replied Robin, "with two great bumps on his forehead, a hook nose, fiery eyes, and, what struck me as the strangest, his face was of two different colors. Do you happen to know such a man, Sir?"

"Not intimately," answered the stranger, "but I chanced to meet him a little time previous to your stopping me. I believe you may trust his word, and that the Major will very shortly pass through this street. In the mean time, as I have a singular curiosity to witness your meeting, I will sit down here upon the steps, and bear you company."

He seated himself accordingly, and soon engaged his companion in animated discourse. It was but of brief continuance, however, for a noise of shouting, which had long been remotely audible, drew so much nearer, that Robin inquired its cause.

"What may be the meaning of this uproar?" asked he. "Truly, if your town be always as noisy, I shall find little sleep, while I am an inhabitant."

"Why, indeed, friend Robin, there do appear to be three or four riotous fellows abroad to-night," replied the gentleman. "You must not expect all the stillness of your native woods, here in our streets. But the watch will shortly be at the heels of these lads, and—"

"Aye, and set them in the stocks by peep of day," interrupted Robin, recollecting his own encounter with the drowsy lantern-bearer. "But, dear Sir, if I may trust my ears, an army of watchmen would never make head against such a multitude of rioters. There were at least a thousand voices went to make up that one shout."

"May not one man have several voices, Robin, as well as two complexions?" said his friend.

"Perhaps a man may; but heaven forbid that a woman should!" responded the shrewd youth, thinking of the seductive tones of the Major's housekeeper.

The sounds of a trumpet in some neighboring street, now became so evident and continual, that Robin's curiosity was strongly excited. In addition to the shouts, he heard frequent bursts from many instruments of discord, and a wild and confused laughter filled up the intervals. Robin rose from the steps, and looked wistfully towards a point, whither several people seemed to be hastening.

"Surely some prodigious merrymaking is going on," exclaimed he. "I have laughed very little since I left home, Sir, and should be sorry to lose an opportunity. Shall we just step round the corner by that darkish house, and take our share of the fun?"

"Sit down again, sit down, good Robin," replied the gentleman, laying his hand on the skirt of the grey coat. "You forget that we must wait here for your kinsman; and there is reason to believe that he will pass by, in the course of a very few moments."

The near approach of the uproar had now disturbed the neighborhood; windows flew open on all sides; and many heads, in the attire of the pillow, and confused by sleep suddenly broken, were protruded to the gaze of whoever had leisure to observe them. Eager voices hailed each other from house to house, all demanding the explanation, which not a soul could give. Half-dressed men hurried towards the unknown commotion, stumbling as they went over the stone steps, that thrust themselves into the narrow foot-walk. The shouts, the laughter, and the tuneless bray, the antipodes of music, came onward with increasing din, till scattered individuals, and then denser bodies, began to appear round a corner, at the distance of a hundred yards.

"Will you recognise your kinsman, Robin, if he passes in this crowd?" inquired the gentleman.

"Indeed, I can't warrant it, Sir; but I'll take my stand here, and keep a bright look out," answered Robin, descending to the outer edge of the pavement.

A mighty stream of people now emptied into the street, and came rolling slowly towards the church. A single horseman wheeled the corner in the midst of them, and close behind him came a band of fearful wind-instruments, sending forth a fresher discord, now that no intervening building kept it from the ear. Then a redder light disturbed the moon-beams, and a dense multitude of torches shone along the street, concealing by their glare whatever object they illuminated. The single horseman, clad in a military dress, and bearing a drawn sword, rode onward as the leader, and, by his fierce and variegated countenance, appeared like war personified; the red of one cheek was an emblem of fire and sword; the blackness of the other betokened the mourning which attends them. In his train, were wild figures in the Indian dress, and many fantastic shapes without a model, giving the whole march a visionary air, as if a dream had broken forth from some feverish brain, and were sweeping visibly through the midnight streets. A mass of people, inactive, except as applauding spectators, hemmed the procession in, and several women ran along the sidewalks, piercing the confusion of heavier sounds, with their shrill voices of mirth or terror.

"The double-faced fellow has his eye upon me," muttered Robin, with an indefinite but uncomfortable idea, that he was himself to bear a part in the pageantry.

The leader turned himself in the saddle, and fixed his glance full upon the country youth, as the steed went slowly by. When Robin had freed his eyes from those fiery ones, the musicians were passing before him, and the torches were close at hand; but the unsteady brightness of the latter formed a veil which he could not penetrate. The rattling of wheels over the stones sometimes found its way to his ear, and confused traces of a human form appeared at intervals, and then melted into the vivid light. A moment more, and the leader thundered a command to halt; the trumpets vomited a horrid breath, and held their peace; the shouts and laughter of the people died away, and there remained only an universal hum, nearly allied to silence. Right before Robin's eyes was an uncovered cart. There the torches blazed the brightest, there the moon shone out like day, and there, in tar-and-feathery dignity, sate his kinsman, Major Molineux!

He was an elderly man, of large and majestic person, and strong, square features betokening a steady soul; but steady as it was, his enemies had found the means to shake it. His face was pale as death, and far more ghastly; the broad forehead was contracted in his agony, so that the eyebrows formed one dark grey line; his eyes were red and wild, and the foam hung white upon his quivering lip. His whole frame was agitated by a quick, and continual tremor, which his pride strove to quell, even in those circumstances of overwhelming humiliation. But perhaps the bitterest pang of all was when his eyes met those of Robin; for he evidently knew him on the instant, as the youth stood witnessing the foul disgrace of a head that had grown grey in honor. They stared at each other in silence, and Robin's knees shook, and his hair bristled, with a mixture of pity and terror. Soon, however, a bewildering excitement began to seize upon his mind; the preceding adventures of the night, the unexpected appearance of the crowd, the torches, the confused din, and the hush that followed, the spectre of his kinsman reviled by that great multitude, all this, and more than all, a perception of tremendous ridicule in the whole scene, affected him with a sort of mental inebreity. At that moment a voice of sluggish merriment saluted Robin's ears; he turned instinctively, and just behind the corner of the church stood the lantern-bearer, rubbing his eyes, and drowsily enjoying the lad's amazement. Then he heard a peal of laughter like the ringing of silvery bells; a woman twitched his arm, a saucy eye met his, and he saw the lady of the scarlet petticoat. A sharp, dry cachinnation appealed to his memory, and standing on tiptoe in the crowd, with his white apron over his head, he beheld the courteous little innkeeper. And lastly, there sailed over the heads of the multitude a great, broad laugh, broken in the midst by two deep sepulchral hems; thus—

"Haw, haw, haw—hem, hem—haw, haw, haw, haw!"

The sound proceeded from the balcony of the opposite edifice, and thither Robin turned his eyes. In front of the Gothic window stood the old citizen, wrapped in a wide gown, his grey periwig exchanged for a nightcap, which was thrust back from his forehead, and his silk stockings hanging down about his legs. He supported himself on his polished cane in a fit of convulsive merriment, which manifested itself on his solemn old features, like a funny inscription on a tomb-stone. Then Robin seemed to hear the voices of the barbers; of the guests of the inn; and of all who had made sport of him that night. The contagion was spreading among the multitude, when, all at once, it seized upon Robin, and he sent forth a shout of laughter that echoed through the street; every man shook his sides, every man emptied his lungs, but Robin's shout was the loudest there. The cloud-spirits peeped from their silvery islands, as the congregated mirth went roaring up the sky! The Man in the Moon heard the far bellow; "Oho," quoth he, "the old Earth is frolicsome to-night!"

When there was a momentary calm in that tempestuous sea of sound, the leader gave the sign, and the procession resumed its march. On they went, like fiends that throng in mockery round some dead potentate, mighty no more, but majestic still in his agony. On they went, in counterfeited pomp, in senseless uproar, in frenzied merriment, trampling all on an old man's heart. On swept the tumult, and left a silent street behind.

"Well, Robin, are you dreaming?" inquired the gentleman, laying his hand on the youth's shoulder.

Robin started, and withdrew his arm from the stone post, to which he had instinctively clung, while the living stream rolled by him. His cheek was somewhat pale, and his eye not quite so lively as in the earlier part of the evening.

"Will you be kind enough to show me the way to the Ferry?" said he, after a moment's pause.

"You have then adopted a new subject of inquiry?" observed his companion, with a smile.

"Why, yes, Sir," replied Robin, rather dryly. "Thanks to you, and to my other friends, I have at last met my kinsman, and he will scarce desire to see my face again. I begin to grow weary of a town life, Sir. Will you show me the way to the Ferry?"

"No, my good friend, Robin, not to-night, at least," said the gentleman. "Some few days hence, if you continue to wish it, I will speed you
on your journey. Or, if you prefer to remain with us, perhaps, as you are
a shrewd youth, you may rise in the world, without the help of your
kinsman, Major Molineux."

EDGAR ALLAN POE

(1809–1849)

*E*dgar Allan Poe was born in Boston. His father disappeared, and his mother, who struggled to make a living as an actress and to care for her young family, succumbed to tuberculosis when Poe was 2. He was taken in and brought up by John Allan. Poe enrolled in 1826 in the University of Virginia, but left after a single term, having incurred heavy gambling debts. He enlisted in the army and served with great distinction, but his resentment of Allan's lack of financial support led to the drunken carousing that occasioned his expulsion from West Point and a severance of all relations with the Allans. Later attempts to patch up relations—Poe hoped to inherit something—failed. Left to fend for himself, he resolved to make his living as a writer. He published poems and short stories, and became, in 1835, the editor of the **Southern Literary Messenger**. He married his cousin, Virginia Clemms, when she was only 13, and worked in various capacities as a journalist. The hundreds of reviews that he wrote show that, despite all the mediocre stuff he had to plough through to make a living, he was a perceptive judge of literary talent when he found it. He is the single greatest practitioner of the gothic tale, and many of his stories and poems are studies in horror brought on by neurotic obsessions with death. He is also the father of the modern detective story and the author of the extraordinary **Eureka** (1848), a scientific treatise-cum–philosophical romance that reveals the range and depth of Poe's mind. He remains pre-eminently important as a contributor to the development of the short story, both as practitioner and theorist, bringing to the genre precisely formulated aesthetic notions that were to change the way short stories were perceived. He insisted that every story must be conceived with a "single effect" in mind and that "in the whole composition there should be no word written of which the tendency, direct or indirect, is not to the one pre-established design."

The Fall of the House of Usher

Son cœur est un luth suspendu;
Sitôt qu'on le touche il résonne.
DE BÉRANGER

During the whole of a dull, dark, and soundless day in the autumn of the year, when the clouds hung oppressively low in the heavens, I had been passing alone, on horseback, through a singularly dreary tract of country; and at length found myself, as the shades of the evening drew on, within view of the melancholy House of Usher. I know not how it was—but, with the first glimpse of the building, a sense of insufferable gloom pervaded my spirit. I say insufferable; for the feeling was unrelieved by any of that half-pleasurable, because poetic, sentiment, with which the mind usually receives even the sternest natural images of the desolate or terrible. I looked upon the scene before me—upon the mere house, and the simple landscape features of the domain—upon the bleak walls—upon the vacant eye-like windows—upon a few rank sedges—and upon a few white trunks of decayed tress—with an utter depression of soul which I can compare to no earthly sensation more properly than to the after-dream of the reveller upon opium—the bitter lapse into everyday life—the hideous dropping off of the veil. There was an iciness, a sinking, a sickening of the heart—an unredeemed dreariness of thought which no goading of the imagination could torture into aught of the sublime. What was it—I paused to think—what was it that so unnerved me in the contemplation of the House of Usher? It was a mystery all insoluble; nor could I grapple with the shadowy fancies that crowded upon me as I pondered. I was forced to fall back upon the unsatisfactory conclusion, that while, beyond doubt, there *are* combinations of very simple natural objects which have the power of thus affecting us, still the analysis of this power lies among considerations beyond our depth. It was possible, I reflected, that a mere different arrangement of the particulars of the scene, of the details of the picture, would be sufficient to modify, or perhaps to annihilate its capacity for sorrowful impression; and, acting upon this idea, I reined my horse to the precipitous brink of a black and lurid tarn that lay in unruffled lustre by the dwelling, and gazed down—but with a shudder even more thrilling than before—upon the remodelled and inverted images of the gray sedge, and the ghastly tree-stems, and the vacant and eye-like windows.

Nevertheless, in this mansion of gloom I now proposed to myself a sojourn of some weeks. Its proprietor, Roderick Usher, had been one of my boon companions in boyhood; but many years had elapsed since our last meeting. A letter, however, had lately reached me in a distant part of the country—a letter from him—which, in its wildly importunate nature, had admitted of no other than a personal reply. The MS. gave evidence of nervous agitation. The writer spoke of acute bodily illness—of a mental disorder which oppressed him—and of an earnest desire to see me, as his best, and indeed his only personal friend, with a view of attempting, by the cheerfulness of my society, some alleviation of his malady. It was the manner in which all this, and much more, was said—it was the apparent *heart* that went with his request—which allowed me no room for hesitation; and I accordingly obeyed forthwith what I still considered a very singular summons.

Although, as boys, we had been even intimate associates, yet I really knew little of my friend. His reserve had been always excessive and habitual. I was aware, however, that his very ancient family had been noted, time out of mind, for a peculiar sensibility of temperament, displaying itself, through long ages, in many works of exalted art, and manifested, of late, in repeated deeds of munificent yet unobtrusive charity, as well as in a passionate devotion to the intricacies, perhaps even more than to the orthodox and easily recognisable beauties, of musical science. I had learned, too, the very remarkable fact, that the stem of the Usher race, all time-honored as it was, had put forth, at no period, any enduring branch; in other words, that the entire family lay in the direct line of descent, and had always, with very trifling and very temporary variation, so lain. It was this deficiency, I considered, while running over in thought the perfect keeping of the character of the premises with the accredited character of the people, and while speculating upon the possible influence which the one, in the long lapse of centuries, might have exercised upon the other—it was this deficiency, perhaps, of collateral issue, and the consequent undeviating transmission, from sire to son, of the patrimony with the name, which had, at length, so identified the two as to merge the original title of the estate in the quaint and equivocal appellation of the "House of Usher"—an appellation which seemed to include, in the minds of the peasantry who used it, both the family and the family mansion.

I have said that the sole effect of my somewhat childish experiment— that of looking down within the tarn—had been to deepen the first singular impression. There can be no doubt that the consciousness of the rapid increase of my superstition—for why should I not so term it?— served mainly to accelerate the increase itself. Such, I have long known, is the paradoxical law of all sentiments having terror as a basis. And it might have been for this reason only, that, when I again uplifted my eyes to the house itself, from its image in the pool, there grew in my mind a strange fancy—a fancy so ridiculous, indeed, that I but mention it to show the vivid force of the sensations which oppressed me. I had so worked upon my imagination as really to believe that about the whole mansion and domain there hung an atmosphere peculiar to themselves and their immediate vicinity—an atmosphere which had no affinity with the air of heaven, but which had reeked up from the decayed trees, and the gray wall, and the silent tarn—a pestilent and mystic vapor, dull, sluggish, faintly discernible, and leaden-hued.

Shaking off from my spirit what *must* have been a dream, I scanned more narrowly the real aspect of the building. Its principal feature seemed to be that of an excessive antiquity. The discoloration of ages had been great. Minute fungi overspread the whole exterior, hanging in a fine tangled web-work from the eaves. Yet all this was apart from any extraordinary dilapidation. No portion of the masonry had fallen; and there appeared to be a wild inconsistency between its still perfect adaptation of parts, and the crumbling condition of the individual stones. In this there was much that reminded me of the specious totality of old wood-work which has rotted for long years in some neglected vault, with no disturbance from the breath of the external air. Beyond this indication of extensive decay, however, the fabric gave little token of instability. Perhaps the eye of a scrutinizing observer might have discovered a barely perceptible fissure, which, extending from the roof of the building in front, made its way down the wall in a zigzag direction, until it became lost in the sullen waters of the tarn.

Noticing these things, I rode over a short causeway to the house. A servant in waiting took my horse, and I entered the Gothic archway of the hall. A valet, of stealthy step, thence conducted me, in silence, through many dark and intricate passages in my progress to the *studio* of his master. Much that I encountered on the way contributed, I know not how, to heighten the vague sentiments of which I have already spoken. While the objects around me—while the carvings of the ceilings, the sombre tapestries of the walls, the ebon blackness of the floors, and the phantasmagoric armorial trophies which rattled as I strode, where but matters to which, or to such as which, I had been accustomed from my infancy—while I hesitated not to acknowledge how familiar was all this—I still wondered to find how unfamiliar were the fancies which ordinary images were stirring up. On one of the staircases, I met the physician of the family. His countenance, I thought, wore a mingled expression of low cunning and perplexity. He accosted me with trepidation and passed on. The valet now threw open a door and ushered me into the presence of his master.

The room in which I found myself was very large and lofty. The windows were long, narrow, and pointed, and at so vast a distance from the black oaken floor as to be altogether inaccessible from within. Feeble gleams of encrimsoned light made their way through the trellissed panes, and served to render sufficiently distinct the more prominent objects around; the eye, however, struggled in vain to reach the remoter angles of the chamber, or the recesses of the vaulted and fretted ceiling. Dark draperies hung upon the walls. The general furniture was profuse, comfortless, antique, and tattered. Many books and musical instruments lay scattered about, but failed to give any vitality to the scene. I felt that I breathed an atmosphere of sorrow. An air of stern, deep, and irredeemable gloom hung over and pervaded all.

Upon my entrance, Usher arose from a sofa on which he had been lying at full length, and greeted me with a vivacious warmth which had much in it, I at first thought, of an overdone cordiality—of the constrained effort of the *ennuyé* man of the world. A glance, however, at his countenance, convinced me of his perfect sincerity. We sat down; and for some moments, while he spoke not, I gazed upon him with a feeling half of pity, half of awe. Surely, man had never before so terribly altered, in so brief a period, as had Roderick Usher! It was with difficulty that I could bring myself to admit the identity of the wan being before me with the companion of my early boyhood. Yet the character of his face had been at all times remarkable. A cadaverousness of complexion; an eye large, liquid, and luminous beyond comparison; lips somewhat thin and very pallid, but of a surpassingly beautiful curve; a nose of delicate Hebrew model, but with a breadth of nostril unusual in similar formations; a finely moulded chin, speaking, in its want of prominence, of a want of moral energy; hair of a more than web-like softness and tenuity; these features, with an inordinate expansion above the regions of the temple, made up altogether a countenance not easily to be forgotten. And now in the mere exaggeration of the prevailing character of these features, and of the expression they were wont to convey, lay so much of change that I doubted to whom I spoke. The now ghastly pallor of the skin, and the now miraculous lustre of the eye, above all things startled and even awed me. The silken hair, too, had been suffered to grow all unheeded, and as, in its wild gossamer texture, it floated rather than fell about the face, I could not, even with effort, connect its Arabesque expression with any idea of simple humanity.

In the manner of my friend I was at once struck with an incoherence—an inconsistency; and I soon found this to arise from a series of feeble and futile struggles to overcome an habitual trepidancy—an excessive nervous agitation. For something of this nature I had indeed been prepared, no less by his letter, than by reminiscences of certain boyish traits, and by conclusions deduced from his peculiar physical conformation and temperament. His action was alternatively vivacious and sullen. His voice varied rapidly from a tremulous indecision (when the animal spirits seemed utterly in abeyance) to that species of energetic concision—that abrupt, weighty, unhurried, and hollow-sounding enunciation—that leaden, self-balanced and perfectly modulated guttural utterance, which may be observed in the lost drunkard, or the irreclaimable eater of opium, during the periods of his most intense excitement.

It was thus that he spoke of the object of my visit, of his earnest desire to see me, and of the solace he expected me to afford him. He entered, at some length, into what he conceived to be the nature of his malady. It was, he said, a constitutional and a family evil, and one for which he despaired to find a remedy—a mere nervous affection, he immediately added, which would undoubtedly soon pass off. It displayed itself in a host of unnatural sensations. Some of these, as he detailed them, interested and bewildered me; although, perhaps, the terms, and the general manner of the narration had their weight. He suffered much from a morbid acuteness of the senses; the most insipid food was alone endurable; he could wear only garments of certain texture; the odors of all flowers were oppressive; his eyes were tortured by even a faint light; and there were but peculiar sounds, and these from stringed instruments, which did not inspire him with horror.

To an anomalous species of terror I found him a bounden slave. "I shall perish," said he, "I *must* perish in this deplorable folly. Thus, thus, and not otherwise, shall I be lost. I dread the events of the future, not in themselves, but in their results. I shudder at the thought of any, even the most trivial, incident, which may operate upon this intolerable agitation of soul. I have, indeed, no abhorrence of danger, except in its absolute effect—in terror. In this unnerved—in this pitiable condition—I feel that the period will sooner or later arrive when I must abandon life and reason together, in some struggle with the grim phantasm, FEAR."

I learned, moreover, at intervals, and through broken and equivocal hints, another singular feature of his mental condition. He was enchained by certain superstitious impressions in regard to the dwelling which he tenanted, and whence, for many years, he had never ventured forth—in regard to an influence whose supposititious force was conveyed in terms too shadowy here to be re-stated—an influence which some peculiarities in the mere form and substance of his family mansion, had, by dint of long sufferance, he said, obtained over his spirit—an effect which the *physique* of the gray walls and turrets, and of the dim tarn into which they all looked down, had, at length, brought about upon the *morale* of his existence.

He admitted, however, although with hesitation, that much of the peculiar gloom which thus afflicted him could be traced to a more natural and far more palpable origin—to the severe and long-continued illness—indeed to the evidently approaching dissolution—of a tenderly beloved sister—his sole companion for long years—his last and only relative on earth. "Her decease," he said, with a bitterness which I can never forget, "would leave him (him the hopeless and the frail) the last of the ancient race of the Ushers." While he spoke, the lady Madeline (for so was she called) passed slowly through a remote portion of the apartment, and, without having noticed my presence, disappeared. I regarded her with an utter astonishment not unmingled with dread—and yet I found it impossible to account for such feelings. A sensation of stupor oppressed me, as my eyes followed her retreating steps. When a door, at length, closed upon her, my glance sought instinctively and eagerly the countenance of the brother—but he had buried his face in his hands, and I could only perceive that a far more than ordinary wanness had overspread the emaciated fingers through which trickled many passionate tears.

The disease of the lady Madeline had long baffled the skill of her physicians. A settled apathy, a gradual wasting away of the person, and frequent although transient affections of a partially cataleptical character, were the unusual diagnosis. Hitherto she had steadily borne up against the pressure of her malady, and had not betaken herself finally to bed; but, on the closing in of the evening of my arrival at the house, she succumbed (as her brother told me at night with inexpressible agitatic ʾ) to the prostrating power of the destroyer; and I learned that the glin ʿse I had obtained of her person would thus probably be the last I should obtain—that the lady, at least while living, would be seen by me no more.

For several days ensuing, her name was unmentioned by either Usher or myself: and during this period I was busied in earnest endeavors to alleviate the melancholy of my friend. We painted and read together; or I listened, as if in a dream, to the wild improvisations of his speaking guitar. And thus, as a closer and still closer intimacy admitted me more unreservedly into the recesses of his spirit, the more bitterly did I perceive the futility of all attempt at cheering a mind from which darkness, as if an inherent positive quality, poured forth upon all objects of the moral and physical universe, in one unceasing radiation of gloom.

I shall ever bear about me a memory of the many solemn hours I thus spent alone with the master of the House of Usher. Yet I should fail in any attempt to convey an idea of the exact character of the studies, or of the occupations, in which he involved me, or led me the way. An excited and highly distempered ideality threw a sulphureous lustre over all. His long improvised dirges will ring forever in my ears. Among other things, I hold painfully in mind a certain singular perversion and amplification of the wild air of the last waltz of Von Weber. From the paintings over which his elaborate fancy brooded, and which grew, touch by touch, into vaguenesses at which I shuddered the more thrillingly, because I shuddered knowing not why;—from these paintings (vivid as their images now are before me) I would in vain endeavor to educe more than a small portion which should lie within the compass of merely written words. By the utter simplicity, by the nakedness of his designs, he arrested and overawed attention. If ever mortal painted an idea, that mortal was

Roderick Usher. For me at least—in the circumstances then surrounding me—there arose out of the pure abstractions which the hypochondriac contrived to throw upon his canvass, an intensity of intolerable awe, no shadow of which felt I ever yet in the contemplation of the certainly glowing yet too concrete reveries of Fuseli.

One of the phantasmagoric conceptions of my friend, partaking not so rigidly of the spirit of abstraction, may be shadowed forth, although feebly, in words. A small picture presented the interior of an immensely long and rectangular vault or tunnel, with low walls, smooth, white, and without interruption or device. Certain accessory points of the design served well to convey the idea that this excavation lay at an exceeding depth below the surface of the earth. No outlet was observed in any portion of its vast extent, and no torch, or other artificial source of light was discernible; yet a flood of intense rays rolled throughout, and bathed the whole in a ghastly and inappropriate splendor.

I have just spoken of that morbid condition of the auditory nerve which rendered all music intolerable to the sufferer, with the exception of certain effects of stringed instruments. It was, perhaps, the narrow limits to which he thus confined himself upon the guitar, which gave birth, in great measure, to the fantastic character of his performances. But the fervid *facility* of his *impromptus* could not be so accounted for. They must have been, and were, in the notes, as well as in the words of his wild fantasias (for he not unfrequently accompanied himself with rhymed verbal improvisations), the result of that intense mental collectedness and concentration to which I have previously alluded as observable only in particular moments of the highest artificial excitement. The words of one of these rhapsodies I have easily remembered. I was, perhaps, the more forcibly impressed with it, as he gave it, because, in the under or mystic current of its meaning, I fancied that I perceived, and for the first time, a full consciousness on the part of Usher, of the tottering of his lofty reason upon her throne. The verses, which were entitled "The Haunted Palace," ran very nearly, if not accurately, thus:

I

> *In the greenest of our valleys,*
> *By good angels tenanted,*
> *Once a fair and stately palace—*
> *Radiant palace—reared its head.*
> *In the monarch Thought's dominion—*
> *It stood there!*
> *Never seraph spread a pinion*
> *Over fabric half so fair.*

II

Banners yellow, glorious, golden,
   On its roof did float and flow;
(This—all this—was in the olden
   Time long ago)
And every gentle air that dallied,
   In that sweet day,
Along the ramparts plumed and pallid,
   A winged odor went away.

III

Wanderers in that happy valley
   Through two luminous windows saw
Spirits moving musically
   To a lute's well-tunéd law,
Round about a throne, where sitting
   (Porphyrogene!)
In state his glory well befitting
   The ruler of the realm was seen.

IV

And all with pearl and ruby glowing
   Was the fair palace door,
Through which came flowing, flowing, flowing,
   And sparkling evermore,
A troop of Echoes whose sweet duty
   Was but to sing,
In voices of surpassing beauty,
   The wit and wisdom of their king.

V

But evil things, in robes of sorrow,
   Assailed the monarch's high estate;
(Ah, let us mourn, for never morrow
   Shall dawn upon him, desolate!)
And, round about his home, the glory
   That blushed and bloomed
Is but a dim-remembered story
   Of the old time entombed.

VI

And travellers now within that valley,
  Through the red-litten windows, see
Vast forms that move fantastically
  To a discordant melody;
While, like a rapid ghastly river,
  Through the pale door,
A hideous throng rush out forever,
  And laugh—but smile no more.

I well remember that suggestions arising from this ballad, led us into a train of thought wherein there became manifest an opinion of Usher's which I mention not so much on account of its novelty, (for other men have thought thus,) as on account of the pertinacity with which he maintained it. This opinion, in its general form, was that of the sentience of all vegetable things. But, in his disordered fancy, the idea had assumed a more daring character, and trespassed, under certain conditions, upon the kingdom of inorganization. I lack words to express the full extent, or the earnest *abandon* of his persuasion. The belief, however, was connected (as I have previously hinted) with the gray stones of the home of his forefathers. The conditions of the sentience had been here, he imagined, fulfilled, in the method of collocation of these stones—in the order of their arrangement, as well as in that of the many *fungi* which overspread them, and of the decayed trees which stood around—above all, in the long undisturbed endurance of his arrangement, and in its reduplication in the still waters of the tarn. Its evidence—the evidence of the sentience— was to be seen, he said, (and I here started as he spoke,) in the gradual yet certain condensation of an atmosphere of their own about the waters and the walls. The result was discoverable, he added, in that silent, yet importunate and terrible influence which for centuries had moulded the destinies of his family, and which made *him* what I now saw him—what he was. Such opinions need no comment, and I will make none.

Our books—the books which, for years, had formed no small portion of the mental existence of the invalid—were, as might be supposed, in strict keeping with this character of phantasm. We pored together over such works as the Ververt et Chartreuse of Gresset; the Belphegor of Machiavelli; the Heaven and Hell of Swedenborg; the Subterranean Voyage of Nicholas Klimm by Holberg; the Chiromancy of Robert Flud, of Jean D'Indaginé, and of De la Chambre; the Journey into the Blue Distance of Tieck; and the City of the Sun of Campanella. One favorite volume was a small octavo edition of the *Directorium Inquisitorium*, by the Dominican Eymeric de Gironne; and there were passages in Pomponius Mela, about the old African Satyrs and Œgipans, over which Usher would sit dreaming for hours. His chief delight, however, was found in the perusal of an exceedingly rare and curious book in quarto Gothic—the manual of a forgotten church—the *Vigiliae Mortuorum secundum Chorum Ecclesiae Maguntinae.*

I could not help thinking of the wild ritual of this work, and of its probable influence upon the hypochondriac, when, one evening, having informed me abruptly that the lady Madeline was no more, he stated his intention of preserving her corpse for a fortnight, (previously to its final interment,) in one of the numerous vaults within the main walls of the building. The worldly reason, however, assigned for this singular proceeding, was one which I did not feel at liberty to dispute. The brother had been led to his resolution (so he told me) by consideration of the unusual character of the malady of the deceased, of certain obtrusive and eager inquiries on the part of her medical men, and of the remote and exposed situation of the burial-ground of the family. I will not deny that when I called to mind the sinister countenance of the person whom I met upon the staircase, on the day of my arrival at the house, I had no desire to oppose what I regarded as at best but a harmless, and by no means an unnatural, precaution.

At the request of Usher, I personally aided him in the arrangements for the temporary entombment. The body having been encoffined, we two alone bore it to its rest. The vault in which we placed it (and which had been so long unopened that our torches, half smothered in its oppressive atmosphere, gave us little opportunity for investigation) was small, damp, and entirely without means of admission for light; lying, at great depth, immediately beneath that portion of the building in which was my own sleeping apartment. It had been used, apparently, in remote feudal times, for the worst purposes of a donjon-keep, and, in later days, as a place of deposit for powder, or some other highly combustible substance, as a portion of its floor, and the whole interior of a long archway through which we reached it, were carefully sheathed with copper. The door, of massive iron, had been, also, similarly protected. Its immense weight caused an unusually sharp grating sound, as it moved upon its hinges.

Having deposited our mournful burden upon tressels within this region of horror, we partially turned aside the yet unscrewed lid of the coffin, and looked upon the face of the tenant. A striking similitude between the brother and sister now first arrested my attention; and Usher, divining, perhaps, my thoughts, murmured out some few words from which I learned that the deceased and himself had been twins, and that sympathies of a scarcely intelligible nature had always existed between them. Our glances, however, rested not long upon the dead—for we could not regard her unawed. The disease which had thus entombed the lady in the maturity of youth, had left, as usual in all maladies of a strictly cataleptical character, the mockery of a faint blush upon the bosom and the face, and that suspiciously lingering smile upon the lip which is so terrible in death. We replaced and screwed down the lid, and, having secured the door of iron, made our way, with toil, into the scarcely less gloomy apartments of the upper portion of the house.

And now, some days of bitter grief having elapsed, an observable change came over the features of the mental disorder of my friend. His ordinary manner had vanished. His ordinary occupations were neglected or forgotten. He roamed from chamber to chamber with hurried, unequal, and objectless step. The pallor of his countenance had assumed, if possible, a more ghastly hue—but the luminousness of his eye had utterly gone out. The once occasional huskiness of his tone was heard no more; and a tremulous quaver, as if of extreme terror, habitually characterized his utterance. There were times, indeed, when I thought his unceasingly agitated mind was laboring with some oppressive secret, to divulge which he struggled for the necessary courage. At times, again, I was obliged to resolve all into the mere inexplicable vagaries of madness, for I beheld him gazing upon vacancy for long hours, in an attitude of the profoundest attention, as if listening to some imaginary sound. It was no wonder that his condition terrified—that it infected me. I felt creeping upon me, by slow yet certain degrees, the wild influences of his own fantastic yet impressive superstitions.

It was, especially, upon retiring to bed late in the night of the seventh or eighth day after the placing of the lady Madeline within the donjon, that I experienced the full power of such feelings. Sleep came not near my couch—while the hours waned and waned away. I struggled to reason off the nervousness which had dominion over me. I endeavored to believe that much, if not all of what I felt, was due to the bewildering influence of the gloomy furniture of the room—of the dark and tattered draperies, which, tortured into motion by the breath of a rising tempest, swayed fitfully to and fro upon the walls, and rustled uneasily about the decorations of the bed. But my efforts were fruitless. An irrepressible tremor gradually pervaded my frame; and, at length, there sat upon my very heart an incubus of utterly causeless alarm. Shaking this off with a gasp and a struggle, I uplifted myself upon the pillows, and, peering earnestly within the intense darkness of the chamber, harkened—I know not why, except that an instinctive spirit prompted me—to certain low and indefinite sounds which came, through the pauses of the storm, at long intervals, I knew not whence. Overpowered by an intense sentiment of horror, unaccountable yet unendurable, I threw on my clothes with haste (for I felt that I should sleep no more during the night), and endeavored to arouse myself from the pitiable condition into which I had fallen, by pacing rapidly to and fro through the apartment.

I had taken but few turns in this manner, when a light step on an adjoining staircase arrested my attention. I presently recognised it as that of Usher. In an instant afterward he rapped, with a gentle touch, at my door, and entered, bearing a lamp. His countenance was, as usual, cadaverously wan—but, moreover, there was a species of mad hilarity in his eyes—an evidently restrained *hysteria* in his whole demeanor. His air appalled me—but anything was preferable to the solitude which I had so long endured, and I even welcomed his presence as a relief.

"And you have not seen it?" he said abruptly, after having stared about him for some moments in silence—"you have not then seen it?— but, stay! you shall." Thus speaking, and having carefully shaded his lamp, he hurried to one of the casements, and threw it freely open to the storm.

The impetuous fury of the entering gust nearly lifted us from our feet. It was, indeed, a tempestuous yet sternly beautiful night, and one wildly singular in its terror and its beauty. A whirlwind had apparently collected its force in our vicinity; for there were frequent and violent alterations in the direction of the wind; and the exceeding density of the clouds (which hung so low as to press upon the turrets of the house) did not prevent our perceiving the life-like velocity with which they flew careering from all points against each other, without passing away into the distance. I say that even their exceeding density did not prevent our perceiving this—yet we had no glimpse of the moon or stars—nor was there any flashing forth of the lightning. But the under surfaces of the huge masses of agitated vapor, as well as all terrestrial objects immediately around us, were glowing in the unnatural light of a faintly luminous and distinctly visible gaseous exhalation which hung about and enshrouded the mansion.

"You must not—you shall not behold this!" said I, shudderingly, to Usher, as I led him, with a gentle violence, from the window to a seat. "These appearances, which bewilder you, are merely electrical phenomena not uncommon—or it may be that they have their ghastly origin in the rank miasma of the tarn. Let us close this casement;—the air is chilling and dangerous to your frame. Here is one of your favorite romances. I will read, and you shall listen;—and so we will pass away this terrible night together."

The antique volume which I had taken up was the "Mad Trist" of Sir Launcelot Canning; but I had called it a favorite of Usher's more in sad jest than in earnest; for, in truth, there is little in its uncouth and unimaginative prolixity which could have had interest for the lofty and spiritual ideality of my friend. It was, however, the only book immediately at hand; and I indulged a vague hope that the excitement which now agitated the hypochondriac, might find relief (for the history of mental disorder is full of similar anomalies) even in the extremeness of the folly which I should read. Could I have judged, indeed, by the wild overstrained air of vivacity with which he harkened, or apparently harkened, to the words of the tale, I might well have congratulated myself upon the success of my design.

I had arrived at that well-known portion of the story where Ethelred, the hero of the Trist, having sought in vain for peaceable admission into the dwelling of the hermit, proceeds to make good an entrance by force. Here, it will be remembered, the words of the narrative run thus:

"And Ethelred, who was by nature of a doughty heart, and who was now mighty withal, on account of the powerfulness of the wine which he had drunken, waited no longer to hold parley with the hermit, who, in sooth, was of an obstinate and maliceful turn, but, feeling the rain upon his shoulders, and fearing the rising of the tempest, uplifted his mace outright, and, with blows, made quickly room in the plankings of the door for his gauntleted hand; and now pulling therewith sturdily, he so cracked, and ripped, and tore all asunder, that the noise of the dry and hollow-sounding wood alarummed and reverberated throughout the forest."

At the termination of this sentence I started, and for a moment, paused; for it appeared to me (although I at once concluded that my excited fancy had deceived me)—it appeared to me that, from some very remote portion of the mansion, there came, indistinctly, to my ears, what might have been, in its exact similarity of character, the echo (but a stifled and dull one certainly) of the very cracking and ripping sound which Sir Launcelot had so particularly described. It was, beyond doubt, the coincidence alone which had arrested my attention; for, amid the rattling of the sashes of the casements, and the ordinary commingled noises of the still increasing storm, the sound, in itself, had nothing, surely, which should have interested or disturbed me. I continued the story:

"But the good champion Ethelred, now entering within the door, was sore enraged and amazed to perceive no signal of the maliceful hermit; but, in the stead thereof, a dragon of a scaly and prodigious demeanor, and of a fiery tongue, which sate in guard before a palace of gold, with a floor of silver; and upon the wall there hung a shield of shining brass with this legend enwritten—

Who entereth herein, a conqueror hath bin;
Who slayeth the dragon, the shield he shall win;

And Ethelred uplifted his mace, and struck upon the head of the dragon, which fell before him, and gave up his pesty breath, with a shriek so horrid and harsh, and withal so piercing, that Ethelred had fain to close his ears with his hands against the dreadful noise of it, the like whereof was never before heard."

Here again I paused abruptly, and now with a feeling of wild amazement—for there could be no doubt whatever that, in this instance, I did actually hear (although from what direction it proceeded I found it impossible to say) a low and apparently distant, but harsh, protracted, and most unusual screaming or grating sound—the exact counterpart of what my fancy had already conjured up for the dragon's unnatural shriek as described by the romancer.

Oppressed, as I certainly was, upon the occurrence of this second and most extraordinary coincidence, by a thousand conflicting sensations, in which wonder and extreme terror were predominant, I still retained sufficient presence of mind to avoid exciting, by any observation, the sensitive nervousness of my companion. I was by no means certain that he had noticed the sounds in question; although, assuredly, a strange alteration had, during the last few minutes, taken place in his demeanor. From a position fronting my own, he had gradually brought round his chair, so as to sit with his face to the door of the chamber; and thus I could but partially perceive his features, although I saw that his lips trembled as if he were murmuring inaudibly. His head had dropped upon his breast—yet I knew that he was not asleep, from the wide and rigid opening of the eye as I caught a glance of it in profile. The motion of his body, too, was at variance with this idea—for he rocked from side to side with a gentle yet constant and uniform sway. Having rapidly taken notice of all this, I resumed the narrative of Sir Launcelot, which thus proceeded:

"And now, the champion, having escaped from the terrible fury of the dragon, bethinking himself of the brazen shield, and of the breaking up of the enchantment which was upon it, removed the carcass from out of the way before him, and approached valorously over the silver pavement of the castle to where the shield was upon the wall; which in sooth tarried not for his full coming, but fell down at his feet upon the silver floor, with a mighty great and terrible ringing sound."

No sooner had these syllables passed my lips, than—as if a shield of brass had indeed, at the moment, fallen heavily upon a floor of silver— I became aware of a distinct, hollow, metallic, and clangorous, yet apparently muffled reverberation. Completely unnerved, I leaped to my feet; but the measured rocking movement of Usher was undisturbed. I rushed to the chair in which he sat. His eyes were bent fixedly before him, and throughout his whole countenance there reigned a stony rigidity. But, as I placed my hand upon his shoulder, there came a strong shudder over his whole person; a sickly smile quivered about his lips; and I saw that he spoke in a low, hurried, and gibbering murmur, as if unconscious of my presence. Bending closely over him, I at length drank in the hideous import of his words.

"Not hear it?—yes, I hear it, and *have* heard it. Long—long—long— many minutes, many hours, many days, have I heard it—yet I dared not—oh, pity me, miserable wretch that I am!—I dared not—I *dared* not speak! *We have put her living in the tomb!* Said I not that my senses were acute? I *now* tell you that I heard her first feeble movements in the hollow coffin. I heard them—many, many days ago—yet I dared not—I *dared not speak!* And now—to-night—Ethelred—ha! ha!—the breaking of the hermit's door, and the death-cry of the dragon, and the clangor of the shield!—say, rather, the rending of her coffin, and the grating of the iron hinges of her prison, and her struggles within the coppered archway of the vault! Oh whither shall I fly? Will she not be here anon? Is she not hurrying to upbraid me for my haste? Have I not heard her footstep on the stair? Do I not distinguish that heavy and horrible beating of her heart? Madman!"—here he sprang furiously to his feet, and shrieked out his syllables, as if in the effort he were giving up his soul—*"Madman! I tell you that she now stands without the door!"*

As if in the superhuman energy of his utterance there had been found the potency of a spell—the huge antique pannels to which the speaker pointed, threw slowly back, upon the instant, their ponderous and ebony jaws. It was the work of the rushing gust—but then without those doors there *did* stand the lofty and enshrouded figure of the lady Madeline of Usher. There was blood upon her white robes, and the evidence of some bitter struggle upon every portion of her emaciated frame. For a moment she remained trembling and reeling to and fro upon the threshold—then, with a low moaning cry, fell heavily inward upon the person of her brother, and in her violent and now final death-agonies, bore him to the floor a corpse, and a victim to the terrors he had anticipated.

From that chamber, and from that mansion, I fled aghast. The storm was still abroad in all its wrath as I found myself crossing the old causeway. Suddenly there shot along the path a wild light, and I turned to see whence a gleam so unusual could have issued; for the vast house and its shadows were alone behind me. The radiance was that of the full, setting, and blood-red moon, which now shone vividly through that once barely-discernible fissure, of which I have before spoken as extending from the roof of the building, in a zigzag direction, to the base. While I gazed, this fissure rapidly widened—there came a fierce breath of the whirlwind—the entire orb of the satellite burst at once upon my sight—my brain reeled as I saw the mighty walls rushing asunder—there was a long tumultuous shouting sound like the voice of a thousand waters—and the deep and dank tarn at my feet closed sullenly and silently over the fragments of the *"House of Usher."*

Ligeia

And the will therein lieth, which dieth not.
Who knoweth the mysteries of the will, with
its vigor? For God is but a great will
pervading all things by nature of its
intentness. Man doth not yield himself to the
angels, nor unto death utterly, save only
through the weakness of his feeble will.
JOSEPH GLANVILL

I cannot, for my soul, remember how, when, or even precisely where, I first became acquainted with the lady Ligeia. Long years have since elapsed, and my memory is feeble through much suffering. Or, perhaps, I cannot *now* bring these points to mind, because, in truth, the character of my beloved, her rare learning, her singular yet placid cast of beauty, and the thrilling and enthralling eloquence of her low musical language, made their way into my heart by paces so steadily and stealthily progressive that they have been unnoticed and unknown. Yet I believe that I met her first and most frequently in some large, old, decaying city near the Rhine. Of her family—I have surely heard her speak. That it is of a remotely ancient date cannot be doubted. Ligeia! Ligeia! Buried in studies of a nature more than all else adapted to deaden impressions of the outward world, it is by that sweet word alone—by Ligeia—that I bring before mine eyes in fancy the image of her who is no more. And now, while I write, a recollection flashes upon me that I have *never known* the paternal name of her who was my friend and my betrothed, and who became the partner of my studies, and finally the wife of my bosom. Was it a playful charge on the part of my Ligeia? or was it a test of my strength of affection, that I should institute no inquiries upon this point? or was it rather a caprice of my own—a wildly romantic offering on the shrine of the most passionate devotion? I but indistinctly recall the fact itself— what wonder that I have utterly forgotten the circumstances which origi- nated or attended it? And, indeed, if ever that spirit which is entitled *Romance* —if ever she, the wan and the misty-winged *Ashtophet* of idola- trous Egypt, presided, as they tell, over marriages ill-omened, then most surely she presided over mine.

There is one dear topic, however, on which my memory fails me not. It is the *person* of Ligeia. In stature she was tall, somewhat slender, and, in her latter days, even emaciated. I would in vain attempt to portray the majesty, the quiet ease, of her demeanor, or the incomprehensible lightness and elasticity of her footfall. She came and departed as a shadow.

I was never made aware of her entrance into my closed study save by the dear music of her low sweet voice, as she placed her marble hand upon my shoulder. In beauty of face no maiden ever equalled her. It was the radiance of an opium dream—an airy and spirit-lifting vision more wildly divine than the phantasies which hovered about the slumbering souls of the daughters of Delos. Yet her features were not of that regular mould which we have been falsely taught to worship in the classical labors of the heathen. "There is no exquisite beauty," says Bacon, Lord Verulam, speaking truly of all the forms and *genera* of beauty, "without some *strangeness* in the proportion." Yet, although I saw that the features of Ligeia were not of a classic regularity—although I perceived that her loveliness was indeed "exquisite," and felt that there was much of "strangeness" pervading it, yet I have tried in vain to detect the irregularity and to trace home my own perception of "the strange." I examined the contour of the lofty and pale forehead—it was faultless—how cold indeed that word when applied to a majesty so divine!—the skin rivalling the purest ivory, the commanding extent and repose, the gentle prominence of the regions above the temples; and then the raven-black, the glossy, the luxuriant and naturally-curling tresses, setting forth the full force of the Homeric epithet, "hyacinthine!" I looked at the delicate outlines of the nose—and nowhere but in the graceful medallions of the Hebrews had I beheld a similar perfection. There were the same luxurious smoothness of surface, the same scarcely perceptible tendency to the aquiline, the same harmoniously curved nostrils speaking the free spirit. I regarded the sweet mouth. Here was indeed the triumph of all things heavenly—the magnificent turn of the short upper lip—the soft, voluptuous slumber of the under—the dimples which sported, and the color which spoke—the teeth glancing back, with a brilliancy almost startling, every ray of the holy light which fell upon them in her serene and placid, yet most exultingly radiant of all smiles. I scrutinized the formation of the chin—and here, too, I found the gentleness of breadth, the softness and the majesty, the fullness and the spirituality, of the Greek—the contour which the God Apollo revealed but in a dream, to Cleomenes, the son of the Athenian. And then I peered into the large eyes of Ligeia.

For eyes we have no models in the remotely antique. It might have been, too, that in these eyes of my beloved lay the secret to which Lord Verulam alludes. They were, I must believe, far larger than the ordinary eyes of our own race. They were even fuller than the fullest of the gazelle eyes of the tribe of the valley of Nourjahad. Yet it was only at intervals— in moments of intense excitement—that this peculiarity became more than slightly noticeable in Ligeia. And at such moments was her beauty— in my heated fancy thus it appeared perhaps—the beauty of beings either above or apart from the earth—the beauty of the fabulous Houri of the Turk. The hue of the orbs was the most brilliant of black, and, far over them, hung jetty lashes of great length. The brows, slightly irregular in outline, had the same tint. The "strangeness," however, which I found in the eyes, was of a nature distinct from the formation, or the color, or the brilliancy of the features, and must, after all, be referred to the *expression*. Ah, word of no meaning! behind whose vast latitude of mere sound we intrench our ignorance of so much of the spiritual. The expression of the eyes of Ligeia! How for long hours have I pondered upon it! How have I, through the whole of a midsummer night, struggled to fathom it! What was it—that something more profound than the well of Democritus—which lay far within the pupils of my beloved? What *was* it? I was possessed with a passion to discover. Those eyes! those large, those shining, those divine orbs! they became to me twin stars of Leda, and I to them devoutest of astrologers.

There is no point, among the many incomprehensible anomalies of the science of mind, more thrillingly exciting than the fact—never, I believe, noticed in the schools—that, in our endeavors to recall to memory something long forgotten, we often find ourselves *upon the very verge* of remembrance, without being able, in the end, to remember. And thus how frequently, in my intense scrutiny of Ligeia's eyes, have I felt approaching the full knowledge of their expression—felt it approaching—yet not quite be mine—and so at length entirely depart! And (strange, oh strangest mystery of all!) I found, in the commonest objects of the universe, a circle of analogies to that expression. I mean to say that, subsequently to the period when Ligeia's beauty passed into my spirit, there dwelling as in a shrine, I derived, from many existences in the material world, a sentiment such as I felt always aroused within me by her large and luminous orbs. Yet not the more could I define that sentiment, or analyze, or even steadily view it. I recognized it, let me repeat, sometimes in the survey of a rapidly-growing vine—in the contemplation of a moth, a butterfly, a chrysalis, a stream of running water. I have felt it in the ocean; in the falling of a meteor. I have felt it in the glances of unusually aged people. And there are one or two stars in heaven—(one especially, a star of the sixth magnitude, double and changeable, to be found near the large star in Lyra) in a telescopic scrutiny of which I have been made aware of the feeling. I have been filled with it by certain sounds from stringed instruments, and not unfrequently by passages from books. Among innumerable other instances, I well remember something in a volume of Joseph Glanvill, which (perhaps merely from its quaintness—who shall say?) never failed to inspire me with the sentiment;—"And the will therein lieth, which dieth not. Who knoweth the mysteries of the will, with its vigor? For God is but a great will pervading all things by nature of its intentness. Man doth not yield him to the angels, nor unto death utterly, save only through the weakness of his feeble will."

Length of years, and subsequent reflection, have enabled me to trace, indeed, some remote connection between this passage in the English moralist and a portion of the character of Ligeia. An *intensity* in thought, action, or speech, was possibly, in her, a result, or at least an index, of that gigantic volition which, during our long intercourse, failed to give other and more immediate evidence of its existence. Of all the women whom I have ever known, she, the outwardly calm, the ever-placid Ligeia, was the most violently a prey to the tumultuous vultures of stern passion. And of such passion I could form no estimate, save by the miraculous expansion of those eyes which at once so delighted and appalled me— by the almost magical melody, modulation, distinctness and placidity of her very low voice—and by the fierce energy (rendered doubly effective by contrast with her manner of utterance) of the wild words which she habitually uttered.

I have spoken of the learning of Ligeia: it was immense—such as I have never known in woman. In the classical tongues was she deeply proficient, and as far as my own acquaintance extended in regard to the modern dialects of Europe, I have never known her at fault. Indeed upon any theme of the most admired, because simply the most abstruse of the boasted erudition of the academy, have I *ever* found Ligeia at fault? How singularly—how thrillingly, this one point in the nature of my wife has forced itself, at this late period only, upon my attention! I said her knowledge was such as I have never known in woman—but where breathes the man who has traversed, and successfully, *all* the wide areas of moral, physical, and mathematical science? I saw not then what I now clearly perceive, that the acquisitions of Ligeia were gigantic, were astounding; yet I was sufficiently aware of her infinite supremacy to resign myself, with a child-like confidence, to her guidance through the chaotic world of metaphysical investigation at which I was most busily occupied during the earlier years of our marriage. With how vast a triumph—with how vivid a delight—with how much of all that is ethereal in hope—did I *feel*, as she bent over me in studies but little sought—but less known—that delicious vista by slow degrees expanding before me, down whose long, gorgeous, and all untrodden path, I might at length pass onward to the goal of a wisdom too divinely precious not to be forbidden!

How poignant, then, must have been the grief with which, after some years, I beheld my well-grounded expectations take wings to themselves and fly away! Without Ligeia I was but as a child groping benighted. Her presence, her readings alone, rendered vividly luminous the many mysteries of the transcendentalism in which we were immersed. Wanting the radiant lustre of her eyes, letters, lambent and golden, grew duller than Saturnian lead. And now those eyes shone less and less frequently upon the pages over which I pored. Ligeia grew ill. The wild eyes blazed with a too—too glorious effulgence; the pale fingers became of the transparent waxen hue of the grave, and the blue veins upon the lofty forehead swelled and sank impetuously with the tides of the most gentle emotion. I saw that she must die—and I struggled desperately in spirit with the grim Azrael. And the struggles of the passionate wife were, to my astonishment, even more energetic than my own. There had been much in her stern nature to impress me with the belief that, to her, death would have come without its terrors;—but not so. Words are impotent to convey any just idea of the fierceness of resistance with which she wrestled with the Shadow. I groaned in anguish at the pitiable spectacle. I would have soothed—I would have reasoned; but, in the intensity of her wild desire for life,—for life—*but* for life—solace and reason were alike the uttermost of folly. Yet not until the last instance, amid the most convulsive writhings of her fierce spirit, was shaken the external placidity of her demeanor. Her voice grew more gentle—grew more low—yet I would not wish to dwell upon the wild meaning of the quietly uttered words. My brain reeled as I hearkened, entranced, to a melody more than mortal—to assumptions and aspirations which mortality had never before known.

That she loved me I should not have doubted; and I might have been easily aware that, in a bosom such as hers, love would have reigned no ordinary passion. But in death only, was I fully impressed with the strength of her affection. For long hours, detaining my hand, would she pour out before me the overflowing of a heart whose more than passion-ate devotion amounted to idolatry. How had I deserved to be so blessed by such confessions?—how had I deserved to be so cursed with the removal of my beloved in the hour of her making them? But upon this subject I cannot bear to dilate. Let me say only, that in Ligeia's more than womanly abandonment to a love, alas! all unmerited, all unworthily bestowed, I at length recognized the principle of her longing with so wildly earnest a desire for the life which was now fleeing so rapidly away. It is this wild longing—it is this eager vehemence of desire for life— *but* for life—that I have no power to portray—no utterance capable of expressing.

At high noon of the night in which she departed, beckoning me, peremptorily, to her side, she bade me repeat certain verses composed by herself not many days before. I obeyed her.—They were these:

> Lo! 'tis a gala night
>   Within the lonesome latter years!
> An angel throng, bewinged, bedight
>   In veils, and drowned in tears,
> Sit in a theatre, to see
>   A play of hopes and fears,
> While the orchestra breathes fitfully
>   The music of the spheres.

Mimes, in the form of God on high,
  Mutter and mumble low,
And hither and thither fly—
  Mere puppets they, who come and go
At bidding of vast formless things
  That shift the scenery to and fro,
Flapping from out their Condor wings
  Invisible Wo!

That motley drama!—oh, be sure
  It shall not be forgot!
With its Phantom chased forevermore,
  By a crowd that seize it not,
Through a circle that ever returneth in
  To the self-same spot,
And much of Madness and more of Sin,
  And Horror the soul of the plot.

But see, amid the mimic rout,
  A crawling shape intrude!
A blood-red thing that writhes from out
  The scenic solitude!
It writhes!—it writhes!—with mortal pangs
  The mimes become its food,
And the seraphs sob at vermin fangs
  In human gore imbued.

Out—out are the lights—out all!
  And over each quivering form,
The curtain, a funeral pall,
  Comes down with the rush of a storm,
And the angels, all pallid and wan,
  Uprising, unveiling, affirm
That the play is the tragedy, "Man,"
  And its hero the Conqueror Worm.

"O God!" half shrieked Ligeia, leaping to her feet and extending her arms aloft with a spasmodic movement, as I made an end of these lines—"O God! O Divine Father!—shall these things be undeviatingly so?—shall this Conqueror be not once conquered? Are we not part and parcel in Thee? Who—who knoweth the mysteries of the will with its vigor? Man doth not yield him to the angels, *nor unto death utterly*, save only through the weakness of his feeble will."

And now, as if exhausted with emotion, she suffered her white arms to fall, and returned solemnly to her bed of Death. And as she breathed her last sighs, there came mingled with them a low murmur from her lips. I bent to them my ear and distinguished, again, the concluding words of the passage in Glanvill—"*Man doth not yield him to the angels, nor unto death utterly, save only through the weakness of his feeble will.*"

She died;—and I, crushed into the very dust with sorrow, could no longer endure the lonely desolation of my dwelling in the dim and decaying city by the Rhine. I had no lack of what the world calls wealth. Ligeia had brought me far more, very far more than ordinarily falls to the lot of mortals. After a few months, therefore, of weary and aimless wandering, I purchased, and put in some repair, an abbey, which I shall not name, in one of the wildest and least frequented portions of fair England. The gloomy and dreary grandeur of the building, the almost savage aspect of the domain, the many melancholy and time-honored memories connected with both, had much in unison with the feelings of utter abandonment which had driven me into that remote and unsocial region of the country. Yet although the external abbey, with its verdant decay hanging about it, suffered but little alteration, I gave way, with a child-like perversity, and perchance with a faint hope of alleviating my sorrows, to a display of more than regal magnificence within. For such follies, even in childhood, I had imbibed a taste, and now they came back to me as if in the dotage of grief. Alas, I feel how much even of incipient madness might have been discovered in the gorgeous and fantastic draperies, in the solemn carvings of Egypt, in the wild cornices and furniture, in the Bedlam patterns of the carpets of tufted gold! I had became a bounden slave in the trammels of opium, and my labors and my orders had taken a coloring from my dreams. But these absurdities I must not pause to detail. Let me speak only of that one chamber, ever accursed, whither in a moment of mental alienation, I led from the altar as my bride—as the successor of the unforgotten Ligeia—the fair-haired and blue-eyed Lady Rowena Trevanion, of Tremaine.

There is no individual portion of the architecture and decoration of that bridal chamber which is not now visibly before me. Where were the souls of the haughty family of the bride, when, through thirst of gold, they permitted to pass the threshold of an apartment *so* bedecked, a maiden and a daughter so beloved? I have said that I minutely remember the details of the chamber—yet I am sadly forgetful on topics of deep moment—and here there was no system, no keeping, in the fantastic display, to take hold upon the memory. The room lay in a high turret of the castellated abbey, was pentagonal in shape, and of capacious size. Occupying the whole southern face of the pentagon was the sole window—an immense sheet of unbroken glass from Venice—a single pane, and tinted of a leaden hue, so that the rays of either the sun or moon, passing through it, fell with a ghastly lustre on the objects within. Over the upper portion of this huge window, extended the trellice-work of an aged vine, which clambered up the massy walls of the turret. The ceiling, of gloomy-looking oak, was excessively lofty, vaulted, and elaborately fretted with the wildest and most grotesque specimens of a semi-Gothic, semi-Druidical device. From out the most central recess of this melancholy vaulting, depended, by a single chain of gold with long links, a huge censer of the same metal, Saracenic in pattern, and with many perforations so contrived that there writhed in and out of them, as if endued with a serpent vitality, a continual succession of parti-colored fires.

Some few ottomans and golden candelabra, of Eastern figure, were in various stations about—and there was the couch, too—the bridal couch—of an Indian model, and low, and sculptured of solid ebony, with a pall-like canopy above. In each of the angles of the chamber stood on end a gigantic sarcophagus of black granite, from the tombs of the kings over against Luxor, with their aged lids full of immemorial sculpture. But in the draping of the apartment lay, alas! the chief phantasy of all. The lofty walls, gigantic in height—even unproportionably so—were hung from summit to foot, in vast folds, with a heavy and massive-looking tapestry—tapestry of a material which was found alike as a carpet on the floor, as a covering for the ottomans and the ebony bed, as a canopy for the bed, and as the gorgeous volutes of the curtains which partially shaded the window. The material was the richest cloth of gold. It was spotted all over, at irregular intervals, with arabesque figures, about a foot in diameter, and wrought upon the cloth in patterns of the most jetty black. But these figures partook of the true character of the arabesque only when regarded from a single point of view. By a contrivance now common, and indeed traceable to a very remote period of antiquity, they were made changeable in aspect. To one entering the room, they bore the appearance of simple monstrosities; but upon a farther advance, this appearance gradually departed; and step by step, as the visitor moved his station in the chamber, he saw himself surrounded by an endless succession of the ghastly forms which belong to the superstition of the Norman, or arise in the guilty slumbers of the monk. The phantasmagoric effect was vastly heightened by the artificial introduction of a strong continual current of wind behind the draperies—giving a hideous and uneasy animation to the whole.

In halls such as these—in a bridal chamber such as this—I passed, with the Lady of Tremaine, the unhallowed hours of the first month of our marriage—passed them with but little disquietude. That my wife dreaded the fierce moodiness of my temper—that she shunned me and loved me but little—I could not help perceiving; but it gave me rather pleasure than otherwise. I loathed her with a hatred belonging more to demon than to man. My memory flew back, (oh, with what intensity of regret!) to Ligeia, the beloved, the august, the beautiful, the entombed. I revelled in recollections of her purity, of her wisdom, of her lofty, her ethereal nature, of her passionate, her idolatrous love. Now, then, did my spirit fully and freely burn with more than all the fires of her own. In the excitement of my opium dreams (for I was habitually fettered in the shackles of the drug) I would call aloud upon her name, during the silence of the night, or among the sheltered recesses of the glens by day, as if, through the wild eagerness, the solemn passion, the consuming ardor of my longing for the departed, I could restore her to the pathway she had abandoned—ah, *could* it be forever?—upon the earth.

About the commencement of the second month of the marriage, the Lady Rowena was attacked with sudden illness, from which her recovery was slow. The fever which consumed her rendered her nights uneasy; and in her perturbed state of half-slumber, she spoke of sounds, and of motions, in and about the chamber of the turret, which I concluded had no origin save in the distemper of her fancy, or perhaps in the phantasmagoric influences of the chamber itself. She became at length convalescent—finally well. Yet but a brief period elapsed, ere a second more violent disorder again threw her upon a bed of suffering; and from this attack her frame, at all times feeble, never altogether recovered. Her illnesses were, after this epoch, of alarming character, and of more alarming recurrence, defying alike the knowledge and the great exertions of her physicians. With the increase of the chronic disease which had thus, apparently, taken too sure hold upon her constitution to be eradicated by human means, I could not fail to observe a similar increase in the nervous irritation of her temperament, and in her excitability by trivial causes of fear. She spoke again, and now more frequently and pertinaciously, of the sounds—of the slight sounds—and of the unusual motions among the tapestries, to which she had formerly alluded.

One night, near the closing in of September, she pressed this distressing subject with more than usual emphasis upon my attention. She had just awakened from an unquiet slumber, and I had been watching, with feelings half of anxiety, half of a vague terror, the workings of her emaciated countenance. I sat by the side of her ebony bed, upon one of the ottomans of India. She partly arose, and spoke, in an earnest low whisper, of sounds which she *then* heard, but which I could not hear—of motions which she *then* saw, but which I could not perceive. The wind was rushing hurriedly behind the tapestries, and I wished to show her (what, let me confess it, I could not *all* believe) that those almost inarticulate breathings, and those very gentle variations of the figures upon the wall, were but the natural effects of that customary rushing of the wind. But a deadly pallor, over-spreading her face, had proved to me that my exertions to reassure her would be fruitless. She appeared to be fainting, and no attendants were within call. I remembered where was deposited a decanter of light wine which had been ordered by her physicians, and hastened across the chamber to procure it. But, as I stepped beneath the light of the censer, two circumstances of a startling nature attracted my attention. I had felt that some palpable although invisible object had passed lightly by my person; and I saw that there lay upon the golden carpet, in the very middle of the rich lustre thrown from the censer, a shadow—a faint, indefinite shadow of angelic aspect—such as might be fancied for the shadow of a shade. But I was wild with the excitement of an immoderate dose of opium, and heeded these things but little, nor spoke of them to Rowena. Having found the wine, I recrossed the chamber, and poured out a goblet-ful, which I held to the lips of the fainting lady. She had now partially recovered, however, and took the vessel herself, while I sank upon an ottoman near me, with my eyes fastened upon her person. It was then that I became distinctly aware of a gentle foot-fall upon the carpet, and near the couch; and in a second thereafter, as Rowena was in the act of raising the wine to her lips, I saw, or may have dreamed that I saw, fall within the goblet, as if from some invisible spring in the atmosphere of the room, three or four large drops of a brilliant and ruby colored fluid. If this I saw—not so Rowena. She swallowed the wine unhesitatingly, and I forbore to speak to her of a circumstance which must, after all, I considered, have been but the suggestion of a vivid imagination, rendered morbidly active by the terror of the lady, by the opium, and by the hour.

Yet I cannot conceal it from my own perception that, immediately subsequent to the fall of the ruby-drops, a rapid change for the worse took place in the disorder of my wife; so that, on the third subsequent night, the hands of her menials prepared her for the tomb, and on the fourth, I sat alone, with her shrouded body, in that fantastic chamber which had received her as my bride. Wild visions, opium-engendered, flitted, shadow-like, before me. I gazed with unquiet eye upon the sarcophagi in the angles of the room, upon the varying figures of the drapery, and upon the writhing of the parti-colored fires in the censer overhead. My eyes then fell, as I called to mind the circumstances of a former night, to the spot beneath the glare of the censer where I had seen the faint traces of the shadow. It was there, however, no longer; and breathing with greater freedom, I turned my glances to the pallid and rigid figure upon the bed. Then rushed upon me a thousand memories of Ligeia— and then came back upon my heart, with the turbulent violence of a flood, the whole of that unutterable wo with which I had regarded *her* thus enshrouded. The night waned; and still, with a bosom full of bitter thoughts of the one only and supremely beloved, I remained gazing upon the body of Rowena.

It might have been midnight, or perhaps earlier, or later, for I had taken no note of time, when a sob, low, gentle, but very distinct, startled me from my revery. I *felt* that it came from the bed of ebony—the bed of death. I listened in an agony of superstitious terror—but there was no repetition of the sound. I strained my vision to detect any motion in the corpse—but there was not the slightest perceptible. Yet I could not have been deceived. I *had* heard the noise, however faint, and my soul was awakened within me. I resolutely and perseveringly kept my attention riveted upon the body. Many minutes elapsed before any circumstances occurred tending to throw light upon the mystery. At length it became evident that a slight, a very feeble, and barely noticeable tinge of color had flushed up within the cheeks, and along the sunken small veins of the eyelids. Through a species of unutterable horror and awe, for which the language of mortality has no sufficiently energetic expression, I felt my heart cease to beat, my limbs grow rigid where I sat. Yet a sense of duty finally operated to restore my self-possession. I could no longer doubt that we had been precipitate in our preparations—that Rowena still lived. It was necessary that some immediate exertion be made; yet the turret was altogether apart from the portion of the abbey tenanted by the servants—there were none within call—I had no means of sum-moning them to my aid without leaving the room for many minutes—and this I could not venture to do. I therefore struggled alone in my endeavors to call back the spirit still hovering. In a short period it was certain, however, that a relapse had taken place; the color disappeared from both eyelid and cheek, leaving a wanness even more than that of marble; the lips became doubly shrivelled and pinched up in the ghastly expression of death; a repulsive clamminess and coldness overspread rapidly the surface of the body; and all the usual rigorous stiffness imme-diately supervened. I fell back with a shudder upon the couch from which I had been so startlingly aroused, and again gave myself up to passionate waking visions of Ligeia.

An hour thus elapsed when (could it be possible?) I was a second time aware of some vague sound issuing from the region of the bed. I listened—in extremity of horror. The sound came again—it was a sigh. Rushing to the corpse, I saw—distinctly saw—a tremor upon the lips. In a minute afterward they relaxed, disclosing a bright line of the pearly teeth. Amazement now struggled in my bosom with the profound awe which had hitherto reigned there alone. I felt that my vision grew dim, that my reason wandered; and it was only by a violent effort that I at length succeeded in nerving myself to the task which duty thus once more had pointed out. There was now a partial glow upon the forehead and upon the cheek and throat; a perceptible warmth pervaded the whole frame; there was even a slight pulsation at the heart. The lady *lived*; and with redoubled ardor I betook myself to the task of restoration. I chafed and bathed the temples and the hands, and used every exertion which experience, and no little medical reading, could suggest. But in vain. Suddenly, the color fled, the pulsation ceased, the lips resumed the expression of the dead, and, in an instant afterward, the whole body took upon itself the icy chilliness, the livid hue, the intense rigidity, the sunken outline, and all the loathsome peculiarities of that which has been, for many days, a tenant of the tomb.

And again I sunk into visions of Ligeia—and again, (what marvel that I shudder while I write?) *again* there reached my ears a low sob from the region of the ebony bed. But why shall I minutely detail the unspeakable horrors of that night? Why shall I pause to relate how, time after time, until near the period of the gray dawn, this hideous drama of revivification was repeated; how each terrific relapse was only into a sterner and apparently more irredeemable death; how each agony wore the aspect of a struggle with some invisible foe; and how each struggle was succeeded by I know not what of wild change in the personal appearance of the corpse? Let me hurry to a conclusion.

The greater part of the fearful night had worn away, and she who had been dead, once again stirred—and now more vigorously than hitherto, although arousing from a dissolution more appalling in its utter hopelessness than any. I had long ceased to struggle or to move, and remained sitting rigidly upon the ottoman, a helpless prey to a whirl of violent emotions, of which extreme awe was perhaps the least terrible, the least consuming. The corpse, I repeat, stirred, and now more vigorously than before. The hues of life flushed up the unwonted energy into the countenance—the limbs relaxed—and, save that the eyelids were yet pressed heavily together, and that the bandages and draperies of the grave still imparted their charnel character to the figure, I might have dreamed that Rowena had indeed shaken off, utterly, the fetters of Death. But if this idea was not, even then, altogether adopted, I could at least doubt no longer, when, arising from the bed, tottering, with feeble steps, with closed eyes, and with the manner of one bewildered in a dream, the thing that was enshrouded advanced bodily and palpably into the middle of the apartment.

I trembled not—I stirred not—for a crowd of unutterable fancies connected with the air, the stature, the demeanor of the figure, rushing hurriedly through my brain, had paralyzed—had chilled me into stone. I stirred not—but gazed upon the apparition. There was a mad disorder in my thoughts—a tumult unappeasable. Could it, indeed, be the *living* Rowena who confronted me? Could it indeed be Rowena *at all*—the fair-haired, the blue-eyed Lady Rowena Trevanion of Tremaine? Why, *why* should I doubt it? The bandage lay heavily about the mouth—but then might it not be the mouth of the breathing Lady of Tremaine? And the cheeks—there were the roses as in her noon of life—yes, these might indeed be the fair cheeks of the living Lady of Tremaine. And the chin, with its dimples, as in health, might it not be hers?—but *had she then grown taller since her malady*? What inexpressible madness seized me with that thought? One bound, and I had reached her feet! Shrinking from my touch, she let fall from her head the ghastly cerements which had confined it, and there streamed forth, into the rushing atmosphere of the chamber, huge masses of long and dishevelled hair; *it was blacker than the wings of the midnight*! And now slowly opened *the eyes* of the figure which stood before me. "Here then, at least," I shrieked aloud, "can I never—can I never be mistaken—these are the full, and the black, and the wild eyes— of my lost love—of the lady—of the LADY LIGEIA!"

NIKOLAY GOGOL

(1809–1852)

N ikolay Gogol was born in Sorochintzy in the province of Poltava
in what is now the Urkraine. His father was a landowner and
an amateur playwright. Gogol worked briefly as a civil servant in
St. Petersburg and as a history teacher at a girls' school. The short stories
he had published in a number of literary journals were collected and
published the same year in Evenings on a Farm near Dikanka. A
second volume followed the next year, and in 1835 Gogol published two
more books of stories and essays, Mivgorod and Arabesques, and his
most famous play, The Government Inspector. He left Russia the
next year and spent most of the next twelve years abroad. In 1842
his masterpiece Dead Souls appeared. Variously described as a comic
masterpiece, an outrageous satire, a lyrical tone poem, and a realistic
depiction of the decadence of nineteenth-century Russian life, it is now
recognized as a classic of world literature. Gogol's most brilliant exponent
in English is Vladimir Nabokov, who describes Gogol's genius for the
irrational this way:

> The sudden slanting of the rational plane of life may be accom-
> plished of course in many ways, and every great writer has his
> own method. With Gogol it was a combination of two move-
> ments: a jerk and a glide. Imagine a trap door that opens under
> your feet with absurd suddenness, and a lyrical gust that sweeps
> you up and then lets you fall with a bang into the next traphole.
> The absurd was Gogol's favorite muse—but when I say "the
> absurd," I do not mean the quaint or the comic. The absurd has
> as many shades and degrees as the tragic has, and moreover, in
> Gogol's case, it borders upon the latter. It would be wrong to
> assert that Gogol placed his characters in absurd situations.
> You cannot place a man in an absurd situation if the whole
> world he lives in is absurd; you cannot do this if you mean by
> "absurd" something provoking a chuckle or a shrug. But if you
> mean the pathetic, the human condition, if you mean all such
> things that in less weird worlds are linked up with the loftiest
> aspirations, the deepest suffering, the strongest passions—then
> of course the necessary breech is there.

The Nose

On March 25th there took place, in Petersburg, an extraordinarily strange occurrence. The barber Ivan Yakovlevich, who lives on Voznesensky Avenue (his family name has been lost and even on his signboard, where a gentleman is depicted with a lathered cheek and the inscription "Also bloodletting," there is nothing else)—the barber Ivan Yakovlevich woke up rather early and smelled fresh bread. Raising himself slightly in bed he saw his spouse, a rather respectable lady who was very fond of drinking coffee, take some newly baked loaves out of the oven.

"I won't have any coffee today, Praskovya Osipovna," said Ivan Yakovlevich. "Instead, I would like to eat a bit of hot bread with onion." (That is to say, Ivan Yakovlevich would have liked both the one and the other, but he knew that it was quite impossible to demand two things at once, for Praskovya Osipovna very much disliked such whims.) "Let the fool eat the bread; all the better for me," the wife thought to herself, "there will be an extra cup of coffee left." And she threw a loaf onto the table.

For the sake of propriety Ivan Yakovlevich put a tailcoat on over his shirt and, sitting down at the table, poured out some salt, got two onions ready, picked up a knife and, assuming a meaningful expression, began to slice the bread. Having cut the loaf in two halves, he looked inside and to his astonishment saw something white. Ivan Yakovlevich poked it carefully with the knife and felt it with his finger. "Solid!" he said to himself. "What could it be?"

He stuck in his finger and extracted—a nose! Ivan Yakovlevich was dumbfounded. He rubbed his eyes and felt the object: a nose, a nose indeed, and a familiar one at that. Ivan Yakovlevich's face expressed horror. But this horror was nothing compared to the indignation which seized his spouse.

"You beast, where did you cut off a nose?" she shouted angrily. "Scoundrel! drunkard! I'll report you to the police myself. What a ruffian! I have already heard from three people that you jerk their noses about so much when shaving that it's a wonder they stay in place."

But Ivan Yakovlevich was more dead than alive. He recognized the nose as that of none other than Collegiate Assessor Kovalyov, whom he shaved every Wednesday and Sunday.

"Hold on, Praskovya Osipovna! I shall put it in a corner, after I've wrapped it in a rag: let it lie there for a while, and later I'll take it away."

"I won't even hear of it. That I should allow a cut-off nose to lie about in my room? You dry stick! All he knows is how to strop his razor, but soon he'll be in no condition to carry out his duty, the rake, the villain! Am I to answer for you to the police? You piece of filth, you blockhead! Away with it! Away! Take it anywhere you like! Out of my sight with it!"

Ivan Yakovlevich stood there as though bereft of senses. He thought and thought—and really did not know what to think. "The devil knows how it happened," he said at last, scratching behind his ear with his hand. "Was I drunk or wasn't I when I came home yesterday, I really can't say. Whichever way you look at it, this is an impossible occurrence. After all, bread is something baked, and a nose is something altogether different. I can't make it out at all."

Ivan Yakovlevich fell silent. The idea that the police might find the nose in his possession and bring a charge against him drove him into a complete frenzy. He was already visualizing the scarlet collar, beautifully embroidered with silver, the saber—and he trembled all over. At last he got out his underwear and boots, pulled on all these tatters and, followed by rather weighty exhortations from Praskovya Osipovna, wrapped the nose in a rag and went out into the street.

He wanted to shove it under something somewhere, either into the hitching-post by the gate—or just drop it as if by accident and then turn off into a side street. But as bad luck would have it, he kept running into people he knew, who at once would ask him, "Where are you going?" or "Whom are you going to shave so early?", so that Ivan Yakovlevich couldn't find the right moment. Once he actually did drop it, but a policeman some distance away pointed to it with his halberd and said: "Pick it up—you've dropped something there," and Ivan Yakovlevich was obliged to pick up the nose and hide it in his pocket. He was seized with despair, all the more so as the number of people in the street constantly increased when the shops began to open.

He decided to go to St. Isaac's Bridge—might he not just manage to toss it into the Neva? But I am somewhat to blame for having so far said nothing about Ivan Yakovlevich, in many ways a respectable man.

Like any self-respecting Russian artisan, Ivan Yakovlevich was a terrible drunkard. And although every day he shaved other people's chins his own was ever unshaven. Ivan Yakovlevich's tailcoat (Ivan Yakovlevich never wore a frockcoat) was piebald, that is to say, it was all black but dappled with brownish-yellow and gray; the collar was shiny, and in place of three of the buttons hung just the ends of thread. Ivan Yakovlevich was a great cynic, and when Collegiate Assessor Kovalyov told him while being shaved, "Your hands, Ivan Yakovlevich, always stink," Ivan Yakovlevich would reply with the question, "Why should they stink?" "I don't know, my dear fellow," the Collegiate Assessor would say, "but they do," and Ivan Yakovlevich, after taking a pinch of snuff, would, in retaliation, lather all over his cheeks and under his nose, and behind his ear, and under his chin—in other words, wherever his fancy took him.

This worthy citizen now found himself on St. Isaac's Bridge. To begin with, he took a good look around, then leaned on the railings as though to look under the bridge to see whether or not there were many fish swimming about, and surreptitiously tossed down the rag containing the nose. He felt as though all of a sudden a ton had been lifted off him: Ivan Yakovlevich even smirked. Instead of going to shave some civil servants' chins he set off for an establishment bearing a sign "Snacks and Tea" to order a glass of punch when he suddenly noticed, at the end of the bridge, a police officer of distinguished appearance, with wide sideburns, wearing a three-cornered hat and with a sword. His heart sank: the officer was wagging his finger at him and saying, "Step this way, my friend."

Knowing the etiquette, Ivan Yakovlevich removed his cap while still some way off, and approaching with alacrity said, "I wish your honor good health."

"No, no, my good fellow, not 'your honor.' Just you tell me, what were you doing over there, standing on the bridge?"

"Honestly, sir, I've been to shave someone and only looked to see if the river were running fast."

"You're lying, you're lying. This won't do. Just be so good as to answer."

"I am ready to shave your worship twice a week, or even three times, and no complaints," replied Ivan Yakovlevich.

"No, my friend, all that's nonsense. I have three barbers who shave me and deem it a great honor, too. Just be so good as to tell me, what were you doing over there?"

Ivan Yakovlevich turned pale. . . . But here the whole episode becomes shrouded in mist, and of what happened subsequently absolutely nothing is known.

II

Collegiate Assessor Kovalyov work up rather early and made a "b-rr-rr" sound with his lips as he was wont to do on awakening, although he could not have explained the reason for it. Kovalyov stretched and asked for the small mirror standing on the table. He wanted to have a look at the pimple which had, the evening before, appeared on his nose. But to his extreme amazement he saw that he had, in the place of his nose, a perfectly smooth surface. Frightened, Kovalyov called for some water and rubbed his eyes with a towel: indeed, no nose! He ran his hand over himself to see whether or not he was asleep. No, he didn't think so. The Collegiate Assessor jumped out of bed and shook himself—no nose! He at once ordered his clothes to be brought to him, and flew off straight to the chief of police.

In the meantime something must be said about Kovalyov, to let the reader see what sort of man this collegiate assessor was. Collegiate assessors who receive their rank on the strength of scholarly diplomas can by no means be equated with those who make the rank in the Caucasus. They are two entirely different breeds. Learned collegiate assessors . . . But Russia is such a wondrous land that if you say something about one collegiate assessor all the collegiate assessors from Riga to Kamchatka will not fail to take it as applying to them, too. The same is true of all our ranks and titles. Kovalyov belonged to the Caucasus variety of collegiate assessors. He had only held that rank for two years and therefore could not forget it for a moment; and in order to lend himself added dignity and weight he never referred to himself as collegiate assessor but always as major. "Listen, my dear woman," he would usually say on meeting in the street a woman selling shirt fronts, "come to my place, my apartment is on Sadovaya; just ask where Major Kovalyov lives, anyone will show you." And if the woman he met happened to be a pretty one, he would also give some confidential instructions, adding, "You just ask, lovey, for Major Kovalyov's apartment."—That is why we, too, will henceforth refer to this collegiate assessor as Major.

Major Kovalyov was in the habit of taking a daily stroll along Nevsky Avenue. The collar of his dress shirt was always exceedingly clean and starched. His sidewhiskers were of the kind you can still see on provincial and district surveyors, or architects (provided they are Russians), as well as on those individuals who perform various police duties, and in general on all those men who have full rosy cheeks and are very good at boston; these sidewhiskers run along the middle of the cheek straight up to the nose. Major Kovalyov wore a great many cornelian seals, some with crests and others with Wednesday, Thursday, Monday, etc., engraved on them. Major Kovalyov had come to Petersburg on business, to wit, to look for a post befitting his rank; if he could arrange it, that of a vice-governor; otherwise, that of a procurement officer in some important government department. Major Kovalyov was not averse to getting married, but only in the event that the bride had a fortune of two hundred thousand. And therefore the reader can now judge for himself what this major's state was when he saw, in the place of a fairly presentable and moderate-sized nose, a most ridiculous flat and smooth surface.

As bad luck would have it, not a single cab showed up in the street, and he was forced to walk, wrapped up in his cloak, his face covered with a handkerchief, pretending that his nose was bleeding. "But perhaps I just imagined all this—a nose cannot disappear in this idiotic way." He stepped into a coffee-house just in order to look at himself in a mirror. Fortunately, there was no one there. Serving boys were sweeping the rooms and arranging the chairs; some of them, sleepy-eyed, were bringing out trays of hot turnovers; yesterday's papers, coffee-stained, lay about on tables and chairs. "Well, thank God, there is no one here," said the Major. "Now I can have a look." Timidly he approached the mirror and glanced at it. "Damnation! How disgusting!" he exclaimed after spitting. "If at least there were something in place of the nose, but there's nothing!"

Biting his lips with annoyance, he left the coffee-house and decided, contrary to his habit, not to look or to smile at anyone. Suddenly he stopped dead in his tracks before the door of a house. An inexplicable phenomenon took place before his very eyes: a carriage drew up to the entrance; the doors opened; a gentleman in uniform jumped out, slightly stooping, and ran up the stairs. Imagine the horror and at the same time the amazement of Kovalyov when he recognized that it was his own nose! At this extraordinary sight everything seemed to whirl before his eyes; he felt that he could hardly keep on his feet. Trembling all over as though with fever, he made up his mind, come what may, to await the gentleman's return to the carriage. Two minutes later the Nose indeed came out. He was wearing a gold-embroidered uniform with a big stand-up collar and doeskin breeches; there was a sword at his side. From his plumed hat one could infer that he held the rank of a state councillor. Everything pointed to his being on the way to pay a call. He looked right and left, shouted to his driver, "Bring the carriage round," got in and was driven off.

Poor Kovalyov almost went out of his mind. He did not even know what to think of this strange occurrence. Indeed, how could a nose which as recently as yesterday had been on his face and could neither ride nor walk—how could it be in uniform? He ran after the carriage, which fortunately had not gone far but had stopped before the Kazan Cathedral.

He hurried into the cathedral, made his way past the ranks of old beggarwomen with bandaged faces and two slits for their eyes, whom he used to make such fun of, and went inside. There were but few worshippers there: they all stood by the entrance. Kovalyov felt so upset that he was in no condition to pray and searched with his eyes for the gentleman in all the church corners. At last he saw him standing to one side. The Nose had completely hidden his face in his big stand-up collar and was praying in an attitude of utmost piety.

"How am I to approach him?" thought Kovalyov. "From everything, from his uniform, from his hat, one can see that he is a state councillor. I'll be damned if I know how to do it."

He started clearing his throat, but the Nose never changed his devout attitude and continued his genuflections.

"My dear sir," said Kovalyov, forcing himself to take courage, "my dear sir . . ."

"What is it you desire?" said the Nose turning round.

"It is strange, my dear sir . . . I think . . . you ought to know your place. And all of a sudden I find you—and where? In church. You'll admit . . ."

"Excuse me, I cannot understand what you are talking about. . . . Make yourself clear."

"How shall I explain to him?" thought Kovalyov and, emboldened, began: "Of course, I . . . however, I am a major. For me to go about without my nose, you'll admit, is unbecoming. It's all right for a peddler woman who sells peeled oranges on Voskresensky Bridge, to sit without a nose. But since I'm expecting—and besides, having many acquaintances among the ladies—Mrs. Chekhtaryova, a state councillor's wife, and others . . . Judge for yourself . . . I don't know, my dear sir . . ." (Here Major Kovalyov shrugged his shoulders.) "Forgive me, if one were to look at this in accordance with rules of duty and honor . . . you yourself can understand. . . ."

"I understand absolutely nothing," replied the Nose. "Make yourself more clear."

"My dear sir," said Kovalyov with a sense of his own dignity, "I don't know how to interpret your words . . . The whole thing seems to me quite obvious . . . Or do you wish . . . After all, you are my own nose!"—

The Nose looked at the major and slightly knitted his brows.

"You are mistaken, my dear sir, I exist in my own right. Besides, there can be no close relation between us. Judging by the buttons on your uniform, you must be employed in the Senate or at least in the Ministry of Justice. As for me, I am in the scholarly line."

Having said this, the Nose turned away and went back to his prayers.

Kovalyov was utterly flabbergasted. He knew not what to do or even what to think. Just then he heard the pleasant rustle of a lady's dress: an elderly lady, all in lace, had come up near him and with her, a slim one, in a white frock which agreeably outlined her slender figure, and in a straw-colored hat, light as a cream-puff. Behind them, a tall footman with huge sidewhiskers and a whole dozen collars, stopped and opened a snuff-box.

Kovalyov stepped closer, pulled out the cambric collar of his dress shirt, adjusted his seals hanging on a golden chain and, smiling in all directions, turned his attention to the ethereal young lady who, like a spring flower, bowed her head slightly and put her little white hand with its translucent fingers to her forehead. The smile on Kovalyov's face grew even wider when from under her hat he caught a glimpse of her little round dazzling-white chin and part of her cheek glowing with the color of the first rose of spring. But suddenly he sprang back as though scalded. He remembered that there was absolutely nothing in the place of his nose, and tears came to his eyes. He turned round, intending without further ado to tell the gentleman in uniform that he was merely pretending to be a state councillor, that he was a rogue and a cad and nothing more than his, the major's, own nose. . . . But the Nose was no longer there; he had managed to dash off, probably to pay another call.

This plunged Kovalyov into despair. He went back, stopped for a moment under the colonnade and looked carefully, this way and that, for the Nose to turn up somewhere. He remembered quite well that the latter had a plumed hat and a gold-embroidered uniform, but he had not noticed his overcoat, or the color of his carriage or of his horses, not even whether he had a footman at the back, and if so in what livery. Moreover, there was such a multitude of carriages dashing back and forth and at such speed that it was difficult to tell them apart; but even if he did pick one of them out, he would have no means of stopping it. The day was fine and sunny. There were crowds of people on Nevsky Avenue. A whole flowery cascade of ladies poured over the sidewalk, all the way down from Police Bridge to Anichkin Bridge. Here came a court councillor he knew, and was used to addressing as lieutenant-colonel, especially in the presence of strangers. Here, too, was Yarygin, a head clerk in the Senate, a great friend of his, who invariably lost at boston when he went up eight. Here was another major who had won his assessorship in the Caucasus, waving to Kovalyov to join him. . . .

"O hell!" said Kovalyov. "Hey, cabby, take me straight to the chief of police!"

Kovalyov got into the cab and kept shouting to the cabman, "Get going as fast you can."

"Is the chief of police at home?" he called out as he entered the hall.

"No sir," answered the doorman, "he has just left."

"You don't say."

"Yes," added the doorman, "he has not been gone long, but he's gone. Had you come in a minute sooner perhaps you might have found him in."

Without removing the handkerchief from his face, Kovalyov got back into the cab and in a voice of despair shouted, "Drive on!"

"Where to?" asked the cabman.

"Drive straight ahead!"

"What do you mean straight ahead? There is a turn here. Right or left?"

This question nonplussed Kovalyov and made him think again. In his plight the first thing for him to do was to apply to the Police Department, not because his case had anything to do directly with the police, but because they could act much more quickly than any other institution; while to seek satisfaction from the superiors of the department by which the Nose claimed to be employed would be pointless because from the Nose's own replies it was obvious that this fellow held nothing sacred, and that he was capable of lying in this case, too, as he had done when he had assured Kovalyov that they had never met. Thus Kovalyov was on the point of telling the cabman to take him to the Police Department when the thought again occurred to him that this rogue and swindler, who had already treated him so shamelessly during their first encounter, might again seize his first chance to slip out of town somewhere, and then all search would be futile or might drag on, God forbid, a whole month. Finally, it seemed, heaven itself brought him to his senses. He decided to go straight to the newspaper office and, before it was too late, place an advertisement with a detailed description of the Nose's particulars, so that anyone coming across him could immediately deliver him or at least give information about his whereabouts. And so, his mind made up, he told the cabby to drive to the newspaper office, and all the way down to it kept whacking him in the back with his fist, saying, "Faster, you villain! faster, you rogue!"—"Ugh, mister!" the cabman would say, shaking his head and flicking his reins at the horse whose coat was as long as a lapdog's. At last the cab drew up to a stop, and Kovalyov, panting, ran into a small reception room where a gray-haired clerk in an old tailcoat and glasses sat at a table and, pen in his teeth, counted newly brought in coppers.

"Who accepts advertisements here?" cried Kovalyov. "Ah, good morning!"

"How do you do," said the gray-haired clerk, raising his eyes for a moment and lowering them again to look at the neat stacks of money.

"I should like to insert—"

"Excuse me. Will you wait a moment," said the clerk as he wrote down a figure on a piece of paper with one hand and moved two beads on the abacus with the fingers of his left hand. A liveried footman, whose appearance suggested his sojourn in an aristocratic house, and who stood by the table with a note in his hand, deemed it appropriate to demonstrate his savoir-faire: "Would you believe it, sir, this little mutt is not worth eighty kopecks, that is, I wouldn't even give eight kopecks for it; but the countess loves it, honestly she does—and so whoever finds it will get one hundred rubles! To put it politely, just as you and I are talking, people's tastes differ: if you're a hunter, keep a pointer or a poodle; don't grudge five hundred, give a thousand, but then let it be a good dog."

The worthy clerk listened to this with a grave expression while at the same time trying to count the number of letters in the note brought to him. All around stood a great many old women, salespeople and house porters with notes. One of them offered for sale a coachman of sober conduct; another, a little-used carriage brought from Paris in 1814; still others, a nineteen-year-old serf girl experienced in laundering work and suitable for other kinds of work; a sound droshky with one spring missing; a young and fiery dappled-gray horse seventeen years old; turnip and radish seed newly received from London; a summer residence with all the appurtenances—to wit, two stalls for horses and a place for planting a grove of birches or firs; there was also an appeal to those wishing to buy old boot soles, inviting them to appear for final bidding every day between eight and three o'clock. The room in which this entire company was crowded was small, and the air in it was extremely thick; but Collegiate Assessor Kovalyov was not in a position to notice the smell, because he kept his handkerchief pressed to his face and because his nose itself was goodness knows where.

"My dear sir, may I ask you . . . It is very urgent," he said at last with impatience.

"Presently, presently! Two rubles forty-three kopecks! Just a moment! One ruble sixty-four kopecks," recited the gray-haired gentleman, tossing the notes into the faces of the old women and the house porters. "What can I do for you?" he said at last, turning to Kovalyov.

"I wish . . .," said Kovalyov. "There has been a swindle or a fraud . . . I still can't find out. I just wish to advertise that whoever hands this scoundrel over to me will receive an adequate reward."

"Allow me to inquire, what is your name?"

"What do you want my name for? I can't give it to you. I have many acquaintances: Mrs. Chekhtaryova, the wife of a state councillor; Pelageya Grigoryevna Podtochina, the wife of a field officer . . . What if they suddenly were to find out? Heaven forbid! You can simply write down: a collegiate assessor or, still better, a person holding the rank of major."

"And was the runaway your household serf?"

"What do you mean, household serf? That wouldn't be such a bad swindle! The runaway was . . . my nose. . . ."

"Hmm! what a strange name! And did this Mr. Nosov rob you of a big sum?"

"My nose, I mean to say—You've misunderstood me. My nose, my very own nose has disappeared goodness knows where. The devil must have wished to play a trick on me!"

"But how did it disappear? I don't quite understand it."

"Well, I can't tell you how; but the main thing is that it is now gallivanting about town and calling itself a state councillor. And that is why I am asking you to advertise that whoever apprehends it should deliver it to me immediately and without delay. Judge for yourself. How, indeed, can I do without such a conspicuous part of my body? It isn't like some little toe which I put into my boot, and no one can see whether it is there or not. On Thursdays I call at the house of Mrs. Chekhtaryova, a state councillor's wife. Mrs. Podtochina, Pelageya Grigoryevna, a field officer's wife, and her very pretty daughter, are also very good friends of mine, and you can judge for yourself how can I now . . . I can't appear at their house now."

The clerk thought hard, his lips pursed tightly in witness thereof.

"No, I can't insert such an advertisement in the papers," he said at last after a long silence.

"How so? Why?"

"Well, the paper might lose its reputation. If everyone were to write that his nose had run away, why . . . As it is, people say that too many absurd stories and false rumors are printed."

"But why is this business absurd? I don't think it is anything of the sort."

"That's what you think. But take last week, there was another such case. A civil servant came in, just as you have, bringing a note, was billed two rubles seventy-three kopecks, and all the advertisement consisted of was that a black-coated poodle had run away. Doesn't seem to amount to much, does it now? But it turned out to be a libel. This so-called poodle was the treasurer of I don't recall what institution."

"But I am not putting in an advertisement about a poodle—it's about my very own nose; that is, practically the same as about myself."

"No, I can't possibly insert such an advertisement."

"But when my nose actually has disappeared!"

"If it has disappeared, then it's a doctor's business. They say there are people who can fix you up with any nose you like. However, I observe that you must be a man of gay disposition and fond of kidding in company."

"I swear to you by all that is holy! Perhaps, if it comes to that, why I'll show you."

"Why trouble yourself?" continued the clerk, taking a pinch of snuff. "However, if it isn't too much trouble," he added, moved by curiosity, "I'd like to have a look."

The collegiate assessor removed the handkerchief from his face.

"Very strange indeed!" said the clerk. "It's absolutely flat, like a pancake fresh off the griddle. Yes, incredibly smooth."

"Well, will you go on arguing after this? You see yourself that you can't refuse to print my advertisement. I'll be particularly grateful and am very glad that this opportunity has given me the pleasure of making your acquaintance. . . ." The major, as we can see, decided this time to use a little flattery.

"To insert it would be easy enough, of course," said the clerk, "but I don't see any advantage to you in it. If you really must, give it to someone who wields a skillful pen and let him describe this as a rare phenomenon of nature and publish this little item in *The Northern Bee*" (here he took another pinch of snuff) "for the benefit of the young" (here he wiped his nose), "or just so, as a matter of general interest."

The collegiate assessor felt completely discouraged. He dropped his eyes to the lower part of the paper where theatrical performances were announced. His face was about to break out into a smile as he came across the name of a pretty actress, and his hand went to his pocket to check whether he had a blue note, because in his opinion field officers ought to sit in the stalls—but the thought of his nose spoiled it all.

The clerk himself seemed to be moved by Kovalyov's embarrassing situation. Wishing at least to ease his distress he deemed it appropriate to express his sympathy in a few words: "I really am grieved that such a thing happened to you. Wouldn't you care for a pinch of snuff? It dispels headaches, and melancholy; it's even good for hemorrhoids." With those words the clerk offered Kovalyov his snuff box, rather deftly snapping open the lid which pictured a lady in a hat.

This unpremeditated action made Kovalyov lose all patience. "I can't understand how you find this a time for jokes," he said angrily. "Can't you see that I lack the very thing one needs to take snuff? To hell with your snuff! I can't bear the sight of it now, even if you offered me some *rapé* itself, let alone your wretched Berezin's." After saying this he left the newspaper office, deeply vexed, and went to visit the district police inspector, a man with a passion for sugar. In his house the entire parlor, which served also as the dining room, was stacked with sugar loaves which local tradesmen brought to him out of friendship. At the moment his cook was pulling off the inspector's regulation topboots; his sword and all his military trappings were already hanging peacefully in the corners, and his three-year-old son was reaching for his redoubtable three-cornered hat, while the inspector himself was preparing to taste the fruits of peace after his day of warlike, martial pursuits.

Kovalyov came in at the moment when the inspector had just stretched, grunted and said, "Oh, for a couple of hours' good snooze!" It was therefore easy to see that the collegiate assessor had come at quite the wrong time. And I wonder whether he would have been welcome even if he had brought several pounds of tea or a piece of cloth. The police inspector was a great patron of all arts and manufacturers, but he preferred a bank note to everything else. "This is the thing," he would usually say. "There can be nothing better than it—it doesn't ask for food, it doesn't take much space, it'll always fit into a pocket, and if you drop it it won't break."

The inspector received Kovalyov rather coolly and said that after dinner was hardly the time to conduct investigations, that nature itself intended that man should rest a little after a good meal (from this the collegiate assessor could see that the aphorisms of the ancient sages were not unknown to the police inspector), that no real gentleman would allow his nose to be pulled off, and that there were many majors in this world who hadn't even decent underwear and hung about in all sorts of disreputable places.

This last was too close for comfort. It must be observed that Kovalyov was extremely quick to take offense. He could forgive whatever was said about himself, but never anything that referred to rank or title. He was even of the opinion that in plays one could allow references to junior officers, but that there should be no criticism of field officers. His reception by the inspector so disconcerted him that he tossed his head and said with an air of dignity, spreading his arms slightly: "I confess that after such offensive remarks on your part, I've nothing more to add. . . ." and left the room.

He came home hardly able to stand on his feet. It was already dusk. After all this fruitless search his apartment appeared to him melancholy or extraordinarily squalid. Coming into the entrance hall he caught sight of his valet Ivan who, lying on his back on the soiled leather sofa, was spitting at the ceiling and rather successfully hitting one and the same spot. Such indifference on the man's part infuriated him; he struck him on the forehead with his hat, saying, "You pig, always doing something stupid!"

Ivan jumped up abruptly and rushed to take off his cloak.

Entering his room the major, tired and sad, sank into an armchair and at last, after several sighs, said:

"O Lord, O Lord! What have I done to deserve such misery? Had I lost an arm or a leg, it would not have been so bad; had I lost my ears, it would have been bad enough but nevertheless bearable; but without a nose a man is goodness knows what; he's not a bird, he's not a human being; in fact, just take him and throw him out the window! And if at least it had been chopped off in battle or in a duel, or if I myself had been to blame; but it disappeared just like that, with nothing, nothing at all to show for it. But no, it can't be," he added after some thought. "It's unbelievable that a nose should disappear; absolutely unbelievable. I must be either dreaming or just imagining it. Maybe, somehow, by mistake instead of water I drank the vodka which I rub on my chin after shaving. That fool Ivan didn't take it away and I probably gulped it down."—To satisfy himself that he was not drunk the major pinched himself so hard that he cried out. The pain he felt fully convinced him that he was wide awake. He stealthily approached the mirror and at first half-closed his eyes, thinking that perhaps the nose would appear in its proper place; but the same moment he sprang back exclaiming, "What a caricature of a face!"

It was indeed incomprehensible. If a button, a silver spoon, a watch, or some such thing had disappeared—but to disappear, and for whom to disappear? and besides in his own apartment, too! . . . After considering all the circumstances, Major Kovalyov was inclined to think that most likely it was the fault of none other than the field officer's wife, Mrs. Podtochina, who wanted him to marry her daughter. He, too, liked to flirt with her but avoided a final showdown. And when the field officer's wife told him point-blank that she wanted to marry her daughter off to him, he eased off on his attentions, saying that he was still young, that he had to serve another five years when he would be exactly forty-two. And so the field officer's wife, presumably in revenge, had decided to put a curse on him and hired for this purpose some old witchwomen, because it was impossible even to suppose that the nose had been simply cut off: no one had entered his room; the barber, Ivan Yakovlevich, had shaved him as recently as Wednesday and throughout that whole day and even on Thursday his nose was all there—he remembered and knew it very well. Besides, he would have felt the pain and no doubt the wound could not have healed so soon and be as smooth as a pancake. Different plans of action occurred to him: should he formally summons Mrs. Podtochina to court or go to her himself and expose her in person? His reflections were interrupted by light breaking through all the cracks in the door, which told him that Ivan had lit the candle in the hall. Soon Ivan himself appeared, carrying it before him and brightly illuminating the whole room. Kovalyov's first gesture was to snatch his handkerchief and cover the place where his nose had been only the day before, so that indeed the silly fellow would not stand there gaping at such an oddity in his master's strange appearance.

Barely had Ivan gone into his cubbyhole when an unfamiliar voice was heard in the hall saying, "Does Collegiate Assessor Kovalyov live here?"

"Come in. Major Kovalyov is here," said Kovalyov, jumping up quickly and opening the door.

In came a police officer of handsome appearance with sidewhiskers that were neither too light nor too dark, and rather full cheeks, the very same who at the beginning of this story was standing at the end of St. Isaac's Bridge.

"Did you happen to mislay your nose?"

"That's right."

"It has been recovered."

"What are you saying!" exclaimed Major Kovalyov. He was tongue-tied with joy. He stared at the police officer standing in front of him, on whose full lips and cheeks the trembling light of the candle flickered. "How?"

"By an odd piece of luck—he was intercepted on the point of leaving town. He was about to board a stagecoach and leave for Riga. He even had a passport made out a long time ago in the name of a certain civil servant. Strangely enough, I also at first took him for a gentleman. But fortunately I had my glasses with me and I saw at once that it was a nose. You see, I am nearsighted and when you stand before me all I can see is that you have a face, but I can't make out if you have a nose or a beard or anything. My mother-in-law, that is, my wife's mother, can't see anything either."

Kovalyov was beside himself. "Where is it? Where? I'll run there at once."

"Don't trouble yourself. Knowing that you need it I have brought it with me. And the strange thing is that the chief villain in this business is that rascally barber from Voznesensky Street who is now in a lockup. I have long suspected him of drunkenness and theft, and as recently as the day before yesterday he stole a dozen buttons from a certain shop. Your nose is quite in order."—With these words the police officer reached into his pocket and pulled out a nose wrapped up in a piece of paper.

"That's it!" shouted Kovalyov. "That's it, all right! Do join me in a little cup of tea today."

"I would consider it a great pleasure, but I simply can't: I have to drop in at a mental asylum. . . . All food prices have gone up enormously. . . . I have my mother-in-law, that's my wife's mother, living with me, and my children; the eldest is particularly promising, a very clever lad, but we haven't the means to educate him."

Kovalyov grasped his meaning and, snatching up a red banknote from the table, thrust it into the hands of the inspector who, clicking his heels, went out the door. Almost the very same instant Kovalyov heard his voice out in the street where he was admonishing with his fist a stupid peasant who had driven his cart onto the boulevard.

After the police officer had left, the collegiate assessor remained for a few minutes in a sort of indefinable state and only after several minutes recovered the capacity to see and feel: his unexpected joy had made him lose his senses. He carefully took the newly found nose in both his cupped hands and once again examined it thoroughly.

"That's it, that's it, all right," said Major Kovalyov. "Here on the left side is the pimple which swelled up yesterday." The major very nearly laughed with joy.

But there is nothing enduring in this world, and that is why even joy is not as keen in the moment that follows the first; and a moment later it grows weaker still and finally merges imperceptibly into one's usual state of mind, just as a ring on the water, made by the fall of a pebble, merges finally into the smooth surface. Kovalyov began to reflect and realized that the whole business was not yet over: the nose was found but it still had to be affixed, put in its proper place.

"And what if it doesn't stick?"

At this question, addressed to himself, the major turned pale.

Seized by unaccountable fear, he rushed to the table and drew the looking-glass closer, to avoid affixing the nose crookedly. His hands trembled. Carefully and deliberately, he put it in its former place. O horror! the nose wouldn't stick. . . . He carried it to his mouth, warmed it slightly with his breath, and again brought it to the smooth place between his two cheeks; but the nose just wouldn't stay on.

"Well, come on, come on, you fool!" he kept saying to it. But the nose was as though made of wood and plopped back on the table with a strange corklike sound. The major's face was twisted in convulsion. "Won't it really grow on?" he said fearfully. But no matter how many times he tried to fit it in its proper place, his efforts were unsuccessful as before.

He called Ivan and sent him for the doctor who occupied the best apartment on the first floor of the same house. The doctor was a fine figure of a man; he had beautiful pitch-black sidewhiskers, a fresh, healthy wife, ate raw apples first thing in the morning, and kept his mouth extraordinarily clean, rinsing it every morning for nearly three quarters of an hour and polishing his teeth with five different kinds of little brushes. The doctor came at once. After asking him how long ago the mishap had occurred, he lifted Major Kovalyov's face by the chin and flicked him with his thumb on the very spot where the nose used to be, so that the major had to throw his head back with such force that he hit the back of it against the wall. The doctor said this didn't matter and, suggesting that he move a little away from the wall, told him first to bend his head to the right, and, after feeling the spot where the nose had been, said "Hmm!" Then he told him to bend his head to the left and said "Hmm!"; and in conclusion he again flicked him with his thumb so that Major Kovalyov jerked his head like a horse whose teeth are being examined. Having carried out this test, the doctor shook his head and said: "No, can't be done. You'd better stay like this, or we might make things even worse. Of course, it can be stuck on. I daresay, I could do it right now for you, but I assure you it'll be worse for you."

"I like that! How am I to remain without a nose?" said Kovalyov. "It couldn't possibly be worse than now. This is simply a hell of a thing! How can I show myself anywhere in such a scandalous state? I have acquaintances in good society; why, this evening, now, I am expected at parties in two houses. I know many people: Mrs. Chekhtaryova, a state councillor's wife, Mrs. Podtochina, a field officer's wife . . . although after what she's done now I'll have nothing more to do with her except through the police. I appeal to you," pleaded Kovalyov, "is there no way at all? Fix it on somehow, even if not very well, just so it stays on; in an emergency, I could even prop it up with my hand. And besides, I don't dance, so I can't do any harm by some careless movement. As regards my grateful acknowledgement of your visits, be assured that as far as my means allow . . ."

"Would you believe it," said the doctor in a voice that was neither loud nor soft but extremely persuasive and magnetic, "I never treat people out of self-interest. This is against my principles and my calling. It is true that I charge for my visits, but solely in order not to offend by my refusal. Of course I could affix your nose; but I assure you on my honor, if you won't take my word for it, that it will be much worse. Rather, let nature take its course. Wash the place more often with cold water, and I assure you that without a nose you'll be as healthy as if you had one. As for the nose itself, I advise you to put the nose in a jar with alcohol, or, better still, pour into the jar two tablespoonfuls of aqua fortis and warmed-up vinegar—and then you can get good money for it. I'll buy it myself, if you don't ask too much."

"No, no! I won't sell it for anything!" exclaimed Major Kovalyov in desperation. "Let it rather go to blazes!"

"Excuse me!" said the doctor, bowing himself out, "I wanted to be of some use to you. . . . Never mind! At least you saw my good will." Having said this the doctor left the room with a dignified air. Kovalyov didn't even notice his face and in his benumbed state saw nothing but the cuffs of his snow-white shirt peeping out of the sleeves of his black tailcoat.

The very next day he decided, before lodging a complaint, to write to Mrs. Podtochina requesting her to restore him his due without a fight. The letter ran as follows:

Dear Madam Alexandra Grigoryevna,

I fail to understand your strange behavior. Be assured that, acting in this way, you gain nothing and certainly will not force me to marry your daughter. Believe me that the incident with my nose is fully known to me, just as is the fact that you—and no one else—are the principal person involved. Its sudden detachment from its place, its flight and its disguise, first as a certain civil servant, then at last in its own shape, is nothing other than the result of a spell cast by you or by those who engage like you in such noble pursuits. I for my part deem it my duty to forewarn you that if the abovementioned nose is not back in its place this very day I shall be forced to resort to the defense and protection of the law.

Whereupon I have the honor to remain, with my full respect,
Your obedient servant
Platon Kovalyov

Dear Sir Platon Kuzmich,

Your letter came as a complete surprise to me. I frankly confess that I never expected it, especially as regards your unjust reproaches. I beg to inform you that I never received in my house the civil servant you mention, neither in disguise nor in his actual shape. It is true that Filipp Ivanovich Potanchikov had been visiting me. And though he did indeed seek my daughter's hand, being himself of good sober conduct and great learning, I never held out any hopes to him. You also mention your nose. If by this you mean that I wanted to put your nose out of joint, that is, to give you a formal refusal, then I am surprised to hear you mention it, for I, as you know, was of the exactly opposite opinion, and if you now seek my daughter in marriage in the lawful way, I am ready to give you immediate satisfaction, for this has always been the object of my keenest desire, in the hope of which I remain always at your service,

Alexandra Podtochina

"No," said Kovalyov, after he had read the letter. "She certainly isn't guilty. Impossible! The letter is written in a way no person guilty of a crime can write."—The collegiate assessor was an expert in this matter, having been sent several times to take part in a judicial investigation while still serving in the Caucasus.—"How then, how on earth could this have happened? The devil alone can make it out," he said at last in utter dejection.

In the meantime rumors about this extraordinary occurrence had spread all over the capital and, as is usual in such cases, not without some special accretions. In those days the minds of everybody were particularly inclined toward things extraordinary: not long before, the whole town had shown an interest in experiments with the effects of hypnotism. Moreover, the story of the dancing chairs in Konyushennaya Street was still fresh in memory, and one should not be surprised therefore that soon people began saying that Collegiate Assessor Kovalyov's nose went strolling along Nevsky Avenue at precisely three o'clock. Throngs of curious people came there very day. Someone said that the Nose was in Junker's store: and such a crowd and jam was created outside Junker's that the police had to intervene. One profit-seeker of respectable appearance, with sidewhiskers, who sold a variety of dry pastries at the entrance to a theater, had specially constructed excellent, sturdy wooden benches, on which he invited the curious to mount for eighty kopecks apiece. One veteran colonel made a point of leaving his house earlier than usual and with much difficulty made his way through the crowd, but to his great indignation saw in the window of the shop instead of the nose an ordinary woolen undershirt and a lithograph showing a young girl straightening her stocking and a dandy, with a lapeled waistcoat and a small beard, peeping at her from behind a tree—a picture which had been hanging in the same place for more than ten years. Moving away he said with annoyance, "How can they confound the people by such silly and unlikely rumors?"—Then a rumor went round that Major Kovalyov's nose was out for a stroll, not on Nevsky Avenue but in Taurida Gardens, that it had been there for ages; that when Khosrev-Mirza lived there he marveled greatly at this strange freak of nature. Some students from the Surgical Academy went there. One aristocratic, respectable lady, in a special letter to the Superintendent of the Gardens, asked him to show her children this rare phenomenon, accompanied, if possible, with an explanation edifying and instructive for the young.

All the men about town, the *habitués* of society parties, who liked to amuse ladies and whose resources had by that time been exhausted, were extremely glad of all these goings-on. A small percentage of respectable and well-meaning people were extremely displeased. One gentleman said indignantly that he could not understand how in this enlightened age such senseless stories could spread and that he was surprised at the government's failure to take heed of it. This gentleman apparently was one of those gentlemen who would like to embroil the government in everything, even in their daily quarrels with their wives. After that . . . but here again the whole incident is shrouded in fog, and what happened afterwards is absolutely unknown.

III

Utterly nonsensical things happen in this world. Sometimes there is absolutely no rhyme or reason in them: suddenly the very nose which had been going around with the rank of a state councillor and created such a stir in the city, found itself again, as though nothing were the matter, in its proper place, that is to say, between the two cheeks of Major Kovalyov. This happened on April 7th. Waking up and chancing to look in the mirror, he sees—his nose! He grabbed it with his hand—his nose indeed! "Aha!" said Kovalyov, and in his joy he very nearly broke into a barefooted dance round the room, but Ivan's entry stopped him. He told Ivan to bring him some water to wash in and, while washing, glanced again at the mirror—his nose! Drying himself with his towel, he again glanced at the mirror—his nose!

"Take a look, Ivan, I think there's a pimple on my nose," he said, and in the meantime thought, "How awful if Ivan says: "Why, no sir, not only there is no pimple but also the nose itself is gone!"

But Ivan said: "Nothing, sir, no pimple—your nose is fine!"

"That's great, damn it!" the major said to himself, snapping his fingers. At that moment the barber Ivan Yakovlevich peeped in at the door but as timidly as a cat which had just been whipped for stealing lard.

"First you tell me—are your hands clean?" Kovalyov shouted to him before he had approached.

"They are."

"You're lying."

"I swear they are, sir."

"Well, we'll see."

Kovalyov sat down. Ivan Yakovlevich draped him with a napkin and instantly, with the help of a shaving brush, transformed his chin and part of his cheek into the whipped cream served at merchants' namesday parties. "Well, I never!" Ivan Yakovlevich said to himself, glancing at his nose, and then cocked his head on the other side and looked at it sideways: "Look at that! Just you try and figure that out," he continued and took a good look at his nose. At last, gently, with the greatest care imaginable, he raised two fingers to grasp it by the tip. Such was Ivan Yakovlevich's method.

"Now, now, now, look out there!" cried Kovalyov. Dumbfounded and confused as never before in his life, Ivan Yakovlevich let his hands drop. At last he began cautiously tickling him with the razor under the chin, and although it wasn't at all handy for him and difficult to shave without holding on to the olfactory portion of the face, nevertheless, somehow bracing his gnarled thumb against the cheek and the lower jaw, he finally overcame all obstacles and finished shaving him.

When everything was ready, Kovalyov hastened to dress, hired a cab and went straight to the coffee-house. Before he was properly inside the door he shouted, "Boy, a cup of chocolate!" and immediately made for the mirror: the nose was there. He turned round cheerfully and looked ironically, slightly screwing up one eye, at two military gentlemen one of whom had a nose no bigger than a waistcoat button. After that he set off for the office of the department where he was trying to obtain the post of a vice-governor, or failing that, of a procurement officer. Passing through the reception room, he glanced in the mirror: the nose was there. Then he went to visit another collegiate assessor or major, a great wag, to whom he often said in reply to various derisive remarks: "Oh, come off it, I know you, you're a kidder." On the way there he thought: "If the major doesn't explode with laughter on seeing me, it's a sure sign that everything is in its proper place." The collegiate assessor did not explode. "That's great, that's great, damn it!" Kovalyov thought to himself. On the street he met Mrs. Podtochina, the field officer's wife, together with her daughter, bowed to them and was hailed with joyful exclamations and so everything was all right, no part of him was missing. He talked with them a very long time and, deliberately taking out his snuffbox, right in front of them kept stuffing his nose with snuff at both entrances for a very long time, saying to himself: "So much for you, you women, you stupid hens! I won't marry the daughter all the same. Anything else, *par amour*—by all means." And from that time on, Major Kovalyov went strolling about as though nothing had happened, both on Nevsky Avenue, and in the theaters, and everywhere. And his nose too, as though nothing had happened, stayed on his face, betraying no sign of having played truant. And thereafter Major Kovalyov was always seen in good humor, smiling, running after absolutely all the pretty ladies, and once even stopping in front of a little shop in Gostinny Dvor and buying himself the ribbon of some order, goodness knows why, for he hadn't been decorated with any order.

That is the kind of affair that happened in the northern capital of our vast empire. Only now, on second thoughts, can we see that there is much that is improbable in it. Without speaking of the fact that the supernatural detachment of the nose and its appearance in various places in the guise of a state councillor is indeed strange, how is it that Kovalyov did not realize that one does not advertise for one's nose through the newspaper office? I do not mean to say that advertising rates appear to me too high: that's nonsense, and I am not at all one of those mercenary people. But it's improper, embarrassing, not nice! And then again—how did the nose come to be in a newly baked loaf, and how about Ivan Yakovlevich? . . . No, this is something I can't understand, positively can't understand. But the strangest, the most incomprehensible thing of all, is how authors can choose such subjects. I confess that this is quite inconceivable; it is indeed . . . no, no, I just can't understand it at all! In the first place, there is absolutely no benefit in it for the fatherland; in the second place . . . but in the second place, there is no benefit either. I simply don't know what to make of it. . . .

And yet, in spite of it all, though, of course, we may assume this and that and the other, perhaps even . . . And after all, where aren't there incongruities?—But all the same, when you think about it, there really is something in all this. Whatever anyone says, such things happen in this world; rarely, but they do.

HERMAN MELVILLE

(1819–1891)

*H*erman Melville was born in New York, the son of Allan Melville, a wholesale merchant, and Maria Gansevoort Melville, the daughter of a hero in the American Revolutionary War. His father lost everything in the panic of 1830, was forced into bankruptcy, and died two years later of worry and overwork. Melville's older brothers repaired the family fortune, and Melville eventually went to work for them in the fur business. It too failed and Melville took a job as ship's apprentice on a boat destined for Liverpool. He returned, taught school for a time, went westward to try his luck, and when nothing turned up took a job in 1841 on a whaling ship bound for the south seas. After eighteen months, he deserted in the Marquesas Islands, subsequently to embark on another whaler, which put him ashore as a mutineer. A third ship took him to Hawaii, where he enlisted as an ordinary seaman on an American warship and set sail for home. He described some of his adventures in Typee (1846), and the novel was an overnight success, as was his next novel, Omoo (1847). Yet Melville was unsure about whether he could gain a sufficient income from writing, and using family connections, applied to the federal government for a post that would give him security. He was unsuccessful, and that failure, in addition to the disappointing reception of his third novel, Mardi (1849), plunged him into despair. Redburn (1849) and Whitejacket (1850) were commercial successes, but Melville felt torn between his desire to write the intellectual fiction that pleased him and his need to gain money by what he regarded as hack work. Moby Dick (1851), the product of his reading of Shakespeare and Carlyle, his friendship with Hawthorne, and two years of intense writing and rewriting confirmed him in his fears: one of the greatest American novels ever written received only mixed reviews, and its author was dismissed by some critics as insane. Pierre (1852) and The Piazza Tales (1856), a collection of short stories, did nothing to halt the decline in his reputation. He toured Europe and the Middle East, went on the American lecture circuit, wrote some startlingly original poetry, but was devastated by his failure to secure a government post. When he finally secured a job as deputy-inspector in New York City in 1866, his writing career was essentially over. His fame revived somewhat near the end of his life, but it was not until this century that his achievement received appropriate recognition. Even in his short fiction, Melville always had large aims. As Richard Fogle suggests, "the purpose of the tales as of all Melville's fiction is to penetrate as deeply as possible into [the world's] metaphysical, theological, moral, psychological, and social truths."

Bartleby the Scrivener

A Story of Wall Street

I am a rather elderly man. The nature of my avocations for the last thirty years has brought me into more than ordinary contact with what would seem an interesting and somewhat singular set of men, of whom as yet nothing that I know of has ever been written:—I mean the law-copyists or scriveners. I have known very many of them, professionally and privately, and if I pleased, could relate divers histories, at which good-natured gentlemen might smile, and sentimental souls might weep. But I waive the biographies of all other scriveners for a few passages in the life of Bartleby, who was a scrivener the strangest I ever saw or heard of. While of other law-copyists I might write the complete life, of Bartleby nothing of that sort can be done. I believe that no materials exist for a full and satisfactory biography of this man. It is an irreparable loss to literature. Bartleby was one of those beings of whom nothing is ascertainable, except from the original sources, and in his case those are very small. What my own astonished eyes saw of Bartleby, *that* is all I know of him, except, indeed, one vague report which will appear in the sequel.

Ere introducing the scrivener, as he first appeared to me, it is fit I make some mention of myself, my *employés*, my business, my chambers, and general surroundings; because some such description is indispensable to an adequate understanding of the chief character about to be presented.

Imprimis: I am a man who, from his youth upward, has been filled with a profound conviction that the easiest way of life is the best. Hence, though I belong to a profession proverbially energetic and nervous, even to turbulence, at times, yet nothing of that sort have I ever suffered to invade my peace. I am one of those unambitious lawyers who never addresses a jury, or in any way draws down public applause; but in the cool tranquillity of a snug retreat, do a snug business among rich men's bonds and mortgages and title-deeds. All who know me, consider me an eminently *safe* man. The late John Jacob Astor, a personage little given to poetic enthusiasm, had no hesitation in pronouncing my first grand point to be prudence; my next, method. I do not speak it in vanity, but simply record the fact, that I was not unemployed in my profession by the late John Jacob Astor; a name which, I admit, I love to repeat, for it hath a rounded and orbicular sound to it, and rings like unto bullion. I will freely add, that I was not insensible to the late John Jacob Astor's good opinion.

Some time prior to the period at which this little history begins, my avocations had been largely increased. The good old office, now extinct in the State of New York, of a Master in Chancery, had been conferred upon me. It was not a very arduous office, but very pleasantly remunerative. I seldom lose my temper; much more seldom indulge in dangerous indignation at wrongs and outrages; but I must be permitted to be rash here and declare, that I consider the sudden and violent abrogation of the office of Master in Chancery, by the new Constitution, as a—premature act; inasmuch as I had counted upon a life-lease of the profits, whereas I only received those of a few short years. But this is by the way.

My chambers were upstairs at No. — Wall Street. At one end they looked upon the white wall of the interior of a spacious sky-light shaft, penetrating the building from top to bottom. This view might have been considered rather tame than otherwise, deficient in what landscape painters call "life." But if so, the view from the other end of my chambers offered, at least, a contrast, if nothing more. In that direction my windows commanded an unobstructed view of a lofty brick wall, black by age and everlasting shade; which wall required no spy-glass to bring out its lurking beauties, but for the benefit of all near-sighted spectators, was pushed up to within ten feet of my window panes. Owing to the great height of the surrounding buildings, and my chambers being on the second floor, the interval between this wall and mine not a little resembled a huge square cistern.

At the period just preceding the advent of Bartleby, I had two persons as copyists in my employment, and a promising lad as an office-boy. First, Turkey; second, Nippers; third, Ginger Nut. These may seem names, the like of which are not usually found in the Directory. In truth they were nicknames, mutually conferred upon each other by my three clerks, and were deemed expressive of their respective persons or characters. Turkey was a short, pursy Englishman of about my own age, that is, somewhere not far from sixty. In the morning, one might say, his face was of a fine florid hue, but after twelve o'clock, meridian—his dinner hour—it blazed like a grate full of Christmas coals; and continued blazing—but, as it were, with a gradual wane—till 6 o'clock P.M. or thereabouts, after which I saw no more of the proprietor of the face, which, gaining its meridian with the sun, seemed to set with it, to rise, culminate, and decline the following day, with the like regularity and undiminished glory. There are many singular coincidences I have known in the course of my life, not the least among which was the fact, that exactly when Turkey displayed his fullest beams from his red and radiant countenance, just then, too, at that critical moment, began the daily period when I considered his business capacities as seriously disturbed for the remainder of the twenty-four hours. Not that he was absolutely idle, or averse to business then; far from it. The difficulty was, he was apt to be altogether too energetic. There was a strange, inflamed, flurried, flighty recklessness of activity about him. He would be incautious in dipping his pen into his inkstand. All his blots upon my documents, were dropped there after twelve o'clock, meridian. Indeed, not only would he be reckless and sadly given to making blots in the afternoon, but some days he went further, and was rather noisy. At such times, too, his face flamed with augmented blazonry, as if cannel coal had been heaped on anthracite. He made an unpleasant racket with his chair; spilled his sand-box; in mending his pens, impatiently split them all to pieces, and threw them on the floor in a sudden passion; stood up and leaned over his table, boxing his papers about in a most indecorous manner, very sad to behold in an elderly man like him. Nevertheless, as he was in many ways a most valuable person to me, and all the time before twelve o'clock, meridian, was the quickest, steadiest creature, too, accomplishing a great deal of work in a style not easy to be matched— for these reasons, I was willing to overlook his eccentricities, though indeed, occasionally, I remonstrated with him. I did this very gently, however, because, though the civilest, nay, the blandest and most reverential of men in the morning, yet in the afternoon he was disposed, upon provocation, to be slightly rash with his tongue, in fact, insolent. Now, valuing his morning services as I did, and resolving not to lose them— yet, at the same time, made uncomfortable by his inflamed ways after twelve o'clock; and being a man of peace, unwilling by my admonitions to call forth unseemly retorts from him—I took upon me, one Saturday noon (he was always worse on Saturdays), to hint to him, very kindly, that perhaps now that he was growing old, it might be well to abridge his labours; in short, he need not come to my chambers after twelve o'clock, but, dinner over, had best go home to his lodgings and rest himself till tea-time. But no; he insisted upon his afternoon devotions. His countenance became intolerably fervid, as he oratorically assured me—gesticulating, with a long ruler, at the other side of the room—that if his services in the morning were useful, how indispensable, then, in the afternoon?

"With submission, sir," said Turkey on this occasion, "I consider myself your right-hand man. In the morning I but marshal and deploy my columns; but in the afternoon I put myself at their head, and gallantly charge the foe, thus!"—and he made a violent thrust with the ruler.

"But the blots, Turkey," intimated I.

"True,—but, with submission, sir, behold these hairs! I am getting old. Surely, sir, a blot or two of a warm afternoon is not to be severely urged against grey hairs. Old age—even if it blot the page—is honourable. With submission, sir, we *both* are getting old."

This appeal to my fellow-feeling was hardly to be resisted. At all events, I saw that go he would not. So I made up my mind to let him stay, resolving, nevertheless, to see to it, that during the afternoon he had to do with my less important papers.

Nippers, the second on my list, was a whiskered, sallow, and, upon the whole, rather piratical-looking young man of about five and twenty. I always deemed him the victim of two evil powers—ambition and indigestion. The ambition was evinced by a certain impatience of the duties of a mere copyist—an unwarrantable usurpation of strictly professional affairs, such as the original drawing up of legal documents. The indigestion seemed betokened in an occasional nervous testiness and grinning irritability, causing the teeth to audibly grind together over mistakes committed in copying; unnecessary maledictions, hissed, rather than spoken, in the heat of business; and especially by a continual discontent with the height of the table where he worked. Though of a very ingenious mechanical turn, Nippers could never get this table to suit him. He put chips under it, blocks of various sorts, bits of pasteboard, and at last went so far as to attempt an exquisite adjustment by final pieces of folded blotting-paper. But no invention would answer. If, for the sake of easing his back, he brought the table lid at a sharp angle well up toward his chin, and wrote there like a man using the steep roof of a Dutch house for his desk—then he declared that it stopped the circulation in his arms. If now he lowered the table to his waistbands, and stooped over it in writing, then there was a sore aching in his back. In short, the truth of the matter was, Nippers knew not what he wanted. Or, if he wanted anything, it was to be rid of a scrivener's table altogether. Among the manifestations of his diseased ambition was a fondness he had for receiving visits from certain ambiguous-looking fellows in seedy coats, whom he called his clients. Indeed I was aware that not only was he, at times, considerable of a ward-politician, but he occasionally did a little business at the Justices' courts, and was not unknown on the steps of the Tombs. I have good reason to believe, however, that one individual who called upon him at my chambers, and who, with a grand air, he insisted was his client, was no other than a dun, and the alleged title-deed, a bill. But with all his failings, and the annoyances he caused me, Nippers, like his compatriot Turkey, was a very useful man to me; wrote a neat, swift hand; and, when he chose, was not deficient in a gentlemanly sort of deportment. Added to this, he always dressed in a gentlemanly sort of way; and so, incidentally, reflected credit upon my chambers. Whereas with respect to Turkey, I had much ado to keep him from being a reproach to me. His clothes were apt to look oily and smell of eating-houses. He wore his pantaloons very loose and baggy in summer. His coats were execrable; his hat not to be handled. But while the hat was a thing of indifference to me, inasmuch as his natural civility and deference, as a dependent Englishman, always led him to doff it the moment he entered the room, yet his coat was another matter. Concerning his coats, I reasoned with him; but with no effect. The truth was, I suppose, that a man with so small an income, could not afford to sport such a lustrous face and a lustrous coat at one and the same time. As Nippers once observed,

Turkey's money went chiefly for red ink. One winter day I presented Turkey with a highly-respectable looking coat of my own, a padded grey coat, of a most comfortable warmth, and which buttoned straight up from the knee to the neck. I thought Turkey would appreciate the favour, and abate his rashness and obstreperousness of afternoons. But no. I verily believe that buttoning himself up in so downy and blanket-like a coat had a pernicious effect upon him; upon the same principle that too much oats are bad for horses. In fact, precisely as a rash, restive horse is said to feel his oats, so Turkey felt his coat. It made him insolent. He was a man whom prosperity harmed.

Though concerning the self-indulgent habits of Turkey I had my own private surmises, yet touching Nippers I was well persuaded that whatever might be his faults in other respects, he was, at least, a temperate young man. But, indeed, nature herself seemed to have been his vintner, and at his birth charged him so thoroughly with an irritable, brandy-like disposition, that all subsequent potations were needless. When I consider how, amid the stillness of my chambers, Nippers would sometimes impatiently rise from his seat, and stooping over this table, spread his arms wide apart, seize the whole desk, and move it, and jerk it, with a grim, grinding motion on the floor, as if the table were a perverse voluntary agent, intent on thwarting and vexing him; I plainly perceive that for Nippers, brandy and water were altogether superfluous.

It was fortunate for me that, owing to its peculiar cause—indigestion—the irritability and consequent nervousness of Nippers, were mainly observable in the morning, while in the afternoon he was comparatively mild. So that Turkey's paroxysms only coming on about twelve o'clock, I never had to do with their eccentricities at one time. Their fits relieved each other like guards. When Nippers's was on, Turkey's was off; and *vice versa*. This was a good natural arrangement under the circumstances.

Ginger Nut, the third on my list, was a lad some twelve years old. His father was a carman, ambitious of seeing his son on the bench instead of a cart, before he died. So he sent him to my office as student at law, errand boy, and cleaner and sweeper, at the rate of one dollar a week. He had a little desk to himself, but he did not use it much. Upon inspection, the drawer exhibited a great array of the shells of various sorts of nuts. Indeed, to this quick-witted youth the whole noble science of the law was contained in a nut-shell. Not the least among the employments of Ginger Nut, as well as one which he discharged with the most alacrity, was his duty as cake and apple purveyor for Turkey and Nippers. Copying law papers being proverbially a dry, husky sort of business, my two scriveners were fain to moisten their mouths very often with Spitzenbergs to be had at the numerous stalls nigh the Custom House and Post Office. Also, they sent Ginger Nut very frequently for that peculiar cake—small, flat, round, and very spicy—after which he had been named by them. Of a cold morning, when business was but dull, Turkey would gobble up scores of these cakes, as if they were mere wafers—indeed they sell them at the rate of six or eight for a penny—the scrape of his pen blending with the crunching of the crisp particles in his mouth. Of all the fiery afternoon blunders and flurried rashness of Turkey, was his once moistening a ginger-cake between his lips, and clapping it on to a mortgage for a seal. I came within an ace of dismissing him then. But he mollified me by making an oriental bow and saying—"With submission, sir, it was generous of me to find you in stationery on my own account."

Now my original business—that of a conveyancer and title hunter, and drawer-up of recondite documents of all sorts—was considerably increased by receiving the master's office. There was now great work for scriveners. Not only must I push the clerks already with me, but I must have additional help. In answer to my advertisement, a motionless young man one morning stood upon my office threshold, the door being open, for it was summer. I can see that figure now—pallidly neat, pitiably respectable, incurably forlorn! It was Bartleby.

After a few words touching his qualifications, I engaged him, glad to have among my corps of copyists a man of so singularly sedate an aspect, which I thought might operate beneficially upon the flighty temper of Turkey, and the fiery one of Nippers.

I should have stated before that ground glass folding-doors divided my premises into two parts, one of which was occupied by my scriveners, the other by myself. According to my humour I threw open these doors, or closed them. I resolved to assign Bartleby a corner by the folding-doors, but on my side of them, so as to have this quiet man within easy call, in case any trifling thing was to be done. I placed his desk close up to a small side-window in that part of the room, a window which originally had afforded a lateral view of certain grimy back-yards and bricks, but which, owing to subsequent erections, commanded at present no view at all, though it gave some light. Within three feet of the panes was a wall, and the light came down from far above, between two lofty buildings, as from a very small opening in a dome. Still further to a satisfactory arrangement, I procured a high green folding screen, which might entirely isolate Bartleby from my sight, though not remove him from my voice. And thus, in a manner, privacy and society were conjoined.

At first Bartleby did an extraordinary quantity of writing. As if long famishing for something to copy, he seemed to gorge himself on my documents. There was no pause for digestion. He ran a day and night line, copying by sun-light and by candle-light. I should have been quite delighted with his application, had he been cheerfully industrious. But he wrote on silently, palely, mechanically.

It is, of course, an indispensable part of a scrivener's business to verify the accuracy of his copy, word by word. Where there are two or more scriveners in an office, they assist each other in this examination, one reading from the copy, the other holding the original. It is a very dull, wearisome, and lethargic affair. I can readily imagine that to some sanguine temperaments it would be altogether intolerable. For example, I cannot credit that the mettlesome poet Byron would have contentedly sat down with Bartleby to examine a law document of, say five hundred pages, closely written in a crimpy hand.

Now and then, in the haste of business, it had been my habit to assist in comparing some brief document myself, calling Turkey or Nippers for this purpose. One object I had in placing Bartleby so handy to me behind the screen, was to avail myself of his services on such trivial occasions. It was on the third day, I think, of his being with me, and before any necessity had arisen for having his own writing examined, that, being much hurried to complete a small affair I had in hand, I abruptly called to Bartleby. In my haste and natural expectancy of instant compliance, I sat with my head bent over the original on my desk, and my right hand sideways, and somewhat nervously extended with the copy, so that immediately upon emerging from his retreat, Bartleby might snatch it and proceed to business without the least delay.

In this very attitude did I sit when I called to him, rapidly stating what it was I wanted him to do—namely, to examine a small paper with me. Imagine my surprise, nay, my consternation, when without moving from his privacy, Bartleby in a singularly mild, firm voice, replied, "I would prefer not to."

I sat awhile in perfect silence, rallying my stunned faculties. Immediately it occurred to me that my ears had deceived me, or Bartleby had entirely misunderstood my meaning. I repeated my request in the clearest tone I could assume. But in quite as clear a one came the previous reply, "I would prefer not to."

"Prefer not to," echoed I, rising in high excitement, and crossing the room with a stride. "What do you mean? Are you moon-struck? I want you to help me compare this sheet here—take it," and I thrust it toward him.

"I would prefer not to," said he.

I looked at him steadfastly. His face was leanly composed; his grey eye dimly calm. Not a wrinkle of agitation rippled him. Had there been the least uneasiness, anger, impatience or impertinence in his manner; in other words, had there been anything ordinarily human about him; doubtless I should have violently dismissed him from the premises. But as it was, I should have as soon thought of turning my pale plaster-of-paris bust of Cicero out of doors. I stood gazing at him awhile, as he went on with his own writing, and then reseated myself at my desk. This is very strange, thought I. What had one best do? But my business hurried me. I concluded to forget the matter for the present, reserving it for my future leisure. So calling Nippers from the other room, the paper was speedily examined.

A few days after this, Bartleby concluded four lengthy documents, being quadruplicates of a week's testimony taken before me in my High Court of Chancery. It became necessary to examine them. It was an important suit, and great accuracy was imperative. Having all things arranged, I called Turkey, Nippers and Ginger Nut from the next room, meaning to place the four copies in the hands of my four clerks, while I should read from the original. Accordingly Turkey, Nippers and Ginger Nut had taken their seats in a row, each with his document in hand, when I called to Bartleby to join this interesting group.

"Bartleby! quick, I am waiting."

I heard a slow scrape of his chair legs on the uncarpeted floor, and soon he appeared standing at the entrance of his hermitage.

"What is wanted?" said he mildly.

"The copies, the copies," said I hurriedly. "We are going to examine them. There"—and I held toward him the fourth quadruplicate.

"I would prefer not to," he said, and gently disappeared behind the screen.

For a few moments I was turned into a pillar of salt, standing at the head of my seated column of clerks. Recovering myself, I advanced toward the screen, and demanded the reason for such extraordinary conduct.

"*Why* do you refuse?"

"I would prefer not to."

With any other man I should have flown outright into a dreadful passion, scorned all further words, and thrust him ignominiously from my presence. But there was something about Bartleby that not only strangely disarmed me, but in a wonderful manner touched and disconcerted me. I began to reason with him.

"These are your own copies we are about to examine. It is labour saving to you, because one examination will answer for your four papers. It is common usage. Every copyist is bound to help examine his copy. Is it not so? Will you not speak? Answer!"

"I prefer not to," he replied in a flute-like tone. It seemed to me that while I had been addressing him, he carefully revolved every statement that I made; fully comprehended the meaning; could not gainsay the irresistible conclusion; but, at the same time, some paramount consideration prevailed with him to reply as he did.

"You are decided, then, not to comply with my request—a request made according to common usage and common sense?"

He briefly gave me to understand that on that point my judgment was sound. Yes: his decision was irreversible.

It is not seldom the case that when a man is browbeaten in some unprecedented and violently unreasonable way, he begins to stagger in his own plainest faith. He begins, as it were, vaguely to surmise that, wonderful as it may be, all the justice and all the reason are on the other side. Accordingly, if any disinterested persons are present, he turns to them for some reinforcement for his own faltering mind.

"Turkey," said I, "what do you think of this? Am I not right?"

"With submission, sir," said Turkey, with his blandest tone, "I think that you are."

"Nippers," said I, "what do *you* think of it?"

"I think I should kick him out of the office."

(The reader of nice perceptions will here perceive that, it being morning, Turkey's answer is couched in polite and tranquil terms but Nippers's reply in ill-tempered ones. Or, to repeat a previous sentence, Nippers's ugly mood was on duty, and Turkey's off.)

"Ginger Nut," said I, willing to enlist the smallest suffrage in my behalf, "what do *you* think of it?"

"I think, sir, he's a little *luny*," replied Ginger Nut, with a grin.

"You hear what they say," said I, turning towards the screen, "come forth and do your duty."

But he vouchsafed no reply. I pondered a moment in sore perplexity. But once more business hurried me. I determined again to postpone the consideration of this dilemma to my future leisure. With a little trouble we made out to examine the papers without Bartleby, though at every page or two, Turkey deferentially dropped his opinion that this proceeding was quite out of the common; while Nippers, twitching in his chair with a dyspeptic nervousness, ground out between his set teeth occasional hissing maledictions against the stubborn oaf behind the screen. And for his (Nippers's) part, this was the first and the last time he would do another man's business without pay.

Meanwhile Bartleby sat in his hermitage, oblivious to everything but his own peculiar business there.

Some days passed, the scrivener being employed upon another lengthy work. His late remarkable conduct led me to regard his ways narrowly. I observed that he never went to dinner; indeed that he never went any where. As yet I had never of my personal knowledge known him to be outside of my office. He was a perpetual sentry in the corner. At about eleven o'clock though, in the morning, I noticed that Ginger Nut would advance towards the opening in Bartleby's screen, as if silently beckoned thither by a gesture invisible to me where I sat. The boy would then leave the office jingling a few pence, and reappear with a handful of ginger-nuts which he delivered in the hermitage, receiving two of the cakes for his trouble.

He lives, then, on ginger-nuts, thought I; never eats a dinner, properly speaking; he must be a vegetarian then; but no; he never eats even vegetables, he eats nothing but ginger-nuts. My mind then ran on in reveries concerning the probable effects upon the human constitution of living entirely on ginger-nuts. Ginger-nuts are so called because they contain ginger as one of their peculiar constituents, and the final flavouring one. Now what was ginger? A hot, spicy thing. Was Bartleby hot and spicy? Not at all. Ginger, then, had no effect upon Bartleby. Probably he preferred it should have none.

Nothing so aggravates an earnest person as a passive resistance. If the individual so resisted be of a not inhumane temper, and the resisting one perfectly harmless in his passivity; then, in the better moods of the former, he will endeavour charitably to construe to his imagination what proves impossible to be solved by his judgment. Even so, for the most part, I regarded Bartleby and his ways. Poor fellow! thought I, he means no mischief; it is plain he intends no insolence; his aspect sufficiently evinces that his eccentricities are involuntary. He is useful to me. I can get along with him. If I turn him away, the chances are he will fall in with some less indulgent employer, and then he will be rudely treated, and perhaps driven forth miserably to starve. Yes. Here I can cheaply purchase a delicious self-approval. To befriend Bartleby; to humour him in his strange wilfulness, will cost me little or nothing, while I lay up in my soul what will eventually prove a sweet morsel for my conscience. But this mood was not invariable with me. The passiveness of Bartleby sometimes irritated me. I felt strangely goaded on to encounter him in new opposition, to elicit some angry spark from him answerable to my own. But indeed I might as well have essayed to strike fire with my knuckles against a bit of Windsor soap. But one afternoon the evil impulse in me mastered me, and the following little scene ensued:

"Bartleby," said I, "when those papers are all copied, I will compare them with you."

"I would prefer not to."

"How? Surely you do not mean to persist in that mulish vagary?"

No answer.

I threw open the folding-doors near by, and turning upon Turkey and Nippers, exclaimed in an excited manner:

"He says, a second time, he won't examine his papers. What do you think of it, Turkey?"

It was afternoon, be it remembered. Turkey sat glowing like a brass boiler, his bald head steaming, his hands reeling among his blotted papers.

"Think of it?" roared Turkey; "I think I'll just step behind his screen, and black his eyes for him!"

So saying, Turkey rose to his feet and threw his arms into a pugilistic position. He was hurrying away to make good his promise, when I detained him, alarmed at the effect of incautiously rousing Turkey's combativeness after dinner.

"Sit down, Turkey," said I, "and hear what Nippers has to say. What do you think of it, Nippers? Would I not be justified in immediately dismissing Bartleby?"

"Excuse me, that is for you to decide, sir. I think his conduct quite unusual, and indeed unjust, as regards Turkey and myself. But it may only be a passing whim."

"Ah," exclaimed I, "you have strangely changed your mind then— you speak very gently of him now."

"All beer," cried Turkey; "gentleness is effects of beer—Nippers and I dined together to-day. You see how gentle *I* am, sir. Shall I go and black his eyes?"

"You refer to Bartleby, I suppose. No, not to-day, Turkey," I replied; "pray, put up your fists."

I closed the doors, and again advanced towards Bartleby. I felt additional incentives tempting me to my fate. I burned to be rebelled against again. I remembered that Bartleby never left the office.

"Bartleby," said I, "Ginger Nut is away; just step round to the Post Office, won't you? (it was but a three minutes' walk), and see if there is anything for me."

"I would prefer not to."

"You *will* not?"

"I *prefer* not."

I staggered to my desk, and sat there in a deep study. My blind inveteracy returned. Was there any other thing in which I could procure myself to be ignominiously repulsed by this lean, penniless wight?—my hired clerk? What added thing is there, perfectly reasonable, that he will be sure to refuse to do?

"Bartleby!"

No answer.

"Bartleby," in a louder tone.

No answer.

"Bartleby," I roared.

Like a very ghost, agreeably to the laws of magical invocation, at the third summons, he appeared at the entrance of his hermitage.

"Go to the next room, and tell Nippers to come to me."

"I prefer not to," he respectfully and slowly said, and mildly disappeared.

"Very good, Bartleby," said I, in a quiet sort of serenely severe self-possessed tone, intimating the unalterable purpose of some terrible retribution very close at hand. At the moment I half intended something of the kind. But upon the whole, as it was drawing towards my dinner-hour, I thought it best to put on my hat and walk home for the day, suffering much from perplexity and distress of mind.

Shall I acknowledge it? The conclusion of this whole business was, that it soon became a fixed fact of my chambers, that a pale young scrivener, by the name of Bartleby, had a desk there; that he copied for me at the usual rate of four cents a folio (one hundred words); but he was permanently exempt from examining the work done by him, that duty being transferred to Turkey and Nippers, out of compliment doubtless to their superior acuteness; moreover, said Bartleby was never on any account to be despatched on the most trivial errand of any sort; and that even if entreated to take upon him such a matter, it was generally understood that he would prefer not to—in other words, that he would refuse point-blank.

As days passed on, I became considerably reconciled to Bartleby. His steadiness, his freedom from all dissipation, his incessant industry (except when he chose to throw himself into a standing revery behind his screen), his great stillness, his unalterableness of demeanour under all circumstances, made him a valuable acquisition. One prime thing was this,— *he was always there;*—first in the morning, continually through the day, and the last at night. I had a singular confidence in his honesty. I felt my most precious papers perfectly safe in his hands. Sometimes to be sure I could not, for the very soul of me, avoid falling into sudden spasmodic passions with him. For it was exceeding difficult to bear in mind all the time those strange peculiarities, privileges, and unheard of exemptions, forming the tacit stipulations on Bartleby's part under which he remained in my office. Now and then, in the eagerness of despatching pressing business, I would inadvertently summon Bartleby, in a short, rapid tone, to put his finger, say, on the incipient tie of a bit of red tape with which I was about compressing some papers. Of course, from behind the screen the usual answer, "I prefer not to," was sure to come; and then, how could a human creature with the common infirmities of our nature, refrain from bitterly exclaiming upon such perverseness—such unreasonableness. However, every added repulse of this sort which I received only tended to lessen the probability of my repeating the inadvertence.

Here it must be said, that according to the custom of most legal gentlemen occupying chambers in densely-populated law buildings, there were several keys to my door. One was kept by a woman residing in the attic, which person weekly scrubbed and daily swept and dusted my apartments. Another was kept by Turkey for convenience sake. The third I sometimes carried in my own pocket. The fourth I knew not who had.

Now, one Sunday morning I happened to go to Trinity Church, to hear a celebrated preacher, and finding myself rather early on the ground, I thought I would walk round to my chambers for awhile. Luckily I had my key with me; but upon applying it to the lock, I found it resisted by something inserted from the inside. Quite surprised, I called out; when to my consternation a key was turned from within; and thrusting his lean visage at me, and holding the door ajar, the apparition of Bartleby appeared, in his shirt sleeves, and otherwise in a strangely tattered dishabille, saying quietly that he was sorry, but he was deeply engaged just then, and—preferred not admitting me at present. In a brief word or two, he moreover added, that perhaps I had better walk round the block two or three times, and by that time he would probably have concluded his affairs.

Now, the utterly unsurmised appearance of Bartleby, tenanting my law-chambers of a Sunday morning, with his cadaverously gentlemanly *nonchalance*, yet withal firm and self-possessed, had such a strange effect upon me, that incontinently I slunk away from my own door, and did as desired. But not without sundry twinges of impotent rebellion against the mild effrontery of this unaccountable scrivener. Indeed, it was his wonderful mildness chiefly, which not only disarmed me, but unmanned me, as it were. For I consider that one, for the time, is in a way unmanned when he tranquilly permits his hired clerk to dictate to him, and order him away from his own premises. Furthermore, I was full of uneasiness as to what Bartleby could possibly be doing in my office in his shirt sleeves, and in an otherwise dismantled condition of a Sunday morning. Was anything amiss going on? Nay, that was out of the question. It was not to be thought of for a moment that Bartleby was an immoral person. But what could he be doing there—copying? Nay again, whatever might be his eccentricities, Bartleby was an eminently decorous person. He would be the last man to sit down to his desk in any state approaching to nudity. Besides, it was Sunday; and there was something about Bartleby that forbade the supposition that he would by any secular occupation violate the proprieties of the day.

Nevertheless, my mind was not pacified; and full of a restless curiosity, at last I returned to the door. Without hindrance I inserted my key, opened it, and entered. Bartleby was not to be seen. I looked round anxiously, peeped behind his screen; but it was very plain that he was gone. Upon more closely examining the place, I surmised that for an indefinite period Bartleby must have ate, dressed, and slept in my office, and that too without plate, mirror, or bed. The cushioned seat of a ricketty old sofa in one corner bore the faint impress of a lean, reclining form. Rolled away under his desk, I found a blanket; under the empty grate, a blacking box and brush; on a chair, a tin basin, with soap and a ragged towel; in a newspaper a few crumbs of ginger-nuts and a morsel of cheese. Yes, thought I, it is evident enough that Bartleby has been making his home here, keeping bachelor's hall all by himself. Immediately then the thought came sweeping across me, What miserable friendlessness and loneliness are here revealed! His poverty is great; but his solitude, how horrible! Think of it. Of a Sunday, Wall street is deserted as Petra; and every night of every day it is an emptiness. This building too, which of week-days hums with industry and life, at nightfall echoes with sheer vacancy, and all through Sunday is forlorn. And here Bartleby makes his home; sole spectator of a solitude which he has seen all populous—a sort of innocent and transformed Marius brooding among the ruins of Carthage!

For the first time in my life a feeling of overpowering stinging melancholy seized me. Before, I had never experienced aught but a not-unpleasing sadness. The bond of a common humanity now drew me irresistibly to gloom. A fraternal melancholy! For both I and Bartleby were sons of Adam. I remembered the bright silks and sparkling faces I had seen that day, in gala trim, swan-like sailing down the Mississippi of Broadway; and I contrasted them with the pallid copyist, and thought to myself, Ah, happiness courts the light, so we deem the world is gay; but misery hides aloof, so we deem that misery there is none. These sad fancyings—chimeras, doubtless, of a sick and silly brain—led on to other and more special thoughts, concerning the eccentricities of Bartleby. Presentiments of strange discoveries hovered round me. The scrivener's pale form appeared to me laid out, among uncaring strangers, in its shivering winding sheet.

Suddenly I was attracted by Bartleby's closed desk, the key in open sight left in the lock.

I mean no mischief, seek the gratification of no heartless curiosity, thought I; besides, the desk is mine, and its contents, too, so I will make bold to look within. Everything was methodically arranged, the papers smoothly placed. The pigeon holes were deep, and, removing the files of documents, I groped into their recesses. Presently I felt something there, and dragged it out. It was an old bandana handkerchief, heavy and knotted. I opened it, and saw it was a savings' bank.

I now recalled all the quiet mysteries which I had noted in the man. I remembered that he never spoke but to answer; that though at intervals he had considerable time to himself, yet I had never seen him reading—no, not even a newspaper; that for long periods he would stand looking out, at his pale window behind the screen, upon the dead brick wall; I was quite sure he never visited any refectory or eating-house; while his pale face clearly indicated that he never drank beer like Turkey, or tea and coffee even, like other men; that he never went anywhere in particular that I could learn; never went out for a walk, unless indeed that was the case at present; that he had declined telling who he was, or whence he came, or whether he had any relatives in the world; that though so thin and pale, he never complained of ill health. And more than all, I remembered a certain unconscious air of pallid—how shall I call it?—of pallid haughtiness, say, or rather an austere reserve about him, which had positively awed me into my tame compliance with his eccentricities, when I had feared to ask him to do the slightest incidental thing for me, even though I might know, from his long-continued motionlessness, that behind his screen he must be standing in one of those dead-wall reveries of his.

Revolving all these things, and coupling them with the recently discovered fact that he made my office his constant abiding place and home, and not forgetful of his morbid moodiness; revolving all these things, a prudential feeling began to steal over me. My first emotions had been those of pure melancholy and sincerest pity; but just in proportion as the forlornness of Bartleby grew and grew to my imagination, did that same melancholy merge into fear, that pity into repulsion. So true it is, and so terrible, too, that up to a certain point the thought or sight of misery enlists our best affections; but, in certain special cases, beyond that point it does not. They err who would assert that invariably this is owing to the inherent selfishness of the human heart. It rather proceeds from a certain hopelessness of remedying excessive and organic ill. To a sensitive being, pity is not seldom pain. And when at least it is perceived that such pity cannot lead to effectual succour, common sense bids the soul be rid of it. What I saw that morning persuaded me that the scrivener was the victim of innate and incurable disorder. I might give alms to his body; but his body did not pain him; it was his soul that suffered, and his soul I could not reach.

I did not accomplish the purpose of going to Trinity Church that morning. Somehow, the things I had seen disqualified me for the time from church-going. I walked homeward, thinking what I would do with Bartleby. Finally, I resolved upon this:—I would put certain calm questions to him the next morning, touching his history, &c., and if he declined to answer them openly and unreservedly (and I supposed he would prefer not), then to give him a twenty dollar bill over and above whatever I might owe him, and tell him his services were no longer required; but that if in any other way I could assist him, I would be happy to do so, especially if he desired to return to his native place, wherever that might be, I would willingly help to defray the expenses. Moreover, if, after reaching home, he found himself at any time in want of aid, a letter from him would be sure of a reply.

The next morning came.

"Bartleby," said I, gently calling to him behind his screen.

No reply.

"Bartleby," said I, in a still gentler tone, "come here; I am not going to ask you to do anything you would prefer not to do—I simply wish to speak to you."

Upon this he noiselessly slid into view.

"Will you tell me, Bartleby, where were you born?"

"I would prefer not to."

"Will you tell me *anything* about yourself?"

"I would prefer not to."

"But what reasonable objection can you have to speak to me? I feel friendly towards you."

He did not look at me while I spoke, but kept his glance fixed upon my bust of Cicero, which, as I then sat, was directly behind me, some six inches above my head.

"What is your answer, Bartleby?" said I, after waiting a considerable time for a reply, during which his countenance remained immovable, only there was the faintest conceivable tremor of the white attenuated mouth.

"At present I prefer to give no answer," he said, and retired into his hermitage.

It was rather weak in me I confess, but his manner on this occasion nettled me. Not only did there seem to lurk in it a certain calm disdain, but his perverseness seemed ungrateful, considering the undeniable good usage and indulgence he had received from me.

Again I sat ruminating what I should do. Mortified as I was at his behaviour, and resolved as I had been to dismiss him when I entered my office, nevertheless I strangely felt something superstitious knocking at my heart, and forbidding me to carry out my purpose, and denouncing me for a villain if I dared to breathe one bitter word against this forlornest of mankind. At last, familiarly drawing my chair behind his screen, I sat down and said: "Bartleby, never mind then about revealing your history; but let me entreat you, as a friend, to comply as far as may be with the usages of this office. Say now you will help to examine papers to-morrow or next day: in short, say now that in a day or two you will begin to be a little reasonable:—say so, Bartleby."

"At present I would prefer not to be a little reasonable," was his mildly cadaverous reply.

Just then the folding-doors opened, and Nippers approached. He seemed suffering from an unusually bad night's rest, induced by severer indigestion than common. He overheard those final words of Bartleby.

"*Prefer not*, eh?" gritted Nippers—"I'd *prefer* him, if I were you, sir," addressing me—"I'd *prefer* him; I'd give him preferences, the stubborn mule! What is it, sir, pray, that he *prefers* not to do now?"

Bartleby moved not a limb.

"Mr. Nippers," said I, "I'd prefer that you would withdraw for the present."

Somehow, of late I had got into the way of involuntarily using this word "prefer" upon all sorts of not exactly suitable occasions. And I trembled to think that my contact with the scrivener had already and seriously affected me in a mental way. And what further and deeper aberration might it not yet produce? This apprehension had not been without efficacy in determining me to summary means.

As Nippers, looking very sour and sulky, was departing, Turkey blandly and deferentially approached.

"With submission, sir," said he, "yesterday I was thinking about Bartleby here, and I think that if he would but prefer to take a quart of good ale every day, it would do much towards mending him, and enabling him to assist in examining his papers."

"So you have got the word, too," said I, slightly excited.

"With submission, what word, sir?" asked Turkey, respectfully crowding himself into the contracted space behind the screen, and by so doing, making me jostle the scrivener. "What word, sir?"

"I would prefer to be left alone here," said Bartleby, as if offended at being mobbed in his privacy.

"*That's* the word, Turkey," said I—"*that's* it."

"Oh, *prefer?* oh, yes—queer word. I never use it myself. But, sir, as I was saying, if he would but prefer—"

"Turkey," interrupted I, "you will please withdraw."

"Oh certainly, sir, if you prefer that I should."

As he opened the folding-door to retire, Nippers at his desk caught a glimpse of me, and asked whether I would prefer to have a certain paper copied on blue paper or white. He did not in the least roguishly accent the word prefer. It was plain that it involuntarily rolled from his tongue. I thought to myself, surely I must get rid of a demented man, who already has in some degree turned the tongues, if not the heads, of myself and clerks. But I thought it prudent not to break the dismission at once.

The next day I noticed that Bartleby did nothing but stand at his window in his dead-wall revery. Upon asking him why he did not write, he said that he had decided upon doing no more writing.

"Why, how now? what next?" exclaimed I, "do no more writing?"

"No more."

"And what is the reason?"

"Do you not see the reason for yourself?" he indifferently replied.

I looked steadfastly at him, and perceived that his eyes looked dull and glazed. Instantly it occurred to me, that his unexampled diligence in copying by his dim window for the first few weeks of his stay with me might have temporarily impaired his vision.

I was touched. I said something in condolence with him. I hinted that, of course, he did wisely in abstaining from writing for a while, and urged him to embrace that opportunity of taking wholesome exercise in the open air. This, however, he did not do. A few days after this, my other clerks being absent, and being in a great hurry to despatch certain letters by the mail, I thought that, having nothing else earthly to do, Bartleby would surely be less inflexible than usual, and carry these letters to the Post Office. But he blankly declined. So, much to my inconvenience, I went myself.

Still added days went by. Whether Bartleby's eyes improved or not, I could not say. To all appearance, I thought they did. But when I asked him if they did, he vouchsafed no answer. At all events, he would do no copying. At last, in reply to my urgings, he informed me that he had permanently given up copying.

"What!" exclaimed I; "suppose your eyes should get entirely well— better than ever before—would you not copy then?"

"I have given up copying," he answered and slid aside.

He remained, as ever, a fixture in my chamber. Nay—if that were possible—he became still more of a fixture than before. What was to be done? He would do nothing in the office: why should he stay there? In plain fact, he had now become a millstone to me, not only useless as a necklace, but afflictive to bear. Yet I was sorry for him. I speak less than truth when I say that, on his own account, he occasioned me uneasiness. If he would but have named a single relative or friend, I would instantly have written, and urged their taking the poor fellow away to some convenient retreat. But he seemed alone, absolutely alone in the universe. A bit of wreckage in the mid-Atlantic. At length, necessities connected with my business tyrannized over all other considerations. Decently as I could, I told Bartleby that in six days' time he must unconditionally leave the office. I warned him to take measures, in the interval, for procuring some other abode. I offered to assist him in this endeavour, if he himself would but take the first step towards a removal. "And when you finally quit me, Bartleby," added I. "I shall see that you go away not entirely unprovided. Six days from this hour, remember."

At the expiration of that period, I peeped behind the screen, and lo! Bartleby was there.

I buttoned up my coat, balanced myself; advanced slowly towards him, touched his shoulder, and said, "The time has come; you must quit this place; I am sorry for you; here is money; but you must go."

"I would prefer not," he replied, with his back still towards me.

"You *must*."

He remained silent.

Now I had an unbounded confidence in this man's common honesty. He had frequently restored to me sixpences and shillings carelessly dropped upon the floor, for I am apt to be very reckless in such shirt-button affairs. The proceeding then which followed will not be deemed extraordinary.

"Bartleby," said I, "I owe you twelve dollars on account; here are thirty-two; the odd twenty are yours.—Will you take it?" and I handed the bills towards him.

But he made no motion.

"I will leave them here then," putting them under a weight on the table. Then taking my hat and cane and going to the door, I tranquilly turned and added—"After you have removed your things from these offices, Bartleby, you will of course lock the door—since every one is now gone for the day but you—and if you please, slip your key underneath the mat, so that I may have it in the morning. I shall not see you again; so good-bye to you. If hereafter in your new place of abode I can be of any service to you, do not fail to advise me by letter. Good-bye, Bartleby, and fare you well."

But he answered not a word; like the last column of some ruined temple, he remained standing mute and solitary in the middle of the otherwise deserted room.

As I walked home in a pensive mood, my vanity got the better of my pity. I could not but highly plume myself on my masterly management in getting rid of Bartleby. Masterly I call it, and such it must appear to any dispassionate thinker. The beauty of my procedure seemed to consist in its perfect quietness. There was no vulgar bullying, no bravado of any sort, no choleric hectoring, no striding to and fro across the apartment, jerking out vehement commands for Bartleby to bundle himself off with his beggarly traps. Nothing of the kind. Without loudly bidding Bartleby depart—as an inferior genius might have done—I *assumed* the ground that depart he must; and upon that assumption built all I had to say. The more I thought over my procedure, the more I was charmed with it. Nevertheless, next morning, upon awakening, I had my doubts,—I had somehow slept off the fumes of vanity. One of the coolest and wisest hours a man has, is just after he awakes in the morning. My procedure seemed as sagacious as ever,—but only in theory. How it would prove in practice—there was the rub. It was truly a beautiful thought to have assumed Bartleby's departure; but, after all, that assumption was simply my own, and none of Bartleby's. The great point was, not whether I had assumed that he would quit me, but whether he would prefer so to do. He was more a man of preferences than assumptions.

After breakfast, I walked down town, arguing the probabilities *pro* and *con*. One moment I thought it would prove a miserable failure, and Bartleby would be found all alive at my office as usual; the next moment it seemed certain that I should see his chair empty. And so I kept veering about. At the corner of Broadway and Canal Street, I saw quite an excited group of people standing in earnest conversation.

"I'll take odds he doesn't," said a voice as I passed.

"Doesn't go?—done!" said I, "put up your money."

I was instinctively putting my hand in my pocket to produce my own, when I remembered that this was an election day. The words I had overheard bore no reference to Bartleby, but to the success or non-success of some candidate for the mayoralty. In my intent frame of mind, I had, as it were, imagined that all Broadway shared in my excitement, and were debating the same question with me. I passed on, very thankful that the uproar of the street screened my momentary absent-mindedness.

As I had intended, I was earlier than usual at my office door. I stood listening for a moment. All was still. He must be gone. I tried the knob. The door was locked. Yes, my procedure had worked to a charm; he indeed must be vanished. Yet a certain melancholy mixed with this: I was almost sorry for my brilliant success. I was fumbling under the door mat for the key, which Bartleby was to have left there for me, when accidentally my knee knocked against a panel, producing a summoning sound, and in response a voice came to me from within—"Not yet; I am occupied."

It was Bartleby.

I was thunderstruck. For an instant I stood like the man who, pipe in mouth, was killed one cloudless afternoon long ago in Virginia, by summer lightening; at his own warm open window he was killed, and remained leaning out there upon the dreamy afternoon, till some one touched him, and he fell.

"Not gone!" I murmured at last. But again obeying that wondrous ascendency which the inscrutable scrivener had over me—and from which ascendency, for all my chafing, I could not completely escape—I slowly went down stairs and out into the street, and while walking round the block, considered what I should next do in this unheard-of perplexity. Turn the man out by an actual thrusting I could not; to drive him away by calling him hard names would not do; calling in the police was an unpleasant idea; and yet, permit him to enjoy his cadaverous triumph over me,—this too I could not think of. What was to be done? or, if nothing could be done, was there anything further that I could *assume* in the matter? Yes, as before I had prospectively assumed that Bartleby would depart, so now I might retrospectively assume that departed he was. In the legitimate carrying out of this assumption, I might enter my office in a great hurry, and pretending not to see Bartleby at all, walk straight against him as if he were air. Such a proceeding would in a singular degree have the appearance of a home-thrust. It was hardly possible that Bartleby could withstand such an application of the doctrine of assumptions. But, upon second thought, the success of the plan seemed rather dubious. I resolved to argue the matter over with him again.

"Bartleby," said I, entering the office, with a quietly severe expression, "I am seriously displeased. I am pained, Bartleby. I had thought better of you. I had imagined you of such a gentlemanly organization, that in any delicate dilemma a slight hint would suffice—in short, an assumption; but it appears I am deceived. Why," I added, unaffectedly starting, "you have not even touched that money yet," pointing to it, just where I had left it the evening previous.

He answered nothing.

"Will you, or will you not, quit me?" I now demanded in a sudden passion, advancing close to him.

"I would prefer *not* to quit you," he replied, gently emphasizing the *not*.

"What earthly right have you to stay here? Do you pay any rent? Do you pay my taxes? Or is this property yours?"

He answered nothing.

"Are you ready to go on and write now? Are your eyes recovered? Could you copy a small paper for me this morning? or help examine a few lines? or step round to the Post Office? In a word, will you do any thing at all, to give a colouring to your refusal to depart the premises?"

He silently retired into his hermitage.

I was now in such a state of nervous resentment that I thought it but prudent to check myself, at present, from further demonstrations. Bartleby and I were alone. I remembered the tragedy of the unfortunate Adams and the still more unfortunate Colt in the solitary office of the latter; and how poor Colt, being dreadfully incensed by Adams, and imprudently permitting himself to get wildly excited, was at unawares hurried into his fatal act—an act which certainly no man could possibly deplore more than the actor himself. Often it had occurred to me in my ponderings upon the subject, that had that altercation taken place in the public street, or at a private residence, it would not have terminated as it did. It was the circumstance of being alone in a solitary office, upstairs, of a building entirely unhallowed by humanizing domestic associations— an uncarpeted office, doubtless, of a dusty, haggard sort of appearance;— this it must have been, which greatly helped to enhance the irritable desperation of the hapless Colt.

But when this old Adam of resentment rose in me and tempted me concerning Bartleby, I grappled him and threw him. How? Why, simply by recalling the divine injunction: "A new commandment give I unto you, that ye love one another." Yes, this it was that saved me. Aside from higher considerations, charity often operates as a vastly wise and prudent principle—a great safeguard to its possessor. Men have committed mur- der for jealousy's sake, and anger's sake, and hatred's sake, and selfish- ness' sake, and spiritual pride's sake; but no man that ever I heard of, ever committed a diabolical murder for sweet charity's sake. Mere self- interest, then, if no better motive can be enlisted, should, especially with high-tempered men, prompt all beings to charity and philanthropy. At any rate, upon the occasion in question, I strove to drown my exasperated feelings toward the scrivener by benevolently construing his conduct. Poor fellow, poor fellow! thought I, he doesn't mean any thing; and besides; he has seen hard times, and ought to be indulged.

I endeavoured also immediately to occupy myself, and at the same time to comfort my despondency. I tried to fancy that in the course of the morning, at such time as might prove agreeable to him, Bartleby, of his own free accord, would emerge from his hermitage, and take up some decided line of march in the direction of the door. But no. Half-past twelve o'clock came; Turkey began to glow in the face, overturn his inkstand, and become generally obstreperous; Nippers abated down into quietude and courtesy; Ginger Nut munched his noon apple; and Bartleby remained standing at his window in one of his profoundest dead-wall reveries. Will it be credited? Ought I to acknowledge it? That afternoon I left the office without saying one further word to him.

Some days now passed, during which at leisure intervals I looked a little into "Edwards on the Will," and "Priestley on Necessity." Under the circumstances, those books induced a salutary feeling. Gradually I slid into the persuasion that these troubles of mine, touching the scrivener, had been all predestinated from eternity, and Bartleby was billeted upon me for some mysterious purpose of an all-wise Providence, which it was not for a mere mortal like me to fathom. Yes, Bartleby, stay there behind your screen, thought I; I shall persecute you no more; you are harmless and noiseless as any of these old chairs; in short, I never feel so private as when I know you are here. At least I see it, I feel it; I penetrate to the predestinated purpose of my life. I am content. Others may have loftier parts to enact; but my mission in this world, Bartleby, is to furnish you with office room for such period as you may see fit to remain.

I believe that this wise and blessed frame of mind would have continued with me had it not been for the unsolicited and uncharitable remarks obtruded upon me by my professional friends who visited the rooms. But thus it often is, that the constant friction of illiberal minds wears out at last the best resolves of the more generous. Though to be sure, when I reflected upon it, it was not strange that people entering my office should be struck by the peculiar aspect of the unaccountable Bartleby, and so be tempted to throw out some sinister observations concerning him. Sometimes an attorney having business with me, and calling at my office, and finding no one but the scrivener there, would undertake to obtain some sort of precise information from him touching my whereabouts; but without heeding his idle talk, Bartleby would remain standing immovable in the middle of the room. So, after contemplating him in that position for a time, the attorney would depart, no wiser than he came.

Also, when a Reference was going on, and the room full of lawyers and witnesses and business was driving fast, some deeply occupied legal gentleman present, seeing Bartleby wholly unemployed, would request him to run round to his (the legal gentleman's) office and fetch some papers for him. Thereupon, Bartleby would tranquilly decline, and yet remain idle as before. Then the lawyer would give a great stare, and turn to me. And what could I say? At last I was made aware that all through the circle of my professional acquaintance, a whisper of wonder was running round, having reference to the strange creature I kept at my office. This worried me very much. And as the idea came upon me of his possibly turning out a long-lived man, and keep occupying my chambers, and denying my authority; and perplexing my visitors; and scandalizing my professional reputation; and casting a general gloom over the premises; keeping soul and body together to the last upon his savings (for doubtless he spent but half a dime a day), and in the end perhaps outlive me, and claim possession of my office by right of his perpetual occupancy: as all these dark anticipations crowded upon me more and more, and my friends continually intruded their relentless remarks upon the apparition in my room, a great change was wrought in me. I resolved to gather all my faculties together, and for ever rid me of this intolerable incubus.

Ere revolving any complicated project, however, adapted to this end, I first simply suggested to Bartleby the propriety of his permanent departure. In a calm and serious tone, I commended the idea to his careful and mature consideration. But having taken three days to meditate upon it, he apprised me that his original determination remained the same; in short, that he still preferred to abide with me.

What shall I do? I now said to myself, buttoning up my coat to the last button. What shall I do? what ought I to do? what does conscience say I *should* do with this man, or rather ghost? Rid myself of him, I must; go, he shall. But how? You will not thrust him, the poor, pale, passive mortal,—you will not thrust such a helpless creature out of your door? you will not dishonour yourself by such cruelty? No, I will not, I cannot do that. Rather would I let him live and die here, and then mason up his remains in the wall. What then will you do? For all your coaxing, he will not budge. Bribes he leaves under your own paper-weight on your table; in short, it is quite plain that he prefers to cling to you.

Then something severe, something unusual must be done. What! surely you will not have him collared by a constable, and commit his innocent pallor to the common jail? And upon what ground could you procure such a thing to be done?—a vagrant, is he? What! he a vagrant, a wanderer, who refuses to budge? It is because he will *not* be a vagrant, then, that you seek to count him *as* a vagrant. That is too absurd. No visible means of support: there I have him. Wrong again: for indubitably he *does* support himself, and that is the only unanswerable proof that any man can show of his possessing the means so to do. No more then. Since he will not quit me, I must quit him. I will change my offices; I will move elsewhere; and give him fair notice, that if I find him on my new premises I will then proceed against him as a common trespasser.

Acting accordingly, next day I thus addressed him: "I find these chambers too far from the City Hall; the air is unwholesome. In a word, I propose to remove my offices next week, and shall no longer require your services. I tell you this now, in order that you may seek another place."

He made no reply, and nothing more was said.

On the appointed day I engaged carts and men, proceeded to my chambers, and having but little furniture, everything was removed in a few hours. Throughout all, the scrivener remained standing behind the screen, which I directed to be removed the last thing. It was withdrawn; and being folded up like a huge folio, left him the motionless occupant of a naked room. I stood in the entry watching him a moment, while something from within me upbraided me.

I re-entered, with my hand in my pocket—and—and my heart in my mouth.

"Good-bye, Bartleby; I am going—good-bye, and God some way bless you; and take that," slipping something in his hand. But it dropped upon the floor and then—strange to say—I tore myself from him whom I had so longed to be rid of.

Established in my new quarters, for a day or two I kept the door locked, and started at every footfall in the passages. When I returned to my rooms after any little absence, I would pause at the threshold for an instant, and attentively listen, ere applying my key. But these fears were needless. Bartleby never came nigh me.

I thought all was going well, when a perturbed looking stranger visited me, inquiring whether I was the person who had recently occupied rooms at No.—Wall Street.

Full of forebodings, I replied that I was.

"Then sir," said the stranger, who proved a lawyer, "you are responsible for the man you left there. He refuses to do any copying, he refuses to do anything; and he says he prefers not to; and he refuses to quit the premises."

"I am very sorry, sir," said I, with assumed tranquillity, but an inward tremor, "but, really, the man you allude to is nothing to me—he is no relation or apprentice of mine, that you should hold me responsible for him."

"In mercy's name, who is he?"

"I certainly cannot inform you. I know nothing about him. Formerly I employed him as a copyist; but he has done nothing for me now for some time past."

"I shall settle him then,—good morning, sir."

Several days passed, and I heard nothing more; and though I often felt a charitable prompting to call at the place and see poor Bartleby, yet a certain squeamishness of I know not what withheld me.

All is over with him, by this time, thought I at last, when through another week no further intelligence reached me. But coming to my room the day after, I found several persons waiting at my door in a high state of nervous excitement.

"That's the man—here he comes," cried the foremost one, whom I recognized as the lawyer who had previously called upon me alone.

"You must take him away, sir, at once," cried a portly person among them, advancing upon me, and whom I knew to be the landlord of No.—Wall Street. "These gentlemen, my tenants, cannot stand it any longer; Mr. B—," pointing to the lawyer, "has turned him out of his room, and he now persists in haunting the building generally, sitting upon the banisters of the stairs by day, and sleeping in the entry by night. Everybody here is concerned; clients are leaving the offices; some fears are entertained of a mob; something you must do, and that without delay."

Aghast at this torrent, I fell back before it, and would fain have locked myself in my new quarters. In vain I persisted that Bartleby was nothing to me—no more than to any one else there. In vain:—I was the last person known to have anything to do with him, and they had me to the terrible account. Fearful then of being exposed in the papers (as one person present obscurely threatened) I considered the matter, and at length said, that if the lawyer would give me a confidential interview with the scrivener, in his (the lawyer's) own room, I would that afternoon strive my best to rid them of the nuisance they complained of.

Going up stairs to my old haunt, there was Bartleby silently sitting upon the banister at the landing.

"What are you doing here, Bartleby?" said I.

"Sitting upon the banister," he mildly replied.

I motioned him into the lawyer's room, who then left us.

"Bartleby," said I, "are you aware that you are the cause of great tribulation to me, by persisting in occupying the entry after being dismissed from the office?"

No answer.

"Now one of two things must take place. Either you must do something, or something must be done to you. Now what sort of business would you like to engage in? Would you like to re-engage in copying for some one?"

"No; I would prefer not to make any change."

"Would you like a clerkship in a dry-goods store?"

"There is too much confinement about that. No, I would not like a clerkship; but I am not particular."

"Too much confinement," I cried, "why you keep yourself confined all the time!"

"I would prefer not to take a clerkship," he rejoined, as if to settle that little item at once.

"How would a bartender's business suit you? There is no trying of the eyesight in that."

"I would not like it at all; though, as I said before, I am not particular."

His unwonted wordiness inspirited me. I returned to the charge.

"Well then, would you like to travel through the country collecting bills for the merchants? That would improve your health."

"No, I would prefer to be doing something else."

"How then would going as a companion to Europe to entertain some young gentleman with your conversation,—how would that suit you?"

"Not at all. It does not strike me that there is anything definite about that. I like to be stationary. But I am not particular."

"Stationary you shall be then," I cried, now losing all patience, and for the first time in all my exasperating connection with him fairly flying into a passion. "If you do not go away from these premises before night, I shall feel bound—indeed I *am* bound—to—to—to quit the premises myself!" I rather absurdly concluded, knowing not with what possible threat to try to frighten his immobility into compliance. Despairing of all further efforts, I was precipitately leaving him, when a final thought occurred to me—one which had not been wholly unindulged before.

"Bartleby," said I, in the kindest tone I could assume under such exciting circumstances, "will you go home with me now—not to my office, but my dwelling—and remain there till we can conclude upon some convenient arrangement for you at our leisure? Come, let us start now, right away."

"No: at present I would prefer not to make any change at all."

I answered nothing; but effectually dodging every one by the suddenness and rapidly of my flight, rushed from the building, ran up Wall Street toward Broadway, and then jumping into the first omnibus was soon removed from pursuit. As soon as tranquillity returned I distinctly perceived that I had now done all that I possibly could, both in respect to the demands of the landlord and his tenants, and with regard to my own desire and sense of duty, to benefit Bartleby, and shield him from rude persecution. I now strove to be entirely care-free and quiescent; and my conscience justified me in the attempt; though indeed it was not so successful as I could have wished. So fearful was I of being again hunted out by the incensed landlord and his exasperated tenants, that, surrendering my business to Nippers, for a few days I drove about the upper part of the town and through the suburbs, in my rockaway; crossed over to Jersey City and Hoboken, and paid fugitive visits to Manhattanville and Astoria. In fact I almost lived in my rockaway for the time.

When again I entered my office, lo, a note from the landlord lay upon the desk. I opened it with trembling hands. It informed me that the writer had sent to the police, and had Bartleby removed to the Tombs as a vagrant. Moreover, since I knew more about him than any one else, he wished me to appear at that place, and make a suitable statement of the facts. These tidings had a conflicting effect upon me. At first I was indignant; but at last almost approved. The landlord's energetic, summary disposition had led him to adopt a procedure which I do not think I would have decided upon myself; and yet as a last resort, under such peculiar circumstances, it seemed the only plan.

As I afterwards learned, the poor scrivener, when told that he must be conducted to the Tombs, offered not the slightest obstacle, but in his own pale, unmoving way silently acquiesced.

Some of the compassionate and curious bystanders joined the party; and headed by one of the constables, arm-in-arm with Bartleby the silent procession filed its way through all the noise, and heat, and joy of the roaring thoroughfares at noon.

The same day I received the note I went to the Tombs, or, to speak more properly, the Halls of Justice. Seeking the right officer, I stated the purpose of my call, and was informed that the individual I described was indeed within. I then assured the functionary that Bartleby was a perfectly honest man, and greatly to be a compassionated (however unaccountable) eccentric. I narrated all I knew, and closed by suggesting the idea of letting him remain in as indulgent confinement as possible till something less harsh might be done—though indeed I hardly knew what. At all events, if nothing else could be decided upon, the alms-house must receive him. I then begged to have an interview.

Being under no disgraceful charge, and quite serene and harmless in all his ways, they had permitted him freely to wander about the prison, and especially in the inclosed grass-platted yards thereof. And so I found him there, standing all alone in the quietest of the yards, his face toward a high wall—while all around, from the narrow slits of the jail windows, I thought I saw peering out upon him the eyes of murderers and thieves.

"Bartleby!"

"I know you," he said, without looking round,—"and I want nothing to say to you."

"It was not I that brought you here, Bartleby," said I, keenly pained at his implied suspicion. "And to you, this should not be so vile a place. Nothing reproachful attaches to you by being here. And see, it is not so sad a place as one might think. Look, there is the sky and here is the grass."

"I know where I am," he replied, but would say nothing more, and so I left him.

As I entered the corridor again a broad, meat-like man in an apron accosted me, and jerking his thumb over his shoulder said—"Is that your friend?"

"Yes."

"Does he want to starve? If he does, let him live on the prison fare, that's all."

"Who are you?" asked I, not knowing what to make of such an unofficially speaking person in such a place.

"I am the grub-man. Such gentlemen as have friends here, hire me to provide them with something good to eat."

"Is this so?" said I, turning to the turnkey.

He said it was.

"Well then," said I, slipping some silver into the grub-man's hands (for so they called him), "I want you to give particular attention to my friend there; let him have the best dinner you can get. And you must be as polite to him as possible."

"Introduce me, will you?" said the grub-man, looking at me with an expression which seemed to say he was all impatience for an opportunity to give a specimen of his breeding.

Thinking it would prove of benefit to the scrivener, I acquiesced; and asking the grub-man his name, went up with him to Bartleby.

"Bartleby, this is Mr. Cutlets; you will find him very useful to you."

"Your sarvant, sir, your sarvant," said the grub-man, making a low salutation behind his apron. "Hope you find it pleasant here, sir;—spacious grounds—cool apartments, sir—hope you'll stay with us some time—try to make it agreeable. May Mrs. Cutlets and I have the pleasure of your company to dinner, sir, in Mrs. Cutlets' private room?"

"I prefer not to dine to-day," said Bartleby, turning away. "It would disagree with me; I am unused to dinners." So saying, he slowly moved to the other side of the inclosure and took up a position fronting the dead-wall.

"How's this?" said the grub-man, addressing me with a stare of astonishment. "He's odd, ain't he?"

"I think he is a little deranged," said I, sadly.

"Deranged? deranged is it? Well now, upon my word, I thought that friend of yourn was a gentleman forger; they are always pale and genteel-like, them forgers. I can't help pity 'em—can't help it, sir. Did you know Monroe Edwards?" he added touchingly, and paused. Then, laying his hand pityingly on my shoulder, sighed, "he died of the consumption at Sing-Sing. So you weren't acquainted with Monroe?"

"No, I was never socially acquainted with any forgers. But I cannot stop longer. Look to my friend yonder. You will not lose by it. I will see you again."

Some few days after this, I again obtained admission to the Tombs, and went through the corridors in quest of Bartleby; but without finding him.

"I saw him coming from his cell not long ago," said a turnkey, "maybe he's gone to loiter in the yards."

So I went in that direction.

"Are you looking for the silent man?" said another turnkey passing me. "Yonder he lies—sleeping in the yard there. 'Tis not twenty minutes since I saw him lie down."

The yard was entirely quiet. It was not accessible to the common prisoners. The surrounding walls, of amazing thickness, kept off all sounds behind them. The Egyptian character of the masonry weighed upon me with its gloom. But a soft imprisoned turf grew under foot. The heart of the eternal pyramids, it seemed, wherein by some strange magic, through the clefts grass-seed, dropped by birds, had sprung.

Strangely huddled at the base of the wall—his knees drawn up, and lying on his side, his head touching the cold stones—I saw the wasted Bartleby. But nothing stirred. I paused; then went close up to him; stooped over, and saw that his dim eyes were open; otherwise he seemed profoundly sleeping. Something prompted me to touch him. I felt his hand, when a tingling shiver ran up my arm and down my spine to my feet.

The round face of the grub-man peered upon me now. "His dinner is ready. Won't he dine to-day, either? Or does he live without dining?"

"Lives without dining," said I, and closed the eyes.

"Eh!—He's asleep, ain't he?"

"With kings and counsellors," murmured I.

*   *   *

There would seem little need for proceeding further in this history. Imagination will readily supply the meagre recital of poor Bartleby's interment. But ere parting with the reader, let me say, that if this little narrative has sufficiently interested him, to awaken curiosity as to who Bartleby was, and what manner of life he led prior to the present narrator's making his acquaintance, I can only reply, that in such curiosity I fully share—but am wholly unable to gratify it. Yet here I hardly know whether I should divulge one little item of rumour, which came to my ear a few months after the scrivener's decease. Upon what basis it rested, I could never ascertain; and hence, how true it is I cannot now tell. But inasmuch as this vague report has not been without a certain strange suggestive interest to me, however sad, it may prove the same with some others; and so I will briefly mention it. The report was this: that Bartleby had been a subordinate clerk in the Dead Letter Office at Washington, from which he had been suddenly removed by a change in the administration.

When I think over this rumour I cannot adequately express the emotions which seize me. Dead letters! does it not sound like dead men? Conceive a man by nature and misfortune prone to a pallid hopelessness: can any business seem more fitted to heighten it than that of continually handling these dead letters, and assorting them for the flames? For by the cart-load they are annually burned. Sometimes from out the folded paper the pale clerk takes a ring:—the finger it was meant for, perhaps, moulders in the grave; a bank-note sent in swiftest charity:—he whom it would relieve, nor eats nor hungers any more; pardon for those who died despairing; hope for those who died unhoping; good tidings for those who died stifled by unrelieved calamities. On errands of life, these letters speed to death.

Ah Bartleby! Ah humanity!

LEO TOLSTOY

(1828–1910)

*L*eo Tolstoy was born to an aristocratic family at Yasnaya Pol-
yana, a large estate in central Russia. He was brought up by two
aunts on what became his lands after his parents' early deaths. A diary
he began to keep as a student gives clear indications of the literary gifts
he was to develop and of the strong moralizing tendencies that made him
such a harsh judge of his own and others' behaviour. He published the
autobiographical Childhood (1851) in the most influential journal in
Russia and followed it with Boyhood (1854) and Youth (1857). His
Sebastopol Sketches (1855), based on his experiences in the Crimean
War, made every literate person in Russia aware of the horrors of war.
All the confident predictions about the great future ahead of him were
fulfilled by War and Peace (1869), a novel he worked on for six years
and into which he poured what he called a "whole life-time's intellectual
activity." Tracing the course of hundreds of lives affected by Russia's
war with Napoleon's France, the novel explores Tolstoy's ideas about
history, freedom, knowledge, and consciousness itself. His other monumental novel, Anna Karenina (1876), plots the course of an adulterous
affair that ends tragically, as well as the story of the Tolstoy-like Levin
and his tortuous pursuit of happiness. Near the end of his life, Tolstoy
became famous for extra-literary reasons—his own version of Christian
anarchism. A suicidal despair caused him to reject the frivolous and self-
indulgent aspects of the life he led, while his fierce criticism of Russia's
institutions alienated him from the Russian Orthodox Church and from
the state. He denounced all Western art (including his own novels) as
decadent and upper class. Only didactic and moral literature that could
be understood by peasants was acceptable, but Tolstoy was such a
supreme artist that even with this fiercely uncompromising aesthetic he
wrote some unforgettable tales. Tracing Tolstoy's intellectual lineage to
Voltaire and Rousseau, Henry Gilford has argued:

> Like most thinkers in the main eighteenth-century stream, he
> clung to the notion of a world stable in its systems, with fixed
> moral foundations, and he wanted to believe in the absolute
> freedom of the individual. . . . He shared no hopes for political
> change in Russia on the way to a millennium. His sole preoccu-
> pation was the cleansing of the conscience, the pursuit not of
> general happiness but of personal rectitude, the recovery of right
> feeling and uncorrupted judgement.

His death in 1910 deprived his country of its most inspiring spiritual
teacher and its most important writer.

The Death of Iván Ilých

I

During an interval in the Melvínski trial in the large building of the Law Courts the members and public prosecutor met in Iván Egórovich Shébek's private room, where the conversation turned on the celebrated Krasóvski case. Fëdor Vasílievich warmly maintained that it was not subject to their jurisdiction, Iván Egórovich maintained the contrary, while Peter Ivánovich, not having entered into the discussion at the start, took no part in it but looked through the *Gazette* which had just been handed in.

"Gentlemen," he said, "Iván Ilých has died!"

"You don't say so!"

"Here, read it yourself," replied Peter Ivánovich, handing Fëdor Vasílievich the paper still damp from the press. Surrounded by a black border were the words: "Praskóvya Fëdorovna Goloviná, with profound sorrow, informs relatives and friends of the demise of her beloved husband Iván Ilých Golovín, Member of the Court of Justice, which occurred on February the 4th of this year 1882. The funeral will take place on Friday at one o'clock in the afternoon."

Iván Ilých had been a colleague of the gentlemen present and was liked by them all. He had been ill for some weeks with an illness said to be incurable. His post had been kept open for him, but there had been conjectures that in case of his death Alexéev might receive his appointment, and that either Vínnikov or Shtábel would succeed Alexéev. So on receiving the news of Iván Ilých's death the first thought of each of the gentlemen in that private room was of the changes and promotions it might occasion among themselves or their acquaintances.

"I shall be sure to get Shtábel's place or Vínnikov's," thought Fëdor Vasílievich. "I was promised that long ago, and the promotion means an extra eight hundred rubles a year for me besides the allowance."

"Now I must apply for my brother-in-law's transfer from Kalúga," thought Peter Ivánovich. "My wife will be very glad, and then she won't be able to say that I never do anything for her relations."

"I thought he would never leave his bed again," said Peter Ivánovich aloud. "It's very sad."

"But what really was the matter with him?"

"The doctors couldn't say—at least they could, but each of them said something different. When last I saw him I thought he was getting better."

"And I haven't been to see him since the holidays. I always meant to go."

"Had he any property?"

"I think his wife had a little—but something quite trifling."

"We shall have to go to see her, but they live so terribly far away."

"Far away from you, you mean. Everything's far away from your place."

"You see, he never can forgive my living on the other side of the river," said Peter Ivánovich, smiling at Shébek. Then, still talking of the distances between different parts of the city, they returned to the Court.

Besides considerations as to the possible transfers and promotions likely to result from Iván Ilých's death, the mere fact of the death of a near acquaintance aroused, as usual, in all who heard of it the complacent feeling that, "it is he who is dead and not I."

Each one thought or felt, "Well, he's dead but I'm alive!" But the more intimate of Iván Ilých's acquaintances, his so-called friends, could not help thinking also that they would now have to fulfil the very tiresome demands of propriety by attending the funeral service and paying a visit of condolence to the widow.

Fëdor Vasílievich and Peter Ivánovich had been his nearest acquaintances. Peter Ivánovich had studied law with Iván Ilých and had considered himself to be under obligations to him.

Having told his wife at dinner-time of Iván Ilých's death, and of his conjecture that it might be possible to get her brother transferred to their circuit, Peter Ivánovich sacrificed his usual nap, put on his evening clothes and drove to Iván Ilých's house.

At the entrance stood a carriage and two cabs. Leaning against the wall in the hall downstairs near the cloak-stand was a coffin-lid covered with cloth of gold, ornamented with gold cord and tassels, that had been polished up with metal powder. Two ladies in black were taking off their fur cloaks. Peter Ivánovich recognized one of them as Iván Ilých's sister, but the other was a stranger to him. His colleague Schwartz was just coming downstairs, but on seeing Peter Ivánovich enter he stopped and winked at him, as if to say: "Iván Ilých has made a mess of things—not like you and me."

Schwartz's face with his Piccadilly whiskers, and his slim figure in evening dress, had as usual an air of elegant solemnity which contrasted with the playfulness of his character and had a special piquancy here, or so it seemed to Peter Ivánovich.

Peter Ivánovich allowed the ladies to precede him and slowly followed them upstairs. Schwartz did not come down but remained where he was, and Peter Ivánovich understood that he wanted to arrange where they should play bridge that evening. The ladies went upstairs to the widow's room, and Schwartz with seriously compressed lips but a playful look in his eyes, indicated by a twist of his eyebrows the room to the right where the body lay.

Peter Ivánovich, like everyone else on such occasions, entered feeling uncertain what he would have to do. All he knew was that at such times it is always safe to cross oneself. But he was not quite sure whether one should make obeisances while doing so. He therefore adopted a middle course. On entering the room he began crossing himself and made a slight movement resembling a bow. At the same time, as far as the motion of his head and arm allowed, he surveyed the room. The young men— apparently nephews, one of whom was a high-school pupil—were leaving the room, crossing themselves as they did so. An old woman was standing motionless, and a lady with strangely arched eyebrows was saying something to her in a whisper. A vigorous, resolute Church Reader, in a frock-coat, was reading something in a loud voice with an expression that precluded any contradiction. The butler's assistant, Gerásim, stepping lightly in front of Peter Ivánovich, was strewing something on the floor. Noticing this, Peter Ivánovich was immediately aware of a faint odour of a decomposing body.

The last time he had called on Iván Ilých, Peter Ivánovich had seen Gerásim in the study. Iván Ilých had been particularly fond of him and he was performing the duty of a sick nurse.

Peter Ivánovich continued to make the sign of the cross slightly inclining his head in an intermediate direction between the coffin, the Reader, and the icons on the table in a corner of the room. Afterwards, when it seemed to him that this movement of his arm in crossing himself had gone on too long, he stopped and began to look at the corpse.

The dead man lay, as dead men always lie, in a specially heavy way, his rigid limbs sunk in the soft cushions of the coffin, with the head forever bowed on the pillow. His yellow waxen brow with bald patches over his sunken temples was thrust up in the way peculiar to the dead, the protruding nose seeming to press on the upper lip. He was much changed and had grown even thinner since Peter Ivánovich had last seen him, but, as is always the case with the dead, his face was handsomer and above all more dignified than when he was alive. The expression on the face said that what was necessary had been accomplished, and accomplished rightly. Besides this there was in that expression a reproach and a warning to the living. This warning seemed to Peter Ivánovich out of place, or at least not applicable to him. He felt a certain discomfort and so he hurriedly crossed himself once more and turned and went out of the door—too hurriedly and too regardless of propriety, as he himself was aware.

Schwartz was waiting for him in the adjoining room with legs spread wide apart and both hands toying with his top-hat behind his back. The mere sight of that playful, well-groomed, and elegant figure refreshed Peter Ivánovich. He felt that Schwartz was above all these happenings and would not surrender to any depressing influences. His very look

said that this incident of a church service for Iván Ilých could not be a
sufficient reason for infringing the order of the session—in other words,
that it would certainly not prevent his unwrapping a new pack of cards
and shuffling them that evening while a footman placed four fresh candles on the table: in fact, that there was no reason for supposing that this
incident would hinder their spending the evening agreeably. Indeed he
said this in a whisper as Peter Ivánovich passed him, proposing that they
should meet for a game at Fëdor Vasílievich's. But apparently Peter
Ivánovich was not destined to play bridge that evening. Praskóvya Fëdorovna (a short, fat woman who despite all efforts to the contrary had
continued to broaden steadily from her shoulders downwards and who
had the same extraordinarily arched eyebrows as the lady who had been
standing by the coffin), dressed all in black, her head covered with lace,
came out of her own room with some other ladies, conducted them to
the room where the dead body lay, and said: "The service will begin
immediately. Please go in."

Schwartz, making an indefinite bow, stood still, evidently neither
accepting nor declining this invitation. Praskóvya Fëdorovna recognizing
Peter Ivánovich, sighed, went close up to him, took his hand, and said:
"I know you were a true friend to Iván Ilých . . ." and looked at him
awaiting some suitable response. And Peter Ivánovich knew that, just as
it had been the right thing to cross himself in that room, so what he had
to do here was to press her hand, sigh, and say, "Believe me . . ." So he
did all this and as he did it felt that the desired result had been achieved:
that both he and she were touched.

"Come with me. I want to speak to you before it begins," said the
widow. "Give me your arm."

Peter Ivánovich gave her his arm and they went to the inner rooms,
passing Schwartz who winked at Peter Ivánovich compassionately.

"That does for our bridge! Don't object if we find another player.
Perhaps you can cut in when you do escape," said his playful look.

Peter Ivánovich sighed still more deeply and despondently, and
Praskóvya Fëdorovna pressed his arm gratefully. When they reached the
drawing-room, upholstered in pink cretonne and lighted by a dim lamp,
they sat down at the table—she on a sofa and Peter Ivánovich on a low
pouffe, the springs of which yielded spasmodically under his weight.
Praskóvya Fëdorovna had been on the point of warning him to take
another seat, but felt that such a warning was out of keeping with her
present condition and so changed her mind. As he sat down on the pouffe
Peter Ivánovich recalled how Iván Ilých had arranged this room and had
consulted him regarding this pink cretonne with green leaves. The whole
room was full of furniture and knick-knacks, and on her way to the sofa
the lace of the widow's black shawl caught on the carved edge of the
table. Peter Ivánovich rose to detach it, and the springs of the pouffe,

relieved of his weight, rose also and gave him a push. The widow began detaching her shawl herself, and Peter Ivánovich again sat down, suppressing the rebellious springs of the pouffe under him. But the widow had not quite freed herself and Peter Ivánovich got up again, and again the pouffe rebelled and even creaked. When this was all over she took out a clean cambric handkerchief and began to weep. The episode with the shawl and the struggle with the pouffe had cooled Peter Ivánovich's emotions and he sat there with a sullen look on his face. This awkward situation was interrupted by Sokolóv, Iván Ilých's butler, who came to report that the plot in the cemetery that Praskóvya Fëdorovna had chosen would cost two hundred rubles. She stopped weeping and, looking at Peter Ivánovich with the air of a victim, remarked in French that it was very hard for her. Peter Ivánovich made a silent gesture signifying his full conviction that it must indeed be so.

"Please smoke," she said in a magnanimous yet crushed voice, and turned to discuss with Sokolóv the price of the plot for the grave.

Peter Ivánovich while lighting his cigarette heard her inquiring very circumstantially into the prices of different plots in the cemetery and finally decide which she would take. When that was done she gave instructions about engaging the choir. Sokolóv then left the room.

"I look after everything myself," she told Peter Ivánovich, shifting the albums that lay on the table; and noticing that the table was endangered by his cigarette-ash, she immediately passed him an ash-tray, saying as she did so: "I consider it an affectation to say that my grief prevents my attending to practical affairs. On the contrary, if anything can—I won't say console me, but—distract me, it is seeing to everything concerning him." She again took out her handkerchief as if preparing to cry, but suddenly, as if mastering her feeling, she shook herself and began to speak calmly. "But there is something I want to talk to you about."

Peter Ivánovich bowed, keeping control of the springs of the pouffe, which immediately began quivering under him.

"He suffered terribly the last few days."

"Did he?" said Peter Ivánovich.

"Oh, terribly! He screamed unceasingly, not for minutes but for hours. For the last three days he screamed incessantly. It was unendurable. I cannot understand how I bore it; you could hear him three rooms off. Oh, what I have suffered!"

"Is it possible that he was conscious all that time?" asked Peter Ivánovich.

"Yes," she whispered. "To the last moment. He took leave of us a quarter of an hour before he died, and asked us to take Volódya away."

The thought of the suffering of this man he had known so intimately, first as a merry little boy, then as a schoolmate, and later as a grown-up colleague, suddenly struck Peter Ivánovich with horror, despite an unpleasant consciousness of his own and this woman's dissimulation. He again saw that brow, and that nose pressing down on the lip, and felt afraid for himself.

"Three days of frightful suffering and the death! Why, that might suddenly, at any time, happen to me," he thought, and for a moment felt terrified. But—he did not himself know how—the customary reflection at once occurred to him that this had happened to Iván Ilých and not to him, and that it should not and could not happen to him, and that to think that it could would be yielding to depression which he ought not to do, as Schwartz's expression plainly showed. After which reflection Peter Ivánovich felt reassured, and began to ask with interest about the details of Iván Ilých's death, as though death was an accident natural to Iván Ilých but certainly not to himself.

After many details of the really dreadful physical sufferings Iván Ilých had endured (which details he learnt only from the effect those sufferings had produced on Praskóvya Fëdorovna's nerves) the widow apparently found it necessary to get to business.

"Oh, Peter Ivánovich, how hard it is! How terribly, terribly hard!" and she again began to weep.

Peter Ivánovich sighed and waited for her to finish blowing her nose. When she had done so he said, "Believe me . . ." and she again began talking and brought out what was evidently her chief concern with him— namely, to question him as to how she could obtain a grant of money from the government on the occasion of her husband's death. She made it appear that she was asking Peter Ivánovich's advice about her pension, but he soon saw that she already knew about that to the minutest detail, more even than he did himself. She knew how much could be got out of the government in consequence of her husband's death, but wanted to find out whether she could not possibly extract something more. Peter Ivánovich tried to think of some means of doing so, but after reflecting for a while and, out of propriety, condemning the government for its niggardliness, he said he thought that nothing more could be got. Then she sighed and evidently began to devise means of getting rid of her visitor. Noticing this, he put out his cigarette, rose, pressed her hand, and went out into the anteroom.

In the dining-room where the clock stood that Iván Ilých had liked so much and had bought at an antique shop, Peter Ivánovich met a priest and a few acquaintances who had come to attend the service, and he recognized Iván Ilých's daughter, a handsome young woman. She was in black and her slim figure appeared slimmer than ever. She had a gloomy, determined, almost angry expression, and bowed to Peter Ivá- novich as though he were in some way to blame. Behind her, with the same offended look, stood a wealthy young man, an examining magistrate whom Peter Ivánovich also knew and who was her fiancé, as he had heard. He bowed mournfully to them and was about to pass into the death-chamber, when from under the stairs appeared the figure of Iván Ilých's schoolboy son, who was extremely like his father. He seemed a little Iván Ilých, such as Peter Ivánovich remembered when they studied law together. His tear-stained eyes had in them the look that is seen in the eyes of boys of thirteen or fourteen who are not pure-minded. When he saw Peter Ivánovich he scowled morosely and shamefacedly. Peter Ivánovich nodded to him and entered the death-chamber. The service began: candles, groans, incense, tears, and sobs. Peter Ivánovich stood looking gloomily down at his feet. He did not look once at the dead man, did not yield to any depressing influence, and was one of the first to leave the room. There was no one in the anteroom, but Gerásim darted out of the dead man's room, rummaged with his strong hands among the fur coats to find Peter Ivánovich's and helped him on with it.

"Well, friend Gerásim," said Peter Ivánovich, so as to say something. "It's a sad affair, isn't it?"

"It's God's will. We shall all come to it some day," said Gerásim, displaying his teeth—the even, white teeth of a healthy peasant—and, like a man in the thick of urgent work, he briskly opened the front door, called the coachman, helped Peter Ivánovich into the sledge, and sprang back to the porch as if in readiness for what he had to do next.

Peter Ivánovich found the fresh air particularly pleasant after the smell of incense, the dead body, and carbolic acid.

"Where to, sir?" asked the coachman.

"It's not too late even now. . . . I'll call round on Fëdor Vasílievich."

He accordingly drove there and found them just finishing the first rubber, so that it was quite convenient for him to cut in.

II

Iván Ilých's life had been most simple and most ordinary and therefore most terrible.

He had been a member of the Court of Justice, and died at the age of forty-five. His father had been an official who after serving in various ministries and departments in Petersburg had made the sort of career which brings men to positions from which by reason of their long service they cannot be dismissed, though they are obviously unfit to hold any responsible position, and for whom therefore posts are specially created, which though fictitious carry salaries of from six to ten thousand rubles that are not fictitious, and in receipt of which they live on to a great age.

Such was the Privy Councillor and superfluous member of various superfluous institutions, Ilyá Epímovich Golovín.

He had three sons, of whom Iván Ilých was the second. The eldest son was following in his father's footsteps only in another department, and was already approaching that stage in the service at which a similar sinecure would be reached. The third son was a failure. He had ruined his prospects in a number of positions and was now serving in the railway department. His father and brothers, and still more their wives, not merely disliked meeting him, but avoided remembering his existence unless compelled to do so. His sister had married Baron Greff, a Petersburg official of her father's type. Iván Ilých was *le phénix de la famille* as people said. He was neither as cold and formal as his elder brother nor as wild as the younger, but was a happy mean between them—an intelligent, polished, lively and agreeable man. He had studied with his younger brother at the School of Law, but the latter had failed to complete the course and was expelled when he was in the fifth class. Iván Ilých finished the course well. Even when he was at the School of Law he was just what he remained for the rest of his life: a capable, cheerful, good-natured, and sociable man, though strict in the fulfilment of what he considered to be his duty: and he considered his duty to be what was so considered by those in authority. Neither as a boy nor as a man was he a toady, but from early youth was by nature attracted to people of high station as a fly is drawn to the light, assimilating their ways and views of life and establishing friendly relations with them. All the enthusiasms of childhood and youth passed without leaving much trace on him; he succumbed to sensuality, to vanity, and latterly among the highest classes to liberalism, but always within limits which his instinct unfailingly indicated to him as correct.

At school he had done things which had formerly seemed to him very horrid and made him feel disgusted with himself when he did them; but when later on he saw that such actions were done by people of good position and that they did not regard them as wrong, he was able not exactly to regard them as right, but to forget about them entirely or not be at all troubled at remembering them.

Having graduated from the School of Law and qualified for the tenth rank of the civil service, and having received money from his father for his equipment, Iván Ilých ordered himself clothes at Scharmer's, the fashionable tailor, hung a medallion inscribed *respice finem* on his watchchain, took leave of his professor and the prince who was patron of the school, had a farewell dinner with his comrades at Donon's first-class restaurant, and with his new and fashionable portmanteau, linen, clothes, shaving and other toilet appliances, and a travelling rug, all purchased at the best shops, he set off for one of the provinces where through his father's influence, he had been attached to the governor as an official for special service.

In the province Iván Ilých soon arranged as easy and agreeable a position for himself as he had had at the School of Law. He performed his official task, made his career, and at the same time amused himself pleasantly and decorously. Occasionally he paid official visits to country districts where he behaved with dignity both to his superiors and inferiors, and performed the duties entrusted to him, which related chiefly to the sectarians, with an exactness and incorruptible honesty of which he could not but feel proud.

In official matters, despite his youth and taste for frivolous gaiety, he was exceedingly reserved, punctilious, and even severe; but in society he was often amusing and witty, and always good-natured, correct in his manner, and *bon enfant*, as the governor and his wife—with whom he was like one of the family—used to say of him.

In the province he had an affair with a lady who made advances to the elegant young lawyer, and there was also a milliner; and there were carousals with aides-de-camp who visited the district, and after-supper visits to a certain outlying street of doubtful reputation; and there was too some obsequiousness to his chief and even to his chief's wife, but all this was done with such a tone of good breeding that no hard names could be applied to it. It all came under the heading of the French saying: *"Il faut que jeunesse se passe."* It was all done with clean hands, in clean linen, with French phrases, and above all among people of the best society and consequently with the approval of people of rank.

So Iván Ilých served for five years and then came a change in his official life. The new and reformed judicial institutions were introduced, and new men were needed. Iván Ilých became such a new man. He was offered the post of examining magistrate, and he accepted it though the post was in another province and obliged him to give up the connexions he had formed and to make new ones. His friends met to give him a send-off; they had a group-photograph taken and presented him with a silver cigarette-case, and he set off to his new post.

As examining magistrate Iván Ilých was just as *comme il faut* and decorous a man, inspiring general respect and capable of separating his official duties from his private life, as he had been when acting as an official on special service. His duties now as examining magistrate were far more interesting and attractive than before. In his former position it had been pleasant to wear an undress uniform made by Scharmer, and to pass through the crowd of petitioners and officials who were timorously awaiting an audience with the governor, and who envied him as with free and easy gait he went straight into his chief's private room to have a cup of tea and a cigarette with him. But not many people had then been directly dependent on him—only police officials and the sectarians when he went on special missions—and he liked to treat them politely, almost as comrades, as if he were letting them feel that he who had the power to crush them was treating them in this simple, friendly way. There were then but few such people. But now, as an examining magistrate, Iván

Ilých felt that everyone without exception, even the most important and self-satisfied, was in his power, and that he need only write a few words on a sheet of paper with a certain heading, and this or that important, self-satisfied person would be brought before him in the role of an accused person or a witness, and if he did not choose to allow him to sit down, would have to stand before him and answer his questions. Iván Ilých never abused his power; he tried on the contrary to soften its expression, but the consciousness of it and of the possibility of softening its effect, supplied the chief interest and attraction of his office. In his work itself, especially in his examinations, he very soon acquired a method of eliminating all considerations irrelevant to the legal aspect of the case, and reducing even the most complicated case to a form in which it would be presented on paper only in its externals, completely excluding his personal opinion of the matter, while above all observing every prescribed formality. The work was new and Iván Ilých was one of the first men to apply the new Code of 1864.

On taking up the post of examining magistrate in a new town, he made new acquaintances and connexions, placed himself on a new footing, and assumed a somewhat different tone. He took up an attitude of rather dignified aloofness towards the provincial authorities, but picked out the best circle of legal gentlemen and wealthy gentry living in the town and assumed a tone of slight dissatisfaction with the government, of moderate liberalism, and of enlightened citizenship. At the same time, without at all altering the elegance of his toilet, he ceased shaving his chin and allowed his beard to grow as it pleased.

Iván Ilých settled down very pleasantly in this new town. The society there, which inclined towards opposition to the governor, was friendly, his salary was larger, and he began to play *vint* [a form of bridge], which he found added not a little to the pleasure of life, for he had a capacity for cards, played good-humouredly, and calculated rapidly and astutely, so that he usually won.

After living there for two years he met his future wife, Praskóvya Fëdorovna Míkhel, who was the most attractive, clever, and brilliant girl of the set in which he moved, and among other amusements and relaxations from his labours as examining magistrate, Iván Ilých established light and playful relations with her.

While he had been an official on special service he had been accustomed to dance, but now as an examining magistrate it was exceptional for him to do so. If he danced now, he did it as if to show that though he served under the reformed order of things, and had reached the fifth official rank, yet when it came to dancing he could do it better than most people. So at the end of an evening he sometimes danced with Praskóvya Fëdorovna, and it was chiefly during these dances that he captivated her. She fell in love with him. Iván Ilých had at first no definite intention of marrying, but when the girl fell in love with him he said to himself: "Really, why shouldn't I marry?"

Praskóvya Fëdorovna came of a good family, was not bad looking, and had some little property. Iván Ilých might have aspired to a more brilliant match, but even this was good. He had his salary, and she, he hoped, would have an equal income. She was well connected, and was a sweet, pretty, and thoroughly correct young woman. To say that Iván Ilých married because he fell in love with Praskóvya Fëdorovna and found that she sympathized with his views of life would be as incorrect as to say that he married because his social circle approved of the match. He was swayed by both these considerations: the marriage gave him personal satisfaction, and at the same time it was considered the right thing by the most highly placed of his associates.

So Iván Ilých got married.

The preparations for marriage and the beginning of married life, with its conjugal caresses, the new furniture, new crockery, and new linen, were very pleasant until his wife became pregnant—so that Iván Ilých had begun to think that marriage would not impair the easy, agreeable, gay and always decorous character of his life, approved of by society and regarded by himself as natural, but would even improve it. But from the first months of his wife's pregnancy, something new, unpleasant, depressing, and unseemly, and from which there was no way of escape, unexpectedly showed itself.

His wife, without any reason—*de gaieté de cœur* as Iván Ilých expressed it to himself—began to disturb the pleasure and propriety of their life. She began to be jealous without any cause, expected him to devote his whole attention to her, found fault with everything, and made coarse and ill-mannered scenes.

At first Iván Ilých hoped to escape from the unpleasantness of this state of affairs by the same easy and decorous relation to life that had served him heretofore: he tried to ignore his wife's disagreeable moods, continued to live in his usual easy and pleasant way, invited friends to his house for a game of cards, and also tried going out to his club or spending his evenings with friends. But one day his wife began upbraiding him so vigorously, using such coarse words, and continued to abuse him every time he did not fulfil her demands, so resolutely and with such evident determination not to give way till he submitted—that is, till he stayed at home and was bored just as she was—that he became alarmed. He now realized that matrimony—at any rate with Praskóvya Fëdorovna—was not always conducive to the pleasures and amenities of life, but on the contrary often infringed both comfort and propriety, and he must therefore entrench himself against such infringement. And Iván Ilých began to seek for means of doing so. His official duties were the one thing that imposed upon Praskóvya Fëdorovna, and by means of his official work and the duties attached to it he began struggling with his wife to secure his own independence.

With the birth of their child, the attempts to feed it and the various failures in doing so, and with the real and imaginary illnesses of mother and child, in which Iván Ilých's sympathy was demanded but about which he understood nothing, the need of securing for himself an existence outside his family life became still more imperative.

As his wife grew more irritable and exacting and Iván Ilých transferred the centre of gravity of his life more and more to his official work, so did he grow to like his work better and became more ambitious than before.

Very soon, within a year of his wedding, Iván Ilých had realized that marriage, though it may add some comforts to life, is in fact a very intricate and difficult affair towards which in order to perform one's duty, that is, to lead a decorous life approved of by society, one must adopt a definite attitude just as towards one's official duties.

And Iván Ilých evolved such an attitude towards married life. He only required of it those conveniences—dinner at home, housewife, and bed—which it could give him, and above all that propriety of external forms required by public opinion. For the rest he looked for lighthearted pleasure and propriety, and was very thankful when he found them, but if he met with antagonism and querulousness he at once retired into his separate fenced-off world of official duties, where he found satisfaction.

Iván Ilých was esteemed a good official, and after three years was made Assistant Public Prosecutor. His new duties, their importance, the possibility of indicting and imprisoning anyone he chose, the publicity his speeches received, and the success he had in all these things, made his work still more attractive.

More children came. His wife became more and more querulous and ill-tempered, but the attitude Iván Ilých had adopted towards his home life rendered him almost impervious to her grumbling.

After seven years' service in that town he was transferred to another province as Public Prosecutor. They moved, but were short of money and his wife did not like the place they moved to. Though the salary was higher the cost of living was greater, besides which two of their children died and family life became still more unpleasant for him.

Praskóvya Fëdorovna blamed her husband for every inconvenience they encountered in their new home. Most of the conversations between husband and wife, especially as to the children's education, led to topics which recalled former disputes, and these disputes were apt to flare up again at any moment. There remained only those rare periods of amorousness which still came to them at times but did not last long. These were islets at which they anchored for a while and then again set out upon that ocean of veiled hostility which showed itself in their aloofness from one another. This aloofness might have grieved Iván Ilých had he considered that it ought not to exist, but he now regarded the position as normal, and even made it the goal at which he aimed in family life. His aim was to free himself more and more from those unpleasantnesses and to give them a semblance of harmlessness and propriety. He attained this by spending less and less time with his family, and when obliged to be at home he tried to safeguard his position by the presence of outsiders. The chief thing however was that he had his official duties. The whole interest of his life now centred in the official world and that interest absorbed him. The consciousness of his power, being able to ruin anybody he wished to ruin, the importance, even the external dignity of his entry into court, or meetings with his subordinates, his success with superiors and inferiors, and above all his masterly handling of cases, of which he was conscious—all this gave him pleasure and filled his life, together with chats with his colleagues, dinners, and bridge. So that on the whole Iván Ilých's life continued to flow as he considered it should do—pleasantly and properly.

So things continued for another seven years. His eldest daughter was already sixteen, another child had died, and only one son was left, a schoolboy and a subject of dissension. Iván Ilých wanted to put him in the School of Law, but to spite him Praskóvya Fëdorovna entered him at the High School. The daughter had been educated at home and had turned out well: the boy did not learn badly either.

III

So Iván Ilých lived for seventeen years after his marriage. He was already a Public Prosecutor of long standing, and had declined several proposed transfers while awaiting a more desirable post, when an unanticipated and unpleasant occurrence quite upset the peaceful course of his life. He was expecting to be offered the post of presiding judge in a University town, but Happe somehow came to the front and obtained the appointment instead. Iván Ilých became irritable, reproached Happe, and quarrelled both with him and with his immediate superiors—who became colder to him and again passed him over when other appointments were made.

This was in 1880, the hardest year of Iván Ilých's life. It was then that it became evident on the one hand that his salary was insufficient for them to live on, and on the other that he had been forgotten, and not only this, but that what was for him the greatest and most cruel injustice appeared to others a quite ordinary occurrence. Even his father did not consider it his duty to help him. Iván Ilých felt himself abandoned by everyone, and that they regarded his position with a salary of 3,500 rubles [about £350] as quite normal and even fortunate. He alone knew that with the consciousness of the injustices done him, with his wife's incessant nagging, and with the debts he had contracted by living beyond his means, this position was far from normal.

In order to save money that summer he obtained leave of absence and went with his wife to live in the country at her brother's place.

In the country, without his work, he experienced *ennui* for the first time in his life, and not only *ennui* but intolerable depression, and he decided that it was impossible to go on living like that, and that it was necessary to take energetic measures.

Having passed a sleepless night pacing up and down the veranda, he decided to go to Petersburg and bestir himself, in order to punish those who had failed to appreciate him and to get transferred to another ministry.

Next day, despite many protests from his wife and her brother, he started for Petersburg with the sole object of obtaining a post with a salary of five thousand rubles a year. He was no longer bent on any particular department, or tendency, or kind of activity. All he now wanted was an appointment to another post with a salary of five thousand rubles, either in the administration, in the banks, with the railways in one of the Empress Márya's Institutions, or even in the customs—but it had to carry with it a salary of five thousand rubles and be in a ministry other than that in which they had failed to appreciate him.

And this quest of Iván Ilých's was crowned with remarkable and unexpected success. At Kursk an acquaintance of his, F. I. Ilyín, got into the first-class carriage, sat down beside Iván Ilých, and told him of a telegram just received by the governor of Kursk announcing that a change was about to take place in the ministry: Peter Ivánovich was to be superseded by Iván Semënovich.

The proposed change, apart from its significance for Russia, had a special significance for Iván Ilých, because by bringing forward a new man, Peter Petróvich, and consequently his friend Zachár Ivánovich, it was highly favourable for Iván Ilých, since Zachár Ivánovich was a friend and colleague of his.

In Moscow this news was confirmed, and on reaching Petersburg Iván Ilých found Zachár Ivánovich and received a definite promise of an appointment in his former Department of Justice.

A week later he telegraphed to his wife: "Zachár in Miller's place. I shall receive appointment on presentation of report."

Thanks to this change of personnel, Iván Ilých had unexpectedly obtained an appointment in his former ministry which placed him two stages above his former colleagues besides giving him five thousand rubles salary and three thousand five hundred rubles for expenses connected with his removal. All his ill humour towards his former enemies and the whole department vanished, and Iván Ilých was completely happy.

He returned to the country more cheerful and contented than he had been for a long time. Praskóvya Fëdorovna also cheered up and a truce was arranged between them. Iván Ilých told of how he had been fêted by everybody in Petersburg, how all those who had been his enemies were put to shame and now fawned on him, how envious they were of his appointment, and how much everybody in Petersburg had liked him.

Praskóvya Fëdorovna listened to all this and appeared to believe it. She did not contradict anything, but only made plans for their life in the town to which they were going. Iván Ilých saw with delight that these plans were his plans, that he and his wife agreed, and that, after a stumble, his life was regaining its due and natural character of pleasant lightheartedness and decorum.

Iván Ilých had come back for a short time only, for he had to take up his new duties on the 10th of September. Moreover, he needed time to settle into the new place, to move all his belongings from the province, and to buy and order many additional things: in a word, to make such arrangements as he had resolved on, which were almost exactly what Praskóvya Fëdorovna too had decided on.

Now that everything had happened so fortunately, and that he and his wife were at one in their aims and moreover saw so little of one another, they got on together better than they had done since the first years of marriage. Iván Ilých had thought of taking his family away with him at once, but the insistence of his wife's brother and her sister-in-law, who had suddenly become particularly amiable and friendly to him and his family, induced him to depart alone.

So he departed, and the cheerful state of mind induced by his success and by the harmony between his wife and himself, the one intensifying the other, did not leave him. He found a delightful house, just the thing both he and his wife had dreamt of. Spacious, lofty reception rooms in the old style, a convenient and dignified study, rooms for his wife and daughter, a study for his son—it might have been specially built for them. Iván Ilých himself superintended the arrangements, chose the wallpapers, supplemented the furniture (preferably with antiques which he considered particularly *comme il faut*), and supervised the upholstering. Everything progressed and progressed and approached the ideal he had set himself: even when things were only half completed they exceeded his expectations. He saw what a refined and elegant character, free from vulgarity, it would all have when it was ready. On falling asleep he pictured to himself how the reception-room would look. Looking at the yet unfinished drawing-room he could see the fireplace, the screen, the what-not, the little chairs dotted here and there, the dishes and plates on the walls, and the bronzes, as they would be when everything was in place. He was pleased by the thought of how his wife and daughter, who shared his taste in this matter, would be impressed by it. They were certainly not expecting as much. He had been particularly successful in finding, and buying cheaply, antiques which gave a particularly aristo-cratic character to the whole place. But in his letters he intentionally understated everything in order to be able to surprise them. All this so absorbed him that his new duties—though he liked his official work—interested him less than he had expected. Sometimes he even had moments of absent-mindedness during the court sessions, and would consider whether he should have straight or curved cornices for his curtains. He was so interested in it all that he often did things himself, rearranging the furniture, or rehanging the curtains. Once when mount-ing a step-ladder to show the upholsterer, who did not understand, how he wanted the hangings draped, he made a false step and slipped, but being a strong and agile man he clung on and only knocked his side against the knob of the window frame. The bruised place was painful but the pain soon passed, and he felt particularly bright and well just then. He wrote: "I feel fifteen years younger." He thought he would have everything ready by September, but it dragged on till mid-October. But the result was charming not only in his eyes but to everyone who saw it.

In reality it was just what is usually seen in the houses of people of moderate means who want to appear rich, and therefore succeed only in resembling others like themselves: there were damasks, dark wood, plants, rugs, and dull and polished bronzes—all the things people of a certain class have in order to resemble other people of that class. His house was so like the others that it would never have been noticed, but to him it all seemed to be quite exceptional. He was very happy when he met his family at the station and brought them to the newly furnished house all lit up, where a footman in a white tie opened the door into the hall decorated with plants, and when they went on into the drawing-room and the study uttering exclamations of delight. He conducted them everywhere, drank in their praises eagerly, and beamed with pleasure. At tea that evening, when Praskóvya Fëdorovna among other things asked him about his fall, he laughed, and showed them how he had gone flying and had frightened the upholsterer.

"It's a good thing I'm a bit of an athlete. Another man might have been killed, but I merely knocked myself, just here; it hurts when it's touched, but it's passing off already—it's only a bruise."

So they began living in their new home—in which, as always hap-pens, when they got thoroughly settled in they found they were just one room short—and with the increased income, which as always was just a little (some five hundred rubles) too little, but it was all very nice.

Things went particularly well at first, before everything was finally arranged and while something had still to be done: this thing bought, that thing ordered, another thing moved, and something else adjusted. Though there were some disputes between husband and wife, they were both so well satisfied and had so much to do that it all passed off without any serious quarrels. When nothing was left to arrange it became rather dull and something seemed to be lacking, but they were then making acquaintances, forming habits, and life was growing fuller.

Iván Ilých spent his mornings at the law court and came home to dinner, and at first he was generally in a good humour, though he occasionally became irritable just on account of his house. (Every spot on the tablecloth or the upholstery, and every broken window-blind string, irritated him. He had devoted so much trouble to arranging it all that every disturbance of it distressed him.) But on the whole his life ran its course as he believed life should do: easily, pleasantly, and decorously.

He got up at nine, drank his coffee, read the paper, and then put on his undress uniform and went to the law courts. There the harness in which he worked had already been stretched to fit him and he donned it without a hitch: petitioners, inquiries at the chancery, the chancery itself, and the sittings public and administrative. In all this the thing was to exclude everything fresh and vital, which always disturbs the regular course of official business, and to admit only official relations with people, and then only on official grounds. A man would come, for instance, wanting some information. Iván Ilých, as one in whose sphere the matter did not lie, would have nothing to do with him: but if the man had some business with him in his official capacity, something that could be expressed on officially stamped paper, he would do everything, positively everything he could within the limits of such relations, and in doing so would maintain the semblance of friendly human relations, that is, would observe the courtesies of life. As soon as the official relations ended, so did everything else. Iván Ilých possessed this capacity to separate his real life from the official side of affairs and not mix the two, in the highest degree, and by long practice and natural aptitude had brought it to such a pitch that sometimes, in the manner of a virtuoso, he would even allow himself to let the human and official relations mingle. He let himself do this just because he felt that he could at any time he chose resume the strictly official attitude again and drop the human relation. And he did it all easily, pleasantly, correctly, and even artistically. In the intervals between the sessions he smoked, drank tea, chatted a little about politics, a little about general topics, a little about cards, but most of all about official appointments. Tired, but with the feelings of a virtuoso—one of the first violins who has played his part in an orchestra with precision— he would return home to find that his wife and daughter had been out paying calls, or had a visitor, and that his son had been to school, had done his homework with his tutor, and was duly learning what is taught at High Schools. Everything was as it should be. After dinner, if they had no visitors, Iván Ilých sometimes read a book that was being much discussed at the time, and in the evening settled down to work, that is, read official papers, compared the depositions of witnesses, and noted paragraphs of the Code applying to them. This was neither dull nor amusing. It was dull when he might have been playing bridge, but if no bridge was available it was at any rate better than doing nothing or sitting with his wife. Iván Ilých's chief pleasure was giving little dinners to which he invited men and women of good social position, and just as his drawing-room resembled all other drawing-rooms so did his enjoyable little parties resemble all other such parties.

Once they even gave a dance. Iván Ilých enjoyed it and everything went off well, except that it led to a violent quarrel with his wife about the cakes and sweets. Praskóvya Fëdorovna had made her own plans, but Iván Ilých insisted on getting everything from an expensive confectioner and ordered too many cakes, and the quarrel occurred because some of those cakes were left over and the confectioner's bill came to forty-five rubles. It was a great and disagreeable quarrel. Praskóvya Fëdorovna called him "a fool and an imbecile," and he clutched at his head and made angry allusions to divorce.

But the dance itself had been enjoyable. The best people were there, and Iván Ilých had danced with Princess Trúfonova, a sister of the distinguished founder of the Society "Bear My Burden."

The pleasures connected with his work were pleasures of ambition; his social pleasures were those of vanity; but Iván Ilých's greatest pleasure was playing bridge. He acknowledged that whatever disagreeable incident happened in his life, the pleasure that beamed like a ray of light above everything else was to sit down to bridge with good players, not noisy partners, and of course to four-handed bridge (with five players it was annoying to have to stand out, though one pretended not to mind), to play a clever and serious game (when the cards allowed it) and then to have supper and drink a glass of wine. After a game of bridge, especially if he had won a little (to win a large sum was unpleasant), Iván Ilých went to bed in specially good humour.

So they lived. They formed a circle of acquaintances among the best people and were visited by people of importance and by young folk. In their views as to their acquaintances, husband, wife and daughter were entirely agreed, and tacitly and unanimously kept at arm's length and shook off the various shabby friends and relations who, with much show of affection, gushed into the drawing-room with its Japanese plates on the walls. Soon these shabby friends ceased to obtrude themselves and only the best people remained in the Golovíns' set.

Young men made up to Lisa, and Petríshchev, an examining magistrate and Dmítri Ivánovich Petríshchev's son and sole heir, began to be so attentive to her that Iván Ilých had already spoken to Praskóvya Fëdorovna about it, and considered whether they should not arrange a party for them, or get up some private theatricals.

So they lived, and all went well, without change, and life flowed pleasantly.

IV

They were all in good health. It could not be called ill health if Iván Ilých sometimes said that he had a queer taste in his mouth and felt some discomfort in his left side.

But this discomfort increased and, though not exactly painful, grew into a sense of pressure in his side accompanied by ill humour. And his irritability became worse and worse and began to mar the agreeable, easy, and correct life that had established itself in the Golovín family. Quarrels between husband and wife became more and more frequent, and soon the ease and amenity disappeared and even the decorum was barely maintained. Scenes again became frequent, and very few of those islets remained on which husband and wife could meet without an explosion. Praskóvya Fëdorovna now had good reason to say that her husband's temper was trying. With characteristic exaggeration she said he had always had a dreadful temper, and that it had needed all her good nature to put up with it for twenty years. It was true that now the quarrels were started by him. His bursts of temper always came just before dinner, often just as he began to eat his soup. Sometimes he noticed that a plate or dish was chipped, or the food was not right, or his son put his elbow on the table, or his daughter's hair was not done as he liked it, and for all this he blamed Praskóvya Fëdorovna. At first she retorted and said disagreeable things to him, but once or twice he fell into such a rage at the beginning of dinner that she realized it was due to some physical derangement brought on by taking food, and so she restrained herself and did not answer, but only hurried to get the dinner over. She regarded this self-restraint as highly praiseworthy. Having come to the conclusion that her husband had a dreadful temper and made her life miserable, she began to feel sorry for herself, and the more she pitied herself the more she hated her husband. She began to wish he would die; yet she did not want him to die because then his salary would cease. And this irritated her against him still more. She considered herself dreadfully unhappy just because not even his death could save her, and though she concealed her exasperation, that hidden exasperation of hers increased his irritation also.

After one scene in which Iván Ilých had been particularly unfair and after which he had said in explanation that he certainly was irritable but that it was due to his not being well, she said that if he was ill it should be attended to, and insisted on his going to see a celebrated doctor.

He went. Everything took place as he had expected and as it always does. There was the usual waiting and the important air assumed by the doctor, with which he was so familiar (resembling that which he himself assumed in court), and the sounding and listening, and the questions which called for answers that were foregone conclusions and were evidently unnecessary, and the look of importance which implied that "if only you put yourself in our hands we will arrange everything—we know indubitably how it has to be done, always in the same way for everybody alike." It was all just as it was in the law courts. The doctor put on just the same air towards him as he himself put on towards an accused person.

The doctor said that so-and-so indicated that there was so-and-so inside the patient, but if the investigation of so-and-so did not confirm this, then he must assume that and that. If he assumed that and that, then . . . and so on. To Iván Ilých only one question was important: was his case serious or not? But the doctor ignored that inappropriate question. From his point of view it was not the one under consideration, the real question was to decide between a floating kidney, chronic catarrh, or appendicitis. It was not a question of Iván Ilých's life or death, but one between a floating kidney and appendicitis. And that question the doctor solved brilliantly, as it seemed to Iván Ilých, in favour of the appendix, with the reservation that should an examination of the urine give fresh indications the matter would be reconsidered. All this was just what Iván Ilých had himself brilliantly accomplished a thousand times in dealing with men on trial. The doctor summed up just as brilliantly, looking over his spectacles triumphantly and even gaily at the accused. From the doctor's summing up Iván Ilých concluded that things were bad, but that for the doctor, and perhaps for everybody else, it was a matter of indifference, though for him it was bad. And this conclusion struck him painfully, arousing in him a great feeling of pity for himself and of bitterness towards the doctor's indifference to a matter of such importance.

He said nothing of this, but rose, placed the doctor's fee on the table, and remarked with a sigh: "We sick people probably often put inappropriate questions. But tell me, in general, is this complaint dangerous, or not? . . ."

The doctor looked at him sternly over his spectacles with one eye, as if to say: "Prisoner, if you will not keep to the questions put to you, I shall be obliged to have you removed from the court."

"I have already told you what I consider necessary and proper. The analysis may show something more." And the doctor bowed.

Iván Ilých went out slowly, seated himself disconsolately in his sledge, and drove home. All the way home he was going over what the doctor had said, trying to translate those complicated, obscure, scientific phrases into plain language and find in them an answer to the question: "Is my condition bad? Is it very bad? Or is there as yet nothing much wrong?" And it seemed to him that the meaning of what the doctor had said was that it was very bad. Everything in the streets seemed depressing. The cabmen, the houses, the passers-by, and the shops, were dismal. His ache, this dull gnawing ache that never ceased for a moment, seemed to have acquired a new and more serious significance from the doctor's dubious remarks. Iván Ilých now watched it with a new and oppressive feeling.

He reached home and began to tell his wife about it. She listened, but in the middle of his account his daughter came in with her hat on, ready to go out with her mother. She sat down reluctantly to listen to this tedious story, but could not stand it long, and her mother too did not hear him to the end.

"Well, I am very glad," she said. "Mind now to take your medicine regularly. Give me the prescription and I'll send Gerásim to the chemist's." And she went to get ready to go out.

While she was in the room Iván Ilých had hardly taken time to breathe, but he sighed deeply when she left it.

"Well," he thought, "perhaps it isn't so bad after all."

He began taking his medicine and following the doctor's directions, which had been altered after the examination of the urine. But then it happened that there was a contradiction between the indications drawn from the examination of the urine and the symptoms that showed themselves. It turned out that what was happening differed from what the doctor had told him, and that he had either forgotten, or blundered, or hidden something from him. He could not, however, be blamed for that, and Iván Ilých still obeyed his orders implicitly and at first derived some comfort from doing so.

From the time of his visit to the doctor, Iván Ilých's chief occupation was the exact fulfillment of the doctor's instructions regarding hygiene and the taking of medicine, and the observation of his pain and his excretions. His chief interests came to be people's ailments and people's health. When sickness, deaths, or recoveries were mentioned in his presence, especially when the illness resembled his own, he listened with agitation which he tried to hide, asked questions, and applied what he heard to his own case.

The pain did not grow less, but Iván Ilých made efforts to force himself to think that he was better. And he could do this so long as nothing agitated him. But as soon as he had any unpleasantness with his wife, any lack of success in his official work, or held bad cards at bridge, he was at once acutely sensible of his disease. He had formerly borne such mischances, hoping soon to adjust what was wrong, to master it and attain success, or to make a grand slam. But now every mischance upset him and plunged him into despair. He would say to himself: "There now, just as I was beginning to get better and the medicine had begun to take effect, comes this accursed misfortune, or unpleasantness . . ." And he was furious with the mishap, or with the people who were causing the unpleasantness and killing him, for he felt that this fury was killing him but he could not restrain it. One would have thought that it should have been clear to him that this exasperation with circumstances and people aggravated his illness, and that he ought therefore to ignore unpleasant occurrences. But he drew the very opposite conclusion: he said that he needed peace, and he watched for everything that might disturb it and became irritable at the slightest infringement of it. His condition was rendered worse by the fact that he read medical books and consulted doctors. The progress of his disease was so gradual that he could deceive himself when comparing one day with another—the difference was so slight. But when he consulted the doctors it seemed to him that he was getting worse, and even very rapidly. Yet despite this he was continually consulting them.

That month he went to see another celebrity, who told him almost the same as the first had done but put his questions rather differently, and the interview with this celebrity only increased Iván Ilých's doubts and fears. A friend of a friend of his, a very good doctor, diagnosed his illness again quite differently from the others, and though he predicted recovery, his questions and suppositions bewildered Iván Ilých still more and increased his doubts. A homeopathist diagnosed the disease in yet another way, and prescribed medicine which Iván Ilých took secretly for a week. But after a week, not feeling any improvement and having lost confidence both in the former doctor's treatment and in this one's, he became still more despondent. One day a lady acquaintance mentioned a cure effected by a wonder-working icon. Iván Ilých caught himself listening attentively and beginning to believe that it had occurred. This incident alarmed him. "Has my mind really weakened to such an extent?" he asked himself. "Nonsense! It's all rubbish. I mustn't give way to nervous fears but having chosen a doctor must keep strictly to his treatment. That is what I will do. Now it's all settled. I won't think about it, but will follow the treatment seriously till summer, and then we shall see. From now there must be no more of this wavering!" This was easy to say but impossible to carry out. The pain in his side oppressed him and seemed to grow worse and more incessant, while the taste in his mouth grew stranger and stranger. It seemed to him that his breath had a disgusting smell, and he was conscious of a loss of appetite and strength. There was no deceiving himself: something terrible, new, and more important than anything before in his life, was taking place within him of which he alone was aware. Those about him did not understand or would not understand it, but thought everything in the world was going on as usual. That tormented Iván Ilých more than anything. He saw that his household, especially his wife and daughter who were in a perfect whirl of visiting, did not understand anything of it and were annoyed that he was so depressed and so exacting, as if he were to blame for it. Though they tried to disguise it he saw that he was an obstacle in their path, and that his wife had adopted a definite line in regard to his illness and kept to it regardless of anything he said or did. Her attitude was this: "You know," she would say to her friends, "Iván Ilých can't do as other people do, and keep to the treatment prescribed for him. One day he'll take his drops and keep strictly to his diet and go to bed in good time, but the next day unless I watch him he'll suddenly forget his medicine, eat sturgeon— which is forbidden—and sit up playing cards till one o'clock in the morning."

"Oh, come, when was that?" Iván Ilých would ask in vexation. "Only once at Peter Ivánovich's."

"And yesterday with Shébek."

"Well, even if I hadn't stayed up, this pain would have kept me awake."

"Be that as it may you'll never get well like that, but will always make us wretched."

Praskóvya Fëdorovna's attitude to Iván Ilých's illness, as she expressed it both to others and to him, was that it was his own fault and was another of the annoyances he caused her. Iván Ilých felt that this opinion escaped her involuntarily—but that did not make it easier for him.

At the law courts too, Iván Ilých noticed, or thought he noticed, a strange attitude towards himself. It sometimes seemed to him that people were watching him inquisitively as a man whose place might soon be vacant. Then again, his friends would suddenly begin to chaff him in a friendly way about his low spirits, as if the awful, horrible, and unheard-of thing that was going on within him, incessantly gnawing at him and irresistibly drawing him away, was a very agreeable subject for jests. Schwartz in particular irritated him by his jocularity, vivacity, and *savoir-faire*, which reminded him of what he himself had been ten years ago.

Friends came to make up a set and they sat down to cards. They dealt, bending the new cards to soften them, and he sorted the diamonds in his hand and found he had seven. His partner said "No trumps" and supported him with two diamonds. What more could be wished for? It ought to be jolly and lively. They would make a grand slam. But suddenly Iván Ilých was conscious of that gnawing pain, that taste in his mouth, and it seemed ridiculous that in such circumstances he should be pleased to make a grand slam.

He looked at his partner Mikháil Mikháylovich, who rapped the table with his strong hand and instead of snatching up the tricks pushed the cards courteously and indulgently towards Iván Ilých that he might have the pleasure of gathering them up without the trouble of stretching out his hand for them. "Does he think I am too weak to stretch out my arm?" thought Iván Ilých, and forgetting what he was doing he over-trumped his partner, missing the grand slam by three tricks. And what was most awful of all was that he saw how upset Mikháil Mikháylovich was about it but did not himself care. And it was dreadful to realize why he did not care.

They all saw that he was suffering, and said: "We can stop if you are tired. Take a rest." Lie down? No, he was not at all tired, and he finished the rubber. All were gloomy and silent. Iván Ilých felt that he had diffused this gloom over them and could not dispel it. They had supper and went away, and Iván Ilých was left alone with the consciousness that his life was poisoned and was poisoning the lives of others, and that this poison did not weaken but penetrated more and more deeply into his whole being.

With this consciousness, and with physical pain besides the terror, he must go to bed, often to lie awake the greater part of the night. Next morning he had to get up again, dress, go to the law courts, speak, and write; or if he did not go out, spend at home those twenty-four hours a day each of which was a torture. And he had to live thus all alone on the brink of an abyss, with no one who understood or pitied him.

V

So one month passed and then another. Just before the New Year his brother-in-law came to town and stayed at their house. Iván Ilých was at the law courts and Praskóvya Fёdorovna had gone shopping. When Iván Ilých came home and entered his study he found his brother-in-law there—a healthy, florid man—unpacking his portmanteau himself. He raised his head on hearing Iván Ilých's footsteps and looked up at him for a moment without a word. That stare told Iván Ilých everything. His brother-in-law opened his mouth to utter an exclamation of surprise but checked himself, and that action confirmed it all.

"I have changed, eh?"

"Yes, there is a change."

And after that, try as he would to get his brother-in-law to return to the subject of his looks, the latter would say nothing about it. Praskóvya Fёdorovna came home and her brother went out to her. Iván Ilých locked the door and began to examine himself in the glass, first full face, then in profile. He took up a portrait of himself taken with his wife, and compared it with what he saw in the glass. The change in him was immense. Then he bared his arms to the elbow, looked at them, drew the sleeves down again, sat down on an ottoman, and grew blacker than night.

"No, no, this won't do!" he said to himself, and jumped up, went to the table, took some law papers and began to read them, but could not continue. He unlocked the door and went into the reception-room. The door leading to the drawing-room was shut. He approached it on tiptoe and listened.

"No, you are exaggerating!" Praskóvya Fëdorovna was saying.

"Exaggerating! Don't you see it? Why, he's a dead man! Look at his eyes—there's no light in them. But what is it that is wrong with him?"

"No one knows. Nikoláevich [that was another doctor] said something, but I don't know what. And Leshchetítsky [this was the celebrated specialist] said quite the contrary . . ."

Iván Ilých walked away, went to his own room, lay down, and began musing: "The kidney, a floating kidney." He recalled all the doctors had told him of how it detached itself and swayed about. And by an effort of imagination he tried to catch that kidney and arrest it and support it. So little was needed for this, it seemed to him. "No, I'll go to see Peter Ivánovich again." [That was the friend whose friend was a doctor.] He rang, ordered the carriage, and got ready to go.

"Where are you going, Jean?" asked his wife, with a specially sad and exceptionally kind look.

This exceptionally kind look irritated him. He looked morosely at her.

"I must go to see Peter Ivánovich."

He went to see Peter Ivánovich, and together they went to see his friend, the doctor. He was in, and Iván Ilých had a long talk with him.

Reviewing the anatomical and physiological details of what in the doctor's opinion was going on inside him, he understood it all.

There was something, a small thing, in the vermiform appendix. It might all come right. Only stimulate the energy of one organ and check the activity of another, then absorption would take place and everything would come right. He got home rather late for dinner, ate his dinner, and conversed cheerfully, but could not for a long time bring himself to go back to work in his room. At last, however, he went to his study and did what was necessary, but the consciousness that he had put something aside—an important, intimate matter which he would revert to when his work was done—never left him. When he had finished his work he remembered that this intimate matter was the thought of his vermiform appendix. But he did not give himself up to it, and went to the drawing-room for tea. There were callers there, including the examining magistrate who was a desirable match for his daughter, and they were conversing, playing the piano, and singing. Iván Ilých, as Praskóvya Fëdorovna remarked, spent that evening more cheerfully than usual, but he never for a moment forgot that he had postponed the important matter of the appendix. At eleven o'clock he said goodnight and went to his bedroom. Since his illness he had slept alone in a small room next to his study. He undressed and took up a novel by Zola, but instead of reading it he fell into thought, and in his imagination that desired improvement in the vermiform appendix occurred. There was the absorption and evacuation and the re-establishment of normal activity. "Yes, that's it!" he said to himself. "One need only assist nature, that's all." He remembered his medicine, rose, took it, and lay down on his back watching for the beneficent action of the medicine and for it to lessen the pain. "I need only take it regularly and avoid all injurious influences. I am already feeling better, much better." He began touching his side: it was not painful to the touch. "There, I really don't feel it. It's much better already." He put out the light and turned on his side . . . "The appendix is getting better, absorption is occurring." Suddenly he felt the old, familiar, dull, gnawing pain, stubborn and serious. There was the same familiar loathsome taste in his mouth. His heart sank and he felt dazed. "My God! My God!" he muttered. "Again, again! And it will never cease." And suddenly the matter presented itself in a quite different aspect. "Vermiform appendix! Kidney! he said to himself. "It's not a question of appendix or kidney, but of life and . . . death. Yes, life was there and now it is going, going and I cannot stop it. Yes. Why deceive myself? Isn't it obvious to everyone but me that I'm dying, and that it's only a question of weeks, days . . . it may happen this moment. There was light and now there is darkness. I was here and now I'm going there! Where?" A chill came over him, his breathing ceased, and he felt only the throbbing of his heart.

"When I am not, what will there be? There will be nothing. Then where shall I be when I am no more? Can this be dying? No, I don't want to!" He jumped up and tried to light the candle, felt for it with trembling hands, dropped candle and candlestick on the floor, and fell back on his pillow.

"What's the use? It makes no difference," he said to himself, staring with wide-open eyes into the darkness. "Death. Yes, death. And none of them knows or wishes to know it, and they have no pity for me. Now they are playing." (He heard through the door the distant sound of a song and its accompaniment.) "It's all the same to them, but they will die too! Fools! I first, and they later, but it will be the same for them. And now they are merry . . . the beasts!"

Anger choked him and he was agonizingly, unbearably miserable. "It is impossible that all men have been doomed to suffer this awful horror!" He raised himself.

"Something must be wrong. I must calm myself—must think it all over from the beginning." And he again began thinking. "Yes, the beginning of my illness: I knocked my side, but I was still quite well that day and the next. It hurt a little, then rather more. I saw the doctors, then followed despondency and anguish, more doctors, and I drew nearer to the abyss. My strength grew less and I kept coming nearer and nearer, and now I have wasted away and there is no light in my eyes. I think of the appendix—but this is death! I think of mending the appendix, and all the while here is death! Can it really be death?" Again terror seized him and he gasped for breath. He leant down and began feeling for the matches, pressing with his elbow on the stand beside the bed. It was in his way and hurt him, he grew furious with it, pressed on it still harder, and upset it. Breathless and in despair he fell on his back, expecting death to come immediately.

Meanwhile the visitors were leaving. Praskóvya Fëdorovna was seeing them off. She heard something fall and came in.

"What has happened?"

"Nothing. I knocked it over accidentally."

She went out and returned with a candle. He lay there panting heavily, like a man who has run a thousand yards, and stared upwards at her with a fixed look.

"What is it, Jean?"

"No . . . o . . . thing. I upset it." ("Why speak of it? She won't understand," he thought.)

And in truth she did not understand. She picked up the stand, lit his candle, and hurried away to see another visitor off. When she came back he still lay on his back looking upwards.

"What is it? Do you feel worse?"

"Yes."

She shook her head and sat down.

"Do you know, Jean, I think we must ask Leshchetítsky to come and see you here."

This meant calling in the famous specialist, regardless of expense. He smiled malignantly and said "No." She remained a little longer and then went up to him and kissed his forehead.

While she was kissing him he hated her from the bottom of his soul and with difficulty refrained from pushing her away.

"Good-night. Please God you'll sleep."

"Yes."

VI

Iván Ilých saw that he was dying, and he was in continual despair.

In the depth of his heart he knew he was dying, but not only was he not accustomed to the thought, he simply did not and could not grasp it.

The syllogism he had learnt from Kiesewetter's Logic: "Caius is a man, men are mortal, therefore Caius is mortal," had always seemed to him correct as applied to Caius, but certainly not as applied to himself. That Caius—man in the abstract—was mortal, was perfectly correct, but he was not Caius, not an abstract man, but a creature quite, quite separate from all others. He had been little Ványa, with a mamma and a papa, with Mítya and Volódya, with the toys, a coachman and a nurse, afterwards with Kátenka and with all the joys, griefs, and delights of childhood, boyhood, and youth. What did Caius know of the smell of that striped leather ball Ványa had been so fond of? Had Caius kissed his mother's hand like that, and did the silk of her dress rustle so for Caius? Had he rioted like that at school when the pastry was bad? Had Caius been in love like that? Could Caius preside at a session as he did? "Caius really was mortal, and it was right for him to die; but for me, little Ványa, Iván Ilých, with all my thoughts and emotions, it's altogether a different matter. It cannot be that I ought to die. That would be too terrible."

Such was his feeling.

"If I had to die like Caius I should have known it was so. An inner voice would have told me so, but there was nothing of the sort in me and I and all my friends felt that our case was quite different from that of Caius. And now here it is!" he said to himself. "It can't be. It's impossible! But here it is. How is this? How is one to understand it?"

He could not understand it, and tried to drive this false, incorrect, morbid thought away and to replace it by other proper and healthy thoughts. But that thought, and not the thought only but the reality itself, seemed to come and confront him.

And to replace that thought he called up a succession of others, hoping to find in them some support. He tried to get back into the former current of thoughts that had once screened the thought of death from him. But strange to say, all that had formerly shut off, hidden, and destroyed his consciousness of death, no longer had that effect. Iván Ilých now spent most of his time in attempting to re-establish that old current. He would say to himself: "I will take up my duties again—after all I used to live by them." And banishing all doubts he would go to the law courts, enter into conversation with his colleagues, and sit carelessly as was his wont, scanning the crowd with a thoughtful look and leaning both his emaciated arms on the arms of his oak chair; bending over as usual to a colleague and drawing his papers nearer he would interchange whispers with him, and then suddenly raising his eyes and sitting erect would pronounce certain words and open the proceedings. But suddenly in the midst of those proceedings the pain in his side, regardless of the stage the proceedings had reached, would begin its own gnawing work. Iván Ilých would turn his attention to it and try to drive the thought of it away, but without success. *It* would come and stand before him and look at him, and he would be petrified and the light would die out of his eyes, and he would again begin asking himself whether *It* alone was true. And his colleagues and subordinates would see with surprise and distress that he, the brilliant and subtle judge, was becoming confused and making mistakes. He would shake himself, try to pull himself together, manage somehow to bring the sitting to a close, and return home with the sorrowful consciousness that his judicial labours could not as formerly hide from him what he wanted them to hide, and could not deliver him from *It*. And what was worst of all was that *It* drew his attention to itself not in order to make him take some action but only that he should look at *It*, look it straight in the face: look at it and without doing anything, suffer inexpressibly.

And to save himself from this condition, Iván Ilých looked for consolations—new screens—and new screens were found and for a while seemed to save him, but then they immediately fell to pieces or rather became transparent, as if *It* penetrated them and nothing could veil *It*.

In these latter days he would go into the drawing-room he had arranged—that drawing-room where he had fallen and for the sake of which (how bitterly ridiculous it seemed) he had sacrificed his life—for he knew that his illness originated with that knock. He would enter and see that something had scratched the polished table. He would look for the cause of this and find that it was the bronze ornamentation of an album, that had got bent. He would take up the expensive album which he had lovingly arranged, and feel vexed with his daughter and her friends for their untidiness—for the album was torn here and there and some of the photographs turned upside down. He would put it carefully in order and bend the ornamentation back into position. Then it would occur to him to place all those things in another corner of the room, near the plants. He would call the footman, but his daughter or wife would come to help him. They would not agree, and his wife would contradict him, and he would dispute and grow angry. But that was all right, for then he did not think about *It*. *It* was invisible.

But then, when he was moving something himself, his wife would say: "Let the servants do it. You will hurt yourself again." And suddenly *It* would flash through the screen and he would see it. It was just a flash, and he hoped it would disappear, but he would involuntarily pay attention to his side. "It sits there as before, gnawing just the same!" And he could no longer forget *It*, but could distinctly see it looking at him from behind the flowers. "What is it all for?"

"It really is so! I lost my life over that curtain as I might have done when storming a fort. Is that possible? How terrible and how stupid. It can't be true! It can't, but it is."

He would go to his study, lie down, and again be alone with *It*: face to face with *It*. And nothing could be done with *It* except to look at it and shudder.

VII

How it happened it is impossible to say because it came about step by step, unnoticed, but in the third month of Iván Ilých's illness, his wife, his daughter, his son, his acquaintances, the doctors, the servants, and above all he himself, were aware that the whole interest he had for other people was whether he would soon vacate his place, and at last release the living from the discomfort caused by his presence and be himself released from his sufferings.

He slept less and less. He was given opium and hypodermic injections of morphine, but this did not relieve him. The dull depression he experienced in a somnolent condition at first gave him a little relief, but only as something new, afterwards it became as distressing as the pain itself or even more so.

Special foods were prepared for him by the doctors' orders, but all those foods became increasingly distasteful and disgusting to him.

For his excretions also special arrangements had to be made, and this was a torment to him every time—a torment from the uncleanliness, the unseemliness, and the smell, and from knowing that another person had to take part in it.

But just through this most unpleasant matter, Iván Ilých obtained comfort. Gerásim, the butler's young assistant, always came in to carry the things out. Gerásim was a clean, fresh peasant lad, grown stout on town food and always cheerful and bright. At first the sight of him, his clean Russian peasant costume, engaged on that disgusting task embarrassed Iván Ilých.

Once when he got up from the commode too weak to draw up his trousers, he dropped into a soft armchair and looked with horror at his bare, enfeebled thighs with the muscles so sharply marked on them.

Gerásim with a firm light tread, his heavy boots emitting a pleasant smell of tar and fresh winter air, came in wearing a clean Hessian apron, the sleeves of his print shirt tucked up over his strong bare young arms; and refraining from looking at his sick master out of consideration for his feelings, and restraining the joy of life that beamed from his face, he went up to the commode.

"Gerásim!" said Iván Ilých in a weak voice.

Gerásim started, evidently afraid he might have committed some blunder, and with a rapid movement turned his fresh, kind, simple young face which just showed the first downy signs of a beard.

"Yes, sir?"

"That must be very unpleasant for you. You must forgive me. I am helpless."

"Oh, why, sir," and Gerásim's eyes beamed and he showed his glistening white teeth, "what's a little trouble? It's a case of illness with you, sir."

And his deft strong hands did their accustomed task, and he went out of the room stepping lightly. Five minutes later he as lightly returned. Iván Ilých was still sitting in the same position in the armchair.

"Gerásim," he said when the latter had replaced the freshly-washed utensil. "Please come here and help me." Gerásim went up to him. "Lift me up. It is hard for me to get up, and I have sent Dmítri away."

Gerásim went up to him, grasped his master with his strong arms deftly but gently, in the same way that he stepped—lifted him, supported him with one hand, and with the other drew up his trousers and would have set him down again, but Iván Ilých asked to be led to the sofa. Gerásim, without an effort and without apparent pressure, led him, almost lifting him, to the sofa and placed him on it.

"Thank you. How easily and well you do it all!"

Gerásim smiled again and turned to leave the room. But Iván Ilých felt his presence such a comfort that he did not want to let him go.

"One thing more, please move up that chair. No, the other one—under my feet. It is easier for me when my feet are raised."

Gerásim brought the chair, set it down gently in place, and raised Iván Ilých's legs on to it. It seemed to Iván Ilých that he felt better while Gerásim was holding up his legs.

"It's better when my legs are higher," he said. "Place that cushion under them."

Gerásim did so. He again lifted the legs and placed them, and again Iván Ilých felt better while Gerásim held his legs. When he set them down Iván Ilých fancied he felt worse.

"Gerásim," he said. "Are you busy now?"

"Not at all, sir," said Gerásim, who had learnt from the townsfolk how to speak to gentlefolk.

"What have you still to do?"

"What have I to do? I've done everything except chopping the logs for to-morrow."

"Then hold my legs up a bit higher, can you?"

"Of course I can. Why not?" And Gerásim raised his master's legs higher and Iván Ilých thought that in that position he did not feel any pain at all.

"And how about the logs?"

"Don't trouble about that, sir. There's plenty of time."

Iván Ilých told Gerásim to sit down and hold his legs, and began to talk to him. And strange to say it seemed to him that he felt better while Gerásim held his legs up.

After that Iván Ilých would sometimes call Gerásim and get him to hold his legs on his shoulders, and he liked talking to him. Gerásim did it all easily, willingly, simply, and with a good nature that touched Iván Ilých. Health, strength, and vitality in other people were offensive to him, but Gerásim's strength and vitality did not mortify but soothed him.

What tormented Iván Ilých most was the deception, the lie, which for some reason they all accepted, that he was not dying but was simply ill, and that he only need keep quiet and undergo a treatment and then something very good would result. He however knew that do what they would nothing would come of it, only still more agonizing suffering and death. This deception tortured him—their not wishing to admit what they all knew and what he knew, but wanting to lie to him concerning his terrible condition, and wishing and forcing him to participate in that lie. Those lies—lies enacted over him on the eve of his death and destined to degrade this awful, solemn act to the level of their visitings, their curtains, their sturgeon for dinner—were a terrible agony for Iván Ilých. And strangely enough, many times when they were going through their antics over him he had been within a hairbreadth of calling out to them: "Stop lying! You know and I know that I am dying. Then at least stop lying about it!" But he had never had the spirit to do it. The awful, terrible act of his dying was, he could see, reduced by those about him to the level of a casual, unpleasant, and almost indecorous incident (as if someone entered a drawing-room diffusing an unpleasant odour) and this was done by that very decorum which he had served all his life long. He saw that no one felt for him, because no one even wished to grasp his position. Only Gerásim recognized it and pitied him. And so Iván Ilých felt at ease only with him. He felt comforted when Gerásim supported his legs (sometimes all night long) and refused to go to bed, saying: "Don't you worry, Iván Ilých. I'll get sleep enough later on," or when he suddenly became familiar and exclaimed: "If you weren't sick it would be another matter, but as it is, why should I grudge a little trouble?" Gerásim alone did not lie; everything showed that he alone understood the facts of the case and did not consider it necessary to disguise them, but simply felt sorry for his emaciated and enfeebled master. Once when Iván Ilých was sending him away he even said straight out: "We shall all of us die, so why should I grudge a little trouble?"—expressing the fact that he did not think his work burdensome, because he was doing it for a dying man and hoped someone would do the same for him when his time came.

Apart from this lying, or because of it, what most tormented Iván Ilých was that no one pitied him as he wished to be pitied. At certain moments after prolonged suffering he wished most of all (though he would have been ashamed to confess it) for someone to pity him as a sick child is pitied. He longed to be petted and comforted. He knew he was an important functionary, that he had a beard turning grey, and that therefore what he longed for was impossible, but still he longed for it.

And in Gerásim's attitude towards him there was something akin to what he wished for, and so that attitude comforted him. Iván Ilých wanted to weep, wanted to be petted and cried over, and then his colleague Shébek would come, and instead of weeping and being petted, Iván Ilých would assume a serious, severe, and profound air, and by force of habit would express his opinion on a decision of the Court of Cassation and would stubbornly insist on that view. This falsity around him and within him did more than anything else to poison his last days.

VIII

It was morning. He knew it was morning because Gerásim had gone, and Peter the footman had come and put out the candles, drawn back one of the curtains, and begun quietly to tidy up. Whether it was morning or evening, Friday or Sunday, made no difference, it was all just the same: the gnawing, unmitigated, agonizing pain, never ceasing for an instant, the consciousness of life inexorably waning but not yet extinguished, the approach of that ever dreaded and hateful Death which was the only reality, and always the same falsity. What were days, weeks, hours, in such a case?

"Will you have some tea, sir?"

"He wants things to be regular, and wishes the gentlefolk to drink tea in the morning," thought Iván Ilých, and only said "No."

"Wouldn't you like to move onto the sofa, sir?"

"He wants to tidy up the room, and I'm in the way. I am uncleanliness and disorder," he thought, and said only:

"No, leave me alone."

The man went on bustling about. Iván Ilých stretched out his hand. Peter came up, ready to help.

"What is it, sir?"

"My watch."

Peter took the watch which was close at hand and gave it to his master.

"Half-past eight. Are they up?"

"No sir, except Vladímir Ivánich" (the son) "who has gone to school. Praskóvya Fëdorovna ordered me to wake her if you asked for her. Shall I do so?"

"No, there's no need to." "Perhaps I'd better have some tea," he thought, and added aloud: "Yes, bring me some tea."

Peter went to the door, but Iván Ilých dreaded being left alone. "How can I keep him here? Oh yes, my medicine." "Peter, give me my medicine." "Why not? Perhaps it may still do me some good." He took a spoonful and swallowed it. "No, it won't help. It's all tomfoolery, all deception," he decided as soon as he became aware of the familiar, sickly, hopeless taste. "No, I can't believe in it any longer. But the pain, why this pain? If it would only cease just for a moment!" And he moaned. Peter turned towards him. "It's all right. Go and fetch me some tea."

Peter went out. Left alone Iván Ilých groaned not so much with pain, terrible though that was, as from mental anguish. Always and for ever the same, always these endless days and nights. If only it would come quicker! If only *what* would come quicker? Death, darkness? . . . No, no! Anything rather than death!

When Peter returned with the tea on a tray, Iván Ilých stared at him for a time in perplexity, not realizing who and what he was. Peter was disconcerted by that look and his embarrassment brought Iván Ilých to himself.

"Oh, tea! All right, put it down. Only help me to wash and put on a clean shirt."

And Iván Ilých began to wash. With pauses for rest, he washed his hands and then his face, cleaned his teeth, brushed his hair, and looked in the glass. He was terrified by what he saw, especially by the limp way in which his hair clung to his pallid forehead.

While his shirt was being changed he knew that he would be still more frightened at the sight of his body, so he avoided looking at it. Finally he was ready. He drew on a dressing-gown, wrapped himself in a plaid, and sat down in the armchair to take his tea. For a moment he felt refreshed, but as soon as he began to drink the tea he was again aware of the same taste, and the pain also returned. He finished it with an effort, and then lay down stretching out his legs, and dismissed Peter.

Always the same. Now a spark of hope flashes up, then a sea of despair rages, and always pain; always pain, always despair, and always the same. When alone he had a dreadful and distressing desire to call someone, but he knew beforehand that with others present it would be still worse. "Another dose of morphine—to lose consciousness. I will tell him, the doctor, that he must think of something else. It's impossible, impossible, to go on like this."

An hour and another pass like that. But now there is a ring at the door bell. Perhaps it's the doctor? It is. He comes in fresh, hearty, plump, and cheerful, with that look on his face that seems to say: "There now, you're in a panic about something, but we'll arrange it all for you directly!" The doctor knows this expression is out of place here, but he has put it on once for all and can't take it off—like a man who has put on a frock-coat in the morning to pay a round of calls.

The doctor rubs his hands vigorously and reassuringly.

"Brr! How cold it is! There's such a sharp frost; just let me warm myself!" he says, as if it were only a matter of waiting till he was warm, and then he would put everything right.

"Well now, how are you?"

Iván Ilých feels that the doctor would like to say: "Well, how are our affairs?" but that even he feels that this would not do, and says instead: "What sort of a night have you had?"

Iván Ilých looks at him as much as to say: "Are you really never ashamed of lying?" But the doctor does not wish to understand this question, and Iván Ilých says: "Just as terrible as ever. The pain never leaves me and never subsides. If only something . . ."

"Yes, you sick people are always like that. . . . There, now I think I am warm enough. Even Praskóvya Fëdorovna, who is so particular, could find no fault with my temperature. Well, now I can say good-morning," and the doctor presses his patient's hand.

Then, dropping his former playfulness, he begins with a most serious face to examine the patient, feeling his pulse and taking his temperature, and then begins the sounding and auscultation.

Iván Ilých knows quite well and definitely that all this is nonsense and pure deception, but when the doctor, getting down on his knee, leans over him, putting his ear first higher then lower, and performs various gymnastic movements over him with a significant expression on his face, Iván Ilých submits to it all as he used to submit to the speeches of the lawyers, though he knew very well that they were all lying and why they were lying.

The doctor, kneeling on the sofa, is still sounding him when Praskóvya Fëdorovna's silk dress rustles at the door and she is heard scolding Peter for not having let her know of the doctor's arrival.

She comes in, kisses her husband, and at once proceeds to prove that she has been up a long time already, and only owing to a misunderstanding failed to be there when the doctor arrived.

Iván Ilých looks at her, scans her all over, sets against her the whiteness and plumpness and cleanness of her hands and neck, the gloss of her hair, and the sparkle of her vivacious eyes. He hates her with his whole soul. And the thrill of hatred he feels for her makes him suffer from her touch.

Her attitude towards him and his disease is still the same. Just as the doctor had adopted a certain relation to his patient which he could not abandon, so had she formed one towards him—that he was not doing something he ought to do and was himself to blame, and that she reproached him lovingly for this—and she could not now change that attitude.

"You see he doesn't listen to me and doesn't take his medicine at the proper time. And above all he lies in a position that is no doubt bad for him—with his legs up."

She described how he made Gerásim hold his legs up.

The doctor smiled with a contemptuous affability that said: "What's to be done? These sick people do have foolish fancies of that kind, but we must forgive them."

When the examination was over the doctor looked at his watch, and then Praskóvya Fëdorovna announced to Iván Ilých that it was of course as he pleased, but she had sent to-day for a celebrated specialist who would examine him and have a consultation with Michael Danílovich (their regular doctor).

"Please don't raise any objections. I am doing this for my own sake," she said ironically, letting it be felt that she was doing it all for his sake and only said this to leave him no right to refuse. He remained silent, knitting his brows. He felt that he was so surrounded and involved in a mesh of falsity that it was hard to unravel anything.

Everything she did for him was entirely for her own sake, and she told him she was doing for herself what she actually was doing for herself, as if that was so incredible that he must understand the opposite.

At half-past eleven the celebrated specialist arrived. Again the sounding began and the significant conversations in his presence and in another room, about the kidneys and the appendix, and the questions and answers, with such an air of importance that again, instead of the real question of life and death which now alone confronted him, the question arose of the kidney and appendix which were not behaving as they ought to and would now be attacked by Michael Danílovich and the specialist and forced to amend their ways.

The celebrated specialist took leave of him with a serious though not hopeless look, and in reply to the timid question Iván Ilých, with eyes glistening with fear and hope, put to him as to whether there was a chance of recovery, said that he could not vouch for it but there was a possibility. The look of hope with which Iván Ilých watched the doctor out was so pathetic that Praskóvya Fëdorovna, seeing it, even wept as she left the room to hand the doctor his fee.

The gleam of hope kindled by the doctor's encouragement did not last long. The same room, the same pictures, curtains, wall-paper, medicine bottles, were all there, and the same aching suffering body, and Iván Ilých began to moan. They gave him a subcutaneous injection and he sank into oblivion.

It was twilight when he came to. They brought him his dinner and he swallowed some beef tea with difficulty, and then everything was the same again and night was coming on.

After dinner, at seven o'clock, Praskóvya Fëdorovna came into the room in evening dress, her full bosom pushed up by her corset, and with traces of powder on her face. She had reminded him in the morning that they were going to the theatre. Sarah Bernhardt was visiting the town and they had a box, which he had insisted on their taking. Now he had forgotten about it and her toilet offended him, but he concealed his vexation when he remembered that he had himself insisted on their securing a box and going because it would be an instructive and aesthetic pleasure for the children.

Praskóvya Fëdorovna came in, self-satisfied but yet with a rather guilty air. She sat down and asked how he was, but, as he saw, only for the sake of asking and not in order to learn about it, knowing that there was nothing to learn—and then went on to what she really wanted to say: that she would not on any account have gone but that the box had been taken and Helen and their daughter were going, as well as Petríshchev (the examining magistrate, their daughter's fiancé) and that it was out of the question to let them go alone; but that she would have much preferred to sit with him for a while; and he must be sure to follow the doctor's orders while she was away.

"Oh, and Fëdor Petróvich" (the fiancé) "would like to come in. May he? And Lisa?"

"All right."

Their daughter came in in full evening dress, her fresh young flesh exposed (making a show of that very flesh which in his own case caused so much suffering), strong, healthy, evidently in love, and impatient with illness, suffering, and death, because they interfered with her happiness.

Fëdor Petróvich came in too, in evening dress, his hair curled *à la Capoul*, a tight stiff collar round his long sinewy neck, an enormous white shirt-front and narrow black trousers tightly stretched over his strong thighs. He had one white glove tightly drawn on, and was holding his opera hat in his hand.

Following him the schoolboy crept in unnoticed, in a new uniform, poor little fellow, and wearing gloves. Terribly dark shadows showed under his eyes, the meaning of which Iván Ilých knew well.

His son had always seemed pathetic to him, and now it was dreadful to see the boy's frightened look of pity. It seemed to Iván Ilých that Vásya was the only one besides Gerásim who understood and pitied him.

They all sat down and again asked how he was. A silence followed. Lisa asked her mother about the opera-glasses, and there was an altercation between mother and daughter as to who had taken them and where they had been put. This occasioned some unpleasantness.

Fëdor Petróvich inquired of Iván Ilých whether he had ever seen Sarah Bernhardt. Iván Ilých did not at first catch the question, but then replied: "No, have you seen her before?"

"Yes, in *Adrienne Lecouvreur*."

Praskóvya Fëdorovna mentioned some rôles in which Sarah Bernhardt was particularly good. Her daughter disagreed. Conversation sprang up as to the elegance and realism of her acting—the sort of conversation that is always repeated and is always the same.

In the midst of the conversation Fëdor Petróvich glanced at Iván Ilých and became silent. The others also looked at him and grew silent. Iván Ilých was staring with glittering eyes straight before him, evidently indignant with them. This had to be rectified, but it was impossible to do so. The silence had to be broken, but for a time no one dared to break it and they all became afraid that the conventional deception would suddenly become obvious and the truth become plain to all. Lisa was the first to pluck up courage and break that silence, but by trying to hide what everybody was feeling, she betrayed it.

"Well, if we are going it's time to start," she said, looking at her watch, a present from her father, and with a faint and significant smile at Fëdor Petróvich relating to something known only to them. She got up with a rustle of her dress.

They all rose, said good-night, and went away.

When they had gone it seemed to Iván Ilých that he felt better; the falsity had gone with them. But the pain remained—that same pain and that same fear that made everything monotonously alike, nothing harder and nothing easier. Everything was worse.

Again minute followed minute and hour followed hour. Everything remained the same and there was no cessation. And the inevitable end of it all became more and more terrible.

"Yes, send Gerásim here," he replied to a question Peter asked.

IX

His wife returned late at night. She came in on tiptoe, but he heard her, opened his eyes, and made haste to close them again. She wished to send Gerásim away and to sit with him herself, but he opened his eyes and said: "No, go away."

"Are you in great pain?"

"Always the same."

"Take some opium."

He agreed and took some. She went away.

Till about three in the morning he was in a state of stupefied misery. It seemed to him that he and his pain were being thrust into a narrow, deep black sack, but though they were pushed further and further in they could not be pushed to the bottom. And this, terrible enough in itself, was accompanied by suffering. He was frightened yet wanted to fall through the sack, he struggled but yet co-operated. And suddenly he broke through, fell, and regained consciousness. Gerásim was sitting at the foot of the bed dozing quietly and patiently, while he himself lay with his emaciated stockinged legs resting on Gerásim's shoulders; the same shaded candle was there and the same unceasing pain.

"Go away, Gerásim," he whispered.

"It's all right, sir. I'll stay a while."

"No. Go away."

He removed his legs from Gerásim's shoulders, turned sideways onto his arm, and felt sorry for himself. He only waited till Gerásim had gone into the next room and then restrained himself no longer but wept like a child. He wept on account of his helplessness, his terrible loneliness, the cruelty of man, the cruelty of God, and the absence of God.

"Why hast Thou done all this? Why hast Thou brought me here? Why, why dost Thou torment me so terribly?"

He did not expect an answer and yet wept because there was no answer and could be none. The pain again grew more acute, but he did not stir and did not call. He said to himself: "Go on! Strike me! But what is it for? What have I done to Thee? What is it for?"

Then he grew quiet and not only ceased weeping but even held his breath and became all attention. It was as though he were listening not to an audible voice but to the voice of his soul, to the current of thoughts arising within him.

"What is it you want?" was the first clear conception capable of expression in words, that he heard.

"What do you want? What do you want?" he repeated to himself.

"What do I want? To live and not to suffer," he answered.

And again he listened with such concentrated attention that even his pain did not distract him.

"To live? How?" asked his inner voice.

"Why, to live as I used to—well and pleasantly."

"As you lived before, well and pleasantly?" the voice repeated.

And in imagination he began to recall the best moments of his pleasant life. But strange to say none of those best moments of his pleasant life now seemed at all what they had then seemed—none of them except the first recollections of childhood. There, in childhood, there had been something really pleasant with which it would be possible to live if it could return. But the child who had experienced that happiness existed no longer, it was like a reminiscence of somebody else.

As soon as the period began which had produced the present Iván Ilých, all that had then seemed joys now melted before his sight and turned into something trivial and often nasty.

And the further he departed from childhood and the nearer he came to the present the more worthless and doubtful were the joys. This began with the School of Law. A little that was really good was still found there—there was light-heartedness, friendship, and hope. But in the upper classes there had already been fewer of such good moments. Then during the first years of his official career, when he was in the service of the governor, some pleasant moments again occurred: they were the memories of love for a woman. Then all became confused and there was still less of what was good; later on again there was still less that was good, and the further he went the less there was. His marriage, a mere accident, then the disenchantment that followed it, his wife's bad breath and the sensuality and hypocrisy: then that deadly official life and those preoccupations about money, a year of it, and two, and ten, and twenty, and always the same thing. And the longer it lasted the more deadly it became. "It is as if I had been going downhill while I imagined I was going up. And that is really what it was. I was going up in public opinion, but to the same extent life was ebbing away from me. And now it is all done and there is only death.

"Then what does it mean? Why? It can't be that life is so senseless and horrible. But if it really has been so horrible and senseless, why must I die and die in agony? There is something wrong!

"Maybe I did not live as I ought to have done," it suddenly occurred to him. "But how could that be, when I did everything properly?" he replied, and immediately dismissed from his mind this, the sole solution of all the riddles of life and death, as something quite impossible.

"Then what do you want now? To live? Live how? Live as you lived in the law courts when the usher proclaimed 'The judge is coming!' The judge is coming, the judge!" he repeated to himself. "Here he is, the judge. But I am not guilty!" he exclaimed angrily. "What is it for?" And he ceased crying, but turning his face to the wall continued to ponder on the same question: Why, and for what purpose, is there all this horror? But however much he pondered he found no answer. And whenever the thought occurred to him, as it often did, that it all resulted from his not having lived as he ought to have done, he at once recalled the correctness of his whole life and dismissed so strange an idea.

X

Another fortnight passed. Iván Ilých now no longer left his sofa. He would not lie in bed but lay on the sofa, facing the wall nearly all the time. He suffered ever the same unceasing agonies and in his loneliness pondered always on the same insoluble question: "What is this? Can it be that it is Death?" And the inner voice answered: "Yes, it is Death."

"Why these sufferings?" And the voice answered, "For no reason— they just are so." Beyond and besides this there was nothing.

From the very beginning of his illness, ever since he had first been to see the doctor, Iván Ilých's life had been divided between two contrary and alternating moods: now it was despair and the expectation of this uncomprehended and terrible death, and now hope and an intently interested observation of the functioning of his organs. Now before his eyes there was only a kidney or an intestine that temporarily evaded its duty, and now only that incomprehensible and dreadful death from which it was impossible to escape.

These two states of mind had alternated from the very beginning of his illness, but the further it progressed the more doubtful and fantastic became the conception of the kidney, and the more real the sense of impending death.

He had but to call to mind what he had been three months before and what he was now, to call to mind with what regularity he had been going downhill, for every possibility of hope to be shattered.

Latterly during that loneliness in which he found himself as he lay facing the back of the sofa, a loneliness in the midst of a populous town and surrounded by numerous acquaintances and relations but that yet could not have been more complete anywhere—either at the bottom of the sea or under the earth—during that terrible loneliness Iván Ilých had lived only in memories of the past. Pictures of his past rose before him one after another. They always began with what was nearest in time and then went back to what was most remote—to his childhood—and rested there. If he thought of the stewed prunes that had been offered him that day, his mind went back to the raw shrivelled French plums of his childhood, their peculiar flavour and the flow of saliva when he sucked their stones, and along with the memory of that taste came a whole series of memories of those days: his nurse, his brother, and their toys. "No, I mustn't think of that. . . . It is too painful," Iván Ilých said to himself, and brought himself back to the present—to the button on the back of the sofa and the creases in its morocco. "Morocco is expensive, but it does not wear well: there had been a quarrel about it. It was a different kind of quarrel and a different kind of morocco that time when we tore father's portfolio and were punished, and mamma brought us some tarts. . . ." And again his thoughts dwelt on his childhood, and again it was painful and he tried to banish them and fix his mind on something else.

Then again together with that chain of memories another series passed through his mind—of how his illness had progressed and grown worse. There also the further back he looked the more life there had been. There had been more of what was good in life and more of life itself. The two merged together. "Just as the pain went on getting worse and worse, so my life grew worse and worse," he thought. "There is one bright spot there at the back, at the beginning of life, and afterwards all becomes blacker and blacker and proceeds more and more rapidly—in inverse ratio to the square of the distance from death," thought Iván Ilých. And the example of a stone falling downwards with increasing velocity entered his mind. Life, a series of increasing sufferings, flies further and further towards its end—the most terrible suffering. "I am flying. . . ." He shuddered, shifted himself, and tried to resist, but was already aware that resistance was impossible, and again with eyes weary of gazing but unable to cease seeing what was before them, he stared at the back of the sofa and waited—awaiting that dreadful fall and shock and destruction.

"Resistance is impossible!," he said to himself. "If I could only understand what it is all for! But that too is impossible. An explanation would be possible if it could be said that I have not lived as I ought to. But it is impossible to say that," and he remembered all the legality, correctitude, and propriety of his life. "That at any rate can certainly not be admitted," he thought, and his lips smiled ironically as if someone could see that smile and be taken in by it. "There is no explanation! Agony, death. . . . What for?"

XI

Another two weeks went by in this way and during that fortnight an event occurred that Iván Ilých and his wife had desired. Petríshchev formally proposed. It happened in the evening. The next day Praskóvya Fëdorovna came into her husband's room considering how best to inform him of it, but that very night there had been a fresh change for the worse in his condition. She found him still lying on the sofa but in a different position. He lay on his back, groaning and staring fixedly straight in front of him.

She began to remind him of his medicines, but he turned his eyes towards her with such a look that she did not finish what she was saying; so great an animosity, to her in particular, did that look express.

"For Christ's sake let me die in peace!" he said.

She would have gone away, but just then their daughter came in and went up to say good morning. He looked at her as he had done at his wife, and in reply to her inquiry about his health said dryly that he would soon free them all of himself. They were both silent and after sitting with him for a while went away.

"Is it our fault?" Lisa said to her mother. "It's as if we were to blame! I am sorry for papa, but why should we be tortured?"

The doctor came at his usual time. Iván Ilých answered "Yes" and "No," never taking his angry eyes from him, and at last said: "You know you can do nothing for me, so leave me alone."

"We can ease your sufferings."

"You can't even do that. Let me be."

The doctor went into the drawing-room and told Praskóvya Fëdorovna that the case was very serious and that the only resource left was opium to allay her husband's sufferings, which must be terrible.

It was true, as the doctor said, that Iván Ilých's physical sufferings were terrible, but worse than the physical sufferings were his mental sufferings which were his chief torture.

His mental sufferings were due to the fact that that night, as he looked at Gerásim's sleepy, good-natured face with its prominent cheek-bones, the question suddenly occurred to him: "What if my whole life has been wrong?"

It occurred to him that what had appeared perfectly impossible before, namely that he had not spent his life as he should have done, might after all be true. It occurred to him that his scarcely perceptible attempts to struggle against what was considered good by the most highly placed people, those scarcely noticeable impulses which he had immediately suppressed, might have been the real thing, and all the rest false. And his professional duties and the whole arrangement of his life and of his family, and all his social and official interests, might all have been false. He tried to defend all those things to himself and suddenly felt the weakness of what he was defending. There was nothing to defend.

"But if that is so," he said to himself, "and I am leaving this life with the consciousness that I have lost all that was given me and it is impossible to rectify it—what then?"

He lay on his back and began to pass his life in review in quite a new way. In the morning when he saw first his footman, then his wife, then his daughter, and then the doctor, their every word and movement confirmed to him the awful truth that had been revealed to him during the night. In them he saw himself—all that for which he had lived—and saw clearly that it was not real at all, but a terrible and huge deception which had hidden both life and death. This consciousness intensified his physical suffering tenfold. He groaned and tossed about, and pulled at his clothing which choked and stifled him. And he hated them on that account.

He was given a large dose of opium and became unconscious, but at noon his sufferings began again. He drove everybody away and tossed from side to side.

His wife came to him and said:

"Jean, my dear, do this for me. It can't do any harm and often helps. Healthy people often do it."

He opened his eyes wide.

"What? Take communion? Why? It's unnecessary! However . . ."

She began to cry.

"Yes, do, my dear. I'll send for our priest. He is such a nice man."

"All right. Very well," he muttered.

When the priest came and heard his confession, Iván Ilých was softened and seemed to feel a relief from his doubts and consequently from his sufferings, and for a moment there came a ray of hope. He again began to think of the vermiform appendix and the possibility of correcting it. He received the sacrament with tears in his eyes.

When they laid him down again afterwards he felt a moment's ease, and the hope that he might live awoke in him again. He began to think of the operation that had been suggested to him. "To live! I want to live!" he said to himself.

His wife came in to congratulate him after his communion, and when uttering the usual conventional words she added:

"You feel better, don't you?"

Without looking at her he said "Yes."

Her dress, her figure, the expression of her face, the tone of her voice, all revealed the same thing. "This is wrong, it is not as it should be. All you have lived for and still live for is falsehood and deception, hiding life and death from you." And as soon as he admitted that thought, his hatred and his agonizing physical suffering again sprang up, and with that suffering a consciousness of the unavoidable, approaching end. And to this was added a new sensation of grinding shooting pain and a feeling of suffocation.

The expression of his face when he uttered that "Yes" was dreadful. Having uttered it, he looked her straight in the eyes, turned on his face with a rapidity extraordinary in his weak state and shouted:

"Go away! Go away and leave me alone!"

XII

From that moment the screaming began that continued for three days, and was so terrible that one could not hear it through two closed doors without horror. At the moment he answered his wife he realized that he was lost, that there was no return, that the end had come, the very end, and his doubts were still unsolved and remained doubts.

"Oh! Oh! Oh!" he cried in various intonations. He had begun by screaming "I won't!" and continued screaming on the letter "O."

For three whole days, during which time did not exist for him, he struggled in that black sack into which he was being thrust by an invisible, resistless force. He struggled as a man condemned to death struggles in the hands of the executioner, knowing that he cannot save himself. And every moment he felt that despite all his efforts he was drawing nearer and nearer to what terrified him. He felt that this agony was due to his being thrust into that black hole and still more to his not being able to get right into it. He was hindered from getting into it by his conviction that his life had been a good one. That very justification of his life held him fast and prevented his moving forward, and it caused him most torment of all.

Suddenly some force struck him in the chest and side, making it still harder to breathe, and he fell through the hole and there at the bottom was a light. What had happened to him was like the sensation one sometimes experiences in a railway carriage when one thinks one is going backwards while one is really going forwards and suddenly becomes aware of the real direction.

"Yes, it was all not the right thing," he said to himself, "but that's no matter. It can be done. But what *is* the right thing?" he asked himself, and suddenly grew quiet.

This occurred at the end of the third day, two hours before his death. Just then his schoolboy son had crept softly in and gone up to the bedside. The dying man was still screaming desperately and waving his arms. His hand fell on the boy's head, and the boy caught it, pressed it to his lips, and began to cry.

At that very moment Iván Ilých fell through and caught sight of the light, and it was revealed to him that though his life had not been what it should have been, this could still be rectified. He asked himself, "What *is* the right thing?" and grew still, listening. Then he felt that someone was kissing his hand. He opened his eyes, looked at his son, and felt sorry for him. His wife came up to him and he glanced at her. She was gazing at him open-mouthed, with undried tears on her nose and cheek and a despairing look on her face. He felt sorry for her too.

"Yes, I am making them wretched," he thought. "They are sorry, but it will be better for them when I die." He wished to say this but had not the strength to utter it. "Besides, why speak? I must act," he thought. With a look at his wife he indicated his son and said: "Take him away . . . sorry for him . . . sorry for you too. . . ." He tried to add, "Forgive me," but said "Forego" and waved his hand, knowing that He whose understanding mattered would understand.

And suddenly it grew clear to him that what had been oppressing him and would not leave him was all dropping away at once from two sides, from ten sides, and from all sides. He was sorry for them, he must act so as not to hurt them: release them and free himself from these sufferings. "How good and how simple!" he thought. "And the pain?" he asked himself. "What has become of it? Where are you, pain?"

He turned his attention to it.

"Yes, here it is. Well, what of it? Let the pain be."

"And death . . . where is it?"

He sought his former accustomed fear of death and did not find it. "Where is it? What death?" There was no fear because there was no death.

In place of death there was light.

"So that's what it is!" he suddenly exclaimed aloud. "What joy!"

To him all this happened in a single instant, and the meaning of that instant did not change. For those present his agony continued for another two hours. Something rattled in his throat, his emaciated body twitched, then the gasping and rattle became less and less frequent.

"It is finished!" said someone near him.

He heard these words and repeated them in his soul.

"Death is finished," he said to himself. "It is no more!"

He drew in a breath, stopped in the midst of a sigh, stretched out, and died.

The Three Hermits

> But when ye pray, use not vain
> repetitions, as the heathen do: for they think
> that they shall be heard for their much
> speaking. Be not ye therefore like unto them:
> for your Father knoweth what things ye have
> need of, before ye ask Him.
> MATT. VI. 7, 8.

A Bishop was sailing from the city of Arkhangelsk to the Solovetsky Islands. On the same vessel there were pilgrims sailing to visit the holy shrines. The wind was favorable, the weather fair, the sea smooth. The pilgrims—some were lying down, some having a bite to eat, some sitting in groups—were talking to each other. The Bishop, too, came out on deck, began to pace the bridge. He approached the bow, saw a group of people gathered together. A peasant was pointing out something in the sea and speaking, and the people were listening. The Bishop stopped, looked where the peasant was pointing: there was nothing to be seen, only the sea gleaming in the sun. The Bishop came closer, began to listen. The peasant saw the Bishop, took off his cap and fell silent. The people also saw the Bishop, also took off their caps, paid their respects.

"Don't mind me, friends," said the Bishop. "I have also come to hear what you, good man, are telling them."

"This fisherman was telling us about the hermits," said one merchant who was bolder than the others.

"What about the hermits?" asked the Bishop, came up to the rail and sat down on a box. "Tell me, too, I'll listen. What were you pointing at?"

"Why, that little island you can just make out," said the peasant and pointed forward to starboard. "On that very island the hermits live, seek salvation."

"But where is the island?" asked the Bishop.

"Here, please look in line with my hand. See that cloud? Just a bit to the left of it, below, showing like a thin streak."

The Bishop looked and looked, the water rippled in the sun, and, for want of practice, he could see nothing.

"I cannot see it," he said. "So, what kind of hermits live on that island?"

"Godly men," answered the peasant. "I had heard of them long ago, but never chanced to see them, and then the summer before last I saw them myself."

And the fisherman began to recount once more how he had gone out fishing, and how he had run aground on that island and didn't know himself where he was. In the morning he wandered off and came upon an earth hut and saw a hermit by the earth hut, and then two more came out; they fed and dried him and helped him repair his boat.

"And what do they look like?" asked the Bishop.

"One of them tiny, bent, quite ancient, in an old little cassock, must be more than a hundred years old, the gray hairs in his beard turning green already; but he keeps smiling and is bright as an angel from Heaven. Another a little taller, also old, in a torn coat, his beard broad, yellowish white, but he is a powerful man: he turned my boat over like a tub, I didn't have a chance to lend him a hand—also joyous. And the third is tall, his beard long, down to his knees—and white as a blue kite, himself gloomy, eyebrows hanging over his eyes, and all naked, only girded with a piece of sacking."

"What did they talk about with you?" asked the Bishop.

"They did everything mostly silently, and they don't talk much to one another. But one looks up and the other understands him. I began to ask the tall one whether they had been living there long. He frowned, began to say something, seemed to get angry; but the little ancient one at once took him by the hand, smiled, and the big one fell silent. The ancient one just said: 'Have mercy on us,' and smiled."

While the peasant spoke the vessel drew still nearer to the island.

"Now you can really see it," said the merchant. "Be so good as to look, your lordship," he said, pointing.

The Bishop looked. And indeed he saw a black streak—the little island. After looking for a while the Bishop went away from the bow to the stern and approached the helmsman.

"What is this little island, showing there?"

"It's nameless. There are many of them here."

"Is it true what they say, that some hermits seek salvation there?"

"So they say, your lordship, but I don't know if it's true. Some fishermen, they say, have seen them. It may be just idle talk."

"I should like to land on that island, to see the hermits," said the Bishop. "How can this be done?"

"The ship cannot come near," said the helmsman. "You can come near in a boat though, but the Captain must be asked."

They called the Captain.

"I should like to have a look at those hermits," said the Bishop. "Can't you row me over?"

The Captain tried to talk him out of it. "It could be done, but we would waste a lot of time, and if I may mention it to your lordship, they are not worth looking at. I have heard from people that these are foolish old men who live there, they understand nothing and can say nothing, like some kind of fish of the sea."

"I want to," said the Bishop. "I'll pay for the trouble, take me there."

There was nothing to be done; the shipmen gave orders, sails were trimmed. The helmsman turned the ship, they sailed toward the island. A chair was brought to the bow for the Bishop. He sat down and watched. And all the people gathered at the bow, all looking at the little island. And those with keener eyes could already see the rocks on the island and point out the earth hut. And one man had already made out the three hermits. The Captain brought out a spyglass, looked through it, handed it to the Bishop. "True enough," he said, "there on the shore, a bit to the right of the large rock, there are three men standing."

The Bishop looked through the glass, trained it in the right direction; true enough, there were three of them standing there: one tall, another a little shorter, and the third quite small; they were standing on the shore, holding hands.

The Captain went up to the Bishop. "Here, your lordship, the ship must stop. If you so wish, you can go on in a boat, while we stand here at anchor."

At once they let out the cable, cast anchor, furled the sail—the ship jerked, shook. A boat was lowered, the oarsmen jumped down, and the Bishop began to descend the ladder. The Bishop descended, sat down on the seat in the boat, the oarsmen pulled at the oars and rowed to the island. They rowed up within a stone's throw; they saw: there stood the three hermits—the tall one, naked, girded with a piece of sacking; the shorter one in a torn coat; and the ancient little bent one, in a little old cassock: they stood, all three of them, holding each other by the hand.

The oarsmen put to the shore, held fast with a boathook. The Bishop got out.

The hermits bowed to him, he blessed them, they bowed to him even lower. And the Bishop spoke to them:

"I have heard," he says, "that you, godly men, seek salvation here, praying for people to Christ the Lord, while I, Christ's unworthy servant, am here by God's grace, called upon to tend His flock, and so I wanted to see you, servants of God, and give you instruction if I can."

The hermits are silent, smile, glance at one another.

"Tell me how you seek salvation and how you serve God," said the Bishop.

The second hermit sighed and looked at the oldest, the ancient one; the tall hermit frowned and looked at the oldest, the ancient one. And the oldest, the ancient hermit, smiled and said: "We don't know, servant of God, how to serve God; we only serve ourselves, feed ourselves."

"How then do you pray to God?" asked the Bishop.

And the ancient hermit said: "We pray thus: three of You, three of us, have mercy on us."

And as soon as the ancient hermit had said this all three hermits raised their eyes to heaven and all three of them said: "Three of You, three of us, have mercy on us."

With an amused smile the Bishop said:

"You must have heard about the Holy Trinity, but you pray in the wrong way. I have come to love you, godly hermits, I can see that you want to please God, but do not know how to serve Him. That's not the way to pray, but listen to me, and I'll teach you. I'll teach you not in some way of my own, but I'll teach you according to the Lord's scripture, the way God commanded all men to pray to Him."

And the Bishop began to expound to the hermits how God had revealed Himself to men; he explained to them about God the Father, God the Son, and God the Holy Ghost, and said:

"God the Son came down on earth to save men and taught them all to pray thus. Listen and repeat after me."

And the Bishop began to recite: "Our Father." And one hermit repeated: "Our Father," the second repeated, too: "Our Father," and the third, too, repeated: "Our Father."—"Which art in Heaven." The hermits, too, repeated: "Which art in Heaven." But the second hermit mixed up the words and said them wrong; and the tall, naked hermit could not pronounce them: his mouth was overgrown with whiskers, he could not pronounce clearly; and the ancient, toothless hermit mumbled indistinctly.

The Bishop repeated once again, and once again the hermits repeated. And down on a little rock sat the Bishop, and the hermits stood near him and stared at his mouth and repeated after him that which he was saying to them. And all day until evening the Bishop labored with them; and ten and twenty and a hundred times he would repeat a single word, and the hermits would repeat it after him. They would get mixed up, and he would correct them and make them repeat it all over again.

And the Bishop did not leave the hermits until he had taught them the whole of the Lord's Prayer. They recited it after him and they recited it by themselves. The first to understand it was the middle hermit and he repeated it all by himself. And the Bishop bade him say it again and again, and repeat again, and the others recited the entire prayer.

It had already begun to grow dark and the young moon was rising out of the sea when the Bishop rose to return to the ship. The Bishop took leave of the hermits, they all bowed to the ground before him. He raised them and embraced each one, bade them pray as he had taught them and got into the boat and went back to the ship.

And as he was going back to the ship the Bishop still heard the hermits loudly reciting in chorus the Lord's Prayer. They were approaching the ship, the hermits' voices were no longer heard, but one could see in the moonlight: standing on the shore, on the same spot, were the three hermits—the smallest one in the middle, and the tall one on the right, and the middle one on the left. The Bishop came up to the ship, climbed on deck, the anchor was weighed, the sails were unfurled, the wind filled them, set the ship in motion, and they sailed on. The Bishop went to the stern and sat down there and kept looking at the little island. At first the hermits could be seen, then they disappeared from view, only the little island could be seen, then the island disappeared, too; only the sea shimmered in the moonlight.

The pilgrims lay themselves down to sleep and all grew quiet on deck. But the Bishop did not feel like sleeping, he sat alone on the stern, gazed toward the place where the island had gone out of sight, and thought about the good hermits. He thought of how they had rejoiced in having learned the prayer and he thanked God for giving him the chance to help those godly hermits, to teach them the word of God.

The Bishop is sitting thus, thinking, gazing at the sea in the direction of the vanished island. And his sight is blurred—now here, now there the moonlight shimmers over the waves. Suddenly he sees something gleaming white in the path of the moon: is it a bird, a gull, or a little sail of a boat showing white? The Bishop peers closer. "A sailing boat," he thinks, "speeding after us. But how fast it is catching up with us. Just now it was far, far away and lo, it is appearing quite near. And the boat is no boat and it doesn't look like a sail. But something is speeding after us and catching up with us." And the Bishop cannot make out what it is: neither a boat, nor a bird, nor a fish! It looks like a man but is too big; and then a man couldn't be in the middle of the sea.—The Bishop rose, went up to the helmsman:

"Look," he said, "what is that?"

"What is that, my friend? What is it?" the Bishop keeps asking; but he can now see for himself—over the sea speed the hermits, their gray beards gleaming white, approaching the vessel as though it were standing still.

The helmsman looked round, was terror-stricken, let go of the helm and shouted in a loud voice:

"O Lord! the hermits are running after us over the sea as over dry land!"

The people heard him, rose, rushed to the stern. They all see: the hermits are speeding, hand in hand, the ones on the outside waving their arms, bidding the ship stop. All three speed over the water as over dry land, without moving their feet.

The vessel had been barely stopped when the hermits drew even with it, came right up alongside, raised their heads and spoke in unison:

"We have forgotten, servant of God, we have forgotten your teaching! As long as we kept reciting it we remembered it, we stopped reciting for an hour, one word escaped us, and we forgot—everything fell apart. We don't remember anything, teach us again."

The Bishop crossed himself, leaned over the side to the hermits and said:

"Your prayer, too, reaches God, godly hermits. It is not for me to teach you. Pray for us sinners!"

And the Bishop bowed to the ground before the hermits. And the hermits stopped, turned and went back over the sea. And until morning a radiance shone in the direction in which the hermits had disappeared.

MARK TWAIN

(1835–1910)

M ark Twain was the pen name of Samuel Clemens, who was born
in the village of Florida, Missouri, and grew up in Hannibal,
the town on the Mississippi River that figures so prominently in The
Adventures of Tom Sawyer *(1876) and* The Adventures of Huckleberry Finn *(1884). His father's death in 1847 forced Clemens to seek
work at an early age. He travelled extensively in the East, earning his
living as a printer hired by the day. In 1856 he became an apprentice
pilot on a Mississippi steamboat and, eighteen months later, a licensed
pilot. In 1861, hoping to profit from the get-rich-quick schemes of various
prospectors and entrepreneurs, he travelled with his brother to Nevada.
But Clemens profited mainly by writing humorous sketches for Nevada
and California newspapers (published under the pseudonym "Mark
Twain," a boatman's term for a sounding of two fathoms). His first book,*
Innocents Abroad *(1869), is Twain's satiric account of the travels of
a group of American tourists in Europe and the Holy Land. In it, Twain
pits the brash confidence of the New World's dynamic new nation against
the aristocratic absurdities of the old, a formula that proved very popular
and that he was to use again in* A Connecticut Yankee at King
Arthur's Court *(1889). The two novels for which Twain is most famous,*
Tom Sawyer *and* Huckleberry Finn, *followed, but they are only
superficially alike. The first is essentially a book for young people, written
in the high style that Twain could affect at will. The latter contains what
Bernard De Voto describes as "a vigor, a depth, and a multiplicity which
no other American novel surpasses," and a central character whom T.S.
Eliot saw as "one of the permanent symbolic figures of fiction not
unworthy to take a place with Ulysses, Faust, Don Quixote, Don Juan,
Hamlet and other discoveries which man has made about himself."
Despite his literary and financial success, Twain became increasingly
pessimistic about humanity in his later years. Losses due to bad investments, the death of a daughter, and his own failing health resulted in the
bitter skepticism articulated in* The Man That Corrupted Hadleyburg
(1900), What Is Man? *(1906) and* The Mysterious Stranger *(1916).
A revered figure to the end of his life, he received honorary doctorates
from Yale and Oxford, and was lionized by the press and the public, who
sought his opinion on every event of public interest. His reputation
endures because his work remains so eminently readable, and because
Twain discovered the vernacular American style that was to convey the
essence of his country's experience.*

The Notorious Jumping Frog of Calaveras County

I n compliance with the request of a friend of mine, who wrote me from the East, I called on good-natured, garrulous old Simon Wheeler, and inquired after my friend's friend, Leonidas W. Smiley, as requested to do, and I hereunto append the result. I have a lurking suspicion that *Leonidas W.* Smiley is a myth; that my friend never knew such a personage; and that he only conjectured that if I asked old Wheeler about him, it would remind him of his infamous *Jim* Smiley, and he would go to work and bore me to death with some exasperating reminiscence of him as long and as tedious as it should be useless to me. If that was the design, it succeeded.

I found Simon Wheeler dozing comfortably by the barroom stove of the dilapidated tavern in the decayed mining camp of Angel's, and I noticed that he was fat and bald-headed, and had an expression of winning gentleness and simplicity upon his tranquil countenance. He roused up, and gave me good day. I told him that a friend of mine had commissioned me to make some inquiries about a cherished companion of his boyhood named *Leonidas W.* Smiley—*Rev. Leonidas W.* Smiley, a young minister of the Gospel, who he had heard was at one time a resident of Angel's Camp. I added that if Mr. Wheeler could tell me anything about this Rev. Leonidas W. Smiley, I would feel under many obligations to him.

Simon Wheeler backed me into a corner and blockaded me there with his chair, and then sat down and reeled off the monotonous narrative which follows this paragraph. He never smiled, he never frowned, he never changed his voice from the gentle-flowing key to which he tuned his initial sentence, he never betrayed the slightest suspicion of enthusiasm; but all through the interminable narrative there ran a vein of impressive earnestness and sincerity, which showed me plainly that, so far from his imagining that there was anything ridiculous or funny about his story, he regarded it as a really important matter, and admired its two heroes as men of transcendent genius in *finesse*. I let him go on in his own way, and never interrupted him once.

"Rev. Leonidas W. H'm, Reverend Le—well, there was a feller here once by the name of *Jim* Smiley, in the winter of '49—or maybe it was the spring of '50—I don't recollect exactly, somehow, though what makes me think it was one or the other is because I remember the big flume warn't finished when he first come to the camp; but anyway, he was the curiousest man about always betting on anything that turned up you ever see, if he could get anybody to bet on the other side; and if he couldn't he'd change sides. Any way that suited the other man would suit *him*—any way just so's he got a bet, *he* was satisfied. But still he was lucky, uncommon lucky; he most always come out winner. He was always ready and laying for a chance; there couldn't be no solit'ry thing mentioned but that feller'd offer to bet on it, and take ary side you please, as I was just telling you. If there was a horse-race, you'd find him flush or you'd find him busted at the end of it; if there was a dog-fight, he'd bet on it; if there was a cat-fight, he'd bet on it; if there was a chicken-fight, he'd bet on it; why, if there was two birds setting on a fence, he would bet you which one would fly first; or if there was a camp-meeting, he would be there reg'lar to bet on Parson Walker, which he judged to be the best exhorter about here, and so he was too, and a good man. If he even see a straddle-bug start to go anywheres, he would bet you how long it would take him to get to—to wherever he was going to, and if you took him up, he would foller that straddle-bug to Mexico but what he would find out where he was bound for and how long he was on the road. Lots of the boys here has seen that Smiley, and can tell you about him. Why, it never made no difference to *him*—he'd bet on *any* thing—the dangdest feller. Parson Walker's wife laid very sick once, for a good while, and it seemed as if they warn't going to save her; but one morning he come in, and Smiley up and asked him how she was, and he said she was considerable better—thank the Lord for his inf'nite mercy—and coming on so smart that with the blessing of Prov'dence she'd get well yet; and Smiley, before he thought, says, 'Well, I'll resk two-and-a-half she don't anyway.'

"Thish-yer Smiley had a mare—the boys called her the fifteen-minute nag, but that was only in fun, you know, because of course she was faster than that—and he used to win money on that horse, for all she was so slow and always had the asthma, or the distemper, or the consumption, or something of that kind. They used to give her two or three hundred yards' start, and then pass her under way; but always at the fag end of the race she'd get excited and desperate like, and come cavorting and straddling up, and scattering her legs around limber, sometimes in the air, and sometimes out to one side among the fences, and kicking up m-o-r-e dust and raising m-o-r-e racket with her coughing and sneezing and blowing her nose—and *always* fetch up at the stand just about a neck ahead, as near as you could cipher it down.

"And he had a little small bull-pup, that to look at him you'd think he warn't worth a cent but to set around and look ornery and lay for a chance to steal something. But as soon as money was up on him he was a different dog; his under-jaw'd begin to stick out like the fo'castle of a steamboat, and his teeth would uncover and shine like the furnaces. And a dog might tackle him and bully-rag him, and bite him, and throw him over his shoulder two or three times, and Andrew Jackson—which was the name of the pup—Andrew Jackson would never let on but what *he* was satisfied, and hadn't expected nothing else—and the bets being doubled and doubled on the other side all the time, till the money was all up; and then all of a sudden he would grab that other dog jest by the j'int of his hind leg and freeze to it—no chaw, you understand, but only just grip and hang on till they throwed up the sponge, if it was a year. Smiley always come out winner on that pup, till he harnessed a dog once that didn't have no hind legs, because they'd been sawed off in a circular saw, and when the thing had gone along far enough, and the money was all up, and he come to make a snatch for his pet holt, he see in a minute how he'd been imposed on, and how the other dog had him in the door, so to speak, and he 'peared surprised, and then he looked sorter discouraged-like, and didn't try no more to win the fight, and so he got shucked out bad. He give Smiley a look, as much as to say his heart was broke, and it was *his* fault, for putting up a dog that hadn't no hind legs for him to take holt of, which was his main dependence in a fight, and then he limped off a piece and laid down and died. It was a good pup, was that Andrew Jackson, and would have made a name for hisself if he'd lived, for the stuff was in him and he had genius—I know it, because he hadn't no opportunities to speak of, and it don't stand to reason that a dog could make such a fight as he could under them circumstances if he hadn't no talent. It always makes me feel sorry when I think of that last fight of his'n, and the way it turned out.

"Well, thish-yer Smiley had rat-tarriers, and chicken cocks, and tom-cats and all them kind of things, till you couldn't rest, and you couldn't fetch nothing for him to bet on but he'd match you. He ketched a frog one day, and took him home, and said he cal'lated to educate him; and so he never done nothing for three months but set in his back yard and learn that frog to jump. And you bet you he *did* learn him, too. He'd give him a little punch behind, and the next minute you'd see that frog whirling in the air like a doughnut—see him turn one summer-set, or maybe a couple, if he got a good start, and come down flat-footed and all right, like a cat. He got him up so in the matter of ketching flies, and kep' him in practice so constant, that he'd nail a fly every time as fur as he could see him. Smiley said all a frog wanted was education, and he could do 'most anything—and I believe him. Why, I've seen him set Dan'l Webster down here on this floor—Dan'l Webster was the name of the frog—and sing out, 'Flies, Dan'l, flies!' and quicker'n you could wink he'd spring straight up and snake a fly off'n the counter there, and flop down on the floor ag'in as solid as a gob of mud, and fall to scratching the side of his head with his hind foot as indifferent as if he hadn't no idea he'd been doin' any more'n any frog might do. You never see a frog so modest and straight-for'ard as he was, for all he was so gifted. And when it come to fair and square jumping on a dead level, he could get over more ground at one straddle than any animal of his breed you ever see. Jumping on a dead level was his strong suit, you understand; and when it come to that, Smiley would ante up money on him as long as he had a red. Smiley was monstrous proud of his frog, and well he might be, for fellers that had traveled and been everywheres all said he laid over any frog that ever *they* see.

"Well, Smiley kep' the beast in a little lattice box, and he used to fetch him downtown sometimes and lay for a bet. One day a feller—a stranger in the camp, he was—come acrost him with his box, and says:

" 'What might it be that you've got in the box?'

"And Smiley says, sorter indifferent-like, 'It might be a parrot, or it might be a canary, maybe, but it ain't—it's only just a frog.'

"And the feller took it, and looked at it careful, and turned it round this way and that, and says, 'H'm—so 'tis. Well, what's *he* good for?'

" 'Well,' Smiley says, easy and careless, 'he's good enough for *one* thing, I should judge—he can outjump any frog in Calaveras County.'

"The feller took the box again, and took another long, particular look, and give it back to Smiley, and says, very deliberate. 'Well,' he says, 'I don't see no p'ints about that frog that's any better'n any other frog.'

" 'Maybe you don't,' Smiley says. 'Maybe you understand frogs and maybe you don't understand 'em; maybe you've had experience, and maybe you ain't only a amature, as it were. Anyways, I've got *my* opinion, and I'll resk forty dollars that he can outjump any frog in Calaveras County.'

"And the feller studied a minute, and then says, kinder sadlike, 'Well, I'm only a stranger here, and I ain't got no frog; but if I had a frog, I'd bet you.'

"And then Smiley says, 'That's all right—that's all right—if you'll hold my box a minute, I'll go and get you a frog.' And so the feller took the box, and put up his forty dollars along with Smiley's and set down to wait.

"So he set there a good while thinking and thinking to himself, and then he got the frog out and prized his mouth open and took a teaspoon and filled him full of quail-shot—filled him pretty near up to his chin—and set him on the floor. Smiley he went to the swamp and slopped around in the mud for a long time, and finally he ketched a frog, and fetched him in, and give him to this feller, and says:

" 'Now, if you're ready, set him alongside of Dan'l, with his fore paws just even with Dan'ls, and I'll give the word.' Then he says, 'One—two—three—*git*!' and him and the feller touched up the frogs from behind, and the new frog hopped off lively, but Dan'l give a heave, and hysted up his shoulders—so—like a Frenchman, but it warn't no use—he couldn't budge; he was planted as solid as a church, and he couldn't no more stir than if he was anchored out. Smiley was a good deal surprised, and he was disgusted too, but he didn't have no idea what the matter was, of course.

"The feller took the money and started away; and when he was going out at the door, he sorter jerked his thumb over his shoulder—so—at Dan'l, and says again, very deliberate, 'Well,' he says, 'I don't see no p'ints about that frog that's any bettern'n any other frog.'

"Smiley he stood scratching his head and looking down at Dan'l a long time, and at last he says, 'I do wonder what in the nation that frog throw'd off for—I wonder if there ain't something the matter with him— he 'pears to look mighty baggy, somehow.' And he ketched Dan'l by the nap of the neck, and hefted him, and says, 'Why blame my cats if he don't weigh five pound!' and turned him upside down and he belched out a double handful of shot. And then he see how it was, and he was the maddest man—he set the frog down and took out after that feller, but he never ketched him. And—"

[Here Simon Wheeler heard his name called from the front yard, and got up to see what was wanted.] And turning to me as he moved away, he said: "Just set where you are, stranger, and rest easy—I ain't going to be gone a second."

But, by your leave, I did not think that a continuation of the history of the enterprising vagabond *Jim* Smiley would be likely to afford me much information concerning the Rev. *Leonidas W.* Smiley, and so I started away.

At the door I met the sociable Wheeler returning, and he buttonholed me and recommenced:

"Well, thish-yer Smiley had a yaller one-eyed cow that didn't have no tail, only just a short stump like a bannanner, and—"

However, lacking both time and inclination, I did not wait to hear about the afflicted cow, but took my leave.

HENRY JAMES

(1843–1916)

*H*enry James was born in New York, the second son in a wealthy and distinguished family. His father inherited a fortune that gave him an income of $10 000 a year. When his sons, worried about what they should tell their friends, asked him how they should describe his occupation, he told them, "Just say I'm a student." His son Henry was educated in a variety of European and American schools. From a young age, he associated with writers. With the publication of his first signed story in the Atlantic Monthly in 1865, he began a professional career that was to span some 50 years. He published many remarkable novels, including masterpieces such as The Portrait of a Lady (1881) and The Ambassadors (1903), as well as distinguished literary criticism (his essays on the novel are essential reading for any student of the genre), a revealing autobiography, and more than 70 stories. He eventually settled in England and, as a result of his extensive travelling and con-tacts, came to be an expert on European literature and culture. His books contain definitive accounts of the encounters between American and European society. As his biographer Leon Edel suggests, "The secret of his enduring fame was simple: he had dealt exclusively with the myth of civilization; he had written about men and women in their struggle to control their emotions and passions within the forms and manners of society. He understood human motive and behavior and was the first of the modern psychological novelists." Edel goes on to note that the entire modern movement "drew upon his explorations of subjective worlds."

The Jolly Corner

I

"Every one asks me what I 'think' of everything," said Spencer Brydon; "and I make answer as I can—begging or dodging the question, putting them off with any nonsense. It wouldn't matter to any of them really," he went on, "for, even were it possible to meet in that stand-and-deliver way so silly a demand on so big a subject, my 'thoughts' would still be almost altogether about something that concerns only myself." He was talking to Miss Staverton, with whom for a couple of months now he had availed himself of every possible occasion to talk; this disposition and this resource, this comfort and support, as the situation in fact presented itself, having promptly enough taken the first place in the considerable array of rather unattenuated surprises attending his so strangely belated return to America. Everything was somehow a surprise; and that might be natural when one had so long and so consistently neglected everything, taken pains to give surprises so much margin for play. He had given them more than thirty years—thirty-three, to be exact; and they now seemed to him to have organised their performance quite on the scale of that licence. He had been twenty-three on leaving New York—he was fifty-six today: unless indeed he were to reckon as he had sometimes, since his repatriation, found himself feeling; in which case he would have lived longer than is often allotted to man. It would have taken a century, he repeatedly said to himself, and said also to Alice Staverton, it would have taken a longer absence and a more averted mind than those even of which he had been guilty, to pile up the differences, the newnesses, the queernesses, above all the bignesses, for the better or the worse, that at present assaulted his vision wherever he looked.

The great fact all the while however had been the incalculability; since he *had* supposed himself, from decade to decade, to be allowing, and in the most liberal and intelligent manner, for brilliancy of change. He actually saw that he had allowed for nothing; he missed what he would have been sure of finding, he found what he would never have imagined. Proportions and values were upside-down; the ugly things he had expected, the ugly things of his far-away youth, when he had too promptly waked up to a sense of the ugly—these uncanny phenomena placed him rather, as it happened, under the charm; whereas the "swagger" things, the modern, the monstrous, the famous things, those he had more particularly, like thousands of ingenuous enquirers every year, come over to see, were exactly his sources of dismay. They were as so many set traps for displeasure, above all for reaction, of which his restless tread was constantly pressing the spring. It was interesting, doubtless, the whole show, but it would have been too disconcerting hadn't a certain finer truth saved the situation. He had distinctly not, in this steadier light, come over *all* for the monstrosities; he had come, not only in the last analysis but quite on the face of the act, under an impulse with which they had nothing to do. He had come—putting the thing pompously— to look at his "property," which he had thus for a third of a century not been within four thousand miles of; or, expressing it less sordidly, he had yielded to the humour of seeing again his house on the jolly corner, as he usually, and quite fondly, described it—the one in which he had first seen the light, in which various members of his family had lived and had died, in which the holidays of his overschooled boyhood had been passed and the few social flowers of his chilled adolescence gathered, and which, alienated then for so long a period, had, through the successive deaths of his two brothers and the termination of old arrangements, come wholly into his hands. He was the owner of another, not quite so "good"—

the jolly corner having been, from far back, superlatively extended and consecrated; and the value of the pair represented his main capital, with an income consisting, in these later years, of their respective rents which (thanks precisely to their original excellent type) had never been depressingly low. He could live in "Europe," as he had been in the habit of living, on the product of these flourishing New York leases, and all the better since, that of the second structure, the mere number in its long row, having within a twelvemonth fallen in, renovation at a high advance had proved beautifully possible.

These were items of property indeed, but he had found himself since his arrival distinguishing more than ever between them. The house within the street, two bristling blocks westward, was already in course of reconstruction as a tall mass of flats; he had acceded, some time before, to overtures for this conversion—in which, now that it was going forward, it had been not the least of his astonishments to find himself able, on the spot, and though without a previous ounce of such experience, to participate with a certain intelligence, almost with a certain authority. He had lived his life with his back so turned to such concerns and his face addressed to those of so different an order that he scarce knew what to make of this lively stir, in a compartment of his mind never yet penetrated, of a capacity for business and a sense for construction. These virtues, so common all round him now, had been dormant in his own organism— where it might be said of them perhaps that they had slept the sleep of the just. At present, in the splendid autumn weather—the autumn at least was a pure boon in the terrible place—he loafed about his "work" undeterred, secretly agitated; not in the least "minding" that the whole proposition, as they said, was vulgar and sordid, and ready to climb ladders, to walk the plank, to handle materials and look wise about them, to ask questions, in fine, and challenge explanations and really "go into" figures.

It amused, it verily quite charmed him; and, by the same stroke, it amused, and even more, Alice Staverton, though perhaps charming her perceptibly less. She wasn't however going to be better off for it, as *he* was—and so astonishingly much: nothing was now likely, he knew, ever to make her better off than she found herself, in the afternoon of life, as the delicately frugal possessor and tenant of the small house in Irving Place to which she had subtly managed to cling through her almost unbroken New York career. If he knew the way to it now better than to any other address among the dreadful multiplied numberings which seemed to him to reduce the whole place to some vast ledger-page, overgrown, fantastic, of ruled and criss-crossed lines and figures—if he had formed, for his consolation, that habit, it was really not a little because of the charm of his having encountered and recognised, in the vast wilderness of the wholesale, breaking through the mere gross generalisation of wealth and force and success, a small still scene where items and shades, all delicate things, kept the sharpness of the notes of a high voice perfectly trained, and where economy hung about like the scent of a garden. His old friend lived with one maid and herself dusted her relics and trimmed her lamps and polished her silver; she stood off, in the awful modern crush, when she could, but she sallied forth and did battle when the challenge was really to "spirit," the spirit she after all confessed to, proudly and a little shyly, as to that of the better time, that of *their* common, their quite far-away and antediluvian social period and order. She made use of the street-cars when need be, the terrible things that people scrambled for as the panic-stricken at sea scramble for the boats; she affronted, inscrutably, under stress, all the public concussions and ordeals; and yet, with that slim mystifying grace of her appearance, which defied you to say if she were a fair young woman who looked older through trouble, or a fine smooth older one who looked young through successful indifference; with her precious reference, above all, to memories and histories into which he could enter, she was as exquisite for him as some pale pressed flower (a rarity to begin with), and, failing other sweetnesses, she was a sufficient reward of his effort. They had communities of knowledge, "their" knowledge (this discriminating possessive was always on her lips) of presences of the other age, presences all overlaid, in his case, by the experience of a man and the freedom of a wanderer, overlaid by pleasure, by infidelity, by passages of life that were strange and dim to her, just by "Europe" in short, but still unobscured, still exposed and cherished, under that pious visitation of the spirit from which she had never been diverted.

She had come with him one day to see how his "apartment-house" was rising; he had helped her over gaps and explained to her plans, and while they were there had happened to have, before her, a brief but lively discussion with the man in charge, the representative of the building-firm that had undertaken his work. He had found himself quite "standing-up" to this personage over a failure on the latter's part to observe some detail of one of their noted conditions, and had so lucidly urged his case that, besides ever so prettily flushing, at the time, for sympathy in his triumph, she had afterwards said to him (though to a slightly greater effect of irony) that he had clearly for too many years neglected a real gift. If he had but stayed at home he would have anticipated the inventor of the sky-scraper. If he had but stayed at home he would have discovered his genius in time really to start some new variety of awful architectural hare and run it till it burrowed in a gold-mine. He was to remember these words, while the weeks elapsed, for the small silver ring they had sounded over the queerest and deepest of his own lately most disguised and most muffled vibrations.

It had begun to be present to him after the first fortnight, it had broken out with the oddest abruptness, this particular wanton wonderment: it met him there—and this was the image under which he himself judged the matter, or at least, not a little, thrilled and flushed with it—very much as he might have been met by some strange figure, some unexpected occupant, at a turn of one of the dim passages of an empty house. The quaint analogy quite hauntingly remained with him, when he didn't indeed rather improve it by a still intenser form: that of his opening a door behind which he would have made sure of finding nothing, a door into a room shuttered and void, and yet so coming, with a great suppressed start, on some quite erect confronting presence, something planted in the middle of the place and facing him through the dusk. After that visit to the house in construction he walked with his companion to see the other and always so much the better one, which in the eastward direction formed one of the corners, the "jolly" one precisely, of the street now so generally dishonoured and disfigured in its westward reaches, and of the comparatively conservative Avenue. The Avenue still had pretensions, as Miss Staverton said, to decency; the old people had mostly gone, the old names were unknown, and here and there an old association seemed to stray, all vaguely, like some very aged person, out too late, whom you might meet and feel the impulse to watch or follow, in kindness, for safe restoration to shelter.

They went in together, our friends; he admitted himself with his key, as he kept no one there, he explained, preferring, for his reasons, to leave the place empty, under a simple arrangement with a good woman living in the neighbourhood and who came for a daily hour to open windows and dust and sweep. Spencer Brydon had his reasons and was growingly aware of them; they seemed to him better each time he was there, though he didn't name them all to his companion, any more than he told her as yet how often, how quite absurdly often, he himself came. He only let her see for the present, while they walked through the great blank rooms, that absolute vacancy reigned and that, from top to bottom, there was nothing but Mrs. Muldoon's broomstick, in a corner, to tempt the burglar. Mrs. Muldoon was then on the premises, and she loquaciously attended the visitors, preceding them from room to room and pushing back shutters and throwing up sashes—all to show them, as she remarked, how little there was to see. There was little indeed to see in the great gaunt shell where the main dispositions and the general apportionment of space, the style of an age of ampler allowances, had nevertheless for its master their honest pleading message, affecting him as some good old servant's, some lifelong retainer's appeal for a character, or even for a retiring-pension; yet it was also a remark of Mrs. Muldoon's that, glad as she was to oblige him by her noonday round, there was a request she greatly hoped he would never make of her. If he should wish her for any reason to come in after dark she would just tell him, if he "plased," that he must ask it of somebody else.

The fact that there was nothing to see didn't militate for the worthy woman against what one *might* see, and she put it frankly to Miss Staverton that no lady could be expected to like, could she? "craping up to thim top storeys in the ayvil hours." The gas and the electric light were off the house, and she fairly evoked a gruesome vision of her march through the great grey rooms—so many of them as there were too!—with her glimmering taper. Miss Staverton met her honest glare with a smile and the profession that she herself certainly would recoil from such an adventure. Spencer Brydon meanwhile held his peace—for the moment; the question of the "evil" hours in his old home had already become too grave for him. He had begun some time since to "crape," and he knew just why a packet of candles addressed to that pursuit had been stowed by his own hand, three weeks before, at the back of a drawer of the fine old sideboard that occupied, as a "fixture," the deep recess in the dining-room. Just now he laughed at his companions—quickly however changing the subject; for the reason that, in the first place, his laugh struck him even at that moment as starting the odd echo, the conscious human resonance (he scarce knew how to qualify it) that sounds made while he was there alone sent back to his ear or his fancy; and that, in the second, he imagined Alice Staverton for the instant on the point of asking him, with a divination, if he ever so prowled. There were divinations he was unprepared for, and he had at all events averted enquiry by the time Mrs. Muldoon had left them, passing on to other parts.

There was happily enough to say, on so consecrated a spot, that could be said freely and fairly; so that a whole train of declarations was precipitated by his friend's having herself broken out, after a yearning look round: "But I hope you don't mean they want you to pull *this* to pieces!" His answer came, promptly, with his re-awakened wrath: it was of course exactly what they wanted, and what they were "at" him for, daily, with the iteration of people who couldn't for their life understand a man's liability to decent feelings. He had found the place, just as it stood and beyond what he could express, an interest and a joy. There were values other than the beastly rent-values, and in short, in short—! But it was thus Miss Staverton took him up. "In short you're to make so good a thing of your sky-scraper that, living in luxury on *those* ill-gotten gains, you can afford for a while to be sentimental here!" Her smile had for him, with the words, the particular mild irony with which he found half her talk suffused; an irony without bitterness and that came, exactly, from her having so much imagination—not, like the cheap sarcasms with which one heard most people, about the world of "society," bid for the reputation of cleverness, from nobody's really having any. It was agreeable to him at this very moment to be sure that when he had answered, after a brief demur, "Well yes: so, precisely, you may put it!" her imagination would still do him justice. He explained that even if never a dollar were to come to him from the other house he would nevertheless cherish this one; and he dwelt, further, while they lingered and wandered, on the fact of the stupefaction he was already exciting, the positive mystification he felt himself create.

He spoke of the value of all he read into it, into the mere sight of the walls, mere shapes of the rooms, mere sound of the floors, mere feel, in his hand, of the old silver-plated knobs of the several mahogany doors, which suggested the pressure of the palms of the dead; the seventy years of the past in fine that these things represented, the annals of nearly three generations, counting his grandfather's, the one that had ended there, and the impalpable ashes of his long-extinct youth, afloat in the very air like microscopic motes. She listened to everything; she was a woman who answered intimately but who utterly didn't chatter. She scattered abroad therefore no cloud of words; she could assent, she could agree, above all she could encourage, without doing that. Only at the last she went a little further than he had done himself. "And then how do you know? You may still, after all, want to live here." It rather indeed pulled him up, for it wasn't what he had been thinking, at least in her sense of the words. "You mean I may decide to stay on for the sake of it?"

"Well, *with* such a home—!" But, quite beautifully, she had too much tact to dot so monstrous an *i*, and it was precisely an illustration of the way she didn't rattle. How could any one—of any wit—insist on any one else's "wanting" to live in New York?

"Oh," he said, "I *might* have lived here (since I had my opportunity early in life); I might have put in here all these years. Then everything would have been different enough—and, I dare say, 'funny' enough. But that's another matter. And then the beauty of it—I mean of my perversity, of my refusal to agree to a 'deal'—is just in the total absence of a reason. Don't you see that if I had a reason about the matter at all it would *have* to be the other way, and would then be inevitably a reason of dollars? There are no reasons here *but* of dollars. Let us therefore have none whatever—not the ghost of one."

They were back in the hall then for departure, but from where they stood the vista was large, through an open door, into the great square main saloon, with its almost antique felicity of brave spaces between windows. Her eyes came back from that reach and met his own a moment. "Are you very sure the 'ghost' of one doesn't, much rather, serve—?"

He had a positive sense of turning pale. But it was as near as they were then to come. For he made answer, he believed, between a glare and a grin: "Oh ghosts—of course the place must swarm with them! I should be ashamed of it if it didn't. Poor Mrs. Muldoon's right, and it's why I haven't asked her to do more than look in."

Miss Staverton's gaze again lost itself, and things she didn't utter, it was clear, came and went in her mind. She might even for the minute, off there in the fine room, have imagined some element dimly gathering. Simplified like the death-mask of a handsome face, it perhaps produced for her just then an effect akin to the stir of an expression in the "set" commemorative plaster. Yet whatever her impression may have been she produced instead a vague platitude. "Well, if it were only furnished and lived in—!"

She appeared to imply that in case of its being still furnished he might have been a little less opposed to the idea of a return. But she passed straight into the vestibule, as if to leave her words behind her, and the next moment he had opened the house-door and was standing with her on the steps. He closed the door and, while he re-pocketed his key, looking and down, they took in the comparatively harsh actuality of the Avenue, which reminded him of the assault of the outer light of the Desert on the traveller emerging from an Egyptian tomb. But he risked before they stepped into the street his gathered answer to her speech. "For me it *is* lived in. For me it *is* furnished." At which it was easy for her to sigh "Ah yes—!" all vaguely and discreetly; since his parents and his favourite sister, to say nothing of other kin, in numbers, had run their course and met their end there. That represented, within the walls, ineffaceable life.

It was a few days after this that, during an hour passed with her again, he had expressed his impatience of the too flattering curiosity—among the people he met—about his appreciation of New York. He had arrived at none at all that was socially producible, and as for that matter of his "thinking" (thinking the better or the worse of anything there) he was wholly taken up with one subject of thought. It was mere vain egoism, and it was moreover, if she liked, a morbid obsession. He found all things come back to the question of what he personally might have been, how he might have led his life and "turned out," if he had not so, at the outset, given it up. And confessing for the first time to the intensity within him of this absurd speculation—which but proved also, no doubt, the habit of too selfishly thinking—he affirmed the impotence there of any other source of interest, any other native appeal. "What would it have made for me, what would it have made of me? I keep for ever wondering, all idiotically; as if I could possibly know! I see what it has made of dozens of others, those I meet, and it positively aches within me, to the point of exasperation, that it would have made something of me as well. Only I can't make out *what*, and the worry of it, the small rage of curiosity never to be satisfied, brings back what I remember to have felt, once or twice, after judging best, for reasons, to burn some important letter unopened. I've been sorry, I've hated it—I've never known what was in the letter. You may of course say it's a trifle—!"

"I don't say it's a trifle," Miss Staverton gravely interrupted.

She was seated by her fire, and before her, on his feet and restless, he turned to and fro between this intensity of his idea and a fitful and unseeing inspection, through his single eye-glass, of the dear little old objects on her chimney-piece. Her interruption made him for an instant look at her harder. "I shouldn't care if you did!" he laughed, however; "and it's only a figure, at any rate, for the way I now feel. *Not* to have followed my perverse young course—and almost in the teeth of my father's curse, as I may say; not to have kept it up, so, 'over there,' from that day to this, without a doubt or a pang; not, above all, to have liked it, to have loved it, so much, loved it, no doubt, with such an abysmal conceit of my own preference: some variation from *that*, I say, must have produced some different effect for my life and for my 'form.' I should have stuck here—if it had been possible; and I was too young, at twenty-three, to judge, *pour deux sous*, whether it *were* possible. If I had waited I might have seen it was, and then I might have been, by staying here, something nearer to one of these types who have been hammered so hard and made so keen by their conditions. It isn't that I admire them so much—the question of any charm in them, or of any charm, beyond that of the rank money-passion, exerted by their conditions *for* them, has nothing to do with the matter: it's only a question of what fantastic, yet perfectly possible, development of my own nature I mayn't have missed. It comes over me that I had then a strange *alter ego* deep down somewhere within me, as the full-blown flower is in the small tight bud, and that I just took the course, I just transferred him to the climate, that blighted him for once and for ever."

"And you wonder about the flower," Miss Staverton said. "So do I, if you want to know; and so I've been wondering these several weeks. I believe in the flower," she continued, "I feel it would have been quite splendid, quite huge and monstrous."

"Monstrous above all!" her visitor echoed; "and I imagine, by the same stroke, quite hideous and offensive."

"You don't believe that," she returned; "if you did you wouldn't wonder. You'd know, and that would be enough for you. What you feel—and what I feel *for* you—is that you'd have had power."

"You'd have liked me that way?" he asked.

She barely hung fire. "How should I not have liked you?"

"I see. You'd have liked me, have preferred me, a billionaire!"

"How should I not have liked you?" she simply again asked.

He stood before her still—her question kept him motionless. He took it in, so much there was of it; and indeed his not otherwise meeting it testified to that. "I know at least what I am," he simply went on; "the other side of the medal's clear enough. I've not been edifying—I believe I'm thought in a hundred quarters to have been barely decent. I've followed strange paths and worshipped strange gods; it must have come to you again and again—in fact you've admitted to me as much—that I was leading, at any time these thirty years, a selfish frivolous scandalous life. And you see what it has made of me."

She just waited, smiling at him. "You see what it has made of *me*."

"Oh you're a person whom nothing can have altered. You were born to be what you are, anywhere, anyway: you've the perfection nothing else could have blighted. And don't you see how, without my exile, I shouldn't have been waiting till now—?" But he pulled up for the strange pang.

"The great thing to see," she presently said, "seems to me to be that it has spoiled nothing. It hasn't spoiled your being here at last. It hasn't spoiled this. It hasn't spoiled your speaking—" She also however faltered.

He wondered at everything her controlled emotion might mean. "Do you believe then—too dreadfully!—that I *am* as good as I might ever have been?"

"Oh no! Far from it!" With which she got up from her chair and was nearer to him. "But I don't care," she smiled.

"You mean I'm good enough?"

She considered a little. "Will you believe it if I say so? I mean will you let that settle your question for you?" And then as if making out in his face that he drew back from this, that he had some idea which, however absurd, he couldn't yet bargain away: "Oh you don't care either—but very differently: you don't care for anything but yourself."

Spencer Brydon recognised it—it was in fact what he had absolutely professed. Yet he importantly qualified. "*He* isn't myself. He's the just so totally other person. But I do want to see him," he added. "And I can. And I shall."

Their eyes met for a minute while he guessed from something in hers that she divined his strange sense. But neither of them otherwise expressed it, and her apparent understanding, with no protesting shock, no easy derision, touched him more deeply than anything yet, constituting for his stifled perversity, on the spot, an element that was like breatheable air. What she said however was unexpected. "Well, *I've* seen him."

"You—?"

"I've seen him in a dream."

"Oh a 'dream'—!" It let him down.

"But twice over," she continued. "I saw him as I see you now."

"You've dreamed the same dream—?"

"Twice over," she repeated. "The very same."

This did somehow a little speak to him, as it also gratified him. "You dream about me at that rate?"

"Ah about *him!*" she smiled.

His eyes again sounded her. "Then you know all about him." And as she said nothing more: "What's the wretch like?"

She hesitated, and it was as if he were pressing her so hard that, resisting for reasons of her own, she had to turn away. "I'll tell you some other time!"

II

It was after this that there was most of a virtue for him, most of a cultivated charm, most of a preposterous secret thrill, in the particular form of surrender to his obsession and of address to what he more and more believed to be his privilege. It was what in these weeks he was living for—since he really felt life to begin but after Mrs. Muldoon had retired from the scene and, visiting the ample house from attic to cellar, making sure he was alone, he knew himself in safe possession and, as he tacitly expressed it, let himself go. He sometimes came twice in the twenty-four hours; the moments he liked best were those of gathering dusk, of the short autumn twilight; this was the time of which, again and again, he found himself hoping most. Then he could, as seemed to him, most intimately wander and wait, linger and listen, feel his fine attention, never in his life before so fine, on the pulse of the great vague place: he preferred the lampless hour and only wished he might have prolonged each day the deep crepuscular spell. Later—rarely much before midnight, but then for a considerable vigil—he watched with his glimmering light; moving slowly, holding it high, playing it far, rejoicing above all, as much as he might, in open vistas, reaches of communication between rooms and by passages; the long straight chance or show, as he would have called it, for the revelation he pretended to invite. It was practice he found he could perfectly "work" without exciting remark; no one was in the least the wiser for it; even Alice Staverton, who was moreover a well of discretion, didn't quite fully imagine.

He let himself in and let himself out with the assurance of calm proprietorship; and accident so far favoured him that, if a fat Avenue "officer" had happened on occasion to see him entering at eleven-thirty, he had never yet, to the best of his belief, been noticed as emerging at two. He walked there on the crisp November nights, arrived regularly at the evening's end; it was as easy to do this after dining out as to take his way to a club or to his hotel. When he left his club, if he hadn't been dining out, it was ostensibly to go to his hotel; and when he left his hotel, if he had spent a part of the evening there, it was ostensibly to go to his club. Everything was easy in fine; everything conspired and promoted: there was truly even in the strain of his experience something that glossed over, something that salved and simplified, all the rest of consciousness. He circulated, talked, renewed, loosely and pleasantly, old relations— met indeed, so far as he could, new expectations and seemed to make out on the whole that in spite of the career, of such different contacts, which he had spoken of to Miss Staverton as ministering so little, for those who might have watched it, to edification, he was positively rather liked than not. He was a dim secondary social success—and all with people who had truly not an idea of him. It was all mere surface sound, this murmur of their welcome, this popping of their corks—just as his gestures of response were the extravagant shadows, emphatic in proportion as they meant little, of some game of *ombres chinoises*. He projected himself all day, in thought, straight over the bristling line of hard unconscious heads and into the other, the real, the waiting life; the life that, as soon as he had heard behind him the click of his great house-door, began for him, on the jolly corner, as beguilingly as the slow opening bars of some rich music follows the tap of the conductor's wand.

He always caught the first effect of the steel point of his stick on the old marble of the hall pavement, large black-and-white squares that he remembered as the admiration of his childhood and that had then made in him, as he now saw, for the growth of an early conception of style. This effect was the dim reverberating tinkle as of some far-off bell hung who should say where?—in the depths of the house, of the past, of that mystical other world that might have flourished for him had he not, for weal or woe, abandoned it. On this impression he did ever the same thing; he put his stick noiselessly away in a corner—feeling the place once more in the likeness of some great glass bowl, all precious concave crystal, set delicately humming by the play of a moist finger round its edge. The concave crystal held, as it were, this mystical other world, and the indescribably fine murmur of its rim was the sigh there, the scarce audible pathetic wail to his strained ear, of all the old baffled forsworn possibilities. What he did therefore by this appeal of his hushed presence was to wake them into such measure of ghostly life as they might still enjoy. They were shy, all but unappeasably shy, but they weren't really sinister; at least they weren't as he had hitherto felt them—before they had taken the Form he so yearned to make them take, the Form he at moments saw himself in the light of fairly hunting on tiptoe, the points of his evening-shoes, from room to room and from storey to storey.

That was the essence of his vision—which was all rank folly, if one would, while he was out of the house and otherwise occupied, but which took on the last verisimilitude as soon as he was placed and posted. He knew what he meant and what he wanted; it was as clear as the figure on a cheque presented in demand for cash. His *alter ego* "walked"—that was the note of his image of him, while his image of his motive for his own odd pastime was the desire to waylay him and meet him. He roamed, slowly, warily, but all restlessly, he himself did—Mrs. Muldoon had been right, absolutely, with her figure of their "craping"; and the presence he watched for would roam restlessly too. But it would be as cautious and as shifty; the conviction of its probable, in fact its already quite sensible, quite audible evasion of pursuit grew for him from night to night, laying on him finally a rigour to which nothing in his life had been comparable. It had been the theory of many superficially-judging persons, he knew, that he was wasting that life in a surrender to sensations, but he had tasted of no pleasure so fine as his actual tension, had been introduced to no sport that demanded at once the patience and the nerve of this stalking of a creature more subtle, yet at bay perhaps more formidable, than any beast of the forest. The terms, the comparisons, the very practices of the chase positively came again into play; there were even moments when passages of his occasional experience as a sportsman, stirred memories, from his younger time, of moor and mountain and desert, revived for him—and to the increase of his keenness—by the tremendous force of analogy. He found himself at moments—once he had placed his single light on some mantel-shelf or in some recess—stepping back into shelter or shade, effacing himself behind a door or in an embrasure, as he had sought of old the vantage of rock and tree; he found himself holding his breath and living in the joy of the instant, the supreme suspense created by big game alone.

He wasn't afraid (though putting himself the question as he believed gentlemen on Bengal tiger-shoots or in close quarters with the great bear of the Rockies had been known to confess to having put it); and this indeed—since here at least he might be frank!—because of the impression, so intimate and so strange, that he himself produced as yet a dread, produced certainly a strain, beyond the liveliest he was likely to feel. They fell for him into categories, they fairly became familiar, the signs, for his own perception, of the alarm his presence and his vigilance created; though leaving him always to remark, portentously, on his probably having formed a relation, his probably enjoying a consciousness, unique in the experience of man. People enough, first and last, had been in terror of apparitions, but who had ever before so turned the tables and become himself, in the apparitional world, an incalculable terror? He might have found this sublime had he quite dared to think of it; but he didn't too much insist, truly, on that side of his privilege. With habit and repetition he gained to an extraordinary degree the power to penetrate the dusk of distances and the darkness of corners, to resolve back into their innocence the treacheries of uncertain light, the evil-looking forms taken in the gloom by mere shadows, by accidents of the air, by shifting effects of perspective; putting down his dim luminary he could still wander on without it, pass into other rooms and, only knowing it was there behind him in case of need, see his way about, visually project for his purpose a comparative clearness. It made him feel, this acquired faculty, like some monstrous stealthy cat; he wondered if he would have glared at these moments with large shining yellow eyes, and what it mightn't verily be, for the poor hard-pressed *alter ego*, to be confronted with such a type.

He liked however the open shutters; he opened everywhere those Mrs. Muldoon had closed, closing them as carefully afterwards, so that she shouldn't notice: he liked—oh this he did like, and above all in the upper rooms!—the sense of the hard silver of the autumn stars through the window-panes, and scarcely less the flare of the street-lamps below, the white electric lustre which it would have taken curtains to keep out. This was human actual social; this was of the world he had lived in, and he was more at his ease certainly for the countenance, coldly general and impersonal, that all the while and in spite of his detachment it seemed to give him. He had support of course mostly in the rooms at the wide front and the prolonged side; it failed him considerably in the central shades and the parts at the back. But if he sometimes, on his rounds, was glad of his optical reach, so none the less often the rear of the house affected him as the very jungle of his prey. The place was there more subdivided; a large "extension" in particular, where small rooms for servants had been multiplied, abounded in nooks and corners, in closets and passages, in the ramifications especially of an ample back staircase over which he leaned, many a time, to look far down—not deterred from his gravity even while aware that he might, for a spectator, have figured some solemn simpleton playing at hide-and-seek. Outside in fact he might himself make that ironic *rapprochement*; but within the walls, and in spite of the clear windows, his consistency was proof against the cynical light of New York.

It had belonged to that idea of the exasperated consciousness of his victim to become a real test for him; since he had quite put it to himself from the first that, oh distinctly! he could "cultivate" his whole perception. He had felt it as above all open to cultivation—which indeed was but another name for his manner of spending his time. He was bringing it on, bringing it to perfection, by practice; in consequence of which it had grown so fine that he was now aware of impressions, attestations of his general postulate, that couldn't have broken upon him at once. This was the case more specifically with a phenomenon at last quite frequent for him in the upper rooms, the recognition—absolutely unmistakeable, and by a turn dating from a particular hour, his resumption of his campaign after a diplomatic drop, a calculated absence of three nights—of his being definitely followed, tracked at a distance carefully taken and to the express end that he should the less confidently, less arrogantly, appear to himself merely to pursue. It worried, it finally quite broke him up, for it proved, of all the conceivable impressions, the one least suited to his book. He was kept in sight while remaining himself—as regards the essence of his position—sightless, and his only recourse then was in abrupt turns, rapid recoveries of ground. He wheeled about, retracing his steps, as if he might so catch in his face at least the stirred air of some other quick revolution. It was indeed true that his fully dislocalised thought of these manoeuvres recalled to him Pantaloon, at the Christmas farce, buffeted and tricked from behind by ubiquitous Harlequin; but it left intact the influence of the conditions themselves each time he was re-exposed to them, so that in fact this association, had he suffered it to become constant, would on a certain side have but ministered to his intenser gravity. He had made, as I have said, to create on the premises the baseless sense of a reprieve, his three absences; and the result of the third was to confirm the after-effect of the second.

On his return, that night—the night succeeding his last intermission—he stood in the hall and looked up the staircase with a certainty more intimate than any he had yet known. "He's *there*, at the top, and waiting—not, as in general, falling back for disappearance. He's holding his ground, and it's the first time—which is a proof, isn't it? that something has happened for him." So Brydon argued with his hand on the banister and his foot on the lowest stair; in which position he felt as never before the air chilled by his logic. He himself turned cold in it, for he seemed of a sudden to know what now was involved. "Harder pressed?—yes, he takes it in, with its thus making clear to him that I've come, as they say, 'to stay.' He finally doesn't like and can't bear it, in the sense, I mean, that his wrath, his menaced interest, now balances with his dread. I've hunted him till he has 'turned': that, up there, is what has happened—he's the fanged or the antlered animal brought at last to bay." There came to him, as I say—but determined by an influence beyond my notation!—the acuteness of this certainty; under which however the next moment he had broken into a sweat that he would as little have consented to attribute to fear as he would have dared immediately to act upon it for enterprise. It marked none the less a prodigious thrill, a thrill that represented sudden dismay, no doubt, but also represented, and with the selfsame throb, the strangest, the most joyous, possibly the next minute almost the proudest, duplication of consciousness.

"He has been dodging, retreating, hiding, but now, worked up to anger, he'll fight!"—this intense impression made a single mouthful, as it were, of terror and applause. But what was wondrous was that the applause, for the felt fact, was so eager, since, if it was his other self he was running to earth, this ineffable identity was thus in the last resort not unworthy of him. It bristled there—somewhere near at hand, however, unseen still—as the hunted thing, even as the trodden worm of the adage *must* at last bristle; and Brydon at this instant tasted probably of a sensation more complex than had ever before found itself consistent with sanity. It was as if it would have shamed him that a character so associated with his own should triumphantly succeed in just skulking, should to the end not risk the open, so that the drop of this danger was, on the spot, a great lift of the whole situation. Yet with another rare shift of the same subtlety he was already trying to measure by how much more he himself might now be in peril of fear; so rejoicing that he could, in another form, actively inspire that fear, and simultaneously quaking for the form in which he might passively know it.

The apprehension of knowing it must after a little have grown in him, and the strangest moment of his adventure perhaps, the most memorable or really most interesting, afterwards, of his crisis, was the lapse of certain instants of concentrated conscious *combat*, the sense of a need to hold on to something, even after the manner of a man slipping and slipping on some awful incline; the vivid impulse, above all, to move, to act, to charge, somehow and upon something—to show himself, in a word, that he wasn't afraid. The state of "holding-on" was thus the state to which he was momentarily reduced; if there had been anything, in the great vacancy, to seize, he would presently have been aware of having clutched it as he might under a shock at home have clutched the nearest chair-back. He had been surprised at any rate—of this he *was* aware— into something unprecedented since his original appropriation of the place; he had closed his eyes, held them tight, for a long minute, as with that instinct of dismay and that terror of vision. When he opened them the room, the other contiguous rooms, extraordinarily, seemed lighter— so light, almost, that at first he took the change for day. He stood firm, however that might be, just where he had paused; his resistance had helped him—it was as if there were something he had tided over. He knew after a little what this was—it had been in the imminent danger of flight. He had stiffened his will against going; without this he would have made for the stairs, and it seemed to him that, still with his eyes closed, he would have descended them, would have known how, straight and swiftly, to the bottom.

Well, as he had held out, here he was—still at the top, among the more intricate upper rooms and with the gauntlet of the others, of all the rest of the house, still to run when it should be his time to go. He would go at his time—only at his time: didn't he go every night very much at the same hour? He took out his watch—there was light for that: it was scarcely a quarter past one, and he had never withdrawn so soon. He reached his lodgings for the most part at two—with his walk of a quarter of an hour. He would wait for the last quarter—he wouldn't stir till then; and he kept his watch there with his eyes on it, reflecting while he held it that this deliberate wait, a wait with an effort, which he recognised, would serve perfectly for the attestation he desired to make. It would prove his courage—unless indeed the latter might most be proved by his budging at last from his place. What he mainly felt now was that, since he hadn't originally scuttled, he had his dignities—which had never in his life seemed so many—all to preserve and to carry aloft. This was before him in truth as a physical image, an image almost worthy of an age of greater romance. That remark indeed glimmered for him only to glow the next instant with a finer light; since what age of romance, after all, could have matched either the state of his mind or, "objectively," as they said, the wonder of his situation? The only difference would have been that, brandishing his dignities over his head as in a parchment scroll, he might then—that is in the heroic time—have proceeded downstairs with a drawn sword in his other grasp.

At present, really, the light he had set down on the mantel of the next room would have to figure his sword; which utensil, in the course of a minute, he had taken the requisite number of steps to possess himself of. The door between the rooms was open, and from the second another door opened to a third. These rooms, as he remembered, gave all three upon a common corridor as well, but there was a fourth, beyond them, without issue save through the preceding. To have moved, to have heard his step again, was appreciably a help; though even in recognising this he lingered once more a little by the chimney-piece on which his light had rested. When he next moved, just hesitating where to turn, he found himself considering a circumstance that, after his first and comparatively vague apprehension of it, produced in him the start that often attends some pang of recollection, the violent shock of having ceased happily to forget. He had come into sight of the door in which the brief chain of communication ended and which he now surveyed from the nearer threshold, the one not directly facing it. Placed at some distance to the left of this point, it would have admitted him to the last room of the four, the room without other approach or egress, had it not, to his intimate conviction, been closed *since* his former visitation, the matter probably of a quarter of an hour before. He stared with all his eyes at the wonder of the fact, arrested again where he stood and again holding his breath while he sounded its sense. Surely it had been *subsequently* closed—that is it had been on his previous passage indubitably open!

He took it full in the face that something had happened between— that he couldn't not have noticed before (by which he meant on his original tour of all the rooms that evening) that such a barrier had exceptionally presented itself. He had indeed since that moment undergone an agitation so extraordinary that it might have muddled for him any earlier view; and he tried to convince himself that he might perhaps then have gone into the room and, inadvertently, automatically, on coming out, have drawn the door after him. The difficulty was that this exactly was what he never did; it was against his whole policy, as he might have said, the essence of which was to keep vistas clear. He had them from the first, as he was well aware, quite on the brain: the strange apparition, at the far end of one of them, of his baffled "prey" (which had become by so sharp an irony so little the term now to apply!) was the form of success his imagination had most cherished, projecting into it always a refinement of beauty. He had known fifty times the start of perception that had afterwards dropped; had fifty times gasped to himself "There!" under some fond brief hallucination. The house, as the case stood, admirably lent itself; he might wonder at the taste, the native architecture of the particular time, which could rejoice so in the multiplication of doors— the opposite extreme to the modern, the actual almost complete proscription of them; but it had fairly contributed to provoke this obsession of the presence encountered telescopically, as he might say, focussed and studied in diminishing perspective and as by a rest for the elbow.

It was with these considerations that his present attention was charged—they perfectly availed to make what he saw portentous. He *couldn't*, by any lapse, have blocked that aperture; and if he hadn't, if it was unthinkable, why what else was clear but that there had been another agent? Another agent?—he had been catching, as he felt, a moment back, the very breath of him; but when had he been so close as in this simple, this logical, this completely personal act? It was so logical, that is, that one might have *taken* it for personal; yet for what did Brydon take it, he asked himself, while, softly panting, he felt his eyes almost leave their sockets. Ah this time at last they *were*, the two, the opposed projections of him, in presence; and this time, as much as one would, the question of danger loomed. With it rose, as not before, the question of courage— for what he knew the blank face of the door to say to him was "Show us how much you have!" It stared, it glared back at him with that challenge; it put to him the two alternatives: should he just push it open or not? Oh to have this consciousness was to *think*—and to think, Brydon knew, as he stood there, was, with the lapsing moments, not to have acted! Not to have acted—that was the misery and the pang—was even still not to act; was in fact *all* to feel the thing in another, in a new and terrible way. How long did he pause and how long did he debate? There was presently nothing to measure it; for his vibration had already changed—as just by the effect of its intensity. Shut up there, at bay, defiant, and with the prodigy of the thing palpably proveably *done*, thus giving notice like some stark signboard—under that accession of accent the situation itself had turned; and Brydon at last remarkably made up his mind on what it had turned to.

It had turned altogether to a different admonition; to a supreme hint, for him, of the value of Discretion! This slowly dawned, no doubt—for it could take its time; so perfectly, on his threshold, had he been stayed, so little as yet had he either advanced or retreated. It was the strangest of all things that now when, by his taking ten steps and applying his hand to a latch, or even his shoulder and his knee, if necessary, to a panel, all the hunger of his prime need might have been met, his high curiosity crowned, his unrest assuaged—it was amazing, but it was also exquisite and rare, that insistence should have, at a touch, quite dropped from him. Discretion—he jumped at that; and yet not, verily, at such a pitch, because it saved his nerves or his skin, but because, much more valuably, it saved the situation. When I say he "jumped" at it I feel the consonance of this term with the fact that—at the end indeed of I know not how long—he did move again, he crossed straight to the door. He wouldn't touch it—it seemed now that he might *if* he would: he would only just wait there a little, to show, to prove, that he wouldn't. He had thus another station, close to the thin partition by which revelation was denied him; but with his eyes bent and his hands held off in a mere intensity of stillness. He listened as if there had been something to hear, but this attitude, while it lasted, was his own communication. "If you won't then—good: I spare you and I give up. You affect me as by the appeal positively for pity: you convince me that for reasons rigid and sublime—what do I know?—we both of us should have suffered. I respect them then, and, though moved and privileged as, I believe, it has never been given to man, I retire, I renounce—never, on my honour, to try again. So rest for ever—and let *me!*"

That, for Brydon was the deep sense of this last demonstration—solemn, measured, directed, as he felt it to be. He brought it to a close, he turned away; and now verily he knew how deeply he had been stirred. He retraced his steps, taking up his candle, burnt, he observed, well-nigh to the socket, and marking again, lighten it as he would, the distinctness of his footfall; after which, in a moment, he knew himself at the other side of the house. He did here what he had not yet done at these hours—he opened half a casement, one of those in the front, and let in the air of the night; a thing he would have taken at any time previous for a sharp rupture of his spell. His spell was broken now, and it didn't matter—broken by his concession and his surrender, which made it idle henceforth that he should ever come back. The empty street—its other life so marked even by the great lamplit vacancy—was within call, within touch; he stayed there as to be in it again, high above it though he was still perched; he watched as for some comforting common fact, some vulgar human note, the passage of a scavenger or a thief, some night-bird however base. He would have blessed that sign of life; he would have welcomed positively the slow approach of his friend the policeman, whom he had hitherto only sought to avoid, and was not sure that if the patrol had come into sight he mightn't have felt the impulse to get into relation with it, to hail it, on some pretext, from his fourth floor.

The pretext that wouldn't have been too silly or too compromising, the explanation that would have saved his dignity and kept his name, in such a case, out of the papers, was not definite to him: he was so occupied with the thought of recording his Discretion—as an effect of the vow he had just uttered to his intimate adversary—that the importance of this loomed large and something had overtaken all ironically his sense of proportion. If there had been a ladder applied to the front of the house, even one of the vertiginous perpendiculars employed by painters and roofers and sometimes left standing overnight, he would have managed somehow, astride of the window-sill, to compass by outstretched leg and arm that mode of descent. If there had been some such uncanny thing as he had found in his room at hotels, a workable fire-escape in the form of notched cable or a canvas shoot, he would have availed himself of it as a proof—well, of his present delicacy. He nursed that sentiment, as the question stood, a little in vain, and even—at the end of he scarce knew, once more, how long—found it, as by the action on his mind of the failure of response of the outer world, sinking back to vague anguish. It seemed to him he had waited an age for some stir of the great grim hush; the life of the town was itself under a spell—so unnaturally, up and down the whole prospect of known and rather ugly objects, the blankness and the silence lasted. Had they ever, he asked himself, the hard-faced houses, which had begun to look livid in the dim dawn, had they ever spoken so little to any need of his spirit? Great builded voids, great crowded still-nesses put on, often, in the heart of cities, for the small hours, a sort of sinister mask, and it was of this large collective negation that Brydon presently became conscious—all the more that the break of day was, almost incredibly, now at hand, proving to him what a night he had made of it.

He looked again at his watch, saw what had become of his time-values (he had taken hours for minutes—not, as in other tense situations, minutes for hours) and the strange air of the streets was but the weak, the sullen flush of a dawn in which everything was still locked up. His choked appeal from his own open window had been the sole note of life, and he could but break off at last as for a worse despair. Yet while so deeply demoralised he was capable again of an impulse denoting—at least by his present measure—extraordinary resolution; of retracing his steps to the spot where he had turned cold with the extinction of his last pulse of doubt as to there being in the place another presence than his own. This required an effort strong enough to sicken him; but he had his reason, which over-mastered for the moment everything else. There was the whole of the rest of the house to traverse, and how should he screw himself to that if the door he had seen closed were at present open? He could hold to the idea that the closing had practically been for him an act of mercy, a chance offered him to descend, depart, get off the ground and never again profane it. This conception held together, it worked; but what it meant for him depended now clearly on the amount of forbearance his recent action, or rather his recent inaction, had engendered. The image of the "presence," whatever it was, waiting there for him to go—this image had not yet been so concrete for his nerves as when he stopped short of the point at which certainty would have come to him. For, with all his resolution, or more exactly with all his dread, he did stop short—he hung back from really seeing. The risk was too great and his fear too definite: it took at this moment an awful specific form.

He knew—yes, as he had never known anything—that, *should* he see the door open, it would all too abjectly be the end of him. It would mean that the agent of his shame—for his shame was the deep abjection—was once more at large and in general possession; and what glared him thus in the face was the act that this would determine for him. It would send him straight about to the window he had left open, and by that window, be long ladder and dangling rope as absent as they would, he saw himself uncontrollably insanely fatally take his way to the street. The hideous chance of this he at least could avert; but he could only avert it by recoiling in time from assurance. He had the whole house to deal with, this fact was still there; only he now knew that uncertainty alone could start him. He stole back from where he had checked himself—merely to do so was suddenly like safety—and, making blindly for the greater staircase, left gaping rooms and sounding passages behind. Here was the top of the stairs, with a fine large dim descent and three spacious landings to mark off. His instinct was all for mildness, but his feet were harsh on the floors, and, strangely, when he had in a couple of minutes become aware of this, it counted somehow for help. He couldn't have spoken, the tone of his voice would have scared him, and the common conceit or resource of "whistling in the dark" (whether literally or figuratively) have appeared basely vulgar; yet he liked none the less to hear himself go, and when he had reached his first landing—taking it all with no rush, but quite steadily—that stage of success drew from him a gasp of relief.

The house, withal, seemed immense, the scale of space again inordinate; the open rooms to no one of which his eyes deflected, gloomed in their shuttered state like mouths of caverns; only the high skylight that formed the crown of the deep well created for him a medium in which he could advance, but which might have been, for queerness of colour, some watery under-world. He tried to think of something noble, as that his property was really grand, a splendid possession; but this nobleness took the form too of the clear delight with which he was finally to sacrifice it. They might come in now, the builders, the destroyers—they might come as soon as they would. At the end of two flights he had dropped to another zone, and from the middle of the third, with only one more left, he recognised the influence of the lower windows, of half-drawn blinds, of the occasional gleam of street-lamps, of the glazed spaces of the vestibule. This was the bottom of the sea, which showed an illumination of its own and which he even saw paved—when at a given moment he drew up to sink a long look over the banisters—with the marble squares of his childhood. By that time indubitably he felt, as he might have said in a commoner cause, better; it had allowed him to stop and draw breath, and the ease increased with the sight of the old black-and-white slabs. But what he most felt was that now surely, with the element of impunity pulling him as by hard firm hands, the case was settled for what he might have seen above had he dared that last look. The closed door, blessedly remote now, was still closed—and he had only in short to reach that of the house.

He came down further, he crossed the passage forming the access to the last flight; and if here again he stopped an instant it was almost for the sharpness of the thrill of assured escape. It made him shut his eyes— which opened again to the straight slope of the remainder of the stairs. Here was impunity still, but impunity almost excessive; inasmuch as the side-lights and the high fan-tracery of the entrance were glimmering straight into the hall; an appearance produced, he the next instant saw, by the fact that the vestibule gaped wide, that the hinged halves of the inner door had been thrown far back. Out of that again the *question* sprang at him, making his eyes, as he felt, half-start from his head, as they had done, at the top of the house, before the sign of the other door. If he had left that one open, hadn't he left this one closed, and wasn't he now in *most* immediate presence of some inconceivable occult activity? It was as sharp, the question, as a knife in his side, but the answer hung fire still and seemed to lose itself in the vague darkness to which the thin admitted dawn, glimmering archwise over the whole outer door, made a semicircu- lar margin, a cold silvery nimbus that seemed to play a little as he looked— to shift and expand and contract.

It was as if there had been something within it, protected by indistinct- ness and corresponding in extent with the opaque surface behind, the painted panels of the last barrier to his escape, of which the key was in his pocket. The indistinctness mocked him even while he stared, affected him as somehow shrouding or challenging certitude, so that after faltering an instant on his step he let himself go with the sense that here *was* at last something to meet, to touch, to take, to know—something all unnatu- ral and dreadful, but to advance upon which was the condition for him either of liberation or of supreme defeat. The penumbra, dense and dark, was the virtual screen of a figure which stood in it as still as some image erect in a niche or as some black-vizored sentinel guarding a treasure. Brydon was to know afterwards, was to recall and make out, the particular thing he had believed during the rest of his descent. He saw, in its great grey glimmering margin, the central vagueness diminish, and he felt it to be taking the very form toward which, for so many days, the passion of his curiosity had yearned. It gloomed, it loomed, it was something, it was somebody, the prodigy of a personal presence.

Rigid and conscious, spectral yet human, a man of his own substance and stature waited there to measure himself with his power to dismay. This only could it be—this only till he recognised, with his advance, that what made the face dim was the pair of raised hands that covered it and in which, so far from being offered in defiance, it was buried as for dark deprecation. So Brydon, before him, took him in; with every fact of him now, in the higher light, hard and acute—his planted stillness, his vivid truth, his grizzled bent head and white masking hands, his queer actuality of evening-dress, of dangling double eye-glass, of gleaming silk lappet and white linen, of pearl button and gold watch-guard and polished shoe. No portrait by a great modern master could have presented him with more intensity, thrust him out of his frame with more art, as if there had been "treatment," of the consummate sort, in his every shade and salience. The revulsion, for our friend, had become, before he knew it, immense— this drop, in the act of apprehension, to the sense of his adversary's inscrutable manoeuvre. That meaning at least, while he gaped, it offered him; for he could but gape at his other self in this other anguish, gape as a proof that *he*, standing there for the achieved, the enjoyed, the triumphant life, couldn't be faced in his triumph. Wasn't the proof in the splendid covering hands, strong and completely spread?—so spread and so intentional that, in spite of a special verity that surpassed every other, the fact that one of these hands had lost two fingers, which were reduced to stumps, as if accidentally shot away, the face was effectually guarded and saved.

"Saved," though, *would* it be?—Brydon breathed his wonder till the very impunity of his attitude and the very insistence of his eyes produced, as he felt, a sudden stir which showed the next instant as a deeper portent, while the head raised itself, the betrayal of a braver purpose. The hands, as he looked, began to move, to open; then, as if deciding in a flash, dropped from the face and left it uncovered and presented. Horror, with the sight, had leaped into Brydon's throat, gasping there in a sound he couldn't utter; for the bared identity was too hideous as *his*, and his glare was the passion of his protest. The face, *that* face, Spencer Brydon's?—he searched it still, but looking away from it in dismay and denial, falling straight from his height of sublimity. It was unknown, inconceivable, awful, disconnected from any possibility—! He had been "sold," he inwardly moaned, stalking such game as this: the presence before him was a presence, the horror within him a horror, but the waste of his nights had been only grotesque and the success of his adventure an irony. Such an identify fitted his at *no* point, made its alternative monstrous. A thousand times yes, as it came upon him nearer now—the face was the face of a stranger. It came upon him nearer now, quite as one of those expanding fantastic images projected by the magic lantern of childhood; for the stranger, whoever he might be, evil, odious, blatant, vulgar, had advanced as for aggression, and he knew himself give ground. Then harder pressed still, sick with the force of his shock, and falling back as under the hot breath and the roused passion of a life larger than his own, a rage of personality before which his own collapsed, he felt the whole vision turn to darkness and his very feet give way. His head went round; he was going; he had gone.

III

What had next brought him back, clearly—though after how long?—was Mrs. Muldoon's voice, coming to him from quite near, from so near that he seemed presently to see her as kneeling on the ground before him while he lay looking up at her; himself not wholly on the ground, but half-raised and upheld—conscious, yes, of tenderness of support and, more particularly, of a head pillowed in extraordinary softness and faintly refreshing fragrance. He considered, he wondered, his wit but half at his service; then another face intervened, bending more directly over him, and he finally knew that Alice Staverton had made her lap an ample and perfect cushion to him, and that she had to this end seated herself on the lowest degree of the staircase, the rest of his long person remaining stretched on his old black-and-white slabs. They were cold, these marble squares of his youth; but *he* somehow was not, in this rich return of consciousness—the most wonderful hour, little by little, that he had ever known, leaving him, as it did, so gratefully, so abysmally passive, and yet as with a treasure of intelligence waiting all round him for quiet appropriation; dissolved, he might call it, in the air of the place and producing the golden glow of a late autumn afternoon. He had come back, yes—come back from further away than any man but himself had ever travelled; but it was strange how with this sense what he had come back *to* seemed really the great thing, and as if his prodigious journey had been all for the sake of it. Slowly but surely his consciousness grew, his vision of his state thus completing itself: he had been miraculously *carried* back—lifted and carefully borne as from where he had been picked up, the uttermost end of an interminable grey passage. Even with this he was suffered to rest, and what had now brought him to knowledge was the break in the long mild motion.

It had brought him to knowledge, to knowledge—yes, this was the beauty of his state; which came to resemble more and more that of a man who has gone to sleep on some news of a great inheritance, and then, after dreaming it away, after profaning it with matters strange to it, has waked up again to serenity of certitude and has only to lie and watch it grow. This was the drift of his patience—that he had only to let it shine on him. He must moreover, with intermissions, still have been lifted and borne; since why and how else should he have known himself, later on, with the afternoon glow intenser, no longer at the foot of his stairs— situated as these now seemed at that dark other end of his tunnel—but on a deep window-bench of his high saloon, over which had been spread, couch-fashion, a mantle of soft stuff lined with grey fur that was familiar to his eyes and that one of his hands kept fondly feeling as for its pledge of truth. Mrs. Muldoon's face had gone, but the other, the second he had recognised, hung over him in a way that showed how he was still propped and pillowed. He took it all in, and the more he took it the more it seemed to suffice: he was as much at peace as if he had had food and drink. It was the two women who had found him, on Mrs. Muldoon's having plied, at her usual hour, her latch-key—and on her having above all arrived while Miss Staverton still lingered near the house. She had been turning away, all anxiety, from worrying the vain bell-handle— her calculation having been the hour of the good woman's visit; but the latter, blessedly, had come up while she was still there, and they had entered together. He had then lain, beyond the vestibule, very much as he was lying now—quite, that is, as he appeared to have fallen, but all so wondrously without bruise or gash; only in a depth of stupor. What he most took in, however, at present, with the steadier clearance, was that Alice Staverton had for a long unspeakable moment not doubted he was dead.

"It must have been that I *was*." He made it out as she held him. "Yes— I can only have died. You brought me literally to life. Only," he wondered, his eyes rising to her, "only, in the name of all the benedictions, how?"

It took her but an instant to bend her face and kiss him, and something in the manner of it, and in the way her hands clasped and locked his head while he felt the cool charity and virtue of her lips, something in all this beatitude somehow answered everything. "And now I keep you," she said.

"Oh keep me, keep me!" he pleaded while her face still hung over him: in response to which it dropped again and stayed close, clingingly close. It was the seal of their situation—of which he tasted the impress for a long blissful moment in silence. But he came back. "Yet how did you know—?"

"I was uneasy. You were to have come, you remember—and you had sent no word."

"Yes, I remember—I was to have gone to you at one today." It caught on to their "old" life and relation—which were so near and so far. "I was still out there in my strange darkness—where was it, what was it? I must have stayed there so long." He could but wonder at the depth and the duration of his swoon.

"Since last night?" she asked with a shade of fear for her possible indiscretion.

"Since this morning—it must have been: the cold dim dawn of today. Where have I been," he vaguely wailed, "where have I been?" He felt her hold him close, and it was as if this helped him now to make in all security his mild moan. "What a long dark day!"

All in her tenderness she had waited a moment. "In the cold dim dawn?" she quavered.

But he had already gone on piecing together the parts of the whole prodigy. "As I didn't turn up you came straight—?"

She barely cast about. "I went first to your hotel—where they told me of your absence. You had dined out last evening and hadn't been back since. But they appeared to know you had been at your club."

"So you had the idea of *this*—?"

"Of what?" she asked in a moment.

"Well—of what has happened."

"I believed at least you'd have been here. I've known, all along," she said, "that you've been coming."

" 'Known' it—?"

"Well, I've believed it. I said nothing to you after that talk we had a month ago—but I felt sure. I knew you *would*," she declared.

"That I'd persist, you mean?"

"That you'd see him."

"Ah but I didn't!" cried Brydon with his long wail. "There's somebody— an awful beast; whom I brought, too horribly, to bay. But it's not me."

At this she bent over him again, and her eyes were in his eyes. "No— it's not you." And it was as if, while her face hovered, he might have made out in it, hadn't it been so near, some particular meaning blurred by a smile. "No, thank heaven," she repeated—"it's not you! Of course it wasn't to have been."

"Ah but it *was*," he gently insisted. And he stared before him now as he had been staring for so many weeks. "I was to have known myself."

"You couldn't!" she returned consolingly. And then reverting, and as if to account further for what she had herself done, "But it wasn't only *that*, that you hadn't been at home," she went on. "I waited till the hour at which we had found Mrs. Muldoon that day of my going with you; and she arrived, as I've told you, while, failing to bring any one to the door, I lingered in my despair on the steps. After a little, if she hadn't come, by such a mercy, I should have found means to hunt her up. But it wasn't, said Alice Staverton, as if once more with her fine intention— "it wasn't only that."

His eyes, as he lay, turned back to her. "What more then?"

She met it, the wonder she had stirred. "In the cold dim dawn, you say? Well, in the cold dim dawn of this morning I too saw you."

"Saw *me*—?"

"Saw *him*," said Alice Staverton. "It must have been at the same moment."

He lay an instant taking it in—as if he wished to be quite reasonable. "At the same moment?"

"Yes—in my dream again, the same one I've named to you. He came back to me. Then I knew it for a sign. He had come to you."

At this Brydon raised himself; he had to see her better. She helped him when she understood his movement, and he sat up, steadying himself beside her there on the window-bench and with his right hand grasping her left. "*He* didn't come to me."

"You came to yourself," she beautifully smiled.

"Ah I've come to myself now—thanks to you, dearest. But this brute, with his awful face—this brute's a black stranger. He's none of *me*, even as I *might* have been," Brydon sturdily declared.

But she kept the clearness that was like the breath of infallibility. "Isn't the whole point that you'd have been different?"

He almost scowled for it. "As different as *that*—?"

Her look again was more beautiful to him than the things of this world. "Haven't you exactly wanted to know *how* different? So this morning," she said, "you appeared to me."

"Like *him*?"

"A black stranger!"

"Then how did you know it was I?"

"Because, as I told you weeks ago, my mind, my imagination, had worked so over what you might, what you mightn't have been—to show you, you see, how I've thought of you. In the midst of that you came to me—that my wonder might be answered. So I knew," she went on; "and believed that, since the question held you too so fast, as you told me that day, you too would see for yourself. And when this morning I again saw I knew it would be because you had—and also then, from the first moment, because you somehow wanted me. *He* seemed to tell me of that. So why," she strangely smiled, "shouldn't I like him?"

It brought Spencer Brydon to his feet. "You 'like' that horror—?"

"I could have liked him. And to me," she said, "he was no horror. I had accepted him."

" 'Accepted'—?" Brydon oddly sounded.

"Before, for the interest of his difference—yes. And as *I* didn't disown him, as *I* knew him—which you at last, confronted with him in his difference, so cruelly didn't, my dear—well, he must have been, you see, less dreadful to me. And it may have pleased him that I pitied him."

She was beside him on her feet, but still holding his hand—still with her arm supporting him. But though it all brought for him thus a dim light, "You 'pitied' him?" he grudgingly, resentfully asked.

"He has been unhappy; he has been ravaged," she said.

"And haven't I been unhappy? Am not I—you've only to look at me!—ravaged?"

"Ah I don't say I like him *better*," she granted after a thought. "But he's grim, he's worn—and things have happened to him. He doesn't make shift, for sight, with your charming monocle."

"No"—it struck Brydon: "I couldn't have sported mine 'downtown.' They'd have guyed me there."

"His great convex pince-nez—I saw it, I recognised the kind—is for his poor ruined sight. And his poor right hand—!"

"Ah!" Brydon winced—whether for his proved identity or for his lost fingers. Then, "He has a million a year," he lucidly added. "But he hasn't you."

"And he isn't—no, he isn't—*you!*" she murmured as he drew her to his breast.

GUY DE MAUPASSANT

(1850–1893)

G uy de Maupassant was born in Normandy near the coastal town of Dieppe. His mother, a childhood friend of Gustave Flaubert, had literary ambitions for her son from the beginning and took charge of his early education. In 1863 de Maupassant was sent to a Catholic boarding school, where he seems to have done well. He wrote poetry from an early age and made the acquaintance of the English poet Algernon Charles Swinburne during a stay at a coastal resort. He worked in Paris as a clerk in the naval ministry and there became part of a literary circle that included Turgenev, Daudet, Zola, and Flaubert. Flaubert greatly admired his young protégé, but he suspected him of being insufficiently dedicated to writing, and advised him to avoid distractions like prostitutes and exercise and to spend more time rewriting. Unfortunately, by this time de Maupassant had already contracted the syphilis that would bring on insanity and death at the age of 42. The influence of Flaubert's hatred of bourgeois stupidity and cruelty combined with de Maupassant's reading of his beloved Schopenhauer to produce the pessimistic view his fiction so often articulates. He believed that most people exist merely on the surface of life, never even suspecting that others see life differently. Those gifted enough to see into the depths feel mostly anguish and fear as a result of the solipsism, banality, and insensitivity of those around them. He wrote more than 300 short stories between 1880 and 1890, and critics agree that what Chekhov did for mood and atmosphere in the short story, de Maupassant did for the well-constructed narrative. Although often thought of as a "surprise ending" writer, de Maupassant is actually responsible for a varied body of work. His reputation in our century has declined somewhat as writers and readers have come to prefer voices less forthright, less confident, less robust than de Maupassant tends to create. But his readable, evocative attempts to tell the truth about the everyday lives he imagined so vividly will retain their perennial fascination.

The Return

T he sea lashes the coast with its short and monotonous waves. Little white clouds pass very quickly across the great blue sky, swept on by the wind, like birds; and the village, in the wrinkle of the little valley sloping toward the ocean, warms itself in the sun.

At the very entrance of it stood the house of Martin Levesque, all alone, by the edge of the road. A humble fisherman's dwelling it was, with walls of clay, and a thatched roof plumed with iris-flowers. It had a garden not bigger than a pocket handkerchief, in which some onions, cabbages, parsley and chervil were growing. A hedge divided it from the road.

The man was away fishing; and his wife, seated by the door, was busy repairing the meshes of a great brown net, spread against the wall like an immense cobweb. A girl of fourteen, seated in a chair propped back so that she could lean her back against the fence, was occupied in mending underwear, poor-man's underwear, already overdarned and patched. Another girl, younger by a year, held in her arms a very young child, not yet able to speak or gesticulate; and two urchins, whose ages might be two and four years, sitting flat upon the ground, face to face, were playing at gardening with their clumsy little hands, and throwing dirt into each other's eyes.

Nobody spoke. Only the child which the young girl was trying to put to sleep cried continuously in a little thin sharp voice. A cat slept in the window; and at the foot of the wall extended a veritable cushion of white gilly flowers, about which buzzed a whole tribe of bees.

All of a sudden the girl sewing near the gate cried out:

"Mamma!"

The mother answered:

"What is it?"

"Here he is again!"

The whole family had been uneasy since early morning because of a man who had kept prowling about the house,—an old man who looked like a beggar. They first saw him while they were going to the boat to see father off. He was then sitting by the ditch, directly in front of the door. When they came back from the beach he was still there, looking at the house.

He seemed sick and very miserable. He had not budged for more than an hour; then, finding that he was being watched like a malefactor, he had risen to his feet and gone away, dragging his legs heavily as he walked.

But after awhile the girls saw him coming back, walking with the same slow and weary step; and he sat down again,—this time a little further off,—and kept watching them.

The mother and her girls began to feel afraid. The mother was particularly worried because she was naturally timid, and, then, her husband, Levesque, would not return until night-fall.

Her husband's real name was Levesque; and hers, Martin; and the neighbours called them the Martin-Levesque folks. This was because she had first married a sailor named Martin, who used to go to Newfoundland every year to engage in the codfisheries.

After two years of married life she had a daughter growing up, and was shortly to become a mother again when the vessel that her husband had shipped on—the *Deux-Sœurs*, a Dieppe three-master,—disappeared.

No news was ever heard of her; none of her crew ever returned; so it was generally believed she had gone down with all hands.

La Martin, as folks called her, waited for her husband ten long years, raising her children with the greatest difficulty;—and then, as she was known to be a good industrious woman, Levesque, a fisherman of the place, and a widower with one son, asked her to marry him. She accepted his proposal; and had two more children by him within three years.

They lived with difficulty by the hardest work. Bread was dear; and meat was almost an unknown luxury in their cottage. Sometimes, during the winter, in the stormy weather, they would get heavily in debt to the baker. Still the children were wonderfully healthy. Folks used to say:

"Them's good people—them Levesques. La Martin—she's a great worker; and there's nobody can beat Levesque fishing."

*   *   *

The girl at the gate continued:

"Looks as if he knew us. P'raps it's some beggar from Epreville or Ausebosc."

But the mother could not be mistaken. No, no!—it wasn't nobody from that part of the country, sure!

As he remained motionless as a stake and kept his eyes persistently fixed on the habitation of the Martin-Levesque people, La Martin became furious at last, and her fear giving her courage, she seized a spade and went out in front of the gate.

"What do you want there?" she screamed to the tramp.

He replied in a wheezy voice:

"I'm just taking a rest in the shade. Why, I ain't doing you any harm—am I?"

She went on:

"What are you spying on my house for?"

The man answered:

"I'm doing no harm to nobody. Ain't a person allowed to sit on the edge of a public road?"

As she could not find any answer to this observation, she went into the house again.

The day passed by very slowly. About noon the man disappeared. But he passed by again about five o'clock in the afternoon. They did not see him again during the evening.

Levesque came in about night-fall. They told him about it. He said: "Must be some sneak or villain."

And he went to bed without feeling the least anxiety, while his wife kept thinking about the prowler who had stared at her with such queer-looking eyes.

When day came around, there was a big wind; and seeing that he could not take his boat out, the sailor began to help his wife to mend the nets.

About nine o'clock the eldest girl—a Martin—who had been sent for bread, came back running, with a frightened face, and cried out:

"Mamma, there he is again!"

The mother almost fainted; and, pale as a ghost, she said to her husband:

"Go out and talk to him, Levesque; and stop this sneaking around,—it just worries me out of my senses."

And Levesque, a burly seaman, whose face was tanned to the colour of brick,—with a rough red beard, blue eyes with a piercing black pupil, and a strong neck always encircled by a woollen scarf to protect him from cold winds and chilly rains at sea,—arose very quietly and walked directly to the prowler.

And the two began to talk.

The mother and the children watched them from a distance, shuddering with anxiety.

All of a sudden the stranger rose up and followed Levesque toward the house.

La Martin shrunk back terrified. Her husband said to her:

"Give him a bite of bread and a glass of cider. He hasn't had anything to eat for two days."

And they both entered the cottage, followed by the mother and her children. The prowler sat down and began to eat, keeping his head down as if to avoid being looked at.

The woman, standing near him, watched him keenly; and the two tall daughters, the Martin girls, leaning against the door posts—one of them carrying the youngest child,—stared at him with curious eyes; and the two little urchins, squatting among the ashes of the fireplace, stopped playing with the pot in order to contemplate the stranger.

Levesque took a chair, and sitting down, asked him:

"So you come from a good ways off?"

"I've come from Cette."

"On foot,—just like you are?"

"Yes, on foot. When one hasn't the means, one has to walk."

"Then where are you going to?"

"Going here."

"Know any folks here?"

"Guess so."

They stopped talking. He ate slowly, hungry as he was; and he drank a little cider after each mouthful of bread. He had a worn face—wrinkled, full of hollows—and seemed to have suffered a great deal.

Levesque roughly asked him:

"What's your name?"

He replied without lifting his eyes.

"My name's Martin."

A strange shiver passed through the mother. She took one long step forward, as if to get a closer view of the tramp, and remained standing in front of him, her arms hanging lifelessly by her sides, her mouth opened as if to cry out. Nobody said a word. At last Levesque resumed.

"Are you from this place?"

He answered:

"I am from this place."

And as he lifted his head at last, the eyes of the woman and his own met and remained fixed, mixed together in a gaze so motionless that it seemed to be interlocked.

And then in a voice wholly changed, low and trembling, she asked:

"Is that you, my man?"

He articulated slowly:

"Yes . . . it's me."

He did not move, and continued to munch his bread.

Levesque, more surprised than moved, stammered out:

"You are . . . Martin?"

The other replied simply:

"Yes; it's me."

And the second husband then asked:

"Where on earth did you come from?"

The first replied:

"From the African coast. We foundered on a shoal. Three of us were saved—Picard and Vatinel and me. And then we were taken by the savages who kept us twelve years. Picard's dead and Vatinel's dead. It was an English traveller passing through who saved me and took me with him to Cette. And here I am."

La Martin was crying, with her apron lifted to her face.

Levesque muttered:

"What will we do, now?"

Martin asked:

"It's you is her man now?"

Levesque answered:

"Yes, it's me."

They looked at each other and remained silent.

Then Martin, looking at the children standing in a ring around him, nodded his head toward the two tall girls and asked:

"Them's mine?"

Levesque replied:

"Them's yourn."

He did not get up; did not kiss them; only observed:

"Good God! how big they've growed!"

Levesque reiterated:

"What's I got to do now?"

Martin, equally puzzled, could not tell. Finally he said:

"Me, I'll fix matters the way you like. I don't want to do you no wrong. Still, it's a bad fix anyhow, when one thinks about the house. I've two children; you've three:—each one can have his own. The mother—is she yourn, or is she mine? I'll agree to anything you want; but the house,—that's mine because my father left it to me, and because I was born in it, and because she's got papers at the notary's to prove it."

La Martin was still crying,—with little sobs she hid behind the blue cotton of her apron. The two tall girls had drawn nearer, and were staring anxiously at their father.

He had finished eating, and exclaimed in his turn:

"What's I got to do now?"

A sudden idea came to Levesque:

"Got to go see the priest—he'll tell."

Martin arose; and as he approached his wife she flung herself sobbing upon his breast.

"My man, my man! it's you! Martin, my poor Martin, it's you!"

And she hugged him tightly, thrilled all suddenly by the memory of other days,—by a great shock of souvenirs that recalled to her the days her own twenty summers and her first love.

Martin, himself affected, kissed her white cap. The two children in the fireplace began to howl simultaneously upon hearing their mother cry, and the baby in the arms of the second Martin girl, clamored in a voice sharp as a squeaky fife.

Levesque stood there, waiting:

"Come," he said, "we've got to settle this matter."

Martin separated from his wife, and as he stood looking at his two daughters the mother said to them:

"Can't you kiss your father?"

They approached him simultaneously, with dry eyes, much astonished and a little afraid. And he kissed them one after the other, on both cheeks, with a loud peasant's kiss. On seeing the stranger draw near, the baby screamed so violently that it nearly took fits.

Then the two men went out together.

As they were about to pass the Café du Commerce, Levesque asked: "S'pose we take a drink."

"Me, I'm willing," declared Martin.

They entered, sat down in the still vacant bar-room, and Levesque cried:

denouement

"Eh! Chicot!—bring two brandies, the good stuff, you know. This here is Martin, who's come back—Martin, you know, my wife's man!— you know, Martin of the *Deux-Sœurs* who was lost."

And the barkeeper, with three glasses in one hand, and a decanter in the other, approached,—stout, sanguine, puffed up with fat, and observed very quietly:

"Well, so you're back again, Martin?"

Martin answered:

"I'm back again."

KATE CHOPIN

(1851–1904)

*K*ate Chopin was born Katherine O'Flaherty in St. Louis, Missouri, the daughter of a prosperous businessman. Her father died when she was just 4. From an early age, she was a voracious reader of classic European literature, and her grandmother told her endless stories of Creole life. She married Oscar Chopin in 1871 and moved to New Orleans. When his cotton business failed, they moved to a plantation near Cloutierville in northwest Louisiana. After he died suddenly in 1883, Kate Chopin returned to St. Louis, determined to raise her six children and to become a writer. She made herself a considerable reputation with two collections of stories, Bayou Folk (1894) and A Night in Acadie (1897). The accuracy with which she depicted the "foreign" world of Creole Louisiana and the evocative, sensual nature of her material impressed many readers. In her novel The Awakening (1899), Chopin wrote frankly about the plight of women, social and economic injustice, and sexuality thwarted by loveless marriage. Ignored for 50 years, the work is a fascinating combination of sharply observed details and compelling characterization, occasionally marred by the triteness of romantic cliché. Its critical reception had a profound effect on Chopin. So upset were the reviewers by the discussion of a woman's sexual desires that they condemned the novel as morbid and unhealthy and applauded its heroine for committing suicide at the end. The book was banned, and Chopin began to have trouble getting publishers to accept her stories. She died of a brain hemorrhage in 1904. Her reputation as one of the most important precursors of twentieth-century feminism continues to grow. As Wendy Martin has written, "In addition to presenting the tensions and conflicts in the life of the emerging new woman in the late nineteenth and early twentieth centuries in American culture," Kate Chopin is the writer whose work gives us an evocative portrait of "the woman whose life bridges two traditions—domestic femininity and romantic individualism."

The Storm

A Sequel to "The 'Cadian Ball"

I

T he leaves were so still that even Bibi thought it was going to rain.
   Bobinôt, who was accustomed to converse on terms of perfect equality with his little son, called the child's attention to certain sombre clouds
that were rolling with sinister intention from the west, accompanied by
a sullen, threatening roar. They were at Friedheimer's store and decided
to remain there till the storm had passed. They sat within the door on
two empty kegs. Bibi was four years old and looked very wise.

"Mama'll be 'fraid, yes," he suggested with blinking eyes.

"She'll shut the house. Maybe she got Sylvie helpin' her this evenin',"
Bobinôt responded reassuringly.

"No; she ent got Sylvie. Sylvie was helpin' her yistiday," piped Bibi.

Bobinôt arose and going across to the counter purchased a can of
shrimps, of which Calixta was very fond. Then he returned to his perch
on the keg and sat stolidly holding the can of shrimps while the storm
burst. It shook the wooden store and seemed to be ripping great furrows
in the distant field. Bibi laid his little hand on his father's knee and was
not afraid.

II

Calixta, at home, felt no uneasiness for their safety. She sat at a side
window sewing furiously on a sewing machine. She was greatly occupied
and did not notice the approaching storm. But she felt very warm and
often stopped to mop her face on which the perspiration gathered in
beads. She unfastened her white sacque at the throat. It began to grow
dark, and suddenly realizing the situation she got up hurriedly and went
about closing windows and doors.

Out on the small front gallery she had hung Bobinôt's Sunday clothes
to air and she hastened out to gather them before the rain fell. As she
stepped outside, Alcée Laballière rode in at the gate. She had not seen
him very often since her marriage, and never alone. She stood there with
Bobinôt's coat in her hands, and the big rain drops began to fall. Alcée
rode his horse under the shelter of a side projection where the chickens
had huddled and there were plows and a harrow piled up in the corner.

"May I come and wait on your gallery till the storm is over, Calixta?" he asked.

"Come 'long in, M'sieur Alcée."

His voice and her own startled her as if from a trance, and she seized Bobinôt's vest; Alcée, mounting to the porch, grabbed the trousers and snatched Bibi's braided jacket that was about to be carried away by a sudden gust of wind. He expressed an intention to remain outside, but it was soon apparent that he might as well have been out in the open: the water beat in upon the boards in driving sheets, and he went inside, closing the door after him. It was even necessary to put something beneath the door to keep the water out.

"My! what a rain! It's good two years sence it rain' like that," exclaimed Calixta as she rolled up a piece of bagging and Alcée helped her to thrust it beneath the crack.

She was a little fuller of figure than five years before when she married; but she had lost nothing of her vivacity. Her blue eyes still retained their melting quality; and her yellow hair, dishevelled by the wind and rain, kinked more stubbornly than ever about her ears and temples.

The rain beat upon the low, shingled roof with a force and clatter that threatened to break an entrance and deluge them there. They were in the dining room—the sitting room—the general utility room. Adjoining was her bed room, with Bibi's couch along side her own. The door stood open, and the room with its white, monumental bed, its closed shutters, looked dim and mysterious.

Alcée flung himself into a rocker and Calixta nervously began to gather up from the floor the lengths of a cotton sheet which she had been sewing.

"If this keeps up, *Dieu sait* if the levees goin' to stan' it!" she exclaimed.

"What have you got to do with the levees?"

"I got enough to do! An' there's Bobinôt with Bibi out in that storm— if he only didn' left Friedheimer's!"

"Let us hope, Calixta, that Bobinôt's got sense enough to come in out of a cyclone."

She went and stood at the window with a greatly disturbed look on her face. She wiped the frame that was clouded with moisture. It was stiflingly hot. Alcée got up and joined her at the window, looking over her shoulder. The rain was coming down in sheets obscuring the view of far-off cabins and enveloping the distant wood in a gray mist. The playing of the lightning was incessant. A bolt struck a tall chinaberry tree at the edge of the field. It filled all visible space with a blinding glare and the crash seemed to invade the very boards they stood upon.

Calixta put her hands to her eyes, and with a cry, staggered backward.

Alcée's arm encircled her, and for an instant he drew her close and spasmodically to him.

"*Bonté!*" she cried, releasing herself from his encircling arm, and retreating from the window, "the house'll go next! If I only knew w'ere Bibi was!" She would not compose herself; she would not be seated. Alcée clasped her shoulders and looked into her face. The contact of her warm, palpitating body when he had unthinkingly drawn her into his arms, had aroused all the old-time infatuation and desire for her flesh.

"Calixta," he said, "don't be frightened. Nothing can happen. The house is too low to be struck, with so many tall trees standing about. There! aren't you going to be quiet? say, aren't you?" He pushed her hair back from her face that was warm and steaming. Her lips were as red and moist as pomegranate seed. Her white neck and a glimpse of her full, firm bosom disturbed him powerfully. As she glanced up at him the fear in her liquid blue eyes had given place to a drowsy gleam that unconsciously betrayed a sensuous desire. He looked down into her eyes and there was nothing for him to do but to gather her lips in a kiss. It reminded him of Assumption.

"Do you remember—in Assumption, Calixta?" he asked in a low voice broken by passion. Oh! she remembered; for in Assumption he had kissed her and kissed and kissed her; until his senses would well nigh fail, and to save her he would resort to a desperate flight. If she was not an immaculate dove in those days, she was still inviolate; a passionate creature whose very defenselessness had made her defense, against which his honor forbade him to prevail. Now—well, now—her lips seemed in a manner free to be tasted, as well as her round, white throat and her whiter breasts.

They did not heed the crashing torrents, and the roar of the elements made her laugh as she lay in his arms. She was a revelation in that dim, mysterious chamber; as white as the couch she lay upon. Her firm, elastic flesh that was knowing for the first time its birthright was like a creamy lily that the sun invites to contribute its breath and perfume to the undying life of the world.

The generous abundance of her passion, without guile or trickery, was like a white flame which penetrated and found response in depths of his own sensuous nature that had never yet been reached.

When he touched her breasts they gave themselves up in quivering ecstasy, inviting his lips. Her mouth was a fountain of delight. And when he possessed her, they seemed to swoon together at the very borderland of life's mystery.

He stayed cushioned upon her, breathless, dazed, enervated, with his heart beating like a hammer upon her. With one hand she clasped his head, her lips lightly touching his forehead. The other hand stroked with a soothing rhythm his muscular shoulders.

The growl of the thunder was distant and passing away. The rain beat softly upon the shingles, inviting them to drowsiness and sleep. But they dared not yield.

The rain was over; and the sun was turning the glistening green world into a palace of gems. Calixta, on the gallery, watched Alcée ride away. He turned and smiled at her with a beaming face; and she lifted her pretty chin in the air and laughed aloud.

III

Bobinôt and Bibi, trudging home, stopped without at the cistern to make themselves presentable.

"My! Bibi, w'at will yo' mama say! You ought to be ashame'. You oughtn' put on those good pants. Look at 'em! An' that mud on yo' collar! How you got that mud on yo' collar, Bibi? I never saw such a boy!" Bibi was the picture of pathetic resignation. Bobinôt was the embodiment of serious solicitude as he strove to remove from his own person and his son's the signs of their tramp over heavy roads and through wet fields. He scraped the mud off Bibi's bare legs and feet with a stick and carefully removed all traces from his heavy brogans. Then, prepared for the worst—the meeting with an over-scrupulous housewife, they entered cautiously at the back door.

Calixta was preparing supper. She had set the table and was dripping coffee at the hearth. She sprang up as they came in.

"On, Bobinôt! You back! My! but I was uneasy. W'ere you been during the rain? An' Bibi? he ain't wet? he ain't hurt?" She had clasped Bibi and was kissing him effusively. Bobinôt explanations and apologies which he had been composing all along the way, died on his lips as Calixta felt him to see if he were dry, and seemed to express nothing but satisfaction at their safe return.

"I brought you some shrimps, Calixta," offered Bobinôt, hauling the can from his ample side pocket and laying it on the table.

"Shrimps! Oh, Bobinôt! you too good fo' anything!" and she gave him a smacking kiss on the cheek that resounded. "*J'vous réponds*, we'll have a feas' to night! umph-umph!"

Bobinôt and Bibi began to relax and enjoy themselves, and when the three seated themselves at table they laughed much and so loud that anyone might have heard them as far away as Laballière's.

IV

Alcée Laballière wrote to his wife, Clarisse, that night. It was a loving letter, full of tender solicitude. He told her not to hurry back, but if she and the babies liked it at Biloxi, to stay a month longer. He was getting on nicely; and though he missed them, he was willing to bear the separation a while longer—realizing that their health and pleasure were the first things to be considered.

V

As for Clarisse, she was charmed upon receiving her husband's letter. She and the babies were doing well. The society was agreeable; many of her old friends and acquaintances were at the bay. And the first free breath since her marriage seemed to restore the pleasant liberty of her maiden days. Devoted as she was to her husband, their intimate conjugal life was something which she was more than willing to forego for a while.

So the storm passed and every one was happy.

JOSEPH CONRAD

(1857–1924)

*J*oseph Conrad—*Jósef Teodor Konrad Nalecz Korzeniowski*—*was born at Berdyczów in the Polish Ukraine. His father worked in a publishing house and edited a literary magazine. Sentenced to exile in Russia for his political activities, he was deported, and 4-year-old Jósef developed pneumonia on the journey. Both his parents eventually died while Conrad was still a boy, and he was raised by his grandmother. He worked in the French merchant navy for a time, travelling to the West Indies and incurring serious gambling debts. From 1878 to 1894, he worked in the British merchant navy, during which time he acquired the experience that he was to transmute into his stories and novels. His first novel,* Almayer's Folly *(1895), written while he was still a seaman, had a kindly critical reception but sold poorly. Now married and committed to pursuing a career as a writer, Conrad settled in southern England.* Heart of Darkness *(1899),* Lord Jim *(1900),* Nostromo *(1904),* The Secret Agent *(1907), and* Under Western Eyes *(1911) secure for him a reputation as one of the most important novelists writing in English. The quality in his fiction that has fascinated generations of readers is admirably summed up by the contemporary Polish writer Jan Józef Szczepanski:*

> *Conrad's heroes—captains of small sailing ships, or white colo-nizers lost in exotic surroundings—are lonely men. True, there was a great power and a great tradition behind them but in solving their immediate conflicts they could only rely on them-selves. This fact gave rise to the entire system of Conradian morality. A morality that functions like the air bubble in the glass tube of a spirit level. Cut off from the world and public opinion, every man is his own judge. And not only a judge. A Conradian man represents a closed, autonomous moral system. This system is a true copy of those ethics that bind merchants and sailors: honesty, fidelity to the given word, self-respect and professional honour, and with a touch of a certain romantic exaltation that bestows upon such virtues a hallmark of chivalric austerity.*

Heart of Darkness

T he *Nellie*, a cruising yawl, swung to her anchor without a flutter of the sails, and was at rest. The flood had made, the wind was nearly calm, and being bound down the river, the only thing for it was to come to and wait for the turn of the tide.

The sea-reach of the Thames stretched before us like the beginning of an interminable waterway. In the offing the sea and the sky were welded together without a joint, and in the luminous space the tanned sails of the barges drifting up with the tide seemed to stand still in red clusters of canvas sharply peaked, with gleams of varnished spirits. A haze rested on the low shores that ran out to sea in vanishing flatness. The air was dark above Gravesend, and farther back still seemed condensed into a mournful gloom, brooding motionless over the biggest, and the greatest, town on earth.

The Director of Companies was our captain and our host. We four affectionately watched his back as he stood in the bows looking to seaward. On the whole river there was nothing that looked half so nautical. He resembled a pilot, which to a seaman is trustworthiness personified. It was difficult to realize his work was not out there in the luminous estuary, but behind him, within the brooding gloom.

Between us there was, as I have already said somewhere, the bond of the sea. Besides holding our hearts together through long periods of separation, it had the effect of making us tolerant of each other's yarns—and even convictions. The Lawyer—the best of old fellows—had, because of his many years and many virtues, the only cushion on deck, and was lying on the only rug. The Accountant had brought out already a box of dominoes, and was toying architecturally with the bones. Marlow sat cross-legged right aft, leaning against the mizzen-mast. He had sunken cheeks, a yellow complexion, a straight back, an ascetic aspect, and, with his arms dropped, the palms of hands outwards, resembled an idol. The director, satisfied the anchor had good hold, made his way aft and sat down amongst us. We exchanged a few words lazily. Afterwards there was silence on board the yacht. For some reason or other we did not begin that game of dominoes. We felt meditative, and fit for nothing but placid staring. The day was ending in a serenity of still and exquisite brilliance. The water shone pacifically; the sky, without a speck, was a benign immensity of unstained light; the very mist on the Essex marshes was like a gauzy and radiant fabric, hung from the wooded rises inland, and draping the low shores in diaphanous folds. Only the gloom to the west, brooding over the upper reaches, became more sombre every minute, as if angered by the approach of the sun.

And at last, in its curved and imperceptible fall, the sun sank low, and from glowing white changed to a dull red without rays and without heat, as if about to go out suddenly, stricken to death by the touch of that gloom brooding over a crowd of men.

Forthwith a change came over the waters, and the serenity became less brilliant but more profound. The old river in its broad reach rested unruffled at the decline of day, after ages of good service done to the race that peopled its banks, spread out in the tranquil dignity of a waterway leading to the uttermost ends of the earth. We looked at the venerable stream not in the vivid flush of a short day that comes and departs for ever, but in the august light of abiding memories. And indeed nothing is easier for a man who has, as the phrase goes, "followed the sea" with reverence and affection, than to evoke the great spirit of the past upon the lower reaches of the Thames. The tidal current runs to and fro in its unceasing service, crowded with memories of men and ships it had borne to the rest of home or to the battles of the sea. It had known and served all the men of whom the nation is proud, from Sir Francis Drake to Sir John Franklin, knights all, titled and untitled—the great knights-errant of the sea. It had borne all the ships whose names are like jewels flashing in the night of time, from the *Golden Hind* returning with her round flanks full of treasure, to be visited by the Queen's Highness and thus pass out of the gigantic tale, to the *Erebus* and *Terror*, bound on other conquests— and that never returned. It had known the ships and the men. They had sailed from Deptford, from Greenwich, from Erith—the adventurers and the settlers; kings' ships and the ships of men on 'Change; captains, admirals, the dark "interlopers" of the Eastern trade, and the commissioned "generals" of East India fleets. Hunters for gold or pursuers of fame, they all had gone out on that stream, bearing the sword, and often the torch, messengers of the might within the land, bearers of a spark from the sacred fire. What greatness had not floated on the ebb of that river into the mystery of an unknown earth! . . . The dreams of men, the seed of commonwealths, the germs of empires.

The sun set; the dusk fell on the stream, and lights began to appear along the shore. The Chapman lighthouse, a three-legged thing erect on a mud-flat, shone strongly. Lights of ships moved in the fairway—a great stir of lights going up and going down. And farther west on the upper reaches the place of the monstrous town was still marked ominously on the sky, a brooding gloom in sunshine, a lurid glare under the stars.

"And this also," said Marlow suddenly, "has been one of the dark places of the earth."

He was the only man of us who still "followed the sea." The worst that could be said of him was that he did not represent his class. He was a seaman, but he was a wanderer, too, while most seamen lead, if one may so express it, a sedentary life. Their minds are of the stay-at-home order, and their home is always with them—the ship; and so is their country—the sea. One ship is very much like another, and the sea is always the same. In the immutability of their surroundings the foreign shores, the foreign faces, the changing immensity of life, glide past, veiled not by a sense of mystery but by a slightly disdainful ignorance; for there is nothing mysterious to a seaman unless it be the sea itself, which is the mistress of his existence and as inscrutable as Destiny. For the rest, after his hours of work, a casual stroll or a casual spree on shore suffices to unfold for him the secret of a whole continent, and generally he finds the secret not worth knowing. The yarns of seamen have a direct simplicity, the whole meaning of which lies within the shell of a cracked nut. But Marlow was not typical (if his propensity to spin yarns be excepted), and to him the meaning of an episode was not inside like a kernel but outside, enveloping the tale which brought it out only as a glow brings out a haze, in the likeness of one of these misty halos that sometimes are made visible by the spectral illumination of moonshine.

His remark did not seem at all surprising. It was just like Marlow. It was accepted in silence. No one took the trouble to grunt even; and presently he said, very slow—

"I was thinking of very old times, when the Romans first came here, nineteen hundred years ago—the other day. . . . Light came out of this river since—you say Knights? Yes; but it is like a running blaze on a plain, like a flash of lightning in the clouds. We live in the flicker—may it last as long as the old earth keeps rolling! But darkness was here yesterday. Imagine the feelings of a commander of a fine—what d'ye call 'em?—trireme in the Mediterranean, ordered suddenly to the north; run over-land across the Gauls in a hurry; put in charge of one of these craft the legionaries—a wonderful lot of handy men they must have been, too—used to build, apparently by the hundred, in a month or two, if we may believe what we read. Imagine him here—the very end of the world, a sea the colour of lead, a sky the colour of smoke, a kind of ship about as rigid as a concertina—and going up this river with stores, or orders, or what you like. Sand-banks, marshes, forests, savages,—precious little to eat fit for a civilized man, nothing but Thames water to drink. No Faler-nian wine here, no going ashore. Here and there a military camp lost in a wilderness, like a needle in a bundle of hay—cold, fog, tempests, disease, exile, and death,—death skulking in the air, in the water, in the bush. They must have been dying like flies here. Oh, yes—he did it. Did it very well, too, no doubt, and without thinking much about it either, except afterwards to brag of what he had gone through in his time, perhaps. They were men enough to face the darkness. And perhaps he was cheered by keeping his eye on a chance of promotion to the fleet at Ravenna by-

and-by, if he had good friends in Rome and survived the awful climate. Or think of a decent young citizen in a toga—perhaps too much dice, you know—coming out here in the train of some prefect, or tax-gatherer, or trader even, to mend his fortunes. Land in a swamp, march through the woods, and in some inland post feel the savagery, the utter savagery, had closed round him,—all that mysterious life of the wilderness that stirs in the forest, in the jungles, in the hearts of wild men. There's no initiation either into such mysteries. He has to live in the midst of the incomprehensible, which is also detestable. And it has a fascination, too, that goes to work upon him. The fascination of the abomination—you know, imagine the growing regrets, the longing to escape, the powerless disgust, the surrender, the hate."

He paused.

"Mind," he began again, lifting one arm from the elbow, the palm of the hand outwards, so that, with his legs folded before him, he had the pose of a Buddha preaching in European clothes and without a lotus-flower—"Mind, none of us would feel exactly like this. What saves us is efficiency—the devotion to efficiency. But these chaps were not much account, really. They were no colonists; their administration was merely a squeeze, and nothing more, I suspect. They were conquerors, and for that you want only brute force—nothing to boast of, when you have it, since your strength is just an accident arising from the weakness of others. They grabbed what they could get for the sake of what was to be got. It was just robbery with violence, aggravated murder on a great scale, and men going at it blind—as is very proper for those who tackle a darkness. The conquest of the earth, which mostly means the taking it away from those who have a different complexion or slightly flatter noses than ourselves, is not a pretty thing when you look into it too much. What redeems it is the idea only. An idea at the back of it; not a sentimental pretence but an idea; and an unselfish belief in the idea—something you can set up, and bow down before, and offer a sacrifice to. . . ."

He broke off. Flames glided in the river, small green flames, red flames, white flames, pursuing, overtaking, joining, crossing each other— then separating slowly or hastily. The traffic of the great city went on in the deepening night upon the sleepless river. We looked on, waiting patiently—there was nothing else to do till the end of the flood; but it was only after a long silence, when he said, in a hesitating voice, "I suppose you fellows remember I did once turn fresh-water sailor for a bit," that we knew we were fated, before the ebb began to run, to hear about one of Marlow's inconclusive experiences.

"I don't want to bother you much with what happened to me person- ally," he began, showing in this remark the weakness of many tellers of tales who seem so often unaware of what their audience would best like to hear; "yet to understand the effect of it on me you ought to know how

I got out there, what I saw, how I went up that river to the place where I first met the poor chap. It was the farthest point of navigation and the culminating point of my experience. It seemed somehow to throw a kind of light on everything about me—and into my thoughts. It was sombre enough, too—and pitiful—not extraordinary in any way—not very clear either. No, not very clear. And yet it seemed to throw a kind of light.

"I had then, as you remember, just returned to London after a lot of Indian Ocean, Pacific, China Seas—a regular dose of the East—six years or so, and I was loafing about, hindering you fellows in your work and invading your homes, just as though I had got a heavenly mission to civilize you. It was very fine for a time, but after a bit I did get tired of resting. Then I began to look for a ship—I should think the hardest work on earth. But the ships wouldn't even look at me. And I got tired of that game, too.

"Now when I was a little chap I had a passion for maps. I would look for hours at South America, or Africa, or Australia, and lose myself in all the glories of exploration. At that time there were many blank spaces on the earth, and when I saw one that looked particularly inviting on a map (but they all look that) I would put my finger on it and say, When I grow up I will go there. The North Pole was one of these places, I remember. Well, I haven't been there yet, and shall not try now. The glamour's off. Other places were scattered about the Equator, and in every sort of latitude all over the two hemispheres. I have been in some of them, and . . . well, we won't talk about that. But there was one yet—the biggest, the most blank, so to speak—that I had a hankering after.

"True, by this time it was not a blank space any more. It had got filled since my boyhood with rivers and lakes and names. It had ceased to be a blank space of delightful mystery—a white patch for a boy to dream gloriously over. It had become a place of darkness. But there was in it one river especially, a mighty big river, that you could see on the map, resembling an immense snake uncoiled, with its head in the sea, its body at rest curving afar over a vast country, and its tail lost in the depths of the land. And as I looked at the map of it in a shop-window, it fascinated me as a snake would a bird—a silly little bird. Then I remembered there was a big concern, a Company for trade on that river. Dash it all! I thought to myself, they can't trade without using some kind of craft on that lot of fresh water—steamboats! Why shouldn't I try to get charge of one? I went on along Fleet Street, but could not shake off the idea. The snake had charmed me.

"You understand it was a Continental concern, that Trading society; but I have a lot of relations living on the Continent, because it's cheap and not so nasty as it looks, they say.

"I am sorry to own I began to worry them. This was already a fresh departure for me. I was not used to get things that way, you know. I always went my own road and on my own legs where I had a mind to go. I wouldn't have believed it of myself; but, then—you see—I felt somehow I must get there by hook or by crook. So I worried them. The men said 'My dear fellow,' and did nothing. Then—would you believe it?—I tried the women. I, Charlie Marlow, set the women to work—to get a job. Heavens! Well, you see, the notion drove me. I had an aunt, a dear enthusiastic soul. She wrote: 'It will be delightful. I am ready to do anything, anything for you. It is a glorious idea. I know the wife of a very high personage in the Administration, and also a man who has lots of influence with,' etc., etc. She was determined to make no end of fuss to get me appointed skipper of a river steamboat, if such was my fancy.

"I got my appointment—of course; and I got it very quick. It appears the Company had received news that one of their captains had been killed in a scuffle with the natives. This was my chance, and it made me the more anxious to go. It was only months and months afterwards, when I made the attempt to recover what was left of the body, that I heard the original quarrel arose from a misunderstanding about some hens. Yes, two black hens. Fresleven—that was the fellow's name, a Dane—thought himself wronged somehow in the bargain, so he went ashore and started to hammer the chief of the village with a stick. Oh, it didn't surprise me in the least to hear this, and at the same time to be told that Fresleven was the gentlest, quietest creature that ever walked on two legs. No doubt he was; but he had been a couple of years already out there engaged in the noble cause, you know, and he probably felt the need at last of asserting his self-respect in some way. Therefore he whacked the old nigger mercilessly, while a big crowd of his people watched him, thunder-struck, till some man—I was told the chief's son—in desperation at hearing the old chap yell, made a tentative jab with a spear at the white man—and of course it went quite easy between the shoulder-blades. Then the whole population cleared into the forest, expecting all kinds of calamities to happen, while, on the other hand, the steamer Fresleven commanded left also in a bad panic, in charge of the engineer, I believe. Afterwards nobody seemed to trouble much about Fresleven's remains, till I got out and stepped into his shoes. I couldn't let it rest, though; but when an opportunity offered at last to meet my predecessor, the grass growing through his ribs was tall enough to hide his bones. They were all there. The supernatural being had not been touched after he fell. And the village was deserted, the huts gaped black, rotting, all askew within the fallen enclosures. A calamity had come to it, sure enough. The people had vanished. Mad terror had scattered them, men, women, and children, through the bush, and they had never returned. What became of the hens I don't know either. I should think the cause of progress got them, anyhow. However, through this glorious affair I got my appointment, before I had fairly begun to hope for it.

"I flew around like mad to get ready, and before forty-eight hours I was crossing the Channel to show myself to my employers, and sign the contract. In a very few hours I arrived in a city that always makes me think of a whited sepulchre. Prejudice no doubt. I had no difficulty in finding the Company's offices. It was the biggest thing in the town, and everybody I met was full of it. They were going to run an over-sea empire, and make no end of coin by trade.

"A narrow and deserted street in deep shadow, high houses, innumerable windows with venetian blinds, a dead silence, grass sprouting between the stones, imposing carriage archways right and left, immense double doors standing ponderously ajar. I slipped through one of these cracks, went up a swept and ungarnished staircase, as arid as a desert, and opened the first door I came to. Two women, one fat and the other slim, sat on straw-bottomed chairs, knitting black wool. The slim one got up and walked straight at me—still knitting with down-cast eyes—and only just as I began to think of getting out of her way, as you would for a somnambulist, stood still, and looked up. Her dress was as plain as an umbrella-cover, and she turned round without a word and preceded me into a waiting-room. I gave my name, and looked about. Deal table in the middle, plain chairs all round the walls, on one end a large shining map, marked with all the colours of a rainbow. There was a vast amount of red—good to see at any time, because one knows that some real work is done in there, a deuce of a lot of blue, a little green, smears of orange, and, on the East Coast, a purple patch, to show where the jolly pioneers of progress drink the jolly lager-beer. However, I wasn't going into any of these. I was going into the yellow. Dead in the centre. And the river was there—fascinating—deadly—like a snake. Ough! A door opened, a white-haired secretarial head, but wearing a compassionate expression, appeared, and a skinny forefinger beckoned me into the sanctuary. Its light was dim, and a heavy writing-desk squatted in the middle. From behind that structure came out an impression of pale plumpness in a frock-coat. The great man himself. He was five feet six, I should judge, and had his grip on the handle-end of ever so many millions. He shook hands, I fancy, murmured vaguely, was satisfied with my French. *Bon voyage.*

"In about forty-five seconds I found myself again in the waiting-room with the compassionate secretary, who, full of desolation and sympathy, made me sign some document. I believe I undertook amongst other things not to disclose any trade secrets. Well, I am not going to.

"I began to feel slightly uneasy. You know I am not used to such ceremonies, and there was something ominous in the atmosphere. It was just as though I had been let into some conspiracy—I don't know—something not quite right; and I was glad to get out. In the outer room the two women knitted black wool feverishly. People were arriving, and the younger one was walking back and forth introducing them. The old one sat on her chair. Her flat cloth slippers were propped up on a foot-warmer, and a cat reposed on her lap. She wore a starched white affair on her head, had a wart on one cheek, and silver-rimmed spectacles hung on the tip of her nose. She glanced at me above the glasses. The swift and indifferent placidity of that look troubled me. Two youths with foolish and cheery countenances were being piloted over, and she threw at them the same quick glance of unconcerned wisdom. She seemed to know all about them and about me, too. An eerie feeling came over me. She seemed uncanny and fateful. Often far away there I thought of these two, guarding the door of Darkness, knitting black wool as for a warm pall, one introducing, introducing continuously to the unknown, the other scrutinizing the cheery and foolish faces with unconcerned old eyes. *Ave!* Old knitter of black wool. *Morituri te salutant.* Not many of those she looked at ever saw her again—not half, by a long way.

"There was yet a visit to the doctor. 'A simple formality,' assured me the secretary, with an air of taking an immense part in all my sorrows. Accordingly a young chap wearing his hat over the left eyebrow, some clerk I suppose,—there must have been clerks in the business, though the house was as still as a house in a city of the dead—came from somewhere up-stairs, and led me forth. He was shabby and careless, with ink-stains on the sleeves of his jacket, and his cravat was large and billowy, under a chin shaped like the toe of an old boot. It was a little too early for the doctor, so I proposed a drink, and thereupon he developed a vein of joviality. As we sat over our vermuths he glorified the Company's business, and by-and-by I expressed casually my surprise at him not going out there. He became very cool and collected all at once. 'I am not such a fool as I look, quoth Plato to his disciples,' he said sententiously, emptied his glass with great resolution, and we rose.

"The old doctor felt my pulse, evidently thinking of something else the while. 'Good, good for there,' he mumbled, and then with a certain eagerness asked me whether I would let him measure my head. Rather surprised, I said Yes, when he produced a thing like calipers and got the dimensions back and front and every way, taking notes carefully. He was an unshaven little man in a threadbare coat like a gaberdine, with his feet in slippers, and I thought him a harmless fool. 'I always ask leave, in the interests of science, to measure the crania of those going out there,' he said. 'And when they come back, too?' I asked. 'Oh, I never see them,' he remarked; 'and, moreover, the changes take place inside, you know.' He smiled, as if at some quiet joke. 'So you are going out there. Famous. Interesting, too.' He gave me a searching glance, and made another note. 'Ever any madness in your family?' he asked, in a matter-of-fact tone. I felt very annoyed. 'Is that question in the interests of science, too?' 'It would be,' he said, without taking notice of my irritation, 'interesting for science to watch the mental changes of individuals, on the spot, but . . .' 'Are you an alienist?' I interrupted. 'Every doctor should be—a little,' answered that original, imperturbably. 'I have a little theory which you Messieurs who go out there must help me to prove. This is my share in the advantages my country shall reap from the possession of such a magnificent dependency. The mere wealth I leave to others. Pardon my questions, but you are the first Englishman coming under my observation . . .' I hastened to assure him I was not in the least typical. 'If I were,' said I, 'I wouldn't be talking like this with you.' 'What you say is rather profound, and probably erroneous,' he said, with a laugh. 'Avoid irritation more than exposure to the sun. Adieu. How do you English say, eh? Good-bye. Ah! Good-bye. Adieu. In the tropics one must before everything keep calm.' . . . He lifted a warning forefinger. . . . *'Du calme, du calme. Adieu.'*

"One thing more remained to do—say good-bye to my excellent aunt. I found her triumphant. I had a cup of tea—the last decent cup of tea for many days—and in a room that most soothingly looked just as you would expect a lady's drawing-room to look, we had a long quiet chat by the fireside. In the course of these confidences it became quite plain to me I had been represented to the wife of the high dignitary, and goodness knows to how many more people besides, as an exceptional and gifted creature—a piece of good fortune for the Company—a man you don't get hold of every day. Good heavens! and I was going to take charge of a two-penny-half-penny river-steamboat with a penny whistle attached! It appeared, however, I was also one of the Workers, with a capital—you know. Something like an emissary of light, something like a lower sort of apostle. There had been a lot of such rot let loose in print and talk just about that time, and the excellent woman, living right in the rush of all that humbug, got carried off her feet. She talked about 'weaning those ignorant millions from their horrid ways,' till, upon my word, she made me quite uncomfortable. I ventured to hint that the Company was run for profit.

" 'You forget, dear Charlie, that the labourer is worthy of his hire,' she said, brightly. It's queer how out of touch with truth women are. They live in a world of their own, and there had never been anything like it, and never can be. It is too beautiful altogether, and if they were to set it up it would go to pieces before the first sunset. Some confounded fact we men have been living contentedly with ever since the day of creation would start up and knock the whole thing over.

"After this I got embraced, told to wear flannel, be sure to write often, and so on—and I left. In the street—I don't know why—a queer feeling came to me that I was an impostor. Odd thing that I, who used to clear out for any part of the world at twenty-four hours' notice, with less thought than most men give to the crossing of a street, had a moment—

I won't say of hesitation, but of startled pause, before this commonplace affair. The best way I can explain it to you is by saying that, for a second or two, I felt as though, instead of going to the centre of a continent, I were about to set off for the centre of the earth.

"I left in a French steamer, and she called in every blamed port they have out there, for, as far as I could see, the sole purpose of landing soldiers and custom-house officers. I watched the coast. Watching a coast as it slips by the ship is like thinking about an enigma. There it is before you—smiling, frowning, inviting, grand, mean, insipid, or savage, and always mute with an air of whispering, come and find out. This one was almost featureless, as if still in the making, with an aspect of monotonous grimness. The edge of a colossal jungle, so dark-green as to be almost black, fringed with white surf, ran straight, like a ruled line, far, far away along a blue sea whose glitter was blurred by a creeping mist. The sun was fierce, the land seemed to glisten and drip with steam. Here and there grayish-whitish specks showed up clustered inside the white surf, with a flag flying above them perhaps. Settlements some centuries old, and still no bigger than pinheads on the untouched expanse of their background. We pounded along, stopped, landed soldiers; went on, landed custom-house clerks to levy toll in what looked like a God-for-saken wilderness, with a tin shed and a flag-pole lost in it; landed more soldiers—to take care of the custom-house clerks, presumably. Some, I heard, got drowned in the surf; but whether they did or not, nobody seemed particularly to care. They were just flung out there, and on we went. Every day the coast looked the same, as though we had not moved; but we passed various places—trading places—with names like Gran' Bassam, Little Popo; names that seemed to belong to some sordid farce acted in front of a sinister back-cloth. The idleness of a passenger, my isolation amongst all these men with whom I had no point of contact, the oily and languid sea, the uniform sombreness of the coast, seemed to keep me away from the truth of things, within the toil of a mournful and senseless delusion. The voice of the surf heard now and then was a positive pleasure, like the speech of a brother. It was something natural, that had its reason, that had a meaning. Now and then a boat from the shore gave one a momentary contact with reality. It was paddled by black fellows. You could see from afar the white of their eyeballs glistening. They shouted, sang; their bodies streamed with perspiration; they had faces like grotesque masks—these chaps; but they had bone, muscle, a wild vitality, an intense energy of movement, that was as natural and true as the surf along their coast. They wanted no excuse for being there. They were a great comfort to look at. For a time I would feel I belonged still to a world of straightforward facts; but the feeling would not last long. Something would turn up to scare it away. Once, I remember, we came upon a man-of-war anchored off the coast. There wasn't even a shed there, and she was shelling the bush. It appears the French had one of their wars going on thereabouts. Her ensign dropped limp like a rag; the muzzles of the long six-inch guns stuck out all over the low hull; the greasy, slimy swell swung her up lazily and let her down, swaying her thin masts. In the empty immensity of earth, sky and water, there she was, incomprehensible, firing into a continent. Pop, would go one of the six-inch guns; a small flame would dart and vanish, a little white smoke would disappear, a tiny projectile would give a feeble screech—and nothing happened. Nothing could happen. There was a touch of insanity in the proceeding, a sense of lugubrious drollery in the sight; and it was not dissipated by somebody on board assuring me earnestly there was a camp of natives—he called them enemies!—hidden out of sight somewhere.

"We gave her her letters (I heard the men in that lonely ship were dying of fever at the rate of three a-day) and went on. We called at some more places with farcical names, where the merry dance of death and trade goes on in a still and earthy atmosphere as of an overheated catacomb; all along the formless coast bordered by dangerous surf, as if Nature herself had tried to ward off intruders; in and out of rivers, streams of death in life, whose banks were rotting into mud, whose waters, thickened into slime, invaded the contorted mangroves, that seemed to writhe at us in the extremity of an impotent despair. Nowhere did we stop long enough to get a particularized impression, but the general sense of vague and oppressive wonder grew upon me. It was like a weary pilgrimage amongst hints for nightmares.

"It was upward of thirty days before I saw the mouth of the big river. We anchored off the seat of the government. But my work would not begin till some two hundred miles farther on. So as soon as I could I made a start for a place thirty miles higher up.

"I had my passage on a little sea-going steamer. Her captain was a Swede, and knowing me for a seaman, invited me on the bridge. He was a young man, lean, fair, and morose, with lanky hair and a shuffling gait. As we left the miserable little wharf, he tossed his head contemptuously at the shore. 'Been living there?' he asked. I said, 'Yes.' 'Fine lot these government chaps—are they not?' he went on, speaking English with great precision and considerable bitterness. 'It is funny what some people will do for a few francs a-month. I wonder what becomes of that kind when it goes up country?' I said to him I expected to see that soon. 'So-o-o!' he exclaimed. He shuffled athwart, keeping one eye ahead vigilantly. 'Don't be too sure,' he continued. 'The other day I took up a man who hanged himself on the road. He was a Swede, too.' 'Hanged himself! Why, in God's name?' I cried. He kept on looking watchfully. 'Who knows? The sun too much for him, or the country perhaps.'

"At last we opened a reach. A rocky cliff appeared, mounds of turned-up earth by the shore, houses on a hill, others with iron roofs, amongst a waste of excavations, or hanging to the declivity. A continuous noise of the rapids above hovered over this scene of inhabited devastation. A lot of people, mostly black and naked, moved about like ants. A jetty projected into the river. A blinding sunlight drowned all this at times in a sudden recrudescence of glare. 'There's your Company's station,' said the Swede, pointing to three wooden barrack-like structures on the rocky slope. 'I will send your things up. Four boxes did you say? So. Farewell.'

"I came upon a boiler wallowing in the grass, then found a path leading up the hill. It turned aside for the boulders, and also for an undersized railway-truck lying there on its back with its wheels in the air. One was off. The thing looked as dead as the carcass of some animal. I came upon more pieces of decaying machinery, a stack of rusty rails. To the left a clump of trees made a shady spot, where dark things seemed to stir feebly. I blinked, the path was steep. A horn tooted to the right, and I saw the black people run. A heavy and dull detonation shook the ground, a puff of smoke came out of the cliff, and that was all. No change appeared on the face of the rock. They were building a railway. The cliff was not in the way or anything; but this objectless blasting was all the work going on.

"A slight clinking behind me made me turn my head. Six black men advanced in a file, toiling up the path. They walked erect and slow, balancing small baskets full of earth on their heads, and the clink kept time with their footsteps. Black rags were wound round their loins, and the short ends behind waggled to and fro like tails. I could see every rib, the joints of their limbs were like knots in a rope; each had an iron collar on his neck, and all were connected together with a chain whose bights swung between them, rhythmically clinking. Another report from the cliff made me think suddenly of that ship of war I had seen firing into a continent. It was the same kind of ominous voice; but these men could by no stretch of imagination be called enemies. They were called criminals, and the outraged law, like the bursting shells, had come to them, an insoluble mystery from the sea. All their meagre breasts panted together, the violently dilated nostrils quivered, the eyes stared stonily up-hill. They passed me within six inches, without a glance, with that complete, deathlike indifference of unhappy savages. Behind this raw matter one of the reclaimed, the product of the new forces at work, strolled despondently, carrying a rifle by its middle. He had a uniform jacket with one button off, and seeing a white man on the path, hoisted his weapon to his shoulder with alacrity. This was simple prudence, white men being so much alike at a distance that he could not tell who I might be. He was speedily reassured, and with a large, white, rascally grin, and a glance at his charge, seemed to take me into partnership in his exalted trust. After all, I also was a part of the great cause of these high and just proceedings.

"Instead of going up, I turned and descended to the left. My idea was to let that chain-gang get out of sight before I climbed the hill. You know I am not particularly tender; I've had to strike and to fend off. I've had to resist and to attack sometimes—that's only one way of resisting—without counting the exact cost, according to the demands of such sort of life as I had blundered into. I've seen the devil of violence, and the devil of greed, and the devil of hot desire; but, by all the stars! these were strong, lusty, red-eyed devils, that swayed and drove men—men, I tell you. But as I stood on this hillside, I foresaw that in the blinding sunshine of that land I would become acquainted with a flabby, pretending, weak-eyed devil of a rapacious and pitiless folly. How insidious he could be, too, I was only to find out several months later and a thousand miles farther. For a moment I stood appalled, as though by a warning. Finally I descended the hill, obliquely, towards the trees I had seen.

"I avoided a vast artificial hole somebody had been digging on the slope, the purpose of which I found it impossible to divine. It wasn't a quarry or a sandpit, anyhow. It was just a hole. It might have been connected with the philanthropic desire of giving the criminals something to do. I don't know. Then I nearly fell into a very narrow ravine, almost no more than a scar in the hillside. I discovered that a lot of imported drainage-pipes for the settlement had been tumbled in there. There wasn't one that was not broken. It was a wanton smash-up. At last I got under the trees. My purpose was to stroll into the shade for a moment; but no sooner within than it seemed to me I had stepped into the gloomy circle of some Inferno. The rapids were near, and an uninterrupted, uniform, headlong, rushing noise filled the mournful stillness of the grove, where not a breath stirred, not a leaf moved, with a mysterious sound—as though the tearing pace of the launched earth had suddenly become audible.

"Black shapes crouched, lay, sat between the trees leaning against the trunks, clinging to the earth, half coming out, half effaced within the dim light, in all the attitudes of pain, abandonment, and despair. Another mine on the cliff went off, followed by a slight shudder of the soil under my feet. The work was going on. The work! And this was the place where some of the helpers had withdrawn to die.

"They were dying slowly—it was very clear. They were not enemies, they were not criminals, they were nothing earthly now,—nothing but black shadows of disease and starvation, lying confusedly in the greenish gloom. Brought from all the recesses of the coast in all the legality of time contracts, lost in uncongenial surroundings, fed on unfamiliar food, they sickened, became inefficient, and were then allowed to crawl away and rest. These moribund shapes were free as air—and nearly as thin. I began to distinguish the gleam of the eyes under the trees. Then, glancing down,

I saw a face near my hand. The black bones reclined at full length with one shoulder against the tree, and slowly the eyelids rose and the sunken eyes looked up at me, enormous and vacant, a kind of blind, white flicker in the depths of the orbs, which died out slowly. The man seemed young—almost a boy—but you know with them it's hard to tell. I found nothing else to do but to offer him one of my good Swede's ship's biscuits I had in my pocket. The fingers closed slowly on it and held—there was no other movement and no other glance. He had tied a bit of white worsted round his neck—Why? Where did he get it? Was it a badge—an ornament—a charm—a propitiatory act? Was there any idea at all connected with it? It looked startling round his black neck, this bit of white thread from beyond the seas.

"Near the same tree two more bundles of acute angles sat with their legs drawn up. One, with his chin propped on his knees, stared at nothing, in an intolerable and appalling manner: his brother phantom rested its forehead, as if overcome with a great weariness; and all about others were scattered in every pose of contorted collapse, as in some picture of a massacre or a pestilence. While I stood horror-struck, one of these creatures rose to his hands and knees, and went off on all-fours towards the river to drink. He lapped out of his hand, then sat up in the sunlight, crossing his shins in front of him, and after a time let his woolly head fall on his breastbone.

"I didn't want any more loitering in the shade, and I made haste towards the station. When near the buildings I met a white man, in such an unexpected elegance of get-up that in the first moment I took him for a sort of vision. I saw a high starched collar, white cuffs, a light alpaca jacket, snowy trousers, a clear necktie, and varnished boots. No hat. Hair parted, brushed, oiled, under a green-lined parasol held in a big white hand. He was amazing, and had a penholder behind his ear.

"I shook hands with this miracle, and I learned he was the Company's chief accountant, and that all the book-keeping was done at this station. He had come out for a moment, he said, 'to get a breath of fresh air.' The expression sounded wonderfully odd, with its suggestion of sedentary desk-life. I wouldn't have mentioned the fellow to you at all, only it was from his lips that I first heard the name of the man who is so indissolubly connected with the memories of that time. Moreover, I respected the fellow. Yes; I respected his collars, his vast cuffs, his brushed hair. His appearance was certainly that of a hairdresser's dummy; but in the great demoralization of the land he kept up his appearance. That's backbone. His starched collars and got-up shirt-fronts were achievements of charac-ter. He had been out nearly three years; and, later, I could not help asking him how he managed to sport such linen. He had just the faintest blush, and said modestly, 'I've been teaching one of the native women about the station. It was difficult. She had a distaste for the work.' Thus this man had verily accomplished something. And he was devoted to his books, which were in apple-pie order.

"Everything else in the station was in a muddle,—heads, things, buildings. Strings of dusty niggers with splay feet arrived and departed; a stream of manufactured goods, rubbishy cottons, beads, and brass-wire set into the depths of darkness, and in return came a precious trickle of ivory.

"I had to wait in the station for ten days—an eternity. I lived in a hut in the yard, but to be out of the chaos I would sometimes get into the accountant's office. It was built of horizontal planks, and so badly put together that, as he bent over his high desk, he was barred from neck to heels with narrow strips of sunlight. There was no need to open the big shutter to see. It was hot there, too; big flies buzzed fiendishly, and did not sting, but stabbed. I sat generally on the floor, while, of faultless appearance (and even slightly scented), perching on a high stool, he wrote, he wrote. Sometimes he stood up for exercise. When a truckle-bed with a sick man (some invalid agent from up-country) was put in there, he exhibited a gentle annoyance. 'The groans of this sick person,' he said, 'distract my attention. And without that it is extremely difficult to guard against clerical errors in this climate.'

"One day he remarked, without lifting his head, 'In the interior you will no doubt meet Mr. Kurtz.' On my asking who Mr. Kurtz was, he said he was a first-class agent; and seeing my disappointment at this information, he added slowly, laying down his pen, 'He is a very remarkable person.' Further questions elicited from him that Mr. Kurtz was at present in charge of a trading post, a very important one, in the true ivory-country, at 'the very bottom of there. Sends in as much ivory as all the others put together . . .' He began to write again. The sick man was too ill to groan. The flies buzzed in a great peace.

"Suddenly there was a growing murmur of voices and a great tramping of feet. A caravan had come in. A violent babble of uncouth sounds burst out on the other side of the planks. All the carriers were speaking together, and in the midst of the uproar the lamentable voice of the chief agent was heard 'giving it up' tearfully for the twentieth time that day. . . . He rose slowly. 'What a frightful row,' he said. He crossed the room gently to look at the sick man, and returning, said to me, 'He does not hear.' 'What! Dead?' I asked, startled. 'No, not yet,' he answered, with great composure. Then, alluding with a toss of the head to the tumult in the station-yard, 'When one has got to make correct entries, one comes to hate those savages—hate them to the death.' He remained thoughtful for a moment. 'When you see Mr. Kurtz,' he went on, 'tell him from me that everything here'—he glanced at the desk—'is very satisfactory. I don't like to write to him—with those messengers of ours you never know who may get hold of your letter—at that Central Station.' He stared at me for a moment with his mild, bulging eyes. 'Oh, he will go far, very far,' he began again. 'He will be a somebody in the Administration before long. They, above—the Council in Europe, you know—mean him to be.'

"He turned to his work. The noise outside had ceased, and presently in going out I stopped at the door. In the steady buzz of flies the home-ward-bound agent was lying flushed and insensible; the other, bent over his books, was making correct entries of perfectly correct transactions; and fifty feet below the doorstep I could see the still tree-tops of the grove of death.

"Next day I left that station at last, with a caravan of sixty men, for a two-hundred-mile tramp.

"No use telling you much about that. Paths, paths, everywhere; a stamped-in network of paths spreading over the empty land, through long grass, through burnt grass, through thickets, down and up chilly ravines, up and down stony hills ablaze with heat; and a solitude, a solitude, nobody, not a hut. The population had cleared out a long time ago. Well, if a lot of mysterious niggers armed with all kinds of fearful weapons suddenly took to travelling on the road between Deal and Gravesend, catching the yokels right and left to carry heavy loads for them, I fancy every farm and cottage thereabouts would get empty very soon. Only here the dwellings were gone, too. Still I passed through several abandoned villages. There's something pathetically childish in the ruins of grass walls. Day after day, with the stamp and shuffle of sixty pair of bare feet behind me, each pair under a 60-lb. load. Camp, cook, sleep, strike camp, march. Now and then a carrier dead in harness, at rest in the long grass near the path, with an empty water-gourd and his long staff lying by his side. A great silence around and above. Perhaps on some quiet night the tremor of far-off drums, sinking, swelling, a tremor vast, faint; a sound weird, appealing, suggestive, and wild—and perhaps with as profound a meaning as the sound of bells in a Christian country. Once a white man in an unbuttoned uniform, camping on the path with an armed escort of lank Zanzibaris, very hospitable and festive—not to say drunk. Was looking after the upkeep of the road, he declared. Can't say I saw any road or any upkeep, unless the body of a middle-aged negro, with a bullet-hole in the forehead, upon which I absolutely stumbled three miles farther on, may be considered as a permanent improvement. I had a white companion, too, not a bad chap, but rather too fleshy and with the exasperating habit of fainting on the hot hillsides, miles away from the least bit of shade and water. Annoying, you know, to hold your own coat like a parasol over a man's head while he is coming-to. I couldn't help asking him once what he meant by coming there at all. 'To make money, of course. What do you think?' he said, scornfully. Then he got fever, and had to be carried in a hammock slung under a pole. As he weighed sixteen stone I had no end of rows with the carriers. They jibbed, ran away, sneaked off with their loads in the night—quite a mutiny. So, one evening, I made a speech in English with gestures, not one of which was lost to the sixty pairs of eyes before me, and the next morning I started the hammock off in front all right. An hour afterwards I came upon the whole concern wrecked in a bush—man, hammock, groans, blankets, horrors. The heavy pole had skinned his poor nose. He was very anxious for me to kill somebody, but there wasn't the shadow of a carrier near. I remember the old doctor,—'It would be interesting for science to watch the mental changes of individuals, on the spot.' I felt I was becoming scientifically interesting. However, all that is to no purpose. On the fifteenth day I came in sight of the big river again, and hobbled into the Central Station. It was on a back water surrounded by scrub and forest, with a pretty border of smelly mud on one side, and on the three others enclosed by a crazy fence of rushes. A neglected gap was all the gate it had, and the first glance at the place was enough to let you see the flabby devil was running that show. White men with long staves in their hands appeared languidly from amongst the buildings, strolling up to take a look at me, and then retired out of sight somewhere. One of them, a stout, excitable chap with black moustaches, informed me with great volubility and many digressions, as soon as I told him who I was, that my steamer was at the bottom of the river. I was thunderstruck. What, how, why? Oh, it was 'all right.' The 'manager himself' was there. All quite correct. 'Everybody had behaved splendidly! splendidly!'—'you must,' he said in agitation, 'go and see the general manager at once. He is waiting!'

"I did not see the real significance of that wreck at once. I fancy I see it now, but I am not sure—not at all. Certainly the affair was too stupid— when I think of it—to be altogether natural. Still . . . But at the moment it presented itself simply as a confounded nuisance. The steamer was sunk. They had started two days before in a sudden hurry up the river with the manager on board, in charge of some volunteer skipper, and before they had been out three hours they tore the bottom out of her on stones, and she sank near the south bank. I asked myself what I was to do there, now my boat was lost. As a matter of fact, I had plenty to do in fishing my command out of the river. I had to set about it the very next day. That, and the repairs when I brought the pieces to the station, took some months.

"My first interview with the manager was curious. He did not ask me to sit down after my twenty-mile walk that morning. He was common-place in complexion, in feature, in manners, and in voice. He was of middle size and of ordinary build. His eyes, of the usual blue, were perhaps remarkably cold, and he certainly could make his glance fall on one as trenchant and heavy as an axe. But even at these times the rest of his person seemed to disclaim the intention. Otherwise there was only an indefinable, faint expression of his lips, something stealthy—a smile—not a smile—I remember it, but I can't explain. It was unconscious, this smile was, though just after he had said something it got intensified for an instant. It came at the end of his speeches like a seal applied on the words to make the meaning of the commonest phrase appear absolutely inscrutable. He was a common trader, from his youth up employed in these parts—nothing more. He was obeyed, yet he inspired neither love nor fear, nor even respect. He inspired uneasiness. That was it! Uneasiness. Not a definite mistrust—just uneasiness—nothing more. You have no idea how effective such a . . . a . . . faculty can be. He had no genius for organizing, for initiative, or for order even. That was evident in such things as the deplorable state of the station. He had no learning, and no intelligence. His position had come to him—why? Perhaps because he was never ill . . . He had served three terms of three years out there . . . Because triumphant health in the general rout of constitutions is a kind of power in itself. When he went home on leave he rioted on a large scale—pompously. Jack ashore—with a difference—in externals only. This one could gather from his casual talk. He originated nothing, he could keep the routine going—that's all. But he was great. He was great by this little thing that it was impossible to tell what could control such a man. He never gave that secret away. Perhaps there was nothing within him. Such a suspicion made one pause—for out there there were no external checks. Once when various tropical diseases had laid low almost every 'agent' in the station, he was heard to say, 'Men who come out here should have no entrails.' He sealed the utterance with that smile of his, as though it had been a door opening into a darkness he had in his keeping. You fancied you had seen things—but the seal was on. When annoyed at meal-times by the constant quarrels of the white men about precedence, he ordered an immense round table to be made, for which a special house had to be built. This was the station's mess-room. Where he sat was the first place—the rest were nowhere. One felt this to be his unalterable conviction. He was neither civil nor uncivil. He was quiet. He allowed his 'boy'—an overfed young negro from the coast—to treat the white men, under his very eyes, with provoking insolence.

"He began to speak as soon as he saw me. I had been very long on the road. He could not wait. Had to start without me. The up-river stations had to be relieved. There had been so many delays already that he did not know who was dead and who was alive, and how they got on—and so on, and so on. He paid no attention to my explanations, and, playing with a stick of sealing-wax, repeated several times that the situation was 'very grave, very grave.' There were rumours that a very important station was in jeopardy, and its chief, Mr. Kurtz, was ill. Hoped it was not true. Mr. Kurtz was . . . I felt weary and irritable. Hang Kurtz, I thought. I interrupted him by saying I had heard of Mr. Kurtz on the coast. 'Ah! So they talk of him down there,' he murmured to himself. Then he began again, assuring me Mr. Kurtz was the best agent he had, an exceptional man, of the greatest importance to the Company; therefore I could understand his anxiety. He was, he said, 'very, very uneasy.' Certainly he fidgeted on his chair a good deal, exclaimed, 'Ah, Mr. Kurtz!' broke the stick of sealing-wax and seemed dumbfounded by the accident. Next think he wanted to know 'how long it would take to' . . . I interrupted him again. Being hungry, you know, and kept on my feet, too, I was getting savage. 'How could I tell?' I said. 'I hadn't even seen the wreck yet—some months, no doubt.' All this talk seemed to me so futile. 'Some months,' he said. 'Well, let us say three months before we can make a start. Yes. That ought to do the affair.' I flung out of his hut (he lived all alone in a clay hut with a sort of verandah) muttering to myself my opinion of him. He was a chattering idiot. Afterwards I took it back when it was borne in upon me startlingly with what extreme nicety he had estimated the time requisite for the 'affair.'

"I went to work the next day, turning, so to speak, my back on that station. In that way only it seemed to me I could keep my hold on the redeeming facts of life. Still, one must look about sometimes; and then I saw this station, these men strolling aimlessly about in the sunshine of the yard. I asked myself sometimes what it all meant. They wandered here and there with their absurd long staves in their hands, like a lot of faithless pilgrims bewitched inside a rotten fence. The word 'ivory' rang in the air, was whispered, was sighed. You would think they were praying to it. A taint of imbecile rapacity blew through it all, like a whiff from some corpse. By Jove! I've never seen anything so unreal in my life. And outside, the silent wilderness surrounding this cleared speck on the earth struck me as something great and invincible, like evil or truth, waiting patiently for the passing away of this fantastic invasion.

"Oh, these months! Well, never mind. Various things happened. One evening a grass shed full of calico, cotton prints, beads, and I don't know what else, burst into a blaze so suddenly that you would have thought the earth had opened to let an avenging fire consume all that trash. I was smoking my pipe quietly by my dismantled steamer, and saw them all cutting capers in the light, with their arms lifted high, when the stout man with moustaches came tearing down to the river, a tin pail in his hand, assured me that everybody was 'behaving splendidly, splendidly,' dipped about a quart of water and tore back again. I noticed there was a hole in the bottom of the pail.

"I strolled up. There was no hurry. You see the thing had gone off like a box of matches. It had been hopeless from the very first. The flame had leaped high, driven everybody back, lighted up everything—and collapsed. The shed was already a heap of embers glowing fiercely. A nigger was being beaten near by. They said he had caused the fire in some way; be that as it may, he was screeching most horribly. I saw him later, for several days, sitting in a bit of shade looking very sick and trying to recover himself: afterwards he arose and went out—and the wilderness without a sound took him into its bosom again. As I approached the glow from the dark I found myself at the back of two men, talking. I heard the name of Kurtz pronounced, then the words, 'take advantage of this unfortunate accident.' One of the men was the manager. I wished him a good evening. 'Did you ever see anything like it—eh? it is incredible,' he said, and walked off. The other man remained. He was a first-class agent, young, gentlemanly, a bit reserved, with a forked little beard and a hooked nose. He was stand-offish with the other agents, and they on their side said he was the manager's spy upon them. As to me, I had hardly ever spoken to him before. We got into talk, and by-and-by we strolled away from the hissing ruins. Then he asked me to his room, which was in the main building of the station. He struck a match, and I perceived that this young aristocrat had not only a silver-mounted dressing-case but also a whole candle all to himself. Just at that time the manager was the only man supposed to have any right to candles. Native mats covered the clay walls; a collection of spears, assegais, shields, knives was hung up in trophies. The business intrusted to this fellow was the making of bricks—so I had been informed; but there wasn't a fragment of a brick anywhere in the station, and he had been there more than a year—waiting. It seems he could not make bricks without something, I don't know what—straw maybe. Anyways, it could not be found there, and as it was not likely to be sent from Europe, it did not appear clear to me what he was waiting for. An act of special creation perhaps. However, they were all waiting—all the sixteen or twenty pilgrims of them—for something; and upon my word it did not seem an uncongenial occupation, from the way they took it, though the only thing that ever came to them was disease—as far as I could see. They beguiled the time by backbiting and intriguing against each other in a foolish kind of way. There was an air of plotting about that station, but nothing came of it, of course. It was as unreal as everything else—as the philanthropic pretence of the whole concern, as their talk, as their government, as their show of work. The only real feeling was a desire to get appointed to a trading-post where ivory was to be had, so that they could earn percentages. They intrigued and slandered and hated each other only on that account,— but as to effectually lifting a little finger—oh, no. By heavens! there is something after all in the world allowing one man to steal a horse while another must not look at a halter. Steal a horse straight out. Very well. He has done it. Perhaps he can ride. But there is a way of looking at a halter that would provoke the most charitable of saints into a kick.

"I had no idea why he wanted to be sociable, but as we chatted in

there it suddenly occurred to me the fellow was trying to get at something—in fact, pumping me. He alluded constantly to Europe, to the
people I was supposed to know there—putting leading questions as to
my acquaintances in the sepulchral city, and so on. His little eyes glittered
like mica discs—with curiousity—though he tried to keep up a bit of
superciliousness. At first I was astonished, but very soon I became awfully
curious to see what he would find out from me. I couldn't possibly
imagine what I had in me to make it worth his while. It was very pretty
to see how he baffled himself, for in truth my body was full only of chills,
and my head had nothing in it but that wretched steamboat business. It
was evident he took me for a perfectly shameless prevaricator. At last he
got angry, and, to conceal a movement of furious annoyance, he yawned.
I rose. Then I noticed a small sketch in oils, on a panel, representing a
woman, draped and blindfolded, carrying a lighted torch. The background was sombre—almost black. The movement of the woman was
stately, and the effect of the torch-light on the face was sinister.

"It arrested me, and he stood by civilly, holding an empty half-pint
champagne bottle (medical comforts) with the candle stuck in it. To my
question he said Mr. Kurtz had painted this—in this very station more
than a year ago—while waiting for means to go to his trading-post. 'Tell
me, pray,' said I, 'who is this Mr. Kurtz?'

" 'The chief of the Inner Station,' he answered in a short tone, looking
away. 'Much obliged,' I said, laughing. 'And you are the brickmaker of
the Central Station. Everyone knows that.' He was silent for a while. 'He
is a prodigy,' he said at last. 'He is an emissary of pity, and science, and
progress, and devil knows what else. We want,' he began to declaim
suddenly, 'for the guidance of the cause intrusted to us by Europe, so to
speak, higher intelligence, wide sympathies, a singleness of purpose.'
'Who says that?' I asked. 'Lots of them,' he replied. 'Some even write that;
and so *he* comes here, a special being, as you ought to know.' 'Why ought
I to know?' I interrupted, really surprised. He paid no attention. 'Yes. Today he is chief of the best station, next year he will be assistant-manager,
two years more and . . . but I daresay you know what he will be in two
years' time. You are of the new gang—the gang of virtue. The same
people who sent him specially also recommended you. Oh, don't say no.
I've my own eyes to trust.' Light dawned upon me. My dear aunt's
influential acquaintances were producing an unexpected effect upon that
young man. I nearly burst into a laugh. 'Do you read the Company's
confidential correspondence?' I asked. He hadn't a word to say. It was
great fun. 'When Mr. Kurtz,' I continued, severely, 'is General Manager,
you won't have the opportunity.'

"He blew the candle out suddenly, and we went outside. The moon
had risen. Black figures strolled about listlessly pouring water on the
glow, whence proceeded a sound of hissing; steam ascended in the

moonlight, the beaten nigger groaned somewhere. 'What a row the brute makes!' said the indefatigable man with the moustaches, appearing near us. 'Serve him right. Transgression—punishment—bang! Pitiless, pitiless. That's the only way. This will prevent all conflagrations for the future. I was just telling the manager . . .' He noticed my companion, and became crestfallen all at once. 'Not in bed yet,' he said, with a kind of servile heartiness; 'it's so natural. Ha! Danger—agitation.' He vanished. I went on to the river-side, and the other followed me. I heard a scathing murmur at my ear, 'Heap of muffs—go to.' The pilgrims could be seen in knots gesticulating, discussing. Several had still their staves in their hands. I verily believe they took these sticks to bed with them. Beyond the fence the forest stood up spectrally in the moonlight, and through the dim stir, through the faint sounds of that lamentable courtyard, the silence of the land went home to one's very heart—its mystery, its greatness, the amazing reality of its concealed life. The hurt nigger moaned feebly somewhere near by, and then fetched a deep sigh that made me mend my pace away from there. I felt a hand introducing itself under my arm. 'My dear sir,' said the fellow, 'I don't want to be misunderstood, and especially by you, who will see Mr. Kurtz long before I can have that pleasure. I wouldn't like him to get a false idea of my disposition. . . .'

"I let him run on, this papier-mâché Mephistopheles, and it seemed to me that if I tried I could poke my forefinger through him, and would find nothing inside but a little loose dirt, maybe. He, don't you see, had been planning to be assistant-manager by-and-by under the present man, and I could see that the coming of that Kurtz had upset them both not a little. He talked precipitately, and I did not try to stop him. I had my shoulders against the wreck of my steamer, hauled up on the slope like a carcass of some big river animal. The smell of mud, of primeval mud, by Jove! was in my nostrils, the high stillness of primeval forest was before my eyes; there were shiny patches on the black creek. The moon had spread over everything a thin layer of silver—over the rank grass, over the mud, upon the wall of matted vegetation standing higher than the wall of a temple, over the great river I could see through a sombre gap glittering, glittering, as it flowed broadly by without a murmur. All this was great, expectant, mute, while the man jabbered about himself. I wondered whether the stillness on the face of the immensity looking at us two were meant as an appeal or as a menace. What were we who had strayed in here? Could we handle that dumb thing, or would it handle us? I felt how big, how confoundedly big, was that thing that couldn't talk, and perhaps was deaf as well. What was in there? I could see a little ivory coming out from there, and I had heard Mr. Kurtz was in there. I had heard enough about it, too—God knows! Yet somehow it didn't bring any image with it—no more than if I had been told an angel or a fiend was in there. I believed it in the same way one of you might believe there are inhabitants in the plant Mars. I knew once a Scotch sailmaker who was certain, dead sure, there were people in Mars. If you asked him for some idea how they looked and behaved, he would get shy and mutter something about 'walking on all-fours.' If you as much as smiled, he would—though a man of sixty—offer to fight you. I would not have gone so far as to fight for Kurtz, but I went for him near enough to a lie. You know I hate, detest, and can't bear a lie, not because I am straighter than the rest of us, but simply because it appalls me. There is a taint of death, a flavour of mortality in lies—which is exactly what I hate and detest in the world—what I want to forget. It makes me miserable and sick, like biting something rotten would do. Temperament, I suppose. Well, I went near enough to it by letting the young fool there believe anything he liked to imagine as to my influence in Europe. I became in an instant as much of a pretence as the rest of the bewitched pilgrims. This simply because I had a notion it somehow would be of help to that Kurtz whom at the time I did not see—you understand. He was just a word for me. I did not see the man in the name any more than you do. Do you see him? Do you see the story? Do you see anything? It seems to me I am trying to tell you a dream—making a vain attempt, because no relation of a dream can convey the dream-sensation, that commingling of absurdity, surprise, and bewilderment in a tremor of struggling revolt, that notion of being captured by the incredible which is of the very essence of dreams. . . ."

He was silent for a while.

" . . . No, it is impossible; it is impossible to convey the life-sensation of any given epoch of one's existence—that which makes its truth, its meaning—its subtle and penetrating essence. It is impossible. We live, as we dream—alone. . . ."

He paused again as if reflecting, then added—

"Of course in this you fellows see more than I could then. You see me, whom you know. . . ."

It had become so pitch dark that we listeners could hardly see one another. For a long time already he, sitting apart, had been no more to us than a voice. There was not a word from anybody. The others might have been asleep, but I was awake. I listened, I listened on the watch for the sentence, for the word, that would give me the clue to the faint uneasiness inspired by this narrative that seemed to shape itself without human lips in the heavy night-air of the river.

" . . . Yes—I let him run on," Marlow began again, "and think what he pleased about the powers that were behind me. I did! And there was nothing behind me! There was nothing but that wretched, old, mangled steamboat I was leaning against, while he talked fluently about 'the necessity for every man to get on.' 'And when one comes out here, you conceive, it is not to gaze at the moon.' Mr. Kurtz was a 'universal genius,' but even a genius would find it easier to work with 'adequate tools— intelligent men.' He did not make bricks—why, there was a physical impossibility in the way—as I was well aware; and if he did secretarial work for the manager, it was because 'no sensible man rejects wantonly the confidence of his superiors.' Did I see it? I saw it. What more did I want? What I really wanted was rivets, by heaven! Rivets. To get on with the work—to stop the hole. Rivets I wanted. There were cases of them down at the coast—cases—piled up—burst—split! You kicked a loose rivet at every second step in that station yard on the hillside. Rivets had rolled into the grove of death. You could fill your pockets with rivets for the trouble of stooping down—and there wasn't one rivet to be found where it was wanted. We had plates that would do, but nothing to fasten them with. And every week the messenger, a lone negro, letter-bag on shoulder and staff in hand, left our station for the coast. And several times a week a coast caravan came in with trade goods—ghastly glazed calico that made you shudder only to look at it, glass beads value about a penny a quart, confounded spotted cotton handkerchiefs. And no rivets. Three carriers could have brought all that was wanted to set that steamboat afloat.

"He was becoming confidential now, but I fancy my unresponsive attitude must have exasperated him at last, for he judged it necessary to inform me he feared neither God nor devil, let alone any mere man. I said I could see that very well, but what I wanted was a certain quantity of rivets—and rivets were what really Mr. Kurtz wanted, if he had only known it. Now letters went to the coast every week. . . . 'My dear sir,' he cried, 'I write from dictation.' I demanded rivets. There was a way— for an intelligent man. He changed his manner; became very cold, and suddenly began to talk about a hippopotamus; wondered whether sleeping on board the steamer (I stuck to my salvage night and day) I wasn't disturbed. There was an old hippo that had the bad habit of getting out on the bank and roaming at night over the station grounds. The pilgrims used to turn out in a body and empty every rifle they could lay hands on at him. Some even had sat up o' nights for him. All this energy was wasted, though. 'That animal has a charmed life,' he said; 'but you can say this only of brutes in this country. No man—you apprehend me?— no man here bears a charmed life.' He stood there for a moment in the moonlight with his delicate hooked nose set a little askew, and his mica eyes glittering without a wink, then, with a curt Good-night, he strode off. I could see he was disturbed and considerably puzzled, which made me feel more hopeful than I had been for days. It was a great comfort to turn from that chap to my influential friend, the battered, twisted, ruined, tin-pot steamboat. I clambered on board. She rang under my feet like an empty Huntley & Palmer biscuit-tin kicked along a gutter; she was nothing so solid in make, and rather less pretty in shape, but I had expended enough hard work on her to make me love her. No influential friend would have served me better. She had given me a chance to come out a bit—to find out what I could do. No, I don't like work. I had rather laze about and think of all the fine things that can be done. I don't like work—no man does—but I like what is in the work,—the chance to find yourself. Your own reality—for yourself, not for others—what no other man can ever know. They can only see the mere show, and never can tell what it really means.

"I was not surprised to see somebody sitting aft, on the deck, with his legs dangling over the mud. You see I rather chummed with the few mechanics there were in that station, whom the other pilgrims naturally despised—on account of their imperfect manners, I suppose. This was the foreman—a boiler-maker by trade—a good worker. He was a lank, bony, yellow-faced man, with big intense eyes. His aspect was worried, and his head was as bald as the palm of my hand; but his hair in falling seemed to have stuck to his chin, and had prospered in the new locality, for his beard hung down to his waist. He was a widower with six young children (he had left them in charge of a sister of his to come out there), and the passion of his life was pigeon-flying. He was an enthusiast and a connoisseur. He would rave about pigeons. After work hours he used sometimes to come over from his hut for a talk about his children and his pigeons; at work, when he had to crawl in the mud under the bottom of the steamboat, he would tie up that beard of his in a kind of white serviette he brought for the purpose. It had loops to go over his ears. In the evening he could be seen squatted on the bank rinsing that wrapper in the creek with great care, then spreading it solemnly on a bush to dry.

"I slapped him on the back and shouted 'We shall have rivets!' He scrambled to his feet exclaiming 'No! Rivets!' as though he couldn't believe his ears. Then in a low voice, 'You . . . eh?' I don't know why we behaved like lunatics. I put my finger to the side of my nose and nodded mysteriously. 'Good for you!' he cried, snapped his fingers above his head, lifting one foot. I tried a jig. We capered on the iron deck. A frightful clatter came out of that hulk, and the virgin forest on the other bank of the creek sent it back in a thundering roll upon the sleeping station. It must have made some of the pilgrims sit up in their hovels. A dark figure obscured the lighted doorway of the manager's hut, vanished, then, a second or so after, the doorway itself vanished, too. We stopped, and the silence driven away by the stamping of our feet flowed back again from the recesses of the land. The great wall of vegetation, an exuberant and entangled mass of trunks, branches, leaves, boughs, festoons, motionless in the moonlight, was like a rioting invasion of soundless life, a rolling wave of plants, piled up, crested, ready to topple over the creek, to sweep every little man of us out of his little existence. And it moved not. A deadened burst of mighty splashes and snorts reached us from afar, as though an ichthyosaurus had been taking a bath of glitter in the great river. 'After all,' said the boiler-maker in a reasonable tone, 'why shouldn't we get the rivets?' Why not, indeed! I did not know of any reason why we shouldn't. They'll come in three weeks,' I said, confidently.

"But they didn't. Instead of rivets there came an invasion, an infliction, a visitation. It came in sections during the next three weeks, each section headed by a donkey carrying a white man in new clothes and tan shoes, bowing from that elevation right and left to the impressed pilgrims. A quarrelsome band of footsore sulky niggers trod on the heels of the donkey; a lot of tents, camp-stools, tin boxes, white cases, brown bales would be shot down in the courtyard, and the air of mystery would deepen a little over the muddle of the station. Five such instalments came, with their absurd air of disorderly flight with the loot of innumerable outfit shops and provision stores, that, one would think, they were lugging, after a raid, into the wilderness for equitable division. It was an inextricable mess of things decent in themselves but that human folly made look like spoils of thieving.

"This devoted band called itself the Eldorado Exploring Expedition, and I believe they were sworn to secrecy. Their talk, however, was the talk of sordid buccaneers: it was reckless without hardihood, greedy without audacity, and cruel without courage; there was not an atom of foresight or of serious intention in the whole batch of them, and they did not seem aware these things are wanted for the work of the world. To tear treasure out of the bowels of the land was their desire, with no more moral purpose at the back of it than there is in burglars breaking into a safe. Who paid the expenses of the noble enterprise I don't know; but the uncle of our manager was leader of that lot.

"In exterior he resembled a butcher in a poor neighbourhood, and his eyes had a look of sleepy cunning. He carried his fat paunch with ostentation on his short legs, and during the time his gang infested the station spoke to no one but his nephew. You could see these two roaming about all day long with their heads close together in an everlasting confab.

"I had given up worrying myself about the rivets. One's capacity for that kind of folly is more limited than you would suppose. I said Hang!—and let things slide. I had plenty of time for meditation, and now and then I would give some thought to Kurtz. I wasn't very interested in him. No. Still, I was curious to see whether this man, who had come out equipped with moral ideas of some sort, would climb to the top after all and how he would set about his work when there."

II

"One evening as I was lying flat on the deck of my steamboat, I heard voices approaching—and there were the nephew and the uncle strolling along the bank. I laid my head on my arm again, and had nearly lost myself in a doze, when somebody said in my ear, as it were: 'I am as harmless as a little child, but I don't like to be dictated to. Am I the manager—or am I not? I was ordered to send him there. It's incredible.' . . . I became aware that the two were standing on the shore alongside the forepart of the steamboat, just below my head. I did not move; it did not occur to me to move: I was sleepy. 'It *is* unpleasant,' grunted the uncle. 'He has asked the Administration to be sent there,' said the other, 'with the idea of showing what he could do; and I was instructed accordingly. Look at the influence that man must have. Is it not frightful?' They both agreed it was frightful, then made several bizarre remarks: 'Make rain and fine weather—one man—the Council—by the nose'—bits of absurd sentences that got the better of my drowsiness, so that I had pretty near the whole of my wits about me when the uncle said, 'The climate may do away with this difficulty for you. Is he alone there?' 'Yes,' answered the manager; 'he sent his assistant down the river with a note to me in these terms: "Clear this poor devil out of the country, and don't bother sending more of that sort. I had rather be alone than have the kind of men you can dispose of with me." It was more than a year ago. Can you imagine such impudence!' 'Anything since then?' asked the other, hoarsely. 'Ivory,' jerked the nephew; 'lots of it—prime sort—lots—most annoying, from him.' 'And with that?' questioned the heavy rumble. 'Invoice,' was the reply fired out, so to speak. Then silence. They had been talking about Kurtz.

"I was broad awake by this time, but, lying perfectly at ease, remained still, having no inducement to change my position. 'How did that ivory come all this way?' growled the elder man, who seemed very vexed. The other explained that it had come with a fleet of canoes in charge of an English half-caste clerk Kurtz had with him; that Kurtz had apparently intended to return himself, the station being by that time bare of goods and stores, but after coming three hundred miles, had suddenly decided to go back, which he started to do alone in a small dugout with four paddlers, leaving the half-caste to continue down the river with the ivory. The two fellows there seemed astounded at anybody attempting such a thing. They were at a loss for an adequate motive. As to me, I seemed to see Kurtz for the first time. It was a distinct glimpse: the dugout, four paddling savages, and the lone white man turning his back suddenly on the headquarters, on relief, on thoughts of home—perhaps; setting his face towards the depths of the wilderness, towards his empty and desolate station. I did not know the motive. Perhaps he was just simply a fine fellow who stuck to his work for its own sake. His name, you understand, had not been pronounced once. He was 'that man.' The half-caste, who, as far as I could see, had conducted a difficult trip with great prudence and pluck, was invariably alluded to as 'that scoundrel.' The 'scoundrel' had reported that the 'man' had been very ill—had recovered imperfectly. . . . The two below me moved away then a few paces, and strolled back and forth at some little distance. I heard: 'Military post—doctor—two hundred miles—quite alone now—unavoidable delays—nine months—no news—strange rumours.' They approached again, just as the manager was saying, 'No one, as far as I know, unless a species of wandering trader—a pestilential fellow, snapping ivory from the natives.' Who was it they were talking about now? I gathered in snatches that this was some man supposed to be in Kurtz's district, and of whom the manager did not approve. 'We will not be free from unfair competition till one of these fellows is hanged for an example,' he said. 'Certainly,' grunted the other; 'get him hanged! Why not? Anything—anything can be done in this country. That's what I say; nobody here, you understand, *here*, can endanger your position. And why? You stand the climate—you outlast them all. The danger is in Europe; but there before I left I took care to——' They moved off and whispered, then their voices rose again. 'The extraordinary series of delays is not my fault. I did my best.' The fat man sighed. 'Very sad.' 'And the pestiferous absurdity of his talk,' continued the other; 'he bothered me enough when he was here. "Each station should be like a beacon on the road towards better things, a centre for trade of course, but also for humanizing, improving, instructing." Conceive you—that ass! And he wants to be manager! No, it's——' Here he got choked by excessive indignation, and I lifted my head the least bit. I was surprised to see how near they were—right under me. I could have spat upon their hats. They were looking on the ground, absorbed in thought. The manager was switching his leg with a slender twig: his sagacious relative lifted his head. 'You have been well since you came out this time?' he asked. The other gave a start. 'Who? I? Oh! Like a charm—like a charm. But the rest—oh, my goodness! All sick. They die so quick, too, that I haven't the time to send them out of the country—it's incredible!' 'H'm. Just so,' grunted the uncle. 'Ah! my boy, trust to this—I say, trust to this.' I saw him extend his short flipper of an arm for a gesture that took in the forest, the creek, the mud, the river,—seemed to beckon with a dishonouring flourish before the sunlit face of the land a treacherous appeal to the lurking death, to the hidden evil, to the profound darkness of its heart. It was so startling that I leaped to my feet and looked back at the edge of the forest, as though I had expected an answer of some sort to that black display of confidence. You know the foolish notions that come to one sometimes. The high stillness confronted these two figures with its ominous patience, waiting for the passing away of a fantastic invasion.

"They swore aloud together—out of sheer fright, I believe—then pretending not to know anything of my existence, turned back to the station. The sun was low; and leaning forward side by side, they seemed to be tugging painfully uphill their two ridiculous shadows of unequal length, that trailed behind them slowly over the tall grass without bending a single blade.

"In a few days the Eldorado Expedition went into the patient wilderness, that closed upon it as the sea closes over a diver. Long afterwards the news came that all the donkeys were dead. I know nothing as to the fate of the less valuable animals. They, no doubt, like the rest of us, found what they deserved. I did not inquire. I was then rather excited at the prospect of meeting Kurtz very soon. When I say very soon I mean it comparatively. It was just two months from the day we left the creek when we came to the bank below Kurtz's station.

"Going up that river was like travelling back to the earliest beginnings of the world, when vegetation rioted on the earth and the big trees were kings. An empty stream, a great silence, an impenetrable forest. The air was warm, thick, heavy, sluggish. There was no joy in the brilliance of sunshine. The long stretches of the waterway ran on, deserted, into the gloom of overshadowed distances. On silvery sandbanks hippos and alligators sunned themselves side by side. The broadening waters flowed through a mob of wooded islands; you lost your way on that river as you would in a desert, and butted all day long against shoals, trying to find the channel, till you thought yourself bewitched and cut off for ever from everything you had known once—somewhere—far away—in another existence perhaps. There were moments when one's past came back to one, as it will sometimes when you have not a moment to spare to yourself; but it came in the shape of an unrestful and noisy dream, remembered with wonder amongst the overwhelming realities of this strange world of plants, and water, and silence. And this stillness of life did not in the least resemble a peace. It was the stillness of an implacable force brooding over an inscrutable intention. It looked at you with a vengeful aspect. I got used to it afterwards; I did not see it any more; I had no time. I had to keep guessing at the channel; I had to discern, mostly by inspiration, the signs of hidden banks; I watched for sunken stones; I was learning to clap my teeth smartly before my heart flew out, when I shaved by a fluke some infernal sly old snag that would have ripped the life out of the tin-pot steamboat and drowned all the pilgrims; I had to keep a look-out for the signs of dead wood we could cut up in the night for next day's steaming. When you have to attend to things of that sort, to the mere incidents of the surface, the reality—the reality, I tell you—fades. The inner truth is hidden—luckily, luckily. But I felt it all the same; I felt often its mysterious stillness watching me at my monkey tricks, just as it watches you fellows performing on your respective tight-ropes for—what is it? half-a-crown a tumble——"

"Try to be civil, Marlow," growled a voice, and I knew there was at least one listener awake besides my self.

"I beg your pardon. I forgot the heartache which makes up the rest of the price. And indeed what does the price matter, if the trick be well done? You do your tricks very well. And I didn't do badly either, since I managed not to sink that steamboat on my first trip. It's a wonder to me yet. Imagine a blindfolded man set to drive a van over a bad road. I sweated and shivered over that business considerably, I can tell you. After all, for a seaman, to scrape the bottom of the thing that's supposed to float all the time under his care is the unpardonable sin. No one may know of it, but you never forget the thump—eh? A blow on the very heart. You remember it, you dream of it, you wake up at night and think of it—years after—and go hot and cold all over. I don't pretend to say that steamboat floated all the time. More than once she had to wade for a bit, with twenty cannibals splashing around and pushing. We had enlisted some of these chaps on the way for a crew. Fine fellows—cannibals—in their place. They were men one could work with, and I am grateful to them. And, after all, they did not eat each other before my face: they had brought along a provision of hippo-meat which went rotten, and made the mystery of the wilderness stink in my nostrils. Phoo! I can sniff it now. I had the manager on board and three or four pilgrims with their staves—all complete. Sometimes we came upon a station close by the bank, clinging to the skirts of the unknown, and the white men rushing out of a tumble-down hovel, with great gestures of joy and surprise and welcome, seemed very strange—had the appearance of being held there captive by a spell. The word ivory would ring in the air for a while—and on we went again into the silence, along empty reaches, round the still bends, between the high walls of our winding way, reverberating in hollow claps the ponderous beat of the stern-wheel. Trees, trees, millions of trees, massive, immense, running up high; and at their foot, hugging the bank against the stream, crept the little begrimed steamboat, like a sluggish beetle crawling on the floor of a lofty portico. It made you feel very small, very lost, and yet it was not altogether depressing, that feeling. After all, if you were small, the grimy beetle crawled on—which was just what you wanted it to do. Where the pilgrims imagined it crawled to I don't know. To some place where they expected to get something, I bet! For me it crawled towards Kurtz—exclusively; but when the steam-pipes started leaking we crawled very slow. The reaches opened before us and closed behind , as if the forest had stepped leisurely across the water to bar the way for our return. We penetrated deeper and deeper into the heart of darkness. It was very quiet there. At night sometimes the roll of drums behind the curtain of trees would run up the river and remain sustained faintly, as if hovering in the air high over our heads, till the first break of day. Whether it meant war, peace, or prayer we could not tell. The dawns were heralded by the descent of a chill stillness; the wood-cutters slept, their fires burned low; the snapping of a twig would make you start. We were wanderers on prehistoric earth, on an earth that wore the aspect of an unknown planet. We could have fancied ourselves the first of men taking possession of an accursed inheritance, to be subdued at the cost of profound anguish and of excessive toil. But suddenly, as we struggled round a bend, there would be a glimpse of rush walls, of peaked grass-roofs, a burst of yells, a whirl of black limbs, a mass of hands clapping, of feet stamping, of bodies swaying, of eyes rolling, under the droop of heavy and motionless foliage. The steamer toiled along slowly on the edge of a black and incomprehensible frenzy. The prehistoric man was cursing us, praying to us, welcoming us—who could tell? We were cut off from the comprehension of our surroundings; we glided past like phantoms, wondering and secretly appalled, as sane men would be before an enthusiastic outbreak in a madhouse. We could not understand because we were too far and could not remember, because we were travelling in the night of first ages, of those ages that are gone, leaving hardly a sign—and no memories.

"The earth seemed unearthly. We are accustomed to look upon the shackled form of a conquered monster, but there—there you could look at a thing monstrous and free. It was unearthly, and the men were—— No, they were not inhuman. Well, you know, that was the worst of it—this suspicion of their not being inhuman. It would come slowly to one. They howled and leaped, and spun, and made horrid faces; but what thrilled you was just the thought of their humanity—like yours—the thought of your remote kinship with this wild and passionate uproar. Ugly. Yes, it was ugly enough; but if you were man enough you would admit to yourself that there was in you just the faintest trace of a response to the terrible frankness of that noise, a dim suspicion of there being a meaning in it which you—you so remote from the night of first ages—could comprehend. And why not? The mind of man is capable of anything—because everything is in it, all the past as well as all the future. What was there after all? Joy, fear, sorrow, devotion, valour, rage—who can tell?—but truth—truth stripped of its cloak of time. Let the fool gape and shudder—the man knows, and can look on without a wink. But he must at least be as much of a man as these on the shore. He must meet that truth with his own true stuff—with his own inborn strength. Principles won't do. Acquisitions, clothes, pretty rags—rags that would fly off at the first good shake. No; you want a deliberate belief. An appeal to me in this fiendish row—is there? Very well; I hear; I admit, but I have a voice, too, and for good or evil mine is the speech that cannot be silenced. Of course, a fool, what with sheer fright and fine sentiments, is always safe. Who's that grunting? You wonder I didn't go ashore for a howl and a dance? Well, no—I didn't. I had no time. I had to mess about with white-lead and strips of woollen blanket helping to put bandages on those leaky steam-pipes—I tell you. I had to watch the steering, and circumvent those snags, and get the tin-pot along by hook or by crook. There was surface-truth enough in these things to save a wiser man. And between whiles I had to look after the savage who was fireman. He was an improved specimen; he could fire up a vertical boiler. He was there below me, and, upon my word, to look at him was as edifying as seeing a dog in a parody of breeches and a feather hat, walking on his hind-legs. A few months of training had done for that really fine chap. He squinted at the steam-gauge and at the water-gauge with an evident effort of intrepidity—and he had filed teeth, too, the poor devil, and the wool of his pate shaved into queer patterns, and three ornamental scars on each of his cheeks. He ought to have been clapping his hands and stamping his feet on the bank, instead of which he was hard at work, a thrall to strange witchcraft, full of improving knowledge. He was useful because he had been instructed; and what he knew was this—that should the water in that transparent thing disappear, the evil spirit inside the boiler would get angry through the greatness of his thirst, and take a terrible vengeance. So he sweated and fired up and watched the glass fearfully (with an impromptu charm, made of rags, tied to his arm, and a piece of polished bone, as big as a watch, stuck flatways through his lower lip), while the wooded banks slipped past us slowly, the short noise was left behind, the interminable miles of silence—and we crept on, towards Kurtz. But the snags were thick, the water was treacherous and shallow, the boiler seemed indeed to have a sulky devil in it, and thus neither that fireman nor I had any time to peer into our creepy thoughts.

"Some fifty miles below the Inner Station we came upon a hut of reeds, an inclined and melancholy pole, with the unrecognizable tatters of what had been a flag of some sort flying from it, and a neatly stacked wood-pile. This was unexpected. We came to the bank, and on the stack of firewood found a flat piece of board with some faded pencil-writing on it. When deciphered it said: 'Wood for you. Hurry up. Approach cautiously.' There was a signature, but it was illegible—not Kurtz—a much longer word. Hurry up. Where? Up the river? 'Approach cautiously.' We had not done so. But the warning could not have been meant for the place where it could be only found after approach. Something was wrong above. But what—and how much? That was the question. We commented adversely upon the imbecility of that telegraphic style. The bush around said nothing, and would not let us look very far, either. A torn curtain of red twill hung in the doorway of the hut, and flapped sadly in our faces. The dwelling was dismantled; but we could see a white man had lived there not very long ago. There remained a rude table—a plank on two posts; a heap of rubbish reposed in a dark corner, and by the door I picked up a book. It had lost its covers, and the pages had been thumbed into a state of extremely dirty softness; but the back had been lovingly stitched afresh with white cotton thread, which looked clean yet. It was an extraordinary find. Its title was, *An Inquiry into some Points of Seamanship*, by a man Tower, Towson—some such name—Master in his Majesty's Navy. The matter looked dreary reading enough, with illustrative diagrams and repulsive tables of figures, and the copy was sixty years old. I handled this amazing antiquity with the greatest possible tenderness, lest it should dissolve in my hands. Within, Towson or Towser was inquiring earnestly into the breaking strain of ships' chains and tackle, and other such matters. Not a very enthralling book; but at the first glance you could see there a singleness of intention, an honest concern for the right way of going to work, which made these humble pages, thought out so many years ago, luminous with another than a professional light. The simple old sailor, with his talk of chains and purchases, made me forget the jungle and the pilgrims in a delicious sensation of having come upon something unmistakably real. Such a book being there was wonderful enough; but still more astounding were the notes pencilled in the margin, and plainly referring to the text. I couldn't believe my eyes! They were in cipher! Yes, it looked like cipher. Fancy a man lugging with him a book of that description into this nowhere and studying it—and making notes—in cipher at that! It was an extravagant mystery.

"I had been dimly aware for some time of a worrying noise, and when I lifted my eyes I saw the wood-pile was gone, and the manager, aided by all the pilgrims, was shouting at me from the river-side. I slipped the book into my pocket. I assure you to leave off reading was like tearing myself away from the shelter of an old and solid friendship.

"I started the lame engine ahead. 'It must be this miserable trader—this intruder,' exclaimed the manager, looking back malevolently at the place we had left. 'He must be English,' I said. 'It will not save him from getting into trouble if he is not careful,' muttered the manager darkly. I observed with assumed innocence that no man was safe from trouble in this world.

"The current was more rapid now, the steamer seemed at her last gasp, the stern-wheel flopped languidly, and I caught myself listening on tiptoe for the next beat of the boat, for in sober truth I expected the wretched thing to give up every moment. It was like watching the last flickers of a life. But still we crawled. Sometimes I would pick out a tree a little way ahead to measure our progress towards Kurtz by, but I lost it invariably before we got abreast. To keep the eyes so long on one thing was too much for human patience. The manager displayed a beautiful resignation. I fretted and fumed and took to arguing with myself whether or no I would talk openly with Kurtz; but before I could come to any conclusion it occurred to me that my speech or my silence, indeed any action of mine, would be a mere futility. What did it matter what any one knew or ignored? What did it matter who was manager? One gets sometimes such a flash of insight. The essentials of this affair lay deep under the surface, beyond my reach, and beyond my power of meddling.

"Towards the evening of the second day we judged ourselves about eight miles from Kurtz's station. I wanted to push on; but the manager looked grave, and told me the navigation up there was so dangerous that it would be advisable, the sun being very low already, to wait where we were till next morning. Moreover, he pointed out that if the warning to approach cautiously were to be followed, we must approach in daylight—not at dusk, or in the dark. This was sensible enough. Eight miles meant nearly three hours' steaming for us, and I could also see suspicious ripples at the upper end of the reach. Nevertheless, I was annoyed beyond expression at the delay, and most unreasonably, too, since one night more could not matter much after so many months. As we had plenty of wood, and caution was the word, I brought up in the middle of the stream. The reach was narrow, straight, with high sides like a railway cutting. The dusk came gliding into it long before the sun had set. The current ran smooth and swift, but a dumb immobility sat on the banks. The living trees, lashed together by the creepers and every living bush of the under-growth, might have been changed into stone, even to the slenderest twig, to the lightest leaf. It was not sleep—it seemed unnatural, like a state of trance. Not the faintest sound of any kind could be heard. You looked on amazed, and began to suspect yourself of being deaf—then the night came suddenly, and struck you blind as well. About three in the morning some large fish leaped, and the loud splash made me jump as though a gun had been fired. When the sun rose there was a white fog, very warm and clammy, and more blinding than the night. It did not shift or drive; it was just there, standing all round you like something solid. At eight or nine, perhaps, it lifted as a shutter lifts. We had a glimpse of the towering multitude of trees, of the immense matted jungle, with the blazing little ball of the sun hanging over it—all perfectly still—and then the white shutter came down again, smoothly, as if sliding in greased grooves. I ordered the chain, which we had begun to heave in, to be paid out again. Before it stopped running with a muffled rattle, a cry, a very loud cry, as of infinite desolation, soared slowly in the opaque air. It ceased. A complaining clamour, modulated in savage discords, filled our ears. The sheer unexpectedness of it made my hair stir under my cap. I don't know how it struck the others: to me it seemed as though the mist itself had screamed, so suddenly, and apparently from all sides at once, did this tumultuous and mournful uproar arise. It culminated in a hurried out-break of almost intolerably excessive shrieking, which stopped short, leaving us stiffened in a variety of silly attitudes, and obstinately listening to the nearly as appalling and excessive silence. 'Good God! What is the meaning——' stammered at my elbow one of the pilgrims,—a little fat man, with sandy hair and red whiskers, who wore side-spring boots, and pink pyjamas tucked into his socks. Two others remained open-mouthed a whole minute, then dashed into the little cabin, to rush out incontinently and stand darting scared glances, with Winchesters at 'ready' in their hands. What we could see was just the steamer we were on, her outlines blurred as though she had been on the point of dissolving, and a misty strip of water, perhaps two feet broad, around her—and that was all. The rest of the world was nowhere, as far as our eyes and ears were concerned. Just nowhere. Gone, disappeared; swept off without leaving a whisper or a shadow behind.

"I went forward, and ordered the chain to be hauled in short, so as to be ready to trip the anchor and move the steamboat at once if necessary. 'Will they attack?' whispered an awed voice. 'We will be all butchered in this fog,' murmured another. The faces twitched with the strain, the hands trembled slightly, the eyes forgot to wink. It was very curious to see the contrast of expressions of the white men and of the black fellows of our crew, who were as much strangers to that part of the river as we, though their homes were only eight hundred miles away. The whites, of course greatly discomposed, had besides a curious look of being painfully shocked by such an outrageous row. The others had an alert, naturally interested expression; but their faces were essentially quiet, even those of the one or two who grinned as they hauled at the chain. Several exchanged short, grunting phrases, which seemed to settle the matter to their satisfaction. Their headman, a young, broad-chested black, severely draped in dark-blue fringed cloths, with fierce nostrils and his hair all done up artfully in oily ringlets, stood near me. 'Aha!' I said, just for good fellowship's sake. 'Catch 'im,' he snapped, with a bloodshot widening of his eyes and a flash of sharp teeth—'catch 'im. Give 'im to us.' 'To you, eh?' I asked; 'what would you do with them?' 'Eat 'im!' he said, curtly, and, leaning his elbow on the rail, looked out into the fog in a dignified and profoundly pensive attitude. I would no doubt have been properly horrified, had it not occurred to me that he and his chaps must be very hungry: that they must have been growing increasingly hungry for at least this month past. They had been engaged for six months (I don't think a single one of them had any clear idea of time, as we at the end of countless ages have. They still belonged to the beginnings of time— had no inherited experience to teach them as it were), and of course, as long as there was a piece of paper written over in accordance with some farcical law or other made down the river, it didn't enter anybody's head to trouble how they would live. Certainly they had brought with them some rotten hippo-meat, which couldn't have lasted very long, anyway, even if the pilgrims hadn't, in the midst of a shocking hullabaloo, thrown a considerable quantity of it overboard. It looked like a high-handed proceeding; but it was really a case of legitimate self-defence. You can't breathe dead hippo waking, sleeping, and eating, and at the same time keep your precarious grip on existence. Besides that, they had given them every week three pieces of brass wire, each about nine inches long; and the theory was they were to buy their provisions with that currency in river-side villages. You can see how *that* worked. There were either no villages, or the people were hostile, or the director, who like the rest of us fed out of tins, with an occasional old he-goat thrown in, didn't want to stop the steamer for some more or less recondite reason. So, unless they swallowed the wire itself, or made loops of it to snare the fishes with, I don't see what good their extravagant salary could be to them. I must say it was paid with a regularity worthy of a large and honourable trading company. For the rest, the only thing to eat—though it didn't look eatable in the least—I saw in their possession was a few lumps of some stuff like half-cooked dough, of a dirty lavender colour, they kept wrapped in leaves, and now and then swallowed a piece of, but so small that it seemed done more for the looks of the thing than for any serious purpose of sustenance. Why in the name of all the gnawing devils of hunger they didn't go for us—they were thirty to five—and have a good tuck in for once, amazes me now when I think of it. They were big powerful men, with not much capacity to weigh the consequences, with courage, with strength, even yet, though their skins were no longer glossy and their muscles no longer hard. And I saw that something restraining, one of those human secrets that baffle probability, had come into play there. I looked at them with a swift quickening of interest—not because it occurred to me I might be eaten by them before very long, though I own to you that just then I perceived—in a new light, as it were—how unwholesome the pilgrims looked, and I hoped, yes, I positively hoped, that my aspect was not so—what shall I say?—so—unappetizing: a touch of fantastic vanity which fitted well with the dream-sensation that pervaded all my days at that time. Perhaps I had a little fever, too. One can't live with one's finger everlastingly on one's pulse. I had often 'a little fever,' or a little touch of other things—the playful paw-strokes of the wilderness, the preliminary trifling before the more serious onslaught which came in due course. Yes; I looked at them as you would on any human being, with a curiosity of their impulses, motives, capacities, weaknesses, when brought to the test of an inexorable physical necessity. Restraint! What possible restraint? Was it superstition, disgust, patience, fear—or some kind of primitive honour? No fear can stand up to hunger, no patience can wear it out, disgust simply does not exist where hunger is; and as to superstition, beliefs, and what you may call principles, they are less than chaff in a breeze. Don't you know the devilry of lingering starvation, its exasperating torment, its black thoughts, its sombre and brooding ferocity? Well, I do. It takes a man all his inborn strength to fight hunger properly. It's really easier to face bereavement, dishonour, and the perdition of one's soul—than this kind of prolonged hunger. Sad, but true. And these chaps, too, had no earthly reason for any kind of scruple. Restraint! I would just as soon have expected restraint from a hyena prowling amongst the corpses of a battlefield. But there was the fact facing me—the fact dazzling, to be seen, like the foam on the depths of the sea, like a ripple on an unfathomable enigma, a mystery greater—when I thought of it—than the curious, inexplicable note of desperate grief in this savage clamour that had swept by us on the river-bank, behind the blind whiteness of the fog.

"Two pilgrims were quarrelling in hurried whispers as to which bank. 'Left.' 'No, no; how can you? Right, right, of course.' 'It is very serious,' said the manager's voice behind me; 'I would be desolated if anything should happen to Mr. Kurtz before we came up.' I looked at him, and had not the slightest doubt he was sincere. He was just the kind of man who would wish to preserve appearances. That was his restraint. But when he muttered something about going on at once, I did not even take the trouble to answer him. I knew, and he knew, that it was impossible. Were we to let go our hold of the bottom, we would be absolutely in the air—in space. We wouldn't be able to tell where we were going to—whether up or down stream, or across—till we fetched against one bank or the other,—and then we wouldn't know at first which it was. Of course I made no move. I had no mind for a smash-up. You couldn't imagine a more deadly place for a shipwreck. Whether drowned at once or not, we were sure to perish speedily in one way or another. 'I authorize you to take all the risks,' he said, after a short silence. 'I refuse to take any,' I said, shortly; which was just the answer he expected, though its tone might have surprised him. 'Well, I must defer to your judgment. You are captain,' he said, with marked civility. I turned my shoulder to him in sign of my appreciation, and looked into the fog. How long would it last? It was the most hopeless look-out. The approach to this Kurtz grubbing for ivory in the wretched bush was beset by as many dangers as though he had been an enchanted princess sleeping in a fabulous castle. 'Will they attack, do you think?' asked the manager, in a confidential tone.

"I did not think they would attack, for several obvious reasons. The thick fog was one. If they left the bank in their canoes they would get lost in it, as we would be if we attempted to move. Still, I had also judged the jungle of both banks quite impenetrable—and yet eyes were in it, eyes that had seen us. The river-side bushes were certainly very thick; but the undergrowth behind was evidently penetrable. However, during the short lift I had seen no canoes anywhere in the reach—certainly not abreast of the steamer. But what made the idea of attack inconceivable to me was the nature of the noise—of the cries we had heard. They had not the fierce character boding of immediate hostile intention. Unexpected, wild, and violent as they had been, they had given me an irresistible impression of sorrow. The glimpse of the steamboat had for some reason filled those savages with unrestrained grief. The danger, if any, I expounded, was from our proximity to a great human passion let loose. Even extreme grief may ultimately vent itself in violence—but more generally take the form of apathy. . . .

"You should have seen the pilgrims stare! They had no heart to grin, or even to revile me: but I believe they thought me gone mad—with fright, maybe. I delivered a regular lecture. My dear boys, it was no good bothering. Keep a look-out? Well, you may guess I watched the fog for the signs of lifting as a cat watches a mouse; but for anything else our eyes were of no more use to us than if we had been buried miles deep in a heap of cotton-wool. It felt like it, too—choking, warm, stifling. Besides, all I said, though it sounded extravagant, was absolutely true to fact. What we afterwards alluded to as an attack was really an attempt at repulse. The action was very far from being aggressive—it was not even defensive, in the usual sense: it was undertaken under the stress of desperation, and in its essence was purely protective.

"It developed itself, I should say, two hours after the fog lifted, and its commencement was at a spot, roughly speaking, about a mile and half below Kurtz's station. We had just floundered and flopped round a bend, when I saw an islet, a mere grassy hummock of bright green, in the middle of the stream. It was the only thing of the kind; but as we opened the reach more, I perceived it was the head of a long sandbank, or rather of a chain of shallow patches stretching down the middle of the river. They were discoloured, just awash, and the whole lot was seen just under the water, exactly as a man's backbone is seen running down the middle of his back under the skin. Now, as far as I did see, I could go to the right or to the left of this. I didn't know either channel, of course. The banks looked pretty well alike, the depth appeared the same; but as I had been informed the station was on the west side, I naturally headed for the western passage.

"No sooner had we fairly entered it than I became aware it was much narrower than I had supposed. To the left of us there was the long uninterrupted shoal, and to the right a high, steep bank heavily over-grown with bushes. Above the bush the trees stood in serried ranks. The twigs overhung the current thickly, and from distance to distance a large limb of some tree projected rigidly over the stream. It was then well on in the afternoon, the face of the forest was gloomy, and a broad strip of shadow had already fallen on the water. In this shadow we steamed up—very slowly, as you may imagine. I sheered her well inshore—the water being deepest near the bank, as the sounding-pole informed me.

"One of my hungry and forbearing friends was sounding in the bows just below me. This steamboat was exactly like a decked scow. On the deck, there were two little teak-wood houses, with doors and windows. The boiler was in the fore-end, and the machinery right astern. Over the whole there was a light roof, supported on stanchions. The funnel projected through that roof, and in front of the funnel a small cabin built of light planks served for a pilot-house. It contained a couch, two camp-stools, a loaded Martini-Henry leaning in one corner, a tiny table, and the steering-wheel. It had a wide door in front and a broad shutter at each side. All these were always thrown open, of course. I spent my days perched up there on the extreme fore-end of that roof, before the door. At night I slept, or tried to, on the couch. An athletic black belonging to some coast tribe, and educated by my poor predecessor, was the helms-man. He sported a pair of brass earrings, wore a blue cloth wrapper from the waist to the ankles, and thought all the world of himself. He was the most unstable kind of fool I had ever seen. He steered with no end of a swagger while you were by; but if he lost sight of you, he became instantly the prey of an abject funk, and would let that cripple of a steamboat get the upper hand of him in a minute.

"I was looking down at the sounding-pole, and feeling much annoyed to see at each try a little more of it stick out of that river, when I saw my poleman give up the business suddenly, and stretch himself flat on the deck, without even taking the trouble to haul his pole in. He kept hold on it though, and it trailed in the water. At the same time the fireman, whom I could also see below me, sat down abruptly before his furnace and ducked his head. I was amazed. Then I had to look at the river mighty quick, because there was a snag in the fairway. Sticks, little sticks, were flying about—thick: they were whizzing before my nose, dropping below me, striking behind me against my pilot-house. All this time the river, the shore, the woods, were very quiet—perfectly quiet. I could only hear the heavy splashing thump of the stern-wheel and the patter of these things. We cleared the snag clumsily. Arrows, by Jove! We were being shot at! I stepped in quickly to close the shutter on the land-side. That fool-helms-man, his hands on the spokes, was lifting his knees high, stamping his feet, champing his mouth, like a reined-in horse. Confound him! And we were staggering within ten feet of the bank. I had to lean right out to swing the heavy shutter, and I saw a face amongst the leaves on the level with my own, looking at me very fierce and steady; and then suddenly, as though a veil had been removed from my eyes, I made out, deep in the tangled gloom, naked breasts, arms, legs, glaring eyes,—the bush was swarming with human limbs in movement, glistening, of bronze colour. The twigs shook, swayed, and rustled, the arrows flew out of them, and then the shutter came to. 'Steer her straight,' I said to the helmsman. He held his head rigid, face forward; but his eyes rolled, he kept on, lifting and setting down his feet gently, his mouth foamed a little. 'Keep quiet!' I said in a fury. I might just as well have ordered a tree not to sway in the wind. I darted out. Below me there was a great scuffle of feet on the iron deck; confused exclamations; a voice screamed, 'Can you turn back?'

I caught sight of a V-shaped ripple on the water ahead. What? Another snag! A fusillade burst out under my feet. The pilgrims had opened with their Winchesters, and were simply squirting lead into that bush. A deuce of a lot of smoke came up and drove slowly forward. I swore at it. Now I couldn't see the ripple or the snag either. I stood in the doorway, peering, and the arrows came in swarms. They might have been poisoned, but they looked as though they wouldn't kill a cat. The bush began to howl. Our wood-cutters raised a warlike whoop; the report of a rifle just at my back deafened me. I glanced over my shoulder, and the pilot-house was yet full of noise and smoke when I made a dash at the wheel. The fool-nigger had dropped everything, to throw the shutter open and let off that Martini-Henry. He stood before the wide opening, glaring, and I yelled at him to come back, while I straightened the sudden twist out of that steamboat. There was no room to turn even if I had wanted to, the snag was somewhere very near ahead in that confounded smoke, there was no time to lose, so I just crowded her into the bank—right into the bank, where I knew the water was deep.

"We tore slowly along the overhanging bushes in a whirl of broken twigs and flying leaves. The fusillade below stopped short, as I had foreseen it would when the squirts got empty. I threw my head back to a glinting whizz that traversed the pilot-house, in at one shutter-hole and out at the other. Looking past that mad helmsman, who was shaking the empty rifle and yelling at the shore, I saw vague forms of men running bent double, leaping, gliding, distinct, incomplete, evanescent. Something big appeared in the air before the shutter, the rifle went overboard, and the man stepped back swiftly, looked at me over his shoulder in an extraordinary, profound, familiar manner, and fell upon my feet. The side of his head hit the wheel twice, and the end of what appeared a long cane clattered round and knocked over a little camp-stool. It looked as though after wrenching that thing from somebody ashore he had lost his balance in the effort. The thin smoke had blown away, we were clear of the snag, and looking ahead I could see that in another hundred yards or so I would be free to sheer off, away from the bank; but my feet felt so very warm and wet that I had to look down. The man had rolled on his back and stared straight up at me; both his hands clutched that cane. It was the shaft of a spear that, either thrown or lunged through the opening, had caught him in the side just below the ribs; the blade had gone in out of sight, after making a frightful gash; my shoes were full; a pool of blood lay very still, gleaming dark-red under the wheel; his eyes shone with an amazing lustre. The fusillade burst out again. He looked at me anxiously, gripping the spear like something precious, with an air of being afraid I would try to take it away from him. I had to make an effort to free my eyes from his gaze and attend to the steering. With one hand I felt above my head for the line of the steam whistle, and jerked out screech after screech hurriedly. The tumult of angry and warlike yells was checked instantly, and then from the depths of the woods went out such a tremulous and prolonged wail of mournful fear and utter despair as may be imagined to follow the flight of the last hope from the earth. There was a great commotion in the bush; the shower of arrows stopped, a few dropping shots rang out sharply—then silence, in which the languid beat of the stern-wheel came plainly to my ears. I put the helm hard a-starboard at the moment when the pilgrim in pink pyjamas, very hot and agitated, appeared in the doorway. 'The manager sends me——' he began in an official tone, and stopped short. 'Good God!' he said, glaring at the wounded man.

"We two whites stood over him, and his lustrous and inquiring glance enveloped us both. I declare it looked as though he would presently put to us some question in an understandable language; but he died without uttering a sound, without moving a limb, without twitching a muscle. Only in the very last moment, as though in response to some sign we could not see, to some whisper we could not hear, he frowned heavily, and that frown gave to his black death-mask an inconceivably sombre, brooding, and menacing expression. The lustre of inquiring glance faded swiftly into vacant glassiness. 'Can you steer?' I asked the agent eagerly. He looked very dubious; but I made a grab at his arm, and he understood at once I meant him to steer whether or no. To tell you the truth, I was morbidly anxious to change my shoes and socks. 'He is dead,' murmured the fellow, immensely impressed. 'No doubt about it,' said I, tugging like mad at the shoe-laces. 'And by the way, I suppose Mr. Kurtz is dead as well by this time.'

"For the moment that was the dominant thought. There was a sense of extreme disappointment, as though I had found out I had been striving after something altogether without a substance. I couldn't have been more disgusted if I had travelled all this way for the sole purpose of talking with Mr. Kurtz. Talking with. . . . I flung one shoe overboard; and became aware that that was exactly what I had been looking forward to— a talk with Kurtz. I made the strange discovery that I had never imagined him as doing, you know, but as discoursing. I didn't say to myself, 'Now I will never see him,' or 'Now I will never shake him by the hand,' but, 'now I will never hear him.' The man presented himself as a voice. Not of course that I did not connect him with some sort of action. Hadn't I been told in all the tones of jealousy and admiration that he had collected, bartered, swindled, or stolen more ivory than all the other agents together? That was not the point. The point was in his being a gifted creature, and that of all his gifts the one that stood out preëminently, that carried with it a sense of real presence, was his ability to talk, his words— the gift of expression, the bewildering, the illuminating, the most exalted and the most contemptible, the pulsating stream of light, or the deceitful flow from the heart of an impenetrable darkness.

"The other shoe went flying unto the devil-god of that river. I thought, By Jove! it's all over. We are too late; he has vanished—the gift has vanished, by means of some spear, arrow, or club. I will never hear that chap speak after all,—and my sorrow had a startling extravagance of emotion, even such as I had noticed in the howling sorrow of these savages in the bush. I couldn't have felt more of lonely desolation some-how, had I been robbed of a belief or had missed my destiny in life. . . . Why do you sigh in this beastly way, somebody? Absurd? Well, absurd. Good Lord! mustn't a man ever—— Here, give me some tobacco." . . .

There was a pause of profound stillness, then a match flared, and Marlow's lean face appeared, worn, hollow, with downward folds and dropped eyelids, with an aspect of concentrated attention; and as he took vigorous draws at his pipe, it seemed to retreat and advance out of the night in the regular flicker of the tiny flame. The match went out.

"Absurd!" he cried. "This is the worst of trying to tell. . . . Here you all are, each moored with two good addresses, like a hulk with two anchors, a butcher round one corner, a policeman round another, excellent appetites, and temperature normal—you hear—normal from year's end to year's end. And you say, Absurd! Absurd be—exploded! Absurd! My dear boys, what can you expect from a man who out of sheer nervousness had just flung overboard a pair of new shoes! Now I think of it, it is amazing I did not shed tears. I am, upon the whole, proud of my fortitude. I was cut to the quick at the idea of having lost the inestimable privilege of listening to the gifted Kurtz. Of course I was wrong. The privilege was waiting for me. Oh, yes, I heard more than enough. And I was right, too. A voice. He was very little more than a voice. And I heard—him—it— this voice—other voices—all of them were so little more than voices— and the memory of that time itself lingers around me, impalpable, like a dying vibration of one immense jabber, silly, atrocious, sordid, savage, or simply mean, without any kind of sense. Voice, voices—even the girl herself—now——"

He was silent for a long time.

"I laid the ghost of his gifts at last with a lie," he began, suddenly. "Girl! What? Did I mention a girl? Oh, she is out of it—completely. They— the women I mean—are out of it—should be out of it. We must help them to stay in that beautiful world of their own, lest ours get worse. Oh, she had to be out of it. You should have heard the disinterred body of Mr. Kurtz saying, 'My Intended.' You would have perceived directly then how completely she was out of it. And the lofty frontal bone of Mr. Kurtz! They say the hair goes on growing sometimes, but this—ah—specimen, was impressively bald. The wilderness had patted him on the head, and,

behold, it was like a ball—an ivory ball; it had caressed him, and—lo!—
he had withered; it had taken him, loved him, embraced him, got into
his veins, consumed his flesh, and sealed his soul to its own by the
inconceivable ceremonies of some devilish initiation. He was its spoiled
and pampered favourite. Ivory? I should think so. Heaps of it, stacks of
it. The old mud shanty was bursting with it. You would think there was
not a single tusk left either above or below the ground in the whole
country. 'Mostly fossil,' the manager had remarked, disparagingly. It was
no more fossil than I am; but they call it fossil when it is dug up. It appears
these niggers do bury the tusks sometimes—but evidently they couldn't
bury this parcel deep enough to save the gifted Mr. Kurtz from his fate.
We filled the steamboat with it, and had to pile a lot on the deck. Thus
he could see and enjoy as long as he could see, because the appreciation
of this favour had remained with him to the last. You should have heard
him say, 'My ivory.' Oh yes, I heard him. 'My Intended, my ivory, my
station, my river, my——' everything belonged to him. It made me hold
my breath in expectation of hearing the wilderness burst into a prodigious
peal of laughter that would shake the fixed stars in their places. Everything belonged to him—but that was a trifle. The thing was to know what
he belonged to, how many powers of darkness claimed him for their own.
That was the reflection that made you creepy all over. It was impossible—
it was not good for one either—trying to imagine. He had taken a high
seat amongst the devils of the land—I mean literally. You can't understand. How could you?—with solid pavement under your feet, surrounded by kind neighbours ready to cheer you or to fall on you, stepping
delicately between the butcher and the policeman, in the holy terror of
scandal and gallows and lunatic asylums—how can you imagine what
particular region of the first ages a man's untrammelled feet may take
him into by the way of solitude—utter solitude without a policeman—by
the way of silence—utter silence, where no warning voice of a kind
neighbour can be heard whispering of public opinion? These little things
make all the great difference. When they are gone you must fall back
upon your own innate strength, upon your own capacity for faithfulness.
Of course you may be too much of a fool to go wrong—too dull even to
know you are being assaulted by the powers of darkness. I take it, no fool
ever made a bargain for his soul with the devil: the fool is too much of
a fool, or the devil too much of a devil—I don't know which. Or you may
be such a thunderingly exalted creature as to be altogether deaf and blind
to anything but heavenly sights and sounds. Then the earth for you is
only a standing place—and whether to be like this is your loss or your
gain I won't pretend to say. But most of us are neither one nor the other.
The earth for us is a place to live in, where we must put up with sights,
with sounds, with smells, too, by Jove!—breathe dead hippo, so to speak,
and not be contaminated. And there, don't you see? your strength comes

in, the faith in your ability for the digging of unostentatious holes to bury the stuff in—your power of devotion, not to yourself, but to an obscure, back-breaking business. And that's difficult enough. Mind, I am not trying to excuse or even explain—I am trying to account to myself for—for— Mr. Kurtz—for the shade of Mr. Kurtz. This initiated wraith from the back of Nowhere honoured me with its amazing confidence before it vanished altogether. This was because it could speak English to me. The original Kurtz had been educated partly in England, and—as he was good enough to say himself—his sympathies were in the right place. His mother was half-English, his father was half-French. All Europe contributed to the making of Kurtz; and by-and-by I learned that, most appropriately, the International Society for the Suppression of Savage Customs had intrusted him with the making of a report, for its future guidance. And he had written it, too. I've seen it. I've read it. It was eloquent, vibrating with eloquence, but too high-strung, I think. Seventeen pages of close writing he had found time for! But this must have been before his—let us say—nerves, went wrong, and caused him to preside at certain midnight dances ending with unspeakable rites, which—as far as I reluctantly gathered from what I heard at various times—were offered up to him— do you understand?—to Mr. Kurtz himself. But it was a beautiful piece of writing. The opening paragraph, however, in the light of later informa- tion, strikes me now as ominous. He began with the argument that we whites, from the point of development we had arrived at, 'must necessar- ily appear to them [savages] in the nature of supernatural beings—we approach them with the might as of a deity,' and so on, and so on. 'By the simple exercise of our will we can exert a power for good practically unbounded,' etc. etc. From that point he soared and took me with him. The peroration was magnificent, though difficult to remember, you know. It gave me the notion of an exotic Immensity ruled by an august Benevo- lence. It made me tingle with enthusiasm. This was the unbounded power of eloquence—of words—of burning noble words. There were no practical hints to interrupt the magic current of phrases, unless a kind of note at the foot of the last page, scrawled evidently much later, in an unsteady hand, may be regarded as the exposition of a method. It was very simple, and at the end of that moving appeal to every altruistic sentiment it blazed at you, luminous and terrifying, like a flash of light- ning in a serene sky: 'Exterminate all the brutes!' The curious part was that he had apparently forgotten all about that valuable postscriptum, because, later on, when he in a sense came to himself, he repeatedly entreated me to take good care of 'my pamphlet' (he called it), as it was sure to have in the future a good influence upon his career. I had full information about all these things, and, besides, as it turned out, I was to have the care of his memory. I've done enough for it to give me the indisputable right to lay it, if I choose, for an everlasting rest in the dustbin of progress, amongst all the sweepings and, figuratively speaking, all the dead cats of civilization. But then, you see, I can't choose. He won't be forgotten. Whatever he was, he was not common. He had the power to charm or frighten rudimentary souls into an aggravated witch-dance in his honour; he could also fill the small souls of the pilgrims with bitter misgivings: he had one devoted friend at least, and he had conquered one soul in the world that was neither rudimentary nor tainted with self-seeking. No; I can't forget him, though I am not prepared to affirm the fellow was exactly worth the life we lost in getting to him. I missed my late helmsman awfully,—I missed him even while his body was still lying in the pilot-house. Perhaps you will think it passing strange this regret for a savage who was no more account than a grain of sand in a black Sahara. Well, don't you see, he had done something, he had steered; for months I had him at my back—a help—an instrument. It was a kind of partnership. He steered for me—I had to look after him, I worried about his deficiencies, and thus a subtle bond had been created, of which I only became aware when it was suddenly broken. And the intimate profundity of that look he gave me when he received his hurt remains to this day in my memory—like a claim of distant kinship affirmed in a supreme moment.

"Poor fool! If he had only left that shutter alone. He had no restraint, no restraint—just like Kurtz—a tree swayed by the wind. As soon as I had put on a dry pair of slippers, I dragged him out, after first jerking the spear out of his side, which operation I confess I performed with my eyes shut tight. His heels leaped together over the little door-step; his shoulders were pressed to my breast; I hugged him from behind desperately. Oh! he was heavy, heavy; heavier than any man on earth, I should imagine. Then without more ado I tipped him overboard. The current snatched him as though he had been a wisp of grass, and I saw the body roll over twice before I lost sight of it for ever. All the pilgrims and the manager were then congregated on the awning-deck about the pilot-house, chattering at each other like a flock of excited magpies, and there was a scandalized murmur at my heartless promptitude. What they wanted to keep that body hanging about for I can't guess. Embalm it, maybe. But I had also heard another, and a very ominous, murmur on the deck below. My friends the wood-cutters were likewise scandalized, and with a better show of reason—though I admit that the reason itself was quite inadmissible. Oh, quite! I had made up my mind that if my late helmsman was to be eaten, the fishes alone should have him. He had been a very second-rate helmsman while alive, but now he was dead he might have become a first-class temptation, and possibly cause some startling trouble. Besides, I was anxious to take the wheel, the man in pink pyjamas showing himself a hopeless duffer at the business.

"This I did directly the simple funeral was over. We were going half-speed, keeping right in the middle of the stream, and I listened to the talk about me. They had given up Kurtz, they had given up the station; Kurtz was dead, and the station had been burnt—and so on—and so on. The red-haired pilgrim was beside himself with the thought that at least this poor Kurtz had been properly avenged. 'Say! We must have made a glorious slaughter of them in the bush. Eh? What do you think? Say?' He positively danced, the bloodthirsty little gingery beggar. And he had nearly fainted when he saw the wounded man! I could not help saying, 'You made a glorious lot of smoke, anyhow.' I had seen, from the way the tops of the bushes rustled and flew, that almost all the shots had gone too high. You can't hit anything unless you take aim and fire from the shoulder; but these chaps fired from the hip with their eyes shut. The retreat, I maintained—and I was right—was caused by the screeching of the steam-whistle. Upon this they forgot Kurtz, and began to howl at me with indignant protests.

"The manager stood by the wheel murmuring confidentially about the necessity of getting well away down the river before dark at all events, when I saw in the distance a clearing on the river-side and the outlines of some sort of building. 'What's this?' I asked. He clapped his hands in wonder. 'The station!' he cried. I edged in at once, still going half-speed.

"Through my glasses I saw the slope of a hill interspersed with rare trees and perfectly free from undergrowth. A long decaying building on the summit was half buried in the high grass; the large holes in the peaked roof gaped black from afar; the jungle and the woods made a background. There was no enclosure or fence of any kind; but there had been one apparently, for near the house half-a-dozen slim posts remained in a row, roughly trimmed, and with their upper ends ornamented with round carved balls. The rails, or whatever there had been between, had disappeared. Of course the forest surrounded all that. The river-bank was clear, and on the water-side I saw a white man under a hat like a cart-wheel beckoning persistently with his whole arm. Examining the edge of the forest above and below, I was almost certain I could see movements—human forms gliding here and there. I steamed past prudently, then stopped the engines and let her drift down. The man on the shore began to shout, urging us to land. 'We have been attacked,' screamed the manager. 'I know—I know. It's all right,' yelled back the other, as cheerful as you please. 'Come along. It's all right. I am glad.'

"His aspect reminded me of something I had seen—something funny I had seen somewhere. As I manoeuvred to get alongside, I was asking myself, 'What does this fellow look like?' Suddenly I got it. He looked like a harlequin. His clothes had been made of some stuff that was brown holland probably, but it was covered with patches all over, with bright patches, blue, red, and yellow,—patches on the back, patches on the front, patches on elbows, on knees; coloured binding around his jacket, scarlet edging at the bottom of his trousers; and the sunshine made him look extremely gay and wonderfully neat withal, because you could see how beautifully all this patching had been done. A beardless, boyish face, very fair, no features to speak of, nose peeling, little blue eyes, smiles and frowns chasing each other over that open countenance like sunshine and shadow on a wind-swept plain. 'Look out, captain!' he cried; 'there's a snag lodged in here last night.' What! Another snag? I confess I swore shamefully. I had nearly holed my cripple, to finish off that charming trip. The harlequin on the bank turned his little pug-nose up to me. 'You English?' he asked, all smiles. 'Are you?' I shouted from the wheel. The smiles vanished, and he shook his head as if sorry for my disappointment. Then he brightened up. 'Never mind!' he cried, encouragingly. 'Are we in time?' I asked. 'He is up there,' he replied, with a toss of the head up the hill, and becoming gloomy all of a sudden. His face was like the autumn sky, overcast one moment and bright the next.

"When the manager, escorted by the pilgrims, all of them armed to the teeth, had gone to the house this chap came on board. 'I say, I don't like this. These natives are in the bush,' I said. He assured me earnestly it was all right. 'They are simple people,' he added; 'well, I am glad you came. It took me all my time to keep them off.' 'But you said it was all right,' I cried. 'Oh, they meant no harm,' he said; and as I stared he corrected himself, 'Not exactly.' Then vivaciously, 'My faith, your pilot-house wants a clean up!' In the next breath he advised me to keep enough steam on the boiler to blow the whistle in case of any trouble. 'One good screech will do more for you than all your rifles. They are simple people,' he repeated. He rattled away at such a rate he quite overwhelmed me. He seemed to be trying to make up for lots of silence, and actually hinted, laughing, that such was the case. 'Don't you talk with Mr. Kurtz?' I said. 'You don't talk with that man—you listen to him,' he exclaimed with severe exaltation. 'But now——' He waved his arm, and in the twinkling of an eye was in the uttermost depths of despondency. In a moment he came up again with a jump, possessed himself of both my hands, shook them continuously, while he gabbled: 'Brother sailor . . . honour . . . pleasure . . . delight . . . introduce myself . . . Russian . . . son of an arch-priest . . . Government of Tambov . . . What? Tobacco! English tobacco; the excellent English tobacco! Now, that's brotherly. Smoke? Where's a sailor that does not smoke?'

"The pipe soothed him, and gradually I made out he had run away from school, had gone to sea in a Russian ship; ran away again; served some time in English ships; was now reconciled with the arch-priest. He made a point of that. 'But when one is young one must see things, gather experience, ideas; enlarge the mind.' 'Here!' I interrupted. 'You can never tell! Here I met Mr. Kurtz,' he said, youthfully solemn and reproachful. I held my tongue after that. It appears he had persuaded a Dutch trading-house on the coast to fit him out with stores and goods, and had started for their interior with a light heart, and no more idea of what would happen to him than a baby. He had been wandering about that river for nearly two years alone, cut off from everybody and everything. 'I am not so young as I look. I am twenty-five,' he said, 'At first old Van Shuyten would tell me to go to the devil,' he narrated with keen enjoyment; 'but I stuck to him, and talked and talked, till at last he got afraid I would talk the hind-leg off his favourite dog, so he gave me some cheap things and a few guns, and told me he hoped he would never see my face again. Good old Dutchman, Van Shuyten. I've sent him one small lot of ivory a year ago, so that he can't call me a little thief when I get back. I hope he got it. And for the rest I don't care. I had some wood stacked for you. That was my old house. Did you see?'

"I gave him Towson's book. He made as though he would kiss me, but restrained himself. 'The only book I had left, and I thought I had lost it,' he said, looking at it ecstatically. 'So many accidents happen to a man going about alone, you know. Canoes get upset sometimes—and sometimes you've got to clear out so quick when the people get angry.' He thumbed the pages. 'You made notes in Russian?' I asked. He nodded. 'I thought they were written in cipher,' I said. He laughed, then became serious. 'I had lots of trouble to keep these people off,' he said. 'Did they want to kill you?' I asked. 'Oh, no!' he cried, and checked himself. 'Why did they attack us?' I pursued. He hesitated, then said shamefacedly, 'They don't want him to go.' 'Don't they?' I said, curiously. He nodded a nod full of mystery and wisdom. 'I tell you,' he cried, 'this man has enlarged my mind.' He opened his arms wide, staring at me with his little blue eyes that were perfectly round."

III

"I looked at him, lost in astonishment. There he was before me, in motley, as though he had absconded from a troupe of mimes, enthusiastic, fabulous. His very existence was improbable, inexplicable, and altogether bewildering. He was an insoluble problem. It was inconceivable how he had existed, how he had succeeded in getting so far, how he had managed to remain—why he did not instantly disappear. 'I went a little farther,' he said, 'then still a little farther—till I had gone so far that I don't know how I'll ever get back. Never mind. Plenty time. I can manage. You take Kurtz away quick—quick—I tell you.' The glamour of youth enveloped his particoloured rags, his destitution, his loneliness, the essential desolation of his futile wanderings. For months—for years—his life hadn't been worth a day's purchase; and there he was gallantly, thoughtlessly alive, to all appearance indestructible solely by the virtue of his few years and of his unreflecting audacity. I was seduced into something like admiration—like envy. Glamour urged him on, glamour kept him unscathed. He surely wanted nothing from the wilderness but space to breathe in and to push on through. His need was to exist, and to move onwards at the greatest possible risk, and with a maximum of privation. If the absolutely pure, uncalculating, unpractical spirit of adventure had ever ruled a human being, it ruled this be-patched youth. I almost envied him the possession of this modest and clear flame. It seemed to have consumed all thought of self so completely, that even while he was talking to you, you forgot that it was he—the man before your eyes—who had gone through these things. I did not envy him his devotion to Kurtz, though. He had not meditated over it. It came to him, and he accepted it with a sort of eager fatalism. I must say that to me it appeared about the most dangerous thing in every way he had come upon so far.

"They had come together unavoidably, like two ships becalmed near each other, and lay rubbing sides at last. I suppose Kurtz wanted an audience, because on a certain occasion, when encamped in the forest, they had talked all night, or more probably Kurtz had talked. 'We talked of everything,' he said, quite transported at the recollection. 'I forgot there was such a thing as sleep. The night did not seem to last an hour. Everything! Everything! . . . Of love, too.' 'Ah, he talked to you of love!' I said, much amused. 'It isn't what you think,' he cried, almost passionately. 'It was in general. He made me see things—things.'

"He threw his arms up. We were on deck at the time, and the headman of my wood-cutters, lounging near by, turned upon him his heavy and glittering eyes. I looked around, and I don't know why, but I assure you that never, never before, did this land, this river, this jungle, the very arch of this blazing sky appear to me so hopeless and so dark, so impenetrable to human thought, so pitiless to human weakness. 'And, ever since, you have been with him, of course?' I said.

"On the contrary. It appears their intercourse had been very much broken by various causes. He had, as he informed me proudly, managed to nurse Kurtz through two illnesses (he alluded to it as you would to some risky feat), but as a rule Kurtz wandered alone, far in the depths of the forest. 'Very often coming to this station, I had to wait days and days before he would turn up,' he said. 'Ah, it was worth waiting for!— sometimes,' 'What was he doing? exploring or what?' I asked. 'Oh, yes, of course;' he had discovered lots of villages, a lake, too—he did not know exactly in what direction; it was dangerous to inquire too much—but mostly his expeditions had been for ivory. 'But he had no goods to trade with by that time,' I objected. 'There's a good lot of cartridges left even yet,' he answered, looking away. 'To speak plainly, he raided the country,' I said. He nodded. 'Not alone, surely!' He muttered something about the villages round that lake. 'Kurtz got the tribe to follow him, did he?' I suggested. He fidgeted a little. 'They adored him,' he said. The tone of these words was so extraordinary that I looked at him searchingly. It was curious to see his mingled eagerness and reluctance to speak of Kurtz. The man filled his life, occupied his thoughts, swayed his emotions. 'What can you expect?' he burst out; 'he came to them with thunder and lightning, you know—and they had never seen anything like it—and very terrible. He could be very terrible. You can't judge Mr. Kurtz as you would an ordinary man. No, no, no! Now—just to give you an idea—I don't mind telling you, he wanted to shoot me, too, one day—but I don't judge him.' 'Shoot you!' I cried. 'What for?' 'Well, I had a small lot of ivory the chief of that village near my house gave me. You see I used to shoot game for them. Well, he wanted it, and wouldn't hear reason. He declared he would shoot me unless I gave him the ivory and then cleared out of the country, because he could do so, and had a fancy for it, and there was nothing on earth to prevent him killing whom he jolly well pleased. And it was true, too. I gave him the ivory. What did I care! But I didn't clear out. No, no. I couldn't leave him. I had to be careful, of course, till we got friendly again for a time. He had his second illness then. Afterwards I had to keep out of the way; but I didn't mind. He was living for the most part in those villages on the lake. When he came down to the river, sometimes he would take to me, and sometimes it was better for me to be careful. This man suffered too much. He hated all this, and somehow he couldn't get away. When I had a chance I begged him to try and leave while there was time; I offered to go back with him. And he would say yes, and then he would remain; go off on another ivory hunt; disappear for weeks; forget himself amongst these people—forget himself—you know.' 'Why! He's mad,' I said. He protested indignantly. Mr. Kurtz couldn't be mad. If I had heard him talk, only two days ago, I wouldn't dare hint at such a thing. . . . I had taken up my binoculars while we talked, and was looking at the shore, sweeping the limit of the forest at each side and at the back of the house. The consciousness of there being people in that bush, so silent, so quiet—as silent and quiet as the ruined house on the hill—made me uneasy. There was no sign on the face of nature of this amazing tale that was not so much told as suggested to me in desolate exclamations, completed by shrugs, in interrupted phrases, in hints ending in deep sighs. The woods were unmoved, like a mask—heavy, like the closed door of a prison—they looked with their air of hidden knowledge, of patient expectation, of unapproachable silence. The Russian was explaining to me that it was only lately that Mr. Kurtz had come down to the river, bringing along with him all the fighting men of that lake tribe. He had been absent for several months—getting himself adored, I suppose—and had come down unexpectedly, with the intention to all appearance of making a raid either across the river or down stream. Evidently the appetite for more ivory had got the better of the—what shall I say?—less material aspirations. However he had got much worse suddenly. 'I heard he was lying helpless, and so I came up—took my chance,' said the Russian. 'Oh, he is bad, very bad.' I directed my glass to the house. There were no signs of life, but there was the ruined roof, the long mud wall peeping above the grass, with three little square window-holes, no two of the same size; all this brought within reach of my hand, as it were. And then I made a brusque movement, and one of the remaining posts of that vanished fence leaped up in the field of my glass. You remember I told you I had been struck at the distance by certain attempts at ornamentation, rather remarkable in the ruinous aspect of the place. Now I had suddenly a nearer view, and its first result was to make me throw my head back as if before a blow. Then I went carefully from post to post with my glass, and I saw my mistake. These round knobs were not ornamental but symbolic; they were expressive and puzzling, striking and disturbing—food for thought and also for the vultures if there had been any looking down from the sky; but at all events for such ants as were industrious enough to ascend the pole. They would have been even more impressive, those heads on the stakes, if their faces had not been turned to the house. Only one, the first I had made out, was facing my way. I was not so shocked as you may think. The start back I had given was really nothing but a movement of surprise. I had expected to see a knob of wood there, you know. I returned deliberately to the first I had seen—and there it was, black, dried, sunken, with closed eyelids,—a head that seemed to sleep at the top of that pole, and, with the shrunken dry lips showing a narrow white line of the teeth, was smiling, too, smiling continuously at some endless and jocose dream of that eternal slumber.

"I am not disclosing any trade secrets. In fact, the manager said afterwards that Mr. Kurtz's methods had ruined the district. I have no opinion on that point, but I want you clearly to understand that there was nothing exactly profitable in these heads being there. They only showed that Mr. Kurtz lacked restraint in the gratification of his various lusts, that there was something wanting in him—some small matter which, when the pressing need arose, could not be found under his magnificent eloquence. Whether he knew of this deficiency himself I can't say. I think the knowledge came to him at last—only at the very last. But the wilderness had found him out early, and had taken on him a terrible vengeance for the fantastic invasion. I think it had whispered to him things about himself which he did not know, things of which he had no conception till he took counsel with this great solitude—and the whisper had proved irresistibly fascinating. It echoed loudly within him because he was hollow at the core. . . . I put down the glass, and the head that had appeared near enough to be spoken to seemed at once to have leaped away from me into inaccessible distance.

"The admirer of Mr. Kurtz was a bit crestfallen. In a hurried, indistinct voice he began to assure me he had not dared to take these—say, symbols—down. He was not afraid of the natives; they would not stir till Mr. Kurtz gave the word. His ascendancy was extraordinary. The camps of these people surrounded the place, and the chiefs came every day to see him. They would crawl. . . . 'I don't want to know anything of the ceremonies used when approaching Mr. Kurtz,' I shouted. Curious, this feeling that came over me that such details would be more intolerable than those heads drying on the stakes under Mr. Kurtz's windows. After all, that was only a savage sight, while I seemed at one bound to have been transported into some lightless region of subtle horrors, where pure, uncomplicated savagery was a positive relief, being something that had a right to exist—obviously—in the sunshine. The young man looked at me with surprise. I suppose it did not occur to him that Mr. Kurtz was no idol of mine. He forgot I hadn't heard any of these splendid monologues on, what was it? on love, justice, conduct of life—or what not. If it had come to crawling before Mr. Kurtz, he crawled as much as the veriest savage of them all. I had no idea of the conditions, he said: these heads were the heads of rebels. I shocked him excessively by laughing. Rebels! What would be the next definition I was to hear? There had been enemies, criminals, workers—and these were rebels. Those rebellious heads looked very subdued to me on their sticks. 'You don't know how such a life tries a man like Kurtz,' cried Kurtz's last disciple. 'Well, and you?' I said. 'I! I! I am a simple man. I have no great thoughts. I want nothing from anybody. How can you compare me to? . . .' His feelings were too much for speech, and suddenly he broke down. 'I don't understand,' he groaned. 'I've been doing my best to keep him alive, and that's enough. I had no hand in all this. I have no abilities. There hasn't been a drop of medicine or a mouthful of invalid food for months here. He was shamefully abandoned. A man like this, with such ideas. Shamefully! Shamefully! I—I—haven't slept for the last ten nights. . .'

"His voice lost itself in the calm of the evening. The long shadows of the forest had slipped down hill while we talked, had gone far beyond the ruined hovel, beyond the symbolic row of stakes. All this was in the gloom, while we down there were yet in the sunshine, and the stretch of the river abreast of the clearing glittered in a still and dazzling splendour, with a murky and overshadowed bend above and below. Not a living soul was seen on the shore. The bushes did not rustle.

"Suddenly round the corner of the house a group of men appeared, as though they had come up from the ground. They waded waist-deep in the grass, in a compact body, bearing an improvised stretcher in their midst. Instantly, in the emptiness of the landscape, a cry arose whose shrillness pierced the still air like a sharp arrow flying straight to the very heart of the land; and, as if by enchantment, streams of human beings— of naked human beings—with spears in their hands, with bows, with shields, with wild glances and savage movements, were poured into the clearing by the dark-faced and pensive forest. The bushes shook, the grass swayed for a time, and then everything stood still in attentive immobility.

" 'Now, if he does not say the right thing to them we are all done for,' said the Russian at my elbow. The knot of men with the stretcher had stopped, too, half-way to the steamer, as if petrified. I saw the man on the stretcher sit up, lank and with an uplifted arm, above the shoulders of the bearers. 'Let us hope that the man who can talk so well of love in general will find some particular reason to spare us this time,' I said. I resented bitterly the absurd danger of our situation, as if to be at the mercy of that atrocious phantom had been a dishonouring necessity. I could not hear a sound, but through my glasses I saw the thin arm extended commandingly, the lower jaw moving, the eyes of that apparition shining darkly far in its bony head that nodded with grotesque jerks. Kurtz—Kurtz—that means short in German—don't it? Well, the name was as true as everything else in his life—and death. He looked at least seven feet long. His covering had fallen off, and his body emerged from it pitiful and appalling as from a winding-sheet. I could see the cage of his ribs all astir, the bones of his arm waving. It was as though an animated image of death carved out of old ivory had been shaking its hand with menaces at a motionless crowd of men made of dark and glittering bronze. I saw him open his mouth wide—it gave him a weirdly voracious aspect, as though he had wanted to swallow all the air, all the earth, all the men before him. A deep voice reached me faintly. He must have been shouting. He fell back suddenly. The stretcher shook as the bearers staggered forward again, and almost at the same time I noticed that the crowd of savages was vanishing without any perceptible movement of retreat, as if the forest that had ejected these beings so suddenly had drawn them in again as the breath is drawn in a long aspiration.

"Some of the pilgrims behind the stretcher carried his arms—two shot-guns, a heavy rifle, and a light revolver-carbine—the thunderbolts of that pitiful Jupiter. The manager bent over him murmuring as he walked beside his head. They laid him down in one of the little cabins— just a room for a bedplace and a camp-stool or two, you know. We had brought his belated correspondence, and a lot of torn envelopes and open letters littered his bed. His hand roamed feebly amongst these papers. I was struck by the fire of his eyes and the composed languor of his expression. It was not so much the exhaustion of disease. He did not seem in pain. This shadow looked satiated and calm, as though for the moment it had had its fill of all the emotions.

"He rustled one of the letters, and looking straight in my face said, 'I am glad.' Somebody had been writing to him about me. These special recommendations were turning up again. The volume of tone he emitted without effort, almost without the trouble of moving his lips, amazed me. A voice! a voice! It was grave, profound, vibrating, while the man did not seem capable of a whisper. However, he had enough strength in him— factitious no doubt—to very nearly make an end of us, as you shall hear directly.

"The manager appeared silently in the doorway; I stepped out at once and he drew the curtain after me. The Russian, eyed curiously by the pilgrims, was staring at the shore. I followed the direction of his glance.

"Dark human shapes could be made out in the distance, flitting indistinctly against the gloomy border of the forest, and near the river two bronze figures, leaning on tall spears, stood in the sunlight under fantastic head-dresses of spotted skins, warlike and still in statuesque repose. And from right to left along the lighted shore moved a wild and gorgeous apparition of a woman.

"She walked with measured steps, draped in striped and fringed cloths, treading the earth proudly, with a slight jingle and flash of barbarous ornaments. She carried her head high; her hair was done in the shape of a helmet; she had brass leggings to the knee, brass wire gauntlets to the elbow, a crimson spot on her tawny cheek, innumerable necklaces of glass beads on her neck; bizarre things, charms, gifts of witch-men, that hung about her, glittered and trembled at every step. She must have had the value of several elephant tusks upon her. She was savage and superb, wild-eyed and magnificent; there was something ominous and stately in her deliberate progress. And in the hush that had fallen suddenly upon the whole sorrowful land, the immense wilderness, the colossal body of the fecund and mysterious life seemed to look at her, pensive, as though it had been looking at the image of its own tenebrous and passionate soul.

"She came abreast of the steamer, stood still, and faced us. Her long shadow fell to the water's edge. Her face had a tragic and fierce aspect of wild sorrow and of dumb pain mingled with the fear of some struggling, half-shaped resolve. She stood looking at us without a stir, and like the wilderness itself, with an air of brooding over an inscrutable purpose. A whole minute passed, and then she made a step forward. There was a low jingle, a glint of yellow metal, a sway of fringed draperies, and she stopped as if her heart had failed her. The young fellow by my side growled. The pilgrims murmured at my back. She looked at us all as if her life had depended upon the unswerving steadiness of her glance. Suddenly she opened her bared arms and threw them up rigid above her head, as though in an uncontrollable desire to touch the sky, and at the same time the swift shadows darted out on the earth, swept around on the river, gathering the steamer into a shadowy embrace. A formidable silence hung over the scene.

"She turned away slowly, walked on, following the bank, and passed into the bushes to the left. Once only her eyes gleamed back at us in the dusk of the thickets before she disappeared.

" 'If she had offered to come aboard I really think I would have tried to shoot her,' said the man of patches, nervously. 'I had been risking my life every day for the last fortnight to keep her out of the house. She got in one day and kicked up a row about those miserable rags I picked up in the storeroom to mend my clothes with. I wasn't decent. At least it must have been that, for she talked like a fury to Kurtz for an hour, pointing at me now and then. I don't understand the dialect of this tribe. Luckily for me, I fancy Kurtz felt too ill that day to care, or there would have been mischief. I don't understand. . . . No—it's too much for me. Ah, well, it's all over now.'

"At this moment I heard Kurtz's deep voice behind the curtain: 'Save me!—save the ivory, you mean. Don't tell me. Save *me*! Why, I've had to save you. Your are interrupting my plans now. Sick! Sick! Not so sick as you would like to believe. Never mind. I'll carry my ideas out yet—I will return. I'll show you what can be done. You with your little peddling notions—you are interfering with me. I will return. I. . . .'

"The manager came out. He did me the honour to take me under the arm and lead me aside. 'He is very low, very low,' he said. He considered it necessary to sigh, but neglected to be consistently sorrowful. 'We have done all we could for him—haven't we? But there is no disguising the fact, Mr. Kurtz had done more harm than good to the Company. He did not see the time was not ripe for vigorous action. Cautiously, cautiously—that's my principle. We must be cautious yet. The district is closed to us for a time. Deplorable! Upon the whole, the trade will suffer. I don't deny there is a remarkable quantity of ivory—mostly fossil. We must save it, at all events—but look how precarious the position is—and why? Because the method is unsound.' 'Do you,' said I, looking at the shore, 'call it "unsound method?" ' 'Without doubt,' he exclaimed, hotly. 'Don't you?' . . . 'No method at all,' I murmured after a while. 'Exactly,' he exulted. 'I anticipated this. Shows a complete want of judgment. It is my duty to point it out in the proper quarter.' 'Oh,' said I, 'that fellow—what's his name?—the brickmaker, will make a readable report for you.' He appeared confounded for a moment. It seemed to me I had never breathed an atmosphere so vile, and I turned mentally to Kurtz for relief—positively for relief. 'Nevertheless I think Mr. Kurtz is a remarkable man,' I said with emphasis. He started, dropped on me a cold heavy glance, said very quietly, 'he *was*,' and turned his back on me. My hour of favour was over; I found myself lumped along with Kurtz as a partisan of methods for which the time was not ripe: I was unsound! Ah! but it was something to have at least a choice of nightmares.

"I had turned to the wilderness really, not to Mr. Kurtz, who, I was ready to admit, was as good as buried. And for a moment it seemed to me as if I also were buried in a vast grave full of unspeakable secrets. I felt an intolerable weight oppressing my breast, the smell of the damp earth, the unseen presence of victorious corruption, the darkness of an impenetrable night. . . . The Russian tapped me on the shoulder. I heard him mumbling and stammering something about 'brother seaman—couldn't conceal—knowledge of matters that would affect Mr. Kurtz's reputation.' I waited. For him evidently Mr. Kurtz was not in his grave; I suspect that for him Mr. Kurtz was one of the immortals. 'Well!' said I at last, 'speak out. As it happens, I am Mr. Kurtz's friend—in a way.'

"He stated with a good deal of formality that had we not been 'of the same profession,' he would have kept the matter to himself without regard to consequences. 'He suspected there was an active ill will towards him on the part of these white men that ——' 'You are right,' I said, remembering a certain conversation I had overheard. 'The manager thinks you ought to be hanged.' He showed a concern at this intelligence which amused me at first. 'I had better get out of the way quietly,' he said, earnestly. 'I can do no more for Kurtz now, and they would soon find some excuse. What's to stop them? There's a military post three hundred miles from here.' 'Well, upon my word,' said I, 'perhaps you had better go if you have any friends amongst the savages near by.' 'Plenty,' he said. 'They are simple people—and I want nothing, you know.' He stood biting his lip, then: 'I don't want any harm to happen to these whites here, but of course I was thinking of Mr. Kurtz's reputation—but you are a brother seaman and——' 'All right,' said I, after a time. 'Mr. Kurtz's reputation is safe with me.' I did not know how truly I spoke.

"He informed me, lowering his voice, that it was Kurtz who had ordered the attack to be made on the steamer. 'He hated sometimes the idea of being taken away—and then again. . . . But I don't understand these matters. I am a simple man. He thought it would scare you away—that you would give it up, thinking him dead. I could not stop him. Oh, I had an awful time of it this last month.' 'Very well,' I said. 'He is all right now.' 'Ye-e-es,' he muttered, not very convinced apparently. 'Thanks,' said I; 'I shall keep my eyes open.' 'But quiet—eh?' he urged, anxiously. 'It would be awful for his reputation if anybody here——' I promised a complete discretion with great gravity. 'I have a canoe and three black fellows waiting not very far. I am off. Could you give me a few Martini-Henry cartridges?' I could, and did, with proper secrecy. He helped himself, with a wink at me, to a handful of my tobacco. 'Between sailors—you know—good English tobacco.' At the door of the pilot-house he turned round—'I say, haven't you a pair of shoes you could spare?' He raised one leg. 'Look.' The soles were tied with knotted strings sandal-wise under his bare feet. I rooted out an old pair, at which he looked with admiration before tucking it under his left arm. One of his pockets (bright red) was bulging with cartridges, from the other (dark blue) peeped 'Towson's Inquiry,' etc., etc. He seemed to think himself excellently well equipped for a renewed encounter with the wilderness. 'Ah! I'll never, never meet such a man again. You ought to have heard him recite poetry—his own, too, it was, he told me. Poetry!' He rolled his eyes at the recollection of these delights. 'Oh, he enlarged my mind!' 'Good-bye,' said I. He shook hands and vanished in the night. Sometimes I ask myself whether I had ever really seen him—whether it was possible to meet such a phenomenon! . . .

"When I woke up shortly after midnight his warning came to my mind with its hint of danger that seemed, in the starred darkness, real enough to make me get up for the purpose of having a look round. On the hill a big fire burned, illuminating fitfully a crooked corner of the station-house. One of the agents with a picket of a few of our blacks, armed for the purpose, was keeping guard over the ivory; but deep within the forest, red gleams that wavered, that seemed to sink and rise from the ground amongst confused columnar shapes of intense blackness, showed the exact position of the camp where Mr. Kurtz's adorers were keeping their uneasy vigil. The monotonous beating of a big drum filled the air with muffled shocks and a lingering vibration. A steady droning sound of many men chanting each to himself some weird incantation came out from the black, flat wall of the woods as the humming of bees comes out of a hive, and had a strange narcotic effect upon my half-awake senses. I believe I dozed off leaning over the rail, till an abrupt burst of yells, an overwhelming outbreak of a pent-up and mysterious frenzy, woke me up in a bewildered wonder. It was cut short all at once, and the low droning went on with an effect of audible and soothing silence. I glanced casually into the little cabin. A light was burning within, but Mr. Kurtz was not there.

"I think I would have raised an outcry if I had believed my eyes. But I didn't believe them at first—the thing seemed so impossible. The fact is I was completely unnerved by a sheer blank fright, pure abstract terror, unconnected with any distinct shape of physical danger. What made this emotion so overpowering was—how shall I define it?—the moral shock I received, as if something altogether monstrous, intolerable to thought and odious to the soul, had been thrust upon me unexpectedly. This lasted of course the merest fraction of a second, and then the usual sense of commonplace, deadly danger, the possibility of a sudden onslaught and massacre, or something of the kind, which I saw impending, was positively welcome and composing. It pacified me, in fact, so much that I did not raise an alarm.

"There was an agent buttoned up inside an ulster and sleeping on a chair on deck within three feet of me. The yells had not awakened him; he snored very slightly; I left him to his slumbers and leaped ashore. I did not betray Mr. Kurtz—it was ordered I should never betray him—it was written I should be loyal to the nightmare of my choice. I was anxious to deal with this shadow by myself alone,—and to this day I don't know why I was so jealous of sharing with any one the peculiar blackness of that experience.

"As soon as I got on the bank I saw a trail—a broad trail through the grass. I remember the exultation with which I said to myself, 'He can't walk—he is crawling on all-fours—I've got him.' The grass was wet with dew. I strode rapidly with clenched fists. I fancy I had some vague notion of falling upon him and giving him a drubbing. I don't know. I had some imbecile thoughts. The knitting old woman with the cat obtruded herself upon my memory as a most improper person to be sitting at the other end of such an affair. I saw a row of pilgrims squirting lead in the air out of Winchesters held to the hip. I thought I would never get back to the steamer, and imagined myself living alone and unarmed in the woods to an advanced age. Such silly things—you know. And I remember I confounded the beat of the drum with the beating of my heart, and was pleased at its calm regularity.

"I kept to the track though—then stopped to listen. The night was very clear; a dark blue space, sparkling with dew and starlight, in which black things stood very still. I thought I could see a kind of motion ahead of me. I was strangely cocksure of everything that night. I actually left the track and ran in a wide semicircle (I verily believe chuckling to myself) so as to get in front of that stir, of that motion I had seen—if indeed I had seen anything. I was circumventing Kurtz as though it had been a boyish game.

"I came upon him, and, if he had not heard me coming, I would have fallen over him, too, but he got up in time. He rose, unsteady, long, pale, indistinct, like a vapour exhaled by the earth, and swayed slightly, misty and silent before me; while at my back the fires loomed between the trees, and the murmur of many voices issued from the forest. I had cut him off cleverly; but when actually confronting him I seemed to come to my senses, I saw the danger in its right proportion. It was by no means over yet. Suppose he began to shout? Though he could hardly stand, there was still plenty of vigour in his voice. 'Go away—hide yourself,' he said, in that profound tone. It was very awful. I glanced back. We were within thirty yards from the nearest fire. A black figure stood up, strode on long black legs, waving long black arms, across the glow. It had horns—antelope horns, I think—on its head. Some sorcerer, some witch-man, no doubt: it looked fiend-like enough. 'Do you know what you are doing?' I whispered. 'Perfectly,' he answered, raising his voice for that single word: it sounded to me far off and yet loud, like a hail though a speaking-trumpet. If he makes a row we are lost, I thought to myself. This clearly was not a case for fisticuffs, even apart from the very natural aversion I had to beat that Shadow—this wandering and tormented thing. 'You will be lost,' I said—'utterly lost.' One gets sometimes such a flash of inspiration, you know. I did say the right thing, though indeed he could not have been more irretrievably lost than he was at this very moment, when the foundations of our intimacy were being laid—to endure—to endure—even to the end—even beyond.

" 'I had immense plans,' he muttered irresolutely. 'Yes,' said I; 'but if you try to shout I'll smash your head with——' There was not a stick or a stone near. 'I will throttle you for good,' I corrected myself. 'I was on the threshold of great things,' he pleaded, in a voice of longing, with a wistfulness of tone that made my blood run cold. 'And now for this stupid scoundrel——' 'Your success in Europe is assured in any case,' I affirmed, steadily. I did not want to have the throttling of him, you understand—and indeed it would have been very little use for any practical purpose. I tried to break the spell—the heavy, mute spell of the wilderness—that seemed to draw him to its pitiless breast by the awakening of forgotten and brutal instincts, by the memory of gratified and monstrous passions. This alone, I was convinced, had driven him out to the edge of the forest, to the bush, towards the gleam of fires, the throb of drums, the drone of weird incantations; this alone had beguiled his unlawful soul beyond the bounds of permitted aspirations. And, don't you see, the terror of the position was not in being knocked on the head—though I had a very lively sense of that danger, too—but in this, that I had to deal with a being to whom I could not appeal in the name of anything high or low. I had, even like the niggers, to invoke him—himself—his own exalted and incredible degradation. There was nothing either above or below him, and I knew it. He had kicked himself loose of the earth. Confound the man! he had kicked the very earth to pieces. He was alone, and I before him did not know whether I stood on the ground or floated in the air. I've been telling you what we said—repeating the phrases we pronounced—but what's the good? They were common everyday words—the familiar, vague sounds exchanged on every waking day of life. But what of that? They had behind them, to my mind, the terrific suggestiveness of words heard in dreams, of phrases spoken in night-mares. Soul! If anybody had ever struggled with a soul, I am the man. And I wasn't arguing with a lunatic either. Believe me or not, his intelligence was perfectly clear—concentrated, it is true, upon himself with horrible intensity, yet clear; and therein was my only chance—barring, of course, the killing him there and then, which wasn't so good, on account of unavoidable noise. But his soul was mad. Being alone in the wilderness, it had looked within itself, and, by heavens! I tell you, it had gone mad. I had—for my sins, I suppose—to go through the ordeal of looking into it myself. No eloquence could have been so withering to one's belief in mankind as his final burst of sincerity. He struggled with himself, too. I saw it,—I heard it. I saw the inconceivable mystery of a soul that knew no restraint, no faith, and no fear, yet struggling blindly with itself. I kept my head pretty well; but when I had him at last stretched on the couch, I wiped my forehead, while my legs shook under me as though I had carried half a ton on my back down that hill. And yet I had only supported him, his bony arm clasped round my neck—and he was not much heavier than a child.

"When next day we left at noon, the crowd, of whose presence behind the curtain of trees I had been acutely conscious all the time, flowed out of the woods again, filled the clearing, covered the slope with a mass of naked, breathing, quivering, bronze bodies. I steamed up a bit, then swung downstream, and two thousand eyes followed the evolutions of the splashing, thumping, fierce river-demon beating the water with its terrible tail and breathing black smoke into the air. In front of the first rank, along the river, three men, plastered with bright red earth from head to foot, strutted to and fro restlessly. When we came abreast again, they faced the river, stamped their feet, nodded their horned heads, swayed their scarlet bodies; they shook towards the fierce river-demon a bunch of black feathers, a mangy skin with a pendent tail—something that looked like a dried gourd; they shouted periodically together strings of amazing words that resembled no sounds of human language; and the deep murmurs of the crowd, interrupted suddenly, were like the responses of some satanic litany.

"We had carried Kurtz into the pilot-house: there was more air there. Lying on the couch, he stared through the open shutter. There was an eddy in the mass of human bodies, and the woman with helmeted head and tawny cheeks rushed out to the very brink of the stream. She put out her hands, shouted something, and all that wild mob took up the shout in a roaring chorus of articulated, rapid, breathless utterance.

" 'Do you understand this?' I asked.

"He kept on looking out past me with fiery, longing eyes, with a mingled expression of wistfulness and hate. He made no answer, but I saw a smile, a smile of indefinable meaning, appear on his colourless lips that a moment after twitched convulsively. 'Do I not?' he said slowly, gasping, as if the words had been torn out of him by a supernatural power.

"I pulled the string of the whistle, and I did this because I saw the pilgrims on deck getting out their rifles with an air of anticipating a jolly lark. At the sudden screech there was a movement of abject terror through that wedged mass of bodies. 'Don't! don't you frighten them away,' cried someone on deck disconsolately. I pulled the string time after time. They broke and ran, they leaped, they crouched, they swerved, they dodged the flying terror of the sound. The three red chaps had fallen flat, face down on the shore, as though they had been shot dead. Only the barbarous and superb woman did not so much as flinch, and stretched tragically her bare arms after us over the sombre and glittering river.

"And then that imbecile crowd down on the deck started their little fun, and I could see nothing more for smoke.

"The brown current ran swiftly out of the heart of darkness, bearing us down towards the sea with twice the speed of our upward progress; and Kurtz's life was running swiftly, too, ebbing, ebbing out of his heart into the sea of inexorable time. The manager was very placid, he had no vital anxieties now, he took us both in with a comprehensive and satisfied glance: the 'affair' had come off as well as could be wished. I saw the time approaching when I would be left alone of the party of 'unsound method.' The pilgrims looked upon me with disfavour. I was, so to speak, numbered with the dead. It is strange how I accepted this unforeseen partnership, this choice of nightmares forced upon me in the tenebrous land invaded by these mean and greedy phantoms.

"Kurtz discoursed. A voice! a voice! It rang deep to the very last. It survived his strength to hide in the magnificent folds of eloquence the barren darkness of his heart. Oh, he struggled! he struggled! The wastes of his weary brain were haunted by shadowy images now—images of wealth and fame revolving obsequiously round his unextinguishable gift of noble and lofty expression. My Intended, my station, my career, my ideas—these were the subjects for the occasional utterances of elevated sentiments. The shade of the original Kurtz frequented the bedside of the hollow sham, whose fate it was to be buried presently in the mould of primeval earth. But both the diabolic love and the unearthly hate of the mysteries it had penetrated fought for the possession of that soul satiated with primitive emotions, avid of lying fame, of sham distinction, of all the appearances of success and power.

"Sometimes he was contemptibly childish. He desired to have kings meet him at railway-stations on his return from some ghastly Nowhere, where he intended to accomplish great things. 'You show them you have in you something that is really profitable, and then there will be no limits to the recognition of your ability,' he would say. 'Of course you must take care of the motives—right motives—always.' The long reaches that were like one and the same reach, monotonous bends that were exactly alike, slipped past the steamer with their multitude of secular trees looking patiently after this grimy fragment of another world, the forerunner of change, of conquest, of trade, of massacres, of blessings. I looked ahead—piloting. 'Close the shutter,' said Kurtz suddenly one day; 'I can't bear to look at this.' I did so. There was a silence. 'Oh, but I will wring your heart yet!' he cried at the invisible wilderness.

"We broke down—as I had expected—and had to lie up for repairs at the head of an island. This delay was the first thing that shook Kurtz's confidence. One morning he gave me a packet of papers and a photograph—the lot tied together with a shoe-string. 'Keep this for me,' he said. 'This noxious fool' (meaning the manager) 'is capable of prying into my boxes when I am not looking.' In the afternoon I saw him. He was lying on his back with closed eyes, and I withdrew quietly, but I heard him mutter, 'Live rightly, die, die . . .' I listened. There was nothing more. Was he rehearsing some speech in his sleep, or was it a fragment of a phrase from some newspaper article? He had been writing for the papers and meant to do so again, 'for the furthering of my ideas. It's a duty.'

"His was an impenetrable darkness. I looked at him as you peer down at a man who is lying at the bottom of a precipice where the sun never shines. But I had not much time to give him, because I was helping the engine-driver to take to pieces the leaky cylinders, to straighten a bent connecting-rod, and in other such matters. I lived in an infernal mess of rust, filings, nuts, bolts, spanners, hammers, ratchet-drills—things I abominate, because I don't get on with them. I tended the little forge we fortunately had aboard; I toiled wearily in a wretched scrap-heap—unless I had the shakes too bad to stand.

"One evening coming in with a candle I was startled to hear him say a little tremulously, 'I am lying here in the dark waiting for death.' The light was within a foot of his eyes. I forced myself to murmur, 'Oh, nonsense!' and stood over him as if transfixed.

"Anything approaching the change that came over his features I have never seen before, and hope never to see again. Oh, I wasn't touched. I was fascinated. It was as though a veil had been rent. I saw on that ivory face the expression of sombre pride, of ruthless power, of craven terror—of an intense and hopeless despair. Did he live his life again in every detail of desire, temptation, and surrender during that supreme moment of complete knowledge? He cried in a whisper at some image, at some vision—he cried out twice, a cry that was no more than a breath—

" 'The horror! The horror!'

"I blew the candle out and left the cabin. The pilgrims were dining in the mess-room, and I took my place opposite the manager, who lifted his eyes to give me a questioning glance, which I successfully ignored. He leaned back, serene, with that peculiar smile of his sealing the unexpressed depths of his meanness. A continuous shower of small flies streamed upon the lamp, upon the cloth, upon our hands and faces. Suddenly the manager's boy put his insolent black head in the doorway, and said in a tone of scathing contempt—

" 'Mistah Kurtz—he dead.'

"All the pilgrims rushed out to see. I remained, and went on with my dinner. I believe I was considered brutally callous. However, I did not eat much. There was a lamp in there—light, don't you know—and outside it was so beastly, beastly dark. I went no more near the remarkable man who had pronounced a judgment upon the adventures of his soul on this earth. The voice was gone. What else had been there? But I am of course aware that next day the pilgrims buried something in a muddy hole.

"And then they very nearly buried me.

"However, as you see, I did not go to join Kurtz there and then. I did not. I remained to dream the nightmare out to the end, and to show my loyalty to Kurtz once more. Destiny. My destiny! Droll thing life is—that mysterious arrangement of merciless logic for a futile purpose. The most you can hope from it is some knowledge of yourself—that comes too late—a crop of unextinguishable regrets. I have wrestled with death. It is the most unexciting contest you can imagine. It takes place in an impalpable grayness, with nothing underfoot, with nothing around, without spectators, without clamour, without glory, without the great desire of victory, without the great fear of defeat, in a sickly atmosphere of tepid scepticism, without much belief in your own right, and still less in that of your adversary. If such is the form of ultimate wisdom, then life is a greater riddle than some of us think it to be. I was within a hair's-breadth of the last opportunity for pronouncement, and I found with humiliation that probably I would have nothing to say. This is the reason why I affirm that Kurtz was a remarkable man. He had something to say. He said it. Since I had peeped over the edge myself, I understand better the meaning of his stare, that could not see the flame of the candle, but was wide enough to embrace the whole universe, piercing enough to penetrate all the hearts that beat in the darkness. He had summed up—he had judged. 'The horror!' He was a remarkable man. After all, this was the expression of some sort of belief; it had candour, it had conviction, it had a vibrating note of revolt in its whisper, it had the appalling face of a glimpsed truth—the strange commingling of desire and hate. And it is not my own extremity I remember best—a vision of grayness without form filled with physical pain, and a careless contempt for the evanescence of all things— even of this pain itself. No! It is his extremity that I seem to have lived through. True, he had made that last stride, he had stepped over the edge, while I had been permitted to draw back my hesitating foot. And perhaps in this is the whole difference; perhaps all the wisdom, and all truth, and all sincerity, are just compressed into that inappreciable moment of time in which we step over the threshold of the invisible. Perhaps! I like to think my summing-up would not have been a word of careless contempt. Better his cry—much better. It was an affirmation, a moral victory paid for by innumerable defeats, by abominable terrors, by abominable satisfactions. But it was a victory! That is why I have remained loyal to Kurtz to the last, and even beyond, when a long time after I heard once more, not his own voice, but the echo of his magnificent eloquence thrown to me from a soul as translucently pure as a cliff of crystal.

"No, they did not bury me, though there is a period of time which I remember mistily, with a shuddering wonder, like a passage through some inconceivable world that had no hope in it and no desire. I found myself back in the sepulchral city resenting the sight of people hurrying through the streets to filch a little money from each other, to devour their infamous cookery, to gulp their unwholesome beer, to dream their insignificant and silly dreams They trespassed upon my thoughts. They were intruders whose knowledge of life was to me an irritating pretence, because I felt so sure they could not possibly know the things I knew. Their bearing, which was simply the bearing of commonplace individuals going about their business in the assurance of perfect safety, was offensive to me like the outrageous flauntings of folly in the face of a danger it is unable to comprehend. I had no particular desire to enlighten them, but I had some difficulty in restraining myself from laughing in their faces, so full of stupid importance. I daresay I was not very well at that time. I tottered about the streets—there were various affairs to settle—grinning bitterly at perfectly respectable persons. I admit my behaviour was inexcusable, but then my temperature was seldom normal in these days. My dear aunt's endeavours to 'nurse up my strength' seemed altogether beside the mark. It was not my strength that wanted nursing, it was my imagination that wanted soothing. I kept the bundle of papers given me by Kurtz, not knowing exactly what to do with it. His mother had died lately, watched over, as I was told, by his Intended. A clean-shaved man, with an official manner and wearing gold-rimmed spectacles, called on me one day and made inquiries, at first circuitous, afterwards suavely pressing, about what he was pleased to denominate certain 'documents.' I was not surprised, because I had had two rows with the manager on the subject out there. I had refused to give up the smallest scrap out of that package, and I took the same attitude with the spectacled man. He became darkly menacing at last, and with much heat argued that the Company had the right to every bit of information about its 'territories.' And said he, 'Mr. Kurtz's knowledge of unexplored regions must have been necessarily extensive and peculiar—owing to his great abilities and to the deplorable circumstances in which he had been placed: there-fore——' I assured him Mr. Kurtz's knowledge, however extensive, did not bear upon the problems of commerce or administration. He invoked then the name of science. 'It would be an incalculable loss if,' etc., etc. I offered him the report on the 'Suppression of Savage Customs,' with the postscriptum torn off. He took it up eagerly, but ended by sniffing at it with an air of contempt. 'This is not what we had a right to expect,' he remarked. 'Expect nothing else,' I said. 'There are only private letters.' He withdrew upon some threat of legal proceedings, and I saw him no more; but another fellow, calling himself Kurtz's cousin, appeared two days later, and was anxious to hear all the details about his dear relative's last moments. Incidentally he gave me to understand that Kurtz had been essentially a great musician. 'There was the making of an immense success,' said the man, who was an organist, I believe, with lank gray hair flowing over a greasy coat-collar. I had no reason to doubt his statement; and to this day I am unable to say what was Kurtz's profession, whether he ever had any—which was the greatest of his talents. I had taken him for a painter who wrote for the papers, or else for a journalist who could paint—but even the cousin (who took snuff during the interview) could not tell me what he had been—exactly. He was a universal genius—on that point I agreed with the old chap, who thereupon blew his nose noisily into a large cotton handkerchief and withdrew in senile agitation, bearing off some family letters and memoranda without importance. Ultimately a journalist anxious to know something of the fate of his 'dear colleague' turned up. This visitor informed me Kurtz's proper sphere ought to have been politics 'on the popular side.' He had furry straight eyebrows, bristly hair cropped short, and eye-glass on a broad ribbon, and, becoming expansive, confessed his opinion that Kurtz really couldn't write a bit—'but heavens! how that man could talk. He electrified large meetings. He had faith—don't you see?—he had the faith. He could get himself to believe anything—anything. He would have been a splendid leader of an extreme party.' 'What party?' I asked. 'Any party,' answered the other. 'He was an—an—extremist.' Did I not think so? I assented. Did I know, he asked, with a sudden flash of curiosity, 'what it was that had induced him to go out there?' 'Yes,' said I, and forthwith handed him the famous Report for publication, if he thought fit. He glanced through it hurriedly, mumbling all the time, judged 'it would do,' and took himself off with this plunder.

"Thus I was left at last with a slim packet of letters and the girl's portrait. She struck me as beautiful—I mean she had a beautiful expression. I know that the sunlight can be made to lie, too, yet one felt that no manipulation of light and pose could have conveyed the delicate shade of truthfulness upon those features. She seemed ready to listen without mental reservation, without suspicion, without a thought for herself. I concluded I would go and give her back her portrait and those letters myself. Curiosity? Yes; and also some other feeling perhaps. All that had been Kurtz's had passed out of my hands: his soul, his body, his station, his plans, his ivory, his career. There remained only his memory and his Intended—and I wanted to give that up, too, to the past, in a way—to surrender personally all that remained of him with me to that oblivion which is the last word of our common fate. I don't defend myself. I had no clear perception of what it was I really wanted. Perhaps it was an impulse of unconscious loyalty, or the fulfilment of one of these ironic necessities that lurk in the facts of human existence. I don't know. I can't tell. But I went.

"I thought his memory was like the other memories of the dead that accumulate in every man's life—a vague impress on the brain of shadows that had fallen on it in their swift and final passage; but before the high and ponderous door, between the tall houses of a street as still and decorous as a well-kept alley in a cemetery, I had a vision of him on the stretcher, opening his mouth voraciously, as if to devour all the earth with all its mankind. He lived then before me; he lived as much as he had ever lived—a shadow insatiable of splendid appearances, of frightful realities; a shadow darker than the shadow of the night, and draped nobly in the folds of a gorgeous eloquence. The vision seemed to enter the house with me—the stretcher, the phantom-bearers, the wild crowd of obedient worshippers, the gloom of the forests, the glitter of the reach between the murky bends, the beat of the drum, regular and muffled like the beating of a heart—the heart of a conquering darkness. It was a moment of triumph for the wilderness, an invading and vengeful rush which, it seemed to me, I would have to keep back alone for the salvation of another soul. And the memory of what I had heard him say afar there, with the horned shapes stirring at my back, in the glow of fires, within the patient woods, those broken phrases came back to me, were heard again in their ominous and terrifying simplicity. I remembered his abject pleading, his abject threats, the colossal scale of his vile desires, the meanness, the torment, the tempestuous anguish of his soul. And later on I seemed to see his collected languid manner, when he said one day, 'This lot of ivory now is really mine. The Company did not pay for it. I collected it myself at a very great personal risk. I am afraid they will try to claim it as theirs though. H'm. It is a difficult case. What do you think I ought to do—resist? Eh? I want no more than justice.' . . . He wanted no more than justice—no more than justice. I rang the bell before a mahogany door on the first floor, and while I waited he seemed to stare at me out of the glassy panel—stare with that wide and immense stare embracing, condemning, loathing all the universe. I seemed to hear the whispered cry, 'The horror! The horror!'

"The dusk was falling. I had to wait in a lofty drawing-room with three long windows from floor to ceiling that were like three luminous and bedraped columns. The bent gilt legs and backs of the furniture shone in indistinct curves. The tall marble fireplace had a cold and monumental whiteness. A grand piano stood massively in a corner; with dark gleams on the flat surfaces like a sombre and polished sarcophagus. A high door opened—closed. I rose.

"She came forward, all in black, with a pale head, floating towards me in the dusk. She was in mourning. It was more than a year since his

death, more than a year since the news came; she seemed as though she would remember and mourn for ever. She took both my hands in hers and murmured, 'I had heard you were coming.' I noticed she was not very young—I mean not girlish. She had a mature capacity for fidelity, for belief, for suffering. The room seemed to have grown darker, as if all the sad light of the cloudy evening had taken refuge on her forehead. This fair hair, this pale visage, this pure brow, seemed surrounded by an ashy halo from which the dark eyes looked out at me. Their glance was guileless, profound, confident, and trustful. She carried her sorrowful head as though she were proud of that sorrow, as though she would say, I—I alone know how to mourn for him as he deserves. But while we were still shaking hands, such a look of awful desolation came upon her face that I perceived she was one of those creatures that are not the playthings of Time. For her he had died only yesterday. And, by Jove! the impression was so powerful that for me, too, he seemed to have died only yesterday—nay, this very minute. I saw her and him in the same instant of time—his death and her sorrow—I saw her sorrow in the very moment of his death. Do you understand? I saw them together—I heard them together. She had said, with a deep catch of the breath, 'I have survived' while my strained ears seemed to hear distinctly, mingled with her tone of despairing regret, the summing up whisper of his eternal condemnation. I asked myself what I was doing there, with a sensation of panic in my heart as though I had blundered into a place of cruel and absurd mysteries not fit for a human being to behold. She motioned me to a chair. We sat down. I laid the packet gently on the little table, and she put her hand over it. . . .
'You knew him well,' she murmured, after a moment of mourning silence.

" 'Intimacy grows quickly out there,' I said. 'I knew him as well as it is possible for one man to know another.'

" 'And you admired him,' she said. 'It was impossible to know him and not to admire him. Was it?'

" 'He was a remarkable man,' I said, unsteadily. Then before the appealing fixity of her gaze, that seemed to watch for more words on my lips, I went on, 'It was impossible not to——'

" 'Love him,' she finished eagerly, silencing me into an appalled dumbness. 'How true! how true! But when you think that no one knew him so well as I! I had all his noble confidence. I knew him best.'

" 'You knew him best,' I repeated. And perhaps she did. But with every word spoken the room was growing darker, and only her forehead, smooth and white, remained illumined by the unextinguishable light of belief and love.

" 'You were his friend,' she went on. 'His friend,' she repeated, a little louder. 'You must have been, if he had given you this, and sent you to me. I feel I can speak to you—and oh! I must speak. I want you—you who have heard his last words—to know I have been worthy of him. . . . It is not pride. . . . Yes! I am proud to know I understood him better than any one on earth—he told me so himself. And since his mother died I have had no one—no one—to—to——'

"I listened. The darkness deepened. I was not even sure whether he had given me the right bundle. I rather suspect he wanted me to take care of another batch of his papers which, after his death, I saw the manager examining under the lamp. And the girl talked, easing her pain in the certitude of my sympathy; she talked as thirsty men drink. I had heard that her engagement with Kurtz had been disapproved by her people. He wasn't rich enough or something. And indeed I don't know whether he had not been a pauper all his life. He had given me some reason to infer that it was his impatience of comparative poverty that drove him out there.

" ' . . . Who was not his friend who had heard him speak once?' she was saying. 'He drew men towards him by what was best in them.' She looked at me with intensity. 'It is the gift of the great,' she went on, and the sound of her low voice seemed to have the accompaniment of all the other sounds, full of mystery, desolation, and sorrow, I had ever heard— the ripple of the river, the soughing of the trees swayed by the wind, the murmurs of the crowds, the faint ring of incomprehensible words cried form afar, the whisper of a voice speaking from beyond the threshold of an eternal darkness. 'But you have heard him! You know!' she cried.

" 'Yes, I know,' I said with something like despair in my heart, but bowing my head before the faith that was in her, before that great and saving illusion that shone with an unearthly glow in the darkness, in the triumphant darkness from which I could not have defended her—from which I could not even defend myself.

" 'What a loss to me—to us!'—she corrected herself with beautiful generosity; then added in a murmur, 'To the world.' By the last gleams of twilight I could see the glitter of her eyes, full of tears—of tears that would not fall.

" 'I have been very happy—very fortunate—very proud,' she went on. 'Too fortunate. Too happy for a little while. And now I am unhappy for—for life.'

"She stood up; her hair seemed to catch all the remaining light in a glimmer of gold. I rose, too.

" 'And of all this,' she went on, mournfully, 'of all his promise, and of all his greatness, of his generous mind, of his noble heart, nothing remains—nothing but a memory. You and I——'

" 'We shall always remember him,' I said, hastily.

" 'No!' she cried. 'It is impossible that all this should be lost—that such a life should be sacrificed to leave nothing—but sorrow. You know

what vast plans he had. I knew of them, too—I could not perhaps understand—but others knew of them. Something must remain. His words, at
least, have not died.'

" 'His words will remain,' I said.

" 'And his example,' she whispered to herself. 'Men looked up to
him—his goodness shone in every act. His example——'

" 'True,' I said; 'his example, too. Yes, his example. I forgot that.'

" 'But I do not. I cannot—I cannot believe—not yet. I cannot believe
that I shall never see him again, that nobody will see him again, never,
never, never.'

"She put out her arms as if after a retreating figure, stretching them
back and with clasped pale hands across the fading and narrow sheen of
the window. Never see him! I saw him clearly enough then. I shall see
this eloquent phantom as long as I live, and I shall see her, too, a tragic
and familiar Shade, resembling in this gesture another one, tragic also,
and bedecked with powerless charms, stretching bare brown arms over
the glitter of the infernal stream, the stream of darkness. She said suddenly
very low, 'He died as he lived.'

" 'His end,' said I, with dull anger stirring in me, 'was in every way
worthy of his life.'

" 'And I was not with him,' she murmured. My anger subsided before
a feeling of infinite pity.

" 'Everything that could be done——' I mumbled.

" 'Ah, but I believed in him more than any one on earth—more than
his own mother, more than—himself. He needed me! Me! I would have
treasured every sigh, every word, every sign, every glance.'

"I felt like a chill grip on my chest. 'Don't,' I said, in a muffled voice.

" 'Forgive me. I—I—have mourned so long in silence—in silence. . . .
You were with him—to the last? I think of his loneliness. Nobody near
to understand him as I would have understood. Perhaps no one to
hear. . . .'

" 'To the very end,' I said, shakily. 'I heard his very last words. . . .' I
stopped in a fright.

" 'Repeat them,' she murmured in a heart-broken tone. 'I want—I
want—something—something—to—to live with.'

"I was on the point of crying at her, 'Don't you hear them?' The dusk
was repeating them in a persistent whisper all around us, in a whisper
that seemed to swell menacingly like the first whisper of a rising wind.
'The horror! the horror!'

" 'His last word—to live with,' she insisted. 'Don't you understand I
loved him—I loved him—I loved him!'

"I pulled myself together and spoke slowly.

" 'The last word he pronounced was—your name.'

"I heard a light sigh and then my heart stood still, stopped dead short by an exulting and terrible cry, by the cry of inconceivable triumph and of unspeakable pain. 'I knew it—I was sure!' . . . She knew. She was sure. I heard her weeping; she had hidden her face in her hands. It seemed to me that the house would collapse before I could escape, that the heavens would fall upon my head. But nothing happened. The heavens do not fall for such a trifle. Would they have fallen, I wonder, if I had rendered Kurtz that justice which was his due? Hadn't he said he wanted only justice? But I couldn't. I could not tell her. It would have been too dark— too dark altogether. . . ."

Marlow ceased, and sat apart, indistinct and silent, in the pose of a meditating Buddha. Nobody moved for a time. "We have lost the first of the ebb," said the Director, suddenly. I raised my head. The offing was barred by a black bank of clouds, and the tranquil waterway leading to the uttermost ends of the earth flowed sombre under an overcast sky— seemed to lead into the heart of an immense darkness.

ANTON CHEKHOV

(1860–1904)

*A*nton Chekhov was born in Taganrog in the south of Russia, the son of a shopkeeper interested in music and literature and the grandson of a serf. He received a medical degree from the University of Moscow but eventually gave up the practice of medicine to dedicate himself full time to writing. His early stories were published while he was still a student. During this time, his earnings as a free-lance journalist and writer of sketches for humorous journals made him the family's principal means of support. In 1890 he journeyed to the penal island of Sakhalin in the far east of Russia, and his account of the prisoners' conditions there is a fine example of the dispassionate objective analysis that informs so much of his fiction. Unlike many Russian writers of the day, Chekhov refused to subordinate his art to some social or ideological purpose, refused to teach people the art of living in his fiction. Yet his approach involved a cool diagnosis of social problems, what Simon Karlinsky has described as a "biological" as opposed to a "sociological humanitarianism." Many of the stories he wrote in the next decade are regarded quite simply as the best examples of the genre: "The Duel," "Ward No. 6," "My Life," "Gooseberries," "The Darling," and the two included here, "A Lady with a Dog" and "In the Hollow." His ear for spoken dialogue is as sharp as Tolstoy's; his ability to suggest a range of subtle emotions with the smallest of observed detail is legendary; the fidelity, compassion, and evocativeness of his portraiture of the various characters of Russian society at the end of the nineteenth century are unequalled. Chekhov married in 1901, when he was already wracked by the tuberculosis that was to kill him at 44. His wife was a young actress who starred in some of the plays that eventually made him world famous as a playwright as well: The Sea Gull *(1896),* Uncle Vanya *(1899),* The Three Sisters *(1901), and* The Cherry Orchard *(1904).*

A Lady with a Dog

I

There was said to be a new arrival on the Esplanade: a lady with a dog.

After spending a fortnight at Yalta, Dmitry Gurov had quite settled in and was now beginning to take an interest in new faces. As he sat outside Vernet's café he saw a fair-haired young woman, not tall, walking on the promenade—wearing a beret, with a white Pomeranian dog trotting after her.

Then he encountered her several times a day in the municipal park and square. She walked alone, always with that beret, always with the white Pomeranian. Who she was no one knew, everyone just called her "the dog lady."

"If she has no husband or friends here she might be worth picking up," calculated Gurov.

He was still in his thirties, but had a twelve-year-old daughter and two schoolboy sons. His marriage had been arranged early—during his second college year—and now his wife seemed half as old again as he. She was a tall, dark-browed woman: outspoken, earnest, stolid and—she maintained—an "intellectual." She was a great reader, she favoured spelling reform, she called her husband "Demetrius" instead of plain "Dmitry," while he privately thought her narrow-minded, inelegant and slow on the uptake. He was afraid of her, and disliked being at home. He had begun deceiving her long ago, and his infidelities were frequent—which is probably why he nearly always spoke so disparagingly of women, calling them an "inferior species" when the subject cropped up.

He was, he felt, sufficiently schooled by bitter experience to call them any name he liked, yet he still couldn't live two days on end without his "inferior species." Men's company bored him, making him ill at ease, tongue-tied and apathetic, whereas with women he felt free. He knew what to talk about, how to behave—he even found it easy to be with them without talking at all. In his appearance and character, in his whole nature, there was an alluring, elusive element which charmed and fascinated women. He knew it, and he was himself strongly attracted in return.

As experience multiple and—in the full sense of the word—bitter had long since taught him, every intimacy which so pleasantly diversifies one's life, which seems so easy, so delightfully adventurous at the outset . . . such an intimacy does, when reasonable people are involved (not least Muscovites—so hesitant and slow off the mark), develop willy-nilly into some vast, extraordinarily complex problem until the whole business finally becomes quite an ordeal. Somehow, though, on every new encounter with an attractive woman all this experience went for nothing—he wanted a bit of excitement and it all seemed so easy and amusing.

Well, he was eating in an open-air restaurant late one afternoon when the lady in the beret sauntered along and took the next table. Her expression, walk, clothes, hair-style . . . all told him that she was socially presentable, married, in Yalta for the first time, alone—and bored.

Much nonsense is talked about the looseness of morals in these parts, and he despised such stories, knowing that they were largely fabricated by people who would have been glad to misbehave themselves, given the aptitude! But when the young woman sat down at the next table, three paces away, he recalled those tales of trips into the mountains and easy conquests. The seductive thought of a swift, fleeting *affaire*—the romance with the stranger whose very name you don't know—suddenly possessed him. He made a friendly gesture to the dog. It came up. He wagged his finger. The dog growled and Gurov shook his finger again.

The lady glanced at him, lowered her eyes at once.

"He doesn't bite." She blushed.

"May I give him a bone?"

She nodded.

"Have you been in Yalta long, madam?" he asked courteously.

"Five days."

"Oh, I've nearly survived my first fortnight."

There was a short pause.

"Time goes quickly, but it *is* so boring," she said, not looking at him.

"That's what they all say, what a bore this place is. Your average tripper from Belyov, Zhizdra or somewhere . . . he doesn't know what boredom means till he comes here. Then it's 'Oh, what a bore! Oh, what dust!' You might think he'd just blown in from sunny Spain!"

She laughed. Then both continued their meal in silence, as strangers. After dinner, though, they left together and embarked on the bantering chat of people who feel free and easy, who don't mind where they go or what they talk about. As they strolled they discussed the strange light on the sea: the water was of a soft, warm, mauve hue, crossed by a stripe of golden moonlight. How sultry it was after the day's heat, they said. Gurov described himself as a Muscovite who had studied literature but worked in a bank. He had once trained as an opera singer but had given that up and owned two houses in Moscow.

From her he learnt that she had grown up in St. Petersburg, but had married in the provincial town where she had now been living for two years, that she was staying in Yalta for another month, that her husband (who also wanted a holiday) might come and fetch her. She was quite unable to explain her husband's job—was it with the County Council or the Rural District?—and even she saw the funny side of this. Gurov also learnt that she was called Anne.

In his hotel room afterwards he thought about her. He was very likely to meet her tomorrow, bound to. As he went to bed he remembered that she had not long left boarding-school, that she had been a schoolgirl like his own daughter—remembered, too, how much shyness and stiffness she still showed when laughing and talking to a stranger. This must be her first time ever alone in such a place, with men following her around, watching her, talking to her: all with a certain privy aim which she could not fail to divine. He remembered her slender, frail neck, her lovely grey eyes.

"You can't help feeling sorry for her, though," he thought. And dozed off.

II

A week had passed since their first meeting. It was a Sunday or some other holiday. Indoors was stifling, and outside flurries of dust swept the streets, whipping off hats. It was a thirsty day, and Gurov kept calling in at the café to fetch Anne a soft drink or an ice-cream. There was no escaping the heat.

In the evening things were a little easier, and they went on the pier to watch a steamer come in. There were a lot of people hanging around on the landing-stage: they were here to meet someone, and held bunches of flowers. Two features of the Yalta smart set were now thrown into sharp relief. The older women dressed like young ones. There were lots of generals.

As the sea was rough the steamer arrived late, after sunset, and manoeuvred for some time before putting in at the jetty. Anne watched boat and passengers through her lorgnette as if seeking someone she knew. Whenever she turned to Gurov her eyes shone. She spoke a lot, asking quick-fire questions and immediately forgetting what they were. Then she lost her lorgnette: dropped it in the crowd.

The gaily-dressed gathering dispersed, no more faces could be seen, and the wind dropped completely while Gurov and Anne stood as if waiting for someone else to disembark. Anne had stopped talking, and sniffed her flowers without looking at Gurov.

"The weather's better now that it's evening," said he. "So where shall we go? How about driving somewhere?"

She did not answer.

Then he stared at her hard, embraced her suddenly and kissed her lips. The scent of her flowers, their dampness, enveloped him, and he immediately glanced around fearfully: had they been observed?

"Let's go to your room," he said softly.

They set off quickly together.

Her room was stuffy and smelt of the scent which she had bought in the Japanese shop.

"What encounters one does have in life," thought Gurov as he looked at her now.

He still retained memories of the easy-going, light-hearted women in his past: women happy in their love and grateful to him for that happiness, however brief. He also recalled those who, like his wife, made love insincerely, with idle chatter, affectations and hysteria, their expressions conveying that this was neither love nor passion but something more significant. He thought of two or three very beautiful frigid women whose faces would suddenly flash a rapacious, stubborn look of lust to seize, to snatch more from life than it can give . . . women no longer young, these: fractious, unreasonable, overbearing and obtuse. When Gurov had cooled towards them their beauty had aroused his hatred, and the lace on their underclothes had looked like a lizard's scales.

In this case, though, all was hesitancy, the awkwardness of inexperienced youth. There was the impression of her being taken aback, too, as by a sudden knock on the door. Anne, this "lady with a dog," had her own special view—a very serious one—of what had happened. She thought of it as her "downfall," it seemed, which was all very strange and inappropriate. Her features had sunk and faded, her long hair dropped sadly down each side of her face. She had struck a pensive, despondent pose, like the Woman Taken in Adultery in an old-fashioned picture.

"This is all wrong," she said. "Now you'll completely despise me."

There was a water-melon on the table. Gurov cut a slice and slowly ate. Half an hour, at least, passed in silence.

He found Anne touching. She had that air of naïve innocence of a thoroughly nice unworldly woman. A solitary candle, burning on the table, barely lit her face, but it was obvious that she was ill at ease.

"Why should I lose respect for you?" asked Gurov. "You don't know what you're saying."

"God forgive me," she said, her eyes brimming with tears. "This is terrible."

"You seem very much on the defensive, Anne."

"How *can* I defend what I've done? I'm a bad, wicked woman, I despise myself and I'm not trying to make excuses. It's not my husband, it is *myself* I've deceived. I don't just mean what happened here, I've been deceiving myself for a long time. My husband may be a good, honourable man, but he *is* such a worm. What he does at that job of his I don't know— all I know is, he's a worm. I was twenty when I married him—I longed to know more of life. Then I wanted something better. There must *be* a different life, mustn't there? Or so I told myself. I wanted a little—well, rather *more* than a little—excitement. I was avid for experience. You won't understand me, I'm sure, but I could control myself no longer, I swear, something had happened to me, there was no holding me. So I told my husband I was ill and I came here. And I've been going round here in a daze as if I was off my head. But now I'm just another vulgar, worthless woman whom everyone is free to despise."

Gurov was bored with all this. He was irritated by the naïve air, the

unexpected, uncalled-for remorse. But for the tears in her eyes he might have thought her to be joking or play-acting.

"I don't understand," said he softly. "What is it you want?"

She hid her face on his breast and clung to him.

"Please, please believe me," she implored. "I long for a decent, moral life. Sin disgusts me, I don't know what I'm doing myself. The common people say the 'Evil One' tempted them, and now I can say the same: I was tempted by the Evil One."

"There there, that's enough," he muttered.

He looked into her staring, frightened eyes, kissed her, spoke softly and gently. She gradually relaxed and cheered up again. Both laughed.

Then they went out. The promenade was deserted, the town with its cypresses looked quite dead, but the sea still roared, breaking on the beach. A single launch with a sleepily glinting lamp tossed on the waves.

They found a cab and drove to Oreanda.

"I've only just discovered your surname, downstairs in your hotel," Gurov told her. " 'Von Diederitz,' it says on the board. Is your husband German?"

"No, his grandfather was, I think, but he's Russian."

They sat on a bench near the church at Oreanda, gazing silently down at the sea. Yalta was barely visible through the dawn mist, white clouds hung motionless on the mountain peaks. Not a leaf stirred on the trees, cicadas chirped. Borne up from below, the sea's monotonous, muffled boom spoke of peace, of the everlasting sleep awaiting us. Before Yalta or Oreanda yet existed that surf had been thundering down there, it was roaring away now, and it will continue its dull booming with the same unconcern when we are no more. This persistence, this utter aloofness from all our lives and deaths . . . do they perhaps hold the secret pledge of our eternal salvation, of life's perpetual motion on earth, of its uninterrupted progress? As he sat there, lulled and entranced by the magic panorama—sea, mountains, clouds, broad sky—beside a young woman who looked so beautiful in the dawn, Gurov reflected that everything on earth is beautiful, really, when you consider it—everything except what we think and do ourselves when we forget the lofty goals of being and our human dignity.

Someone—a watchman, no doubt—came up, looked at them, went away. Even this incident seemed mysterious—beautiful, too. In the dawn they saw a steamer arrive from Feodosiya, its lights already extinguished.

"There's dew on the grass," Anne said, after a pause.

"Yes, time to go home."

They went back to town.

After this they met on the promenade each noon, lunched, dined, strolled, enthused about the sea together. She complained of sleeping badly, of palpitations. Disturbed by jealousy, and by the fear that he did

not respect her enough, she kept repeating the same old questions. And often in the Square or Gardens, when there was nobody near them, he would suddenly draw her to him and kiss her ardently. This utter idleness, these kisses in broad daylight, these glances over the shoulder, this fear of being seen, the heat, the sea's smell, the repeated glimpses of idle, elegant, sleek persons . . . it all seemed to revitalize him. He told Anne how pretty she was, how provocative. He was impetuous, he was passionate, he never left her side, while she was for ever brooding and begging him to admit that he did not respect her, that he loved her not at all, that he could see in her no more than a very ordinary woman. Late almost every evening they would drive out of town: to Oreanda or the waterfall. These trips were invariably a great success, leaving an impression of majesty and beauty.

They had been expecting the husband to arrive, but he sent a letter to say that he had eye trouble, and begged his wife to come home soon. Anne bestirred herself.

"It's just as well I *am* leaving," she told Gurov. "This is fate."

She left by carriage and he drove with her. This part of her journey took all day. When she took her seat in the express train, which was due to leave in five minutes, she asked to look at him once more.

"One last look—that's right."

She did not cry, but was so sad that she seemed ill. Her face quivered.

"I'll think of you, I'll remember you," she said. "God bless and keep you. Don't think ill of me. We're parting for ever. We must, because we should never have met at all. God bless you."

The train departed swiftly, its lights soon vanishing and its noise dying away within a minute, as though everything had conspired to make a quick end of that sweet trance, that madness. Alone on the platform, gazing into the dark distance, Gurov heard the chirp of grasshoppers and the hum of telegraph wires, feeling as if he had just awoken. Well, there went another adventure or episode in his life, he reflected. It too had ended, now only the memory was left.

He was troubled, sad, somewhat penitent. This young woman whom he would never see again . . . she hadn't been happy with him, now, had she? He had treated her kindly and affectionately. And yet his attitude to her, his tone, his caresses had betrayed a faint irony: the rather crude condescension of your conquering male—of a man nearly twice her age into the bargain. She had kept calling him kind, exceptional, noble—so she hadn't seen him as he really was, obviously, and he must have been deceiving her without meaning to.

Here at the station there was already a whiff of autumn in the air, and the evening was cool.

"It's time I went north too," thought Gurov, leaving the platform. "High time."

III

Back home in Moscow it was already like winter. The stoves were alight. It was dark when his children breakfasted and got ready for school in the mornings, so their nanny lit the light for a short time. The frosts had begun. It is always such a joy to see the white ground and white roofs when the snow first falls, on that first day of sleigh-riding. The air is so fresh and good to breathe, and you remember the years of your youth. White with frost, the old limes and birches have a kindly look, they are dearer to your heart than any cypresses or palm-trees, and near them you no longer hanker after mountains and sea.

A Moscow man himself, Gurov had come home on a fine frosty day. He put on his fur coat and warm gloves and strolled down the Petrovka, he heard church bells pealing on Saturday evening . . . and his recent trip, all the places he had visited, lost all charm for him. He gradually plunged into Moscow life. He was zealously reading his three newspapers a day, now—while claiming to read no Moscow newspapers on principle! He felt that lure of restaurants, clubs, dinner parties, anniversary celebrations; he was flattered to be visited by famous lawyers and actors, flattered to play cards with a professor at the Doctors' Club. He could tackle a large helping of "Moscow hot-pot" straight from the pan.

In a month or two's time the memory of Anne would become blurred, thought he—he would just dream of her, of her adorable smile, occasionally as he used to dream of those other ones. But more than a month passed, real winter set in, and yet everything was still as clear in his mind as if they had parted only yesterday. His memories flared up ever more brightly. When, in the quiet of evening, his children's voices reached his study as they did their homework, when he heard a sentimental song or a barrel organ in a restaurant, when a blizzard howled in his chimney . . . it would all suddenly come back to him: that business on the pier, the early morning with the mist on the mountains, the Feodosiya steamer, the kisses. He would pace the room for hours, remembering and smiling until these recollections merged into fantasies: until, in his imagination, past fused with future. Though he did not dream of Anne, she pursued him everywhere like his shadow, watching him. If he closed his eyes he could see her vividly—younger, gentler, more beautiful than she really was. He even saw himself as a better man than he had been back in Yalta. She gazed at him from the book-case in the evenings, from the hearth, from a corner of the room. He heard her breathing, heard the delightful rustle of her dress. In the street he followed women with his eyes, seeking one like her.

He was plagued, now, by the urge to share his memories. But he could not talk about his love at home, and outside his home there was no one to tell—he couldn't very well discuss it with his tenants or at the bank! What was there to say, anyway? Had he really been in love? Had there really been anything beautiful or idyllic, anything edifying—anything merely interesting, even—in his relations with Anne? He was reduced to vague remarks about love and women, and no one guessed what he had in mind. His wife just twitched those dark eyebrows and told him that "the role of lady-killer doesn't suit you at all, Demetrius."

As he was leaving the Doctors' Club one night with his partner, a civil servant, he could not help saying that he had "met such an enchanting woman in Yalta—did you but know!"

The civil servant climbed into his sledge and drove off, but suddenly turned round and shouted Gurov's name.

"What is it?"

"You were quite right just now, the sturgeon *was* a bit off."

For some reason these words, humdrum though they were, suddenly infuriated Gurov, striking him as indelicate and gross. What barbarous manners, what faces, what meaningless nights, what dull, featureless days! Frantic card-playing, guzzling, drunkenness, endless chatter always on one and the same topic. Futile activities, repetitious talk, talk, talk . . . they engross most of your time, your best efforts, and you end up with a sort of botched, pedestrian life: a form of imbecility from which there's no way out, no escape. You might as well be in jail or in a madhouse!

Gurov lay awake all night, fuming—then had a headache all next day. He slept badly on the following nights, too, sitting up in bed thinking, or pacing the room. He was fed up with his children, fed up with his bank, there was nowhere he wanted to go, nothing he wanted to talk about.

Towards Christmas he prepared for a journey. He told his wife that he was going to St. Petersburg on a certain young man's business—but he actually went to the town where Anne lived. Why? He didn't really know himself. He wanted to see her, speak to her—make an assignation if he could.

He reached the town one morning and put up at a hotel, in the "best" room with wall-to-wall carpeting in coarse field-grey material. On the table stood an inkstand, grey with dust and shaped as a horseman holding his hat up in one hand and minus a head. The porter told him what he needed to know: von Diederitz lived in Old Pottery Street in his own house near the hotel. He did things in style, kept his own horses, was known to everyone in town. The porter pronounced the name as "Drearydits." Gurov sauntered off to Old Pottery Street, found the house. Immediately facing it was a long, grey fence crowned with nails: "a fence to run away from," thought Gurov, looking from windows to fence and back.

Local government offices were closed today, so the husband was probably at home, Gurov reckoned. In any case it would be tactless to go into the house and create a disturbance. If he sent a note, though, it might fall into the husband's hands and ruin everything. Better trust to chance. He paced the street near the fence, awaiting this chance. He saw a beggar go through the gate, saw him set upon by dogs. An hour later he heard the faint, muffled sound of a piano—that must be Anne playing. Suddenly the front door opened, and out came an old woman with the familiar white Pomeranian running after her. Gurov wanted to call the dog, but his heart suddenly raced and he was too excited to remember its name.

He paced about, loathing that grey fence more and more. In his irritation, he fancied that Anne had forgotten him and might be amusing herself with another man—what else could be expected of a young woman compelled to contemplate this confounded fence morning, noon and night? He went back to his room, sat on the sofa for hours not knowing what to do, then lunched and dozed for hours.

"It's all so stupid and distressing," he thought, waking up and seeing the dark windows—it was already evening. "Now I've had a good sleep for some reason, but what shall I do tonight?"

He sat on the bed—it was covered with a cheap, grey hospital blanket.

"So much for your ladies with dogs!" said he in petulant self-mockery. "So much for your holiday romances—now you're stuck in this dump."

In the station that morning his eye had been caught by a poster in bold lettering advertising the opening of *The Geisha*. Recalling this, he drove to the theatre, reflecting that she very probably attended first nights.

The theatre was full. As usual in provincial theatres a mist hung above the chandelier, while the gallery was restive and rowdy. In the first row before the performance began stood the local gallants, hands clasped behind their backs. In the Governor's box, in front, sat that worthy's daughter complete with feather boa, while the Governor himself lurked modestly behind a *portière*, only his hands showing. The curtain shook, the orchestra tuned up protractedly. As the audience came in and took its seats, Gurov peered frantically around.

In came Anne. She sat down in the third row, and when Gurov glimpsed her his heart seemed to miss a beat. He saw clearly, now, that she was nearer, dearer, more important to him than anyone in the whole world. Lost in the provincial crowd, this very ordinary little woman carrying her vulgar lorgnette now absorbed his whole being. She was his grief, his joy—the only happiness he wanted, now. To the strains of that abominable orchestra with its atrocious, tasteless fiddling he thought how lovely she was . . . thought and brooded.

A young man with short dundrearies, very tall, round-shouldered, had come in with Anne and sat down beside her. He kept bobbing his head as if making obeisance with every step he took. It must be the husband whom, in that bitter outburst back in Yalta, she had dubbed a "worm." His lanky figure, his side-whiskers, his small bald patch . . . there actually *was* something menial and flunkey-like about them. He gave an ingratiating smile, the emblem of some learned society glinting in his buttonhole like a hotel servant's number.

The husband went for a smoke in the first interval, while she remained seated. Gurov—his seat was also in the stalls—approached her. His voice trembling, forcing a smile, he wished her good evening.

She glanced at him, she blenched. The she looked again—aghast, not believing her eyes, crushing fan and lorgnette together in her hands in an obvious effort to prevent herself from fainting. Neither spoke. She sat, he remained standing—alarmed by her discomfiture, not venturing to sit down beside her. Fiddles and flute started tuning up, and he suddenly panicked: from all the boxes eyes seemed to be staring at them. Then she stood up and quickly made for the exit, while he followed, both walking at random along corridors, up and down stairways, glimpsing men in the uniforms of the courts, the schools and and administration of crown lands, all wearing their decorations. There were glimpses of ladies and fur coats on pegs. A draught enveloped them with the smell of cigarette ends.

"Oh God—why all these people, this orchestra?" wondered Gurov, his heart pounding.

Suddenly he recalled the evening when he had seen Anne off at the station, when he had told himself that it was all over and that they would never meet again. How far they were now, though, from any ending!

On a narrow, gloomy staircase labelled ENTRANCE TO CIRCLE she stopped.

"How you did scare me," she panted, still pale and dazed. "I nearly died, you scared me so. Why, why, why are you here?"

"Try and understand, Anne," he said in a rapid undertone. "Understand, I implore you——"

She looked at him—fearfully, pleadingly, lovingly. She stared, trying to fix his features in her memory.

"I'm so miserable," she went on, not hearing him. "I've thought only of you all this time, my thoughts of you have kept me alive. Oh, I did so want to forget you—why, why, why are you here?"

On a landing higher up two schoolboys were smoking and looking down, but Gurov did not care. He pulled Anne to him, kissed her face, cheek, hands.

"Whatever are you doing?" she asked—horrified, pushing him from her. "We must be out of our minds. You must go away today—leave this very instant, I implore you, I beg you in the name of all that is holy. Someone's coming."

Someone indeed was coming upstairs.

"You *must* leave," Anne went on in a whisper. "Do you hear me, Gurov? I'll visit you in Moscow. I've never been happy, I'm unhappy now, and I shall never, never, never be happy. So don't add to my sufferings. I'll come to Moscow, I swear it, but we must part now. We must say good-bye, my good, kind darling."

She pressed his hand and went quickly downstairs, looking back at him, and he could see from her eyes that she really was unhappy. Gurov waited a little, cocked an ear and, when all was quiet, found the peg with his coat and left the theatre.

IV

Anne took to visiting him in Moscow. Once every two or three months she would leave her home town, telling her husband that she was going to consult a professor about a female complaint. The husband neither believed nor disbelieved her. In Moscow she would put up at the Slav Fair Hotel, and at once send a red-capped messenger to Gurov. Gurov would visit her hotel, and no one in Moscow knew anything about it.

It thus chanced that he was on his way to see her one winter morning—her messenger had called on the previous evening, but had not found him at home. He was walking with his daughter, wanting to take her to her school, which was on his way. There was a heavy downpour of sleet.

"It's three degrees above zero, yet look at the sleet," said Gurov to his daughter. "But it's only the ground which is warm, you see—the temperature in the upper strata of the atmosphere is quite different."

"Why doesn't it thunder in winter, Daddy?"

He explained this too, reflecting as he spoke that he was on his way to an assignation. Not a soul knew about it—or ever would know, probably. He was living two lives. One of them was open to view by—and known to—the people concerned. It was full of stereotyped truths and stereotyped untruths, it was identical with the life of his friends and acquaintances. The other life proceeded in secret. Through some strange and possibly arbitrary chain of coincidences everything vital, interesting and crucial to him, everything which called his sincerity and integrity into play, everything which made up the core of his life . . . all that took place in complete secrecy, whereas everything false about him, the façade behind which he hid to conceal the truth—his work at the bank, say, his arguments at the club, that "inferior species" stuff, attending anniversary celebrations with his wife—all that was in the open. He judged others by himself, disbelieving the evidence of his eyes, and attributing to everyone a real, fascinating life lived under the cloak of secrecy as in the darkness of the night. Each individual existence is based on mystery, which is perhaps why civilized man makes such a neurotic fuss about having his privacy respected.

After taking his daughter to school, Gurov made for the Slav Fair. He removed his coat downstairs, went up, tapped on the door. Anne was wearing his favourite grey dress, she was tired by the journey—and by the wait, after expecting him since the previous evening. She was pale, she looked at him without smiling, and no sooner was he in the room than she flung herself against his chest. Their kiss was as protracted and lingering as if they had not met for two years.

"Well, how are things with you?" he asked. "What's the news?"

"Wait, I'll tell you in a moment—I can't now."

Unable to speak for crying, she turned away and pressed a handkerchief to her eyes.

"Let her cry, I'll sit down for a bit," thought he, and sat in the armchair.

Then he rang and ordered tea. Then he drank it while she still stood with her back to him, facing the window.

She wept as one distressed and woefully aware of the melancholy turn which their lives had taken. They met only in secret, they hid from other people like thieves. Their lives were in ruins, were they not?

"Now, do stop it," he said.

He could see that this was no fleeting affair—there was no telling when it would end. Anne was growing more and more attached to him. She adored him, and there was no question of telling her that all this must finish one day. Besides, she would never believe him.

He went up to her, laid his hands on her shoulders, meaning to soothe her with a little banter—and then caught sight of himself in the mirror.

His hair was turning grey. He wondered why he had aged so much in the last few years and lost his looks. The shoulders on which his hands rested were warm and trembling. He pitied this life—still so warm and beautiful, but probably just about to fade and wither like his own. Why did she love him so? Women had never seen him as he really was. What they loved in him was not his real self but a figment of their own imaginations—someone whom they had dreamed of meeting all their lives. Then, when they realized their mistake, they had loved him all the same. Yet none of them had been happy with him. Time had passed, he had met new ones, been intimate with them, parted from them. Not once had he been in love, though. He had known everything conceivable—except love, that is.

Only now that his head was grey had he well and truly fallen in love: for the first time in his life.

Anne and he loved each other very, very dearly, like man and wife or bosom friends. They felt themselves predestined for each other. That he should have a wife, and she a husband . . . it seemed to make no sense. They were like two migratory birds, a male and a female, caught and put in separate cages. They had forgiven each other the shameful episodes of their past, they forgave each other for the present too, and they felt that their love had transformed them both.

Once, in moments of depression, he had tried to console himself with any argument which came into his head—but now he had no use for arguments. His deepest sympathies were stirred, he only wanted to be sincere and tender.

"Stop, darling," he said. "You've had your cry—that's enough. Now let's talk, let's think of something."

Then they consulted at length about avoiding the need for concealment and deception, for living in different towns, for meeting only at rare intervals. How could they break these intolerable bonds? How, how, how?

He clutched his head and asked the question again and again.

Soon, it seemed, the solution would be found and a wonderful new life would begin. But both could see that they still had a long, long way to travel—and that the most complicated and difficult part was only just beginning.

In the Hollow

I

U kleyevo village was at the bottom of a hollow. Only its belfry and the chimneys of its calico-printing factories could be seen from the main road and railway station. When travellers asked what village it was, they would be told "where the sexton ate all the caviare at the funeral."

Once, after a funeral at factory-owner Kostyukov's place, an elderly sexton had spotted some unpressed caviare among the eatables and begun gulping it down. People jostled him, tugged his sleeve, but he was in a sort of ecstatic trance: felt nothing, just went on eating. He wolfed the lot, and the jar had held about four pounds! This had been some time ago and the sexton had long since died, yet they still remembered that caviare. Was life there really so miserable? Or were people just incapable of noticing anything but this trivial episode, now ten years old? Anyway, it was all one ever heard about Ukleyevo village.

Malaria was endemic in the place. There was gluey mud, even in summer: especially beneath the fences broadly overshadowed by ancient stooping willows. It always smelt of factory waste, and of acetic acid as used in processing cotton. The factories—three calico print-works, one tannery—were not in the actual village, but on the outskirts or some distance away. They were small concerns, employing no more than four hundred workers all told. The tannery often made the stream stink, its waste polluted the meadow, the villagers' cattle suffered from anthrax. There had been an order to close it down, and it did indeed rate as closed. But it functioned clandestinely—the police inspector and the county health officer were in the know, and each was paid his ten roubles a month by the owner. There were only two decent stone-built, iron-roofed houses in the whole village. One contained the local council offices, while the other—two-storeyed, right opposite the church—was the home of Gregory Tsybukin, a shopkeeper from Yepifan.

Gregory kept a grocery store, but only as a cover for dealing in vodka, cattle, skins, grain, pigs and whatever else was going. For instance, when there was a demand to export peasant bonnets as ladies' headgear, he made thirty copecks a pair on the deal. He bought standing timber, lent money at interest. He was, by and large, a resourceful old boy.

He had two sons. The elder, Anisim, was in the police detective branch, and was seldom at home. The younger, Stephen, had gone into the business, and assisted his father, but they didn't expect real help from him as he was deaf and ailing. His wife Aksinya was a beautiful, well-built woman. She sported her hat and sunshade of a Sunday, rose early, went to bed late, and was on the go all day in barn, cellar and shop—skirts hitched up, keys jingling. It made old man Tsybukin happy to look at her, and his eyes would light up—yet he was sorry that she was not married to his elder son, but to the younger: deaf and clearly no connoisseur of feminine beauty!

The old boy had always been domestically inclined, and loved his family more than anything on earth: especially his elder, detective son and his other son's wife. No sooner had Aksinya married her deaf husband than she was already showing an unusual head for business. She knew who could and could not be given credit, she kept her keys on her, not trusting even her husband with them, she clicked away at her counting-frame. She looked horses in the mouth like a peasant, and she was always laughing or shouting. Whatever she did or said, the old man just doted on her.

"Good for you, daughter!" he would mutter. "Well done, my lovely darling——"

He had been a widower, but one year after his son's marriage had again succumbed to wedlock. They found him a girl of good family, called Barbara, twenty miles from Ukleyevo. Though not in her first youth, she was a fine figure of a woman. And no sooner had she settled into her little first-floor room than everything in the house was sparkling like a new pin. Lamps burned before icons, tables were covered with snow-white table-cloths, red-eyed flowers appeared on window-sills and in the front garden, meals were no longer eaten from a common bowl—everyone had his own little dish. Barbara's warm, friendly smile seemed to make the whole house smile. Also—and this was new—beggars and various pilgrims began to call. The piteous whining of the Ukleyevo women was heard outside the windows, as also was the apologetic coughing of their frail, haggard menfolk dismissed from the works for drunkenness. Barbara gave them money, food, old clothes. When she was a bit more sure of herself she also took to fetching them odd things from the shop. The deaf man once saw her taking two two-ounce packets of tea, which disconcerted him.

"Mum just took two packets of tea," he informed his father later. "Who shall I charge it to?"

The old man made no answer—just stood and thought, twitching his eyebrows—then went upstairs to his wife.

"Barbara, dear," said he affectionately, "if you want something in the shop you take it. Take as much as you like, don't you hesitate."

Next day the deaf man ran across the yard shouting "if you want something, Mum, you take it."

There was something fresh, cheerful and light-hearted about her alms-giving, just as there was in those icon-lamps and little red flowers. Just before fasts, or on the village saint's-day (it actually lasted three days), they used to palm off putrid salt beef on the villagers: stuff with so vile a stench that you could hardly go near the barrel. And they let drunks pawn their scythes, their caps and their women's kerchiefs, while millhands—befuddled by foul vodka—sprawled in the mud, the very air seeming clogged by a dense miasma of sin . . . at which times it rather helped to remember that over there in the house was a neat, quiet woman who had nothing to do with that beef or vodka. On such oppressive, hazy occasions her charity operated as a safety valve.

These were busy days at the Tsybukins'. Aksinya would be spluttering as she washed herself in the passage before sun-up, while the kitchen samovar hissed and droned like a prophet of doom. Gregory—a nice, clean little old fellow in his long black frock-coat, nankeen trousers and sparkling jack-boots—paced the rooms, tapping his heels like "My Husband's Dear Old Dad" in the popular song. They would open the shop. When it was light the fast droshky would be brought to the porch, and in the old man would jump, jauntily, pulling his large peaked cap down over his ears. No one looking at him would have thought him fifty-six years old. His wife and daughter-in-law would see him off. Now, at such times, when he wore his nice, clean frock-coat and the great black three-hundred-rouble stallion was hitched to the droshky, the old man disliked the yokels coming up to complain and beg favours. He hated peasants, they riled him.

"Why are you hanging round? You clear off," he would yell wrathfully if he saw one waiting by the gate. Or, if it was a beggar, he would shout that God would "pervide."

When he was away on business his wife, in her dark clothes and black apron, would tidy the house or help in the kitchen. Aksinya served in the shop, and you could hear the jingle of bottles and coins out in the yard while she laughed or shouted and her offended customers raged. That the clandestine vodka trade was in full swing in the shop was also evident.

The deaf husband would also sit in the shop, or pace the street bareheaded, hands in pockets, looking absently at huts and sky. They drank tea half a dozen times a day in the house and sat down to about four meals. In the evening they counted the takings and entered them, after which they slept soundly.

All three Ukleyevo print-works were connected by telephone, as were the homes of the owners: Khrymins, Khrymin Sons and Kostyukov. The parish offices had been connected up too, but that instrument soon stopped working, having become infested with bugs and cockroaches. The parish chairman could hardly read, and he began every word in his documents with a capital letter, but when the telephone stopped working he said, yes, it was going to be "a bit difficult, like, without that there telephone."

Khrymins were always suing Khrymin Sons, while Khrymin Sons sometimes quarrelled among themselves and went to law, whereupon their works would stand idle for a month or two until they made it up again—which amused the Ukleyevites, seeing that each squabble provoked much discussion and tittle-tattle. On Sundays Kostyukov and Khrymin Sons would go out driving and career through Ukleyevo running down the calves. Rustling her starched skirts and dressed up to the nines, Aksinya would parade in the street near her shop until Khrymin Sons swooped down and whisked her off as if abducting her by force. Then old Tsybukin would drive out too, to show off his new horse, taking Barbara with him.

In the evening, when the driving was over and folk were going to bed, an expensive-sounding accordion would be played in Khrymin Sons' grounds, and if there was a moon these sounds thrilled and gladdened the heart. No longer did Ukleyevo seem quite such a dump.

II

The elder son Anisim came back very seldom, only on the major saints' days, but he often got people from the village to take home presents and letters beautifully written in some else's hand. They were always on a good-quality paper, they had an official look about them, and they abounded in expressions never used by Anisim in conversation, such as "dearest Mum and Dad, I send you a pound of herbal tea for the gratification of your physical requirements."

At the foot of each letter was scratched ANISIM TSYBUKIN, as if with a cross-nibbed pen, and beneath this, in the same ornate hand as before, the word AGENT.

The letters were read aloud several times.

"Ah well, he wouldn't stay at home, he would be a scholar," said the old man, much moved and crimson with excitement. "So be it then. Everyone should go his own way."

Once, just before Shrovetide, there was heavy rain and sleet. The old man and Barbara went to the window for a look—and behold Anisim sleighing in from the station. Completely unexpected, he entered anxiously as if he had something on his mind, and kept this up during the rest of his time there. He seemed a bit off-hand too, and was in no hurry to leave. Could he have lost his job? That's what it looked like. Barbara was glad to see him and kept giving him rather arch looks, sighing and shaking her head.

"Now, goodness me, this won't do at all," she clucked. "Here's a lad turned twenty-seven—and he's still the gay bachelor! Goodness gracious me!"

From another room her quiet, level speech sounded like a continuous susurration. She took to whispering to the old man and Aksinya, and their faces also adopted that arch, mysteriously conspiratorial look.

They decided to marry Anisim off.

"Your younger brother's been wed long since," clucked Barbara. "But you're unspliced still, like a cockerel at market—it ain't right, that. You can marry, God willing, and then do as you please: go back to work, and your wife can stay at home and help. You've got into bad ways, my lad, I can see that. Forgotten what's what, you have. Proper shockers you town folks are, goodness gracious me!"

When Tsybukins married they had the pick of the best-looking girls, seeing that they were rich. For Anisim too a beautiful bride was found. His own looks were drab and unprepossessing. His build was frail and sickly, he was short of stature, he had plump, bulging cheeks which looked as if he was puffing them out. He had a sharp, unwinking stare and a sparse, gingery beard which, in pensive mood, he was always chewing at. He liked his dram, too—that showed in his face and walk. But when informed that a very beautiful bride had been found for him, he said that he was, "well, not exactly misshapen" himself.

"We Tsybukins are a good-looking breed, and that's a fact."

Adjoining the local town was the village of Torguyevo, half of which had recently been amalgamated with the town, the other half remaining a village. In the town part lived a certain widow in a cottage which she owned. She had a sister who was very poor and went out to work by the day. This sister had a daughter, Lipa, who was a hired drudge like her mother. Lipa's beauty was the talk of Torguyevo. The trouble was, though, she was so terribly poor. The view was that some elderly man or widower would marry her, overlooking her poverty—or else, "you know, just live with her"—and then the mother would be provided for as well. Hearing of Lipa from local marriage-brokers, Barbara went over to Torguyevo.

Then a bride-showing was laid on at the aunt's house—it was all done properly with the usual snacks and drinks. Lipa wore a new pink dress specially made for the occasion, and a crimson ribbon flamed in her hair. She was a frail, slim, pale little thing with fine, delicate, features, sunburnt from work in the open air. A sad, nervous smile played on her face. And there was a childlike look, trustful and inquisitive, about her eyes.

She was young—no more than a little girl, her bosom barely developed—but already of marriageable age. She really was beautiful, having only one feature which might seem unattractive: large arms, like a man's, now dangling idly like two great claws.

"There's no dowry, but that don't bother us," the old man told the aunt. "We took a girl from a poor family for our son Stephen too, and we're as pleased as could be. About the house, in the shop . . . oh, she's a real treasure."

Lipa stood by the door, and seemed to be trying to tell them to "do what you like with me, I trust you."

Her mother Praskovya, the hired hand, skulked in the kitchen almost too shy to breathe. In her youth a merchant whose floors she was scrubbing once flew into a rage and stamped his feet at her. She had been terribly frightened, it had given her rather a turn, and that terror had remained with her all her life: a terror which kept her arms and legs for ever trembling—her cheeks too. From her seat in the kitchen she tried to hear what the guests were saying, and she kept crossing herself, pressing her fingers to her forehead and glancing at the icon. Slightly drunk, Anisim kept opening the kitchen door.

"Why sit out here, dearest Mum?" he would ask jauntily. "We've been missing you."

Praskovya timidly pressed her hands to her gaunt, emaciated bosom.

"Oh, you shouldn't sir, really," she answered. "It's far too good of you, sir."

They inspected the bride, they named the wedding day—after which Anisim kept pacing the rooms at home and whistling. Or he would suddenly remember something, start brooding and fix a piercing stare on the floor as if his eyes sought to penetrate deep into the earth. He evinced neither pleasure at the prospect of marrying soon (the week after Easter) nor any wish to see his bride either, he only whistled. He was only marrying because his father and stepmother wanted him to, that was obvious—and because it's a village custom: the son takes a wife to help in the house. When he left for town again he did so without haste. This time his whole conduct had differed from that of his previous visits: he had been particularly offhand and said all the wrong things.

III

In Shikalovo village lived two dressmakers—sisters, belonging to the Flagellant sect. They were given the order for the wedding clothes, they often came over for fittings, and they drank tea for hours. For Barbara they made a brown dress trimmed with black lace and bugles, and for Aksinya a light green one with a train and a yellow bodice. When the dressmakers had finished, Tsybukin paid them: not in cash, but in goods from his shop. They went away sadly, holding bundles of tallow candles and sardines for which they had no use at all, and when they came out of the village into open country they sat on a tussock and wept.

Three days before the wedding Anisim turned up in a completely new outfit: shiny rubber galoshes, a red cord with bobbles instead of a tie. A greatcoat, also new, was slung loosely over his shoulders.

He prayed solemnly before the icon, greeted his father—and gave him ten silver roubles and ten fifty-copeck pieces. He gave the same to Barbara, and he gave Aksinya twenty quarter-roubles. The main charm of these gifts was this: the coins were all brand new, in mint condition, and glinted in the sunlight. Trying to look solemn and earnest, Anisim pulled a long face, puffed out his cheeks and gave off a whiff of spirits. He'd popped into the bar at every station, very likely. Once again there was something off-hand, something rather otiose, about the fellow. Then Anisim and the old man had tea while Barbara fingered the bright new roubles and asked about folk from their village who had gone to live in town.

"They're all right, praise the Lord—doing well, they are," said Anisim. "Oh, there has been an incident, though, in Ivan Yegorov's domestic life. His old woman Sophia passed on. The consumption, it was. The caterers handled the wake at two-and-a-half roubles a head. There was wine too. There was peasants there—some of our lot—and they charged two-and-a-half roubles for them too, though they never ate nothing. What do them bumpkins know about sauce?"

"Two-and-a-half roubles each!" The old man shook his head.

"What else do you expect? It ain't like a village. You go into a restaurant for a bite, you order a few things, a few of your pals look in, you have a drink—and then, lo and behold, it's already dawn, and it's fork

out your three or four roubles a head if you please. And when Samorodov's there, he wants his coffee and brandy after everything—and with
brandy at 'sixty copecks the glass, sir'!"

The old man was ecstatic. "What nonsense he does talk!"

"I spend all my time with Samorodov these days. He's the one who
writes my letters to you—oh, he's a great writer, is Samorodov."

Anisim turned to Barbara. "You'd never believe me, Mum," he went
on cheerfully, "if I told you what Samorodov's like. We call him Mukhtar
because he looks like an Armenian: black all over. Read him like a book,
I do—I know all his business like the palm of my hand, Mum. And don't
he feel it! He's always making up to me, won't leave me alone, we're
thick as thieves now, we are. He's a bit scared of me, but he can't do
without me. Where I go he goes. I've got a real good eye, Mum, that I
have. Like when I see a peasant selling a shirt in the flea-market. 'Hey
there,' says I, 'that's stolen property!' And I'm always right, the shirt *is*
stolen, it turns out——"

"But how can you tell?" asked Barbara.

"I *can't* tell, I've just got the eye for it. I don't know nothing about
that shirt, I somehow just feel it's stolen, and that's that. That's what they
say in the office. 'Anisim's gone sniping,' say they: looking for stolen
goods, that is. True enough, anyone can steal things—it's keeping them
that counts. Big as the world is, there ain't nowhere to hide the swag."

"Last week a ram and two ewes were stolen from the Guntorevs here
in the village," sighed Barbara. "Goodness gracious me! There was no
one to look for them."

"Very well, I might take it on—I wouldn't mind."

The wedding day arrived. It was a cool April day, but bright and
brisk. Troikas and two-horse carriages—harness-bells jingling, with
gaudy ribbons on yokes and manes—had been driving round Ukleyevo
since early morning. Disturbed by all the coming and going, rooks chattered in the willows and starlings nearly burst their lungs, seeming to
celebrate the Tsybukin wedding with their non-stop singing.

Indoors the tables were already groaning with long fishes, hams,
stuffed birds, boxes of sprats, various salted and pickled items, and an
array of vodka and wine bottles. There was a smell of salami and stale
lobster. Near those tables, clattering his heels and sharpening knife on
knife, paraded the old man. They kept calling Barbara and asking for
something, and she—panting, looking distracted—would run into the
kitchen where Kostyukov's chef and Khrymin Sons' cook had been hard
at work since dawn. Hair curled, in corsets but no dress, new boots
squeaking, Aksinya whirled round the yard with flashes of bare knee and
breast. It was noisy, there was cursing and swearing. Passers-by paused
at the wide open gate, and could sense that something most unusual was
afoot.

"They've gone for the bride."

Harness-bells jingled, then died away far beyond the village.

At about half-past two a crowd ran up, and the bells were heard again. They were bringing the bride!

The church was full, the candelabra blazed, the choristers sang from sheet music—old Tsybukin's wish, this. The glittering lights, the bright dresses blinded Lipa, the choir's loud voices rang like hammers in her head. Her corset—the first she had ever worn—and her shoes were pinching her: she looked as if she had just come out of a faint, gazing about her but not understanding. Anisim, in his black frock-coat with his bit of red cord for a tie, was plunged in thought, staring fixedly and hastily crossing himself whenever a great shout came from the choir. He was deeply moved, to the point of tears. He had known this church since he was a little boy. His mother of blessed memory had brought him here for the sacraments, he had once sung in the boys' choir. Each little nook, each icon . . . he remembered them all so well. Now he was being married here because that was the done thing, but his mind was elsewhere, he no longer thought of his wedding, somehow—had forgotten it entirely. He could not see the icons for tears, there was a lump in his throat. He was praying, he was begging God that those fell disasters about to burst on him any day now . . . that they might somehow pass him by as clouds pass over a village in time of drought without shedding one drop of rain. And what of the weight of accumulated sin in his past—the many sins which had ensnared him beyond redemption, sins past praying forgiveness for, even? Pray forgiveness, though, he did—he even sobbed aloud, but no one heeded.

They just thought he'd had a drop too much.

A child's tearful cry rang out. "Mummy, darling! Take me away from here!"

"Silence there!" the priest shouted.

On their way back from church the peasants thronged after them, and there were more crowds near shop and gate, and beneath the windows facing the yard. Village women had come to sing the bridal songs. No sooner had the young couple crossed the threshold than the choristers, waiting ready in the hall with that sheet music, shrieked for all they were worth. The band, specially hired from town, struck up. Tall goblets of Cossack "bubbly" were offered round, and the jobbing carpenter Yelizarov—a tall, lean old man with brows so bushy that they nearly masked his eyes—addressed the newly-weds.

"Anisim and you, child, love each other and lead godly lives, my children, and the Holy Mother will not forsake you." He leant on the old man's shoulder and sobbed.

"Gregory Tsybukin, let us weep aloud, let us weep tears of joy!" he said in a reedy little voice followed by a sudden loud guffaw.

"And this new daughter-in-law of yours is a real good-looker too," he went on in a loud, deep voice. "She has everything in the right place, like: all smooth stuff, it won't rattle, the whole mechanics is in tip-top order—plenty of screws."

He came from out Yegoryevsk way, but had worked in the Ukleyevo mills and near-by parts since youth—he'd settled down. He had looked just as old, lean and lanky as he was now for as long as folk remembered. For years he had had the nickname "Lofty." For over forty years he had done nothing but maintenance work at the mills, which is perhaps why he judged everyone and everything solely in terms of their durability: did they need repair? Before sitting down at table he had tested a few chairs for soundness, also prodding the cold salmon.

After the "bubbly" they all took their places at table. The guests spoke and moved their chairs, the choir sang in the hall, the band played, while the women in the yard simultaneously sang their folk songs in unison: a ghastly, grotesque medley of noise which made your head spin.

Now crying, now laughing aloud, Lofty fidgeted in his chair, elbowed his neighbours, wouldn't let them get a word in edgeways.

"Children, children, children," he muttered rapidly. "Aksinya, my dear, and Barbara, let us all live in peace and harmony, my darling little hatchets——"

No great drinker, he was quite merry, now, on one glass of "English bitters." This revolting brew, made of God knows what, stunned all who drank it as if they had been slugged. Tongues became entwined.

There were clergy here, there were clerks from the mills with their wives, there were traders and pub-keepers from other villages. The parish chairman and his clerk—they'd been working together for fourteen years now, and never during all that time had they signed a single document, nor let a soul leave their office, without cheating and insulting somebody—sat side by side: fat and smug, both of them . . . and seemingly so steeped in skulduggery that the very skin of their faces had a curiously depraved texture. The clerk's scrawny, cross-eyed wife had brought all her children along. She was squinting vulture-like at the bowls, grabbing whatever came her way and putting it in her own and the children's pockets.

Lipa sat there like a statue with the same look on her face as in church. Not having exchanged a single word with her since their first meeting, Anisim still didn't know what her voice sounded like. Now, as they sat side by side, he still wasn't speaking, but drank those "English bitters." Then, when he was tipsy, he addressed Lipa's aunt—sitting opposite.

"I have a friend, name of Samorodov. He's rather special, like. He's a cut above the rank and file, and he has something to say for himself. But I read him like a book, Aunty—and don't he feel it! May we now drink Samorodov's health together, Aunty dear?"

Barbara hovered round the table pressing the guests to eat—puffed, flustered, obviously glad that there were so many dishes. It was all on so lavish a scale that no one could sneer at them now. The sun went down, but the meal went on. No longer did they know what they were eating or drinking, nor could they hear what was said, but now and then when the band was quiet some village woman's shout carried clearly from the yard.

"Rotten swine, grinding the faces of the poor! May you rot in hell!"

In the evening they danced to the band. Khrymin Sons had brought their own drink, and during the quadrille one of them held a bottle in each hand and a glass in his mouth, which was all great fun. In mid-quadrille they suddenly launched into a squatting dance. Green Aksinya kept flashing past with a breath of wind from her train. Someone had trodden on one of her flounces.

"Hey, her skirting board's come loose, children!" shouted Lofty.

Aksinya had naïve grey eyes which rarely blinked and a naïve smile for ever playing on her face. In those unblinking eyes, in the small head on the long neck, in her litheness, there was something of the snake. Dressed in green, yellow-bodiced, smiling, she looked like a viper: coiled, head uplifted in the young rye, as it watches someone go past in spring time. The Khrymins took liberties with her, and it was only too obvious that she had long been on the closest terms with the eldest. The deaf husband sensed nothing, though—he wasn't looking at her, but sat with his legs crossed, eating nuts and cracking them loudly with his teeth. It sounded like pistol shots.

Out came old Tsybukin himself into the middle and flipped a handkerchief to show that he too wanted to do the squat-dance. A roar of approval ran through the crowded house and yard.

" 'Tis the old gaffer himself going to dance!"

Barbara danced, while the old man only waved his handkerchief and shuffled his heels, but the folk out in the yard—clinging to each other as they peered through the windows—were in ecstasy and straightway forgave him everything: his money, his insults. Voices were heard in the crowd.

"Good old Gregory!" they laughed. "That's it, you have a go! So you ain't past it, eh? Ha, Ha."

It all ended late, after one in the morning. Anisim staggered round choir and band, giving everyone a new half-rouble as a parting gift, while the old man—steady on his feet, but vaguely limping—saw his guests off, telling everyone that the wedding had "cost me a cool two thousand."

As they were dispersing it turned out that someone had taken the Shikalovo pub-keeper's new jacket, leaving an old one behind in its place. Anisim flared up.

"Stop, everyone! I'm going to make a search," he shouted. "I know who took that. Hold it!"

He ran out into the street, started chasing someone.

They caught Anisim, they dragged him back by the arms. They thrust him—drunk, crimson with rage, wet with sweat—into the room where Aunty had been undressing Lipa. And locked him in.

IV

Five days passed. Anisim was ready to leave, and went upstairs to say good-bye to Barbara. Her icon-lamps were all lit, there was a smell of incense and she sat by the window knitting a red woolen stocking.

"You didn't stay long," said she. "Got bored, eh? Goodness gracious me. We do ourselves well, we don't want for anything. And your wedding was done right and proper—two thousand it cost, the old man said. We live off the fat of the land in fact, but it's a dull life, this is. Too hard on them peasants, we are. It grieves me so, dear, to think how we wrong them. Bartering horses, buying things, hiring workmen . . . it's all fraud, fraud, fraud, Lord help us. The olive oil in the shop's sour and rancid— no better than tar, it isn't. How come we can't sell proper oil, eh? You tell me that."

"None of my business, Mum."

"But we all die in the end, don't we? You really should talk to your father, dear me you should."

"Talk to him yourself."

"Not me. If I do he only answers same as you: it ain't none of my business. Whose business it is . . . that'll be settled in the next world. God's judgement is righteous."

"Of course it won't be settled," sighed Anisim. "There ain't no such thing as God anyway, is there, Mum? So much for your next world!"

Barbara looked at him in amazement, laughed and threw up her arms. That she so genuinely marvelled at his words, that she really did think him a freak . . . it quite disconcerted him.

"Perhaps there is a God, and it's just me that can't believe," he said. "I felt a bit funny at the wedding—like when you take an egg from the hen, and there's a chick squeaking in it. It was that way with my conscience—it suddenly started squeaking, and during the service I kept thinking that God does exist. Then I come out of church and the feeling's gone. Anyway, how can *I* tell if there's a God or not? That's not what they taught us as kids. From when we was babes in arms we was taught only one thing: you keep your place. Now, Dad don't believe in God either, do he? You once mentioned some sheep being stolen from Guntorevs'. It was a Shikalovo peasant stole 'em, I discovered. He stole them, but it's Dad who's got the skins. There's your religion for you!"

Anisim winked and shook his head.

"The parish chairman don't believe in God either," he went on. "Nor does the clerk, nor does the sexton. If they go to church, if they keep the fasts, they only do it so folks won't speak badly of them, and to be on the safe side—what if there should really be a Judgement Day? Folk are so feeble nowadays, don't respect their parents and all that—so people think it's the end of the world. Nonsense! The way I see it is this, Mum: all this grief, it comes from folk not having enough conscience. I read 'em like a book, Mum, I know what's what. If a man has a stolen shirt, I can tell. Or take someone sitting in a pub—all you can see is him drinking his tea, no more than that. But *I* see that, tea or no tea, he ain't got no conscience. You can search all day and still not see one man with a conscience. And for why? Because they don't know if there's a God or not. Well, good-bye, Mum. Long life and good health to you, don't think too badly of me."

Anisim bowed low to Barbara.

"We thanks you for everything, Mum," he added. "You've been real good to our family, you have. You're a very proper sort of a woman, and I'm real pleased with you."

Deeply touched, Anisim went out, but came back again.

"Samorodov's got me involved in some deal," said he. "It's riches or ruination for me. If it don't go right, do comfort the old man, won't you, Mum?"

"Oh dear, whatever next! Goodness gracious me! God have mercy on us!" she clucked. "Now, you be nice to your wife, Anisim. You look as if you'd taken agin each other. You might at least laugh a bit, really!"

"Yes, she's a strange one," sighed Anisim. "Doesn't understand nothing, never says nothing. She's very young, though—wait till she grows up."

Near the porch stood a tall, sleek, white stallion harnessed to a dog-cart. Old Tsybukin took a run up, jumped jauntily aboard, seized the reins. Anisim kissed Barbara, Aksinya and his brother. Lipa too stood in the porch—stock still, eyes averted, looking as if she hadn't come out to see him off but had just somehow happened to be there. Anisim went up, lightly brushed her cheek with his lips, and said good-bye.

Not looking at him, she gave a somewhat strange smile. Her face trembled, and everyone felt rather sorry for her. Anisim too leapt aboard, and sat with arms akimbo, thinking himself handsome.

As they drove up out of the hollow Anisim kept looking back at the village. It was a warm, bright day. The cattle had been driven out for the first time, girls and women were walking about near the herd wearing holiday dresses. A brown bull bellowed, enjoying his freedom and pawing the ground with his front hooves. Larks sang everywhere, both above and below. Anisim looked round at the church so neat and white—it had just been whitewashed—and remembered worshipping there five days ago. He looked round at the school with its green roof, at the stream where he had once bathed and fished—and joy stirred within his breast. If only the earth would suddenly throw up a wall to bar his way and leave him alone with his memories.

They went into the station buffet for a glass of sherry. Wanting to pay, the old man felt in his pocket for his purse.

"This one's on me," said Anisim.

Delighted, the old man clapped him on the shoulder, and winked at the barman to show what a fine son he had.

"Why don't you stay at home and join the business, Anisim," he asked. "You'd be a real asset. I'd make you a mint of money, son."

"It's quite out of the question, Dad."

The sherry was rather bitter and smelt of sealing-wax, but they had another glass.

When the old man arrived home from the station he at first failed to recognize his younger daughter-in-law. No sooner had her husband left the premises than Lipa became transformed, suddenly cheering up. Barefoot, in a worn old skirt, sleeves rolled up to her shoulders, she was washing the staircase in the hall and singing in a thin, silvery little voice. And when she carried out the great pail of dirty water, looking into the sun with her childlike smile, she might have been another lark herself.

Walking past the porch, an old labourer shook his head and cleared his throat. "Fine women, Mr. Gregory, your son's wives. God has blessed you with real treasures, sir."

V

On Friday the eighth of July "Lofty" Yelizarov and Lipa were on their way back from making a pilgrimage to Kazanskoye village in honour of Our Lady of Kazan, whose festival this was. Far behind walked Lipa's mother Praskovya—being ailing and short of breath, she always did lag behind. It was late afternoon. Listening admiringly to Lipa, Lofty kept sighing and mumbling.

"I'm very fond of jam, I am, Mr. Yelizarov," said Lipa. "I sit in my own little corner drinking my tea and jam. Or Barbara and I have it together, and she tells some sad story, like. They have lots of jam—four jars at a time. 'You have some, Lipa,' they tell me. 'You help yourself.' "

"Aha! Four jars, eh?"

"They do themselves proud. They have white rolls with their tea, and there's as much beef as you like. They live well, but it's so frightening there, Mr. Yelizarov—it don't half scare me."

"What have you to fear, child?" asked Lofty, looking round to see if Praskovya was very far behind.

"At first, after the wedding, I was scared of Mr. Anisim. He never done nothing, he weren't nasty to me—it's just that when he comes near me a shudder goes through every bone in me body. And I don't sleep a wink at nights, just keep shivering and praying. Now I'm a-feared of Aksinya, Mr. Yelizarov. She seems all right, she's always laughing—it's just that you see her look out of the window sometimes with them angry green eyes afire, like a sheep's in the shed. Them Khrymin Sons are always on at her. Your old man has a bit of land at Butyokino—over a hundred acres, they tell her. There's sand, they tell her, and water too. So you build a brickyard on it in your own name, say they, and we'll go shares with you. Bricks fetch twenty roubles a thousand now—it's good business, that is. Well, at dinner yesterday Aksinya tells the old man she wants to start this brickyard at Butyokino—wants to go into business for herself. She's laughing as she says it, but Mr. Gregory gives her a black look—he don't like it, that's clear enough. 'So long as I'm alive,' says he, 'we ain't going to split up, we must stick together.' Well, she flashes them eyes and kind of grinds her teeth. We had pancakes, but she wouldn't eat none."

"Oh, so she wouldn't eat none?" Lofty was surprised.

"And another thing—when does she sleep if you please?" Lipa went on. "She'll sleep half an hour, then up she'll jump, rummage round everywhere to see if the peasants have set anything on fire or stolen anything. She scares me, Mr. Yelizarov. And after the wedding them Khrymin Sons never went to bed. They went to town to have the law on each other, and it was all Aksinya's doing—or so folks say. Two of them brothers promised to build her the works, but that annoyed the third one and their mill was shut for a month—my uncle Prokhor was out of work and had to go round begging for scraps. 'Why don't you go a-ploughing for a bit, Uncle,' I ask him. 'Or saw some wood. Why bring shame on yourself?' 'I've lost the habit of farm work,' says he. 'There ain't nothing I can do, Lipa dear.' "

They paused near a grove of young aspens to rest and wait for Praskovya. Yelizarov had been doing contract work for years, but he didn't keep a horse. He travelled the whole county on foot with a little bag of bread and onions—walked with long strides, swinging his arms, so that he was hard to keep up with.

At the entrance to the copse was a boundary post, and Yelizarov touched it to see if it was sound. Up came Praskovya, panting. Her wrinkled face, with its perpetual look of fear, beamed happiness. She had been to church today like a real person, then she had visited the fair and drunk pear kvass. It was such a rare treat, she even felt as if she had enjoyed herself today for the first time in her life. After a rest the three of them went on together. The sun was setting, its rays piercing ahead of them. The Ukleyevo girls had gone a long way in front, but had tarried in this copse—to pick mushrooms, probably.

"Hey there, lasses!" shouted Yelizarov. "Hallo my beauties."

"That's old Lofty, that is," they laughed in reply. "Silly old geezer!" The laughter echoed after them.

The copse was behind them, now, the tops of the mill chimneys had come into view, the belfry cross glittered. Here was the village "where the sexton ate all the caviare at the funeral." They were nearly home, they only had to go down into that great ravine. Lipa and Praskovya, who had been walking barefoot, sat on the grass to put their shoes on, and the carpenter sat down beside them. From up here Ukleyevo—with its willows, white church and stream—seemed pretty and peaceful. The only eyesores were the mill roofs, painted a gloomy greyish colour for economy reasons. On the far slope they could see rye: stooks and sheaves of it here and there, as if scattered by a storm, and newly reaped swathes. The oats were ripe and gleamed like mother-of-pearl in the sun. It was harvest time, but today was a day off. Tomorrow, Saturday, they would get in the rye and cart hay. Then it would be Sunday, another holiday. There was a rumbling of distant thunder every day, it was steamy and looked like rain. Gazing at the fields, now, they all hoped to harvest their crops in time, God willing. It was a cheerful, joyous—yet uneasy—feeling.

"Reapers come dear nowadays," said Praskovya. "One rouble forty a day."

More and more folk were rolling in from Kazanskoye fair: peasant women, mill-hands in new caps, beggars, children.

A cart would drive past, raising the dust, with an unsold horse trotting behind it and seeming glad not to have been bought. Someone would drag a reluctant cow by the horns. Or another cart would come along with drunken peasants dangling their legs. An old woman led a little boy in a large hat and large boots. Exhausted by the heat and his heavy boots, which stopped him bending his knees, he was yet blowing non-stop for all he was worth at a toy trumpet. Even when they had reached the bottom and turned into the village street that trumpet could still be heard.

"There's something wrong with our mill-owners," said Yelizarov. "Real vexing, it is. Kostyukov's annoyed with me. 'You used too many laths on them cornices,' says he. 'What do you mean, too many?' says I. 'I used what I needed, Mr. Kostyukov,' I tells him. 'I don't eat 'em with me porridge, them laths.' 'How dare you talk to me like that?' he asks. 'You oaf, you so-and-so! You forget your place. It was me at first set you up in business,' he shouts. 'You think you're very clever,' says I. 'But I still drank tea every day even when I didn't have me own business.' 'You're all swindlers,' says he. I says nothing. 'Oho!' I thinks. 'We may be swindlers in this world, but you'll be swindlers in the next!' On the day after that he caves in. 'Don't you be vexed, my good man,' says he. 'Don't you mind what I said. If,' says he, 'I said a bit too much—well, I'm a member of the chamber of commerce, so I'm a better man than you are, and you'd better not answer me back.' 'You,' says I, 'may well be a member of the chamber of commerce, while I'm just a carpenter. True enough. But Saint Joseph was a carpenter too,' says I. 'It's righteous, our work is, and pleasing to God. And if,' says I, 'you think you're a better man than me, Mr. Kostyukov, then the best of good luck to you, sir.' After this—after this here talk, I mean—I get to thinking: what *is* better: big businessman or carpenter? I reckon it's the carpenter, children.

"That's the way of it," Lofty added after a moment's thought. "It's the one as labours and puts up with things as is better."

The sun had gone down, and a dense, milk-white mist was rising over the river, in the churchyard and in the clearings near the mills. Now, with darkness so quickly descending, with the lights flashing down there, with the mist seeming to cloak a bottomless abyss, Lipa and her mother, who had been born beggars and were ready to live as such to the end—sacrificing to others everything but their frightened, gentle souls—briefly fancied perhaps that in the unnumbered, never-ending catalogue of lives in this vast, mysterious universe, they too amounted to something. Perhaps even they were "better" than someone? It was good to be sitting up here, and they smiled merrily, forgetting that they did, after all, have to go back down to the bottom.

They reached home at last. By the gate, near the shop, reapers sat around on the ground. Tsybukin's fellow-Ukleyevites usually refused to work for him, so he had to hire strangers—now, in the darkness, they all seemed to have long black beards. The shop was open, and through the door the deaf man could be seen playing draughts with a boy. The reapers sang softly, barely audibly, or loudly demanded yesterday's pay, but that had been kept back to stop them leaving before the morning. Old Tsybukin—minus his frock-coat, in waistcoat and shirt sleeves—was having tea with Aksinya beneath the birch-tree by the porch. There was a lighted lamp on the table.

"Hey there, Gaffer!" drawled a teasing voice behind the gate—one of the reapers. "At least pay us the half, Gaffer!"

There was laughter, after which they again sang, barely audibly. Lofty sat down to tea as well, and began a yarn.

"Well, there we are at the fair. We're having a good time, children—a real good time, praise be—when a rather nasty thing happens. Blacksmith Sashka buys some tobacco, and he gives the shopkeeper a half-rouble piece, like. But it was a bad one."

Lofty glanced round. He was trying to whisper, but spoke in a hoarse, strangled voice which everyone could hear.

"It was a bad half-rouble, that. 'Where did you get it?' they ask. 'Anisim Tsybukin give it me when I was a guest at his wedding,' says he. They call the sergeant, they take him off. You'd better watch out, old Gregory—there might be talk or summat——"

"Gaffer," drawled the same teasing voice behind the gate. "Hey there, Gaffer!"

Silence followed.

"Ah, children, children," muttered Lofty rapidly, and stood up. He was practically dozing off. "Well, thanks for the tea and sugar, children. Time for bed. I'm a-mouldering away, I am—me joists are all a-rotting, ho, ho, ho!

"Time I was in me grave," he said as he left. And sobbed.

Old Tsybukin did not finish his tea, but sat brooding and looking as if he was listening to Lofty's footsteps, though he was now far down the street.

"He was lying, was Blacksmith Sashka, I reckon," said Aksinya, guessing his thoughts.

Gregory went indoors and came back a bit later with a bundle which he untied. The brand-new roubles glinted, and he took one, bit it, threw it down on the tray. Then he threw down another.

"Them roubles really are forged," said he, looking at Aksinya as if in a quandary. "It's the same ones—them as Anisim brought from town that time, the ones he gave us. Now, you take them, my girl," he whispered, thrusting the bundle in her hands. "Take them and throw them down the well, confound them. And mind there ain't no talk! I hope it's going to be all right. Now clear away the samovar and put that light out."

Sitting in the shed, Lipa and Praskovya saw the lights going out one after the other. Only from Barbara's upstairs room did the blue and red icon-lamps still shed a glow of peace and blissful ignorance. Praskovya just couldn't accept her daughter's marriage to a rich man. She would cringe timidly in the passage during her visits, and smile pleadingly—and they would send tea and sugar out. Lipa couldn't resign herself to it either. After her husband had left she stopped using her bed, and would just lie down any old where in kitchen or shed. Every day she scrubbed floors or laundered, feeling like a charwoman. Now, after having returned from their pious mission, they had had tea in the kitchen with the cook, and had then gone into the shed and lain down on the straw between sledge and wall. It was dark and smelt of horse-collars. The lights round the house went out. Then they heard the deaf man locking up the shop and the reapers dossing down in the yard. Far away, at Khrymin Sons', someone was playing that expensive-sounding accordion.

Praskovya and Lipa began to doze off.

The moon was already bright when they were woken by footsteps. By the entrance to the shed stood Aksinya carrying her bedding.

"Perhaps it's cooler out here," she said, coming in and lying down almost on the threshold, all bathed in moonlight.

Unable to sleep, she breathed heavily, tossing and turning about in the heat and throwing almost all the clothes off her. What a fine, proud beast she looked in the magical moonlight! A little later more steps were heard, and the old man showed up in the doorway, entirely white.

"You in here, Aksinya?" he called.

"Yes," she responded angrily.

"Remember me telling you to throw them coins down the well just now? Did you do it?"

"Throw good money down a well—no fear! I gave it to them reapers."

"God, oh God!" exclaimed the old man, horror-struck. "You *are* a wild woman, God you are!"

With a gesture of annoyance he went muttering on his way. Not long afterwards Aksinya sat up with a deep, exasperated sigh, got to her feet and went out with an armful of bedding.

"Oh, Mother dear, why did you make me marry into this house?" Lipa asked.

"Folks must get wed, child. It ain't us decides these things."

Grief and despair seemed about to overwhelm them. But they could sense someone looking down on them from heaven's height, from that starry dark-blue vault: someone who saw all that went on in Ukleyevo, and kept watch. However great the evil, the night was still calm and splendid. God's truth—no less calm, no less splendid—still stood, and would remain, in his creation. All things on earth were only waiting to mingle with that truth, as the moonlight mingles with the night.

Comforted, they fell asleep in each other's arms.

VI

News of Anisim's arrest for coining and uttering counterfeit money had arrived long ago. Months—more than half a year—went by, the long winter ended, spring came on, and Anisim's imprisonment became an accepted fact in his house and village. Anyone passing the house or shop at night would remember that he was in jail. The tolling of the bells in the parish church was also a reminder, somehow, that he was in prison awaiting trial.

A shadow seemed to lie over the premises. The house looked dirtier, the roof was rusty, the heavy, iron-bound, green-painted shop door had shrivelled until it was "proper mortified," according to the deaf man. Old Tsybukin seemed a bit dingy himself. He had long stopped trimming his hair and beard, he looked shaggy, he was no longer leaping jauntily aboard that four-wheeler, nor did he shout at beggars that God would "pervide." His powers were waning, that was abundantly clear. Folk feared him less, now, and the local police sergeant sent in a report on the shop—even though he was still getting his usual cut. Three times the old man was summoned to town to stand trial for illicit vodka-dealing, but the case was repeatedly adjourned because of the witnesses' non-appearance. He was worn to a shadow.

He was for ever visiting his son, hiring lawyers, making submissions, presenting churches with banners. On the chief warder of Anisim's prison he bestowed a silver glass-holder with an enamelled inscription—MODERATION IN ALL THINGS—and a long spoon.

"There's no one, no one to put in a proper word for us," clucked Barbara. "Gracious me, you should get one of the nobs to write to the powers that be. They might at least give him bail—why torment the lad?"

She too was grieved, but she had put on weight, her complexion was whiter, and she still lit the icon-lamps, still kept the house clean, still regaled her guests with jam and apple-cheese.

The deaf man and Aksinya served in the shop. That new business—the Butyokino brickyard—had been started up, and Aksinya went over almost daily in the four-wheeler. She always drove herself, and when she met anyone she knew she would stretch up her neck like a snake in the young rye, smiling her naïve, enigmatic smile.

Lipa was always playing with her baby, born just before Lent. He was a tiny, emaciated, pathetic little thing. How strange that he could cry and see, that he rated as a human being and was even called Nikifor! As he lay in his cradle Lipa would go towards the door, bow and wish "a very good day to you, Master Nikifor Tsybukin!" Then she would rush headlong to him and kiss him, before going back to the door, bowing and again wishing a very good day to "Master Nikifor Tsybukin." He would kick up his little red legs—crying and chuckling at the same time, like Yelizarov the carpenter.

A date had been fixed for the trial at last, and the old man left five days early. Then they heard that some peasants from the village had been called as witnesses. Their old labourer went too, having also had a summons.

The trial was on a Thursday. But Sunday passed and the old man still wasn't back, there was still no news. Late on the Tuesday afternoon Barbara sat by an open window listening for his return. Lipa was playing with her baby in the next room.

"You're going to be a big, big man," she gleefully exclaimed, throwing him up in her arms. "You'll be a peasant and we'll go and work in the fields together, that we shall!"

"Well, really!" Barbara was offended. " 'Work in the fields!' What do you mean, you silly girl? We'll make a merchant of him."

Lipa started singing softly, but forgot herself a little later and repeated that he would grow up to be a big, big man and a peasant, and that they would go and work in the fields together.

"Oh, really! You're at it again!"

Carrying Nikifor in her arms, Lipa paused in the doorway.

"Why do I love him so much, Mother?" she asked. "Why do I feel so sorry for him?" she went on in a quavering voice, her eyes shining with tears. "Who is he? What's he really like? He's light as a feather or a crumb, but I love him—I love him as a real person. He can't do anything, see, he can't speak, but I always know what he wants by the look in his dear little eyes."

Barbara pricked up her ears, and a distant sound was heard: the evening train coming into the station. Might the old man be on it? She no longer heard what Lipa was saying, she couldn't take it in, she was not conscious of the passage of time, she just shook all over: not from fear, from overwhelming curiosity. She saw a cartful of peasants clatter swiftly by: the witnesses on their way home from the station. As the cart sped past the shop their old labourer jumped off it and came into the yard. Folk were heard greeting him out there, asking questions.

"Deprived of rights and property," he said loudly. "And six years' hard labour in Siberia."

Aksinya was heard coming out of the shop by the back door. She had been serving paraffin, she had a bottle in one hand and a can in the other, and there were silver coins in her mouth.

"Where's Father?" she mumbled.

"At the station," answered the labourer. "Says he'll come on later when it's dark."

When the news of Anisim's hard-labour sentence spread through the household, the cook suddenly started keening out in the kitchen— supposing this to be what propriety dictated.

"Why, oh why, have you forsaken us, Anisim, son of Gregory, light of our lives——"

The dogs, disturbed, started barking. Barbara ran to the window.

"Stop it, Stepanida, do!" she shouted to the cook in an anguished paroxysm, straining her voice to the limit. "For Christ's sake stop torment-ing us!"

They forgot to put on the samovar, they couldn't keep their minds on anything any more. Lipa alone had no idea what it was all about, but went on nursing her baby.

When the old man arrived from the station they asked him no ques-tions. He greeted them, then paced the house in silence. He ate no supper.

"There ain't no one to put in a word for us," clucked Barbara when they were alone together. "I told you to see some of the nobs, but you wouldn't listen. We should make an application——"

"I *have* been putting in a word for us!" said the old man with an impatient gesture. "When Anisim was sentenced I went to the gent as was defending him. 'There's nothing to be done now,' says he. 'It's too late.' Anisim himself says it's too late. Still, I did speak to one lawyer when I came out of court, gave him something in advance. I'll wait another week and then go back again. It's all God's will."

Again the old man paced about the house in silence, then returned to Barbara.

"I must be unwell," said he. "In my head there's an–er, a sort of a fog. I can't think straight."

He closed the door so that Lipa should not hear.

"It's money that's troubling me," he went on quietly. "Remember Anisim bringing me some new rouble and half-rouble coins? Before his wedding it was, the week after Easter. I hid one packet of 'em, but I got the others all mixed up with me own. Now, me Uncle Dmitry, God rest his soul . . . used to fetch merchandise from Moscow and the Crimea in his time. He had a wife, did Uncle. And while he was a-fetching of his goods, this wife of his would be having fun with other men. Six children she bore. How dear old Uncle used to laugh when he'd had a drop to drink! 'I can't make out them kids,' says he. 'Which of 'em is true coin and which is the counterfeit?' A bit of a light-weight was Uncle. Now it's the same with me: I can't make out which of me money's true coin and which is the counterfeit. It all seems counterfeit."

"Oh, really, get away with you!"

"I buy a ticket at the station in town, I pay me three roubles—and then I feel they must be bad ones. It don't half scare me. Unwell, I must be."

"None of us will last for ever, goodness me, it stands to reason," declared Barbara with a shake of her head. "That's what you should be thinking of, Gregory. Something might happen to you—you never know, you're not young any more. You watch they don't harm your grandson when you're dead and gone—oh, they'll do that child an injury, I fear, that they will. He ain't got no father, properly speaking, and his mother's young and silly. You might put the little lad down for something, Gregory, if only some land: that Butyokino, say. You think about it," Barbara pressed him. "He's a pretty little lad, it's such a shame. You go and write the paper tomorrow. No sense in waiting."

"Now, I'd quite forgotten my little grandson," said Tsybukin. "I must say hallo to him. The boy's all right, you tell me? Well well, so may he grow up, God willing!"

He opened the door and beckoned Lipa, who came up with the baby in her arms.

"Lipa dear, you ask for anything you need," said he. "And you must eat whatever you like—we don't grudge you nothing so long as you keep well!" He made the sign of the cross over the child. "And you look after my little grandson. My son's gone, so there's only my grandson left."

Tears coursed down his cheeks. He sobbed and moved away. Soon afterwards he went to bed and slept soundly after seven sleepless nights.

VII

The old man had made a short visit to town. Someone told Aksinya that he had gone to a lawyer's to make a will—and that he was leaving Butyokino, that same Butyokino where she was firing bricks, to his grandson Nikifor. She learnt this one morning when the old man and Barbara were sitting under the birch-tree drinking tea. She locked the shop doors, front and back, collected all the keys, and flung them at the old man's feet.

"I ain't a-going to work for you no longer!" she shouted, and suddenly burst out sobbing. "I ain't no daughter of yours, it seems, I'm your servant. Everyone's laughing at me: 'See what a good maid them Tsybukins have found!' I never asked you for no job. I ain't no beggar— I ain't common, like, I do have a father and mother."

Not wiping her tears, she glared at the old man—eyes swimming, vicious, squinting with rage. Her face and neck were red with strain.

"I ain't going to be your servant no longer," she went on, yelling for all she was worth. "Worn to a shred, I am! Oh yes, when it comes to work, minding the shop day in day out, and sneaking out to fetch the vodka of a night—then *I* can do it! But when there's land going begging you give it to that jail-bird's woman and her brat! She's the mistress, she's the fine lady round here, and I'm her drudge. Give her the lot, the convict's woman! May it choke her! I'm going home. And you can find yourself some other ninny, you rotten swine!"

Never in his life had the old man used bad language or punished children. That any member of his family could be rude to him, or treat him disrespectfully . . . the very idea was inconceivable. Absolutely terrified, he rushed into the house and hid behind a cupboard, while Barbara was so flabbergasted that she couldn't get up from her chair, but just waved both arms about as if trying to ward off a bee.

"Dear, oh dear, what can this be?" she muttered in horror. "Why does she shout like this? Goodness gracious me! Folks may hear. Not so loud, oh dear, less noise, please!"

"They've given Butyokino to the jail-bird's moll!" Aksinya shouted. "Well, you can give her the lot now, I don't want nothing from you! You can go to hell! A lot of gangsters, you are. I've seen enough, I don't care. Rich and poor, old and young . . . they've robbed all who came their way, the crooks! Who sold vodka without a licence? And what of them forgeries? They stuff their coffers with false coin, and now they don't need me no more!"

By now a crowd had gathered at the open gates, and folk were staring into the yard.

"Let 'em stare!" shouted Aksinya. "I'll disgrace you yet, I'll make you burn with shame, you'll crawl to me, you will!

"Hey, Stephen," she called the deaf man. "Come on—we're going home this instant: home to me father and me mother. I ain't living with no jail-birds! You get your things together."

Washing was hanging on the clothes lines in the yard. Snatching down her skirts and blouses, she threw them, still damp, into the deaf man's arms. Then she charged round the washing in the yard in a towering fury, tearing off everything—other people's clothes too—hurling it to the ground and trampling on it.

"Gracious, can't someone stop her?" groaned Barbara. "What on earth is she at? Let her have Butyokino—give it her, for Christ's sake!"

"Well, well, well!" said people by the gate. "What a woman! Gone berserk she has, and no mistake!"

Aksinya ran into the kitchen where the washing was being done. Lipa was working on her own, the cook having gone down to the stream to do some rinsing.

The tub and the copper near the stove gave off steam, misting and darkening the stuffy kitchen. On the floor was a heap of clothes still unwashed, and Nikifor had been put near it on a bench so that he wouldn't hurt himself if he fell. He was kicking up his little red legs. When Aksinya came in Lipa had just taken a shift of hers out of the pile, put it in the tub, and was reaching for the large can of boiling water on the table.

"You give that here!" said Aksinya, glaring her hatred, and snatched the shift from the tub. "You take your dirty hands off my underclothes! You're a jail-bird's woman, that's what you are, and you should know your place."

Lipa looked at her, utterly taken aback, not understanding. But she suddenly caught the look which Aksinya gave the baby . . . and then she *did* understand and turned pale as death.

"You stole my land, now take that!"

Thus speaking, Aksinya seized the can and splashed the boiling water on Nikifor.

There followed a yell like none ever heard in Ukleyevo—that a small, weak creature like Lipa could make such a noise was incredible. A sudden silence fell on the premises. Aksinya went wordlessly into the house with her usual naïve smile.

The deaf man was still out in the yard holding an armful of washing. Then he started hanging it up again—silently, without haste. Not until the cook came back from the stream did anyone dare go in the kitchen and see what was there.

VIII

Nikifor was taken to the local hospital, but was dead by evening. Not waiting to be fetched, Lipa wrapped the body in a little blanket and started to carry him home.

The hospital—newly built, with large windows—stood high on a hill and shone in the setting sun, seeming to be on fire inside. At the foot of the hill was a small village. Lipa walked down the road and sat by a little pond before reaching the village. A woman led a horse to the pond, but it would not drink.

"What more do you want?" asked the woman softly, quite bewildered. "Ain't that good enough for you?"

A red-shirted boy sat at the water's edge washing his father's boots. Neither in the village nor on the hill was another soul to be seen.

"Won't drink," said Lipa, looking at the horse.

The woman and the boy with the boots left, and there was no one to be seen at all. The sun went to his rest under a coverlet of purple and gold brocade, while long red and mauve clouds watched over his sleep, straddling the sky. From some unknown far-away spot came the doleful, muffled boom of a bittern—it sounded like a cow shut in a shed. Each spring the cry of this mysterious bird was heard, but no one knew what it was or where it lived. Up the hill near the hospital, in the bushes right here by the pond, beyond the village, in the fields all round, nightingales were trilling. A cuckoo was counting someone's age, but kept losing count and going back to the beginning. In the pond frogs bandied enraged croaks, straining their lungs, and you could even hear what they said: "Hark at *her*! Hark at *her*!" What a racket! All these creatures seemed to be crying and singing with the express aim of making sleep impossible on this spring evening, and of ensuring that all—even those angry frogs— might relish and savour each passing minute. We do only live once, after all.

A silver crescent moon shone in the sky, and there were many stars. Lipa could not remember how long she had been sitting by the pond, but when she got up to go everyone in the little village was asleep, and there was not a light anywhere. It must be eight miles to her home, but she was worn out and had no idea of the way. The moon shone—now in front, now on the right—while that cuckoo, hoarse by now, still teased her with its mocking laughter and a "Yoo-hoo—you fool—you'll lose— your route!"

Lipa walked quickly, and the kerchief had fallen from her head.

She looked at the sky and wondered: where might her little boy's soul now be—following her, or floating up there with the stars, unmindful of his mother? How lonely it was in the open country at night amid all the singing when you couldn't sing yourself, amid those non-stop cries of joy when you couldn't rejoice yourself . . . with the moon—also solitary—looking down from the sky and not caring whether it was spring or winter, whether people were alive or dead.

It is hard to have no one near you when your heart is broken. If only her mother Praskovya had been there! Or Lofty, or the cook, or one of the peasants.

The bittern gave a slow, protracted boom.

Then, suddenly, a man's voice was distinctly heard. "Put them horses in, Vavila."

Ahead of her a bonfire was burning on the roadside. The flames had died down, and there was only a glow of red embers. She heard horses munching. Two carts loomed up in the darkness—one containing a barrel, and another, lower one, with sacks—and two men. One was taking a horse to put it in the shafts, the other stood stock-still near the fire with his hands behind his back. A dog growled near the cart.

The man leading the horse stopped. "Seems to be someone on the road."

"Sharik, quiet!" the other shouted to the dog in what sounded like an old man's voice.

Lipa stood still and said, "God be with you."

The old man came up to her, paused briefly, and wished her good evening.

"Your dog won't bite, will he, Grandpa?"

"It's all right, come on—he won't hurt you."

"I've been to hospital," said Lipa after a short silence, "My little son died there. Now I'm taking him home."

The old man must have disliked hearing this because he stepped back. "Never mind, dear, it's God's will," he said rapidly.

He turned to his companion. "Don't waste time, lad—get a move on."

"Your yoke ain't here—can't see it," said the lad.

"You're a proper so-and-so, Vavila."

Picking up an ember, the old man blew on it, but lit up only his eyes and nose. Then, when the yoke had been found, he took the light over to Lipa and gazed at her. His look expressed sympathy and tenderness.

"You're a mother," he sighed, shaking his head. "Every mother loves her child."

Vavila threw something on the fire, trod it down—and it suddenly grew very dark. The scene disappeared, and they were left with the same old fields, the starlit sky and the racket of the birds preventing each other from sleeping. A corncrake's cry came: from the very spot, seemingly, where the fire had been.

A minute later, though, carts, old man and tall Vavila were seen again. The carts creaked as they came out on to the road.

"Are you holy men?" Lipa asked the old fellow.

"No. We're from Firsanovo."

"When you looked at me just now my heart melted. And the lad's so quiet—so I thought these must be holy men."

"Have you far to go?"

"Ukleyevo."

"Get in, then, we'll take you to Kuzmyonki. You go straight on there, we turn left."

Vavila got into the cart with the barrel, the old man and Lipa into the other. They set off at a walk, Vavila in front.

"My little boy was in agony all day," said Lipa. "He looks at me with them little eyes and says nothing. He wants to tell me, but he can't. Lord God above us! Holy Mother! I keep falling on the floor, I'm so grieved. I stand near his bed and just can't keep me feet. Tell me, Grandpa, why should a little baby suffer so before he dies? When a grown person is in pain, man or woman, their sins are forgiven, but why, oh why should it happen to a baby which ain't never sinned at all?"

"Who knows?" the old man answered.

They drove for half an hour in silence.

"You can't know the rights and wrongs of everything," the old man said. "Birds are made with two wings, not four. And for why? Because two's enough to fly with. Man's the same—he ain't made to know every-thing—only the half or the quarter. What he needs to live . . . that's what he knows."

"I'd rather walk, now, Grandpa. Me heart's trembling, like."

"Never mind, you sit tight."

The old man yawned and made the sign of the cross over his mouth.

"Never mind," he repeated. "Your grief ain't so bad. Life is long. There's good and bad, there's all kind of things to come.

"Great is Mother Russia," said he, looking about him. "I've been all over Russia, my dear—I've seen it all, I have, believe you me. There's good to come, and there's bad too. I been on village business to Siberia, I been on the Amur, in the Altay. I settled in Siberia—farmed land there—but then I got homesick for Mother Russia and I came back to me native village. We came back home on foot. We're on a ferry once, as I recall, and I'm thin as a rake. All tattered, barefoot and frozen, I am, and I'm sucking a crust, when a gentleman as was going through on the same ferry—if he's passed on since, may he rest in peace—looks at me in pity and his tears start flowing. 'Ah me!' says he. 'Your bread is black—and so's your prospects.' And when I get back home I've nothing to bless meself with, as they say. I did have a wife once, but I left her behind in Siberia—she was buried there. So I worked as a farm-hand. And then what? I'll tell you. There was bad times and good times both, my dear. And now I don't want to die, see—I'd like to live another twenty year. So there must have been more good than bad.

"Great is Mother Russia!" he said, again looking around and glancing back.

"Grandpa, when someone dies . . . how long does his soul wander the earth? How many days?"

"Who can tell? Let's ask Vavila—he's been to school. They teach them everything nowadays.

"Vavila!" called the old man.

"What?"

"When someone dies, Vavila, how many days does his soul walk the earth?"

Vavila stopped the horse before answering. "Nine days, I reckon. When me Uncle Cyril died, his soul lived on in our hut for thirteen days."

"How do you know?"

"There were a banging in the stove for thirteen days."

"Oh well. Drive on," said the old man, obviously not believing a word.

Near Kuzmyonki the carts turned on to the metalled road and Lipa walked straight on. It was growing light. As she descended into the canyon the huts and church of Ukleyevo were hidden in mist. It was cold, and she still seemed to hear that same cuckoo calling.

Lipa reached home before they had driven the cattle out. Everyone was asleep. She sat on the steps and waited. First to appear was the old man, who took in what had happened at a glance but could not utter a word for a long time: only smacked his lips.

"Ah, Lipa," said he. "You didn't save him then, my little grandson."

They woke Barbara. She threw up her arms, burst out sobbing, and at once started laying out the baby.

"Such a pretty little boy he was," said she. "Goodness me, she couldn't even keep the one baby she had—silly little thing!"

They held a requiem in the morning and again in the evening, and buried him next day. At the wake the guests and clergy stuffed themselves—you'd have thought they were starving, they were so greedy! Lipa helped to serve at table.

"Grieve not for the babe, for of such," said the priest picking up a fork with a pickled mushroom on it, "is the Kingdom of Heaven."

Only when they had all left did it really come home to Lipa that Nikifor was—and would be—no more, and she burst out sobbing. But she didn't know what room to go and sob in, for she felt out of place in this house after the child's death—she counted for nothing here, she felt, she was only in the way. And others felt so too.

"Hey, what's all this hullabaloo?" shouted Aksinya, suddenly appearing in the doorway. She was wearing an entirely new outfit for the funeral, and had powdered her face. "Shut up, you!"

Lipa tried to stop crying, but could not—only sobbed louder than ever.

"Do you hear me?" shouted Aksinya, stamping her foot in a mighty rage. "Who do you think *you* are? You clear out of here! Don't you never show your face again, you convict scum! Away with you!"

"There, there," fussed the old man. "Calm down, Aksinya dear. It's only natural for her to cry—her baby died."

" '*Only natural*'!" sneered Aksinya. "She can spend tonight here, but tomorrow she can clear out lock stock and barrel!

" '*Only natural*'!" she sneered again, and went off to the shop with a laugh.

Early next morning Lipa went to her mother's at Torguyevo.

IX

Today the shop roof and door have been painted and shine like new. The usual cheerful geraniums bloom in the windows, and what happened at the Tsybukins' three years ago is almost forgotten.

Old Gregory Tsybukin still rates as head of the house, but in fact everything has passed into Aksinya's hands. She does the buying and selling, and nothing goes without her say-so. The brickyard is doing well. Bricks are needed for the railway, so the price has gone up to twenty-four roubles a thousand. The local women and girls cart bricks to the station, and load the wagons—all for a quarter of a rouble a day.

Aksinya has gone into partnership with Khrymins, and their works is now called "Khrymin Sons & Co." They have opened a pub near the station, and it's here—not at the works—that the expensive-sounding accordion is played nowadays. The regulars include the postmaster—who has also started up some business of his own—and the stationmaster. Khrymin Sons have given deaf Stephen a gold watch, and he keeps taking it out of his pocket and holding it to his ear.

In the village Aksinya is said to have "come on mighty powerful." And it's true enough that when she drives to the works of a morning—naïvely smiling, handsome and happy—and when she is running that works, she indeed does convey a great air of power. At home, in the village, at the works . . . they're all scared of her. When she goes to the post-office the postmaster jumps to his feet with an "I humbly beg you to be seated, Mrs. Tsybukin, ma'am."

A certain dandified squire in his jerkin of fine cloth and patent-leather jack-boots—a middle-aged man—was once selling her a horse, and was so taken with her as they spoke that he let her have it on her own terms. He held her hand for some time, looking into her merry, artful, naïve eyes.

"For a woman like you, madam, there's no pleasure I wouldn't provide," said he. "Only tell me when we can meet without interruption."

"Why, whenever you like."

Ever since that the middle-aged dandy has driven to the shop almost daily for his glass of beer. The beer is atrocious—bitter as wormwood—but the squire shakes his head and drinks it.

Old Tsybukin takes no more part in business. He keeps no cash on him, for he simply can't tell true coin from false. But he holds his peace, never mentioning this infirmity. He has become rather absent-minded and if they don't give him his meals he never asks for them. They are used to eating without him by now, and Barbara often remarks that her "old man went to bed without his supper again last night." She speaks as if it didn't matter because she takes it for granted.

For some reason he goes about in his fur coat, summer and winter alike—it is only on the very hottest days that he doesn't go out at all, but stays at home. After donning that coat, raising the collar and wrapping up well, he usually potters round the village and the road to the station. Or sits on the bench near the church gate from morn till eve. There he sits, not moving. Folk bow as they pass, but he makes no reply: he still dislikes peasants as much as ever. If anyone asks him a question he answers quite rationally and politely—but briefly.

Village gossip says that his son's wife has driven him out of house and home, that she won't feed him, that he lives on what people give him. Some are glad, others are sorry for him.

Barbara is even plumper and paler, and she still goes about doing good—unhampered by Aksinya. They make so much jam nowadays that there's no time to eat it all before the new season's berries are ripe. It candies, and Barbara almost weeps for not knowing what to do with it.

They are beginning to forget Anisim. A letter did once arrive from him—written in verse on a large sheet of paper resembling an official document, and in the same imposing handwriting as before. Obviously he and his friend Samorodov were doing time in the same place. Beneath the verses a single line had been added in an ugly, barely legible hand: "I'm always ill here, I'm miserable, for Christ's sake help me."

Late one fine autumn afternoon old Tsybukin was sitting by the church gate with his coat collar up and only his nose and cap peak showing. At the other end of the long bench sat the carpenter Yelizarov, and beside him the school caretaker Jacob: a toothless old fellow of about seventy. Lofty and the caretaker were talking.

"Children should give old folks their food and drink—honour thy father and thy mother," said Jacob testily. "But that young woman has thrown her husband's old dad out of his own house, like. Nothing to eat nor drink, the old fellow has—where's he to go now? Three days he ain't had no food."

Lofty was surprised. "Three days!"

"Aye, there he sits, never says a word. Proper weak, he is. Why keep quiet about it? They ought to take her to court—she wouldn't get off lightly!"

"Who got off lightly?" asked Lofty, not hearing.

"Eh?"

"The woman's all right. A hard worker, she is. In their line of business you can't manage without it—not without cutting corners, I mean."

"Out of his own home!" Jacob went on testily. "Let her build a house herself before she starts throwing folks out of it. What a woman, though! A proper plague, she is."

Tsybukin listened, but made no move.

"His own house or someone else's . . . what's the difference so long as it's warm and womenfolk don't quarrel?" laughed Lofty. "Very fond of my Nastasya, I was as a young fellow. She was a quiet little woman. 'You buy a house, Eli,' says she—kept on at me all the time, she did with this 'you buy a house, Eli' stuff. And when she was a-dying she was on about 'you buy yourself a good fast droshky, Eli, so you don't need to walk.' But all I ever buys her is gingerbread, that's all."

"That deaf husband of hers is a fool," went on Jacob, not hearing. "A proper dunce he is, a real old goose. Can the likes of him understand? Hit a goose on the head with a stick—it still won't understand."

Lofty stood up to go home to the works. Jacob got up too, and they set off together, still talking. When they had gone about fifty yards old Tsybukin also stood up and doddered after them, treading gingerly as if walking on ice.

Now the village was plunged in twilight. The sun sparkled only on the top part of the road snaking up the hillside from below. Old women were on their way back from the woods bringing the children and carrying baskets of pink and yellow-white mushrooms. From the station, where they had been loading wagons with bricks, came a group of women and girls, their noses and their cheeks under the eyes red with brick dust. They were singing. In front of all walked Lipa singing in a reedy voice— carolling away as she looked up at the sky and seeming to exult and rejoice that the day, thank God, was over and that she could rest. In the group was her mother Praskovya, the hired drudge, carrying a bundle in her hand and panting as usual.

"Good day, Eli, my dear," said Lipa, seeing Lofty.

"Good day, Lipa darling." Lofty was delighted. "Hey, you women and girls, be nice to the rich carpenter.

"My children, my dear children," he sobbed. "Oho, my darling little hatchets!"

Lofty and Jacob were heard talking to each other as they moved off. Then old Tsybukin came up with the crowd, and silence suddenly fell. Lipa and Praskovya had lagged behind a little.

"Good day, Mr. Tsybukin," said Lipa with a low bow as the old man drew level.

Her mother bowed too. The old man stopped, looked at them both wordlessly, lips shaking, eyes full of tears. Lipa got a piece of buckwheat pasty from her mother's bundle and gave it to him. He took it and started eating.

Now the sun had completely set—even from the top part of the road the fire had faded. It was growing dark and chilly. Lipa and Praskovya went on their way, crossing themselves for a long time afterwards.

Sara Jeannette Duncan

(1861–1922)

Sara Jeannette Duncan was born in Brantford, Ontario. In the 1880s, she became the first woman journalist employed regularly by the Toronto Globe (subsequently working also for The Montreal Star and The Washington Post, and contributing articles to numerous North American magazines). She travelled throughout the world, living for 25 years in India and ending her life in England. Of her 22 books, 2 are set in Canada, with the best known being the novel The Imperialist (1904). That novel traces the political fortunes of an idealistic young Canadian politician campaigning for the Imperialist cause—for closer ties between Canada and Britain and among the colonies of the British Empire—in a turn-of-the-century Ontario town based on Brantford. Duncan's skills as a recorder of ordinary experience made her one of North America's earliest practitioners of literary realism. Also one of Canada's premier essayists, she offered this reason for her country's lack of a literary culture towards the end of the nineteenth century:

> In our character as colonists we find the root of all our sins of omission in letters. . . . Our enforced political humility is the distinguishing characteristic of every phase of our national life. We are ignored, and we ignore ourselves. A nation's development is like a plant's, unattractive under ground. So long as Canada remains in political obscurity, content to thrive only at the roots, so long will the leaves and blossoms of art and literature be scanty and stunted products of our national energy. . . .
>
> A national literature cannot be looked for as an outcome of anything less than a complete national existence.

In her novels, stories, and essays, Sara Jeannette Duncan contributed much to the first flourishing of the Canadian culture she analyzed and wrote about so astutely.

A Mother in India

Chapter I

There were times when we had to go without puddings to pay John's uniform bills, and always I did the facings myself with a cloth-ball to save getting new ones. I would have polished his sword, too, if I had been allowed; I adored his sword. And once, I remember, we painted and varnished our own dogcart, and very smart it looked, to save fifty rupees. We had nothing but our pay—John had his company when we were married, but what is that?—and life was made up of small knowing economies, much more amusing in recollection than in practise. We were sodden poor, and that is a fact, poor and conscientious, which was worse. A big fat spider of a money-lender came one day into the veranda and tempted us—we lived in a hut, but it had a veranda—and John threatened to report him to the police. Poor when everybody else had enough to live in the open-handed Indian fashion, that was what made it so hard; we were alone in our sordid little ways. When the expectation of Cecily came to us we made out to be delighted, knowing that the whole station pitied us, and when Cecily came herself, with a swamping burst of expense, we kept up the pretense splendidly. She was peevish, poor little thing, and she threatened convulsions from the beginning, but we both knew that it was abnormal not to love her a great deal, more than life, immediately and increasingly; and we applied ourselves honestly to do it, with the thermometer at a hundred and two, and the nurse leaving at the end of a fortnight because she discovered that I had only six of everything for the table. To find out a husband's virtues, you must marry a poor man. The regiment was under-officered as usual, and John had to take parade at daylight quite three times a week; but he walked up and down the veranda with Cecily constantly till two in the morning, when a little coolness came. I usually lay awake the rest of the night in the fear that a scorpion would drop from the ceiling on her. Nevertheless, we were of excellent mind towards Cecily; we were in such terror, not so much of failing in our duty towards her as towards the ideal standard of mankind. We were very anxious indeed not to come short. To be found too small for one's place in nature would have been odious. We would talk about her for an hour at a time, even when John's charger was threatening glanders and I could see his mind perpetually wandering to the stable. I would say to John that she had brought a new element into our lives— she had indeed!—and John would reply, "I know what you mean," and go on to prophesy that she would "bind us together." We didn't need binding together; we were more to each other, there in the desolation of that arid frontier outpost, than most husbands and wives; but it seemed a proper and hopeful thing to believe, so we believed it. Of course, the real experience would have come, we weren't monsters; but fate curtailed the opportunity. She was just five weeks old when the doctor told us that we must either pack her home immediately or lose her, and the very next day John went down with enteric. So Cecily was sent to England with a sergeant's wife who had lost her twins, and I settled down under the direction of a native doctor, to fight for my husband's life, without ice or proper food, or sickroom comforts of any sort. Ah! Fort Samila, with the sun glaring up from the sand!—however, it is a long time ago now. I trusted the baby willingly to Mrs Berry and to Providence, and did not fret; my capacity for worry, I suppose, was completely absorbed. Mrs Berry's letter, describing the child's improvement on the voyage and safe arrival came, I remember, the day on which John was allowed his first solid mouthful; it had been a long siege. "Poor little wretch!" he said when I read it aloud; and after that Cecily became an episode.

She had gone to my husband's people; it was the best arrangement. We were lucky that it was possible; so many children had to be sent to strangers and hirelings. Since an unfortunate infant must be brought into the world and set adrift, the haven of its grandmother and its Aunt Emma and its Aunt Alice certainly seemed providential. I had absolutely no cause for anxiety, as I often told people, wondering that I did not feel a little all the same. Nothing, I knew, could exceed the conscientious devotion of all three Farnham ladies to the child. She would appear upon their somewhat barren horizon as a new and interesting duty, and the small additional income she also represented would be almost nominal compensation for the care she would receive. They were excellent persons of the kind that talk about matins and vespers, and attend both. They helped little charities and gave little teas, and wrote little notes, and made deprecating allowance for the eccentricities of their titled or moneyed acquaintances. They were the subdued, smiling, unimaginatively dressed women on a small definite income that you meet at every rectory garden-party in the country, a little snobbish, a little priggish, wholly conventional, but apart from these weaknesses, sound and simple and dignified, managing their two small servants with a display of the most exact traditions, and keeping a somewhat vague and belated but constant eye upon the doings of their country as chronicled in a bi-weekly paper. They were all immensely interested in royalty, and would read paragraphs aloud to each other about how the Princess Beatrice or the Princess Maud had opened a fancy bazaar, looking remarkably well in plain grey poplin trimmed with Irish lace—an industry which, as is well known, the Royal Family has set its heart on rehabilitating. Upon which Mrs Farnham's comment invariably would be, "How thoughtful of them, dear!" and Alice would usually say, "Well, if I were a princess, I should like something nicer than plain grey poplin." Alice, being the youngest, was not always expected to think before she spoke. Alice painted in water-colours, but Emma was supposed to have the most common sense.

They took turns in writing to us with the greatest regularity about Cecily; only once, I think, did they miss the weekly mail, and that was when she threatened diphtheria and they thought we had better be kept in ignorance. The kind and affectionate terms of these letters never altered except with the facts they described—teething, creeping, measles, cheeks growing round and rosy, all were conveyed in the same smooth, pat, and proper phrases, so absolutely empty of any glimpse of the child's personality that after the first few months it was like reading about a somewhat uninteresting infant in a book. I was sure Cecily was not uninteresting, but her chroniclers were. We used to wade through the long, thin sheets and saw how much more satisfactory it would be when Cecily could write to us herself. Meanwhile we noted her weekly progress with much the feeling one would have about a far-away little bit of property that was giving no trouble and coming on exceedingly well. We would take possession of Cecily at our convenience; till then, it was gratifying to hear of our unearned increment in dear little dimples and sweet little curls.

She was nearly four when I saw her again. We were home on three months' leave; John had just got his first brevet for doing something which he does not allow me to talk about in the Black Mountain country; and we were fearfully pleased with ourselves. I remember that excitement lasted well up to Port Said. As far as the Canal, Cecily was only one of the pleasures and interests we were going home to: John's majority was the thing that really gave savour to life. But the first faint line of Europe brought my child to my horizon; and all the rest of the way she kept her place, holding out her little arms to me, beckoning me on. Her four motherless years brought compunction to my heart and tears to my eyes; she should have all the compensation that could be. I suddenly realized how ready I was—how ready!—to have her back. I rebelled fiercely against John's decision that we must not take her with us on our return to the frontier; privately, I resolved to dispute it, and, if necessary, I saw myself abducting the child—my own child. My days and nights as the ship crept on were full of a long ache to possess her; the defrauded tenderness of the last four years rose up in me and sometimes caught at my throat. I could think and talk and dream of nothing else. John indulged me as much as was reasonable, and only once betrayed by a yawn that the subject was not for him endlessly absorbing. Then I cried and he apologized. "You know," he said, "it isn't exactly the same thing. I'm not her mother." At which I dried my tears and expanded, proud and pacified. I was her mother!

Then the rainy little station and Alice, all-embracing in a damp waterproof, and the drive in the fly, and John's mother at the gate and a necessary pause while I kissed John's mother. Dear thing, she wanted to hold our hands and look into our faces and tell us how little we had changed for all our hardships; and on the way to the house she actually stopped to point out some alterations in the flower-borders. At last the drawing-room door and the smiling housemaid turning the handle and the unforgettable picture of a little girl, a little girl unlike anything we had imagined, starting bravely to trot across the room with the little speech that had been taught her. Half-way she came; I suppose our regards were too fixed, too absorbed, for there she stopped with a wail of terror at the strange faces, and ran straight back to the outstretched arms of her Aunt Emma. The most natural thing in the world, no doubt. I walked over to a chair opposite with my hand-bag and umbrella and sat down—a spectator, aloof and silent. Aunt Emma fondled and quieted the child, apologizing for her to me, coaxing her to look up, but the little figure still shook with sobs, hiding its face in the bosom that it knew. I smiled politely, like any other stranger, at Emma's deprecations, and sat impassive, looking at my alleged baby breaking her heart at the sight of her mother. It is not amusing even now to remember the anger that I felt. I did not touch her or speak to her; I simply sat observing my alien possession, in the frock I had not made and the sash I had not chosen, being coaxed and kissed and protected and petted by its Aunt Emma. Presently I asked to be taken to my room, and there I locked myself in for two atrocious hours. Just once my heart beat high, when a tiny knock came and a timid, docile little voice said that tea was ready. But I heard the rustle of a skirt, and guessed the directing angel in Aunt Emma, and responded, "Thank you, dear, run away and say that I am coming," with a pleasant visitor's inflection which I was able to sustain for the rest of the afternoon.

"She goes to bed at seven," said Emma.

"Oh, does she?" said I. "A very good hour, I should think."

"She sleeps in my room," said Mrs Farnham.

"We give her mutton broth very often, but seldom stock soup," said Aunt Emma. "Mamma thinks it is too stimulating."

"Indeed?" said I, to all of it.

They took me up to see her in her crib, and pointed out, as she lay asleep, that though she had "a general look" of me, her features were distinctively Farnham.

"Won't you kiss her?" asked Alice. "You haven't kissed her yet, and she is used to so much affection."

"I don't think I could take such an advantage of her," I said.

They looked at each other, and Mrs Farnham said that I was plainly worn out. I mustn't sit up to prayers.

If I had been given anything like reasonable time I might have made a fight for it, but four weeks—it took a month each way in those days—was too absurdly little; I could do nothing. But I would not stay at mamma's. It was more than I would ask of myself, that daily disappointment under the mask of gratified discovery, for long.

I spent an approving, unnatural week, in my farcical character, bridling my resentment and hiding my mortification with pretty phrases; and then I went up to town and drowned my sorrows in the summer sales. I took John with me. I may have been Cecily's mother in theory, but I was John's wife in fact.

We went back to the frontier, and the regiment saw a lot of service. That meant medals and fun for my husband, but economy and anxiety for me, though I managed to be allowed as close to the firing line as any woman.

Once the Colonel's wife and I, sitting in Fort Samila, actually heard the rifles of a punitive expedition cracking on the other side of the river—that was a bad moment. My man came in after fifteen hours' fighting, and went sound asleep, sitting before his food with his knife and fork in his hands. But service makes heavy demands besides those on your wife's nerves. We had saved two thousand rupees, I remember, against another run home, and it all went like powder, in the Mirzai expedition; and the run home diminished to a month in a boarding-house in the hills.

Meanwhile, however, we had begun to correspond with our daughter, in large round words of one syllable, behind which, of course, was plain the patient guiding hand of Aunt Emma. One could hear Aunt Emma suggesting what would be nice to say, trying to instil a little pale affection for the far-off papa and mamma. There was so little Cecily and so much Emma—of course, it could not be otherwise—that I used to take, I fear, but a perfunctory joy in these letters. When we went home again I stipulated absolutely that she was to write to us without any sort of supervision—the child was ten.

"But the spelling!" cried Aunt Emma, with lifted eyebrows.

"Her letters aren't exercises," I was obliged to retort; "she will do the best she can."

We found her a docile little girl, with nice manners, a thoroughly unobjectionable child. I saw quite clearly that I could not have brought her up so well; indeed, there were moments when I fancied that Cecily, contrasting me with her aunts, wondered a little what my bringing up could have been like. With this reserve of criticism on Cecily's part, however, we got on very tolerably, largely because I found it impossible to assume any responsibility towards her, and in moments of doubt or discipline referred her to her aunts. We spent a pleasant summer with a little girl in the house whose interest in us was amusing, and whose outings it was gratifying to arrange; but when we went back, I had no desire to take her with us. I thought her very much better where she was.

Then came the period which is filled, in a subordinate degree, with Cecily's letters. I do not wish to claim more than I ought; they were not my only or even my principal interest in life. It was a long period; it lasted till she was twenty-one. John had had promotion in the meantime, and there was rather more money, but he had earned his second brevet with a bullet through one lung, and the doctors ordered our leave to be spent in South Africa. We had photographs, we knew she had grown tall and athletic and comely, and the letters were always very creditable. I had the unusual and qualified privilege of watching my daughter's development from ten to twenty-one, at a distance of four thousand miles, by means of the written word. I wrote myself as provocatively as possible; I sought for every string, but the vibration that came back across the seas to me was always other than the one I looked for, and sometimes there was none. Nevertheless, Mrs Farnham wrote me that Cecily very much valued my communications. Once when I had described an unusual excursion in a native state, I learned that she had read my letter aloud to the sewing circle. After that I abandoned description, and confined myself to such intimate personal details as no sewing circle could find amusing. The child's own letters were simply a mirror of the ideas of the Farnham ladies; that must have been so, it was not altogether my jaundiced eye. Alice and Emma and grandmamma paraded the pages in turn. I very early gave up hope of discoveries in my daughter, though as much of the original as I could detect was satisfactorily simple and sturdy. I found little things to criticize, of course, tendencies to correct; and by return post I criticized and corrected, but the distance and the deliberation seemed to touch my maxims with a kind of arid frivolity, and sometimes I tore them up. One quick, warm-blooded scolding would have been worth a sheaf of them. My studied little phrases could only inoculate her with a dislike for me without protecting her from anything under the sun.

However, I found she didn't dislike me, when John and I went home at last to bring her out. She received me with just a hint of kindness, perhaps, but on the whole very well.

Chapter II

John was recalled, of course, before the end of our furlough, which knocked various things on the head; but that is the sort of thing one learned to take with philosophy in any lengthened term of Her Majesty's service. Besides, there is usually sugar for the pill; and in this case it was a Staff command bigger than anything we expected for at least five years to come. The excitement of it when it was explained to her gave Cecily a charming colour. She took a good deal of interest in the General, her papa; I think she had an idea that his distinction would alleviate the situation in India, however it might present itself. She accepted that prospective situation calmly; it had been placed before her all her life. There would always be a time when she should go and live with papa and mamma in India, and so long as she was of an age to receive the idea with rebel tears she was assured that papa and mamma would give her a pony. The pony was no longer added to the prospect; it was absorbed no doubt in the general list of attractions calculated to reconcile a young lady to a parental roof with which she had no practical acquaintance. At all events, when I feared the embarrassment and dismay of a pathetic parting with darling grandmamma and the aunties, and the sweet cat and the dear vicar and all the other objects of affection, I found an agreeable unexpected philosophy.

I may add that while I anticipated such broken-hearted farewells I was quite prepared to take them easily. Time, I imagined, had brought philosophy to me also, equally agreeable and equally unexpected.

It was a Bombay ship, full of returning Anglo-Indians. I looked up and down the long saloon tables with a sense of relief and of solace; I was again among my own people. They belonged to Bengal and to Burma, to Madras and to the Punjab, but they were all my people. I could pick out a score that I knew in fact, and there were none that in imagination I didn't know. The look of wider seas and skies, the casual experienced glance, the touch of irony and of tolerance, how well I knew it and how well I liked it! Dear Old England, sitting in our wake, seemed to hold by comparison a great many soft, unsophisticated people, immensely occupied about very particular trifles. How difficult it had been, all the summer, to be interested! These of my long acquaintance belonged to my country's Executive, acute, alert, with the marks of travail on them. Gladly I went in and out of the women's cabins and listened to the argot of the men; my own ruling, administering, soldiering little lot.

Cecily looked at them askance. To her the atmosphere was alien, and I perceived that gently and privately she registered objections. She cast a disapproving eye upon the wife of a Conservator of Forests, who scanned with interest a distant funnel and laid a small wager that it belonged to the Messageries Maritimes. She looked with a straightened lip at the crisply stepping women who walked the deck in short and rather shabby skirts with their hands in their jacket-pockets talking transfers and promotions; and having got up at six to make a water-colour sketch of the sunrise, she came to me in profound indignation to say that she had met a man in his pyjamas; no doubt, poor wretch, on his way to be shaved. I was unable to convince her that he was not expected to visit the barber in all his clothes.

At the end of the third day she told me that she wished these people wouldn't talk to her; she didn't like them. I had turned in the hour we left the Channel and had not left my berth since, so possibly I was not in the most amiable mood to receive a douche of cold water. "I must try to remember, dear," I said, "that you have been brought up altogether in the society of pussies and vicars and elderly ladies, and of course you miss them. But you must have a little patience. I shall be up tomorrow, if this beastly sea continues to go down; and then we will try to find somebody suitable to introduce to you."

"Thank you, mamma," said my daughter, without a ray of suspicion. Then she added consideringly, "Aunt Emma and Aunt Alice do seem quite elderly ladies beside you, and yet you are older than either of them, aren't you? I wonder how that is."

It was so innocent, so admirable, that I laughed at my own expense; while Cecily, doing her hair, considered me gravely. "I wish you would tell me why you laugh, mamma," quoth she; "you laugh so often."

We had not to wait after all for my good offices of the next morning. Cecily came down at ten o'clock that night quite happy and excited; she had been talking to a bishop, such a dear bishop. The bishop had been showing her his collection of photographs, and she had promised to play the harmonium for him at the eleven-o'clock service in the morning. "Bless me!" said I, "is it Sunday?" It seemed she had got on very well indeed with the bishop, who knew the married sister, at Tunbridge, of her very greatest friend. Cecily herself did not know the married sister, but that didn't matter—it was a link. The bishop was charming. "Well, my love," said I—I was teaching myself to use these forms of address for fear she would feel an unkind lack of them, but it was difficult—"I am glad that somebody from my part of the world has impressed you favourably at last. I wish we had more bishops."

"Oh, but my bishop doesn't belong to your part of the world," responded my daughter sleepily. "He is travelling for his health."

It was the most unexpected and delightful thing to be packed into one's chair next morning by Dacres Tottenham. As I emerged from the music saloon after breakfast—Cecily had stayed below to look over her hymns and consider with her bishop the possibility of an anthem—Dacres's face was the first I saw; it simply illuminated, for me, that portion of the deck. I noticed with pleasure the quick toss of the cigar overboard as he recognized and bore down upon me. We were immense friends; John liked him too. He was one of those people who make a tremendous difference; in all our three hundred passengers there could be no one like him, certainly no one whom I could be more glad to see. We plunged at once into immediate personal affairs, we would get at the heart of them later. He gave his vivid word to everything he had seen and done; we laughed and exclaimed and were silent in a concert of admirable understanding. We were still unravelling, still demanding and explaining when the ship's bell began to ring for church, and almost simultaneously

Cecily advanced towards us. She had a proper Sunday hat on, with flowers under the brim, and a church-going frock; she wore gloves and clasped a prayer-book. Most of the women who filed past to the summons of the bell were going down as they were, in cotton blouses and serge skirts, in tweed caps or anything, as to a kind of family prayers. I knew exactly how they would lean against the pillars of the saloon during the psalms. This young lady would be little less than a rebuke to them. I surveyed her approach; she positively walked as if it were Sunday.

"My dear," I said, "how *endimanchée* you look! The bishop will be very pleased with you. This gentleman is Mr Tottenham, who administers Her Majesty's pleasure in parts of India about Allahabad. My daughter, Dacres." She was certainly looking very fresh, and her calm grey eyes had the repose in them that has never known itself to be disturbed about anything. I wondered whether she bowed so distantly also because it was Sunday, and then I remembered that Dacres was a young man, and that the Farnham ladies had probably taught her that it was right to be very distant with young men.

"It is almost eleven, mamma."

"Yes, dear. I see you are going to church."

"Are you not coming, mamma?"

I was well wrapped up in an extremely comfortable corner. I had *La Duchesse Bleue* uncut in my lap, and an agreeable person to talk to. I fear that in any case I should not have been inclined to attend the service, but there was something in my daughter's intonation that made me distinctly hostile to the idea. I am putting things down as they were, extenuating nothing.

"I think not, dear."

"I've turned up two such nice seats."

"Stay, Miss Farnham, and keep us in countenance," said Dacres, with his charming smile. The smile displaced a look of discreet and amused observation. Dacres had an eye always for a situation, and this one was even newer to him than to me.

"No, no. She must run away and not bully her mamma," I said. "When she comes back we will see how much she remembers of the sermon;" and as the flat tinkle from the companion began to show signs of diminishing, Cecily, with one grieved glance, hastened down.

"You amazing lady!" said Dacres. "A daughter—and such a tall daughter! I somehow never—"

"You knew we had one?"

"There was theory of that kind, I remember, about ten years ago. Since then—excuse me—I don't think you've mentioned her."

"You talk as if she were a skeleton in the closet!"

"You *didn't* talk—as if she were."

"I think she was, in a way, poor child. But the resurrection day hasn't confounded me as I deserved. She's a very good girl."

"If you had asked me to pick out your daughter—"

"She would have been the last you would indicate! Quite so," I said. "She is like her father's people. I can't help that."

"I shouldn't think you would if you could," Dacres remarked absently; but the sea air, perhaps, enabled me to digest his thoughtlessness with a smile.

"No," I said, "I am just as well pleased. I think a resemblance to me would confuse me, often."

There was a trace of scrutiny in Dacres's glance. "Don't you find yourself in sympathy with her?" he asked.

"My dear boy, I have seen her just twice in twenty-one years! You see, I've always stuck to John."

"But between mother and daughter—I may be old-fashioned, but I had an idea that there was an instinct that might be depended on."

"I am depending on it," I said, and let my eyes follow the little blue waves that chased past the hand-rail. "We are making very good speed, aren't we? Thirty-five knots since last night at ten. Are you in the sweep?"

"I never bet on the way out—can't afford it. Am I old-fashioned?" he insisted.

"Probably. Men are very slow in changing their philosophy about women. I fancy their idea of the maternal relation is firmest fixed of all."

"We see it a beatitude!" he cried.

"I know," I said wearily, "and you never modify the view."

Dacres contemplated the portion of the deck that lay between us. His eyes were discreetly lowered, but I saw embarrassment and speculation and a hint of criticism in them.

"Tell me more about it," said he.

"Oh, for heaven's sake don't be sympathetic!" I exclaimed. "Lend me a little philosophy instead. There is nothing to tell. There she is and there I am, in the most intimate relation in the world, constituted when she is twenty-one and I am forty." Dacres started slightly at the ominous word; so little do men realize that the women they like can ever pass out of the constated years of attraction. "I find the young lady very tolerable, very creditable, very nice. I find the relation atrocious. There you have it. I would like to break the relation into pieces," I went on recklessly, "and throw it into the sea. Such things should be tempered to one. I should feel it much less if she occupied another cabin, and would consent to call me Elizabeth or Jane. It is not as if I had been her mother always. One grows fastidious at forty—new intimacies are only possible then on a basis of temperament—"

I paused; it seemed to me that I was making excuses, and I had not the least desire in the world to do that.

"How awfully rough on the girl!" said Dacres Tottenham.

"That consideration has also occurred to me," I said candidly, "though I have perhaps been even more struck by its converse."

"You had no earthly business to be her mother," said my friend, with irritation.

I shrugged my shoulders—what would you have done?—and opened *La Duchesse Bleue.*

Chapter III

Mrs Morgan, wife of a judge of the High Court of Bombay, and I sat amidships on the cool side in the Suez Canal. She was outlining "Soiled Linen" in chain-stitch on a green canvas bag; I was admiring the Egyptian sands. "How charming," said I, "is this solitary desert in the endless oasis we are compelled to cross!"

"Oasis in the desert, you mean," said Mrs Morgan; "I haven't noticed any, but I happened to look up this morning as I was putting on my stockings, and I saw through my port-hole the most lovely mirage."

I had been at school with Mrs Morgan more than twenty years agone, but she had come to the special enjoyment of the dignities of life while I still liked doing things. Mrs Morgan was the kind of person to make one realize how distressing a medium is middle age. Contemplating her precipitous lap, to which conventional attitudes were certainly more becoming, I crossed my own knees with energy, and once more resolved to be young until I was old.

"How perfectly delightful for you to be taking Cecily out!" said Mrs Morgan placidly.

"Isn't it?" I responded, watching the gliding sands.

"But she was born in sixty-nine—that makes her twenty-one. Quite time, I should say."

"Oh, we couldn't put it off any longer. I mean—her father has such a horror of early débuts. He simply would not hear of her coming before."

"Doesn't want her to marry in India, I dare say—the only one," purred Mrs Morgan.

"Oh, I don't know. It isn't such a bad place. I was brought out there to marry, and I married. I've found it very satisfactory."

"You always did say exactly what you thought, Helena," said Mrs Morgan excusingly.

"I haven't much patience with people who bring their daughters out to give them the chance they never would have in England, and then go about devoutly hoping they won't marry in India," I said. "I shall be very pleased if Cecily does as well as your girls have done."

"Mary in the Indian Civil and Jessie in the Imperial Service Troops," sighed Mrs Morgan complacently. "And both, my dear, within a year. It *was* a blow."

"Oh, it must have been!" I said civilly.

There was no use in bandying words with Emily Morgan.

"There is nothing in the world like the satisfaction and pleasure one takes in one's daughters," Mrs Morgan went on limpidly. "And one can be in such *close* sympathy with one's girls. I have never regretted having no sons."

"Dear me, yes. To watch oneself growing up again—call back the lovely April of one's prime, etcetera—to read every thought and anticipate every wish—there is no more golden privilege in life, dear Emily. Such a direct and natural avenue for affection, such a wide field for interest!"

I paused, lost in the volume of my admirable sentiments.

"How beautifully you talk, Helena! I wish I had the gift."

"It doesn't mean very much," I said truthfully.

"Oh, I think it's everything! And how companionable a girl is! I quite envy you, this season, having Cecily constantly with you and taking her about everywhere. Something quite new for you, isn't it?"

"Absolutely," said I; "I am looking forward to it immensely. But it is likely she will make her own friends, don't you think?" I added anxiously.

"Hardly the first season. My girls didn't. I was practically their only intimate for months. Don't be afraid; you won't be obliged to go shares in Cecily with anybody for a good long while," added Mrs Morgan kindly. "I know just how you feel about *that*."

The muddy water of the Ditch chafed up from under us against its banks with a smell that enabled me to hide the emotions Mrs Morgan evoked behind my handkerchief. The pale desert was pictorial with the drifting, deepening purple shadows of clouds, and in the midst a blue glimmer of the Bitter Lakes, with a white sail on them. A little frantic Arab boy ran alongside keeping pace with the ship. Except for the smell, it was like a dream, we moved so quietly; on, gently on and on between the ridgy clay banks and the rows of piles. Peace was on the ship; you could hear what the Fourth in his white ducks said to the quartermaster in his blue denims; you could count the strokes of the electric bell in the wheelhouse; peace was on the ship as she pushed on, an ever-venturing, double-funneled impertinence, through the sands of the ages. My eyes wandered along a plank-line in the deck till they were arrested by a petticoat I knew, when they returned of their own accord. I seemed to be always seeing that petticoat.

"I think," resumed Mrs Morgan, whose glance had wandered in the same direction, "that Cecily is a very fine type of our English girls. With those dark grey eyes, a *little* prominent possibly, and that good colour—it's rather high now perhaps, but she will lose quite enough of it in India—and those regular features, she would make a splendid Britannia. Do you know, I fancy she must have a great deal of character. Has she?"

"Any amount. And all of it good," I responded, with private dejection.

"No faults at all?" chaffed Mrs Morgan.

I shook my head. "Nothing," I said sadly, "that I can put my finger on. But I hope to discover a few later. The sun may bring them out."

"Like freckles. Well, you are a lucky woman. Mine had plenty, I assure you. Untidiness was no name for Jessie, and Mary—I'm *sorry* to say that Mary sometimes fibbed."

"How lovable of her! Cecily's neatness is a painful example to me, and I don't believe she would tell a fib to save my life."

"Tell me," said Mrs Morgan, as the lunch-bell rang and she gathered her occupation into her work-basket, "who is that talking to her?"

"Oh, an old friend," I replied easily; "Dacres Tottenham, a dear fellow, and most benevolent. He is trying on my behalf to reconcile her to the life she'll have to lead in India."

"She won't need much reconciling, if she's like most girls," observed Mrs Morgan, "but he seems to be trying very hard."

That was quite the way I took it—on my behalf—for several days. When people have understood you very adequately for ten years you do not expect them to boggle at any problem you may present at the end of the decade. I thought Dacres was moved by a fine sense of compassion. I thought that with his admirable perception he had put a finger on the little comedy of fruitfulness in my life that laughed so bitterly at the tragedy of the barren woman, and was attempting, by delicate manipulation, to make it easier. I really thought so. Then I observed that myself had preposterously deceived me, that it wasn't like that at all. When Mr Tottenham joined us, Cecily and me, I saw that he listened more than he talked, with an ear specially cocked to register any small irony which might appear in my remarks to my daughter. Naturally he registered more than there were, to make up perhaps for dear Cecily's obviously not registering any. I could see, too, that he was suspicious of any flavour of kindness; finally, to avoid the strictures of his upper lip, which really, dear fellow, began to bore me, I talked exclusively about the distant sails and the Red Sea littoral. When he no longer joined us as we sat or walked together, I perceived that his hostility was fixed and his *parti pris*. He was brimful of compassion, but it was all for Cecily, none for the situation or for me. (She would have marvelled, placidly, why he pitied her. I am glad I can say that.) The primitive man in him rose up as Pope of nature and excommunicated me as a creature recusant to her functions. Then deliberately Dacres undertook an office of consolation; and I fell to wondering, while Mrs Morgan spoke her convictions plainly out, how far an impulse of reparation for a misfortune with which he had nothing to do might carry a man.

I began to watch the affair with an interest which even to me seemed queer. It was not detached, but it was semi-detached, and, of course, on the side for which I seem, in this history, to be perpetually apologizing. With certain limitations it didn't matter an atom whom Cecily married.

So that he was sound and decent, with reasonable prospects, her simple requirements and ours for her would be quite met. There was the ghost of a consolation in that; one needn't be anxious or exacting.

I could predict with a certain amount of confidence that in her first season she would probably receive three or four proposals, any one of which she might accept with as much propriety and satisfaction as any other one. For Cecily, it was so simple; prearranged by nature like her digestion, one could not see any logical basis for difficulties. A nice upstanding sapper, a dashing Bengal Lancer—oh, I could think of a half a dozen types that would answer excellently. She was the kind of young person, and that was the summing up of it, to marry a type and be typically happy. I hoped and expected that she would. But Dacres!

Dacres should exercise the greatest possible discretion. He was not a person who could throw the dice indifferently with fate. He could respond to so much, and he would inevitably, sooner or later, demand so much response! He was governed by a preposterously exacting temperament, and he wore his nerves outside. And what vision he had! How he explored the world he lived in and drew out of it all there was, all there was! I could see him in the years to come ranging alone the fields that were sweet and the horizons that lifted for him, and ever returning to pace the common dusty mortal road by the side of a purblind wife. On general principles, as a case to point at, it would be conspicuous pity. Nor would it lack the aspect of a particular, a personal misfortune. Dacres was occupied in quite the natural normal degree with his charming self; he would pass his misery on, and who would deserve to escape it less than this mother-in-law?

I listened to Emily Morgan, who gleaned in the ship more information about Dacres Tottenham's people, pay, and prospects than I had ever acquired, and I kept an eye upon the pair which was, I flattered myself, quite maternal. I watched them without acute anxiety, deploring the threatening destiny, but hardly nearer to it than one is in the stalls to the stage. My moments of real concern for Dacres were mingled more with anger than with sorrow—it seemed inexcusable that he, with his infallible divining-rod for temperament, should be on the point of making such an ass of himself. Though I talk of the stage there was nothing at all dramatic to reward my attention, mine and Emily Morgan's. To my imagination, excited by its idea of what Dacres Tottenham's courtship ought to be, the attentions he paid to Cecily were most humdrum. He threw rings into buckets with her—she was good at that—and quoits upon the "bull" board; he found her chair after the decks were swabbed in the morning and established her in it; he paced the deck with her at convenient times and seasons. They were humdrum, but they were constant and cumulative. Cecily took them with an even breath that perfectly matched. There was hardly anything, on her part, to note—a little discreet observation of his comings and goings, eyes scarcely lifted from her book, and later just a hint of proprietorship, as the evening she came up to me on deck, our first night in the Indian Ocean. I was lying in my long chair looking at the thick, low stars and thinking it was a long time since I had seen John.

"Dearest mamma, out here and nothing over your shoulders! You *are* imprudent. Where is your wrap? Mr Tottenham, will you please fetch mamma's wrap for her?"

"If mamma so instructs me," he said audaciously.

"Do as Cecily tells you," I laughed, and he went and did it, while I by the light of a quartermaster's lantern distinctly saw my daughter blush.

Another time, when Cecily came down to undress, she bent over me as I lay in the lower berth with unusual solicitude. I had been dozing, and I jumped.

"What is it, child?" I said. "Is the ship on fire?"

"No, mamma, the ship is not on fire. There is nothing wrong. I'm so sorry I startled you. But Mr Tottenham has been telling me all about what you did for the soldiers the time plague broke out in the lines at Mian-Mir. I think it was splendid, mamma, and so does he."

"Oh, *Lord!*" I groaned. "Good night."

Chapter IV

It remained in my mind, that little thing that Dacres had taken the trouble to tell my daughter; I thought about it a good deal. It seemed to me the most serious and convincing circumstance that had yet offered itself to my consideration. Dacres was no longer content to bring solace and support to the more appealing figure of the situation; he must set to work, bless him! to improve the situation itself. He must try to induce Miss Farnham, by telling her everything he could remember to my credit, to think as well of her mother as possible, in spite of the strange and secret blows which that mother might be supposed to sit up at night to deliver to her. Cecily thought very well of me already; indeed, with private reservations as to my manners and—no, *not* my morals, I believe I exceeded her expectations of what a perfectly new and untrained mother would be likely to prove. It was my theory that she found me all she could understand me to be. The maternal virtues of the outside were certainly mine; I put them on with care every morning and wore them with patience all day. Dacres, I assured myself, must have allowed his preconception to lead him absurdly by the nose not to see that the girl was satisfied, that my impatience, my impotence, did not at all make her miserable. Evidently, however, he had created our relations differently; evidently he had set himself to their amelioration. There was portent in it; things seemed to be closing in. I bit off a quarter of an inch of wooden pen-handle in considering whether or not I should mention it in my letter to John, and decided that it would be better just perhaps to drop a hint. Though I could not expect John to receive it with any sort of perturbation. Men are different; he would probably think Tottenham well enough able to look after himself.

I had embarked on my letter, there at the end of a corner-table of the saloon, when I saw Dacres saunter through. He wore a very conscious and elaborately purposeless air; and it jumped with my mood that he had nothing less than the crisis of his life in his pocket, and was looking for me. As he advanced towards me between the long tables doubt left me and alarm assailed me. "I'm glad to find you in a quiet corner," said he, seating himself, and confirmed my worst anticipations.

"I'm writing to John," I said, and again applied myself to my pen-handle. It is a trick Cecily has since done her best in vain to cure me of.

"I am going to interrupt you," he said. "I have not had an opportunity of talking to you for some time."

"I like that!" I exclaimed derisively.

"And I want to tell you that I am very much charmed with Cecily."

"Well," I said, "I am not going to gratify you by saying anything against her."

"You don't deserve her, you know."

"I won't dispute that. But, if you don't mind—I'm not sure that I'll stand being abused, dear boy."

"I quite see it isn't any use. Though one spoke with the tongues of men and of angels—"

"And had not charity," I continued for him. "Precisely. I won't go on, but your quotation is very apt."

"I so bow down before her simplicity. It makes a wide and beautiful margin for the rest of her character. She is a girl Ruskin would have loved."

"I wonder," said I. "He did seem fond of the simple type, didn't he?"

"Her mind is so clear, so transparent. The motive spring of everything she says and does is so direct. Don't you find you can most completely depend upon her?"

"Oh yes," I said; "certainly. I nearly always know what she is going to say before she says it, and under given circumstances I can tell precisely what she will do."

"I fancy her sense of duty is very beautifully developed."

"It is," I said. "There is hardly a day when I do not come in contact with it."

"Well, that is surely a good thing. And I find that calm poise of hers very restful."

"I would not have believed that so many virtues could reside in one young lady," I said, taking refuge in flippancy, "and to think that she should be my daughter!"

"As I believe you know, that seems to me rather a cruel stroke of destiny, Mrs Farnham."

"Oh yes, I know! You have a constructive imagination, Dacres. You don't seem to see that the girl is protected by her limitations, like a tortoise. She lives within them quite secure and happy and content. How determined you are to be sorry for her!"

Mr Tottenham looked at the end of his lively exchange as though he sought for a polite way of conveying to me that I rather was the limited person. He looked as if he wished he could say things. The first of them would be, I saw, that he had quite a different conception of Cecily, that it was illuminated by many trifles, nuances of feeling and expression, which he had noticed in his talks with her whenever they had skirted the subject of her adoption by her mother. He knew her, he was longing to say, better than I did; when it would have been natural to reply that one could not hope to compete in such a direction with an intelligent young man, and we should at once have been upon delicate and difficult ground. So it was as well perhaps that he kept silence until he said, as he had come prepared to say, "Well, I want to put that beyond a doubt— her happiness—if I'm good enough. I want her, please, and I only hope that she will be half as willing to come as you are likely to be to let her go."

It was a shock when it came, plump, like that; and I was horrified to feel how completely every other consideration was lost for the instant in the immense relief that it prefigured. To be my whole complete self again, without the feeling that a fraction of me was masquerading about in Cecily! To be freed at once, or almost, from an exacting condition and an impossible ideal! "Oh!" I exclaimed, and my eyes positively filled. "You *are* good, Dacres, but I couldn't let you do that."

His undisguised stare brought me back to a sense of the proportion of things. I saw that in the combination of influences that had brought Mr Tottenham to the point of proposing to marry my daughter consideration for me, if it had a place, would be fantastic. Inwardly I laughed at the egotism of raw nerves that had conjured it up, even for an instant, as a reason for gratitude. The situation was not so peculiar, not so interesting, as that. But I answered his stare with a smile; what I had said might very well stand.

"Do you imagine," he said, seeing that I did not mean to amplify it, "that I want to marry her out of any sort of *good*ness?"

"Benevolence is your weakness, Dacres."

"I see. You think one's motive is to withdraw her from a relation which ought to be the most natural in the world, but which is, in her particular and painful case, the most equivocal."

"Well, come," I remonstrated. "You have dropped one or two things, you know, in the heat of your indignation, not badly calculated to give one that idea. The eloquent statement you have just made, for instance— it carries all the patness of old conviction. How often have you rehearsed it?"

I am a fairly long-suffering person, but I began to feel a little annoyed with my would-be son-in-law. If the relation were achieved it would give him no prescriptive right to bully me; and we were still in very early anticipation of that.

"Ah!" he said disarmingly. "Don't let us quarrel. I'm sorry you think that; because it isn't likely to bring your favour to my project, and I want you friendly and helpful. Oh, confound it!" he exclaimed, with sudden temper. "You ought to be. I don't understand this aloofness, I half suspect it's pose. You undervalue Cecily—well, you have no business to under-value me. You know me better than anybody in the world. Now are you going to help me to marry your daughter?"

"I don't think so," I said slowly, after a moment's silence, which he sat through like a mutinous schoolboy. "I might tell you that I don't care a button whom you marry, but that would not be true. I do care more or less. As you say, I know you pretty well. I'd a little rather you didn't make a mess of it; and if you must I should distinctly prefer not to have the spectacle under my nose for the rest of my life. I can't hinder you, but I won't help you."

"And what possesses you to imagine that in marrying Cecily I should make a mess of it? Shouldn't your first consideration be whether *she* would?"

"Perhaps it should, but, you see, it isn't. Cecily would be happy with anybody who made her comfortable. You would ask a good deal more than that, you know."

Dacres, at this, took me up promptly. Life, he said, the heart of life, had particularly little to say to temperament. By the heart of life I suppose he meant married love. He explained that its roots asked other sustenance, and that it throve best of all on simple elemental goodness. So long as a man sought in women mere casual companionship, perhaps the most exquisite thing to be experienced was the stimulus of some spiritual feminine counterpart; but when he desired of one woman that she should be always and intimately with him, the background of his life, the mother of his children, he was better advised to avoid nerves and sensibilities, and try for the repose of the common—the uncommon—domestic virtues. Ah, he said, they were sweet, like lavender. (Already, I told him, he smelled the housekeeper's linen-chest.) But I did not interrupt him much; I couldn't, he was too absorbed. To temperamental pairing, he declared, the century owed its breed of decadents. I asked him if he had ever really recognized one; and he retorted that if he hadn't he didn't wish to make a beginning in his own family. In a quarter of an hour he repudiated the theories of a lifetime, a gratifying triumph for simple elemental goodness. Having denied the value of the subtler pretensions to charm in woman as you marry her, he went artless on to endow Cecily with as many of them as could possibly be desirable. He actually persuaded himself to say that it was lovely to see the reflections of life in her tranquil spirit; and when I looked at him incredulously he grew angry, and hinted that Cecily's sensitiveness to reflections and other things might be a trifle beyond her mother's ken. "She responds instantly, intimately, to the beautiful everywhere," he declared.

"Aren't the opportunities of life on board ship rather limited to demonstrate that?" I inquired. "I know—you mean sunsets. Cecily is very fond of sunsets. She is always asking me to come and look at them."

"I was thinking of last night's sunset," he confessed. "We looked at it together."

"What did she say?" I asked idly.

"Nothing very much. That's just the point. Another girl would have raved and gushed."

"Oh, well, Cecily never does that," I responded. "Nevertheless she is a very ordinary human instrument. I hope I shall have no temptation ten years hence to remind you that I warned you of her quality."

"I wish, not in the least for my own profit, for I am well convinced already, but simply to win your cordiality and your approval—never did an unexceptional wooer receive such niggard encouragement!—I wish there were some sort of test for her quality. I would be proud to stand by it, and you would be convinced. I can't find words to describe my objection to your state of mind."

The thing seemed to me to be a foregone conclusion. I saw it accomplished, with all its possibilities of disastrous commonplace. I saw all that I have here taken the trouble to foreshadow. So far as I was concerned, Dacres's burden would add itself to my philosophies, *voilà tout*. I should always be a little uncomfortable about it, because it had been taken from my back; but it would not be a matter for the wringing of hands. And yet—the hatefulness of the mistake! Dacres's bold talk of a test made no suggestion. Should my invention be more fertile? I thought of something.

"You have said nothing to her yet?" I asked.

"Nothing. I don't think she suspects for a moment. She treats me as if no such fell design were possible. I'm none too confident, you know," he added, with longer face.

"We go straight to Agra. Could you come to Agra?"

"Ideal!" he cried. "The memory of Mumtaz! The garden of the Taj! I've always wanted to love under the same moon as Shah Jehan. How thoughtful of you!"

"You must spend a few days with us in Agra," I continued. "And as you say, it is the very place to shrine your happiness, if it comes to pass there."

"Well, I am glad to have extracted a word of kindness from you at last," said Dacres, as the stewards came to lay the table. "But I wish," he added regretfully, "you could have thought of a test."

Chapter V

Four days later we were in Agra. A time there was when the name would have been the key of dreams to me; now it stood for John's headquarters. I was rejoiced to think I would look again upon the Taj; and the prospect of living with it was a real enchantment; but I pondered most of the kind of house that would be provided for the General Commanding the District, how many the dining-room would seat, and whether it would have a roof of thatch or of corrugated iron—I prayed against corrugated iron. I confess these my preoccupations. I was forty, and at forty the practical considerations of life hold their own even against domes of marble, world-renowned, and set about with gardens where the bulbul sings to the rose. I smiled across the years at the raptures of my first vision of the place at twenty-one, just Cecily's age. Would I now sit under Arjamand's cypresses till two o'clock in the morning to see the wonder of her tomb at a particular angle of the moon? Would I climb one of her tall white ministering minarets to see anything whatever? I very greatly feared that I would not. Alas for the aging of sentiment, of interest! Keep your touch with life and your seat in the saddle as long as you will, the world is no new toy at forty. But Cecily was twenty-one, Cecily who sat stolidly finishing her lunch while Dacres Tottenham talked about Akbar and his philosophy. "The sort of man," he said, "that Carlyle might have smoked a pipe with."

"But surely," said Cecily reflectively, "tobacco was not discovered in England then. Akbar came to the throne in 1526."

"Nor Carlyle either for that matter," I hastened to observe. "Nevertheless, I think Mr Tottenham's proposition must stand."

"Thanks, Mrs Farnham," said Dacres. "But imagine Miss Farnham's remembering Akbar's date! I'm sure you didn't!"

"Let us hope she doesn't know too much about him," I cried gaily, "or there will be nothing to tell!"

"Oh, really and truly very little!" said Cecily, "but as soon as we heard papa would be stationed here Aunt Emma made me read up about those old Moguls and people. I think I remember the dynasty. Baber, wasn't he the first? and then Humayon, and after him Akbar, and then Jehangir, and then Shah Jehan. But I've forgotten every date but Akbar's."

She smiled her smile of brilliant health and even spirits as she made the damaging admission, and she was so good to look at, sitting there simple and wholesome and fresh, peeling her banana with her well-shaped fingers, that we swallowed the dynasty as it were whole, and smiled back upon her. John, I may say, was extremely pleased with Cecily; he said she was a very satisfactory human accomplishment. One would have thought, positively, the way he plumed himself over his handsome daughter, that he alone was responsible for her. But John, having received his family, straightway set off with his Staff on a tour of inspection, and thereby takes himself out of this history. I sometimes think that if he had stayed—but there has never been the lightest recrimination between us about it, and I am not going to hint one now.

"Did you read," asked Dacres, "what he and the Court poet wrote over the entrance gate to the big mosque at Fattehpur-Sikri? It's rather nice. 'The world is a looking-glass, wherein the image has come and is gone—take as thine own nothing more than what thou lookest upon.' "

My daughter's thoughtful gaze was, of course, fixed upon the speaker, and in his own glance I saw a sudden ray of consciousness; but Cecily transferred her eyes to the opposite wall, deeply considering, and while Dacres and I smiled across the table, I saw that she had perceived no reason for blushing. It was a singularly narrow escape.

"No," she said, "I didn't; what a curious proverb for an emperor to make! He couldn't possibly have been able to see all his possessions at once."

"If you have finished," Dacres addressed her, "do let me show you what your plain and immediate duty is to the garden. The garden waits for you—all the roses expectant—"

"Why, there isn't one!" cried Cecily, pinning on her hat. It was pleasing, and just a trifle pathetic, the way he hurried her out of the scope of any little dart; he would not have her even within range of amused observation. Would he continue, I wondered vaguely, as, with my elbows on the table, I tore into strips the lemon-leaf that floated in my finger-bowl—would he continue, through life, to shelter her from his other clever friends as now he attempted to shelter her from her mother? In that case he would have to domicile her, poor dear, behind the curtain, like the native ladies—a good price to pay for a protection of which, bless her heart! she would be all unaware. I had quite stopped bemoaning the affair; perhaps the comments of my husband, who treated it with broad approval and satisfaction, did something to soothe my sensibilities. At all events, I had gradually come to occupy a high fatalistic ground towards the pair. If it was written upon their foreheads that they should marry, the inscription was none of mine; and, of course, it was true, as John had indignantly stated, that Dacres might do very much worse. One's interest in Dacres Tottenham's problematical future had in no way diminished;

but the young man was so positive, so full of intention, so disinclined to discussion—he had not reopened the subject since that morning in the saloon of the Caledonia—that one's feeling about it rather took the attenuated form of a shrug. I am afraid, too, that the pleasurable excitement of such an impending event had a little supervened; even at forty there is no disallowing the natural interests of one's sex. As I sat there pulling my lemon-leaf to pieces, I should not have been surprised or in the least put about if the two had returned radiant from the lawn to demand my blessing. As to the test of quality that I had obligingly invented for Dacres on the spur of the moment without his knowledge or connivance, it had some time ago faded into what he apprehended it to be—a mere idyllic opportunity, a charming background, a frame for his project, of prettier sentiment than the funnels and the hand-rails of a ship.

Mr Tottenham had ten days to spend with us. He knew the place well; it belonged to the province to whose service he was dedicated, and he claimed with impressive authority the privilege of showing it to Cecily by degrees—the Hall of Audience to-day, the Jessamine Tower to-morrow, the tomb of Akbar another, and the Deserted City yet another day. We arranged the expeditions in conference, Dacres insisting only upon the order of them, which I saw was to be cumulative, with the Taj at the very end, on the night precisely of the full of the moon, with a better chance of roses. I had no special views, but Cecily contributed some; that we should do the Hall of Audience in the morning, so as not to interfere with the club tennis in the afternoon, that we should bicycle to Akbar's tomb and take a cold luncheon—if we were sure there would be no snakes—to the Deserted City, to all of which Dacres gave loyal assent. I endorsed everything; I was the encouraging chorus, only stipulating that my number should be swelled from day to day by the addition of such persons as I should approve. Cecily, for instance, wanted to invite the Bakewells because we had come out in the same ship with them; but I could not endure the Bakewells, and it seemed to me that our having made the voyage with them was the best possible reason for declining to lay eyes on them for the rest of our natural lives. "Mamma has such strong prejudices," Cecily remarked, as she reluctantly gave up the idea; and I waited to see whether the graceless Tottenham would unmurmuringly take down the Bakewells. How strong must be the sentiment that turns a man into a boa-constrictor without a pang of transmigration! But no, this time he was faithful to the principles of his pre-Cecilian existence. "They are rather Boojums," he declared. "You would think so, too, if you knew them better. It is that kind of excellent person that makes the real burden of India." I could have patted him on the back.

Thanks to the rest of the chorus, which proved abundantly available, I was no immediate witness to Cecily's introduction to the glorious fragments which sustain in Agra the memory of the Moguls. I may as well say that I arranged with care that if anybody must be standing by when Dacres disclosed them, it should not be I. If Cecily had squinted, I should have been sorry, but I would have found in it no personal humiliation. There were other imperfections of vision, however, for which I felt responsible and ashamed; and with Dacres, though the situation, Heaven knows, was none of my seeking, I had a little the feeling of a dealer who offers a defective *bibelot* to a connoisseur. My charming daughter—I was fifty times congratulated upon her appearance and her manners—had many excellent qualities and capacities which she never inherited from me; but she could see no more than the bulk, no further than the perspective; she could register exactly as much as a camera.

This was a curious thing, perhaps, to displease my maternal vanity, but it did; I had really rather she squinted; and when there was anything to look at I kept out of the way. I can not tell precisely, therefore, what the incidents were that contributed to make Mr Tottenham, on our return from these expeditions, so thoughtful, with a thoughtfulness which increased, towards the end of them, to a positive gravity. This would disappear during dinner under the influence of food and drink. He would talk nightly with new enthusiasm and fresh hope—or did I imagine it?— of the loveliness he had arranged to reveal on the following day. If again my imagination did not lead me astray, I fancied this occurred later and later in the course of the meal as the week went on; as if his state required more stimulus as time progressed. One evening, when I expected it to flag altogether, I had a whim to order champagne and observe the effect; but I am glad to say that I reproved myself, and refrained.

Cecily, meanwhile, was conducting herself in a manner which left nothing to be desired. If, as I sometimes thought, she took Dacres very much for granted, she took him calmly for granted; she seemed a prey to none of those fluttering uncertainties, those suspended judgements and elaborate indifferences which translate themselves so plainly in a young lady receiving addresses. She turned herself out very freshly and very well; she was always ready for everything, and I am sure that no glance of Dacres Tottenham's found aught but direct and decorous response. His society on these occasions gave her solid pleasure; so did the drive and the lunch; the satisfactions were apparently upon the same plane. She was aware of the plum, if I may be permitted a brusque but irresistible simile; and with her mouth open, her eyes modestly closed, and her head in a convenient position, she waited, placidly, until it should fall in. The Farnham ladies would have been delighted with the result of their labours in the sweet reason and eminent propriety of this attitude. Thinking of my idiotic sufferings when John began to fix himself upon my horizon, I pondered profoundly the power of nature in differentiation.

One evening, the last, I think, but one, I had occasion to go to my daughter's room, and found her writing in her commonplace-book. She had a commonplace-book, as well as a Where Is It? an engagement-book, an account-book, a diary, a Daily Sunshine, and others with purposes too various to remember. "Dearest mamma," she said, as I was departing, "there is only one 'p' in 'opulence,' isn't there?"

"Yes," I replied, with my hand on the door-handle, and added curiously, for it was an odd word in Cecily's mouth, "Why?"

She hardly hesitated. "Oh," she said, "I am just writing down one or two things Mr Tottenham said about Agra before I forget them. They seemed so true."

"He has a descriptive touch," I remarked.

"I think he describes beautifully. Would you like to hear what he said to-day?"

"I would," I replied, sincerely.

" 'Agra,' " read this astonishing young lady, " 'is India's one pure idyll. Elsewhere she offers other things, foolish opulence, tawdry pageant, treachery of eunuchs and jealousies of harems, thefts of kings' jewels and barbaric retributions; but they are all actual, visualized, or part of a past that shows to the backward glance hardly more relief and vitality than a Persian painting'—I should like to see a Persian painting—'but here the immortal tombs and pleasure-houses rise out of color delicate and subtle; the vision holds across three hundred years; the print of the court is still in the dust of the city.' "

"Did you really let him go on like that?" I exclaimed. "It has the license of a lecture!"

"I encouraged him to. Of course he didn't say it straight off. He said it naturally; he stopped now and then to cough. I didn't understand it all; but I think I have remembered every word."

"You have a remarkable memory. I'm glad he stopped to cough. Is there any more?"

"One little bit. 'Here the Moguls wrought their passions into marble, and held them up with great refrains from their religion, and set them about with gardens; and here they stand in the twilight of the glory of those kings and the noonday splendour of their own.' "

"How clever of you!" I exclaimed. "How wonderfully clever of you to remember!"

"I had to ask him to repeat one or two sentences. He didn't like that. But this is nothing. I used to learn pages letter-perfect for Aunt Emma. She was very particular. I think it is worth preserving, don't you?"

"Dear Cecily," I responded, "you have a frugal mind."

There was nothing else to respond. I could not tell her just how practical I thought her, or how pathetic her little book.

Chapter VI

We drove together, after dinner, to the Taj. The moonlight lay in an empty splendor over the broad sandy road, with the acacias pricking up on each side of it and the gardens of the station bungalows stretching back into clusters of crisp shadows. It was an exquisite February night, very still. Nothing seemed abroad but two or three pariah dogs, upon vague and errant business, and the Executive Engineer going swiftly home from the club on his bicycle. Even the little shops of the bazaar were dark and empty; only here and there a light showed barred behind the carved balconies of the upper rooms, and there was hardly any tom-tomming. The last long slope of the road showed us the river curving to the left, through a silent white waste that stretched indefinitely into the moonlight on one side, and was crowned by Akbar's fort on the other. His long high line of turrets and battlements still guarded a hint of their evening rose, and dim and exquisite above them hovered the three dome-bubbles of the Pearl Mosque. It was a night of perfect illusion, and the illusion was mysterious, delicate, and faint. I sat silent as we rolled along, twenty years nearer to the original joy of things when John and I drove through the same old dream.

Dacres, too, seemed preoccupied; only Cecily was, as they say, herself. Cecily was really more than herself, she exhibited an unusual flow of spirits. She talked continually, she pointed out this and that, she asked who lived here and who lived there. At regular intervals of about four minutes she demanded if it wasn't simply too lovely. She sat straight up with her vigorous profile and her smart hat; and the silhouette of her personality sharply refused to mingle with the dust of any dynasty. She was a contrast, a protest; positively she was an indignity. "Do lean back, dear child," I exclaimed at last. "You interfere with the landscape."

She leaned back, but she went on interfering with it in terms of sincerest enthusiasm.

When we stopped at the great archway of entrance I begged to be left in the carriage. What else could one do, when the golden moment had come, but sit in the carriage and measure it? They climbed the broad stone steps together and passed under the lofty gravures into the garden, and I waited. I waited and remembered. I am not, as perhaps by this time is evident, a person of overwhelming sentiment, but I think the smile upon my lips was gentle. So plainly I could see, beyond the massive archway and across a score of years, all that they saw at that moment—Arjamand's garden, and the long straight tank of marble cleaving it full of sleeping water and the shadows of the marshaling cypresses; her wide dark garden of roses and of pomegranates, and at the end the Vision, marvellous, aerial, the soul of something—is it beauty? is it sorrow?—that great white pride of love in mourning such as only here in all the round of our little world lifts itself to the stars, the unpaintable, indescribable Taj Mahal. A gentle breath stole out with a scent of jessamine and such a memory! I closed my eyes and felt the warm luxury of a tear.

Thinking of the two in the garden, my mood was very kind, very conniving. How foolish after all were my cherry-stone theories of taste and temperament before that uncalculating thing which sways a world and builds a Taj Mahal! Was it probable that Arjamand and her Emperor had loved fastidiously, and yet how they had loved! I wandered away into consideration of the blind forces which move the world, in which comely young persons like my daughter Cecily had such a place; I speculated vaguely upon the value of the subtler gifts of sympathy and insight which seemed indeed, at that enveloping moment, to be mere flowers strewn upon the tide of deeper emotions. The garden sent me a fragrance of roses; the moon sailed higher and picked out the little kiosks set along the wall. It was a charming, charming thing to wait, there at the portal of the silvered, scented garden, for an idyll to come forth.

When they reappeared, Dacres and my daughter, they came with casual steps and cheerful voices. They might have been a couple of tourists. The moonlight fell full upon them on the platform under the arch. It showed Dacres measuring with his stick the length of the Sanskrit letters which declared the stately texts, and Cecily's expression of polite, perfunctory interest. They looked up at the height above them; they looked back at the vision behind. Then they sauntered towards the carriage, he offering a formal hand to help her down the uncertain steps, she gracefully accepting it.

"You—you have not been long," said I. "I hope you didn't hurry on my account."

"Miss Farnham found the marble a little cold under foot," replied Dacres, putting Miss Farnham in.

"You see," explained Cecily, "I stupidly forgot to change into thicker soles. I have only my slippers. But, mamma, how lovely it is! Do let us come again in the daytime. I am dying to make a sketch of it."

Mr Tottenham was to leave us on the following day. In the morning, after "little breakfast," as we say in India, he sought me in the room I had set aside to be particularly my own.

Again I was writing to John, but this time I waited for precisely his interruption. I had got no further than "My dearest husband," and my pen-handle was a fringe.

"Another fine day," I said, as if the old, old Indian joke could give him ease, poor man!

"Yes," said he, "we are having lovely weather."

He had forgotten that it was a joke. Then he lapsed into silence while I renewed my attentions to my pen.

"I say," he said at last, with so strained a look about his mouth, that it was almost a contortion, "I haven't done it, you know."

"No," I responded, cheerfully, "and you're not going to. Is that it? Well!"

"Frankly—" said he.

"Dear me, yes! Anything else between you and me would be grotesque," I interrupted, "after all these years."

"I don't think it would be a success," he said, looking at me resolutely with his clear blue eyes, in which still still lay, alas! the possibility of many delusions.

"No," I said, "I never did, you know. But the prospect had begun to impose upon me."

"To say how right you were would seem, under the circumstances, the most hateful form of flattery."

"Yes," I said, "I think I can dispense with your verbal endorsement." I felt a little bitter. It was, of course, better that the connoisseur should have discovered the flaw before concluding the transaction; but although I had pointed it out myself I was not entirely pleased to have the article returned.

"I am infinitely ashamed that it should have taken me all these days— day after day and each contributory—to discover what you saw so easily and so completely."

"You forget that I am her mother," I could not resist the temptation of saying.

"Oh, for God's sake don't jeer! Please be absolutely direct, and tell me if you have reason to believe that to the extent of a thought, of a breath—to any extent at all—she cares."

He was, I could see, very deeply moved; he had not arrived at this point without trouble and disorder not lightly to be put on or off. Yet I did not hurry to his relief, I was still possessed by a vague feeling of offense. I reflected that any mother would be, and I quite plumed myself upon my annoyance. It was so satisfactory, when one had a daughter, to know the sensations of even any mother. Nor was it soothing to remember that the young man's whole attitude towards Cecily had been based upon criticism of me, even though he sat before me whipped with his own lash. His temerity had been stupid and obstinate; I could not regret his punishment.

I kept him waiting long enough to think all this, and then I replied, "I have not the least means of knowing."

I can not say what he expected, but he squared his shoulders as if he had received a blow and might receive another. Then he looked at me with a flash of the old indignation. "You are not near enough to her for that!" he exclaimed.

"I am not near enough to her for that."

Silence fell between us. A crow perched upon an opened venetian and cawed lustily. For years afterward I never heard a crow caw without a sense of vain, distressing experiment. Dacres got up and began to walk about the room. I very soon put a stop to that. "I can't talk to a pendulum," I said, but I could not persuade him to sit down again.

"Candidly," he said at length, "do you think she would have me?"

"I regret to say that I think she would. But you would not dream of asking her."

"Why not? She is a dear girl," he responded inconsequently.

"You could not possibly stand it."

Then Mr Tottenham delivered himself of this remarkable phrase: "I could stand it," he said, "as well as you can."

There was far from being any joy in the irony with which I regarded him and under which I saw him gather up his resolution to go; nevertheless I did nothing to make it easy for him. I refrained from imparting my private conviction that Cecily would accept the first presentable substitute that appeared, although it was strong. I made no reference to my daughter's large fund of philosophy and small balance of sentiment. I did not even—though this was reprehensible—confess the test, the test of quality in these ten days with the marble archives of the Moguls, which I had almost wantonly suggested, which he had so unconsciously accepted, so disastrously applied. I gave him quite fifteen minutes of his bad quarter of an hour, and when it was over I wrote truthfully but furiously to John. . . .

That was ten years ago. We have since attained the shades of retirement, and our daughter is still with us when she is not with Aunt Emma and Aunt Alice—grandmamma has passed away. Mr Tottenham's dumb departure that day in February—it was the year John got his C.B.—was followed, I am thankful to say, by none of the symptoms of unrequited affection on Cecily's part. Not for ten minutes, so far as I was aware, was she the maid forlorn. I think her self-respect was of too robust a character, thanks to the Misses Farnham. Still less, of course, had she any reproaches to serve upon her mother, although for a long time I thought I detected— or was it my guilty conscience?—a spark of shrewdness in the glance she bent upon me when the talk was of Mr Tottenham and the probabilities of his return to Agra. So well did she sustain her experience, or so little did she feel it, that I believe the impression went abroad that Dacres had been sent disconsolate away. One astonishing conversation I had with her some six months later, which turned upon the point of a particularly desirable offer. She told me something then, without any sort of embarrassment, but quite lucidly and directly, that edified me much to hear. She said that while she was quite sure that Mr Tottenham thought of her only as a friend—she had never had the least reason for any other impression—he had done her a service for which she could not thank him enough—in showing her what a husband might be. He had given her a standard; it might be high, but it was unalterable. She didn't know whether she could describe it, but Mr Tottenham was different from the kind of man you seemed to meet in India. He had his own ways of looking at things, and he talked so well. He had given her an ideal, and she intended to profit by it. To know that men like Mr Tottenham existed, and to marry any other kind would be an act of folly which she did not intend to commit. No, Major the Hon. Hugh Taverel did not come near it—very far short, indeed! He had talked to her during the whole of dinner the night before about jackal-hunting with a bobbery pack—not at all an elevated mind. Yes, he might be a very good fellow, but as a companion for life she was sure he would not be at all suitable. She would wait.

And she has waited. I never thought she would, but she has. From time to time men have wished to take her from us, but the standard has been inexorable, and none of them have reached it. When Dacres married the charming American whom he caught like a butterfly upon her Eastern tour, Cecily sent them as a wedding present an alabaster model of the Taj, and I let her do it—the gift was so exquisitely appropriate. I suppose he never looks at it without being reminded that he didn't marry Miss Farnham, and I hope that he remembers that he owes it to Miss Farnham's mother. So much I think I might claim; it is really very little considering what it stands for. Cecily is permanently with us—I believe she considers herself an intimate. I am very reasonable about lending her to her aunts, but she takes no sort of advantage of my liberality; she says she knows her duty is at home. She is growing into a firm and solid English maiden lady, with a good colour and great decision of character. That she always had.

I point out to John, when she takes our crumpets away from us, that she gets it from him. I could never take away anybody's crumpets, merely because they were indigestible, least of all my own parents'. She has acquired a distinct affection for us, by some means best known to herself; but I should have no objection to that if she would not rearrange my bonnet-strings. That is a fond liberty to which I take exception; but it is one thing to take exception and another to express it.

Our daughter is with us, permanently with us. She declares that she intends to be the prop of our declining years; she makes the statement often, and always as if it were humorous. Nevertheless I sometimes notice a spirit of inquiry, a note of investigation in her encounters with the opposite sex that suggests an expectation not yet extinct that another and perhaps a more appreciative Dacres Tottenham may flash across her field of vision—alas, how improbable! Myself I can not imagine why she should wish it; I have grown in my old age into a perfect horror of cultivated young men; but if such a person should by a miracle at any time appear, I think it is extremely improbable that I will interfere on his behalf.

EDITH WHARTON

(1862–1937)

*E*dith Wharton was born Edith Jones into a rich New York family. *She did not attend school but was educated by governesses, from whom she learned foreign languages, as well as by browsing in her father's library and travelling extensively in Europe. She was not allowed to read American children's books because, as she says in her autobiography, they "spoke bad English without the author's knowing it." She published her first stories in 1891, but her first major collections of stories,* The Greek Inclination *(1899),* Crucial Instances *(1902), and* The Descent of Man *(1904), mark her coming of age as a writer. She also published important nonfiction on art, history, travel, and general culture. In* Italian Villas and Their Gardens *(1904), for example, she provided readers with so much meticulous detail that landscape gardeners used it as a manual. Her novels include* Valley of Decision *(1902),* The House of Mirth *(1905),* Ethan Frome *(1911),* The Reef *(1912), and* The Age of Innocence *(1920). She moved to France in 1905, and during the war she organized war relief and worked tirelessly for the Allied cause, for which she was made a member of France's Légion d'honneur. Her best stories convey the New York society into which she was born. As Richard Lawson points out: "The vanity, the rigidity, the inconsistency of this society and its extended membership all receive their full measure of disapproval. She treats cultural pretentiousness with a special disdain. She makes us see the cruelty—even if it is unconscious cruelty—that accompanies the vices of her society."*

Roman Fever

I

From the table at which they had been lunching two American ladies of ripe but well-cared-for middle age moved across the lofty terrace of the Roman restaurant and, leaning on its parapet, looked first at each other, and then down on the outspread glories of the Palatine and the Forum, with the same expression of vague but benevolent approval.

As they leaned there a girlish voice echoed up gaily from the stairs leading to the court below. "Well, come along, then," it cried, not to them but to an invisible companion, "and let's leave the young things to their knitting"; and a voice as fresh laughed back: "Oh, look here, Babs, not actually knitting—" "Well, I mean figuratively," rejoined the first. "After all, we haven't left our poor parents much else to do . . ." and at that point the turn of the stairs engulfed the dialogue.

The two ladies looked at each other again, this time with a tinge of smiling embarrassment, and the smaller and paler one shook her head and coloured slightly.

"Barbara!" she murmured, sending an unheard rebuke after the mocking voice in the stairway.

The other lady, who was fuller, and higher in colour, with a small determined nose supported by vigorous black eyebrows, gave a good-humoured laugh. "That's what our daughters think of us!"

Her companion replied by a deprecating gesture. "Not of us individually. We must remember that. It's just the collective modern idea of Mothers. And you see—" Half guiltily she drew from her handsomely mounted black hand-bag a twist of crimson silk run through by two fine knitting needles. "One never knows," she murmured. "The new system has certainly given us a good deal of time to kill; and sometimes I get tired just looking—even at this." Her gesture was now addressed to the stupendous scene at their feet.

The dark lady laughed again, and they both relapsed upon the view, contemplating it in silence, with a sort of diffused serenity which might have been borrowed from the spring effulgence of the Roman skies. The luncheon-hour was long past, and the two had their end of the vast terrace to themselves. At its opposite extremity a few groups, detained by a lingering look at the outspread city, were gathering up guide-books and fumbling for tips. The last of them scattered, and the two ladies were alone on the air-washed height.

"Well, I don't see why we shouldn't just stay here," said Mrs. Slade, the lady of the high colour and energetic brows. Two derelict basketchairs stood near, and she pushed them into the angle of the parapet, and settled herself in one, her gaze upon the Palatine. "After all, it's still the most beautiful view in the world."

"It always will be, to me," assented her friend Mrs. Ansley, with so slight a stress on the "me" that Mrs. Slade, though she noticed it, wondered if it were not merely accidental, like the random underlinings of old-fashioned letter-writers.

"Grace Ansley was always old-fashioned," she thought; and added aloud, with a retrospective smile: "It's a view we've both been familiar with for a good many years. When we first met here we were younger than our girls are now. You remember?"

"Oh, yes, I remember," murmured Mrs. Ansley, with the same undefinable stress.—"There's that head-waiter wondering," she interpolated. She was evidently far less sure than her companion of herself and of her rights in the world.

"I'll cure him of wondering," said Mrs. Slade, stretching her hand toward a bag as discreetly opulent-looking as Mrs. Ansley's. Signing to the head-waiter, she explained that she and her friend were old lovers of Rome, and would like to spend the end of the afternoon looking down on the view—that is, if it did not disturb the service? The head-waiter, bowing over her gratuity, assured her that the ladies were most welcome, and would be still more so if they would condescend to remain for dinner. A full moon night, they would remember . . .

Mrs. Slade's black brows drew together, as though references to the moon were out-of-place and even unwelcome. But she smiled away her frown as the headwaiter retreated. "Well, why not? We might do worse. There's no knowing, I suppose, when the girls will be back. Do you even know back from *where*? I don't!"

Mrs. Ansley again coloured slightly. "I think those young Italian aviators we met at the Embassy invited them to fly to Tarquinia for tea. I suppose they'll want to wait and fly back by moonlight."

"Moonlight—moonlight! What a part it still plays. Do you suppose they're as sentimental as we were?"

"I've come to the conclusion that I don't in the least know what they are," said Mrs. Ansley. "And perhaps we didn't know much more about each other."

"No; perhaps we didn't."

Her friend gave her a shy glance. "I never should have supposed you were sentimental, Alida."

"Well, perhaps I wasn't." Mrs. Slade drew her lids together in retrospect; and for a few moments the two ladies, who had been intimate since childhood, reflected how little they knew each other. Each one, of course, had a label ready to attach to the other's name; Mrs. Delphin Slade, for instance, would have told herself, or any one who asked her, that Mrs. Horace Ansley, twenty-five years ago, had been exquisitely lovely—no, you wouldn't believe it, would you? . . . though, of course, still charming, distinguished . . . Well, as a girl she had been exquisite; far more beautiful than her daughter Barbara, though certainly Babs, according to the new standards at any rate, was more effective—had more *edge*, as they say. Funny where she got it, with those two nullities as parents. Yes; Horace Ansley was—well, just the duplicate of his wife. Museum specimens of old New York. Goodlooking, irreproachable, exemplary. Mrs. Slade and Mrs. Ansley had lived opposite each other—actually as well as figuratively—for years. When the drawing-room curtains in No. 20 East 73rd Street were renewed, No. 23, across the way, was always aware of it. And of all the movings, buyings, travels, anniversaries, illnesses—the tame chronicle of an estimable pair. Little of it escaped Mrs. Slade. But she had grown bored with it by the time her husband made his big *coup* in Wall Street, and when they bought in upper Park Avenue had already begun to think: "I'd rather live opposite a speak-easy for a change;

at least one might see it raided." The idea of seeing Grace raided was so amusing that (before the move) she launched it at a woman's lunch. It made a hit, and went the rounds—she sometimes wondered if it had crossed the street, and reached Mrs. Ansley. She hoped not, but didn't much mind. Those were the days when respectability was at a discount, and it did the irreproachable no harm to laugh at them a little.

A few years later, and not many months apart, both ladies lost their husbands. There was an appropriate exchange of wreaths and condolences, and a brief renewal of intimacy in the half-shadow of their mourning; and now, after another interval, they had run across each other in Rome, at the same hotel, each of them the modest appendage of a salient daughter. The similarity of their lot had again drawn them together, lending itself to mild jokes, and the mutual confession that, if in old days it must have been tiring to "keep up" with daughters, it was now, at times, a little dull not to.

No doubt, Mrs. Slade reflected, she felt her unemployment more than poor Grace ever would. It was a big drop from being the wife of Delphin Slade to being his widow. She had always regarded herself (with a certain conjugal pride) as his equal in social gifts, as contributing her full share to the making of the exceptional couple they were: but the difference after his death was irremediable. As the wife of the famous corporation lawyer, always with an international case or two on hand, every day brought its exciting and unexpected obligation: the impromptu entertaining of eminent colleagues from abroad, the hurried dashes on legal business to London, Paris or Rome, where the entertaining was so handsomely reciprocated; the amusement of hearing in her wake: "What, that handsome woman with the good clothes and the eyes is Mrs. Slade—*the* Slade's wife? Really? Generally the wives of celebrities are such frumps."

Yes; being *the* Slade's widow was a dullish business after that. In living up to such a husband all her faculties had been engaged; now she had only her daughter to live up to, for the son who seemed to have inherited his father's gifts had died suddenly in boyhood. She had fought through that agony because her husband was there, to be helped and to help; now, after the father's death, the thought of the boy had become unbearable. There was nothing left but to mother her daughter; and dear Jenny was such a perfect daughter that she needed no excessive mothering. "Now with Babs Ansley I don't know that I *should* be so quiet," Mrs. Slade sometimes half-enviously reflected; but Jenny, who was younger than her brilliant friend, was that rare accident, an extremely pretty girl who somehow made youth and prettiness seem as safe as their absence. It was all perplexing—and to Mrs. Slade a little boring. She wished that Jenny would fall in love—with the wrong man, even; that she might have to be watched, out-manoeuvred, rescued. And instead, it was Jenny who watched her mother, kept her out of draughts, made sure that she had taken her tonic . . .

Mrs. Ansley was much less articulate than her friend, and her mental portrait of Mrs. Slade was slighter, and drawn with fainter touches. "Alida Slade's awfully brilliant; but not as brilliant as she thinks," would have summed it up; though she would have added, for the enlightenment of strangers, that Mrs. Slade had been an extremely dashing girl; much more so than her daughter, who was pretty, of course, and clever in a way, but had none of her mother's—well, "vividness," some one had once called it. Mrs. Ansley would take up current words like this, and cite them in quotation marks, as unheard-of-audacities. No; Jenny was not like her mother. Sometimes Mrs. Ansley thought Alida Slade was disappointed; on the whole she had had a sad life. Full of failures and mistakes; Mrs. Ansley had always been rather sorry for her . . .

So these two ladies visualized each other, each through the wrong end of her little telescope.

II

For a long time they continued to sit side by side without speaking. It seemed as though, to both, there was a relief in laying down their somewhat futile activities in the presence of the vast Memento Mori which faced them. Mrs. Slade sat quite still, her eyes fixed on the golden slope of the Palace of the Caesars, and after a while Mrs. Ansley ceased to fidget with her bag, and she too sank into meditation. Like many intimate friends, the two ladies had never before had occasion to be silent together, and Mrs. Ansley was slightly embarrassed by what seemed, after so many years, a new stage in their intimacy, and one with which she did not yet know how to deal.

Suddenly the air was full of that deep clangour of bells which periodically covers Rome with a roof of silver. Mrs. Slade glanced at her wristwatch. "Five o'clock already," she said, as though surprised.

Mrs. Ansley suggested interrogatively: "There's bridge at the Embassy at five." For a long time Mrs. Slade did not answer. She appeared to be lost in contemplation, and Mrs. Ansley thought the remark had escaped her. But after a while she said, as if speaking out of a dream: "Bridge, did you say? Not unless you want to . . . But I don't think I will, you know."

"Oh, no," Mrs. Ansley hastened to assure her. "I don't care to at all. It's so lovely here; and so full of old memories, as you say." She settled herself in her chair, and almost furtively drew forth her knitting. Mrs. Slade took sideway note of this activity, but her own beautifully cared-for hands remained motionless on her knee.

"I was just thinking," she said slowly, "what different things Rome stands for to each generation of travellers. To our grandmothers, Roman fever; to our mothers, sentimental dangers—how we used to be guarded!—to our daughters, no more dangers than the middle of Main Street. They don't know it—but how much they're missing!"

The long golden light was beginning to pale, and Mrs. Ansley lifted her knitting a little closer to her eyes. "Yes; how we were guarded!"

"I always used to think," Mrs. Slade continued, "that our mothers had a much more difficult job than our grandmothers. When Roman fever stalked the streets it must have been comparatively easy to gather in the girls at the danger hour; but when you and I were young, with such beauty calling us, and the spice of disobedience thrown in, and no worse risk than catching cold during the cool hour after sunset, the mothers used to be put to it to keep us in—didn't they?"

She turned again toward Mrs. Ansley, but the latter had reached a delicate point in her knitting. "One, two, three—slip two; yes, they must have been," she assented, without looking up.

Mrs. Slade's eyes rested on her with a deepened attention. "She can knit—in the face of *this*! How like her . . ."

Mrs. Slade leaned back, brooding, her eyes ranging from the ruins which faced her to the long green hollow of the Forum, the fading glow of the church fronts beyond it, and the outlying immensity of the Colosseum. Suddenly she thought: "It's all very well to say that our girls have done away with sentiment and moonlight. But if Babs Ansley isn't out to catch that young aviator—the one who's a Marchese—then I don't know anything. And Jenny has no chance beside her. I know that too. I wonder if that's why Grace Ansley likes the two girls to go everywhere together? My poor Jenny as a foil—!" Mrs. Slade gave a hardly audible laugh, and at the sound Mrs. Ansley dropped her knitting.

"Yes—?"

"I—oh, nothing. I was only thinking how your Babs carries everything before her. That Campolieri boy is one of the best matches in Rome. Don't look so innocent, my dear—you know he is. And I was wondering, ever so respectfully, you understand . . . wondering how two such exemplary characters as you and Horace had managed to produce anything quite so dynamic." Mrs. Slade laughed again, with a touch of asperity.

Mrs. Ansley's hands lay inert across her needles. She looked straight out at the great accumulated wreckage of passion and splendour at her feet. But her small profile was almost expressionless. At length she said: "I think you overrate Babs, my dear."

Mrs. Slade's tone grew easier. "No; I don't. I appreciate her. And perhaps envy you. Oh, my girl's perfect; if I were a chronic invalid I'd—well, I think I'd rather be in Jenny's hands. There must be times . . . but there! I always wanted a brilliant daughter . . . and never quite understood why I got an angel instead."

Mrs. Ansley echoed her laugh in a faint murmur. "Babs is an angel too."

"Of course—of course! But she's got rainbow wings. Well, they're wandering by the sea with their young men; and here we sit . . . and it all brings back the past a little too acutely."

Mrs. Ansley had resumed her knitting. One might almost have imagined (if one had known her less well, Mrs. Slade reflected) that, for her also, too many memories rose from the lengthening shadows of those august ruins. But no; she was simply absorbed in her work. What was there for her to worry about? She knew that Babs would almost certainly come back engaged to the extremely eligible Campolieri. "And she'll sell the New York house, and settle down near them in Rome, and never be in their way . . . she's much too tactful. But she'll have an excellent cook, and just the right people in for bridge and cocktails . . . and a perfectly peaceful old age among her grandchildren."

Mrs. Slade broke off this prophetic flight with a recoil of self-disgust. There was one of whom she had less right to think unkindly than of Grace Ansley. Would she ever cure herself of envying her? Perhaps she had begun too long ago.

She stood up and leaned against the parapet, filling her troubled eyes with the tranquillizing magic of the hour. But instead of tranquillizing her the sight seemed to increase her exasperation. Her gaze turned toward the Colosseum. Already its golden flank was drowned in purple shadow, and above it the sky curved crystal clear, without light or colour. It was the moment when afternoon and evening hang balanced in mid-heaven.

Mrs. Slade turned back and laid her hand on her friend's arm. The gesture was so abrupt that Mrs. Ansley looked up, startled.

"The sun's set. You're not afraid, my dear?"

"Afraid—"

"Of Roman fever or pneumonia? I remember how ill you were that winter. As a girl you had a very delicate throat, hadn't you?"

"Oh, we're all right up here. Down below, in the Forum, it does get deathly cold, all of a sudden . . . but not here."

"Ah, of course you know because you had to be so careful." Mrs. Slade turned back to the parapet. She thought: "I must make one more effort not to hate her." Aloud she said: "Whenever I look at the Forum from up here, I remember that story about a great-aunt of yours, wasn't she? A dreadfully wicked great-aunt?"

"Oh, yes; Great-aunt Harriet. The one who was supposed to have sent her young sister out to the Forum after sunset to gather a night-blooming flower for her album. All our great-aunts and grand-mothers used to have albums of dried flowers."

Mrs. Slade nodded. "But she really sent her because they were in love with the same man—"

"Well, that was the family tradition. They said Aunt Harriet confessed it years afterward. At any rate, the poor little sister caught the fever and died. Mother used to frighten us with the story when we were children."

"And you frightened *me* with it, that winter when you and I were here as girls. The winter I was engaged to Delphin."

Mrs. Ansley gave a faint laugh. "Oh, did I? Really frightened you? I don't believe you're easily frightened."

"Not often; but I was then. I was easily frightened because I was too happy. I wonder if you know what that means?"

"I—yes . . ." Mrs. Ansley faltered.

"Well, I suppose that was why the story of your wicked aunt made such an impression on me. And I thought: 'There's no more Roman fever, but the Forum is deathly cold after sunset—especially after a hot day. And the Colosseum's even colder and damper.' "

"The Colosseum—?"

"Yes. It wasn't easy to get in, after the gates were locked for the night. Far from easy. Still, in those days it could be managed; it *was* managed, often. Lovers met there who couldn't meet elsewhere. You knew that?"

"I—I daresay. I don't remember."

"You don't remember? You don't remember going to visit some ruins or other one evening, just after dark, and catching a bad chill? You were supposed to have gone to see the moon rise. People always said that expedition was what caused your illness."

There was a moment's silence; then Mrs. Ansley rejoined: "Did they? It was all so long ago."

"Yes. And you got well again—so it didn't matter. But I suppose it struck your friends—the reason given for your illness, I mean—because everybody knew you were so prudent on account of your throat, and your mother took such care of you . . . You *had* been out late sight-seeing, hadn't you, that night?"

"Perhaps I had. The most prudent girls aren't always prudent. What made you think of it now?"

Mrs. Slade seemed to have no answer ready. But after a moment she broke out: "Because I simply can't bear it any longer—!"

Mrs. Ansley lifted her head quickly. Her eyes were wide and very pale. "Can't bear what?"

"Why—your not knowing that I've always known why you went."

"Why I went—?"

"Yes. You think I'm bluffing, don't you? Well, you went to meet the man I was engaged to—and I can repeat every word of the letter that took you there."

While Mrs. Slade spoke Mrs. Ansley had risen unsteadily to her feet. Her bag, her knitting and gloves, slid in a panic-stricken heap to the ground. She looked at Mrs. Slade as though she were looking at a ghost.

"No, no—don't," she faltered out.

"Why not? Listen, if you don't believe me. 'My one darling, things can't go on like this. I must see you alone. Come to the Colosseum immediately after dark tomorrow. There will be somebody to let you in. No one whom you need fear will suspect'—but perhaps you've forgotten what the letter said?"

Mrs. Ansley met the challenge with an unexpected composure. Steadying herself against the chair she looked at her friend, and replied: "No; I know it by heart too."

"And the signature? 'Only *your* D.S.' Was that it? I'm right, am I? That was the letter that took you out that evening after dark?"

Mrs. Ansley was still looking at her. It seemed to Mrs. Slade that a slow struggle was going on behind the voluntarily controlled mask of her small quiet face. "I shouldn't have thought she had herself so well in hand," Mrs. Slade reflected, almost resentfully. But at this moment Mrs. Ansley spoke. "I don't know how you knew. I burnt that letter at once."

"Yes; you would, naturally—you're so prudent!" The sneer was open now. "And if you burnt the letter you're wondering how on earth I know what was in it. That's it, isn't it?"

Mrs. Slade waited, but Mrs. Ansley did not speak.

"Well, my dear, I know what was in that letter because I wrote it!"

"You wrote it?"

"Yes."

The two women stood for a minute staring at each other in the last golden light. Then Mrs. Ansley dropped back into her chair. "Oh," she murmured, and covered her face with her hands.

Mrs. Slade waited nervously for another word or movement. None came, and at length she broke out: "I horrify you."

Mrs. Ansley's hands dropped to her knee. The face they uncovered was streaked with tears. "I wasn't thinking of you. I was thinking—it was the only letter I ever had from him!"

"And I wrote it. Yes; I wrote it! But I was the girl he was engaged to. Did you happen to remember that?"

Mrs. Ansley's head drooped again. "I'm not trying to excuse myself . . . I remembered . . ."

"And still you went?"

"Still I went."

Mrs. Slade stood looking down on the small bowed figure at her side. The flame of her wrath had already sunk, and she wondered why she had ever thought there would be any satisfaction in inflicting so purposeless a wound on her friend. But she had to justify herself.

"You do understand? I'd found out—and I hated you, hated you. I knew you were in love with Delphin—and I was afraid; afraid of you, of your quiet ways, your sweetness . . . your . . . well, I wanted you out of the way, that's all. Just for a few weeks; just till I was sure of him. So in a blind fury I wrote that letter . . . I don't know why I'm telling you now."

"I suppose," said Mrs. Ansley slowly, "it's because you've always gone on hating me."

"Perhaps. Or because I wanted to get the whole thing off my mind." She paused. "I'm glad you destroyed the letter. Of course I never thought you'd die."

Mrs. Ansley relapsed into silence, and Mrs. Slade, leaning above her, was conscious of a strange sense of isolation, of being cut off from the warm current of human communion. "You think me a monster!"

"I don't know . . . It was the only letter I had, and you say he didn't write it?"

"Ah, how you care for him still!"

"I cared for that memory," said Mrs. Ansley.

Mrs. Slade continued to look down on her. She seemed physically reduced by the blow—as if, when she got up, the wind might scatter her like a puff of dust. Mrs. Slade's jealousy suddenly leapt up again at the sight. All these years the woman had been living on that letter. How she must have loved him, to treasure the mere memory of its ashes! The letter of the man her friend was engaged to. Wasn't it she who was the monster?

"You tried your best to get him away from me, didn't you? But you failed; and I kept him. That's all."

"Yes. That's all."

"I wish now I hadn't told you. I'd no idea you'd feel about it as you do; I thought you'd be amused. It all happened so long ago, as you say; and you must do me the justice to remember that I had no reason to think you'd ever taken it seriously. How could I, when you were married to Horace Ansley two months afterward? As soon as you could get out of bed your mother rushed you off to Florence and married you. People were rather surprised—they wondered at its being done so quickly; but I thought I knew. I had an idea you did it out of *pique*—to be able to say you'd got ahead of Delphin and me. Girls have such silly reasons for doing the most serious things. And your marrying so soon convinced me that you'd never really cared."

"Yes. I suppose it would," Mrs. Ansley assented.

The clear heaven overhead was emptied of all its gold. Dusk spread over it, abruptly darkening the Seven Hills. Here and there lights began to twinkle through the foliage at their feet. Steps were coming and going on the deserted terrace—waiters looking out of the doorway at the head of the stairs, then reappearing with trays and napkins and flasks of wine. Tables were moved, chairs straightened. A feeble string of electric lights flickered out. Some vases of faded flowers were carried away, and brought back replenished. A stout lady in a dust-coat suddenly appeared, asking in broken Italian if any one had seen the elastic band which held together her tattered Baedeker. She poked with her stick under the table at which she had lunched, the waiters assisting.

The corner where Mrs. Slade and Mrs. Ansley sat was still shadowy and deserted. For a long time neither of them spoke. At length Mrs. Slade began again: "I suppose I did it as a sort of joke—"

"A joke?"

"Well, girls are ferocious sometimes, you know. Girls in love especially. And I remember laughing to myself all that evening at the idea that you were waiting around there in the dark, dodging out of sight, listening for every sound, trying to get in—. Of course I was upset when I heard you were so ill afterward."

Mrs. Ansley had not moved for a long time. But now she turned slowly toward her companion. "But I didn't wait. He'd arranged everything. He was there. We were let in at once," she said.

Mrs. Slade sprang up from her leaning position. "Delphin there? They let you in?—Ah, now you're lying!" She burst out with violence.

Mrs. Ansley's voice grew clearer, and full of surprise. "But of course he was there. Naturally he came—"

"Came? How did he know he'd find you there? You must be raving!"

Mrs. Ansley hesitated, as though reflecting. "But I answered the letter. I told him I'd be there. So he came."

Mrs. Slade flung her hands up to her face. "Oh, God—you answered! I never thought of your answering . . ."

"It's odd you never thought of it, if you wrote the letter."

"Yes. I was blind with rage."

Mrs. Ansley rose, and drew her fur scarf about her. "It is cold here. We'd better go . . . I'm sorry for you," she said, as she clasped the fur about her throat.

The unexpected words sent a pang through Mrs. Slade. "Yes; we'd better go." She gathered up her bag and cloak. "I don't know why you should be sorry for me," she muttered.

Mrs. Ansley stood looking away from her toward the dusky secret mass of the Colosseum. "Well—because I didn't have to wait that night."

Mrs. Slade gave an unquiet laugh. "Yes; I was beaten there. But I oughtn't to begrudge it to you, I suppose. At the end of all these years. After all, I had everything; I had him for twenty-five years. And you had nothing but that one letter that he didn't write."

Mrs. Ansley was again silent. At length she turned toward the door of the terrace. She took a step, and turned back, facing her companion.

"I had Barbara," she said, and began to move ahead of Mrs. Slade toward the stairway.

DUNCAN CAMPBELL SCOTT

(1862–1947)

*D*uncan Campbell Scott was born and raised in Ottawa. He worked in the civil service, first as a clerk in what was then called the Indian Branch, eventually rising to become the deputy superintendent of the Department of Indian Affairs. He was elected to the Royal Society of Canada in 1899 and became its president in 1921. As a poet, Scott is best known for a number of lyrics and longer narrative poems that depict the difficulties Indians endured during the period of transition from their aboriginal way of life to an accommodation with European-Christian civilization. As one of his Department's formulators of policy and as a major treaty negotiator, Scott's first-hand exposure to the Indians' way of life helped him to portray his subjects with a knowledge and sympathy unusual for the time. Nonetheless, his depiction of the problems faced by Indians remains, of necessity, that of the outsider, of an administrator who was responsible for putting into place the policies that were largely the cause of the dilemma. Scott's short stories, the best of which comprise the story cycle In the Village of Viger (1896), from which "The Little Milliner" is taken, often deal with wilderness themes and, as in Viger, small-town Quebec life at the turn of the century. Like many of the half-breed subjects who populate the poems, the village of Viger is also in a period of transition, and "The Little Milliner" illustrates one moment of contact between the small community and the neighbouring city that is reaching out to subsume it. The stories of Viger are based on Scott's boyhood experiences travelling with his minister father throughout the small towns of western Quebec. Scott's books of poetry include The Magic House and Other Poems (1893), Labor and the Angel (1898), New World Lyrics and Ballads (1905), Via Borealis (1906), Lundy's Lane and Other Poems (1916), Beauty and Life (1921), The Poems of Duncan Campbell Scott (1926), The Green Cloister and Other Poems (1935), and The Circle of Affection, and Other Pieces in Prose and Verse (1947). As well as in Viger, his stories are collected in The Witching of Elspie (1923) and Selected Stories of Duncan Campbell Scott (1972). Scott also wrote biographies, a play, essays, and an untitled novel published in 1979, and he was the chief author of The Administration of Indian Affairs in Canada (1931).

The Little Milliner

I t was too true that the city was growing rapidly. As yet its arms were not long enough to embrace the little village of Viger, but before long they would be, and it was not a time that the inhabitants looked forward to with any pleasure. It was not to be wondered at, for few places were more pleasant to live in. The houses, half-hidden amid the trees, clustered around the slim steeple of St. Joseph's, which flashed like a naked poniard in the sun. They were old, and the village was sleepy, almost dozing, since the mill, behind the rise of land, on the Blanche had shut down. The miller had died; and who would trouble to grind what little grist came to the mill, when flour was so cheap? But while the beech-groves lasted, and the Blanche continued to run, it seemed impossible that any change could come. The change was coming, however, rapidly enough. Even now, on still nights, above the noise of the frogs in the pools, you could hear the rumble of the street-cars and the faint tinkle of their bells, and when the air was moist the whole southern sky was luminous with the reflection of thousands of gas-lamps. But when the time came for Viger to be mentioned in the city papers as one of the outlying wards, what a change there would be! There would be no unfenced fields, full of little inequalities and covered with short grass; there would be no deep pools, where the quarries had been, and where the boys pelted the frogs; there would be no more beech-groves, where the children could gather nuts; and the dread pool, which had filled the shaft where old Daigneau, years ago, mined for gold, would cease to exist. But in the meantime, the boys of Viger roamed over the unclosed fields and pelted the frogs, and the boldest ventured to roll huge stones into Daigneau's pit, and only waited to see the green slime come working up to the surface before scampering away, their flesh creeping with the idea that it was old Daigneau himself who was stirring up the water in a rage.

New houses had already commenced to spring up in all directions, and there was a large influx of the labouring population which overflows from large cities. Even on the main street of Viger, on a lot which had been vacant ever since it was a lot, the workmen had built a foundation. After a while it was finished, when men from the city came and put up the oddest wooden house that one could imagine. It was perfectly square; there was a window and a door in front, a window at the side, and a window upstairs. There were many surmises as to the probable occupant of such a diminutive habitation; and the widow Laroque, who made dresses and trimmed hats, and whose shop was directly opposite, and next door to the Post Office, suffered greatly from unsatisfied curiosity. No one who looked like the proprietor was ever seen near the place. The foreman of the labourers who were working at the house seemed to know nothing; all that he said, in answer to questions, was: "I have my orders."

At last the house was ready; it was painted within and without, and Madame Laroque could scarcely believe her eyes when, one morning, a man came from the city with a small sign under his arm and nailed it above the door. It bore these words: "Mademoiselle Viau, Milliner." "Ah!" said Madame Laroque, "the bread is to be taken out of my mouth." The next day came a load of furniture—not a very large load, as there was only a small stove, two tables, a bedstead, three chairs, a sort of lounge, and two large boxes. The man who brought the things put them in the house, and locked the door on them when he went away; then nothing happened for two weeks, but Madame Laroque watched. Such a queer little house it was, as it stood there so new in its coat of gum-coloured paint. It looked just like a square bandbox which some Titan had made for his wife; and there seemed no doubt that if you took hold of the chimney and lifted the roof off, you would see the gigantic bonnet, with its strings and ribbons, which the Titaness could wear to church on Sundays.

Madame Laroque wondered how Mademoiselle Viau would come, whether in a cab, with her trunks and boxes piled around her, or on foot, and have her belongings on a cart. She watched every approaching vehicle for two weeks in vain; but one morning she saw that a curtain had been put up on the window opposite, that it was partly raised, and that a geranium was standing on the sill. For one hour she never took her eyes off the door, and at last had the satisfaction of seeing it open. A trim little person, not very young, dressed in grey, stepped out on the platform with her apron full of crumbs and cast them down for the birds. Then, without looking around, she went in and closed the door. It was Mademoiselle Viau. "The bird is in its nest," thought the old postmaster, who lived alone with his mother. All that Madame Laroque said was: "Ah!"

Mademoiselle Viau did not stir out that day, but on the next day she went to the baker's and the butcher's, and came over the road to Monsieur Cuerrier, the postmaster, who also kept a grocery.

That evening, according to her custom, Madame Laroque called on Madame Cuerrier.

"We have a neighbour," she said.

"Yes."

"She was making purchases today."

"Yes."

"Tomorrow she will expect people to make purchases."

"Without doubt."

"It is very tormenting, this, to have these irresponsible girls, that no one knows anything about, setting up shops under our very noses. Why does she live alone?"

"I did not ask her," answered Cuerrier, to whom the question was addressed.

"You are very cool, Monsieur Cuerrier; but if it was a young man and a postmaster, instead of a young woman and a milliner, you would not relish it."

"There can be only one postmaster," said Cuerrier.

"In Paris, where I practised my art," said Monsieur Villeblanc, who was a retired hairdresser, "there were whole rows of tonsorial parlours, and everyone had enough to do." Madame Laroque sniffed, as she always did in his presence.

"Did you see her hat?" she asked.

"I did, and it was very nice."

"Nice! with the flowers all on one side? I wouldn't go to St. Thérèse with it on." St. Thérèse was the postmaster's native place.

"The girl has no taste," she continued.

"Well, if she hasn't, you needn't be afraid of her."

"There will be no choice between you," said the retired hairdresser, maliciously.

But there was a choice between them, and all the young girls of Viger chose Mademoiselle Viau. It was said she had such an eye; she would take a hat and pin a bow on here, and loop a ribbon there, and cast a flower on somewhere else, all the time surveying her work with her head on one side and her mouth bristling with pins. "There, how do you like that?—put it on—no, it is not becoming—wait!" and in a trice the desired change was made. She had no lack of work from the first; soon she had too much to do. At all hours of the day she could be seen sitting at her window, working, and "she must be making money fast," argued Madame Laroque, "for she spends nothing." In truth, she spent very little—she lived so plainly. Three times a week she took a fresh twist from the baker, once a day the milkman left a pint of milk, and once every week mademoiselle herself stepped out to the butcher's and bought a pound of steak. Occasionally she mailed a letter, which she always gave into the hands of the postmaster; if he was not there she asked for a pound of tea or something else that she needed. She was fast friends with Cuerrier, but with no one else, as she never received visitors. Once only did a young man call on her. It was young Jourdain, the clerk in the dry-goods store. He had knocked at the door and was admitted. "Ah!" said Madame Laroque, "it is the young men who can conquer." But the next moment Monsieur Jourdain came out, and, strangely enough, was so bewildered as to forget to put on his hat. It was not this young man who could conquer.

"There is something mysterious about that young person," said Madame Laroque between her teeth.

"Yes," replied Cuerrier, "very mysterious—she minds her own business."

"Bah!" said the widow, "who can tell what her business is, she who comes from no one knows where? But I'll find out what all this secrecy means, trust me!"

So the widow watched the little house and its occupant very closely, and these are some of the things she saw: every morning an open door and crumbs for the birds, the watering of the geranium, which was just going to flower, a small figure going in and out, dressed in grey, and, oftener than anything else, the same figure sitting at the window, working. This continued for a year with little variation, but still the widow watched. Everyone else had accepted the presence of the new resident as a benefaction. They had got accustomed to her. They called her "the little milliner." Old Cuerrier called her "the little one in grey." But she was not yet adjusted in the widow's system of things. She laid a plot with her second cousin, which was that the cousin should get a hat made by Mademoiselle Viau, and that she should ask her some questions.

"Mademoiselle Viau, were you born in the city?"

"I do not think, Mademoiselle, that green will become you."

"No, perhaps not. Where did you live before you came here?"

"Mademoiselle, this grey shape is very pretty." And so on.

That plan would not work.

But before long something very suspicious happened. One evening, just about dusk, as Madame Laroque was walking up and down in front of her door, a man of a youthful appearance came quickly up the street, stepped upon Mademoiselle Viau's platform, opened the door without knocking, and walked in. Mademoiselle was working in the last vestige of daylight, and the widow watched her like a lynx. She worked on unconcernedly, and when it became so dark that she could not see she lit her lamp and pulled down the curtain. That night Madame Laroque did not go into Cuerrier's. It commenced to rain, but she put on a large frieze coat of the deceased Laroque and crouched in the dark. She was very much interested in this case, but her interest brought no additional knowledge. She had seen the man go in; he was rather young and about the medium height, and had a black moustache; she could remember him distinctly, but she did not see him come out.

The next morning Mademoiselle Viau's curtain went up as usual, and as it was her day to go to the butcher's she went out. While she was away Madame Laroque took a long look in at the side window, but there was nothing to see except the lounge and the table.

While Madame Laroque had been watching in the rain, Cuerrier was reading to Villeblanc from *Le Monde*. "Hello!" said he, and then went on reading to himself.

"Have you lost your voice?" asked Villeblanc, getting nettled.

"No, no; listen to this—'Daring Jewel Robbery. A Thief in the Night.' " These were the headings of the column, and then followed the particulars. In the morning the widow borrowed the paper, as she had been too busy the night before to come and hear it read. She looked over the front page, when her eye caught the heading, "Daring Jewel Robbery," and she read the whole story. As she neared the end her eyebrows commenced to travel up her forehead, as if they were going to hide in her hair, and with an expression of surprise she tossed the paper to her second cousin.

"Look here!" she said, "read this out to me."

The second cousin commenced to read at the top.

"No, no! right here."

" 'The man Durocher, who is suspected of the crime, is not tall, wears a heavy moustache, has grey eyes, and wears an ear-ring in his left ear. He has not been seen since Saturday.' "

"I told you so!" exclaimed the widow.

"You told me nothing of the kind," said the second cousin.

"He had no ear-ring in his ear," said the widow—"but—but—but it was the *right* ear that I saw. Hand me my shawl!"

"Where are you going?"

"I have business; never mind!" She took the paper with her and went straight to the constable.

"But," said he, "I cannot come."

"There is no time to be lost; you must come now."

"But he will be desperate; he will face me like a lion."

"Never mind! you will have the reward."

"Well, wait!" And the constable went upstairs to get his pistol.

He came down with his blue coat on. He was a very fat man, and was out of breath when he came to the little milliner's.

"But who shall I ask for?" he inquired of Madame Laroque.

"Just search the house, and I will see that he does not escape by the back door." She had forgotten that there was no back door.

"Do you want a bonnet?" asked Mademoiselle Viau. She was on excellent terms with the constable.

"No!" said he, sternly. "You have a man in this house, and I have come to find him."

"Indeed?" said mademoiselle, very stiffly. "Will you be pleased to proceed?"

"Yes," said he, taking out his pistol and cocking it. "I will first look downstairs." He did so, and only frightened a cat from under the stove. No one knew that Mademoiselle Viau had a cat.

"Lead the way upstairs!" commanded the constable.

"I am afraid of your pistol, will you not go first?"

He went first and entered at once the only room, for there was no hall. In the meantime Madame Laroque had found out that there was no back door, and had come into the lower flat and reinspected it, looking under everything.

"Open that closet!" said the constable, as he levelled his pistol at the door.

Mademoiselle threw open the door and sprang away, with her hands over her ears. There was no one there; neither was there anyone under the bed.

"Open that trunk!" eyeing the little leather-covered box.

"Monsieur, you will respect—but—as you will." She stooped over the trunk and threw back the lid; on the top was a dainty white skirt, embroidered beautifully. The little milliner was blushing violently.

"That will do!" said the constable. "There is no one there."

"Get out of the road!" he cried to the knot of people who had collected at the door. "I have been for my wife's bonnet; it is not finished." But the people looked at his pistol, which he had forgotten to put away. He went across to the widow's.

"Look here!" he said, "you had better stop this or I'll have the law on you—no words now! Making a fool of me before the people—getting me to put on my coat and bring my pistol to frighten a cat from under the stove. No words now!"

"Monsieur Cuerrier," inquired Madame Laroque that night, "who is it that Mademoiselle Viau writes to?"

"I am an official of the government. I do not tell state secrets."

"State secrets, indeed! Depend upon it, there are secrets in those letters which the state would like to know."

"That is not my business. I only send the letters where they are posted, and refuse to tell amiable widows where they go."

The hairdresser, forgetting his constant fear of disarranging his attire, threw back his head and laughed wildly.

"Trust a barber to laugh," said the widow. Villeblanc sobered up and looked sadly at Cuerrier; he could not bear to be called a barber.

"And you uphold her in this—a person who comes from no one knows where, and writes to no one knows whom—"

"I know whom she writes to—" The widow got furious.

"Yes, whom she writes to—yes, of course you do—that person who comes out of her house without ever having gone into it, and who is visited by men who go in and never come out—"

"How do you know he went in?"

"I saw him."

"How do you know he never came out?"

"I didn't see him."

"Ah! then you were watching?"

"Well, what if I was! The devil has a hand in it."

"I have no doubt," said Cuerrier, insinuatingly.

"Enough, fool!" exclaimed the widow—"but wait, I have not done yet!"

"You had better rest, or you will have the law on you."

The widow was afraid of the law.

About six months after this, when the snow was coming on, a messenger came from the city with a telegram for Monsieur Cuerrier—at least, it was in his care. He very seldom went out, but he got his boots and went across to Mademoiselle Viau's. The telegram was for her. When she had read it she crushed it in her hand and leaned against the wall. But she recovered herself.

"Monsieur Cuerrier, you have always been a good friend to me— help me! I must go away—you will watch my little place when I am gone!"

The postmaster was struck with pity, and he assisted her. She left that night.

"*Accomplice!*" the widow hissed in his ear the first chance she got.

About three weeks after this, when Madame Laroque asked for *Le Monde*, Cuerrier refused to give it to her.

"Where is it?"

"It has been lost."

"*Lost!*" said the widow, derisively. "Well, I will find it." In an hour she came back with the paper.

"There!" said she, thrusting it under the postmaster's nose so that he could not get his pipe back to his mouth. Cuerrier looked consciously at the paragraph which she had pointed out. He had seen it before.

"Our readers will remember that the police, while attempting to arrest one Ellwell for the jewel-robbery which occurred in the city some time ago, were compelled to fire on the man in self-defence. He died last night in the arms of a female relative, who had been sent for at his request. He was known by various names—Durocher, Gillet, etc.—and the police have had much trouble with him."

"There!" said the widow.

"Well, what of that?"

"He died in the arms of a female relative."

"Well, were you the relative?"

"Indeed! my fine fellow, be careful! Do you think I would be the female relative of a convict? Do you not know any of these names?" The postmaster felt guilty; he did know one of the names.

"They are common enough," he replied. "The name of my aunt's second husband was Durocher."

"It will not do!" said the widow. "Somebody builds a house, no one knows who; people come and go, no one knows how; and you, a stupid postmaster, shut your eyes and help things along."

Three days after this, Mademoiselle Viau came home. She was no longer the little one in grey; she was the little one in black. She came straight to Monsieur Cuerrier to get her cat. Then she went home. The widow watched her go in. "Now," she said, "we will not see her come out again."

Mademoiselle Viau refused to take any more work. She was sick, she said; she wanted to rest. She rested for two weeks, and Monsieur Cuerrier brought her food ready cooked. Then he stopped; she was better. One evening Madame Laroque peeped in at the side window. She saw the little milliner quite distinctly. She was on her knees, her face was hidden in her arms. The fire was very bright, and the lamp was lighted.

Two days after that the widow said to Cuerrier: "It is very strange there is no smoke. Has Mademoiselle Viau gone away?"

"Yes, she has gone."

"Did you see her go?"

"No."

"It is as I said—no one has seen her go. But wait, she will come back; and no one will see her come."

That was three years ago, and she has not come back. All the white curtains are pulled down. Between the one that covers the front window and the sash stands the pot in which grew the geranium. It only had one blossom all the time it was alive, and it is dead now and looks like a dry stick. No one knows what will become of the house. Madame Laroque thinks that Monsieur Cuerrier knows. She expects, some morning, to look across and see the little milliner cast down crumbs for the birds. In the meantime, in every corner of the house the spiders are weaving webs, and an enterprising caterpillar has blocked up the key-hole with his cocoon.

STEPHEN LEACOCK

(1869–1944)

S *tephen Leacock was born in Swanmore, Hampshire, England, and
came with his family to Canada as a child to live on a farm in the
Lake Simcoe district of Ontario. He was educated at the private school
Upper Canada College (where he also taught from 1889 to 1899), the
University of Toronto, and the University of Chicago, where he received
a Ph.D. in political economy in 1903. He had a long and distinguished
career as Professor of Economics and Political Science at McGill University, eventually assuming the chairmanship of the department. Throughout his career, Leacock divided his time between academic years in
Montreal and summers at the lavish home he built on the shores of Lake
Couchiching near Orillia, Ontario. He was able to do so because his
writings made him comparatively wealthy; in fact, for the period roughly
from 1915 to 1925, he was the English-speaking world's best-selling
humorist, achieving a fame that has been enjoyed only by such other
Canadian writers as Thomas Chandler Haliburton, Bliss Carman, and
Margaret Atwood. In total he published some 80 books and pamphlets
on as wide a range of subjects as can be imagined: economics, history,
the British Empire, political science, biography, teaching, humour, writing, and so forth. And though in recent years he has come to be better
appreciated for his contributions to these fields, it is as a writer of
humorous fiction that Leacock will be remembered. His first, and still
one of his most inspired, collections of humour was* Literary Lapses
(1910). He followed this with Nonsense Novels *(1911), a book of
parodies,* Sunshine Sketches of a Little Town *(1912), from which
"The Hostelry of Mr. Smith" is taken,* Behind the Beyond *(1913),*
Arcadian Adventures with the Idle Rich *(1914), and so on, averaging
about a book of humour a year—some of it tired and forced, but a
remarkable proportion still as fresh in its verbal play and nonsense as
any written anywhere at any time. Of all his fiction, however, it is*
Sunshine Sketches *and* Arcadian Adventures *that guarantee Leacock
literary immortality; these two form a coherent whole and, taken together,
constitute companion volumes. The* Sketches *takes a long ironic and
affectionate look at small-town Canada at the turn of the century; The*
Adventures *brings Leacock's gently satiric, though no less satiric for
being gentle, vision to bear on a big American city at about the same
time. Whatever the subject of his humour, Leacock can always be seen to
be subtly and ironically expressing the values that are associated with
the words "humanist" and "tory," chief among which, for Leacock, is
the charm of an interdependent community, as the following introduction
to the* Sketches' *Mariposa suggests.*

The Hostelry of Mr. Smith

I don't know whether you know Mariposa. If not, it is of no consequence, for if you know Canada at all, you are probably well
acquainted with a dozen towns just like it.

There it lies in the sunlight, sloping up from the little lake that spreads
out at the foot of the hillside on which the town is built. There is a wharf
beside the lake, and lying alongside of it a steamer that is tied to the
wharf with two ropes of about the same size as they use on the Lusitania.
The steamer goes nowhere in particular, for the lake is land-locked and
there is no navigation for the Mariposa Belle except to "run trips" on the
first of July and the Queen's Birthday, and to take excursions of the
Knights of Pythias and the Sons of Temperance to and from the Local
Option Townships.

In point of geography the lake is called Lake Wissanotti and the river
running out of it the Ossawippi, just as the main street of Mariposa is
called Missinaba Street and the county Missinaba County. But these
names do not really matter. Nobody uses them. People simply speak of
the "lake" and the "river" and the "main street," much in the same way
as they always call the Continental Hotel, "Pete Robinson's" and the
Pharmaceutical Hall, "Eliot's Drug Store." But I suppose this is just the
same in every one else's town as in mine, so I need lay no stress on it.

The town, I say, has one broad street that runs up from the lake,
commonly called the Main Street. There is no doubt about its width.
When Mariposa was laid out there was none of that shortsightedness
which is seen in the cramped dimensions of Wall Street and Piccadilly.
Missinaba Street is so wide that if you were to roll Jeff Thorpe's barber
shop over on its face it wouldn't reach half way across. Up and down the
Main Street are telegraph poles of cedar of colossal thickness, standing at
a variety of angles and carrying rather more wires than are commonly
seen at a transatlantic cable station.

On the Main Street itself are a number of buildings of extraordinary
importance,—Smith's Hotel and the Continental and the Mariposa House,
and the two banks (the Commercial and the Exchange), to say nothing
of McCarthy's Block (erected in 1878), and Glover's Hardware Store with
the Oddfellows' Hall above it. Then on the "cross" street that intersects
Missinaba Street at the main corner there is the Post Office and the Fire
Hall and the Young Men's Christian Association and the office of the
Mariposa Newspacket,—in fact, to the eye of discernment a perfect jostle
of public institutions comparable only to Threadneedle Street or Lower
Broadway. On all the side streets there are maple trees and broad sidewalks, trim gardens with upright calla lilies, houses with verandahs,
which are here and there being replaced by residences with piazzas.

To the careless eye the scene on the Main Street of a summer afternoon is one of deep and unbroken peace. The empty street sleeps in the sunshine. There is a horse and buggy tied to the hitching post in front of Glover's hardware store. There is, usually and commonly, the burly figure of Mr. Smith, proprietor of Smith's Hotel, standing in his chequered waistcoat on the steps of his hostelry, and perhaps, further up the street, Lawyer Macartney going for his afternoon mail, or the Rev. Mr. Drone, the Rural Dean of the Church of England Church, going home to get his fishing rod after a mothers' auxiliary meeting.

But this quiet is mere appearance. In reality, and to those who know it, the place is a perfect hive of activity. Why, at Netley's butcher shop (established in 1882) there are no less than four men working on the sausage machines in the basement; at the Newspacket office there are as many more job-printing; there is a long distance telephone with four distracting girls on high stools wearing steel caps and talking incessantly; in the offices in McCarthy's block are dentists and lawyers with their coats off, ready to work at any moment; and from the big planing factory down beside the lake where the railroad siding is, you may hear all through the hours of the summer afternoon the long-drawn music of the running saw.

Busy—well, I should think so! Ask any of its inhabitants if Mariposa isn't a busy, hustling, thriving town. Ask Mullins, the manager of the Exchange Bank, who comes hustling over to his office from the Mariposa House every day at 10.30 and has scarcely time all morning to go out and take a drink with the manager of the Commercial; or ask—well, for the matter of that, ask any of them if they ever knew a more rushing go-a-head town than Mariposa.

Of course if you come to the place fresh from New York, you are deceived. Your standard of vision is all astray. You do think the place is quiet. You do imagine that Mr. Smith is asleep merely because he closes his eyes as he stands. But live in Mariposa for six months or a year and then you will begin to understand it better; the buildings get higher and higher; the Mariposa House grows more and more luxurious; McCarthy's block towers to the sky; the 'buses roar and hum to the station; the trains shriek; the traffic multiplies; the people move faster and faster; a dense crowd swirls to and fro in the post-office and the five and ten cent store— and amusements! well, now! lacrosse, baseball, excursions, dances, the Fireman's Ball every winter and the Catholic picnic every summer; and music—the town band in the park every Wednesday evening, and the Oddfellows' brass band on the street every other Friday; the Mariposa Quartette, the Salvation Army—why, after a few months' residence you begin to realize that the place is a mere mad round of gaiety.

In point of population, if one must come down to figures, the Canadian census puts the numbers every time at something round five thousand. But it is very generally understood in Mariposa that the census is largely the outcome of malicious jealousy. It is usual that after the census the editor of the Mariposa Newspacket makes a careful re-estimate (based on the data of relative non-payment of subscriptions), and brings the population up to 6,000. After that the Mariposa Times-Herald makes an estimate that runs the figures up to 6,500. Then Mr. Gingham, the undertaker, who collects the vital statistics for the provincial government, makes an estimate from the number of what he calls the "demised" as compared with the less interesting persons who are still alive, and brings the population to 7,000. After that somebody else works it out that it's 7,500; then the man behind the bar of the Mariposa House offers to bet the whole room that there are 9,000 people in Mariposa. That settles it, and the population is well on the way to 10,000, when down swoops the federal census taker on his next round and the town has to begin all over again.

Still, it is a thriving town and there is no doubt of it. Even the transcontinental railways, as any townsman will tell you, run through Mariposa. It is true that the trains mostly go through at night and don't stop. But in the wakeful silence of the summer night you may hear the long whistle of the through train for the west as it tears through Mariposa, rattling over the switches and past the semaphores and ending in a long, sullen roar as it takes the trestle bridge over the Ossawippi. Or, better still, on a winter evening about eight o'clock you will see the long row of the Pullmans and diners of the night express going north to the mining country, the windows flashing with brilliant light, and within them a vista of cut glass and snow-white table linen, smiling negroes and millionaires with napkins at their chins whirling past in the driving snowstorm.

I can tell you the people of Mariposa are proud of the trains, even if they don't stop! The joy of being on the main line lifts the Mariposa people above the level of their neighbours in such places as Tecumseh and Nichols Corners into the cosmopolitan atmosphere of through traffic and the larger life. Of course, they have their own train, too—the Mariposa Local, made up right there in the station yard, and running south to the city a hundred miles away. That, of course, is a real train, with a box stove on end in the passenger car, fed with cordwood upside down, and with seventeen flat cars of pine lumber set between the passenger car and the locomotive so as to give the train its full impact when shunting.

Outside of Mariposa there are farms that begin well but get thinner and meaner as you go on, and end sooner or later in bush and swamp and the rock of the north country. And beyond that again, as the background of it all, though it's far away, you are somehow aware of the great pine woods of the lumber country reaching endlessly into the north.

Not that the little town is always gay or always bright in the sunshine. There never was such a place for changing its character with the season.

Dark enough and dull it seems of a winter night, the wooden sidewalks creaking with the frost, and the lights burning dim behind the shop windows. In olden times the lights were coal oil lamps; now, of course, they are, or are supposed to be, electricity,—brought from the power house on the lower Ossawippi nineteen miles away. But, somehow, though it starts off as electricity from the Ossawippi rapids, by the time it gets to Mariposa and filters into the little bulbs behind the frosty windows of the shops, it has turned into coal oil again, as yellow and bleared as ever.

After the winter, the snow melts and the ice goes out of the lake, the sun shines high and the shanty-men come down from the lumber woods and lie round drunk on the sidewalk outside of Smith's Hotel—and that's spring time. Mariposa is then a fierce, dangerous lumber town, calculated to terrorize the soul of a newcomer who does not understand that this also is only an appearance and that presently the rough-looking shanty-men will change their clothes and turn back again into farmers.

Then the sun shines warmer and the maple trees come out and Lawyer Macartney puts on his tennis trousers, and that's summer time. The little town changes to a sort of summer resort. There are visitors up from the city. Every one of the seven cottages along the lake is full. The Mariposa Belle churns the waters of the Wissanotti into foam as she sails out from the wharf, in a cloud of flags, the band playing and the daughters and sisters of the Knights of Pythias dancing gaily on the deck.

That changes too. The days shorten. The visitors disappear. The golden rod beside the meadow droops and withers on its stem. The maples blaze in glory and die. The evening close dark and chill, and in the gloom of the main corner of Mariposa the Salvation Army around a naphtha lamp lift up the confession of their sins—and that is autumn. Thus the year runs its round, moving and changing in Mariposa, much as it does in other places.

If, then, you feel that you know the town well enough to be admitted into the inner life and movement of it, walk down this June afternoon half way down the Main Street—or, if you like, half way up from the wharf—to where Mr. Smith is standing at the door of his hostelry. You will feel as you draw near that it is no ordinary man that you approach. It is not alone the huge bulk of Mr. Smith (two hundred and eighty pounds as tested on Netley's scales). It is not merely his costume, though the chequered waistcoat of dark blue with a flowered pattern forms, with his shepherd's plaid trousers, his grey spats and patent-leather boots, a colour scheme of no mean order. Nor is it merely Mr. Smith's finely mottled face. The face, no doubt, is a notable one,—solemn, inexpressible, unreadable, the face of the heaven-born hotel keeper. It is more than that. It is the strange dominating personality of the man that somehow holds you captive. I know nothing in history to compare with the position of Mr. Smith among those who drink over his bar, except, though in a lesser degree, the relation of the Emperor Napoleon to the Imperial Guard.

When you meet Mr. Smith first you think he looks like an over-dressed pirate. Then you begin to think him a character. You wonder at his enormous bulk. Then the utter hopelessness of knowing what Smith is thinking by merely looking at his features gets on your mind and makes the Mona Lisa seem an open book and the ordinary human countenance as superficial as a puddle in the sunlight. After you have had a drink in Mr. Smith's bar, and he has called you by your Christian name, you realize that you are dealing with one of the greatest minds in the hotel business.

Take, for instance, the big sign that sticks out into the street above Mr. Smith's head as he stands. What is on it? "JOS. SMITH, PROP." Nothing more, and yet the thing was a flash of genius. Other men who had had the hotel before Mr. Smith had called it by such feeble names as the Royal Hotel and the Queen's and the Alexandria. Every one of them failed. When Mr. Smith took over the hotel he simply put up the sign with "JOS. SMITH, PROP.," and then stood underneath in the sunshine as a living proof that a man who weighs nearly three hundred pounds is the natural king of the hotel business.

But on this particular afternoon, in spite of the sunshine and deep peace, there was something as near to profound concern and anxiety as the features of Mr. Smith were ever known to express.

The moment was indeed an anxious one. Mr. Smith was awaiting a telegram from his legal adviser who had that day journeyed to the county town to represent the proprietor's interest before the assembled License Commissioners. If you know anything of the hotel business at all, you will understand that as beside the decisions of the License Commissioners of Missinaba County, the opinions of the Lords of the Privy Council are mere trifles.

The matter in question was very grave. The Mariposa Court had just fined Mr. Smith for the second time for selling liquors after hours. The Commissioners, therefore, were entitled to cancel the license.

Mr. Smith knew his fault and acknowledged it. He had broken the law. How he had come to do so, it passed his imagination to recall. Crime always seems impossible in retrospect. By what sheer madness of the moment could he have shut up the bar on the night in question, and shut Judge Pepperleigh, the district judge in Missinaba County, outside of it? The more so inasmuch as the closing up of the bar under the rigid license law of the province was a matter that the proprietor never trusted to any hands but his own. Punctually every night at 11 o'clock Mr. Smith strolled from the desk of the "rotunda" to the door of the bar. If it seemed properly full of people and all was bright and cheerful, then he closed it. If not, he kept it open a few minutes longer till he had enough people inside to warrant closing. But never, never unless he was assured that Pepperleigh, the judge of the court, and Macartney, the prosecuting attorney, were both safely in the bar, or the bar parlour, did the proprietor venture to close up. Yet on this fatal night Pepperleigh and Macartney had been shut out—actually left on the street without a drink, and compelled to hammer and beat at the street door of the bar to gain admittance.

This was the kind of thing not to be tolerated. Either a hotel must be run decently or quit. An information was laid next day and Mr. Smith convicted in four minutes, his lawyers practically refusing to plead. The Mariposa court, when the presiding judge was cold sober, and it had the force of public opinion behind it, was a terrible engine of retributive justice.

So no wonder that Mr. Smith awaited with anxiety the message of his legal adviser.

He looked alternately up the street and down it again, hauled out his watch from the depths of his embroidered pocket, and examined the hour hand and the minute hand and the second hand with frowning scrutiny.

Then wearily, and as one mindful that a hotel man is ever the servant of the public, he turned back into the hotel.

"Billy," he said to the desk clerk, "if a wire comes bring it into the bar parlour."

The voice of Mr. Smith is of a deep guttural such as Plancon or Edouard de Reske might have obtained had they had the advantages of the hotel business. And with that, Mr. Smith, as was his custom in off moments, joined his guests in the back room. His appearance, to the untrained eye, was merely that of an extremely stout hotel-keeper walking from the rotunda to the back bar. In reality, Mr. Smith was on the eve of one of the most brilliant and daring strokes ever effected in the history of licensed liquor. When I say that it was out of the agitation of this situation that Smith's Ladies' and Gent's Café originated, anybody who knows Mariposa will understand the magnitude of the moment.

Mr. Smith, then, moved slowly from the doorway of the hotel through the "rotunda," or more simply the front room with the desk and the cigar case in it, and so to the bar and thence to the little room or back bar behind it. In this room, as I have said, the brightest minds of Mariposa might commonly be found in the quieter part of a summer afternoon.

To-day there was a group of four who looked up as Mr. Smith entered, somewhat sympathetically, and evidently aware of the perplexities of the moment.

Henry Mullins and George Duff, the two bank managers, were both present. Mullins is a rather short, rather round, smooth-shaven man of less than forty, wearing one of those round banking suits of pepper and salt, with a round banking hat of hard straw, and with the kind of gold tie-pin and heavy watch-chain and seals necessary to inspire confidence in matters of foreign exchange. Duff is just as round and just as short, and equally smoothly shaven, while his seals and straw hat are calculated to prove that the Commercial is just as sound a bank as the Exchange. From the technical point of view of the banking business, neither of them had any objection to being in Smith's Hotel or to taking a drink as long as the other was present. This, of course, was one of the cardinal principles of Mariposa banking.

Then there was Mr. Diston, the high school teacher, commonly known as the "one who drank." None of the other teachers ever entered a hotel unless accompanied by a lady or protected by a child. But as Mr. Diston was known to drink beer on occasions and to go in and out of the Mariposa House and Smith's Hotel, he was looked upon as a man whose life was a mere wreck. Whenever the School Board raised the salaries of the other teachers, fifty or sixty dollars per annum at one lift, it was well understood that public morality wouldn't permit of an increase for Mr. Diston.

Still more noticeable, perhaps, was the quiet, sallow looking man dressed in black, with black gloves and with black silk hat heavily craped and placed hollow-side-up on a chair. This was Mr. Golgotha Gingham, the undertaker of Mariposa, and his dress was due to the fact that he had just come from what he called an "interment." Mr. Gingham had the true spirit of his profession, and such words as "funeral" or "coffin" or "hearse" never passed his lips. He spoke always of "interments," of "caskets," and "coaches," using terms that were calculated rather to bring out the majesty and sublimity of death than to parade its horrors.

To be present at the hotel was in accord with Mr. Gingham's general conception of his business. No man had ever grasped the true principles of undertaking more thoroughly than Mr. Gingham. I have often heard him explain that to associate with the living, uninteresting though they appear, is the only way to secure the custom of the dead.

"Get to know people really well while they are alive," said Mr. Gingham; "be friends with them, close friends, and then when they die you don't need to worry. You'll get the order every time."

So, naturally, as the moment was one of sympathy, it was Mr. Gingham who spoke first.

"What'll you do, Josh," he said, "if the Commissioners go against you?"

"Boys," said Mr. Smith, "I don't rightly know. If I have to quit, the next move is to the city. But I don't reckon that I will have to quit. I've got an idee that I think's good every time."

"Could you run a hotel in the city?" asked Mullins.

"I could," said Mr. Smith. "I'll tell you. There's big things doin' in the hotel business right now, big chances if you go into it right. Hotels in the city is branching out. Why, you take the dining-room side of it," continued Mr. Smith, looking round at the group, "there's thousands in it. The old plan's all gone. Folks won't eat now in an ordinary dining-room with a high ceiling and windows. You have to get 'em down underground in a room with no windows and lots of sawdust round and waiters that can't speak English. I seen them places last time I was in the city. They call 'em Rats' Coolers. And for light meals they want a Caff, a real French Caff, and for folks that come in late another place that they call a Girl Room that don't shut up at all. If I go to the city that's the kind of place I mean to run. What's yours, Gol? It's on the house."

And it was just at the moment when Mr. Smith said this that Billy, the desk-clerk, entered the room with the telegram in his hand.

But stop—it is impossible for you to understand the anxiety with which Mr. Smith and his associates awaited the news from the Commissioners, without first realizing the astounding progress of Mr. Smith in the three past years, and the pinnacle of public eminence to which he had attained.

Mr. Smith had come down from the lumber country of the Spanish River, where the divide is toward the Hudson Bay,—"back north" as they called it in Mariposa.

He had been, it was said, a cook in the lumber shanties. To this day Mr. Smith can fry an egg on both sides with a lightness of touch that is the despair of his own "help."

After that, he had run a river driver's boarding-house.

After that, he had taken a food contract for a gang of railroad navvies on the transcontinental.

After that, of course, the whole world was open to him.

He came down to Mariposa and bought out the "inside" of what had been the Royal Hotel.

Those who are educated understand that by the "inside" of a hotel is meant everything except the four outer walls of it—the fittings, the furniture, the bar, Billy the desk-clerk, the three dining-room girls, and above all the license granted by King Edward VII., and ratified further by King George, for the sale of intoxicating liquors.

Till then the Royal had been a mere nothing. As "Smith's Hotel" it broke into a blaze of effulgence.

From the first, Mr. Smith, as a proprietor, was a wild, rapturous success.

He had all the qualifications.

He weighed two hundred and eighty pounds.

He could haul two drunken men out of the bar each by the scruff of the neck without the faintest anger or excitement.

He carried money enough in his trousers pockets to start a bank, and spent it on anything, bet it on anything, and gave it away in handfuls.

He was never drunk, and, as a point of chivalry to his customers, never quite sober. Anybody was free of the hotel who cared to come in. Anybody who didn't like it could go out. Drinks of all kinds cost five cents, or six for a quarter. Meals and beds were practically free. Any persons foolish enough to go the desk and pay for them, Mr. Smith charged according to the expression of their faces.

At first the loafers and the shanty men settled down on the place in a shower. But that was not the "trade" that Mr. Smith wanted. He knew how to get rid of them. An army of charwomen, turned into the hotel, scrubbed it from top to bottom. A vacuum cleaner, the first seen in Mariposa, hissed and screamed in the corridors. Forty brass beds were imported from the city, not, of course, for the guests to sleep in, but to keep them out. A bar-tender with a starched coat and wicker sleeves was put behind the bar.

The loafers were put out of business. The place had become too "high toned" for them.

To get the high class trade, Mr. Smith set himself to dress the part. He wore wide cut coats of filmy serge, light as gossamer; chequered waistcoats with a pattern for every day in the week; fedora hats light as autumn leaves; four-in-hand ties of saffron and myrtle green with a diamond pin the size of a hazel nut. On his fingers there were as many gems as would grace a native prince of India; across his waistcoat lay a gold watch-chain in huge square links and in his pocket a gold watch that weighed a pound and a half and marked minutes, seconds and quarter seconds. Just to look at Josh Smith's watch brought at least ten men to the bar every evening.

Every morning Mr. Smith was shaved by Jefferson Thorpe, across the way. All that art could do, all that Florida water could effect, was lavished on his person.

Mr. Smith became a local character. Mariposa was at his feet. All the reputable business-men drank at Mr. Smith's bar, and in the little parlour behind it you might find at any time a group of the brightest intellects in the town.

Not but what there was opposition at first. The clergy, for example, who accepted the Mariposa House and the Continental as a necessary and useful evil, looked askance at the blazing lights and the surging crowd of Mr. Smith's saloon. They preached against him. When the Rev. Dean Drone led off with a sermon on the text "Lord be merciful even unto this publican Matthew Six," it was generally understood as an invitation to strike Mr. Smith dead. In the same way the sermon at the Presbyterian church the week after was on the text "Lo what now doeth Abiram in the land of Melchisideck Kings Eight and Nine?" and it was perfectly plain that what was meant was, "Lo, what is Josh Smith doing in Mariposa?"

But this opposition had been countered by a wide and sagacious philanthropy. I think Mr. Smith first got the idea of that on the night when the steam merry-go-round came to Mariposa. Just below the hostelry, on an empty lot, it whirled and whistled, steaming forth its tunes on the summer evening while the children crowded round it in hundreds. Down the street strolled Mr. Smith, wearing a soft fedora to indicate that it was evening.

"What d'you charge for a ride, boss?" said Mr. Smith.

"Two for a nickel," said the man.

"Take that," said Mr. Smith, handing out a ten-dollar bill from a roll of money, "and ride the little folks free all evening."

That night the merry-go-round whirled madly till after midnight, freighted to capacity with Mariposa children, while up in Smith's Hotel, parents, friends and admirers, as the news spread, were standing four deep along the bar. They sold forty dollars' worth of lager alone that night, and Mr. Smith learned, if he had not already suspected it, the blessedness of giving.

The uses of philanthropy went further. Mr. Smith subscribed to everything, joined everything, gave to everything. He became an Oddfellow, a Forester, A Knight of Pythias and a Workman. He gave a hundred dollars to the Mariposa Hospital and a hundred dollars to the Young Men's Christian Association.

He subscribed to the Ball Club, the Lacrosse Club, the Curling Club, to anything, in fact, and especially to all those things which needed premises to meet in and grew thirsty in their discussions.

As a consequence the Oddfellows held their annual banquet at Smith's Hotel and the Oyster Supper of the Knights of Pythias was celebrated in Mr. Smith's dining-room.

Even more effective, perhaps, were Mr. Smith's secret benefactions, the kind of giving done by stealth of which not a soul in town knew anything, often, for a week after it was done. It was in this way that Mr. Smith put the new font in Dean Drone's church, and handed over a hundred dollars to Judge Pepperleigh for the unrestrained use of the Conservative party.

So it came about that, little by little, the antagonism had died down. Smith's Hotel became an accepted institution in Mariposa. Even the temperance people were proud of Mr. Smith as a sort of character who added distinction to the town. There were moments, in the earlier quiet of the morning, when Dean Drone would go so far as to step in to the "rotunda" and collect a subscription. As for the Salvation Army, they ran in and out all the time unreproved.

On only one point difficulty still remained. That was the closing of the bar. Mr. Smith could never bring his mind to it,—not as a matter of profit, but as a point of honour. It was too much for him to feel that Judge

Pepperleigh might be out on the sidewalk thirsty at midnight, that the night hands of the Times-Herald on Wednesday might be compelled to go home dry. On this point Mr. Smith's moral code was simplicity itself,—do what is right and take the consequences. So the bar stayed open.

Every town, I suppose, has its meaner spirits. In every genial bosom some snake is warmed,—or, as Mr. Smith put it to Golgotha Gingham—"there are some fellers even in this town skunks enough to inform."

At first the Mariposa court quashed all indictments. The presiding judge, with his spectacles on and a pile of books in front of him, threatened the informer with the penitentiary. The whole bar of Mariposa was with Mr. Smith. But by sheer iteration the informations had proved successful. Judge Pepperleigh learned that Mr. Smith had subscribed a hundred dollars for the Liberal party and at once fined him for keeping open after hours. That made one conviction. On the top of this had come the untoward incident just mentioned and that made two. Beyond that was the deluge. This then was the exact situation when Billy, the desk clerk, entered the back bar with the telegram in his hand.

"Here's your wire, sir," he said.

"What does it say?" said Mr. Smith.

He always dealt with written documents with a fine air of detachment. I don't suppose there were ten people in Mariposa who knew that Mr. Smith couldn't read.

Billy opened the message and read, "Commissioners give you three months to close down."

"Let me read it," said Mr. Smith, "that's right, three months to close down."

There was dead silence when the message was read. Everybody waited for Mr. Smith to speak. Mr. Gingham instinctively assumed the professional air of hopeless melancholy.

As it was afterwards recorded, Mr. Smith stood and "studied" with the tray in his hand for at least four minutes. Then he spoke.

"Boys," he said, "I'll be darned if I close down till I'm ready to close down. I've got an idee. You wait and I'll show you."

And beyond that, not another word did Mr. Smith say on the subject.

But within forty-eight hours the whole town knew that something was doing. The hotel swarmed with carpenters, bricklayers and painters. There was an architect up from the city with a bundle of blue prints in his hand. There was an engineer taking the street level with a theodolite, and a gang of navvies with shovels digging like fury as if to dig out the back foundations of the hotel.

"That'll fool 'em," said Mr. Smith.

Half the town was gathered round the hotel crazy with excitement. But not a word would the proprietor say.

Great dray loads of square timber, and two-by-eight pine joists kept arriving from the planing mill. There was a pile of matched spruce sixteen feet high lying by the sidewalk.

Then the excavation deepened and the dirt flew, and the beams went up and the joists across, and all the day from dawn till dusk the hammers of the carpenters clattered away, working overtime at time and a half.

"It don't matter what it costs," said Mr. Smith; "get it done."

Rapidly the structure took form. It extended down the side street, joining the hotel at a right angle. Spacious and graceful it looked as it reared its uprights into the air.

Already you could see the place where the row of windows was to come, a veritable palace of glass, it must be, so wide and commodious were they. Below it, you could see the basement shaping itself, with a low ceiling like a vault and big beams running across, dressed, smoothed, and ready for staining. Already in the street there were seven crates of red and white awning.

And even then nobody knew what it was, and it was not till the seventeenth day that Mr. Smith, in the privacy of the back bar, broke the silence and explained.

"I tell you, boys," he says, "it's a caff—like what they have in the city—a ladies' and gent's caff, and that underneath (what's yours, Mr. Mullins?) is a Rats' Cooler. And when I get her started, I'll hire a French Chief to do the cooking, and for the winter I will put in a 'girl room,' like what they have in the city hotels. And I'd like to see who's going to close her up then."

Within two more weeks the plan was in operation. Not only was the caff built but the very hotel was transformed. Awnings had broken out in a red and white cloud upon its face, its every window carried a box of hanging plants, and above in glory floated the Union Jack. The very stationery was changed. The place was now Smith's Summer Pavilion. It was advertised in the city as Smith's Tourists' Emporium, and Smith's Northern Health Resort. Mr. Smith got the editor of the Times-Herald to write up a circular all about ozone and the Mariposa pine woods, with illustrations of the maskinonge (piscis mariposis) of Lake Wissanotti.

The Saturday after that circular hit the city in July, there were men with fishing rods and landing nets pouring in on every train, almost too fast to register. And if, in the face of that, a few little drops of whiskey were sold over the bar, who thought of it?

But the caff! that, of course, was the crowning glory of the thing, that and the Rats' Cooler below.

Light and cool, with swinging windows open to the air, tables with marble tops, palms, waiters in white coats—it was the standing marvel of Mariposa. Not a soul in the town except Mr. Smith, who knew it by instinct, ever guessed that waiters and palms and marble tables can be rented over the long distance telephone.

Mr. Smith was as good as his word. He got a French Chief with an aristocratic saturnine countenance, and a moustache and imperial that recalled the late Napoleon III. No one knew where Mr. Smith got him. Some people in the town said he was a French marquis. Others said he was a count and explained the difference.

No one in Mariposa had ever seen anything like the caff. All down the side of it were the grill fires, with great pewter dish covers that went up and down on a chain, and you could walk along the row and actually pick out your own cutlet and then see the French marquis throw it on to the broiling iron; you could watch a buckwheat pancake whirled into existence under your eyes and see fowls' legs devilled, peppered, grilled, and tormented till they lost all semblance of the original Mariposa chicken.

Mr. Smith, of course, was in his glory.

"What have you got to-day, Alf?" he would say, as he strolled over to the marquis. The name of the Chief was, I believe Alphonse, but "Alf" was near enough for Mr. Smith.

The marquis would extend to the proprietor the menu, "Voilà, m'sieu, la carte du jour."

Mr. Smith, by the way, encouraged the use of the French language in the caff. He viewed it, of course, solely in its relation to the hotel business, and, I think, regarded it as a recent invention.

"It's comin' in all the time in the city," he said, "and y'aint expected to understand it."

Mr. Smith would take the carte between his finger and thumb and stare at it. It was all covered with such devices as Potage à la Mariposa—Filet Mignon à la propriétaire—Côtelette à la Smith, and so on.

But the greatest thing about the caff were the prices. Therein lay, as everybody saw at once, the hopeless simplicity of Mr. Smith.

The prices stood fast at 25 cents a meal. You could come in and eat all they had in the caff for a quarter.

"No, sir," Mr. Smith said stoutly, "I ain't going to try to raise no prices on the public. The hotel's always been a quarter and the caff's a quarter."

Full? Full of people?

Well, I should think so! From the time the caff opened at 11 till it closed at 8.30, you could hardly find a table. Tourists, visitors, travellers, and half the people of Mariposa crowded at the little tables; crockery rattling, glasses tinkling on trays, corks popping, the waiters in their white coats flying to and fro, Alphonse whirling the cutlets and pancakes into the air, and in and through it all, Mr. Smith, in a white flannel suit and a broad crimson sash about his waist. Crowded and gay from morning to night, and even noisy in its hilarity.

Noisy, yes; but if you wanted deep quiet and cool, if you wanted to step from the glare of a Canadian August to the deep shadow of an enchanted glade,—walk down below into the Rats' Cooler. There you had it; dark old beams (who could believe they were put there a month ago?), great casks set on end with legends such as Amontillado Fino done in gilt on a black ground, tall steins filled with German beer soft as moss, and a German waiter noiseless as moving foam. He who entered the Rats' Cooler at three of a summer afternoon was buried there for the day. Mr. Golgotha Gingham spent anything from four to seven hours there of every day. In his mind the place had all the quiet charm of an interment, with none of its sorrows.

But at night, when Mr. Smith and Billy, the desk clerk, opened up the cash register and figured out the combined losses of the caff and the Rats' Cooler, Mr. Smith would say:

"Billy, just wait till I get the license renood, and I'll close up this damn caff so tight they'll never know what hit her. What did that lamb cost? Fifty cents a pound, was it? I figure it, Billy, that every one of them hogs eats about a dollar's worth a grub for every twenty-five cents they pay on it. As for Alf—by gosh, I'm through with him."

But that, of course, was only a confidential matter as between Mr. Smith and Billy.

I don't know at what precise period it was that the idea of a petition to the License Commissioners first got about the town. No one seemed to know just who suggested it. But certain it was that public opinion began to swing strongly towards the support of Mr. Smith. I think it was perhaps on the day after the big fish dinner that Alphonse cooked for the Mariposa Canoe Club (at twenty cents a head) that the feeling began to find open expression. People said it was a shame that a man like Josh Smith should be run out of Mariposa by three license commissioners. Who were the license commissioners, anyway? Why, look at the license system they had in Sweden; yes, and in Finland and in South America. Or, for the matter of that, look at the French and Italians, who drink all day and all night. Aren't they all right? Aren't they a musical people? Take Napoleon, and Victor Hugo; drunk half the time, and yet look what they did.

I quote these arguments not for their own sake, but merely to indicate the changing temper of public opinion in Mariposa. Men would sit in the caff at lunch perhaps for an hour and a half and talk about the license question in general, and then go down into the Rats' Cooler and talk about it for two hours more.

It was amazing the way the light broke in the case of particular individuals, often the most unlikely, and quelled their opposition.

Take, for example, the editor of the Newspacket. I suppose there wasn't a greater temperance advocate in town. Yet Alphonse queered him with an Omelette à la License in one meal.

Or take Pepperleigh himself, the judge of the Mariposa court. He was put to the bad with a game pie,—pâté normand aux fines herbes—the real thing, as good as a trip to Paris in itself. After eating it, Pepperleigh had the common sense to realize that it was sheer madness to destroy a hotel that could cook a thing like that.

In the same way, the secretary of the School Board was silenced with a stuffed duck à la Ossawippi.

Three members of the town council were converted with a Dindon farci à la Josh Smith.

And then, finally, Mr. Diston persuaded Dean Drone to come, and as soon as Mr. Smith and Alphonse saw him they landed him with a fried flounder that even the apostles would have appreciated.

After that, every one knew that the license question was practically settled. The petition was all over the town. It was printed in duplicate at the Newspacket and you could see it lying on the counter of every shop in Mariposa. Some of the people signed it twenty or thirty times.

It was the right kind of document too. It began—"Whereas in the bounty of providence the earth putteth forth her luscious fruits and her vineyards for the delight and enjoyment of mankind—" It made you thirsty just to read it. Any man who read that petition over was wild to get to the Rats' Cooler.

When it was all signed up they had nearly three thousand names on it.

Then Nivens, the lawyer, and Mr. Gingham (as a provincial official) took it down to the county town, and by three o'clock that afternoon the news had gone out from the long distance telephone office that Smith's license was renewed for three years.

Rejoicings! Well, I should think so! Everybody was down wanting to shake hands with Mr. Smith. They told him that he had done more to boom Mariposa than any ten men in town. Some of them said he ought to run for the town council, and others wanted to make him the Conservative candidate for the next Dominion election. The caff was a mere babel of voices, and even the Rats' Cooler was almost floated away from its moorings.

And in the middle of it all. Mr. Smith found time to say to Billy, the desk clerk: "Take the cash registers out of the caff and the Rats' Cooler and start counting up the books."

And Billy said: "Will I write the letters for the palms and the tables and the stuff to go back?"

And Mr. Smith said: "Get 'em written right away."

So all evening the laughter and the clatter and the congratulations went on, and it wasn't till long after midnight that Mr. Smith was able to join Billy in the private room behind the "rotunda." Even when he did, there was a quiet and a dignity about his manner that had never been there before. I think it must have been the new halo of the Conservative candidacy that already radiated from his brow. It was, I imagine, at this very moment that Mr. Smith first realised that the hotel business formed the natural and proper threshold of the national legislature.

"Here's the account of the cash registers," said Billy.

"Let me see it," said Mr. Smith. And he studied the figures without a word.

"And here's the letters about the palms, and here's Alphonse up to yesterday—"

And then an amazing thing happened.

"Billy," said Mr. Smith, "tear 'em up. I ain't going to do it. It ain't right and I won't do it. They got me the license for to keep the caff and I'm going to keep the caff. I don't need to close her. The bar's good for anything from forty to a hundred a day now, with the Rats' Cooler going good, and that caff will stay right here."

And stay it did.

There it stands, mind you, to this day. You've only to step round the corner of Smith's Hotel on the side street and read the sign: LADIES' AND GENT'S CAFÉ, just as large and as imposing as ever.

Mr. Smith said that he'd keep the caff, and when he said a thing he meant it!

Of course there were changes, small changes.

I don't say, mind you, that the fillet de beef that you get there now is perhaps quite up to the level of the filet de boeufs aux champignons of the days of glory.

No doubt the lamb chops in Smith's Caff are often very much the same, nowadays, as the lamb chops of the Mariposa House or the Continental.

Of course, things like Omelette aux Trufles practically died out when Alphonse went. And, naturally, the leaving of Alphonse was inevitable. No one knew just when he went, or why. But one morning he was gone. Mr. Smith said that "Alf had to go back to his folks in the old country."

So, too, when Alf left, the use of the French language, as such, fell off tremendously in the caff. Even now they use it to some extent. You can still get fillet de beef, and saucisson au juice, but Billy the desk clerk has considerable trouble with the spelling.

The Rats' Cooler, of course, closed down, or rather Mr. Smith closed it for repairs, and there is every likelihood that it will hardly open for three years. But the caff is there. They don't use the grills, because there's no need to, with the hotel kitchen so handy.

The "girl room," I may say, was never opened. Mr. Smith promised it, it is true, for the winter, and still talks of it. But somehow there's been a sort of feeling against it. Every one in town admits that every big hotel in the city has a "girl room" and that it must be all right. Still, there's a certain—well, you know how sensitive opinion is in a place like Mariposa.

STEPHEN CRANE

(1871–1900)

S tephen Crane was born in Newark, New Jersey, the son of a
Methodist minister. His father died when Crane, the last of fourteen
children, was only 9, and his mother was left to bring up the family. He
was an indifferent student at Lafayette College and Syracuse University.
He paid for the publication of his first novel, Maggie: A Girl of the
Streets (1893). His best-known work, The Red Badge of Courage,
followed two years later and made him a celebrity. His most important
book of short stories, The Open Boat, was published in 1898. During
these years, he wrote a good deal of journalism, including his memorable
dispatches during the Spanish-American War (1898). His life was one
long struggle against poverty and ill health, and he died of tuberculosis
at the age of 28. He once wrote an editor, "Of all human lots for a person
of sensibility that of obscure free lance in literature or journalism is, I
think, the most discouraging." Even when he was renowned as a writer,
romantic entanglements made him the subject of vicious gossip, and the
debts he amassed forced him to take on a crippling amount of work when
his health was all but broken. Despite these hindrances, in novels such
as Maggie he became one of the founders of American naturalism, the
literary theory that considers humans as animals subject to their drives
and desires, caught up in an environment that further controls and
determines their fate. In The Red Badge of Courage, Crane charts
how the context of modern war has altered humanity's understanding
of nature and fate. R.W. Stallman compares Crane to Chekhov and
Mansfield, two of the supreme practitioners of the short story:

> All three artists had essentially the same theory and method:
> intensity of vision, objectivity in rendering it. All three aimed at
> a depersonalization of art: they aimed to get outside themselves
> completely in order "to find the greatest truth of the idea" and
> "see the thing as it really is"; to keep themselves aloof from
> their characters, not to become emotionally involved with their
> subjects, and to comment on them not by statement, but by
> evocation in picture and tone.

P. 448 Theme of the story

The Open Boat

A Tale Intended to be after the Fact:
Being the Experience of Four Men
From the Sunk Steamer *Commodore*.

I

N one of them knew the color of the sky. Their eyes glanced level, and were fastened upon the waves that swept toward them. These waves were of the hue of slate, save for the tops, which were of foaming white, and all of the men knew the colors of the sea. The horizon narrowed and widened, and dipped and rose, and at all times its edge was jagged with waves that seemed thrust up in points like rocks.

Many a man ought to have a bath-tub larger than the boat which here rode upon the sea. These waves were most wrongfully and barbarously abrupt and tall, and each froth-top was a problem in small-boat navigation.

The cook squatted in the bottom, and looked with both eyes at the six inches of gunwale which separated him from the ocean. His sleeves were rolled over his fat forearms, and the two flaps of his unbuttoned vest dangled as he bent to bail out the boat. Often he said, "Gawd! that was a narrow clip." As he remarked it, he invariably gazed eastward over the broken sea.

The oiler, steering with one of the two oars in the boat, sometimes raised himself suddenly to keep clear of water that swirled in over the stern. It was a thin little oar, and it seemed often ready to snap.

The correspondent, pulling at the other oar, watched the waves and wondered why he was there.

The injured captain, lying in the bow, was at this time buried in that profound dejection and indifference which comes, temporarily at least, to even the bravest and most enduring when, willy-nilly, the firm fails, the army loses, the ship goes down. The mind of the master of a vessel is rooted deep in the timbers of her, though he command for a day or a decade; and this captain had on him the stern impression of a scene in the grays of dawn of seven turned faces, and later a stump of a topmast with a white ball on it, that slashed to and fro at the waves, went low and lower, and down. Thereafter there was something strange in his voice. Although steady, it was deep with mourning, and of a quality beyond oration or tears.

"Keep 'er a little more south, Billie," said he.

"A little more south, sir," said the oiler in the stern.

A seat in this boat was not unlike a seat upon a bucking broncho, and, by the same token, a broncho is not much smaller. The craft pranced and reared and plunged like an animal. As each wave came, and she rose for it, she seemed like a horse making at a fence outrageously high. The manner of her scramble over these walls of water is a mystic thing, and, moreover, at the top of them were ordinarily these problems in white water, the foam racing down from the summit of each wave, requiring a new leap, and a leap from the air. Then, after scornfully bumping a crest, she would slide and race and splash down a long incline, and arrive bobbing and nodding in front of the next menace.

A singular disadvantage of the sea lies in the fact that, after successfully surmounting one wave, you discover that there is another behind it, just as important and just as nervously anxious to do something effective in the way of swamping boats. In a ten-foot dinghy one can get an idea of the resources of the sea in the line of waves that is not probable to the average experience, which is never at sea in a dinghy. As each salty wall of water approached, it shut all else from the view of the men in the boat, and it was not difficult to imagine that this particular wave was the final outburst of the ocean, the last effort of the grim water. There was a terrible grace in the move of the waves, and they came in silence, save for the snarling of the crests.

In the wan light the faces of the men must have been gray. Their eyes must have glinted in strange ways as they gazed steadily astern. Viewed from a balcony, the whole thing would, doubtless, have been weirdly picturesque. But the men in the boat had no time to see it, and if they had had leisure, there were other things to occupy their minds. The sun swung steadily up the sky, and they knew it was broad day because the color of the sea changed from slate to emerald-green streaked with amber lights, and the foam was like tumbling snow. The process of the breaking day was unknown to them. They were aware only of this effect upon the color of the waves that rolled toward them.

In disjointed sentences the cook and the correspondent argued as to the difference between a life-saving station and a house of refuge. The cook had said: "There's a house of refuge just north of the Mosquito Inlet Light, and as soon as they see us they'll come off in their boat and pick us up."

"As soon as who see us?" said the correspondent.

"The crew," said the cook.

"Houses of refuge can't have crews," said the correspondent. "As I understand them, they are only places where clothes and grub are stored for the benefit of shipwrecked people. They don't carry crews."

"Oh, yes, they do," said the cook.

"No, they don't," said the correspondent.

"Well, we're not there yet, anyhow," said the oiler in the stern.

"Well," said the cook, "perhaps it's not a house of refuge that I'm thinking of as being near Mosquito Inlet Light; perhaps it's a life-saving station."

"We're not there yet," said the oiler in the stern.

II

As the boat bounced from the top of each wave the wind tore through the hair of the hatless men, and as the craft plopped her stern down again the spray slashed past them. The crest of each of these waves was a hill, from the top of which the men surveyed for a moment a broad, tumultuous expanse, shining and wind-riven. It was probably splendid, it was probably glorious, this play of the free sea, wild with lights of emerald and white and amber.

"Bully good thing it's an on-shore wind," said the cook. "If not, where would we be? Wouldn't have a show."

"That's right," said the correspondent.

The busy oiler nodded his assent.

Then the captain, in the bow, chuckled in a way that expressed humor, contempt, tragedy, all in one. "Do you think we've got much of a show now, boys?" said he.

Whereupon the three were silent, save for a trifle of hemming and hawing. To express any particular optimism at this time they felt to be childish and stupid, but they all doubtless possessed this sense of the situation in their minds. A young man thinks doggedly at such times. On the other hand, the ethics of their condition was decidedly against any open suggestion of hopelessness. So they were silent.

"Oh, well," said the captain, soothing his children, "we'll get ashore all right."

But there was that in his tone which made them think; so the oiler quoth, "Yes! if this wind holds."

The cook was bailing. "Yes! if we don't catch hell in the surf."

Canton-flannel gulls flew near and far. Sometimes they sat down on the sea, near patches of brown seaweed that rolled over the waves with a movement like carpets on a line in a gale. The birds sat comfortably in groups, and they were envied by some in the dinghy, for the wrath of the sea was no more to them than it was to a covey of prairie-chickens a thousand miles inland. Often they came very close and stared at the men with black, bead-like eyes. At these times they were uncanny and sinister in their unblinking scrutiny, and the men hooted angrily at them, telling them to be gone. One came, and evidently decided to alight on the top of the captain's head. The bird flew parallel to the boat, and did not circle, but made short sidelong jumps in the air in chicken fashion. His black eyes were wistfully fixed upon the captain's head. "Ugly brute," said the oiler to the bird. "You look as if you were made with a jack-knife." The cook and the correspondent swore darkly at the creature. The captain naturally wished to knock it away with the end of the heavy painter, but he did not dare do it, because anything resembling an emphatic gesture would have capsized this freighted boat; and so, with his open hand, the captain gently and carefully waved the gull away. After it had been discouraged from the pursuit the captain breathed easier on account of his hair, and others breathed easier because the bird struck their minds at this time as being somehow gruesome and ominous.

In the meantime the oiler and the correspondent rowed; and also they rowed. They sat together in the same seat, and each rowed an oar. Then the oiler took both oars; then the correspondent took both oars; then the oiler; then the correspondent. They rowed and they rowed. The very ticklish part of the business was when the time came for the reclining one in the stern to take his turn at the oars. By the very last star of truth, it is easier to steal eggs from under a hen than it was to change seats in the dinghy. First the man in the stern slid his hand along the thwart and moved with care, as if he were of Sèvres. Then the man in the rowing-seat slid his hand along the other thwart. It was all done with the most extraordinary care. As the two sidled past each other, the whole party kept watchful eyes on the coming wave, and the captain cried: "Look out, now! Steady, there!"

The brown mats of seaweed that appeared from time to time were like islands, bits of earth. They were traveling, apparently, neither one way nor the other. They were, to all intents, stationary. They informed the men in the boat that it was making progress slowly toward the land.

The captain, rearing cautiously in the bow after the dinghy soared on a great swell, said that he had seen the lighthouse at Mosquito Inlet. Presently the cook remarked that he had seen it. The correspondent was at the oars then, and for some reason he too wished to look at the lighthouse; but his back was toward the far shore, and the waves were important, and for some time he could not seize an opportunity to turn his head. But at last there came a wave more gentle than the others, and when at the crest of it he swiftly scoured the western horizon.

"See it?" said the captain.

"No," said the correspondent, slowly; "I didn't see anything."

"Look again," said the captain. He pointed. "It's exactly in that direction."

At the top of another wave the correspondent did as he was bid, and this time his eyes chanced on a small, still thing on the edge of the swaying horizon. It was precisely like the point of a pin. It took an anxious eye to find a lighthouse so tiny.

"Think we'll make it, Captain?"

"If this wind holds and the boat don't swamp, we can't do much else," said the captain.

The little boat, lifted by each towering sea and splashed viciously by the crests, made progress that in the absence of seaweed was not apparent to those in her. She seemed just a wee thing wallowing miraculously, top up, at the mercy of five oceans. Occasionally a great spread of water, like white flames, swarmed into her.

"Bail her, cook," said the captain, serenely.

"All right, Captain," said the cheerful cook.

III

It would be difficult to describe the subtle brotherhood of men that was here established on the seas. No one said that it was so. No one mentioned it. But it dwelt in the boat, and each man felt it warm him. They were a captain, an oiler, a cook, and a correspondent, and they were friends— friends in a more curiously iron-bound degree than may be common. The hurt captain, lying against the water-jar in the bow, spoke always in a low voice and calmly; but he could never command a more ready and swiftly obedient crew than the motley three of the dinghy. It was more than a mere recognition of what was best for the common safety. There was surely in it a quality that was personal and heartfelt. And after this devotion to the commander of the boat, there was this comradeship, that the correspondent, for instance, who had been taught to be cynical of men, knew even at the time was the best experience of his life. But no one said that it was so. No one mentioned it.

"I wish we had a sail," remarked the captain. "We might try my overcoat on the end of an oar, and give you two boys a chance to rest." So the cook and the correspondent held the mast and spread wide the overcoat; the oiler steered; and the little boat made good way with her new rig. Sometimes the oiler had to scull sharply to keep a sea from breaking into the boat, but otherwise sailing was a success.

Meanwhile the lighthouse had been growing slowly larger. It had now almost assumed color, and appeared like a little gray shadow on the sky. The man at the oars could not be prevented from turning his head rather often to try for a glimpse of this little gray shadow.

At last, from the top of each wave, the men in the tossing boat could see land. Even as the lighthouse was an upright shadow on the sky, this land seemed but a long black shadow on the sea. It certainly was thinner than paper. "We must be about opposite New Smyrna," said the cook, who had coasted this shore often in schooners. "Captain, by the way, I believe they abandoned that life-saving station there about a year ago."

"Did they?" said the captain.

The wind slowly died away. The cook and the correspondent were not now obliged to slave in order to hold high the oar; but the waves continued their old impetuous swooping at the dinghy, and the little craft, no longer under way, struggled woundily over them. The oiler or the correspondent took the oars again.

Shipwrecks are *apropos* of nothing. If men could only train for them and have them occur when the men had reached pink condition, there would be less drowning at sea. Of the four in the dinghy none had slept any time worth mentioning for two days and two nights previous to embarking in the dinghy, and in the excitement of clambering about the deck of a foundering ship they had also forgotten to eat heartily.

For these reasons, and for others, neither the oiler nor the correspondent was fond of rowing at this time. The correspondent wondered ingenuously how in the name of all that was sane could there be people who thought it amusing to row a boat. It was not amusement; it was a diabolical punishment, and even a genius of mental aberrations could never conclude that it was anything but a horror to the muscles and a crime against the back. He mentioned to the boat in general how the amusement of rowing struck him, and the weary-faced oiler smiled in full sympathy. Previously to the foundering, by the way, the oiler had worked double watch in the engine-room of the ship.

"Take her easy now, boys," said the captain. "Don't spend yourselves. If we have to run a surf you'll need all your strength, because we'll sure have to swim for it. Take your time."

Slowly the land arose from the sea. From a black line it became a line of black and a line of white—trees and sand. Finally the captain said that he could make out a house on the shore. "That's the house of refuge, sure," said the cook. "They'll see us before long, and come out after us."

The distant lighthouse reared high. "The keeper ought to be able to make us out now, if he's looking through a glass," said the captain. "He'll notify the life-saving people."

"None of those other boats could have got ashore to give word of the wreck," said the oiler, in a low voice, "else the lifeboat would be out hunting us."

Slowly and beautifully the land loomed out of the sea. The wind came again. It had veered from the northeast to the southeast. Finally a new sound struck the ears of the men in the boat. It was the low thunder of the surf on the shore. "We'll never be able to make the lighthouse now," said the captain. "Swing her head a little more north, Billie."

"A little more north, sir," said the oiler.

Whereupon the little boat turned her nose once more down the wind, and all but the oarsman watched the shore grow. Under the influence of this expansion doubt and direful apprehension were leaving the minds of the men. The management of the boat was still most absorbing, but it could not prevent a quiet cheerfulness. In an hour, perhaps, they would be ashore.

Their backbones had become thoroughly used to balancing in the boat, and they now rode this wild colt of a dinghy like circus men. The correspondent thought that he had been drenched to the skin, but happening to feel in the top pocket of his coat, he found therein eight cigars. Four of them were soaked with sea-water; four were perfectly scatheless. After a search, somebody produced three dry matches; and thereupon the four waifs rode in their little boat and, with an assurance of an impending rescue shining in their eyes, puffed at the big cigars, and judged well and ill of all men. Everybody took a drink of water.

IV

"Cook," remarked the captain, "there don't seem to be any signs of life about your house of refuge."

"No," replied the cook. "Funny they don't see us!"

A broad stretch of lowly coast lay before the eyes of the men. It was of low dunes topped with dark vegetation. The roar of the surf was plain, and sometimes they could see the white lip of a wave as it spun up the beach. A tiny house was blocked out black upon the sky. Southward, the slim lighthouse lifted its little gray length.

Tide, wind, and waves were swinging the dinghy northward. "Funny they don't see us," said the men.

The surf's roar was here dulled, but its tone was nevertheless thunder-ous and mighty. As the boat swam over the great rollers the men sat listening to this roar. "We'll swamp sure," said everybody.

It is fair to say here that there was not a life-saving station within twenty miles in either direction; but the men did not know this fact, and in consequence they made dark and opprobrious remarks concerning the eyesight of the nation's life-savers. Four scowling men sat in the dinghy, and surpassed records in the invention of epithlets.

"Funny they don't see us."

The light-heartedness of a former time had completely faded. To their sharpened minds it was easy to conjure pictures of all kinds of incompetency and blindness and, indeed, cowardice. There was the shore of the populous land, and it was bitter and bitter to them that from it came no sign.

"Well," said the captain, ultimately, "I suppose we'll have to make a try for ourselves. It we stay out here too long, we'll none of us have strength left to swim after the boat swamps."

And so the oiler, who was at the oars, turned the boat straight for the shore. There was a sudden tightening of muscles. There was some thinking.

"If we don't all get ashore," said the captain—"if we don't all get ashore, I suppose you fellows know where to send news of my finish?"

They then briefly exchanged some addresses and admonitions. As for the reflections of the men, there was a great deal of rage in them. Perchance they might be formulated thus: "If I am going to be drowned— if I am going to be drowned—if I am going to be drowned, why, in the name of the seven mad gods who rule the sea, was I allowed to come thus far and contemplate sand and trees? Was I brought here merely to have my nose dragged away as I was about to nibble the sacred cheese of life? It is preposterous! If this old ninny-woman, Fate, cannot do better than this, she should be deprived of the management of men's fortunes. She is an old hen who knows not her intention. If she has decided to drown me, why did she not do it in the beginning, and save me all this trouble? The whole affair is absurd. . . . But no; she cannot mean to drown me. She dare not drown me. She cannot drown me. Not after all this work!" Afterward the man might have had an impulse to shake his fist at the clouds. "Just you drown me, now, and then hear what I call you!"

The billows that came at this time were more formidable. They seemed always just about to break and roll over the little boat in a turmoil of foam. There was a preparatory and long growl in the speech of them. No mind unused to the sea would have concluded that the dinghy could ascend these sheer heights in time. The shore was still afar. The oiler was a wily surfman. "Boys," he said swiftly, "she won't live three minutes more, and we're too far out to swim. Shall I take her to sea again, Captain?"

"Yes; go ahead!" said the captain.

This oiler, by a series of quick miracles and fast and steady oarsmanship, turned the boat in the middle of the surf and took her safely to sea again.

There was a considerable silence as the boat bumped over the furrowed sea to deeper water. Then somebody in gloom spoke: "Well, anyhow, they must have seen us from the shore by now."

The gulls went in slanting flight up the wind toward the gray, desolate east. A squall, marked by dingy clouds, and clouds brick-red, like smoke from a burning building, appeared from the southeast.

"What do you think of those life-saving people? Ain't they peaches?"

"Funny they haven't seen us."

"Maybe they think we're out here for sport! Maybe they think we're fishin'. Maybe they think we're damned fools."

It was a long afternoon. A changed tide tried to force them southward, but wind and wave said northward. Far ahead, where coast-line, sea, and sky formed their mighty angle, there were little dots which seemed to indicate a city on the shore.

"St. Augustine?"

The captain shook his head. "Too near Mosquito Inlet."

And the oiler rowed, and then the correspondent rowed; then the oiler rowed. It was a weary business. The human back can become the seat of more aches and pains than are registered in books for the composite anatomy of a regiment. It is a limited area, but it can become the theater of innumerable muscular conflicts, tangles, wrenches, knots, and other comforts.

"Did you ever like to row, Billie?" asked the correspondent.

"No," said the oiler; "hang it!"

When one exchanged the rowing-seat for a place in the bottom of the boat, he suffered a bodily depression that caused him to be careless of everything save an obligation to wiggle one finger. There was cold sea-water swashing to and fro in the boat, and he lay in it. His head, pillowed on a thwart, was within an inch of the swirl of a wave-crest, and sometimes a particularly obstreperous sea came inboard and drenched him once more. But these matters did not annoy him. It is almost certain that if the boat had capsized he would have trembled comfortably out upon the ocean as if he felt sure that it was a great, soft mattress.

"Look! There's a man on the shore!"

"Where?"

"There! See 'im? See 'im?"

"Yes, sure! He's walking along."

"Now he's stopped. Look! He's facing us!"

"He's waving at us!"

"So he is! By thunder!"

"Ah, now we're all right! Now we're all right! There'll be a boat out here for us in half an hour.

"He's going on. He's running. He's going up to that house there."

The remote beach seemed lower than the sea, and it required a searching glance to discern the little black figure. The captain saw a floating stick, and they rowed to it. A bath towel was by some weird chance in the boat, and tying this on the stick, the captain waved it. The oarsman did not dare turn his head, so he was obliged to ask questions.

"What's he doing now?"

"He's standing still again. He's looking, I think. . . . There he goes again—toward the house. . . . Now he's stopped again."

"Is he waving at us?"

"No, not now; he was, though."

"Look! There comes another man!"

"He's running."

"Look at him go, would you!"

"Why, he's on a bicycle. Now he's met the other man. They're both waving at us. Look!"

"There comes something up the beach."

"What the devil is that thing?"

"Why, it looks like a boat."

"Why, certainly, it's a boat."

"No; it's on wheels."

"Yes, so it is. Well, that must be the life-boat. They drag them along shore on a wagon."

"That's the life-boat, sure."

"No, by——, it's—it's an omnibus."

"I tell you it's a life-boat."

"It is not! It's an omnibus. I can see it plain. See? One of these big hotel omnibuses."

"By thunder, you're right. It's an omnibus, sure as fate. What do you suppose they are doing with an omnibus? Maybe they are going around collecting the life-crew, hey?"

"That's it, likely. Look! There's a fellow waving a little black flag. He's standing on the steps of the omnibus. There come those other two fellows. Now they're all talking together. Look at the fellow with the flag. Maybe he ain't waving it!"

"That ain't a flag, is it? That's his coat. Why, certainly, that's his coat."

"So it is; it's his coat. He's taken it off and is waving it around his head. But would you look at him swing it!"

"Oh, say, there isn't any life-saving station there. That's just a winter-resort hotel omnibus that has brought over some of the boarders to see us drown."

"What's that idiot with the coat mean? What's he signaling, anyhow?"

"It looks as if he were trying to tell us to go north. There must be a life-saving station up there."

"No; he thinks we're fishing. Just giving us a merry hand. See? Ah, there, Willie!"

"Well, I wish I could make something out of those signals. What do you suppose he means?"

"He don't mean anything; he's just playing."

"Well, if he'd just signal us to try the surf again, or to go to sea and wait, or go north, or go south, or go to hell, there would be some reason in it. But look at him! He just stands there and keeps his coat revolving like a wheel. The ass!"

"There come more people."

"Now there's quite a mob. Look! Isn't that a boat?"

"Where? Oh, I see where you mean. No, that's no boat."

"That fellow is still waving his coat."

"He must think we like to see him do that. Why don't he quit it? It don't mean anything."

"I don't know. I think he is trying to make us go north. It mus
that there's a life-saving station there somewhere."

"Say, he ain't tired yet. Look at 'im wave!"

"Wonder how long he can keep that up. He's been revolving his coat
ever since he caught sight of us. He's an idiot. Why aren't they getting
men to bring a boat out? A fishing-boat—one of those big yawls—could
come out here all right. Why don't he do something?"

"Oh, it's all right now."

"They'll have a boat out here for us in less than no time, now that
they've seen us."

A faint yellow tone came into the sky over the low land. The shadows
on the sea slowly deepened. The wind bore coldness with it, and the men
began to shiver.

"Holy smoke!" said one, allowing his voice to express his impious
mood, "if we keep on monkeying out here! If we've got to flounder out
here all night!"

"Oh, we'll never have to stay here all night! Don't you worry. They've
seen us now, and it won't be long before they'll come chasing out after
us."

The shore grew dusky. The man waving a coat blended gradually
into this gloom, and it swallowed in the same manner the omnibus and
the group of people. The spray, when it dashed uproariously over the
side, made the voyagers shrink and swear like men who were being
branded.

"I'd like to catch the chump who waved the coat. I feel like soaking
him one, just for luck."

"Why? What did he do?"

"Oh, nothing, but then he seemed so damned cheerful."

In the meantime the oiler rowed, and then the correspondent rowed,
and then the oiler rowed. Gray-faced and bowed forward, they mechanically, turn by turn, plied the leaden oars. The form of the lighthouse had
vanished from the southern horizon, but finally a pale star appeared, just
lifting from the sea. The streaked saffron in the west passed before the
all-merging darkness, and the sea to the east was black. The land had
vanished, and was expressed only by the low and drear thunder of the
surf.

"If I am going to be drowned—if I am going to be drowned—if I am
going to be drowned, why, in the name of the seven mad gods who rule
the sea, was I allowed to come thus far and contemplate sand and trees?
Was I brought here merely to have my nose dragged away as I was about
to nibble the sacred cheese of life?"

The patient captain, drooped over the water-jar, was sometimes
obliged to speak to the oarsman.

"Keep her head up! Keep her head up!"

"Keep her head up, sir." The voices were weary and low.

This was surely a quiet evening. All save the oarsman lay heavily and listlessly in the boat's bottom. As for him, his eyes were just capable of noting the tall black waves that swept forward in a most sinister silence, save for an occasional subdued growl of a crest.

The cook's head was on a thwart, and he looked without interest at the water under his nose. He was deep in other scenes. Finally he spoke. "Billie," he murmured dreamfully, "what kind of pie do you like best?"

V

"Pie!" said the oiler and the correspondent, agitatedly. "Don't talk about those things, blast you!"

"Well," said the cook, "I was just thinking about ham sandwiches, and—"

A night on the sea in an open boat is a long night. As darkness settled finally, the shine of the light, lifting from the sea in the south, changed to full gold. On the northern horizon a new light appeared, a small bluish gleam on the edge of the waters. These two lights were the furniture of the world. Otherwise there was nothing but waves.

Two men huddled in the stern, and distances were so magnificent in the dinghy that the rower was enabled to keep his feet partly warm by thrusting them under his companions. Their legs indeed extended far under the rowing-seat until they touched the feet of the captain forward. Sometimes, despite the efforts of the tired oarsman, a wave came piling into the boat, an icy wave of the night, and the chilling water soaked them anew. They would twist their bodies for a moment and groan, and sleep the dead sleep once more, while the water in the boat gurgled about them as the craft rocked.

The plan of the oiler and the correspondent was for one to row until he lost the ability, and then arouse the other from his sea-water couch in the bottom of the boat.

The oiler plied the oars until his head drooped forward and the overpowering sleep blinded him; and he rowed yet afterward. Then he touched a man in the bottom of the boat, and called his name. "Will you spell me for a little while?" he said meekly.

"Sure, Billie," said the correspondent, awaking and dragging himself to a sitting position. They exchanged places carefully, and the oiler, cuddling down in the sea-water at the cook's side, seemed to go to sleep instantly.

The particular violence of the sea had ceased. The waves came without snarling. The obligation of the man at the oars was to keep the boat headed so that the tilt of the rollers would not capsize her, and to preserve her from filling when the crests rushed past. The black waves were silent and hard to be seen in the darkness. Often one was almost upon the boat before the oarsman was aware.

In a low voice the correspondent addressed the captain. He was not sure that the captain was awake, although this iron man seemed to be always awake. "Captain, shall I keep her making for that light north, sir?"

The same steady voice answered him. "Yes. Keep it about two points off the port bow."

The cook had tied a life-belt around himself in order to get even the warmth which this clumsy cork contrivance could donate, and he seemed almost stove-like when a rower, whose teeth invariably chattered wildly as soon as he ceased his labor, dropped down to sleep.

The correspondent, as he rowed, looked down at the two men sleeping under foot. The cook's arm was around the oiler's shoulders, and, with their fragmentary clothing and haggard faces, they were the babes of the sea—a grotesque rendering of the old babes in the wood.

Later he must have grown stupid at his work, for suddenly there was a growling of water, and a crest came with a roar and a swash into the boat, and it was a wonder that it did not set the cook afloat in his life-belt. The cook continued to sleep, but the oiler sat up, blinking his eyes and shaking with the new cold.

"Oh, I'm awful sorry, Billie," said the correspondent contritely.

"That's all right, old boy," said the oiler, and lay down again and was asleep.

Presently it seemed that even the captain dozed, and the correspondent thought that he was the one man afloat on all the oceans. The wind had a voice as it came over the waves, and it was sadder than the end.

There was a long, loud swishing astern of the boat, and a gleaming trail of phosphorescence, like blue flame, was furrowed on the black waters. It might have been made by a monstrous knife.

Then there came a stillness, while the correspondent breathed with open mouth and looked at the sea.

Suddenly there was another swish and another long flash of bluish light, and this time it was alongside the boat, and might almost have been reached with an oar. The correspondent saw an enormous fin speed like a shadow through the water, hurling the crystalline spray and leaving the long glowing trail.

The correspondent looked over his shoulder at the captain. His face was hidden, and he seemed to be asleep. He looked at the babes of the sea. They certainly were asleep. So, being bereft of sympathy, he leaned a little way to one side and swore softly into the sea.

But the thing did not then leave the vicinity of the boat. Ahead or astern, on one side or the other, at intervals long or short, fled the long sparkling streak, and there was to be heard the *whirroo* of the dark fin. The speed and power of the thing was greatly to be admired. It cut the water like a gigantic and keen projectile.

The presence of this biding thing did not affect the man with the same horror that it would if he had been a picnicker. He simply looked at the sea dully and swore in an undertone.

Nevertheless, it is true that he did not wish to be alone with the thing. He wished one of his companions to awake by chance and keep him company with it. But the captain hung motionless over the water-jar, and the oiler and the cook in the bottom of the boat were plunged in slumber.

VI

"If I am going to be drowned—if I am going to be drowned—if I am going to be drowned, why, in the name of the seven mad gods who rule the sea, was I allowed to come thus far and contemplate sand and trees?"

During this dismal night, it may be remarked that a man would conclude that it was really the intention of the seven mad gods to drown him, despite the abominable injustice of it. For it was certainly an abominable injustice to drown a man who had worked so hard, so hard. The man felt it would be a crime most unnatural. Other people had drowned at sea since galleys swarmed with painted sails, but still—

When it occurs to a man that nature does not regard him as important, and that she feels she would not maim the universe by disposing of him, he at first wishes to throw bricks at the temple, and he hates deeply the fact that there are no bricks and no temples. Any visible expression of nature would surely be pelleted with his jeers.

Then, if there be no tangible thing to hoot, he feels, perhaps, the desire to confront a personification and indulge in pleas, bowed to one knee, and with hands supplicant, saying, "Yes, but I love myself."

A high cold star on a winter's night is the word he feels that she says to him. Thereafter he knows the pathos of his situation.

The men in the dinghy had not discussed these matters, but each had, no doubt, reflected upon them in silence and according to his mind. There was seldom any expression upon their faces save the general one of complete weariness. Speech was devoted to the business of the boat.

To chime the notes of his emotion, a verse mysteriously entered the correspondent's head. He had even forgotten that he had forgotten this verse, but it suddenly was in his mind.

A soldier of the Legion lay dying in Algiers;
There was lack of woman's nursing, there was dearth of woman's tears;
But a comrade stood beside him, and he took that comrade's hand,

And he said, "I never more shall see my own, my native land."

In his childhood the correspondent had been made acquainted with the fact that a soldier of the Legion lay dying in Algiers, but he had never regarded it as important. Myriads of his school-fellows had informed him of the soldier's plight, but the dinning had naturally ended by making him perfectly indifferent. He had never considered it his affair that a soldier of the Legion lay dying in Algiers, nor had it appeared to him as a matter for sorrow. It was less to him than the breaking of a pencil's point.

Now, however, it quaintly came to him as a human, living thing. It was no longer merely a picture of a few throes in the breast of a poet, meanwhile drinking tea and warming his feet at the grate; it was an actuality—stern, mournful, and fine.

The correspondent plainly saw the soldier. He lay on the sand with his feet out straight and still. While his pale left hand was upon his chest in an attempt to thwart the going of his life, the blood came between his fingers. In the far Algerian distance, a city of low square forms was set against a sky that was faint with the last sunset hues. The correspondent, plying the oars and dreaming of the slow and slower movements of the lips of the soldier, was moved by a profound and perfectly impersonal comprehension. He was sorry for the soldier of the Legion who lay dying in Algiers.

The thing which had followed the boat and waited had evidently grown bored at the delay. There was no longer to be heard the slash of the cutwater, and there was no longer the flame of the long trail. The light in the north still glimmered, but it was apparently no nearer to the boat. Sometimes the boom of the surf rang in the correspondent's ears, and he turned the craft seaward then and rowed harder. Southward, some one had evidently built a watch-fire on the beach. It was too low and too far to be seen, but it made a shimmering, roseate reflection upon the bluff back of it, and this could be discerned from the boat. The wind came stronger, and sometimes a wave suddenly raged out like a mountain-cat, and there was to be seen the sheen and sparkle of a broken crest.

The captain, in the bow, moved on his water-jar and sat erect. "Pretty long night," he observed to the correspondent. He looked at the shore. "Those life-saving people take their time."

"Did you see that shark playing around?

"Yes, I saw him. He was a big fellow, all right."

"Wish I had known you were awake."

Later the correspondent spoke into the bottom of the boat.

"Billie!" There was a slow and gradual disentanglement. "Billie, will you spell me?"

"Sure," said the oiler.

As soon as the correspondent touched the cold, comfortable sea-water in the bottom of the boat and had huddled close to the cook's life-belt he was deep in sleep, despite the fact that his teeth played all the popular airs. This sleep was so good to him that it was but a moment before he heard a voice call his name in a tone that demonstrated the last stages of exhaustion. "Will you spell me?"

"Sure, Billie."

The light in the north had mysteriously vanished, but the correspondent took his course from the wide-awake captain.

Later in the night they took the boat farther out to sea, and the captain directed the cook to take one oar at the stern and keep the boat facing the seas. He was to call out if he should hear the thunder of the surf. This plan enabled the oiler and the correspondent to get respite together. "We'll give those boys a chance to get into shape again," said the captain. They curled down and, after a few preliminary chatterings and trembles, slept once more the dead sleep. Neither knew they had bequeathed to the cook the company of another shark, or perhaps the same shark.

As the boat caroused on the waves, spray occasionally bumped over the side and gave them a fresh soaking, but this had no power to break their repose. The ominous slash of the wind and the water affected them as it would have affected mummies.

"Boys," said the cook, with the notes of every reluctance in his voice, "she's drifted in pretty close. I guess one of you had better take her to sea again." The correspondent, aroused, heard the crash of the toppled crests.

As he was rowing, the captain gave him some whisky and water, and this steadied the chills out of him. "If I ever get ashore and anybody shows me even a photograph of an oar—"

At last there was a short conversation.

"Billie! . . . Billie, will you spell me?"

"Sure," said the oiler.

VII

When the correspondent again opened his eyes, the sea and the sky were each of the gray hue of the dawning. Later, carmine and gold was painted upon the waters. The morning appeared finally, in its splendor, with a sky of pure blue, and the sunlight flamed on the tips of the waves.

On the distant dunes were set many little black cottages, and a tall white windmill reared above them. No man, nor dog, nor bicycle appeared on the beach. The cottages might have formed a deserted village.

The voyagers scanned the shore. A conference was held in the boat. "Well," said the captain, "if no help is coming, we might better try a run through the surf right away. If we stay out here much longer we will be too weak to do anything for ourselves at all." The others silently acquiesced in this reasoning. The boat was headed for the beach. The correspondent wondered if none ever ascended the tall wind-tower, and if then they never looked seaward. This tower was a giant, standing with its back to the plight of the ants. It represented in a degree, to the correspondent, the serenity of nature amid the struggles of the individual—nature in the wind, and nature in the vision of men. She did not seem cruel to him then, nor beneficent, nor treacherous, nor wise. But she was indifferent, flatly indifferent. It is, perhaps, plausible that a man in this situation, impressed with the unconcern of the universe, should see the innumerable flaws of his life and have them taste wickedly in his mind and wish for another chance. A distinction between right and wrong seems absurdly clear to him, then, in this new ignorance of the grave-edge, and he understands that if he were given another opportunity he would mend his conduct and his words, and be better and brighter during an introduction or at a tea.

"Now, boys," said the captain, "she is going to swamp sure. All we can do is to work her in as far as possible, and then when she swamps, pile out and scramble for the beach. Keep cool now, and don't jump until she swamps sure."

The oiler took the oars. Over his shoulders he scanned the surf. "Captain," he said, "I think I'd better bring her about, and keep her head-on to the seas, and back her in."

"All right, Billie," said the captain. "Back her in." The oiler swung the boat then, and, seated in the stern, the cook and the correspondent were obliged to look over their shoulders to contemplate the lonely and indifferent shore.

The monstrous inshore rollers heaved the boat high until the men were again enabled to see the white sheets of water scudding up the slanted beach. "We won't get in very close," said the captain. Each time a man could wrest his attention from the rollers, he turned his glance toward the shore, and in the expression of the eyes during this contemplation there was a singular quality. The correspondent, observing the others, knew that they were not afraid, but the full meaning of their glances was shrouded.

As for himself, he was too tired to grapple fundamentally with the fact. He tried to coerce his mind into thinking of it, but the mind was dominated at this time by the muscles, and the muscles said they did not care. It merely occurred to him that if he should drown it would be a shame.

There were no hurried words, no pallor, no plain agitation. The men simply looked at the shore. "Now, remember to get well clear of the boat when you jump," said the captain.

Seaward the crest of a roller suddenly fell with a thunderous crash, and the long white comber came roaring down upon the boat.

"Steady now," said the captain. The men were silent. They turned their eyes from the shore to the comber and waited. The boat slid up the incline, leaped at the furious top, bounced over it, and swung down the long back of the wave. Some water had been shipped, and the cook bailed it out.

But the next crest crashed also. The tumbling, boiling flood of white water caught the boat and whirled it almost perpendicular. Water swarmed in from all sides. The correspondent had his hands on the gunwale at this time, and when the water entered at that place he swiftly withdrew his fingers, as if he objected to wetting them.

The little boat, drunken with this weight of water, reeled and snuggled deeper into the sea.

"Bail her out, cook! Bail her out!" said the captain.

"All right, Captain," said the cook.

"Now, boys, the next one will do for us sure," said the oiler. "Mind to jump clear of the boat."

The third wave moved forward, huge, furious, implacable. It fairly swallowed the dinghy, and almost simultaneously the men tumbled into the sea. A piece of life-belt had lain in the bottom of the boat, and as the correspondent went overboard he held this to his chest with his left hand.

The January water was icy, and he reflected immediately that it was colder than he had expected to find it off the coast of Florida. This appeared to his dazed mind as a fact important enough to be noted at the time. The coldness of the water was sad; it was tragic. This fact was somehow mixed and confused with his opinion of his own situation so that it seemed almost a proper reason for tears. The water was cold.

When he came to the surface he was conscious of little but the noisy water. Afterward he saw his companions in the sea. The oiler was ahead in the race. He was swimming strongly and rapidly. Off to the correspondent's left, the cook's great white and corked back bulged out of the water, and in the rear the captain was hanging with his one good hand to the keel of the overturned dinghy.

There is a certain immovable quality to a shore, and the correspondent wondered at it amid the confusion of the sea.

It seemed also very attractive; but the correspondent knew that it was a long journey, and he paddled leisurely. The piece of life-preserver lay under him, and sometimes he whirled down the incline of a wave as if he were on a hand-sled.

But finally he arrived at a place in the sea where travel was beset with difficulty. He did not pause swimming to inquire what manner of current had caught him, but there his progress ceased. The shore was set before him like a bit of scenery on a stage, and he looked at it, and understood with his eyes each detail of it.

As the cook passed, much farther to the left, the captain was calling to him, "Turn over on your back, cook! Turn over on your back and use the oar."

"All right, sir." The cook turned on his back, and, paddling with an oar, went ahead as if he were a canoe.

Presently the boat also passed to the left of the correspondent, with the captain clinging with one hand to the keel. He would have appeared like a man raising himself to look over a board fence if it were not for the extraordinary gymnastics of the boat. The correspondent marveled that the captain could still hold to it.

They passed on nearer to shore,—the oiler, the cook, the captain,— and following them went the water-jar, bouncing gaily over the seas.

The correspondent remained in the grip of this strange new enemy, a current. The shore, with its white slope of sand and its green bluff, topped with little silent cottages, was spread like a picture before him. It was near to him then, but he was impressed as one who, in a gallery, looks at a scene from Brittany or Algiers.

He thought: "I'm going to drown? Can it be possible? Can it be possible? Can it be possible?" Perhaps an individual must consider his own death to be the final phenomenon of nature.

But later a wave perhaps whirled him out of this small deadly current, for he found suddenly that he could again make progress toward the shore. Later still he was aware that the captain, clinging with one hand to the keel of the dinghy, had his face turned away from the shore and toward him, and was calling his name. "Come to the boat! Come to the boat!"

In his struggle to reach the captain and the boat, he reflected that when one gets properly wearied drowning must really be a comfortable arrangement—a cessation of hostilities accompanied by a large degree of relief; and he was glad of it, for the main thing in his mind for some moments had been horror of the temporary agony; he did not wish to be hurt.

Presently he saw a man running along the shore. He was undressing with most remarkable speed. Coat, trousers, shirt, everything flew magically off him.

"Come to the boat!" called the captain.

"All right, Captain." As the correspondent paddled, he saw the captain let himself down to bottom and leave the boat. Then the correspondent performed his one little marvel of the voyage. A large wave caught him and flung him with ease and supreme speed completely over the boat and far beyond it. It struck him even then as an event in gymnastics and a true miracle of the sea. An overturned boat in the surf is not a plaything to a swimming man.

The correspondent arrived in water that reached only to his waist, but his condition did not enable him to stand for more than a moment. Each wave knocked him into a heap, and the undertow pulled at him.

Then he saw the man who had been running and undressing, and undressing and running, come bounding into the water. He dragged ashore the cook, and then waded toward the captain; but the captain waved him away and sent him to the correspondent. He was naked— naked as a tree in winter; but a halo was about his head, and he shone like a saint. He gave a strong pull, and a long drag, and a bully heave at the correspondent's hand. The correspondent, schooled in the minor formulae, said, "Thanks, old man." But suddenly the man cried, "What's that?" He pointed a swift finger. The correspondent said, "Go."

In the shallows, face downward, lay the oiler. His forehead touched sand that was periodically, between each wave, clear of the sea.

The correspondent did not know all that transpired afterward. When he achieved safe ground he fell, striking the sand with each particular part of his body. It was as if he had dropped from a roof, but the thud was grateful to him.

It seems that instantly the beach was populated with men with blankets, clothes, and flasks, and women with coffee-pots and all the remedies sacred to their minds. The welcome of the land to the men from the sea was warm and generous; but a still and dripping shape was carried slowly up the beach, and the land's welcome for it could only be the different and sinister hospitality of the grave.

When it came night, the white waves paced to and fro in the moonlight, and the wind brought the sound of the great sea's voice to the men on shore, and they felt that they could then be interpreters.

Sherwood Anderson

(1876–1941)

S *herwood Anderson was born in Camden, Ohio. His father was a harness dealer whose fortunes were in decline. Anderson attended public school and worked in various jobs to help make ends meet. He served in Cuba as a private in the Spanish-American War, spent a semester at a college in the Midwest, and then worked in a Chicago advertising office. He tried his hand at running a paint factory as well. Aspiring to be a writer, to turn the lives of the people around him into fiction, Anderson staged a dramatic exit from the world of work. One of his accounts of this break runs like this:*

> I did it one day—walked into my office and called the stenographer—It was a bright warm day in summer. I closed the door in my office and spoke to her. A startled look came into her eyes. "My feet are cold and wet," I said. "I have been walking too long on the bed of a river." Saying these words I walked out the door leaving her staring after me with frightened eyes. I walked eastward along a railroad track. There were five or six dollars in my pocket.

He left regular employment in November 1912 and eventually began to move in Chicago's avant-garde literary circles, publishing his first two novels in 1916 and 1917. But it was his three collections of short stories, **Winesburg, Ohio** *(1919),* **The Triumph of the Egg** *(1921), and* **Horses and Men** *(1923), that secured him his reputation as a major writer. Anderson did for small-town life in America what Turgenev and Zola had done for peasant life in the nineteenth century; that is, he stripped away the sentimentalized, bucolic image created by previous literature and revealed the pettiness, repressiveness, and powerful instincts that characterized the lives of ordinary men and women. As one of the first of the American modernists, he liberated prose for the next generation; as the chronicler of the poignancy of simple lives and simple memories, the rich strain of melancholy that runs through the most ordinary and uneventful life, he has few equals.*

Death in the Woods

She was an old woman and lived on a farm near the town in which I lived. All country and small-town people have seen such old women, but no one knows much about them. Such an old woman comes into town driving an old worn-out horse or she comes afoot carrying a basket. She may own a few hens and have eggs to sell. She brings them in a basket and takes them to a grocer. There she trades them in. She gets some salt pork and some beans. Then she gets a pound or two of sugar and some flour.

Afterwards she goes to the butcher's and asks for some dog-meat. She may spend ten or fifteen cents, but when she does she asks for something. Formerly the butchers gave liver to anyone who wanted to carry it away. In our family we were always having it. Once one of my brothers got a whole cow's liver at the slaughterhouse near the fair grounds in our town. We had it until we were sick of it. It never cost a cent. I have hated the thought of it ever since.

The old farm woman got some liver and a soup-bone. She never visited with anyone, and as soon as she got what she wanted she lit out for home. It made quite a load for such an old body. No one gave her a lift. People drive right down a road and never notice an old woman like that.

There was such an old woman who used to come into town past our house one summer and fall when I was a young boy and was sick with what was called inflammatory rheumatism. She went home later carrying a heavy pack on her back. Two or three large gaunt-looking dogs followed at her heels.

The old woman was nothing special. She was one of the nameless ones that hardly anyone knows, but she got into my thoughts. I have just suddenly now, after all these years, remembered her and what happened. It is a story. Her name was Grimes, and she lived with her husband and son in a small unpainted house on the bank of a small creek four miles from town.

The husband and son were a tough lot. Although the son was but twenty-one, he had already served a term in jail. It was whispered about that the woman's husband stole horses and ran them off to some other county. Now and then, when a horse turned up missing, the man had also disappeared. No one ever caught him. Once, when I was loafing at Tom Whitehead's livery-barn, the man came there and sat on the bench in front. Two or three other men were there, but no one spoke to him. He sat for a few minutes and then got up and went away. When he was leaving he turned around and stared at the men. There was a look of defiance in his eyes. "Well, I have tried to be friendly. You don't want to talk to me. It has been so wherever I have gone in this town. If, some day, one of your fine horses turns up missing, well, then what?" He did not say anything actually. "I'd like to bust one of you on the jaw," was about what his eyes said. I remember how the look in his eyes made me shiver.

The old man belonged to a family that had had money once. His name was Jake Grimes. It all comes back clearly now. His father, John Grimes, had owned a sawmill when the country was new, and had made money. Then he got to drinking and running after women. When he died there wasn't much left.

Jake blew in the rest. Pretty soon there wasn't any more lumber to cut and his land was nearly all gone.

He got his wife off a German farmer, for whom he went to work one June day in the wheat harvest. She was a young thing then and scared to death. You see, the farmer was up to something with the girl—she was, I think, a bound girl and his wife had her suspicions. She took it out on the girl when the man wasn't around. Then, when the wife had to go off to town for supplies, the farmer got after her. She told young Jake that nothing really ever happened, but he didn't know whether to believe it or not.

He got her pretty easy himself, the first time he was out with her. He wouldn't have married her if the German farmer hadn't tried to tell him where to get off. He got her to go riding with him in his buggy one night when he was threshing on the place, and then he came for her the next Sunday night.

She managed to get out of the house without her employer's seeing, but when she was getting into the buggy he showed up. It was almost dark, and he just popped up suddenly at the horse's head. He grabbed the horse by the bridle and Jake got out his buggy-whip.

They had it out all right! The German was a tough one. Maybe he didn't care whether his wife knew or not. Jake hit him over the face and shoulders with the buggy-whip, but the horse got to acting up and he had to get out.

Then the two men went for it. The girl didn't see it. The horse started to run away and went nearly a mile down the road before the girl got him stopped. Then she managed to tie him to a tree beside the road. (I wonder how I know all this. It must have stuck in my mind from small-town tales when I was a boy.) Jake found her there after he got through with the German. She was huddled up in the buggy seat, crying, scared to death. She told Jake a lot of stuff, how the German had tried to get her, how he chased her once into the barn, how another time, when they happened to be alone in the house together, he tore her dress open clear down the front. The German, she said, might have got her that time if he hadn't heard his old woman drive in at the gate. She had been off to town for supplies. Well, she would be putting the horse in the barn. The German managed to sneak off to the fields without his wife seeing. He told the girl he would kill her if she told. What could she do? She told a lie about ripping her dress in the barn when she was feeding the stock. I remember now that she was a bound girl and did not know where her father and mother were. Maybe she did not have any father. You know what I mean.

Such bound children were often enough cruelly treated. They were children who had no parents, slaves really. There were very few orphan homes then. They were legally bound into some home. It was a matter of pure luck how it came out.

II

She married Jake and had a son and daughter, but the daughter died.

Then she settled down to feed stock. That was her job. At the German's place she had cooked the food for the German and his wife. The wife was a strong woman with big hips and worked most of the time in the fields with her husband. She fed them and fed the cows in the barn, fed the pigs, the horses and the chickens. Every moment of every day, as a young girl, was spent feeding something.

Then she married Jake Grimes and he had to be fed. She was a slight thing, and when she had been married for three or four years, and after the two children were born, her slender shoulders became stooped.

Jake always had a lot of big dogs around the house, that stood near the unused sawmill near the creek. He was always trading horses when he wasn't stealing something and had a lot of poor bony ones about. Also he kept three or four pigs and a cow. They were all pastured in the few acres left of the Grimes place and Jake did little enough work.

He went into debt for a threshing outfit and ran it for several years, but it did not pay. People did not trust him. They were afraid he would steal the grain at night. He had to go a long way off to get work and it cost too much to get there. In the winter he hunted and cut a little firewood, to be sold in some nearby town. When the son grew up he was just like the father. They got drunk together. If there wasn't anything to eat in the house when they came home the old man gave his old woman a cut over the head. She had a few chickens of her own and had to kill one of them in a hurry. When they were all killed she wouldn't have any eggs to sell when she went to town, and then what would she do?

She had to scheme all her life about getting things fed, getting the pigs fed so they would grow fat and could be butchered in the fall. When they were butchered her husband took most of the meat off to town and sold it. If he did not do it first the boy did. They fought sometimes and when they fought the old woman stood aside trembling.

She had got the habit of silence anyway—that was fixed. Sometimes, when she began to look old—she wasn't forty yet—and when the husband and son were both off, trading horses or drinking or hunting or stealing, she went around the house and the barnyard muttering to herself.

How was she going to get everything fed?—that was her problem. The dogs had to be fed. There wasn't enough hay in the barn for the horses and the cow. If she didn't feed the chickens how could they lay eggs? Without eggs to sell how could she get things in town, things she had to have to keep the life of the farm going? Thank heaven, she did not have to feed her husband—in a certain way. That hadn't lasted long after their marriage and after the babies came. Where he went on his long trips she did not know. Sometimes he was gone from home for weeks, and after the boy grew up they went off together.

They left everything at home for her to manage and she had no money. She knew no one. No one ever talked to her in town. When it was winter she had to gather sticks of wood for her fire, had to try to keep the stock fed with very little grain.

The stock in the barn cried to her hungrily, the dogs followed her about. In the winter the hens laid few enough eggs. They huddled in the corners of the barn and she kept watching them. If a hen lays an egg in the barn in the winter and you do not find it, it freezes and breaks.

One day in winter the old woman went off to town with a few eggs and the dogs followed her. She did not get started until nearly three o'clock and the snow was heavy. She hadn't been feeling very well for several days and so she went muttering along, scantily clad, her shoulders stooped. She had an old grain bag in which she carried her eggs, tucked away down in the bottom. There weren't many of them, but in winter the price of eggs is up. She would get a little meat in exchange for the eggs, some salt pork, a little sugar, and some coffee perhaps. It might be the butcher would give her a piece of liver.

When she had got to town and was trading in her eggs the dogs lay by the door outside. She did pretty well, got the things she needed, more than she had hoped. Then she went to the butcher and he gave her some liver and some dog-meat.

It was the first time anyone had spoken to her in a friendly way for a long time. The butcher was alone in his shop when she came in and was annoyed by the thought of such a sick-looking old woman out on such a day. It was bitter cold and the snow, that had let up during the afternoon, was falling again. The butcher said something about her husband and her son, swore at them, and the old woman stared at him, a look of mild surprise in her eyes as he talked. He said that if either the husband or the son were going to get any of the liver or the heavy bones with scraps of meat hanging to them that he had put into the grain bag, he'd see him starve first.

Starve, eh? Well, things had to be fed. Men had to be fed, and the horses that weren't any good but maybe could be traded off, and the poor thin cow that hadn't given any milk for three months.

Horses, cows, pigs, dogs, men.

III

The old woman had to get back before darkness came if she could. The dogs followed at her heels, sniffing at the heavy grain bag she had fastened on her back. When she got to the edge of town she stopped by a fence and tied the bag on her back with a piece of rope she had carried in her dress-pocket for just that purpose. That was an easier way to carry it. Her arms ached. It was hard when she had to crawl over fences and once she fell over and landed in the snow. The dogs went frisking about. She had to struggle to get to her feet again, but she made it. The point of climbing over the fences was that there was a short cut over a hill and through a woods. She might have gone around by the road, but it was a mile farther that way. She was afraid she couldn't make it. And then, besides, the stock had to be fed. There was a little hay left and a little corn. Perhaps her husband and son would bring some home when they came. They had driven off in the only buggy the Grimes family had, a rickety thing, a rickety horse hitched to the buggy, two other rickety horses led by halters. They were going to trade horses, get a little money if they could. They might come home drunk. It would be well to have something in the house when they came back.

The son had an affair on with a woman at the county seat, fifteen miles away. She was a rough enough woman, a tough one. Once, in the summer, the son had brought her to the house. Both she and the son had been drinking. Jake Grimes was away and the son and his woman ordered the old woman about like a servant. She didn't mind much; she was used to it. Whatever happened she never said anything. That was her way of getting along. She had managed that way when she was a young girl at the German's and ever since she had married Jake. That time her son brought his woman to the house they stayed all night, sleeping together just as though they were married. It hadn't shocked the old woman, not much. She had got past being shocked early in life.

With the pack on her back she went painfully along across an open field, wading in the deep snow, and got into the woods.

There was a path, but it was hard to follow. Just beyond the top of the hill, where the woods was thickest, there was a small clearing. Had someone once thought of building a house there? The clearing was as large as a building lot in town, large enough for a house and a garden. The path ran along the side of the clearing, and when she got there the old woman sat down to rest at the foot of a tree.

It was a foolish thing to do. When she got herself placed, the pack against the tree's trunk, it was nice, but what about getting up again? She worried about that for a moment and then quietly closed her eyes.

She must have slept for a time. When you are about so cold you can't get any colder. The afternoon grew a little warmer and the snow came thicker than ever. Then after a time the weather cleared. The moon even came out.

There were four Grimes dogs that had followed Mrs. Grimes into town, all tall gaunt fellows. Such men as Jake Grimes and his son always keep just such dogs. They kick and abuse them, but they stay. The Grimes dogs, in order to keep from starving, had to do a lot of foraging for themselves, and they had been at it while the old woman slept with her back to the tree at the side of the clearing. They had been chasing rabbits in the woods and in adjoining fields and in their ranging had picked up three other farm dogs.

After a time all the dogs came back to the clearing. They were excited about something. Such nights, cold and clear and with a moon, do things to dogs. It may be that some old instinct, come down from the time when they were wolves and ranged the woods in packs on winter nights, comes back into them.

The dogs in the clearing, before the old woman, had caught two or three rabbits and their immediate hunger had been satisfied. They began to play, running in circles in the clearing. Round and round they ran, each dog's nose at the tail of the next dog. In the clearing under the snow-laden trees and under the wintry moon they made a strange picture, running thus silently, in a circle their running had beaten in the soft snow. The dogs made no sound. They ran around and around in the circle.

It may have been that the old woman saw them doing that before she died. She may have awakened once or twice and looked at the strange sight with dim old eyes.

She wouldn't be very cold now, just drowsy. Life hangs on a long time. Perhaps the old woman was out of her head. She may have dreamed of her girlhood, at the German's, and before that, when she was a child and before her mother lit out and left her.

Her dreams couldn't have been very pleasant. Not many pleasant things had happened to her. Now and then one of the Grimes dogs left the running circle and came to stand before her. The dog thrust his face close to her face. His red tongue was hanging out.

The running of the dogs may have been a kind of death ceremony.

It may have been that the primitive instinct of the wolf, having been aroused in the dogs by the night and the running, made them somehow afraid.

"Now we are no longer wolves. We are dogs, the servants of men. Keep alive, man! When man dies we become wolves again."

When one of the dogs came to where the old woman sat with her back against the tree and thrust his nose close to her face he seemed satisfied and went back to run with the pack. All the Grimes dogs did it at some time during the evening, before she died. I knew all about it afterward, when I grew to be a man, because once in a woods in Illinois, on another winter night, I saw a pack of dogs act just like that. The dogs were waiting for me to die as they had waited for the old woman that night when I was a child, but when it happened to me I was a young man and had no intention whatever of dying.

The old woman died softly and quietly. When she was dead and when one of the Grimes dogs had come to her and had found her dead all the dogs stopped running.

They gathered about her.

Well, she was dead now. She had fed the Grimes dogs when she was alive, what about now?

There was the pack on her back, the grain bag containing the piece of salt pork, the liver the butcher had given her, the dog-meat, the soup bones. The butcher in town, having been suddenly overcome with a feeling of pity, had loaded her grain bag heavily. It had been a big haul for the old woman.

It was a big haul for the dogs now.

IV

One of the Grimes dogs sprang suddenly out from among the others and began worrying the pack on the old woman's back. Had the dogs really been wolves that one would have been the leader of the pack. What he did, all the others did.

All of them sank their teeth into the grain bag the old woman had fastened with ropes to her back.

They dragged the old woman's body out into the open clearing. The worn-out dress was quickly torn from her shoulders. When she was found, a day or two later, the dress had been torn from her body clear to the hips, but the dogs had not touched her body. They had got the meat out of the grain bag, that was all. Her body was frozen stiff when it was found, and the shoulders were so narrow and the body so slight that in death it looked like the body of some charming young girl.

Such things happened in towns of the Middle West, on farms near town, when I was a boy. A hunter out after rabbits found the old woman's body and did not touch it. Something, the beaten round path in the little snow-covered clearing, the silence of the place, the place where the dogs had worried the body trying to pull the grain bag away or tear it open— something startled the man and he hurried off to town.

I was in Main Street with one of my brothers who was town newsboy and who was taking the afternoon papers to the stores. It was almost night.

The hunter came into a grocery and told his story. Then he went to a hardware shop and into a drugstore. Men began to gather on the sidewalks. Then they started out along the road to the place in the woods.

My brother should have gone on about his business of distributing papers but he didn't. Everyone was going to the woods. The undertaker went and the town marshal. Several men got on a dray and rode out to where the path left the road and went into the woods, but the horses weren't very sharply shod and slid about on the slippery roads. They made no better time than those of us who walked.

The town marshal was a large man whose leg had been injured in the Civil War. He carried a heavy cane and limped rapidly along the road. My brother and I followed at his heels, and as we went other men and boys joined the crowd.

It had grown dark by the time we got to where the old woman had left the road but the moon had come out. The marshal was thinking there might have been a murder. He kept asking the hunter questions. The hunter went along with his gun across his shoulders, a dog following at his heels. It isn't often a rabbit hunter has a chance to be so conspicuous. He was taking full advantage of it, leading the procession with the town marshal. "I didn't see any wounds. She was a beautiful young girl. Her face was buried in the snow. No, I didn't know her." As a matter of fact, the hunter had not looked closely at the body. He had been frightened. She might have been murdered and someone might spring out from behind a tree and murder him. In a woods, in the late afternoon, when the trees are all bare and there is white snow on the ground, when all is silent, something creepy steals over the mind and body. If something strange or uncanny has happened in the neighborhood all you think about is getting away from there as fast as you can.

The crowd of men and boys had got to where the old woman had crossed the field and went, following the marshal and the hunter, up the slight incline and into the woods.

My brother and I were silent. He had his bundle of papers in a bag slung across his shoulder. When he got back to town he would have to go on distributing his papers before he went home to supper. If I went along, as he had no doubt already determined I should, we would both be late. Either mother or our older sister would have to warm our supper.

Well, we would have something to tell. A boy did not get such a chance very often. It was lucky we just happened to go into the grocery when the hunter came in. The hunter was a country fellow. Neither of us had ever seen him before.

Now the crowd of men and boys had got to the clearing. Darkness comes quickly on such winter nights, but the full moon made everything clear. My brother and I stood near the tree, beneath which the old woman had died.

She did not look old, lying there in that light, frozen and still. One of the men turned her over in the snow and I saw everything. My body trembled with some strange mystical feeling and so did my brother's. It might have been the cold.

Neither of us had ever seen a woman's body before. It may have been the snow, clinging to the frozen flesh, that made it look so white and lovely, so like marble. No woman had come with the party from town; but one of the men, he was the town blacksmith, took off his overcoat and spread it over her. Then he gathered her into his arms and started off to town, all the others following silently. At that time no one knew who she was.

V

I had seen everything, had seen the oval in the snow, like a miniature race track, where the dogs had run, had seen how the men were mystified, had seen the white bare young-looking shoulders, had heard the whispered comments of the men.

The men were simply mystified. They took the body to the undertaker's, and when the blacksmith, the hunter, the marshal and several others had got inside they closed the door. If father had been there perhaps he could have got in, but we boys couldn't.

I went with my brother to distribute the rest of his papers and when we got home it was my brother who told the story.

I kept silent and went to bed early. It may have been I was not satisfied with the way he told it.

Later, in the town, I must have heard other fragments of the old woman's story. She was recognized the next day and there was an investigation.

The husband and son were found somewhere and brought to town and there was an attempt to connect them with the woman's death, but it did not work. They had perfect enough alibis.

However, the town was against them. They had to get out. Where they went I never heard.

I remember only the picture there in the forest, the men standing about, the naked girlish-looking figure, face down in the snow, the tracks made by the running dogs and the clear cold winter sky above. White fragments of clouds were drifting across the sky. They went racing across the little open space among the trees.

The scene in the forest had become for me, without my knowing it, the foundation for the real story I am now trying to tell. The fragments, you see, had to be picked up slowly, long afterwards.

Things happened. When I was a young man I worked on the farm of a German. The hired-girl was afraid of her employer. The farmer's wife hated her.

I saw things at that place. Once later, I had a half-uncanny, mystical adventure with dogs in an Illinois forest on a clear, moonlit winter night. When I was a schoolboy, and on a summer day, I went with a boy friend out along a creek some miles from town and came to the house where the old woman had lived. No one had lived in the house since her death. The doors were broken from the hinges; the window lights were all broken. As the boy and I stood in the road outside, two dogs, just roving farm dogs no doubt, came running around the corner of the house. The dogs were tall, gaunt fellows and came down to the fence and glared through at us, standing in the road.

The whole thing, the story of the old woman's death, was to me as I grew older like music heard from far off. The notes had to be picked up slowly one at a time. Something had to be understood.

The woman who died was one destined to feed animal life. Anyway, that is all she ever did. She was feeding animal life before she was born, as a child, as a young woman working on the farm of the German, after she married, when she grew old and when she died. She fed animal life in cows, in chickens, in pigs, in horses, in dogs, in men. Her daughter had died in childhood and with her one son she had no articulate relations. On the night when she died she was hurrying homeward, bearing on her body food for animal life.

She died in the clearing in the woods and even after her death continued feeding animal life.

You see it is likely that, when my brother told the story, that night when we got home and my mother and sister sat listening, I did not think he got the point. He was too young and so was I. A thing so complete has its own beauty.

I shall not try to emphasize the point. I am only explaining why I was dissatisfied then and have been ever since. I speak of that only that you may understand why I have been impelled to try to tell the simple story over again.

E.M. FORSTER

(1879–1970)

E. M. *Forster was born in London. After his father died, his mother brought him up in the country near Stevenage, Hertfordshire. A legacy of 8000 pounds from an aunt made it possible for him to attend Cambridge and to dedicate himself to writing. At university he acquired the humanistic values that he defended all his life. The Apostles Group that he joined included Lytton Strachey, John Maynard Keynes, Leonard Woolf, and Roger Fry, men who were later active in the famous Blooms-bury group, along with Virginia Stephen (Woolf), Vanessa Stephen (Bell), and Duncan Grant. As Frederick McDowell points out, "most of what Bloomsbury came to represent, Forster also valued: friendship, love of discussion, irreverence toward tradition and convention, agnosticism, the inevitability of social change, an appreciation of the new and innovative in the arts, and a questioning of ready-made concepts." Forster travelled in Italy and Greece after university, returning to found* The Independent Review, *to which he contributed a number of essays. His first novel was published when he was 26, and four others quickly followed. His masterpiece,* A Passage to India, *was completed in 1924. Forster's career as a novelist was over, but he went on to become an astute and tireless commentator on social and cultural issues.* Abinger Harvest *(1936) and* Two Cheers for Democracy *(1951) are books of essays that make clear just how helpful Forster's sane and compassionate views are as an aid to understanding both his time and our own. In "What I Believe," he reluctantly formulates a creed to supplement the trio of "tolerance, good temper and sympathy," which, on the eve of the Second World War, he recognizes as insufficient. In the essay, he praises democracy "because it admits variety" and "permits criticism," recognizes the fears and power of violence and its perpetrators, but maintains that "what is good in people—and consequently in the world—is their insistence on connection, their belief in friendship and loyalty for their own sakes." More exalted and more demanding visions of humanity and its potential have been formulated, but few have proved to be as useful and life-sustaining as the simple truths Forster articulates here and in his fiction.*

The Road from Colonus

For no very intelligible reason, Mr Lucas had hurried ahead of his party. He was perhaps reaching the age at which independence becomes valuable, because it is so soon to be lost. Tired of attention and consideration, he liked breaking away from the younger members, to ride by himself, and to dismount unassisted. Perhaps he also relished that more subtle pleasure of being kept waiting for lunch, and of telling the others on their arrival that it was of no consequence.

So, with childish impatience, he battered the animal's sides with his heels, and made the muleteer bang it with a thick stick and prick it with a sharp one, and jolted down the hill sides through clumps of flowering shrubs and stretches of anemones and asphodel, till he heard the sound of running water, and came in sight of the group of plane trees where they were to have their meal.

Even in England those trees would have been remarkable, so huge were they, so interlaced, so magnificently clothed in quivering green. And here in Greece they were unique, the one cool spot in that hard brilliant landscape, already scorched by the heat of an April sun. In their midst was hidden a tiny Khan or country inn, a frail mud building with a broad wooden balcony in which sat an old woman spinning, while a small brown pig, eating orange peel, stood beside her. On the wet earth below squatted two children, playing some primeval game with their fingers; and their mother, none too clean either, was messing with some rice inside. As Mrs Forman would have said, it was all very Greek, and the fastidious Mr Lucas felt thankful that they were bringing their own food with them, and should eat it in the open air.

Still, he was glad to be there—the muleteer had helped him off—and glad that Mrs Forman was not there to forestall his opinions—glad even that he should not see Ethel for quite half an hour. Ethel was his youngest daughter, still unmarried. She was unselfish and affectionate, and it was generally understood that she was to devote her life to her father, and be the comfort of his old age. Mrs Forman always referred to her as Antigone, and Mr Lucas tried to settle down to the role of Oedipus, which seemed the only one that public opinion allowed him.

He had this in common with Oedipus, that he was growing old. Even to himself it had become obvious. He had lost interest in other people's affairs, and seldom attended when they spoke to him. He was fond of talking himself but often forgot what he was going to say, and even when he succeeded, it seldom seemed worth the effort. His phrases and gestures had become stiff and set, his anecdotes, once so successful, fell flat, his silence was as meaningless as his speech. Yet he had led a healthy, active life, had worked steadily, made money, educated his children. There was nothing and no one to blame: he was simply growing old.

At the present moment, here he was in Greece, and one of the dreams of his life was realized. Forty years ago he had caught the fever of Hellenism, and all his life he had felt that could he but visit that land, he would not have lived in vain. But Athens had been dusty, Delphi wet, Thermopylae flat, and he had listened with amazement and cynicism to the rapturous exclamations of his companions. Greece was like England: it was a man who was growing old, and it made no difference whether that man looked at the Thames or the Eurotas. It was his last hope of contradicting that logic of experience, and it was failing.

Yet Greece had done something for him, though he did not know it. It had made him discontented, and there are stirrings of life in discontent. He knew that he was not the victim of continual ill-luck. Something great was wrong, and he was pitted against no mediocre or accidental enemy. For the last month a strange desire had possessed him to die fighting.

"Greece is the land for young people," he said to himself as he stood under the plane trees, "but I will enter into it, I will possess it. Leaves shall be green again, water shall be sweet, the sky shall be blue. They were so forty years ago, and I will win them back. I do mind being old, and I will pretend no longer."

He took two steps forward, and immediately cold waters were gurgling over his ankle.

"Where does the water come from?" he asked himself. "I do not even know that." He remembered that all the hill sides were dry; yet here the road was suddenly covered with flowing streams.

He stopped still in amazement, saying: "Water out of a tree—out of a hollow tree? I never saw nor thought of that before."

For the enormous plane that leant towards the Khan was hollow—it had been burnt out for charcoal—and from its living trunk there gushed an impetuous spring, coating the bark with fern and moss, and flowing over the mule track to create fertile meadows beyond. The simple country folk had paid to beauty and mystery such tribute as they could, for in the rind of the tree a shrine was cut, holding a lamp and a little picture of the Virgin, inheritor of the Naiad's and Dryad's joint abode.

"I never saw anything so marvellous before," said Mr Lucas. "I could even step inside the trunk and see where the water comes from."

For a moment he hesitated to violate the shrine. Then he remembered with a smile his own thought—"the place shall be mine; I will enter it and possess it"—and leapt almost aggressively on to a stone within.

The water pressed up steadily and noiselessly from the hollow roots and hidden crevices of the plane, forming a wonderful amber pool ere it spilt over the lip of bark on to the earth outside. Mr Lucas tasted it and it was sweet, and when he looked up the black funnel of the trunk he saw sky which was blue, and some leaves which were green; and he remembered, without smiling, another of his thoughts.

Others had been before him—indeed he had a curious sense of companionship. Little votive offerings to the presiding Power were fastened on to the bark—tiny arms and legs and eyes in tin; grotesque models of the brain or the heart—all tokens of some recovery of strength or wisdom or love. There was no such thing as the solitude of nature, for the sorrows and joys of humanity had pressed even into the bosom of a tree. He spread out his arms and steadied himself against the soft charred wood, and then slowly leant back, till his body was resting on the trunk behind. His eyes closed, and he had the strange feeling of one who is moving, yet at peace—the feeling of the swimmer, who, after long struggling with chopping seas, finds that after all the tide will sweep him to his goal.

So he lay motionless, conscious only of the stream below his feet, and that all things were a stream, in which he was moving.

He was aroused at last by a shock—the shock of an arrival perhaps, for when he opened his eyes, something unimagined, indefinable, had passed over all things, and made them intelligible and good.

There was meaning in the stoop of the old woman over her work, and in the quick motions of the little pig, and in her diminishing globe of wool. A young man came singing over the streams on a mule, and there was a beauty in his pose and sincerity in his greeting. The sun made no accidental patterns upon the spreading roots of the trees, and there was intention in the nodding clumps of asphodel, and in the music of the water. To Mr Lucas, who, in a brief space of time, had discovered not only Greece, but England and all the world and life, there seemed nothing ludicrous in the desire to hang within the tree another votive offering— a little model of an entire man.

"Why, here's papa, playing at being Merlin."

All unnoticed they had arrived—Ethel, Mrs Forman, Mr Graham, and the English-speaking dragoman. Mr Lucas peered out at them suspiciously. They had suddenly become unfamiliar, and all that they did seemed strained and coarse.

"Allow me to give you a hand," said Mr Graham, a young man who was always polite to his elders.

Mr Lucas felt annoyed. "Thank you, I can manage perfectly well by myself," he replied. His foot slipped as he stepped out of the tree, and went into the spring.

"Oh papa, my papa!" said Ethel, "what are you doing? Thank goodness I have got a change for you on the mule."

She tended him carefully, giving him clean socks and dry boots, and then sat him down on the rug beside the lunch basket, while she went with the others to explore the grove.

They came back in ecstasies, in which Mr Lucas tried to join. But he found them intolerable. Their enthusiasm was superficial, commonplace, and spasmodic. They had no perception of the coherent beauty that was flowering around them. He tried at least to explain his feelings, and what he said was:

"I am altogether pleased with the appearance of this place. It impresses me very favourably. The trees are fine, remarkably fine for Greece, and there is something very poetic in the spring of clear running water. The people too seem kindly and civil. It is decidedly an attractive place."

Mrs Forman upbraided him for his tepid praise.

"Oh, it is a place in a thousand!" she cried, "I could live here and die here! I really would stop if I had not to be back at Athens! It reminds me of the Colonus of Sophocles."

"Well, *I* must stop," said Ethel. "I positively must."

"Yes, do! You and your father! Antigone and Oedipus. Of course you must stop at Colonus!"

Mr Lucas was almost breathless with excitement. When he stood within the tree, he had believed that his happiness would be independent of locality. But these few minutes' conversation had undeceived him. He no longer trusted himself to journey through the world, for old thoughts, old wearinesses might be waiting to rejoin him as soon as he left the shade of the planes, and the music of the virgin water. To sleep in the Khan with the gracious, kind-eyed country people, to watch the bats flit about within the globe of shade, and see the moon turn the golden patterns into silver—one such night would place him beyond relapse, and confirm him for ever in the kingdom he had regained. But all his lips could say was: "I should be willing to put in a night here."

"You mean a week, papa! It would be sacrilege to put in less."

"A week then, a week," said his lips, irritated at being corrected, while his heart was leaping with joy. All through lunch he spoke to them no more, but watched the place he should know so well, and the people who would so soon be his companions and friends. The inmates of the Khan only consisted of an old woman, a middle-aged woman, a young man and two children, and to none of them had he spoken, yet he loved them as he loved everything that moved or breathed or existed beneath the benedictory shade of the planes.

"*En route!*" said the shrill voice of Mrs Forman. "Ethel! Mr Graham! The best of things must end."

"To-night," thought Mr Lucas, "they will light the little lamp by the shrine. And when we all sit together on the balcony, perhaps they will tell me which offerings they put up."

"I beg your pardon, Mr Lucas," said Graham, "but they want to fold up the rug you are sitting on."

Mr Lucas got up, saying to himself: "Ethel shall go to bed first, and then I will try to tell them about my offering too—for it is a thing I must do. I think they will understand if I am left with them alone."

Ethel touched him on the cheek. "Papa! I've called you three times. All the mules are here."

"Mules? What mules?"

"Our mules. We're all waiting. Oh, Mr Graham, do help my father on."

"I don't know what you're talking about, Ethel."

"My dearest papa, we must start. You know we have to get to Olympia to-night."

Mr Lucas in pompous, confident tones replied: "I always did wish, Ethel, that you had a better head for plans. You know perfectly well that we are putting in a week here. It is your own suggestion."

Ethel was startled into impoliteness. "What a perfectly ridiculous idea. You must have known I was joking. Of course I meant I wished we could."

"Ah! if we could only do what we wished!" sighed Mrs Forman, already seated on her mule.

"Surely," Ethel continued in calmer tones, "you didn't think I meant it."

"Most certainly I did. I have made all my plans on the supposition that we are stopping here, and it will be extremely inconvenient, indeed, impossible for me to start."

He delivered this remark with an air of great conviction, and Mrs Forman and Mr Graham had to turn away to hide their smiles.

"I am sorry I spoke so carelessly; it was wrong of me. But, you know, we can't break up our party, and even one night here would make us miss the boat at Patras."

Mrs Forman, in an aside, called Mr Graham's attention to the excellent way in which Ethel managed her father.

"I don't mind about the Patras boat. You said that we should stop here, and we are stopping."

It seemed as if the inhabitants of the Khan had divined in some mysterious way that the altercation touched them. The old woman stopped her spinning, while the young man and the two children stood behind Mr Lucas, as if supporting him.

Neither arguments nor entreaties moved him. He said little, but he was absolutely determined, because for the first time he saw his daily life aright. What need had he to return to England? Who would miss him? His friends were dead or cold. Ethel loved him in a way, but, as was right, she had other interests. His other children he seldom saw. He had only one other relative, his sister Julia, whom he both feared and hated. It was no effort to struggle. He would be a fool as well as a coward if he stirred from the place which brought him happiness and peace.

At last Ethel, to humour him, and not disinclined to air her modern Greek, went into the Khan with the astonished dragoman to look at the rooms. The woman inside received them with loud welcomes, and the young man, when no one was looking, began to lead Mr Lucas' mule to the stable.

"Drop it, you brigand!" shouted Graham, who always declared that foreigners could understand English if they chose. He was right, for the man obeyed, and they all stood waiting for Ethel's return.

She emerged at last, with close-gathered skirts, followed by the dragoman bearing the little pig, which he had bought at a bargain.

"My dear papa, I will do all I can for you, but stop in that Khan—no."

"Are there—fleas?" asked Mrs Forman.

Ethel intimated that "fleas" was not the word.

"Well, I am afraid that settles it," said Mrs Forman, "I know how particular Mr Lucas is."

"It does not settle it," said Mr Lucas. "Ethel, you go on. I do not want you. I don't know why I ever consulted you. I shall stop here alone."

"That is absolute nonsense," said Ethel, losing her temper. "How can you be left alone at your age? How would you get your meals or your bath? All your letters are waiting for you at Patras. You'll miss the boat. That means missing the London operas, and upsetting all your engagements for the month. And as if you could travel by yourself!"

"They might knife you," was Mr Graham's contribution.

The Greeks said nothing; but whenever Mr Lucas looked their way, they beckoned him towards the Khan. The children would even have drawn him by the coat, and the old woman on the balcony stopped her almost completed spinning, and fixed him with mysterious appealing eyes. As he fought, the issue assumed gigantic proportions, and he believed that he was not merely stopping because he had regained youth or seen beauty or found happiness, but because in that place and with those people a supreme event was awaiting him which would transfigure the face of the world. The moment was so tremendous that he abandoned words and arguments as useless, and rested on the strength of his mighty unrevealed allies: silent men, murmuring water, and whispering trees. For the whole place called with one voice, articulate to him, and his garrulous opponents became every minute more meaningless and absurd.

Soon they would be tired and go chattering away into the sun, leaving him to the cool grove and the moonlight and the destiny he foresaw.

Mrs Forman and the dragoman had indeed already started, amid the piercing screams of the little pig, and the struggle might have gone on indefinitely if Ethel had not called in Mr Graham.

"Can you help me?" she whispered. "He is absolutely un-manageable."

"I'm no good at arguing—but if I could help you in any other way——" and he looked down complacently at his well-made figure.

Ethel hesitated. Then she said: "Help me in any way you can. After all, it is for his good that we do it."

"Then have his mule led up behind him."

So when Mr Lucas thought he had gained the day, he suddenly felt himself lifted off the ground, and sat sideways on the saddle, and at the same time the mule started off at a trot. He said nothing, for he had nothing to say, and even his face showed little emotion as he felt the shade pass and heard the sound of the water cease. Mr Graham was running at his side, hat in hand, apologizing.

"I know I had no business to do it, and I do beg your pardon awfully. But I do hope that some day you too will feel that I was—damn!"

A stone had caught him in the middle of the back. It was thrown by the little boy, who was pursuing them along the mule track. He was followed by his sister, also throwing stones.

Ethel screamed to the dragoman, who was some way ahead with Mrs Forman, but before he could rejoin them, another adversary appeared. It was the young Greek, who had cut them off in front, and now dashed down at Mr Lucas' bridle. Fortunately Graham was an expert boxer, and it did not take him a moment to beat down the youth's feeble defence, and to send him sprawling with a bleeding mouth into the asphodel. By this time the dragoman had arrived, the children, alarmed at the fate of their brother, had desisted, and the rescue party, if such it is to be consid-ered, retired in disorder to the trees.

"Little devils!" said Graham, laughing with triumph. "That's the modern Greek all over. Your father meant money if he stopped, and they consider we were taking it out of their pocket."

"Oh, they are terrible—simple savages! I don't know how I shall ever thank you. You've saved my father."

"I only hope you didn't think me brutal."

"No," replied Ethel with a little sigh. "I admire strength."

Meanwhile the cavalcade reformed, and Mr Lucas, who, as Mrs Forman said, bore his disappointment wonderfully well, was put comfort-ably on to his mule. They hurried up the opposite hillside, fearful of another attack, and it was not until they had left the eventful place far behind that Ethel found an opportunity to speak to her father and ask his pardon for the way she had treated him.

"You seemed so different, dear father, and you quite frightened me. Now I feel that you are your old self again."

He did not answer, and she concluded that he was not unnaturally offended at her behaviour.

By one of those curious tricks of mountain scenery, the place they had left an hour before suddenly reappeared far below them. The Khan was hidden under the green dome, but in the open there still stood three figures, and through the pure air rose up a faint cry of defiance or farewell.

Mr Lucas stopped irresolutely, and let the reins fall from his hand.

"Come, father dear," said Ethel gently.

He obeyed, and in another moment a spur of the hill hid the dangerous scene for ever.

II

It was breakfast time, but the gas was alight, owing to the fog. Mr Lucas was in the middle of an account of a bad night he had spent. Ethel, who was to be married in a few weeks, had her arms on the table, listening.

"First the door bell rang, then you came back from the theatre. Then the dog started, and after the dog the cat. And at three in the morning a young hooligan passed by singing. Oh yes: then there was the water gurgling in the pipe above my head."

"I think that was only the bath water running away," said Ethel, looking rather worn.

"Well, there's nothing I dislike more than running water. It's perfectly impossible to sleep in the house. I shall give it up. I shall give notice next quarter. I shall tell the landlord plainly, 'The reason I am giving up the house is this: it is perfectly impossible to sleep in it.' If he says—says— well, what has he got to say?"

"Some more toast, father?"

"Thank you, my dear." He took it, and there was an interval of peace.

But he soon recommenced. "I'm not going to submit to the practising next door as tamely as they think. I wrote and told them so—didn't I?"

"Yes," said Ethel, who had taken care of that the letter should not reach. "I have seen the governess, and she has promised to arrange it differently. And Aunt Julia hates noise. It will be sure to be all right."

Her aunt, being the only unattached member of the family, was coming to keep house for her father when she left him. The reference was not a happy one, and Mr Lucas commenced a series of half articulate sighs, which was only stopped by the arrival of the post.

"Oh, what a parcel!" cried Ethel. "For me! What can it be! Greek stamps. This is most exciting!"

It proved to be some asphodel bulbs, sent by Mrs Forman from Athens for planting in the conservatory.

"Doesn't it bring it all back! You remember the asphodels, father. And all wrapped up in Greek newspapers. I wonder if I can read them still. I used to be able to, you know."

She rattled on, hoping to conceal the laughter of the children next door—a favourite source of querulousness at breakfast time.

"Listen to me! 'A rural disaster.' Oh, I've hit on something sad. But never mind. 'Last Tuesday at Plataniste, in the province of Messenia, a shocking tragedy occurred. A large tree'—aren't I getting on well?—'blew down in the night and'—wait a minute—oh dear! 'crushed to death the five occupants of the little Khan there, who had apparently been sitting in the balcony. The bodies of Maria Rhomaides, the aged proprietress, and of her daughter, aged forty-six, were easily recognizable, whereas that of her grandson'—oh, the rest is really too horrid; I wish I had never tried it, and what's more I feel to have heard the name Plataniste before. We didn't stop there, did we, in the spring?"

"We had lunch," said Mr Lucas, with a faint expression of trouble on his vacant face. "Perhaps it was where the dragoman bought the pig."

"Of course," said Ethel in a nervous voice. "Where the dragoman bought the little pig. How terrible!"

"Very terrible!" said her father, whose attention was wandering to the noisy children next door. Ethel suddenly started to her feet with genuine interest.

"Good gracious!" she exclaimed. "This is an old paper. It happened not lately but in April—the night of Tuesday the eighteenth—and we—we must have been there in the afternoon."

"So we were," said Mr Lucas. She put her hand to her heart, scarcely able to speak.

"Father, dear father, I must say it: you wanted to stop there. All those people, those poor half savage people, tried to keep you, and they're dead. The whole place, it says, is in ruins, and even the stream has changed its course. Father, dear, if it had not been for me, and if Arthur had not helped me, you must have been killed."

Mr Lucas waved his hand irritably. "It is not a bit of good speaking to the governess, I shall write to the landlord and say, "The reason I am giving up the house is this: the dog barks, the children next door are intolerable, and I cannot stand the noise of running water."

Ethel did not check his babbling. She was aghast at the narrowness of the escape, and for a long time kept silence. At last she said: "Such a marvellous deliverance does make one believe in Providence."

Mr Lucas, who was still composing his letter to the landlord, did not reply.

JAMES JOYCE

(1882–1941)

J ames Joyce was born in Dublin and educated at Clongowes Wood
College and Belvedere College, two of the best Jesuit schools in
Ireland. At University College, he was taught by teachers obliged to
make religion the basis of science and the humanities. Reacting against
what he saw as censorship, Joyce found himself in conflict with college
authorities. Attracted to Ibsen's plays, he wrote an essay in which he
praised the Norwegian dramatist for his exposure of middle-class corruption and hypocrisy. In 1902 he journeyed to Paris to enrol at the Berlitz
School in Trieste. Having tried his hand at drama and poetry, Joyce
turned to prose fiction and wrote the short stories that were eventually
to be collected in his first major work, **Dubliners** *(1914). In his short
fiction, Joyce created what is generally regarded as a new, more carefully
crafted type of story, in which he expressed his ambivalent feelings
about his city and countrymen. Documentary realism, the "slice of life"
technique, and the development of a style used to create a narrative
mediated through the consciousness of the characters—*Dubliners *marks
an important advance in all of these areas. In* A Portrait of the Artist
as a Young Man *(1916), Joyce refined the techniques that enabled him
to become the artist who, "like the God of creation, remains within or
behind or beyond or above his handiwork, invisible, refined out of existence." As a portrait of the writer as exile, it became one of the definitive
works of the modernist movement. In* Ulysses *(1922), Joyce's fascination
with Dublin, contemporary history, myth, the texture of society, the
role of the individual, and the process of writing itself finds its fullest
expression. The encyclopaedic nature of Joyce's eccentric genius mani-
fests itself most clearly in* **Finnegans Wake** *(1939), a book on which
Joyce worked for seventeen years, written in a language, and by a
language that constitutes its own representation of the "monomyth"
that is human life. Its defenders have made Joyce's daunting erudition
the subject of endlessly ingenious exegetical works, while its critics have
dismissed it as a "petrified superpun." His dedication to his craft and
his exuberant imagination have made him the modern writer whose work
sets the standards by which others are judged.*

Araby

N orth Richmond Street, being blind, was a quiet street except at the hour when the Christian Brothers' School set the boys free. An uninhabited house of two storeys stood at the blind end, detached from its neighbours in a square ground. The other houses of the street, conscious of decent lives within them, gazed at one another with brown imperturbable faces.

The former tenant of our house, a priest, had died in the back drawing-room. Air, musty from having been long enclosed, hung in all the rooms, and the waste room behind the kitchen was littered with old useless papers. Among these I found a few paper-covered books, the pages of which were curled and damp: *The Abbot*, by Walter Scott, *The Devout Communicant* and *The Memoirs of Vidocq*. I liked the last best because its leaves were yellow. The wild garden behind the house contained a central apple-tree and a few straggling bushes under one of which I found the late tenant's rusty bicycle-pump. He had been a very charitable priest; in his will he had left all his money to institutions and the furniture of his house to his sister.

When the short days of winter came dusk fell before we had well eaten our dinners. When we met in the street the houses had grown sombre. The space of sky above us was the colour of ever-changing violet and towards it the lamps of the street lifted their feeble lanterns. The cold air stung us and we played till our bodies glowed. Our shouts echoed in the silent street. The career of our play brought us through the dark muddy lanes behind the houses where we ran the gauntlet of the rough tribes from the cottages, to the back doors of the dark dripping gardens where odours arose from the ashpits, to the dark odorous stables where a coachman smoothed and combed the horse or shook music from the buckled harness. When we returned to the street light from the kitchen windows had filled the areas. If my uncle was seen turning the corner we hid in the shadow until we had seen him safely housed. Or if Mangan's sister came out on the doorstep to call her brother in to his tea we watched her from our shadow peer up and down the street. We waited to see whether she would remain or go in and, if she remained, we left our shadow and walked up to Mangan's steps resignedly. She was waiting for us, her figure defined by the light from the half-opened door. Her brother always teased her before he obeyed and I stood by the railings looking at her. Her dress swung as she moved her body and the soft rope of her hair tossed from side to side.

Every morning I lay on the floor in the front parlour watching her door. The blind was pulled down to within an inch of the sash so that I could not be seen. When she came out on the doorstep my heart leaped. I ran to the hall, seized my books and followed her. I kept her brown figure always in my eye and, when we came near the point at which our ways diverged, I quickened my pace and passed her. This happened morning after morning. I had never spoken to her, except for a few casual words, and yet her name was like a summons to all my foolish blood.

Her image accompanied me even in places the most hostile to romance. On Saturday evenings when my aunt went marketing I had to go to carry some of the parcels. We walked through the flaring streets, jostled by drunken men and bargaining women, amid the curses of labourers, the shrill litanies of shop-boys who stood on guard by the barrels of pigs' cheeks, the nasal chanting of street-singers, who sang a *come-all-you* about O'Donovan Rossa, or a ballad about the troubles in our native land. These noises converged in a single sensation of life for me: I imagined that I bore my chalice safely through a throng of foes. Her name sprang to my lips at moments in strange prayers and praises which I myself did not understand. My eyes were often full of tears (I could not tell why) and at times a flood from my heart seemed to pour itself out into my bosom. I thought little of the future. I did not know whether I would ever speak to her or not or, if I spoke to her, how I could tell her of my confused adoration. But my body was like a harp and her words and gestures were like fingers running upon the wires.

One evening I went into the back drawing-room in which the priest had died. It was a dark rainy evening and there was no sound in the house. Through one of the broken panes I heard the rain impinge upon the earth, the fine incessant needles of water playing in the sodden beds. Some distant lamp or lighted window gleamed below me. I was thankful that I could see so little. All my senses seemed to desire to veil themselves and, feeling that I was about to slip from them, I pressed the palms of my hands together until they trembled, murmuring: "*O love! O love!*" many times.

At last she spoke to me. When she addressed the first words to me I was so confused that I did not know what to answer. She asked me was I going to *Araby*. I forgot whether I answered yes or no. It would be a splendid bazaar, she said she would love to go.

"And why can't you?" I asked.

While she spoke she turned a silver bracelet round and round her wrist. She could not go, she said, because there would be a retreat that week in her convent. Her brother and two other boys were fighting for their caps and I was alone at the railings. She held one of the spikes, bowing her head towards me. The light from the lamp opposite our door caught the white curve of her neck, lit up her hair that rested there and, falling, lit up the hand upon the railing. It fell over one side of her dress and caught the white border of a petticoat, just visible as she stood at ease.

"It's well for you," she said.

"If I go," I said, "I will bring you something."

What innumerable follies laid waste my waking and sleeping thoughts after that evening! I wished to annihilate the tedious intervening days. I chafed against the work of school. At night in my bedroom and by day in the classroom her image came between me and the page I strove to read. The syllables of the word *Araby* were called to me through the silence in which my soul luxuriated and cast an Eastern enchantment over me. I asked for leave to go to the bazaar on Saturday night. My aunt was surprised and hoped it was not some Freemason affair. I answered few questions in class. I watched my master's face pass from amiability to sternness; he hoped I was not beginning to idle. I could not call my wandering thoughts together. I had hardly any patience with the serious work of life which, now that it stood between me and my desire, seemed to me child's play, ugly monotonous child's play.

On Saturday morning I reminded my uncle that I wished to go to the bazaar in the evening. He was fussing at the hallstand, looking for the hat-brush, and answered me curtly:

"Yes, boy, I know."

As he was in the hall I could not go into the front parlour and lie at the window. I left the house in bad humour and walked slowly towards the school. The air was pitilessly raw and already my heart misgave me.

When I came home to dinner my uncle had not yet been home. Still it was early. I sat staring at the clock for some time and, when its ticking began to irritate me, I left the room. I mounted the staircase and gained the upper part of the house. The high cold empty gloomy rooms liberated me and I went from room to room singing. From the front window I saw my companions playing below in the street. Their cries reached me weakened and indistinct and, leaning my forehead against the cool glass, I looked over at the dark house where she lived. I may have stood there for an hour, seeing nothing but the brown-clad figure cast by my imagination, touched discreetly by the lamplight at the curved neck, at the hand upon the railings and at the border below the dress.

When I came downstairs again I found Mrs. Mercer sitting at the fire. She was an old garrulous woman, a pawnbroker's widow, who collected used stamps for some pious purpose. I had to endure the gossip of the tea-table. The meal was prolonged beyond an hour and still my uncle did not come. Mrs. Mercer stood up to go: she was sorry she couldn't wait any longer, but it was after eight o'clock and she did not like to be out late, as the night air was bad for her. When she had gone I began to walk up and down the room, clenching my fists. My aunt said:

"I'm afraid you may put off your bazaar for this night of Our Lord."

At nine o'clock I heard my uncle's latchkey in the halldoor. I heard him talking to himself and heard the hallstand rocking when it had received the weight of his overcoat. I could interpret these signs. When he was midway through his dinner I asked him to give me the money to go to the bazaar. He had forgotten.

"The people are in bed and after their first sleep now," he said.

I did not smile. My aunt said to him energetically:

"Can't you give him the money and let him go? You've kept him late enough as it is."

My uncle said he was very sorry he had forgotten. He said he believed in the old saying: "All work and no play makes Jack a dull boy." He asked me where I was going and, when I had told him a second time he asked me did I know *The Arab's Farewell to his Steed*. When I left the kitchen he was about to recite the opening lines of the piece to my aunt.

I held a florin tightly in my hand as I strode down Buckingham Street towards the station. The sight of the streets thronged with buyers and glaring with gas recalled to me the purpose of my journey. I took my seat in a third-class carriage of a deserted train. After an intolerable delay the train moved out of the station slowly. It crept onward among ruinous houses and over the twinkling river. At Westland Row Station a crowd of people pressed to the carriage doors; but the porters moved them back, saying that it was a special train for the bazaar. I remained alone in the bare carriage. In a few minutes the train drew up beside an improvised wooden platform. I passed out on to the road and saw by the lighted dial of a clock that it was ten minutes to ten. In front of me was a large building which displayed the magical name.

I could not find any sixpenny entrance and, fearing that the bazaar would be closed, I passed in quickly through a turnstile, handing a shilling to a weary-looking man. I found myself in a big hall girdled at half its height by a gallery. Nearly all the stalls were closed and the greater part of the hall was in darkness. I recognised a silence like that which pervades a church after a service. I walked into the centre of the bazaar timidly. A few people were gathered about the stalls which were still open. Before a curtain, over which the words *Café Chantant* were written in coloured lamps, two men were counting money on a salver. I listened to the fall of the coins.

Remembering with difficulty why I had come I went over to one of the stalls and examined porcelain vases and flowered tea-sets. At the door of the stall a young lady was talking and laughing with two young gentlemen. I remarked their English accents and listened vaguely to their conversation.

"O, I never said such a thing!"

"O, but you did!"

"O, but I didn't!"

"Didn't she say that?"

"Yes. I heard her."

"O, there's a . . . fib!"

Observing me the young lady came over and asked me did I wish to buy anything. The tone of her voice was not encouraging; she seemed to have spoken to me out of a sense of duty. I looked humbly at the great jars that stood like eastern guards at either side of the dark entrance to the stall and murmured:

"No, thank you."

The young lady changed the position of one of the vases and went back to the two young men. They began to talk of the same subject. Once or twice the young lady glanced at me over her shoulder.

I lingered before her stall, though I knew my stay was useless, to make my interest in her wares seem the more real. Then I turned away slowly and walked down the middle of the bazaar. I allowed the two pennies to fall against the sixpence in my pocket. I heard a voice call from one end of the gallery that the light was out. The upper part of the hall was now completely dark.

Gazing up into the darkness I saw myself as a creature driven and derided by vanity; and my eyes burned with anguish and anger.

The Boarding House

Mrs. Mooney was a butcher's daughter. She was a woman who was quite able to keep things to herself: a determined woman. She had married her father's foreman and opened a butcher's shop near Spring Gardens. But as soon as his father-in-law was dead Mr. Mooney began to go to the devil. He drank, plundered the till, ran headlong into debt. It was no use making him take the pledge: he was sure to break out again a few days after. By fighting his wife in the presence of customers and by buying bad meat he ruined his business. One night he went for his wife with the cleaver and she had to sleep in a neighbour's house.

After that they lived apart. She went to the priest and got a separation from him with care of the children. She would give him neither money nor food nor house-room; and so he was obliged to enlist himself as a sheriff's man. He was a shabby stooped little drunkard with a white face and a white moustache and white eyebrows, pencilled above his little eyes, which were pink-veined and raw; and all day long he sat in the bailiff's room, waiting to be put on a job. Mrs. Mooney, who had taken what remained of her money out of the butcher business and set up a boarding house in Hardwicke Street, was a big imposing woman. Her house had a floating population made up of tourists from Liverpool and the Isle of Man and, occasionally, *artistes* from the music halls. Its resident population was made up of clerks from the city. She governed the house cunningly and firmly, knew when to give credit, when to be stern and when to let things pass. All the resident young men spoke of her as *The Madam*.

Mrs. Mooney's young men paid fifteen shillings a week for board and lodgings (beer or stout at dinner excluded). They shared in common tastes and occupations and for this reason they were very chummy with one another. They discussed with one another the chances of favourites and outsiders. Jack Mooney, the Madam's son, who was clerk to a commission agent in Fleet Street, had the reputation of being a hard case. He was fond of using soliders' obscenities: usually he came home in the small hours. When he met his friends he had always a good one to tell them and he was always sure to be on to a good thing—that is to say, a likely horse or a likely *artiste*. He was also handy with the mits and sang comic songs. On Sunday nights there would often be a reunion in Mrs. Mooney's front drawing-room. The music-hall *artistes* would oblige; and Sheridan played waltzes and polkas and vamped accompaniments. Polly Mooney, the Madam's daughter, would also sing. She sang:

> *I'm a . . . naughty girl.*
> *You needn't sham:*
> *You know I am.*

Polly was a slim girl of nineteen; she had light soft hair and a small full mouth. Her eyes, which were grey with a shade of green through them, had a habit of glancing upwards when she spoke with anyone, which made her look like a little perverse madonna. Mrs. Mooney had first sent her daughter to be a typist in a corn-factor's office but, as a disreputable sheriff's man used to come every other day to the office, asking to be allowed to say a word to his daughter, she had taken her daughter home again and set her to do housework. As Polly was very lively the intention was to give her the run of the young men. Besides, young men like to feel that there is a young woman not very far away. Polly, of course, flirted with the young men but Mrs. Mooney, who was a shrewd judge, knew that the young men were only passing the time away: none of them meant business. Things went on so for a long time and Mrs. Mooney began to think of sending Polly back to typewriting when she noticed that something was going on between Polly and one of the young men. She watched the pair and kept her own counsel.

Polly knew that she was being watched, but still her mother's persistent silence could not be misunderstood. There had been no open complicity between mother and daughter, no open understanding but, though people in the house began to talk of the affair, still Mrs. Mooney did not intervene. Polly began to grow a little strange in her manner and the young man was evidently perturbed. At last, when she judged it to be the right moment, Mrs. Mooney intervened. She dealt with moral problems as a cleaver deals with meat: and in this case she had made up her mind.

It was a bright Sunday morning of early summer, promising heat, but with a fresh breeze blowing. All the windows of the boarding house were open and the lace curtains ballooned gently towards the street beneath the raised sashes. The belfry of George's Church sent out constant peals and worshippers, singly or in groups, traversed the little circus before the church, revealing their purpose by their self-contained demeanour no less than by the little volumes in their gloved hands. Breakfast was over in the boarding house and the table of the breakfast-room was covered with plates on which lay yellow streaks of eggs with morsels of bacon-fat and bacon-rind. Mrs. Mooney sat in the straw arm-chair and watched the servant Mary remove the breakfast things. She made Mary collect the crusts and pieces of broken bread to help to make Tuesday's bread-pudding. When the table was cleared, the broken bread collected, the sugar and butter safe under lock and key, she began to reconstruct the interview which she had had the night before with Polly. Things were as she had suspected: she had been frank in her questions and Polly had been frank in her answers. Both had been somewhat awkward, of course. She had been made awkward by her not wishing to receive the news in too cavalier a fashion or to seem to have connived and Polly had been made awkward not merely because allusions of that kind always made her awkward but also because she did not wish it to be thought that in her wise innocence she had divined the intention behind her mother's tolerance.

Mrs. Mooney glanced instinctively at the little gilt clock on the mantel-piece as soon as she had become aware through her revery that the bells of George's Church had stopped ringing. It was seventeen minutes past eleven: she would have lots of time to have the matter out with Mr. Doran and then catch short twelve at Marlborough Street. She was sure she would win. To begin with she had all the weight of social opinion on her side: she was an outraged mother. She had allowed him to live beneath her roof, assuming that he was a man of honour, and he had simply abused her hospitality. He was thirty-four or thirty-five years of age, so that youth could not be pleaded as his excuse; nor could ignorance be his excuse since he was a man who had seen something of the world. He had simply taken advantage of Polly's youth and inexperience: that was evident. The question was: What reparation would he make?

There must be reparation made in such case. It is all very well for the man: he can go his ways as if nothing had happened, having had his moment of pleasure, but the girl has to bear the brunt. Some mothers would be content to patch up such an affair for a sum of money; she had known cases of it. But she would not do so. For her only one reparation could make up for the loss of her daughter's honour: marriage.

She counted all her cards again before sending Mary up to Mr. Doran's room to say that she wished to speak with him. She felt sure she would win. He was a serious young man, not rakish or loud-voiced like the others. If it had been Mr. Sheridan or Mr. Meade or Bantam Lyons her task would have been much harder. She did not think he would face publicity. All the lodgers in the house knew something of the affair; details had been invented by some. Besides, he had been employed for thirteen years in a great Catholic wine-merchant's office and publicity would mean for him, perhaps, the loss of his job. Whereas if he agreed all might be well. She knew he had a good screw for one thing and she suspected he had a bit of stuff put by.

Nearly the half-hour! She stood up and surveyed herself in the pier-glass. The decisive expression of her great florid face satisfied her and she thought of some mothers she knew who could not get their daughters off their hands.

Mr. Doran was very anxious indeed this Sunday morning. He had made two attempts to shave but his hand had been so unsteady that he had been obliged to desist. Three days' reddish beard fringed his jaws and every two or three minutes a mist gathered on his glasses so that he had to take them off and polish them with his pocket-handkerchief. The recollection of his confession of the night before was a cause of acute pain to him; the priest had drawn out every ridiculous detail of the affair and in the end had so magnified his sin that he was almost thankful at being afforded a loophole of reparation. The harm was done. What could he do now but marry her or run away? He could not brazen it out. The affair would be sure to be talked of and his employer would be certain to hear of it. Dublin is such a small city: everyone knows everyone else's business. He felt his heart leap warmly in his throat as he heard in his excited imagination old Mr. Leonard calling out in his rasping voice: "Send Mr. Doran here, please."

All his long years of service gone for nothing! All his industry and diligence thrown away! As a young man he had sown his wild oats, of course; he had boasted of his free-thinking and denied the existence of God to his companions in public-houses. But that was all passed and done with . . . nearly. He still bought a copy of *Reynolds's Newspaper* every week but he attended to his religious duties and for nine-tenths of the year lived a regular life. He had money enough to settle down on; it was not that. But the family would look down on her. First of all there was her disreputable father and then her mother's boarding house was beginning to get a certain fame. He had a notion that he was being had.

He could imagine his friends talking of the affair and laughing. She *was* a little vulgar; some times she said "I seen" and "If I had've known." But what would grammar matter if he really loved her? He could not make up his mind whether to like her or despise her for what she had done. Of course he had done it too. His instinct urged him to remain free, not to marry. Once you are married you are done for, it said.

While he was sitting helplessly on the side of the bed in shirt and trousers she tapped lightly at his door and entered. She told him all, that she had made a clean breast of it to her mother and that her mother would speak with him that morning. She cried and threw her arms round his neck, saying:

"O Bob! Bob! What am I to do? What am I to do at all?"

She would put an end to herself, she said.

He comforted her feebly, telling her not to cry, that it would be all right, never fear. He felt against his shirt the agitation of her bosom.

It was not altogether his fault that it had happened. He remembered well, with the curious patient memory of the celibate, the first casual caresses her dress, her breath, her fingers had given him. Then late one night as he was undressing for bed she had tapped at his door, timidly. She wanted to relight her candle at his for hers had been blown out by a gust. It was her bath night. She wore a loose open combing-jacket of printed flannel. Her white instep shone in the opening of her furry slippers and the blood glowed warmly behind her perfumed skin. From her hands and wrists too as she lit and steadied her candle a faint perfume arose.

On nights when he came in very late it was she who warmed up his dinner. He scarcely knew what he was eating feeling her beside him alone, at night, in the sleeping house. And her thoughtfulness! If the night was anyway cold or wet or windy there was sure to be a little tumbler of punch ready for him. Perhaps they could be happy together. . . .

They used to go upstairs together on tiptoe, each with a candle, and on the third landing exchange reluctant good-nights. They used to kiss. He remembered well her eyes, the touch of her hand and his delirium. . . .

But delirium passes. He echoed her phrase, applying it to himself: *"What am I to do?"* The instinct of the celibate warned him to hold back. But the sin was there; even his sense of honour told him that reparation must be made for such a sin.

While he was sitting with her on the side of the bed Mary came to the door and said that the missus wanted to see him in the parlour. He stood up to put on his coat and waistcoat, more helpless than ever. When he was dressed he went over to her to comfort her. It would be all right, never fear. He left her crying on the bed and moaning softly: *"O my God!"*

Going down the stairs his glasses became so dimmed with moisture that he had to take them off and polish them. He longed to ascend through the roof and fly away to another country where he would never hear again of his trouble, and yet a force pushed him downstairs step by step. The implacable faces of his employer and of the Madam stared upon his discomfiture. On the last flight of stairs he passed Jack Mooney who was coming up from the pantry nursing two bottles of *Bass*. They saluted coldly; and the lover's eyes rested for a second or two on a thick bulldog face and a pair of thick short arms. When he reached the foot of the staircase he glanced up and saw Jack regarding him from the door of the return-room.

Suddenly he remembered the night when one of the music-hall *artistes*, a little blond Londoner, had made a rather free allusion to Polly. The reunion had been almost broken up on account of Jack's violence. Everyone tried to quiet him. The music-hall *artiste*, a little paler than usual, kept smiling and saying that there was no harm meant: but Jack kept shouting at him that if any fellow tried that sort of a game on with his sister he'd bloody well put his teeth down his throat, so he would.

Polly sat for a little time on the side of the bed, crying. Then she dried her eyes and went over to the looking-glass. She dipped the end of the towel in the water-jug and refreshed her eyes with the cool water. She looked at herself in profile and readjusted a hairpin above her ear. Then she went back to the bed again and sat at the foot. She regarded the pillows for a long time and the sight of them awakened in her mind secret, amiable memories. She rested the nape of her neck against the cool iron bed-rail and fell into a reverie. There was no longer any perturbation visible on her face.

She waited on patiently, almost cheerfully, without alarm, her memories gradually giving place to hopes and visions of the future. Her hopes and visions were so intricate that she no longer saw the white pillows on which her gaze was fixed or remembered that she was waiting for anything.

At last she heard her mother calling. She started to her feet and ran to the banisters.

"Polly! Polly!"

"Yes, mamma?"

"Come down, dear. Mr. Doran wants to speak to you."

Then she remembered what she had been waiting for.

Virginia Woolf

(1882–1941)

V irginia Woolf was born in London, the daughter of Sir Leslie Stephen, a distinguished man of letters and editor of the Diction-ary of National Biography. *She educated herself in her father's library and through her contacts with the London intelligentsia. After her father's death in 1904, she moved with her sister and two brothers to Bloomsbury, a fashionable district in the heart of London. The "Blooms-bury group" that congregated there included Lytton Strachey, J.M. Keynes, Roger Fry, E.M. Forster, and Clive Bell, the most famous of a group of gifted intellectual and artistic people who enjoyed each other's company and the witty and erudite conversation their gatherings pro-duced. Virginia married Leonard Woolf in 1912 and found in him the emotional and intellectual support that was to help her through a series of crises. Her most important novels mark a significant break with the novels popular in England at that time. In a famous essay, "Mr. Bennett and Mrs. Brown," Woolf argues that novelists such as Arnold Bennett and John Galsworthy convey only a limited aspect of reality in bombard-ing readers with its facts and minute particulars. The novelist, Woolf argues, has a duty to tell another truth, one that revolves around human perceptions and consciousness, the ebb and flow of ideas and impressions that characterize the workings of "an ordinary mind on an ordinary day." In* Jacob's Room (1922), Mrs. Dalloway (1925), To the Lighthouse (1927), *and* The Waves (1931), *she explored a variety of ways in which this aim might be accomplished, and revolutionized the modern novel in the process. Her writings on the plight of women—*A Room of One's Own (1929) *and* Three Guineas (1938)—*have been enormously influ-ential. Her literary criticism, collected in* The Common Reader (1925) *and* The Second Common Reader (1932), *established a new standard for other writers' critical forays. The eleven volumes of* Letters and Diaries *give us some idea of the astounding indefatigability of this "frail" woman, and a keen sense of how totally she devoted herself to the practice of her craft. Fearing that recurring madness would make her a burden to her husband, she drowned herself near her home in Sussex in 1941.*

Kew Gardens

F rom the oval-shaped flower-bed there rose perhaps a hundred stalks spreading into heart-shaped or tongue-shaped leaves half-way up and unfurling at the tip red or blue or yellow petals marked with spots of colour raised upon the surface; and from the red, blue or yellow gloom of the throat emerged a straight bar, rough with gold dust and slightly clubbed at the end. The petals were voluminous enough to be stirred by the summer breeze, and when they moved, the red, blue and yellow lights passed one over the other, staining an inch of the brown earth beneath with a spot of the most intricate colour. The light fell either upon the smooth, grey back of a pebble, or, the shell of a snail with its brown, circular veins, or falling into a raindrop, it expanded with such intensity of red, blue and yellow the thin walls of water that one expected them to burst and disappear. Instead, the drop was left in a second silver grey once more, and the light now settled upon the flesh of a leaf, revealing the branching thread of fibre beneath the surface, and again it moved on and spread its illumination in the vast green spaces beneath the dome of the heart-shaped and tongue-shaped leaves. Then the breeze stirred rather more briskly overhead and the colour was flashed into the air above, into the eyes of the men and women who walk in Kew Gardens in July.

The figures of these men and women straggled past the flower-bed with a curiously irregular movement not unlike that of the white and blue butterflies who crossed the turf in zig-zag flights from bed to bed. The man was about six inches in front of the woman, strolling carelessly, while she bore on with greater purpose, only turning her head now and then to see that the children were not too far behind. The man kept this distance in front of the woman purposely, though perhaps unconsciously, for he wished to go on with his thoughts.

"Fifteen years ago I came here with Lily," he thought. "We sat somewhere over there by a lake and I begged her to marry me all through the hot afternoon. How the dragonfly kept circling round us: how clearly I see the dragonfly and her shoe with the square silver buckle at the toe. All the time I spoke I saw her shoe and when it moved impatiently I knew without looking up what she was going to say: the whole of her seemed to be in her shoe. And my love, my desire, were in the dragonfly; for some reason I thought that if it settled there, on that leaf, the broad one with the red flower in the middle of it, if the dragonfly settled on the leaf she would say 'Yes' at once. But the dragonfly went round and round: it never settled anywhere—of course not, happily not, or I shouldn't be walking here with Eleanor and the children. Tell me, Eleanor. D'you ever think of the past?"

"Why do you ask, Simon?"

"Because I've been thinking of the past. I've been thinking of Lily, the woman I might have married. . . . Well, why are you silent? Do you mind my thinking of the past?"

"Why should I mind, Simon? Doesn't one always think of the past, in a garden with men and women lying under the trees? Aren't they one's past, all that remains of it, those men and women, those ghosts lying under the trees, . . . one's happiness, one's reality?"

"For me, a square silver shoe buckle and a dragonfly—"

"For me, a kiss. Imagine six little girls sitting before their easels twenty years ago, down by the side of a lake, painting the water-lilies, the first red water-lilies I'd ever seen. And suddenly a kiss, there on the back of my neck. And my hand shook all the afternoon so that I couldn't paint. I took out my watch and marked the hour when I would allow myself to think of the kiss for five minutes only—it was so precious—the kiss of an old grey-haired woman with a wart on her nose, the mother of all my kisses all my life. Come, Caroline, come, Hubert."

They walked on past the flower-bed, now walking four abreast, and soon diminished in size among the trees and looked half transparent as the sunlight and shade swam over their backs in large trembling irregular patches.

In the oval flower-bed the snail, whose shell had been stained red, blue and yellow for the space of two minutes or so, now appeared to be moving very slightly in its shell, and next began to labour over the crumbs of loose earth which broke away and rolled down as it passed over them. It appeared to have a definite goal in front of it, differing in this respect from the singular high stepping angular green insect who attempted to cross in front of it, and waited for a second with its antennae trembling as if in deliberation, and then stepped off as rapidly and strangely in the opposite direction. Brown cliffs with deep green lakes in the hollows, flat, blade-like trees that waved from root to tip, round boulders of grey stone, vast crumpled surfaces of a thin crackling texture—all these objects lay across the snail's progress between one stalk and another to his goal. Before he had decided whether to circumvent the arched tent of a dead leaf or to breast it there came past the bed the feet of other human beings.

This time they were both men. The younger of the two wore an expression of perhaps unnatural calm; he raised his eyes and fixed them very steadily in front of him while his companion spoke, and directly his companion had done speaking he looked on the ground again and sometimes opened his lips only after a long pause and sometimes did not open them at all. The elder man had a curiously uneven and shaky method of walking, jerking his hand forward and throwing up his head abruptly, rather in the manner of an impatient carriage horse tired of waiting outside a house; but in the man these gestures were irresolute and pointless. He talked almost incessantly; he smiled to himself and again began to talk, as if the smile had been an answer. He was talking about spirits—the spirits of the dead, who, according to him, were even now telling him all sorts of odd things about their experiences in Heaven.

"Heaven was known to the ancients as Thessaly, William, and now, with this war, the spirit matter is rolling between the hills like thunder." He paused, seemed to listen, smiled, jerked his head and continued:

"You have a small electric battery and a piece of rubber to insulate the wire—isolate?—insulate?—well, we'll skip the details, no good going into details that wouldn't be understood—and in short the little machine stands in any convenient position by the head of the bed, we will say, on a neat mahogany stand. All arrangements being properly fixed by workmen under my direction, the widow applies her ear and summons the spirit by sign as agreed. Women! Widows! Women in black—"

Here he seemed to have caught sight of a woman's dress in the distance, which in the shade looked a purple black. He took off his hat, placed his hand upon his heart, and hurried towards her muttering and gesticulating feverishly. But William caught him by the sleeve and touched a flower with the tip of his walking-stick in order to divert the old man's attention. After looking at it for a moment in some confusion the old man bent his ear to it and seemed to answer a voice speaking from it, for he began talking about the forests of Uruguay which he had visited hundreds of years ago in company with the most beautiful young woman in Europe. He could be heard murmuring about forests of Uruguay blanketed with the wax petals of tropical roses, nightingales, sea beaches, mermaids, and women drowned at sea, as he suffered himself to be moved on by William, upon whose face the look of stoical patience grew slowly deeper and deeper.

Following his steps so closely as to be slightly puzzled by his gestures came two elderly women of the lower middle class, one stout and ponderous, the other rosy cheeked and nimble. Like most people of their station they were frankly fascinated by any signs of eccentricity betokening a disordered brain, especially in the well-to-do; but they were too far off to be certain whether the gestures were merely eccentric or genuinely mad. After they had scrutinized the old man's back in silence for a moment and given each other a queer, sly look, they went on energetically piecing together their very complicated dialogue:

"Nell, Bert, Lot, Cess, Phil, Pa, he says, I says, she says, I says, I says—"

"My Bert, Sis, Bill, Grandad, the old man, sugar,

Sugar, flour, kippers, greens,
Sugar, sugar, sugar."

The ponderous woman looked through the pattern of falling words at the flowers standing cool, firm, and upright in the earth, with a curious expression. She saw them as a sleeper waking from a heavy sleep sees a brass candlestick reflecting the light in an unfamiliar way, and closes his eyes and opens them, and seeing the brass candlestick again, finally starts broad awake and stares at the candlestick with all his powers. So the heavy woman came to a standstill opposite the oval-shaped flower-bed, and ceased even to pretend to listen to what the other woman was saying. She stood there letting the words fall over her, swaying the top part of her body slowly backwards and forwards, looking at the flowers. Then she suggested that they should find a seat and have their tea.

The snail had now considered every possible method of reaching his goal without going round the dead leaf or climbing over it. Let alone the effort needed for climbing a leaf, he was doubtful whether the thin texture which vibrated with such an alarming crackle when touched even by the tips of his horns would bear his weight; and this determined him finally to creep beneath it, for there was a point where the leaf curved high enough from the ground to admit him. He had just inserted his head in the opening and was taking stock of the high brown roof and was getting used to the cool brown light when two other people came past outside on the turf. This time they were both young, a young man and a young woman. They were both in the prime of youth, or even in that season which precedes the prime of youth, the season before the smooth pink folds of the flower have burst their gummy case, when the wings of the butterfly, though fully grown, are motionless in the sun.

"Lucky it isn't Friday," he observed.

"Why? D'you believe in luck?"

"They make you pay sixpence on Friday."

"What's sixpence anyway? Isn't it worth sixpence?"

"What's 'it'—what do you mean by 'it'?"

"O, anything—I mean—you know what I mean."

Long pauses came between each of these remarks; they were uttered in toneless and monotonous voices. The couple stood still on the edge of the flower-bed, and together pressed the end of her parasol deep down into the soft earth. The action and the fact that his hand rested on the top of hers expressed their feelings in a strange way, as these short insignificant words also expressed something, words with short wings for their heavy body of meaning, inadequate to carry them far and thus alighting awkwardly upon the very common objects that surrounded them, and were to their inexperienced touch so massive; but who knows (so they thought as they pressed the parasol into the earth) what precipices aren't concealed in them, or what slopes of ice don't shine in the sun on the other side? Who knows? Who has ever seen this before? Even when she wondered what sort of tea they gave you at Kew, he felt that something loomed up behind her words, and stood vast and solid behind them; and the mist very slowly rose and uncovered—O, Heavens, what were those shapes?—little white tables, and waitresses who looked first at her and then at him; and there was a bill that he would pay with a real two shilling piece, and it was real, all real, he assured himself, fingering the coin in his pocket, real to everyone except to him and to her; even to him it began to seem real; and then—but it was too exciting to stand and think any longer, and he pulled the parasol out of the earth with a jerk and was impatient to find the place where one had tea with other people, like other people.

"Come along, Trissie; it's time we had our tea."

"Wherever *does* one have one's tea?" she asked with the oddest thrill of excitement in her voice, looking vaguely round and letting herself be drawn on down the grass path, trailing her parasol; turning her head this way and that way forgetting her tea, wishing to go down there and then down there, remembering orchids and cranes among wild flowers, a Chinese pagoda and a crimson crested bird; but he bore her on.

Thus one couple after another with much the same irregular and aimless movement passed the flower-bed and were enveloped in layer after layer of green blue vapour, in which at first their bodies had substance and a dash of colour, but later both substance and colour dissolved in the green-blue atmosphere. How hot it was! So hot that even the thrush chose to hop, like a mechanical bird, in the shadow of the flowers, with long pauses between one movement and the next; instead of rambling vaguely the white butterflies danced one above another, making with their white shifting flakes the outline of a shattered marble column above the tallest flowers; the glass roofs of the palm house shone as if a whole market full of shiny green umbrellas had opened in the sun; and in the drone of the aeroplane the voice of the summer sky murmured its fierce soul. Yellow and black, pink and snow white, shapes of all these colours, men, women, and children were spotted for a second upon the horizon, and then, seeing the breadth of yellow that lay upon the grass, they wavered and sought shade beneath the trees, dissolving like drops of water in the yellow and green atmosphere, staining it faintly with red and blue. It seemed as if all gross and heavy bodies had sunk down in the heat motionless and lay huddled upon the ground, but their voices went wavering from them as if they were flames lolling from the thick waxen bodies of candles. Voices. Yes, voices. Wordless voices, breaking the silence suddenly with such depth of contentment, such passion of desire, or, in the voices of children, such freshness of surprise; breaking the silence? But there was no silence; all the time the motor omnibuses were turning their wheels and changing their gear; like a vast nest of Chinese boxes all of wrought steel turning ceaselessly one within another the city murmured; on the top of which the voices cried aloud and the petals of myriads of flowers flashed their colours into the air.

Franz Kafka

(1883–1924)

F *ranz Kafka was born in Prague, the son of a prosperous Jewish*
merchant. Kafka was later to recall that he saw his father only at
mealtimes and therefore learned only table manners from him. But
this authoritarian and domineering figure loomed large in his son's
imagination, giving Kafka the sense of living in a separate world, sub-
jected to laws he was unable to satisfy, while other people occupied a
permanently inaccessible realm in which they led happy lives. He was
educated in a German grammar school, where he read Goethe, Schiller,
Nietzsche, and Haeckel, and came to declare himself an atheist and a
socialist. He received his doctorate in law in 1906, but his studies bored
him. As he put it: "I fed my mind on sawdust which thousands of others
had chewed over before me. It was a tremendous strain on my nerves."
He took a job at the Workers' Accident Insurance Institute and worked
there for the next fourteen years. Meanwhile he was writing. Though he
published only a few short stories during his life, other stories and the
three novels, The Trial *(1925),* The Castle *(1926), and* Amerika *(1927),*
published posthumously by his friend Max Brod (despite Kafka's instruc-
tions to burn all the unpublished work), have earned him a reputation
as one of the most important modernist writers. Kafka translated a life
of ill health, insecurity, frustration in love, into some of our century's
most haunting and compelling literature. Humanist, psychoanalytical,
Marxist, and deconstructive critics have shown us many different Kafkas,
and no doubt others will be discovered because his work, as one critic
has said, by its very nature "validates a thousand keys and authorizes
none."

The Metamorphosis

I

A s Gregor Samsa awoke one morning from uneasy dreams he found
himself transformed in his bed into a gigantic insect. He was lying
on his hard, as it were armor-plated, back and when he lifted his head a
little he could see his domelike brown belly divided into stiff arched
segments on top of which the bed quilt could hardly keep in position and
was about to slide off completely. His numerous legs, which were pitifully
thin compared to the rest of his bulk, waved helplessly before his eyes.

What has happened to me? he thought. It was no dream. His room, a regular human bedroom, only rather too small, lay quiet between the four familiar walls. Above the table on which a collection of cloth samples was unpacked and spread out—Samsa was a commercial traveler—hung the picture which he had recently cut out of an illustrated magazine and put into a pretty gilt frame. It showed a lady, with a fur cap on and a fur stole, sitting upright and holding out to the spectator a huge fur muff into which the whole of her forearm had vanished!

Gregor's eyes turned next to the window, and the overcast sky—one could hear raindrops beating on the window gutter—made him quite melancholy. What about sleeping a little longer and forgetting all this nonsense, he thought, but it could not be done, for he was accustomed to sleep on his right side and in his present condition he could not turn himself over. However violently he forced himself toward his right side he always rolled onto his back again. He tried it at least a hundred times, shutting his eyes to keep from seeing his struggling legs, and only desisted when he began to feel in his side a faint dull ache he had never experienced before.

Oh God, he thought, what an exhausting job I've picked on! Traveling about day in, day out. It's much more irritating work than doing the actual business in the office, and on top of that there's the trouble of constant traveling, of worrying about train connections, the bed and irregular meals, casual acquaintances that are always new and never become intimate friends. The devil take it all! He felt a slight itching up on his belly; slowly pushed himself on his back nearer to the top of the bed so that he could lift his head more easily; identified the itching place which was surrounded by many small white spots the nature of which he could not understand and made to touch it with a leg, but drew the leg back immediately, for the contact made a cold shiver run through him.

He slid down again into his former position. This getting up early, he thought, makes one quite stupid. A man needs his sleep. Other commercials live like harem women. For instance, when I come back to the hotel of a morning to write up the orders I've got, these others are only sitting down to the breakfast. Let me just try that with my chief; I'd be sacked on the spot. Anyhow, that might be quite a good thing for me, who can tell? If I didn't have to hold my hand because of my parents I'd have given notice long ago, I'd have gone to the chief and told him exactly what I think of him. That would knock him endways from his desk! It's a queer way of doing, too, this sitting on high at a desk and talking down to employees, especially when they have to come quite near because the chief is hard of hearing. Well, there's still hope; once I've saved enough money to pay back my parents' debts to him—that should take another five or six years—I'll do it without fail. I'll cut myself completely loose then. For the moment, though, I'd better get up, since my train goes at five.

He looked at the alarm clock ticking on the chest. Heavenly Father! he thought. It was half-past six o'clock and the hands were quietly moving on, it was even past the half-hour, it was getting on toward a quarter to seven. Had the alarm clock not gone off? From the bed one could see that it had been properly set for four o'clock; of course it must have gone off. Yes, but was it possible to sleep quietly through that ear-splitting noise? Well, he had not slept quietly, yet apparently all the more soundly for that. But what was he to do now? The next train went at seven o'clock; to catch that he would need to hurry like mad and his samples weren't even packed up, and he himself wasn't feeling particularly fresh and active. And even if he did catch the train he wouldn't avoid a row with the chief, since the firm's porter would have been waiting for the five o'clock train and would have long since reported his failure to turn up. The porter was a creature of the chief's, spineless and stupid. Well, supposing he were to say he was sick? But that would be most unpleasant and would look suspicious, since during his five years' employment he had not been ill once. The chief himself would be sure to come with the sick-insurance doctor, would reproach his parents with their son's laziness, and would cut all excuses short by referring to the insurance doctor, who of course regarded all mankind as perfectly healthy malingerers. And would he be so far wrong on this occasion? Gregor really felt quite well, apart from a drowsiness that was utterly superfluous after such a long sleep, and he was even unusually hungry.

As all this was running through his mind at top speed without his being able to decide to leave his bed—the alarm clock had just struck a quarter to seven—there came a cautious tap at the door behind the head of his bed. "Gregor," said a voice—it was his mother's—"it's a quarter to seven. Hadn't you a train to catch?" That gentle voice! Gregor had a shock as he heard his own voice answering hers, unmistakably his own voice, it was true, but with a persistent horrible twittering squeak behind it like an undertone, which left the words in their clear shape only for the first moment and then rose up reverberating around them to destroy their sense, so that one could not be sure one had heard them rightly. Gregor wanted to answer at length and explain everything, but in the circumstances he confined himself to saying: "Yes, yes, thank you, Mother, I'm getting up now." The wooden door between them must have kept the change in his voice from being noticeable outside, for his mother contented herself with this statement and shuffled away. Yet this brief exchange of words had made the other members of the family aware that Gregor was still in the house, as they had not expected, and at one of the side doors his father was already knocking, gently, yet with his fist.

"Gregor, Gregor," he called, "What's the matter with you?" And after a little while he called again in a deeper voice: "Gregor! Gregor!" At the other side door his sister was saying in a low, plaintive tone: "Gregor? Aren't you well? Are you needing anything?" He answered them both at once. "I'm just ready," and did his best to make his voice sound as normal as possible by enunciating the words very clearly and leaving long pauses between them. So his father went back to his breakfast, but his sister whispered: "Gregor, open the door, do." However, he was not thinking of opening the door, and felt thankful for the prudent habit he had acquired in traveling of locking all doors during the night, even at home.

His immediate intention was to get up quietly without being disturbed, to put on his clothes and above all eat his breakfast, and only then consider what else was to be done, since in bed, he was well aware, his meditations would come to no sensible conclusion. He remembered that often enough in bed he had felt small aches and pains, probably caused by awkward postures, which had proved purely imaginary once he got up, and he looked forward eagerly to seeing this morning's delusions gradually fall away. That the change in his voice was nothing but the precursor of a severe chill, a standing ailment of commercial travelers, he had not the least possible doubt.

To get rid of the quilt was quite easy; he had only to inflate himself a little and it fell off by itself. But the next move was difficult, especially because he was so uncommonly broad. He would have needed arms and hands to hoist himself up; instead he had only the numerous little legs which never stopped waving in all directions and which he could not control in the least. When he tried to bend one of them it was the first to stretch itself straight; and did he succeed at last in making it do what he wanted, all the other legs meanwhile waved the more wildly in a high degree of unpleasant agitation. "But what's the use of lying idle in bed," said Gregor to himself.

He thought that he might get out of bed with the lower part of his body first, but his lower part, which he had not yet seen and of which he could form no clear conception, proved too difficult to move; it shifted so slowly; and when finally, almost wild with annoyance, he gathered his forces together and thrust out recklessly, he had miscalculated the direction and bumped heavily against the lower end of the bed, and the stinging pain he felt informed him that precisely this lower part of his body was at the moment probably the most sensitive.

So he tried to get the top of himself out first, and cautiously moved his head toward the edge of the bed. That proved easy enough, and despite its breadth and mass the bulk of his body at last slowly followed the movement of his head. Still, when he finally got his head free over the edge of the bed he felt too scared to go on advancing, for after all if he let himself fall in this way it would take a miracle to keep his head from being injured. And at all costs he must not lose consciousness now, precisely now; he would rather stay in bed.

But when after a repetition of the same efforts he lay in his former position again, sighing, and watched his little legs struggling against each other more wildly than ever, if that were possible, and saw no way of bringing any order into this arbitrary confusion, he told himself again that it was impossible to stay in bed and that the most sensible course was to risk everything for the smallest hope of getting away from it. At the same time he did not forget to remind himself occasionally that cool reflection, the coolest possible, was much better than desperate resolves. In such moments he focused his eyes as sharply as possible on the window, but, unfortunately, the prospect of the morning fog, which muffled even the other side of the narrow street, brought him little encouragement and comfort. "Seven o'clock already," he said to himself when the alarm clock chimed again, "seven o'clock already and still such a thick fog." And for a little while he lay quiet, breathing lightly, as if perhaps expecting such complete repose to restore all things to their real and normal condition.

But then he said to himself: "Before it strikes a quarter past seven I must be quite out of this bed, without fail. Anyhow, by that time someone will have come from the office to ask for me, since it opens before seven." And he set himself to rocking his whole body at once in a regular rhythm, with the idea of swinging it out of the bed. If he tipped himself out in that way he could keep his head from injury by lifting it at an acute angle when he fell. His back seemed to be hard and was not likely to suffer from a fall on the carpet. His biggest worry was the loud crash he would not be able to help making, which would probably cause anxiety, if not terror, behind all the doors. Still, he must take the risk.

When he was already half out of the bed—the new method was more a game than an effort, for he needed only to hitch himself across by rocking to and fro—it struck him how simple it would be if he could get help. Two strong people—he thought of his father and the servant girl—would be amply sufficient; they would only have to thrust their arms under his convex back, lever him out of the bed, bend down with their burden, and then be patient enough to let him turn himself right over onto the floor, where it was to be hoped his legs would then find their proper function. Well, ignoring the fact that the doors were all locked, ought he really to call for help? In spite of his misery he could not suppress a smile at the very idea of it.

He had got so far that he could barely keep his equilibrium when he rocked himself strongly, and he would have to nerve himself very soon for the final decision since in five minutes' time it would be quarter past seven—when the front doorbell rang. "That's someone from the office," he said to himself, and grew almost rigid, while his little legs only jigged about all the faster. For a moment everything stayed quiet. "They're not going to open the door," said Gregor to himself, catching at some kind of irrational hope. But then of course the servant girl went as usual to the door with her heavy tread and opened it. Gregor needed only to hear the first good morning of the visitor to know immediately who it was— the chief clerk himself. What a fate, to be condemned to work for a firm where the smallest omission at once gave rise to the gravest suspicion! Were all employees in a body nothing but scoundrels, was there not among them one single devoted man who, had he wasted only an hour or so of the firm's time in a morning, was so tormented by conscience as to be driven out of his mind and actually incapable of leaving his bed? Wouldn't it really have been sufficient to send an apprentice to inquire— if any inquiry were necessary at all—did the chief clerk himself have to come and thus indicate to the entire family, an innocent family, that this suspicious circumstance could be investigated by no one less versed in affairs than himself? And more through the agitation caused by these reflections than through any act of will Gregor swung himself out of bed with all his strength. There was a loud thump, but it was not really a crash. His fall was broken to some extent by the carpet, his back, too, was less stiff than he thought, and so there was merely a dull thud, not so very startling. Only he had not lifted his head carefully enough and had hit it; he turned it and rubbed it on the carpet in pain and irritation.

"That was something falling down in there," said the chief clerk in the next room to the left. Gregor tried to suppose to himself that something like what had happened to him today might someday happen to the chief clerk; one really could not deny that it was possible. But as if in brusque reply to this supposition the chief clerk took a couple of firm steps in the next-door room and his patent leather boots creaked. From the right-hand room his sister was whispering to inform him of the situation: "Gregor, the chief clerk's here." "I know," muttered Gregor to himself; but he didn't dare to make his voice loud enough for his sister to hear it.

"Gregor," said his father now from the left-hand room, "the chief clerk has come and wants to know why you didn't catch the early train. We don't know what to say to him. Besides, he wants to talk to you in person. So open the door, please. He will be good enough to excuse the untidiness of your room." "Good morning, Mr. Samsa," the chief clerk was calling amiably meanwhile. "He's not well," said his mother to the visitor, while his father was still speaking through the door, "he's not well, sir, believe me. What else would make him miss a train! The boy thinks about nothing but his work. It makes me almost cross the way he never goes out in the evenings; he's been here the last eight days and has stayed at home every single evening. He just sits there quietly at the table reading a newspaper or looking through railway timetables. The only amusement he gets is doing fretwork. For instance, he spent two or three evenings cutting out a little picture frame; you would be surprised to see how pretty it is; it's hanging in his room; you'll see it in a minute when Gregor opens the door. I must say I'm glad you've come, sir; we should never have got him to unlock the door by ourselves; he's so obstinate; and I'm sure he's unwell, though he wouldn't have it to be so this morning." "I'm just coming," said Gregor slowly and carefully, not moving an inch for fear of losing one word of the conversation. "I can't think of any other explanation, madame," said the chief clerk, "I hope it's nothing serious. Although on the other hand I must say that we men of business—fortunately or unfortunately—very often simply have to ignore any slight indisposition, since business must be attended to." "Well, can the chief clerk come in now?" asked Gregor's father impatiently, again knocking on the door. "No," said Gregor. In the left-hand room a painful silence followed this refusal, in the right-hand room his sister began to sob.

Why didn't his sister join the others? She was probably newly out of bed and hadn't even begun to put on her clothes yet. Well, why was she crying? Because he wouldn't get up and let the chief clerk in, because he was in danger of losing his job, and because the chief would begin dunning his parents again for the old debts? Surely these were things one didn't need to worry about for the present. Gregor was still at home and not in the least thinking of deserting the family. At the moment, true, he was lying on the carpet and no one who knew the condition he was in could seriously expect him to admit the chief clerk. But for such a small discourtesy, which could plausibly he explained away somehow later on, Gregor could hardly be dismissed on the spot. And it seemed to Gregor that it would be much more sensible to leave him in peace for the present than to trouble him with tears and entreaties. Still, of course, their uncertainty bewildered them all and excused their behavior.

"Mr. Samsa," the chief clerk called now in a louder voice, "what's the matter with you? Here you are, barricading yourself in your room, giving only 'yes' and 'no' for answers, causing your parents a lot of unnecessary trouble and neglecting—I mention this only in passing—neglecting your business duties in an incredible fashion. I am speaking here in the name of your parents and of your chief, and I beg you quite seriously to give me an immediate and precise explanation. You amaze me, you amaze me. I thought you were a quiet, dependable person, and now all at once you seem bent on making a disgraceful exhibition of yourself. The chief did hint to me early this morning a possible explanation for your disappearance—with reference to the cash payments that were entrusted to you recently—but I almost pledged my solemn word of honor that this could not be so. But now that I see how incredibly obstinate you are, I no longer have the slightest desire to take your part at all. And your position in the firm is not so unassailable. I came with the intention of telling you all this in private, but since you are wasting my time so needlessly I don't see why your parents shouldn't hear it too. For some time past your work has been most unsatisfactory; this is not the season of the year for a business boom, of course, we admit that, but a season of the year for doing no business at all, that does not exist, Mr. Samsa, must not exist."

"But, sir," cried Gregor, beside himself and in his agitation forgetting everything else, "I'm just going to open the door this very minute. A slight illness, an attack of giddiness, has kept me from getting up. I'm still lying in bed. But I feel all right again. I'm getting out of bed now. Just give me a moment or two longer! I'm not quite so well as I thought. But I'm all right, really. How a thing like that can suddenly strike one down! Only last night I was quite well, my parents can tell you, or rather I did have a slight presentiment. I must have showed some sign of it. Why didn't I report it at the office! But one always thinks that an indisposition can be got over without staying in the house. Oh sir, do spare my parents! All that you're reproaching me with now has no foundation; no one has ever said a word to me about it. Perhaps you haven't looked at the last orders I sent in. Anyhow, I can still catch the eight o'clock train, I'm much the better for my few hours' rest. Don't let me detain you here, sir; I'll be attending to business very soon, and do be good enough to tell the chief so and to make my excuses to him!"

And while all this was tumbling out pell-mell and Gregor hardly knew what he was saying, he had reached the chest quite easily, perhaps because of the practice he had had in bed, and was now trying to lever himself upright by means of it. He meant actually to open the door, actually to show himself and speak to the chief clerk; he was eager to find out what the others, after all their insistence, would say at the sight of him. If they were horrified then the responsibility was no longer his and he could stay quiet. But if they took it calmly, then he had no reason either to be upset, and could really get to the station for the eight o'clock train if he hurried. At first he slipped down a few times from the polished surface of the chest, but at length with a last heave he stood upright; he paid no more attention to the pains in the lower part of his body, however they smarted. Then he let himself fall against the back of a nearby chair, and clung with his little legs to the edges of it. That brought him into control of himself again and he stopped speaking, for now he could listen to what the chief clerk was saying.

"Did you understand a word of it?" the chief clerk was asking, "surely he can't be trying to make fools of us?" "Oh dear," cried his mother, in tears, "perhaps he's terribly ill and we're tormenting him. Grete! Grete!" she called out then. "Yes Mother?" called his sister from the other side. They were calling to each other across Gregor's room. "You must go this minute for the doctor. Gregor is ill. Go for the doctor, quick. Did you hear how he was speaking?" "That was no human voice," said the chief clerk in a voice noticeably low beside the shrillness of the mother's. "Anna! Anna!" his father was calling through the hall to the kitchen, clapping his hands, "get a locksmith at once!" And the two girls were already running through the hall with a swish of skirts—how could his sister have got dressed so quickly?—and were tearing the front door open. There was no sound of its closing again; they had evidently left it open, as one does in houses where some great misfortune has happened.

But Gregor was now much calmer. The words he uttered were no longer understandable, apparently, although they seemed clear enough to him, even clearer than before, perhaps because his ear had grown accustomed to the sound of them. Yet at any rate people now believed that something was wrong with him, and were ready to help him. The positive certainty with which these first measures had been taken comforted him. He felt himself drawn once more into the human circle and hoped for great and remarkable results from both the doctor and the locksmith, without really distinguishing precisely between them. To make his voice as clear as possible for the decisive conversation that was now imminent he coughed a little, as quietly as he could, of course, since this noise too might not sound like a human cough for all he was able to judge. In the next room meanwhile there was complete silence. Perhaps his parents were sitting at the table with the chief clerk, whispering, perhaps they were all leaning against the door and listening.

Slowly Gregor pushed the chair toward the door, then let go of it, caught hold of the door for support—the soles at the end of his little legs were somewhat sticky—and rested against it for a moment after his efforts. Then he set himself to turning the key in the lock with his mouth. It seemed, unhappily, that he hadn't really any teeth—what could he grip the key with?—but on the other hand his jaws were certainly very strong; with their help he did manage to set the key in motion, heedless of the fact that he was undoubtedly damaging them somewhere, since a brown fluid issued from his mouth, flowed over the key, and dripped on the floor. "Just listen to that," said the chief clerk next door; "he's turning the key." That was a great encouragement to Gregor; but they should all have shouted encouragement to him, his father and mother too: "Go on, Gregor," they should have called out, "keep going, hold on to that key!" And in the belief that they were all following his efforts intently, he clenched his jaws recklessly on the key with all the force at his command. As the turning of the key progressed he circled around the lock, holding on now only with his mouth, pushing on the key, as required, or pulling it down again with all the weight of his body. The louder click of the finally yielding lock literally quickened Gregor. With a deep breath of relief he said to himself: "So I didn't need the locksmith," and laid his head on the handle to open the door wide.

Since he had to pull the door toward him, he was still invisible when it was really wide open. He had to edge himself slowly round the near half of the double door, and to do it very carefully if he was not to fall plump upon his back just on the threshold. He was still carrying out this difficult maneuver, with no time to observe anything else, when he heard the chief clerk utter a loud "Oh!"—it sounded like a gust of wind—and now he could see the man, standing as he was nearest to the door, clapping one hand before his open mouth and slowly backing away as if driven by some invisible steady pressure. His mother—in spite of the chief clerk's being there her hair was still undone and sticking up in all directions—first clasped her hands and looked at his father, then took two steps toward Gregor and fell on the floor among her outspread skirts, her face quite hidden on her breast. His father knotted his fist with a fierce expression on his face as if he meant to knock Gregor back into his room, then looked uncertainly around the living room, covered his eyes with his hands, and wept till his great chest heaved.

Gregor did not go now into the living room, but leaned against the inside of the firmly shut wing of the door, so that only half his body was visible and his head above it bending sideways to look at the others. The light had meanwhile strengthened; on the other side of the street one could see clearly a section of the endlessly long, dark gray building opposite—it was a hospital—abruptly punctuated by its row of regular windows; the rain was still falling, but only in large singly discernible and literally singly splashing drops. The breakfast dishes were set out on the table lavishly, for breakfast was the most important meal of the day to Gregor's father, who lingered it out for hours over various newspapers. Right opposite Gregor on the wall hung a photograph of himself in military service, as a lieutenant, hand on sword, a carefree smile on his face, inviting one to respect his uniform and military bearing. The door leading to the hall was open, and one could see that the front door stood open too, showing the landing beyond and the beginning of the stairs going down.

"Well," said Gregor, knowing perfectly that he was the only one who had retained any composure, "I'll put my clothes on at once, pack up my samples, and start off. Will you only let me go? You see, sir, I'm not obstinate, and I'm willing to work; traveling is a hard life, but I couldn't live without it. Where are you going, sir? To the office? Yes? Will you give a true account of all this? One can be temporarily incapacitated, but that's just the moment for remembering former services and bearing in mind that later on, when the incapacity has been got over, one will certainly work with all the more industry and concentration. I'm loyally bound to serve the chief, you know that very well. Besides, I have to provide for my parents and my sister. I'm in great difficulties, but I'll get out of them again. Don't make things any worse for me than they are.

Stand up for me in the firm. Travelers are not popular there, I know. People think they earn sacks of money and just have a good time. A prejudice there's no particular reason for revising. But you, sir, have a more comprehensive view of affairs than the rest of the staff, yes, let me tell you in confidence, a more comprehensive view than the chief himself, who, being the owner, lets his judgment easily be swayed against one of his employees. And you know very well that the traveler, who is never seen in the office almost the whole year around, can so easily fall a victim to gossip and ill luck and unfounded complaints, which he mostly knows nothing about, except when he comes back exhausted from his rounds, and only then suffers in person from their evil consequences, which he can no longer trace back to the original causes. Sir, sir, don't go away without a word to me to show that you think me in the right at least to some extent!"

But at Gregor's very first words the chief clerk had already backed away and only stared at him with parted lips over one twitching shoulder. And while Gregor was speaking he did not stand still one moment but stole away toward the door, without taking his eyes off Gregor, yet only an inch at a time, as if obeying some secret injunction to leave the room. He was already at the hall, and the suddenness with which he took his last step out of the living room would have made one believe he had burned the sole of his foot. Once in the hall he stretched his right arm before him toward the staircase, as if some supernatural power were waiting there to deliver him.

Gregor perceived that the chief clerk must on no account be allowed to go away in this frame of mind if his position in the firm were not to be endangered to the utmost. His parents did not understand this so well; they had convinced themselves in the course of years that Gregor was settled for life in this firm, and besides they were so preoccupied with their immediate troubles that all foresight had forsaken them. Yet Gregor had this foresight. The chief clerk must be detained, soothed, persuaded, and finally won over; the whole future of Gregor and his family depended on it! If only his sister had been there! She was intelligent; she had begun to cry while Gregor was still lying quietly on his back. And no doubt the chief clerk, so partial to ladies, would have been guided by her; she would have shut the door of the flat and in the hall talked him out of his horror. But she was not there, and Gregor would have to handle the situation himself. And without remembering that he was still unaware what powers of movement he possessed, without even remembering that his words in all possibility, indeed in all likelihood, would again be unintelligible, he let go the wing of the door, pushed himself through the opening, started to walk toward the chief clerk, who was already ridiculously clinging with both hands to the railing on the landing; but immediately, as he was feeling for a support, he fell down with a little cry upon all his numerous legs. Hardly was he down when he experienced for the first time this morning a sense of physical comfort; his legs had firm ground under them; they were completely obedient, as he noted with joy; they even strove to carry him forward in whatever direction he chose; and he was inclined to believe that a final relief from all his sufferings was at hand. But in the same moment as he found himself on the floor, rocking with suppressed eagerness to move, not far from his mother, indeed just in front of her, she, who had seemed so completely crushed, sprang all at once to her feet, her arms and fingers outspread, cried: "Help, for God's sake, help!" bent her head down as if to see Gregor better, yet on the contrary kept backing senselessly away; had quite forgotten that the laden table stood behind her; sat upon it hastily, as if in absence of mind, when she bumped into it; and seemed altogether unaware that the big coffeepot beside her was upset and pouring coffee in a flood over the carpet.

"Mother, Mother," said Gregor in a low voice, and looked up at her. The chief clerk, for the moment, had quite slipped from his mind; instead, he could not resist snapping his jaws together at the sight of the streaming coffee. That made his mother scream again, she fled from the table and fell into the arms of his father, who hastened to catch her. But Gregor had now no time to spare for his parents; the chief clerk was already on the stairs; with his chin on the banisters he was taking one last backward look. Gregor made a spring, to be as sure as possible of overtaking him; the chief clerk must have divined his intention, for he leaped down several steps and vanished; he was still yelling "Ugh!" and it echoed through the whole staircase.

Unfortunately, the flight of the chief clerk seemed completely to upset Gregor's father, who had remained relatively calm until now, for instead of running after the man himself, or at least not hindering Gregor in his pursuit, he seized in his right hand the walking stick that the chief clerk had left behind on a chair, together with a hat and greatcoat, snatched in his left hand a large newspaper from the table, and began stamping his feet and flourishing the stick and the newspaper to drive Gregor back into his room. No entreaty of Gregor's availed, indeed no entreaty was even understood, however humbly he bent his head his father only stamped on the floor the more loudly. Behind his father his mother had torn open a window, despite the cold weather, and was leaning far out of it with her face in her hands. A strong draught set in from the street to the staircase, the window curtains blew in, the newspapers on the table fluttered, stray pages whisked over the floor. Pitilessly Gregor's father drove him back, hissing and crying "Shoo!" like a savage. But Gregor was quite unpracticed in walking backwards, it really was a slow business. If he only had a chance to turn around he could get back to his room at once, but he was afraid of exasperating his father by the slowness of such a rotation and at any moment the stick in his father's hand might hit him a fatal blow on the back or on the head. In the end, however, nothing else was left for him to do since to his horror he observed that in moving backward he could not even control the direction he took; and so, keeping an anxious eye on his father all the time over his shoulder, he began to turn around as quickly as he could, which was in reality very slowly. Perhaps his father noted his good intentions, for he did not interfere except every now and then to help him in the maneuver from a distance with the point of the stick. If only he would have stopped making that unbearable hissing noise! It made Gregor quite lose his head. He had turned almost completely around when the hissing noise so distracted him that he even turned a little the wrong way again. But when at last his head was fortunately right in front of the doorway, it appeared that his body was too broad simply to get through the opening. His father, of course, in his present mood was far from thinking of such a thing as opening the other half of the door, to let Gregor have enough space. He had merely the fixed idea of driving Gregor back into his room as quickly as possible. He would never have suffered Gregor to make the circumstantial preparations for standing up on end and perhaps slipping his way through the door. Maybe he was now making more noise than ever to urge Gregor forward, as if no obstacle impeded him; to Gregor, anyhow, the noise in his rear sounded no longer like the voice of one single father; this was really no joke, and Gregor thrust himself—come what might— into the doorway. One side of his body rose up, he was tilted at an angle in the doorway, his flank was quite bruised, horrid blotches stained the white door, soon he was stuck fast and, left to himself, could not have moved at all, his legs on one side fluttered trembling in the air, those on the other were crushed painfully to the floor—when from behind his father gave him a strong push which was literally a deliverance and he flew far into the room, bleeding freely. The door was slammed behind him with the stick, and then at last there was silence.

II

Not until it was twilight did Gregor awake out of a deep sleep, more like a swoon than a sleep. He would certainly have waked up of his own accord not much later, for he felt himself sufficiently rested and well slept, but it seemed to him as if a fleeting step and a cautious shutting of the door leading into the hall had aroused him. The electric lights in the street cast a pale sheen here and there on the ceiling and the upper surfaces of the furniture, but down below, where he lay, it was dark. Slowly, awkwardly trying out his feelers, which he now first learned to appreciate, he pushed his way to the door to see what had been happening there.

His left side felt like one single long, unpleasantly tense scar, and he had actually to limp on his two rows of legs. One little leg, moreover, had been severely damaged in the course of that morning's events—it was almost a miracle that only one had been damaged—and trailed uselessly behind him.

He had reached the door before he discovered what had really drawn him to it: the smell of food. For there stood a basin filled with fresh milk in which floated little sops of white bread. He could almost have laughed with joy, since he was now still hungrier than in the morning, and he dipped his head almost over the eyes straight into the milk. But soon in disappointment he withdrew it again; not only did he find it difficult to feed because of his tender left side—and he could only feed with the palpitating collaboration of his whole body—he did not like the milk either, although milk had been his favorite drink and that was certainly why his sister had set it there for him, indeed it was almost with repulsion that he turned away from the basin and crawled back to the middle of the room.

He could see through the crack of the door that the gas was turned on in the living room, but while usually at this time his father made a habit of reading the afternoon newspaper in a loud voice to his mother and occasionally to his sister as well, not a sound was now to be heard. Well, perhaps his father had recently given up this habit of reading aloud, which his sister had mentioned so often in conversation and in her letters. But there was the same silence all around, although the flat was certainly not empty of occupants. "What a quiet life our family has been leading," said Gregor to himself, and as he sat there motionless staring into the darkness he felt great pride in the fact that he had been able to provide such a life for his parents and sister in such a fine flat. But what if all the quiet, the comfort, the contentment were now to end in horror? To keep himself from being lost in such thoughts Gregor took refuge in movement and crawled up and down the room.

Once during the long evening one of the side doors was opened a little and quickly shut again, later the other side door too; someone had apparently wanted to come in and then thought better of it. Gregor now stationed himself immediately before the living-room door, determined to persuade any hesitating visitor to come in or at least to discover who it might be; but the door was not opened again and he waited in vain. In the early morning, when the doors were locked, they had all wanted to come in, now that he had opened one door and the other had apparently been opened during the day, no one came in and even the keys were on the other side of the doors.

It was late at night before the gas went out in the living room, and Gregor could easily tell that his parents and his sister had all stayed awake until then, for he could clearly hear the three of them stealing away on tiptoe. No one was likely to visit him, not until the morning, that was certain; so he had plenty of time to meditate at his leisure on how he was to arrange his life afresh. But the lofty, empty room in which he had to lie flat on the floor filled him with an apprehension he could not account for, since it had been his very own room for the past five years—and with a half-unconscious action, not without a slight feeling of shame, he scuttled under the sofa, where he felt comfortable at once, although his back was a little cramped and he could not lift his head up, and his only regret was that his body was too broad to get the whole of it under the sofa.

He stayed there all night, spending the time partly in a light slumber, from which his hunger kept waking him up with a start, and partly in worrying and sketching vague hopes, which all led to the same conclusion, that he must lie low for the present and, by exercising patience and the utmost consideration, help the family to bear the inconvenience he was bound to cause them in his present condition.

Very early in the morning, it was still almost night, Gregor had the chance to test the strength of his new resolutions, for his sister, nearly fully dressed, opened the door from the hall and peered in. She did not see him at once, yet when she caught sight of him under the sofa—well, he had to be somewhere, he couldn't have flown away, could he?—she was so startled that without being able to help it she slammed the door shut again. But as if regretting her behavior she opened the door again immediately and came in on tiptoe, as if she were visiting an invalid or even a stranger. Gregor had pushed his head forward to the very edge of the sofa and watched her. Would she notice that he had left the milk standing, and not for lack of hunger, and would she bring in some other kind of food more to his taste? If she did not do it of her own accord, he would rather starve than draw her attention to the fact, although he felt a wild impulse to dart out from under the sofa, throw himself at her feet, and beg her for something to eat. But his sister at once noticed, with surprise, that the basin was still full, except for a little milk that had been spilled all around it, she lifted it immediately, not with her bare hands, true, but with a cloth and carried it away. Gregor was wildly curious to know what she would bring instead, and made various speculations about it. Yet what she actually did next, in the goodness of her heart, he could never have guessed at. To find out what he liked she brought him a whole selection of food, all set out on an old newspaper. There were old, half-decayed vegetables, bones from last night's supper covered with a white sauce that had thickened; some raisins and almonds; a piece of cheese that Gregor would have called uneatable two days ago; a dry roll of bread, a buttered roll, and a roll both buttered and salted. Besides all that, she set down again the same basin, into which she had poured some water, and which was apparently to be reserved for his exclusive use.

And with fine tact, knowing that Gregor would not eat in her presence, she withdrew quickly and even turned the key, to let him understand that he could take his ease as much as he liked. Gregor's legs all whizzed toward the food. His wounds must have healed completely, moreover, for he felt no disability, which amazed him and made him reflect how more than a month ago he had cut one finger a little with a knife and had still suffered pain from the wound only the day before yesterday. Am I less sensitive now? he thought, and sucked greedily at the cheese, which above all the other edibles attracted him at once and strongly. One after another and with tears of satisfaction in his eyes he quickly devoured the cheese, the vegetables, and the sauce; the fresh food, on the other hand, had no charms for him, he could not even stand the smell of it and actually dragged away to some little distance the things he could eat. He had long finished his meal and was only lying lazily on the same spot when his sister turned the key slowly as a sign for him to retreat. That roused him at once, although he was nearly asleep, and he hurried under the sofa again. But it took considerable self-control for him to stay under the sofa, even for the short time his sister was in the room, since the large meal had swollen his body somewhat and he was so cramped he could hardly breathe. Slight attacks of breathlessness afflicted him and his eyes were starting a little out of his head as he watched his unsuspecting sister sweeping together with a broom not only the remains of what he had eaten but even the things he had not touched, as if these were now of no use to anyone, and hastily shoveling it all into a bucket, which she covered with a wooden lid and carried away. Hardly had she turned her back when Gregor came from under the sofa and stretched and puffed himself out.

In this manner Gregor was fed, once in the early morning while his parents and the servant girl were still asleep, and a second time after they had all had their midday dinner, for then his parents took a short nap and the servant girl could be sent out on some errand or other by his sister. Not that they would have wanted him to starve, of course, but perhaps they could not have borne to know more about his feeding than from hearsay, perhaps too his sister wanted to spare them such little anxieties wherever possible, since they had quite enough to bear as it was.

Under what pretext the doctor and the locksmith had been got rid of on that first morning Gregor could not discover, for since what he said was not understood by the others it never struck any of them, not even his sister, that he could understand what they said, and so whenever his sister came into his room he had to content himself with hearing her utter only a sigh now and then and an occasional appeal to the saints. Later on, when she had got a little used to it—she sometimes threw out a remark which was kindly meant or could be so interpreted. "Well, he liked his dinner today," she would say when Gregor had made a good clearance of his food; and when he had not eaten, which gradually happened more and more often, she would say almost sadly: "Everything's been left standing again."

But although Gregor could get no news directly, he overheard a lot from the neighboring rooms, and as soon as voices were audible, he would run to the door of the room concerned and press his whole body against it. In the first few days especially there was no conversation that did not refer to him somehow, even if only indirectly. For two whole days there were family consultations at every mealtime about what should be done; but also between meals the same subject was discussed, for there were always at least two members of the family at home, since no one wanted to be alone in the flat and to leave it quite empty was unthinkable. And on the very first of these days the household cook—it was not quite clear what and how much she knew of the situation—went down on her knees to his mother and begged leave to go, and when she departed, a quarter of an hour later, gave thanks for her dismissal with tears in her eyes as if for the greatest benefit that could have been conferred on her, and without any prompting swore a solemn oath that she would never say a single word to anyone about what had happened.

Now Gregor's sister had to cook too, helping her mother; true, the cooking did not amount to much, for they ate scarcely anything. Gregor was always hearing one of the family vainly urging another to eat and getting no answer but: "Thanks, I've had all I want," or something similar. Perhaps they drank nothing either. Time and again his sister kept asking his father if he wouldn't like some beer and offered kindly to go and fetch it herself, and when he made no answer suggested that she could ask the concierge to fetch it, so that he need feel no sense of obligation, but then a round "No" came from his father and no more was said about it.

In the course of that very first day Gregor's father explained the family's financial position and prospects to both his mother and his sister. Now and then he rose from the table to get some voucher or memorandum out of the small safe he had rescued from the collapse of his business five years earlier. One could hear him opening the complicated lock and rustling papers out and shutting it again. This statement made by his father was the first cheerful information Gregor had heard since his imprisonment. He had been of the opinion that nothing at all was left over from his father's business, at least his father had never said anything to the contrary, and of course he had not asked him directly. At that time Gregor's sole desire was to do his utmost to help the family to forget as soon as possible the catastrophe that had overwhelmed the business and thrown them all into a state of complete despair. And so he had set to work with unusual ardor and almost overnight had become a commercial traveler instead of a little clerk, with of course much greater chances of earning money, and his success was immediately translated into good round coin which he could lay on the table for his amazed and happy family. These had been fine times, and they had never recurred, at least not with the same sense of glory, although later on Gregor had earned so much money that he was able to meet the expenses of the whole household and did so. They had simply got used to it, both the family and Gregor; the money was gratefully accepted and gladly given, but there was no special uprush of warm feeling. With his sister alone had he remained intimate, and it was a secret plan of his that she, who loved music, unlike himself, and could play movingly on the violin, should be sent next year to study at the Conservatorium, despite the great expense that would entail, which must be made up in some other way. During his brief visits home the Conservatorium was often mentioned in the talks he had with his sister, but always merely as a beautiful dream which could never come true, and his parents discouraged even these innocent references to it; yet Gregor had made up his mind firmly about it and meant to announce the fact with due solemnity on Christmas Day.

Such were the thoughts, completely futile in his present condition, that went through his head as he stood clinging upright to the door and listening. Sometimes out of sheet weariness he had to give up listening and let his head fall negligently against the door, but he always had to pull himself together again at once, for even the slight sound his head made was audible next door and brought all conversation to a stop. "What can he be doing now?" his father would say after a while, obviously turning toward the door, and only then would the interrupted conversation gradually be set going again.

Gregor was now informed as amply as he could wish—for his father tended to repeat himself in his explanations, partly because it was a long time since he had handled such matters and partly because his mother could not always grasp things at once—that a certain amount of investments, a very small amount it was true, had survived the wreck of their fortunes and had even increased a little because the dividends had not been touched meanwhile. And besides that, the money Gregory brought home every month—he had kept only a few dollars for himself—had never been quite used up and now amounted to a small capital sum. Behind the door Gregor nodded his head eagerly, rejoiced at this evidence of unexpected thrift and foresight. True, he could really have paid off some more of his father's debts to the chief with this extra money, and so brought much nearer the day on which he could quit his job, but doubtless it was better the way his father had arranged it.

Yet this capital was by no means sufficient to let the family live on the interest of it; for one year, perhaps, or at the most two, they could live on the principal, that was all. It was simply a sum that ought not to be touched and should be kept for a rainy day; money for living expenses would have to be earned. Now his father was still hale enough but an old man, and he had done no work for the past five years and could not be expected to do much; during these five years, the first years of leisure in his laborious though unsuccessful life, he had grown rather fat and become sluggish. And Gregor's old mother, how was she to earn a living with her asthma, which troubled her even when she walked through the flat and kept her lying on a sofa every other day panting for breath beside an open window? And was his sister to earn her bread, she who was still a child of seventeen and whose life hitherto had been so pleasant, consisting as it did in dressing herself nicely, sleeping long, helping in the housekeeping, going out to a few modest entertainments, and above all playing the violin? At first whenever the need for earning money was mentioned Gregor let go his hold on the door and threw himself down on the cool leather sofa beside it, he felt so hot with shame and grief.

Often he just lay there the long nights through without sleeping at all, scrabbling for hours on the leather. Or he nerved himself to the great effort of pushing an armchair to the window, then crawled up over the window sill and, braced against the chair, leaned against the window-panes, obviously in some recollection of the sense of freedom that looking out of a window always used to give him. For in reality day by day things that were even a little way off were growing dimmer to his sight; the hospital across the street, which he used to execrate for being all too often before his eyes, was now quite beyond his range of vision, and if he had not known that he lived in Charlotte Street, a quiet street but still a city street, he might have believed that his window gave on a desert waste where gray sky and gray land blended indistinguishably into each other. His quick-witted sister only needed to observe twice that the armchair stood by the window; after that whenever she had tidied the room she always pushed the chair back to the same place at the window and even left the inner casements open.

If he could have spoken to her and thanked her for all she had to do for him, he could have borne her ministrations better; as it was, they oppressed him. She certainly tried to make as light as possible of whatever was disagreeable in her task, and as time went on she succeeded, of course, more and more, but time brought more enlightenment to Gregor too. The very way she came in distressed him. Hardly was she in the room when she rushed to the window, without even taking time to shut the door, careful as she was usually to shield the sight of Gregor's room from the others, and as if she were almost suffocating tore the casements open with hasty fingers, standing then in the open draught for a while even in the bitterest cold and drawing deep breaths. This noisy scurry of hers upset Gregor twice a day; he would crouch trembling under the sofa all the time, knowing quite well that she would certainly have spared him such a disturbance had she found it at all possible to stay in his presence without opening the window.

On one occasion, about a month after Gregor's metamorphosis, when there was surely no reason for her to be still startled at his appearance, she came a little earlier than usual and found him gazing out of the window, quite motionless, and thus well placed to look like a bogey. Gregor would not have been surprised had she not come in at all, for she could not immediately open the window while he was there, but not only did she retreat, she jumped back as if in alarm and banged the door shut; a stranger might well have thought that he had been lying in wait for her there meaning to bite her. Of course he hid himself under the sofa at once, but he had to wait until midday before she came again, and she seemed more ill at ease than usual. This made him realize how repulsive the sight of him still was to her, and that it was bound to go on being repulsive, and what an effort it must cost her not to run away even from the sight of the small portion of his body that stuck out from under the sofa. In order to spare her that, therefore, one day he carried a sheet on his back to the sofa—it cost him four hours' labor—and arranged it there in such a way as to hide him completely, so that even if she were to bend down she could not see him. Had she considered the sheet unnecessary, she would certainly have stripped it off the sofa again, for it was clear enough that this curtaining and confining of himself was not likely to conduce to Gregor's comfort, but she left it where it was, and Gregor even fancied that he caught a thankful glance from her eye when he lifted the sheet carefully a very little with his head to see how she was taking the new arrangement.

For the first fortnight his parents could not bring themselves to the point of entering his room, and he often heard them expressing their appreciation of his sister's activities, whereas formerly they had frequently scolded her for being as they thought a somewhat useless daughter. But now, both of them often waited outside the door, his father and his mother, while his sister tidied his room, and as soon as she came out she had to tell them exactly how things were in the room, what Gregor had eaten, how he had conducted himself this time, and whether there was not perhaps some slight improvement in his condition. His mother, moreover, began relatively soon to want to visit him, but his father and sister dissuaded her at first with arguments which Gregor listened to very attentively and altogether approved. Later, however, she had to be held back by main force, and when she cried out: "Do let me in to Gregor, he is my unfortunate son! Can't you understand that I must go to him?" Gregor thought that it might be well to have her come in, not every day, of course, but perhaps once a week; she understood things, after all, much better than his sister, who was only a child despite the efforts she was making and had perhaps taken on so difficult a task merely out of childish thoughtlessness.

Gregor's desire to see his mother was soon fulfilled. During the daytime he did not want to show himself at the window, out of consideration for his parents, but he could not crawl very far around the few square yards of floor space he had, nor could he bear lying quietly at rest all during the night, while he was fast losing any interest he had ever taken in food, so that for mere recreation he had formed the habit of crawling crisscross over the walls and ceiling. He especially enjoyed hanging suspended from the ceiling; it was much better than lying on the floor; one could breathe more freely; one's body swung and rocked lightly; and in the almost blissful absorption induced by this suspension it could happen to his own surprise that he let go and fell plump on the floor. Yet he now had his body much better under control than formerly, and even such a big fall did him no harm. His sister at once remarked the new distraction Gregor had found for himself—he left traces behind him of the sticky stuff on his soles wherever he crawled—and she got the idea in her head of giving him as wide a field as possible to crawl in and of removing the pieces of furniture that hindered him, above all the chest of drawers and the writing desk. But that was more than she could manage all by herself; she did not dare ask her father to help her; and as for the servant girl, a young creature of sixteen who had had the courage to stay on after the cook's departure, she could not be asked to help, for she had begged as a special favor that she might keep the kitchen door locked and open it only on a definite summons; so there was nothing left but to apply to her mother at an hour when her father was out. And the old lady did come, with exclamations of joyful eagerness, which, however, died away at the door of Gregor's room. Gregor's sister, of course, went in first, to see that everything was in order before letting his mother enter. In great haste Gregor pulled the sheet lower and rucked it more in folds so that it really looked as if it had been thrown accidentally over the sofa. And this time he did not peer out from under it; he renounced the pleasure of seeing his mother on this occasion and was only glad that she had come at all. "Come in, he's out of sight," said his sister, obviously leading her mother in by the hand. Gregor could now hear the two women struggling to shift the heavy old chest from its place, and his sister claiming the greater part of the labor for herself, without listening to the admonitions of her mother, who feared she might overstrain herself. It took a long time. After at least a quarter of an hour's tugging his mother objected that the chest had better be left where it was, for in the first place it was too heavy and could never be got out before his father came home, and standing in the middle of the room like that it would only hamper Gregor's movements, while in the second place it was not at all certain that removing the furniture would be doing a service to Gregor. She was inclined to think to the contrary; the sight of the naked walls made her own heart heavy, and why shouldn't Gregor have the same feeling, considering that he had been used to his furniture for so long and might feel forlorn without it. "And doesn't it look," she concluded in a low voice—in fact she had been almost whispering all the time as if to avoid letting Gregor, whose exact whereabouts she did not know, hear even the tones of her voice, for she was convinced that he could not understand her words—"doesn't it look as if we were showing him, by taking away his furniture, that we have given up hope of his ever getting better and are just leaving him coldly to himself? I think it would be best to keep his room exactly as it has always been, so that when he comes back to us he will find everything unchanged and be able all the more easily to forget what has happened in between."

On hearing these words from his mother Gregor realized that the lack of all direct human speech for the past two months together with the monotony of family life must have confused his mind, otherwise he could not account for the fact that he had quite earnestly looked forward to having his room emptied of furnishing. Did he really want his warm room, so comfortably fitted with old family furniture, to be turned into a naked den in which he would certainly be able to crawl unhampered in all directions but at the price of shedding simultaneously all recollection of his human background? He had indeed been so near the brink of forgetfulness that only the voice of his mother, which he had not heard for so long, had drawn him back from it. Nothing should be taken out of his room; everything must stay as it was; he could not dispense with the good influence of the furniture on his state of mind; and even if the furniture did hamper him in his senseless crawling around and around, that was no drawback but a great advantage.

Unfortunately his sister was of the contrary opinion; she had grown accustomed, and not without reason, to consider herself an expert in Gregor's affairs as against her parents, and so her mother's advice was now enough to make her determined on the removal not only of the chest and the writing desk, which had been her first intention, but of all the furniture except the indispensable sofa. This determination was not, of course, merely the outcome of childish recalcitrance and of the self-confidence she had recently developed so unexpectedly and at such cost; she had in fact perceived that Gregor needed a lot of space to crawl about in, while on the other hand he never used the furniture at all, so far as could be seen. Another factor might also have been the enthusiastic temperament of an adolescent girl, which seeks to indulge itself on every opportunity and which now tempted Grete to exaggerate the horror of her brother's circumstances in order that she might do all the more for him. In a room where Gregor lorded it all alone over empty walls no one save herself was likely ever to set foot.

And so she was not to be moved from her resolve by her mother, who seemed moreover to be ill at ease in Gregor's room and therefore unsure of herself, was soon reduced to silence, and helped her daughter as best she could to push the chest outside. Now, Gregor could do without the chest, if need be, but the writing desk he must retain. As soon as the two women had got the chest out of his room, groaning as they pushed it, Gregor stuck his head out from under the sofa to see how he might intervene as kindly and cautiously as possible. But as bad luck would have it, his mother was the first to return, leaving Grete clasping the chest in the room next door where she was trying to shift it all by herself, without of course moving it from the spot. His mother however was not accustomed to the sight of him, it might sicken her and so in alarm Gregor backed quickly to the other end of the sofa, yet could not prevent the sheet from swaying a little in front. That was enough to put her on the alert. She paused, stood still for a moment, and then went back to Grete.

Although Gregor kept reassuring himself that nothing out of the way was happening, but only a few bits of furniture were being changed around, he soon had to admit that all this trotting to and fro of the two women, their little ejaculations, and the scraping of furniture along the floor affected him like a vast disturbance coming from all sides at once, and however much he tucked in his head and legs and cowered to the very floor he was bound to confess that he would not be able to stand it for long. They were clearing his room out; taking away everything he loved; the chest in which he kept his fret saw and other tools was already dragged off; they were now loosening the writing desk which had almost sunk into the floor, the desk at which he had done all his homework when he was at the commercial academy, at the grammar school before that, and yes, even at the primary school—he had no more time to waste in weighing the good intentions of the two women, whose existence he had by now almost forgotten, for they were so exhausted that they were laboring in silence and nothing could be heard but the heavy scuffling of their feet.

And so he rushed out—the women were just leaning against the writing desk in the next room to give themselves a breather—and four times changed his direction, since he really did not know what to rescue first, then on the wall opposite, which was already otherwise cleared, he was struck by the picture of the lady muffled in so much fur and quickly crawled up to it and pressed himself to the glass, which was a good surface to hold on to and comforted his hot belly. This picture at least, which was entirely hidden beneath him, was going to be removed by nobody. He turned his head toward the door of the living room so as to observe the women when they came back.

They had not allowed themselves much of a rest and were already coming; Grete had twined her arm around her mother and was almost supporting her. "Well, what shall we take now?" said Grete, looking around. Her eyes met Gregor's from the wall. She kept her composure, presumably because of her mother, bent her head down to her mother, to keep her from looking up, and said, although in a fluttering, unpremeditated voice: "Come, hadn't we better go back to the living room for a moment?" Her intentions were clear enough to Gregor, she wanted to bestow her mother in safety and then chase him down from the wall. Well, just let her try it! He clung to his picture and would not give it up. He would rather fly in Grete's face.

But Grete's words had succeeded in disquieting her mother, who took a step to one side, caught sight of the huge brown mass on the flowered wallpaper, and before she was really conscious that what she saw was Gregor, screamed in a loud, hoarse voice: "Oh God, oh God!" fell with outspread arms over the sofa as if giving up, and did not move. "Gregor!" cried his sister, shaking her fist and glaring at him. This was the first time she had directly addressed him since his metamorphosis. She ran into the next room for some aromatic essence with which to rouse her mother from her fainting fit. Gregor wanted to help too—there was still time to rescue the picture—but he was stuck fast to the glass and had to tear himself loose; he then ran after his sister into the next room as if he could advise her, as he used to do; but then had to stand helplessly behind her; she meanwhile searched among various small bottles and when she turned around started in alarm at the sight of him; one bottle fell on the floor and broke; a splinter of glass cut Gregor's face and some kind of corrosive medicine splashed him; without pausing a moment longer Grete gathered up all the bottles she could carry and ran to her mother with them; she banged the door shut with her foot. Gregor was now cut off from his mother, who was perhaps nearly dying because of him; he dared not open the door for fear of frightening away his sister, who had to stay with her mother; there was nothing he could do but wait; and harassed by self-reproach and worry he began now to crawl to and fro, over everything, walls, furniture, and ceiling, and finally in his despair, when the whole room seemed to be reeling around him, fell down onto the middle of the big table.

A little while elapsed, Gregor was still lying there feebly and all around was quiet, perhaps that was a good omen. Then the doorbell rang. The servant girl was of course locked in her kitchen, and Grete would have to open the door. It was his father. "What's been happening?" were his first words; Grete's face must have told him everything. Grete answered in a muffled voice, apparently hiding her head on his breast: "Mother has been fainting, but she's better now. Gregor's broken loose." "Just what I expected," said his father, "just what I've been telling you, but you women would never listen." It was clear to Gregor that his father had taken the worst interpretation of Grete's all too brief statement and was assuming that Gregor had been guilty of some violent act. Therefore Gregor must now try to propitiate his father, since he had neither time nor means for an explanation. And so he fled to the door of his own room and crouched against it, to let his father see as soon as he came in from the hall that his son had the good intention of getting back into his room immediately and that it was not necessary to drive him there, but that if only the door were opened he would disappear at once.

Yet his father was not in the mood to perceive such fine distinctions. "Ah!" he cried as soon as he appeared, in a tone that sounded at once angry and exultant. Gregor drew his head back from the door and lifted it to look at his father. Truly, this was not the father he had imagined to himself; admittedly he had been too absorbed of late in his new recreation of crawling over the ceiling to take the same interest as before in what was happening elsewhere in the flat, and he ought really to be prepared for some changes. And yet, and yet, could that be his father? The man who used to lie wearily sunk in bed whenever Gregor set out on a business journey; who welcomed him back of an evening lying in a long chair in a dressing gown; who could not really rise to his feet but only lifted his arms in greeting, and on the rare occasions when he did go out with his family, on one or two Sundays a year and on highest holidays, walked between Gregor and his mother, who were slow walkers anyhow, even more slowly than they did, muffled in his old greatcoat, shuffling laboriously forward with the help of his crook-handled stick which he set down most cautiously at every step and, whenever he wanted to say anything, nearly always came to a full stop and gathered his escort around him? Now he was standing there in fine shape; dressed in a smart blue uniform with gold buttons, such as bank messengers wear; his strong double chin bulged over the stiff high collar of his jacket; from under his bushy eyebrows his black eyes darted fresh and penetrating glances; his onetime tangled white hair had been combed flat on either side of a shining and carefully exact parting. He pitched his cap, which bore a gold monogram, probably the badge of some bank, in a wide sweep across the whole room onto a sofa and with the tail-ends of his jacket thrown back, his hands in his trouser pockets, advanced with a grim visage toward Gregor. Likely enough he did not himself know what he meant to do; at any rate he lifted his feet uncommonly high, and Gregor was dumbfounded at the enormous size of his shoe soles. But Gregor could not risk standing up to him, aware as he had been from the very first day of his new life that his father believed only the severest measures suitable for dealing with him. And so he ran before his father, stopping when he stopped and scuttling forward again when his father made any kind of move. In this way they circled the room several times without anything decisive happening, indeed the whole operation did not even look like a pursuit because it was carried out so slowly. And so Gregor did not leave the floor, for he feared that his father might take as a piece of peculiar wickedness any excursion of his over the walls or the ceiling. All the same, he could not stay this course much longer, for while his father took one step he had to carry out a whole series of movements. He was already beginning to feel breathless, just as in his former life his lungs had not been very dependable. As he was staggering along, trying to concentrate his energy on running, hardly keeping his eyes open; in his dazed state never even thinking of any other escape than simply going forward; and having almost forgotten that the walls were free to him, which in this room were well provided with finely carved pieces of furniture full of knobs and crevices—suddenly something lightly flung landed close behind him and rolled before him. It was an apple; a second apple followed immediately; Gregor came to a stop in alarm; there was no point in running on, for his father was determined to bombard him. He had filled his pockets with fruit from the dish on the sideboard and was now shying apple after apple, without taking particularly good aim for the moment. The small red apples rolled about the floor as if magnetized and cannoned into each other. An apple thrown without much force grazed Gregor's back and glanced off harmlessly. But another following immediately landed right on his back and sank in; Gregor wanted to drag himself forward, as if this startling, incredible pain could be left behind him; but he felt as if nailed to the spot and flattened himself out in a complete derangement of all his senses. With his last conscious look he saw the door of his room being torn open and his mother rushing out ahead of his screaming sister, in her underbodice, for her daughter had loosened her clothing to let her breathe more freely and recover from her swoon, he saw his mother rushing toward his father, leaving one after another behind her on the floor her loosened petticoats, stumbling over her petticoats straight to his father and embracing him, in complete union with him—but here Gregor's sight began to fail—with her hands clasped around his father's neck as she begged for her son's life.

III

The serious injury done to Gregor, which disabled him for more than a month—the apple went on sticking in his body as a visible reminder, since no one ventured to remove it—seemed to have made even his father recollect that Gregor was a member of the family, despite his present unfortunate and repulsive shape, and ought not to be treated as an enemy, that, on the contrary, family duty required the suppression of disgust and the exercise of patience, nothing but patience.

And although his injury had impaired, probably forever, his powers of movement, and for the time being it took him long, long minutes to creep across his room like an old invalid—there was no question now of crawling up the wall—yet in his own opinion he was sufficiently compensated for this worsening of his condition by the fact that toward evening the living-room door, which he used to watch intently for an hour or two beforehand, was always thrown open, so that lying in the darkness of his room, invisible to the family, he could see them all at the lamp-lit table and listen to their talk, by general consent as it were, very different from his earlier eavesdropping.

True, their intercourse lacked the lively character of former times, which he had always called to mind with a certain wistfulness in the small hotel bedrooms where he had been wont to throw himself down, tired out, on damp bedding. They were now mostly very silent. Soon after supper his father would fall asleep in his armchair; his mother and sister would admonish each other to be silent; his mother, bending low over the lamp, stitched at fine sewing for an underwear firm; his sister, who had taken a job as a salesgirl, was learning shorthand and French in the evenings on the chance of bettering herself. Sometimes his father woke up, and as if quite unaware that he had been sleeping said to his mother: "What a lot of sewing you're doing today!" and at once fell asleep again, while the two women exchanged a tired smile.

With a kind of mulishness his father persisted in keeping his uniform on even in the house; his dressing gown hung uselessly on its peg and he slept fully dressed where he sat, as if he were ready for service at any moment and even here only at the beck and call of his superior. As a result, his uniform, which was not brand-new to start with, began to look dirty, despite all the loving care of the mother and sister to keep it clean, and Gregor often spent whole evenings gazing at the many greasy spots on the garment, gleaming with gold buttons always in a high state of polish, in which the old man sat sleeping in extreme discomfort and yet quite peacefully.

And soon as the clock struck ten his mother tried to rouse his father with gentle words and to persuade him after that to get into bed, for sitting there he could not have a proper sleep and that was what he needed most, since he had to go on duty at six. But with the mulishness that had obsessed him since he became a bank messenger he always insisted on staying longer at the table, although he regularly fell asleep again and in the end only with the greatest trouble could be got out of his armchair and into his bed. However insistently Gregor's mother and sister kept urging him with gentle reminders, he would go on slowly shaking his head for a quarter of an hour, keeping his eyes shut, and refuse to get to his feet. The mother plucked at his sleeve, whispering endearments in his ear, the sister left her lessons to come to her mother's help, but Gregor's father was not to be caught. He would only sink down deeper in his chair. Not until the two women hoisted him up by the armpits did he open his eyes and look at them both, one after the other, usually with the remark: "This is a life. This is the peace and quiet of my old age." And leaning on the two of them he would heave himself up, with difficulty, as if he were a great burden to himself, suffer them to lead him as far as the door and then wave them off and go on alone, while the mother abandoned her needlework and the sister her pen in order to run after him and help him farther.

Who could find time, in this overworked and tired-out family, to bother about Gregor more than was absolutely needful? The household was reduced more and more; the servant girl was turned off; a gigantic bony charwoman with white hair flying around her head came in morning and evening to do the rough work; everything else was done by Gregor's mother, as well as great piles of sewing. Even various family ornaments, which his mother and sister used to wear with pride at parties and celebrations, had to be sold, as Gregor discovered of an evening from hearing them all discuss the prices obtained. But what they lamented most was the fact that they could not leave the flat which was much too big for their present circumstances, because they could not think of any way to shift Gregor. Yet Gregor saw well enough that consideration for him was not the main difficulty preventing the removal, for they could have easily shifted him in some suitable box with a few air holes in it; what really kept them from moving into another flat was rather their own complete hopelessness and the belief that they had been singled out for a misfortune such as had never happened to any of their relations or acquaintances. They fulfilled to the uttermost all that the world demands of poor people, the father fetched breakfast for the small clerks in the bank, the mother devoted her energy to making underwear for strangers, the sister trotted to and fro behind the counter at the behest of customers, but more than this they had not the strength to do. And the wound in Gregor's back began to nag at him afresh when his mother and sister, after getting his father into bed, came back again, left their work lying, drew close to each other, and sat cheek by cheek; when his mother, pointing toward his room, said: "Shut that door now, Grete," and he was left again in darkness, while next door the women mingled their tears or perhaps sat dry-eyed staring at the table.

Gregor hardly slept at all by night or by day. He was often haunted by the idea that next time the door opened he would take the family's affairs in hand again just as he used to do; once more, after this long interval, there appeared in his thoughts the figures of the chief and the chief clerk, the commercial travelers and the apprentices, the porter who was so dull-witted, two or three friends in other firms, a chambermaid in one of the rural hotels, a sweet and fleeting memory, a cashier in a milliner's shop, whom he had wooed earnestly but too slowly—they all appeared, together with strangers or people he had quite forgotten, but instead of helping him and his family they were one and all unapproachable and he was glad when they vanished. At other times he would not be in the mood to bother about his family, he was only filled with rage at the way they were neglecting him, and although he had no clear idea of what he might care to eat he would make plans for getting into the larder to take the food that was after all his due, even if he were not hungry. His sister no longer took thought to bring him what might especially please him, but in the morning and at noon before she went to business hurriedly pushed into his room with her foot any food that was available, and in the evening cleared it out again with one sweep of the broom, heedless of whether it had been merely tasted, or—as most frequently happened—left untouched. The cleaning of his room, which she now did always in the evenings, could not have been more hastily done. Streaks of dirt stretched along the walls, here and there lay balls of dust and filth. At first Gregor used to station himself in some particularly filthy corner when his sister arrived, in order to reproach her with it, so to speak. But he could have sat there for weeks without getting her to make any improvement; she could see the dirt as well as he did, but she had simply made up her mind to leave it alone. And yet, with a touchiness that was new to her, which seemed anyhow to have infected the whole family, she jealously guarded her claim to be the sole caretaker of Gregor's room. His mother once subjected his room to a thorough cleaning, which was achieved only by means of several buckets of water—all this dampness of course upset Gregor too and he lay widespread, sulky, and motionless on the sofa—but she was well punished for it. Hardly had his sister noticed the changed aspect of his room that evening when she rushed in high dudgeon into the living room and, despite the imploringly raised hands of her mother, burst into a storm of weeping, while her parents—her father had of course been startled out of his chair—looked on at first in helpless amazement; then they too began to go into action; the father reproached the mother on his right for not having left the cleaning of Gregor's room to his sister; shrieked at the sister on his left that never again was she to be allowed to clean Gregor's room; while the mother tried to pull the father into his bedroom, since he was beyond himself with agitation; the sister, shaken with sobs, then beat upon the table with her small fists; and Gregor hissed loudly with rage because not one of them thought of shutting the door to spare him such a spectacle and so much noise.

Still, even if the sister, exhausted by her daily work, had grown tired of looking after Gregor as she did formerly, there was no need for his mother's intervention or for Gregor's being neglected at all. The charwoman was there. This old widow, whose strong bony frame had enabled her to survive the worst a long life could offer, by no means recoiled from Gregor. Without being in the least curious she had once by chance opened the door of his room and at the sight of Gregor, who, taken by surprise, began to rush to and fro although no one was chasing him, merely stood there with her arms folded. From that time she never failed to open his door a little for a moment, morning and evening, to have a look at him. At first she even used to call him to her, with words which apparently she took to be friendly, such as: "Come along, then, you old dung beetle!" or "Look at the old dung beetle, then!" To such allocutions Gregor made no answer, but stayed motionless where he was, as if the door had never been opened. Instead of being allowed to disturb him so senselessly whenever the whim took her, she should rather have been ordered to clean out his room daily, that charwoman! Once, early in the morning— heavy rain was lashing on the windowpanes, perhaps a sign that spring was on the way—Gregor was so exasperated when she began addressing him again that he ran at her, as if to attack her, although slowly and feebly enough. But the charwoman instead of showing fright merely lifted high a chair that happened to be beside the door, and as she stood there with her mouth wide open it was clear that she meant to shut it only when she brought the chair down on Gregor's back. "So you're not coming any nearer?" she asked, as Gregor turned away again, and quietly put the chair back into the corner.

Gregor was now eating hardly anything. Only when he happened to pass the food laid out for him did he take a bit of something in his mouth as a pastime, kept it there for an hour at a time, and usually spat it out again. At first he thought it was chagrin over the state of his room that prevented him from eating, yet he soon got used to the various changes in his room. It had become a habit in the family to push into his room things there was no room for elsewhere, and there were plenty of these now, since one of the rooms had been let to three lodgers. These serious gentlemen—all three of them with full beards, as Gregor once observed through a crack in the door—had a passion for order, not only in their own room but, since they were now members of the household, in all its arrangements, especially in the kitchen. Superfluous, not to say dirty, objects they could not bear. Besides, they had brought with them most of the furnishings they needed. For this reason many things could be dispensed with that it was no use trying to sell but that should not be thrown away either. All of them found their way into Gregor's room. The ash can likewise and the kitchen garbage can. Anything that was not needed for the moment was simply flung into Gregor's room by the charwoman, who did everything in a hurry; fortunately Gregor usually saw only the object, whatever it was, and the hand that held it. Perhaps she intended to take the things away again as time and opportunity offered, or to collect them until she could throw them all out in a heap, but in fact they just lay wherever she happened to throw them, except when Gregor pushed his way through the junk heap and shifted it somewhat, at first out of necessity, because he had not room enough to crawl, but later with increasing enjoyment, although after such excursions, being sad and weary to death, he would lie motionless for hours. And since the lodgers often ate their supper at home in the common living room, the living-room door stayed shut many an evening, yet Gregor reconciled himself quite easily to the shutting of the door, for often enough on evenings when it was opened he had disregarded it entirely and lain in the darkest corner of his room, quite unnoticed by the family. But on one occasion the charwoman left the door open a little and it stayed ajar even when the lodgers came in for supper and the lamp was lit. They set themselves at the top end of the table where formerly Gregor and his father and mother had eaten their meals, unfolded their napkins, and took knife and fork in hand. At once his mother appeared in the other doorway with a dish of meat and close behind her his sister with a dish of potatoes piled high. The food steamed with a thick vapor. The lodgers bent over the food set before them as if to scrutinize it before eating, in fact the man in the middle, who seemed to pass for an authority with the other two, cut a piece of meat as it lay on the dish, obviously to discover if it were tender or should be sent back to the kitchen. He showed satisfaction, and Gregor's mother and sister, who had been watching anxiously, breathed freely and began to smile.

The family itself took its meals in the kitchen. Nonetheless, Gregor's father came into the living room before going into the kitchen and with one prolonged bow, cap in hand, made a round of the table. The lodgers all stood up and murmured something in their beards. When they were alone again they ate their food in almost complete silence. It seemed remarkable to Gregor that among the various noises coming from the table he could always distinguish the sound of their masticating teeth, as if this were a sign to Gregor that one needed teeth in order to eat, and that with toothless jaws even of the finest make one could do nothing. "I'm hungry enough," said Gregor sadly to himself, "but not for that kind of food. How these lodgers are stuffing themselves, and here am I dying of starvation!"

On that very evening—during the whole of his time there Gregor could not remember ever having heard the violin—the sound of violin-playing came from the kitchen. The lodgers had already finished their supper, the one in the middle had brought out a newspaper and given the other two a page apiece, and now they were leaning back at ease reading and smoking. When the violin began to play they pricked up their ears, got to their feet, and went on tiptoe to the hall door where they stood huddled together. Their movements must have been heard in the kitchen, for Gregor's father called out: "Is the violin-playing disturbing you, gentlemen? It can be stopped at once." "On the contrary," said the middle lodger, "could not Fräulein Samsa come and play in this room, beside us, where it is much more convenient and comfortable? "Oh certainly," cried Gregor's father, as if he were the violin-player. The lodgers came back into the living room and waited. Presently Gregor's father arrived with the music stand, his mother carrying the music and his sister with the violin. His sister quietly made everything ready to start playing; his parents, who had never let rooms before and so had an exaggerated idea of the courtesy due to lodgers, did not venture to sit down on their own chairs; his father leaned against the door, the right hand thrust between two buttons of his livery coat, which was formally buttoned up; but his mother was offered a chair by one of the lodgers and, since she left the chair just where he had happened to put it, sat down in a corner to one side.

Gregor's sister began to play; the father and mother, from either side, intently watched the movements of her hands. Gregor, attracted by the playing, ventured to move forward a little until his head was actually inside the living room. He felt hardly any surprise at his growing lack of consideration for the others; there had been a time when he prided himself on being considerate. And yet just on this occasion he had more reason than ever to hide himself, since, owing to the amount of dust that lay thick in his room and rose into the air at the slightest movement, he too was covered with dust; fluff and hair and remnants of food trailed with him, caught on his back and along his sides; his indifference to everything was much too great for him to turn on his back and scrape himself clean on the carpet, as once he had done several times a day. And in spite of his condition, no shame deterred him from advancing a little over the spotless floor of the living room.

To be sure, no one was aware of him. The family was entirely absorbed in the violin-playing; the lodgers, however, who first of all had stationed themselves, hands in pockets, much too close behind the music stand so that they could all have read the music, which must have bothered his sister, had soon retreated to the window, half whispering with downbent heads, and stayed there while his father turned an anxious eye on them. Indeed, they were making it more than obvious that they had been disappointed in their expectation of hearing good or enjoyable violin-playing, that they had had more than enough of the performance and only out of courtesy suffered a continued disturbance of their peace. From the way they all kept blowing the smoke of their cigars high in the air through nose and mouth one could divine their irritation. And yet Gregor's sister was playing so beautifully. Her face leaned sideways, intently and sadly her eyes followed the notes of music. Gregor crawled a little farther forward and lowered his head to the ground so that it might be possible for his eyes to meet hers. Was he an animal, that music had such an effect upon him? He felt as if the way were opening before him to the unknown nourishment he craved. He was determined to push forward till he reached his sister, to pull at her skirt and so let her know that she was to come into his room with her violin, for no one here appreciated her playing as he would appreciate it. He would never let her out of his room, at least, not so long as he lived; his frightful appearance would become, for the first time, useful to him; he would watch all the doors of his room at once and spit at intruders; but his sister should need no constraint, she should stay with him of her own free will; she should sit beside him on the sofa, bend down her ear to him, and hear him confide that he had had the firm intention of sending her to the Conservatorium, and that, but for his mishap, last Christmas—surely Christmas was long past?—he would have announced it to everybody without allowing a single objection. After this confession his sister would be so touched that she would burst into tears, and Gregor would then raise himself to her shoulder and kiss her on the neck, which, now that she went to business, she kept free of any ribbon or collar.

"Mr. Samsa!" cried the middle lodger to Gregor's father, and pointed, without wasting any more words, at Gregor, now working himself slowly forward. The violin fell silent, the middle lodger first smiled to his friends with a shake of the head and then looked at Gregor again. Instead of driving Gregor out, his father seemed to think it more needful to begin by soothing down the lodgers, although they were not at all agitated and apparently found Gregor more entertaining than the violin-playing. He hurried toward them and, spreading out his arms, tried to urge them back into their own room and at the same time to block their view of Gregor. They now began to be really a little angry, one could not tell whether because of the old man's behavior or because it had just dawned on them that all unwittingly they had such a neighbor as Gregor next door. They demanded explanations of his father, they waved their arms like him, tugged uneasily at their beards, and only with reluctance backed toward their room. Meanwhile Gregor's sister, who stood there as if lost when her playing was so abruptly broken off, came to life again, pulled herself together all at once after standing for a while holding violin and bow in nervelessly hanging hands and staring at her music, pushed her violin into the lap of her mother, who was still sitting in her chair fighting asthmatically for breath, and ran into the lodgers' room to which they were now being shepherded by her father rather more quickly than before. One could see the pillows and blankets on the beds flying under her accustomed fingers and being laid in order. Before the lodgers had actually reached their room she had finished making the beds and slipped out.

The old man seemed once more to be so possessed by his mulish self-assertiveness that he was forgetting all the respect he should show to his lodgers. He kept driving them on and driving them on until in the very door of the bedroom the middle lodger stamped his foot loudly on the floor and so brought him to a halt. "I beg to announce," said the lodger, lifting one hand and looking also at Gregor's mother and sister, "that because of the disgusting conditions prevailing in this household and family"—here he spat on the floor with emphatic brevity—"I give you notice on the spot. Naturally I won't pay you a penny for the days I have lived here, on the contrary I shall consider bringing an action for damages against you, based on claims—believe me—that will be easily susceptible of proof." He ceased and stared straight in front of him, as if he expected something. In fact his two friends at once rushed into the breach with these words: "And we too give notice on the spot." On that he seized the door handle and shut the door with a slam.

Gregor's father, groping with his hands, staggered forward and fell into his chair; it looked as if he were stretching himself there for his ordinary evening nap, but the marked jerkings of his head, which were as if uncontrollable, showed that he was far from asleep. Gregor had simply stayed quietly all the time on the spot where the lodgers had espied him. Disappointment at the failure of his plan, perhaps also the weakness arising from extreme hunger, made it impossible for him to move. He feared, with a fair degree of certainty, that at any moment the general tension would discharge itself in a combined attack upon him, and he lay waiting. He did not react even to the noise made by the violin as it fell off his mother's lap from under her trembling fingers and gave out a resonant note.

"My dear parents," said his sister, slapping her hand on the table by way of introduction, "things can't go on like this. Perhaps you don't realize that, but I do. I won't utter my brother's name in the presence of this creature, and so all I say is: we must try to get rid of it. We've tried to look after it and to put up with it as far as is humanly possible, and I don't think anyone could reproach us in the slightest."

"She is more than right," said Gregor's father to himself. His mother, who was still choking for lack of breath, began to cough hollowly into her hand with a wild look in her eyes.

His sister rushed over to her and held her forehead. His father's thoughts seemed to have lost their vagueness at Grete's words, he sat more upright, fingering his service cap that lay among the plates still lying on the table from the lodgers' supper, and from time to time looked at the still form of Gregor.

"We must try to get rid of it," his sister now said explicitly to her father, since her mother was coughing too much to hear a word, "it will be the death of both of you, I can see that coming. When one has to work as hard as we do, all of us, one can't stand this continual torment at home on top of it. At least I can't stand it any longer." And she burst into such a passion of sobbing that her tears dropped on her mother's face, where she wiped them off mechanically.

"My dear," said the old man sympathetically, and with evident understanding, "but what can we do?"

Gregor's sister merely shrugged her shoulders to indicate the feeling of helplessness that had now overmastered her during her weeping fit, in contrast to her former confidence.

"If he could understand us," said her father, half questioningly; Grete, still sobbing, vehemently waved a hand to show how unthinkable that was.

"If he could understand us," repeated the old man, shutting his eyes to consider his daughter's conviction that understanding was impossible, "then perhaps we might come to some agreement with him. But as it is——"

"He must go," cried Gregor's sister, "that's the only solution, Father. You must just try to get rid of the idea that this is Gregor. The fact that we've believed it for so long is the root of all our trouble. But how can it be Gregor? If this were Gregor, he would have realized long ago that human beings can't live with such a creature, and he'd have gone away on his own accord. Then we wouldn't have any brother, but we'd be able to go on living and keep his memory in honor. As it is, this creature persecutes us, drives away our lodgers, obviously wants the whole apartment to himself, and would have us all sleep in the gutter. Just look, Father," she shrieked all at once, "he's at it again!" And in an access of panic that was quite incomprehensible to Gregor she even quitted her mother, literally thrusting the chair from her as if she would rather sacrifice her mother than stay so near to Gregor, and rushed behind her father, who also rose up, being simply upset by her agitation, and half spread his arms out as if to protect her.

Yet Gregor had not the slightest intention of frightening anyone, far less his sister. He had only begun to turn around in order to crawl back to his room, but it was certainly a startling operation to watch, since because of his disabled condition he could not execute the difficult turning movements except by lifting his head and then bracing it against the floor over and over again. He paused and looked around. His good intentions seemed to have been recognized; the alarm had only been momentary. Now they were all watching him in melancholy silence. His mother lay in her chair, her legs stiffly outstretched and pressed together, her eyes almost closing for sheer weariness; his father and his sister were sitting beside each other, his sister's arm around the old man's neck.

Perhaps I can go on turning around now, thought Gregor, and began his labors again. He could not stop himself from panting with the effort, and had to pause now and then to take breath. Nor did anyone harass him, he was left entirely to himself. When he had completed the turn-around he began at once to crawl straight back. He was amazed at the distance separating him from his room and could not understand how in his weak state he had managed to accomplish the same journey so recently, almost without remarking it. Intent on crawling as fast as possible, he barely noticed that not a single word, not an ejaculation from his family, interfered with his progress. Only when he was already in the doorway did he turn his head around, not completely, for his neck muscles were getting stiff, but enough to see that nothing had changed behind him except that his sister had risen to her feet. His last glance fell on his mother, who was not quite overcome by sleep.

Hardly was he well inside his room when the door was hastily pushed shut, bolted, and locked. The sudden noise in his rear startled him so much that his little legs gave beneath him. It was his sister who had shown such haste. She had been standing ready waiting and had made a light spring forward, Gregor had not even heard her coming, and she cried "At last!" to her parents as she turned the key in the lock.

"And what now?" said Gregor to himself, looking around in the darkness. Soon he made the discovery that he was now unable to stir a limb. This did not surprise him, rather it seemed unnatural that he should ever actually have been able to move on these feeble little legs. Otherwise he felt relatively comfortable. True, his whole body was aching, but it seemed that the pain was gradually growing less and would finally pass away. The rotting apple in his back and the inflamed area around it, all covered with soft dust, already hardly troubled him. He thought of his family with tenderness and love. The decision that he must disappear was one that he held to even more strongly than his sister, if that were possible. In this state of vacant and peaceful meditation he remained until the tower clock struck three in the morning. The first broadening of light in the world outside the window entered his consciousness once more. Then his head sank to the floor of its own accord and from his nostrils came the last faint flicker of his breath.

When the charwoman arrived in the morning—what between her strength and her impatience she slammed all the doors so loudly, never mind how often she had been begged not to do so, that no one in the whole apartment could enjoy any quiet sleep after her arrival—she noticed nothing unusual as she took her customary peep into Gregor's room. She thought he was lying motionless on purpose, pretending to be in the sulks; she credited him with every kind of intelligence. Since she happened to have the long-handled broom in her hand she tried to tickle him up with it from the doorway. When that too produced no reaction she felt provoked and poked at him a little harder, and only when she had pushed him along the floor without meeting any resistance was her attention aroused. It did not take her long to establish the truth of the matter, and her eyes widened, she let out a whistle, yet did not waste much time over it but tore open the door of the Samsas' bedroom and yelled into the darkness at the top of her voice: "Just look at this, it's dead; it's lying here dead and done for!"

Mr. and Mrs. Samsa started up in their double bed and before they realized the nature of the charwoman's announcement had some difficulty in overcoming the shock of it. But then they got out of bed quickly, one on either side, Mr. Samsa throwing a blanket over his shoulders, Mrs. Samsa in nothing but her nightgown; in this array they entered Gregor's room. Meanwhile the door of the living room opened, too, where Grete had been sleeping since the advent of the lodgers; she was completely dressed as if she had not been to bed, which seemed to be confirmed also by the paleness of her face. "Dead?" said Mrs. Samsa, looking questioningly at the charwoman, although she would have investigated for herself, and the fact was obvious enough without investigation. "I should say so," said the charwoman, proving her words by pushing Gregor's corpse a long way to one side with her broomstick. Mrs. Samsa made a movement as if to stop her, but checked it. "Well," said Mr. Samsa, "now thanks be to God." He crossed himself, and the three women followed his example. Grete, whose eyes never left the corpse, said: "Just see how thin he was. It's such a long time since he's eaten anything. The food came out again just as it went in." Indeed, Gregor's body was completely flat and dry, as could only now be seen when it was no longer supported by the legs and nothing prevented one from looking closely at it.

"Come in beside us, Grete, for a little while," said Mrs. Samsa with a tremulous smile, and Grete, not without looking back at the corpse, followed her parents into their bedroom. The charwoman shut the door and opened the window wide. Although it was so early in the morning a certain softness was perceptible in the fresh air. After all, it was already the end of March.

The three lodgers emerged from their room and were surprised to see no breakfast; they had been forgotten. "Where's our breakfast?" said the middle lodger peevishly to the charwoman. But she put her finger to her lips and hastily, without a word, indicated by gestures that they should go into Gregor's room. They did so and stood, their hands in the pockets of their somewhat shabby coats, around Gregor's corpse in the room where it was now fully light.

At that the door of the Samsas's bedroom opened and Mr. Samsa appeared in his uniform, his wife on one arm, his daughter on the other. They all looked a little as if they had been crying; from time to time Grete hid her face on her father's arm.

"Leave my house at once!" said Mr. Samsa, and pointed to the door without disengaging himself from the women. "What do you mean by that?" said the middle lodger, taken somewhat aback, with a feeble smile. The two others put their hands behind them and kept rubbing them together, as if in gleeful expectation of a fine set-to in which they were bound to come off the winners. "I mean just what I say," answered Mr. Samsa, and advanced in a straight line with his two companions toward the lodger. He stood his ground at first quietly, looking at the floor as if his thoughts were taking a new pattern in his head. "Then let us go, by all means," he said, and looked up at Mr. Samsa as if in a sudden access of humility he was expecting some renewed sanction for this decision. Mr. Samsa merely nodded briefly once or twice with meaning eyes. Upon that the lodger really did go with long strides into the hall, his two friends had been listening and had quite stopped rubbing their hands for some moments and now went scuttling after him as if afraid that Mr. Samsa might get into the hall before them and cut them off from their leader. In the hall they all three took their hats from the rack, their sticks from the umbrella stand, bowed in silence, and quitted the apartment. With a suspiciousness that proved quite unfounded Mr. Samsa and the two women followed them out to the landing; leaning over the banister they watched the three figures slowly but surely going down the long stairs, vanishing from sight at a certain turn of the staircase on every floor and coming into view again after a moment or so; the more they dwindled, the more the Samsa family's interest in them dwindled, and when a butcher's boy met them and passed them on the stairs coming up proudly with a tray on his head, Mr. Samsa and the two women soon left the landing and as if a burden had been lifted from them went back into their apartment.

They decided to spend this day in resting and going for a stroll; they had not only deserved such a respite from work, but absolutely needed it. And so they sat down at the table and wrote three notes of excuse, Mr. Samsa to his board of management, Mrs. Samsa to her employer, and Grete to the head of her firm. While they were writing, the charwoman came in to say that she was going now, since her morning's work was finished. At first they only nodded without looking up, but as she kept hovering there they eyed her irritably. "Well?" said Mr. Samsa. The charwoman stood grinning in the doorway as if she had good news to impart to the family but meant not to say a word unless properly questioned. The small ostrich feather standing upright on her hat, which had annoyed Mr. Samsa ever since she was engaged, was waving gaily in all directions. "Well, what is it then?" asked Mrs. Samsa, who obtained more respect from the charwoman than the others. "Oh," said the charwoman, giggling so amiably that she could not at once continue, "just this, you don't need to bother about how to get rid of the thing next door. It's been seen to already," Mrs. Samsa and Grete bent over their letters again, as if preoccupied; Mr. Samsa, who perceived that she was eager to begin describing it all in detail, stopped her with a decisive hand. But since she was not allowed to tell her story, she remembered the great hurry she was in, obviously deeply huffed: "Bye, everybody," she said, whirling off violently, and departed with a frightful slamming of doors.

"She'll be given notice tonight," said Mr. Samsa, but neither from his wife nor his daughter did he get any answer, for the charwoman seemed to have shattered again the composure they had barely achieved. They rose, went to the window and stayed there, clasping each other tight. Mr. Samsa turned in his chair to look at them and quietly observed them for a little. Then he called out: "Come along, now, do. Let bygones be bygones. And you might have some consideration for me." The two of them complied at once, hastened to him, caressed him, and quickly finished their letters.

Then they all three left the apartment together, which was more than they had done for months, and went by tram into the open country outside the town. The tram, in which they were the only passengers, was filled with warm sunshine. Leaning comfortably back in their seats they canvassed their prospects for the future, and it appeared on closer inspection that these were not at all bad, for the jobs they had got, which so far they had never really discussed with each other, were all three admirable and likely to lead to better things later on. The greatest immediate improvement in their condition would of course arise from moving to another house; they wanted to take a smaller and cheaper but also better situated and more easily run apartment than the one they had, which Gregor had selected. While they were thus conversing, it struck both Mr. and Mrs. Samsa, almost at the same moment, as they became aware of their daughter's increasing vivacity, that in spite of all the sorrow of recent times, which had made her cheeks pale, she had bloomed into a pretty girl with a good figure. They grew quieter and half unconsciously exchanged glances of complete agreement, having come to the conclusion that it would soon be time to find a good husband for her. And it was like a confirmation of their new dreams and excellent intentions that at the end of their journey their daughter sprang to her feet first and stretched her young body.

D.H. LAWRENCE

(1885–1930)

D. H. (David Herbert) Lawrence was born at Eastwood, a small village near Nottingham in the English Midlands. His father was a miner, his mother an educated woman who dominated his early life and helped him escape what she saw as the vulgarity and coarseness of the working class. He did well at high school and at Nottingham University College, where he obtained his teacher's certificate in 1908. After four years as a teacher, he went to Germany with Frieda von Richtofen, the wife of his French professor at Nottingham. His first major novel, Sons and Lovers (1913), is an autobiographical account of Lawrence's attempt to find his own calling and fight free of all the forces that threatened to stultify and restrict him. His revulsion for the war, his conviction that the industrial revolution had dehumanized modern man, and his belief that human relations had gone badly wrong made him embark on what he called "a savage enough pilgrimage." With his wife, he travelled to Italy, Ceylon, Australia, Mexico, and New Mexico, searching for the place where they could escape the censoriousness, the stupidity, the shallowness of the modern world. The major novels, The Rainbow (1915) and Women in Love (1920), record the nature of the struggle and of the vision that Lawrence passionately believed in. Like all writers with something new to say, he was often misunderstood or judged by the wrong criteria. As he once explained in a letter to Edward Garnett:

> You musn't look in my novel for the old stable ego—of the character. There is another ego, according to whose action the individual is unrecognisable. . . . (Like as diamond and coal are the same pure single element of carbon. The ordinary novel would trace the history of a diamond—but I say, "Diamond, what! This is carbon." And my diamond might be coal or soot, and my theme is carbon.)

The novels that followed include Aaron's Rod (1922), Kangaroo (1923), The Plumed Serpent (1926), and the once notorious Lady Chatterley's Lover (1928). E.M. Forster called Lawrence the greatest imaginative genius of his age, and history has confirmed the judgement. Lawrence's short fiction shows what a splendid craftsman he could be in a different form. He was also a prolific poet, an amateur painter, a fascinating travel writer, and a lively, insightful, prophetic, outrageous literary critic. He died of tuberculosis in Vence in the south of France.

The Horse Dealer's Daughter

"Well, Mabel, and what are you going to do with yourself?" asked Joe, with foolish flippancy. He felt quite safe himself. Without listening for an answer, he turned aside, worked a grain of tobacco to the tip of his tongue, and spat it out. He did not care about anything, since he felt safe himself.

The three brothers and the sister sat round the desolate breakfast-table, attempting some sort of desultory consultation. The morning's post had given the final tap to the family fortunes, and all was over. The dreary dining-room itself, with its heavy mahogany furniture, looked as if it were waiting to be done away with.

But the consultation amounted to nothing. There was a strange air of ineffectuality about the three men, as they sprawled at table, smoking and reflecting vaguely on their own condition. The girl was alone, a rather short, sullen-looking young woman of twenty-seven. She did not share the same life as her brothers. She would have been good-looking, save for the impressive fixity of her face, "bull-dog," as her brothers called it.

There was a confused tramping of horses' feet outside. The three men all sprawled round in their chairs to watch. Beyond the dark holly bushes that separated the strip of lawn from the high-road, they could see a cavalcade of shire horses swinging out of their own yard, being taken for exercise. This was the last time. These were the last horses that would go through their hands. The young men watched with critical, callous look. They were all frightened at the collapse of their lives, and the sense of disaster in which they were involved left them no inner freedom.

Yet they were three fine, well-set fellows enough. Joe, the eldest, was a man of thirty-three, broad and handsome in a hot, flushed way. His face was red, he twisted his black moustache over a thick finger, his eyes were shallow and restless. He had a sensual way of uncovering his teeth when he laughed, and his bearing was stupid. Now he watched the horses with a glazed look of helplessness in his eye, a certain stupor of downfall.

The great draught-horses swung past. They were tied head to tail, four of them, and they heaved along to where a lane branched off from the high-road, planting their great hoofs floutingly in the fine black mud, swinging their great rounded haunches sumptuously, and trotting a few sudden steps as they were led into the lane, round the corner. Every movement showed a massive, slumbrous strength, and a stupidity which held them in subjection. The groom at the head looked back, jerking the leading rope. And the cavalcade moved out of sight up the lane, the tail of the last horse, bobbed up tight and stiff, held out taut from the swinging great haunches as they rocked behind the hedges in a motion-like sleep.

Joe watched with glazed hopeless eyes. The horses were almost like his own body to him. He felt he was done for now. Luckily he was engaged to a woman as old as himself, and therefore her father, who was steward of a neighbouring estate, would provide him with a job. He would marry and go into harness. His life was over, he would be a subject animal now.

He turned uneasily aside, the retreating steps of the horses echoing in his ears. Then, with foolish restlessness, he reached for the scraps of bacon-rind from the plates, and making a faint whistling sound, flung them to the terrier that lay against the fender. He watched the dog swallow them, and waited till the creature looked into his eyes. Then a faint grin came on his face, and in a high, foolish voice he said:

"You won't get much more bacon, shall you, you little b——?"

The dog faintly and dismally wagged its tail, then lowered its haunches, circled round, and lay down again.

There was another helpless silence at the table. Joe sprawled uneasily in his seat, not willing to go till the family conclave was dissolved. Fred Henry, the second brother, was erect, clean-limbed, alert. He had watched the passing of the horses with more sang-froid. If he was an animal, like Joe, he was an animal which controls, not one which is controlled. He was master of any horse, and he carried himself with a well-tempered air of mastery. But he was not master of the situations of life. He pushed his coarse brown moustache upwards, off his lip, and glanced irritably at his sister, who sat impassive and inscrutable.

"You'll go and stop with Lucy for a bit, shan't you?" he asked. The girl did not answer.

"I don't see what else you can do," persisted Fred Henry.

"Go as a skivvy," Joe interpolated laconically.

The girl did not move a muscle.

"If I was her, I should go in for training for a nurse," said Malcolm, the youngest of them all. He was the baby of the family, a young man of twenty-two, with a fresh, jaunty *museau*.

But Mabel did not take any notice of him. They had talked at her and round her for so many years, that she hardly heard them at all.

The marble clock on the mantelpiece softly chimed the half-hour, the dog rose uneasily from the hearth-rug and looked at the party at the breakfast-table. But still they sat on in ineffectual conclave.

"Oh, all right," said Joe suddenly, apropos of nothing. "I'll get a move on."

He pushed back his chair, straddled his knees with a downward jerk, to get them free, in horsey fashion, and went to the fire. Still, he did not go out of the room; he was curious to know what the others would do or say. He began to charge his pipe, looking down at the dog and saying in a high, affected voice:

"Going wi' me? Going wi' me are ter? Tha'rt goin' further than tha counts on just now, dost hear?"

The dog faintly wagged its tail, the man stuck out his jaw and covered his pipe with his hands, and puffed intently, losing himself in the tobacco, looking down all the while at the dog with an absent brown eye. The dog looked up at him in mournful distrust. Joe stood with his knees stuck out, in real horsey fashion.

"Have you had a letter from Lucy?" Fred Henry asked of his sister.

"Last week," came the neutral reply.

"And what does she say?"

There was no answer.

"Does she *ask* you to go and stop there?" persisted Fred Henry.

"She says I can if I like."

"Well, then, you'd better. Tell her you'll come on Monday."

This was received in silence.

"That's what you'll do then, is it?" said Fred Henry, in some exasperation.

But she made no answer. There was a silence of futility and irritation in the room. Malcolm grinned fatuously.

"You'll have to make up your mind between now and next Wednesday," said Joe loudly, "or else find yourself lodgings on the kerbstone."

The face of the young woman darkened, but she sat on immutable.

"Here's Jack Fergusson!" exclaimed Malcolm, who was looking aimlessly out of the window.

"Where?" exclaimed Joe loudly.

"Just gone past."

"Coming in?"

Malcolm craned his neck to see the gate.

"Yes," he said.

There was a silence. Mabel sat on like one condemned, at the head of the table. Then a whistle was heard from the kitchen. The dog got up and barked sharply. Joe opened the door and shouted:

"Come on."

After a moment a young man entered. He was muffled up in overcoat and a purple woollen scarf, and his tweed cap, which he did not remove, was pulled down on his head. He was of medium height, his face was rather long and pale, his eyes looked tired.

"Hello, Jack! Well, Jack!" exclaimed Malcolm and Joe. Fred Henry merely said: "Jack."

"What's doing?" asked the newcomer, evidently addressing Fred Henry.

"Same. We've got to be out by Wednesday. Got a cold?"

"I have – got it bad, too."

"Why don't you stop in?"

"*Me* stop in? When I can't stand on my legs, perhaps I shall have a chance." The young man spoke huskily. He had a slight Scotch accent.

"It's a knock-out, isn't it," said Joe, boisterously, "if a doctor goes round croaking with a cold. Looks bad for the patients, doesn't it?"

The young doctor looked at him slowly.

"Anything the matter with *you*, then?" he asked sarcastically.

"Not as I know of. Damn your eyes, I hope not. Why?"

"I thought you were very concerned about the patients, wondered if you might be one yourself."

"Damn it, no, I've never been patient to no flaming doctor, and hope I never shall be," returned Joe.

At this point Mabel rose from the table, and they all seemed to become aware of her existence. She began putting the dishes together. The young doctor looked at her, but did not address her. He had not greeted her. She went out of the room with the tray, her face impassive and unchanged.

"When are you off then, all of you?" asked the doctor.

"I'm catching the eleven-forty," replied Malcolm. "Are you goin' down wi' th' trap, Joe?"

"Yes, I've told you I'm going down wi' th' trap, haven't I?"

"We'd better be getting her in then. So long, Jack, if I don't see you before I go," said Malcolm, shaking hands.

He went out, followed by Joe, who seemed to have his tail between his legs.

"Well, this is the devil's own," exclaimed the doctor, when he was left alone with Fred Henry. "Going before Wednesday, are you?"

"That's the orders," replied the other.

"Where, to Northampton?"

"That's it."

"The devil!" exclaimed Fergusson, with quiet chagrin.

And there was silence between the two.

"All settled up, are you?" asked Fergusson.

"About."

There was another pause.

"Well, I shall miss yer, Freddy, boy," said the young doctor.

"And I shall miss thee, Jack," returned the other.

"Miss you like hell," mused the doctor.

Fred Henry turned aside. There was nothing to say. Mabel came in again, to finish clearing the table.

"What are *you* going to do, then, Miss Pervin?" asked Fergusson. "Going to your sister's, are you?"

Mabel looked at him with her steady, dangerous eyes, that always made him uncomfortable, unsettling his superficial ease.

"No," she said.

"Well, what in the name of fortune *are* you going to do? Say what you mean to do," cried Fred Henry, with futile intensity.

But she only averted her head, and continued her work. She folded the white table-cloth, and put on the chenille cloth.

"The sulkiest bitch that ever trod!" muttered her brother.

But she finished her task with perfectly impassive face, the young doctor watching her interestedly all the while. Then she went out.

Fred Henry stared after her, clenching his lips, his blue eyes fixing in sharp antagonism, as he made a grimace of sour exasperation.

"You could bray her into bits, and that's all you'd get out of her," he said, in a small, narrowed tone.

The doctor smiled faintly.

"What's she *going* to do, then?" he asked.

"Strike me if *I* know!" returned the other.

There was a pause. Then the doctor stirred.

"I'll be seeing you to-night, shall I?" he said to his friend.

"Ay – where's it to be? Are we going over to Jessdale?"

"I don't know, I've got such a cold on me. I'll come round to the 'Moon and Stars,' anyway."

"Let Lizzie and May miss their night for once, eh?"

"That's it – if I feel as I do now."

"All's one—"

The two young men went through the passage and down to the back door together. The house was large, but it was servantless now, and desolate. At the back was a small bricked house-yard and beyond that a big square, gravelled fine and red, and having stables on two sides. Sloping, dank, winter-dark fields stretched away on the open sides.

But the stables were empty. Joseph Pervin, the father of the family, had been a man of no education, who had become a fairly large horse dealer. The stables had been full of horses, there was a great turmoil and come-and-go of horses and of dealers and grooms. Then the kitchen was full of servants. But of late things had declined. The old man had married a second time, to retrieve his fortunes. Now he was dead and everything was gone to the dogs, there was nothing but debt and threatening.

For months, Mabel had been servantless in the big house, keeping the home together in penury for her ineffectual brothers. She had kept house for ten years. But previously it was with unstinted means. Then, however brutal and coarse everything was, the sense of money had kept her proud, confident. The men might be foul-mouthed, the women in the kitchen might have bad reputations, her brothers might have illegitimate children. But so long as there was money, the girl felt herself established, and brutally proud, reserved.

No company came to the house, save dealers and coarse men. Mabel had no associates of her own sex, after her sister went away. But she did

´not mind. She went regularly to church, she attended to her father. And she lived in the memory of her mother, who had died when she was fourteen, and whom she had loved. She had loved her father, too, in a different way, depending upon him, and feeling secure in him, until at the age of fifty-four he married again. And then she had set hard against him. Now he had died and left them all hopelessly in debt.

She had suffered badly during the period of poverty. Nothing, however, could shake the curious, sullen, animal pride that dominated each member of the family. Now, for Mabel, the end had come. Still she would not cast about her. She would follow her own way just the same. She would always hold the keys of her own situation. Mindless and persistent, she endured from day to day. Why should she think? Why should she answer anybody? It was enough that this was the end, and there was no way out. She need not pass any more darkly along the main street of the small town, avoiding every eye. She need not demean herself any more, going into the shops and buying the cheapest food. This was at an end. She thought of nobody, not even of herself. Mindless and persistent, she seemed in a sort of ecstasy to be coming nearer to her fulfilment, her own glorification, approaching her dead mother, who was glorified.

In the afternoon she took a little bag, with shears and sponge and a small scrubbing-brush, and went out. It was a grey, wintry day, with saddened, dark green fields and an atmosphere blackened by the smoke of foundries not far off. She went quickly, darkly along the causeway, heeding nobody, through the town to the churchyard.

There she always felt secure, as if no one could see her, although as a matter of fact she was exposed to the stare of everyone who passed along under the churchyard wall. Nevertheless, once under the shadow of the great looming church, among the graves, she felt immune from the world, reserved within the thick churchyard wall as in another country.

Carefully she clipped the grass from the grave, and arranged the pinky white, small chrysanthemums in the tin cross. When this was done, she took an empty jar from a neighbouring grave, brought water, and carefully, most scrupulously sponged the marble headstone and the coping-stone.

It gave her sincere satisfaction to do this. She felt in immediate contact with the world of her mother. She took minute pains, went through the park in a state bordering on pure happiness, as if in performing this task she came into a subtle, intimate connection with her mother. For the life she followed here in the world was far less real than the world of death she inherited from her mother.

The doctor's house was just by the church. Fergusson, being a mere hired assistant, was slave to the country-side. As he hurried now to attend to the out-patients in the surgery, glancing across the graveyard with his quick eye, he saw the girl at her task at the grave. She seemed so intent and remote, it was like looking into another world. Some mystical element was touched in him. He slowed down as he walked, watching her as if spellbound.

She lifted her eyes, feeling him looking. Their eyes met. And each looked again at once, each feeling, in some way, found out by the other. He lifted his cap and passed on down the road. There remained distinct in his consciousness, like a vision, the memory of her face, lifted from the tombstone in the churchyard, and looking at him with slow, large, portentous eyes. It *was* portentous, her face. It seemed to mesmerise him. There was a heavy power in her eyes which laid hold of his whole being, as if he had drunk some powerful drug. He had been feeling weak and done before. Now the life came back into him, he felt delivered from his own fretted, daily self.

He finished his duties at the surgery as quickly as might be, hastily filling up the bottles of the waiting people with cheap drugs. Then, in perpetual haste, he set off again to visit several cases in another part of his round, before tea-time. At all times he preferred to walk if he could, but particularly when he was not well. He fancied the motion restored him.

The afternoon was falling. It was grey, deadened, and wintry, with a slow, moist, heavy coldness sinking in and deadening all the faculties. But why should he think or notice? He hastily climbed the hill and turned across the dark green fields, following the black cinder-track. In the distance, across a shallow dip in the country, the small town was clustered like smouldering ash, a tower, a spire, a heap of low, raw, extinct houses. And on the nearest fringe of the town, sloping into the dip, was Oldmeadow, the Pervins' house. He could see the stables and the outbuildings distinctly, as they lay towards him on the slope. Well, he would not go there many more times! Another resource would be lost to him, another place gone: the only company he cared for in the alien, ugly little town he was losing. Nothing but work, drudgery, constant hastening from dwelling to dwelling among the colliers and the iron-workers. It wore him out, but at the same time he had a craving for it. It was a stimulant to him to be in the homes of the working people, moving, as it were, through the innermost body of their life. His nerves were excited and gratified. He could come so near, into the very lives of the rough, inarticulate, powerfully emotional men and women. He grumbled, he said he hated the hellish hole. But as a matter of fact it excited him, the contact with the rough, strongly-feeling people was a stimulant applied direct to his nerves.

Below Oldmeadow, in the green, shallow, soddened hollow of fields, lay a square, deep pond. Roving across the landscape, the doctor's quick eye detected a figure in black passing through the gate of the field, down towards the pond. He looked again. It would be Mabel Pervin. His mind suddenly became alive and attentive.

Why was she going down there? He pulled up on the path on the slope above, and stood staring. He could just make sure of the small black figure moving in the hollow of the failing day. He seemed to see her in the midst of such obscurity, that he was like a clairvoyant, seeing rather with the mind's eye than with ordinary sight. Yet he could see her positively enough, whilst he kept his eye attentive. He felt, if he looked away from her, in the thick, ugly falling dusk, he would lose her altogether.

He followed her minutely as she moved, direct and intent, like something transmitted rather than stirring in voluntary activity, straight down the fields towards the pond. There she stood on the bank for a moment. She never raised her head. Then she waded slowly into the water.

He stood motionless as the small black figure walked slowly and deliberately towards the centre of the pond, very slowly, gradually moving deeper into the motionless water, and still moving forward as the water got up to her breast. Then he could see her no more in the dusk of the dead afternoon.

"There!" he exclaimed. "Would you believe it?"

And he hastened straight down, running over the wet, soddened fields, pushing through the hedges, down into the depression of callous wintry obscurity. It took him several minutes to come to the pond. He stood on the bank, breathing heavily. He could see nothing. His eyes seemed to penetrate the dead water. Yes, perhaps that was the dark shadow of her black clothing beneath the surface of the water.

He slowly ventured into the pond. The bottom was deep, soft clay, he sank in, and the water clasped dead cold round his legs. As he stirred he could smell the cold, rotten clay that fouled up into the water. It was objectionable in his lungs. Still, repelled and yet not heeding, he moved deeper into the pond. The cold water rose over his thighs, over his loins, upon his abdomen. The lower part of his body was all sunk in the hideous cold element. And the bottom was so deeply soft and uncertain, he was afraid of pitching with his mouth underneath. He could not swim, and was afraid.

He crouched a little, spreading his hands under the water and moving them round, trying to feel for her. The dead cold pond swayed upon his chest. He moved again, a little deeper, and again, with his hands underneath, he felt all around under the water. And he touched her clothing. But it evaded his fingers. He made a desperate effort to grasp it.

And so doing he lost his balance and went under, horribly, suffocating in the foul earthy water, struggling madly for a few moments. At last, after what seemed an eternity, he got his footing, rose again into the air and looked around. He gasped, and knew he was in the world. Then he looked at the water. She had risen near him. He grasped her clothing, and drawing her nearer, turned to take his way to land again.

He went very slowly, carefully, absorbed in the slow process. He rose higher, climbing out of the pond. The water was now only about his legs; he was thankful, full of relief to be out of the clutches of the pond. He lifted her and staggered on to the bank, out of the horror of wet, grey clay.

He laid her down on the bank. She was quite unconscious and running with water. He made the water come from her mouth, he worked to restore her. He did not have to work very long before he could feel the breathing begin again in her; she was breathing naturally. He worked a little longer. He could feel her live beneath his hands; she was coming back. He wiped her face, wrapped her in his overcoat, looked round into the dim, dark grey world, then lifted her and staggered down the bank and across the fields.

It seemed an unthinkably long way, and his burden so heavy he felt he would never get to the house. But at last he was in the stable-yard, and then in the house-yard. He opened the door and went into the house. In the kitchen he laid her down on the hearth-rug and called. The house was empty. But the fire was burning in the grate.

Then again he kneeled to attend to her. She was breathing regularly, her eyes were wide open and as if conscious, but there seemed something missing in her look. She was conscious in herself, but unconscious of her surroundings.

He ran upstairs, took blankets from a bed, and put them before the fire to warm. Then he removed her saturated, earthy-smelling clothing, rubbed her dry with a towel, and wrapped her naked in the blankets. Then he went into the dining-room, to look for spirits. There was a little whisky. He drank a gulp himself, and put some into her mouth.

The effect was instantaneous. She looked full into his face, as if she had been seeing him for some time, and yet had only just become conscious of him.

"Dr. Fergusson?" she said.

"What?" he answered.

He was divesting himself of his coat, intending to find some dry clothing upstairs. He could not bear the smell of the dead, clayey water, and he was mortally afraid for his own health.

"What did I do?" she asked.

"Walked into the pond," he replied. He had begun to shudder like one sick, and could hardly attend to her. Her eyes remained full on him, he seemed to be going dark in his mind, looking back at her helplessly.

The shuddering became quieter in him, his life came back to him, dark and unknowing, but strong again.

"Was I out of my mind?" she asked, while her eyes were fixed on him all the time.

"Maybe, for the moment," he replied. He felt quiet, because his strength had come back. The strange fretful strain had left him.

"Am I out of my mind now?" she asked.

"Are you?" he reflected a moment. "No," he answered truthfully, "I don't see that you are." He turned his face aside. He was afraid now, because he felt dazed, and felt dimly that her power was stronger than his, in this issue. And she continued to look at him fixedly all the time. "Can you tell me where I shall find some dry things to put on?" he asked.

"Did you dive into the pond for me?" she asked.

"No," he answered. "I walked in. But I went in overhead as well."

There was silence for a moment. He hesitated. He very much wanted to go upstairs to get into dry clothing. But there was another desire in him. And she seemed to hold him. His will seemed to have gone to sleep, and left him, standing there slack before her. But he felt warm inside himself. He did not shudder at all, though his clothes were sodden on him.

"Why did you?" she asked.

"Because I didn't want you to do such a foolish thing," he said.

"It wasn't foolish," she said, still gazing at him as she lay on the floor, with a sofa cushion under her head. "It was the right thing to do. *I* knew best, then."

"I'll go and shift these wet things," he said. But still he had not the power to move out of her presence, until she sent him. It was as if she had the life of his body in her hands, and he could not extricate himself. Or perhaps he did not want to.

Suddenly she sat up. Then she became aware of her own immediate condition. She felt the blankets about her, she knew her own limbs. For a moment it seemed as if her reason were going. She looked around, with wild eye, as if seeking something. He stood still with fear. She saw her clothing lying scattered.

"Who undressed me?" she asked, her eyes resting full and inevitable on his face.

"I did," he replied, "to bring you round."

For some moments she sat and gazed at him awfully, her lips parted.

"Do you love me, then?" she asked.

He only stood and stared at her, fascinated. His soul seemed to melt.

She shuffled forward on her knees, and put her arms round him, round his legs, as he stood there, pressing her breasts against his knees and thighs, clutching him with strange, convulsive certainty, pressing his thighs against her, drawing him to her face, her throat, as she looked up at him with flaring, humble eyes and transfiguration, triumphant in first possession.

"You love me," she murmured, in strange transport, yearning and triumphant and confident. "You love me. I know you love me, I know."

And she was passionately kissing his knees, through the wet clothing, passionately and indiscriminately kissing his knees, his legs, as if unaware of everything.

He looked down at the tangled wet hair, the wild, bare, animal shoulders. He was amazed, bewildered, and afraid. He had never thought of loving her. He had never wanted to love her. When he rescued her and restored her, he was a doctor, and she was a patient. He had had no single personal thought of her. Nay, this introduction of the personal element was very distasteful to him, a violation of his professional honour. It was horrible to have her there embracing his knees. It was horrible. He revolted from it, violently. And yet – and yet – he had not the power to break away.

She looked at him again, with the same supplication of powerful love, and that same transcendent, frightening light of triumph. In view of the delicate flame which seemed to come from her face like a light, he was powerless. And yet he had never intended to love her. He had never intended. And something stubborn in him could not give way.

"You love me," she repeated, in a murmur of deep, rhapsodic assurance. "You love me."

Her hands were drawing him, drawing him down to her. He was afraid, even a little horrified. For he had, really, no intention of loving her. Yet her hands were drawing him towards her. He put out his hand quickly to steady himself, and grasped her bare shoulder. A flame seemed to burn the hand that grasped her soft shoulder. He had no intention of loving her: his whole will was against his yielding. It was horrible. And yet wonderful was the touch of her shoulders, beautiful the shining of her face. Was she perhaps mad? He had a horror of yielding to her. Yet something in him ached also.

He had been staring away at the door, away from her. But his hand remained on her shoulder. She had gone suddenly very still. He looked down at her. Her eyes were now wide with fear, with doubt, the light was dying from her face, a shadow of terrible greyness was returning. He could not bear the touch of her eyes' question upon him, and the look of death behind the question.

With an inward groan he gave way, and let his heart yield towards her. A sudden gentle smile came on his face. And her eyes, which never left his face, slowly, slowly filled with tears. He watched the strange water rise in her eyes, like some slow fountain coming up. And his heart seemed to burn and melt away in his breast.

He could not bear to look at her any more. He dropped on his knees and caught her head with his arms and pressed her face against his throat. She was very still. His heart, which seemed to have broken, was burning with a kind of agony in his breast. And he felt her slow, hot tears wetting his throat. But he could not move.

He felt the hot tears wet his neck and the hollows of his neck, and he remained motionless, suspended through one of man's eternities. Only now it had become indispensable to him to have her face pressed close to him; he could never let her go again. He could never let her head go away from the close clutch of his arm. He wanted to remain like that for ever, with his heart hurting him in a pain that was also life to him. Without knowing, he was looking down on her damp, soft brown hair.

Then, as it were suddenly, he smelt the horrid stagnant smell of that water. And at the same moment she drew away from him and looked at him. Her eyes were wistful and unfathomable. He was afraid of them, and he fell to kissing her, not knowing what he was doing. He wanted her eyes not to have that terrible, wistful, unfathomable look.

When she turned her face to him again, a faint delicate flush was glowing, and there was again dawning that terrible shining of joy in her eyes, which really terrified him, and yet which he now wanted to see, because he feared the look of doubt still more.

"You love me?" she said, rather faltering.

"Yes." The word cost him a painful effort. Not because it wasn't true. But because it was too newly true, the *saying* seemed to tear open again his newly-torn heart. And he hardly wanted it to be true, even now.

She lifted her face to him, and he bent forward and kissed her on the mouth, gently, with the one kiss that is an eternal pledge. And as he kissed her his heart strained again in his breast. He never intended to love her. But now it was over. He had crossed over the gulf to her, and all that he had left behind had shrivelled and become void.

After the kiss, her eyes again slowly filled with tears. She sat still, away from him, with her face drooped aside, and her hands folded in her lap. The tears fell very slowly. There was complete silence. He too sat there motionless and silent on the hearth-rug. The strange pain of his heart that was broken seemed to consume him. That he should love her? That this was love! That he should be ripped open in this way! Him, a doctor! How they would all jeer if they knew! It was agony to him to think they might know.

In the curious naked pain of the thought he looked again to her. She was sitting there drooped into a muse. He saw a tear fall, and his heart flared hot. He saw for the first time that one of her shoulders was quite uncovered, one arm bare, he could see one of her small breasts; dimly, because it had become almost dark in the room.

"Why are you crying?" he asked, in an altered voice.

She looked up at him, and behind her tears the consciousness of her situation for the first time brought a dark look of shame to her eyes.

"I'm not crying, really," she said, watching him, half frightened.

He reached his hand, and softly closed it on her bare arm.

"I love you! I love you!" he said in a soft, low vibrating voice, unlike himself.

She shrank, and dropped her head. The soft, penetrating grip of his hand on her arm distressed her. She looked up at him.

"I want to go," she said. "I want to go and get you some dry things."

"Why?" he said. "I'm all right."

"But I want to go," she said. "And I want you to change your things."

He released her arm, and she wrapped herself in the blanket, looking at him rather frightened. And still she did not rise.

"Kiss me," she said wistfully.

He kissed her, but briefly, half in anger.

Then, after a second, she rose nervously, all mixed up in the blanket. He watched her in her confusion as she tried to extricate herself and wrap herself up so that she could walk. He watched her relentlessly, as she knew. And as she went, the blanket trailing, and as he saw a glimpse of her feet and her white leg, he tried to remember her as she was when he had wrapped her in the blanket. But then he didn't want to remember, because she had been nothing to him then, and his nature revolted from remembering her as she was when she was nothing to him.

A tumbling, muffled noise from within the dark house startled him. Then he heard her voice: "There are clothes." He rose and went to the foot of the stairs, and gathered up the garments she had thrown down. Then he came back to the fire, to rub himself down and dress. He grinned at his own appearance when he had finished.

The fire was sinking, so he put on coal. The house was now quite dark, save for the light of a street-lamp that shone in faintly from beyond the holly trees. He lit the gas with matches he found on the mantelpiece. Then he emptied the pockets of his own clothes, and threw all his wet things in a heap into the scullery. After which he gathered up her sodden clothes, gently, and put them in a separate heap on the copper-top in the scullery.

It was six o'clock on the clock. His own watch had stopped. He ought to go back to the surgery. He waited, and still she did not come down. So he went to the foot of the stairs and called:

"I shall have to go."

Almost immediately he heard her coming down. She had on her best dress of black voile, and her hair was tidy, but still damp. She looked at him – and in spite of herself, smiled.

"I don't like you in those clothes," she said.

"Do I look a sight?" he answered.

They were shy of one another.

"I'll make you some tea," she said.

"No, I must go."

"Must you?" And she looked at him again with the wide, strained, doubtful eyes. And again, from the pain of his breast, he knew how he loved her. He went and bent to kiss her, gently, passionately, with his heart's painful kiss.

"And my hair smells so horrible," she murmured in distraction. "And I'm so awful, I'm so awful! Oh no, I'm too awful." And she broke into bitter, heart-broken sobbing. "You can't want to love me, I'm horrible."

"Don't be silly, don't be silly," he said, trying to comfort her, kissing her, holding her in his arms. "I want you, I want to marry you, we're going to be married, quickly, quickly – to-morrow if I can."

But she only sobbed terribly, and cried:

"I feel awful. I feel awful. I feel I'm horrible to you."

"No, I want you, I want you," was all he answered, blindly, with that terrible intonation which frightened her almost more than her horror lest he should *not* want her.

Odour of Chrysanthemums

I

The small locomotive engine, Number 4, came clanking, stumbling down from Selston with seven full wagons. It appeared round the corner with loud threats of speed, but the colt that it startled from among the gorse, which still flickered indistinctly in the raw afternoon, out-distanced it at a canter. A woman, walking up the railway line to Underwood, drew back into the hedge, held her basket aside, and watched the footplate of the engine advancing. The trucks thumped heavily past, one by one, with slow inevitable movements, as she stood insignificantly trapped between the jolting black wagons and the hedge; then they curved away towards the coppice where the withered oak leaves dropped noiselessly, while the birds, pulling at the scarlet hips beside the track, made off into the dusk that had already crept into the spinney. In the open, the smoke from the engine sank and cleaved to the rough grass. The fields were dreary and forsaken, and in the marshy strip that led to the whimsey, a reedy pit-pond, the fowls had already abandoned their run among the alders, to roost in the tarred fowl-house. The pit-bank looked up beyond the pond, flames like red sores licking its ashy sides, in the afternoon's stagnant light. Just beyond rose the tapering chimneys and the clumsy black headstocks of Brinsley Colliery. The two wheels were spinning fast up against the sky, and the winding engine rapped out its little spasms. The miners were being turned up.

The engine whistled as it came into the wide bay of railway lines beside the colliery, where rows of trucks stood in harbour.

Miners, single, trailing and in groups, passed like shadows diverging home. At the edge of the ribbed level of sidings squat a low cottage, three steps down from the cinder track. A large bony vine clutched at the house, as if to claw down the tiled roof. Round the bricked yard grew a few wintry primroses. Beyond, the long garden sloped down to a bush-covered brook course. There were some twiggy apple trees, winter-crack trees, and ragged cabbages. Beside the path hung dishevelled pink chrysanthemums, like pink cloths hung on bushes. A woman came stooping out of the felt-covered fowlhouse, half-way down the garden. She closed and padlocked the door, then drew herself erect, having brushed some bits from her white apron.

She was a tall woman of imperious mien, handsome, with definite black eyebrows. Her smooth black hair was parted exactly. For a few moments she stood steadily watching the miners as they passed along the railway: then she turned towards the brook course. Her face was calm and set, her mouth was closed with disillusionment. After a moment she called:

"John!" There was no answer. She waited, and then said distinctly: "Where are you?"

"Here!" replied a child's sulky voice from among the bushes. The woman looked piercingly through the dusk.

"Are you at that brook?" she asked sternly.

For answer the child showed himself before the raspberry-canes that rose like whips. He was a small, sturdy boy of five. He stood quite still, defiantly.

"Oh!" said the mother, conciliated. "I thought you were down at that wet brook – and you remember what I told you—"

The boy did not move or answer.

"Come, come on in," she said more gently, "it's getting dark. There's your grandfather's engine coming down the line!"

The lad advanced slowly, with resentful, taciturn movement. He was dressed in trousers and waistcoat of cloth that was too thick and hard for the size of the garments. They were evidently cut down from a man's clothes.

As they went slowly towards the house he tore at the ragged wisps of chrysanthemums and dropped the petals in handfuls along the path.

"Don't do that – it does look nasty," said his mother. He refrained, and she, suddenly pitiful, broke off a twig with three or four wan flowers and held them against her face. When mother and son reached the yard her hand hesitated, and instead of laying the flower aside, she pushed it in her apron-band. The mother and son stood at the foot of the three steps looking across the bay of lines at the passing home of the miners. The trundle of the small train was imminent. Suddenly the engine loomed past the house and came to a stop opposite the gate.

The engine-driver, a short man with round grey beard, leaned out of the cab high above the woman.

"Have you got a cup of tea?" he said in a cheery, hearty fashion.

It was her father. She went in, saying she would mash. Directly, she returned.

"I didn't come to see you on Sunday," began the little grey-bearded man.

"I didn't expect you," said his daughter.

The engine-driver winced; then, reassuming his cheery, airy manner, he said:

"Oh, have you heard then? Well, and what do you think—"

"I think it is soon enough," she replied.

At her brief censure the little man made an impatient gesture, and said coaxingly, yet with dangerous coldness:

"Well, what's a man to do? It's no sort of life for a man of my years, to sit at my own hearth like a stranger. And if I'm going to marry again it may as well be soon as late – what does it matter to anybody?"

The woman did not reply, but turned and went into the house. The man in the engine-cab stood assertive, till she returned with a cup of tea and a piece of bread and butter on a plate. She went up the steps and stood near the footplate of the hissing engine.

"You needn't 'a' brought me bread an' butter," said her father. "But a cup of tea" – he sipped appreciatively – "it's very nice." He sipped for a moment or two, then: "I hear as Walter's got another bout on," he said.

"When hasn't he?" said the woman bitterly.

"I heerd tell of him in the 'Lord Nelson' braggin' as he was going to spend that b—— afore he went: half a sovereign that was."

"When?" asked the woman.

"A' Sat'day night – I know that's true."

"Very likely," she laughed bitterly. "He gives me twenty-three shillings."

"Aye, it's a nice thing, when a man can do nothing with his money but make a beast of himself!" said the grey-whiskered man. The woman turned her head away. Her father swallowed the last of his tea and handed her the cup.

"Aye," he sighed, wiping his mouth. "It's a settler, it is—"

He put his hand on the lever. The little engine strained and groaned, and the train rumbled towards the crossing. The woman again looked across the metals. Darkness was settling over the spaces of the railway and trucks: the miners, in grey sombre groups, were still passing home. The winding engine pulsed hurriedly, with brief pauses. Elizabeth Bates looked at the dreary flow of men, then she went indoors. Her husband did not come.

The kitchen was small and full of firelight; red coals piled glowing up the chimney mouth. All the life of the room seemed in the white, warm hearth and the steel fender reflecting the red fire. The cloth was laid for tea; cups glinted in the shadows. At the back, where the lowest stairs protruded into the room, the boy sat struggling with a knife and a piece of white wood. He was almost hidden in the shadow. It was half-past four. They had but to await the father's coming to begin tea. As the mother watched her son's sullen little struggle with the wood, she saw herself in his silence and pertinacity; she saw the father in her child's indifference to all but himself. She seemed to be occupied by her husband. He had probably gone past his home, slunk past his own door, to drink before he came in, while his dinner spoiled and wasted in waiting. She glanced at the clock, then took the potatoes to strain them in the yard. The garden and fields beyond the brook were closed in uncertain darkness. When she rose with the saucepan, leaving the drain steaming into the night behind her, she saw the yellow lamps were lit along the high road that went up the hill away beyond the space of the railway lines and the field.

Then again she watched the men trooping home, fewer now and fewer.

Indoors the fire was sinking and the room was dark red. The woman put her saucepan on the hob, and set a batter-pudding near the mouth of the oven. Then she stood unmoving. Directly, gratefully, came quick young steps to the door. Something hung on the latch a moment, then a little girl entered and began pulling off her outdoor things, dragging a mass of curls, just ripening from gold to brown, over her eyes with her hat.

Her mother chid her for coming late from school, and said she would have to keep her at home the dark winter days.

"Why, mother, it's hardly a bit dark yet. The lamp's not lighted, and my father's not home."

"No, he isn't. But it's a quarter to five! Did you see anything of him?"

The child became serious. She looked at her mother with large, wistful blue eyes.

"No, mother, I've never seen him. Why? Has he come up an' gone past, to Old Brinsley? He hasn't, mother, 'cos I never saw him."

"He'd watch that," said the mother bitterly, "he'd take care as you didn't see him. But you may depend upon it, he's seated in the 'Prince o' Wales.' He wouldn't be this late."

The girl looked at her mother piteously.

"Let's have our teas, mother, should we?" said she.

The mother called John to table. She opened the door once more and looked out across the darkness of the lines. All was deserted: she could not hear the winding-engines.

"Perhaps," she said to herself, "he's stopped to get some ripping done."

They sat down to tea. John, at the end of the table near the door, was almost lost in the darkness. Their faces were hidden from each other. The girl crouched against the fender slowly moving a thick piece of bread before the fire. The lad, his face a dusky mark on the shadow, sat watching her who was transfigured in the red glow.

"I do think it's beautiful to look in the fire," said the child.

"Do you?" said her mother. "Why?"

"It's so red, and full of little caves – and it feels so nice, and you can fair smell it."

"It'll want mending directly," replied her mother, "and then if your father comes he'll carry on and say there never is a fire when a man comes home sweating from the pit. A public-house is always warm enough."

There was silence till the boy said complainingly: "Make haste, our Annie."

"Well, I am doing! I can't make the fire do it no faster, can I?"

"She keeps wafflin' it about so's to make 'er slow," grumbled the boy.

"Don't have such an evil imagination, child," replied the mother.

Soon the room was busy in the darkness with the crisp sound of crunching. The mother ate very little. She drank her tea determinedly, and sat thinking. When she rose her anger was evident in the stern unbending of her head. She looked at the pudding in the fender, and broke out:

"It is a scandalous thing as a man can't even come home to his dinner! If it's crozzled up to a cinder I don't see why I should care. Past his very door he goes to get to a public-house, and here I sit with his dinner waiting for him—"

She went out. As she dropped piece after piece of coal on the red fire, the shadows fell on the walls, till the room was almost in total darkness.

"I canna see," grumbled the invisible John. In spite of herself, the mother laughed.

"You know the way to your mouth," she said. She set the dust-pan outside the door. When she came again like a shadow on the hearth, the lad repeated, complaining sulkily:

"I canna see."

"Good gracious!" cried the mother irritably, "you're as bad as your father if it's a bit dusk!"

Nevertheless, she took a paper spill from a sheaf on the mantelpiece and proceeded to light the lamp that hung from the ceiling in the middle of the room. As she reached up, her figure displayed itself just rounding with maternity.

"Oh, mother—!" exclaimed the girl.

"What?" said the woman, suspended in the act of putting the lamp-glass over the flame. The copper reflector shone handsomely on her, as she stood with uplifted arm, turning to face her daughter.

"You've got a flower in your apron!" said the child, in a little rapture at this unusual event.

"Goodness me!" exclaimed the woman, relieved. "One would think the house was afire." She replaced the glass and waited a moment before turning up the wick. A pale shadow was seen floating vaguely on the floor.

"Let me smell!" said the child, still rapturously, coming forward and putting her face to her mother's waist.

"Go along, silly!" said the mother, turning up the lamp. The light revealed their suspense so that the woman felt it almost unbearable. Annie was still bending at her waist. Irritably, the mother took the flowers out from her apron-band.

"Oh, mother – don't take them out!" Annie cried catching her hand and trying to replace the sprig.

"Such nonsense!" said the mother, turning away. The child put the pale chrysanthemums to her lips, murmuring:

"Don't they smell beautiful!"

Her mother gave a short laugh.

"No," she said, "not to me. It was chrysanthemums when I married him, and chrysanthemums when you were born, and the first time they ever brought him home drunk, he'd got brown chrysanthemums in his button-hole."

She looked at the children. Their eyes and their parted lips were wondering. The mother sat rocking in silence for some time. Then she looked at the clock.

"Twenty minutes to six!" In a tone of fine bitter carelessness she continued: "Eh, he'll not come now till they bring him. There he'll stick! But he needn't come rolling in here in his pit-dirt, for *I* won't wash him. He can lie on the floor—Eh, what a fool I've been, what a fool! And this is what I came here for, to this dirty hole, rats and all, for him to slink past his very door. Twice last week – he's begun now—" She silenced herself, and rose to clear the table.

While for an hour or more the children played, subduedly intent, fertile of imagination, united in fear of the mother's wrath, and in dread of their father's home-coming, Mrs. Bates sat in her rocking-chair making a "singlet" of thick cream-coloured flannel, which gave a dull wounded sound as she tore off the grey edge. She worked at her sewing with energy, listening to the children, and her anger wearied itself, lay down to rest, opening its eyes from time to time and steadily watching, its ears raised to listen. Sometimes even her anger quailed and shrank, and the mother suspended her sewing, tracing the footsteps that thudded along the sleepers outside; she would lift her head sharply to bid the children "hush," but she recovered herself in time, and the footsteps went past the gate, and the children were not flung out of their play-world.

But at last Annie sighed, and gave in. She glanced at her wagon of slippers, and loathed the game. She turned plaintively to her mother.

"Mother!" – but she was inarticulate.

John crept out like a frog from under the sofa. His mother glanced up.

"Yes," she said, "just look at those shirt-sleeves!"

The boy held them out to survey them, saying nothing. Then somebody called in a hoarse voice away down the line, and suspense bristled in the room, till two people had gone by outside, talking.

"It is time for bed," said the mother.

"My father hasn't come," wailed Annie plaintively. But her mother was primed with courage.

"Never mind. They'll bring him when he does come – like a log." She meant there would be no scene. "And he may sleep on the floor till he wakes himself. I know he'll not go to work to-morrow after this!"

The children had their hands and faces wiped with a flannel. They were very quiet. When they had put on their nightdresses, they said their prayers, the boy mumbling. The mother looked down at them, at the brown silken bush of intertwining curls in the nape of the girl's neck, at the little black head of the lad, and her heart burst with anger at their father, who caused all three such distress. The children hid their faces in her skirts for comfort.

When Mrs. Bates came down, the room was strangely empty, with a tension of expectancy. She took up her sewing and stitched for some time without raising her head. Meantime her anger was tinged with fear.

II

The clock struck eight and she rose suddenly, dropping her sewing on her chair. She went to the stair-foot door, opened it, listening. Then she went out, locking the door behind her.

Something scuffled in the yard, and she started, though she knew it was only the rats with which the place was over-run. The night was very dark. In the great bay of railway lines, bulked with trucks, there was no trace of light, only away back she could see a few yellow lamps at the pit-top, and the red smear of the burning pit-bank on the night. She hurried along the edge of the track, then, crossing the converging lines, came to the stile by the white gates, whence she emerged on the road. Then the fear which had led her shrank. People were walking up to New Brinsley; she saw the lights in the houses; twenty yards farther on were the broad windows of the "Prince of Wales," very warm and bright, and the loud voices of men could be heard distinctly. What a fool she had been to imagine that anything had happened to him! He was merely drinking over there at the "Prince of Wales." She faltered. She had never yet been to fetch him, and she never would go. So she continued her walk towards the long straggling line of houses, standing back on the highway. She entered a passage between the dwellings.

"Mr. Rigley? – yes! Did you want him? No, he's not in at this minute."

The raw-boned woman leaned forward from her dark scullery and peered at the other, upon whom fell a dim light through the blind of the kitchen window.

"Is it Mrs. Bates?" She asked in a tone tinged with respect.

"Yes. I wondered if your Master was at home. Mine hasn't come yet."

" 'Asn't e! Oh, Jack's been 'ome an' 'ad 'is dinner an' gone out. 'E's just gone for 'alf an hour afore bed-time. Did you call at the 'Prince of Wales'?"

"No—"

"No, you didn't like—! It's not very nice." The other woman was indulgent. There was an awkward pause. "Jack never said nothink about– about your Master," she said.

"No! – I expect he's stuck in there!"

Elizabeth Bates said this bitterly, and with recklessness. She knew that the woman across the yard was standing at her door listening, but she did not care. As she turned:

"Stop a minute! I'll just go an' ask Jack if 'e knows anythink," said Mrs. Rigley.

"Oh no – I wouldn't like to put—!"

"Yes, I will, if you'll just step inside an' see as th' childer doesn't come downstairs and set theirselves afire."

Elizabeth Bates, murmuring a remonstrance, stepped inside. The other woman apologised for the state of the room.

The kitchen needed apology. There were little frocks and trousers and childish undergarments on the squab and on the floor, and a litter of playthings everywhere. On the black American cloth of the table were pieces of bread and cake, crusts, slops, and a teapot with cold tea.

"Eh, ours is just as bad," said Elizabeth Bates, looking at the woman, not at the house. Mrs. Rigley put a shawl over her head and hurried out, saying:

"I shanna be a minute."

The other sat, noting with faint disapproval the general untidiness of the room. Then she fell to counting the shoes of various sizes scattered over the floor. There were twelve. She sighed and said to herself: "No wonder!" – glancing at the litter. There came the scratching of two pairs of feet on the yard, and the Rigleys entered. Elizabeth Bates rose. Rigley was a big man, with very large bones. His head looked particularly bony. Across his temple was a blue scar, caused by a wound got in the pit, a wound in which the coal-dust remained blue like tattooing.

" 'Asna 'e come whoam yit?" asked the man, without any form of greeting, but with deference and sympathy. "I couldn'a say wheer he is – 'e's non ower theer!" – he jerked his head to signify the "Prince of Wales."

" 'E's 'appen gone up to th' 'Yew,' " said Mrs. Rigley.

There was another pause. Rigley had evidently something to get off his mind:

"Ah left 'im finishin' a stint," he began. "Loose-all 'ad bin gone about ten minutes when we com'n away, an' I shouted: 'Are ter comin', Walt?' an' 'e said: 'Go on, Ah shanna be but a'ef a minnit,' so we com'n ter th' bottom, me an' Bowers, thinkin' as 'e wor just behint, an' 'ud come up i' the' next bantle—"

He stood perplexed, as if answering a charge of deserting his mate. Elizabeth Bates, now again certain of disaster, hastened to reassure him:

"I expect 'e's gone up to th' 'Yew Tree,' as you say. It's not the first time. I've fretted myself into a fever before now. He'll come home when they carry him."

"Ay, isn't it too bad!" deplored the other woman.

"I'll just step up to Dick's an' see if 'e *is* theer," offered the man, afraid of appearing alarmed, afraid of taking liberties.

"Oh, I wouldn't think of bothering you that far," said Elizabeth Bates, with emphasis, but he knew she was glad of his offer.

As they stumbled up the entry, Elizabeth Bates heard Rigley's wife run across the yard and open her neighbour's door. At this, suddenly all the blood in her body seemed to switch away from her heart.

"Mind!" warned Rigley. "Ah've said many a time as Ah'd fill up them ruts in this entry, sumb'dy 'll be breakin' their legs yit."

She recovered herself and walked quickly along with the miner.

"I don't like leaving the children in bed, and nobody in the house," she said.

"No, you dunna!" he replied courteously. They were soon at the gate of the cottage.

"Well, I shanna be many minnits. Dunna you be frettin' now, 'e'll be all right," said the butty.

"Thank you very much, Mr. Rigley," she replied.

"You're welcome!" he stammered, moving away. "I shanna be many minnits."

The house was quiet. Elizabeth Bates took off her hat and shawl, and rolled back the rug. When she had finished, she sat down. It was a few minutes past nine. She was startled by the rapid chuff of the winding-engine at the pit, and the sharp whirr of the brakes on the rope as it descended. Again she felt the painful sweep of her blood, and she put her hand to her side, saying aloud: "Good gracious! – it's only the nine o'clock deputy going down," rebuking herself.

She sat still, listening. Half an hour of this, and she was wearied out.

"What am I working myself up like this for?" she said pitiably to herself. "I s'll only be doing myself some damage."

She took out her sewing again.

At a quarter to ten there were footsteps. One person! She watched for the door to open. It was an elderly woman, in a black bonnet and a black woollen shawl – his mother. She was about sixty years old, pale, with blue eyes, and her face all wrinkled and lamentable. She shut the door and turned to her daughter-in-law peevishly.

"Eh, Lizzie, whatever shall we do, whatever shall we do!" she cried.

Elizabeth drew back a little, sharply.

"What is it, mother?" she said.

The elder woman seated herself on the sofa.

"I don't know, child, I can't tell you!"—she shook her head slowly. Elizabeth sat watching her, anxious and vexed.

"I don't know," replied the grandmother, sighing very deeply. "There's no end to my troubles, there isn't. The things I've gone through, I'm sure it's enough—!" She wept without wiping her eyes, the tears running.

"But, mother," interrupted Elizabeth, "what do you mean? What is it?"

The grandmother slowly wiped her eyes. The fountains of her tears were stopped by Elizabeth's directness. She wiped her eyes slowly.

"Poor child! Eh, you poor thing!" she moaned. "I don't know what we're going to do, I don't – and you as you are – it's a thing, it is indeed!"

Elizabeth waited.

"Is he dead?" she asked, and at the words her heart swung violently, though she felt a slight flush of shame at the ultimate extravagance of the question. Her words sufficiently frightened the old lady, almost brought her to herself.

"Don't say so, Elizabeth! We'll hope it's not as bad as that; no, may the Lord spare us that, Elizabeth. Jack Rigley, came just as I was sittin' down to a glass afore going to bed, an' 'e said: ' 'Appen you'll go down th' line, Mrs. Bates. Walt's had an accident. 'Appen you'll go an' sit wi' 'er till we can get him home.' I hadn't time to ask him a word afore he was gone. An' I put my bonnet on an' come straight down, Lizzie. I thought to myself: 'Eh, that poor blessed child, if anybody should come an' tell her of a sudden, there's no knowin' what'll 'appen to 'er.' You mustn't let it upset you, Lizzie – or you know what to expect. How long is it, six months – or is it five, Lizzie? Ay!" – the old woman shook her head – "time slips on, it slips on! Ay!"

Elizabeth's thoughts were busy elsewhere. If he was killed – would she be able to manage on the little pension and what she could earn? – she counted up rapidly. If he was hurt – they wouldn't take him to the hospital – how tiresome he would be to nurse! – but perhaps she'd be able to get him away from the drink and his hateful ways. She would – while he was ill. The tears offered to come to her eyes at the picture. But what sentimental luxury was this she was beginning? She turned to consider the children. At any rate she was absolutely necessary for them. They were her business.

"Ay!" repeated the old woman, "it seems but a week or two since he brought me his first wages. Ay – he was a good lad, Elizabeth, he was, in his way. I don't know why he got to be such a trouble, I don't. He was a happy lad at home, only full of spirits. But there's no mistake he's been a handful of trouble, he has! I hope the Lord'll spare him to mend his ways. I hope so, I hope so. You've had a sight o' trouble with him, Elizabeth, you have indeed. But he was a jolly enough lad wi' me, he was, I can assure you. I don't know how it is. . . ."

The old woman continued to muse aloud, a monotonous irritating sound, while Elizabeth thought concentratedly, startled once, when she heard the winding-engine chuff quickly, and the brakes skirr with a shriek. Then she heard the engine more slowly, and the brakes made no sound. The old woman did not notice. Elizabeth waited in suspense. The mother-in-law talked, with lapses into silence.

"But he wasn't your son, Lizzie, an' it makes a difference. Whatever he was, I remember him when he was little, an' I learned to understand him and to make allowances. You've got to make allowances for them—"

It was half-past ten, and the old woman was saying: "But it's trouble from beginning to end; you're never too old for trouble, never too old for that—" when the gate banged back, and there were heavy feet on the steps.

"I'll go, Lizzie, let me go," cried the old woman, rising. But Elizabeth was at the door. It was a man in pit-clothes.

"They're bringin' 'im, Missis," he said. Elizabeth's heart halted a moment. Then it surged on again, almost suffocating her.

"Is he – is it bad?" she asked.

The man turned away, looking at the darkness:

"The doctor says 'e'd been dead hours. 'E saw 'im i' th' lamp-cabin."

The old woman, who stood just behind Elizabeth, dropped into a chair, and folded her hands crying: "Oh, my boy, my boy!"

"Hush!" said Elizabeth, with a sharp twitch of a frown. "Be still, mother, don't waken th' children: I wouldn't have them down for anything!"

The old woman moaned softly, rocking herself. The man was drawing away. Elizabeth took a step forward.

"How was it?" she asked.

"Well, I couldn't say for sure," the man replied, very ill at ease. " 'E wor finishin' a stint an' th' butties 'ad gone, an' a lot o'stuff come down atop 'n 'im."

"And crushed him?" cried the widow, with a shudder.

"No," said the man, "it fell at th' back of 'im. 'E wor under th' face, an' it niver touched 'im. It shut 'im in. It seems 'e wor smothered."

Elizabeth shrank back. She heard the old woman behind her cry:

"What? – what did 'e say it was?"

The man replied, more loudly: " 'E wor smothered!"

Then the old woman wailed aloud, and this relieved Elizabeth.

"Oh, mother," she said, putting her hand on the old woman, "don't waken th' children, don't waken th' children."

She wept a little, unknowing, while the old mother rocked herself and moaned. Elizabeth remembered that they were bringing him home, and she must be ready. "They'll lay him in the parlour," she said to herself, standing a moment pale and perplexed.

Then she lighted a candle and went into the tiny room. The air was cold and damp, but she could not make a fire, there was no fireplace. She set down the candle and looked round. The candlelight glittered on the lustre-glasses, on two vases that held some of the pink chrysanthemums, and on the dark mahogany. There was a cold, deathly smell of chrysanthemums in the room. Elizabeth stood looking at the flowers. She turned away, and calculated whether there would be room to lay him on the floor, between the couch and the chiffonier. She pushed the chairs aside. There would be room to lay him down and to step round him. Then she fetched the old red tablecloth, and another old cloth, spreading them down to save her bit of carpet. She shivered on leaving the parlour; so, from the dresser drawer she took a clean shirt and put it at the fire to air. All the time her mother-in-law was rocking herself in the chair and moaning.

"You'll have to move from there, mother," said Elizabeth. "They'll be bringing him in. Come in the rocker."

The old mother rose mechanically, and seated herself by the fire, continuing to lament. Elizabeth went into the pantry for another candle, and there, in the little pent-house under naked tiles, she heard them coming. She stood still in the pantry doorway, listening. She heard them pass the end of the house, and come awkwardly down the three steps, a jumble of shuffling footsteps and muttering voices. The old woman was silent. The men were in the yard.

Then Elizabeth heard Matthews, the manager of the pit, say: "You go in first, Jim. Mind!"

The door came open, and the two women saw a collier backing into the room, holding one end of a stretcher, on which they could see the nailed pit-boots of the dead man. The two carriers halted, the man at the head stooping to the lintel of the door.

"Wheer will you have him?" asked the manager, a short, white-bearded man.

Elizabeth roused herself and came from the pantry carrying the unlighted candle.

"In the parlour," she said.

"In there, Jim!" pointed the manager, and the carriers backed round into the tiny room. The coat with which they had covered the body fell off as they awkwardly turned through the two doorways, and the women saw their man, naked to the waist, lying stripped for work. The old woman began to moan in a low voice of horror.

"Lay th' stretcher at th' side," snapped the manager, "an' put 'im on th' cloths. Mind now, mind! Look you now—!"

One of the men had knocked off a vase of chrysanthemums. He stared awkwardly, then they set down the stretcher. Elizabeth did not look at her husband. As soon as she could get in the room, she went and picked up the broken vase and the flowers.

"Wait a minute!" she said.

The three men waited in silence while she mopped up the water with a duster.

"Eh, what a job, what a job, to be sure!" the manager was saying, rubbing his brow with trouble and perplexity. "Never knew such a thing in my life, never! He'd no business to ha' been left. I never knew such a thing in my life! Fell over him clean as a whistle, an' shut him in. Not four foot of space, there wasn't – yet it scarce bruised him."

He looked down at the dead man, lying prone, half naked, all grimed with coal-dust.

"''Sphyxiated,' the doctor said. It *is* the most terrible job I've ever known. Seems as if it was done o' purpose. Clean over him, an' shut 'im in, like a mouse-trap" – he made a sharp, descending gesture with his hand.

The colliers standing by jerked aside their heads in hopeless comment.

The horror of the thing bristled upon them all.

Then they heard the girl's voice upstairs calling shrilly: "Mother, mother – who is it? Mother, who is it?"

Elizabeth hurried to the foot of the stairs and opened the door:

"Go to sleep!" She commanded sharply. "What are you shouting about? Go to sleep at once – there's nothing—"

Then she began to mount the stairs. They could hear her on the boards, and on the plaster floor of the little bedroom. They could hear her distinctly:

"What's the matter now?–what's the matter with you, silly thing?"– her voice was much agitated, with an unreal gentleness.

"I thought it was some men come," said the plaintive voice of the child. "Has he come?"

"Yes, they've brought him. There's nothing to make a fuss about. Go to sleep now, like a good child."

They could hear her voice in the bedroom, they waited whilst she covered the children under the bedclothes.

"Is he drunk?" asked the girl, timidly, faintly.

"No! No – he's not! He's asleep."

"Is he asleep downstairs?"

"Yes – and don't make a noise."

There was silence for a moment, then the men heard the frightened child again:

"What's that noise?"

"It's nothing, I tell you, what are you bothering for?"

The noise was the grandmother moaning. She was oblivious of everything, sitting on her chair rocking and moaning. The manager put his hand on her arm and bade her "Sh–sh!!"

The old woman opened her eyes and looked at him. She was shocked by this interruption, and seemed to wonder.

"What time is it?" the plaintive thin voice of the child, sinking back unhappily into sleep, asked this last question.

"Ten o'clock," answered the mother more softly. Then she must have bent down and kissed the children.

Matthews beckoned to the men to come away. They put on their caps and took up the stretcher. Stepping over the body, they tiptoed out of the house. None of them spoke till they were far from the wakeful children.

When Elizabeth came down she found her mother alone on the parlour floor, leaning over the dead man, the tears dropping on him.

"We must lay him out," the wife said. She put on the kettle, then returning knelt at the feet, and began to unfasten the knotted leather laces. The room was clammy and dim with only one candle, so that she had to bend her face almost to the floor. At last she got off the heavy boots and put them away.

"You must help me now," she whispered to the old woman. Together they stripped the man.

When they arose, saw him lying in the naïve dignity of death, the women stood arrested in fear and respect. For a few moments they remained still, looking down, the old mother whimpering. Elizabeth felt countermanded. She saw him, how utterly inviolable he lay in himself.

She had nothing to do with him. She could not accept it. Stooping, she laid her hand on him, in claim. He was still warm, for the mine was hot where he had died. His mother had his face between her hands, and was murmuring incoherently. The old tears fell in succession as drops from wet leaves; the mother was not weeping, merely her tears flowed. Elizabeth embraced the body of her husband, with cheek and lips. She seemed to be listening, inquiring, trying to get some connection. But she could not. She was driven away. He was impregnable.

She rose, went into the kitchen, where she poured warm water into a bowl, brought soap and flannel and a soft towel.

"I must wash him," she said.

Then the old mother rose stiffly, and watched Elizabeth as she carefully washed his face, carefully brushing the big blond moustache from his mouth with the flannel. She was afraid with a bottomless fear, so she ministered to him. The old woman, jealous, said:

"Let me wipe him!" – and she kneeled on the other side drying slowly as Elizabeth washed, her big black bonnet sometimes brushing the dark head of her daughter-in-law. They worked thus in silence for a long time. They never forgot it was death, and the touch of the man's dead body gave them strange emotions, different in each of the women; a great dread possessed them both, the mother felt the lie was given to her womb, she was denied; the wife felt the utter isolation of the human soul, the child within her was a weight apart from her.

At last it was finished. He was a man of handsome body, and his face showed no traces of drink. He was blond, full-fleshed, with fine limbs. But he was dead.

"Bless him," whispered his mother, looking always at his face, and speaking out of sheer terror. "Dear lad – bless him!" She spoke in a faint, sibilant ecstasy of fear and mother love.

Elizabeth sank down again to the floor, and put her face against his neck, and trembled and shuddered. But she had to draw away again. He was dead, and her living flesh had no place against his. A great dread and weariness held her: she was so unavailing. Her life was gone like this.

"White as milk he is, clear as a twelve-month baby, bless him, the darling!" the old mother murmured to herself. "Not a mark on him, clear and clean and white, beautiful as ever a child was made," she murmured with pride. Elizabeth kept her face hidden.

"He went peaceful, Lizzie – peaceful as sleep. Isn't he beautiful, the lamb? Ay – he must ha' made his peace, Lizzie. 'Appen he made it all right, Lizzie, shut in there. He'd have time. He wouldn't look like this if he hadn't made his peace. The lamb, the dear lamb. Eh, but he had a hearty laugh. I loved to hear it. He had the heartiest laugh, Lizzie, as a lad—"

Elizabeth looked up. The man's mouth was fallen back, slightly open under the cover of the moustache. The eyes, half shut, did not show glazed in the obscurity. Life with its smoky burning gone from him, had left him apart and utterly alien to her. And she knew what a stranger he was to her. In her womb was ice of fear, because of this separate stranger with whom she had been living as one flesh. Was this what it all meant – utter, intact separateness, obscured by heat of living? In dread she turned her face away. The fact was too deadly. There had been nothing between them, and yet they had come together, exchanging their nakedness repeatedly. Each time he had taken her, they had been two isolated beings, far apart as now. He was no more responsible than she. The child was like ice in her womb. For as she looked at the dead man, her mind, cold and detached, said clearly: "Who am I? What have I been doing? I have been fighting a husband who did not exist. *He* existed all the time. What wrong have I done? What was that I have been living with? There lies the reality, this man." And her soul died in her for fear: she knew she had never seen him, and he had never seen her, they had met in the dark and had fought in the dark, not knowing whom they met nor whom they fought. And now she saw, and turned silent in seeing. For she had been wrong. She had said he was something he was not; she had felt familiar with him. Whereas he was apart all the while, living as she never lived, feeling as she never felt.

In fear and shame she looked at his naked body, that she had known falsely. And he was the father of her children. Her soul was torn from her body and stood apart. She looked at his naked body and was ashamed, as if she had denied it. After all, it was itself. It seemed awful to her. She looked at his face, and she turned her own face to the wall. For his look was other than hers, his way was not her way. She had denied him what he was – she saw it now. She had refused him as himself. And this had been her life, and his life. She was grateful to death, which restored the truth. And she knew she was not dead.

And all the while her heart was bursting with grief and pity for him. What had he suffered? What stretch of horror for this helpless man! She was rigid with agony. She had not been able to help him. He had been cruelly injured, this naked man, this other being, and she could make no reparation. There were the children – but the children belonged to life. This dead man had nothing to do with them. He and she were only channels through which life had flowed to issue in the children. She was a mother – but how awful she knew it now to have been a wife. And he, dead now, how awful he must have felt it to be a husband. She felt that in the next world he would be a stranger to her. If they met, there in the beyond, they would only be ashamed of what had been before. The children had come, for some mysterious reason, out of both of them. But the children did not unite them. Now he was dead, she knew how eternally he was apart from her, how eternally he had nothing more to do with her. She saw this episode of her life closed. They had denied each other in life. Now he had withdrawn. An anguish came over her. It was finished then: it had become hopeless between them long before he died. Yet he had been her husband. But how little!

"Have you got his shirt, 'Lizabeth?"

Elizabeth turned without answering, though she strove to weep and behave as her mother-in-law expected. But she could not, she was silenced. She went into the kitchen and returned with the garment.

"It is aired," she said, grasping the cotton shirt here and there to try. She was almost ashamed to handle him; what right had she or anyone to lay hands on him; but her touch was humble on his body. It was hard work to clothe him. He was so heavy and inert. A terrible dread gripped her all the while: that he could be so heavy and utterly inert, unresponsive, apart. The horror of the distance between them was almost too much for her – it was so infinite a gap she must look across.

At last it was finished. They covered him with a sheet and left him lying, with his face bound. And she fastened the door of the little parlour, lest the children should see what was lying there. Then, with peace sunk heavy on her heart, she went about making tidy the kitchen. She knew she submitted to life, which was her immediate master. But from death, her ultimate master, she winced with fear and shame.

ISAK DINESEN

(1885–1962)

*I*sak Dinesen is the pseudonym for Karen, Baroness von Blixen-
Finecke, who was born on her parents' estate near Copenhagen. Her
father was a gifted and restless man who fought the Prussians in two
wars, abandoned Europe to live with the Indians in North America,
and hanged himself when his daughter was 10. Karen Blixen grew up
wondering how a girl "living in this deadly boring twentieth century"
could gain access to the heroic world represented by those who had
participated in the French Revolution. She published a number of short
stories in Danish literary reviews, enrolled as a student at the Danish
Royal Academy of Art, and maintained a lifelong interest in the visual
arts. In 1914 she married her Swedish cousin and went to live on a farm
in Kenya. Although she soon separated from her husband, she ran her
farm until forced to sell it in 1931, and in the process came to love the
land and its people. Some of her experiences are recounted in her 1937
memoir Out of Africa. When she returned to Denmark, she began to
write in English, stories that were published as Seven Gothic Tales, a
book that was an enormous popular success, as was her Winter Tales
(1942). Other works include Angelic Avengers (1947), Last Tales
(1957), Anecdotes of Destiny (1958), Shadows on the Grass (1961),
and Ehrengard (1963). Robert Langbaum summarizes her stories by
suggesting that in them

> Isak Dinesen recapitulates the change in European perceptions
> of reality during the last three or four centuries. By imposing
> upon each other, in the same story, at least three different
> judgments of the same events, she shows how we lost unity of
> perception and how we may regain it. For when we look at life
> with single vision, with the one analytic eye that cuts facts off
> from value, then life is meaningless and depressing. When we
> look at it with both eyes, with the understanding and sympathy
> that enables us to project ourselves into events and other people,
> then life is beautiful and sad. But when, using more than our
> eyes, using also the resources of cultural and biological memory,
> we look through life, seeing in it a transforming vision that
> collapses the single person and event into a pattern of recurrence
> and our highest aspiration into our most primitive instinct,
> then we see how every part of life is necessary, how we could
> not have what we call the highest without what we call the
> lowest. Then we see life as the storyteller does, as we may
> imagine God does.

Babette's Feast

I. Two Ladies of Berlevaag

In Norway there is a Fjord—a long narrow arm of the sea between tall mountains—named Berlevaag Fjord. At the foot of the mountains the small town of Berlevaag looks like a child's toy-town of little wooden pieces painted grey, yellow, pink and many other colours.

Sixty-five years ago two elderly ladies lived in one of the yellow houses. Other ladies at that time wore a bustle, and the two sisters might have worn it as gracefully as any of them, for they were tall and willowy. But they had never possessed any article of fashion, they had dressed demurely in grey or black all their lives. They were christened Martine and Philippa, after Martin Luther and his friend Philip Melanchthon. Their father had been a Dean and a Prophet, the founder of a pious ecclesiastic party or sect, which was known and looked up to in all the country of Norway. Its members renounced the pleasures of this world, for the earth and all that it held to them was but a kind of illusion, and the true reality was the New Jerusalem towards which they were longing. They swore not at all, but their communication was yea yea and nay nay, and they called one another Brother and Sister.

The Dean had married late in life and by now had long been dead. His disciples were becoming fewer in number every year, whiter or balder and harder of hearing, they were even becoming somewhat querulous and quarrelsome, so that sad little schisms would arise in the congregation. But they still gathered together to read and interpret the Word. They had all known the Dean's daughters as little girls, to them they were even now very small sisters, precious for their dear Father's sake. In the yellow house they felt that their Master's spirit was with them, here they were at home and at peace.

These two ladies had got a French maid-of-all-work, Babette.

It was a strange thing in a couple of puritan women in a small Norwegian town, it might even seem to call for an explanation. The people of Berlevaag found the explanation in the sisters' piety and kindness of heart. For the old Dean's daughters spent their time and their small income in works of charity, no sorrowful or distressed creature knocked on their door in vain. And Babette had come to that door twelve years ago as a friendless fugitive, almost mad with grief and fear.

But the reason for Babette's presence in the two sisters' house was to be found further back in time and deeper down in the domain of human hearts.

II. Martine's Lover

As young girls Martine and Philippa had been extraordinarily pretty, with the almost supernatural fairness of flowering fruit-trees or perpetual snow. They were never to be seen at balls or parties, but people turned when they passed in the streets, and the young men of Berlevaag went to church to watch them walk up the aisle. The younger sister also had a lovely voice, which on Sundays filled the church with sweetness. To the Dean's congregation earthly love, and marriage with it, were trivial matters, in themselves nothing but illusions, still it is possible that more than one of the elderly Brothers had been prizing the maidens far above rubies and had suggested as much to their Father. But the Dean had declared that to him in his calling his daughters were his right and left hand—who could want to bereave him of them? And the fair girls had been brought up to an ideal of heavenly love, they were all filled with it and did not let themselves be touched by the flames of this world.

All the same they had upset the peace of heart of two gentlemen from the great world outside Berlevaag.

There was a young officer named Lorens Loewenhielm, who had led a gay life in his garrison-town and had run into debt. In the year of 1854, when Martine was eighteen and Philippa seventeen, his angry Father sent him on a month's visit to his Aunt in her old country-house of Fossum near Berlevaag, where he would have time to meditate and to better his ways. One day he rode into town and met Martine in the market-place. He looked down at the pretty girl, and she looked up at the fine horseman. When she had passed him and disappeared he was not certain whether he was to believe his own eyes.

In the Loewenhielm family there existed a legend to the effect that long ago a gentleman of the name had married a Huldre, a female mountain spirit of Norway, who is so fair that the air round her shines and quivers. Since then from time to time members of the family had been second-sighted. Young Lorens till now had not been aware of any particular spiritual gift in his own nature. But at this one moment there rose before his eyes a sudden, mighty vision of a higher and purer life, with no creditors, dunning-letters or parental lectures, with no secret, unpleasant pangs of conscience and with a gentle, golden-haired angel to guide and reward him.

Through his pious Aunt he got admission to the Dean's house, and saw that Martine was even lovelier without a bonnet. He followed her slim figure with adoring eyes, but he loathed and despised the figure which he himself cut in her nearness. He was amazed and shocked by the fact that he could find nothing at all to say, and no inspiration in the glass of water before him. "Mercy and Truth, dear brethren, have met together," said the Dean. "Righteousness and Bliss have kissed one another." And the young man's thoughts were with the moment when Lorens and Martine should be kissing one another. He repeated his visit time after time, and each time seemed to himself to grow smaller and more insignificant and contemptible.

When in the evening he came back to his Aunt's house he kicked his shining riding-boots to the corners of his room, he even laid his head on the table and wept.

On the last day of his stay he made a last attempt to communicate his feelings to Martine. Till now it had been easy to him to tell a pretty girl that he loved her, but the tender words stuck in his throat as he looked into this maiden's face. When he had said good-bye to the party, Martine saw him to the door with a candlestick in her hand. The light shone on her mouth and threw upwards the shadows of her long eye-lashes. He was about to leave in dumb despair when on the threshold he suddenly seized her hand and pressed it to his lips.

"I am going away for ever!" he cried, "I shall never, never see you again! For I have learned here that Fate is hard, and that in this world there are things which are impossible!"

When he was once more back in his garrison-town he thought his adventure over, and found that he did not like to think of it at all. While the other young officers talked of their love-affairs he was silent upon his. For seen from the officers' mess, and so to say with its eyes, it was a pitiful business. How had it come to pass that a lieutenant of the hussars had let himself be defeated and frustrated by a set of long-faced sectarians, in the bare-floored rooms of an old Dean's house?

Then he got afraid, a panic came upon him. Was it the family-madness which made him still carry with him the dream-like picture of a maiden so fair that she made the air round her shine with purity and holiness? He did not want to be a dreamer, he wanted to be like his brother-officers.

So he pulled himself together, and in the greatest effort of his young life made up his mind to forget what happened to him in Berlevaag. From now, he resolved, he would look forward, not back. He would concentrate on his career, and the day was to come when he would cut a brilliant figure in a brilliant world.

His mother was pleased with the result of his visit to Fossum, and in her letters expressed her gratitude to his Aunt. She did not know by what queer, winding roads her son had reached this happy moral standpoint.

The ambitious young officer soon caught the attention of his superiors and made unusually quick advancement. He was sent to France and Russia, and on his return he married a lady-in-waiting to Queen Sophia. In these high circles he moved with grace and ease, pleased with his surroundings and with himself. He even in course of time benefited from words and turns which had stuck in his mind from the Dean's house, for piety was now in fashion at Court.

In the yellow house of Berlevaag Philippa sometimes turned the talk to the handsome, silent young man who had so suddenly made his appearance, and so suddenly disappeared again. Her elder sister would then answer her gently, with a still, clear face, and find other things to discuss.

III. Philippa's Lover

A year later a more distinguished person even than Lieutenant Loewen-hielm came to Berlevaag.

The great singer Achille Papin of Paris for a week had sung at the Royal Opera of Stockholm, and had carried away his audience there as everywhere. One evening a lady of the Court, who had been dreaming of a romance with the artist, had described to him the wild, grandiose scenery of Norway. His own romantic nature was stirred by the narration, and he had laid his way back to France round the Norwegian coast. But he felt small in the sublime surroundings, with nobody to talk to he fell into that melancholy in which he saw himself as an old man, at the end of his career—till on a Sunday, when he could think of nothing else to do, he went to church and heard Philippa sing.

Then in one single moment he knew and understood all. For here were the snowy summits, the wild flowers and the white Nordic nights, translated into his own language of music, and brought him in a young woman's voice. Like Lorens Loewenhielm he had a vision.

"Almighty God," he thought, "thy power is without end, and thy mercy reacheth into the clouds! And here is a Primadonna of the Opera who will lay Paris at her feet."

Achille Papin at this time was a handsome man of forty, with curly black hair and a red mouth. The idolisation of nations had not spoilt him, he was a kind-hearted person and honest towards himself.

He went straight to the yellow house, gave his name—which told the Dean nothing—and explained that he was staying in Berlevaag for his health, and the while would be happy to take on the young lady as a pupil.

He did not mention the Opera of Paris, but described at length how beautifully Miss Philippa would come to sing in church, to the glory of God.

For a moment he forgot himself, for when the Dean asked whether he was a Roman Catholic he answered according to truth, and the old clergyman, who had never seen a live Roman Catholic, grew a little pale.

All the same the Dean was pleased to speak French, which reminded him of his young days, when he had studied the works of the great French Lutheran writer Lefèvre d'Etaples. And as nobody could long withstand Achille Papin when he had really set his heart on a matter, in the end the Father gave his consent, and remarked to his daughter: "God's paths run across the Sea and the snowy mountains, where man's eye sees no track."

So the great French singer and the young Norwegian novice set to work together. Achille's expectation grew into certainty and his certainty into ecstasy. He thought: "I have been wrong in believing that I was growing old. My greatest triumphs are before me! The world will once more believe in miracles when she and I sing together!"

After a while he could not keep his dreams to himself, but told Philippa about them.

She would, he said, rise like a star above any Diva of the past or present. The Emperor and Empress, the Princess, great ladies and bel-esprits of Paris would listen to her, and shed tears. The common people too would worship her, and she would bring consolation and strength to the wronged and oppressed. When she left the Grand Opera upon her master's arm the crowd would unharness her horses, and themselves draw her to the Café Anglais, where a magnificent supper awaited her.

Philippa did not repeat these prospects to her Father or her Sister, and this was the first time in her life that she had had a secret from them.

The teacher now gave his pupil the part of Zerlina in Mozart's Opera "Don Giovanni" to study. He himself, as often before, sang Don Giovanni's part.

He had never in his life sung as now. In the duet of the second act— which is called the seduction duet—he was swept off his feet by the heavenly music and the heavenly voices. As the last melting note died away he seized Philippa's hands, drew her towards him and kissed her solemnly, as a bridegroom might kiss his bride before the altar. Then he let her go. For the moment was too sublime for any further word or movement, Mozart himself was looking down on the two.

Philippa went home, told her Father that she did not want any more singing-lessons and asked him to write and tell Monsieur Papin so.

The Dean said: "And God's paths run across the rivers, my child."

When Achille got the Dean's letter he sat immovable for an hour. He thought: "I have been wrong. My day is over. Never again shall I be the divine Papin. And this poor weedy garden of the world has lost its nightingale!"

A little later he thought: "I wonder what is the matter with that hussy? Did I kiss her, by any chance?"

In the end he thought: "I have lost my life for a kiss, and I have no remembrance at all of the kiss! Don Giovanni kissed Zerlina, and Achille Papin pays for it! Such is the fate of the artist!"

In the Dean's house Martine felt that the matter was deeper than it looked, and searched her sister's face. For a moment, slightly trembling, she too imagined that the Roman Catholic gentleman might have tried to kiss Philippa. She did not imagine that her sister might have been surprised and frightened by something in her own nature.

Achille Papin took the first boat from Berlevaag.

Of this visitor from the great world the sisters spoke but little, they lacked the words in which to discuss him.

IV. A Letter from Paris

Fifteen years later, on a rainy June night of 1871, the bellrope of the yellow house was pulled violently three times. The mistresses of the house opened the door to a massive, dark, deadly pale woman with a bundle on her arm, who stared at them, took a step forward and fell down on the doorstep in a dead swoon. When the frightened ladies had restored her to life she sat up, gave them one more glance from her sunken eyes and, all the time without a word, fumbled in her wet clothes and brought out a letter which she handed to them.

The letter was addressed to them all right, but it was written in French. The sisters put their heads together and read it. It ran as follows:

> Ladies!
>
> Do you remember me? Ah, when I think of you I have the heart filled with wild lilies-of-the-valley! Will the memory of a Frenchman's devotion bend your hearts to save the life of a Frenchwoman?
>
> The bearer of this letter, Madame Babette Hersant, like my divine Empress herself has had to flee from Paris. Civil war has raged in our streets. French hands have shed French blood. The noble Communards, standing up for the Rights of Man have been crushed and annihilated. Madame Hersant's husband and son, both eminent ladies' hairdressers, have been shot. She herself was arrested as a Pétroleuse—(which word is used here for women who set fire to houses with paraffin)—and has narrowly escaped the bloodstained hands of General Galliffet. She has lost all she possessed and dares not remain in France.
>
> A nephew of hers is Cook to the boat *Anna Colbioernsson*, bound for Christiania—(as I believe the capital of Norway)—and he has obtained shipping opportunity for his Aunt. This is now her last sad resort!
>
> Knowing that I was once a visitor to your magnificent country she comes to me, asks me if there be any good people in Norway

and begs me, if it be so, to supply her with a letter to them. The two words of "good people" immediately bring before my eyes your picture, sacred to my heart. I send her to you. How she is to get from Christiania to Berlevaag I know not, having forgotten the map of Norway. But she is a Frenchwoman, and you will find that in her misery she has still got resourcefulness, majesty and true stoicism.

I envy her in her despair; she is to see your faces.

As you receive her mercifully, send a merciful thought back to France.

For fifteen years, Miss Philippa, I have grieved that your voice should never fill the Grand Opera of Paris. When tonight I think of you, no doubt surrounded by a gay and loving family, and of myself: grey, lonely, forgotten by those who once applauded and adored me, I feel that you may have chosen the better part in life. What is fame? What is glory?—The grave awaits us all!

And yet, my lost Zerlina, and yet, soprano of the snow!—as I write this I feel that the grave is not the end. In Paradise I shall hear your voice again. There you will sing, without fears or scruples, as God meant you to sing. There you will be the great artist that God meant you to be. Ah! how you will enchant the angels.

Babette can cook.

Deign to receive, my ladies, the humble homage of the friend who was once

Achille Papin

At the bottom of the page, as a P.S. were neatly printed the first two bars of the duet between Don Giovanni and Zerlina like this:

The two sisters till now had only kept a small servant of fifteen to help them in the house, and they felt that they could not possibly afford to take on an elderly, experienced housekeeper. But Babette told them that she would serve Monsieur Papin's good people for nothing, and that she would take service with nobody else. If they sent her away she must die.

Babette now remained in the house of the Dean's daughters for twelve years, until the time of this tale.

V. Still Life

Babette had arrived haggard and wild-eyed like a hunted animal, but in her new, friendly surroundings she soon acquired all the appearance of a respectable and trusted servant. She had appeared to be a beggar, she turned out to be a conqueror. Her quiet countenance and her steady, deep glance had magnetic qualities: under her eyes things moved, noiselessly, into their proper places.

Her mistresses at first had trembled a little, just as the Dean had once done, at the idea of receiving a Papist under their roof. But they did not like to worry a hard-tried fellow creature with catechisation, neither were they quite sure of their French. They silently agreed that the example of a good Lutheran life would be the best means of converting their servant. In this way Babette's presence in the house became so as to say a moral spur to its inhabitants.

They had distrusted Monsieur Papin's assertion that Babette could cook. In France, they knew, people ate frogs. They showed Babette how to prepare a split cod and an ale-and-bread-soup: during the demonstration the Frenchwoman's face became absolutely expressionless. But within a week Babette cooked a split cod and an ale-and-bread-soup as well as anybody born and bred in Berlevaag.

The idea of French luxury and extravagance next alarmed and dismayed the Dean's daughters. The first day after Babette had entered their service they took her before them and explained to her that they were poor, and that to them luxurious fare was sinful. Their own food must be as plain as possible, it was the soup-pails and baskets for their poor that signified. Babette nodded her head: as a girl, she informed her ladies, she had been Cook to an old priest who was a saint. Upon this the sisters resolved to surpass the French priest in ascetism. And they soon found that from the day when Babette took over the housekeeping its cost was miraculously reduced, and the soup-pails and baskets acquired a new, mysterious power to stimulate and strengthen their poor and sick.

The world outside the yellow house too came to acknowledge Babette's excellence. The refugee never learned to speak the language of her new country, but in her broken Norwegian she beat down the prices of Berlevaag's flintiest tradesmen. She was held in awe on the quay and in the market-place.

The old Brothers and Sisters, who had first looked askance at the foreign woman in their midst, felt a happy change in their little Sisters' life, rejoiced at it and benefited by it. They found that troubles and cares had been conjured away from their existence, and that now they had money to give away, time for the confidences and complaints of their old friends and peace for meditating on heavenly matters. In course of time not a few of the Brotherhood included Babette's name in their prayers, and thanked God for the speechless stranger, the dark Martha in the house of their two fair Marys. The stone which the builders had almost refused had become the head-stone of the corner.

The ladies in the yellow house were the only ones to know that their corner-stone had a mysterious and alarming feature to it, as if it was somehow related to the Black Stone of Mecca, the Kaaba itself.

Hardly ever did Babette refer to her past life. When in early days the sisters had gently condoled her upon her losses, they had been met with that majesty and stoicism of which Monsieur Papin had written. "What will you ladies?" she had answered, shrugging her shoulders, "it is Fate."

But one day she suddenly informed them that she had for many years held a ticket in a French lottery, and that a faithful friend in Paris was still renewing it for her every year. Some time she might win the grand prix of ten thousand francs. At that they felt that their Cook's old carpet-bag was made from a magic carpet, at a given moment she might mount it, and be carried off, back to Paris.

And it happened when Martine and Philippa spoke to Babette that they would get no answer, and would wonder if she had even heard what they said. They would find her in the kitchen, her elbows on the table and her temples on her hands, lost in the study of a heavy black book which they secretly suspected to be a popish prayer-book. Or she would sit immovable on the three-legged kitchen-chair, her strong hands in her lap and her dark eyes wide open, as enigmatical and fatal as a Pythia upon her tripod. At such moments they realised that Babette was deep, and that in the soundings of her being there were passions, there were memories and longings of which they knew nothing at all.

A little cold shiver ran through them, and in their hearts they thought: "Perhaps after all she had indeed been a Pétroleuse."

VI. Babette's Good Luck

The fifteenth of December was the Dean's hundredth anniversary.

His daughters had long been looking forward to this day and had wished to celebrate it, as if their dear father were still among his disciples. Therefore it had been to them a sad and incomprehensible thing that in this last year discord and dissension had been raising their heads in his flock. They had endeavoured to make peace, but they were aware that they had failed. It was as if the fine and lovable vigour of their father's personality had been evaporating, such as Hoffmann's anodyne will evaporate when left on the shelf in a bottle without a cork. And his departure had left the door ajar to things hitherto unknown to the two sisters, much younger than his spiritual children. From a past half a century back, when the unshepherded sheep had been running astray in the mountains, uninvited dismal guests pressed through the opening on the heels of the worshippers and seemed to darken the little rooms and to let in the cold. The sins of the old brothers and sisters came, with late piercing repentance like a toothache, and the sins of others against them came back with bitter resentment, like a poisoning of the blood.

There were in the congregation two old women who before their conversion had spread slander upon one another, and thereby to one another ruined a marriage and an inheritance. Today they could not remember happenings of yesterday or a week ago, but they remembered these forty year old wrongs and kept going through the ancient accounts—they scowled at one another. There was an old brother who suddenly called to mind how another brother, forty-five years ago, had cheated him in a deal, he could have wished to dismiss the matter from his mind, but it stuck there like a deep-seated, festering splinter. There was a grey, honest skipper and a furrowed, pious widow, who in their young days, while she was the wife of another man, had been sweethearts. Of late each had begun to grieve, while shifting the burden of guilt from his own shoulders to those of the other and back again, and to worry about the possible terrible consequences, through all eternity, brought upon him by one who had pretended to hold him dear. They grew pale at the meetings in the yellow house and avoided one another's eyes.

As the birthday drew nearer, Martine and Philippa felt the responsibility growing heavier. Would their ever faithful father look down to his daughters and call them by name as unjust stewards? Between them they talked matters over and repeated their father's saying, that God's paths were running even across the salt sea and the snowclad mountains, where man's eye sees no track.

One day of this summer the post brought a letter from France to Madame Babette Hersant. This in itself was a surprising thing, for during these twelve years Babette had received no letter. What, her mistresses wondered, could it contain? They took it into the kitchen to watch her open and read it. Babette opened it, read it, lifted her eyes from it to her ladies' faces and told them that her number in the French lottery had come out. She had won ten thousand francs.

The news made such an impression on the two sisters that for a full minute they could not speak a word. They themselves were used to receiving their modest pension in small instalments, it was difficult to them even to imagine the sum of ten thousand francs in a pile. Then they pressed Babette's hand, their own hands trembling a little. They had never before pressed the hand of a person who the moment before had come into possession of ten thousand francs.

After a while they realised that the happenings concerned themselves as well as Babette. The country of France, they felt, was slowly rising before their servant's horizon, and correspondingly their own existence was sinking beneath their feet. The ten thousand francs which made her rich—how poor did they not make the house she had served! One by one old forgotten cares and worries began to peep out at them from the four corners of the kitchen. The congratulations died on their lips, and the two pious women were ashamed of their own silence.

During the following days they announced the news to their friends, with joyous faces, but it did them good to see these friends' faces grow sad as they listened to them. Nobody, it was felt in the Brotherhood, could really blame Babette: birds will return to their nests and human beings to the country of their birth. But did that good and faithful servant realise that in going away from Berlevaag she would be leaving many old and poor people in distress? Their little sisters would have no more time for the sick and sorrowful. Indeed, indeed, lotteries were ungodly affairs.

In due time the money arrived through offices in Christiania and Berlevaag. The two ladies helped Babette to count it, and gave her a box to keep it in. They handled, and became familiar with, the ominous bits of paper.

They dared not question Babette upon the date of her departure. Dared they hope that she would remain with them over the fifteenth of December?

The mistresses had never been quite certain how much of their private conversation the Cook followed or understood. So they were surprised when on a September evening Babette came into the drawing-room, more humble or subdued than they had ever seen her, to ask a favour. She begged them, she said, to let her cook a celebration-dinner on the Dean's birthday.

The ladies had not intended to have any dinner at all. A very plain supper with a cup of coffee was the most sumptuous meal to which they had ever asked any guest to sit down. But Babette's dark eyes were as eager and pleading as a dog's, they agreed to let her have her way. At this the Cook's face lighted up.

But she had got more to say. She wanted, she said, to cook a French dinner, a real French dinner, for this one time. Martine and Philippa looked at one another. They did not like the idea, they felt that they did not know what it might imply. But the very strangeness of the request disarmed them. They had no arguments wherewith to meet the proposition of cooking a real French dinner.

Babette drew a long sigh of happiness, but still she did not move. She had got one more prayer to make. She begged that her mistresses would allow her to pay for the French dinner with her own money.

"No Babette!" the ladies exclaimed. How could she imagine such a thing? Did she believe that they would allow her to spend her precious money on food and drink—or on them? No Babette, indeed.

Babette took a step forward. There was something formidable in the move, like a wave rising. Had she stepped forth like this, in 1871, to plant a red flag on a barricade? She spoke, in her queer Norwegian, with classical French eloquence, her voice was like a song.

Ladies! Had she ever, during twelve years, asked you a favour? No! And why not?—ladies, you who say your prayers every day, can you imagine what it means to a human heart to have no prayer to make? What would Babette have had to pray for? Nothing! Tonight she had got a prayer to make, from the bottom of her heart. Do you not then feel tonight, my ladies, that it becomes you to grant it her, with such joy as that with which the good God has granted you your own?

The ladies for a while said nothing. Babette was right, it was her first request these twelve years, very likely it would be her last. They thought the matter over. After all, they told themselves, their Cook was now better off than they, and a dinner could make no difference to a person who owned ten thousand francs.

Their consent in the end completely changed Babette. They saw that as a young woman she had been beautiful. And they wondered whether in this hour they themselves had not, for the very first time, become to her the "good people" of Achille Papin's letter.

VII. The Turtle

In November Babette went for a journey.

She had preparations to make, she told her mistresses, and would need a leave of a week or ten days. Her nephew, who had once got to her to Christiania, was still sailing to that town, she must see him and talk things over with him. Babette was a bad sailor, she had spoken of her one sea-voyage, from France to Norway, as of the most horrible experience of her life. Now she was strangely collected, the ladies felt that her heart was already in France.

After ten days she came back to Berlevaag.

Had she got things arranged as she wished? the ladies asked. Yes, she answered, she had seen her nephew and given him a list of the goods which he was to bring her from France. To Martine and Philippa this was a dark saying, but they did not care to talk of her departure, so they asked her no more questions.

Babette was somewhat nervous during the next weeks. But one December day she triumphantly announced to her mistresses that the goods had come to Christiania, had been trans-shipped there, and on this very day had arrived at Berlevaag. She had, she added, engaged an old man with a wheelbarrow to have them conveyed from the harbour to the house.

But what goods, Babette? the ladies asked. Why, Mesdames, Babette replied, the ingredients for the birthday-dinner. Praise be to God, they had all arrived in good condition from Paris.

By this time Babette, like the bottled demon of the fairy-tale, had swelled and grown to such dimensions that her mistresses felt smaller before her. They now saw the French dinner coming upon them, a thing of incalculable nature and range. But they had never in their life broken a promise, they gave themselves into their Cook's hands.

All the same when Martine saw a barrow-load of bottles wheeled into the kitchen, she stood still. She touched the bottles and lifted up one. "What is there in this bottle, Babette?" she asked in a low voice, "not wine?" "Wine, Madame!" Babette answered, "no, Madame, it is a Clos Vougeout 1846!" After a moment she added: "From Philippe, in Rue Montorgueil!" Martine had never suspected that wines could have names to them, and was put to silence.

Later in the evening she opened the door to a ring, and was once more faced with the wheelbarrow, this time with a red-haired sailor-boy behind it, as if the old man had by this time been worn out. The youth grinned at her as he lifted a big, undefinable object from the barrow. In the light of the lamp it looked like some greenish-black stone, but when sat down on the kitchen floor it suddenly shot out a snake-like head and moved it slightly from side to side. Martine had seen pictures of tortoises, and had even as a child owned a pet tortoise, but this thing was monstrous in size and terrible to behold. She backed out of the kitchen without a word.

She dared not tell her sister what she had seen. She passed an almost sleepless night, she thought of her Father and felt that on his very birthday she and her sister were lending his house to a witches' sabbath. When at last she fell asleep she had a terrible dream, in which she saw Babette poisoning the old Brothers and Sisters, Philippa and herself.

Early in the morning she got up, put on her grey cloak and went out in the dark street. She walked from house to house, opened her heart to her Brothers and Sisters, and confessed her guilt. She and Philippa, she said, had meant no harm, they had granted their servant a prayer and had not foreseen what might come of it. Now she could not tell what, on her Father's birthday, her guests would be given to eat or drink. She did not actually mention the turtle, but it was present in her face and voice.

The old people, as has already been told, had all known Martine and Philippa as little girls, they had seen them cry bitterly over a broken doll. Martine's tears brought tears into their own eyes. They gathered in the afternoon and talked the problem over.

Before they again parted they promised one another that for their little sisters' sake they would, on the great day, be silent upon all matters of food and drink. Nothing that might be set before them, be it even frogs or snails, should wring a word from their lips.

"Even so," said a white-bearded brother, "the tongue is a little member and boasteth great things. The tongue can no man tame, it is an unruly evil, full of deadly poison. On the day of our master we will cleanse our tongues of all taste and purify them of all delight or disgust of the senses, keeping and preserving them for the higher functions of praise and thanksgiving."

So few things ever happened in the quiet existence of the Berlevaag brotherhood that they were at this moment deeply moved and elevated. They shook hands on their vow, and it was to them as if they were doing so before the face of their master.

VIII. The Hymn

On Sunday morning it began to snow. The white flakes fell fast and thick, the small window-panes of the yellow house pasted with snow.

Early in the day a groom from Fossum brought the two sisters a note. Old Mrs Loewenhielm still resided in her country-house. She was now ninety years old and stone-deaf, and she had lost all sense of smell or taste. But she had been one of the Dean's first supporters, and neither her infirmity nor the sledge-journey would keep her from doing honour to his memory. Now, she wrote, her nephew, General Lorens Loewenhielm, had unexpectedly come on a visit, he had spoken with deep veneration of the Dean, and she begged permission to bring him with her. It would do him good, for the dear boy seemed to be in somewhat low spirits.

Martine and Philippa at this remembered the young officer and his visits, it relieved their present anxiety to talk of old happy days. They wrote back that General Loewenhielm would be welcome. They also called in Babette to inform her that there would now be twelve for dinner, they added that their latest guest had lived in Paris for several years. Babette seemed pleased with the news, and assured them that there would be food enough.

The hostesses made their little preparations in the sitting-room. They dared not set foot in the kitchen, for Babette had mysteriously nosed out a cook's mate from a ship in the harbour—the same boy, Martine realised, who had brought in the turtle—to assist her in the kitchen and to wait at table, and now the dark woman and the red-haired boy, like some witch with her familiar spirit, had taken possession of these regions. The ladies could not tell what fires had been burning or what cauldrons bubbling there from before daybreak.

Table-linen and plate had been magically ironed and polished, glasses and decanters brought, Babette only knew from where. The Dean's house did not possess twelve dining-room chairs, the long horse-hair covered sofa had been moved from the parlour to the dining-room, and the parlour, ever sparsely furnished, now looked strangely bare and big without it.

Martine and Philippa did their best to embellish the domain left to them. Whatever troubles might be in wait for their guests, in any case they should not be cold, all day the sisters fed the towering old stove with birch-knots. They hung a garland of juniper round their father's portrait on the wall, and placed candlesticks on their mother's small working-table beneath it, they burned juniper-twigs to make the room smell nice. The while they wondered if in this weather the sledge from Fossum would get through. In the end they put on their old black best frocks and their confirmation gold crosses. They sat down, folded their hands in their laps and committed themselves unto God.

The old Brothers and Sisters arrived in small groups, and entered the room slowly and solemnly.

This low room with its bare floor and scanty furniture was dear to the Dean's disciples. Outside its windows lay the great world. Seen from in here the great world in its winter-whiteness was ever prettily bordered in pink, blue and red by the row of hyacinths on the window-sills. And in summer, when the windows were open, the great world had a softly moving frame of white muslin curtains to it.

Tonight the guests were met on the doorstep with warmth and sweet smell, and they were looking into the face of their beloved Master, wreathed with evergreen. Their hearts like their numb fingers thawed.

One very old Brother after a few moments' silence in his trembling voice struck up one of the Master's own hymns:

> *"Jerusalem, my happy home*
> *name ever dear to me . . ."*

One by one the other voices fell in, thin quivering women's voices, ancient seafaring Brothers' deep growls, and above them all Philippa's clear soprano, a little worn with age but still angelic. Unwittingly the choir had seized one another's hands. They sang the hymn to the end, but could not bear to cease and joined in another:

> *"Take not thought for food or raiment*
> *careful one, so anxiously . . ."*

The mistresses of the house were somewhat reassured by it, the words of the third verse:

> "Wouldst thou give a stone, a reptile
> to thy pleading child for food? . . ."

went straight to Martine's heart and inspired her with hope.

In the middle of this hymn sledge-bells were heard outside, the guests from Fossum had arrived.

Martine and Philippa went to receive them and saw them into the parlour. Mrs Loewenhielm with age had become quite small, her face colourless like parchment, and very still. By her side General Loewenhielm, tall, broad and ruddy, in his bright uniform, his breast covered with decorations, strutted and shone like an ornamental bird, a golden pheasant or a peacock, in this sedate party of black crows and jackdaws.

IX. General Loewenhielm

General Loewenhielm had been driving from Fossum to Berlevaag in a strange mood. He had not visited this part of the country for thirty years, he had come now to get a rest from his busy life at Court, and he had found no rest. The old house of Fossum was peaceful enough and seemed somehow pathetically small after the Tuileries and the Winter Palace. But it held one disquieting figure: young Lieutenant Loewenhielm walked in its rooms.

General Loewenhielm saw the handsome, slim figure pass close by him. And as he passed the boy gave the elder man a short glance and a smile, the haughty, arrogant smile which youth gives to age. The General might have smiled back, kindly and a little sadly, such as age smiles at youth, if it had not been that he was really in no mood to smile, he was, as his Aunt had written, in low spirits.

General Loewenhielm had obtained everything that he had striven for in life and was admired and envied by everyone. Only he himself knew of a queer fact, which jarred with his prosperous existence: that he was not perfectly happy. Something was wrong somewhere, and he carefully felt his mental self all over, as one feels a finger over to determine the place of a deep-seated, invisible thorn.

He was in high favour with Royalty, he had done well in his calling, he had friends everywhere. The thorn sat in none of these places.

His wife was a brilliant woman and still good looking. Perhaps she neglected her own house a little for her visits and parties, she changed her servants every three months and the General's meals at home were served unpunctually. The General, who valued good food highly in life, here felt a slight bitterness against his lady, and secretly blamed her for the indigestion from which he sometimes suffered. Still the thorn was not here either.

Nay, but an absurd thing had lately been happening to General Loewenhielm: he would find himself worrying about his immortal soul. Did he have any reason for doing so? He was a moral person, loyal to his king, his wife and his friends, an example to everybody. But there were moments when it seemed to him that the world was not a moral, but a mystic, concern. He looked into the mirror, examined the row of decorations on his breast and sighed to himself: "Vanity, vanity, all is vanity!"

The strange meeting at Fossum had compelled him to make out the balance sheet of his life.

Young Lorens Loewenhielm had attracted dreams and fancies as a flower attracts bees and butterflies. He had fought to free himself of them, he had fled and they had followed. He had been scared of the Huldre of the family legend and had declined her invitation to come into the mountain, he had firmly refused the gift of second-sight.

The elderly Lorens Loewenhielm found himself wishing that one little dream would come his way, and a grey moth of dusk look him up before nightfall. He found himself longing for the faculty of second sight, as a blind man will long for the normal faculty of vision.

Can the sum of a row of victories in many years and in many countries be a defeat? General Loewenhielm had fulfilled Lieutenant Loewenhielm's wishes and had more than satisfied his ambitions. It might be held that he had gained the whole world to him. And it had come to this, that the stately, worldly-wise older man now turned towards the naïve young figure to ask him, gravely, even bitterly, in what he had profited? Somewhere something had been lost.

When Mrs Loewenhielm had told her nephew of the Dean's anniversary and he had made up his mind to go with her to Berlevaag, his decision had not been an ordinary acception of a dinner invitation.

He would, he resolved, tonight make up his account with young Lorens Loewenhielm, who had felt himself to be a shy and sorry figure in the house of the Dean, and who in the end had shaken its dust off his riding-boots. He would let the youth prove to him, once and for all, that thirty-one years ago he had made the right choice. The low rooms, the haddock and the glass water on the table before him should all be called in to bear evidence that in their milieu the existence of Lorens Loewenhielm would soon have become sheer misery.

He let his mind stray far away. In Paris he had once won a *concours hippique* and had been fêted by high French cavalry officers, princes and dukes among them. A dinner had been given in his honour at the finest restaurant of the city. Opposite him at table was a noble lady, a famous beauty whom he had long been courting. In the midst of dinner she had lifted her dark velvet eyes above the rim of her champagne glass and without words had promised to make him happy. In the sledge he now all of a sudden remembered that he had then, for a second, seen Martine's face before him and had rejected it.

For a while he listened to the tinkling of the sledge-bells, then he smiled a little as he reflected how he would tonight come to dominate the conversation round that same table by which young Lorens Loewenhielm had sat mute.

Large snowflakes fell densely, behind the sledge the tracks were wiped out quickly. General Loewenhielm sat immovable by the side of his aunt, his chin sunk in the high fur-collar of his coat.

X. Babette's Dinner

As Babette's red-haired familiar opened the door to the dining-room, and the guests slowly crossed the threshold, they let go one another's hands and became silent. But the silence was sweet, for in spirit they still held hands and were still singing.

Babette had set a row of candles down the middle of the table, the small flames shone on the black coats and frocks and on the one scarlet uniform, and were reflected in the clear, moist eyes.

General Loewenhielm saw Martine's face in the candlelight as he had seen it when the two parted, thirty years ago. What traces would thirty years of Berlevaag-life have left on it? The golden hair was now streaked with silver, the flower-like face had slowly been turned into alabaster. But how serene was the forehead, how quietly trustful the eyes, how pure and sweet the mouth, as if no hasty word had ever passed its lips.

When all were seated, the eldest member of the congregation said grace in the Dean's own words:

> *"May my food my body maintain,*
> *may my body my soul sustain,*
> *may my soul in deed and word*
> *give thanks for all things to the Lord."*

At the word of "food" the guests, with their old heads bent over their folded hands, remembered how they had vowed not to utter a word about the subject, and in their hearts they reinforced the vow: they would not even give it a thought! They were sitting down to a meal, well, so had people done at the wedding of Cana. And grace had chosen to manifest itself there, in the very wine, as fully as anywhere.

Babette's boy filled a small glass before each of the party. They lifted it to their lips gravely, in confirmation of their resolution.

General Loewenhielm, somewhat suspicious of his wine, took a sip of it, startled, raised the glass first to his nose and then to his eyes, and sat down bewildered. "This is very strange!" he thought, "Amontillado! And the finest Amontillado that I have ever tasted." After a moment, in order to test his senses, he took a small spoonful of his soup, took a second spoonful and laid down his spoon. "This is exceedingly strange!" he said to himself, "for surely I am eating turtle-soup—and what turtle-soup!" He was seized by a queer kind of panic and emptied his glass.

Usually in Berlevaag people did not speak much while they were eating. But somehow this evening tongues had been loosened. An old Brother told the story of his first meeting with the Dean. Another went through that sermon which sixty years ago had brought about his conversion. An aged woman, the one to whom Martine had first confided her distress, reminded her friends how in all afflictions any Brother or Sister was ready to share the burden of any other.

General Loewenhielm, who was to dominate the conversation of the dinner-table, related how the Dean's collection of sermons was a favourite book of the Queen's. But as a new dish was served he was silenced. "Incredible!" he told himself, "it is Blinis Demidoff!" He looked round at his fellow-diners. They were all quietly eating their Blinis Demidoff, without any sign of either surprise or approval, as if they had been doing so every day for thirty years.

A Sister on the other side of the table opened on the subject of strange happenings which had taken place while the Dean was still amongst his children, and which one might venture to call miracles. Did they remember, she asked, the time when he had promised a Christmas sermon in the village the other side of the Fiord? For a fortnight the weather had been so bad that no skipper or fisherman would risk the crossing. The villagers were giving up hope, but the Dean told them that if no boat would take him, he would come to them walking upon the waves. And behold! Three days before Christmas the storm stopped, hard frost set in, and the Fiord froze from shore to shore—and this was a thing which had not happened within the memory of man!

The boy once more filled the glasses. This time the Brothers and Sisters knew that what they were given to drink was not wine, for it sparkled. It must be some kind of lemonade. The lemonade agreed with their exalted state of mind and seemed to lift them off the ground into a higher and purer sphere.

General Loewenhielm again set down his glass, turned to his neighbour on the right and said to him: "But surely this is a Veuve Cliquot 1860?" His neighbour looked at him kindly, smiled at him and made a remark about the weather.

Babette's boy had got his instructions, he filled the glasses of the Brotherhood only once, but he refilled the General's glass as soon as it was emptied. The General emptied it quickly time after time. For how is a man of sense to behave when he cannot trust his senses? It is better to be drunk than mad.

Most often the people in Berlevaag during the course of a good meal would come to feel a little heavy. Tonight it was not so. The convives grew lighter in weight and lighter of heart the more they ate and drank. They no longer needed to remind themselves of their vow. It was, they realised, when man has not only altogether forgotten but has firmly renounced all ideas of food and drink that he eats and drinks in the right spirit.

General Loewenhielm stopped eating and sat immovable. Once more he was carried back to that dinner in Paris of which he had thought in the sledge. An incredibly recherché and palatable dish had been served there, he had asked its name from his fellow diner, Colonel Galliffet, and the Colonel had smilingly told him that it was named "Cailles en Sarcophage." He had further told him that the dish had been invented by the chef of the very café in which they were dining, a person known all over Paris as the greatest culinary genius of the age, and—most surprisingly—a woman! "And indeed," said Colonel Galliffet, "this woman is now turning a dinner at the Café Anglais into a kind of love-affair—into a love-affair of the noble and romantic category in which one no longer distinguishes between bodily and spiritual appetite or satiety! I have, before now, fought a duel for the sake of a fair lady. For no woman in all Paris, my young friend, would I more willingly shed my blood!" General Loewenhielm turned to his neighbour on the left and said to him: "But this is Cailles en Sarcophage!" The neighbour, who had been listening to the description of a miracle, looked at him absent-mindedly, then nodded his head and answered: "Yes, Yes, certainly. What else would it be?"

From the Master's miracles the talk round the table had turned to the smaller miracles of kindliness and helpfulness daily performed by his daughters. The old Brother who had first struck up the hymn quoted the Dean's saying: "The only things which we may take with us from our life on earth are those which we have given away!" The guests smiled—what Nabobs would not the poor, simple maidens become in the next world!

General Loewenhielm no longer wondered at anything. When a few minutes later he saw grapes, peaches and fresh figs before him, he laughed to his neighbour across the table and remarked: "Beautiful grapes!" His neighbour replied: "And they came on to the brook of Eshcol, and cut down a branch with one cluster of grapes. And they bare it two upon a staff."

Then the General felt that the time had come to make a speech. He rose and stood up very straight.

Nobody else by the dinner-table had stood up to speak. The old people lifted their eyes to the face above them in high, happy expectation.

They were used to seeing sailors and vagabonds dead drunk with the crass gin of the country, but they did not recognise in a warrior and courtier the intoxication brought about by the noblest wine of the world.

XI. General Loewenhielm's Speech

"Mercy and truth, my friends, have met together," said the General. "Righteousness and bliss shall kiss one another."

He spoke in a clear voice which had been trained in drill-grounds and had echoed sweetly in royal halls, and yet he was speaking in a manner so new to himself and so strangely moving that after his first sentence he had to make a pause. For he was in the habit of forming his speeches with care, conscious of his purpose, but here, in the midst of the Dean's simple congregation, it was as if the whole figure of General Loewenhielm, his breast covered with decorations, were but a mouth-piece for a message which meant to be brought forth.

"Man, my friends," said General Loewenhielm, "is frail and foolish. We have all of us been told that grace is to be found in the universe. But in our human foolishness and short-sightedness we imagine divine grace to be finite. For this reason we tremble—" Never till now had the General stated that he trembled, he was genuinely surprised and even shocked at hearing his own voice proclaim the fact. "We tremble before making our choice in life, and after having made it again tremble in fear of having chosen wrong. But the moment comes when our eyes are opened, and we see and realise that grace is infinite. Grace, my friends, demands nothing from us but that we shall await it with confidence and acknowl-edge it in gratitude. Grace, brothers, makes no conditions and singles out none of us in particular, grace takes us all to its bosom and proclaims general amnesty. See! that which we have chosen is given us, and that which we have refused is, also and at the same time, granted us. Ay, that which we have rejected is poured upon us abundantly. For mercy and truth have met together, and righteousness and bliss have kissed one another!"

The Brothers and Sisters had not altogether understood the General's speech, but his collected and inspired face and the sound of well-known and cherished words had seized and moved all hearts. In this way, after thirty-one years, General Loewenhielm succeeded in dominating the conversation at the Dean's dinner-table.

Of what happened later in the evening nothing definite can here be stated. None of the guests later on had any clear remembrance of it. They only knew that the rooms had been filled with a heavenly light, as if a number of small haloes had blended into one glorious radiance. Taciturn old people received the gift of tongues, ears that for years had been almost deaf were opened to it. Time itself had merged into eternity. Long after midnight the windows of the house shone like gold, and golden song flowed out into the winter air.

The two old women who had once slandered one another now in their hearts went back a long way, past the evil period in which they had been stuck, to those days of their early girlhood when together they had been preparing for confirmation and hand in hand had filled the roads round Berlevaag with singing. A brother in the congregation gave another a knock in the ribs, like a rough caress between boys, and cried out: "You cheated me on that timber, you old scoundrel!" The brother thus addressed almost collapsed in a heavenly burst of laughter, but tears ran from his eyes. "Yes, I did so, beloved brother," he answered. "I did so." Skipper Halvorsen and Madam Oppegaarden suddenly found themselves close together in a corner and gave one another that long, long kiss for which the secret uncertain love-affair of their youth had never left them time.

The old Dean's flock were humble people. When later in life they thought of this evening it never occurred to any of them that they might have been exalted by their own merit. They realised that the infinite grace of which General Loewenhielm had spoken had been allotted to them, and they did not even wonder at the fact, for it had been but the fulfilment of an ever-present hope. The vain illusions of this earth had dissolved before their eyes like smoke, and they had seen the universe as it really is. They had been given one hour of the millennium.

Old Mrs Loewenhielm was the first to leave. Her nephew accompanied her, and their hostesses lighted them out. While Philippa was helping the old lady into her many wraps, the General seized Martine's hand and held it for a long time without a word. At last he said:

"I have been with you every day of my life. You know, do you not, that it has been so?"

"Yes," said Martine, "I know that it has been so."

"And," he continued, "I shall be with you every day that is left to me. Every evening I shall sit down, if not in the flesh, which means nothing, in spirit, which is all, to dine with you, just like tonight. For tonight I have learned, dear sister, that in this world anything is possible."

"Yes, it is so, dear brother," said Martine. "In this world anything is possible."

Upon this they parted.

When at last the company broke up it had ceased to snow. The town and the mountains lay in white, unearthly splendour and the sky was bright with thousands of stars. In the street the snow was lying so deep that it had become difficult to walk. The guests from the yellow house wavered on their feet, staggered, sat down abruptly or fell forward on their knees and hands and were covered with snow, as if they had indeed had their sins washed white as wool, and in this regained innocent attire were gambolling like little lambs. It was, to each of them, blissful to have become as a small child, it was also a blessed joke to watch old brothers and sisters, who had been taking themselves so seriously, in this kind of celestial second childhood. They stumbled and got up, walked on or stood still, bodily as well as spiritually hand in hand, at moments performing the great chain of a beatified lanciers.

"Bless you, bless you, bless you," like an echo of the harmony of the spheres rang to all sides.

Martine and Philippa stood for a long time on the stone steps outside the house. They did not feel the cold. "The stars have come nearer," said Philippa.

"They will come every night," said Martine quietly. "Quite possibly it will never snow again."

In this, however, she was mistaken. An hour later it again began to snow, and such a heavy snowfall had never been known in Berlevaag. The next morning people could hardly push open their doors against the tall snowdrifts. The windows of the houses were so thickly covered with snow, it was told for years afterwards, that many good citizens of the town did not realise that daybreak had come, but slept on till late in the afternoon.

XII. The Great Artist

When Martine and Philippa locked the door they remembered Babette. A little wave of tenderness and pity swept through them: Babette alone had had no share in the bliss of the evening.

So they went out into the kitchen, and Martine said to Babette: "It was quite a nice dinner, Babette."

Their hearts suddenly filled with gratitude. They realised that none of their guests had said a single word about the food. Indeed, try as they might, they could not themselves remember any of the dishes which had been served. Martine bethought herself of the turtle. It had not appeared at all, and now seemed very vague and far away—it was quite possible that it had been nothing but a nightmare.

Babette sat on the chopping-block, surrounded by more black and greasy pots and pans than her mistresses had ever seen in their life. She was as white and as deadly exhausted as on the night when she had first appeared and had fainted on their doorstep.

After a long time she looked straight at them and said: "I was once Cook at the Café Anglais."

Martine said again: "They all thought that it was a nice dinner." And when Babette did not answer a word she added: "We will all remember this evening when you have gone back to Paris, Babette."

Babette said: "I am not going back to Paris."

"You are not going back to Paris?" Martine exclaimed.

"No," said Babette. "What will I do in Paris? They have all gone, I have lost them all, Mesdames."

The sisters' thoughts went to Monsieur Hersant and his son, and they said: "Oh, my poor Babette."

"Yes, they have all gone," said Babette. "The Duke of Morny, the Duke of Decazes, Prince Narishkine, General Galliffet, Aurélien Scholl, Paul Daru, the Princes Pauline! All!"

The strange names and titles of people lost to Babette faintly confused the two ladies, but there was such an infinite perspective of tragedy in her announcement that in their responsive state of mind they felt her losses as their own, and their eyes filled with tears.

At the end of another long silence Babette suddenly smiled slightly at them and said: "And how would I go back to Paris, Mesdames? I have no money."

"No money?" the sisters cried as with one mouth.

"No," said Babette.

"But the ten thousand francs?" the sisters asked in a horrified gasp.

"The ten thousand francs have been spent, Mesdames," said Babette.

The sisters sat down. For a full minute they could not speak.

"But ten thousand francs?" Martine slowly whispered.

"What will you, Mesdames," said Babette with great dignity. "A dinner for twelve at the Café Anglais would cost ten thousand francs."

The ladies still did not find a word to say. The piece of news was incomprehensible to them, but then many things tonight in one way or another had been beyond comprehension.

Martine remembered a tale told by a friend of her father's who had been a missionary in Africa. He had saved the life of an old chief's favourite wife, and to show his gratitude the chief had treated him to a rich meal. Only long afterwards the missionary learned from his own black servant that what he had partaken of was a small fat grandchild of the chief's, cooked in honour of the great Christian medicine man. She shuddered.

But Philippa's heart was melting in her bosom. It seemed that an unforgettable evening was to be finished off with an unforgettable proof of human loyalty and self-sacrifice.

"Dear Babette," she said softly, "you ought not to have given away all you had for our sake."

Babette gave her mistress a deep glance, a strange glance—was there not pity, even scorn, at the bottom of it?

"For your sake," she replied. "No. For my own."

She rose from the chopping-block and stood up before the two sisters. "I am a great artist!" she said.

She waited a moment and then repeated: "I am a great artist, Mesdames."

Again for a long time there was deep silence in the kitchen.

Then Martine said: "So you will be poor now all your life, Babette?"

"Poor?" said Babette. She smiled as if to herself. "No. I shall never be poor. I told you that I am a great artist. A great artist, Mesdames, is never poor. We have got something, Mesdames, of which other people know nothing."

While the elder sister found nothing more to say, in Philippa's heart deep, forgotten chords vibrated. For she had heard, before now, long ago, of the Café Anglais. She had heard, before now, long ago, the names on Babette's tragic list. She rose and took a step towards her servant.

"But all those people whom you have mentioned," she said, "those princes and great people of Paris whom you named, Babette? You yourself fought against them. You were a Communard! The General you named had your husband and son shot! How can you grieve over them?"

Babette's dark eyes met Philippa's.

"Yes," she said, "I was a Communard. Thanks be to God, I was a Communard! And those people whom I named, Mesdames, were evil and cruel. They let the people of Paris starve, they oppressed and wronged the poor. Thanks be to God, I stood upon a barricade, I loaded the gun for my men-folk! But all the same, Mesdames, I shall not go back to Paris, now that those people of whom I have spoken are no longer there."

She stood immovable, lost in thought.

"You see, Mesdames," she said, at last, "those people belonged to me, they were mine. They had been brought up and trained, with greater expense than you, my little ladies, could ever imagine or believe, to understand what a great artist I am. I could make them happy. When I did my very best I could make them perfectly happy."

She paused for a moment.

"It was like that with Monsieur Papin too," she said.

"With Monsieur Papin?" Philippa asked.

"Yes, with your Monsieur Papin, my poor lady," said Babette. "He told me so himself: 'It is terrible and unbearable to an artist,' he said, 'to be encouraged to do, to be applauded for doing, his second best.' He said: 'Through all the world there goes one long cry from the heart of the artist: Give me leave to do my utmost!' "

Philippa went up to Babette and put her arms round her. She felt the Cook's body like a marble monument against her own, but she herself shook and trembled from head to foot.

For a while she could not speak. Then she whispered:

"Yet this is not the end! I feel, Babette, that this is not the end. In

Paradise you will be the great artist that God meant you to be! Ah!"she added, the tears streaming down her cheeks, "ah, how you will enchant the angels!"

KATHERINE MANSFIELD

(1888–1923)

*K*atherine Mansfield was the pen name of Kathleen Mansfield Beau-
champ, who was born in Wellington, New Zealand, the daughter
of a wealthy, self-made business tycoon, a figure she portrayed as overbearing and frightening in her autobiographical fiction, and an invalid
mother who taught her courage in the face of adversity. She was a lonely,
withdrawn, rebellious child who had only mixed success at school because
of her attitude. She went to England with her family to study music at
Queen's College, London. Forced to return to New Zealand after three
years, Mansfield reacted against the stifling parochialism and conven-
tionality of her native land and yearned for England. She read writers
such as Ruskin, Morris, Shaw, and Whitman, writers who passionately
believed that creative art could change the world, as well as Tolstoy,
Dostoevsky, and Chekhov. Back in England, she gave up music, married
one man while pregnant by another (she later miscarried), and eventually
left for Germany, almost certainly suffering from the gonorrhea that,
along with tuberculosis, was to cause her death at 34. Her first volume
of stories, **In a German Pension** (1911), received favourable reviews in
English newspapers. In that same year, she met John Middleton Murry,
the editor-critic who moved in with her in April 1912. In the years of
poverty, squalor, but intense literary excitement (such as a tumultuous,
searing contact with D.H. Lawrence and his wife Frieda), Katherine
Mansfield wrote the stories that secured her a reputation as the pre-
eminent writer of such collections of short fiction as Bliss (1920), **The
Garden Party** (1922), and The Dove's Nest (1923). Claire Tomalin
has summarized her perennial appeal this way:

> It was not only the delicacy, charm and pathos attributed to her
> by Lawrence. The sharp impersonality, the clarity and concision
> of the best stories made them genuinely startling. Her voice
> was the voice of modernity, bright, short-winded, sometimes
> whimsical, often ambiguous. . . . Her territory was that of the
> fragile emotions, half-understood feelings, the fine edge between
> the ridiculous and the stirrings of the sick, the jealous, the
> powerless, those who make animals or inanimate objects the
> focus of their feelings.

The Daughters of the Late Colonel

1

The week after was one of the busiest weeks of their lives. Even when they went to bed it was only their bodies that lay down and rested; their minds went on, thinking things out, talking things over, wondering, deciding, trying to remember where . . .

Constantia lay like a statue, her hands by her sides, her feet just overlapping each other, the sheet up to her chin. She stared at the ceiling.

"Do you think father would mind if we gave his top-hat to the porter?"

"The porter?" snapped Josephine. "Why ever the porter? What a very extraordinary idea!"

"Because," said Constantia slowly, "he must often have to go to funerals. And I noticed at—at the cemetery that he only had a bowler." She paused. "I thought then how very much he'd appreciate a top-hat. We ought to give him a present, too. He was always very nice to father."

"But," cried Josephine, flouncing on her pillow and staring across the dark at Constantia, "father's head!" And suddenly, for one awful moment, she nearly giggled. Not, of course, that she felt in the least like giggling. It must have been habit. Years ago, when they had stayed awake at night talking, their beds had simply heaved. And now the porter's head, disappearing, popped out, like a candle, under father's hat. . . . The giggle mounted, mounted; she clenched her hands; she fought it down; she frowned fiercely at the dark and said "Remember" terribly sternly.

"We can decide to-morrow," she sighed.

Constantia had noticed nothing; she sighed.

"Do you think we ought to have our dressing-gowns dyed as well?"

"Black?" almost shrieked Josephine.

"Well, what else?" said Constantia. "I was thinking—it doesn't seem quite sincere, in a way, to wear black out of doors and when we're fully dressed, and then when we're at home—"

"But nobody sees us," said Josephine. She gave the bedclothes such a twitch that both her feet became uncovered, and she had to creep up the pillows to get them well under again.

"Kate does," said Constantia. "And the postman very well might."

Josephine thought of her dark-red slippers, which matched her dressing-gown, and of Constantia's favourite indefinite green ones which went with hers. Black! Two black dressing-gowns and two pairs of black woolly slippers, creeping off to the bathroom like black cats.

"I don't think it's absolutely necessary," said she.

Silence. Then Constantia said, "We shall have to post the papers with the notice in them to-morrow to catch the Ceylon mail. . . . How many letters have we had up till now?"

"Twenty-three."

Josephine had replied to them all, and twenty-three times when she came to "We miss our dear father so much" she had broken down and had to use her handkerchief, and on some of them even to soak up a very light-blue tear with an edge of blotting-paper. Strange! She couldn't have put it on—but twenty-three times. Even now, though, when she said over to herself sadly. "We miss our dear father *so* much" she could have cried if she'd wanted to.

"Have you got enough stamps?" came from Constantia.

"Oh, how can I tell?" said Josephine crossly. "What's the good of asking me that now?"

"I was just wondering," said Constantia mildly.

Silence again. There came a little rustle, a scurry, a hop.

"A mouse," said Constantia.

"It can't be a mouse because there aren't any crumbs," said Josephine.

"But it doesn't know there aren't," said Constantia.

A spasm of pity squeezed her heart. Poor little thing! She wished she'd left a tiny piece of biscuit on the dressing-table. It was awful to think of it not finding anything. What would it do?

"I can't think how they manage to live at all," she said slowly.

"Who?" demanded Josephine.

And Constantia said more loudly than she meant to, "Mice."

Josephine was furious. "Oh, what nonsense, Con!" she said. "What have mice got to do with it? You're asleep."

"I don't think I am," said Constantia. She shut her eyes to make sure. She was.

Josephine arched her spine, pulled up her knees, folded her arms so that her fists came under her ears, and pressed her cheek hard against the pillow.

2

Another thing which complicated matters was they had Nurse Andrews staying on with them that week. It was their own fault; they had asked her. It was Josephine's idea. On the morning—well, on the last morning, when the doctor had gone, Josephine had said to Constantia, "Don't you think it would be rather nice if we asked Nurse Andrews to stay on for a week as our guest?"

"Very nice," said Constantia.

"I thought," went on Josephine quickly, "I should just say this afternoon, after I've paid her, 'My sister and I would be very pleased, after all you've done for us, Nurse Andrews, if you would stay on for a week as our guest.' I'd have to put that in about being our guest in case—"

"Oh, but she could hardly expect to be paid!" cried Constantia.

"One never knows," said Josephine sagely.

Nurse Andrews had, of course, jumped at the idea. But it was a bother. It meant they had to have regular sit-down meals at the proper times, whereas if they'd been alone they could just have asked Kate if she wouldn't have minded bringing them a tray wherever they were. And meal-times now that the strain was over were rather a trial.

Nurse Andrews was simply fearful about butter. Really they couldn't help feeling that about butter, at least, she took advantage of their kindness. And she had that maddening habit of asking for just an inch more bread to finish what she had on her plate, and then, at the last mouthful, absent-mindedly—of course it wasn't absent-mindedly—taking another helping. Josephine got very red when this happened, and she fastened her small, bead-like eyes on the tablecloth as if she saw a minute strange insect creeping through the web of it. But Constantia's long, pale face lengthened and set, and she gazed away—away—far over the desert, to where that line of camels unwound like a thread of wool. . . .

"When I was with Lady Tukes," said Nurse Andrews, "she had such a dainty little contrayvance for the buttah. It was a silvah Cupid balanced on the—on the bordah of a glass dish, holding a tayny fork. And when you wanted some buttah you simply pressed his foot and he bent down and spread you a piece. It was quite a gayme."

Josephine could hardly bear that. But "I think those things are very extravagant" was all she said.

"But whey?" asked Nurse Andrews, beaming through her eye-glasses. "No one, surely, would take more buttah than one wanted—would one?"

"Ring, Con," cried Josephine. She couldn't trust herself to reply.

And proud young Kate, the enchanted princess, came in to see what the old tabbies wanted now. She snatched away their plates of mock something or other and slapped down a white, terrified blancmange.

"Jam, please, Kate," said Josephine kindly.

Kate knelt and burst open the sideboard, lifted the lid of the jam-pot, saw it was empty, put it on the table, and stalked off.

"I'm afraid," said Nurse Andrews a moment later, "there isn't any."

"Oh, what a bother!" said Josephine. She bit her lip. "What had we better do?"

Constantia looked dubious. "We can't disturb Kate again," she said softly.

Nurse Andrews waited, smiling at them both. Her eyes wandered, spying at everything behind her eye-glasses. Constantia in despair went back to her camels. Josephine frowned heavily—concentrated. If it hadn't been for this idiotic woman she and Con would, of course, have eaten their blancmange without. Suddenly the idea came.

"I know," she said. "Marmalade. There's some marmalade in the sideboard. Get it, Con."

"I hope," laughed Nurse Andrews, and her laugh was like a spoon tinkling against a medicine-glass—"I hope it's not very bittah marmalayde."

3

But, after all, it was not long now, and then she'd be gone for good. And there was no getting over the fact that she had been very kind to father. She had nursed him day and night at the end. Indeed, both Constantia and Josephine felt privately she had rather overdone the not leaving him at the very last. For when they had gone in to say good-bye Nurse Andrews had sat beside his bed the whole time, holding his wrist and pretending to look at her watch. It couldn't have been necessary. It was so tactless, too. Supposing father had wanted to say something— something private to them. Not that he had. Oh, far from it! He lay there, purple, a dark, angry purple in the face, and never even looked at them when they came in. Then, as they were standing there, wondering what to do, he had suddenly opened one eye. Oh, what a difference it would have made, what a difference to their memory of him, how much easier to tell people about it, if he had only opened both! But no—one eye only. It glared at them a moment and then . . . went out.

4

It had made it very awkward for them when Mr. Farolles, of St. John's, called the same afternoon.

"The end was quite peaceful, I trust?" were the first words he said as he glided towards them through the dark drawing-room.

"Quite," said Josephine faintly. They both hung their heads. Both of them felt certain that eye wasn't at all a peaceful eye.

"Won't you sit down?" said Josephine.

"Thank you, Miss Pinner," said Mr. Farolles gratefully. He folded his coat-tails and began to lower himself into father's armchair, but just as he touched it he almost sprang up and slid into the next chair instead.

He coughed. Josephine clasped her hands; Constantia looked vague.

"I want you to feel, Miss Pinner," said Mr. Farolles, "and you, Miss Constantia, that I'm trying to be helpful. I want to be helpful to you both, if you will let me. These are the times," said Mr. Farolles, very simply and earnestly, "when God means us to be helpful to one another."

"Thank you very much, Mr. Farolles," said Josephine and Constantia.

"Not at all," said Mr. Farolles gently. He drew his kid gloves through his fingers and leaned forward. "And if either of you would like a little Communion, either or both of you, here *and* now, you have only to tell me. A little Communion is often very help—a great comfort," he added tenderly.

But the idea of a little Communion terrified them. What! in the drawing-room by themselves—with no—no altar or anything! The piano would be much too high, thought Constantia, and Mr. Farolles could not possibly lean over it with the chalice. And Kate would be sure to come bursting in and interrupt them, thought Josephine. And supposing the bell rang in the middle? It might be somebody important—about their mourning. Would they get up reverently and go out, or would they have to wait . . . in torture?

"Perhaps you will send round a note by your good Kate if you would care for it later," said Mr. Farolles.

"Oh yes, thank you very much!" they both said.

Mr. Farolles got up and took his black straw hat from the round table.

"And about the funeral," he said softly. "I may arrange that—as your dear father's old friend and yours, Miss Pinner—and Miss Constantia?"

Josephine and Constantia got up too.

"I should like it to be quite simple," said Josephine firmly, "and not too expensive. At the same time, I should like—"

"A good one that will last," thought dreamy Constantia, as if Josephine were buying a nightgown. But of course Josephine didn't say that. "One suitable to our father's position." She was very nervous.

"I'll run round to our good friend Mr. Knight," said Mr. Farolles soothingly. "I will ask him to come and see you. I am sure you will find him very helpful indeed."

5

Well, at any rate, all that part of it was over, though neither of them could possibly believe that father was never coming back. Josephine had had a moment of absolute terror at the cemetery, while the coffin was lowered, to think that she and Constantia had done this thing without asking his permission. What would father say when he found out? For he was bound to find out sooner or later. He always did. "Buried. You two girls had me *buried!*" She heard his stick thumping. Oh, what would they say? What possible excuse could they make? It sounded such an appallingly heartless thing to do. Such a wicked advantage to take of a person because he happened to be helpless at the moment. The other people seemed to treat it all as a matter of course. They were strangers; they couldn't be expected to understand that father was the very last person for such a thing to happen to. No, the entire blame for it all would fall on her and Constantia. And the expense, she thought, stepping into the tight-buttoned cab. When she had to show him the bills. What would he say then?

She heard him absolutely roaring, "And do you expect me to pay for this gimcrack excursion of yours?"

"Oh," groaned poor Josephine aloud, "we shouldn't have done it, Con!"

And Constantia, pale as a lemon in all that blackness, said in a frightened whisper, "Done what, Jug?"

"Let them bu-bury father like that," said Josephine, breaking down and crying into her new, queer-smelling mourning handkerchief.

"But what else could we have done?" asked Constantia wonderingly. "We couldn't have kept him, Jug—we couldn't have kept him unburied. At any rate, not in a flat that size."

Josephine blew her nose; the cab was dreadfully stuffy.

"I don't know,"she said forlornly. "It is all so dreadful. I feel we ought to have tried to, just for a time at least. To make perfectly sure. One thing's certain"—and her tears sprang out again—"father will never forgive us for this—never!"

6

Father would never forgive them. That was what they felt more than ever when, two mornings later, they went into his room to go through his things. They had discussed it quite calmly. It was even down on Josephine's list of things to be done. *Go through father's things and settle about them.* But that was a very different matter from saying after breakfast:

"Well, are you ready, Con?"

"Yes, Jug—when you are."

"Then I think we'd better get it over."

It was dark in the hall. It had been a rule for years never to disturb father in the morning, whatever happened. And now they were going to open the door without knocking even. . . . Constantia's eyes were enormous at the idea; Josephine felt weak in the knees.

"You—you go first," she gasped, pushing Constantia.

But Constantia said, as she always had said on those occasions, "No, Jug, that's not fair. You're eldest."

Josephine was just going to say—what at other times she wouldn't have owned to for the world—what she kept for her very last weapon,

"But you're tallest," when they noticed that the kitchen door was open, and there stood Kate. . . .

"Very stiff," said Josephine, grasping the door-handle and doing her best to turn it. As if anything ever deceived Kate!

It couldn't be helped. That girl was . . . Then the door was shut behind them, but—but they weren't in father's room at all. They might have suddenly walked through the wall by mistake into a different flat together. Was the door just behind them? They were too frightened to look. Josephine knew that if it was it was holding itself tight shut; Constantia felt that, like the doors in dreams, it hadn't any handle at all. It was the coldness which made it so awful. Or the whiteness—which? Everything was covered. The blinds were down, a cloth hung over the mirror, a sheet hid the bed; a huge fan of white paper filled the fireplace. Constantia timidly put out her hand; she almost expected a snowflake to fall. Josephine felt a queer tingling in her nose, as if her nose was freezing. Then a cab klop-klopped over the cobbles below, and the quiet seemed to shake into little pieces.

"I had better pull up a blind," said Josephine bravely.

"Yes, it might be a good idea," whispered Constantia.

They only gave the blind a touch, but it flew up and the cord flew after, rolling round the blindstick, and the little tassel tapped as if trying to get free. That was too much for Constantia.

"Don't you think—don't you think we might put it off for another day?" she whispered.

"Why?" snapped Josephine, feeling, as usual, much better now that she knew for certain that Constantia was terrified. "It's got to be done. But I do wish you wouldn't whisper, Con."

"I didn't know I was whispering," whispered Constantia.

"And why do you keep on staring at the bed?" said Josephine, raising her voice almost defiantly. "There's nothing *on* the bed."

"Oh, Jug, don't say so!" said poor Connie. "At any rate, not so loudly."

Josephine felt herself that she had gone too far. She took a wide swerve over to the chest of drawers, put out her hand, but quickly drew it back again.

"Connie!" she gasped, and she wheeled round and leaned with her back against the chest of drawers.

"Oh, Jug—what?"

Josephine could only glare. She had the most extraordinary feeling that she had just escaped something simply awful. But how could she explain to Constantia that father was in the chest of drawers? He was in the top drawer with his handkerchiefs and neckties, or in the next with his shirts and pyjamas, or in the lowest of all with his suits. He was watching there, hidden away—just behind the door-handle—ready to spring.

She pulled a funny old-fashioned face at Constantia, just as she used to in the old days when she was going to cry.

"I can't open," she nearly wailed.

"No, don't, Jug," whispered Constantia earnestly. "It's much better not to. Don't let's open anything. At any rate, not for a long time."

"But—but it seems so weak," said Josephine, breaking down.

"But why not be weak for once, Jug?" argued Constantia, whispering quite fiercely. "If it is weak." And her pale stare flew from the locked writing-table—so safe—to the huge glittering wardrobe, and she began to breathe in a queer, panting way. "Why shouldn't we be weak for once in our lives, Jug? It's quite excusable. Let's be weak—be weak, Jug. It's much nicer to be weak than to be strong."

And then she did one of those amazingly bold things that she'd done about twice before in their lives; she marched over to the wardrobe, turned the key, and took it out of the lock. Took it out of the lock and held it up to Josephine, showing Josephine by her extraordinary smile that she knew what she'd done, she'd risked deliberately father being in there among his overcoats.

If the huge wardrobe had lurched forward, had crashed down on Constantia, Josephine wouldn't have been surprised. On the contrary, she would have thought it the only suitable thing to happen. But nothing happened. Only the room seemed quieter than ever, and bigger flakes of cold air fell on Josephine's shoulders and knees. She began to shiver.

"Come, Jug," said Constantia, still with that awful callous smile, and Josephine followed just as she had that last time, when Constantia had pushed Benny into the round pond.

7

But the strain told on them when they were back in the dining-room. They sat down, very shaky, and looked at each other.

"I don't feel I can settle to anything," said Josephine, "until I've had something. Do you think we could ask Kate for two cups of hot water?"

"I really don't see why we shouldn't," said Constantia carefully. She was quite normal again. "I won't ring. I'll go to the kitchen door and ask her."

"Yes, do" said Josephine, sinking down into a chair. "Tell her, just two cups, Con, nothing else—on a tray."

"She needn't even put the jug on, need she?" said Constantia, as though Kate might very well complain if the jug had been there.

"Oh no, certainly not! The jug's not at all necessary. She can pour it direct out of the kettle," cried Josephine, feeling that would be a labour-saving indeed.

Their cold lips quivered at the greenish brims. Josephine curved her small red hands round the cup; Constantia sat up and blew on the wavy stream, making it flutter from one side to the other.

"Speaking of Benny," said Josephine.

And though Benny hadn't been mentioned Constantia immediately looked as though he had.

"He'll expect us to send him something of father's, of course. But it's so difficult to know what to send to Ceylon."

"You mean things get unstuck so on the voyage," murmured Constantia.

"No, lost," said Josephine sharply. "You know there's no post. Only runners."

Both paused to watch a black man in white linen drawers running through the pale fields for dear life, with a large brown-paper parcel in his hands. Josephine's black man was tiny; he scurried along glistening like an ant. But there was something blind and tireless about Constantia's tall, thin fellow, which made him, she decided, a very unpleasant person indeed. . . . On the veranda, dressed all in white and wearing a cork helmet, stood Benny. His right hand shook up and down, as father's did when he was impatient. And behind him, not in the least interested, sat Hilda, the unknown sister-in-law. She swung in a cane rocker and flicked over the leaves of the *Tatler*.

"I think his watch would be the most suitable present," said Josephine.

Constantia looked up; she seemed surprised.

"Oh, would you trust a gold watch to a native?"

"But of course I'd disguise it," said Josephine. "No one would know it was a watch." She liked the idea of having to make a parcel such a curious shape that no one could possibly guess what it was. She even thought for a moment of hiding the watch in a narrow cardboard corset-box that she'd kept by her for a long time, waiting for it to come in for something. It was such beautiful firm cardboard. But, no, it wouldn't be appropriate for this occasion. It had lettering on it: *Medium Women's 28. Extra Firm Busks.* It would be almost too much of a surprise for Benny to open that and find father's watch inside.

"And of course it isn't as though it would be going—ticking, I mean," said Constantia, who was still thinking of the native love of jewellery. "At least," she added, "it would be very strange if after all that time it was."

8

Josephine made no reply. She had flown off on one of her tangents. She had suddenly thought of Cyril. Wasn't it more usual for the only grandson to have the watch? And then dear Cyril was so appreciative, and a gold watch meant so much to a young man. Benny, in all probability, had quite got out of the habit of watches; men so seldom wore waistcoats in those hot climates. Whereas Cyril in London wore them from year's end to year's end. And it would be so nice for her and Constantia, when he came to tea, to know it was there. "I see you've got on grandfather's watch, Cyril." It would be somehow so satisfactory.

Dear boy! What a blow his sweet, sympathetic little note had been! Of course they quite understood; but it was most unfortunate.

"It would have been such a point, having him," said Josephine.

"And he would have enjoyed it so," said Constantia, not thinking what she was saying.

However, as soon as he got back he was coming to tea with his aunties. Cyril to tea was one of their rare treats.

"Now, Cyril, you mustn't be frightened of our cakes. Your Auntie Con and I bought them at Buszard's this morning. We know what a man's appetite is. So don't be ashamed of making a good tea."

Josephine cut recklessly into the rich dark cake that stood for her winter gloves or the soling and heeling of Constantia's only respectable shoes. But Cyril was most unmanlike in appetite.

"I say, Aunt Josephine, I simply can't. I've only just had lunch, you know."

"Oh, Cyril, that can't be true! It's after four," cried Josephine. Constantia sat with her knife poised over the chocolate-roll.

"It is, all the same," said Cyril. "I had to meet a man at Victoria, and he kept me hanging about till . . . there was only time to get lunch and to come on here. And he gave me—phew"—Cyril put his hand to his forehead—"a terrific blow-out," he said.

It was disappointing—to-day of all days. But still he couldn't be expected to know.

"But you'll have a meringue, won't you, Cyril?" said Aunt Josephine. "These meringues were bought specially for you. Your dear father was so fond of them. We were sure you are, too."

"I *am*, Aunt Josephine," cried Cyril ardently. "Do you mind if I take half to begin with?"

"Not at all, dear boy; but we mustn't let you off with that."

"Is your dear father still so fond of meringues?" asked Auntie Con gently. She winced faintly as she broke through the shell of hers.

"Well, I don't quite know, Auntie Con," said Cyril breezily. At that they both looked up.

"Don't know?" almost snapped Josephine. "Don't know a thing like that about your own father, Cyril?"

"Surely," said Auntie Con softly.

Cyril tried to laugh it off. "Oh, well," he said, "it's such a long time since—" He faltered. He stopped. Their faces were too much for him.

"Even *so*," said Josephine.

And Auntie Con looked.

Cyril put down his teacup. "Wait a bit," he cried. "Wait a bit, Aunt Josephine. What am I thinking of?"

He looked up. They were beginning to brighten. Cyril slapped his knee.

"Of course," he said, "it was meringues. How could I have forgotten? Yes, Aunt Josephine, you're perfectly right. Father's most frightfully keen on meringues."

They didn't only beam. Aunt Josephine went scarlet with pleasure; Auntie Con gave a deep, deep sigh.

"And now, Cyril, you must come and see father," said Josephine. "He knows you were coming to-day."

"Right," said Cyril, very firmly and heartily. He got up from his chair; suddenly he glanced at the clock.

"I say, Auntie Con, isn't your clock a bit slow? I've got to meet a man at—at Paddington just after five. I'm afraid I shan't be able to stay very long with grandfather."

"Oh, he won't expect you to stay *very* long!" said Aunt Josephine.

Constantia was still gazing at the clock. She couldn't make up her mind if it was fast or slow. It was one or the other, she felt almost certain of that. At any rate, it had been.

Cyril still lingered. "Aren't you coming along, Auntie Con?"

"Of course," said Josephine, "we shall all go. Come on, Con."

9

They knocked at the door, and Cyril followed his aunts into grandfather's hot, sweetish room.

"Come on," said Grandfather Pinner. "Don't hang about. What is it? What've you been up to?"

He was sitting in front of a roaring fire, clasping his stick. He had a thick rug over his knees. On his lap there lay a beautiful pale yellow silk handkerchief.

"It's Cyril, father," said Josephine shyly. And she took Cyril's hand and led him forward.

"Good afternoon, grandfather," said Cyril, trying to take his hand out of Aunt Josephine's. Grandfather Pinner shot his eyes at Cyril in the way he was famous for. Where was Auntie Con? She stood on the other side of Aunt Josephine; her long arms hung down in front of her; her hands were clasped. She never took her eyes off grandfather.

"Well," said Grandfather Pinner, beginning to thump, "What have you got to tell me?"

.

What had he, what had he got to tell him? Cyril felt himself smiling like a perfect imbecile. The room was stifling, too.

But Aunt Josephine came to his rescue. She cried brightly, "Cyril says his father is still very fond of meringues, father dear."

"Eh?" said Grandfather Pinner, curving his hand like a purple meringue-shell over one ear.

Josephine repeated, "Cyril says his father is still very fond of meringues."

"Can't hear," said old Colonel Pinner. And he waved Josephine away with his stick, then pointed with his stick to Cyril. "Tell me what she's trying to say," he said.

(My God!) "Must I?" said Cyril, blushing and staring at Aunt Josephine.

"Do, dear," she smiled. "It will please him so much."

"Come on, out with it!" cried Colonel Pinner testily, beginning to thump again.

And Cyril leaned forward and yelled, "Father's still very fond of meringues."

At that Grandfather Pinner jumped as though he had been shot.

"Don't shout!" he cried. "What's the matter with the boy? *Meringues!* What about 'em?"

"Oh, Aunt Josephine, must we go on?" groaned Cyril desperately.

"It's quite all right, dear boy," said Aunt Josephine, as though he and she were at the dentist's together. "He'll understand in a minute." And she whispered to Cyril, "He's getting a bit deaf, you know." Then she leaned forward and really bawled at Grandfather Pinner, "Cyril only wanted to tell you, father dear, that *his* father is still very fond of meringues."

Colonel Pinner heard that time, heard and brooded, looking Cyril up and down.

"What an esstrordinary thing!" said old Grandfather Pinner. "What an esstrordinary thing to come all this way here to tell me!"

And Cyril felt it *was*.

"Yes, I shall send Cyril the watch," said Josephine.

"That would be very nice," said Constantia. "I seem to remember last time he came there was some little trouble about the time."

10

They were interrupted by Kate bursting through the door in her usual fashion, as though she had discovered some secret panel in the wall.

"Fried or boiled?" asked the bold voice.

Fried or boiled? Josephine and Constantia were quite bewildered for the moment. They could hardly take it in.

"Fried or boiled what, Kate?" asked Josephine, trying to begin to concentrate.

Kate gave a loud sniff. "Fish."

"Well, why didn't you say so immediately?" Josephine reproached her gently. "How could you expect us to understand, Kate? There are a great many things in this world, you know, which are fried or boiled." And after such a display of courage she said quite brightly to Constantia, "Which do you prefer, Con?"

"I think it might be nice to have it fried," said Constantia. "On the other hand, of course boiled fish is very nice. I think I prefer both equally well . . . Unless you . . . In that case—"

"I shall fry it," said Kate, and she bounced back, leaving their door open and slamming the door of her kitchen.

Josephine gazed at Constantia; she raised her pale eyebrows until they rippled away into her pale hair. She got up. She said in a very lofty, imposing way, "Do you mind following me into the drawing-room, Constantia? I've something of great importance to discuss with you."

For it was always to the drawing-room they retired when they wanted to talk over Kate.

Josephine closed the door meaningly. "Sit down, Constantia," she said, still very grand. She might have been receiving Constantia for the first time. And Con looked round vaguely for a chair, as though she felt indeed quite a stranger.

"Now the question is," said Josephine, bending forward, "whether we shall keep her or not."

"That is the question," agreed Constantia.

"And this time," said Josephine firmly, "we must come to a definite decision."

Constantia looked for a moment as though she might begin going over all the other times, but she pulled herself together and said, "Yes, Jug."

"You see, Con," explained Josephine, "everything is so changed now." Constantia looked up quickly. "I mean," went on Josephine, "we're not dependent on Kate as we were." And she blushed faintly. "There's not father to cook for."

"That is perfectly true," agreed Constantia. "Father certainly doesn't want any cooking now, whatever else—"

Josephine broke in sharply. "You're not sleepy, are you, Con?"

"Sleepy, Jug?" Constantia was wide-eyed.

"Well, concentrate more," said Josephine sharply, and she returned to the subject. "What it comes to is, if we did"—and this she barely breathed, glancing at the door—"give Kate notice"—she raised her voice again—"we could manage our own food."

"Why not?" cried Constantia. She couldn't help smiling. The idea was so exciting. She clasped her hands. "What should we live on, Jug?"

"Oh, eggs in various forms!" said Jug, lofty again. "And, besides, there are all the cooked foods."

"But I've always heard," said Constantia, "they are considered so very expensive."

"Not if one buys them in moderation," said Josephine. But she tore herself away from this fascinating bypath and dragged Constantia after her.

"What we've got to decide now, however, is whether we really do trust Kate or not."

Constantia leaned back. Her flat little laugh flew from her lips.

"Isn't it curious, Jug," said she, "that just on this one subject I've never been able to quite make up my mind?"

11

She never had. The whole difficulty was to prove anything. How did one prove things, how could one? Suppose Kate had stood in front of her and deliberately made a face. Mightn't she very well have been in pain? Wasn't it impossible, at any rate, to ask Kate if she was making a face at her? If Kate answered "No"—and of course she would say "No"—what a position! How undignified! Then again Constantia suspected, she was almost certain that Kate went to her chest of drawers when she and Josephine were out, not to take things but to spy. Many times she had come back to find her amethyst cross in the most unlikely places, under her lace ties or on top of her evening Bertha. More than once she had laid a trap for Kate. She had arranged things in a special order and then called Josephine to witness.

"You see, Jug?"

"Quite, Con."

"Now we shall be able to tell."

But, oh dear, when she did go to look, she was as far off from a proof as ever! If anything was displaced, it might so very well have happened as she closed the drawer; a jolt might have done it so easily.

"You come, Jug, and decide. I really can't. It's too difficult."

But after a pause and a long glare Josephine would sigh, "Now you've put the doubt into my mind, Con, I'm sure I can't tell myself."

"Well, we can't postpone it again," said Josephine. "If we postpone it this time—"

12

But at that moment in the street below a barrel-organ struck up. Josephine and Constantia sprang to their feet together.

"Run, Con," said Josephine. "Run quickly. There's sixpence on the—"

Then they remembered. It didn't matter. They would never have to stop the organ-grinder again. Never again would she and Constantia be told to make that monkey take his noise somewhere else. Never would sound that loud, strange bellow when father thought they were not hurrying enough. The organ-grinder might play there all day and the stick would not thump.

> *It never will thump again,*
> *It never will thump again,*

played the barrel-organ.

What was Constantia thinking? She had such a strange smile; she looked different. She couldn't be going to cry.

"Jug, Jug," said Constantia softly, pressing her hands together. "Do you know what day it is? It's Saturday. It's a week to-day, a whole week."

> *A week since father died,*
> *A week since father died,*

cried the barrel-organ. And Josephine, too, forgot to be practical and sensible; she smiled faintly, strangely. On the Indian carpet there fell a square of sunlight, pale red; it came and went and came—and stayed, deepened—until it shone almost golden.

"The sun's out," said Josephine, as though it really mattered.

A perfect fountain of bubbling notes shook from the barrel-organ, round, bright notes, carelessly scattered.

Constantia lifted her big, cold hands as if to catch them, and then her hands fell again. She walked over to the mantelpiece to her favourite Buddha. And the stone and gilt image, whose smile always gave her such a queer feeling, almost a pain and yet a pleasant pain, seemed to-day to be more than smiling. He knew something; he had a secret. "I know something that you don't know," said her Buddha. Oh, what was it, what could it be? And yet she had always felt there was . . . something.

The sunlight pressed through the windows, thieved its way in, flashed its light over the furniture and the photographs. Josephine watched it. When it came to mother's photograph, the enlargement over the piano, it lingered as though puzzled to find so little remained of mother, except the earrings shaped like tiny pagodas and a black feather boa. Why did the photographs of dead people always fade so? wondered Josephine. As soon as a person was dead their photograph died too. But, of course, this one of mother was very old. It was thirty-five years old. Josephine remembered standing on a chair and pointing out that feather boa to Constantia and telling her that it was a snake that had killed their mother in Ceylon. . . . Would everything have been different if mother hadn't died? She didn't see why. Aunt Florence had lived with them until they had left school, and they had moved three times and had their yearly holiday and . . . and there'd been changes of servants, of course.

Some little sparrows, young sparrows they sounded, chirped on the window-ledge. *Yeep—eyeep—yeep.* But Josephine felt they were not sparrows, not on the window-ledge. It was inside her, that queer little crying noise. *Yeep—eyeep—yeep.* Ah, what was it crying, so weak and forlorn?

If mother had lived, might they have married? But there had been nobody for them to marry. There had been father's Anglo-Indian friends before he quarrelled with them. But after that she and Constantia never met a single man except clergymen. How did one meet men? Or even if they'd met them, how could they have got to know men well enough to be more than strangers? One read of people having adventures, being followed, and so on. But nobody had ever followed Constantia and her. Oh yes, there had been one year at Eastbourne a mysterious man at their boarding-house who had put a note on the jug of hot water outside their bedroom door! But by the time Connie had found it the steam had made the writing too faint to read; they couldn't even make out to which of them it was addressed. And he had left next day. And that was all. The rest had been looking after father, and at the same time keeping out of father's way. But now? But now? The thieving sun touched Josephine gently. She lifted her face. She was drawn over to the window by gentle beams. . . .

Until the barrel-organ stopped playing Constantia stayed before the Buddha, wondering, but not as usual, not vaguely. This time her wonder was like longing. She remembered the times she had come in here, crept out of bed in her nightgown when the moon was full, and lain on the floor with her arms outstretched, as though she was crucified. Why? The big, pale moon had made her do it. The horrible dancing figures on the carved screen had leered at her and she hadn't minded. She remembered too how, whenever they were at the seaside, she had gone off by herself and got as close to the sea as she could, and sung something, something she had made up, while she gazed all over that restless water. There had been this other life, running out, bringing things home in bags, getting things on approval, discussing them with Jug, and taking them back to get more things on approval, and arranging father's trays and trying not to annoy father. But it all seemed to have happened in a kind of tunnel. It wasn't real. It was only when she came out of the tunnel into the moonlight or by the sea or into a thunderstorm that she really felt herself. What did it mean? What was it she was always wanting? What did it all lead to? Now? Now?

She turned away from the Buddha with one of her vague gestures. She went over to where Josephine was standing. She wanted to say something to Josephine, something frightfully important, about—about the future and what . . .

"Don't you think perhaps—" she began.

But Josephine interrupted her. "I was wondering if now—" she murmured. They stopped; they waited for each other.

"Go on, Con," said Josephine.

"No, no Jug; after you," said Constantia.

"No, say what you were going to say. You began," said Josephine.

"I . . . I'd rather hear what you were going to say first," said Constantia.

"Don't be absurd, Con."

"Really, Jug."

"Connie!"

"Oh, *Jug!*"

A pause. Then Constantia said faintly, "I can't say what I was going to say, Jug, because I've forgotten what it was . . . that I was going to say."

Josephine was silent for a moment. She stared at a big cloud where the sun had been. Then she replied shortly, "I've forgotten too."

ETHEL WILSON

(1888–1980)

E thel Wilson was born in Port Elizabeth, South Africa, where her mother died when she was only 18 months old. She emigrated to England with her father, where at the age of 9 she was orphaned, and subsequently moved at age 10 to Vancouver to live with relatives. For thirteen years Wilson taught in Vancouver's public school system, and as a young woman she took painting lessons from (as she describes her teacher) "a forthright woman named Emily Carr who lived upstairs on Granville St. at that time." Wilson herself has had an influence on the generation of Canadian women writers who came of age in the 1950s and 1960s, including Margaret Laurence and Alice Munro. Although Wilson encouraged the image of herself as the befuddled housewife-writer, David Stouck has shown that she wanted to be a writer from an early age and served a lengthy apprenticeship in the craft, that she was ambitious for book publication, and that she was as serious as any high modernist when it came to matters of style and revision. In her fiction— six novels and numerous short stories—the early instability of her life finds expression in an atmosphere of the unsettled, of lonely heroines searching for connection and community in a world always just one step ahead of dissolution and chaos. The natural scenery of British Columbia also figures largely in her work, both as an area for the struggle between people and their physical environment and as a provider of a wealth of metaphoric illustrations of the workings of indifferent natural law. Her books include the novels Hetty Dorval (1947), Swamp Angel (1954), and Love and Salt Water (1956) and the story collection Mrs. Golightly and Other Stories (1961). She is also the author of The Innocent Traveler (1949), a book that combines fact and fiction in its portrayal of the fortunes of a number of English women in British Columbia.

A Visit to the Frontier

L ucy turned from looking out of the window of the train.

The appearance of the country has changed since we left Saskatoon, hasn't it? she said, but Charles did not answer. He remained concealed by the weekend review which he was reading; so, since the question was of the kind which neither requires nor demands an answer, Lucy returned her gaze to the window.

Rivers flow through, or near, four of the five cities of the Canadian

north and middle west. The fifth city, which has no large adjacent body
of water, has courageously made itself a spacious lake in the dry prairies,
and planted trees. The small northern city of Saskatoon on the high banks
of the Saskatchewan River had given Lucy a great deal of pleasure. True,
in summer the weather was very hot and in winter the weather was very
cold. But the far spread of prairie, the vast span of sky with wildness of
sunrise and sunset and aurora, the felt nearness of the northland, the
grave majestic sweep of the tawny Saskatchewan River, the clarity and
stimulation of the air delighted her—a dweller by the western ocean. So
did the neatness of the heart of the small city; the dignity of the surprisingly large hotel upon the high river bank; the austere elegance of the
large red brick churches on the river road, outlined clean against the
clean sky as by some northern Canaletto; and those churches which
terminated, also with elegance, in Byzantine onions.

By this time the train had left behind the flat prairies, and any suggestion of a town or even a dwelling was so improbable as to make one
wonder, Will the curve of any small hill or valley here ever become home
and significant and a part of memory to people who will live here and
die here—all so empty of life now? (Yet see, a hawk!) Lucy sat wondering.
The broad land slid behind them and now the country was broken,
curved, into innumerable forested or bushy valleys and headlands, with
stretches of intermediate green. Streams appeared around distant curves
or near at hand, and vanished again, left behind. Was it the same stream?
Were they many streams? And beyond the horizon disclosed by the
speeding train, was there more of this softly moulded, recklessly planted
and treed, mildly watered greenish brownish country, or did it change
with suddenness into the true north? And what did the true north look
like? she wondered. Perhaps this was the true north, momentarily kind,
just before the end of autumn.

It is impossible to guess, so why guess, said Lucy, partly to herself
and partly aloud and unheeded, whether this everlasting empty country
will ever be settled with people and activity, will ever, in fact, be covered
with towns and cities? We haven't seen a dwelling for hours. There are
a great many factors of climate, water, soil, oil, minerals, transportation
that must enter, of course. If you and I, two hundred years ago—which
is nothing at all in time—should have found ourselves on the empty
banks of the Saskatchewan River where Saskatoon now stands, we would
have seen nothing to suggest the establishment of a town or city there,
and the same is true now, and here.

A quiver of the weekend review caused Lucy to stop her soliloquy
for the moment. There was nothing in what she had to say just then to
warrant Charles's breaking off his reading and coming out of his private
world to listen.

She turned her attention to him, and away from the window. How heavenly fortunate I am, she thought—and this time she kept her soliloquy to herself, as there are many things that do not translate into mutual speech, and this was one—that ever since we first loved each other, every day has renewed our love. Never never have we taken it for granted but have always known, without saying, that it is our greatest thing and that it might be removed at any moment (although not in essence) by death, which comes once and forever to each person on earth, on this continent, on this train, and we are no exception. And so, now, as I sit across from Charlie and see him lounging there, and see his elbows sticking out each side of his paper, and his legs sprawled across, one boot touching my shoe, the contentment and joy of his presence is greater than when my heart first leapt to see him. And one wonders why most of the books that have ever been written and most of the tales that have been told (for the oldest tales were tales of fighting or of love) have been of nascent love, tragic love, deceived, faithless or unlawful love, but not of perfect and lasting fulfilment. There is no literature of perfect and lasting fulfilment of happy love. That must be because continuing fulfilment does not lend itself to the curiosity that is impelled to read a story and because in any case this fulfilment can never be revealed.

Charles came out from behind the paper. Listen to this, he said, it's funny. He had come to the end of the paper where the competitions are. He read, and his French was pleasantly bad. "An English Member of Parliament who belonged to the M.R.A. related his confessions at a house party in France. He said '*Quand je regarde mon derrière, je vois qu'il est divisé en deux parties.*' " Lucy laughed a lot at this and at some similar stories in the competition, and Charles turned to the serious beginning of the review again and fell silent. Lucy now saw his face above the paper, intent and grown serious again.

The scenery had slipped behind the train unobserved, and the rather spectacular changes in the nature of the scenery had escaped Lucy's notice as she sat, still smiling at the derrière which was divisé. The roadbed appeared to be rough here and so the train gave the impression of hurrying. It was actually slower and rocked a good deal, and soap and glasses and bags and coats slipped and rattled and swayed in the compartment as the train ran on.

I'm glad, said Lucy out loud and still amused at the story, that now I've discovered—

Charles came up over the top of his paper again and looked at her. What on earth are you chunnering about now? he said.

I'm not chunnering, said Lucy. I'm simply saying—but she never said what she was simply saying because of the crash.

If it was a crash. It was a shattering, a physical impact, a screeching, a settling, a cessation in which she was seized and shaken and lost. It was for a millionth of a second—or forever—fear and helpless panic to the obliteration of everything that had been Lucy. There was at last this settling down again to the irregular motion of the train and the assumption that something had happened and something was over. Lucy, who had so lately been in the middle of her laughing, had been banged about (it seemed), with sudden pain like thunder and lightning, and sat now with her eyes closed because she was afraid to open them. She remembered like a quick dream that once, in the sage-brush country, the train had run into a small herd of cattle. The train, at that time, had stopped, and there was a long wait while the poor beasts were removed from the rails. Evidently—and her first emotion was gladness—they had not run over anybody or any animal because they still kept on their way; probably one of the large boulders which so often overhang the railway cuttings had timed its falling to the vibrations of the train passing below and had knocked them about. Still a little fearful, Lucy opened her eyes and saw, but hazily, Charles sitting on the opposite seat, still reading. Really, Charlie, this is carrying imperturbability too far.

Darling, what was that? she said.

What was what? said Charles indifferently.

That crash, said his wife.

I don't know, said Charles and went on reading.

Sometimes you do infuriate me! said Lucy, and now I'm sure that you just pretend when you put it over me as you often do—being imperturbable like that. What *did* happen?

Charles looked up at her and the familiar look flowed between them. He said amiably, The train is slowing up. And it was.

Lucy still felt shaken. It's possible, she thought, that nothing happened at all, except inside my head. Dear me, I hope I'm not starting to have fits like a cat. Do people? she said out loud.

Do people what? asked Charles who had got up and was putting on his tweed jacket over his sweater.

Start having fits, she said.

At that moment the conductor put his head in at the compartment door. Cut Off. This stop is Cut Off, he said. An hour and a half at Cut Off. You'll have time to go up to the settlement. They say it's worth seeing. And he went on and made his announcement along the train.

Lucy put on her leather jacket because they were pretty far north and the air would no doubt be nippy. They both went out.

She stepped on to the platform, glad to be free of the train for a long prospect of time, and stood before the sign of the railway station. The station, was wooden, primitive, and so was the sign. It spelled CUT OFF. Lucy turned to the coloured porter who stood beside the steps. He was particularly nice and seemed to know the answers to all railroad questions.

Porter, she said, what an odd name. What does it mean?

The porter shrugged and regarded her with his slow gentle smile. Ah doan know, lady, he said. They's mighty odd names all over this country. They's The Leavings and Ah guess that kinda speaks for itself, n they's Dog Pound n Jumpn Pound n Ghost River n Spirit River but Ah doan no nuthn about Cut Off. Tell you the truth lady, it's the first time Ah done this run. And he helped down another passenger.

The air was brilliantly fresh after the train smell. Lucy breathed deep. She noticed the passenger who had followed them off the train. He was tall. His face was serious and perhaps sad. He regarded his surroundings with slow sweeping glances which were also inward glances and he appeared anxious.

Who's that, Charles? breathed Lucy. I've seen him or seen his picture and why is he so sad?

That is Proker, said Charles, and he has lost his fountain pen. Perhaps he lost it when we changed trains.

Changed trains? said Lucy. (Changed trains *changed trains changed trains* changed trains.) Her head clanged. She put her hand to her eyes, closing them, and then it was better and she stepped out with Charlie because they had no time to waste.

They left behind the little wooden station and the people standing about and walked into the open space to see what they could of the settlement of Cut Off.

Impressions flowed in on Lucy like a newly tasted wine, and yet taste was the only faculty unemployed. Simultaneously, simultaneously, they flowed in, ravishing her. The prospect revealed itself to the north towards which they looked as an open stretch of brisk grass in front of them, crossed by paths and wagon trails and sloping down to a near river which cut foaming across the landscape. This river which was large enough to be spectacular and powerful and yet not useful for navigation was of water so whitely brilliant as to be quite dazzling in its motion. It had a strange peculiarity which Lucy had never seen before in picture or story; and now she marvelled that this attribute of the river had not already become famous. At intervals in the course of the river, both on its banks and springing up through the waters of the river itself, were fountains, rising buoyantly and joyously several feet in the air. Only to look at these fountains of bright perpetual water refreshed and revived Lucy—and perhaps other watchers too, for some of the other passengers were standing, gazing—so that her sense of well-being was beyond anything she had ever felt before. They stood, and then looked beyond the river, where lay the settlement proper. The river was crossed by two simple wooden bridges that led to the settlement.

Wood seemed to be abundant here. Spreading trees which still held their leaves and large dark comely firs and shapely cedars grew, not very crowded, on either side of the sloping river banks. Indians and other people walked here, separately or together, or stood looking at the fountains of springing waters, or sat upon the pine and cedar scented earth. A look to right and left showed the country folded away and away further and further into hills and valleys behind hills and valleys, wild yet embowered in trees; away until soft brown and green hills of wiry tawny grass and light and dark trees became dun-coloured, mauve, and then deeply purple. Lucy turned back to look at the river. Across the river flew one after another of small western blue-birds, bluer than forget-me-nots in flight, and there came continuous bird-song from the trees.

She was soon aware that the air which they were breathing was different from the air she customarily breathed and whose quality she used not to notice particularly unless it was exceptionally bad. This air, at Cut Off, was vigorous, so vigorous that Lucy felt herself different, stronger, and gayer. She said to Charles, Don't you feel as if the air we used to breathe was more like earth and stone than air—solid and heavy, I mean—and I feel as if it was only water that I used to have in my veins. This must be the true north.

But Charles did not answer.

She turned and looked up but he was not there. She looked back. Perhaps he had gone to hunt for the fountain pen. Or was it possible—but not likely—that Charles had walked on alone or with some other people?

Charles! Darling! Charlie! she called, but he cannot have heard her.

Well, she thought, how strange, but he must have gone on ahead. I'll hurry after, I mustn't wait here, we'll meet at the train. She found it much easier than usual not to worry. She was aware as she walked on quickly, and with a delight in walking, that she had shed some accompanying emotion (the emotion was anxiety). Even the unaccountable absence of Charles did not make her anxious.

This delicious air, strong and pine-scented, which she drew in gave her active pleasure. It *was* like water or wine compared to earth or stone. She came to the nearer footbridge and stood for a few moments watching the lively river and the strange crystalline fountains that shot vertically upwards and sprayed down again into the rushing sparkling stream whose noise was strangely agreeable. She watched, too, some of the people who seemed to be inhabitants enjoying the river and its banks. These people walked quickly, or strolled, or sat on the ground. But whether they walked or wandered or rested, whether moving or in repose, there was a lively look of well-being and pleasure upon them. They talked to each other in passing and laughed spontaneously. Even a crippled man whom she saw making his way on crutches by the river-bank seemed to swing along in an easy debonair fashion and whistled as he swung. They feel as I do, thought Lucy; this is certainly a very healthy place.

On the footbridge as she stopped to look down at the water racing radiant and broken under the bridge, a man and woman leaned upon the railing. Lucy heard them talking and found that their language was strange to her; but she had a vague sentiment of knowing what they were talking about, although she did not understand the words, only the feeling. They looked at her in friendly fashion and seemed as if they would include her in the conversation only that they knew she could not converse with them. Lucy wondered if this were one of the many foreign settlements to be found in the Canadian northwest—Ukrainians, Hutterites. No, not Hutterites; these people had no uniformity of dress.

She realized that time (was it time?) was passing, and that if she were to climb the far slope and see the buildings which the trees partly disclosed, she could no longer stand there water-gazing. So she crossed the footbridge, and leaving the river bank she climbed the gradual slope of the hill, following a trail which led up among the trees.

She felt no shortness of breath, as she sometimes did, but an increased exhilaration in this climbing. People in twos and threes climbed, too, or walked down the hill and towards the river. She was struck by the freedom and elasticity of their steps, and the certainty and serenity of their faces. They were not like the crowds she knew. She did not recognize the absence of anxiety or preoccupation in them or in herself, because there was no anxiety to recognize. This is a country of truth! she thought, surprised. We are free like birds.

She now saw through the trees, which had become fewer, a long low building of dark stained rough wood. The building was pleasing in its simple proportions. There was a long verandah which faced west. The settlement of Cut Off must be unexpectedly large, she thought, for already she had seen more people than would usually constitute a village, and she found that more were coming and going in and out of the unusually large doors of the building which was perhaps some kind of lodge or village centre. As she went up to the broad, shallow, wooden steps towards the entrance, she saw that there were, higher up the trail, other buildings among the trees. Is there a church? she wondered. If I could see a church, that would tell me something.

She was about to cross the threshold of the lodge quite eagerly, without any customary shyness, and to mingle with the people amongst whom friendliness seemed to blow like a breeze—although no-one appeared to notice her—when there sounded the very loud ringing of a bell. She turned quickly. Something in her spirit and spirits descended and became confused, and she remembered the time, and the train, and above all she remembered Charles. Without looking further inside the lodge she went with an attempt at haste down the hill. So far from buoying her up as the bright air had heretofore done, the bright air was too strong for her and now pressed her down, so that she made her way with some difficulty until she reached a low rectangular stone, seat high. She looked down upon the stone, and on it was chiselled a finely sweeping double curve. She bent down and followed this curve with her finger, murmuring The Line of Beauty, The Line of Beauty. She thought, I must sit down for a moment on this stone for I am very tired and I am confused. So she sank down and sat on the stone, and looked towards the dazzling jets of water which no longer invigorated her but were far too strong, as some strong drink might be too strong. A man walked up to her and stood over her, and she looked up at him and was grateful for something in his face. He spoke to her, and although she could not understand his words she knew that he wished to be kind. I am like a dog who is lost, she thought, and he is like a man who is kind to the dog and powerful; but because he is a man and I am a dog, however kind and powerful he is, we cannot communicate except on the level of pity. He helped her to rise, and she hurried on, labouring as she ran.

After she crossed the footbridge, her mind and body freshened a little, and some of her calm and pleasure seemed to be restored, so that she did not race and press on to the railway station with anxiety. There were new sounds in the air. She heard from her right, behind the brow of a curving hill, the galloping of hooves. And there was this peculiarity in this air, that one sound did not overlay or drown out another sound; so that the sound of galloping hooves which drew nearer and nearer did not at all drown the sound of light and laughing voices calling to one another.

Around the curve swept into view one, two, seven, twelve horses and their riders. Lucy stood entranced.

The girls who raced their horses round the concealing curve of the hill, into the clearing and across the clearing to a spinney of thin trees, turned to each other as they galloped, and seemed to be in a kind of laughing harmony. They wore bright scarves which fluttered behind them in the wind; so that these merry riders galloping towards the spinney with their bright scarves flowing behind them were a beautiful sight. The heavy hooves pounded, the gay voices sounded, the scarves streamed and fluttered, all in the brilliant air. Lucy stood like a radiant statue, watching. When the riders reached the spinney, they slid down off their horses, while the sound of their light voices crossed and crisscrossed. They threw the reins forward over their horses' heads and the horses stood, tossing their long manes, switching their tails, and moving only a step or two towards a patch of grass or a green bough.

Lucy was so enchanted with the girl riders that she had again forgotten her urgency. Some of the girls wore full divided skirts such as a riding gypsy might wear (but they were not gypsies), and walking lightly, talking and laughing together, they set out quickly for the footbridge by which Lucy had just crossed the river, some in blue jeans, some in gypsy skirts, all with their scarves fluttering. One bright-eyed Indian girl saw Lucy standing there and waved to her as they passed. Lucy waved back, very much pleased at this. Where do they come from behind those hills? What is it, there? Why do they come? But the girls had gone towards the bridge and only the horses remained in the spinney, resting, pawing, and shaking their heads. Lucy heard again the loud station bell. The train was pulling out. Oh! she gasped, and began to run.

She ran, and caught a handle beside a step; a hand from a dark blue sleeve clutched her and she swung onto the train.

Oh thank you, she gasped to the conductor, and made her way into the train. There was no-one there. The train was very old. Not a single passenger. There was no sign at all that Charles had ever been there. It was not the same train. Oh! she cried desperately, and found her way to the conductor. I'm on the wrong train! Where is my husband?

The conductor said You must have changed trains (changed trains *changed trains changed trains* changed trains).

If you want to get off, said the conductor, you'd better jump before the train gets up speed. Her one desire was to get off. She stood on the lowest step of this old-fashioned train, still holding on and—divided between the desire to leave the train at once before it got up speed, and the desire to choose a good place on which to jump out so that she would not disable herself—she jumped, onto a soft grassy mound. She scrambled up, and in raising herself she leaned her weight on a soft but firm object that moved beneath her hand. She looked down in a hurry and saw that her hand rested upon the flat head of a large polar bear. She drew her hand away in alarm, but not before she had felt the texture of the crisp, coarse, gleaming, cream-coloured hair. The bear looked at her with humourless animal eyes and extended its head this way that way—this way, that way—and then paid her no attention. She thought as she regained her equilibrium and started to run the short distance back to the station, yes, this must be the true north, yet something is wrong about that bear.

And as she ran she began to be aware that living in this country would, of itself, inescapably exclude the memory of much sorrow and much joy that made up the uneven fabric of her life as she had known it. She began to pray as she ran, panting, stumbling. Oh God just this. Let me find him. Where is he? Let me find him. Just to be together. Only that. Oh God, oh God!

When she reached the station she saw that their own train was beside the little platform. She stood and scanned the windows anxiously. There, looking out of a window was the serious face of the passenger who had lost his fountain pen. She mounted the steps and hurried to their compartment. Charles was not there. The weekend review lay upon the seat where he had put it down. For some reason she clutched the paper and held it tightly crumpled in her hand. She made her way down the car—the train had begun to move—to where their fellow-passenger sat. She supported herself at his open compartment door.

Please, she said to the poet—for she felt somehow that he was a poet or kin to a poet—have you seen my husband? I have lost him.

I saw him, said the passenger, but he is not here now. He came back to the train and looked for you. He told me, She always likes water and she must have followed the river. So he took the far footbridge and followed down the stream. I am very sorry, said the passenger deliberately and with compassion.

Lucy turned and went back with great difficulty to the steps. It seemed as though she fell, and lay there, on the tawny prairie.

In the course of time, or of time and a time, all memory and strange pictures and confusion of human experience left her, and she died.

When those who were killed in the train wreck had at last recovered from the fatigues of death, it may be that some of them met again with a transfigured delight in that beautiful and happy country, with death past and over. We do not know.

KATHERINE ANNE PORTER

(1890–1980)

K atherine Anne Porter was born in Indian Creek, Texas, the first native of the state ever to become a professional writer, as she once put it. Her mother died when she was just 2, and the family moved in with her paternal grandmother. An early marriage ended in divorce, but soon she made herself a successful and peripatetic career as a journalist. Her first book of stories, Flowering Judas, was published in 1930. Other collections of fiction include Noon Wine (1937), Pale Horse, Pale Rider (1939), and The Leaning Tower (1944). Her allegorical novel Ship of Fools appeared in 1962. Commenting on the symbolic quality of her stories, V.S. Pritchett notes: "To every human being there eventually comes—Miss Porter seems to say—the shock of perception of something violent or rock-like in themselves, in others, or in circumstances. We awaken to primitive knowledge and become impersonal in our tragedies. . . . It is something out of one's control scarcely belonging to one, and that has to be borne as if one were a stone." She has been extravagantly praised by critics such as Robert Penn Warren, but her fiction has never had particularly broad appeal. Yet the artistry she displays in a dozen or so short stories should be enough to secure her a permanent place in American literature.

That Tree

H e had really wanted to be a cheerful bum lying under a tree in a good climate, writing poetry. He wrote bushel basketsful of poetry and it was all no good and he knew it, even while he was writing it. Knowing his poetry was no good did not take away much from his pleasure in it. He would have enjoyed just that kind of life: no respectability, no responsibility, no money to speak of, wearing worn-out sandals and a becoming, if probably ragged, blue shirt, lying under a tree writing poetry. That was why he had come to Mexico in the first place. He had felt in his bones that it was the country for him. Long after he had become quite an important journalist, an authority on Latin-American revolutions and a best seller, he confessed to any friends and acquaintances who would listen to him—he enjoyed this confession, it gave him a chance to talk about the thing he believed he loved best, the idle free romantic life of a poet—that the day Miriam kicked him out was the luckiest day of his life. She had left him, really, packing up suddenly in a cold quiet fury, stabbing him with her elbows when he tried to get his arms around her, now and again cutting him to the bone with a short sentence expelled through her clenched teeth; but he felt that he had been, as he always explained, kicked out. She had kicked him out and it had served him right.

The shock had brought him to himself as if he had been surprised out of a long sleep. He had sat quite benumbed in the bare clean room, among the straw mats and the painted Indian chairs Miriam hated, in the sudden cold silence, his head in his hands, nearly all night. It hadn't even occurred to him to lie down. It must have been almost daylight when he got up stiff in every joint from sitting still so long, and though he could not say he had been thinking yet he had formed a new resolution. He had started out, you might almost say that very day, to make a career for himself in journalism. He couldn't say why he had hit on that, except that the word would impress his wife, the work was just intellectual enough to save his self-respect, such as it was, and even to him it seemed a suitable occupation for a man such as he had suddenly become, bent on getting on in the world of affairs. Nothing ever happens suddenly to anyone, he observed, as if the thought had just occurred to him; it had been coming on probably for a long time, sneaking up on him when he wasn't looking. His wife had called him "Parasite!" She had said "Ne'er-do-well!" and as she repeated these things for what proved to be the last time, it struck him she had said them often before, when he had not listened to her with the ear of his mind. He translated these relatively harmless epithets instantly into their proper synonyms of Loafer! and Bum! Miriam had been a schoolteacher, and no matter what her disappointments and provocations may have been, you could not expect her easily to forget such discipline. She had got into a professional habit of primness; besides, she was a properly brought-up girl, not a prissy bore, not at all, but a—well, there you are, a nicely brought-up Middle-Western girl, who took life seriously. And what can you do about that? She was sweet and gay and full of little crazy notions, but she never gave way to them honestly, or at least never at the moment when they might have meant something. She was never able to see the amusing side of a threatening situation which, taken solemnly, would ruin everything. No, her sense of humor never worked for salvation. It was just an extra frill on what would have been a good time anyhow.

He wondered if anybody had ever thought—oh, well, of course everybody else had, he was always making marvelous discoveries that other people had known all along—how impossible it is to explain or to make other eyes see the special qualities in the person you love. There was such a special kind of beauty in Miriam. In certain lights and moods he simply got a clutch in the pit of his stomach when he looked at her. It was something that could happen at any hour of the day, in the midst of the most ordinary occupations. He thought there was something to be said for living with one person day and night the year round. It brings out the worst, but it brings out the best, too, and Miriam's best was pretty damn swell. He couldn't describe it. It was easy to talk about her faults. He remembered all of them, he could add them up against her like rows of figures in a vast unpaid debt. He had lived with her for four years, and even now sometimes he woke out of a sound sleep in a sweating rage with himself, asking himself again why he had ever wasted a minute on her. She wasn't beautiful in his style. He confessed to a weakness for the kind that knocks your eye out. Her notion of daytime dress was a tailored suit with a round-collared blouse and a little felt hat like a bent shovel pulled down over her eyes. In the evening she put on a black dinner dress, positively disappeared into it. But she did her hair well and had the most becoming nightgowns he ever saw. You could have put her mind in a peanut shell. She hadn't temperament of the kind he had got used to in the Mexican girls. She did not approve of his use of the word temperament, either. She thought it was a kind of occupational disease among artists, or a trick they practiced to make themselves interesting. In any case, she distrusted artists and she distrusted temperament. But there was something about her. In cold blood he could size her up to himself, but it made him furious if anyone even hinted a criticism against her. His second wife had made a point of being catty about Miriam. In the end he could almost be willing to say this had led to his second divorce. He could not bear hearing Miriam called a mousy little nit-wit— at least not by *that* woman . . .

They both jumped nervously at an explosion in the street, the backfire of an automobile.

"Another revolution," said the fat scarlet young man in the tight purplish suit, at the next table. He looked like a parboiled sausage ready to burst from its skin. It was the oldest joke since the Mexican Independence, but he was trying to look as if he had invented it. The journalist glanced back at him over a sloping shoulder. "Another of those smart-cracking newspaper guys," he said in a tough voice, too loudly on purpose, "sitting around the Hotel Regis lobby wearing out the spittoons."

The smart-cracker swelled visibly and turned a darker red. "Who do you think you're talking about, you banjo-eyed chinless wonder, you?" he asked explicitly, spreading his chest across the table.

"Somebody way up, no doubt," said the journalist, in his natural voice, "somebody in with the government, I'll bet."

"Dyuhwana fight?" asked the newspaper man, trying to unwedge himself from between the table and his chair, which sat against the wall.

"Oh, I don't mind," said the journalist, "if you don't."

The newspaper man's friends laid soothing paws all over him and held him down. "Don't start anything with that shrimp," said one of them, his wet pink eyes trying to look sober and responsible. "For crisesake, Joe, can't you see he's about half your size and a feeb to boot? You wouldn't hit a feeb, now, Joe, would you?"

"I'll feeb him," said the newspaper man, wiggling faintly under restraint.

"*Señores'n, señores'n,*" urged the little Mexican waiter, "there are respectable ladies and gentlemen present. Please, a little silence and correct behavior, please."

"Who the hell are *you,* anyhow?" the newspaper man asked the journalist, from under his shelter of hands, around the thin form of the waiter.

"Nobody you'd wanta know, Joe," said another of his pawing friends. "Pipe down now before these greasers turn in a general alarm. You know how liable they are to go off when you least expect it. Pipe down, now, Joe, now you just remember what happened the last time, Joe. Whaddayah *care,* anyhow?"

"*Señores'n,*" said the little waiter, working his thin outspread mahogany-colored hands up and down alternately as if they were on sticks, "it is necessary it must cease or the *señores'n* must remove themselves."

It did cease. It seemed to evaporate. The four newspaper men at the next table subsided, cluttered in a circle with their heads together, muttering into their highballs. The journalist turned back, ordered another round of drinks, and went on talking, in a low voice.

He had never liked this café, never had any luck in it. Something always happened here to spoil his evening. If there was one brand of bum on earth he despised, it was a newspaper bum. Or anyhow the drunken illiterates the United Press and Associated Press seemed to think were good enough for Mexico and South America. They were always getting mixed up in affairs that were none of their business, and they spent their time trying to work up trouble somewhere so they could get a story out of it. They were always having to be thrown out on their ears by the government. He just happened to know that the bum at the next table was about due to be deported. It had been pretty safe to make that crack about how he was no doubt way up in Mexican official esteem. . . . He thought that would remind him of something, all right.

One evening he had come here with Miriam for dinner and dancing, and at the very next table sat four fat generals from the North, with oxhorn mustaches and big bellies and big belts full of cartridges and pistols. It was in the old days just after Obregón had taken the city, and the town was crawling with generals. They infested the steam baths, where they took off their soiled campaign harness and sweated away the fumes of tequila and fornication, and they infested the cafés to get drunk again on champagne, and pick up the French whores who had been imported for the festivities of the presidential inauguration. These four were having an argument very quietly, their mean little eyes boring into each other's faces. He and his wife were dancing within arm's length of the table when one of the generals got up suddenly, tugging at his pistol, which stuck, and the other three jumped and grabbed him, all without a word; everybody in the place saw it at once. So far there was nothing unusual. The point was, every right-minded Mexican girl just seized her man firmly by the waist and spun him around until his back was to the generals, holding him before her like a shield, and there the whole roomful had stood frozen for a second, the music dead. His wife Miriam had broken from him and hidden under a table. He had to drag her out by the arm before everybody. "Let's have another drink," he said, and paused, looking around him as if he saw again the place as it had been on that night nearly ten years before. He blinked, and went on. It had been the most utterly humiliating moment of his whole blighted life. He had thought he couldn't survive to pick up their things and get her out of there. The generals had all sat down again and everybody went on dancing as though nothing had happened. . . . Indeed, nothing had happened to anyone except himself.

He tried, for hours that night and on and on for nearly a year, to explain to her how he felt about it. She could not understand at all. Sometimes she said it was all perfect nonsense. Or she remarked complacently that it had never occurred to her to save her life at his expense. She thought such tricks were all very well for the Mexican girls who had only one idea in their heads, and any excuse would do to hold a man closer than they should, but she could not, could *not*, see why he should expect her to imitate them. Besides, she had felt safer under the table. It was her first and only thought. He told her a bullet might very well have gone through the wood; a plank was no protection at all, a human torso was as good as a feather pillow to stop a bullet. She kept saying it simply had not occurred to her to do anything else, and that it really had nothing at all to do with him. He could never make her see his point of view for one moment. It should have had something to do with him. All those Mexican girls were born knowing what they should do and they did it instantly, and Miriam had merely proved once for all that her instincts were out of tune. When she tightened her mouth to bite her lip and say "Instincts!" she could make it sound like the most obscene word in any language. It was a shocking word. And she did not stop there. At last she said, she hadn't the faintest interest in what Mexican girls were born for, but she had no intention of wasting her life flattering male vanity. "Why should I trust you in anything?" she asked. "What reason have you given me to trust you?"

He was surprised at the change in her since he had first met her in Minneapolis. He chose to believe this change had been caused by her teaching school. He told her he thought it the most deadly occupation there was and a law should be passed prohibiting pretty women under thirty-five years of age from taking it up. She reminded him they were living on the money she had earned at it. They had been engaged for three years, a chaste long-distance engagement which he considered morbid and unnatural. Of course he had to do something to wear away the time, so while she was in Minneapolis saving her money and filling a huge trunk with household linen, he had been living in Mexico City with an Indian girl who posed for a set of painters he knew. He had a job teaching English in one of the technical schools—damned odd, he had been a schoolteacher too, but he never thought of it just that way until this minute—and he lived very comfortably with the Indian girl on his wages, for naturally the painters did not pay her for posing. The Indian girl divided her time cheerfully between the painters, the cooking pot, and his bed, and she managed to have a baby without interrupting any of these occupations for more than a few days. Later on she was taken up by one of the more famous and successful painters, and grew very sophisticated and a "character," but at the time she was still simple and nice. She took, later on, to wearing native art-jewelry and doing native dances in costume, and learned to paint almost as well as a seven-year-old child; "you know," he said, "the primitive style." Well, by that time, he was having troubles of his own. When the time came for Miriam to come out and marry him—the whole delay, he realized afterward, was caused by Miriam's expansive notions of what a bride's outfit should be—the Indian girl had gone away very cheerfully, too cheerfully, in fact, with a new man. She had come back in three days to say she was at last going to get married honestly, and she felt he should give her the furniture for a dowry. He had helped her pile the stuff on the backs of two Indian carriers, and the girl had walked away with the baby's head dangling out of her shawl. For just a moment when he saw the baby's face, he had an odd feeling. "That's mine," he said to himself, and added at once, "perhaps." There was no way of knowing, and it certainly looked like any other little shock-haired Indian baby. Of course the girl had not got married; she had never even thought of it.

When Miriam arrived, the place was almost empty, because he had not been able to save a peso. He had a bed and a stove, and the walls were decorated with drawings and paintings by his Mexican friends, and there was a litter of painted gourds and carved wood and pottery in beautiful colors. It didn't seem so bad to him, but Miriam's face, when she stepped into the first room, was, he had to admit, pretty much of a study. She said very little, but she began to be unhappy about a number of things. She cried intermittently for the first few weeks, for the most mysterious and farfetched causes. He would wake in the night and find her crying hopelessly. When she sat down to coffee in the morning she would lean her head on her hands and cry. "It's nothing, nothing really," she would tell him. "I don't know what is the matter. I just want to cry."

He knew now what was the matter. She had come all that way to marry after three years' planning, and she couldn't see herself going back and facing the music at home. This mood had not lasted, but it made a fairly dreary failure of their honeymoon. She knew nothing about the Indian girl, and believed, or professed to believe, that he was a virgin as she was at their marriage. She hadn't much curiosity and her moral standards were severe, so it was impossible for him ever to take her into his confidence about his past. She simply took it for granted in the most irritating way that he hadn't any past worth mentioning except the three years they were engaged, and that, of course, they shared already. He had believed that all virgins, however austere their behavior, were palpitating to learn about life, were you might say hanging on by an eyelash until they arrived safely at initiation within the secure yet libertine advantage of marriage. Miriam upset this theory as in time she upset most of his theories. His intention to play the rôle of a man of the world educating an innocent but interestingly teachable bride was nipped in the bud. She was not at all teachable and she took no trouble to make herself interesting. In their most intimate hours her mind seemed elsewhere, gone into some darkness of its own, as if a prior and greater shock of knowledge had forestalled her attention. She was not to be won, for reasons of her own which she would not or could not give. He could not even play the rôle of a poet. She was not interested in his poetry. She preferred Milton, and she let him know it. She let him know also that she believed their mutual sacrifice of virginity was the most important act of their marriage, and this sacred rite once achieved, the whole affair had descended to a pretty low plane. She had a terrible phrase about "walking the chalk line" which she applied to all sorts of situations. One walked, as never before, the chalk line in marriage; there seemed to be a chalk line drawn between them as they lay together. . . .

The thing that finally got him down was Miriam's devilish inconsistency. She spent three mortal years writing him how dull and dreadful and commonplace her life was, how sick and tired she was of petty little conventions and amusements, how narrow-minded everybody around her was, how she longed to live in a beautiful dangerous place among interesting people who painted and wrote poetry, and how his letters came into her stuffy little world like a breath of free mountain air, and all that. "For God's sake," he said to his guest, "let's have another drink." Well, he had something of a notion he was freeing a sweet bird from a cage. Once freed, she would perch gratefully on his hand. He wrote a poem about a caged bird set free, dedicated it to her and sent her a copy. She forgot to mention it in her next letter. Then she came out with a two-hundred-pound trunk of linen and enough silk underwear to last her a lifetime, you might have supposed, expecting to settle down in a modern steam-heated flat and have nice artistic young couples from the American colony in for dinner Wednesday evenings. No wonder her face had changed at the first glimpse of her new home. His Mexican friends had scattered flowers all over the place, tied bunches of carnations on the door knobs, almost carpeted the floor with red roses, pinned posies of small bright blooms on the sagging cotton curtains, spread a coverlet of gardenias on the lumpy bed, and had disappeared discreetly, leaving gay reassuring messages, scribbed here and there, even on the white plastered walls. . . . She had walked through with a vague look of terror in her eyes, pushing back the wilting flowers with her advancing feet. She swept the gardenias aside to sit on the edge of the bed, and she had said not a word. Hail, Hymen! What next?

He had lost his teaching job almost immediately. The Minister of Education, who was a patron of the school superintendent, was put out of office suddenly, and naturally every soul in his party down to the school janitors went out with him, and there you were. After a while you learn to take such things calmly. You wait until your man gets back in the saddle or you work up an alliance with the new one. . . . Whichever . . . Meanwhile the change and movement made such a good show you almost forgot the effect it had on your food supply. Miriam was not interested in politics or the movement of local history. She could see nothing but that he had lost his job. They lived on Miriam's savings eked out with birthday checks and Christmas checks from her father, who threatened constantly to come for a visit, in spite of Miriam's desperate letters warning him that the country was appalling, and the climate would most certainly ruin his health. Miriam went on holding her nose when she went to the markets, trying to cook wholesome civilized American food over a charcoal brasier, and doing the washing in the patio over a stone tub with a cold water tap; and everything that had seemed so jolly and natural and inexpensive with the Indian girl was too damnifying and costly for words with Miriam. Her money melted away and they got nothing for it.

She would not have an Indian servant near her: they were dirty and besides how could she afford it? He could not see why she despised and resented housework so, especially since he offered to help. He had thought it rather a picnic to wash a lot of gayly colored Indian crockery outdoors in the sunshine, with the bougainvillea climbing up the wall and the heaven tree in full bloom. Not Miriam. She despised him for thinking it a picnic. He remembered for the first time his mother doing the housework when he was a child. There were half a dozen assorted children, her work was hard and endless, but she went about it with a quiet certainty, a happy absorbed look on her face, as if her hands were working automatically while her imagination was away playing somewhere. "Ah, your mother," said his wife, without any particular emphasis. He felt horribly injured, as if she were insulting his mother and calling down a curse on her head for bringing such a son into the world. No doubt about it, Miriam had force. She could make her personality, which no one need really respect, felt in a bitter, sinister way. She had a background, and solid earth under her feet, and a point of view and a strong spine: even when she danced with him he could feel her tense controlled hips and her locked knees, which gave her dancing a most attractive strength and lightness without any yielding at all. She had her points, all right, like a good horse, but she had missed being beautiful. It wasn't in her. He began to cringe when she reminded him that if he were an invalid she would cheerfully work for him and take care of him, but he appeared to be in the best of health, he was not even looking for a job, and he was still writing that poetry, which was the last straw. She called him a failure. She called him worthless and shiftless and trifling and faithless. She showed him her ruined hands and asked him what she had to look forward to, and told him again, and again, that she was not used to associating with the simply indescribably savage and awful persons who kept streaming through the place. Moreover, she had no intention of getting used to it. He tried to tell her that these persons were the best painters and poets and what-alls in Mexico, that she should try to appreciate them; these were the artists he had told her about in his letters. She wanted to know why Carlos never changed his shirt. "I told her," said the journalist, "it was because probably he hadn't got any other shirt." And why was Jaime such a glutton, leaning over his plate and wolfing his food? Because he was famished, no doubt. It was precisely that she could not understand. Why didn't they go to work and make a living? It was no good trying to explain to her his Franciscan notions of holy Poverty as being the natural companion for the artist. She said, "So you think they're being poor on purpose? Nobody but you would be such a fool." Really, the things that girl said. And his general impression of her was that she was silent as a cat. He went on in his pawky way trying to make clear to her his mystical faith in these men who went ragged and hungry because they had chosen once for all between what he called in all seriousness their souls, and this world. Miriam knew better. She knew they were looking for the main chance. "She was abominably, obscenely right. How I hate that woman, I hate her as I hate no one else. She assured me they were not so stupid as I thought; and I lived to see Jaime take up with a rich old woman, and Ricardo decide to turn film actor, and Carlos sitting easy with a government job, painting revolutionary frescoes to order, and I asked myself, Why shouldn't a man survive in any way he can?" But some fixed point of feeling in him refused to be convinced, he had a sackful of romantic notions about artists and their destiny and he was left holding it. Miriam had seen through them with half an eye, and how he wished he might have thought of a trick to play on her that would have finished her for life. But he had not. They all in turn ran out on him and in the end he had run out too. "So you see, I don't feel any better about doing what I did finally do, but I can say I am not unusual. That I can say. The trouble was that Miriam was right, damn her. I am not a poet, my poetry is filthy, and I had notions about artists that I must have got out of books. . . . You know, a race apart, dedicated men much superior to common human needs and ambitions. . . . I mean I thought art was a religion. . . . I mean that when Miriam kept saying . . ."

What he meant was that all this conflict began to damage him seriously. Miriam had become an avenging fury, yet he could not condemn her. Hate her, yes, that was almost too simple. His old-fashioned respectable middle-class hard-working American ancestry and training rose up in him and fought on Miriam's side. He felt he had broken about every bone in him to get away from them and live them down, and here he had been overtaken at last and beaten into resignation that had nothing to do with his mind or heart. It was as if his blood stream had betrayed him. The prospect of taking a job and being a decent little clerk with shiny pants and elbows—for he couldn't think of a job in any other terms—seemed like a kind of premature death which would not even compensate him with loss of memory. He didn't do anything about it at all. He did odd jobs and picked up a little money, but never enough. He could see her side of it, at least he tried hard to see it. When it came to a showdown, he hadn't a single argument in favor of his way of life that would hold water. He had been trying to live and think in a way that he hoped would end by making a poet of him, but it hadn't worked. That was the long and short of it. So he might have just gone on to some unimaginably sordid end if Miriam, after four years: four years? yes, good God, four years and one month and eleven days, had not written home for money, packed up what was left of her belongings, called him a few farewell names, and left. She had been shabby and thin and wild-looking for so long he could not remember ever having seen her any other way, yet all at once her profile in the doorway was unrecognizable to him.

So she went, and she did him a great favor without knowing it. He had fallen into the cowardly habit of thinking their marriage was permanent, no matter how evil it might be, that they loved each other, and so it did not matter what cruelties they committed against each other, and he had developed a real deafness to her words. He was unable, towards the end, either to see her or hear her. He realized this afterward, when remembered phrases and expressions of her eyes and mouth began to eat into his marrow. He was grateful to her. If she had not gone, he might have loitered on, wasting his time trying to write poetry, hanging around dirty picturesque little cafés with a fresh set of clever talkative poverty-stricken young Mexicans who were painting or writing or talking about getting ready to paint or write. His faith had renewed itself; these fellows were pure artists—they would never sell out. They were not bums, either. They worked all the time at something to do with Art. "Sacred Art," he said, "our glasses are empty again."

But try telling anything of the kind to Miriam. Somehow he had never got to that tree he meant to lie down under. If he had, somebody would certainly have come around and collected rent for it, anyhow. He had spent a good deal of time lying under tables at Dinty Moore's or the Black Cat with a gang of Americans like himself who were living a free life and studying the native customs. He was rehearsing, he explained to Miriam, hoping for once she would take a joke, for lying under a tree later on. It didn't go over. She would have died with her boots on before she would have cracked a smile at that. So then . . . He had gone in for a career in the hugest sort of way. It had been easy. He hardly could say now just what his first steps were, but it had been easy. Except for Miriam, he would have been a lousy failure, like those bums at Dinty Moore's, still rolling under the tables, studying the native customs. He had gone in for a career in journalism and he had made a good thing of it. He was a recognized authority on revolutions in twenty-odd Latin-American countries, and his sympathies happened to fall in exactly right with the high-priced magazines of a liberal humanitarian slant which paid him well for telling the world about the oppressed peoples. He could really write, too; if he did say so, he had a prose style of his own. He had made the kind of success you can clip out of newspapers and paste in a book, you can count it and put it in the bank, you can eat and drink and wear it, and you can see it in other people's eyes at tea and dinner parties. Fine, and now what? On the strength of all this he had got married again. Twice, in fact, and divorced twice. That made three times, didn't it? That was plenty. He had spent a good deal of time and energy doing all sorts of things he didn't care for in the least to prove to his first wife, who had been a twenty-three-year-old schoolteacher in Minneapolis, Minnesota, that he was not just merely a bum, fit for nothing but lying under a tree— if he had ever been able to locate that ideal tree he had in his mind's eye—writing poetry and enjoying his life.

Now he had done it. He smoothed out the letter he had been turning in his hands and stroked it as if it were a cat. He said, "I've been working up the climax all this time. You know, good old surprise technique. Now then, get ready."

Miriam had written to him, after these five years, asking him to take her back. And would you believe it, he was going to break down and do that very thing. Her father was dead, she was terribly lonely, she had had time to think everything over, she believed herself to blame for a great many things, she loved him truly and she always had, truly; she regretted, oh, everything, and hoped it was not too late for them to make a happy life together once more. . . . She had read everything she could find of his in print, and she loved all of it. He had that very morning sent by cable the money for her to travel on, and he was going to take her back. She was going to live again in a Mexican house without any conveniences and she was not going to have a modern flat. She was going to take whatever he chose to hand her, and like it. And he wasn't going to marry her again, either. Not he. If she wanted to live with him on these terms, well and good. If not, she could just go back once more to that school of hers in Minneapolis. If she stayed, she would walk a chalk line, all right, one she hadn't drawn for herself. He picked up a cheese knife and drew a long sharp line in the checkered table-cloth. She would, believe him, walk *that*.

The hands of the clock pointed half past two. The journalist swallowed the last of his drink and went on drawing more crosshatches on the table-cloth with a relaxed hand. His guest wished to say, "Don't forget to invite me to your wedding," but thought better of it. The journalist raised his twitching lids and swung his half-focused eyes upon the shadow opposite and said, "I suppose you think I don't know—"

His guest moved to the chair edge and watched the orchestra folding up for the night. The café was almost empty. The journalist paused, not for an answer, but to give weight to the important statements he was about to make.

"I don't know what's happening, this time," he said, "don't deceive yourself. This time, I know." He seemed to be admonishing himself before a mirror.

Isaac Babel

(1894–1941)

I saac Babel was born in Odessa, a city in the south of Russia, which Babel thought might serve in literature as symbolic complement— sun-drenched, genial, material, fecund, erotic—to the bleak, savage, misty, abstract world created by other Russian writers. His merchant father was ambitious for his son and set out to educate him as well as possible. Given Hebrew lessons and Talmudic training from an early age, Babel was also taught French, German, and English at Russian schools. The quota for Jews kept him out of the University of Odessa, and he enrolled in a finance and business institute in Kiev. He went to Petrograd in 1916, published two stories, and was befriended by Gorky, Shklovsky, and Mayakovsky. He welcomed the October Revolution and fought with the Reds in the Civil War, recording his fascination and horror of war in his account of his experiences with Marshal Budyonny's First Cavalry in the Ukraine and Byelorussia in a volume of stories called **Red Calvary** *(1926) that made him a Soviet celebrity. But Babel was too imaginative, too unorthodox a writer to produce the "socialist realism" demanded in Stalinist Russia, and he refused to write what he regarded as propaganda. Attacked for his lack of output, he defended himself as best he could. At the first Congress of Soviet Writers, he said: "I spoke of respect for the reader. I perhaps suffer from hypertrophy of that feeling. I have such an unbounded respect for him I am struck dumb," and he described himself as "a master of the genre of silence" in an age when everybody was speaking "unbearably loudly." Babel was arrested in 1939. His death certificate reads 17 March 1941, but the exact circumstances of his death remain unknown. He shared the modernists' ideas about the importance of craftsmanship (one of his short stories he rewrote 22 times) and maintained that form and content were indivisible. One of his friends records him on the subject this way: "My motto is* authenticity. . . . *What I do is get hold of some trifle, some little anecdote, a piece of market gossip, and turn it into a short story I cannot tear myself away from. It's alive, it plays. . . . And people will read the story, they'll remember it, they'll laugh, not because it's funny but because one always feels like laughing in the presence of human good fortune."*

The Story of My Dovecot

To M. Gorky

W hen I was a kid I longed for a dovecot. Never in all my life have I wanted a thing more. But not till I was nine did father promise the wherewithal to buy the wood to make one and three pairs of pigeons to stock it with. It was then 1904, and I was studying for the entrance exam to the preparatory class of the secondary school at Nikolayev in the Province of Kherson, where my people were at that time living. This province of course no longer exists, and our town has been incorporated in the Odessa Region.

I was only nine, and I was scared stiff of the exams. In both subjects, Russian language and arithmetic, I couldn't afford to get less than top marks. At our secondary school the *numerus clausus* was stiff: a mere five percent. So that out of forty boys only two that were Jews could get into the preparatory class. The teachers used to put cunning questions to Jewish boys; no one else was asked such devilish questions. So when father promised to buy the pigeons he demanded top marks with distinction in both subjects. He absolutely tortured me to death. I fell into a state of permanent daydream, into an endless, despairing, childish reverie. I went to the exam deep in this dream, and nevertheless did better than everybody else.

I had a knack for book-learning. Even though they asked cunning questions, the teachers could not rob me of my intelligence and my avid memory. I was good at learning, and got top marks in both subjects. But then everything went wrong. Khariton Efrussi, the corn-dealer who exported wheat to Marseille, slipped someone a 500-rouble bribe. My mark was changed from A to A −, and Efrussi Junior went to the secondary school instead of me. Father took it very badly. From the time I was six he had been cramming me with every scrap of learning he could, and that A − drove him to despair. He wanted to beat Efrussi up, or at least bribe two longshoremen to beat Efrussi up, but mother talked him out of the idea, and I started studying for the second exam the following year, the one for the lowest class. Behind my back my people got the teacher to take me in one year through the preparatory and first-year courses simultaneously, and conscious of the family's despair, I got three whole books by heart. These were Smirnovsky's *Russian Grammar*, Yevtushevsky's *Problems*, and Putsykovich's *Manual of Early Russian History*. Children no longer cram from these books, but I learned them by heart line upon line, and the following year in the Russian exam Karavayev gave me an unrivaled A +.

This Karavayev was a red-faced, irritable fellow, a graduate of Moscow University. He was hardly more than thirty. Crimson glowed in his manly cheeks as it does in the cheeks of peasant children. A wart sat perched on one cheek, and from it there sprouted a tuft of ash-colored cat's whiskers. At the exam, besides Karavayev, there was the Assistant Curator Pyatnitsky, who was reckoned a big noise in the school and throughout the province. When the Assistant Curator asked me about Peter the Great a feeling of complete oblivion came over me, an awareness that the end was near: an abyss seemed to yawn before me, an arid abyss lined with exultation and despair.

About Peter the Great I knew things by heart from Putsykovich's book and Pushkin's verses. Sobbing, I recited these verses, while the faces before me suddenly turned upside down, were shuffled as a pack of cards is shuffled. This card-shuffling went on, and meanwhile, shivering, jerking my back straight, galloping headlong, I was shouting Pushkin's stanzas at the top of my voice. On and on I yelled them, and no one broke into my crazy mouthings. Through a crimson blindness, through the sense of absolute freedom that had filled me, I was aware of nothing but Pyatnitsky's old face with its silver-touched beard bent toward me. He didn't interrupt me, and merely said to Karavayev, who was rejoicing for my sake and Pushkin's:

"What a people," the old man whispered, "those little Jews of yours! There's a devil in them!"

And when at last I could shout no more, he said:

"Very well, run along, my little friend."

I went out from the classroom into the corridor, and there, leaning against a wall that needed a coat of whitewash, I began to awake from my trance. About me Russian boys were playing, the school bell hung not far away above the stairs, the caretaker was snoozing on a chair with a broken seat. I looked at the caretaker, and gradually woke up. Boys were creeping toward me from all sides. They wanted to give me a jab, or perhaps just have a game, but Pyatnitsky suddenly loomed up in the corridor. As he passed me he halted for a moment, the frock coat flowing down his back in a slow heavy wave. I discerned embarrassment in that large, fleshy, upper-class back, and got closer to the old man.

"Children," he said to the boys, "don't touch this lad." And he laid a fat hand tenderly on my shoulder.

"My little friend," he went on, turning me towards him, "tell your father that you are admitted to the first class."

On his chest a great star flashed, and decorations jingled in his lapel. His great black uniformed body started to move away on its stiff legs. Hemmed in by the shadowy walls, moving between them as a barge moves through a deep canal, it disappeared in the doorway of the head-master's study. The little servingman took in a tray of tea, clinking solemnly, and I ran home to the shop.

In the shop a peasant customer, tortured by doubt, sat scratching himself. When he saw me my father stopped trying to help the peasant make up his mind, and without a moment's hesitation believed everything I had to say. Calling to the assistant to start shutting up shop, he dashed out into Cathedral Street to buy me a school cap with a badge on it. My poor mother had her work cut out getting me away from the crazy fellow. She was pale at that moment, she was experiencing destiny. She kept smoothing me, and pushing me away as though she hated me. She said there was always a notice in the paper about those who had been admitted to the school and that God would punish us, and that folk would laugh at us if we bought a school cap too soon. My mother was pale; she was experiencing destiny through my eyes. She looked at me with bitter compassion as one might look at a little cripple boy, because she alone knew what a family ours was for misfortunes.

All the men in our family were trusting by nature, and quick to ill-considered actions. We were unlucky in everything we undertook. My grandfather had been a rabbi somewhere in the Belaya Tserkov region. He had been thrown out for blasphemy, and for another forty years he lived noisily and sparsely, teaching foreign languages. In his eightieth year he started going off his head. My Uncle Leo, my father's brother, had studied at the Talmudic Academy in Volozhin. In 1892 he ran away to avoid doing military service, eloping with the daughter of someone serving in the commissariat in the Kiev military district. Uncle Leo took this woman to California, to Los Angeles, and there he abandoned her, and died in a house of ill fame among Negroes and Malays. After his death the American police sent us a heritage from Los Angeles, a large trunk bound with brown iron hoops. In this trunk there were dumbbells, locks of women's hair, uncle's talith, horsewhips with gilt handles, scented tea in boxes trimmed with imitation pearls. Of all the family there remained only crazy Uncle Simon-Wolf, who lived in Odessa, my father, and I. But my father had faith in people, and he used to put them off with the transports of first love. People could not forgive him for this, and used to play him false. So my father believed that his life was guided by an evil fate, an inexplicable being that pursued him, a being in every respect unlike him. And so I alone of all our family was left to my mother. Like all Jews I was short, weakly, and had headaches from studying. My mother saw all this. She had never been dazzled by her husband's pauper pride, by his incomprehensible belief that our family would one day be richer and more powerful than all others on earth. She desired no success for us, was scared of buying a school jacket too soon, and all she would consent to was that I should have my photo taken.

On September 20, 1905, a list of those admitted to the first class was hung up at the school. In the list my name figured too. All our kith and kin kept going to look at this paper, and even Shoyl, my granduncle, went along. I loved that boastful old man, for he sold fish at the market.

His fat hands were moist, covered with fish-scales, and smelt of worlds chill and beautiful. Shoyl also differed from ordinary folk in the lying stories he used to tell about the Polish Rising of 1861. Years ago Shoyl had been a tavern-keeper at Skvira. He had seen Nicholas I's soldiers shooting Count Godlevski and other Polish insurgents. But perhaps he hadn't. *Now* I know that Shoyl was just an old ignoramus and a simple-minded liar, but his cock-and-bull stories I have never forgotten: they were good stories. Well now, even silly old Shoyl went along to the school to read the list with my name on it, and that evening he danced and pranced at our pauper ball.

My father got up the ball to celebrate my success, and asked all his pals—grain-dealers, real-estate brokers, and the traveling salesmen who sold agricultural machinery in our parts. These salesmen would sell a machine to anyone. Peasants and landowners went in fear of them: you couldn't break loose without buying something or other. Of all Jews, salesmen are the widest-awake and the jolliest. At our party they sang Hasidic songs consisting of three words only but which took an awful long time to sing, songs performed with endless comical intonations. The beauty of these intonations may only be recognized by those who have had the good fortune to spend Passover with the Hasidim or who have visited their noisy Volhynian synagogues. Besides the salesmen, old Lieberman who had taught me the Torah and ancient Hebrew honored us with his presence. In our circle he was known as Monsieur Lieberman. He drank more Bessarabian wine than he should have. The ends of the traditional silk tassels poked out from beneath his waistcoat, and in ancient Hebrew he proposed my health. In this toast the old man congratulated my parents and said that I had vanquished all my foes in single combat: I had vanquished the Russian boys with their fat cheeks, and I had vanquished the sons of our own vulgar parvenus. So too in ancient times David King of Judah had overcome Goliath, and just as I had triumphed over Goliath, so too would our people by the strength of their intellect conquer the foes who had encircled us and were thirsting for our blood. Monsieur Lieberman started to weep as he said this, drank more wine as he wept, and shouted *"Vivat!"* The guests formed a circle and danced an old-fashioned quadrille with him in the middle, just as at a wedding in a little Jewish town. Everyone was happy at our ball. Even mother took a sip of vodka, though she neither liked the stuff nor understood how anyone else could—because of this she considered all Russians cracked, and just couldn't imagine how women managed with Russian husbands.

But our happy days came later. For mother they came when of a morning, before I set off for school, she would start making me sand-wiches; when we went shopping to buy my school things—pencil box, money box, satchel, new books in cardboard bindings, and exercise books in shiny covers. No one in the world has a keener feeling for new things than children have. Children shudder at the smell of newness as a dog does when it scents a hare, experiencing the madness which later, when we grow up, is called inspiration. And mother acquired this pure and childish sense of the ownership of new things. It took us a whole month to get used to the pencil box, to the morning twilight as I drank my tea on the corner of the large, brightly-lit table and packed my books in my satchel. It took us a month to grow accustomed to our happiness, and it was only after the first half-term that I remembered about the pigeons.

I had everything ready for them: one rouble fifty and a dovecot made from a box by Grandfather Shoyl, as we called him. The dovecot was painted brown. It had nests for twelve pairs of pigeons, carved strips on the roof, and a special grating that I had devised to facilitate the capture of strange birds. All was in readiness. On Sunday, October 20, I set out for the bird market, but unexpected obstacles arose in my path.

The events I am relating, that is to say my admission to the first class at the secondary school, occurred in the autumn of 1905. The Emperor Nicholas was then bestowing a constitution on the Russian people. Orators in shabby overcoats were clambering onto tall curbstones and haranguing the people. At night shots had been heard in the streets, and so mother didn't want me to go to the bird market. From early morning on October 20 the boys next door were flying a kite right by the police station, and our water carrier, abandoning all his buckets, was walking about the streets with a red face and brilliantined hair. Then we saw baker Kalistov's sons drag a leather vaulting-horse out into the street and start doing gym in the middle of the roadway. No one tried to stop them: Semernikov the policeman even kept inciting them to jump higher. Semernikov was girt with a silk belt his wife had made him, and his boots had been polished that day as they had never been polished before. Out of his customary uniform, the policeman frightened my mother more than anything else. Because of him she didn't want me to go out, but I sneaked out by the back way and ran to the bird market, which in our town was behind the station.

At the bird market Ivan Nikodimych, the pigeon-fancier, sat in his customary place. Apart from pigeons, he had rabbits for sale too, and a peacock. The peacock, spreading its tail, sat on a perch moving a passionless head from side to side. To its paw was tied a twisted cord, and the other end of the cord was caught beneath one leg of Ivan Nikodimych's wicker chair. The moment I got there I bought from the old man a pair of cherry-colored pigeons with luscious tousled tails, and a pair of crowned pigeons, and put them away in a bag on my chest under my shirt. After these purchases I had only forty copecks left, and for this price the old man was not prepared to let me have a male and female pigeon of the Kryukov breed. What I liked about Kryukov pigeons was their short, knobbly, good-natured beaks. Forty copecks was the proper price, but the fancier insisted on haggling, averting from me a yellow face scorched by the unsociable passions of bird-snarers. At the end of our bargaining, seeing that there were no other customers, Ivan Nikodimych beckoned me closer. All went as I wished, and all went badly.

Toward twelve o'clock, or perhaps a bit later, a man in felt boots passed across the square. He was stepping lightly on swollen feet, and in his worn-out face lively eyes glittered.

"Ivan Nikodimych," he said as he walked past the bird-fancier, "pack up your gear. In town the Jerusalem aristocrats are being granted a constitution. On Fish Street Grandfather Babel has been constitutioned to death."

He said this and walked lightly on between the cages like a barefoot ploughman walking along the edge of a field.

"They shouldn't," murmured Ivan Nikodimych in his wake. "They shouldn't!" he cried more sternly. He started collecting his rabbits and his peacock, and shoved the Kryukov pigeons at me for forty copecks. I hid them in my bosom and watched the people running away from the bird market. The peacock on Ivan Nikodimych's shoulder was last of all to depart. It sat there like the sun in a raw autumnal sky; it sat as July sits on a pink riverbank, a white-hot July in the long cool grass. No one was left in the market, and not far off shots were rattling. Then I ran to the station, cut across a square that had gone topsy-turvy, and flew down an empty lane of trampled yellow earth. At the end of the lane, in a little wheeled armchair, sat the legless Makarenko, who rode about town in his wheel-chair selling cigarettes from a tray. The boys in our street used to buy smokes from him, children loved him, I dashed toward him down the lane.

"Makarenko," I gasped, panting from my run, and I stroked the legless one's shoulder, "have you seen Shoyl?"

The cripple did not reply. A light seemed to be shining through his coarse face built up of red fat, clenched fists, chunks of iron. He was fidgeting on his chair in his excitement, while his wife Kate, presenting a wadded behind, was sorting out some things scattered on the ground.

"How far have you counted?" asked the legless man, and moved his whole bulk away from the woman, as though aware in advance that her answer would be unbearable.

"Fourteen pair of leggings," said Kate, still bending over, "six under-sheets. Now I'm a-counting the bonnets."

"Bonnets!" cried Makarenko, with a choking sound like a sob, "it's clear, Catherine, that God has picked on me, that I must answer for all. People are carting off whole rolls of cloth, people have everything they should, and we're stuck with bonnets."

And indeed a woman with a beautiful burning face ran past us down the lane. She was clutching an armful of fezzes in one arm and a piece of cloth in the other, and in a voice of joyful despair she was yelling for her children, who had strayed. A silk dress and a blue blouse fluttered after her as she flew, and she paid no attention to Makarenko who was rolling his chair in pursuit of her. The legless man couldn't catch up. His wheels clattered as he turned the handles for all he was worth.

"Little lady," he cried in a deafening voice, "where did you get that striped stuff?"

But the woman with the fluttering dress was gone. Round the corner to meet her leaped a rickety cart in which a peasant lad stood upright.

"Where've they all run to?" asked the lad, raising a red rein above the nags jerking in their collars.

"Everybody's on Cathedral Street," said Makarenko pleadingly, "everybody's there, sonny. Anything you happen to pick up, bring it along to me. I'll give you a good price."

The lad bent down over the front of the cart and whipped up his piebald nags. Tossing their filthy croups like calves, the horses shot off at a gallop. The yellow lane was once more yellow and empty. Then the legless man turned his quenched eyes upon me.

"God's picked on me, I reckon," he said lifelessly, "I'm a son of man, I reckon."

And he stretched a hand spotted with leprosy toward me.

"What's that you've got in your sack?" he demanded, and took the bag that had been warming my heart.

With his fat hand the cripple fumbled among the tumbler pigeons and dragged to light a cherry-colored she-bird. Jerking back its feet, the bird lay still on his palm.

"Pigeons," said Makarenko, and squeaking his wheels he rode right up to me. "Damned pigeons," he repeated, and struck me on the cheek.

He dealt me a flying blow with the hand that was clutching the bird. Kate's wadded back seemed to turn upside down, and I fell to the ground in my new overcoat.

"Their spawn must be wiped out," said Kate, straightening up over the bonnets. "I can't a-bear their spawn, nor their stinking menfolk."

She said more things about our spawn, but I heard nothing of it. I lay on the ground, and the guts of the crushed bird trickled down from my temple. They flowed down my cheek, winding this way and that, splashing, blinding me. The tender pigeon-guts slid down over my forehead, and I closed my solitary unstopped-up eye so as not to see the world that spread out before me. This world was tiny, and it was awful. A stone lay just before my eyes, a little stone so chipped as to resemble the face of an old woman with a large jaw. A piece of string lay not far away, and a bunch of feathers that still breathed. My world was tiny, and it was awful. I closed my eyes so as not to see it, and pressed myself tight into the ground that lay beneath me in soothing dumbness. This trampled earth in no way resembled real life, waiting for exams in real life. Somewhere far away Woe rode across it on a great steed, but the noise of the hoofbeats grew weaker and died away, and silence, the bitter silence that sometimes overwhelms children in their sorrow, suddenly deleted the boundary between my body and the earth that was moving nowhither. The earth smelled of raw depths, of the tomb, of flowers. I smelled its smell and started crying, unafraid. I was walking along an unknown street set on either side with white boxes, walking in a getup of blood-stained feathers, alone between the pavements swept clean as on Sunday, weeping bitterly, fully and happily as I never wept again in all my life. Wires that had grown white hummed above my head, a watchdog trotted on in front, in the lane on one side a young peasant in a waistcoat was smashing a window frame in the house of Khariton Efrussi. He was smashing it with a wooden mallet, striking out with his whole body. Sighing, he smiled all around with the amiable grin of drunkenness, sweat, and spiritual power. The whole street was filled with a splitting, a snapping, the song of flying wood. The peasant's whole existence consisted in bending over, sweating, shouting queer words in some unknown, non-Russian language. He shouted the words and sang, shot out his blue eyes; till in the street there appeared a procession bearing the Cross and moving from the Municipal Building. Old men bore aloft the portrait of the neatly-combed Tsar, banners with graveyard saints swayed above their heads, inflamed old women flew on in front. Seeing the procession, the peasant pressed his mallet to his chest and dashed off in pursuit of the banners, while I, waiting till the tail-end of the procession had passed, made my furtive way home. The house was empty. Its white doors were open, the grass by the dovecot had been trampled down. Only Kuzma was still in the yard. Kuzma the yardman was sitting in the shed laying out the dead Shoyl.

"The wind bears you about like an evil wood-chip," said the old man when he saw me. "You've been away ages. And now look what they've done to granddad."

Kuzma wheezed, turned away from me, and started pulling a fish out of a rent in grandfather's trousers. Two pike perch had been stuck into grandfather: one into the rent in his trousers, the other into his mouth. And while grandfather was dead, one of the fish was still alive, and struggling.

"They've done grandfather in, but nobody else," said Kuzma, tossing the fish to the cat. "He cursed them all good and proper, a wonderful damning and blasting it was. You might fetch a couple of pennies to put on his eyes."

But then, at ten years of age, I didn't know what need the dead had of pennies.

"Kuzma," I whispered, "save us."

And I went over to the yardman, hugged his crooked old back with its one shoulder higher than the other, and over his back I saw grandfather. Shoyl lay in the sawdust, his chest squashed in, his beard twisted upwards, battered shoes on his bare feet. His feet, thrown wide apart, were dirty, lilac-colored, dead. Kuzma was fussing over him. He tied the dead man's jaws and kept glancing over the body to see what else he could do. He fussed as though over a newly-purchased garment, and only cooled down when he had given the dead man's beard a good combing.

"He cursed the lot of 'em right and left," he said, smiling, and cast a loving look over the corpse. "If Tartars had crossed his path he'd have sent them packing, but Russians came, and their women with them, Rooski women. Russians just can't bring themselves to forgive, I know what Rooskis are."

The yardman spread some more sawdust beneath the body, threw off his carpenter's apron, and took me by the hand.

"Let's go to father," he mumbled, squeezing my hand tighter and tighter. "Your father has been searching for you since morning, sure as fate you was dead."

And so with Kuzma I went to the house of the tax-inspector, where my parents, escaping the pogrom, had sought refuge.

F. SCOTT FITZGERALD

(1896–1940)

F. Scott Fitzgerald was born in St. Paul, Minnesota, the son of
sensitive, genteel, but impractical parents. His father was dismissed from his job in 1908, and the family was forced to move from one
part of St. Paul to another as poverty threatened. Fitzgerald's time at
Princeton meant intellectual stimulation and his first contacts with real
culture, but helped develop his obsession with social climbing and his
fascination with the good life. In 1920 he married Zelda Sayre, the
beautiful and charming girl he had met in Montgomery, Alabama, while
stationed at an army camp, and he published his first novel, This Side
of Paradise, which was something of a bestseller (40 000 books in less
than a year) and a success with the critics. The parties and lavish lifestyle
that ensued made the Fitzgeralds the quintessential Jazz Age couple. His
stories commanded fabulous amounts in American magazines. In New
York, Paris, and Rome, Fitzgerald was known for his prodigal habits and
his drunken exploits. The Great Gatsby (1925) established him as one
of the great American novelists, but Fitzgerald was disappointed by its
sales. His third collection of stories, All the Sad Young Men (1926),
did not solve his growing financial problems. Zelda's nervous break-
downs and his troubles with alcoholism brought on his own great depression in the early 1930s. The party was over. Tender Is the Night (1934)
was only a limited success. In 1937 Fitzgerald moved to Hollywood,
where he worked on film scripts that were never produced, and struggled
to rediscover his vocation. But as he wrote in the notes for his posthumously published novel, The Last Tycoon (1941), "there are no second
acts in American lives." He began drinking again, quarrelled with those
who had befriended him, and died of a heart attack. As Sergio Perosa has
argued, Fitzgerald's parables "on the two themes of love and money,
indissolubly connected," his "modern tragicomedy of manners," still
make him essential reading for students of American literature.

Babylon Revisited

"*A* nd where's Mr. Campbell?" Charlie asked.
        "Gone to Switzerland. Mr. Campbell's a pretty sick man,
Mr. Wales."
    "I'm sorry to hear that. And George Hardt?" Charlie inquired.
    "Back in America, gone to work."
    "And where is the Snow Bird?"

"He was in here last week. Anyway, his friend, Mr. Schaeffer, is in Paris."

Two familiar names from the long list of a year and a half ago. Charlie scribbled an address in his notebook and tore out the page.

"If you see Mr. Schaeffer, give him this," he said. "It's my brother-in-law's address. I haven't settled on a hotel yet."

He was not really disappointed to find Paris was so empty. But the stillness in the Ritz bar was strange and portentous. It was not an American bar any more—he felt polite in it, and not as if he owned it. It had gone back into France. He felt the stillness from the moment he got out of the taxi and saw the doorman, usually in a frenzy of activity at this hour, gossiping with a *chasseur* by the servants' entrance.

Passing through the corridor, he heard only a single, bored voice in the once-clamorous women's room. When he turned into the bar he traveled the twenty feet of green carpet with his eyes fixed straight ahead by old habit; and then, with his foot firmly on the rail, he turned and surveyed the room, encountering only a single pair of eyes that fluttered up from a newspaper in the corner. Charlie asked for the head barman, Paul, who in the latter days of the bull market had come to work in his own custom-built car—disembarking, however, with due nicety at the nearest corner. But Paul was at his country house today and Alix giving him information.

"No, no more," Charlie said, "I'm going slow these days."

Alix congratulated him: "You were going pretty strong a couple of years ago."

"I'll stick to it all right," Charlie assured him. "I've stuck to it for over a year and a half now."

"How do you find conditions in America?"

"I haven't been to America for months. I'm in business in Prague, representing a couple of concerns there. They don't know about me down there."

Alix smiled.

"Remember the night of George Hardt's bachelor dinner here?" said Charlie. "By the way, what's become of Claude Fessenden?"

Alix lowered his voice confidentially: "He's in Paris, but he doesn't come here any more. Paul doesn't allow it. He ran up a bill of thirty thousand francs, charging all his drinks and his lunches, and usually his dinner, for more than a year. And when Paul finally told him he had to pay, he gave him a bad check."

Alix shook his head sadly.

"I don't understand it, such a dandy fellow. Now he's all bloated up—" He made a plump apple of his hands.

Charlie watched a group of strident queens installing themselves in a corner.

"Nothing affects them," he thought. "Stocks rise and fall, people loaf or work, but they go on forever." The place oppressed him. He called for the dice and shook with Alix for the drink.

"Here for long, Mr. Wales?"

"I'm here for four or five days to see my little girl."

"Oh-h! You have a little girl?"

Outside, the fire-red, gas-blue, ghost-green signs shone smokily through the tranquil rain. It was late afternoon and the streets were in movement; the *bistros* gleamed. At the corner of the Boulevard des Capucines he took a taxi. The Place de la Concorde moved by in pink majesty; they crossed the logical Seine, and Charlie felt the sudden provincial quality of the left bank.

Charlie directed his taxi to the Avenue de l'Opera, which was out of his way. But he wanted to see the blue hour spread over the magnificent façade, and imagine that the cab horns, playing endlessly the first few bars of *Le Plus que Lent*, were the trumpets of the Second Empire. They were closing the iron grill in front of Brentano's Book-store, and people were already at dinner behind the trim little bourgeois hedge of Duval's. He had never eaten at a really cheap restaurant in Paris. Five-course dinner, four francs fifty, eighteen cents, wine included. For some odd reason he wished that he had.

As they rolled on to the Left Bank and he felt its sudden provincialism, he thought, "I spoiled this city for myself. I didn't realize it, but the days came along one after another, and then two years were gone, and everything was gone, and I was gone."

He was thirty-five, and good to look at. The Irish mobility of his face was sobered by a deep wrinkle between his eyes. As he rang his brother-in-law's bell in the Rue Palatine, the wrinkle deepened till it pulled down his brows; he felt a cramping sensation in his belly. From behind the maid who opened the door darted a lovely little girl of nine who shrieked "Daddy!" and flew up, struggling like a fish, into his arms. She pulled his head around by one ear and set her cheek against his.

"My old pie," he said.

"Oh, daddy, daddy, daddy, daddy, dads, dads, dads!"

She drew him into the salon, where the family waited, a boy and a girl his daughter's age, his sister-in-law and her husband. He greeted Marion with his voice pitched carefully to avoid either feigned enthusiasm or dislike, but her response was more frankly tepid, though she minimized her expression of unalterable distrust by directing her regard toward his child. The two men clasped hands in a friendly way and Lincoln Peters rested his for a moment on Charlie's shoulder.

The room was warm and comfortably American. The three children moved intimately about, playing through the yellow oblongs that led to other rooms; the cheer of six o'clock spoke in the eager smacks of the fire and the sounds of French activity in the kitchen. But Charlie did not relax; his heart sat up rigidly in his body and he drew confidence from his daughter, who from time to time came close to him, holding in her arms the doll he had brought.

"Really extremely well," he declared in answer to Lincoln's question. "There's a lot of business there that isn't moving at all, but we're doing even better than ever. In fact, damn well. I'm bringing my sister over from America next month to keep house for me. My income last year was bigger than it was when I had money. You see, the Czechs—"

His boasting was for a specific purpose; but after a moment, seeing a faint restiveness in Lincoln's eye, he changed the subject:

"Those are fine children of yours, well brought up, good manners."

"We think Honoria's a great little girl too."

Marion Peters came back from the kitchen. She was a tall woman with worried eyes, who had once possessed a fresh American loveliness. Charlie had never been sensitive to it and was always surprised when people spoke of how pretty she had been. From the first there had been an instinctive antipathy between them.

"Well, how do you find Honoria?" she asked.

"Wonderful. I was astonished how much she's grown in ten months. All the children are looking well."

"We haven't had a doctor for a year. How do you like being back in Paris?"

"It seems very funny to see so few Americans around."

"I'm delighted," Marion said vehemently. "Now at least you can go into a store without their assuming you're a millionaire. We've suffered like everybody, but on the whole it's a good deal pleasanter."

"But it was nice while it lasted," Charlie said. "We were a sort of royalty, almost infallible, with a sort of magic around us. In the bar this afternoon"—he stumbled, seeing his mistake—"there wasn't a man I knew."

She looked at him keenly. "I should think you'd have had enough of bars."

"I only stayed a minute. I take one drink every afternoon, and no more."

"Don't you want a cocktail before dinner?" Lincoln asked.

"I take only one drink every afternoon, and I've had that."

"I hope you keep to it," said Marion.

Her dislike was evident in the coldness with which she spoke, but Charlie only smiled; he had larger plans. Her very aggressiveness gave him an advantage, and he knew enough to wait. He wanted them to initiate the discussion of what they knew had brought him to Paris.

At dinner he couldn't decide whether Honoria was most like him or her mother. Fortunate if she didn't combine the traits of both that had brought them to disaster. A great wave of protectiveness went over him. He thought he knew what to do for her. He believed in character; he wanted to jump back a whole generation and trust in character again as the eternally valuable element. Everything else wore out.

He left soon after dinner, but not to go home. He was curious to see Paris by night with clearer and more judicious eyes than those of other days. He bought a *strapontin* for the Casino and watched Josephine Baker go through her chocolate arabesques.

After an hour he left and strolled toward Montmartre, up the Rue Pigalle into the Place Blanche. The rain had stopped and there were a few people in evening clothes disembarking from taxis in front of cabarets, and *cocottes* prowling singly or in pairs, and many Negroes. He passed a lighted door from which issued music, and stopped with the sense of familiarity; it was Bricktop's, where he had parted with so many hours and so much money. A few doors farther on he found another ancient rendezvous and incautiously put his head inside. Immediately an eager orchestra burst into sound, a pair of professional dancers leaped to their feet and a maître d'hôtel swooped toward him, crying, "Crowd just arriving, sir!" But he withdrew quickly.

"You have to be damn drunk," he thought.

Zelli's was closed, the bleak and sinister cheap hotels surrounding it were dark; up in the Rue Blanche there was more light and a local, colloquial French crowd. The Poet's Cave had disappeared, but the two great mouths of the Café of Heaven and the Café of Hell still yawned— even devoured, as he watched, the meager contents of a tourist bus—a German, a Japanese, and an American couple who glanced at him with frightened eyes.

So much for the effort and ingenuity of Montmartre. All the catering to vice and waste was on an utterly childish scale, and he suddenly realized the meaning of the word "dissipate"—to dissipate into thin air; to make nothing out of something. In the little hours of the night every move from place to place was an enormous human jump, an increase of paying for the privilege of slower and slower motion.

He remembered thousand-franc notes given to an orchestra for playing a single number, hundred-franc notes tossed to a doorman for calling a cab.

But it hadn't been given for nothing.

It had been given, even the most wildly squandered sum, as an offering to destiny that he might not remember the things most worth remembering, the things that now he would always remember—his child taken from his control, his wife escaped to a grave in Vermont.

In the glare of a *brasserie* a woman spoke to him. He bought her some eggs and coffee, and then, eluding her encouraging stare, gave her a twenty-franc note and took a taxi to his hotel.

II

He woke upon a fine fall day—football weather. The depression of yesterday was gone and he liked the people on the streets. At noon he sat opposite Honoria at Le Grand Vatel, the only restaurant he could think of not reminiscent of champagne dinners and long luncheons that began at two and ended in a blurred and vague twilight.

"Now, how about vegetables? Oughtn't you to have some vegetables?"

"Well, yes."

"Here's *épinards* and *chou-fleur* and carrots and *haricots.*"

"I'd like *chou-fleur.*"

"Wouldn't you like to have two vegetables?"

"I usually only have one at lunch."

The waiter was pretending to be inordinately fond of children. *"Qu'elle est mignonne la petite! Elle parle exactement comme une Française."*

"How about dessert? Shall we wait and see?"

The waiter disappeared. Honoria looked at her father expectantly.

"What are we going to do?"

"First, we're going to that toy store in the Rue Saint-Honoré and buy you anything you like. And then we're going to the vaudeville at the Empire."

She hesitated. "I like it about the vaudeville, but not the toy store."

"Why not?"

"Well, you brought me this doll." She had it with her. "And I've got lots of things. And we're not rich any more, are we?"

"We never were. But today you are to have anything you want."

"All right, " she agreed resignedly.

When there had been her mother and a French nurse he had been inclined to be strict; now he extended himself, reached out for a new tolerance; he must be both parents to her and not shut any of her out of communication.

"I want to get to know you," he said gravely. "First let me introduce myself. My name is Charles J. Wales, of Prague."

"Oh, daddy!" her voice cracked with laughter.

"And who are you, please?" he persisted, and she accepted a rôle immediately: "Honoria Wales, Rue Palatine, Paris."

"Married or single?"

"No, not married. Single."

He indicated the doll. "But I see you have a child, madame."

Unwilling to disinherit it, she took it to her heart and thought quickly: "Yes, I've been married, but I'm not married now. My husband is dead."

He went on quickly, "And the child's name?"

"Simone. That's after my best friend at school."

"I'm very pleased that you're doing so well at school."

"I'm third this month," she boasted. "Elsie"—that was her cousin—"is only about eighteenth, and Richard is about at the bottom."

"You like Richard and Elsie, don't you?"

"Oh, yes. I like Richard quite well and I like her all right."

Cautiously and casually he asked: "And Aunt Marion and Uncle Lincoln—which do you like best?"

"Oh, Uncle Lincoln, I guess."

He was increasingly aware of her presence. As they came in, a murmur of ". . . adorable" followed them, and now the people at the next table bent all their silences upon her, staring as if she were something no more conscious than a flower.

"Why don't I live with you?" she asked suddenly. "Because mamma's dead?"

"You must stay here and learn more French. It would have been hard for daddy to take care of you so well."

"I don't really need much taking care of any more. I do everything for myself."

Going out of the restaurant, a man and a woman unexpectedly hailed him.

"Well, the old Wales!"

"Hello there, Lorraine. . . . Dunc."

Sudden ghosts out of the past: Duncan Schaeffer, a friend from college. Lorraine Quarrles, a lovely, pale blonde of thirty; one of a crowd who had helped them make months into days in the lavish times of three years ago.

"My husband couldn't come this year," she said, in answer to his question. "We're poor as hell. So he gave me two hundred a month and told me I could do my worst on that. . . . This your little girl?"

"What about coming back and sitting down?" Duncan asked.

"Can't do it." He was glad for an excuse. As always, he felt Lorraine's passionate, provocative attraction, but his own rhythm was different now.

"Well, how about dinner?" she asked.

"I'm not free. Give me your address and let me call you."

"Charlie, I believe you're sober," she said judicially. "I honestly believe he's sober, Dunc. Pinch him and see if he's sober."

Charlie indicate Honoria with his head. They both laughed.

"What's your address?" said Duncan skeptically.

He hesitated, unwilling to give the name of his hotel.

"I'm not settled yet. I'd better call you. We're going to see the vaudeville at the Empire."

"There! That's what I want to do," Lorraine said. "I want to see some clowns and acrobats and jugglers. That's just what we'll do, Dunc."

"We've got to do an errand first," said Charlie. "Perhaps we'll see you there."

"All right, you snob. . . . Good-by, beautiful little girl."

"Good-by."

Honoria bobbed politely.

Somehow, an unwelcome encounter. They liked him because he was functioning, because he was serious; they wanted to see him, because he was stronger than they were now, because they wanted to draw a certain sustenance from his strength.

At the Empire, Honoria proudly refused to sit upon her father's folded coat. She was already an individual with a code of her own, and Charlie was more and more absorbed by the desire of putting a little of himself into her before she crystallized utterly. It was hopeless to try to know her in so short a time.

Between the acts they came upon Duncan and Lorraine in the lobby where the band was playing.

"Have a drink?"

"All right, but not up at the bar. We'll take a table."

"The perfect father."

Listening abstractedly to Lorraine, Charlie watched Honoria's eyes leave their table, and he followed them wistfully about the room, wondering what they saw. He met her glance and she smiled.

"I liked that lemonade," she said.

What had she said? What had he expected? Going home in a taxi afterward, he pulled her over until her head rested against his chest.

"Darling, do you ever think about your mother?"

"Yes, sometimes," she answered vaguely.

"I don't want you to forget her. Have you got a picture of her?"

"Yes, I think so. Anyhow, Aunt Marion has. Why don't you want me to forget her?"

"She loved you very much."

"I loved her too."

They were silent for a moment.

"Daddy, I want to come and live with you," she said suddenly. His heart leaped; he had wanted it to come like this.

"Aren't you perfectly happy?"

"Yes, but I love you better than anybody. And you love me better than anybody, don't you, now that mummy's dead?"

"Of course I do. But you won't always like me best, honey. You'll grow up and meet somebody your own age and go marry him and forget you ever had a daddy."

"Yes, that's true," she agreed tranquilly.

He didn't go in. He was coming back at nine o'clock and he wanted to keep himself fresh and new for the thing he must say then.

"When you're safe inside, just show yourself in that window."

"All right. Good-by, dads, dads, dads, dads."

He waited in the dark street until she appeared, all warm and glowing, in the window above and kissed her fingers out into the night.

III

They were waiting. Marion sat behind the coffee service in a dignified black dress that just faintly suggested mourning. Lincoln was walking up and down with the animation of one who had already been talking. They were as anxious as he was to get into the question. He opened it almost immediately:

"I suppose you know what I want to see you about—why I really came to Paris."

Marion played with the black stars on her necklace and frowned.

"I'm awfully anxious to have a home," he continued. "And I'm awfully anxious to have Honoria in it. I appreciate your taking in Honoria for her mother's sake, but things have changed now"—he hesitated and then continued more forcibly—"changed radically with me, and I want to ask you to reconsider the matter. It would be silly for me to deny that about three years ago I was acting badly——"

Marion looked up at him with hard eyes.

"—but all that's over. As I told you, I haven't had more than a drink a day for over a year, and I take that drink deliberately, so that the idea of alcohol won't get too big in my imagination. You see the idea?"

"No," said Marion succinctly.

"It's a sort of stunt I set myself. It keeps the matter in proportion."

"I get you," said Lincoln. "You don't want to admit it's got any attraction for you."

"Something like that. Sometimes I forget and don't take it. But I try to take it. Anyhow, I couldn't afford to drink in my position. The people I represent are more than satisfied with what I've done, and I'm bringing my sister over from Burlington to keep house for me, and I want awfully to have Honoria too. You know that even when her mother and I weren't getting along well we never let anything that happened touch Honoria. I know she's fond of me and I know I'm able to take care of her and—well, there you are. How do you feel about it?"

He knew that now he would have to take a beating. It would last an hour or two hours, and it would be difficult, but if he modulated his inevitable resentment to the chastened attitude of the reformed sinner, he might win his point in the end.

Keep your temper, he told himself. You don't want to be justified. You want Honoria.

Lincoln spoke first: "We've been talking it over ever since we got your letter last month. We're happy to have Honoria here. She's a dear little thing, and we're glad to be able to help her, but of course that isn't the question——"

Marion interrupted suddenly. "How long are you going to stay sober, Charlie?" she asked.

"Permanently, I hope."

"How can anybody count on that?"

"You know I never did drink heavily until I gave up business and came over here with nothing to do. Then Helen and I began to run around with——"

"Please leave Helen out of it. I can't bear to hear you talk about her like that."

He stared at her grimly; he had never been certain how fond of each other the sisters were in life.

"My drinking only lasted about a year and half—from the time we came over until I—collapsed."

"It was time enough."

"It was time enough," he agreed.

"My duty is entirely to Helen," she said. "I try to think what she would have wanted me to do. Frankly, from the night you did that terrible thing you haven't really existed for me. I can't help that. She was my sister."

"Yes."

"When she was dying she asked me to look out for Honoria. If you hadn't been in a sanitarium then, it might have helped matters."

He had no answer.

"I'll never in my life be able to forget the morning when Helen knocked at my door, soaked to the skin and shivering, and said you'd locked her out."

Charlie gripped the sides of the chair. This was more difficult than he expected; he wanted to launch out into a long expostulation and explanation, but he only said: "The night I locked her out—" and she interrupted, "I don't feel up to going over that again."

After a moment's silence Lincoln said: "We're getting off the subject. You want Marion to set aside her legal guardianship and give you Honoria. I think the main point for her is whether she has confidence in you or not."

"I don't blame Marion," Charlie said slowly, "but I think she can have entire confidence in me. I had a good record up to three years ago. Of course, it's within human possibilities I might go wrong any time. But if we wait much longer I'll lose Honoria's childhood and my chance for a home." He shook his head, "I'll simply lose her, don't you see?"

"Yes, I see," said Lincoln.

"Why didn't you think of all this before?" Marion asked.

"I suppose I did, from time to time, but Helen and I were getting along badly. When I consented to the guardianship, I was flat on my back in a sanitarium and the market had cleaned me out. I knew I'd acted badly, and I thought if it would bring any peace to Helen, I'd agree to anything. But now it's different. I'm functioning, I'm behaving damn well, so far as——"

"Please don't swear at me," Marion said.

He looked at her, startled. With each remark the force of her dislike became more and more apparent. She had built up all her fear of life into one wall and faced it toward him. This trivial reproof was possibly the result of some trouble with the cook several hours before. Charlie became increasingly alarmed at leaving Honoria in this atmosphere of hostility against himself; sooner or later it would come out, in a word here, a shake of the head there, and some of that distrust would be irrevocably implanted in Honoria. But he pulled his temper down out of his face and shut it up inside him; he had won a point, for Lincoln realized the absurdity of Marion's remark and asked her lightly since when she had objected to the word "damn."

"Another thing," Charlie said: "I'm able to give her certain advantages now. I'm going to take a French governess to Prague with me. I've got a lease on a new apartment——"

He stopped, realizing that he was blundering. They couldn't be expected to accept with equanimity the fact that his income was again twice as large as their own.

"I suppose you can give her more luxuries than we can," said Marion. "When you were throwing away money we were living along watching every ten francs. . . . I suppose you'll start doing it again."

"Oh, no," he said. "I've learned. I worked hard for ten years, you know—until I got lucky in the market, like so many people. Terribly lucky. It didn't seem any use working any more, so I quit."

There was a long silence. All of them felt their nerves straining, and for the first time in a year Charlie wanted a drink. He was sure now that Lincoln Peters wanted him to have his child.

Marion shuddered suddenly; part of her saw that Charlie's feet were planted on the earth now, and her own maternal feeling recognized the naturalness of his desire; but she had lived for a long time with a prejudice—a prejudice founded on a curious disbelief in her sister's happiness, and which, in the shock of one terrible night, had turned to hatred for him. It had all happened at a point in her life where the discouragement of ill health and adverse circumstances made it necessary for her to believe in tangible villainy and a tangible villain.

"I can't help what I think!" she cried out suddenly. "How much you were responsible for Helen's death, I don't know. It's something you'll have to square with your own conscience."

An electric current of agony surged through him; for a moment he was almost on his feet, an unuttered sound echoing in his throat. He hung on to himself for a moment, another moment.

"Hold on there," said Lincoln uncomfortably. "I never thought you were responsible for that."

"Helen died of heart trouble," Charlie said dully.

"Yes, heart trouble." Marion spoke as if the phrase had another meaning for her.

Then, in the flatness that followed her outburst, she saw him plainly and she knew he had somehow arrived at control over the situation. Glancing at her husband, she found no help from him, and as abruptly as if it were a matter of no importance, she threw up the sponge.

"Do what you like!" she cried, springing up from her chair. "She's your child. I'm not the person to stand in your way. I think if it were my child I'd rather see her—" She managed to check herself. "You two decide it. I can't stand this. I'm sick. I'm going to bed."

She hurried from the room; after a moment Lincoln said:

"This has been a hard day for her. You know how strongly she feels—" His voice was almost apologetic: "When a woman gets an idea in her head."

"Of course."

"It's going to be all right. I think she sees now that you—can provide for the child, and so we can't very well stand in your way or Honoria's way."

"Thank you, Lincoln."

"I'd better go along and see how she is."

"I'm going."

He was still trembling when he reached the street, but a walk down the Rue Bonaparte to the *quais* set him up, and as he crossed the Seine, fresh and new by the *quai* lamps, he felt exultant. But back in his room he couldn't sleep. The image of Helen haunted him. Helen whom he had loved so until they had senselessly begun to abuse each other's love, tear it into shreds. On that terrible February night that Marion remembered so vividly, a slow quarrel had gone on for hours. There was a scene at the Florida, and then he attempted to take her home, and then she kissed young Webb at a table; after that there was what she had hysterically said. When he arrived home alone he turned the key in the lock in wild anger. How could he know she would arrive an hour later alone, that there would be a snowstorm in which she wandered about in slippers, too confused to find a taxi? Then the aftermath, her escaping pneumonia by a miracle, and all the attendant horror. They were "reconciled," but that was the beginning of the end, and Marion, who had seen with her own eyes and who imagined it to be one of many scenes from her sister's martyrdom, never forgot.

Going over it again brought Helen nearer, and in the white, soft light that steals upon half sleep near morning he found himself talking to her again. She said that he was perfectly right about Honoria and that she wanted Honoria to be with him. She said she was glad he was being good and doing better. She said a lot of other things—very friendly things—but she was in a swing in a white dress, and swinging faster and faster all the time, so that at the end he could not hear clearly all that she said.

IV

He woke up feeling happy. The door of the world was open again. He made plans, vistas, futures for Honoria and himself, but suddenly he grew sad, remembering all the plans he and Helen had made. She had not planned to die. The present was the thing—work to do and someone to love. But not to love too much, for he knew the injury that a father can do to a daughter or a mother to a son by attaching them too closely: afterward, out in the world, the child would seek in the marriage partner the same blind tenderness and, failing probably to find it, turn against love and life.

It was a bright, crisp day. He called Lincoln Peters at the bank where he worked and asked if he could count on taking Honoria when he left for Prague. Lincoln agreed that there was no reason for delay. One thing—the legal guardianship. Marion wanted to retain that a while longer. She was upset by the whole matter, and it would oil things if she felt that the situation was still in her control for another year. Charlie agreed, wanting only the tangible, visible child.

Then the question of a governess. Charles sat in a gloomy agency and talked to a cross Béarnaise and to a buxom Breton peasant, neither of whom he could have endured. There were others whom he would see tomorrow.

He lunched with Lincoln Peters at Griffons, trying to keep down his exultation.

"There's nothing quite like your own child," Lincoln said. "But you understand how Marion feels too."

"She's forgotten how hard I worked for seven years there," Charlie said. "She just remembers one night."

"There's another thing." Lincoln hesitated. "While you and Helen were tearing around Europe throwing money away, we were just getting along. I didn't touch any of the prosperity because I never got ahead enough to carry anything but my insurance. I think Marion felt there was some kind of injustice in it—you not even working toward the end, and getting richer and richer."

"It went just as quick as it came," said Charlie.

"Yes, a lot of it stayed in the hands of *chasseurs* and saxophone players and maîtres d'hôtel—well, the big party's over now. I just said that to explain Marion's feeling about those crazy years. If you drop in about six o'clock tonight before Marion's too tired, we'll settle the details on the spot."

Back at his hotel, Charlie found a *pneumatique* that had been redirected from the Ritz bar where Charlie had left his address for the purpose of finding a certain man.

> DEAR CHARLIE: You were so strange when we saw you the other day that I wondered if I did something to offend you. If so, I'm not conscious of it. In fact, I have thought about you too much for the last year, and it's always been in the back of my mind that I might see you if I came over here. We *did* have such good times that crazy spring, like the night you and I stole the butcher's tricycle, and the time we tried to call on the president and you had the old derby rim and the wire cane. Everybody seems so old lately, but I don't feel old a bit. Couldn't we get together some time today for old time's sake? I've got a vile hang-over for the moment, but will be feeling better this afternoon and will look for you about five in the sweatshop at the Ritz.
>
> Always devotedly,
>
> LORRAINE.

His first feeling was one of awe that he had actually, in his mature years, stolen a tricycle and pedaled Lorraine all over the Étoile between the small hours and dawn. In retrospect it was a nightmare. Locking out Helen didn't fit in with any other act of his life, but the tricycle incident did—it was one of many. How many weeks or months of dissipation to arrive at that condition of utter irresponsibility?

He tried to picture how Lorraine had appeared to him then—very attractive; Helen was unhappy about it, though she said nothing. Yesterday, in the restaurant, Lorraine had seemed trite, blurred, worn away. He emphatically did not want to see her, and he was glad Alix had not given away his hotel address. It was a relief to think, instead, of Honoria, to think of Sundays spent with her and of saying good morning to her and of knowing she was there in his house at night, drawing her breath in the darkness.

At five he took a taxi and bought presents for all the Peters—a piquant cloth doll, a box of Roman soldiers, flowers for Marion, big linen handkerchiefs for Lincoln.

He saw, when he arrived in the apartment, that Marion had accepted the inevitable. She greeted him now as though he were a recalcitrant member of the family, rather than a menacing outsider. Honoria had been told she was going; Charlie was glad to see that her tact made her conceal her excessive happiness. Only on his lap did she whisper her delight and the question "When?" before she slipped away with the other children.

He and Marion were alone for a minute in the room, and on an impulse he spoke out boldly:

"Family quarrels are bitter things. They don't go according to any rules. They're not like aches or wounds; they're more like splits in the skin that won't heal because there's not enough material. I wish you and I could be on better terms."

"Some things are hard to forget," she answered. "It's a question of confidence." There was no answer to this and presently she asked, "When do you propose to take her?"

"As soon as I can get a governess. I hoped the day after tomorrow."

"That's impossible. I've got to get her things in shape. Not before Saturday."

He yielded. Coming back into the room, Lincoln offered him a drink.

"I'll take my daily whisky," he said.

It was warm here, it was a home, people together by a fire. The children felt very safe and important; the mother and father were serious, watchful. They had things to do for the children more important than his visit here. A spoonful of medicine was, after all, more important than the strained relations between Marion and himself. They were not dull people, but they were very much in the grip of life and circumstances. He wondered if he couldn't do something to get Lincoln out of his rut at the bank.

A long peal at the door-bell; the *bonne à tout faire* passed through and went down the corridor. The door opened upon another long ring, and then voices, and the three in the salon looked up expectantly; Richard moved to bring the corridor within his range of vision, and Marion rose. Then the maid came back along the corridor, closely followed by the voices, which developed under the light into Duncan Schaeffer and Lorraine Quarrles.

They were gay, they were hilarious, they were roaring with laughter. For a moment Charlie was astounded; unable to understand how they ferreted out the Peters' address.

"Ah-h-h!" Duncan wagged his finger roguishly at Charlie. "Ah-h-h!"

They both slid down another cascade of laughter. Anxious and at a loss, Charlie shook hands with them quickly and presented them to Lincoln and Marion. Marion nodded, scarcely speaking. She had drawn back a step toward the fire; her little girl stood beside her, and Marion put an arm about her shoulder.

With growing annoyance at the intrusion, Charlie waited for them to explain themselves. After some concentration Duncan said:

"We came to invite you out to dinner. Lorraine and I insist that all this chi-chi, cagy business 'bout your address got to stop."

Charlie came closer to them, as if to force them backward down the corridor.

"Sorry, but I can't. Tell me where you'll be and I'll phone you in half an hour."

This made no impression. Lorraine sat down suddenly on the side of a chair, and focusing her eyes on Richard, cried, "Oh, what a nice little boy! Come here, little boy." Richard glanced at his mother, but did not move. With a perceptible shrug of her shoulders, Lorraine turned back to Charlie:

"Come and dine. Sure your cousins won' mine. See you so sel'om. Or solemn."

"I can't," said Charlie sharply. "You two have dinner and I'll phone you."

Her voice became suddenly unpleasant. "All right, we'll go. But I remember once when you hammered on my door at four A.M. I was enough of a good sport to give you a drink. Come on, Dunc."

Still in slow motion, with blurred, angry faces, with uncertain feet, they retired along the corridor.

"Good night," Charlie said.

"Good night!" responded Lorraine emphatically.

When he went back into the salon Marion had not moved, only now her son was standing in the circle of her other arm. Lincoln was still swinging Honoria back and forth like a pendulum from side to side.

"What an outrage!" Charlie broke out. "What an absolute outrage!"

Neither of them answered. Charlie dropped into an armchair, picked up his drink, set it down again and said:

"People I haven't seen for two years having the colossal nerve——"

He broke off. Marion had made the sound "Oh!" in one swift, furious breath, turned her body from him with a jerk and left the room.

Lincoln set down Honoria carefully.

"You children go in and start your soup," he said, and when they obeyed, he said to Charlie:

"Marion's not well and she can't stand shocks. That kind of people make her really physically sick."

"I didn't tell them to come here. They wormed your name out of somebody. They deliberately——"

"Well, it's too bad. It doesn't help matters. Excuse me a minute."

Left alone, Charlie sat tense in his chair. In the next room he could hear the children eating, talking in monosyllables, already oblivious to the scene between their elders. He heard a murmur of conversation from a farther room and then the ticking bell of a telephone receiver picked up, and in a panic he moved to the other side of the room and out of earshot.

In a minute Lincoln came back. "Look here, Charlie. I think we'd better call off dinner for tonight. Marion's in bad shape."

"Is she angry with me?"

"Sort of," he said, almost roughly. "She's not strong and ——"

"You mean she's changed her mind about Honoria?"

"She's pretty bitter right now. I don't know. You phone me at the bank tomorrow."

"I wish you'd explain to her I never dreamed these people would come here. I'm just as sore as you are."

"I couldn't explain anything to her now."

Charlie got up. He took his coat and hat and started down the corridor. Then he opened the door of the dining room and said in a strange voice, "Good night, children."

Honoria rose and ran around the table to hug him.

"Good night, sweetheart," he said vaguely, and then trying to make his voice more tender, trying to conciliate something, "Good night, dear children."

V

Charlie went directly to the Ritz bar with the furious idea of finding Lorraine and Duncan, but they were not there, and he realized that in any case there was nothing he could do. He had not touched his drink at the Peters', and now he ordered a whisky-and-soda. Paul came over to say hello.

"It's a great change," he said sadly. "We do about half the business we did. So many fellows I hear about back in the States lost everything, maybe not in the first crash, but then in the second. Your friend George Hardt lost every cent, I hear. Are you back in the States?"

"No, I'm in business in Prague."

"I heard that you lost a lot in the crash."

"I did," and he added grimly, "but I lost everything I wanted in the boom."

"Selling short."

"Something like that."

Again the memory of those days swept over him like a nightmare— the people they had met travelling; then people who couldn't add a row of figures or speak a coherent sentence. The little man Helen had consented to dance with at the ship's party, who had insulted her ten feet from the table; the women and girls carried screaming with drink or drugs out of public places——

—The men who locked their wives out in the snow, because the snow of twenty-nine wasn't real snow. If you didn't want it to be snow, you just paid some money.

He went to the phone and called the Peters' apartment; Lincoln answered.

"I called up because this thing is on my mind. Has Marion said anything definite?"

"Marion's sick," Lincoln answered shortly. "I know this thing isn't altogether your fault, but I can't have her go to pieces about it. I'm afraid we'll have to let it slide for six months; I can't take the chance of working her up to this state again."

"I see."

"I'm sorry, Charlie."

He went back to his table. His whisky glass was empty, but he shook his head when Alix looked at it questioningly. There wasn't much he could do now except send Honoria some things; he would send her a lot of things tomorrow. He thought rather angrily that this was just money— he had given so many people money. . . .

"No, no more," he said to another waiter. "What do I owe you?"

He would come back some day; they couldn't make him pay forever. But he wanted his child, and nothing was much good now, beside that fact. He wasn't young any more, with a lot of nice thoughts and dreams to have by himself. He was absolutely sure Helen wouldn't have wanted him to be so alone.

William Faulkner

(1897–1962)

Willliam Faulkner *was born in New Albany, Mississippi, and named after a great-grandfather who was a colonel in the Civil War. In 1902 the family moved to Oxford, a town of 1800. He was bored with school in Oxford but read avidly on his own: Melville's* Moby Dick *was a particular favourite. Phil Stone, a young lawyer, became both friend and mentor, introducing him to all sorts of great literature and providing him with an outlet for his own ideas about becoming a writer. Swinburne and Housman were two of his favourite poets. Faulkner went to Canada near the end of the First World War and enlisted in the Royal Canadian Flying Corps. He studied literature and language at the University of Mississippi and distinguished himself as both poet and artist in the student newspaper. After working in a bookstore in New York, he returned to Mississippi in 1921 to become postmaster at the University of Mississippi post office. He was fired for drunkenness and neglect of his duties. His uncle said at the time: "That damn Billy is not worth a Mississippi goddamn—and never will be." He continued to work on his writing, and spent a memorable six months in Europe in 1925. His first novel,* Soldier's Pay, *was published the next year, and* Mosquitoes *followed in 1927. Two years later, settled in Oxford and married to Estelle Oldham Franklin, Faulkner published* Sartoris *and* The Sound and the Fury, *the first of a series of novels that were to tell the story of the imaginary Yoknapatawpha County. His 13 novels, along with 100 short stories, were to make him one of the most famous American writers of the century. Shocked by his gloomy portrayal of the decadent remains of aristocratic southern society, and by the violence and sexuality in his fiction, American readers in particular were slow to grant him the recognition he deserved. He was awarded the Nobel Prize in 1950, and the tribute to man's indomitable spirit in his acceptance speech became as famous as the pessimism and despair in some of the novels. He routinely deprecated his own importance as a writer of stories, but as James Carothers points out, Faulkner's "short stories feature the same distinctions which earned him the title of innovator in the novel: the exploration of unusual points-of-view, the radical manipulation of narrative time, the sensitive and forceful evocation of an identifiable region, and the masterful delineation of the heroic, tragic, comic or pathetic characters for whom he created a world."*

Dry September

I

Through the bloody September twilight, aftermath of sixty-two rainless days, it had gone like a fire in dry grass—the rumor, the story, whatever it was. Something about Miss Minnie Cooper and a Negro. Attacked, insulted, frightened: none of them, gathered in the barber shop on that Saturday evening where the ceiling fan stirred, without freshening it, the vitiated air, sending back upon them, in recurrent surges of stale pomade and lotion, their own stale breath and odors, knew exactly what had happened.

"Except it wasn't Will Mayes," a barber said. He was a man of middle age; a thin, sand-colored man with a mild face, who was shaving a client. "I know Will Mayes. He's a good nigger. And I know Miss Minnie Cooper, too."

"What do you know about her?" a second barber said.

"Who is she?" the client said. "A young girl?"

"No," the barber said. "She's about forty, I reckon. She aint married. That's why I dont believe—"

"Believe, hell!" a hulking youth in a sweat-stained silk shirt said. "Wont you take a white woman's word before a nigger's?"

"I dont believe Will Mayes did it," the barber said. "I know Will Mayes."

"Maybe you know who did it, then. Maybe you already got him out of town, you damn niggerlover."

"I dont believe anybody did anything. I dont believe anything happened. I leave it to you fellows if them ladies that get old without getting married dont have notions that a man cant—"

"Then you are a hell of a white man," the client said. He moved under the cloth. The youth had sprung to his feet.

"You dont?" he said. "Do you accuse a white woman of lying?"

The barber held the razor poised above the half-risen client. He did not look around.

"It's this durn weather," another said. "It's enough to make a man do anything. Even to her."

Nobody laughed. The barber said in his mild, stubborn tone: "I aint accusing nobody of nothing. I just know and you fellows know how a woman that never—"

"You damn niggerlover!" the youth said.

"Shut up, Butch," another said. "We'll get the facts in plenty of time to act."

"Who is? Who's getting them?" the youth said. "Facts, hell! I—"

"You're a fine white man," the client said. "Aint you?" In his frothy beard he looked like a desert rat in the moving pictures. "You tell them, Jack," he said to the youth. "If there aint any white men in this town, you can count on me, even if I aint only a drummer and a stranger."

"That's right, boys," the barber said. "Find out the truth first. I know Will Mayes."

"Well, by God!" the youth shouted. "To think that a white man in this town—"

"Shut up, Butch," the second speaker said. "We got plenty of time."

The client sat up. He looked at the speaker. "Do you claim that anything excuses a nigger attacking a white woman? Do you mean to tell me you are a white man and you'll stand for it? You better go back North where you came from. The South dont want your kind here."

"North what?" the second said. "I was born and raised in this town."

"Well, by God!" the youth said. He looked about with a strained, baffled gaze, as if he was trying to remember what it was he wanted to say or to do. He drew his sleeve across his sweating face. "Damn if I'm going to let a white woman—"

"You tell them, Jack," the drummer said. "By God, if they—"

The screen door crashed open. A man stood in the floor, his feet apart and his heavy-set body poised easily. His white shirt was open at the throat; he wore a felt hat. His hot, bold glance swept the group. His name was McLendon. He had commanded troops at the front in France and had been decorated for valor.

"Well," he said, "are you going to sit there and let a black son rape a white woman on the streets of Jefferson?"

Butch sprang up again. The silk of his shirt clung flat to his heavy shoulders. At each armpit was a dark halfmoon. "That's what I been telling them! That's what I—"

"Did it really happen?" a third said. "This aint the first man scare she ever had, like Hawkshaw says. Wasn't there something about a man on the kitchen roof, watching her undress, about a year ago?"

"What?" the client said. "What's that?" The barber had been slowly forcing him back into the chair; he arrested himself reclining, his head lifted, the barber still pressing him down.

McLendon whirled on the third speaker. "Happen? What the hell difference does it make? Are you going to let the black sons get away with it until one really does it?"

"That's what I'm telling them!" Butch shouted. He cursed, long and steady, pointless.

"Here, here," a fourth said. "Not so loud. Dont talk so loud."

"Sure," McLendon said; "no talking necessary at all. I've done my talking. Who's with me?" He poised on the balls of his feet, roving his gaze.

The barber held the drummer's face down, the razor poised. "Find

out the facts first, boys. I know Willy Mayes. It wasn't him. Let's get the
sheriff and do this thing right."

McLendon whirled upon him his furious, rigid face. The barber did
not look away. They looked like men of different races. The other barbers
had ceased also above their prone clients. "You mean to tell me," McLendon said, "that you'd take a nigger's word before a white woman's? Why,
you damn niggerloving—"

The third speaker rose and grasped McLendon's arm; he too had
been a soldier. "Now, now. Let's figure this thing out. Who knows anything about what really happened?"

"Figure out hell!" McLendon jerked his arm free. "All that're with
me get up from there. The ones that aint—" He roved his gaze, dragging
his sleeve across his face.

Three men rose. The drummer in the chair sat up. "Here," he said,
jerking at the cloth about his neck; "get this rag off me. I'm with him. I
dont live here, but by God, if our mothers and wives and sisters—" He
smeared the cloth over his face and flung it to the floor. McLendon stood
in the floor and cursed the others. Another rose and moved toward him.
The remainder sat uncomfortable, not looking at one another, then one
by one they rose and joined him.

The barber picked the cloth from the floor. He began to fold it neatly.
"Boys, dont do that. Will Mayes never done it. I know."

"Come on," McLendon said. He whirled. From his hip pocket protruded the butt of a heavy automatic pistol. They went out. The screen
door crashed behind them reverberant in the dead air.

The barber wiped the razor carefully and swiftly, and put it away,
and ran to the rear, and took his hat from the wall. "I'll be back as soon
as I can," he said to the other barbers. "I cant let—" He went out, running.
The two other barbers followed him to the door and caught it on the
rebound, leaning out and looking up the street after him. The air was flat
and dead. It had a metallic taste at the base of the tongue.

"What can he do?" the first said. The second one was saying "Jees
Christ, Jees Christ" under his breath. "I'd just as lief be Will Mayes as
Hawk, if he gets McLendon riled."

"Jees Christ, Jees Christ," the second whispered.

"You reckon he really done it to her?" the first said.

II

She was thirty-eight or thirty-nine. She lived in a small frame house
with her invalid mother and a thin, sallow, unflagging aunt, where each
morning between ten and eleven she would appear on the porch in a

lace-trimmed boudoir cap, to sit swinging in the porch swing until noon. After dinner she lay down for a while, until the afternoon began to cool. Then, in one of the three or four new voile dresses which she had each summer, she would go downtown to spend the afternoon in the stores with the other ladies, where they would handle the goods and haggle over the prices in cold, immediate voices, without any intention of buying.

She was of comfortable people—not the best in Jefferson, but good people enough—and she was still on the slender side of ordinary looking, with a bright, faintly haggard manner and dress. When she was young she had had a slender, nervous body and a sort of hard vivacity which had enabled her for a time to ride upon the crest of the town's social life as exemplified by the high school party and church social period of her contemporaries while still children enough to be unclassconscious.

She was the last to realize that she was losing ground; that those among whom she had been a little brighter and louder flame than any other were beginning to learn the pleasure of snobbery—male—and retaliation—female. That was when her face began to wear that bright, haggard look. She still carried it to parties on shadowy porticoes and summer lawns, like a mask or a flag, with that bafflement of furious repudiation of truth in her eyes. One evening at a party she heard a boy and two girls, all schoolmates, talking. She never accepted another invitation.

She watched the girls with whom she had grown up as they married and got homes and children, but no man ever called on her steadily until the children of the other girls had been calling her "aunty" for several years, the while their mothers told them in bright voices about how popular Aunt Minnie had been as a girl. Then the town began to see her driving on Sunday afternoons with the cashier in the bank. He was a widower of about forty—a high-colored man, smelling always faintly of the barber shop or of whisky. He owned the first automobile in town, a red runabout; Minnie had the first motoring bonnet and veil the town ever saw. Then the town began to say: "Poor Minnie." "But she is old enough to take care of herself," others said. That was when she began to ask her old schoolmates that their children call her "cousin" instead of "aunty."

It was twelve years now since she had been relegated into adultery by public opinion, and eight years since the cashier had gone to a Memphis bank, returning for one day each Christmas, which he spent at an annual bachelors' party at a hunting club on the river. From behind their curtains the neighbors would see the party pass, and during the over-the-way Christmas day visiting they would tell her about him, about how well he looked, and how they heard that he was prospering in the city, watching with bright, secret eyes her haggard, bright face. Usually by

[handwritten margin notes: "social outcast"; "drunk choleric nervous"; "affair ended"; "town's cruelty"]

that hour there would be the scent of whisky on her breath. It was supplied her by a youth, a clerk at the soda fountain: "Sure; I buy it for the old gal. I reckon she's entitled to a little fun."

Her mother kept to her room altogether now; the gaunt aunt ran the house. Against that background Minnie's bright dresses, her idle and empty days, had a quality of furious unreality. She went out in the evenings only with women now, neighbors, to the moving pictures. Each afternoon she dressed in one of the new dresses and went downtown alone, where her young "cousins" were already strolling in the late afternoons with their delicate, silken heads and thin, awkward arms and conscious hips, clinging to one another or shrieking and giggling with paired boys in the soda fountain when she passed and went on along the serried store fronts, in the doors of which the sitting and lounging men did not even follow her with their eyes any more.

III

The barber went swiftly up the street where the sparse lights, insect-swirled, glared in rigid and violent suspension in the lifeless air. The day had died in a pall of dust; above the darkened square, shrouded by the spent dust, the sky was as clear as the inside of a brass bell. Below the east was a rumor of the twice-waxed moon.

When he overtook them McLendon and three others were getting into a car parked in an alley. McLendon stooped his thick head, peering out beneath the top. "Changed your mind, did you?" he said. "Damn good thing; by God, tomorrow when this town hears about how you talked tonight—"

"Now, now," the other ex-soldier said. "Hawkshaw's all right. Come on, Hawk; jump in."

"Will Mayes never done it, boys," the barber said. "If anybody done it. Why, you all know well as I do there aint any town where they got better niggers than us. And you know how a lady will kind of think things about men when there aint any reason to, and Miss Minnie anyway—"

"Sure, sure," the soldier said. "We're just going to talk to him a little; that's all."

"Talk hell!" Butch said. "When we're through with the —"

"Shut up, for God's sake!" the soldier said. "Do you want everybody in town—"

"Tell them, by God!" McLendon said. "Tell every one of the sons that'll let a white woman—"

"Let's go; let's go: here's the other car." The second car slid squealing out of a cloud of dust at the alley mouth. McLendon started his car and took the lead. Dust lay like fog in the street. The street lights hung nimbused, as in water. They drove on out of town.

A rutted lane turned at right angles. Dust hung above it too, and above all the land. The dark bulk of the ice plant, where the Negro Mayes was night watchman, rose against the sky. "Better stop here, hadn't we?" the soldier said. McLendon did not reply. He hurled the car up and slammed to a stop, the headlights glaring on the blank wall.

"Listen here, boys," the barber said: "if he's here, dont that prove he never done it? Dont it? If it was him, he would run. Dont you see he would?" The second car came up and stopped. McLendon got down; Butch sprang down beside him. "Listen, boys," the barber said.

"Cut the lights off!" McLendon said. The breathless dark rushed down. There was no sound in it save their lungs as they sought air in the parched dust in which for two months they had lived; then the diminishing crunch of McLendon's and Butch's feet, and a moment later McLendon's voice:

"Will! . . .Will!"

Below the east the wan hemorrhage of the moon increased. It heaved above the ridge, silvering the air, the dust, so that they seemed to breathe, live, in a bowl of molten lead. There was no sound of nightbird nor insect, no sound save their breathing and a faint ticking of contracting metal about the cars. Where their bodies touched one another they seemed to sweat dryly, for no more moisture came. "Christ!" a voice said; "let's get out of here."

But they didn't move until vague noises began to grow out of the darkness ahead; then they got out and waited tensely in the breathless dark. There was another sound: a blow, a hissing expulsion of breath and McLendon cursing in undertone. They stood a moment longer, then they ran forward. They ran in a stumbling clump, as though they were fleeing something. "Kill him, kill the son," a voice whispered. McLendon flung them back.

"Not here," he said. "Get him into the car." "Kill him, kill the black son!" the voice murmured. They dragged the Negro to the car. The barber had waited beside the car. He could feel himself sweating and he knew he was going to be sick at the stomach.

"What is it, captains?" the Negro said. "I aint done nothing. 'Fore God, Mr John." Someone produced handcuffs. They worked busily about the Negro as though he were a post, quiet, intent, getting in one another's way. He submitted to the handcuffs, looking swiftly and constantly from dim face to dim face. "Who's here, captains?" he said, leaning to peer into the faces until they could feel his breath and smell his sweaty reek. He spoke a name or two. "What you all say I done, Mr John?"

McLendon jerked the car door open. "Get in!" he said.

The Negro did not move. "What you all going to do with me, Mr

John? I aint done nothing. White folks, captains, I aint done nothing: I swear 'fore God." He called another name.

"Get in!" McLendon said. He struck the Negro. The others expelled their breath in a dry hissing and struck him with random blows and he whirled and cursed them, and swept his manacled hands across their faces and slashed the barber upon the mouth, and the barber struck him also. "Get him in there," McLendon said. They pushed at him. He ceased struggling and got in and sat quietly as the others took their places. He sat between the barber and the soldier, drawing his limbs in so as not to touch them, his eyes going swiftly and constantly from face to face. Butch clung to the running board. The car moved on. The barber nursed his mouth with his handkerchief.

"What's the matter, Hawk?" the soldier said.

"Nothing," the barber said. They regained the highroad and turned away from town. The second car dropped back out of the dust. They went on, gaining speed; the final fringe of houses dropped behind.

"Goddamn, he stinks!" the soldier said.

"We'll fix that," the drummer in front beside McLendon said. On the running board Butch cursed into the hot rush of air. The barber leaned suddenly forward and touched McLendon's arm.

"Let me out, John," he said.

"Jump out, niggerlover," McLendon said without turning his head. He drove swiftly. Behind them the sourceless lights of the second car glared in the dust. Presently McLendon turned into a narrow road. It was rutted with disuse. It led back to an abandoned brick kiln—a series of reddish mounds and weed- and vine-choked vats without bottom. It had been used for pasture once, until one day the owner missed one of his mules. Although he prodded carefully in the vats with a long pole, he could not even find the bottom of them.

"John," the barber said.

"Jump out, then," McLendon said, hurling the car along the ruts. Beside the barber the Negro spoke:

"Mr Henry."

The barber sat forward. The narrow tunnel of the road rushed up and past. Their motion was like an extinct furnace blast: cooler, but utterly dead. The car bounded from rut to rut.

"Mr Henry," the Negro said.

The barber began to tug furiously at the door. "Look out, there!" the soldier said, but the barber had already kicked the door open and swung onto the running board. The soldier leaned across the Negro and grasped at him, but he had already jumped. The car went on without checking speed.

The impetus hurled him crashing through dust-sheathed weeds, into the ditch. Dust puffed about him, and in a thin, vicious crackling of sapless stems he lay choking and retching until the second car passed and died away. Then he rose and limped on until he reached the highroad and turned toward town, brushing at his clothes with his hands. The moon was higher, riding high and clear of the dust at last, and after a while the town began to glare beneath the dust. He went on, limping. Presently he heard cars and the glow of them grew in the dust behind him and he left the road and crouched again in the weeds until they passed. McLendon's car came last now. There were four people in it and Butch was not on the running board.

They went on; the dust swallowed them; the glare and the sound died away. The dust of them hung for a while, but soon the eternal dust absorbed it again. The barber climbed back onto the road and limped on toward town.

IV

As she dressed for supper on that Saturday evening, her own flesh felt like fever. Her hands trembled among the hooks and eyes, and her eyes had a feverish look, and her hair swirled crisp and crackling under the comb. While she was still dressing the friends called for her and sat while she donned her sheerest underthings and stockings and a new voile dress. "Do you feel strong enough to go out?" they said, their eyes bright too, with a dark glitter. "When you have had time to get over the shock, you must tell us what happened. What he said and did; everything."

In the leafed darkness, as they walked toward the square, she began to breathe deeply, something like a swimmer preparing to dive, until she ceased trembling, the four of them walking slowly because of the terrible heat and out of solicitude for her. But as they neared the square she began to tremble again, walking with her head up, her hands clenched at her sides, their voices about her murmurous, also with that feverish, glittering quality of the eyes.

They entered the square, she in the center of the group, fragile in her fresh dress. She was trembling worse. She walked slower and slower, as children eat ice cream, her head up and her eyes bright in the haggard banner of her face, passing the hotel and the coatless drummers in chairs along the curb looking around at her: "That's the one: see? The one in pink in the middle." "Is that her? What did they do with the nigger? Did they—?" "Sure. He's all right." "All right, is he?" "Sure. He went on a little trip." Then the drug store, where even the young men lounging in the doorway tipped their hats and followed with their eyes the motion of her hips and legs when she passed.

They went on, passing the lifted hats of the gentlemen, the suddenly ceased voices, deferent, protective. "Do you see?" the friends said. Their voices sounded like long, hovering sighs of hissing exultation. "There's not a Negro on the square. Not one."

They reached the picture show. It was like a miniature fairyland with its lighted lobby and colored lithographs of life caught in its terrible and beautiful mutations. Her lips began to tingle. In the dark, when the picture began, it would be all right; she could hold back the laughing so it would not waste away so fast and so soon. So she hurried on before the turning faces, the undertones of low astonishment, and they took their accustomed places where she could see the aisle against the silver glare and the young men and girls coming in two and two against it.

The lights flicked away; the screen glowed silver, and soon life began to unfold, beautiful and passionate and sad, while still the young men and girls entered, scented and sibilant in the half dark, their paired backs in silhouette delicate and sleek, their slim, quick bodies awkward, divinely young, while beyond them the silver dream accumulated, inevitably on and on. She began to laugh. In trying to suppress it, it made more noise than ever; heads began to turn. Still laughing, her friends raised her and led her out, and she stood at the curb, laughing on a high, sustained note, until the taxi came up and they helped her in.

They removed the pink voile and the sheer underthings and the stockings, and put her to bed, and cracked ice for her temples, and sent for the doctor. He was hard to locate, so they ministered to her with hushed ejaculations, renewing the ice and fanning her. While the ice was fresh and cold she stopped laughing and lay still for a time, moaning only a little. But soon the laughing welled again and her voice rose screaming.

"Shhhhhhhhhhh! Shhhhhhhhhhhhhhh!" they said, freshening the icepack, smoothing her hair, examining it for gray; "poor girl!" Then to one another: "Do you suppose anything really happened?" their eyes darkly aglitter, secret and passionate. "Shhhhhhhhhh! Poor girl! Poor Minnie!"

V

It was midnight when McLendon drove up to his neat new house. It was trim and fresh as a birdcage and almost as small, with its clean, green-and-white paint. He locked the car and mounted the porch and entered. His wife rose from a chair beside the reading lamp. McLendon stopped in the floor and stared at her until she looked down.

"Look at that clock," he said, lifting his arm, pointing. She stood before him, her face lowered, a magazine in her hands. Her face was pale, strained, and weary-looking. "Haven't I told you about sitting up like this, waiting to see when I come in?"

"John," she said. She laid the magazine down. Poised on the balls of his feet, he glared at her with his hot eyes, his sweating face.

"Didn't I tell you?" He went toward her. She looked up then. He caught her shoulder. She stood passive, looking at him.

"Don't, John. I couldn't sleep . . . The heat; something. Please, John. You're hurting me."

"Didn't I tell you?" He released her and half struck, half flung her across the chair, and she lay there and watched him quietly as he left the room.

He went on through the house, ripping off his shirt, and on the dark, screened porch at the rear he stood and mopped his head and shoulders with the shirt and flung it away. He took the pistol from his hip and laid it on the table beside the bed, and sat on the bed and removed his shoes, and rose and slipped his trousers off. He was sweating again already, and he stooped and hunted furiously for the shirt. At last he found it and wiped his body again, and, with his body pressed against the dusty screen, he stood panting. There was no movement, no sound, not even an insect. The dark world seemed to lie stricken beneath the cold moon and the lidless stars.

ERNEST HEMINGWAY

(1899–1961)

E rnest Hemingway was born in Oak Park, Illinois, the son of a doctor who loved the outdoors and a music teacher who taught him an admiration for high culture. Unable to enlist in the army, he joined the ambulance corps in 1917 and served in Northern Italy until he was seriously wounded by shrapnel while evacuating wounded soldiers. Characteristically, having served with great bravery and distinction, Hemingway, when recounting his war experiences, embroidered and actually lied to make himself seem that much more brave. This ability to act with high courage, and his conviction that it somehow should have been higher, is an essential trait in his character. He served in Paris as correspondent for the Toronto Star, and the "telegraphic style" required of a foreign correspondent helped him to perfect his own distinctive prose. In Our Time (1925), a collection of stories and journalistic "interchapters," and The Sun Also Rises (1926) made him the spokesman for the "Lost Generation," those who were appalled by the murderous killing of the First World War and turned to a frenzied hedonism as a result. They also marked the most important advances in American fiction in a generation. The Hemingway style, with its resonant and deceptive simplicity ("I always try to write on the principle of the iceberg. There is seven-eighths of it under water for every part that shows," he told one interviewer); the idea that life is a game, played against an imperturbable and invincible adversary, that requires dignity and "grace under pressure"; the macho hero who loves war, blood sports, good booze, and good women (in roughly that order)—all of these had the most profound influence on the millions of readers who made him (and continue to make him) the most popular American writer of his generation. Haunted by the pressures put upon him by celebrity status and by the legend he worked so hard to create, he spent the last half of his life searching for the intensity of experience that the war years had provided him. For Whom the Bell Tolls (1940) and The Old Man and the Sea (1952) proved how much talent he still had. He received the Nobel Prize in 1954. His physical and mental health suffered in his final years, and he shot himself in 1961, a day after being released from a hospital that had pronounced him cured.

Soldier's Home

K rebs went to the war from a Methodist college in Kansas. There is a picture which shows him among his fraternity brothers, all of them wearing exactly the same height and style collar. He enlisted in the Marines in 1917 and did not return to the United States until the second division returned from the Rhine in the summer of 1919.

There is a picture which shows him on the Rhine with two German girls and another corporal. Krebs and the corporal look too big for their uniforms. The German girls are not beautiful. The Rhine does not show in the picture.

By the time Krebs returned to his home town in Oklahoma the greeting of heroes was over. He came back much too late. The men from the town who had been drafted had all been welcomed elaborately on their return. There had been a great deal of hysteria. Now the reaction had set in. People seemed to think it was rather ridiculous for Krebs to be getting back so late, years after the war was over.

At first Krebs, who had been at Belleau Wood, Soissons, the Champagne, St. Mihiel and in the Argonne did not want to talk about the war at all. Later he felt the need to talk but no one wanted to hear about it. His town had heard too many atrocity stories to be thrilled by actualities. Krebs found that to be listened to at all he had to lie, and after he had done this twice he, too, had a reaction against the war and against talking about it. A distaste for everything that had happened to him in the war set in because of the lies he had told. All of the times that had been able to make him feel cool and clear inside himself when he thought of them; the times so long back when he had done the one thing, the only thing for a man to do, easily and naturally, when he might have done something else, now lost their cool, valuable quality and then were lost themselves.

His lies were quite unimportant lies and consisted in attributing to himself things other men had seen, done or heard of, and stating as facts certain apocryphal incidents familiar to all soldiers. Even his lies were not sensational at the pool room. His acquaintances, who had heard detailed accounts of German women found chained to machine guns in the Argonne forest and who could not comprehend, or were barred by their patriotism from interest in, any German machine gunners who were not chained, were not thrilled by his stories.

Krebs acquired the nausea in regard to experience that is the result of untruth or exaggeration, and when he occasionally met another man who had really been a soldier and they talked a few minutes in the dressing room at a dance he fell into the easy pose of the old soldier among other soldiers: that he had been badly, sickeningly frightened all the time. In this way he lost everything.

During this time, it was late summer, he was sleeping late in bed, getting up to walk down town to the library to get a book, eating lunch at home, reading on the front porch until he became bored and then walking down through the town to spend the hottest hours of the day in the cool dark of the pool room. He loved to play pool.

In the evening he practised on his clarinet, strolled down town, read and went to bed. He was still a hero to his two young sisters. His mother would have given him breakfast in bed if he had wanted it. She often came in when he was in bed and asked him to tell her about the war, but her attention always wandered. His father was non-committal.

Before Krebs went away to the war he had never been allowed to drive the family motor car. His father was in the real estate business and always wanted the car to be at his command when he required it to take clients out into the country to show them a piece of farm property. The car always stood outside the First National Bank building where his father had an office on the second floor. Now, after the war, it was still the same car.

Nothing was changed in the town except that the young girls had grown up. But they lived in such a complicated world of already defined alliances and shifting feuds that Krebs did not feel the energy or the courage to break into it. He liked to look at them, though. There were so many good-looking young girls. Most of them had their hair cut short. When he went away only little girls wore their hair like that or girls that were fast. They all wore sweaters and shirt waists with round Dutch collars. It was a pattern. He liked to look at them from the front porch as they walked on the other side of the street. He liked to watch them walking under the shade of the trees. He liked the round Dutch collars above their sweaters. He liked their silk stockings and flat shoes. He liked their bobbed hair and the way they walked.

When he was in town their appeal to him was not very strong. He did not like them when he saw them in the Greek's ice cream parlor. He did not want them themselves really. They were too complicated. There was something else. Vaguely he wanted a girl but he did not want to have to work to get her. He would have liked to have a girl but he did not want to have to spend a long time getting her. He did not want to get into the intrigue and the politics. He did not want to have to do any courting. He did not want to tell any more lies. It wasn't worth it.

He did not want any consequences. He did not want any consequences ever again. He wanted to live along without consequences. Besides he did not really need a girl. The army had taught him that. It was all right to pose as though you had to have a girl. Nearly everybody did that. But it wasn't true. You did not need a girl. That was the funny thing. First a fellow boasted how girls mean nothing to him, that he never thought of them, that they could not touch him. Then a fellow boasted that he could not get along without girls, that he had to have them all the time, that he could not go to sleep without them.

That was all a lie. It was all a lie both ways. You did not need a girl unless you thought about them. He learned that in the army. Then sooner or later you always got one. When you were really ripe for a girl you always got one. You did not have to think about it. Sooner or later it would come. He had learned that in the army.

Now he would have liked a girl if she had come to him and not wanted to talk. But here at home it was all too complicated. He knew he could never get through it all again. It was not worth the trouble. That was the thing about French girls and German girls. There was not all this talking. You couldn't talk much and you did not need to talk. It was simple and you were friends. He thought about France and then he began to think about Germany. On the whole he had liked Germany better. He did not want to leave Germany. He did not want to come home. Still, he had come home. He sat on the front porch.

He liked the girls that were walking along the other side of the street. He liked the look of them much better than the French girls or the German girls. But the world they were in was not the world he was in. He would like to have one of them. But it was not worth it. They were such a nice pattern. He liked the pattern. It was exciting. But he would not go through all the talking. He did not want one badly enough. He liked to look at them all, though. It was not worth it. Not now when things were getting good again.

He sat there on the porch reading a book on the war. It was a history and he was reading about all the engagements he had been in. It was the most interesting reading he had ever done. He wished there were more maps. He looked forward with a good feeling to reading all the really good histories when they would come out with good detail maps. Now he was really learning about the war. He had been a good soldier. That made a difference.

One morning after he had been home about a month his mother came into his bedroom and sat on the bed. She smoothed her apron.

"I had a talk with your father last night, Harold," she said, "and he is willing for you to take the car out in the evenings."

"Yeah?" said Krebs, who was not fully awake. "Take the car out? Yeah?"

"Yes. Your father has felt for some time that you should be able to take the car out in the evenings whenever you wished but we only talked it over last night."

"I'll bet you made him," Krebs said.

"No. It was your father's suggestion that we talk the matter over."

"Yeah. I'll bet you made him," Krebs sat up in bed.

"Will you come down to breakfast, Harold?" his mother said.

"As soon as I get my clothes on," Krebs said.

His mother went out of the room and he could hear her frying something downstairs while he washed, shaved and dressed to go down into the dining-room for breakfast. While he was eating breakfast his sister brought in the mail.

"Well, Hare," she said. "You old sleepy-head. What do you ever get up for?"

Krebs looked at her. He liked her. She was his best sister.

"Have you got the paper?" he asked.

She handed him *The Kansas City Star* and he shucked off its brown wrapper and opened it to the sporting page. He folded *The Star* open and propped it against the water pitcher with his cereal dish to steady it, so he could read while he ate.

"Harold," his mother stood in the kitchen doorway, "Harold, please don't muss up the paper. Your father can't read his *Star* if it's been mussed."

"I won't muss it," Krebs said.

His sister sat down at the table and watched him while he read.

"We're playing indoor over at school this afternoon," she said. "I'm going to pitch."

"Good," said Krebs. "How's the old wing?"

"I can pitch better than lots of the boys. I tell them all you taught me. The other girls aren't much good."

"Yeah?" said Krebs.

"I tell them all you're my beau. Aren't you my beau, Hare?"

"You bet."

"Couldn't your brother really be your beau just because he's your brother?"

"I don't know."

"Sure you know. Couldn't you be my beau, Hare, if I was old enough and if you wanted to?"

"Sure. You're my girl now."

"Am I really your girl?"

"Sure."

"Do you love me?"

"Uh, huh."

"Will you love me always?"

"Sure."

"Will you come over and watch me play indoor?"

"Maybe."

"Aw, Hare, you don't love me. If you loved me, you'd want to come over and watch me play indoor."

Krebs's mother came into the dining-room from the kitchen. She carried a plate with two fried eggs and some crisp bacon on it and a plate of buckwheat cakes.

"You run along, Helen," she said. "I want to talk to Harold."

She put the eggs and bacon down in front of him and brought in a jug of maple syrup for the buckwheat cakes. Then she sat down across the table from Krebs.

"I wish you'd put down the paper a minute, Harold," she said.

Krebs took down the paper and folded it.

"Have you decided what you are going to do yet, Harold?" his mother said, taking off her glasses.

"No," said Krebs.

"Don't you think it's about time?" His mother did not say this in a mean way. She seemed worried.

"I hadn't thought about it," Krebs said.

"God has some work for every one to do," his mother said. "There can be no idle hands in His Kingdom."

"I'm not in His Kingdom," Krebs said.

"We are all of us in His Kingdom."

Krebs felt embarrassed and resentful as always.

"I've worried about you so much, Harold," his mother went on. "I know the temptations you must have been exposed to. I know how weak men are. I know what your own dear grandfather, my own father, told us about the Civil War and I have prayed for you. I pray for you all day long, Harold."

Krebs looked at the bacon fat hardening on his plate.

"Your father is worried, too," his mother went on. "He thinks you have lost your ambition, that you haven't got a definite aim in life. Charley Simmons, who is just your age, has a good job and is going to be married. The boys are all settling down; they're all determined to get somewhere; you can see that boys like Charley Simmons are on their way to being really a credit to the community."

Krebs said nothing.

"Don't look that way, Harold," his mother said. "You know we love you and I want to tell you for your own good how matters stand. Your father does not want to hamper your freedom. He thinks you should be allowed to drive the car. If you want to take some of the nice girls out riding with you, we are only too pleased. We want you to enjoy yourself. But you are going to have to settle down to work, Harold. Your father doesn't care what you start in at. All work is honorable as he says. But you've got to make a start at something. He asked me to speak to you this morning and then you can stop in and see him at his office."

"Is that all?" Krebs said.

"Yes. Don't you love your mother, dear boy?"

"No," Krebs said.

His mother looked at him across the table. Her eyes were shiny. She started crying.

"I don't love anybody," Krebs said.

It wasn't any good. He couldn't tell her, he couldn't make her see it. It was silly to have said it. He had only hurt her. He went over and took hold of her arm. She was crying with her head in her hands.

"I didn't mean it," he said. "I was just angry at something. I didn't mean I didn't love you."

His mother went on crying. Krebs put his arm on her shoulder.

"Can't you believe me, mother?"

His mother shook her head.

"Please, please, mother. Please believe me."

"All right," his mother said chokily. She looked up at him. "I believe you, Harold."

Krebs kissed her hair. She put her face up to him.

"I'm your mother," she said. "I held you next to my heart when you were a tiny baby."

Krebs felt sick and vaguely nauseated.

"I know, Mummy," he said. "I'll try and be a good boy for you."

"Would you kneel and pray with me, Harold?" his mother asked.

They knelt down beside the dining-room table and Krebs's mother prayed.

"Now, you pray, Harold," she said.

"I can't," Krebs said.

"Try, Harold."

"I can't."

"Do you want me to pray for you?"

"Yes."

So his mother prayed for him and then they stood up and Krebs kissed his mother and went out of the house. He had tried so to keep his life from being complicated. Still, none of it had touched him. He had felt sorry for his mother and she had made him lie. He would go to Kansas City and get a job and she would feel all right about it. There would be one more scene maybe before he got away. He would not go down to his father's office. He would miss that one. He wanted his life to go smoothly. It had just gotten going that way. Well, that was all over now, anyway. He would go over to the schoolyard and watch Helen play indoor baseball.

VLADIMIR NABOKOV

(1899–1977)

V *ladimir Nabokov was born in St. Petersburg, the Russian capital* *that was to become Leningrad after the Revolution in 1917. Like* *most of the liberal intelligentsia, the Nabokovs left Russia soon after* *the Bolsheviks took power and established themselves in Berlin, where* *Nabokov's father edited the newspaper* Rul' *until he was murdered by* *Russian right-wing extremists. Vladimir, the eldest and most gifted son,* *took an honours degree in French and Russian at Cambridge and then* *returned to Berlin, where he stayed until 1935, making a living by* *writing poetry, criticism, short stories, plays, and novels, as well as by* *giving tennis, boxing, and English lessons. Nabokov wrote nine novels* *in Russian, including* Mary *(1926),* Camera Obscura *(1933),* Despair *(1936), and* The Gift *(1952). He escaped with his wife and son from* *France when it was invaded by the Nazis in 1940, and sailed to America.* *There, he taught courses in European and Russian literature at Wellesley* *and Cornell, and became one of America's foremost writers. The anglo-* *phile inclinations of his family and a trilingual childhood helped prepare* *him for the shift into English. The* succès de scandale *that resulted* *from the publication of* Lolita *(1955) enabled him to retire from teaching* *and devote himself full time to writing. In works like* Pale Fire *(1962)* *and* Ada *(1969), he forced his readers to question many of the traditional* *assumptions about what constitutes a novel and made himself a reputa-* *tion as one of the leading postmodernist novelists. Nabokov was also an* *accomplished poet and an insightful critic, as his idiosyncratic study of* Gogol *(1944) and his* Lectures on Literature *(1980) and* Lectures on Russian Literature *(1981) attest. His short fiction features the same* *technical virtuosity, black humour, and complex formal play that charac-* *terize his fiction. Collections of his stories include* The Return of Chorb *(1930),* Spring in Fialta and Other Stories *(1956),* Nabokov's Dozen *(1958),* Nabokov's Quartet *(1966), and* A Russian Beauty and Other Stories *(1973).*

Spring in Fialta

S pring in Fialta is cloudy and dull. Everything is damp: the piebald
trunks of the plane trees, the juniper shrubs, the railings, the gravel.
Far away, in a watery vista between the jagged edges of pale bluish
houses, which have tottered up from their knees to climb the slope (a
cypress indicating the way), the blurred Mount St. George is more than
ever remote from its likeness on the picture post cards which since 1910,
say (those straw hats, those youthful cabmen), have been courting the
tourist from the sorry-go-round of their prop, among amethyst-toothed
lumps of rock and the mantelpiece dreams of sea shells. The air is windless
and warm, with a faint tang of burning. The sea, its salt drowned in a
solution of rain, is less glaucous than gray with waves too sluggish to
break into foam.

It was on such a day in the early thirties that I found myself, all my
senses wide open, on one of Fialta's steep little streets, taking in everything at once, that marine rococo on the stand, and the coral crucifixes in
a shopwindow, and the dejected poster of a visiting circus, one corner of
its drenched paper detached from the wall, and a yellow bit of unripe
orange peel on the old, slate-blue sidewalk, which retained here and
there a fading memory of ancient mosaic design. I am fond of Fialta; I am
fond of it because I feel in the hollow of those violaceous syllables the
sweet dark dampness of the most rumpled of small flowers, and because
the altolike name of a lovely Crimean town is echoed by its viola; and
also because there is something in the very somnolence of its humid Lent
that especially anoints one's soul. So I was happy to be there again, to
trudge uphill in inverse direction to the rivulet of the gutter, hatless, my
head wet, my skin already suffused with warmth although I wore only
a light mackintosh over my shirt.

I had come on the Capparabella express, which, with that reckless
gusto peculiar to trains in mountainous country, had done its thundering
best to collect throughout the night as many tunnels as possible. A day
or two, just as long as a breathing spell in the midst of a business trip
would allow me, was all I expected to stay. I had left my wife and children
at home, and that was an island of happiness always present in the clear
north of my being, always floating beside me, and even through me, I
dare say, but yet keeping on the outside of me most of the time.

A pantless infant of the male sex, with a taut mud-gray little belly,
jerkily stepped down from a doorstep and waddled off, bowlegged, trying
to carry three oranges at once, but continuously dropping the variable
third, until he fell himself, and then a girl of twelve or so, with a string

of heavy beads around her dusky neck and wearing a skirt as long as that of a gypsy, promptly took away the whole lot with her more nimble and more numerous hands. Nearby, on the wet terrace of a café, a waiter was wiping the slabs of tables; a melancholy brigand hawking local lollipops, elaborate-looking things with a lunar gloss, had placed a hopelessly full basket on the cracked balustrade, over which the two were conversing. Either the drizzle had stopped or Fialta had got so used to it that she herself did not know whether she was breathing moist air or warm rain. Thumb-filling his pipe from a rubber pouch as he walked, a plus-foured Englishman of the solid exportable sort came from under an arch and entered a pharmacy, where large pale sponges in a blue vase were dying a thirsty death behind their glass. What luscious elation I felt rippling through my veins, how gratefully my whole being responded to the flutters and effluvia of that gray day saturated with a vernal essence which itself it seemed slow in perceiving! My nerves were unusually receptive after a sleepless night; I assimilated everything: the whistling of a thrush in the almond trees beyond the chapel, the peace of the crumbling houses, the pulse of the distant sea, panting in the mist, all this together with the jealous green of bottle glass bristling along the top of a wall and the fast colors of a circus advertisement featuring a feathered Indian on a rearing horse in the act of lassoing a boldly endemic zebra, while some thoroughly fooled elephants sat brooding upon their star-spangled thrones.

Presently the same Englishman overtook me. As I absorbed him along with the rest, I happened to notice the sudden side-roll of his big blue eyes straining at its crimson canthus, and the way he rapidly moistened his lips—because of the dryness of those sponges, I thought; but then I followed the direction of his glance, and saw Nina.

Every time I had met her during the fifteen years of our—well, I fail to find the precise term for our kind of relationship—she had not seemed to recognize me at once; and this time too she remained quite still for a moment, on the opposite sidewalk, half turning toward me in sympathetic incertitude mixed with curiosity, only her yellow scarf already on the move like those dogs that recognize you before their owners do—and then she uttered a cry, her hands up, all her ten fingers dancing, and in the middle of the street, with merely the frank impulsiveness of an old friendship (just as she would rapidly make the sign of the cross over me every time we parted), she kissed me thrice with more mouth than meaning, and then walked beside me, hanging on to me, adjusting her stride to mine, hampered by her narrow brown skirt perfunctorily slit down the side.

"Oh yes, Ferdie is here too," she replied and immediately in her turn inquired nicely after Elena.

"Must be loafing somewhere around with Segur," she went on in reference to her husband. "And I have some shopping to do; we leave after lunch. Wait a moment, where are you leading me, Victor dear?"

Back into the past, back into the past, as I did every time I met her, repeating the whole accumulation of the plot from the very beginning up to the last increment—thus in Russian fairy tales the already told is bunched up again at every new turn of the story. This time we had met in warm and misty Fialta, and I could not have celebrated the occasion with greater art, could not have adorned with brighter vignettes the list of fate's former services, even if I had known that this was to be the last one; the last one, I maintain, for I cannot imagine any heavenly firm of brokers that might consent to arrange me a meeting with her beyond the grave.

My introductory scene with Nina had been laid in Russia quite a long time ago, around 1917 I should say, judging by certain left-wing theater rumblings backstage. It was at some birthday party at my aunt's on her country estate, near Luga, in the deepest folds of winter (how well I remember the first sign of nearing the place: a red barn in a white wilderness). I had just graduated from the Imperial Lyceum; Nina was already engaged: although she was of my age and of that of the century, she looked twenty at least, and this in spite or perhaps because of her neat slender build, whereas at thirty-two that very slightness of hers made her look younger. Her fiancé was a guardsman on leave from the front, a handsome heavy fellow, incredibly well-bred and stolid, who weighed every word on the scales of the most exact common sense and spoke in a velvety baritone, which grew even smoother when he addressed her; his decency and devotion probably got on her nerves; and he is now a successful if somewhat lonesome engineer in a most distant tropical country.

Windows light up and stretch their luminous lengths upon the dark billowy snow, making room for the reflection of the fan-shaped light above the front door between them. Each of the two side-pillars is fluffily fringed with white, which rather spoils the lines of what might have been a perfect ex libris for the book of our two lives. I cannot recall why we had all wandered out of the sonorous hall into the still darkness, peopled only with firs, snow-swollen to twice their size; did the watchmen invite us to look at a sullen red glow in the sky, portent of nearing arson? Possibly. Did we go to admire an equestrian statue of ice sculptured near the pond by the Swiss tutor of my cousins? Quite as likely. My memory revives only on the way back to the brightly symmetrical mansion towards which we tramped in single file along a narrow furrow between snow-banks, with that crunch-crunch-crunch which is the only comment that a taciturn winter night makes upon humans. I walked last; three singing steps ahead of me walked a small bent shape; the firs gravely showed their burdened paws. I slipped and dropped the dead flashlight someone had forced upon me; it was devilishly hard to retrieve; and instantly attracted by my curses, with an eager, low laugh in anticipation of fun, Nina dimly veered toward me. I call her Nina, but I could hardly have known her name yet, hardly could we have had time, she and I, for any preliminary; "Who's that?" she asked with interest—and I was already kissing her neck, smooth and quite fiery hot from the long fox fur of her coat collar, which kept getting into my way until she clasped my shoulder, and with the candor so peculiar to her gently fitted her generous, dutiful lips to mine.

But suddenly parting us by its explosion of gaiety, the theme of a snowball fight started in the dark, and someone, fleeing, falling, crunching, laughing and panting, climbed a drift, tried to run, and uttered a horrible groan: deep snow had performed the amputation of an arctic. And soon after, we all dispersed to our respective homes, without my having talked with Nina, nor made any plans about the future, about those fifteen itinerant years that had already set out toward the dim horizon, loaded with the parts of our unassembled meetings; and as I watched her in the maze of gestures and shadows of gestures of which the rest of that evening consisted (probably parlor games—with Nina persistently in the other camp), I was astonished, I remember, not so much by her inattention to me after that warmth in the snow as by the innocent naturalness of that inattention, for I did not yet know that had I said a word it would have changed at once into a wonderful sunburst of kindness, a cheerful, compassionate attitude with all possible co-operation, as if a woman's love were spring water containing salubrious salts which at the least notice she ever so willingly gave anyone to drink.

"Let me see, where did we last meet," I began (addressing the Fialta version of Nina) in order to bring to her small face with prominent cheekbones and dark-red lips a certain expression I knew; and sure enough, the shake of her head and the puckered brow seemed less to imply forgetfulness than to deplore the flatness of an old joke; or to be more exact, it was as if all those cities where fate had fixed our various rendezvous without ever attending them personally, all those platforms and stairs and three-walled rooms and dark back alleys, were trite settings remaining after some other lives all brought to a close long before and were so little related to the acting out of our own aimless destiny that it was almost bad taste to mention them.

I accompanied her into a shop under the arcades; there, in the twilight beyond a beaded curtain, she fingered some red leather purses stuffed with tissue paper, peering at the price tags, as if wishing to learn their museum names. She wanted, she said, exactly that shape but in fawn, and when after ten minutes of frantic rustling the old Dalmatian found such a freak by a miracle that has puzzled me ever since, Nina, who was about to pick some money out of my hand, changed her mind and went through the streaming beads without having bought anything.

Outside it was just as milky dull as before; the same smell of burning, stirring my Tartar memories, drifted from the bare windows of the pale houses; a small swarm of gnats was busy darning the air above a mimosa, which bloomed listlessly, her sleeves trailing to the very ground; two workmen in broad-brimmed hats were lunching on cheese and garlic, their backs against a circus billboard, which depicted a red hussar and an orange tiger of sorts; curious—in his effort to make the beast as ferocious as possible, the artist had gone so far that he had come back from the other side, for the tiger's face looked positively human.

"*Au fond*, I wanted a comb," said Nina with belated regret.

How familiar to me were her hesitations, second thoughts, third thoughts mirroring first ones, ephemeral worries between trains. She had always either just arrived or was about to leave, and of this I find it hard to think without feeling humiliated by the variety of intricate routes one feverishly follows in order to keep that final appointment which the most confirmed dawdler knows to be unavoidable. Had I to submit before judges of our earthly existence a specimen of her average pose, I would have perhaps placed her leaning upon a counter at Cook's, left calf crossing right shin, left toe tapping floor, sharp elbows and coin-spilling bag on the counter, while the employee, pencil in hand, pondered with her over the plan of an eternal sleeping car.

After the exodus from Russia, I saw her—and that was the second time—in Berlin at the house of some friends. I was about to get married; she had just broken with her fiancé. As I entered that room I caught sight of her at once and, having glanced at the other guests, I instinctively determined which of the men knew more about her than I. She was sitting in the corner of a couch, her feet pulled up, her small comfortable body folded in the form of a Z; an ash tray stood aslant on the couch near one of her heels; and, having squinted at me and listened to my name, she removed her stalklike cigarette holder from her lips and proceeded to utter slowly and joyfully, "Well of all people—" and at once it became clear to everyone, beginning with her, that we had long been on intimate terms; unquestionably, she had forgotten all about the actual kiss, but somehow because of that trivial occurrence she found herself recollecting a vague stretch of warm, pleasant friendship, which in reality had never existed between us. Thus the whole cast of our relationship was fraudulently based upon an imaginary amity—which had nothing to do with her random good will. Our meeting proved quite insignificant in regard to the words we said, but already no barriers divided us; and when that night I happened to be seated beside her at supper, I shamelessly tested the extent of her secret patience.

Then she vanished again; and a year later my wife and I were seeing my brother off to Posen, and when the train had gone, and we were moving toward the exit along the other side of the platform, suddenly near a car of the Paris express I saw Nina, her face buried in the bouquet she held, in the midst of a group of people whom she had befriended without my knowledge and who stood in a circle gaping at her as idlers gape at a street row, a lost child, or the victim of an accident. Brightly she signaled to me with her flowers; I introduced her to Elena, and in that life-quickening atmosphere of a big railway station where everything is something trembling on the brink of something else, thus to be clutched and cherished, the exchange of a few words was enough to enable two totally dissimilar women to start calling each other by their pet names that very next time they met. That day, in the blue shade of the Paris car, Ferdinand was first mentioned: I learned with a ridiculous pang that she was about to marry him. Doors were beginning to slam; she quickly but piously kissed her friends, climbed into the vestibule, disappeared; and then I saw her through the glass settling herself in her compartment, having suddenly forgotten about us or passed into another world, and we all, our hands in our pockets, seemed to be spying upon an utterly unsuspecting life moving in that aquarium dimness, until she grew aware of us and drummed on the windowpane, then raised her eyes, fumbling at the frame as if hanging a picture, but nothing happened; some fellow passenger helped her, and she leaned out, audible and real, beaming with pleasure; one of us, keeping up with the stealthily gliding car, handed her a magazine and a Tauchnitz (she read English only when traveling); all was slipping away with beautiful smoothness, and I held a platform ticket crumpled beyond recognition, while a song of the last century (connected, it has been rumored, with some Parisian drama of love) kept ringing and ringing in my head, having emerged, God knows why, from the music box of memory, a sobbing ballad which often used to be sung by an old maiden aunt of mine, with a face as yellow as Russian church wax, but whom nature had given such a powerful, ecstatically full voice that it seemed to swallow her up in the glory of a fiery cloud as soon as she would begin:

> *On dit que tu te maries,*
> *tu sais que j'en vais mourir,*

and that melody, the pain, the offense, the link between hymen and death evoked by the rhythm, and the voice itself of the dead singer, which accompanied the recollection as the sole owner of the song, gave me no rest for several hours after Nina's departure and even later arose at increasing intervals like the last flat little waves sent to the beach by a passing ship, lapping ever more infrequently and dreamily, or like the bronze agony of a vibrating belfry after the bell ringer has already reseated himself in the cheerful circle of his family. And another year or two later, I was in Paris on business; and one morning on the landing of a hotel, where I had been looking up a film-actor fellow, there she was again, clad in a gray tailored suit, waiting for the elevator to take her down, a key dangling from her fingers. "Ferdinand has gone fencing," she said conversationally; her eyes rested on the lower part of my face as if she were lip reading, and after a moment of reflection (her amatory comprehension was matchless), she turned and rapidly swaying on slender ankles led me along the sea-blue carpeted passage. A chair at the door of her room supported a tray with the remains of breakfast—a honeystained knife, crumbs on the gray porcelain; but the room had already been done, and because of our sudden draft a wave of muslin embroidered with white dahlias got sucked in, with a shudder and knock, between the responsive halves of the French window, and only when the door had been locked did they let go that curtain with something like a blissful sigh; and a little later I stepped out on the diminutive cast-iron balcony beyond to inhale a combined smell of dry maple leaves and gasoline—the dregs of the hazy blue morning street; and as I did not yet realize the presence of that growing morbid pathos which was to embitter so my subsequent meetings with Nina, I was probably quite as collected and carefree as she was, then from the hotel I accompanied her to some office or other to trace a suitcase she had lost, and thence to the café where her husband was holding session with his court of the moment.

I will not mention the name (and what bits of it I happen to give here appear in decorous disguise) of that man, that Franco-Hungarian writer. . . . I would rather not dwell upon him at all, but I cannot help it— he is surging up from under my pen. Today one does not hear much about him; and this is good, for it proves that I was right in resisting his evil spell, right in experiencing a creepy chill down my spine whenever this or that new book of his touched my hand. The fame of his likes circulates briskly but soon grows heavy and stale; and as for history it will limit his life story to the dash between two dates. Lean and arrogant, with some poisonous pun ever ready to fork out and quiver at you, and with a strange look of expectancy in his dull brown veiled eyes, the false wag had, I daresay, an irresistible effect on small rodents. Having mastered the art of verbal invention to perfection, he particularly prided himself on being a weaver of words, a title he valued higher than that of a writer; personally, I never could understand what was the good of thinking up books, of penning things that had not really happened in some way or other; and I remember once saying to him as I braved the mockery of his encouraging nods that, were I a writer, I should allow only my heart to have imagination, and for the rest rely upon memory, that long-drawn sunset shadow of one's personal truth.

I had known his books before I knew him; a faint disgust was already replacing the aesthetic pleasure which I had suffered his first novel to give me. At the beginning of his career, it had been possible perhaps to distinguish some human landscape, some old garden, some dream-familiar disposition of trees through the stained glass of his prodigious prose . . . but with every new book the tints grew still more dense, the gules and purpure still more ominous; and today one can no longer see anything at all through that blazoned, ghastly rich glass, and it seems that were one to break it, nothing but a perfectly black void would face one's shivering soul. But how dangerous he was in his prime, what venom he squirted, with what whips he lashed when provoked! The tornado of his passing satire left a barren waste where felled oaks lay in a row, and the dust still twisted, and the unfortunate author of some adverse review, howling with pain, spun like a top in the dust.

At the time we met, his *"Passage à niveau"* was being acclaimed in Paris; he was, as they say, "surrounded," and Nina (whose adaptability was an amazing substitute for the culture she lacked) had already assumed if not the part of a muse at least that of a soul mate and subtle adviser, following Ferdinand's creative convolutions and loyally sharing his artistic tastes; for although it is wildly improbable that she had ever waded through a single volume of his, she had a magic knack of gleaning all the best passages from the shop talk of literary friends.

An orchestra of women was playing when we entered the café; first I noted the ostrich thigh of a harp reflected in one of the mirror-faced pillars, and then I saw the composite table (small ones drawn together to form a long one) at which, with his back to the plush wall, Ferdinand was presiding; and for a moment his whole attitude, the position of his parted hands, and the faces of his table companions all turned toward him reminded me in a grotesque, nightmarish way of something I did not quite grasp, but when I did so in retrospect, the suggested comparison struck me as hardly less sacrilegious than the nature of his art itself. He wore a white turtle-neck sweater under a tweed coat; his glossy hair was combed back from the temples, and above it cigarette smoke hung like a halo; his bony, Pharaohlike face was motionless: the eyes alone roved this way and that, full of dim satisfaction. Having forsaken the two or three obvious haunts where naïve amateurs of Montparnassian life would have expected to find him, he had started patronizing this perfectly bourgeois establishment because of his peculiar sense of humor, which made him derive ghoulish fun from the pitiful *specialité de la maison*—this orchestra composed of half a dozen weary-looking, self-conscious ladies interlacing mild harmonies on a crammed platform and not knowing, as he put it, what to do with their motherly bosoms, quite superfluous in the world of music. After each number he would be convulsed by a fit of epileptic applause, which the ladies had stopped acknowledging and which was already arousing, I thought, certain doubts in the minds of the proprietor of the café and its fundamental customers, but which seemed highly diverting to Ferdinand's friends. Among these I recall: an artist with an impeccably bald though slightly chipped head, which under various pretexts he constantly painted into his eye-and-guitar canvases; a poet, whose special gag was the ability to represent, if you asked him, Adam's Fall by means of five matches; a humble business man who financed surrealist ventures (and paid for the *apéritifs*) if permitted to print in a corner eulogistic allusions to the actress he kept; a pianist, presentable insofar as the face was concerned, but with a dreadful expression of the fingers; a jaunty but linguistically impotent Soviet writer fresh from Moscow, with an old pipe and a new wrist watch, who was completely and ridiculously unaware of the sort of company he was in; there were several other gentlemen present who have become confused in my memory, and doubtless two or three of the lot had been intimate with Nina. She was the only woman at the table; there she stooped, eagerly sucking at a straw, the level of her lemonade sinking with a kind of childish celerity, and only when the last drop had gurgled and squeaked, and she had pushed away the straw with her tongue, only then did I finally catch her eye, which I had been obstinately seeking, still not being able to cope with the fact that she had had time to forget what had occurred earlier in the morning—to forget it so thoroughly that upon meeting my glance, she replied with a blank questioning smile, and only after peering more closely did she remember suddenly what kind of answering smile I was expecting. Meanwhile, Ferdinand (the ladies having temporarily left the platform after pushing away their instruments like so many pieces of furniture) was juicily drawing his cronies' attention to the figure of an elderly luncher in a far corner of the café, who had, as some Frenchmen for some reason or other have, a little red ribbon or something on his coat lapel and whose gray beard combined with his mustaches to form a cosy yellowish nest for his sloppily munching mouth. Somehow the trappings of old age always amused Ferdie.

I did not stay long in Paris, but that week proved sufficient to engender between him and me that fake chumminess the imposing of which he had such a talent for. Subsequently I even turned out to be of some use to him: my firm acquired the film rights of one of his more intelligible stories, and then he had a good time pestering me with telegrams. As the years passed, we found ourselves every now and then beaming at each other in some place, but I never felt at ease in his presence, and that day in Fialta, too, I experienced a familiar depression upon learning that he was on the prowl nearby; one thing, however, considerably cheered me up: the flop of his recent play.

And here he was coming toward us, garbed in an absolutely waterproof coat with belt and pocket flaps, a camera across his shoulder, double rubber soles to his shoes, sucking with an imperturbability that was meant to be funny a long stick of moonstone candy, that specialty of Fialta's. Beside him, walked the dapper, doll-like, rosy Segur, a lover of art and a perfect fool; I never could discover for what purpose Ferdinand needed him; and I still hear Nina exclaiming with a moaning tenderness that did not commit her to anything: "Oh, he is such a darling, Segur!" They approached; Ferdinand and I greeted each other lustily, trying to crowd into hand shake and back slap as much fervor as possible, knowing by experience that actually that was all but pretending it was only a preface; and it always happened like that: after every separation we met to the accompaniment of strings being excitedly tuned, in a bustle of geniality, in the hubbub of sentiments taking their seats; but the ushers would close the doors, and after that no one was admitted.

Segur complained to me about the weather, and at first I did not understand what he was talking about; even if the moist, gray, greenhouse essence of Fialta might be called "weather," it was just as much outside of anything that could serve us as a topic of conversation as was, for instance, Nina's slender elbow, which I was holding between finger and thumb, or a bit of tin foil someone had dropped, shining in the middle of the cobbled street in the distance.

We four moved on, vague purchases still looming ahead. "God, what an Indian!" Ferdinand suddenly exclaimed with fierce relish, violently nudging me and pointing at a poster. Further on, near a fountain, he gave his stick of candy to a native child, a swarthy girl with beads round her pretty neck; we stopped to wait for him: he crouched saying something to her, addressing her sooty-black lowered eyelashes, and then he caught up with us, grinning and making one of those remarks with which he loved to spice his speech. Then his attention was drawn by an unfortunate object exhibited in a souvenir shop: a dreadful marble imitation of Mount St. George showing a black tunnel at its base, which turned out to be the mouth of an inkwell, and with a compartment for pens in the semblance of railroad tracks. Open-mouthed, quivering, all agog with sardonic triumph, he turned that dusty, cumbersome, and perfectly irresponsible thing in his hands, paid without bargaining, and with his mouth still open came out carrying the monster. Like some autocrat who surrounds himself with hunchbacks and dwarfs, he would become attached to this or that hideous object; this infatuation might last from five minutes to several days or even longer if the thing happened to be animate.

Nina wistfully alluded to lunch, and seizing the opportunity when Ferdinand and Segur stopped at a post office, I hastened to lead her away. I still wonder what exactly she meant to me, that small dark woman of the narrow shoulders and "lyrical limbs" (to quote the expression of a mincing émigré poet, one of the few men who had sighed platonically after her), and still less do I understand what was the purpose of fate in bringing us constantly together. I did not see her for quite a long while after my sojourn in Paris, and then one day when I came home from my office I found her having tea with my wife and examining on her silk-hosed hand, with her wedding ring gleaming through, the texture of some stockings bought cheap in Tauentzienstrasse. Once I was shown her photograph in a fashion magazine full of autumn leaves and gloves and wind-swept golf links. On a certain Christmas she sent me a picture post card with snow and stars. On a Riviera beach she almost escaped my notice behind her dark glasses and terracotta tan. Another day, having dropped in on an ill-timed errand at the house of some strangers where a party was in progress, I saw her scarf and fur coat among alien scare-crows on a coat rack. In a bookshop she nodded to me from a page of one of her husband's stories, a page referring to an episodic servant girl, but smuggling in Nina in spite of the author's intention: "Her face," he wrote, "was rather nature's snapshot than a meticulous portrait, so that when . . . tried to imagine it, all he could visualize were fleeting glimpses of disconnected features: the downy outline of her pommettes in the sun, the amber-tinted brown darkness of quick eyes, lips shaped into a friendly smile which was always ready to change into an ardent kiss."

Again and again she hurriedly appeared in the margins of my life, without influencing in the least its basic text. One summer morning (Friday—because housemaids were thumping out carpets in the sun-dusted yard), my family was away in the country and I was lolling and smoking in bed when I heard the bell ring with tremendous violence—and there she was in the hall having burst in to leave (incidentally) a hairpin and (mainly) a trunk illuminated with hotel labels, which a fort-night later was retrieved for her by a nice Austrian boy, who (according to intangible but sure symptoms) belonged to the same very cosmopolitan association of which I was a member. Occasionally, in the middle of a conversation her name would be mentioned, and she would run down the steps of a chance sentence, without turning her head. While traveling in the Pyrenees, I spent a week at the château belonging to people with whom she and Ferdinand happened to be staying, and I shall never forget my first night there: how I waited, how certain I was that without my having to tell her she would steal to my room, how she did not come, and the din thousands of crickets made in the delirious depth of the rocky garden dripping with moonlight, the mad bubbling brooks, and my struggle between blissful southern fatigue after a long day of hunting on the screes and the wild thirst for her stealthy coming, low laugh, pink ankles above the swan's-down trimming of high-heeled slippers; but the night raved on, and she did not come, and when next day, in the course of a general ramble in the mountains, I told her of my waiting, she clasped her hands in dismay—and at once with a rapid glance estimated whether the backs of the gesticulating Ferd and his friend had sufficiently receded.

I remember talking to her on the telephone across half of Europe (on her husband's business) and not recognizing at first her eager barking voice; and I remember once dreaming of her: I dreamt that my eldest girl had run in to tell me the doorman was sorely in trouble—and when I had gone down to him, I saw lying on a trunk, a roll of burlap under her head, pale-lipped and wrapped in a woolen kerchief, Nina fast asleep, as miserable refugees sleep in Godforsaken railway stations. And regardless of what happened to me or to her, in between, we never discussed anything, as we never thought of each other during the intervals in our destiny, so that when we met the pace of life altered at once, all its atoms were recombined, and we lived in another, lighter time-medium, which was measured not by the lengthy separations but by those few meetings of which a short, supposedly frivolous life was thus artificially formed. And with each new meeting I grew more and more apprehensive; no— I did not experience any inner emotional collapse, the shadow of tragedy did not haunt our revels, my married life remained unimpaired, while on the other hand her eclectic husband ignored her casual affairs although deriving some profit from them in the way of pleasant and useful connections. I grew apprehensive because something lovely, delicate, and unrepeatable was being wasted: something which I abused by snapping off poor bright bits in gross haste while neglecting the modest but true core which perhaps it kept offering me in a pitiful whisper. I was apprehensive because, in the long run, I was somehow accepting Nina's life, the lies, the futility, the gibberish of that life. Even in the absence of any sentimental discord, I felt myself bound to seek for a rational, if not moral, interpretation of my existence, and this meant choosing between the world in which I sat for my portrait, with my wife, my young daughters, the Doberman pinscher (idyllic garlands, a signet ring, a slender cane), between that happy, wise, and good world . . . and what? Was there any practical chance of life together with Nina, life I could barely imagine, for it would be penetrated, I knew, with a passionate, intolerable bitterness and every moment of it would be aware of a past, teeming with protean partners. No, the thing was absurd. And moreover was she not chained to her husband by something stronger than love—the staunch friendship between two convicts? Absurd! But then what should I have done with you, Nina, how should I have disposed of the store of sadness that had gradually accumulated as a result of our seemingly carefree, but really hopeless meetings?

Fialta consists of the old town and of the new one; here and there, past and present are interlaced, struggling either to disentangle themselves or to thrust each other out; each one has its own methods: the newcomer fights honestly—importing palm trees, setting up smart tourist agencies, painting with creamy lines the red smoothness of tennis courts; whereas the sneaky old-timer creeps out from behind a corner in the shape of some little street on crutches or the steps of stairs leading nowhere. On our way to the hotel, we passed a half-built white villa, full of litter within, on a wall of which again the same elephants, their monstrous baby knees wide apart, sat on huge, gaudy drums; in ethereal bundles the equestrienne (already with a penciled mustache) was resting on a broad-backed steed; and a tomato-nosed clown was walking a tightrope, balancing an umbrella ornamented with those recurrent stars—a vague symbolic recollection of the heavenly fatherland of circus performers. Here, in the Riviera part of Fialta, the wet gravel crunched in a more luxurious manner, and the lazy sighing of the sea was more audible. In the back yard of the hotel, a kitchen boy armed with a knife was pursuing a hen which was clucking madly as it raced for its life. A bootblack offered me his ancient throne with a toothless smile. Under the plane trees stood a motorcycle of German make, a mud-bespattered limousine, and a yellow long-bodied Icarus that looked like a giant scarab: ("That's ours—Segur's, I mean," said Nina, adding "Why don't you come with us, Victor?" although she knew very well that I could not come); in the lacquer of its elytra a gouache of sky and branches was engulfed; in the metal of one of the bomb-shaped lamps we ourselves were momentarily reflected, lean filmland pedestrians passing along the convex surface; and then, after a few steps, I glanced back and foresaw, in an almost optical sense, as it were, what really happened an hour or so later: the three of them wearing motoring helmets, getting in, smiling and waving to me, transparent to me like ghosts, with the color of the world shining through them, and then they were moving, receding, diminishing (Nina's last ten-fingered farewell); but actually the automobile was still standing quite motionless, smooth and whole like an egg, and Nina under my outstretched arm was entering a laurel-flanked doorway, and as we sat down we could see through the window Ferdinand and Segur, who had come by another way, slowly approaching.

There was no one on the veranda where we lunched except the Englishman I had recently observed; in front of him, a long glass containing a bright crimson drink threw an oval reflection on the tablecloth. In his eyes, I noticed the same bloodshot desire, but now it was in no sense related to Nina; that avid look was not directed at her at all, but was fixed on the upper right-hand corner of the broad window near which he was sitting.

Having pulled the gloves off her small thin hands, Nina, for the last time in her life, was eating the shellfish of which she was so fond. Ferdinand also busied himself with food, and I took advantage of his hunger to begin a conversation which gave me the semblance of power over him: to be specific, I mentioned his recent failure. After a brief period of fashionable religious conversion, during which grace descended upon him and he undertook some rather ambiguous pilgrimages, which ended in a decidedly scandalous adventure, he had turned his dull eyes toward barbarous Moscow. Now, frankly speaking, I have always been irritated by the complacent conviction that a ripple of stream consciousness, a few healthy obscenities, and a dash of communism in any old slop pail will alchemically and automatically produce ultramodern literature; and I will contend until I am shot that art as soon as it is brought into contact with politics inevitably sinks to the level of any ideological trash. In Ferdinand's case, it is true, all this was rather irrelevant: the muscles of his muse were exceptionally strong, to say nothing of the fact that he didn't care a damn for the plight of the underdog; but because of certain obscurely mischievous undercurrents of that sort, his art had become still more repulsive. Except for a few snobs none had understood the play; I had not seen it myself, but could well imagine that elaborate Kremlinesque night along the impossible spirals of which he spun various wheels of dismembered symbols; and now, not without pleasure, I asked him whether he had read a recent bit of criticism about himself.

"Criticism!" he exclaimed, "Fine criticism! Every slick jackanapes sees fit to read me a lecture. Ignorance of my work is their bliss. My books are touched gingerly, as one touches something that may go bang. Criticism! They are examined from every point of view except the essential one. It is as if a naturalist, in describing the equine genus, started to jaw about saddles or Mme. de V. (he named a well-known literary hostess who indeed strongly resembled a grinning horse). I would like some of that pigeon's blood, too," he continued in the same loud, ripping voice, addressing the waiter, who understood his desire only after he had looked in the direction of the long-nailed finger which unceremoniously pointed at the Englishman's glass. For some reason or other, Segur mentioned Ruby Rose, the lady who painted flowers on her breast, and the conversation took on a less insulting character. Meanwhile the big Englishman suddenly made up his mind, got up on a chair, stepped from there on to the window sill, and stretched up till he reached that coveted corner of the frame where rested a compact furry moth, which he deftly slipped into a pillbox.

" . . . rather like Wouwerman's white horse," said Ferdinand, in regard to something he was discussing with Segur.

"*Tu es très hippique ce matin,*" remarked the latter.

Soon they both left to telephone. Ferdinand was particularly fond of long-distance calls, and particularly good at endowing them, no matter what the distance, with a friendly warmth when it was necessary, as for instance now, to make sure of free lodgings.

From afar came the sounds of music—a trumpet, a zither. Nina and I set out to wander again. The circus on its way to Fialta had apparently sent out runners: an advertising pageant was tramping by; but we did not catch its head, as it had turned uphill into a side alley: the gilded back of some carriage was receding, a man in a burnoose led a camel, a file of four mediocre Indians carried placards on poles, and behind them, by special permission, a tourist's small son in a sailor suit sat reverently on a tiny pony.

We wandered by a café where the tables were now almost dry but still empty; the waiter was examining (I hope he adopted it later) a horrible foundling, the absurd inkstand affair, stowed by Ferdinand on the banisters in passing. At the next corner we were attracted by an old stone stairway, and we climbed up, and I kept looking at the sharp angle of Nina's step as she ascended, raising her skirt, its narrowness requiring the same gesture as formerly length had done; she diffused a familiar warmth, and going up beside her, I recalled the last time we had come together. It had been in a Paris house, with many people around, and my dear friend Jules Darboux, wishing to do me a refined aesthetic favor, had touched my sleeve and said, "I want you to meet—" and led me to Nina, who sat in the corner of a couch, her body folded Z-wise, with an ash tray at her heel, and she took a long turquoise cigarette holder from her lips and joyfully, slowly exclaimed, "Well, of all people—" and then all evening my heart felt like breaking, as I passed from group to group with a sticky glass in my fist, now and then looking at her from a distance (she did not look . . .), and listened to scraps of conversation, and overheard one man saying to another, "Funny, how they all smell alike, burnt leaf through whatever perfume they use, those angular dark-haired girls," and as it often happens, a trivial remark related to some unknown topic coiled and clung to one's own intimate recollection, a parasite of its sadness.

At the top of the steps, we found ourselves on a rough kind of terrace. From here one could see the delicate outline of the dove-colored Mount St. George with a cluster of bone-white flecks (some hamlet) on one of its slopes; the smoke of an indiscernible train undulated along its rounded base—and suddenly disappeared; still lower, above the jumble of roofs, one could perceive a solitary cypress, resembling the moist-twirled black tip of a water-color brush; to the right, one caught a glimpse of the sea, which was gray, with silver wrinkles. At our feet lay a rusty old key, and on the wall of the half-ruined house adjoining the terrace, the ends of some wire still remained hanging . . . I reflected that formerly there had been life here, a family had enjoyed the coolness at nightfall, clumsy children had colored pictures by the light of a lamp . . . We lingered there as if listening to something; Nina, who stood on higher ground, put a hand on my shoulder and smiled, and carefully, so as not to crumple her smile, kissed me. With an unbearable force, I relived (or so it now seems to me) all that had ever been between us beginning with a similar kiss; and I said (substituting for our cheap, formal "thou" that strangely full and expressive "you" to which the circumnavigator, enriched all around, returns), "Look here—what if I love you?" Nina glanced at me, I repeated those words, I wanted to add . . . but something like a bat passed swiftly across her face, a quick, queer, almost ugly expression, and she, who would utter coarse words with perfect simplicity, became embarrassed; I also felt awkward . . . "Never mind, I was only joking," I hastened to say, lightly encircling her waist. From somewhere a firm bouquet of small dark, unselfishly smelling violets appeared in her hands, and before she returned to her husband and car, we stood for a little while longer by the stone parapet, and our romance was even more hopeless than it had ever been. But the stone was as warm as flesh, and suddenly I understood something I had been seeing without understanding—why a piece of tin foil had sparkled so on the pavement, why the gleam of a glass had trembled on a tablecloth, why the sea was ashimmer: somehow, by imperceptible degrees, the white sky above Fialta had got saturated with sunshine, and now it was sun-pervaded throughout, and this brimming white radiance grew broader and broader, all dissolved in it, all vanished, all passed, and I stood on the station platform of Mlech with a freshly bought newspaper, which told me that the yellow car I had seen under the plane trees had suffered a crash beyond Fialta, having run at full speed into the truck of a traveling circus entering the town, a crash from which Ferdinand and his friend, those invulnerable rogues, those salamanders of fate, those basilisks of good fortune, had escaped with local and temporary injury to their scales, while Nina, in spite of her long-standing, faithful imitation of them, had turned out after all to be mortal.

JORGE LUIS BORGES

(1899–1986)

J orge Luis Borges was born in Buenos Aires into a well-established and financially secure family. An English tutor and his father's library helped develop his early interest in English literature. Travelling with his family in Europe in 1914 at the outbreak of the war, he found himself forced to remain in Geneva for four years. Here he read widely in French and German and began to develop an interest in thinkers as disparate as Schopenhauer and G.K. Chesterton. Returning to Buenos Aires in 1921, Borges worked with a group of young writers to produce a literary review, and the "Ultraist Manifesto," which he helped publish, defined their modernist goals. The group was apolitical, viewing literature as a pleasant game for an intellectual elite. Borges's early poetry was praised extravagantly in Spain, and he published numerous books of verse and essays in the next two decades. He began to write the fantasies that are commonly associated with his name in 1939. The rise of Argentina's populist dictator Perón created problems for Borges, whose reputation was growing in his native country. When Borges spoke out against what he saw as incipient tyranny, he lost his job as a municipal librarian. After Perón's government fell in 1955, Borges was made director of the National Library, and in 1956 Professor of English Literature at the University of Buenos Aires. In the 1960s came international renown, visiting professorships, reading tours, literary prizes, and translation into numerous languages, and all the while the writing of poetry and fiction continued unabated. He characterized his own approach to literature in numerous interviews. The following comment is typical:

> Literature is a dream, a controlled dream. Now, I believe we owe literature almost everything we are and what we have been, also what we will be. Our past is nothing but a sequence of dreams. What difference can there be between dreaming and remembering the past? Books are the great memory of all centuries. Their function, therefore, is irreplaceable. If books disappear, surely history would disappear, and man would also disappear.

Borges's radical aestheticism does not turn its back on the world but absorbs it, makes it part of an enormous work of art which it is man's task to create and to decipher.

The Garden of Forking Paths

For Victoria Ocampo

On page 22 of Liddell Hart's *History of World War I* you will read that an attack against the Serre-Montauban line by thirteen British divisions (supported by 1,400 artillery pieces), planned for the 24th of July, 1916, had to be postponed until the morning of the 29th. The torrential rains, Captain Liddell Hart comments, caused this delay, an insignificant one, to be sure.

The following statement, dictated, reread and signed by Dr. Yu Tsun, former professor of English at the *Hochschule* at Tsingtao, throws an unsuspected light over the whole affair. The first two pages of the document are missing.

" . . . and I hung up the receiver. Immediately afterwards, I recognized the voice that had answered in German. It was that of Captain Richard Madden. Madden's presence in Viktor Runeberg's apartment meant the end of our anxieties and—but this seemed, *or should have seemed*, very secondary to me—also the end of our lives. It meant that Runeberg had been arrested or murdered.[1] Before the sun set on that day, I would encounter the same fate. Madden was implacable. Or rather, he was obliged to be so. An Irishman at the service of England, a man accused of laxity and perhaps of treason, how could he fail to seize and be thankful for such a miraculous opportunity: the discovery, capture, maybe even the death of two agents of the German Reich? I went up to my room; absurdly I locked the door and threw myself on my back on the narrow iron cot. Through the window I saw the familiar roofs and the cloud-shaded six o'clock sun. It seemed incredible to me that the day without premonitions or symbols should be the one of my inexorable death. In spite of my dead father, in spite of having been a child in a symmetrical garden of Hai Feng, was I—now—going to die? Then I reflected that everything happens to a man precisely, precisely *now*. Centuries of centuries and only in the present do things happen; countless men in the air, on the face of the earth and the sea, and all that really is happening is happening to me . . . The almost intolerable recollection of Madden's horselike face banished these wanderings. In the midst of my hatred and terror (it means nothing to me now to speak of terror, now that I have mocked Richard Madden, now that my throat yearns for the noose) it

---

[1] An hypothesis both hateful and odd. The Prussian spy Hans Rabener, alias Viktor Runeberg, attacked with drawn automatic the bearer of the warrant for his arrest, Captain Richard Madden. The latter, in self-defense, inflicted the wound which brought about Runeberg's death. (Editor's note.)

occurred to me that that tumultuous and doubtless happy warrior did not suspect that I possessed the Secret. The name of the exact location of the new British artillery park on the River Ancre. A bird streaked across the gray sky and blindly I translated it into an airplane and that airplane into many (against the French sky) annihilating the artillery station with vertical bombs. If only my mouth, before a bullet shattered it, could cry out that secret name so it could be heard in Germany . . . My human voice was very weak. How might I make it carry to the ear of the Chief? To the ear of that sick and hateful man who knew nothing of Runeberg and me save that we were in Staffordshire and who was waiting in vain for our report in his arid office in Berlin, endlessly examining newspapers . . . I said out loud: *I must flee.* I sat up noiselessly, in a useless perfection of silence, as if Madden were already lying in wait for me. Something— perhaps the mere vain ostentation of proving my resources were nil— made me look through my pockets. I found what I knew I would find. The American watch, the nickel chain and the square coin, the key ring with the incriminating useless keys to Runeberg's apartment, the note-book, a letter which I resolved to destroy immediately (and which I did not destroy), a crown, two shillings and a few pence, the red and blue pencil, the handkerchief, the revolver with one bullet. Absurdly, I took it in my hand and weighed it in order to inspire courage within myself. Vaguely I thought that a pistol report can be heard at a great distance. In ten minutes my plan was perfected. The telephone book listed the name of the only person capable of transmitting the message; he lived in a suburb of Fenton, less than a half hour's train ride away.

I am a cowardly man. I say it now, now that I have carried to its end a plan whose perilous nature no one can deny. I know its execution was terrible. I didn't do it for Germany, no. I care nothing for a barbarous country which imposed upon me the abjection of being a spy. Besides, I know of a man from England—a modest man—who for me is no less great than Goethe. I talked with him for scarcely an hour, but during that hour he was Goethe . . . I did it because I sensed that the Chief somehow feared people of my race—for the innumerable ancestors who merge within me. I wanted to prove to him that a yellow man could save his armies. Besides, I had to flee from Captain Madden. His hands and his voice could call at my door at any moment. I dressed silently, bade farewell to myself in the mirror, went downstairs, scrutinized the peaceful street and went out. The station was not far from my home, but I judged it wise to take a cab. I argued that in this way I ran less risk of being recognized; the fact is that in the deserted street I felt myself visible and vulnerable, infinitely so. I remember that I told the cab driver to stop a short distance before the main entrance. I got out with voluntary, almost painful slowness; I was going to the village of Ashgrove but I bought a ticket for a more distant station. The train left within a very few minutes, at eight-fifty. I hurried; the next one would leave at nine-thirty. There was hardly a soul on the platform. I went through the coaches; I remember a few farmers, a woman dressed in mourning, a young boy who was reading with fervor the *Annals* of Tacitus, a wounded and happy soldier. The coaches jerked forward at last. A man whom I recognized ran in vain to the end of the platform. It was Captain Richard Madden. Shattered, trembling, I shrank into the far corner of the seat, away from the dreaded window.

From this broken state I passed into an almost abject felicity. I told myself that the duel had already begun and that I had won the first encounter by frustrating, even if for forty minutes, even if by a stroke of fate, the attack of my adversary. I argued that this slightest of victories foreshadowed a total victory. I argued (no less fallaciously) that my cowardly felicity proved that I was a man capable of carrying out the adventure successfully. From this weakness I took strength that did not abandon me. I foresee that man will resign himself each day to more atrocious undertakings; soon there will be no one but warriors and brigands; I give them this counsel: *The author of an atrocious undertaking ought to imagine that he has already accomplished it, ought to impose upon himself a future as irrevocable as the past.* Thus I proceeded as my eyes of a man already dead registered the elapsing of that day, which was perhaps the last, and the diffusion of the night. The train ran gently along, amid ash trees. It stopped, almost in the middle of the fields. No one announced the name of the station. "Ashgrove?" I asked a few lads on the platform. "Ashgrove," they replied. I got off.

A lamp enlightened the platform but the faces of the boys were in shadow. One questioned me, "Are you going to Dr. Stephen Albert's house?" Without waiting for my answer, another said, "The house is a long way from here, but you won't get lost if you take this road to the left and at every crossroads turn again to your left." I tossed them a coin (my last), descended a few stone steps and started down the solitary road. It went downhill, slowly. It was of elemental earth; overhead the branches were tangled; the low, full moon seemed to accompany me.

For an instant, I thought that Richard Madden in some way had penetrated my desperate plan. Very quickly, I understood that that was impossible. The instructions to turn always to the left reminded me that such was the common procedure for discovering the central point of certain labyrinths. I have some understanding of labyrinths: not for nothing am I the great grandson of that Ts'ui Pên who was governor of Yunnan and who renounced worldly power in order to write a novel that might be even more populous than the *Hung Lu Meng* and to construct a labyrinth in which all men would become lost. Thirteen years he dedicated to these heterogeneous tasks, but the hand of a stranger murdered him—and his novel was incoherent and no one found the labyrinth.

Beneath English trees I meditated on that lost maze: I imagined it inviolate and perfect at the secret crest of a mountain; I imagined it erased by rice fields or beneath the water; I imagined it infinite, no longer composed of octagonal kiosks and returning paths, but of rivers and provinces and kingdoms . . . I thought of a labyrinth of labyrinths, of one sinuous spreading labyrinth that would encompass the past and the future and in some way involve the stars. Absorbed in these illusory images, I forgot my destiny of one pursued. I felt myself to be, for an unknown period of time, an abstract perceiver of the world. The vague, living countryside, the moon, the remains of the day worked on me, as well as the slope of the road which eliminated any possibility of weariness. The afternoon was intimate, infinite. The road descended and forked among the now confused meadows. A high-pitched, almost syllabic music approached and receded in the shifting of the wind, dimmed by leaves and distance. I thought that a man can be an enemy of other men, of the moments of other men, but not of a country: not of fireflies, words, gardens, streams of water, sunsets. Thus I arrived before a tall, rusty gate. Between the iron bars I made out a poplar grove and a pavilion. I understood suddenly two things, the first trivial, the second almost unbelievable: the music came from the pavilion, and the music was Chinese. For precisely that reason I had openly accepted it without paying it any heed. I do not remember whether there was a bell or whether I knocked with my hand. The sparkling of the music continued.

From the rear of the house within a lantern approached: a lantern that the trees sometimes striped and sometimes eclipsed, a paper lantern that had the form of a drum and the color of the moon. A tall man bore it. I didn't see his face for the light blinded me. He opened the door and said slowly, in my own language: "I see that the pious Hsi P'êng persists in correcting my solitude. You no doubt wish to see the garden?"

I recognized the name of one of our consuls and I replied, disconcerted, "The garden?"

"The garden of forking paths."

Something stirred in my memory and I uttered with incomprehensible certainty, "The garden of my ancestor Ts'ui Pên."

"Your ancestor? Your illustrious ancestor? Come in."

The damp path zigzagged like those of my childhood. We came to a library of Eastern and Western books. I recognized bound in yellow silk several volumes of the Lost Encyclopedia, edited by the Third Emperor of the Luminous Dynasty but never printed. The record on the phonograph revolved next to a bronze phoenix. I also recall a *famille rose* vase and another, many centuries older, of that shade of blue which our craftsmen copied from the potters of Persia . . .

Stephen Albert observed me with a smile. He was, as I have said, very tall, sharp-featured, with gray eyes and a gray beard. He told me that he had been a missionary in Tientsin "before aspiring to become a Sinologist."

We sat down—I on a long, low divan, he with his back to the window and a tall circular clock. I calculated that my pursuer, Richard Madden, could not arrive for at least an hour. My irrevocable determination could wait.

"An astounding fate, that of Ts'ui Pên," Stephen Albert said. "Governor of his native province, learned in astronomy, in astrology and in the tireless interpretation of the canonical books, chess player, famous poet and calligrapher—he abandoned all this in order to compose a book and a maze. He renounced the pleasures of both tyranny and justice, of his populous couch, of his banquets and even of erudition—all to close himself up for thirteen years in the Pavilion of the Limpid Solitude. When he died, his heirs found nothing save chaotic manuscripts. His family, as you may be aware, wished to condemn them to the fire; but his executor— a Taoist or Buddhist monk—insisted on their publication."

"We descendants of Ts'ui Pên," I replied, "continue to curse that monk. Their publication was senseless. The book is an indeterminate heap of contradictory drafts. I examined it once: in the third chapter the hero dies, in the fourth he is alive. As for the other undertaking of Ts'ui Pên, his labyrinth . . ."

"Here is Ts'ui Pên's labyrinth," he said, indicating a tall lacquered desk.

"An ivory labyrinth!" I exclaimed. "A minimum labyrinth."

"A labyrinth of symbols," he corrected. "An invisible labyrinth of time. To me, a barbarous Englishman, has been entrusted the revelation of this diaphanous mystery. After more than a hundred years, the details are irretrievable; but it is not hard to conjecture what happened. Ts'ui Pên must have said once: *I am withdrawing to write a book.* And another time: *I am withdrawing to construct a labyrinth.* Every one imagined two works; to no one did it occur that the book and the maze were one and the same thing. The Pavilion of the Limpid Solitude stood in the center of a garden that was perhaps intricate; that circumstance could have suggested to the heirs a physical labyrinth. Ts'ui Pên died; no one in the vast territories that were his came upon the labyrinth; the confusion of the novel suggested to me that *it* was the maze. Two circumstances gave me the correct solution of the problem. One: the curious legend that Ts'ui Pên had planned to create a labyrinth which would be strictly infinite. The other: a fragment of a letter I discovered."

Albert rose. He turned his back on me for a moment; he opened a drawer of the black and gold desk. He faced me and in his hands he held a sheet of paper that had once been crimson, but was now pink and tenuous and cross-sectioned. The fame of Ts'ui Pên as a calligrapher had been justly won. I read, uncomprehendingly and with fervor, these words written with a minute brush by a man of my blood: *I leave to the various futures (not to all) my garden of forking paths*. Wordlessly, I returned the sheet. Albert continued:

"Before unearthing this letter, I had questioned myself about the ways in which a book can be infinite. I could think of nothing other than a cyclic volume, a circular one. A book whose last page was identical with the first, a book which had the possibility of continuing indefinitely. I remembered too that night which is at the middle of the Thousand and One Nights when Scheherazade (through a magical oversight of the copyist) begins to relate word for word the story of the Thousand and One Nights, establishing the risk of coming once again to the night when she must repeat it, and thus on to infinity. I imagined as well a Platonic, hereditary work, transmitted from father to son, in which each new individual adds a chapter or corrects with pious care the pages of his elders. These conjectures diverted me; but none seemed to correspond, not even remotely, to the contradictory chapters of Ts'ui Pên. In the midst of this perplexity, I received from Oxford the manuscript you have examined. I lingered, naturally, on the sentence: *I leave to the various futures (not to all) my garden of forking paths*. Almost instantly, I understood: 'the garden of forking paths' was the chaotic novel; the phrase 'the various futures (not to all)' suggested to me the forking in time, not in space. A broad rereading of the work confirmed the theory. In all fictional works, each time a man is confronted with several alternatives, he chooses one and eliminates the others; in the fiction of Ts'ui Pên, he chooses—simultaneously—all of them. *He creates*, in this way, diverse futures, diverse times which themselves also proliferate and fork. Here, then, is the explanation of the novel's contradictions. Fang, let us say, has a secret; a stranger calls at his door; Fang resolves to kill him. Naturally, there are several possible outcomes: Fang can kill the intruder, the intruder can kill Fang, they both can escape, they both can die, and so forth. In the work of Ts'ui Pên, all possible outcomes occur; each one is the point of departure for other forkings. Sometimes, the paths of this labyrinth converge: for example, you arrive at this house, but in one of the possible pasts you are my enemy, in another, my friend. If you will resign yourself to my incurable pronunciation, we shall read a few pages."

His face, within the vivid circle of the lamplight, was unquestionably that of an old man, but with something unalterable about it, even immortal. He read with slow precision two versions of the same epic chapter. In the first, an army marches to a battle across a lonely mountain; the horror of the rocks and shadows makes the men undervalue their lives and they gain an easy victory. In the second, the same army traverses a palace where a great festival is taking place; the resplendent battle seems to them a continuation of the celebration and they win the victory. I listened with proper veneration to these ancient narratives, perhaps less admirable in themselves than the fact that they had been created by my blood and were being restored to me by a man of a remote empire, in the course of a desperate adventure, on a Western isle. I remember the last words, repeated in each version like a secret commandment: *Thus fought the heroes, tranquil their admirable hearts, violent their swords, resigned to kill and to die.*

From that moment on, I felt about me and within my dark body an invisible, intangible swarming. Not the swarming of the divergent, parallel and finally coalescent armies, but a more inaccessible, more intimate agitation that they in some manner prefigured. Stephen Albert continued:

"I don't believe that your illustrious ancestor played idly with these variations. I don't consider it credible that he would sacrifice thirteen years to the infinite execution of a rhetorical experiment. In your country, the novel is a subsidiary form of literature; in Ts'ui Pên's time it was a despicable form. Ts'ui Pên was a brilliant novelist, but he was also a man of letters who doubtless did not consider himself a mere novelist. The testimony of his contemporaries proclaims—and his life fully confirms—his metaphysical and mystical interests. Philosophic controversy usurps a good part of the novel. I know that of all problems, none disturbed him so greatly nor worked upon him so much as the abysmal problem of time. Now then, the latter is the only problem that does not figure in the pages of the *Garden*. He does not even use the word that signifies *time*. How do you explain this voluntary omission?"

I proposed several solutions—all unsatisfactory. We discussed them. Finally, Stephen Albert said to me:

"In a riddle whose answer is chess, what is the only prohibited word?"

I thought a moment and replied, "The word *chess*."

"Precisely," said Albert. "*The Garden of Forking Paths* is an enormous riddle, or parable, whose theme is time; this recondite cause prohibits its mention. To omit a word always, to resort to inept metaphors and obvious periphrases, is perhaps the most emphatic way of stressing it. That is the tortuous method preferred, in each of the meanderings of his indefatigable novel, by the oblique Ts'ui Pên. I have compared hundreds of manuscripts, I have corrected the errors that the negligence of the copyists has introduced, I have guessed the plan of this chaos, I have re-established—I believe I have re-established—the primordial organization, I have translated the entire work; it is clear to me that not once does he employ the word 'time.' The explanation is obvious: *The Garden of Forking Paths* is an incomplete, but not false, image of the universe as Ts'ui Pên conceived it. In contrast to Newton and Schopenhauer, your ancestor did not believe in a uniform, absolute time. He believed in an infinite series of times, in a growing, dizzying net of divergent, convergent and parallel times. This network of times which approached one another, forked, broke off, or were unaware of one another for centuries, embraces *all* possibilities of time. We do not exist in the majority of these times; in some you exist, and not I; in others I, and not you; in others, both of us. In the present one, which a favorable fate has granted me, you have arrived at my house; in another, while crossing the garden, you found me dead; in still another, I utter these same words, but I am a mistake, a ghost."

"In every one," I pronounced, not without a tremble to my voice, "I am grateful to you and revere you for your re-creation of the garden of Ts'ui Pên."

"Not in all," he murmured with a smile. "Time forks perpetually toward innumerable futures. In one of them I am your enemy."

Once again I felt the swarming sensation of which I have spoken. It seemed to me that the humid garden that surrounded the house was infinitely saturated with invisible persons. Those persons were Albert and I, secret, busy and multiform in other dimensions of time. I raised my eyes and the tenuous nightmare dissolved. In the yellow and black garden there was only one man; but this man was as strong as a statue . . . this man was approaching along the path and he was Captain Richard Madden.

"The future already exists," I replied, "but I am your friend. Could I see the letter again?"

Albert rose. Standing tall, he opened the drawer of the tall desk; for the moment his back was to me. I had readied the revolver. I fired with extreme caution. Albert fell uncomplainingly, immediately. I swear his death was instantaneous—a lightning stroke.

The rest is unreal, insignificant. Madden broke in, arrested me. I have been condemned to the gallows. I have won out abominably; I have communicated to Berlin the secret name of the city they must attack. They bombed it yesterday; I read it in the same papers that offered to England the mystery of the learned Sinologist Stephen Albert who was murdered by a stranger, one Yu Tsun. The Chief had deciphered this mystery. He knew my problem was to indicate (through the uproar of the war) the city called Albert, and that I had found no other means to do so than to kill a man of that name. He does not know (no one can know) my innumerable contrition and weariness.

Elizabeth Bowen

(1899–1973)

E lizabth Bowen was born in Dublin. She grew up an only child on the family estate, Bowen's Court, but when her father was afflicted by a debilitating brain disease, she went to England with her mother. Her mother died when Bowen was 13, leaving her to shuttle between the houses of different relatives in Ireland and England. Bowen says of this period in her life: "I was, it seemed, at everyone's disposition. Though quite happy, I lived with a submerged fear that I might fail to establish grown-up status. That fear, it may be, egged me on to writing: an author, a grown-up, must they not be synonymous? As far as I now see, I must have been anxious to approximate my elders, yet to demolish them." She published her first collection of short stories, Encounter, *in 1923, and more than a dozen books of fiction followed, including* To the North *(1932),* The Death of the Heart *(1938),* The Demon Lover *(1945), and* A World of Love *(1955). She befriended some of the most important members of the famous Bloomsbury circle during her time in London— Virginia Woolf, E.M. Forster—and their dedication to the world of letters had a marked influence on her approach to her craft. She has been called "an oblique social historian," "a romantic up against the despotism of reality," "a critic of the English middle-classes," and a novelist limited by her "fluttery concern with a miniature world." In her best fiction, she creates a sense of place and an emotional resonance, and provides a penetrating analysis of the modern malaise.*

The Demon Lover

T owards the end of her day in London Mrs Drover went round to her shut-up house to look for several things she wanted to take away. Some belonged to herself, some to her family, who were by now used to their country life. It was late August; it had been a steamy, showery day: at the moment the trees down the pavement glittered in an escape of humid yellow afternoon sun. Against the next batch of clouds, already piling up ink-dark, broken chimneys and parapets stood out. In her once familiar street, as in any unused channel, an unfamiliar queerness had silted up; a cat wove itself in and out of railings, but no human eye watched Mrs Drover's return. Shifting some parcels under her arm, she slowly forced round her latchkey in an unwilling lock, then gave the door, which had warped, a push with her knee. Dead air came out to meet her as she went in.

The staircase window having been boarded up, no light came down into the hall. But one door, she could just see, stood ajar, so she went quickly through into the room and unshuttered the big window in there. Now the prosaic woman, looking about her, was more perplexed than she knew by everything that she saw, by traces of her long former habit of life—the yellow smoke-stain up the white marble mantelpiece, the ring left by a vase on the top of the escritoire; the bruise in the wallpaper where, on the door being thrown open widely, the china handle had always hit the wall. The piano, having gone away to be stored, had left what looked like claw-marks on its part of the parquet. Though not much dust had seeped in, each object wore a film of another kind; and, the only ventilation being the chimney, the whole drawing-room smelled of the cold hearth. Mrs Drover put down her parcels on the escritoire and left the room to proceed upstairs; the things she wanted were in a bedroom chest.

She had been anxious to see how the house was—the part-time caretaker she shared with some neighbours was away this week on his holiday, known to be not yet back. At the best of times he did not look in often, and she was never sure that she trusted him. There were some cracks in the structure, left by the last bombing, on which she was anxious to keep an eye. Not that one could do anything—

A shaft of refracted daylight now lay across the hall. She stopped dead and stared at the hall table—on this lay a letter addressed to her.

She thought first—then the caretaker *must* be back. All the same, who, seeing the house shuttered, would have dropped a letter in at the box? It was not a circular, it was not a bill. And the post office redirected, to the address in the country, everything for her that came through the post. The caretaker (even if he *were* back) did not know she was due in London today—her call here had been planned to be a surprise—so his negligence in the manner of this letter, leaving it to wait in the dusk and the dust, annoyed her. Annoyed, she picked up the letter, which bore no stamp. But it cannot be important, or they would know . . . She took the letter rapidly upstairs with her, without a stop to look at the writing till she reached what had been her bedroom, where she let in light. The room looked over the garden and other gardens: the sun had gone in; as the clouds sharpened and lowered, the trees and rank lawns seemed already to smoke with dark. Her reluctance to look again at the letter came from the fact that she felt intruded upon—and by someone contemptuous of her ways. However, in the tenseness preceding the fall of rain she read it: it was a few lines.

Dear Kathleen: You will not have forgotten that today is our anniversary, and the day we said. The years have gone by at once slowly and fast. In view of the fact that nothing has changed, I shall rely upon you to keep your promise. I was sorry to see you leave London, but was satisfied that you would be back in time. You may expect me, therefore, at the hour arranged. Until then . . .

K.

Mrs Drover looked for the date: it was today's. She dropped the letter on to the bed-springs, then picked it up to see the writing again—her lips, beneath the remains of lipstick, beginning to go white. She felt so much the change in her own face that she went to the mirror, polished a clear patch in it and looked at once urgently and stealthily in. She was confronted by a woman of forty-four, with eyes starting out under a hat-brim that had been rather carelessly pulled down. She had not put on any more powder since she left the shop where she ate her solitary tea. The pearls her husband had given her on their marriage hung loose round her now rather thinner throat, slipping in the V of the pink wool jumper her sister knitted last autumn as they sat round the fire. Mrs Drover's most normal expression was one of controlled worry, but of assent. Since the birth of the third of her little boys, attended by a quite serious illness, she had had an intermittent muscular flicker to the left of her mouth, but in spite of this she could always sustain a manner that was at once energetic and calm.

Turning from her own face as precipitately as she had gone to meet it, she went to the chest where the things were, unlocked it, threw up the lid and knelt to search. But as rain began to come crashing down she could not keep from looking over her shoulder at the stripped bed on which the letter lay. Behind the blanket of rain the clock of the church that still stood struck six—with rapidly heightening apprehension she counted each of the slow strokes. "The hour arranged . . . My God," she said, "*what* hour? How should I . . .? After twenty-five years . . ."

The young girl talking to the soldier in the garden had not ever completely seen his face. It was dark; they were saying goodbye under a tree. Now and then—for it felt, from not seeing him at this intense moment, as though she had never seen him at all—she verified his presence for these few moments longer by putting out a hand, which he each time pressed, without very much kindness, and painfully, on to one of the breast buttons of his uniform. That cut of the button on the palm of her hand was, principally what she was to carry away. This was so near the end of a leave from France that she could only wish him already gone. It was August 1916. Being not kissed, being drawn away from and looked at intimidated Kathleen till she imagined spectral glitters in the place of his eyes. Turning away and looking back up the lawn she saw, through branches of trees, the drawing-room window alight: she caught a breath for the moment when she could go running back there into the safe arms of her mother and sister, and cry: "What shall I do, what shall I do? He has gone."

Hearing her catch her breath, her fiancé said, without feeling: "Cold?"

"You're going away such a long way."

"Not so far as you think."

"I don't understand?"

"You don't have to," he said. "You will. You know what we said."

"But that was—suppose you—I mean, suppose."

"I shall be with you," he said, "sooner or later. You won't forget that. You need do nothing but wait."

Only a little more than a minute later she was free to run up the silent lawn. Looking in through the window at her mother and sister, who did not for the moment perceive her, she already felt that unnatural promise drive down between her and the rest of all human kind. No other way of having given herself could have made her feel so apart, lost and foresworn. She could not have plighted a more sinister troth.

Kathleen behaved well when, some months later, her fiancé was reported missing, presumed killed. Her family not only supported her but were able to praise her courage without stint because they could not regret, as a husband for her, the man they knew almost nothing about. They hoped she would, in a year or two, console herself—and had it been only a question of consolation things might have gone much straighter ahead. But her trouble, behind just a little grief, was a complete dislocation from everything. She did not reject other lovers, for these failed to appear: for years she failed to attract men—and with the approach of her 'thirties she became natural enough to share her family's anxiousness on this score. She began to put herself out, to wonder; and at thirty-two she was very greatly relieved to find herself being courted by William Drover. She married him, and the two of them settled down in this quiet, arboreal part of Kensington: in this house the years piled up, her children were born and they all lived till they were driven out by the bombs of the next war. Her movements as Mrs Drover were circumscribed, and she dismissed any idea that they were still watched.

As things were—dead or living the letter-writer sent her only a threat. Unable, for some minutes, to go on kneeling with her back exposed to the empty room, Mrs Drover rose from the chest to sit on an upright chair whose back was firmly against the wall. The desuetude of her former bedroom, her married London home's whole air of being a cracked cup from which memory, with its reassuring power, had either evaporated or leaked away, made a crisis—and at just this crisis the letter-writer had, knowledgeably, struck. The hollowness of the house this evening cancelled years on years of voices, habits and steps. Through the shut windows she only heard rain fall on the roofs around. To rally herself, she said she was in a mood—and for two or three seconds shutting her eyes, told herself that she had imagined the letter. But she opened them—there it lay on the bed.

On the supernatural side of the letter's entrance she was not permitting her mind to dwell. Who, in London, knew she meant to call at the house today? Evidently, however, this had been known. The caretaker, *had* he come back, had had no cause to expect her: he would have taken the letter in his pocket, to forward it, at his own time, through the post. There was no other sign that the caretaker had been in—but, if not? Letters dropped in at doors of deserted houses do not fly or walk to tables in halls. They do not sit on the dust of empty tables with the air of certainty that they will be found. There is needed some human hand—but nobody but the caretaker had a key. Under circumstances she did not care to consider, a house can be entered without a key. It was possible that she was not alone now. She might be being waited for, downstairs. Waited for—until when? Until "the hour arranged." At least that was not six o'clock: six has struck.

She rose from the chair and went over and locked the door.

The thing was, to get out. To fly? No, not that: she had to catch her train. As a woman whose utter dependability was the keystone of her family life she was not willing to return to the country, to her husband, her little boys and her sister, without the objects she had come up to fetch. Resuming work at the chest she set about making up a number of parcels in a rapid, fumbling-decisive way. These, with her shopping parcels, would be too much to carry; these meant a taxi—at the thought of the taxi her heart went up and her normal breathing resumed. I will ring up the taxi now; the taxi cannot come too soon: I shall hear the taxi out there running its engine, till I walk calmly down to it through the hall. I'll ring up—But no: the telephone is cut off . . . She tugged at a knot she had tied wrong.

The idea of flight . . . He was never kind to me, not really. I don't remember him kind at all. Mother said he never considered me. He was set on me, that was what it was—not love. Not love, not meaning a person well. What did he do, to make me promise like that? I can't remember—But she found that she could.

She remembered with such dreadful acuteness that the twenty-five years since then dissolved like smoke and she instinctively looked for the weal left by the button on the palm of her hand. She remembered not only all that he said and did but the complete suspension of *her* existence during that August week. I was not myself—they all told me so at the time. She remembered—but with one white burning blank as where acid has dropped on a photograph: *under no conditions* could she remember his face.

So, wherever he may be waiting, I shall not know him. You have no time to run from a face you do not expect.

The thing was to get to the taxi before any clock struck what could be the hour. She would slip down the street and round the side of the square to where the square gave on the main road. She would return in the taxi, safe, to her own door, and bring the solid driver into the house with her to pick up the parcels from room to room. The idea of the taxi driver made her decisive, bold: she unlocked her door, went to the top of the staircase and listened down.

She heard nothing—but while she was hearing nothing the *passé* air of the staircase was disturbed by a draught that travelled up to her face. It emanated from the basement: down there a door or window was being opened by someone who chose this moment to leave the house.

The rain had stopped; the pavements steamily shone as Mrs Drover let herself out by inches from her own front door into the empty street. The unoccupied houses opposite continued to meet her look with their damaged stare. Making towards the thoroughfare and the taxi, she tried not to keep looking behind. Indeed, the silence was so intense—one of those creeks of London silence exaggerated this summer by the damage of war—that no tread could have gained on hers unheard. Where her street debouched on the square where people went on living, she grew conscious of, and checked, her unnatural pace. Across the open end of the square two buses impassively passed each other: women, a perambulator, cyclists, a man wheeling a barrow signalized, once again, the ordinary flow of life. At the square's most populous corner should be—and was— the short taxi rank. This evening, only one taxi—but this, although it presented its blank rump, appeared already to be alertly waiting for her. Indeed, without looking round the driver started his engine as she panted up from behind and put her hand on the door. As she did so, the clock struck seven. The taxi faced the main road: to make the strip back to her house it would have to turn—she had settled back on the seat and the taxi *had* turned before she, surprised by its knowing movement, recol- lected that she had not 'said where'. She leaned forward to scratch at the glass panel that divided the driver's head from her own.

The driver braked to what was almost a stop, turned round and slid the glass panel back: the jolt of this flung Mrs Drover forward till her face was almost into the glass. Through the aperture driver and passenger, not six inches between them, remained for an eternity eye to eye. Mrs Drover's mouth hung open for some seconds before she could issue her first scream. After that she continued to scream freely and to beat with her gloved hands on the glass all round as the taxi, accelerating without mercy, made off with her into the hinterland of deserted streets.

Seán O'Faoláin

(b. 1900)

S eán O'Faoláin was the pen name of John Whelan, who was born
in Cork, Ireland, the son of straight-laced parents who demanded
hard work, absolute obedience and strict adherence to the teachings of
the Catholic Church. He served in the Irish Republican Army from 1918
to 1924 and eventually became its publicity director, although he didn't
see much actual fighting. He received two degrees in English from
University College Cork and a degree in philology from Harvard.
Although he lectured at universities in England and at various American
universities, including Northwestern, Princeton, and Boston College, he
dedicated most of his adult life to writing. In an introduction to a
collection of his stories published by Penguin in 1970, O'Faoláin helpfully summarizes his development as a writer of fiction. He describes his
first stories, **Midsummer Night Madness** (1932), as full of "ands"
and "buts," as luxuriating expansions of "the essential thing." The
inexperienced writer "goes on with the echoes of his first image or idea.
His emotions and his thoughts dilate, the style dilates with them, and in
the end he is trying to write a kind of verbal music to convey feelings
that the mere sense of words cannot give." By the time **A Purse of
Coppers** (1938), his second volume of stories, appeared, O'Faoláin had
learned detachment and had adopted the attitude of gentle mockery of
both himself and his country that figures prominently in his work. With
The Man Who Invented Sin and Other Stories (1948), he notes that
he had found his theme: the ambivalence of the Irish, whose romantic-
idealistic way of considering themselves was at odds with their ruthless
thinking. "When it comes to writing about people who, like the Irish of
our day, combine beautiful, palpitating tea-rose souls with hard, coolly
calculating heads, there does not seem to be any way at all of writing
about them except satirically or angrily." Of the 30 stories he thought
worth preserving, he doubted if even 3 or 4 would be remembered. The
future will almost certainly reveal that O'Faoláin's characteristic self-
deprecation made him far too harsh a judge.

Admiring the Scenery

F rom between the little wayside platforms the railway shot two shining arrows off into the vast bogland where they vanished over a rise that might have been imperceptible without them. It was just before sunset in early spring, a soft evening of evaporating moisture and tentative bird song; for the birds seemed to be practising rather than singing, twirling and stopping, and twirling and stopping, and when the bold thrush rolled out a whirl of sound he might have been mocking all the other eager, stupid little fellows, like the bullfinch or the tits, who had not yet learned their songs.

The three men, leaning on the wooden railing along the platform, looked at the blush of the sun on the last drifted snow of the mountains, and though every rail was cut into an A shape on top, uncomfortable for arm or elbow, they found it restful to lean and look over the bog, speaking hardly at all. They had been walking all day and now were dog tired. They were waiting for the last train to take them into the country town where they all three taught in the diocesan college.

The priest stood in the middle, a young man, too fat for his years, with drooping lids, puffed lips, and a red face as if he suffered from blood pressure. The same features on another man might have suggested a sensual nature, but there was in his heavily lidded eyes a look that was sometimes whimsical and sometimes sad, and that look, with the gentle turn to his mouth when he smiled, gave him the appearance of a man who had gone through many struggles and finally solved his problems in a spirit of good-humoured regret. So, now, as he pulled at his pipe and looked down into a cold bog stream that flowed beneath them, his chin and his piggy jowls rested on his Roman collar, expanded around his little mouth as if he might at any moment break into a little, silent chuckle. Only, you might have felt, those tired eyes would not even then have changed: they would have mocked his own smile.

On his left, carrying the haversack, was a small dark man, with a slim small body and a button of a head and clipped dark moustaches. The main thing about him was that he did break occasionally into sudden talk, and when he did he banged the hard railings repeatedly or lifted his two fists in the air and slapped his forehead. He did all these things, suddenly, when he cried out:

"Why on earth is this ten-thousand-times-accursed station three miles from the village? What's it here for at all? My God, what a country! What—is—it—for?"

"To take us home," said the third man, and the priest's belly shook a little, too tired to expel laughter.

There was nothing remarkable about this third man except that he had handlebar moustaches and a long black coat and a black hat that came down low on his forehead and shaded his melancholy face; when he spoke, however, his face was gentle as the fluting of a dove. There was nothing resigned about him; his oblong face was blackberry-coloured where he shaved and delicate as a woman's where he did not. His eyes were lined with a myriad of fine wrinkles. They were cranky, tormented eyes, and his mouth was thin and cold and hard.

"I know," cried the small man. "It's some bloody czar that did it. Some fool of an undersecretary long ago or some ass of a flaming lord-lieutenant who took a ruler and drew a line across Ireland and said, 'That shall be the route of the new railway!' God, what a flaming country!"

"I wonder," said the sad man, Hanafan, in his slow voice, "do the common people ever admire scenery?"

"Now that's very interesting, Hanafan," cried the small man across the priest's chest. "That's a most extraordinary thing. I often thought of that. Isn't that a coincidence!"

"Well," said the sad Hanafan, blushing modestly, "it's a common enough idea, you know."

"Of course they do," said the deep basso of the priest.

"But do they, do they?" shouted the little man, hammering the railing.

The priest nodded, never taking his eyes from the stream or his pipe from his little mouth.

"How do you know?" demanded the small man, leaping backward and whirling his head left, right, and up in the air, as if the answer were a bird.

"Why wouldn't they?" grunted the priest.

"I know what you mean," interrupted the small man, and he wagged his finger into the priest's face. "I know. I met men like that. Our gardener at home, for example. I'd say to him—he was an awful old drunkard—he'd be lying of a hot summer's afternoon under an apple tree—a lazy old ruffian—'Grand day, Murphy,' I'd say. 'Oh, a grand day, God bless it,' he'd say, 'and isn't it good to be alive?' But that's not admiring the scenery," went on the small man. "It's not being *conscious* of it. It isn't, if you understand me, projecting the idea of the beauty of the scene, the idea, into one's own consciousness. Is it, now, Hanafan? And that's what you mean by admiring the scenery."

"Well," said Hanafan, and his words were like prize pigeons that he released one by one from his hands, "I don't know. I'm not sure I mean that."

"Then what the hell *do* you mean?"

"If a man said to me," went on Hanafan, in his downy voice, "I do be sometimes sitting here, Mr. Hanafan, enjoying the cool of the evening,' I'd say that that man was enjoying the scenery even though he might not know he was doing so at all."

The priest nodded. The small man looked contemptuously at Hanafan, who now began to quote from Gray's 'Elegy' in his round, womanly voice, all the time looking sadly at the warmth of the sun fading from the distant grains of snow, and the mountains becoming black and cold:

> *"The lowing herd winds slowly o'er the lea . . ."*

"I know, I know," interrupted the other, but Hanafan went on quietly:

> *"The ploughman homeward plods his weary way,*
> *And leaves the world to darkness and to me."*

"You see, I feel," he said, "that the ploughman responded to the sense of the end of the day, and the way the fields were all gentle, and dark, and quiet. Just like that bog there . . . is . . . all . . ."

His voice died out.

"Ah, damn it," said the small man in disgust, "that has nothing to do with it."

"It has, Mr Governey," murmured the priest. "In a sense it has."

"Every man," cried Hanafan, aroused with such vigour that the other two glanced at him, "lives out his own imagination of himself. And every imagination must have a background. I'll tell you a queer thing. It's about the stationmaster in this station a few years ago."

The priest nodded and chuckled aloud.

"He was nearly sixty-five," said Hanafan. "And he was married, and had a grown-up son in New York, and a daughter, a nun in South America."

"I sent her there," said the priest. "A nice poor girl she was, God rest her."

"Did she die?" asked Hanafan, and when the priest said, "Yes," he fell silent and forgot his story until the other teacher reminded him crossly.

"Yes," said Hanafan. But, again, he stopped because the station porter came out with two oil lamps, one of which he put into the frame of the standard near them.

"It's a grand evening, Father," he said as he turned up the wick.

"Is she late again?" asked the priest, and the porter looked up the line at the signal, and said:

"Aye, she's a trifle behindhand, I'm thinking."

He got down and drew a great silver watch from his corduroy vest and held it up to the setting sun, peering through the yellow celluloid guard.

"She's due, bedad. Ah, she'll be here in a quarter of an hour all right."

The small man groaned and said, "What a country!" The other two looked up at the lamp and then away, and Hanafan said:

"Isn't it dark!"

The porter had walked away.

"Well," resumed Hanafan suddenly, "this old stationmaster! His name was Boyhan. He thought he had a great voice for singing. He was stationed at Newtown and he used to come and sing in the choir with us. That was before your time, Mr Governey. And he sang in the parish choir. And he'd have sung in the Protestant choir and the Wesleyan choir and the tin-hut choir if they let him. There was not a concert in Newtown that he wasn't the head and tail of it, and he always sang twice and three times, and it was all they could do to keep him from giving encores all night long. For," sighed the teacher, "he had no sense and the people used to make a hare of him. He couldn't sing any more than I could. He had a small little voice, a small range too, but it had no strength or sweetness; there was no richness in it."

The teacher said these words, *strength, sweetness, richness*, with a luscious curl of his thin lips around the fruit of sound. His eyes widened. Clearly he was seeing nothing but the old stationmaster. Earnestly he went on, a small glow on each cheek:

"That was all right until they shifted poor Boyhan to this Godforsaken place. And if Newtown is a lonely hole, this is the back of beyond. At the same time they started the new broadcasting station in Dublin and Boyhan conceived a great ambition to sing there. He formed the idea that some day or other a passenger would be on his way to Dublin, or from Dublin, and he would hear him singing and say, 'My heavens, who is that with the grand voice?' And he would make inquiries—some director or government official—and stop the train and seek out Boyhan and say to him, 'What's the meaning of this neglect? Why haven't you been asked to sing over the radio?' Then there would be paragraphs in the newspapers about Discovery of Great Irish Baritone, and Romance of a Chance-heard Voice, and so on.

"The result of this was that whenever a train rolled in, Boyhan used always to come out of his office singing. He'd be singing little trills up and down the scale, or a bar of 'The Moon Hath Raised Her Lamp Above.' He was known to all the passengers and, sure, they used to be looking out for him. And there he would always be, rubbing his hands and pretending he was doing his do-sol-mi-do just for delight and jollity.

"Well, one hard, moonlight night in December, I was here, like this, waiting for the last train back to Newtown. The snow was white on the hills. It was blazing. There wasn't a sound but the wind in the telegraph wires. The clouds were in flitters, in bits. I well remember it. A rich night. A deep, rich night, and no harm in the winds, but they puffing and blowing."

Again Hanafan's cold thin lips sucked the sound of those words, *rich, deep*, and his eyes dilated under his black hat with the image of his memory. His eyes were not cranky now, but soft and big.

"I was here with a—a—I was here with a—friend."

He stopped for a second. The small man's eyes pounced on him, observing at once his strange embarrassment. He glanced at the priest, but he had lowered his face and his mouth was clamped. In that hesitant second he saw at once a piece of Hanafan's secret life revealed, a memory of something known also to the priest; the thought of a dead friend—or perhaps a woman—something or somebody that made the memory of that night so precious to Hanafan that he could not speak of it openly.

"Was this long ago?" probed the small man inquisitively.

"We walked up and down," said Hanafan, "looking at the snow under the moon and the clouds tumbling. Then Boyhan came out and he took us across the line. He had a fire and we sat around it. The smell of the peat, thick and slab, was stuck into everything in the room."

"Was it only two of you?" prodded the small man, eager to know if it was a woman.

"He showed us photographs of his daughter, the nun, and of his son, Timsy, with, as he said, a lawn tennis in his hand. He had no wife. She was dead. And there he was living alone, in the station, three miles from the village and his only two children in the world away in exile. I quoted Sir Thomas Browne for him, the passage in *The Quincunx*. We all looked out the little window at the stars of the Plough. "Think!" said I. *"The quincunx of heaven runs low and 'tis time to close the five ports of knowledge . . . The huntsmen are up in America and they are already past their first sleep in Persia. But who can be drowsy at that hour which freed us from everlasting sleep, or have slumbering thoughts at that time, when sleep itself must end . . ."*

"Then, by way of no harm, he began to talk about music and singing and he gave us one song after another. He sang us 'Oft in the Stilly Night'—and, you know, he sang it well. He sang 'The Moon Hath Raised Her Lamp Above.' I heard the signal bell ring as he was in the middle of it and far away the train began to purr. He was singing it so heartily we didn't like to interrupt him, and as the train became a roar across the bog and the lights went flashing across the window, he rose and went out to the platform. By heavens, that man saw the trainload as a vast audience whirled before him. He stood out on the platform singing to them.

"We rushed for the bridge, we had no tickets, he gave us no tickets, and as I ran I shouted back to him, 'Hold the train!' He paid no heed, and when we were up on the middle of the bridge he got to the grand burst, the last crescendo, of 'I come! . . . My heart's delight . . .' and waved the train on. We were left looking at it vanishing up the line. I roared at him for a fool, and a vain fool, but he only bowed to us, and he bowed to the porter, and he bowed his way backward to the office like a Caruso. The train purred into the distance and there we two were with the wind in the wires and the white moon on mountains.

"I went back to abuse him—it was the last train—but he only looked at me like a child you'd strike and said he couldn't hold back a train for anyone. The porter paid no heed to us. He outed the lamps and locked the place up. We left the old fellow alone in the station. We had to walk home. It was a grand, bright night. A lovely, thick night . . ."

Hanafan's voice broke. Just then a signal bell rang. It was dark over the bog where far away the train murmured and it could easily be heard because the birds had stopped singing. There was nothing but the deep scent of the night air, and below them in a marsh, still deep from the March rains, a prattling as of a thousand tiny frogs.

"This is a lonely place he lived in," whispered Hanafan. "A lonely life. No children. No wife."

The priest rose up and knocked out the ashes of his pipe as the train roared nearer.

"Yes," he agreed.

"But," cried Governey, "what has all that got to do with admiring the scenery?"

"He sang to the night," cried Hanafan passionately. "He sang to the whole night. The moon was up."

His voice fell and they barely heard him over the rumbling train at the end of the platform.

"We saw the moon in the flags of the Liffey as we left the station. In the flags of the river, through the trees."

"Still and all," cried the small man, "he didn't form any intellectual concept . . ."

The train drowned his voice and its lights flitted across their faces. When they climbed into a carriage the windows were speckled with rain and the three men inside, who leaned back to let them pass, had a cold, damp look. They had been talking when the train stopped, but when they saw the priest they fell silent; looked at him under their brows; and shyly tipped their hats.

"Raining up the line?" asked the priest in a friendly voice.

"Oh, pouring in Dublin, Father," said one of the three men—an elderly, soldierly-looking man, probably a warder in the jail at Maryborough.

The three teachers fell silent, sensing that they had interrupted a conversation. Then they were rolling through the night, looking at the lights racing along the little hedges beside the line. Suddenly the rain that had hit Dublin half an hour before swept down on them across the mountains, slapping the windows like a bucket of water. It kept trickling and shining on the windows.

"He died there last year," said Hanafan suddenly, looking at the trickle outside the pane.

"I once asked him," the priest leaned forward to say to the small man, "what his favourite song was. Do you know what he said? 'Scenes That Are Brightest.' "

The priest leaned back and gave a merry little laugh.

"Still," cried the small man, thumping his knee, "I can't see what this has to do with the question we were discussing!"

The priest looked at him, and kept looking at him as he swayed with the carriage, but he said nothing. Angrily the small man looked back, and then he looked angrily at Hanafan, whose eyes had become cranky and tormented once more. He began to wonder why Hanafan was always so sour, and why he remained on in Newtown if he didn't like the place, and why he had never married. His eye lit up a bit at that and he determined to get it all out of the priest when they were next alone. He tapped Hanafan on the knee and he began to ask him some question, but when he saw that Hanafan's eyes were closed he leaned back again. The priest was still looking at him, so he nodded towards Hanafan and winked. The priest's lidded eyes were as immovable as an owl's.

As they rolled on through the bog the small man kept looking around him restlessly, and at last he shifted over to the three countrymen, determined to find out if the common people really do admire the scenery. He started a conversation about turf cutting, but before he could lead up to the question the train halted at a small station and the strangers got out. Then the three friends were left alone in the cold, damp carriage, listening to the battering rain. Tired and sleepy, nobody noticed that, in his corner, Hanafan was weeping to himself, the drops creeping through his tightly closed eyes.

JOHN STEINBECK

(1902–1968)

*J*ohn Steinbeck was born and raised in the rich agricultural valley of Salinas, California. His father was a flour mill manager and his mother was a teacher. He grew to know the entire Salinas Valley intimately, and its residents later provided the inspiration for the characters of much of his best fiction, a fiction as distinctively Californian as William Faulkner's is Mississippian and Margaret Laurence's is Manitoban. His education included a drawn-out six years at Stanford University because he was forced to spend time working at various low-paying jobs to finance the next term of schooling. These stints, however, exposed him to the lives he would write about. Although Steinbeck was already writing and publishing stories while at Stanford, his first novel, Cup of Gold, a fictionalized treatment of the life of pirate Henry Morgan, was not published until 1929. His second book of fiction was a collection of related stories centred on the town of Corral de Tierra, California, The Pastures of Heaven (1932). He was to return to the form of the story cycle in such works as Tortilla Flat (1935), about a group of down-and-out inhabitants of the Monterey Peninsula, The Red Pony (1937), and The Long Valley (1938). But it was as a novelist that Steinbeck earned his international reputation as the champion of ordinary men and women struggling against the powerful socio-economic forces of unregulated capitalism in hope of building decent lives for themselves and their families. In Dubious Battle (1936) courageously indicted the California land barons who exploited the small farmer and the farm labourer. The Grapes of Wrath (1939) is the epic story of one family of migrant workers who travel from Depression-era Oklahoma to California. In 1937 Steinbeck wrote the novel Of Mice and Men and a version for the stage (produced by George S. Kaufman); the huge success of the two won him a national audience. The pathetic and tragic story of the dreamer, George, and the simpleton, Lennie, epitomizes Steinbeck's lifelong interest in the workings of human consciousness and embodies his vision of fallible humanity in a fallen world—and of man as potentially noble nonetheless, as capable of realizing, in Steinbeck's words, "his proven capacity for greatness of heart and spirit." Of his over 30 books of fiction, drama, travel, chronicle, and marine exploration, particular mention should be made of the novels Cannery Row (1945), again about the lives of vagabonds on the Monterey waterfront; East of Eden (1952), a family saga set in the Salinas Valley; and The Winter of Our Discontent (1961), his pointed attack on American materialism and the book that Steinbeck considered his greatest work, though it has had a mixed reception among his critics. In addition to numerous other awards *and honours, Steinbeck won the Pulitzer Prize for* The Grapes of Wrath *and the 1962 Nobel Prize for Literature.*

The Chrysanthemums

T he high gray-flannel fog of winter closed off the Salinas Valley from the sky and from all the rest of the world. On every side it sat like a lid on the mountains and made of the great valley a closed pot. On the broad, level land floor the gang plows bit deep and left the black earth shining like metal where the shares had cut. On the foothill ranches across the Salinas River, the yellow stubble fields seemed to be bathed in pale cold sunshine, but there was no sunshine in the valley now in December. The thick willow scrub along the river flamed with sharp and positive yellow leaves.

It was a time of quiet and of waiting. The air was cold and tender. A light wind blew up from the southwest so that the farmers were mildly hopeful of a good rain before long; but fog and rain do not go together.

Across the river, on Henry Allen's foothill ranch there was little work to be done, for the hay was cut and stored and the orchards were plowed up to receive the rain deeply when it should come. The cattle on the higher slopes were becoming shaggy and rough-coated.

Elisa Allen, working in her flower garden, looked down across the yard and saw Henry, her husband, talking to two men in business suits. The three of them stood by the tractor shed, each man with one foot on the side of the little Fordson. They smoked cigarettes and studied the machine as they talked.

Elisa watched them for a moment and then went back to her work. She was thirty-five. Her face was lean and strong and her eyes were as clear as water. Her figure looked blocked and heavy in her gardening costume, a man's black hat pulled low down over her eyes, clodhopper shoes, a figured print dress almost completely covered by a big corduroy apron with four big pockets to hold the snips, the trowel and scratcher, the seeds and the knife she worked with. She wore heavy leather gloves to protect her hands while she worked.

She was cutting down the old year's chrysanthemum stalks with a pair of short and powerful scissors. She looked down toward the men by the tractor shed now and then. Her face was eager and mature and handsome; even her work with the scissors was over-eager, over-powerful. The chrysanthemum stems seemed too small and easy for her energy.

She brushed a cloud of hair out of her eyes with the back of her glove, and left a smudge of earth on her cheek in doing it. Behind her stood the neat white farm house with red geraniums close-banked around it as high as the windows. It was a hard-swept looking little house, with hard-polished windows, and a clean mud-mat on the front steps.

Elisa cast another glance toward the tractor shed. The strangers were getting into their Ford coupe. She took off a glove and put her strong fingers down into the forest of new green chrysanthemum sprouts that were growing around the old roots. She spread the leaves and looked down among the close-growing stems. No aphids were there, no sowbugs or snails or cutworms. Her terrier fingers destroyed such pests before they could get started.

Elisa started at the sound of her husband's voice. He had come near quietly, and he leaned over the wire fence that protected her flower garden from cattle and dogs and chickens.

"At it again," he said. "You've got a strong new crop coming."

Elisa straightened her back and pulled on the gardening glove again. "Yes. They'll be strong this coming year." In her tone and on her face there was a little smugness.

"You've got a gift with things," Henry observed. "Some of those yellow chrysanthemums you had this year were ten inches across. I wish you'd work out in the orchard and raise some apples that big."

Her eyes sharpened. "Maybe I could do it, too. I've a gift with things, all right. My mother had it. She could stick anything in the ground and make it grow. She said it was having planters' hands that knew how to do it."

"Well, it sure works with flowers," he said.

"Henry, who were those men you were talking to?"

"Why, sure, that's what I came to tell you. They were from the Western Meat Company. I sold those thirty head of three-year-old steers. Got nearly my own price, too."

"Good," she said. "Good for you."

"And I thought," he continued, "I thought how it's Saturday after-noon, and we might go into Salinas for dinner at a restaurant, and then to a picture show—to celebrate, you see."

"Good," she repeated. "Oh, yes. That will be good."

Henry put on his joking tone. "There's fights tonight. How'd you like to go to the fights?"

"Oh, no," she said breathlessly. "No, I wouldn't like fights."

"Just fooling, Elisa. We'll go to a movie. Let's see. It's two now. I'm going to take Scotty and bring down those steers from the hill. It'll take us maybe two hours. We'll go in town about five and have dinner at the Cominos Hotel. Like that?"

"Of course I'll like it. It's good to eat away from home."

"All right, then. I'll go get up a couple of horses."

She said, "I'll have plenty of time to transplant some of these sets, I guess."

She heard her husband calling Scotty down by the barn. And a little later she saw the two men ride up the pale yellow hillside in search of the steers.

There was a little square sandy bed kept for rooting the chrysanthemums. With her trowel she turned the soil over and over, and smoothed it and patted it firm. Then she dug ten parallel trenches to receive the sets. Back at the chrysanthemum bed she pulled out the little crisp shoots, trimmed off the leaves of each one with her scissors and laid it on a small orderly pile.

A squeak of wheels and plod of hoofs came from the road. Elisa looked up. The country road ran along the dense bank of willows and cottonwoods that bordered the river, and up this road came a curious vehicle, curiously drawn. It was an old spring-wagon, with a round canvas top on it like the cover of a prairie schooner. It was drawn by an old bay horse and a little gray-and-white burro. A big stubble-bearded man sat between the cover flaps and drove the crawling team. Underneath the wagon, between the hind wheels, a lean and rangy mongrel dog walked sedately. Words were painted on the canvas, in clumsy, crooked letters. "Pots, pans, knives, sisors, lawn mores, Fixed." Two rows of articles, and the triumphantly definitive "Fixed" below. The black paint had run down in little sharp points beneath each letter.

Elisa, squatting on the ground, watched to see the crazy, loose-jointed wagon pass by. But it didn't pass. It turned into the farm road in front of her house, crooked old wheels skirling and squeaking. The rangy dog darted from between the wheels and ran ahead. Instantly the two ranch shepherds flew out at him. Then all three stopped, and with stiff and quivering tails, with taut straight legs, with ambassadorial dignity, they slowly circled, sniffing daintily. The caravan pulled up to Elisa's wire fence and stopped. Now the newcomer dog, feeling out-numbered, lowered his tail and retired under the wagon with raised hackles and bared teeth.

The man on the wagon seat called out, "That's a bad dog in a fight when he gets started."

Elisa laughed. "I see he is. How soon does he generally get started?"

The man caught up her laughter and echoed it heartily. "Sometimes not for weeks and weeks," he said. He climbed stiffly down, over the wheel. The horse and the donkey drooped like unwatered flowers.

Elisa saw that he was a very big man. Although his hair and beard were graying, he did not look old. His worn black suit was wrinkled and spotted with grease. The laughter had disappeared from his face and eyes the moment his laughing voice ceased. His eyes were dark, and they were full of the brooding that gets in the eyes of teamsters and of sailors. The calloused hands he rested on the wire fence were cracked, and every crack was a black line. He took off his battered hat.

"I'm off my general road, ma'am," he said. "Does this dirt road cut over across the river to the Los Angeles highway?"

Elisa stood up and shoved the thick scissors in her apron pocket. "Well, yes, it does, but it winds around and then fords the river. I don't think your team could pull through the sand."

He replied with some asperity, "It might surprise you what them beasts can pull through."

"When they get started?" she asked.

He smiled for a second. "Yes. When they get started."

"Well," said Elisa, "I think you'll save time if you go back to the Salinas road and pick up the highway there."

He drew a big finger down the chicken wire and made it sing. "I ain't in any hurry, ma'am. I go from Seattle to San Diego and back every year. Takes all my time. About six months each way. I aim to follow nice weather."

Elisa took off her gloves and stuffed them in the apron pocket with the scissors. She touched the under edge of her man's hat, searching for fugitive hairs. "That sounds like a nice kind of way to live," she said.

He leaned confidentially over the fence. "Maybe you noticed the writing on my wagon. I mend pots and sharpen knives and scissors. You got any of them things to do?"

"Oh, no," she said quickly. "Nothing like that." Her eyes hardened with resistance.

"Scissors is the worst thing," he explained. "Most people just ruin scissors trying to sharpen 'em, but I know how. I got a special tool. It's a little bobbit kind of thing, and patented. But it sure does the trick."

"No. My scissors are all sharp."

"All right, then. Take a pot," he continued earnestly, "a bent pot, or a pot with a hole. I can make it like new so you don't have to buy no new ones. That's a saving for you."

"No," she said shortly. "I tell you I have nothing like that for you to do."

His face fell to an exaggerated sadness. His voice took on a whining undertone. "I ain't had a thing to do today. Maybe I won't have no supper tonight. You see I'm off my regular road. I know folks on the highway clear from Seattle to San Diego. They save their things for me to sharpen up because they know I do it so good and save them money."

"I'm sorry," Elisa said irritably. "I haven't anything for you to do."

His eyes left her face and fell to searching the ground. They roamed about until they came to the chrysanthemum bed where she had been working. "What's them plants, ma'am?"

The irritation and resistance melted from Elisa's face.

"Oh, those are chrysanthemums, giant whites and yellows. I raise them every year, bigger than anybody around here."

"Kind of a long-stemmed flower? Looks like a quick puff of colored smoke?" he asked.

"That's it. What a nice way to describe them."

"They smell kind of nasty till you get used to them," he said.

"It's a good bitter smell," she retorted, "not nasty at all."

He changed his tone quickly. "I like the smell myself."

"I had ten-inch blooms this year," she said.

The man leaned farther over the fence. "Look. I know a lady down the road a piece, has got the nicest garden you ever seen. Got nearly every kind of flower but no chrysanthemums. Last time I was mending a copper-bottom washtub for her (that's a hard job but I do it good), she said to me, 'If you ever run acrost some nice chrysanthemums I wish you'd try to get me a few seeds.' That's what she told me."

Elisa's eyes grew alert and eager. "She couldn't have known much about chrysanthemums. You *can* raise them from seed, but it's much easier to root the little sprouts you see there."

"Oh," he said. "I s'pose I can't take none to her, then."

"Why yes you can," Elisa cried. "I can put some in damp sand, and you can carry them right along with you. They'll take root in the pot if you keep them damp. And then she can transplant them."

"She'd sure like to have some, ma'am. You say they're nice ones?"

"Beautiful," she said. "Oh, beautiful." Her eyes shone. She tore off the battered hat and shook out her dark pretty hair. "I'll put them in a flower pot, and you can take them right with you. Come into the yard."

While the man came through the picket gate Elisa ran excitedly along the geranium-bordered path to the back of the house. And she returned carrying a big red flower pot. The gloves were forgotten now. She kneeled on the ground by the starting bed and dug up the sandy soil with her fingers and scooped it into the bright new flower pot. Then she picked up the little pile of shoots she had prepared. With her strong fingers she pressed them into the sand and tamped around them with her knuckles. The man stood over her. "I'll tell you what to do," she said. "You remember so you can tell the lady."

"Yes, I'll try to remember."

"Well, look. These will take root in about a month. Then she must set them out, about a foot apart in good rich earth like this, see?" She lifted a handful of dark soil for him to look at. "They'll grow fast and tall. Now remember this: In July tell her to cut them down, about eight inches from the ground."

"Before they bloom?" he asked.

"Yes, before they bloom." Her face was tight with eagerness. "They'll grow right up again. About the last of September the buds will start."

She stopped and seemed perplexed. "It's the budding that takes the most care," she said hesitantly. "I don't know how to tell you." She looked deep into his eyes, searchingly. Her mouth opened a little, and she seemed to be listening. "I'll try to tell you," she said. "Did you ever hear of planting hands?"

"Can't say I have, ma'am."

"Well, I can only tell you what it feels like. It's when you're picking off the buds you don't want. Everything goes right down into your fingertips. You watch your fingers work. They do it themselves. You can feel how it is. They pick and pick the buds. They never make a mistake. They're with the plant. Do you see? Your fingers and the plant. You can feel that, right up your arm. They know. They never make a mistake. You can feel it. When you're like that you can't do anything wrong. Do you see that? Can you understand that?"

She was kneeling on the ground looking up at him. Her breast swelled passionately.

The man's eyes narrowed. He looked away self-consciously. "Maybe I know," he said. "Sometimes in the night in the wagon there——"

Elisa's voice grew husky. She broke in on him, "I've never lived as you do, but I know what you mean. When the night is dark—why, the stars are sharp-pointed, and there's quiet. Why, you rise up and up! Every pointed star gets driven into your body. It's like that. Hot and sharp and—lovely."

Kneeling there, her hand went out toward his legs in the greasy black trousers. Her hesitant fingers almost touched the cloth. Then her hand dropped to the ground. She crouched low like a fawning dog.

He said, "It's nice, just like you say. Only when you don't have no dinner, it ain't."

She stood up then, very straight, and her face was ashamed. She held the flower pot out to him and placed it gently in his arms. "Here. Put it in your wagon, on the seat, where you can watch it. Maybe I can find something for you to do."

At the back of the house she dug in the can pile and found two old and battered aluminum saucepans. She carried them back and gave them to him. "Here, maybe you can fix these."

His manner changed. He became professional. "Good as new I can fix them." At the back of his wagon he set a little anvil, and out of an oily tool box dug a small machine hammer. Elisa came through the gate to watch him while he pounded out the dents in the kettles. His mouth grew sure and knowing. At a difficult part of the work he sucked his under-lip.

"You sleep right in the wagon?" Elisa asked.

"Right in the wagon, ma'am. Rain or shine I'm dry as a cow in there."

"It must be nice," she said. "It must be very nice. I wish women could do such things."

"It ain't the right kind of a life for a woman."

Her upper lip raised a little, showing her teeth. "How do you know? How can you tell?" she said.

"I don't know, ma'am," he protested. "Of course I don't know. Now here's your kettles, done. You don't have to buy no new ones."

"How much?"

"Oh, fifty cents'll do. I keep my prices down and my work good. That's why I have all them satisfied customers up and down the highway."

Elisa brought him a fifty-cent piece from the house and dropped it in his hand. "You might be surprised to have a rival some time. I can sharpen scissors, too. And I can beat the dents out of little pots. I could show you what a woman might do."

He put his hammer back in the oily box and shoved the little anvil out of sight. "It would be a lonely life for a woman, ma'am, and a scarey life, too, with animals creeping under the wagon all night." He climbed over the singletree, steadying himself with a hand on the burro's white rump. He settled himself in the seat, picked up the lines. "Thank you kindly, ma'am," he said. "I'll do like you told me; I'll go back and catch the Salinas road."

"Mind," she called, "if you're long in getting there, keep the sand damp."

"Sand, ma'am? . . . Sand? Oh, sure. You mean around the chrysanthemums. Sure I will." He clucked his tongue. The beasts leaned luxuriously into their collars. The mongrel dog took his place between the back wheels. The wagon turned and crawled out the entrance road and back the way it had come, along the river.

Elisa stood in front of her wire fence watching the slow progress of the caravan. Her shoulders were straight, her head thrown back, her eyes half-closed, so that the scene came vaguely into them. Her lips moved silently, forming the words "Good-bye—good-bye." Then she whispered, "That's a bright direction. There's a glowing there." The sound of her whisper startled her. She shook herself free and looked about to see whether anyone had been listening. Only the dogs had heard. They lifted their heads toward her from their sleeping in the dust, and then stretched out their chins and settled asleep again. Elisa turned and ran hurriedly into the house.

In the kitchen she reached behind the stove and felt the water tank. It was full of hot water from the noonday cooking. In the bathroom she tore off her soiled clothes and flung them into the corner. And then she scrubbed herself with a little block of pumice, legs and thighs, loins and chest and arms, until her skin was scratched and red. When she had dried herself she stood in front of a mirror in her bedroom and looked at her body. She tightened her stomach and threw out her chest. She turned and looked over her shoulder at her back.

After a while she began to dress, slowly. She put on her newest underclothing and her nicest stockings and the dress which was the symbol of her prettiness. She worked carefully on her hair, penciled her eyebrows and rouged her lips.

Before she was finished she heard the little thunder of hoofs and the shouts of Henry and his helper as they drove the red steers into the corral. She heard the gate bang shut and set herself for Henry's arrival.

His step sounded on the porch. He entered the house calling, "Elisa, where are you?"

"In my room, dressing. I'm not ready. There's hot water for your bath. Hurry up. It's getting late."

When she heard him splashing in the tub, Elisa laid his dark suit on the bed, and shirt and socks and tie beside it. She stood his polished shoes on the floor beside the bed. Then she went to the porch and sat primly and stiffly down. She looked toward the river road where the willow-line was still yellow with frosted leaves so that under the high gray fog they seemed a thin band of sunshine. This was the only color in the gray afternoon. She sat unmoving for a long time. Her eyes blinked rarely.

Henry came banging out of the door, shoving his tie inside his vest as he came. Elisa stiffened and her face grew tight. Henry stopped short and looked at her. "Why—why, Elisa. You look so nice!"

"Nice? You think I look nice? What do you mean by 'nice'?"

Henry blundered on. "I don't know. I mean you look different, strong and happy."

"I am strong? Yes, strong. What do you mean 'strong'?"

He looked bewildered. "You're playing some kind of a game," he said helplessly. "It's a kind of a play. You look strong enough to break a calf over your knee, happy enough to eat it like a watermelon."

For a second she lost her rigidity. "Henry! Don't talk like that. You didn't know what you said." She grew complete again. "I'm strong," she boasted. "I never knew before how strong."

Henry looked down toward the tractor shed, and when he brought his eyes back to her, they were his own again. "I'll get out the car. You can put on your coat while I'm starting."

Elisa went into the house. She heard him drive to the gate and idle down his motor, and then she took a long time to put on her hat. She pulled it here and pressed it there. When Henry turned the motor off she slipped into her coat and went out.

The little roadster bounced along on the dirt road by the river, raising the birds and driving the rabbits into the brush. Two cranes flapped heavily over the willow-line and dropped into the river-bed.

Far ahead on the road Elisa saw a dark speck. She knew.

She tried not to look as they passed it, but her eyes would not obey. She whispered to herself sadly, "He might have thrown them off the road. That wouldn't have been much trouble, not very much. But he kept the pot," she explained. "He had to keep the pot. That's why he couldn't get them off the road."

The roadster turned a bend and she saw the caravan ahead. She swung full around toward her husband so she could not see the little covered wagon and the mismatched team as the car passed them.

In a moment it was over. The thing was done. She did not look back.

She said loudly, to be heard above the motor, "It will be good, tonight, a good dinner."

"Now you're changed again," Henry complained. He took one hand from the wheel and patted her knee. "I ought to take you in to dinner oftener. It would be good for both of us. We get so heavy out on the ranch."

"Henry," she asked, "could we have wine at dinner?"

"Sure we could. Say! That will be fine."

She was silent for a while; then she said, "Henry, at those prize fights, do the men hurt each other very much?"

"Sometimes a little, not often. Why?"

"Well, I've read how they break noses, and blood runs down their chests. I've read how the fighting gloves get heavy and soggy with blood."

He looked around at her. "What's the matter, Elisa? I didn't know you read things like that." He brought the car to a stop, then turned to the right over the Salinas River bridge.

"Do any women ever go to the fights?" she asked.

"Oh, sure, some. What's the matter, Elisa? Do you want to go? I don't think you'd like it, but I'll take you if you really want to go."

She relaxed limply in the seat. "Oh, no. No. I don't want to go. I'm sure I don't." Her face was turned away from him. "It will be enough if we can have wine. It will be plenty." She turned up her coat collar so he could not see that she was crying weakly—like an old woman.

Frank O'Connor

(1903–1966)

*F*rank O'Connor was the pseudonym of Michael O'Donovan, who
was born in Cork, Ireland, the son of an alcoholic soldier and a
cleaning woman. The family's poverty caused him to leave school at 14,
but by then he had already immersed himself in poetry and fiction. He
said later that in his youth he saw everything "through the veil of
literature," by which he meant Gogol, Balzac, Tolstoy, Turgenev, Chekhov, and Babel, all masters of the short story. He took a number of jobs
when he left school but was fired from them all for daydreaming. O'Connor fought with the Irish Republican Army against the British during
the civil war and was taken prisoner. In Guests of the Nation (1931),
his first collection of short stories, he summed up everything about war
that appalled him. He went on to publish many other collections of
stories, as well as novels, dramatizations, a biography, travel books, an
autobiography, literary criticism, and journalistic articles. He left Ireland
in 1951 for America and lectured at Harvard, Northwestern, and Stanford. Richard Ellmann has noted that much of O'Connor's fiction moves
between two poles, "fixity" and "accommodation." A favourite O'Connor theme is "that flexible people can suddenly become fixed, that the
other side may be less the enemy than one's own incrustation." On the
other hand, Ireland's "secret understandings" result in a great deal of
collusion, and "what interests O'Connor is not the question of illegality
or immortality but the personal warmth that renders collusion inevitable
and implies that most offences are venial anyway and trivial beyond
communal bonds." Of course, the prime reason for his appeal is the
brilliant re-creation of Ireland, its people, language, and mores, in stories
that are rooted in time and place while evoking the perennial concerns
of humanity.

Guests of the Nation

*A*t dusk the big Englishman, Belcher, would shift his long legs out
of the ashes and say "Well, chums, what about it?" and Noble or
me would say "All right, chum" (for we had picked up some of their
curious expressions), and the little Englishman, Hawkins, would light the
lamp and bring out the cards. Sometimes Jeremiah Donovan would come
up and supervise the game and get excited over Hawkins's cards, which
he always played badly, and shout at him as if he was one of our own
"Ah, you divil, you, why didn't you play the tray?"

But ordinarily Jeremiah was a sober and contented poor devil like the big Englishman, Belcher, and was looked up to only because he was a fair hand at documents, though he was slow enough even with them. He wore a small cloth hat and big gaiters over his long pants, and you seldom saw him with his hands out of his pockets. He reddened when you talked to him, tilting from toe to heel and back, and looking down all the time at his big farmer's feet. Noble and me used to make fun of his broad accent, because we were from the town.

I couldn't at the time see the point of me and Noble guarding Belcher and Hawkins at all, for it was my belief that you could have planted that pair down anywhere from this to Claregalway and they'd have taken root there like a native weed. I never in my short experience seen two men to take to the country as they did.

They were handed on to us by the Second Battalion when the search for them became too hot, and Noble and myself, being young, took over with a natural feeling of responsibility, but Hawkins made us look like fools when he showed that he knew the country better than we did.

"You're the bloke they calls Bonaparte," he says to me. "Mary Brigid O'Connell told me to ask you what you done with the pair of her brother's socks you borrowed."

For it seemed, as they explained it, that the Second used to have little evenings, and some of the girls of the neighbourhood turned in, and, seeing they were such decent chaps, our fellows couldn't leave the two Englishmen out of them. Hawkins learned to dance "The Walls of Limerick," "The Siege of Ennis," and "The Waves of Tory" as well as any of them, though, naturally, he couldn't return the compliment, because our lads at that time did not dance foreign dances on principle.

So whatever privileges Belcher and Hawkins had with the Second they just naturally took with us, and after the first day or two we gave up all pretense of keeping a close eye on them. Not that they could have got far, for they had accents you could cut with a knife and wore khaki tunics and overcoats with civilian pants and boots. But it's my belief that they never had any idea of escaping and were quite content to be where they were.

It was a treat to see how Belcher got off with the old woman of the house where we were staying. She was a great warrant to scold, and cranky even with us, but before ever she had a chance of giving our guests, as I may call them, a lick of her tongue, Belcher had made her his friend for life. She was breaking sticks, and Belcher, who hadn't been more than ten minutes in the house, jumped up from his seat and went over to her.

"Allow me, madam," he says, smiling his queer little smile, "please allow me"; and he takes the bloody hatchet. She was struck too paralytic to speak, and after that, Belcher would be at her heels, carrying a bucket, a basket, or a load of turf, as the case might be. As Noble said, he got into looking before she leapt, and hot water, or any little thing she wanted, Belcher would have it ready for her. For such a huge man (and though I am five foot ten myself I had to look up at him) he had an uncommon shortness—or should I say lack?—of speech. It took us some time to get used to him, walking in and out, like a ghost, without a word. Especially because Hawkins talked enough for a platoon, it was strange to hear big Belcher with his toes in the ashes come out with a solitary "Excuse me, chum," or "That's right, chum." His one and only passion was cards, and I will say for him that he was a good card-player. He could have fleeced myself and Noble, but whatever we lost to him Hawkins lost to us, and Hawkins played with the money Belcher gave him.

Hawkins lost to us because he had too much old gab, and we probably lost to Belcher for the same reason. Hawkins and Noble would spit at one another about religion into the early hours of the morning, and Hawkins worried the soul out of Noble, whose brother was a priest, with a string of questions that would puzzle a cardinal. To make it worse, even in treating of holy subjects, Hawkins had a deplorable tongue. I never in all my career met a man who could mix such a variety of cursing and bad language into an argument. He was a terrible man, and a fright to argue. He never did a stroke of work, and when he had no one else to talk to, he got stuck in the old woman.

He met his match in her, for one day when he tried to get her to complain profanely of the drought, she gave him a great come-down by blaming it entirely on Jupiter Pluvius (a deity neither Hawkins nor I had ever heard of, though Noble said that among the pagans it was believed that he had something to do with the rain). Another day he was swearing at the capitalists for starting the German war when the old lady laid down her iron, puckered up her little crab's mouth, and said: "Mr. Hawkins, you can say what you like about the war, and think you'll deceive me because I'm only a simple poor countrywoman, but I know what started the war. It was the Italian Count that stole the heathen divinity out of the temple in Japan. Believe me, Mr. Hawkins, nothing but sorrow and want can follow the people that disturb the hidden powers."

A queer old girl, all right.

II

We had our tea one evening, and Hawkins lit the lamp and we all sat into cards. Jeremiah Donovan came in too, and sat down and watched us for a while, and it suddenly struck me that he had no great love for the two Englishmen. It came as a great surprise to me, because I hadn't noticed anything about him before.

Late in the evening a really terrible argument blew up between Hawkins and Noble, about capitalists and priests and love of your country.

"The capitalists," says Hawkins with an angry gulp, "pays the priests to tell you about the next world so as you won't notice what the bastards are up to in this."

"Nonsense, man!" says Noble, losing his temper. "Before ever a capitalist was thought of, people believed in the next world."

Hawkins stood up as though he was preaching a sermon.

"Oh, they did, did they?" he says with a sneer. "They believed all the things you believe, isn't that what you mean? And you believe that God created Adam, and Adam created Shem, and Shem created Jehoshophat. You believe all that silly old fairytale about Eve and Eden and the apple. Well, listen to me, chum. If you're entitled to hold a silly belief like that, I'm entitled to hold my silly belief—which is that the first thing your God created was a bleeding capitalist, with morality and Rolls-Royce complete. Am I right, chum?" he says to Belcher.

"You're right, chum," says Belcher with his amused smile, and got up from the table to stretch his long legs into the fire and stroke his moustache. So, seeing that Jeremiah Donovan was going, and that there was no knowing when the argument about religion would be over, I went out with him. We strolled down to the village together, and then he stopped and started blushing and mumbling and saying I ought to be behind, keeping guard on the prisoners. I didn't like the tone he took with me, and anyway I was bored with life in the cottage, so I replied by asking him what the hell we wanted guarding them at all for. I told him I'd talked it over with Noble, and that we'd both rather be out with a fighting column.

"What use are those fellows to us?" says I.

He looked at me in surprise and said: "I thought you knew we were keeping them as hostages."

"Hostages?" I said.

"The enemy have prisoners belonging to us," he says, "and now they're talking of shooting them. If they shoot our prisoners, we'll shoot theirs."

"Shoot them?" I said.

"What else did you think we were keeping them for?" he says.

"Wasn't it very unforeseen of you not to warn Noble and myself of that in the beginning?" I said.

"How was it?" says he. "You might have known it."

"We couldn't know it, Jeremiah Donovan," says I. "How could we when they were on our hands so long?"

"The enemy have our prisoners as long and longer," says he.

"That's not the same thing at all," says I.

"What difference is there?" says he.

I couldn't tell him, because I knew he wouldn't understand. If it was only an old dog that was going to the vet's, you'd try and not get too fond of him, but Jeremiah Donovan wasn't a man that would ever be in danger of that.

"And when is this thing going to be decided?" says I.

"We might hear tonight," he says. "Or tomorrow or the next day at latest. So if it's only hanging round here that's a trouble to you, you'll be free soon enough."

It wasn't the hanging round that was a trouble to me at all by this time. I had worse things to worry about. When I got back to the cottage the argument was still on. Hawkins was holding forth in his best style, maintaining that there was no next world, and Noble was maintaining that there was; but I could see that Hawkins had had the best of it.

"Do you know what, chum?" he was saying with a saucy smile. "I think you're just as big a bleeding unbeliever as I am. You say you believe in the next world, and you know just as much about the next world as I do, which is sweet damn-all. What's heaven? You don't know. Where's heaven? You don't know. You know sweet damn-all! I ask you again, do they wear wings?"

"Very well, then," says Noble, "they do. Is that enough for you? They do wear wings."

"Where do they get them, then? Who makes them? Have they a factory for wings? Have they a sort of store where you hands in your chit and takes your bleeding wings?"

"You're an impossible man to argue with," says Noble. "Now, listen to me—" And they were off again.

It was long after midnight when we locked up and went to bed. As I blew out the candle I told Noble what Jeremiah Donovan was after telling me. Noble took it very quietly. When we'd been in bed about an hour he asked me did I think we ought to tell the Englishmen. I didn't think we should, because it was more than likely that the English wouldn't shoot our men, and even if they did, the brigade officers, who were always up and down with the Second Battalion and knew the Englishmen well, wouldn't be likely to want them plugged. "I think so too," says Noble. "It would be great cruelty to put the wind up them now."

"It was very unforeseen of Jeremiah Donovan anyhow," says I.

It was next morning that we found it so hard to face Belcher and Hawkins. We went about the house all day scarcely saying a word. Belcher didn't seem to notice; he was stretched into the ashes as usual, with his usual look of waiting in quietness for something unforeseen to happen, but Hawkins noticed and put it down to Noble's being beaten in the argument of the night before.

"Why can't you take a discussion in the proper spirit?" he says severely. "You and your Adam and Eve! I'm a Communist, that's what I am. Communist or anarchist, it all comes to much the same thing." And for hours he went round the house, muttering when the fit took him. "Adam and Eve! Adam and Eve! Nothing better to do with their time than picking bleeding apples!"

III

I don't know how we got through that day, but I was very glad when it was over, the tea things were cleared away, and Belcher said in his peaceable way: "Well, chums, what about it?" We sat round the table and Hawkins took out the cards, and just then I heard Jeremiah Donovan's footstep on the path and a dark presentiment crossed my mind. I rose from the table and caught him before he reached the door.

"What do you want?" I asked.

"I want those two soldier friends of yours," he says, getting red.

"Is that the way, Jeremiah Donovan?" I asked.

"That's the way. There were four of our lads shot this morning, one of them a boy of sixteen."

"That's bad," I said.

At that moment Noble followed me out, and the three of us walked down the path together, talking in whispers. Feeney, the local intelligence officer, was standing by the gate.

"What are you going to do about it?" I asked Jeremiah Donovan.

"I want you and Noble to get them out; tell them they're being shifted again; that'll be the quietest way."

"Leave me out of that," says Noble under his breath.

Jeremiah Donovan looks at him hard.

"All right," he says. "You and Feeney get a few tools from the shed and dig a hole by the far end of the bog. Bonaparte and myself will be after you. Don't let anyone see you with the tools. I wouldn't like it to go beyond ourselves."

We saw Feeney and Noble go round to the shed and went in ourselves. I left Jeremiah Donovan to do the explanations. He told them that he had orders to send them back to the Second Battalion. Hawkins let out a mouthful of curses, and you could see that though Belcher didn't say anything, he was a bit upset too. The old woman was for having them stay in spite of us, and she didn't stop advising them until Jeremiah Donovan lost his temper and turned on her. He had a nasty temper, I noticed. It was pitch-dark in the cottage by this time, but no one thought of lighting the lamp, and in the darkness the two Englishmen fetched their topcoats and said good-bye to the old woman.

"Just as a man makes a home of a bleeding place, some bastard at headquarters thinks you're too cushy and shunts you off," says Hawkins, shaking her hand.

"A thousand thanks, madam," says Belcher. "A thousand thanks for everything"—as though he'd made it up.

We went round to the back of the house and down towards the bog. It was only then that Jeremiah Donovan told them. He was shaking with excitement.

"There were four of our fellows shot in Cork this morning and now you're to be shot as a reprisal."

"What are you talking about?" snaps Hawkins. "It's bad enough being mucked about as we are without having to put up with your funny jokes."

"It isn't a joke," says Donovan. "I'm sorry, Hawkins, but it's true," and begins on the usual rigmarole about duty and how unpleasant it is.

I never noticed that people who talk a lot about duty find it much of a trouble to them.

"Oh, cut it out!" says Hawkins.

"Ask Bonaparte," says Donovan, seeing that Hawkins isn't taking him seriously. "Isn't it true, Bonaparte?"

"It is," I say, and Hawkins stops.

"Ah, for Christ's sake, chum!"

"I mean it, chum," I say.

"You don't sound as if you meant it."

"If he doesn't mean it, I do," says Donovan, working himself up.

"What have you against me, Jeremiah Donovan?"

"I never said I had anything against you. But why did your people take out four of our prisoners and shoot them in cold blood?"

He took Hawkins by the arm and dragged him on, but it was impossible to make him understand that we were in earnest. I had the Smith and Wesson in my pocket and I kept fingering it and wondering what I'd do if they put up a fight for it or ran, and wishing to God they'd do one or the other. I knew if they did run for it, that I'd never fire on them. Hawkins wanted to know was Noble in it, and when we said yes, he asked us why Noble wanted to plug him. Why did any of us want to plug him? What had he done to us? Weren't we all chums? Didn't we understand him and didn't he understand us? Did we imagine for an instant that he'd shoot us for all the so-and-so officers in the so-and-so British Army?

By this time we'd reached the bog, and I was so sick I couldn't even answer him. We walked along the edge of it in the darkness, and every now and then Hawkins would call a halt and begin all over again, as if he was wound up, about our being chums, and I knew that nothing but the sight of the grave would convince him that we had to do it. And all the time I was hoping that something would happen; that they'd run for it or that Noble would take over the responsibility from me. I had the feeling that it was worse on Noble than on me.

IV

At last we saw the lantern in the distance and made towards it. Noble was carrying it, and Feeney was standing somewhere in the darkness behind him, and the picture of them so still and silent in the bogland brought it home to me that we were in earnest, and banished the last bit of hope I had.

Belcher, on recognizing Noble, said: "Hallo, chum," in his quiet way, but Hawkins flew at him at once, and the argument began all over again, only this time Noble had nothing to say for himself and stood with his head down, holding the lantern between his legs.

It was Jeremiah Donovan who did the answering. For the twentieth time, as though it was haunting his mind, Hawkins asked if anybody thought he'd shoot Noble.

"Yes, you would," says Jeremiah Donovan.

"No, I wouldn't, damn you!"

"You would, because you'd know you'd be shot for not doing it."

"I wouldn't, not if I was to be shot twenty times over. I wouldn't shoot a pal. And Belcher wouldn't—isn't that right, Belcher?"

"That's right, chum," Belcher said, but more by way of answering the question than of joining in the argument. Belcher sounded as though whatever unforeseen thing he'd always been waiting for had come at last.

"Anyway, who says Noble would be shot if I wasn't? What do you think I'd do if I was in his place, out in the middle of a blasted bog?"

"What would you do?" asked Donovan.

"I'd go with him wherever he was going, of course. Share my last bob with him and stick by him through thick and thin. No one can ever say of me that I let down a pal."

"We had enough of this," says Jeremiah Donovan, cocking his revolver. "Is there any message you want to send?"

"No, there isn't."

"Do you want to say your prayers?"

Hawkins came out with a cold-blooded remark that even shocked me and turned on Noble again.

"Listen to me, Noble," he says. "You and me are chums. You can't come over to my side, so I'll come over to your side. That show you I mean what I say? Give me a rifle and I'll go along with you and the other lads."

Nobody answered him. We knew that was no way out.

"Hear what I'm saying?" he says. "I'm through with it. I'm a deserter or anything else you like. I don't believe in your stuff, but it's no worse than mine. That satisfy you?"

Noble raised his head, but Donovan began to speak and he lowered it again without replying.

"For the last time, have you any messages to send?" says Donovan in a cold, excited sort of voice.

"Shut up, Donovan! You don't understand me, but these lads do. They're not the sort to make a pal and kill a pal. They're not the tools of any capitalist."

I alone of the crowd saw Donovan raise his Webley to the back of Hawkins's neck, and as he did so I shut my eyes and tried to pray. Hawkins had begun to say something else when Donovan fired, and as I opened my eyes at the bang, I saw Hawkins stagger at the knees and lie out flat at Noble's feet, slowly and as quiet as a kid falling asleep, with the lantern-light on his lean legs and bright farmer's boots. We all stood very still, watching him settle out in the last agony.

Then Belcher took out a handkerchief and began to tie it about his own eyes (in our excitement we'd forgotten to do the same for Hawkins), and, seeing it wasn't big enough, turned and asked for the loan of mine. I gave it to him and he knotted the two together and pointed with his foot at Hawkins.

"He's not quite dead," he says. "Better give him another."

Sure enough, Hawkins's left knee is beginning to rise. I bend down and put my gun to his head; then, recollecting myself, I get up again. Belcher understands what's in my mind.

"Give him his first," he says. "I don't mind. Poor bastard, we don't know what's happening to him now."

I knelt and fired. By this time I didn't seem to know what I was doing. Belcher, who was fumbling a bit awkwardly with the handkerchiefs, came out with a laugh as he heard the shot. It was the first time I heard him laugh and it sent a shudder down my back; it sounded so unnatural.

"Poor bugger!" he said quietly. "And last night he was so curious about it all. It's very queer, chums, I always think. Now he knows as much about it as they'll ever let him know, and last night he was all in the dark."

Donovan helped him to tie the handkerchiefs about his eyes. "Thanks, chum," he said. Donovan asked if there were any messages he wanted sent.

"No, chum," he says. "Not for me. If any of you would like to write to Hawkins's mother, you'll find a letter from her in his pocket. He and his mother were great chums. But my missus left me eight years ago.

Went away with another fellow and took the kid with her. I like the feeling of a home, as you may have noticed, but I couldn't start again after that."

It was an extraordinary thing, but in those few minutes Belcher said more than in all the weeks before. It was just as if the sound of the shot had started a flood of talk in him and he could go on the whole night like that, quite happily, talking about himself. We stood round like fools now that he couldn't see us any longer. Donovan looked at Noble, and Noble shook his head. Then Donovan raised his Webley, and at that moment Belcher gives his queer laugh again. He may have thought we were talking about him, or perhaps he noticed the same thing I'd noticed and couldn't understand it.

"Excuse me, chums," he says. "I feel I'm talking the hell of a lot, and so silly, about my being so handy about a house and things like that. But this thing came on me suddenly. You'll forgive me, I'm sure."

"You don't want to say a prayer?" asks Donovan.

"No, chum," he says. "I don't think it would help. I'm ready, and you boys want to get it over."

"You understand that we're only doing our duty?" says Donovan.

Belcher's head was raised like a blind man's, so that you could only see his chin and the tip of his nose in the lantern-light.

"I never could make out what duty was myself," he said. "I think you're all good lads, if that's what you mean. I'm not complaining."

Noble, just as if he couldn't bear any more of it, raised his fist at Donovan, and in a flash Donovan raised his gun and fired. The big man went over like a sack of meal, and this time there was no need of a second shot.

I don't remember much about the burying, but that it was worse than all the rest because we had to carry them to the grave. It was all mad lonely with nothing but a patch of lantern-light between ourselves and the dark, and birds hooting and screeching all round, disturbed by the guns. Noble went through Hawkins's belongings to find the letter from his mother, and then joined his hands together. He did the same with Belcher. Then, when we'd filled in the grave, we separated from Jeremiah Donovan and Feeney and took our tools back to the shed. All the way we didn't speak a word. The kitchen was dark and cold as we'd left it, and the old woman was sitting over the hearth, saying her beads. We walked past her into the room, and Noble struck a match to light the lamp. She rose quietly and came to the doorway with all her cantankerousness gone.

"What did ye do with them?" she asked in a whisper, and Noble started so that the match went out in his hand.

"What's that?" he asked without turning round.

"I heard ye," she said.

"What did you hear?" asked Noble.

"I heard ye. Do ye think I didn't hear ye, putting the spade back in the houseen?"

Noble struck another match and this time the lamp lit for him.

"Was that what ye did to them?" she asked.

Then, by God, in the very doorway, she fell on her knees and began praying, and after looking at her for a minute or two Noble did the same by the fireplace. I pushed my way out past her and left them at it. I stood at the door, watching the stars and listening to the shrieking of the birds dying out over the bogs. It is so strange what you feel at times like that that you can't describe it. Noble says he saw everything ten times the size, as though there were nothing in the whole world but that little patch of bog with the two Englishmen stiffening into it, but with me it was as if the patch of bog where the Englishmen were was a million miles away, and even Noble and the old woman, mumbling behind me, and the birds and the bloody stars were all far away, and I was somehow very small and very lost and lonely like a child astray in the snow. And anything that happened me afterwards, I never felt the same about again.

First Confession

A ll the trouble began when my grandfather died and my grand-mother—my father's mother—came to live with us. Relations in the one house are a strain at the best of times, but, to make matters worse, my grandmother was a real old countrywoman and quite unsuited to the life in town. She had a fat, wrinkled old face, and, to Mother's great indignation, went round the house in bare feet—the boots had her crippled, she said. For dinner she had a jug of porter and a pot of potatoes with—sometimes—a bit of salt fish, and she poured out the potatoes on the table and ate them slowly, with great relish, using her fingers by way of a fork.

Now, girls are supposed to be fastidious, but I was the one who suffered most from this. Nora, my sister, just sucked up to the old woman for the penny she got every Friday out of the old-age pension, a thing I could not do. I was too honest, that was my trouble; and when I was playing with Bill Connell, the sergeant-major's son, and saw my grandmother steering up the path with the jug of porter sticking out from beneath her shawl, I was mortified. I made excuses not to let him come into the house, because I could never be sure what she would be up to when we went in.

When Mother was at work and my grandmother made the dinner I wouldn't touch it. Nora once tried to make me, but I hid under the table from her and took the bread-knife with me for protection. Nora let on to be very indignant (she wasn't, of course, but she knew Mother saw through her, so she sided with Gran) and came after me. I lashed out at her with the bread-knife, and after that she left me alone. I stayed there till Mother came in from work and made my dinner, but when Father came in later Nora said in a shocked voice: "Oh, Dadda, do you know what Jackie did at dinner-time?" Then, of course, it all came out; Father gave me a flaking; Mother interfered, and for days after that he didn't speak to me and Mother barely spoke to Nora. And all because of that old woman! God knows, I was heart-scalded.

Then, to crown my misfortunes, I had to make my first confession and communion. It was an old woman called Ryan who prepared us for these. She was about the one age with Gran; she was well-do-to, lived in a big house on Montenotte, wore a black cloak and bonnet, and came every day to school at three o'clock when we should have been going home, and talked to us of hell. She may have mentioned the other place as well, but that could only have been by accident, for hell had the first place in her heart.

She lit a candle, took out a new half-crown, and offered it to the first boy who would hold one finger—only one finger!—in the flame for five minutes by the school clock. Being always very ambitious I was tempted to volunteer, but I thought it might look greedy. Then she asked were we afraid of holding one finger—only one finger!—in a little candle flame for five minutes and not afraid of burning all over in roasting hot furnaces for all eternity. "All eternity! Just think of that! A whole lifetime goes by and it's nothing, not even a drop in the ocean of your sufferings." The woman was really interesting about hell, but my attention was all fixed on the half-crown. At the end of the lesson she put it back in her purse. It was a great disappointment; a religious woman like that, you wouldn't think she'd bother about a thing like a half-crown.

Another day she said she knew a priest who woke one night to find a fellow he didn't recognize leaning over the end of his bed. The priest was a bit frightened—naturally enough—but he asked the fellow what he wanted, and the fellow said in a deep, husky voice that he wanted to go to confession. The priest said it was an awkward time and wouldn't it do in the morning, but the fellow said that last time he went to confession, there was one sin he kept back, being ashamed to mention it, and now it was always on his mind. Then the priest knew it was a bad case, because the fellow was after making a bad confession and committing a mortal sin. He got up to dress, and just then the cock crew in the yard outside, and—lo and behold!—when the priest looked round there was no sign of the fellow, only a smell of burning timber, and when the priest looked at his bed didn't he see the print of two hands burned in it? That was because the fellow had made a bad confession. This story made a shocking impression on me.

But the worst of all was when she showed us how to examine our conscience. Did we take the name of the Lord, our God, in vain? Did we honour our father and our mother? (I asked her did this include grandmothers and she said it did.) Did we love our neighbours as ourselves? Did we covet our neighbour's goods? (I thought of the way I felt about the penny that Nora got every Friday.) I decided that, between one thing and another, I must have broken the whole ten commandments, all on account of that old woman, and so far as I could see, so long as she remained in the house I had no hope of ever doing anything else.

I was scared to death of confession. The day the whole class went I let on to have a toothache, hoping my absence wouldn't be noticed; but at three o'clock, just as I was feeling safe, along comes a chap with a message from Mrs Ryan that I was to go to confession myself on Saturday and be at the chapel for communion with the rest. To make it worse, Mother couldn't come with me and sent Nora instead.

Now, that girl had ways of tormenting me that Mother never knew of. She held my hand as we went down the hill, smiling sadly and saying how sorry she was for me, as if she were bringing me to the hospital for an operation.

"Oh, God help us!" she moaned. "Isn't it a terrible pity you weren't a good boy? Oh, Jackie, my heart bleeds for you! How will you ever think of all your sins? Don't forget you have to tell him about the time you kicked Gran on the shin."

"Lemme go!" I said, trying to drag myself free of her. "I don't want to go to confession at all."

"But sure, you'll have to go to confession, Jackie," she replied in the same regretful tone. "Sure, if you didn't, the parish priest would be up to the house, looking for you. 'Tisn't, God knows, that I'm not sorry for you. Do you remember the time you tried to kill me with the bread-knife under the table? And the language you used to me? I don't know what he'll do with you at all, Jackie. He might have to send you up to the bishop."

I remember thinking bitterly that she didn't know the half of what I had to tell—if I told it. I knew I couldn't tell it, and understood perfectly why the fellow in Mrs Ryan's story made a bad confession; it seemed to me a great shame that people wouldn't stop criticizing him. I remember that steep hill down to the church, and the sunlit hillsides beyond the valley of the river, which I saw in the gaps between the houses like Adam's last glimpse of Paradise.

Then, when she had manoeuvred me down the long flight of steps to the chapel yard, Nora suddenly changed her tone. She became the raging malicious devil she really was.

"There you are!" she said with a yelp of triumph, hurling me through the church door. "And I hope he'll give you the penitential psalms, you dirty little caffler."

I knew then I was lost, given up to eternal justice. The door with the coloured-glass panels swung shut behind me, the sunlight went out and gave place to deep shadow, and the wind whistled outside so that the silence within seemed to crackle like ice under my feet. Nora sat in front of me by the confession box. There were a couple of old women ahead of her, and then a miserable-looking poor devil came and wedged me in at the other side, so that I couldn't escape even if I had the courage. He joined his hands and rolled his eyes in the direction of the roof, muttering aspirations in an anguished tone, and I wondered had he a grandmother too. Only a grandmother could account for a fellow behaving in that heart-broken way, but he was better off than I, for he at least could go and confess his sins; while I would make a bad confession and then die in the night and be continually coming back and burning people's furniture.

Nora's turn came, and I heard the sound of something slamming, and then her voice as if butter wouldn't melt in her mouth, and then another slam, and out she came. God, the hypocrisy of women! Her eyes were lowered, her head was bowed, and her hands were joined very low down on her stomach, and she walked up the aisle to the side altar looking like a saint. You never saw such an exhibition of devotion; and I remembered the devilish malice with which she had tormented me all the way from our door, and wondered were all religious people like that, really. It was my turn now. With the fear of damnation in my soul I went in, and the confessional door closed of itself behind me.

It was pitch-dark and I couldn't see priest or anything else. Then I really began to be frightened. In the darkness it was a matter between God and me, and He had all the odds. He knew what my intentions were before I even started; I had no chance. All I had ever been told about confession got mixed up in my mind, and I knelt to one wall and said: "Bless me, father, for I have sinned; this is my first confession." I waited for a few minutes, but nothing happened, so I tried it on the other wall. Nothing happened there either. He had me spotted all right.

It must have been then that I noticed the shelf at about one height with my head. It was really a place for grown-up people to rest their elbows, but in my distracted state I thought it was probably the place you were supposed to kneel. Of course, it was on the high side and not very deep, but I was always good at climbing and managed to get up all right. Staying up was the trouble. There was room only for my knees, and nothing you could get a grip on but a sort of wooden moulding a bit above it. I held on to the moulding and repeated the words a little louder, and this time something happened all right. A slide was slammed back; a little light entered the box, and a man's voice said: "Who's there?"

" 'Tis me, father," I said for fear he mightn't see me and go away again. I couldn't see him at all. The place the voice came from was under the moulding, about level with my knees, so I took a good grip of the moulding and swung myself down till I saw the astonished face of a young priest looking up at me. He had to put his head on one side to see me, and I had to put mine on one side to see him, so we were more or less talking to one another upside-down. It struck me as a queer way of hearing confessions, but I didn't feel it my place to criticize.

"Bless me, father, for I have sinned; this is my first confession," I rattled off all in one breath, and swung myself down the least shade more to make it easier for him.

"What are you doing up there?" he shouted in an angry voice, and the strain the politeness was putting on my hold of the moulding, and the shock of being addressed in such an uncivil tone, were too much for me. I lost my grip, tumbled, and hit the door an unmerciful wallop before I found myself flat on my back in the middle of the aisle. The people who had been waiting stood up with their mouths open. The priest opened the door of the middle box and came out, pushing his biretta back from his forehead; he looked something terrible. Then Nora came scampering down the aisle.

"Oh, you dirty little caffler!" she said. "I might have known you'd do it. I might have known you'd disgrace me. I can't leave you out of my sight for one minute."

Before I could even get to my feet to defend myself she bent down and gave me a clip across the ear. This reminded me that I was so stunned I had even forgotten to cry, so that people might think I wasn't hurt at all, when in fact I was probably maimed for life. I gave a roar out of me.

"What's all this about?" the priest hissed, getting angrier than ever and pushing Nora off me. "How dare you hit the child like that, you little vixen?"

"But I can't do my penance with him, father," Nora cried, cocking an outraged eye up at him.

"Well, go and do it, or I'll give you some more to do," he said, giving me a hand up. "Was it coming to confession you were, my poor man?" he asked me.

" 'Twas, father," said I with a sob.

"Oh," he said respectfully, "a big hefty fellow like you must have terrible sins. Is this your first?"

" 'Tis, father," said I.

"Worse and worse," he said gloomily. "The crimes of a lifetime. I don't know will I get rid of you at all today. You'd better wait now till

I'm finished with these old ones. You can see by the looks of them they haven't much to tell."

"I will, father," I said with something approaching joy.

The relief of it was really enormous. Nora stuck out her tongue at me from behind his back, but I couldn't even be bothered retorting. I knew from the very moment that man opened his mouth that he was intelligent above the ordinary. When I had time to think, I saw how right I was. It only stood to reason that a fellow confessing after seven years would have more to tell than people that went every week. The crimes of a lifetime, exactly as he said. It was only what he expected, and the rest was the cackle of old women and girls with their talk of hell, the bishop, and the penitential psalms. That was all they knew. I started to make my examination of conscience, and barring the one bad business of my grandmother it didn't seem so bad.

The next time, the priest steered me into the confession box himself and left the shutter back the way I could see him get in and sit down at the further side of the grille from me.

"Well, now," he said "what do they call you?"

"Jackie, father," said I.

"And what's a-trouble to you, Jackie?"

"Father," I said, feeling I might as well get it over while I had him in good humour, "I had it all arranged to kill my grandmother."

He seemed a bit shaken by that, all right, because he said nothing for quite a while.

"My goodness," he said at last, "that'd be a shocking thing to do. What put that into your head?"

"Father," I said, feeling very sorry for myself, "she's an awful woman."

"Is she?" he asked. "What way is she awful?"

"She takes porter, father," I said, knowing well from the way Mother talked of it that this was a mortal sin, and hoping it would make the priest take a more favourable view of my case.

"Oh, my!" he said, and I could see he was impressed.

"And snuff, father," said I.

"That's a bad case, sure enough, Jackie," he said.

"And she goes round in her bare feet, father," I went on in a rush of self-pity, "and she knows I don't like her, and she gives pennies to Nora and none to me, and my da sides with her and flakes me, and one night I was so heart-scalded I made up my mind I'd have to kill her."

"And what would you do with the body?" he asked with great interest.

"I was thinking I could chop that up and carry it away in a barrow I have," I said.

"Begor, Jackie," he said, "do you know you're a terrible child?"

"I know, father," I said, for I was just thinking the same thing myself. "I tried to kill Nora too with a bread-knife under the table, only I missed her."

"Is that the little girl that was beating you just now?" he asked.

" 'Tis, father."

"Someone will go for her with a bread-knife one day, and he won't miss her," he said rather cryptically. "You must have great courage. Between ourselves, there's a lot of people I'd like to do the same to but I'd never have the nerve. Hanging is an awful death."

"Is it, father?" I asked with the deepest interest—I was always very keen on hanging. "Did you ever see a fellow hanged?"

"Dozens of them," he said solemnly. "And they all died roaring."

"Jay!" I said.

"Oh, a horrible death!" he said with great satisfaction. "Lots of the fellows I saw killed their grandmothers too, but they all said 'twas never worth it."

He had me there for a full ten minutes talking, and then walked out the chapel yard with me. I was genuinely sorry to part with him, because he was the most entertaining character I'd ever met in the religious line. Outside, after the shadow of the church, the sunlight was like the roaring of waves on a beach; it dazzled me; and when the frozen silence melted and I heard the screech of the trams on the road my heart soared. I knew now I wouldn't die in the night and come back, leaving marks on my mother's furniture. It would be a great worry to her, and the poor soul had enough.

Nora was sitting on the railing, waiting for me, and she put on a very sour puss when she saw the priest with me. She was mad jealous because a priest had never come out of the church with her.

"Well," she asked coldly, after he left me, "what did he give you?"

"Three Hail Marys," I said.

"Three Hail Marys," she repeated incredulously. "You mustn't have told him anything."

"I told him everything," I said confidently.

"About Gran and all?"

"About Gran and all."

(All she wanted was to be able to go home and say I'd made a bad confession.)

"Did you tell him you went for me with the bread-knife?" she asked with a frown.

"I did to be sure."

"And he only gave you three Hail Marys?"

"That's all."

She slowly got down from the railing with a baffled air. Clearly, this was beyond her. As we mounted the steps back to the main road she looked at me suspiciously.

"What are you sucking?" she asked.

"Bullseyes."

"Was it the priest gave them to you?"

" 'Twas."

"Lord God," she wailed bitterly, "some people have all the luck! 'Tis no advantage to anybody trying to be good. I might just as well be a sinner like you."

MORLEY CALLAGHAN

(1903–1990)

*M*orley Callaghan was born in Toronto, the city in which he lived his whole life. He was educated at the University of Toronto and Osgoode Hall Law School. He was called to the bar in 1928 but never practised, finding instead early success as a writer the same year with the novel **Strange Fugitive** and, the following year, with the short-story collection **A Native Argosy**. For a period he worked as a reporter on the Toronto Star, where he met Ernest Hemingway. Hemingway encouraged Callaghan to pursue a literary career and, judging from the first books, profoundly influenced his prose style. In 1929 Callaghan and his wife went to Paris, where they participated in the literary scene that revolved around Hemingway, the Fitzgeralds, and James Joyce. (A scene that involved more than literary matters: Callaghan's friendship with Hemingway ended on a sour note when, in a sparring match that included Fitzgerald as timekeeper, the smaller Canadian knocked down the pugilistic "Papa.") Callaghan's account of this period in **That Summer in Paris** (1963) makes for fascinating reading. The book also provides a needed corrective to other reminiscences of the Left Bank scene in the Paris of the 1920s. Callaghan's career was characterized by periods of high productivity and years of silence. His novels of the 1930s are still his best known and most studied, Canadian classics such as **Such Is My Beloved** (1934), **They Shall Inherit the Earth** (1935), and **More Joy in Heaven** (1937). In these novels, Callaghan grapples with religious themes, such as the difficulties of exercising free will within the confines of an authoritarian church and in the presence of a seemingly indifferent creator, or at least of a god whose love appears to be a mixed blessing at best and is more often a trial by fire. Callaghan's next productive period was the 1950s, which saw the appearance of novels dealing with social and psychological concerns, such as **The Loved and the Lost** (1951), which won the Governor General's Award. Callaghan's productivity continued unabated to contemporary times with the novels **The Many Colored Coat** (1960), **A Passion in Rome** (1961), **A Fine and Private Place** (1975), **Close to the Sun Again** (1977), **A Time for Judas** (1983) and **An Old Man on the Road** (1989). This selective list attests to a remarkable achievement by any standard. To the novels can be added the short-story collections: **Now That April's Here** (1936), **Morley Callaghan's Stories** (1950), and **The Lost and Found Stories of Morley Callaghan** (1985). The American critic Edmund Wilson has described Morley Callaghan as "perhaps the most unjustly neglected novelist in the English-speaking world . . . a writer whose work may be mentioned without absurdity in association with Chekhov's and Turgenev's."

Ancient Lineage

T he young man from the Historical Club with a green magazine under his arm got off the train at Clintonville. It was getting dark but the station lights were not lit. He hurried along the platform and jumped down on the sloping cinder path to the sidewalk.

Trees were on the lawns alongside the walk, branches drooping low, leaves scraping occasionally against the young man's straw hat. He saw a cluster of lights, bluish-white in the dusk across a river, many lights for a small town. He crossed the lift-lock bridge and turned on to the main street. A hotel was at the corner.

At the desk a bald-headed man in a blue shirt, the sleeves rolled up, looked critically at the young man while he registered. "All right, Mr. Flaherty," he said, inspecting the signature carefully.

"Do you know many people around here?" Mr. Flaherty asked.

"Just about everybody."

"The Rowers?"

"The old lady?"

"Yeah, an old lady."

"Sure, Mrs. Anna Rower. Around the corner to the left, then turn to the right on the first street, the house opposite the Presbyterian church on the hill."

"An old family," suggested the young man.

"An old-timer all right." The hotel man made it clear by a twitching of his lips that he was a part of the new town, canal, water power, and factories.

Mr. Flaherty sauntered out and turned to the left. It was dark and the street had the silence of small towns in the evening. Turning a corner he heard girls giggling in a doorway. He looked at the church on the hill, the steeple dark against the sky. He had forgotten whether the man had said beside the church or across the road, but could not make up his mind to ask the fellow who was watering the wide church lawn. No lights in the shuttered windows of the rough-cast house beside the church. He came down the hill and had to yell three times at the man because the water swished strongly against the grass.

"All right, thanks. Right across the road," Mr. Flaherty repeated.

Tall trees screened the square brick house. Looking along the hall to a lighted room, Mr. Flaherty saw an old lady standing at a sideboard. "She's in all right," he thought, rapping on the screen door. A large woman of about forty, dressed in blue skirt and blue waist, came down the stairs. She did not open the screen door.

"Could I speak to Mrs. Anna Rower?"

"I'm Miss Hilda Rower."

"I'm from the University Historical Club."

"What did you want to see Mother for?"

Mr. Flaherty did not like talking through the screen door. "I wanted to talk to her," he said firmly.

"Well, maybe you'd better come in."

He stood in the hall while the large woman lit the gas in the front room. The gas flared up, popped, showing fat hips and heavy lines on her face. Mr. Flaherty, disappointed, watched her swaying down the hall to get her mother. He carefully inspected the front room, the framed photographs of dead Conservative politicians, the group of military men hanging over the old-fashioned piano, the faded greenish wallpaper and the settee in the corner.

An old woman with a knot of white hair and good eyes came into the room, walking erectly. "This is the young man who wanted to see you, Mother," Miss Hilda Rower said. They all sat down. Mr. Flaherty explained he wanted to get some information concerning the Rower genealogical tree for the next meeting of his society. The Rowers, he knew, were a pioneer family in the district, and descended from William the Conqueror, he had heard.

The old lady laughed thinly, swaying from side to side. "It's true enough, but I don't know who told you. My father was Daniel Rower, who came to Ontario from Cornwall in 1830."

Miss Hilda Rower interrupted. "Wait, Mother, you may not want to tell about it." Brusque and businesslike, she turned to the young man. "You want to see the family tree, I suppose."

"Oh, yes."

"My father was a military settler here," the old lady said.

"I don't know but what we might be able to give you some notes," Miss Hilda spoke generously.

"Thanks awfully, if you will."

"Of course you're prepared to pay something if you're going to print it," she added, smugly adjusting her big body in the chair.

Mr. Flaherty got red in the face; of course he understood, but to tell the truth he had merely wanted to chat with Mrs. Rower. Now he knew definitely he did not like the heavy nose and unsentimental assertiveness of the lower lip of this big woman with the wide shoulders. He couldn't stop looking at her thick ankles. Rocking back and forth in the chair she was primly conscious of lineal superiority; a proud unmarried woman, surely she could handle a young man, half-closing her eyes, a young man from the University indeed. "I don't want to talk to her about the University," he thought.

Old Mrs. Rower went into the next room and returned with a framed genealogical tree of the house of Rower. She handed it graciously to Mr.

Flaherty, who read, "The descent of the family of Rower, from William the Conqueror, from Malcolm 1st, and from the Capets, Kings of France." It bore the *imprimatur* of the College of Arms, 1838.

"It's wonderful to think you have this," Mr. Flaherty said, smiling at Miss Hilda, who watched him suspiciously.

"A brother of mine had it all looked up," old Mrs. Rower said.

"You don't want to write about that," Miss Hilda said, crossing her ankles. The ankles looked much thicker crossed. "You just want to have a talk with Mother."

"That's it," Mr. Flaherty smiled agreeably.

"We may write it up ourselves some day." Her heavy chin dipped down and rose again.

"Sure, why not?"

"But there's no harm in you talking to Mother if you want to, I guess."

"You could write a good story about that tree," Mr. Flaherty said, feeling his way.

"We may do it some day but it'll take time," she smiled complacently at her mother, who mildly agreed.

Mr. Flaherty talked pleasantly to this woman, who was so determined he would not learn anything about the family tree without paying for it. He tried talking about the city, then tactfully asked old Mrs. Rower what she remembered of the Clintonville of seventy years ago. The old lady talked willingly, excited a little. She went into the next room to get a book of clippings. "My father, Captain Rower, got a grant of land from the Crown and cleared it," she said, talking over her shoulder. "A little way up the Trent River. Clintonville was a small military settlement then . . ."

"Oh, Mother, he doesn't want to know all about that," Miss Hilda said impatiently.

"It's very interesting indeed."

The old woman said nervously, "My dear, what difference does it make? You wrote it all up for the evening at the church."

"So I did too," she hesitated, thinking the young man ought to see how well it was written. "I have an extra copy." She looked at him thoughtfully. He smiled. She got up and went upstairs.

The young man talked very rapidly to the old lady and took many notes.

Miss Rower returned. "Would you like to see it?" She handed Mr. Flaherty a small gray booklet. Looking quickly through it, he saw it contained valuable information about the district.

"The writing is simply splendid. You must have done a lot of work on it."

"I worked hard on it," she said, pleased and more willing to talk.

"Is this an extra copy?"

"Yes, it's an extra copy."

"I suppose I might keep it," he said diffidently.

She looked at him steadily. "Well . . . I'll have to charge you twenty-five cents."

"Sure, sure, of course, that's fine." He blushed.

"Just what it costs to get them out," the old lady explained apologetically.

"Can you change a dollar?" He fumbled in his pocket, pulling the dollar out slowly.

They could not change it but Miss Rower would be pleased to go down to the corner grocery store. Mr. Flaherty protested. No trouble, he would go. She insisted on asking the next-door neighbour to change it. She went across the room, the dollar in hand.

Mr. Flaherty chatted with the nice old lady and carefully examined the family tree, and wrote quickly in a small book till the screen door banged, the curtains parted, and Miss Hilda Rower came into the room. He wanted to smirk, watching her walking heavily, so conscious of her ancient lineage, a virginal mincing sway to her large hips, seventy-five cents change held loosely in drooping fingers.

"Thank you," he said, pocketing the change, pretending his work was over. Sitting back in the chair he praised the way Miss Rower had written the history of the neighbourhood and suggested she might write a splendid story of the family tree, if she had the material, of course.

"I've got the material, all right," she said, trying to get comfortable again. How would Mr. Flaherty arrange it and where should she try to sell it? The old lady was dozing in the rocking-chair. Miss Rower began to talk rather nervously about her material. She talked of the last title in the family and the Sir Richard who had been at the court of Queen Elizabeth.

Mr. Flaherty chimed in gaily, "I suppose you know the O'Flahertys were kings in Ireland, eh?"

She said vaguely, "I daresay, I daresay," conscious only of an interruption to the flow of her thoughts. She went on talking with hurried eagerness, all the fine talk about her ancestors bringing her peculiar satisfaction. A soft light came into her eyes and her lips were moist.

Mr. Flaherty started to rub his cheek, and looked at her big legs, and felt restive, and then embarrassed, watching her closely, her firm lower lip hanging loosely. She was talking slowly, lazily, relaxing in her chair, a warm fluid oozing through her veins, exhausting but satisfying her.

He was uncomfortable. She was liking it too much. He did not know what to do. There was something immodest about it. She was close to forty, her big body relaxed in the chair. He looked at his watch and suggested he would be going. She stretched her legs graciously, pouting, inviting him to stay a while longer, but he was standing up, tucking his magazine under his arm. The old lady was still dozing. "I'm so comfortable," Miss Rower said, "I hate to move."

The mother woke up and shook hands with Mr. Flaherty. Miss Rower got up to say good-bye charmingly.

Half-way down the path Mr. Flaherty turned. She was standing in the doorway, partly shadowed by the tall trees, bright moonlight filtering through leaves touching soft lines on her face and dark hair.

He went down the hill to the hotel unconsciously walking with a careless easy stride, wondering at the change that had come over the heavy, strong woman. He thought of taking a walk along the river in the moonlight, the river on which old Captain Rower had drilled troops on the ice in the winter of 1837 to fight the rebels. Then he thought of having a western sandwich in the café across the road from the hotel. That big woman in her own way had been hot stuff.

In the hotel he asked to be called early so he could get the first train to the city. For a long time he lay awake in the fresh, cool bed, the figure of the woman whose ancient lineage had taken the place of a lover in her life, drifting into his thoughts and becoming important while he watched on the wall the pale moonlight that had softened the lines of her face, and wondered if it was still shining on her bed, and on her throat, and on her contented, lazily relaxed body.

GRAHAM GREENE

(1904–1991)

G raham Greene was born in Berkhamsted, England, the son of a headmaster at the famous public (that is, private) school in the village, which Greene attended. From a young age, he was fascinated by religious ritual, and he records that he believed in hell because he had seen a version of it in the school dormitories and in the menacing of the masters. He converted to Catholicism as a young man, convinced that in doing so he "had taken up the thread of life from very far back, from so far back as innocence." He worked as a journalist in Nottingham and London, and published his first novel in 1929. Greene's early writing is characterized by morbidity, violence, and melodrama. He shared the intellectual's conviction in the 1930s that modern man was spiritually destitute, the victim of powers over which he had lost control. Yet he was skeptical about the Communists' confidence in the future as a workers' paradise, finding instead a more rigorous and more ambiguous answer in the Catholic Church. His novels ask probing questions about the nature of sin and evil, and in them he explores the idea that someone capable of great evil may be more admirable than a benevolent atheist because he is "man enough to be damned." He muses about how sin can mean not only alienation from God but also the first step in the sequence of guilt, confession, repentance, and redemption. His fiction is as particular as it is universal; as John Spurling has noted, "No European writer since Conrad has put the hot, poor, and foully governed places of the earth as vividly as Greene." His more than twenty novels include Brighton Rock (1938), The Power and the Glory (1940), The Heart of the Matter (1948), The End of the Affair (1951), A Burnt-Out Case (1961), The Honorary Consul (1973), and Doctor Fischer of Geneva (1980). "Across the Bridge" is taken from his story collection Twenty-one Stories (1954).

Across the Bridge

"T hey say he's worth a million," Lucia said. He sat there in the little hot damp Mexican square, a dog at his feet, with an air of immense and forlorn patience. The dog attracted your attention at once; for it was very nearly an English setter, only something had gone wrong with the tail and the feathering. Palms wilted over his head, it was all shade and stuffiness round the bandstand, radios talked loudly in Spanish from the little wooden sheds where they changed your pesos into dollars at a loss. I could tell he didn't understand a word from the way he read his newspaper—as I did myself picking out the words which were like English ones. "He's been here a month," Lucia said. "They turned him out of Guatemala and Honduras."

You couldn't keep any secrets for five hours in this border town. Lucia had only been twenty-four hours in the place, but she knew all about Mr. Joseph Calloway. The only reason I didn't know about him (and I'd been in the place two weeks) was because I couldn't talk the language any more than Mr. Calloway could. There wasn't another soul in the place who didn't know the story—the whole story of the Halling Investment Trust and the proceedings for extradition. Any man doing dusty business in any of the wooden booths in the town is better fitted by long observation to tell Mr. Calloway's tale than I am, except that I was in—literally—at the finish. They all watched the drama proceed with immense interest, sympathy and respect. For, after all, he had a million.

Every once in a while through the long steamy day, a boy came and cleaned Mr. Calloway's shoes: he hadn't the right words to resist them— they pretended not to know his English. He must have had his shoes cleaned the day Lucia and I watched him at least half a dozen times. At midday he took a stroll across the square to the Antonio Bar and had a bottle of beer, the setter sticking to heel as if they were out for a country walk in England (he had, you may remember, one of the biggest estates in Norfolk). After his bottle of beer, he would walk down between the money changers' huts to the Rio Grande and look across the bridge into the United States: people came and went constantly in cars. Then back to the square till lunch-time. He was staying in the best hotel, but you don't get good hotels in this border town: nobody stays in them more than a night. The good hotels were on the other side of the bridge: you could see their electric signs twenty storeys high from the little square at night, like light-houses marking the United States.

You may ask what I'd been doing in so drab a spot for a fortnight. There was no interest in the place for anyone; it was just damp and dust and poverty, a kind of shabby replica of the town across the river: both had squares in the same spots; both had the same number of cinemas. One was cleaner than the other, that was all, and more expensive, much more expensive. I'd stayed across there a couple of nights waiting for a man a tourist bureau said was driving down from Detroit to Yucatan and would sell a place in his car for some fantastically small figure—twenty dollars, I think it was. I don't know if he existed or was invented by the optimistic half-caste in the agency; anyway, he never turned up and so I waited, not much caring, on the cheap side of the river. It didn't much matter; I was living. One day I meant to give up the man from Detroit and go home or go south, but it was easier not to decide anything in a hurry. Lucia was just waiting for a car going the other way, but she didn't have to wait so long. We waited together and watched Mr. Calloway waiting—for God knows what.

I don't know how to treat this story—it was a tragedy for Mr. Calloway, it was poetic retribution, I suppose, in the eyes of the shareholders he'd ruined with his bogus transactions, and to Lucia and me, at this stage, it was pure comedy—except when he kicked the dog. I'm not a sentimentalist about dogs, I prefer people to be cruel to animals rather than to human beings, but I couldn't help being revolted at the way he'd kick that animal—with a hint of cold-blooded venom, not in anger but as if he were getting even for some trick it had played him a long while ago. That generally happened when he returned from the bridge: it was the only sign of anything resembling emotion he showed. Otherwise he looked a small, set, gentle creature with silver hair and a silver moustache, and gold-rimmed glasses, and one gold tooth like a flaw in character.

Lucia hadn't been accurate when she said he'd been turned out of Guatemala and Honduras; he'd left voluntarily when the extradition proceedings seemed likely to go through and moved north. Mexico is still not a very centralised state, and it is possible to get round governors as you can't get round cabinet ministers or judges. And so he waited there on the border for the next move. That earlier part of the story is, I suppose, dramatic, but I didn't watch it and I can't invent what I haven't seen— the long waiting in ante-rooms, the bribes taken and refused, the growing fear of arrest, and then the flight—in gold-rimmed glasses—covering his tracks as well as he could, but this wasn't finance and he was an amateur at escape. And so he'd washed up here, under my eyes and Lucia's eyes, sitting all day under the bandstand, nothing to read but a Mexican paper, nothing to do but look across the river at the United States, quite unaware, I suppose, that everyone knew everything about him, once a day kicking his dog. Perhaps in its semi-setter way it reminded him too much of the Norfolk estate—though that, too, I suppose, was the reason he kept it.

And the next act again was pure comedy. I hesitate to think what this man worth a million was costing his country as they edged him out from this land and that. Perhaps somebody was getting tired of the business, and careless; anyway, they sent across two detectives, with an old photograph. He'd grown his silvery moustache since that had been taken, and he'd aged a lot, and they couldn't catch sight of him. They hadn't been across the bridge two hours when everybody knew that there were two foreign detectives in town looking for Mr. Calloway—everybody knew, that is to say, except Mr. Calloway, who couldn't talk Spanish. There were plenty of people who could have told him in English, but they didn't. It wasn't cruelty, it was a sort of awe and respect: like a bull, he was on show, sitting there mournfully in the plaza with his dog, a magnificent spectacle for which we all had ring-side seats.

I ran into one of the policemen in the Bar Antonio. He was disgusted;

he had had some idea that when he crossed the bridge life was going to be different, so much more colour and sun, and—I suspect—love, and all he found were wide mud streets where the nocturnal rain lay in pools, and mangy dogs, smells and cockroaches in his bedroom, and the nearest to love, the open door of the Academia Comercial, where pretty mestizo girls sat all the morning learning to typewrite. Tip-tap-tip-tap-tip—perhaps they had a dream, too—jobs on the other side of the bridge, where life was going to be so much more luxurious, refined and amusing.

We got into conversation; he seemed surprised that I knew who they both were and what they wanted. He said, "We've got information this man Calloway's in town."

"He's knocking around somewhere," I said.

"Could you point him out?"

"Oh, I don't know him by sight," I said.

He drank his beer and thought a while. "I'll go out and sit in the plaza. He's sure to pass sometime."

I finished my beer and went quickly off and found Lucia. I said, "Hurry, we're going to see an arrest." We didn't care a thing about Mr. Calloway, he was just an elderly man who kicked his dog and swindled the poor, and who deserved anything he got. So we made for the plaza; we knew Calloway would be there, but it had never occurred to either of us that the detectives wouldn't recognise him. There was quite a surge of people round the place; all the fruit-sellers and boot-blacks in town seemed to have arrived together; we had to force our way through, and there in the little green stuffy centre of the place, sitting on adjoining seats, were the two plain-clothes men and Mr. Calloway. I've never known the place so silent; everybody was on tiptoe, and the plain-clothes men were staring at the crowd looking for Mr. Calloway, and Mr. Calloway sat on his usual seat staring out over the money-changing booths at the United States.

"It can't go on. It just can't," Lucia said. But it did. It got more fantastic still. Somebody ought to write a play about it. We sat as close as we dared. We were afraid all the time we were going to laugh. The semi-setter scratched for fleas and Mr. Calloway watched the U.S.A. The two detectives watched the crowd, and the crowd watched the show with solemn satisfaction. Then one of the detectives got up and went over to Mr. Calloway. That's the end, I thought. But it wasn't, it was the beginning. For some reason they had eliminated him from their list of suspects. I shall never know why. The man said:

"You speak English?"

"I *am* English," Mr. Calloway said.

Even that didn't tear it, and the strangest thing of all was the way Mr. Calloway came alive. I don't think anybody had spoken to him like that for weeks. The Mexicans were too respectful—he was a man with a million—and it had never occurred to Lucia and me to treat him casually like a human being; even in our eyes he had been magnified by the colossal theft and the world-wide pursuit.

He said, "This is rather a dreadful place, don't you think?"

"It is," the policeman said.

"I can't think what brings anybody across the bridge."

"Duty," the policeman said gloomily. "I suppose you are passing through."

"Yes," Mr. Calloway said.

"I'd have expected over here there'd have been—you know what I mean—life. You read things about Mexico."

"Oh, life," Mr. Calloway said. He spoke firmly and precisely, as if to a committee of shareholders. "That begins on the other side."

"You don't appreciate your own country until you leave it."

"That's very true," Mr. Calloway said. "Very true."

At first it was difficult not to laugh, and then after a while there didn't seem to be much to laugh at; an old man imagining all the fine things going on beyond the international bridge. I think he thought of the town opposite as a combination of London and Norfolk—theatres and cocktail bars, a little shooting and a walk round the field at evening with the dog—that miserable imitation of a setter—poking the ditches. He'd never been across, he couldn't know that it was just the same thing over again—even the same layout; only the streets were paved and the hotels had ten more storeys, and life was more expensive, and everything was a little bit cleaner. There wasn't anything Mr. Calloway would have called living—no galleries, no book-shops, just *Film Fun* and the local paper, and *Click* and *Focus* and the tabloids.

"Well," said Mr. Calloway, "I think I'll take a stroll before lunch. You need an appetite to swallow the food here. I generally go down and look at the bridge about now. Care to come, too?"

The detective shook his head. "No," he said, "I'm on duty. I'm looking for a fellow." And that, of course, gave *him* away. As far as Mr. Calloway could understand, there was only one "fellow" in the world anyone was looking for—his brain had eliminated friends who were seeking their friends, husbands who might be waiting for their wives, all objectives of any search but just the one. The power of elimination was what had made him a financier—he could forget the people behind the shares.

That was the last we saw of him for a while. We didn't see him going into the Botica Paris to get his aspirin, or walking back from the bridge with his dog. He simply disappeared, and when he disappeared, people began to talk, and the detectives heard the talk. They looked silly enough, and they got busy after the very man they'd been sitting next to in the garden. Then they, too, disappeared. They, as well as Mr. Calloway, had gone to the state capital to see the Governor and the Chief of Police, and it must have

been an amusing sight there, too, as they bumped into Mr. Calloway and
sat with him in the waiting-rooms. I suspect Mr. Calloway was generally
shown in first, for everyone knew he was worth a million. Only in Europe
is it possible for a man to be a criminal as well as a rich man.

Anyway, after about a week the whole pack of them returned by
the same train. Mr. Calloway travelled Pullman, and the two policemen
travelled in the day coach. It was evident that they hadn't got their
extradition order.

Lucia had left by that time. The car came and went across the bridge.
I stood in Mexico and watched her get out at the United States Customs.
She wasn't anything in particular, but she looked beautiful at a distance
as she gave me a wave out of the United States and got back into the car.
And I suddenly felt sympathy for Mr. Calloway, as if there were something over there which you couldn't find here, and turning round I saw
him back on his old beat, with the dog at his heels.

I said "Good afternoon," as if it had been all along our habit to greet
each other. He looked tired and ill and dusty, and I felt sorry for him—
to think of the kind of victory he'd been winning, with so much expendi-
ture of cash and care—the prize this dirty and dreary town, the booths
of the money-changers, the awful little beauty parlours with their wicker
chairs and sofas looking like the reception rooms of brothels, that hot and
stuffy garden by the bandstand.

He replied gloomily "Good morning," and the dog started to sniff at
some ordure and he turned and kicked it with fury, with depression,
with despair.

And at that moment a taxi with the two policemen in it passed us on
its way to the bridge. They must have seen that kick; perhaps they
were cleverer than I had given them credit for, perhaps they were just
sentimental about animals, and thought they'd do a good deed, and the
rest happened by accident. But the fact remains—those two pillars of the
law set about the stealing of Mr. Calloway's dog.

He watched them go by. Then he said, "Why don't you go across?"

"It's cheaper here," I said.

"I mean just for an evening. Have a meal at that place we can see at
night in the sky. Go to the theatre."

"There isn't a chance."

He said angrily, sucking his gold tooth, "Well, anyway, get away from
here." He stared down the hill and up the other side. He couldn't see
that the street climbing up from the bridge contained only the same
money-changers' booths as this one.

I said, "Why don't *you* go?"

He said evasively, "Oh—business."

I said, "It's only a question of money. You don't *have* to pass by the
bridge."

He said with faint interest, "I don't talk Spanish."

"There isn't a soul here," I said, "who doesn't talk English."

He looked at me with surprise. "Is that so?" he said. "Is that so?"

It's as I have said; he'd never tried to talk to anyone, and they respected him too much to talk to him—he was worth a million. I don't know whether I'm glad or sorry that I told him that. If I hadn't, he might be there now, sitting by the bandstand having his shoes cleaned—alive and suffering.

Three days later his dog disappeared. I found him looking for it, calling it softly and shamefacedly between the palms of the garden. He looked embarrassed. He said in a low angry voice, "I *hate* that dog. The beastly mongrel," and called "Rover, Rover" in a voice which didn't carry five yards. He said, "I bred setters once. I'd have shot a dog like that." It reminded him, I *was* right, of Norfolk, and he lived in the memory, and he hated it for its imperfection. He was a man without a family and without friends, and his only enemy was that dog. You couldn't call the law an enemy; you have to be intimate with an enemy.

Late that afternoon someone told him they'd seen the dog walking across the bridge. It wasn't true, of course, but we didn't know that then—they'd paid a Mexican five pesos to smuggle it across. So all that afternoon and the next Mr. Calloway sat in the garden having his shoes cleaned over and over again, and thinking how a dog could just walk across like that, and a human being, an immortal soul, was bound here in the awful routine of the little walk and the unspeakable meals and the aspirin at the botica. That dog was seeing things he couldn't see—that hateful dog. It made him mad—I think literally mad. You must remember the man had been going on for months. He had a million and he was living on two pounds a week, with nothing to spend his money on. He sat there and brooded on the hideous injustice of it. I think he'd have crossed over one day in any case, but the dog was the last straw.

Next day when he wasn't to be seen, I guessed he'd gone across and I went too. The American town is as small as the Mexican. I knew I couldn't miss him if he was there, and I was still curious. A little sorry for him, but not much.

I caught sight of him first in the only drug-store, having a coca-cola, and then once outside a cinema looking at the posters; he had dressed with extreme neatness, as if for a party, but there was no party. On my third time round, I came on the detectives—they were having coca-colas in the drug-store, and they must have missed Mr. Calloway by inches. I went in and sat down at the bar.

"Hello," I said, "you still about." I suddenly felt anxious for Mr. Calloway, I didn't want them to meet.

One of them said, "Where's Calloway?"

"Oh," I said, "he's hanging on."

"But not his dog," he said, and laughed. The other looked a little shocked, he didn't like anyone to *talk* cynically about a dog. Then they got up—they had a car outside.

"Have another?" I said.

"No thanks. We've got to keep moving."

The men bent close and confided to me, "Calloway's on this side."

"No!" I said.

"And his dog."

"He's looking for it," the other said.

"I'm damned if he is," I said, and again one of them looked a little shocked, as if I'd insulted the dog.

I don't think Mr. Calloway was looking for his dog, but his dog certainly found him. There was a sudden hilarious yapping from the car and out plunged the semi-setter and gambolled furiously down the street. One of the detectives—the sentimental one—was into the car before we got to the door and was off after the dog. Near the bottom of the long road to the bridge was Mr. Calloway—I do believe he'd come down to look at the Mexican side when he found there was nothing but the drug-store and the cinemas and the paper shops on the American. He saw the dog coming and yelled at it to go home—"home, home, home," as if they were in Norfolk—it took no notice at all, pelting towards him. Then he saw the police car coming, and ran. After that, everything happened too quickly, but I think the order of events was this—the dog started across the road right in front of the car, and Mr. Calloway yelled, at the dog or the car, I don't know which. Anyway, the detective swerved—he said later, weakly, at the enquiry, that he couldn't run over a dog, and down went Mr. Calloway, in a mess of broken glass and gold rims and silver hair, and blood. The dog was on to him before any of us could reach him, licking and whimpering and licking. I saw Mr. Calloway put up his hand, and down it went across the dog's neck and the whimper rose to a stupid bark of triumph, but Mr. Calloway was dead—shock and a weak heart.

"Poor old geezer," the detective said, "I bet he really loved that dog," and it's true that the attitude in which he lay looked more like a caress than a blow. I thought it was meant to be a blow, but the detective may have been right. It all seemed to me a little too touching to be true as the old crook lay there with his arm over the dog's neck, dead with his million between the moneychangers' huts, but it's as well to be humble in the face of human nature. He had come across the river for something, and it may, after all, have been the dog he was looking for. It sat there, baying its stupid and mongrel triumph across his body, like a piece of sentimental statuary: the nearest he could get to the fields, the ditches, the horizon of his home. It was comic and it was pitiable, but it wasn't less comic because the man was dead. Death doesn't change comedy to tragedy, and if the last gesture was one of affection, I suppose it was only one more indication of a human being's capacity for self-deception, our baseless optimism that is so much more appalling than our despair.

ISAAC BASHEVIS SINGER

(b. 1904)

*I*saac Bashevis Singer was born in Leoncin, Poland, the son of an
impoverished rabbi and of a mother who was a descendant of rabbis.
*He was educated in the pious tradition of the Jewish religion and isolated
from the world. Against his family's wishes, he decided to become a
Yiddish writer. He worked as a Hebrew teacher and as a proofreader for
a Yiddish literary magazine, and translated writers such as Knut Ham-
sun and Thomas Mann into Yiddish. Meanwhile his own stories were
beginning to appear in literary journals. Emigrating to the United States
in 1935 induced a culture shock so severe that he gave up writing
altogether, but in 1943 five new stories appeared.* The Family Moskat
*(1950) sold 35 000 copies, and in 1953 Saul Bellow translated one of
Singer's best short stories, "Gimpel the Fool," for the* Partisan Review.
*Eighteen volumes of fiction were to follow, along with a worldwide
reputation and readership. He won the Nobel Prize for Literature in
1978. His* Collected Stories *(1982) confirmed his reputation as one of
the contemporary masters of the genre. He describes his own aesthetic
this way: "Genuine literature informs while it entertains. It manages to
be both clear and profound. It has the magical power of merging causality
with purpose, doubt with faith, the passions of the flesh with the yearn-
ings of the soul. It is unique and general, national and universal, realistic
and mystical." Although he insists that art must never try to explain
itself, he has described his own fiction as rooted in "a humanism and
ethics the basis of which would be a refusal to justify all the evils the
Almighty has sent us and is preparing to bestow upon us in the future."
Though modestly suggesting that his stories are simply a means of
"forgetting the human disaster" for a while, Singer cannot disguise the
fact that he celebrates, in the face of the most monstrous adversity, the
triumph and the glory of the human spirit.*

The Spinoza of Market Street

I

Dr. Nahum Fischelson paced back and forth in his garret room in
Market Street, Warsaw. Dr. Fischelson was a short, hunched man
with a grayish beard, and was quite bald except for a few wisps of hair
remaining at the nape of the neck. His nose was as crooked as a beak and
his eyes were large, dark, and fluttering like those of some huge bird. It

was a hot summer evening, but Dr. Fischelson wore a black coat which reached to his knees, and he had on a stiff collar and a bow tie. From the door he paced slowly to the dormer window set high in the slanting room and back again. One had to mount several steps to look out. A candle in a brass holder was burning on the table and a variety of insects buzzed around the flame. Now and again one of the creatures would fly too close to the fire and sear its wings, or one would ignite and glow on the wick for an instant. At such moments Dr. Fischelson grimaced. His wrinkled face would twitch and beneath his disheveled mustache he would bite his lips. Finally he took a handkerchief from his pocket and waved it at the insects.

"Away from there, fools and imbeciles," he scolded. "You won't get warm here; you'll only burn yourself."

The insects scattered but a second later returned and once more circled the trembling flame. Dr. Fischelson wiped the sweat from his wrinkled forehead and sighed, "Like men they desire nothing but the pleasure of the moment." On the table lay an open book written in Latin, and on its broad-margined pages were notes and comments printed in small letters by Dr. Fischelson. The book was Spinoza's *Ethics* and Dr. Fischelson had been studying it for the last thirty years. He knew every proposition, every proof, every corollary, every note by heart. When he wanted to find a particular passage, he generally opened to the place immediately without having to search for it. But, nevertheless, he continued to study the *Ethics* for hours every day with a magnifying glass in his bony hand, murmuring and nodding his head in agreement. The truth was that the more Dr. Fischelson studied, the more puzzling sentences, unclear passages, and cryptic remarks he found. Each sentence contained hints unfathomed by any of the students of Spinoza. Actually the philosopher had anticipated all of the criticisms of pure reason made by Kant and his followers. Dr. Fischelson was writing a commentary on the *Ethics*. He had drawers full of notes and drafts, but it didn't seem that he would ever be able to complete his work. The stomach ailment which had plagued him for years was growing worse from day to day. Now he would get pains in his stomach after only a few mouthfuls of oatmeal. "God in Heaven, it's difficult, very difficult," he would say to himself, using the same intonation as had his father, the late Rabbi of Tishevitz. "It's very, very hard."

Dr. Fischelson was not afraid of dying. To begin with, he was no longer a young man. Secondly, it is stated in the fourth part of the *Ethics* that "a free man thinks of nothing less than of death and his wisdom is a meditation not of death, but of life." Thirdly, it is also said that "the human mind cannot be absolutely destroyed with the human body but there is some part of it that remains eternal." And yet Dr. Fischelson's ulcer (or perhaps it was a cancer) continued to bother him. His tongue was always coated. He belched frequently and emitted a different foul-smelling gas each time. He suffered from heartburn and cramps. At times he felt like vomiting and at other times he was hungry for garlic, onions, and fried foods. He had long ago discarded the medicines prescribed for him by the doctors and had sought his own remedies. He found it beneficial to take grated radish after meals and lie on his bed, belly down, with his head hanging over the side. But these home remedies offered only temporary relief. Some of the doctors he consulted insisted there was nothing the matter with him. "It's just nerves," they told him. "You could live to be a hundred."

But on this particular hot summer night, Dr. Fischelson felt his strength ebbing. His knees were shaky, his pulse weak. He sat down to read and his vision blurred. The letters on the page turned from green to gold. The lines became waved and jumped over each other, leaving white gaps as if the text had disappeared in some mysterious way. The heat was unbearable, flowing down directly from the tin roof; Dr. Fischelson felt he was inside of an oven. Several times he climbed the four steps to the window and thrust his head out into the cool of the evening breeze. He would remain in that position for so long his knees would become wobbly. "Oh it's a fine breeze," he would murmur, "really delightful," and he would recall that according to Spinoza, morality and happiness were identical, and that the most moral deed a man could perform was to indulge in some pleasure which was not contrary to reason.

II

Dr. Fischelson, standing on the top step at the window and looking out, could see into two worlds. Above him were the heavens, thickly strewn with stars. Dr. Fischelson had never seriously studied astronomy but he could differentiate between the planets, those bodies which like the earth, revolve around the sun, and the fixed stars, themselves distant suns, whose light reaches us a hundred or even a thousand years later. He recognized the constellations which mark the path of the earth in space and that nebulous sash, the Milky Way. Dr. Fischelson owned a small telescope he had bought in Switzerland where he had studied and he particularly enjoyed looking at the moon through it. He could clearly make out on the moon's surface the volcanoes bathed in sunlight and the dark, shadowy craters. He never wearied of gazing at these cracks and crevasses. To him they seemed both near and distant, both substantial and insubstantial. Now and then he would see a shooting star trace a wide arc across the sky and disappear, leaving a fiery trail behind it. Dr. Fischelson would know then that a meteorite had reached our atmosphere, and perhaps some unburned fragment of it had fallen into the ocean or had landed in the desert or perhaps even in some inhabited region. Slowly the stars which had appeared from behind Dr. Fischelson's roof rose until they were shining above the house across the street. Yes, when Dr. Fischelson looked up into the heavens, he became aware of that infinite extension which is, according to Spinoza, one of God's attributes. It comforted Dr. Fischelson to think that although he was only a weak, puny man, a changing mode of the absolutely infinite Substance, he was nevertheless a part of the cosmos, made of the same matter as the celestial bodies; to the extent that he was a part of the Godhead, he knew he could not be destroyed. In such moments, Dr. Fischelson experienced the *Amor Dei Intellectualis* which is, according to the philosopher of Amsterdam, the highest perfection of the mind. Dr. Fischelson breathed deeply, lifted his head as high as his stiff collar permitted and actually felt he was whirling in company with the earth, the sun, the stars of the Milky Way, and the infinite host of galaxies known only to infinite thought. His legs became light and weightless and he grasped the window frame with both hands as if afraid he would lose his footing and fly out into eternity.

When Dr. Fischelson tired of observing the sky, his glance dropped to Market Street below. He could see a long strip extending from Yanash's market to Iron Street with the gas lamps lining it merged into a string of fiery dots. Smoke was issuing from the chimneys on the black, tin roofs; the bakers were heating their ovens, and here and there sparks mingled with the black smoke. The street never looked so noisy and crowded as on a summer evening. Thieves, prostitutes, gamblers, and fences loafed in the square which looked from above like a pretzel covered with poppy seeds. The young men laughed coarsely and the girls shrieked. A peddler with a keg of lemonade on his back pierced the general din with his intermittent cries. A watermelon vendor shouted in a savage voice, and the long knife which he used for cutting the fruit dripped with the blood-like juice. Now and again the street became even more agitated. Fire engines, their heavy wheels clanging, sped by; they were drawn by sturdy black horses which had to be tightly curbed to prevent them from running wild. Next came an ambulance, its siren screaming. Then some thugs had a fight among themselves and the police had to be called. A passerby was robbed and ran about shouting for help. Some wagons loaded with firewood sought to get through into the courtyards where the bakeries were located but the horses could not lift the wheels over the steep curbs and the drivers berated the animals and lashed them with their whips. Sparks rose from the clanging hoofs. It was now long after seven, which was the prescribed closing time for stores, but actually business had only begun. Customers were led in stealthily through back doors. The Russian policemen on the street, having been paid off, noticed nothing of this. Merchants continued to hawk their wares, each seeking to outshout the others.

"Gold, gold, gold," a woman who dealt in rotten oranges shrieked.

"Sugar, sugar, sugar," croaked a dealer of overripe plums.

"Heads, heads, heads," a boy who sold fishheads roared.

Through the window of a Hasidic study house across the way, Dr. Fischelson could see boys with long sidelocks swaying over holy volumes, grimacing and studying aloud in sing-song voices. Butchers, porters, and fruit dealers were drinking beer in the tavern below. Vapor drifted from the tavern's open door like steam from a bathhouse, and there was the sound of loud music. Outside of the tavern, streetwalkers snatched at drunken soldiers and at workers on their way home from the factories. Some of the men carried bundles of wood on their shoulders, reminding Dr. Fischelson of the wicked who are condemned to kindle their own fires in Hell. Husky record players poured out their raspings through open windows. The liturgy of the high holidays alternated with vulgar vaudeville songs.

Dr. Fischelson peered into the half-lit bedlam and cocked his ears. He knew that the behavior of this rabble was the very antithesis of reason. These people were immersed in the vainest of passions, were drunk with emotions, and, according to Spinoza, emotion was never good. Instead of the pleasure they ran after, all they succeeded in obtaining was disease and prison, shame and the suffering that resulted from ignorance. Even the cats which loitered on the roofs here seemed more savage and passionate than those in other parts of the town. They caterwauled with the voices of women in labor, and like demons scampered up walls and leaped onto eaves and balconies. One of the toms paused at Dr. Fischelson's window and let out a howl which made Dr. Fischelson shudder. The doctor stepped from the window and, picking up a broom, brandished it in front of the black beast's glowing, green eyes. "Scat, begone, you ignorant savage!"—and he rapped the broom handle against the roof until the tom ran off.

II

When Dr. Fischelson had returned to Warsaw from Zurich, where he had studied philosophy, a great future had been predicted for him. His friends had known that he was writing an important book on Spinoza. A Jewish Polish journal had invited him to be a contributor; he had been a frequent guest at several wealthy households and he had been made head librarian at the Warsaw synagogue. Although even then he had been considered an old bachelor, the matchmakers had proposed several rich girls for him.

But Dr. Fischelson had not taken advantage of these opportunities. He had wanted to be as independent as Spinoza himself. And he had been. But because of his heretical ideas he had come into conflict with the rabbi and had had to resign his post as librarian. For years after that, he had supported himself by giving private lessons in Hebrew and German. Then, when he had become sick, the Berlin Jewish community had voted him a subsidy of five hundred marks a year. This had been made possible through the intervention of the famous Dr. Hildesheimer with whom he corresponded about philosophy. In order to get by on so small a pension, Dr. Fischelson had moved into the attic room and had begun cooking his own meals on a kerosene stove. He had a cupboard which had many drawers, and each drawer was labeled with the food it contained— buckwheat, rice, barley, onions, carrots, potatoes, mushrooms. Once a week Dr. Fischelson put on his wide brimmed black hat, took a basket in one hand and Spinoza's *Ethics* in the other, and went off to the market for his provisions. While he was waiting to be served, he would open the *Ethics*. The merchants knew him and would motion him to their stalls.

"A fine piece of cheese, Doctor—just melts in your mouth."

"Fresh mushrooms, Doctor, straight from the woods."

"Make way for the doctor, ladies," the butcher would shout. "Please don't block the entrance."

During the early years of his sickness, Dr. Fischelson had still gone in the evening to a café which was frequented by Hebrew teachers and other intellectuals. It had been his habit to sit there and play chess while drinking a half a glass of black coffee. Sometimes he would stop at the bookstores on Holy Cross Street where all sorts of old books and magazines could be purchased cheap. On one occasion a former pupil of his had arranged to meet him at a restaurant one evening. When Dr. Fischelson arrived, he had been surprised to find a group of friends and admirers who forced him to sit at the head of the table while they made speeches about him. But these were things that had happened long ago. Now people were no longer interested in him. He had isolated himself completely and had become a forgotten man. The events of 1905 when the boys of Market Street had begun to organize strikes, throw bombs at police stations, and shoot strike breakers so that the stores were closed even on weekdays had greatly increased his isolation. He began to despise everything associated with the modern Jew—Zionism, socialism, anarchism. The young men in question seemed to him nothing but an ignorant rabble intent on destroying society, society without which no reasonable existence was possible. He still read a Hebrew magazine occasionally, but he felt contempt for modern Hebrew, which had no roots in the Bible or the Mishnah. The spelling of Polish words had changed also. Dr. Fischelson concluded that even the so-called spiritual men had abandoned reason and were doing their utmost to pander to the mob. Now and again he still visited a library and browsed through some of the modern histories of philosophy, but he found that the professors did not understand Spinoza, quoted him incorrectly, attributed their own muddled ideas to the philosopher. Although Dr. Fischelson was well aware that anger was an emotion unworthy of those who walk the path of reason, he would become furious, and would quickly close the book and push it from him. "Idiots," he would mutter, "asses, upstarts." And he would vow never again to look at modern philosophy.

IV

Every three months a special mailman who only delivered money orders brought Dr. Fischelson eighty rubles. He expected his quarterly allotment at the beginning of July but as day after day passed and the tall man with the blond mustache and the shiny buttons did not appear, the doctor grew anxious. He had scarcely a groschen left. Who knows—possibly the Berlin community had rescinded his subsidy; perhaps Dr. Hildesheimer had died, God forbid; the post office might have made a mistake. Every event has its cause, Dr. Fischelson knew. All was determined, all necessary, and a man of reason had no right to worry. Nevertheless, worry invaded his brain, and buzzed about like the flies. If the worst came to the worst, it occurred to him, he could commit suicide, but then he remembered that Spinoza did not approve of suicide and compared those who took their own lives to the insane.

One day when Dr. Fischelson went out to a store to purchase a composition book, he heard people talking about war. In Serbia somewhere, an Austrian prince had been shot and the Austrians had delivered an ultimatum to the Serbs. The owner of the store, a young man with a yellow beard and shifty yellow eyes, announced, "We are about to have a small war," and he advised Dr. Fischelson to store up food because in the near future there was likely to be a shortage.

Everything happened so quickly. Dr. Fischelson had not even decided whether it was worthwhile to spend four groschen on a newspaper, and already posters had been hung up announcing mobilization. Men were to be seen walking on the street with round, metal tags on their lapels, a sign that they were being drafted. They were followed by their crying wives. One Monday when Dr. Fischelson descended to the street to buy some food with his last kopecks, he found the stores closed. The owners and their wives stood outside and explained that merchandise was unobtainable. But certain special customers were pulled to one side and let in through back doors. On the street all was confusion. Policemen with swords unsheathed could be seen riding on horseback. A large crowd had gathered around the tavern where, at the command of the czar, the tavern's stock of whiskey was being poured into the gutter.

Dr. Fischelson went to his old café. Perhaps he would find some acquaintances there who would advise him. But he did not come across a single person he knew. He decided, then, to visit the rabbi of the synagogue where he had once been librarian, but the sexton with the six-sided skullcap informed him that the rabbi and his family had gone off to the spas. Dr. Fischelson had other old friends in town but he found no one at home. His feet ached from so much walking; black and green spots appeared before his eyes and he felt faint. He stopped and waited for the giddiness to pass. The passers-by jostled him. A dark-eyed high-school girl tried to give him a coin. Although the war had just started, soldiers eight abreast were marching in full battle dress—the men were covered with dust and were sunburnt. Canteens were strapped to their sides and they wore rows of bullets across their chests. The bayonets on their rifles gleamed with a cold, green light. They sang with mournful voices. Along with the men came cannons, each pulled by eight horses; their blind muzzles breathed gloomy terror. Dr. Fischelson felt nauseous. His stomach ached; his intestines seemed about to turn themselves inside out. Cold sweat appeared on his face.

"I'm dying," he thought. "This is the end." Nevertheless, he did manage to drag himself home where he lay down on the iron cot and remained, panting and gasping. He must have dozed off because he imagined that he was in his home town, Tishevitz. He had a sore throat and his mother was busy wrapping a stocking stuffed with hot salt around his neck. He could hear talk going on in the house; something about a candle and about how a frog had bitten him. He wanted to go out into the street but they wouldn't let him because a Catholic procession was passing by. Men in long robes, holding double-edged axes in their hands, were intoning in Latin as they sprinkled holy water. Crosses gleamed; sacred pictures waved in the air. There was an odor of incense and corpses. Suddenly the sky turned a burning red and the whole world started to burn. Bells were ringing; people rushed madly about. Flocks of birds flew overhead, screeching. Dr. Fischelson awoke with a start. His body was covered with sweat and his throat was now actually sore. He tried to meditate about his extraordinary dream, to find its rational connection with what was happening to him and to comprehend it *sub specie eternitatis*, but none of it made sense. "Alas, the brain is a receptacle for nonsense," Dr. Fischelson thought. "This earth belongs to the mad."

And he once more closed his eyes; once more he dozed; once more he dreamed.

V

The eternal laws, apparently, had not yet ordained Dr. Fischelson's end. There was a door to the left of Dr. Fischelson's attic room which opened off a dark corridor, cluttered with boxes and baskets, in which the odor of fried onions and laundry soap was always present. Behind this door lived a spinster whom the neighbors called Black Dobbe. Dobbe was tall and lean, and as black as a baker's shovel. She had a broken nose and there was a mustache on her upper lip. She spoke with the hoarse voice of a man and she wore men's shoes. For years Black Dobbe had sold breads, rolls, and bagels which she had bought from the baker at the gate of the house. But one day she and the baker had quarreled and she had moved her business to the marketplace and now she dealt in what were called "wrinklers," which was a synonym for cracked eggs. Black Dobbe had no luck with men. Twice she had been engaged to baker's apprentices but in both instances they had returned the engagement contract to her. Some time afterwards she had received an engagement contract from an old man, a glazier who claimed that he was divorced, but it had later come to light that he still had a wife. Black Dobbe had a cousin in America, a shoemaker, and repeatedly she boasted that this cousin was sending her passage, but she remained in Warsaw. She was constantly being teased by the women who would say, "There's no hope for you, Dobbe. You're fated to die an old maid." Dobbe always answered, "I don't intend to be a slave for any man. Let them all rot."

That afternoon Dobbe received a letter from America. Generally she would go to Leizer the tailor and have him read it to her. However, that day Leizer was out and so Dobbe thought of Dr. Fischelson, whom the other tenants considered a convert since he never went to prayer. She knocked on the door of the doctor's room but there was no answer. "The heretic is probably out," Dobbe thought but, nevertheless, she knocked once more, and this time the door moved slightly. She pushed her way in and stood there frightened. Dr. Fischelson lay fully clothed on his bed; his face was as yellow as wax; his Adam's apple stuck out prominently; his beard pointed upward. Dobbe screamed; she was certain that he was dead, but—no—his body moved. Dobbe picked up a glass which stood on the table, ran into the corridor, filled the glass with water from the faucet, hurried back, and threw the water into the face of the unconscious man. Dr. Fischelson shook his head and opened his eyes.

"What's wrong with you?" Dobbe asked. "Are you sick?"

"Thank you very much. No."

"Have you a family? I'll call them."

"No family," Dr. Fischelson said.

Dobbe wanted to fetch the barber from across the street but Dr. Fischelson signified that he didn't wish the barber's assistance. Since Dobbe was not going to the market that day, no "wrinklers" being available, she decided to do a good deed. She assisted the sick man to get off the bed and smoothed down the blanket. Then she undressed Dr. Fischelson and prepared some soup for him on the kerosene stove. The sun never entered Dobbe's room, but here squares of sunlight shimmered on the faded walls. The floor was painted red. Over the bed hung a picture of a man who was wearing a broad frill around his neck and had long hair. "Such an old fellow and yet he keeps his place so nice and clean," Dobbe thought approvingly. Dr. Fischelson asked for the *Ethics*, and she gave it to him disapprovingly. She was certain it was a Gentile prayer book. Then she began bustling about, brought in a pail of water, swept the floor. Dr. Fischelson ate; after he had finished, he was much stronger and Dobbe asked him to read her the letter.

He read it slowly, the paper trembling in his hands. It came from New York, from Dobbe's cousin. Once more he wrote that he was about to send her a "really important letter" and a ticket to America. By now, Dobbe knew the story by heart and she helped the old man decipher her cousin's scrawl. "He's lying," Dobbe said. "He forgot about me a long time ago." In the evening, Dobbe came again. A candle in a brass holder was burning on the chair next to the bed. Reddish shadows trembled on the walls and ceiling. Dr. Fischelson sat propped up in bed, reading a book. The candle threw a golden light on his forehead which seemed as if cleft in two. A bird had flown in through the window and was perched on the table. For a moment Dobbe was frightened. This man made her think of witches, of black mirrors and corpses wandering around at night and terrifying women. Nevertheless, she took a few steps toward him and inquired, "How are you? Any better?"

"A little, thank you."

"Are you really a convert?" she asked although she wasn't quite sure what the word meant.

"Me, a convert? No, I'm a Jew like any other Jew," Dr. Fischelson answered.

The doctor's assurances made Dobbe feel more at home. She found the bottle of kerosene and lit the stove, and after that she fetched a glass of milk from her room and began cooking kasha. Dr. Fischelson continued to study the *Ethics*, but that evening he could make no sense of the theorems and proofs with their many references to axioms and definitions and other theorems. With trembling hand he raised the book to his eyes and read, "The idea of each modification of the human body does not involve adequate knowledge of the human body itself . . . The idea of the idea of each modification of the human mind does not involve adequate knowledge of the human mind."

VI

Dr. Fischelson was certain he would die any day now. He made out his will, leaving all of his books and manuscripts to the synagogue library.

His clothing and furniture would go to Dobbe since she had taken care of him. But death did not come. Rather his health improved. Dobbe returned to her business in the market, but she visited the old man several times a day, prepared soup for him, left him a glass of tea, and told him news of the war. The Germans had occupied Kalish, Bendin, and Cestechow, and they were marching on Warsaw. People said that on a quiet morning one could hear the rumblings of the cannon. Dobbe reported that the casualties were heavy. "They're falling like flies," she said. "What a terrible misfortune for the women."

She couldn't explain why, but the old man's attic room attracted her. She liked to remove the gold-rimmed books from the bookcase, dust them, and then air them on the windowsill. She would climb the few steps to the window and look out through the telescope. She also enjoyed talking to Dr. Fischelson. He told her about Switzerland, where he had studied, of the great cities he had passed through, of the high mountains that were covered with snow even in the summer. His father had been a rabbi, he said, and before he, Dr. Fischelson, had become a student, he had attended a yeshiva. She asked him how many languages he knew and it turned out that he could speak and write Hebrew, Russian, German, and French, in addition to Yiddish. He also knew Latin. Dobbe was astonished that such an educated man should live in an attic room on Market Street. But what amazed her most of all was that although he had the title "Doctor," he couldn't write prescriptions. "Why don't you become a real doctor?" she would ask him. "I am a doctor," he would answer. "I'm just not a physician." "What kind of a doctor?" "A doctor of philosophy." Although she had no idea of what this meant, she felt it must be very important. "Oh, my blessed mother," she would say, "where did you get such a brain?"

Then one evening after Dobbe had given him his crackers and his glass of tea with milk, he began questioning her about where she came from, who her parents were, and why she had not married. Dobbe was surprised. No one had ever asked her such questions. She told him her story in a quiet voice and stayed until eleven o'clock. Her father had been a porter at the kosher butcher shops. Her mother had plucked chickens in the slaughterhouse. The family had lived in a cellar at No. 19 Market Street. When she had been ten, she had become a maid. The man she had worked for had been a fence who bought stolen goods from thieves on the square. Dobbe had had a brother who had gone into the Russian army and had never returned. Her sister had married a coachman in Praga and had died in childbirth. Dobbe told of the battles between the underworld and the revolutionaries in 1905, of blind Itche and his gang and how they collected protection money from the stores, of the thugs who attacked young boys and girls out on Saturday afternoon strolls if they were not paid money for security. She also spoke of the pimps who drove about in carriages and abducted women to be sold in Buenos Aires. Dobbe swore that some men had even sought to inveigle her into a brothel, but that she had run away. She complained of a thousand evils done to her. She had been robbed; her boy friend had been stolen; a competitor had once poured a pint of kerosene into her basket of bagels; her own cousin, the shoemaker, had cheated her out of a hundred rubles before he had left for America. Dr. Fischelson listened to her attentively. He asked her questions, shook his head, and grunted.

"Well, do you believe in God?" he finally asked her.

"I don't know," she answered. "Do you?"

"Yes, I believe."

"Then why don't you go to synagogue?" she asked.

"God is everywhere," he replied. "In the synagogue. In the market-place. In this very room. We ourselves are parts of God."

"Don't say such things," Dobbe said. "You frighten me."

She left the room and Dr. Fischelson was certain she had gone to bed. But he wondered why she had not said good night. "I probably drove her away with my philosophy," he thought. The very next moment he heard her footsteps. She came in carrying a pile of clothing like a peddler.

"I wanted to show you these," she said. "They're my trousseau." And she began to spread out, on the chair, dresses—woolen, silk, velvet. Taking each dress up in turn, she held it to her body. She gave him an account of every item in her trousseau—underwear, shoes, stockings.

"I'm not wasteful," she said. "I'm a saver. I have enough money to go to America."

Then she was silent and her face turned brick-red. She looked at Dr. Fischelson out of the corner of her eyes, timidly, inquisitively. Dr. Fischelson's body suddenly began to shake as if he had the chills. He said, "Very nice, beautiful things." His brow furrowed and he pulled at his beard with two fingers. A sad smile appeared on his toothless mouth and his large fluttering eyes, gazing into the distance through the attic window, also smiled sadly.

VII

The day that Black Dobbe came to the rabbi's chambers and announced that she was to marry Dr. Fischelson, the rabbi's wife thought she had gone mad. But the news had already reached Leizer the tailor, and had spread to the bakery, as well as to other shops. There were those who thought that the "old maid" was very lucky; the doctor, they said, had a vast hoard of money. But there were others who took the view that he was a run-down degenerate who would give her syphilis. Although Dr. Fischelson had insisted that the wedding be a small, quiet one, a host of guests assembled in the rabbi's rooms. The baker's apprentices who generally went about barefoot, and in their underwear, with paper bags on the tops of their heads, now put on light-colored suits, straw hats, yellow shoes, gaudy ties, and they brought with them huge cakes and pans filled with cookies. They had even managed to find a bottle of vodka although liquor was forbidden in wartime. When the bride and groom entered the rabbi's chamber, a murmur arose from the crowd. The women could not believe their eyes. The woman that they saw was not the one they had known. Dobbe wore a wide-brimmed hat which was amply adorned with cherries, grapes, and plumes, and the dress that she had on was of white silk and was equipped with a train; on her feet were high-heeled shoes, gold in color, and from her thin neck hung a string of imitation pearls. Nor was this all: her fingers sparkled with rings and glittering stones. Her face was veiled. She looked almost like one of those rich brides who were married in the Vienna Hall. The bakers' apprentices whistled mockingly. As for Dr. Fischelson, he was wearing his black coat and broad-toed shoes. He was scarcely able to walk; he was leaning on Dobbe. When he saw the crowd from the doorway, he became frightened and began to retreat, but Dobbe's former employer approached him saying, "Come in, come in, bridegroom. Don't be bashful. We are all brethren now."

The ceremony proceeded according to the law. The rabbi, in a worn satin gaberdine, wrote the marriage contract and then had the bride and groom touch his handkerchief as a token of agreement; the rabbi wiped the point of the pen on his skullcap. Several porters who had been called from the street to make up the quorum supported the canopy. Dr. Fischelson put on a white robe as a reminder of the day of his death and Dobbe walked around him seven times as custom required. The light from the braided candles flickered on the walls. The shadows wavered. Having poured wine into a goblet, the rabbi chanted the benedictions in a sad melody. Dobbe uttered only a single cry. As for the other women, they took out their lace handkerchiefs and stood with them in their hands, grimacing. When the bakers' boys began to whisper wisecracks to each other, the rabbi put a finger to his lips and murmured, *"Eh nu oh,"* as a sign that talking was forbidden. The moment came to slip the wedding ring on the bride's finger, but the bridegroom's hand started to tremble and he had trouble locating Dobbe's index finger. The next thing, according to custom, was the smashing of the glass, but though Dr. Fischelson kicked the goblet several times, it remained unbroken. The girls lowered their heads, pinched each other gleefully, and giggled. Finally one of the apprentices struck the goblet with his heel and it shattered. Even the rabbi could not restrain a smile. After the ceremony the guests drank vodka and ate cookies. Dobbe's former employer came up to Dr. Fischelson and said, *"Mazel tov,* bridegroom. Your luck should be as good as your wife." "Thank you, thank you," Dr. Fischelson murmured, "but I don't look forward to any luck." He was anxious to return as quickly as possible to his attic room. He felt a pressure in his stomach and his chest ached. His face had become greenish. Dobbe had suddenly become angry. She pulled back her veil and called out to the crowd, "What are you laughing at? This isn't a show." And without picking up the cushion cover in which the gifts were wrapped, she returned with her husband to their rooms on the fifth floor.

Dr. Fischelson lay down on the freshly made bed in his room and began reading the *Ethics*. Dobbe had gone back to her own room. The doctor had explained to her that he was an old man, that he was sick and without strength. He had promised her nothing. Nevertheless she returned wearing a silk nightgown, slippers with pompoms, and with her hair hanging down over her shoulders. There was a smile on her face, and she was bashful and hesitant. Dr. Fischelson trembled and the *Ethics* dropped from his hands. The candle went out. Dobbe groped for Dr. Fischelson in the dark and kissed his mouth. "My dear husband," she whispered to him, *"Mazel tov."*

What happened that night could be called a miracle. If Dr. Fischelson hadn't been convinced that every occurrence is in accordance with the laws of nature, he would have thought that Black Dobbe had bewitched him. Powers long dormant awakened in him. Although he had only a sip of the benediction wine, he was as if intoxicated. He kissed Dobbe and spoke to her of love. Long-forgotten quotations from Klopstock, Lessing, Goethe, rose to his lips. The pressures and aches stopped. He embraced Dobbe, pressed her to himself, was again a man as in his youth. Dobbe was faint with delight; crying, she murmured things to him in a Warsaw slang which he did not understand. Later, Dr. Fischelson slipped off into the deep sleep young men know. He dreamed that he was in Switzerland and that he was climbing mountains—running, falling, flying. At dawn he opened his eyes; it seemed to him that someone had blown into his ears. Dobbe was snoring. Dr. Fischelson quietly got out of bed. In his long nightshirt he approached the window, walked up the steps and looked out in wonder. Market Street was asleep, breathing with a deep stillness. The gas lamps were flickering. The black shutters on the stores were fastened with iron bars. A cool breeze was blowing. Dr. Fischelson looked up at the sky. The black arch was thickly sown with stars—there were green, red, yellow, blue stars; there were large ones and small ones, winking and steady ones. There were those that were clustered in dense groups and those that were alone. In the higher sphere, apparently, little notice was taken of the fact that a certain Dr. Fischelson had in his declining days married someone called Black Dobbe. Seen from above even the Great War was nothing but a temporary play of the modes. The myriads of fixed stars continued to travel their destined courses in unbounded space. The comets, planets, satellites, asteroids kept circling these shining centres. Worlds were born and died in cosmic upheavals. In the chaos of nebulae, primeval matter was being formed. Now and again a star tore loose, and swept across the sky, leaving behind it a fiery streak. It was the month of August when there are showers of meteors. Yes, the divine substance was extended and had neither beginning nor end; it was absolute, indivisible, eternal, without duration, infinite in its attributes. Its waves and bubbles danced in the universal cauldron, seething with change, following the unbroken chain of causes and effects, and he, Dr. Fischelson, with his unavoidable fate, was part of this. The doctor closed his eyelids and allowed the breeze to cool the sweat on his forehead and stir the hair of his beard. He breathed deeply of the midnight air, supported his shaky hands on the windowsill and murmured, "Divine Spinoza, forgive me. I have become a fool."

SINCLAIR ROSS

(b. 1908)

S inclair Ross was born on a farm near Prince Albert, Saskatchewan. His working life, apart from his writing, was spent as a bank clerk for the Union Bank of Canada (which has since been absorbed by the Royal Bank) throughout Saskatchewan, in Winnipeg, and in Montreal. He retired in 1968, lived for a time in Greece and Spain, and currently resides in Vancouver. Ross has written four novels, As for Me and My House (1941), The Well (1958), Whir of Gold (1970), and Sawbones Memorial (1974). The first of these novels, in the form of a woman's journal covering one of the dust-bowl years on the Prairies in a small town during the 1930s, has attained the status of a Canadian classic. Ross's short stories have been collected in The Lamp at Noon and Other Stories (1968) and The Race and Other Stories (1982). Like As for Me and My House, the best of these stories are set on the Prairies during the "dirty thirties." Like "One's a Heifer," they often deal with the frustrations caused by poverty and loneliness. Ross's stories are highly symbolic, and the impressions they leave readers with are ones of sadness for the determined victims and admiration for those who persist after such ordeals.

One's a Heifer

M y uncle was laid up that winter with sciatica, so when the blizzard stopped and still two of the yearlings hadn't come home with the other cattle, Aunt Ellen said I'd better saddle Tim and start out looking for them.

"Then maybe I'll not be back tonight," I told her firmly. "Likely they've drifted as far as the sandhills. There's no use coming home without them."

I was thirteen, and had never been away like that all night before, but, busy with the breakfast, Aunt Ellen said yes, that sounded sensible enough, and while I ate, hunted up a dollar in silver for my meals.

"Most people wouldn't take it from a lad, but they're strangers up towards the hills. Bring it out independent-like, but don't insist too much. They're more likely to grudge you a feed of oats for Tim."

After breakfast I had to undress again, and put on two suits of underwear and two pairs of thick, home-knitted stockings. It was a clear, bitter morning. After the storm the drifts lay clean and unbroken to the horizon. Distant farm-buildings stood out distinct against the prairie as if the thin sharp atmosphere were a magnifying glass. As I started off Aunt Ellen peered cautiously out of the door a moment through a cloud of steam, and waved a red and white checkered dish-towel. I didn't wave back, but conscious of her uneasiness rode erect, as jaunty as the sheepskin and two suits of underwear would permit.

We took the road straight south about three miles. The calves, I reasoned, would have by this time found their way home if the blizzard hadn't carried them at least that far. Then we started catercornering across fields, riding over to straw-stacks where we could see cattle sheltering, calling at farmhouses to ask had they seen any strays. "Yearlings," I said each time politely. "Red with white spots and faces. The same almost except that one's a heifer and the other isn't."

Nobody had seen them. There was a crust on the snow not quite hard enough to carry Tim, and despite the cold his flanks and shoulders soon were steaming. He walked with his head down, and sometimes, taking my sympathy for granted, drew up a minute for breath.

My spirits, too, began to flag. The deadly cold and the flat white silent miles of prairie asserted themselves like a disapproving presence. The cattle round the straw-stacks stared when we rode up as if we were intruders. The fields stared, and the sky stared. People shivered in their doorways, and said they'd seen no strays.

At about one o'clock we stopped at a farmhouse for dinner. It was a single oat sheaf half thistles for Tim, and fried eggs and bread and tea for me. Crops had been poor that year, they apologized, and though they shook their heads when I brought out my money I saw the woman's eyes light greedily a second, as if her instincts of hospitality were struggling hard against some urgent need. We too, I said, had had poor crops lately. That was why it was so important that I find the calves.

We rested an hour, then went on again. "Yearlings," I kept on describing them. "Red with white spots and faces. The same except that one's a heifer and the other isn't."

Still no one had seen them, still it was cold, still Tim protested what a fool I was.

The country began to roll a little. A few miles ahead I could see the first low line of sandhills. "They'll be there for sure," I said aloud, more to encourage myself than Tim. "Keeping straight to the road it won't take a quarter as long to get home again."

But home now seemed a long way off. A thin white sheet of cloud spread across the sky, and though there had been no warmth in the sun the fields looked colder and bleaker without the glitter on the snow. Straw-stacks were fewer here, as if the land were poor, and every house we stopped at seemed more dilapidated than the one before.

A nagging wind rose as the afternoon wore on. Dogs yelped and bayed at us, and sometimes from the hills, like the signal of our approach, there was a thin, wavering howl of a coyote. I began to dread the miles home again almost as much as those still ahead. There were so many cattle straggling across the fields, so many yearlings just like ours. I saw them for sure a dozen times, and as often choked my disappointment down and clicked Tim on again.

And then at last I really saw them. It was nearly dusk, and along with fifteen or twenty other cattle they were making their way towards some buildings that lay huddled at the foot of the sandhills. They passed in single file less than fifty yards away, but when I pricked Tim forward to turn them back he floundered in a snowed-in water-cut. By the time we were out they were a little distance ahead, and on account of the drifts it was impossible to put on a spurt of speed and pass them. All we could do was take our place at the end of the file, and proceed at their pace towards the buildings.

It was about half a mile. As we drew near I debated with Tim whether we should ask to spend the night or start off right away for home. We were hungry and tired, but it was a poor, shiftless-looking place. The yard was littered with old wagons and machinery; the house was scarcely distinguishable from the stables. Darkness was beginning to close in, but there was no light in the windows.

Then as we crossed the yard we heard a shout, "Stay where you are," and a man came running towards us from the stable. He was tall and ungainly, and, instead of the short sheepskin that most farmers wear, had on a long black overcoat nearly to his feet. He seized Tim's bridle when he reached us, and glared for a minute as if he were going to pull me out of the saddle. "I told you to stay out," he said in a harsh, excited voice. "You heard me, didn't you? What do you want coming round here anyway?"

I steeled myself and said, "Our two calves."

The muscles of his face were drawn together threateningly, but close to him like this and looking straight into his eyes I felt that for all their fierce look there was something about them wavering and uneasy. "The two red ones with the white faces." I continued. "They've just gone into the shed over there with yours. If you'll give me a hand getting them out again I'll start for home now right away."

He peered at me a minute, let go the bridle, then clutched it again. "They're all mine," he countered. "I was over by the gate. I watched them coming in."

His voice was harsh and thick. The strange wavering look in his eyes steadied itself for a minute to a dare. I forced myself to meet it and insisted, "I saw them back a piece in the field. They're ours all right. Let me go over a minute and I'll show you."

With a crafty tilt of his head he leered, "You didn't see any calves. And now, if you know what's good for you, you'll be on your way."

"You're trying to steal them," I flared rashly. "I'll go home and get my uncle and the police after you—then you'll see whether they're our calves or not."

My threat seemed to impress him a little. With a shifty glance in the direction of the stable he said, "All right, come along and look them over. Then maybe you'll be satisfied." But all the way across the yard he kept his hand on Tim's bridle, and at the shed made me wait a few minutes while he went inside.

The cattle shed was a lean-to on the horse stable. It was plain enough: he was hiding the calves before letting me inside to look around. While waiting for him, however, I had time to reflect that he was a lot bigger and stronger than I was, and that it might be prudent just to keep my eyes open, and not give him too much insolence.

He reappeared carrying a smoky lantern. "All right," he said pleasantly enough, "come in and look around. Will your horse stand, or do you want to tie him?"

We put Tim in an empty stall in the horse stable, then went through a narrow doorway with a bar across it to the cattle shed. Just as I expected, our calves weren't there. There were two red ones with white markings that he tried to make me believe were the ones I had seen, but, positive I hadn't been mistaken, I shook my head and glanced at the doorway we had just come through. It was narrow, but not too narrow. He read my expression and said. "You think they're in there. Come on, then, and look around."

The horse stable consisted of two rows of open stalls with a passage down the centre like an aisle. At the far end were two box-stalls, one with a sick colt in it, the other closed. They were both boarded up to the ceiling, so that you could see inside them only through the doors. Again he read my expression, and with a nod towards the closed one said, "It's just a kind of harness room now. Up till a year ago I kept a stallion."

But he spoke furtively, and seemed anxious to get me away from that end of the stable. His smoky lantern threw great swaying shadows over us; and the deep clefts and triangles of shadow on his face sent a little chill through me, and made me think what a dark and evil face it was.

I was afraid, but not too afraid. "If it's just a harness room," I said recklessly, "why not let me see inside? Then I'll be satisfied and believe you."

He wheeled at my question, and sidled over swiftly to the stall. He stood in front of the door, crouched down a little, the lantern in front of him like a shield. There was a sudden stillness through the stable as we faced each other. Behind the light from his lantern the darkness hovered vast and sinister. It seemed to hold its breath, to watch and listen. I felt a clutch of fear now at my throat, but I didn't move. My eyes were fixed on him so intently that he seemed to lose substance, to loom up close a moment, then recede. At last he disappeared completely, and there was only the lantern like a hard hypnotic eye.

It held me. It held me rooted, against my will. I wanted to run from the stable, but I wanted even more to see inside the stall. Wanting to see and yet afraid of seeing. So afraid that it was a relief when at last he gave a shame-faced laugh and said, "There's a hole in the floor—that's why I keep the door closed. If you didn't know, you might step into it—twist your foot. That's what happened to one of my horses a while ago."

I nodded as if I believed him, and went back tractably to Tim. But regaining control of myself as I tried the saddle girths, beginning to feel that my fear had been unwarranted, I looked up and said, "It's ten miles home, and we've been riding hard all day. If we could stay a while—have something to eat, and then get started—"

The wavering light came into his eyes again. He held the lantern up to see me better, such a long, intent scrutiny that it seemed he must discover my designs. But he gave a nod finally, as if reassured, brought oats and hay for Tim, and suggested, companionably, "After supper we can have a game of checkers."

Then, as if I were a grown-up, he put out his hand and said, "My name is Arthur Vickers."

Inside the house, rid of his hat and coat, he looked less forbidding. He had a white nervous face, thin lips, a large straight nose, and deep uneasy eyes. When the lamp was lit I fancied I could still see the wavering expression in them, and decided it was what you called a guilty look.

"You won't think much of it," he said apologetically, following my glance around the room. "I ought to be getting things cleaned up again. Come over to the stove. Supper won't take long."

It was a large, low-ceilinged room that for the first moment or two struck me more like a shed or granary than a house. The table in the centre was littered with tools and harness. On a rusty cook-stove were two big steaming pots of bran. Next to the stove stood a grindstone, then a white iron bed covered with coats and horse blankets. At the end opposite the bed, weasel and coyote skins were drying. There were guns and traps on the wall, a horse collar, a pair of rubber boots. The floor was bare and grimy. Ashes were littered around the stove. In a corner squatted a live owl with a broken wing.

He walked back and forth a few times looking helplessly at the disorder, then cleared off the table and lifted the pots of bran to the back of the stove. "I've been mending harness," he explained. "You get careless, living alone like this. It takes a woman anyway."

My presence, apparently, was making him take stock of the room. He picked up a broom and swept for a minute, made an ineffective attempt to straighten the blankets on the bed, brought another lamp out of a cupboard and lit it. There was an ungainly haste to all his movements. He started unbuckling my sheepskin for me, then turned away suddenly to take off his own coat. "Now we'll have supper," he said with an effort at self-possession. "Coffee and beans is all I can give you—maybe a little molasses."

I replied diplomatically that that sounded pretty good. It didn't seem right, accepting hospitality this way from a man trying to steal your calves, but theft, I reflected, surely justified deceit. I held my hands out to the warmth and asked if I could help.

There was a kettle of plain navy beans already cooked. He dipped out enough for our supper into a frying pan, and on top laid rashers of fat salt pork. While I watched that they didn't burn he rinsed off a few dishes. Then he set out sugar and canned milk, butter, molasses, and dark heavy biscuits that he had baked himself the day before. He kept glancing at me so apologetically all the while that I leaned over and sniffed the beans, and said at home I ate a lot of them.

"It takes a woman," he repeated as we sat down to the table. "I don't often have anyone here to eat with me. If I'd known, I'd have cleaned things up a little."

I was too intent on my plateful of beans to answer. All through the meal he sat watching me, but made no further attempts at conversation. Hungry as I was, I noticed that the wavering, uneasy look was still in his eyes. A guilty look, I told myself again, and wondered what I was going to do to get the calves away. I finished my coffee and he continued:

"It's worse even than this in the summer. No time for meals—and the heat and flies. Last summer I had a girl cooking for a few weeks, but it didn't last. Just a cow she was—just a big stupid cow—and she wanted to stay on. There's a family of them back in the hills. I had to send her home."

I wondered should I suggest starting now, or ask to spend the night. Maybe when he's asleep, I thought, I can slip out of the house and get away with the calves. He went on, "You don't know how bad it is sometimes. Weeks on end and no one to talk to. You're not yourself—you're not sure what you're going to say or do."

I remembered hearing my uncle talk about a man who had gone crazy living alone. And this fellow Vickers had queer eyes all right. And there was the live owl over in the corner, and the grindstone standing right beside the bed. "Maybe I'd better go now," I decided aloud. "Tim'll be rested, and it's ten miles home."

But he said no, it was colder now, with the wind getting stronger, and seemed so kindly and concerned that I half forgot my fears. "Likely he's just starting to go crazy, " I told myself, "and it's only by staying that I'll have a chance to get the calves away."

When the table was cleared and the dishes washed he said he would go out and bed down the stable for the night. I picked up my sheepskin to go with him, but he told me sharply to stay inside. Just for a minute he looked crafty and forbidding as when I first rode up on Tim, and to allay his suspicions I nodded compliantly and put my sheepskin down again. It was better like that anyway, I decided. In a few minutes I could follow him, and perhaps, taking advantage of the shadows and his smoky lantern, make my way to the box-stall unobserved.

But when I reached the stable he had closed the door after him and hooked it from the inside. I walked round a while, tried to slip in by way of the cattle shed, and then had to go back to the house. I went with a vague feeling of relief again. There was still time, I told myself, and it would be safer anyway when he was sleeping.

So that it would be easier to keep from falling asleep myself I planned to suggest coffee again just before we went to bed. I knew that the guest didn't ordinarily suggest such things, but it was no time to remember manners when there was someone trying to steal your calves.

When he came in from the stable we played checkers. I was no match for him, but to encourage me he repeatedly let me win. "It's long time now since I've had a chance to play," he kept on saying, trying to convince me that his short-sighted moves weren't intentional. "Sometimes I used to ask her to play, but I had to tell her every move to make. If she didn't win she'd upset the board and go off and sulk."

"My aunt is a little like that too," I said. "She cheats sometimes when we're playing cribbage—and, when I catch her, says her eyes aren't good."

"Women talk too much ever to make good checker players. It takes concentration. This one, though, couldn't even talk like anybody else."

After my long day in the cold I was starting to yawn already. He noticed it, and spoke in a rapid, earnest voice, as if afraid I might lose interest soon and want to go to bed. It was important for me too to stay awake, so I crowned a king and said, "Why don't you get someone, then, to stay with you?"

"Too many of them want to do that." His face darkened a little, almost as if warning me. "Too many of the kind you'll never get rid of again. She did, last summer when she was here. I had to put her out."

There was silence for a minute, his eyes flashing, and wanting to placate him I suggested, "She liked you, maybe."

He laughed a moment, harshly. "She liked me all right. Just two weeks ago she came back—walked over with an old suitcase and said she was going to stay. It was cold at home, and she had to work too hard, and she didn't mind even if I couldn't pay her wages."

I was getting sleepier. To keep awake I sat on the edge of the chair where it was uncomfortable and said, "Hadn't you asked her to come?"

His eyes narrowed. "I'd had trouble enough getting rid of her the first time. There were six of them at home, and she said her father thought it time that someone married her."

"Then she must be a funny one," I said. "Everybody knows that the man's supposed to ask the girl."

My remark seemed to please him. "I told you didn't I?" he said, straightening a little, jumping two of my men. "She was so stupid that at checkers she'd forget whether she was black or red."

We stopped playing now. I glanced at the owl in the corner and the ashes littered on the floor, and thought that keeping her would maybe have been a good idea after all. He read it in my face and said, "I used to think that too sometimes. I used to look at her and think nobody knew now anyway and that she'd maybe do. You need a woman on a farm all right. And night after night she'd be sitting there where you are—right there where you are, looking at me, not even trying to play—"

The fire was low, and we could hear the wind. "But then I'd go up in the hills, away from her for a while, and start thinking back the way things used to be, and it wasn't right even for the sake of your meals ready and your house kept clean. When she came back I tried to tell her that, but all the family are the same, and I realized it wasn't any use. There's nothing you can do when you're up against that sort of thing. The mother talks just like a child of ten. When she sees you coming she runs and hides. There are six of them, and it's come out in every one."

It was getting cold, but I couldn't bring myself to go over to the stove. There was the same stillness now as when he was standing at the box-stall door. And I felt the same illogical fear, the same powerlessness to move. It was the way his voice had sunk, the glassy, cold look in his eyes. The rest of his face disappeared; all I could see were his eyes. And they filled me with a vague and overpowering dread. My own voice a whisper, I asked, "And when you wouldn't marry her—what happened then?"

He remained motionless a moment, as if answering silently; then with an unexpected laugh like a breaking dish said, "Why, nothing happened. I just told her she couldn't stay. I went to town for a few days—and when I came back she was gone."

"Has she been back to bother you since?" I asked.

He made a little silo of checkers. "No—she took her suitcase with her."

To remind him that the fire was going down I went over to the stove and stood warming myself. He raked the coals with the lifter and put in poplar, two split pieces for a base and a thick round log on top. I yawned again. He said maybe I'd like to go to bed now, and I shivered and asked him could I have a drink of coffee first. While it boiled he stood stirring the two big pots of bran. The trouble with coffee, I realized, was that it would keep him from getting sleepy too.

I undressed finally and got into bed, but he blew out only one of the lamps, and sat on playing checkers with himself. I dozed a while, then sat up with a start, afraid it was morning already and that I'd lost my chance to get the calves away. He came over and looked at me a minute, then gently pushed my shoulders back on the pillow. "Why don't you come to bed too?" I asked, and he said, "Later I will—I don't feel sleepy yet."

It was like that all night. I kept dozing on and off, wakening in a fright each time to find him still there sitting at his checker board. He would raise his head sharply when I stirred, then tiptoe over to the bed and stand close to me listening till satisfied again I was asleep. The owl kept wakening too. It was down in the corner still where the lamplight scarcely reached, and I could see its eyes go on and off like yellow bulbs. The wind whistled drearily around the house. The blankets smelled like an old granary. He suspected what I was planning to do, evidently, and was staying awake to make sure I didn't get outside.

Each time I dozed I dreamed I was on Tim again. The calves were in sight, but far ahead of us, and with the drifts so deep we couldn't overtake them. Then instead of Tim it was the grindstone I was straddling, and that was the reason, not the drifts, that we weren't making better progress.

I wondered what would happen to the calves if I didn't get away with them. My uncle had sciatica, and it would be at least a day before I could be home and back again with some of the neighbours. By then Vickers might have butchered the calves, or driven them up to a hiding place in the hills where we'd never find them. There was a possibility, too, that Aunt Ellen and the neighbours wouldn't believe me. I dozed and woke—dozed and woke—always he was sitting at the checker board. I could hear the dry tinny ticking of an alarm clock, but from where I was lying couldn't see it. He seemed to be listening to it too. The wind would sometimes creak the house, and then he would give a start and sit rigid a moment with his eyes fixed on the window. It was always the window, as if there was nothing he was afraid of that could reach him by the door.

Most of the time he played checkers with himself, moving his lips, muttering words I couldn't hear, but once I woke to find him staring fixedly across the table as if he had a partner sitting there. His hands were clenched in front of him, there was a sharp, metallic glitter in his eyes. I lay transfixed, unbreathing. His eyes as I watched seemed to dilate, to brighten, to harden like a bird's. For a long time he sat contracted, motionless, as if gathering himself to strike, then furtively he slid his hand an inch or two along the table towards some checkers that were piled beside the board. It was as if he were reaching for a weapon, as if his invisible partner were an enemy. He clutched the checkers, slipped slowly from his chair and straightened. His movements were sure, stealthy, silent like a cat's. His face had taken on a desperate, contorted look. As he raised his hand the tension was unbearable.

It was a long time—a long time watching him the way you watch a finger tightening slowly in the trigger of a gun—and then suddenly wrenching himself to action he hurled the checkers with such vicious fury that they struck the wall and clattered back across the room.

And everything was quiet again. I started a little, mumbled to myself as if half-awakened, lay quite still. But he seemed to have forgotten me, and after standing limp and dazed a minute got down on his knees and started looking for the checkers. When he had them all, he put more wood in the stove, then returned quietly to the table and sat down. We were alone again; everything was exactly as before. I relaxed gradually, telling myself that he'd just been seeing things.

The next time I woke he was sitting with his head sunk forward on the table. It looked as if he had fallen asleep at last, and huddling alert among the bed-clothes I decided to watch a minute to make sure, then dress and try to slip out to the stable.

While I watched, I planned exactly every movement I was going to make. Rehearsing it in my mind as carefully as if I were actually doing it, I climbed out of bed, put on my clothes, tiptoed stealthily to the door and slipped outside. By this time, though, I was getting drowsy, and relaxing among the blankets I decided that for safety's sake I should rehearse it still again. I rehearsed it four times altogether, and the fourth time dreamed that I hurried on successfully to the stable.

I fumbled with the door a while, then went inside and felt my way through the darkness to the box-stall. There was a bright light suddenly and the owl was sitting over the door with his yellow eyes like a pair of lanterns. The calves, he told me, were in the other stall with the sick colt. I looked and they were there all right, but Tim came up and said it might be better not to start for home till morning. He reminded me that I hadn't paid for his feed or my own supper yet, and that if I slipped off this way it would mean that I was stealing, too. I agreed, realizing now that it wasn't the calves I was looking for after all, and that I still had to see inside the stall that was guarded by the owl. "Wait here," Tim said, "I'll tell you if he flies away," and without further questioning I lay down in the straw and went to sleep again. . . . When I woke coffee and beans were on the stove already, and though the lamp was still lit I could tell by the window that it was nearly morning.

We were silent during breakfast. Two or three times I caught him watching me, and it seemed his eyes were shiftier than before. After his sleepless night he looked tired and haggard. He left the table while I was still eating and fed raw rabbit to the owl, then came back and drank another cup of coffee. He had been friendly and communicative the night before, but now, just as when he first came running out of the stable in his long black coat, his expression was sullen and resentful. I began to feel that he was in a hurry to be rid of me.

I took my time, however, racking my brains to outwit him still and get the calves away. It looked pretty hopeless now, his eyes on me so suspiciously, my imagination at low ebb. Even if I did get inside the box-stall to see the calves—was he going to stand back then and let me start off home with them? Might it not more likely frighten him, make him do something desperate, so that I couldn't reach my uncle or the police? There was the owl over in the corner, the grindstone by the bed. And with such a queer fellow you could never tell. You could never tell, and you had to think about your own skin too. So I said politely, "Thank you, Mr. Vickers, for letting me stay all night," and remembering what Tim had told me took out my dollar's worth of silver.

He gave a short dry laugh and wouldn't take it. "Maybe you'll come back," he said, "and next time stay longer. We'll go shooting up in the hills if you like—and I'll make a trip to town for things so that we can have better meals. You need company sometimes for a change. There's been no one here now quite a while."

His face softened again as he spoke. There was an expression in his eyes as if he wished that I could stay on now. It puzzled me. I wanted to be indignant, and it was impossible. He held my sheepskin for me while I put it on, and tied the scarf around the collar with a solicitude and determination equal to Aunt Ellen's. And then he gave his short dry laugh again, and hoped I'd find my calves all right.

He had been out to the stable before I was awake, and Tim was ready for me, fed and saddled. But I delayed a few minutes, pretending to be interested in his horses and the sick colt. It would be worth something after all, I realized, to get just a glimpse of the calves. Aunt Ellen was going to be sceptical enough of my story as it was. It could only confirm her doubts to hear me say I hadn't seen the calves in the box-stall, and was just pretty sure that they were there.

So I went from stall to stall, stroking the horses and making comparisons with the ones we had at home. The door, I noticed, he had left wide open, ready for me to lead out Tim. He was walking up and down the aisle, telling me which horses were quiet, which to be careful of. I came to a nervous chestnut mare, and realized she was my only chance.

She crushed her hips against the side of the stall as I slipped up to her manger, almost pinning me, then gave her head a toss and pulled back hard on the halter shank. The shank, I noticed, was tied with an easy slip-knot that the right twist and a sharp tug would undo in half a second. And the door was wide open, ready for me to lead out Tim—and standing as she was with her body across the stall diagonally, I was for the moment screened from sight.

It happened quickly. There wasn't time to think of consequences. I just pulled the knot, in the same instant struck the mare across the nose. With a snort she threw herself backwards, almost trampling Vickers, then flung up her head to keep from tripping on the shank and plunged outside.

It worked as I hoped it would. "Quick," Vickers yelled to me, "the gate's open—try and head her off"—but instead I just waited till he himself was gone, then leaped to the box-stall.

The door was fastened with two tight-fitting slide-bolts, one so high that I could scarcely reach it standing on my toes. It wouldn't yield. There was a piece of broken whiffle-tree beside the other box-stall door. I snatched it up and started hammering on the pin. Still it wouldn't yield. The head of the pin was small and round, and the whiffle-tree kept glancing off. I was too terrified to pause a moment and take careful aim.

Terrified of the stall though, not of Vickers. Terrified of the stall, yet compelled by a frantic need to get inside. For the moment I had forgotten Vickers, forgotten even the danger of his catching me. I worked blindly, helplessly, as if I were confined and smothering. For a moment I yielded to panic, dropped the piece of whiffle-tree and started kicking at the door. Then, collected again, I forced back the lower bolt, and picking up the whiffle-tree to pry the door out a little at the bottom. But I had wasted too much time. Just as I dropped to my knees to peer through the opening Vickers seized me. I struggled to my feet and fought a moment, but it was such a hard, strangling clutch at my throat that I felt myself go limp and blind. In desperation then I kicked him, and with a blow like a reflex he sent me staggering to the floor.

But it wasn't the blow that frightened me. It was the fierce, wild light in his eyes.

Stunned as I was, I looked up and saw him watching me, and, sick with terror, made a bolt for Tim. I untied him with hands that moved incredibly, galvanized for escape. I knew now for sure that Vickers was crazy. He followed me outside, and, just as I mounted, seized Tim again by the bridle. For a second or two it made me crazy too. Gathering up the free ends of the rein I lashed him hard across the face. He let go of the bridle, and, frightened and excited too now, Tim made a dash across the yard and out of the gate. Deep as the snow was, I kept him galloping for half a mile, pommelling him with my fists, kicking my heels against his sides. Then of his own accord he drew up short for breath, and I looked around to see whether Vickers was following. He wasn't—there was only snow and the hills, his buildings a lonely little smudge against the whiteness—and the relief was like a stick pulled out that's been holding up tomato vines or peas. I slumped across the saddle weakly, and till Tim started on again lay there whimpering like a baby.

We were home by noon. We didn't have to cross fields or stop at houses now, and there had been teams on the road packing down the snow so that Tim could trot part of the way and even canter. I put him in the stable without taking time to tie or unbridle him, and ran to the house to tell Aunt Ellen. But I was still frightened, cold and a little hysterical, and it was a while before she could understand how everything had happened. She was silent a minute, indulgent, then helping me off with my sheepskin said kindly, "You'd better forget about it now, and come over and get warm. The calves came home themselves yesterday. Just about an hour after you set out."

I looked up at her. "But the stall, then—just because I wanted to look inside he knocked me down—and if it wasn't the calves in there—"

She didn't answer. She was busy building up the fire and looking at the stew.

GABRIELLE ROY

(1909–1983)

G abrielle Roy was born in St-Boniface, Manitoba, and lived most of her life in Quebec City. She was elected to the Royal Society of Canada in 1947 (the first woman to be so honoured), made a Companion of the Order of Canada in 1967, and awarded the Molson Prize and the Prix David. Before settling in Quebec City, Roy lived for a period in Montreal, whose environs provided material for her first two novels, Bonheur d'occasion (1945) and Alexandre Chênevert (1955). Bonheur d'occasion, which was translated into English as The Tin Flute (1947), won the Governor General's Award and was the first Canadian work to win a major French literary prize, the Prix Fémina. Her numerous collections of short stories and tales include La petite poule d'eau (1950; Where Nests the Water Hen); Rue Deschambault (1955; Street of Riches, 1957), winner of the Governor General's Award; La route d'Altamont (1966; The Road past Altamont); Un jardin au bout du monde (1975; Garden in the Wind, 1977); and Ces enfants de ma vie (1977; Children of My Heart, 1979). She is also a delightfully unconventional children's author and an essayist whose nonfictional prose has been collected in Fragiles lumières de la terre (1978; Fragile Lights of Earth, 1982). Like the prairie novelist and story writer Rudy Wiebe, Roy demonstrates in her fiction an interest in the fate of those living on the periphery of white, middle-class Canadian society. M.G. Hesse has remarked the connection between Roy's life and humanitarian fiction:

> The conviction that every human being has a distinct dignity is based on the author's personal contacts from early childhood on with representatives of the many nationalities that sought a new home in Canada. Her extraordinary empathy and love for her fellow men are coupled with profound psychologic insights and a writing talent so that she conveys through her books her belief that the differences separating people are superficial since at heart all people are the same.

Roy described the following story as "a fairly just account . . . of the chimerical dreams that guided so many immigrants of Eastern and Central Europe in their settlement in the lands of the Canadian West: poor people who, because they had tried to follow their star, ended in the most total disillusionment."

Hoodoo Valley

The group of Doukhobors newly arrived in Verigin, a prairie hamlet, were living for the time being in the round tents and converted railway cars that had been provided for them: a melancholy encampment on a hostile terrain invested by marshes, mosquitoes and, worse still, every evening, by boredom. Then, gathered like an immense family around a fire of branches, you could hear them intoning, all with the same low-pitched, afflicted voice, some song of their people.

No Doukhobor was ready to say it right out loud, but they were desolate.

"It's nothing like our Humid Mountains."

"Oh, no! Far it is from our green Caucasus!"

From the very start the plain had set about rebuffing them with its flat immensity, naked under the sky, this endless space, this too-vast exaggeration of a land where in winter, they said, it was cold enough to freeze your breath in your throat, and in summer hot enough to put an end to your days. And the people here, the ones who'd been living in this solitude awhile, what strange ones they were! Eaters of meat and other forbidden foods, they squabbled among themselves as if life wasn't hard enough already; or, carried away by a different madness, they'd dance till the tavern tables jumped. They couldn't be Christians, these folk who used alcohol and tobacco and never seemed to tire of spatting viciously among themselves.

The Doukhobor women, their blond hair carefully hidden under kerchiefs doubled to a point, had perhaps less time for boredom than their men. They cooked over little piles of embers, did the washing, laid it to dry on the grass, and went off across the naked plain, sometimes quite a distance, searching for bits of wood to burn. But their husbands, these great stalwarts, upright as oaks, with heavy moustaches, their blue eyes childlike and astonished, had all the leisure they needed for sighing and lamenting.

Their leaders, Streliov, Zibinov and Strekov, went out every day with their guide McPherson, the settlement agent, sometimes to the north, sometimes to the south, in search of land for their community. Up to now they had nowhere found a concession that in their eyes combined the qualities they obscurely felt would suit them.

The man McPherson, an ambitious and enterprising little Scot, had wagered that he'd settle his Doukhobors in no time, intending to use their success on Canadian soil as a stepping stone to promotion in his career.

The women, the children, the old men, would surround the three leaders on their return to the encampment and ask: "What did you see today, Zibinov, Streliov, Strekov?"

And these three, the men in whom they had placed their confidence, would reply: "Just the flat land. The same as here."

"And that was all?"

"Just prairie, I tell you. Nothing but prairie."

McPherson was fuming. What else did they expect to find here in the flattest stretch of all Canada?

A strange folk, gentle, dreaming, with only one foot in this world; but in their refusal, their disillusion, they had a tenacity that could outlast the most energetic. The people of the village, a handful of neighbours, immigrants themselves but resigned with good grace to their new land, began to grow impatient with these long-faced Doukhobors whose incessant plaintive songs reached them night after night in their scattered shacks. As if singing could change the prairie! It had heard other sighs, seen other regrets, this plain of exile and homesickness. In the end it always brought people around. Others, many others, had been through the same thing. The Doukhobors too would have to give in.

They didn't want to break up or settle in small groups as others did. That would have solved many problems, for the good land was by no means all in one place. Most often it was a patchwork created by ancient alluvia or waterways. But they absolutely refused to separate. They insisted on settling in a single region, old and young, grandchildren and grandparents together, along with nephews, cousins and friends—in short, the whole lost folk in one place.

So they sought a big stretch of arable land. At some distance from the camp such tracts of land were still to be found. McPherson took Strekov, Streliov and Zibinov to see them, across miles and miles of silent plain, often serene and inviting under the high, clear sky. Where the road stopped the wagon made its own trail through the grasses. In this way they'd seen a good part of the countryside: sandy, desert-like spaces overrun by the wind; others with a stubby growth like wire twisted and rolled together; others made almost livable by pretty groups of trees that showed from afar the presence of water. Nowhere did the Doukhobor leaders consent to stop.

"Nyet, nyet."

Here the country seemed too wild, too isolated; there they would spy tents or trappers' huts and suddenly were unwilling to have neighbours.

"Nyet, nyet!"

They shook their heads. Their eyes, blue and candid, wide with astonishment, always expressed the same tenacious estrangement.

And this had been going on for weeks.

The women were constantly on the lookout for the party's return.

"Come now, you must have seen something today that would suit us!"

"Nyet. We saw nothing but the flat land. Always the same."

They could find no other way to express their disappointment. Before they left the Caucasus, someone must have told them a very fancy story to attract them to the Canadian West, and they'd swallowed it whole. They always ended up singing their songs of lamentation. At such times the gentle landscape they had left behind, the land of acacias, of lemon trees and tender grass, came to life again behind their closed eyelids. For each new evil chases out the last; having forgotten the persecutions that had forced them to leave their native soil, their hearts retained nothing of it but the most tender recollections.

Oh, what nostalgia!

By now even the women were almost all infected by it.

This wretched plain all around! (At times you could see one of them stoop to pick up a pebble and hurl it violently as if to strike the immense countryside and take vengeance on its numb expanse.)

"What did you see today, Streliov?" asked Makaroff, the oldest and wisest, who thought the time had come to make the best of a bad job. Life wasn't so long, he often said. If we have to use up so much of it regretting the past, what's left for doing what's still to be done?

And Streliov, the oldest of the three leaders, a solid man with all the strength of his thirty years, began to sigh like a stripling.

"The same thing as here, Grandfather. The naked plain, always. And always, it seems, the same cruel indifference."

The old man drew nearer to poke the fire.

"I remember when I was young and we'd just been exiled to the Caucasus, life didn't seem so easy there either at the start. Did you say 'indifference,' Streliov? Do you have any idea how many trees—lemon trees and cherry trees and acacias—we had to plant there for every one that lived? Do you know that, Streliov?"

The immigrants, seated in a circle in the growing dark, were suddenly as struck by his words as they had been by their recurrent longing for their lost homeland. At once their eyes turned outward toward the plain which their imagination saw as endless: the mute, the enigmatic land. They did their best to see it covered with little whitewashed houses, with pens for the chickens, vegetable gardens, fences, milk pails upside down on the fence posts, busy comings and goings, and even their seesaw wells like the ones at home in the Caucasus, punctuating the prairie with the long strokes of their lever poles drawn dark against the sky. For awhile they were all comforted by the vision of the tremendous work to be redone and they burned with impatience to get started.

"True enough, you know," some of the more realistic women grumbled, "it's more than time we started in somewhere. You leaders, go off on your search again. And try to come back with some good news. It's high time to get on with our work."

But others, lulling their babies, held them tight to their breast as if defying the dark plain to steal them away. And suddenly they would begin to weep, doubtless because of some vague perception that the plain would finally take their children, would take thousands of others, would absorb as many lives as there were grains of sand, before this would even show. Still others, a few about to bear children, had an even stronger hatred of the stark land and the giant sky which their eyes probed in terror.

The ones with the most common sense were the very old women, tottering babushkas, come to this country with just enough time left to die and sleep in its foreign soil.

They scolded the younger ones: "What would our holy little father Verigin think, and him in exile in the wilds of Siberia, if he saw you now, downcast and fearful and always snivelling?"

And the others would reply: "Our little father Verigin promised we'd find peace at the end of the world, and harmony, and that in the place we went to we'd be of one heart and mind. Perhaps we didn't understand his orders. Did he really mean us to come to Canada?"

A very angry babushka scolded back: "There's no such thing as a country where we can be of one mind unless we try, each one of us, to make it so. Our little father Verigin promised us a land where they'd let us live in peace according to our ideal of non-violence and free conscience. He didn't promise the grass would be trimmed and the house all built and the bread on the table. Have you all gone mad? Tell me! The old Doukhobors of my time put more heart in their work and whined less. And they'd seen something of cruelty and injustice, before our good Loukeria, in those dark years when they wandered over Russia. What about those who fell under the knout of the Czarist soldiers rather than take arms against their brothers? Did you ever hear that they grumbled? Shame to these Doukhobors around me!"

In the end they prayed together under the great starlit sky. At least the stars were still familiar. Their eyes raised on high, they asked for a light to guide them on their earthly path.

"Little mother, it's not the work we're afraid of. It's the silence here. It's as if God no longer wanted to give us a sign. As if from now on he would be silent forever."

The wrinkled face, furrowed by life, was absorbed in contemplation of the flames.

"It is true. Since we came to Canada he has seldom spoken to us. But he is there, behind all that silence. Just wait, my lambs. Tomorrow, the next day, one day soon, he will surely give us a sign."

II

Forty miles north of the railway a great stretch of grassy plain, formerly pastureland to a herd of buffalo, was still there for the taking. That was the destination of the expedition that set out on a certain July morning.

The heavy wagon lumbered along at the trot—often a slow one—of the four prairie horses, all small but solidly built. Six men were in the party: the three Doukhobor leaders, then McPherson, flanked by his interpreter, James Craig, and the half-breed driver. They had left at dawn accompanied by particularly fervent women's voices raised in song, for after the long evening of prayer everyone had risen with the conviction that this day, at last, would be marked by divine favour.

At first they drove across the plain where a reddish grass waved as far as you could see; then others where a thick growth of weeds rose to the wagon's axles; saline patches harboured the noxious smells of many carcasses of young deer and dead birds; brushwood country, and muskegs where everyone had to get off and help the horses; morose landscapes where there was nothing living but the wind; and, from time to time, fresh little stands of elder trees or poplar. Almost everywhere the plain seemed uninhabited and silent.

Each patch of green in this limitless landscape could be seen for miles around, and this was all that kept the tired beasts going or altered the men's unblinking stare.

Evening was not far off. Still nothing hinted that they might be nearing the former buffalo pasture. McPherson was growing worried. Had they taken the wrong fork at the last faint crossing of the ways?

No path was visible now. They were navigating by guesswork across rocky soil or through virgin grass. The half-breed driver seemed as uncertain as the little horses themselves. Their ears pricked up anxiously from time to time. The leaders, impassive in the back, pretended to ignore these disturbing developments.

Suddenly McPherson exclaimed loudly in vexation. The land was changing without warning. For in fact, on emerging from a gulley of shadows that had hemmed them in for several minutes, they were met by an intense and gleaming light. There a new landscape stood revealed, one of surprising beauty, unsuspected even a moment ago.

It was Hoodoo Valley, so named by the Indians who were frightened of its strangeness and the curious power it had—precisely at this hour of day—over the unstable souls of men.

With an exotic splendour, more reminiscent of the Orient than of the plain with its assortment of quiet shades, it flamed up before them in the floods of copper light the sun spilled over it at this day's end. Countless flowers, pushing up through brambles and tall, sharp-bladed grass, gave off a glow in that light almost not to be borne. Flowers among which not one, so people said, was without its sting, its poison sap, its capacity to wound; but all strangely sumptuous, in umbels of garnet velvet, bunched heads of sombre gold, purple or milky corollas with stiff, smooth leaves shining with their lacquer.

In the distance clouds tinted blazing red enclosed this odd valley, surrounding it as with a chain of hills whose folds held an indefinable attraction. Each one appeared to open into the reddened sky a secret and mysterious passage toward a place where certainty and happiness must reign at last. From one minute to the next, moreover, beneath the constant flaming of the sky, the more distant clouds took on further depth and issued their silent call.

McPherson, almost caught in the spell for a moment, though he'd have been the last to admit it, got hold of himself. He hated this place above all others. He was about to give the order to leave at once when the three leaders, on their feet in the back of the wagon, began encouraging each other excitedly: "Da, da!"'

This was the first time McPherson had heard them say yes.

Further words seemed torn from them by their excess of emotion and the infinite joy of being there together, all three unanimous.

"What's that they're saying?" asked McPherson.

The interpreter smiled with some commiseration.

"They want to get off here. They're talking about the Humid Mountains, something about receiving a sign at last . . . and I don't know what-all, it doesn't make much sense. . . ."

As if under a spell, they were barely recognizable, their faces lit up and transformed, their eyes gleaming. With one accord they leapt from the wagon and advanced toward the valley. Stones rolled beneath their feet, a fine dust rose from the earth where they walked, and this alone should have told them of the poverty of the soil; but the Doukhobors paid no attention, their eyes dazzled, advancing in the line toward the brilliance the setting sun had managed to extract from an inextricable tangle of thorn and thistle.

They stopped. One raised his arm and pointed to the mass of clouds resting on the sky's edge, forming enchanting hills that rolled back to beyond this world. Another pointed at the long streak of light that wound across the valley like a river of pale waters. The third fervently stared out at the fiery horizon.

"What do they say?"

"That there's all you need here to rejoice the heart of man," the interpreter said. "Mountains in the distance, a river in the grass, a rare kind of peace and birds everywhere."

True enough, for look! The burning air was filled with the presence of birds! Nesting in the serried thickets, calling from bush to bush, then, all at once, with great cries and whirring of wings, bursting into flight; creatures with flaming throats, crested with red or light yellow, thronged into the air. But these were unsociable birds and fled from men: their presence here, like that of the strange flowers, spoke further of the wildness of the place.

"But those aren't mountains yonder," McPherson tried to explain, "and that's no river in the valley. Tell them, Craig, that it's all mirage and trumpery. It's the sun and the time of day that make the cursed valley turn this way at sunset!"

But it was no use. The three Doukhobors had removed their hats as if to salute one of the most moving encounters of their lives. They stayed motionless a long time, their eyes moist, contemplating the landscape and listening to their conquered hearts.

"They know, at least I think they do," the interpreter reported, "that the mountains and rivers aren't real, but they say, 'What's the difference, as long as we can see them? And if the three of us, by God's grace, can see again in this place the mountains and rivers of our sweet homeland, why should it be any different for our wives and children and old men? Won't they see these things too? And when they've seen them, won't they be reassured, as we are?' "

Then McPherson, forgetting that they couldn't understand him, shouted: "Just scratch that soil! See how poor it is! Look at that confounded brush, it's all that'll grow here. I can give you a hundred times better, a thousand times better! I can give you lively flat fields where the grass is so tasty your horses'll whinny a mile away. Or if you want I'll find you land that's half woods and a real river running through it. Just a few hours from here, all that's waiting for you!"

But the Doukhobors would hear none of it. Beyond the call of reason now, exiled in elation, assured that they alone understood the world's mystery, they stood there, hat in hand, imagining that they had perhaps been shown an infallible sign of destiny. They took one pace forward and struck up a song of thanksgiving. The song found its way down the valley and echoed back twice, three times. The great, wild birds, and the dry leaves rustling at their passage, seemed shaken with surprise at hearing an old, exalted hymn rolling all the way from ancient Russia.

At last the three men ended their song. McPherson saw that they were weeping. Tears rushed impetuously from their eyes, washing the dust from their cheeks and disappearing in their blond moustaches. They wept without raising a hand to wipe their cheeks, in abandon and confidence, relieved once and for all of the cruelty of expectation.

McPherson waited yet awhile. Soon there would be an end to the fugitive beauty of the place. In a moment now it would be left bare: when the great footlight on the horizon dimmed, perhaps they would see that this was nothing but a wasteland under false, flamboyant colours.

But now the Doukhobors were showing their impatience to be gone. They were in a hurry to bring the good news to the others.

They sat on one side of the wagon, facing the same way. They were looking back when suddenly the valley dimmed into twilight and what was perhaps its true and poignant gloom. But in the shadow there still glowed on their inscrutable faces the flaming sky that their eyes had seen and their souls now bore away.

SHEILA WATSON

(b. 1909)

*S*heila Watson was born in New Westminster, British Columbia.
She received her B.A. (1931), teaching certificate (1932), and M.A.
(1933) from the University of British Columbia. Returning to literary
studies some 30 years later, she received her doctorate from the University of Toronto in 1965, having written her dissertation on the experimental novelist Wyndham Lewis under the supervision of the innovative
communications theorist Marshall McLuhan. From 1961 to 1975, Watson was an English professor at the University of Alberta. She is best
known for her novel **The Double Hook** (1959), which has been credited
by such postmodernist writers as Robert Kroetsch and George Bowering
with having broken new ground for writers of the Canadian West.
Watson has said that she wanted in that novel to find a technique that
would allow her fiction to be regional without sacrificing universality,
while at the same time demythologizing mistaken notions of western
Canadian society, such as the clichés of Hollywood and "Western"
novels. She succeeded in telling the story of a small western community
struggling to rediscover cohesion under the related curses of drought
and murder, in an elliptical prose that reads more like poetry than
conventional fiction. Here and in the stories of **Four Stories** (1979) can
be traced the influence of experimental prose writers such as James Joyce,
Lewis, and McLuhan. More particularly, in the content of a story like
"Antigone" can be seen the influence of Watson's early experience living
at British Columbia's Provincial Mental Hospital in New Westminster,
where her father was superintendent. Watson shows herself to be fully
committed to experimental writing in "Antigone," where both the subject
and the prose style are unconventional. As the title of this story suggests,
Watson's fiction frequently relies on a deep structure of classical Greek
myth (**The Double Hook** utilizes the **Oresteia** of Aeschylus), though
her aesthetic remains determinedly anti-realistic—less concerned with
character and narrative than with image, tone, and the more figurative,
less representational, uses of language. She has also published **And the
Four Animals** (1980), a single story distributed as a manuscript edition.

Antigone

My father ruled a kingdom on the right bank of the river. He ruled it with a firm hand and a stout heart though he was often more troubled than Moses, who was simply trying to bring a stubborn and moody people under God's yoke. My father ruled men who thought they were gods or the instruments of gods or, at very least, god-afflicted and god-pursued. He ruled Atlas who held up the sky, and Hermes who went on endless messages, and Helen who'd been hatched from an egg, and Pan the gardener, and Kallisto the bear, and too many others to mention by name. Yet my father had no thunderbolt, no trident, no helmet of darkness. His subjects were delivered bound into his hands. He merely watched over them as the hundred-handed ones watched over the dethroned Titans so that they wouldn't bother Hellas again.

Despite the care which my father took to maintain an atmosphere of sober common sense in his whole establishment, there were occasional outbursts of self-indulgence which he could not control. For instance, I have seen Helen walking naked down the narrow cement path under the chestnut trees for no better reason, I suppose, than that the day was hot and the white flowers themselves lay naked and expectant in the sunlight. And I have seen Atlas forget the sky while he sat eating the dirt which held him up. These were things which I was not supposed to see.

If my father had been as sensible through and through as he was thought to be, he would have packed me off to boarding school when I was old enough to be disciplined by men. Instead he kept me at home with my two cousins who, except for the accident of birth, might as well have been my sisters. Today I imagine people concerned with our welfare would take such an environment into account. At the time I speak of most people thought us fortunate—especially the girls whose fathers' affairs had come to an unhappy issue. I don't like to revive old scandal and I wouldn't except to deny it; but it takes only a few impertinent newcomers in any community to force open cupboards which had been decently sealed by time. However, my father was so busy setting his kingdom to rights that he let weeds grow up in his own garden.

As I said, if my father had had all his wits about him he would have sent me to boarding school—and Antigone and Ismene too. I might have fallen in love with the headmaster's daughter and Antigone might have learned that no human being can be right always. She might have found out besides that from the seeds of eternal justice grow madder flowers than any which Pan grew in the gardens of my father's kingdom.

Between the kingdom which my father ruled and the wilderness flows a river. It is this river which I am crossing now. Antigone is with me.

How often can we cross the same river, Antigone asks.

Her persistence annoys me. Besides, Heraklitos made nonsense of her question years ago. He saw a river too—the Inachos, the Kephissos, the Lethaios. The name doesn't matter. He said: See how quickly the water flows. However agile a man is, however nimbly he swims, or runs, or flies, the water slips away before him. See, even as he sets down his foot the water is displaced by the stream which crowds along in the shadow of its flight.

But after all, Antigone says, one must admit that it is the same kind of water. The oolichans run in it as they ran last year and the year before. The gulls cry above the same banks. Boats drift towards the Delta and circle back against the current to gather up the catch.

At any rate, I tell her, we're standing on a new bridge. We are standing so high that the smell of mud and river weeds passes under us out to the straits. The unbroken curve of the bridge protects the eye from details of river life. The bridge is foolproof as a clinic's passport to happiness.

The old bridge still spans the river, but the cat-walk with its cracks and knot-holes, with its gap between planking and hand-rail has been torn down. The centre arch still grinds open to let boats up and down the river, but a child can no longer be walked on it or swung out on it beyond the watergauge at the very centre of the flood.

I've known men who scorned any kind of bridge, Antigone says. Men have walked into the water, she says, or, impatient, have jumped from the bridge into the river below.

But these, I say, didn't really want to cross the river. They went Persephone's way, cradled in the current's arms, down the long halls under the pink feet of the gulls, under the booms and tow-lines, under the soft bellies of the fish.

Antigone looks at me.

There's no coming back, she says, if one goes far enough.

I know she's going to speak of her own misery and I won't listen. Only a god has the right to say: Look what I suffer. Only a god should say: What more ought I to have done for you that I have not done?

Once in winter, she says, a man walked over the river.

Taking advantage of nature, I remind her, since the river had never frozen before.

Yet he escaped from the penitentiary, she says. He escaped from the guards walking round the walls or standing with their guns in the sentry-boxes at the four corners of the enclosure. He escaped.

Not without risk, I say. He had to test the strength of the ice himself. Yet safer perhaps than if he had crossed by the old bridge where he might have slipped through a knot-hole or tumbled out through the railing.

He did escape, she persists, and lived forever on the far side of the river in the Alaska tea and bulrushes. For where, she asks, can a man go farther than to the outermost edge of the world?

The habitable world, as I've said, is on the right bank of the river.

Here is the market with its market stalls— the coops of hens, the long-tongued geese, the haltered calf, the bearded goat, the shoving pigs, and the empty bodies of cows and sheep and rabbits hanging on iron hooks. My father's kingdom provides asylum in the suburbs. Near it are the convent, the churches, and the penitentiary. Above these on the hill the cemetery looks down and on the river itself.

It is a world spread flat, tipped up into the sky so that men and women bend forward, walking as men walk when they board a ship at high tide. This is the world I feel with my feet. It is the world I see with my eyes.

I remember standing once with Antigone and Ismene in the square just outside the gates of my father's kingdom. Here from a bust set high on a cairn the stone eyes of Simon Fraser look from his stone face over the river that he found.

It is the head that counts, Ismene said.

It's no better than an urn, Antigone said, one of the urns we see when we climb to the cemetery above.

And all I could think was that I didn't want an urn, only a flat green grave with a chain about it.

A chain won't keep out the dogs, Antigone said.

But his soul could swing on it, Ismene said, like a bird blown on a branch in the wind.

And I remember Antigone's saying: The cat drags its belly on the ground and the rat sharpens its tooth in the ivy.

I should have loved Ismene, but I didn't. It was Antigone I loved. I should have loved Ismene because, although she walked the flat world with us, she managed somehow to see it round.

The earth is an oblate spheroid, she'd say. And I knew that she saw it there before her comprehensible and whole like a tangerine spiked through and held in place while it rotated on the axis of one of Nurse's steel sock needles. The earth was a tangerine and she saw the skin peeled off and the world parcelled out into neat segments, each segment sweet and fragrant in its own skin.

It's the head that counts, she said.

In her own head she made diagrams to live by, cut and fashioned after the eternal patterns spied out by Plato as he rummaged about in the sewing basket of the gods.

I should have loved Ismene. She would live now in some prefabricated and perfect chrysolite by some paradigm which made love round and whole. She would simply live and leave destruction in the purgatorial ditches outside her own walled paradise.

Antigone is different. She sees the world flat as I do and feels it tip beneath her feet. She has walked in the market and seen the living animals penned and the dead hanging stiff on their hooks. Yet she defies what she sees with a defiance which is almost denial. Like Atlas she tries to keep the vaulted sky from crushing the flat earth. Like Hermes she brings a message that there is life if one can escape to it in the brush and bulrushes in some dim Hades beyond the river. It is defiance not belief and I tell her that this time we walk the bridge to a walled cave where we can deny death no longer.

Yet she asks her questions still. And standing there I tell her that Heraklitos has made nonsense of her question. I should have loved Ismene for she would have taught me what Plato meant when he said in all earnest that the union of the soul with the body is in no way better than dissolution. I expect that she understood things which Antigone is too proud to see.

I turn away from here and flatten my elbows on the high wall of the bridge. I look back at my father's kingdom. I see the terraces rolling down from the red-brick buildings with their barred windows. I remember hands shaking the bars and hear fingers tearing up paper and stuffing it through the meshes. Diktynna, mother of nets and high leaping fear. O Artemis, mistress of wild beasts and wild men.

The inmates are beginning to come out on the screened verandas. They pace up and down in straight lines or stand silent like figures which appear at the same time each day from some depths inside a clock.

On the upper terrace Pan the gardener is shifting sprinklers with a hooked stick. His face is shadowed by the brim of his hat. He moves as economically as an animal between the beds of lobelia and geranium. It is high noon.

Antigone has cut out a piece of sod and has scooped out a grave. The body lies in a coffin in the shade of the magnolia tree. Antigone and I are standing. Ismene is sitting between two low angled branches of the monkey puzzle tree. Her lap is filled with daisies. She slits the stem of one daisy and pulls the stem of another through it. She is making a chain for her neck and a crown for her hair.

Antigone reaches for a branch of the magnolia. It is almost beyond her grip. The buds flame above her. She stands on a small fire of daisies which smoulder in the roots of grass.

I see the magnolia buds. They brood above me, whiteness feathered on whiteness. I see Antigone's face turned to the light. I hear the living birds call to the sun. I speak private poetry to myself: Between four trumpeting angels at the four corners of the earth a bride stands before the altar in a gown as white as snow.

Yet I must have been speaking aloud because Antigone challenges me: You're mistaken. It's the winds the angels hold, the four winds of the earth. After the just are taken to paradise the winds will destroy the earth. It's a funeral, she says, not a wedding.

She looks towards the building.

Someone is coming down the path from the matron's house, she says.

I notice that she has pulled one of the magnolia blossoms from the branch. I take it from her. It is streaked with brown where her hands have bruised it. The sparrow which she has decided to bury lies on its back. Its feet are clenched tight against the feathers of its breast. I put the flower in the box with it.

Someone is coming down the path. She is wearing a blue cotton dress. Her cropped head is bent. She walks slowing carrying something in a napkin.

It's Kallisto the bear, I say. Let's hurry. What will my father say if he sees us talking to one of his patients?

If we live here with him, Antigone says, what can he expect? If he spends his life trying to tame people he can't complain if you behave as if they were tame. What would your father think, she says, if he saw us digging in the Institution lawn?

Pan comes closer. I glower at him. There's no use speaking to him. He's deaf and dumb.

Listen, I say to Antigone, my father's not unreasonable. Kallisto thinks she's a bear and he thinks he's a bear tamer, that's all. As for the lawn, I say quoting my father without conviction, a man must have order among his own if he is to keep order in the state.

Kallisto has come up to us. She is smiling and laughing to herself. She gives me her bundle.

Fish, she says.

I open the napkin.

Pink fish sandwiches, I say.

For the party, she says.

But it isn't a party, Antigone says. It's a funeral.

For the funeral breakfast, I say.

Ismene is twisting two chains of daisies into a rope. Pan has stopped pulling the sprinkler about. He is standing beside Ismene resting himself on his hooked stick. Kallisto squats down beside her. Ismene turns away, preoccupied, but she can't turn far because of Pan's legs.

> *Father said we never should*
> *Play with madmen in the wood.*

I look at Antigone.

It's my funeral, she says.

I go over to Ismene and gather up a handful of loose daisies from her lap. The sun reaches through the shadow of the magnolia tree.

It's my funeral, Antigone says. She moves possessively toward the body.

An ant is crawling into the bundle of sandwiches which I've put on the ground. A file of ants is marching on the sparrow's box.

I go over and drop daisies on the bird's stiff body. My voice speaks ritual words: Deliver me, O Lord, from everlasting death on this dreadful day. I tremble and am afraid.

The voice of a people comforts me. I look at Antigone. I look her in the eye.

It had better be a proper funeral then, I say.

Kallisto is crouched forward on her hands. Tears are running down her cheeks and she is licking them away with her tongue.

My voice rises again: I said in the midst of my days, I shall not see—

Antigone just stands there. She looks frightened, but her eyes defy me with their assertion.

It's my funeral, she says. It's my bird. I was the one who wanted to bury it.

She is looking for a reason. She will say something which sounds eternally right.

Things have to be buried, she says. They can't be left lying around anyhow for people to see.

Birds shouldn't die, I tell her. They have wings. Cats and rats haven't wings.

Stop crying, she says to Kallisto. It's only a bird.

It has a bride's flower in its hand, Kallisto says.

We shall rise again, I mutter, but we shall not all be changed.

Antigone does not seem to hear me.

Behold, I say in a voice she must hear, in a moment, in the twinkling of an eye, the trumpet shall sound.

Ismene turns to Kallisto and throws the daisy chain about her neck.

Shall a virgin forget her adorning or a bride the ornament of her breast?

Kallisto is lifting her arms towards the tree.

The bridegroom has come, she says, white as a fall of snow. He stands above me in a great ring of fire.

Antigone looks at me now.

Let's cover the bird up, she says. Your father will punish us all for making a disturbance.

He has on his garment, Kallisto says, and on his thigh is written King of Kings.

I look at the tree. If I could see with Kallisto's eyes I wouldn't be afraid of death, or punishment, or the penitentiary guards. I wouldn't be afraid of my father's belt or his honing strap or his bedroom slipper. I wouldn't be afraid of falling into the river through a knot-hole in the bridge.

But, as I look, I see the buds falling like burning lamps and I hear the sparrow twittering in its box: Woe, woe, woe because of the three trumpets which are yet to sound.

Kallisto is on her knees. She is growling like a bear. She lumbers over to the sandwiches and mauls them with her paw.

Ismene stands alone for Pan the gardener has gone.

Antigone is fitting a turf in place above the coffin. I go over and press the edge of the turf with my feet. Ismene has caught me by the hand.

Go away, Antigone says.

I see my father coming down the path. He has an attendant with him. In front of them walks Pan holding the sprinkler hook like a spear.

What are you doing here? my father asks.

Burying a bird, Antigone says.

Here? my father asks again.

Where else could I bury it? Antigone says.

My father looks at her.

This ground is public property, he says. No single person has any right to an inch of it.

I've taken six inches, Antigone says. Will you dig the bird up again?

Some of his subjects my father restrained since they were moved to throw themselves from high places or to tear one another to bits from jealousy or rage. Others who disturbed the public peace he taught to walk in the airing courts or to work in the kitchen or in the garden.

If men live at all, my father said, it is because discipline saves their life for them.

From Antigone he simply turned away.

Eudora Welty

(b. 1909)

E udora Welty was born in Jackson, Mississippi. She was educated at Mississippi State College and the University of Wisconsin, where she studied English literature and from which she received a B.A. in 1929. She enrolled in the School of Business at Columbia and worked writing advertisements in New York, but the Depression forced her to return to Mississippi in 1931. Her jobs in journalism and with various government agencies enabled her to acquire the experience that she began to transpose into stories. By 1940 she had published in The Southern Review and The Atlantic Monthly; in 1941 her first book of stories, A Curtain of Green, was published. The next collection followed in 1946, as did her first novel, Delta Wedding. Her reputation has grown apace since that time. Her Collected Stories (1980) and One Writer's Beginnings (1984) have enabled younger readers to become acquainted with this writer, who is, as one of her critics has said, "in happy possession of a supple, clear, and sympathetic mind and sensibility," and who has used that mind to fashion a body of work that has gained the world's attention and respect. She has been writer-in-residence at numerous universities and has published helpful commentary on others' fiction and her own work. Here is an excerpt from a discussion of the following story, "No Place for You, My Love":

> I did my best to merge, or even to identify, the abstract with the concrete as it became possible in this story. . . . Above all, I had no wish to sound mystical, but I admit that I did expect to sound mysterious now and then, if I could: this was a circumstantial, realistic story in which the reality was mystery. . . . Relationship is a pervading and changing mystery; it is not words that make it so in life, but words have to make it so in a story. Brutal or lovely, the mystery waits for people wherever they go, whatever extreme they run to.

No Place for You, My Love

They were strangers to each other, both fairly well strangers to the place, now seated side by side at luncheon—a party combined in a free-and-easy way when the friends he and she were with recognized each other across Galatoire's. The time was a Sunday in summer—those hours of afternoon that seem Time Out in New Orleans.

The moment he saw her little blunt, fair face, he thought that here was a woman who was having an affair. It was one of those odd meetings when such an impact is felt that it has to be translated at once into some sort of speculation.

With a married man, most likely, he supposed, slipping quickly into a groove—he was long married—and feeling more conventional, then, in his curiosity as she sat there, leaning her cheek on her hand, looking no further before her than the flowers on the table, and wearing that hat.

He did not like her hat, any more than he liked tropical flowers. It was the wrong hat for her, thought this Eastern businessman who had no interest whatever in women's clothes and no eye for them; he thought the unaccustomed thing crossly.

It must stick out all over me, she thought, so people think they can love me or hate me just by looking at me. How did it leave us—the old, safe, slow way people used to know of learning how one another feels, and the privilege that went with it of shying away if it seemed best? People in love like me, I suppose, give away the short cuts to everybody's secrets.

Something, though, he decided, had been settled about her predica-ment—for the time being, anyway; the parties to it were all still alive, no doubt. Nevertheless, her predicament was the only one he felt so sure of here, like the only recognizable shadow in that restaurant, where mirrors and fans were busy agitating the light, as the very local talk drawled across and agitated the peace. The shadow lay between her fingers, between her little square hand and her cheek, like something always best carried about the person. Then suddenly, as she took her hand down, the secret fact was still there—it lighted her. It was a bold and full light, shot up under the brim of that hat, as close to them all as the flowers in the center of the table.

Did he dream of making her disloyal to that hopelessness that he saw very well she'd been cultivating down here? He knew very well that he did not. What they amounted to was two Northerners keeping each other company. She glanced up at the big gold clock on the wall and smiled. He didn't smile back. She had that naïve face that he associated, for no good reason, with the Middle West—because it said "Show me," perhaps.

It was a serious, now-watch-out-everybody face, which orphaned her entirely in the company of these Southerners. He guessed her age, as he could not guess theirs: thirty-two. He himself was further along.

Of all human moods, deliberate imperviousness may be the most quickly communicated—it may be the most successful, most fatal signal of all. And two people can indulge in imperviousness as well as in anything else. "You're not very hungry either," he said.

The blades of fan shadows came down over their two heads, as he saw inadvertently in the mirror, with himself smiling at her now like a villain. His remark sounded dominant and rude enough for everybody present to listen back a moment; it even sounded like an answer to a question she might have just asked him. The other women glanced at him. The Southern look—Southern mask—of life-is-a-dream irony, which could turn to pure challenge at the drop of a hat, he could wish well away. He liked naïveté better.

"I find the heat down here depressing," she said, with the heart of Ohio in her voice.

"Well—I'm in somewhat of a temper about it, too," he said.

They looked with grateful dignity at each other.

"I have a car here, just down the street," he said to her as the luncheon party was rising to leave, all the others wanting to get back to their houses and sleep. "If it's all right with— Have you ever driven down south of here?"

Out on Bourbon Street, in the bath of July, she asked at his shoulder, "South of New Orleans? I didn't know there was any south to *here*. Does it just go on and on?" She laughed, and adjusted the exasperating hat to her head in a different way. It was more than frivolous, it was conspicuous, with some sort of glitter or flitter tied in a band around the straw and hanging down.

"That's what I'm going to show you."

"Oh—you've been there?"

"No!"

His voice rang out over the uneven, narrow sidewalk and dropped back from the walls. The flaked-off, colored houses were spotted like the hides of beasts faded and shy, and were hot as a wall of growth that seemed to breathe flower-like down onto them as they walked to the car parked there.

"It's just that it couldn't be any worse—we'll see."

"All right, then," she said. "We will."

So, their actions reduced to amiability, they settled into the car—a faded-red Ford convertible with a rather threadbare canvas top, which had been standing in the sun for all those lunch hours.

"It's rented," he explained. "I asked to have the top put down, and was told I'd lost my mind."

"It's out of this world. *Degrading* heat," she said and added, "Doesn't matter."

The stranger in New Orleans always sets out to leave it as though following the clue in a maze. They were threading through the narrow and one-way streets, past the pale-violet bloom of tired squares, the brown steeples and statues, the balcony with the live and probably famous black monkey dipping along the railing as over a ballroom floor, past the grillework and the lattice-work to all the iron swans painted flesh color on the front steps of bungalows outlying.

Driving, he spread his new map and put his finger down on it. At the intersection marked Arabi, where their road led out of the tangle and he took it, a small Negro seated beneath a black umbrella astride a box chalked "Shou Shine" lifted his pink-and-black hand and waved them languidly good-by. She didn't miss it, and waved back.

Below New Orleans there was a raging of insects from both sides of the concrete highway, not quite together, like the playing of separated marching bands. The river and the levee were still on her side, waste and jungle and some occasional settlements on his—poor houses. Families bigger than housefuls thronged the yards. His nodding, driving head would veer from side to side, looking and almost lowering. As time passed and the distance from New Orleans grew, girls ever darker and younger were disposing themselves over the porches and the porch steps, with jet-black hair pulled high, and ragged palm-leaf fans rising and falling like rafts of butterflies. The children running forth were nearly always naked ones.

She watched the road. Crayfish constantly crossed in front of the wheels, looking firm and bonneted, in a great hurry.

"How the Old Woman Got Home," she murmured to herself.

He pointed, as it flew by, at a saucepan full of cut zinnias which stood waiting on the open lid of a mailbox at the roadside, with a little note tied onto the handle.

They rode mostly in silence. The sun bore down. They met fishermen and other men bent on some local pursuits, some in sulphur-colored pants, walking and riding; met wagons, trucks, boats in trucks, autos, boats on top of autos—all coming to meet them, as though something of high moment were doing back where the car came from, and he and she were determined to miss it. There was nearly always a man lying with his shoes off in the bed of any truck otherwise empty—with the raw, red look of a man sleeping in the daytime, being jolted about as he slept. Then there was a sort of dead man's land, where nobody came. He loosened his collar and tie. By rushing through the heat at high speed, they brought themselves the effect of fans turned onto their cheeks.

Clearing alternated with jungle and canebrake like something tried, tried again. Little shell roads led off on both sides; now and then a road of planks led into the yellow-green.

"Like a dance floor in there." She pointed.

He informed her, "In there's your oil, I think."

There were thousands, millions of mosquitoes and gnats—a universe of them, and on the increase.

A family of eight or nine people on foot strung along the road in the same direction the car was going, beating themselves with the wild palmettos. Heels, shoulders, knees, breasts, back of the heads, elbows, hands, were touched in turn—like some game, each playing it with himself.

He struck himself on the forehead, and increased their speed. (His wife would not be at her most charitable if he came bringing malaria home to the family.)

More and more crayfish and other shell creatures littered their path, scuttling or dragging. These little samples, little jokes of creation, persisted and sometimes perished, the more of them the deeper down the road went. Terrapins and turtles came up steadily over the horizons of the ditches.

Back there in the margins were worse—crawling hides you could not penetrate with bullets or quite believe, grins that had come down from the primeval mud.

"Wake up." Her Northern nudge was very timely on his arm. They had veered toward the side of the road. Still driving fast, he spread his map.

Like a misplaced sunrise, the light of the river flowed up; they were mounting the levee on a little shell road.

"Shall we cross here?" he asked politely.

He might have been keeping track over years and miles of how long they could keep that tiny ferry waiting. Now skidding down the levee's flank, they were the last-minute car, the last possible car that could squeeze on. Under the sparse shade of one willow tree, the small, amateurish-looking boat slapped the water, as, expertly, he wedged on board.

"Tell him we put him on hub cap!" shouted one of the numerous olive-skinned, dark-eyed young boys standing dressed up in bright shirts at the railing, hugging each other with delight that that last straw was on board. Another boy drew his affectionate initials in the dust of the door on her side.

She opened the door and stepped out, and, after only a moment's standing at bay, started up a little iron stairway. She appeared above the car, on the tiny bridge beneath the captain's window and the whistle.

From there, while the boat still delayed in what seemed a trance—as if it were too full to attempt the start—she could see the panlike deck below, separated by its rusty rim from the tilting, polished water.

The passengers walking and jostling about there appeared oddly amateurish, too—amateur travelers. They were having such a good time. They all knew each other. Beer was being passed around in cans, bets were being loudly settled and new bets made, about local and special subjects on which they all doted. One red-haired man in a burst of wildness even tried to give away his truckload of shrimp to a man on the other side of the boat—nearly all the trucks were full of shrimp—causing taunts and then protests of "They good! They good!" from the giver. The young boys leaned on each other thinking of what next, rolling their eyes absently.

A radio pricked the air behind her. Looking like a great tomcat just above her head, the captain was digesting the news of a fine stolen automobile.

At last a tremendous explosion burst—the whistle. Everything shuddered in outline from the sound, everybody said something—everybody else.

They started with no perceptible motion, but her hat blew off. It went spiraling to the deck below, where he, thank heaven, sprang out of the car and picked it up. Everybody looked frankly up at her now, holding her hands to her head.

The little willow tree receded as its shade was taken away. The heat was like something falling on her head. She held the hot rail before her. It was like riding a stove. Her shoulders dropping, her hair flying, her skirt buffeted by the sudden strong wind, she stood there, thinking they all must see that with her entire self all she did was wait. Her set hands, with the bag that hung from her wrist and rocked back and forth—all three seemed objects bleaching there, belonging to no one; she could not feel a thing in the skin of her face; perhaps she was crying, and not knowing it. She could look down and see him just below her, his black shadow, her hat, and his black hair. His hair in the wind looked unreasonably long and rippling. Little did he know that from here it had a red undergleam like an animal's. When she looked up and outward, a vortex of light drove through and over the brown waves like a star in the water.

He did after all bring the retrieved hat up the stairs to her. She took it back—useless—and held it to her skirt. What they were saying below was more polite than their searchlight faces.

"Where you think he come from, that man?"

"I bet he come from Lafitte."

"Lafitte? What you bet, eh?"—all crouched in the shade of trucks, squatting and laughing.

Now his shadow fell partly across her; the boat had jolted into some other strand of current. Her shaded arm and shaded hand felt pulled out from the blaze of light and water, and she hoped humbly for more shade for her head. It had seemed so natural to climb up and stand in the sun.

The boys had a surprise—an alligator on board. One of them pulled it by a chain around the deck, between the cars and trucks, like a toy— a hide that could walk. He thought, Well they had to catch one sometime. It's Sunday afternoon. So they have him on board now, riding him across the Mississippi River. . . . The playfulness of it beset everybody on the ferry. The hoarseness of the boat whistle, commenting briefly, seemed part of the general appreciation.

"Who want to rassle him? Who want to, eh?" two boys cried, looking up. A boy with shrimp-colored arms capered from side to side, pretending to have been bitten.

What was there so hilarious about jaws that could bite? And what danger was there once in this repulsiveness—so that the last worldly evidence of some old heroic horror of the dragon had to be paraded in capture before the eyes of country clowns?

He noticed that she looked at the alligator without flinching at all. Her distance was set—the number of feet and inches between herself and it mattered to her.

Perhaps her measuring coolness was to him what his bodily shade was to her, while they stood pat up there riding the river, which felt like the sea and looked like the earth under them—full of the red-brown earth, charged with it. Ahead of the boat it was like an exposed vein of ore. The river seemed to swell in the vast middle with the curve of the earth. The sun rolled under them. As if in memory of the size of things, uprooted trees were drawn across their path, sawing at the air and tumbling one over the other.

When they reached the other side, they felt that they had been racing around an arena in their chariot, among lions. The whistle took and shook the stairs as they went down. The young boys, looking taller, had taken out colored combs and were combing their wet hair back in solemn pompadour above their radiant foreheads. They had been bathing in the river themselves not long before.

The cars and trucks, then the foot passengers and the alligator, wad- dling like a child to school, all disembarked and wound up the weed- sprung levee.

Both respectable and merciful, their hides, she thought, forcing her- self to dwell on the alligator as she looked back. Deliver us all from the naked in heart. (As she had been told.)

When they regained their paved road, he heard her give a little sigh and saw her turn her straw-colored head to look back once more. Now that she rode with her hat in her lap, her earrings were conspicuous too. A little metal ball set with small pale stones danced beside each square, faintly downy cheek.

Had she felt a wish for someone else to be riding with them? He thought it was more likely that she would wish for her husband if she had one (his wife's voice) than for the lover in whom he believed. Whatever people liked to think, situations (if not scenes) were usually three-way—there was somebody else always. The one who didn't—couldn't—understand the two made the formidable third.

He glanced down at the map flapping on the seat between them, up at his wristwatch, out at the road. Out there was the incredible brightness of four o'clock.

On this side of the river, the road ran beneath the brow of the levee and followed it. Here was a heat that ran deeper and brighter and more intense than all the rest—its nerve. The road grew one with the heat as it was one with the unseen river. Dead snakes stretched across the concrete like markers—inlaid mosaic bands, dry as feathers, which their tires licked at intervals that began to seem clocklike.

No, the heat faced them—it was ahead. They could see it waving at them, shaken in the air above the white of the road, always at a certain distance ahead, shimmering finely as a cloth, with running edges of green and gold, fire and azure.

"It's never anything like this in Syracuse," he said.

"Or in Toledo, either," she replied with dry lips.

They were driving through greater waste down here, through fewer and even more insignificant towns. There was water under everything. Even where a screen of jungle had been left to stand, splashes could be heard from under the trees. In the vast open, sometimes boats moved inch by inch through what appeared endless meadows of rubbery flowers.

Her eyes overcome with brightness and size, she felt a panic rise, as sudden as nausea. Just how far below questions and answers, concealment and revelation, they were running now—that was still a new question, with a power of its own, waiting. How dear—how costly—could this ride be?

"It looks to me like your road can't go much further," she remarked cheerfully. "Just over there, it's all water."

"Time out," he said, and with that he turned the car into a sudden road of white shells that rushed at them narrowly out of the left.

They bolted over a cattle guard, where some rayed and crested purple flowers burst out of the vines in the ditch, and rolled onto a long, narrow, green, mowed clearing: a churchyard. A paved track ran between two short rows of raised tombs, all neatly white-washed and now brilliant as faces against the vast flushed sky.

The track was the width of the car with a few inches to spare. He passed between the tombs slowly but in the manner of a feat. Names took their places on the walls slowly at a level with the eye, names as near as the eyes of a person stopping in conversation, and as far away in origin, and in all their music and dead longing, as Spain. At intervals were set packed bouquets of zinnias, oleanders, and some kind of purple flowers, all quite fresh, in fruit jars, like nice welcomes on bureaus.

They moved on into an open plot beyond, of violent-green grass, spread before the green-and-white frame church with worked flower beds around it, flowerless poinsettias growing up to the windowsills. Beyond was a house, and left on the doorstep of the house a fresh caught catfish the size of a baby—a fish wearing whiskers and bleeding. On a clothesline in the yard, a priest's black gown on a hanger hung airing, swaying at man's height, in a vague, trainlike, ladylike sweep along an evening breath that might otherwise have seemed imaginary from the unseen, felt river.

With the motor cut off, with the raging of the insects about them, they sat looking out at the green and white and black and red and pink as they leaned against the sides of the car.

"What is your wife like?" she asked. His right hand came up and spread—iron, wooden, manicured. She lifted her eyes to his face. He looked at her like that hand.

Then he lit a cigarette, and the portrait, and the right-hand testimonial it made, were blown away. She smiled, herself as unaffected as by some stage performance; and he was annoyed in the cemetery. They did not risk going on to her husband—if she had one.

Under the supporting posts of the priest's house, where a boat was, solid ground ended and palmettos and what hyacinths could not wait to begin; suddenly the rays of the sun, from behind the car, reached that lowness and struck the flowers. The priest came out onto the porch in his underwear, stared at the car a moment as if he wondered what time it was, then collected his robe off the line and his fish off the doorstep and returned inside. Vespers was next, for him.

After backing out between the tombs he drove on still south, in the sunset. They caught up with an old man walking in a sprightly way in their direction, all by himself, wearing a clean bright shirt printed with a pair of palm trees fanning green over his chest. It might better be a big colored woman's shirt, but she didn't have it. He flagged the car with gestures like hoops.

"You're coming to the end of the road," the old man told them. He pointed ahead, tipped his hat to the lady, and pointed again. "End of the road." They didn't understand that he meant, "Take me."

They drove on. "If we do go any further, it'll have to be by water— is that it?" he asked her, hesitating at this odd point.

"You know better than I do," she replied politely.

The road had for some time ceased to be paved; it was made of shells. It was leading into a small, sparse settlement like the others a few miles back, but with even more of the camp about it. On the lip of the clearing, directly before a green willow blaze with the sunset gone behind it, the row of houses and shacks faced out on broad, colored, moving water that stretched to reach the horizon and looked like an arm of the sea. The houses on their shaggy posts, patchily built, some with plank runways instead of steps, were flimsy and alike, and not much bigger than the boats tied up at the landing.

"Venice," she heard him announce, and he dropped the crackling map in her lap.

They coasted down the brief remainder. The end of the road—she could not remember ever seeing a road simply end—was a spoon shape, with a tree stump in the bowl to turn around by.

Around it, he stopped the car, and they stepped out, feeling put down in the midst of a sudden vast pause or subduement that was like a yawn. They made their way on foot toward the water, where at an idle-looking landing men in twos and threes stood with their backs to them.

The nearness of darkness, the still uncut trees, bright water partly under a sheet of flowers, shacks, silence, dark shapes of boats tied up, then the first sounds of people just on the other side of thin walls—all this reached them. Mounds of shells like day-old snow, pink-tinted, lay around a central shack with a beer sign on it. An old man up on the porch there sat holding an open newspaper, with a fat white goose sitting opposite him on the floor. Below, in the now shadowless and sunless open, another old man, with a colored pencil bright under his hat brim, was late mending a sail.

When she looked clear around, thinking they had a fire burning somewhere now, out of the heat had risen the full moon. Just beyond the trees, enormous, tangerine-colored, it was going solidly up. Other lights just striking into view, looking farther distant, showed moss shapes hanging, or slipped and broke matchlike on the water that so encroached upon the rim of ground they were standing on.

There was a touch at her arm—his, accidental.

"We're at the jumping-off place," he said.

She laughed, having thought his hand was a bat, while her eyes rushed downward toward a great pale drift of water hyacinths—still partly open, flushed and yet moonlit, level with her feet—through which paths of water for the boats had been hacked. She drew her hands up to her face under the brim of her hat; her own cheeks felt like the hyacinths to her, all her skin still full of too much light and sky, exposed. The harsh vesper bell was ringing.

"I believe there must be something wrong with me, that I came on this excursion to begin with," she said, as if he had already said this and she were merely in hopeful, willing, maddening agreement with him.

He took hold of her arm, and said, "Oh come on—I see we can get something to drink here, at least."

But there was a beating, muffled sound from over the darkening water. One more boat was coming in, making its way through the tenacious, tough, dark flower traps, by the shaken light of what first appeared to be torches. He and she waited for the boat, as if on each other's patience. As if borne in on a mist of twilight or a breath, a horde of mosquitoes and gnats came singing and striking at them first. The boat bumped, men laughed. Somebody was offering somebody else some shrimp.

Then he might have cocked his dark city head down at her; she did not look up at him, only turned when he did. Now the shell mounds, like the shacks and trees, were solid purple. Lights had appeared in the not-quite-true window squares. A narrow neon sign, the lone sign, had come out in bright blush on the beer shack's roof: "Baba's Place." A light was on on the porch.

The barnlike interior was brightly lit and unpainted, looking not quite finished, with a partition dividing this room from what lay behind. One of the four cardplayers at a table in the middle of the floor was the newspaper reader; the paper was in his pants pocket. Midway along the partition was a bar, in the form of a pass-through to the other room, with a varnished, second-hand fretwork overhang. They crossed the floor and sat, alone there, on wooden stools. An eruption of humorous signs, newspaper cutouts and cartoons, razor-blade cards, and personal messages of significance to the owner or his friends decorated the overhang, framing where Baba should have been but wasn't.

Through there came a smell of garlic and cloves and red pepper, a blast of hot cloud escaped from a cauldron they could see now on a stove at the back of the other room. A massive back, presumably female, with a twist of gray hair on top, stood with a ladle akimbo. A young man joined her and with his fingers stole something out of the pot and ate it. At Baba's they were boiling shrimp.

When he got ready to wait on them, Baba strolled out to the counter, young, black-headed, and in very good humor.

"Coldest beer you've got. And food—What will you have?"

"Nothing for me, thank you," she said. "I'm not sure I could eat, after all."

"Well, I could," he said, shoving his jaw out. Baba smiled. "I want a good solid ham sandwich."

"I could have asked him for some water," she said, after he had gone.

While they sat waiting, it seemed very quiet. The bubbling of the shrimp, the distant laughing of Baba, and the slap of cards, like the beating of moths on the screens, seemed to come in fits and starts. The steady breathing they heard came from a big rough dog asleep in the corner. But it was bright. Electric lights were strung riotously over the room from a kind of spider web of old wires in the rafters. One of the written messages tacked before them read, "Joe! At the boyy!!" It looked very yellow, older than Baba's Place. Outside, the world was pure dark.

Two little boys, almost alike, almost the same size, and just cleaned up, dived into the room with a double bang of the screen door, and circled around the card game. They ran their hands into the men's pockets.

"Nickel for some pop!"

"Nickel for some pop!"

"Go 'way and let me play, you!"

They circled around and shrieked at the dog, ran under the lid of the counter and raced through the kitchen and back, and hung over the stools at the bar. One child had a live lizard on his shirt, clinging like a breast pin—like lapis lazuli.

Bringing in a strong odor of geranium talcum, some men had come in now—all in bright shirts. They drew near the counter, or stood and watched the game.

When Baba came out bringing the beer and sandwich, "Could I have some water?" she greeted him.

Baba laughed at everybody. She decided the woman back there must be Baba's mother.

Beside her, he was drinking his beer and eating his sandwich—ham, cheese, tomato, pickle, and mustard. Before he finished, one of the men who had come in beckoned from across the room. It was the old man in the palm-tree shirt.

She lifted her head to watch him leave her, and was looked at, from all over the room. As a minute passed, no cards were laid down. In a far-off way, like accepting the light from Arcturus, she accepted it that she was more beautiful or perhaps more fragile than the women they saw every day of their lives. It was just this thought coming into a woman's face, and at this hour, that seemed familiar to them.

Baba was smiling. He had set an opened, frosted brown bottle before her on the counter, and a thick sandwich, and stood looking at her. Baba made her eat some supper, for what she was.

"What the old fellow wanted," said he when he came back at last, "was to have a friend of his apologize. Seems church is just out. Seems the friend made a remark coming in just now. His pals told him there was a lady present."

"I see you bought him a beer," she said.

"Well, the old man looked like he wanted *something.*"

All at once the juke box interrupted from back in the corner, with the same old song as anywhere. The half-dozen slot machines along the wall were suddenly all run to like Maypoles, and thrown into action—taken over by further battalions of little boys.

There were three little boys to each slot machine. The local custom appeared to be that one pulled the lever for the friend he was holding up to put the nickel in, while the third covered the pictures with the flat of his hand as they fell into place, so as to surprise them all if anything happened.

The dog lay sleeping on in front of the raging juke box, his ribs working fast as a concertina's. At the side of the room a man with a cap on his white thatch was trying his best to open a side screen door, but it was stuck fast. It was he who had come in with the remark considered ribald; now he was trying to get out the other way. Moths as thick as ingots were trying to get in. The cardplayers broke into shouts of derision, then joy, then tired derision among themselves; they might have been here all afternoon—they were the only ones not cleaned up and shaved. The original pair of little boys ran in once more, with the hyphenated bang. They got nickels this time, then were brushed away from the table like mosquitoes, and they rushed under the counter and on to the cauldron behind, clinging to Baba's mother there. The evening was at the threshold.

They were quite unnoticed now. He was eating another sandwich, and she, having finished part of hers, was fanning her face with her hat. Baba had lifted the flap of the counter and come out into the room. Behind his head there was a sign lettered in orange crayon: "Shrimp Dance Sun. PM." That was tonight, still to be.

And suddenly she made a move to slide down from her stool, maybe wishing to walk out into that nowhere down the front steps to be cool a moment. But he had hold of her hand. He got down from his stool, and, patiently, reversing her hand in his own—just as she had had the look of being about to give up, faint—began moving her, leading her. They were dancing.

"I get to thinking this is what we get—what you and I deserve," she whispered, looking past his shoulder into the room. "And all the time, it's real. It's a real place—away off down here. . . ."

They danced gratefully, formally, to some song carried on in what must be the local patois, while no one paid any attention as long as they were together, and the children poured the family nickels steadily into the slot machines, walloping the handles down with regular crashes and troubling nobody with winning.

She said rapidly, as they began moving together too well, "One of those clippings was an account of a shooting right here. I guess they're proud of it. And that awful knife Baba was carrying . . . I wonder what he called me," she whispered in his ear.

"Who?"

"The one who apologized to you."

If they had ever been going to overstep themselves, it would be now as he held her closer and turned her, when she became aware that he could not help but see the bruise at her temple. It would not be six inches from his eyes. She felt it come out like an evil star. (Let it pay him back, then, for the hand he had stuck in her face when she'd tried once to be sympathetic, when she'd asked about his wife.) They danced on still as the record changed, after standing wordless and motionless, linked together in the middle of the room, for the moment between.

Then, they were like a matched team—like professional, Spanish dancers wearing masks—while the slow piece was playing.

Surely even those immune from the world, for the time being, need the touch of one another, or all is lost. Their arms encircling each other, their bodies circling the odorous, just-nailed-down floor, they were, at last, imperviousness in motion. They had found it, and had almost missed it: they had had to dance. They were what their separate hearts desired that day, for themselves and each other.

They were so good together that once she looked up and half smiled. "For whose benefit did we have to show off?"

Like people in love, they had a superstition about themselves almost as soon as they came out on the floor, and dared not think the words "happy" or "unhappy," which might strike them, one or the other, like lightning.

In the thickening heat they danced on while Baba himself sang with the mosquito-voiced singer in the chorus of *"Moi pas l'aimez ça,"* enumerating the *ça's* with a hot shrimp between his fingers. He was counting over the platters the old woman now set out on the counter, each heaped with shrimp in their shells boiled to iridescence, like mounds of honeysuckle flowers.

The goose wandered in from the back room under the lid of the counter and hitched itself around the floor among the table legs and people's legs, never seeing that it was neatly avoided by two dancers—who nevertheless vaguely thought of this goose as learned, having earlier heard an old man read to it. The children called Mimi, and lured it away. The old thatched man was again drunkenly trying to get out by the stuck side door; now he gave it a kick, but was prevailed on to remain. The sleeping dog shuddered and snored.

It was left up to the dancers to provide nickels for the juke box; Baba kept a drawerful for every use. They had grown fond of all the selections by now. This was the music you heard out of the distance at night—out of the roadside taverns you fled past, around the late corners in cities half asleep, drifting up from the carnival over the hill, with one odd little strain always managing to repeat itself. This seemed a homey place.

Bathed in sweat, and feeling the false coolness that brings, they stood finally on the porch in the lapping night air for a moment before leaving. The first arrivals of the girls were coming up the steps under the porch light—all flowered fronts, their black pompadours giving out breathlike feelers from sheer abundance. Where they'd resprinkled it since church, the talcum shone like mica on their downy arms. Smelling solidly of geranium, they filed across the porch with short steps and fingers joined, just timed to turn their smiles loose inside the room. He held the door open for them.

"Ready to go?" he asked her.

Going back, the ride was wordless, quiet except for the motor and the insects driving themselves against the car. The windshield was soon blinded. The headlights pulled in two other spinning storms, cones of flying things that, it seemed, might ignite at the last minute. He stopped the car and got out to clean the windshield thoroughly with his brisk, angry motions of driving. Dust lay thick and cratered on the roadside scrub. Under the now ash-white moon, the world traveled through very faint stars—very many slow stars, very high, very low.

It was a strange land, amphibious—and whether water-covered or grown with jungle or robbed entirely of water and trees, as now, it had the same loneliness. He regarded the great sweep—like steppes, like moors, like deserts (all of which were imaginary to him); but more than it was like any likeness, it was South. The vast, thin, wide-thrown, pale, unfocused star-sky, with its veils of lightning adrift, hung over this land as it hung over the open sea. Standing out in the night alone, he was struck as powerfully with recognition of the extremity of this place as if all other bearings had vanished—as if snow had suddenly started to fall.

He climbed back inside and drove. When he moved to slap furiously at his shirtsleeves, she shivered in the hot, licking night wind that their speed was making. Once the car lights picked out two people—a Negro couple, sitting on two facing chairs in the yard outside their lonely cabin—half undressed, each battling for self against the hot night, with long white rags in endless, scarflike motions.

In peopleless open places there were lakes of dust, smudge fires burning at their hearts. Cows stood in untended rings around them, motionless in the heat, in the night—their horns standing up sharp against that glow.

At length, he stopped the car again, and this time he put his arm under her shoulder and kissed her—not knowing even whether gently or harshly. It was the loss of that distinction that told him this was now. Then their faces touched unkissing, unmoving, dark, for a length of time. The heat came inside the car and wrapped them still, and the mosquitoes had begun to coat their arms and even their eyelids.

Later, crossing a large open distance, he saw at the same time two fires. He had the feeling that they had been riding for a long time across a face—great, wide, and upturned. In its eyes and open mouth were those fires they had had glimpses of, where the cattle had drawn together: a face, a head, far down here in the South—south of South, below it. A whole giant body sprawled downward then, on and on, always, constant as a constellation or an angel. Flaming and perhaps falling, he thought.

She appeared to be sound asleep, lying back flat as a child, with her hat in her lap. He drove on with her profile beside his, behind his, for he bent forward to drive faster. The earrings she wore twinkled with their rushing motion in an almost regular beat. They might have spoken like tongues. He looked straight before him and drove on, at a speed that, for the rented, overheated, not at all new Ford car, was demoniac.

It seemed often now that a barnlike shape flashed by, roof and all outlined in lonely neon—a movie house at a crossroads. The long white flat road itself, since they had followed it to the end and turned around to come back, seemed able, this far up, to pull them home.

A thing is incredible, if ever, only after it is told—returned to the world it came out of. For their different reasons, he thought, neither of them would tell this (unless something was dragged out of them): that, strangers, they had ridden down into a strange land together and were getting safely back—by a slight margin, perhaps, but margin enough. Over the levee wall now, like an aurora borealis, the sky of New Orleans, across the river, was flickering gently. This time they crossed by bridge, high above everything, merging onto a long light-stream of cars turned cityward.

For a time afterward he was lost in the streets, turning almost at random with the noisy traffic until he found his bearings. When he stopped the car at the next sign and leaned forward frowning to make it out, she sat up straight on her side. It was Arabi. He turned the car right around.

"We're all right now," he muttered, allowing himself a cigarette.

Something that must have been with them all along suddenly, then, was not. In a moment, tall as panic, it rose, cried like a human, and dropped back.

"I never got my water," she said.

She gave him the name of her hotel, he drove her there, and he said good night on the sidewalk. They shook hands.

"Forgive . . ." For, just in time, he saw she expected it of him.

And that was just what she did, forgive him. Indeed, had she waked in time from a deep sleep, she would have told him her story. She disappeared through the revolving door, with a gesture of smoothing her hair, and he thought a figure in the lobby strolled to meet her. He got back in the car and sat there.

He was not leaving for Syracuse until early in the morning. At length, he recalled the reason; his wife had recommended that he stay where he was this extra day so that she could entertain some old, unmarried college friends without him underfoot.

As he started up the car, he recognized in the smell of exhausted, body-warm air in the streets, in which the flow of drink was an inextricable part, the signal that the New Orleans evening was just beginning. In Dickie Grogan's, as he passed, the well-known Josefina at her organ was charging up and down with *"Clair de Lune."* As he drove the little Ford safely to its garage, he remembered for the first time in years when he was young and brash, a student in New York, and the shriek and horror and unholy smother of the subway had its original meaning for him as the lilt and expectation of love.

JOHN CHEEVER

(1912–1982)

J ohn Cheever was born in Quincy, Massachusetts. He was expelled
*from Thayer Academy for smoking, and described that and other
experiences at the school in his first short story, published when he was
18. By the time he was 23,* The New Yorker *had accepted one of his
stories. For the rest of his life he devoted himself to writing, eventually
becoming one of America's most admired writers. His reputation was
slow to develop, though, and critics have responded variously to the
unique blend of realism and surrealism, social content and gestures
toward the otherworldly that characterizes his fiction. His first collection
of stories,* The Way Some People Live *(1943), was followed by many
others, including* The Enormous Room and Other Stories *(1953),*
The Brigade and the Golf Widow *(1964), and* The Stories of John
Cheever *(1978). He also wrote novels, among them* The Wapshot
Chronicle *(1957),* The Wapshot Scandal *(1964), and* Falconer
*(1977). He has been called "a satirist, a Transcendentalist, an existential-
ist, a social critic, a religious writer, a trenchant moralist, an enlightened
Puritan, an Episcopalian anarch, a suburban surrealist, Ovid in Ossin-
ing [Cheever's adopted home town], the American Chekhov, the American Trollope for an age of angst, a toothless Thurber." What is more to
the point is that Cheever's popularity rests securely on his being "one
of us." As Robert G. Collins wrote in 1982, the year of Cheever's death:*

> *It is probably because the state of domestic life and personal
> emotional needs in America in the past four decades have been
> at the very center of our insecurity and regret; as the prose poet
> of the middle decades of our century, while we were losing our
> old world, Cheever has been our guide, our conscience, our court
> fool, and our prosecutor. He is one of those writers that we meet
> with a sense that he knows all about us in advance; he has
> thought many of our thoughts already, uttered many phrases
> that we had assumed were safely buried in our thoughts. Yet,
> he has done it with so graceful a manner, so mocking and yet
> gentle a ridicule, that we are teased into acceptance.*

Goodbye, My Brother

W e are a family that has always been very close in spirit. Our father was drowned in a sailing accident when we were young, and our mother has always stressed the fact that our familial relationships have a kind of permanence that we will never meet with again. I don't think about the family much, but when I remember its members and the coast where they lived and the sea salt that I think is in our blood, I am happy to recall that I am a Pommeroy—that I have the nose, the coloring, and the promise of longevity—and that while we are not a distinguished family, we enjoy the illusion, when we are together, that the Pommeroys are unique. I don't say any of this because I'm interested in family history or because this sense of uniqueness is deep or important to me but in order to advance the point that we are loyal to one another in spite of our differences, and that any rupture in this loyalty is a source of confusion and pain.

We are four children; there is my sister Diana and the three men— Chaddy, Lawrence, and myself. Like most families in which the children are out of their twenties, we have been separated by business, marriage, and war. Helen and I live on Long Island now, with our four children. I teach in a secondary school, and I am past the age where I expect to be made headmaster—or principal, as we say—but I respect the work. Chaddy, who has done better than the rest of us, lives in Manhattan, with Odette and their children. Mother lives in Philadelphia, and Diana, since her divorce, has been living in France, but she comes back to the States in the summer to spend a month at Laud's Head. Laud's Head is a summer place on the shore of one of the Massachusetts islands. We used to have a cottage there, and in the twenties our father built the big house. It stands on a cliff above the sea and, excepting St. Tropez and some of the Apennine villages, it is my favorite place in the world. We each have an equity in the place and we contribute some money to help keep it going.

Our youngest brother, Lawrence, who is a lawyer, got a job with a Cleveland firm after the war, and none of us saw him for four years. When he decided to leave Cleveland and go to work for a firm in Albany, he wrote Mother that he would, between jobs, spend ten days at Laud's Head, with his wife and their two children. This was when I had planned to take my vacation—I had been teaching summer school—and Helen and Chaddy and Odette and Diana were all going to be there, so the family would be together. Lawrence is the member of the family with whom the rest of us have least in common. We have never seen a great deal of him, and I suppose that's why we still call him Tifty—a nickname he was given when he was a child, because when he came down the hall toward the dining room for breakfast, his slippers made a noise that sounded like "Tifty, tifty, tifty." That's what Father called him, and so did everyone else. When he grew older, Diana sometimes used to call him Little Jesus, and Mother often called him the Croaker. We had disliked Lawrence, but we looked forward to his return with a mixture of apprehension and loyalty, and with some of the joy and delight of reclaiming a brother.

Lawrence crossed over from the mainland on the four-o'clock boat one afternoon late in the summer, and Chaddy and I went down to meet him. The arrivals and departures of the summer ferry have all the outward signs that suggest a voyage—whistles, bells, hand trucks, reunions, and the smell of brine—but it is a voyage of no import, and when I watched the boat come into the blue harbor that afternoon and thought that it was completing a voyage of no import, I realized that I had hit on exactly the kind of observation that Lawrence would have made. We looked for his face behind the windshields as the cars drove off the boat, and we had no trouble in recognizing him. And we ran over and shook his hand and clumsily kissed his wife and the children. "Tifty!" Chaddy shouted. "Tifty!" It is difficult to judge changes in the appearance of a brother, but both Chaddy and I agreed, as we drove back to Laud's Head, that Lawrence still looked very young. He got to the house first, and we took the suitcases out of his car. When I came in, he was standing in the living room, talking with Mother and Diana. They were in their best clothes and all their jewelry, and they were welcoming him extravagantly, but even then, when everyone was endeavoring to seem most affectionate and at a time when these endeavors come easiest, I was aware of a faint tension in the room. Thinking about this as I carried Lawrence's heavy suitcases up the stairs, I realized that our dislikes are as deeply ingrained as our better passions, and I remembered that once, twenty-five years ago, when I had hit Lawrence on the head with a rock, he had picked himself up and gone directly to our father to complain.

I carried the suitcases up to the third floor, where Ruth, Lawrence's wife, had begun to settle her family. She is a thin girl, and she seemed very tired from the journey, but when I asked her if she didn't want me to bring a drink upstairs to her, she said she didn't think she did.

When I got downstairs, Lawrence wasn't around, but the others were all ready for cocktails, and we decided to go ahead. Lawrence is the only member of the family who has never enjoyed drinking. We took our cocktails onto the terrace, so that we could see the bluffs and the sea and the islands in the east, and the return of Lawrence and his wife, their presence in the house, seemed to refresh our responses to the familiar view; it was as if the pleasure they would take in the sweep and the color of that coast, after such a long absence, had been imparted to us. While we were there, Lawrence came up the path from the beach.

"Isn't the beach fabulous, Tifty?" Mother asked. "Isn't it fabulous to be back? Will you have a Martini?"

"I don't care," Lawrence said. "Whiskey, gin—I don't care what I drink. Give me a little rum."

"We don't have any *rum*," Mother said. It was the first note of asperity. She had taught us never to be indecisive, never to reply as Lawrence had. Beyond this, she is deeply concerned with the propriety of her house, and anything irregular by her standards, like drinking straight rum or bringing a beer can to the dinner table, excites in her a conflict that she cannot, even with her capacious sense of humor, surmount. She sensed the asperity and worked to repair it. "Would you like some Irish, Tifty dear?" she said. "Isn't Irish what you've always liked? There's some Irish on the sideboard. Why don't you get yourself some Irish?" Lawrence said that he didn't care. He poured himself a Martini, and then Ruth came down and we went in to dinner.

In spite of the fact that we had, through waiting for Lawrence, drunk too much before dinner, we were all anxious to put our best foot forward and to enjoy a peaceful time. Mother is a small woman whose face is still a striking reminder of how pretty she must have been, and whose conversation is unusually light, but she talked that evening about a soil-reclamation project that is going on up-island. Diana is as pretty as Mother must have been; she is an animated and lovely woman who likes to talk about the dissolute friends that she has made in France, but she talked that night about the school in Switzerland where she had left her two children. I could see that the dinner had been planned to please Lawrence. It was not too rich, and there was nothing to make him worry about extravagance.

After supper, when we went back onto the terrace, the clouds held that kind of light that looks like blood, and I was glad that Lawrence had such a lurid sunset for his homecoming. When we had been out there a few minutes, a man named Edward Chester came to get Diana. She had met him in France, or on the boat home, and he was staying for ten days at the inn in the village. He was introduced to Lawrence and Ruth, and then he and Diana left.

"Is that the one she's sleeping with now?" Lawrence asked.

"What a horrid thing to say!" Helen said.

"You ought to apologize for that, Tifty," Chaddy said.

"I don't know," Mother said tiredly. "I don't know, Tifty. Diana is in a position to do whatever she wants, and I don't ask sordid questions. She's my only daughter. I don't see her often."

"Is she going back to France?"

"She's going back the week after next."

Lawrence and Ruth were sitting at the edge of the terrace, not in the chairs, not in the circle of chairs. With his mouth set, my brother looked to me then like a Puritan cleric. Sometimes, when I try to understand his frame of mind, I think of the beginnings of our family in this country, and his disapproval of Diana and her lover reminded me of this. The branch of the Pommeroys to which we belong was founded by a minister who was eulogized by Cotton Mather for his untiring abjuration of the Devil. The Pommeroys were ministers until the middle of the nineteenth century, and the harshness of their thought—man is full of misery, and all earthly beauty is lustful and corrupt—has been preserved in books and sermons. The temper of our family changed somewhat and became more lighthearted, but when I was of school age, I can remember a cousinage of old men and women who seemed to hark back to the dark days of the ministry and to be animated by perpetual guilt and the deification of the scourge. If you are raised in this atmosphere—and in a sense we were—I think it is a trial of the spirit to reject its habits of guilt, self-denial, taciturnity, and penitence, and it seemed to me to have been a trial of the spirit in which Lawrence had succumbed.

"Is that Cassiopeia?" Odette asked.

"No, dear," Chaddy said. "That isn't Cassiopeia."

"Who was Cassiopeia?" Odette said.

"She was the wife of Cepheus and the mother of Andromeda," I said.

"The cook is a Giants fan," Chaddy said. "She'll give you even money that they win the pennant."

It had grown so dark that we could see the passage of light through the sky from the lighthouse at Cape Heron. In the dark below the cliff, the continual detonations of the surf sounded. And then, as she often does when it is getting dark and she has drunk too much before dinner, Mother began to talk about the improvements and additions that would someday be made on the house, the wings and bathrooms and gardens.

"This house will be in the sea in five years," Lawrence said.

"Tifty the Croaker," Chaddy said.

"Don't call me Tifty," Lawrence said.

"Little Jesus," Chaddy said.

"The sea wall is badly cracked," Lawrence said. "I looked at it this afternoon. You had it repaired four years ago, and it cost eight thousand dollars. You can't do that every four years."

"Please, Tifty," Mother said.

"Facts are facts," Lawrence said, "and it's a damned-fool idea to build a house at the edge of the cliff on a sinking coastline. In my lifetime, half the garden has washed away and there's four feet of water where we used to have a bathhouse."

"Let's have a very *general* conversation," Mother said bitterly. "Let's talk about politics or the boat-club dance."

"As a matter of fact," Lawrence said, "the house is probably in some danger now. If you had an unusually high sea, a hurricane sea, the wall would crumble and the house would go. We could all be drowned."

"I can't *bear* it," Mother said. She went into the pantry and came back with a full glass of gin.

I have grown too old now to think that I can judge the sentiments of others, but I was conscious of the tension between Lawrence and Mother, and I knew some of the history of it. Lawrence couldn't have been more than sixteen years old when he decided that Mother was frivolous, mischievous, destructive, and overly strong. When he had determined this, he decided to separate himself from her. He was at boarding school then, and I remember that he did not come home for Christmas. He spent Christmas with a friend. He came home very seldom after he had made his unfavorable judgment on Mother, and when he did come home, he always tried, in his conversation, to remind her of his estrangement. When he married Ruth, he did not tell Mother. He did not tell her when his children were born. But in spite of these principled and lengthy exertions he seemed, unlike the rest of us, never to have enjoyed any separation, and when they are together, you feel at once a tension, an unclearness.

And it was unfortunate, in a way, that Mother should have picked that night to get drunk. It's her privilege, and she doesn't get drunk often, and fortunately she wasn't bellicose, but we were all conscious of what was happening. As she quietly drank her gin, she seemed sadly to be parting from us; she seemed to be in the throes of travel. Then her mood changed from travel to injury, and the few remarks she made were petulant and irrelevant. When her glass was nearly empty, she stared angrily at the dark air in front of her nose, moving her head a little, like a fighter. I knew that there was not room in her mind then for all the injuries that were crowding into it. Her children were stupid, her husband was drowned, her servants were thieves, and the chair she sat in was uncomfortable. Suddenly she put down her empty glass and interrupted Chaddy, who was talking about baseball. "I know one *thing*," she said hoarsely. "I know that if there is an afterlife, I'm going to have a very different kind of family. I'm going to have nothing but fabulously rich, witty, and enchanting children." She got up and, starting for the door, nearly fell. Chaddy caught her and helped her up the stairs. I could hear their tender good-nights, and then Chaddy came back. I thought that Lawrence by now would be tired from his journey and his return, but he remained on the terrace, as if he were waiting to see the final malfeasance, and the rest of us left him there and went swimming in the dark.

When I woke the next morning, or half woke, I could hear the sound of someone rolling the tennis court. It is a fainter and a deeper sound than the iron buoy bells off the point—an unrhythmic iron chiming—that belongs in my mind to the beginnings of a summer day, a good portent. When I went downstairs, Lawrence's two kids were in the living room, dressed in ornate cowboy suits. They are frightened and skinny children. They told me their father was rolling the tennis court but that they did not want to go out because they had seen a snake under the doorstep. I explained to them that their cousins—all the other children—ate breakfast in the kitchen and that they'd better run along in there. At this announcement, the boy began to cry. Then his sister joined him. They cried as if to go in the kitchen and eat would destroy their most precious rights. I told them to sit down with me. Lawrence came in, and I asked him if he wanted to play some tennis. He said no, thanks, although he thought he might play some singles with Chaddy. He was in the right here, because both he and Chaddy play better tennis than I, and he did play some singles with Chaddy after breakfast, but later on, when the others came down to play family doubles, Lawrence disappeared. This made me cross—unreasonably so, I suppose—but we play darned interesting family doubles and he could have played in a set for the sake of courtesy.

Late in the morning, when I came up from the court alone, I saw Tifty on the terrace, prying up a shingle from the wall with his jackknife. "What's the matter, Lawrence?" I said. "Termites?" There are termites in the wood and they've given us a lot of trouble.

He pointed out to me, at the base of each row of shingles, a faint blue line of carpenter's chalk. "This house is about twenty-two years old," he said. "These shingles are about two hundred years old. Dad must have bought shingles from all the farms around here when he built the place, to make it look venerable. You can still see the carpenter's chalk put down where these antiques were nailed into place."

It was true about the shingles, although I had forgotten it. When the house was built, our father, or his architect, had ordered it covered with lichened and weather-beaten shingles. I didn't follow Lawrence's reasons for thinking that this was scandalous.

"And look at these doors," Lawrence said. "Look at these doors and window frames." I followed him over to a big Dutch door that opens onto the terrace and looked at it. It was a relatively new door, but someone had worked hard to conceal its newness. The surface had been deeply scored with some metal implement, and white paint had been rubbed into the incisions to imitate brine, lichen, and weather rot. "Imagine spending thousands of dollars to make a sound house look like a wreck," Lawrence said. "Imagine the frame of mind this implies. Imagine wanting to live so much in the past that you'll pay men carpenters' wages to disfigure your front door." Then I remembered Lawrence's sensitivity to time and his sentiments and opinions about our feelings for the past. I had heard him say, years ago, that we and our friends and our part of the nation, finding ourselves unable to cope with the problems of the present, had, like a wretched adult, turned back to what we supposed was a happier and a simpler time, and that our taste for reconstruction and candlelight was a measure of this irremediable failure. The faint blue line of chalk had reminded him of these ideas, the scarified door had reinforced them, and now clue after clue presented itself to him—the stern light at the door, the bulk of the chimney, the width of the floorboards and the pieces set into them to resemble pegs. While Lawrence was lecturing me on these frailties, the others came up from the court. As soon as Mother saw Lawrence, she responded, and I saw that there was little hope of any rapport between the matriarch and the changeling. She took Chaddy's arm. "Let's go swimming and have Martinis on the beach," she said. "Let's have a *fabulous* morning."

The sea that morning was a solid color, like verd stone. Everyone went to the beach but Tifty and Ruth. "I don't mind *him*," Mother said. She was excited, and she tipped her glass and spilled some gin into the sand. "I don't mind *him*. It doesn't matter to me how *rude* and *horrid* and *gloomy* he is, but what I can't bear are the faces of his wretched little children, those fabulously unhappy little children." With the height of the cliff between us, everyone talked wrathfully about Lawrence; about how he had grown worse instead of better, how unlike the rest of he was, how he endeavored to spoil every pleasure. We drank our gin; the abuse seemed to reach a crescendo, and then, one by one, we went swimming in the solid green water. But when we came out no one mentioned Lawrence unkindly; the line of abusive conversation had been cut, as if swimming had the cleansing force claimed for baptism. We dried our hands and lighted cigarettes, and if Lawrence was mentioned, it was only to suggest, kindly, something that might please him. Wouldn't he like to sail to Barin's cove, or go fishing?

And now I remember that while Lawrence was visiting us, we went swimming oftener than we usually do, and I think there was a reason for this. When the irritability that accumulated as a result of his company began to lessen our patience, not only with Lawrence but with one another, we would all go swimming and shed our animus in the cold water. I can see the family now, smarting from Lawrence's rebukes as they sat on the sand, and I can see them wading and diving and surface-diving and hear in their voices the restoration of patience and the redis-covery of inexhaustible good will. If Lawrence noticed this change—this illusion of purification—I suppose that he would have found in the vocabulary of psychiatry, or the mythology of the Atlantic, some circumspect name for it, but I don't think he noticed the change. He neglected to name the curative powers of the open sea, but it was one of the few chances for diminution that he missed.

The cook we had that year was a Polish woman named Anna Ostrovick, a summer cook. She was first-rate—a big, fat, hearty, industrious woman who took her work seriously. She liked to cook and to have the food she cooked appreciated and eaten, and whenever we saw her, she always urged us to eat. She cooked hot bread—crescents and brioches— for breakfast two or three times a week, and she would bring these into the dining room herself and say, "Eat, eat, eat!" When the maid took the serving dishes back into the pantry, we could sometimes hear Anna, who was standing there, say, "Good! They eat." She fed the garbage man, the milkman, and the gardener. "Eat!" she told them. "Eat, eat!" On Thursday afternoons, she went to the movies with the maid, but she didn't enjoy the movies, because the actors were all so thin. She would sit in the dark theatre for an hour and a half watching the screen anxiously for the appearance of someone who had enjoyed his food. Bette Davis merely left with Anna the impression of a woman who has not eaten well. "They are all so skinny," she would say when she left the movies. In the evenings, after she had gorged all of us, and washed the pots and pans, she would collect the table scraps and go out to feed the creation. We had a few chickens that year, and although they would have roosted by then, she would dump food into their troughs and urge the sleeping fowl to eat. She fed the songbirds in the orchard and the chipmunks in the yard. Her appearance at the edge of the garden and her urgent voice— we could hear her calling "East, eat, eat"—had become, like the sunset gun at the boat club and the passage of light from Cape Heron, attached to that hour. "East, eat, eat," we could hear Anna say. "Eat, eat . . ." Then it would be dark.

When Lawrence had been there three days, Anna called me into the kitchen. "You tell your mother," she said, "that *he* doesn't come into my kitchen. If *he* comes into my kitchen all the time, I go. *He* is always coming into my kitchen to tell me what a sad woman I am. He is always telling me that I work too hard and that I don't get paid enough and that I should belong to a union with vacations. Ha! He is so skinny but he is always coming into my kitchen when I am busy to pity me, but I am as good as him, I am as good as *anybody*, and I do not have to have people like that getting into my way all the time and feeling sorry for me. I am a famous and wonderful cook and I have jobs everywhere and the only reason I come here to work this summer is because I was never before on an island, but I can have other jobs tomorrow, and if he is always coming into my kitchen to pity me, you tell your mother I am going. I am as good as *anybody* and I do not have to have that skinny all the time telling how poor I am."

I was pleased to find that the cook was on our side, but I felt that the situation was delicate. If Mother asked Lawrence to stay out of the kitchen, he would make a grievance out of the request. He could make a grievance out of anything, and it sometimes seemed that as he sat darkly at the dinner table, every word of disparagement, wherever it was aimed, came home to him. I didn't mention the cook's complaint to anyone, but somehow there wasn't any more trouble from that quarter.

The next cause for contention that I had from Lawrence came over our backgammon games.

When we are at Laud's Head, we play a lot of backgammon. At eight o'clock, after we have drunk our coffee, we usually get out the board. In a way, it is one of our pleasantest hours. The lamps in the room are still unlighted, Anna can be seen in the dark garden, and in the sky above her head there are continents of shadow and fire. Mother turns on the light and rattles the dice as a signal. We usually play three games apiece, each with the others. We play for money, and you can win or lose a hundred dollars on a game, but the stakes are usually much lower. I think that Lawrence used to play—I can't remember—but he doesn't play any more. He doesn't gamble. This is not because he is poor or because he has any principles about gambling but because he thinks the game is foolish and a waste of time. He was ready enough, however, to waste his time watching the rest of us play. Night after night, when the game began, he pulled a chair up beside the board, and watched the checkers and the dice. His expression was scornful, and yet he watched carefully. I wondered why he watched us night after night, and, through watching his face, I think that I may have found out.

Lawrence doesn't gamble, so he can't understand the excitement of winning and losing money. He has forgotten how to play the game, I think, so that its complex odds can't interest him. His observations were bound to include the facts that backgammon is an idle game and a game of chance, and that the board, marked with points, was a symbol of our worthlessness. And since he doesn't understand gambling or the odds of the game, I thought that what interested him must be the members of his family. One night when I was playing with Odette—I had won thirty-seven dollars from Mother and Chaddy—I think I saw what was going on in his mind.

Odette has black hair and black eyes. She is careful never to expose her white skin to the sun for long, so the striking contrast of blackness and pallor is not changed in the summer. She needs and deserves admiration—it is the element that contents her—and she will flirt, unseriously, with any man. Her shoulders were bare that night, her dress was cut to show the division of her breasts and to show her breasts when she leaned over the board to play. She kept losing and flirting and making her losses seem like a part of the flirtation. Chaddy was in the other room. She lost three games, and when the third game ended, she fell back on the sofa and, looking at me squarely, said something about going out on the dunes to settle the score. Lawrence heard her. I looked at Lawrence. He seemed shocked and gratified at the same time, as if he had suspected all along that we were not playing for anything so insubstantial as money. I may be wrong, of course, but I think that Lawrence felt that in watching our backgammon he was observing the progress of a mordant tragedy in which the money we won and lost served as a symbol for more vital forfeits. It is like Lawrence to try to read significance and finality into every gesture that we make, and it is certain of Lawrence that when he finds the inner logic to our conduct, it will be sordid.

Chaddy came in to play with me. Chaddy and I have never liked to lose to each other. When we were younger, we used to be forbidden to play games together, because they always ended in a fight. We think we know each other's mettle intimately. I think he is prudent; he thinks I am foolish. There is always bad blood when we play anything—tennis or backgammon or softball or bridge—and it does seem at times as if we were playing for the possession of each other's liberties. When I lose to Chaddy, I can't sleep. All this is only half the truth of our competitive relationship, but it was the half-truth that would be discernible to Lawrence, and his presence at the table made me so self-conscious that I lost two games. I tried not to seem angry when I got up from the board. Lawrence was watching me. I went out onto the terrace to suffer there in the dark the anger I always feel when I lose to Chaddy.

When I came back into the room, Chaddy and Mother were playing. Lawrence was still watching. By his lights, Odette had lost her virtue to me, I had lost my self-esteem to Chaddy, and now I wondered what he saw in the present match. He watched raptly, as if the opaque checkers and the marked board served for an exchange of critical power. How dramatic the board, in its ring of light, and the quiet players and the crash of the sea outside must have seemed to him! Here was spiritual cannibalism made visible; here, under his nose, were the symbols of the rapacious use human beings make of one another.

Mother plays a shrewd, an ardent, and an interfering game. She always has her hands in her opponent's board. When she plays with Chaddy, who is her favorite, she plays intently. Lawrence would have noticed this. Mother is a sentimental woman. Her heart is good and easily moved by tears and frailty, a characteristic that, like her handsome nose, has not been changed at all by age. Grief in another provokes her deeply, and she seems at times to be trying to divine in Chaddy some grief, some loss, that she can succor and redress, and so re-establish the relationship that she enjoyed with him when he was sickly and young. She loves defending the weak and the childlike, and now that we are old, she misses it. The world of debts and business, men and war, hunting and fishing has on her an exacerbating effect. (When Father drowned, she threw away his fly rods and his guns.) She has lectured us all endlessly on self-reliance, but when we come back to her for comfort and for help—particularly Chaddy—she seems to feel most like herself. I suppose

Lawrence thought that the old woman and her son were playing for each other's soul.

She lost. "Oh *dear*," she said. She looked stricken and bereaved, as she always does when she loses. "Get me my glasses, get me my checkbook, get me something to drink." Lawrence got up at last and stretched his legs. He looked at us all bleakly. The wind and the sea had risen, and I thought that if he heard the waves, he must hear them only as a dark answer to all his dark questions; that he would think that the tide had expunged the embers of our picnic fires. The company of a lie is unbearable, and he seemed like the embodiment of a lie. I couldn't explain to him the simple and intense pleasures of playing for money, and it seemed to me hideously wrong that he should have sat at the edge of the board and concluded that we were playing for one another's soul. He walked restlessly around the room two or three times and then, as usual, gave us a parting shot. "I should think you'd go crazy," he said, "cooped up with one another like this, night after night. Come on, Ruth. I'm going to bed."

That night, I dreamed about Lawrence, I saw his plain face magnified into ugliness, and when I woke in the morning, I felt sick, as if I had suffered a great spiritual loss while I slept, like the loss of courage and heart. It was foolish to let myself be troubled by my brother. I needed a vacation. I needed to relax. At school, we live in one of the dormitories, we eat at the house table, and we never get away. I not only teach English winter and summer but I work in the principal's office and fire the pistol at track meets. I needed to get away from this and from every other form of anxiety, and I decided to avoid my brother. Early that day, I took Helen and the children sailing, and we stayed out until suppertime. The next day, we went on a picnic. Then I had to go to New York for a day, and when I got back, there was the costume dance at the boat club. Lawrence wasn't going to this, and it's a party where I always have a wonderful time.

The invitations that year said to come as you wish you were. After several conversations, Helen and I had decided what to wear. The thing she most wanted to be again, she said, was a bride, and so she decided to wear her wedding dress. I thought this was a good choice—sincere, lighthearted, and inexpensive. Her choice influenced mine, and I decided to wear an old football uniform. Mother decided to go as Jenny Lind, because there was an old Jenny Lind costume in the attic. The others decided to rent costumes, and when I went to New York, I got the clothes. Lawrence and Ruth didn't enter into any of this.

Helen was on the dance committee, and she spent most of Friday decorating the club. Diana and Chaddy and I went sailing. Most of the sailing that I do these days is in Manhasset, and I am used to setting a homeward course by the gasoline barge and the tin roofs of the boat shed, and it was a pleasure that afternoon, as we returned, to keep the bow on a white church spire in the village and to find even the inshore water green and clear. At the end of our sail, we stopped at the club to get Helen. The committee had been trying to give a submarine appearance to the ballroom, and the fact that they had nearly succeeded in accomplishing this illusion made Helen very happy. We drove back to Laud's Head. It had been a brilliant afternoon, but on the way home we could smell the east wind—the dark wind, as Lawrence would have said—coming in from the sea.

My wife, Helen, is thirty-eight, and her hair would be gray, I guess, if it were not dyed, but it is dyed an unobtrusive yellow—a faded color—and I think it becomes her. I mixed cocktails that night while she was dressing, and when I took a glass upstairs to her, I saw her for the first time since our marriage in her wedding dress. There would be no point in saying that she looked to me more beautiful than she did on our wedding day, but because I have grown older and have, I think, a greater depth of feeling, and because I could see in her face that night both youth and age, both her devotion to the young woman that she had been and the positions that she had yielded graciously to time, I think I have never been so deeply moved. I had already put on the football uniform, and the weight of it, the heaviness of the pants and the shoulder guards, had worked a change in me, as if in putting on these old clothes I had put off the reasonable anxieties and troubles of my life. It felt as if we had both returned to the years before our marriage, the years before the war.

The Collards had a big dinner party before the dance, and our family—excepting Lawrence and Ruth—went to this. We drove over to the club, through the fog, at about half past nine. The orchestra was playing a waltz. While I was checking my raincoat, someone hit me on the back. It was Chucky Ewing, and the funny thing was that Chucky had on a football uniform. This seemed comical as hell to both of us. We were laughing when we went down the hall to the dance floor. I stopped at the door to look at the party, and it was beautiful. The committee had hung fish nets around the sides and over the high ceiling. The nets on the ceiling were filled with colored balloons. The light was soft and uneven, and the people—our friends and neighbors—dancing in the soft light to "Three O'Clock in the Morning" made a pretty picture. Then I noticed the number of women dressed in white, and I realized that they, like Helen, were wearing wedding dresses. Patsy Hewitt and Mrs. Gear and the Lackland girl waltzed by, dressed as brides. Then Pep Talcott came over to where Chucky and I were standing. He was dressed to be Henry VIII, but he told us that the Auerbach twins and Henry Barrett and Dwight MacGregor were all wearing football uniforms, and that by the last count there were ten brides on the floor.

This coincidence, this funny coincidence, kept everybody laughing, and made this one of the most lighthearted parties we've ever had at the club. At first I thought that the women had planned with one another to wear wedding dresses, but the ones that I danced with said it was a coincidence and I'm sure that Helen had made her decision alone. Everything went smoothly for me until a little before midnight. I saw Ruth standing at the edge of the floor. She was wearing a long red dress. It was all wrong. It wasn't the spirit of the party at all. I danced with her, but no one cut in, and I was darned if I'd spend the rest of the night dancing with her and I asked her where Lawrence was. She said he was out on the dock, and I took her over to the bar and left her and went out to get Lawrence.

The east fog was thick and wet, and he was alone on the dock. He was not in costume. He had not even bothered to get himself up as a fisherman or a sailor. He looked particularly saturnine. The fog blew around us like a cold smoke. I wished that it had been a clear night, because the easterly fog seemed to play into my misanthropic brother's hands. And I knew that the buoys—the groaners and bells that we could hear then—would sound to him like half-human, half-drowned cries, although every sailor knows that buoys are necessary and reliable fixtures, and I knew that the foghorn at the lighthouse would mean wanderings and losses to him and that he could misconstrue the vivacity of the dance music. "Come on in, Tifty," I said, "and dance with your wife or get her some partners."

"Why should I?" he said. "Why should I?" And he walked to the window and looked in at the party. "Look at it," he said. "Look at that . . ."

Chucky Ewing had got hold of a balloon and was trying to organize a scrimmage line in the middle of the floor. The others were dancing a samba. And I knew that Lawrence was looking bleakly at the party as he had looked at the weather-beaten shingles on our house, as if he saw here an abuse and a distortion of time; as if in wanting to be brides and football players we exposed the fact that, the lights of youth having been put out in us, we had been unable to find other lights to go by and, destitute of faith and principle, had become foolish and sad. And that he was thinking this about so many kind and happy and generous people made me angry, made me feel for him such an unnatural abhorrence that I was ashamed, for he is my brother and a Pommeroy. I put my arm around his shoulders and tried to force him to come in, but he wouldn't.

I got back in time for the Grand March, and after the prizes had been given out for the best costumes, they let the balloons down. The room was hot, and someone opened the big doors onto the dock, and the easterly wind circled the room and went out, carrying across the dock and out onto the water most of the balloons. Chucky Ewing went running out after the balloons, and when he saw them pass the dock and settle on the water, he took off his football uniform and dove in. Then Eric Auerbach dove in and Lew Phillips dove in and I dove in, and you know how it is at a party after midnight when people start jumping into the water. We recovered most of the balloons and dried off and went on dancing, and we didn't get home until morning.

The next day was the day of the flower show. Mother and Helen and Odette all had entries. We had a pickup lunch, and Chaddy drove the women and children over to the show. I took a nap, and in the middle of the afternoon I got some trunks and a towel and, on leaving the house, passed Ruth in the laundry. She was washing clothes. I don't know why she should seem to have so much more work to do than anyone else, but she is always washing or ironing or mending clothes. She may have been taught, when she was young, to spend her time like this, or she may be at the mercy of an expiatory passion. She seems to scrub and iron with a penitential fervor, although I can't imagine what it is that she thinks she's done wrong. Her children were with her in the laundry. I offered to take them to the beach, but they didn't want to go.

It was late in August, and the wild grapes that grow profusely all over the island made the land wind smell of wine. There is a little grove of holly at the end of the path, and then you climb the dunes, where nothing grows but that coarse grass. I could hear the sea, and I remember thinking how Chaddy and I used to talk mystically about the sea. When we were young, we had decided that we could never live in the West because we would miss the sea. "It is very nice here," we used to say politely when we visited people in the mountains, "but we miss the Atlantic." We used to look down our noses at people from Iowa and Colorado who had been denied this revelation, and we scorned the Pacific. Now I could hear the waves, whose heaviness sounded like a reverberation, like a tumult, and it pleased me as it had pleased me when I was young, and it seemed to have a purgative force, as if it had cleared my memory of, among other things, the penitential image of Ruth in the laundry.

But Lawrence was on the beach. There he sat. I went in without speaking. The water was cold, and when I came out, I put on a shirt. I told him that I was going to walk up to Tanners Point, and he said that he would come with me. I tried to walk beside him. His legs are no longer than mine, but he always likes to stay a little ahead of his companion. Walking along behind him, looking at his bent head and his shoulders, I wondered what he could make of that landscape.

There were the dunes and cliffs, and then, where they declined, there were some fields that had begun to turn from green to brown and yellow. The fields were used for pasturing sheep, and I guess Lawrence would have noticed that the soil was eroded and that the sheep would accelerate this decay. Beyond the fields there are a few coastal farms, with square and pleasant buildings, but Lawrence could have pointed out the hard lot of an island farmer. The sea, at our other side, was the open sea. We always tell guests that there, to the east, lies the coast of Portugal, and for Lawrence it would be an easy step from the coast of Portugal to the tyranny in Spain. The waves broke with a noise like a "hurrah, hurrah, hurrah," but to Lawrence they would say *"Vale, vale."* I suppose it would have occurred to his baleful and incisive mind that the coast was terminal moraine, the edge of the prehistoric world, and it must have occurred to him that we walked along the edge of the known world in spirit as much as in fact. If he should otherwise have overlooked this, there were some Navy planes bombing an uninhabited island to remind him.

That beach is a vast and preternaturally clean and simple landscape. It is like a piece of the moon. The surf had pounded the floor solid, so it was easy walking, and everything left on the sand had been twice changed by the waves. There was the spine of a shell, a broomstick, part of a bottle and part of a brick, both of them milled and broken until they were nearly unrecognizable, and I suppose Lawrence's sad frame of mind—for he kept his head down—went from one broken thing to another. The company of his pessimism began to infuriate me, and I caught up with him and put a hand on his shoulder. "It's only a summer day, Tifty," I said. "It's only a summer day. What's the matter? Don't you like it here?"

"I don't like it here," he said blandly, without raising his eyes. "I'm going to sell my equity in the house to Chaddy. I didn't expect to have a good time. The only reason I came back was to say goodbye."

I let him get ahead again and I walked behind him, looking at his shoulders and thinking of all the goodbyes he had made. When Father drowned, he went to church and said goodbye to Father. It was only three years later that he concluded that Mother was frivolous and said goodbye to her. In his freshman year at college, he had been very good friends with his roommate, but the man drank too much, and at the beginning of the spring term Lawrence changed roommates and said goodbye to his friend. When he had been in college for two years, he concluded that the atmosphere was too sequestered and he said goodbye to Yale. He enrolled at Columbia and got his law degree there, but he found his first employer dishonest, and at the end of six months he said goodbye to a good job. He married Ruth in City Hall and said goodbye to the Protestant Episcopal Church; they went to live on a back street in Tuckahoe and said goodbye to the middle class. In 1938, he went to Washington to work as a government lawyer, saying goodbye to private enterprise, but after eight months in Washington he concluded that the Roosevelt administration was sentimental and he said goodbye to it. They left Washington for a suburb of Chicago, where he said goodbye to his neighbors, one by one, on counts of drunkenness, boorishness, and stupidity. He said goodbye to Chicago and went to Kansas; he said goodbye to Kansas and went to Cleveland. Now he had said goodbye to Cleveland and come East again, stopping at Laud's Head long enough to say goodbye to the sea.

It was elegiac and it was bigoted and narrow, it mistook circumspection for character, and I wanted to help him. "Come out of it," I said. "Come out of it, Tifty."

"Come out of what?"

"Come out of this gloominess. Come out of it. It's only a summer day. You're spoiling your own good time and you're spoiling everyone else's. We need a vacation, Tifty. I need one. I need to rest. We all do. And you've made everything tense and unpleasant. I only have two weeks in the year. Two weeks. I need to have a good time and so do all the others. We need to rest. You think that your pessimism is an advantage, but it's nothing but an unwillingness to grasp realities."

"What are the realities?" he said. "Diana is a foolish and a promiscuous woman. So is Odette. Mother is an alcoholic. If she doesn't discipline herself, she'll be in a hospital in a year or two. Chaddy is dishonest. He always has been. The house is going to fall into the sea." He looked at me and added, as an afterthought, "You're a fool."

"You're a gloomy son of a bitch," I said. "You're a gloomy son of a bitch."

"Get your fat face out of mine," he said. He walked along.

Then I picked up a root and, coming at his back—although I have never hit a man from the back before—I swung the root, heavy with sea water, behind me, and the momentum sped my arm and I gave him, my brother, a blow on the head that forced him to his knees on the sand, and I saw the blood come out and begin to darken his hair. Then I wished that he was dead, dead and about to be buried, not buried but about to be buried, because I did not want to be denied ceremony and decorum in putting him away, in putting him out of my consciousness, and I saw the rest of us—Chaddy and Mother and Diana and Helen—in mourning in the house on Belvedere Street that was torn down twenty years ago, greeting our guests and our relatives at the door and answering their mannerly condolences with mannerly grief. Nothing decorous was lacking so that even if he had been murdered on a beach, one would feel before the tiresome ceremony ended that he had come into the winter of his life and that it was a law of nature, and a beautiful one, that Tifty should be buried in the cold, cold ground.

He was still on his knees. I looked up and down. No one had seen us. The naked beach, like a piece of the moon, reached to invisibility. The spill of a wave, in a glancing run, shot up to where he knelt. I would still have liked to end him, but now I had begun to act like two men, the murderer and the Samaritan. With a swift roar, like hollowness made sound, a white wave reached him and encircled him, boiling over his shoulders, and I held him against the undertow. Then I led him to a higher place. The blood had spread all through his hair, so that it looked black. I took off my shirt and tore it to bind up his head. He was conscious, and I didn't think he was badly hurt. He didn't speak. Neither did I. Then I left him there.

I walked a little way down the beach and turned to watch him, and I was thinking of my own skin then. He had got to his feet and he seemed steady. The daylight was still clear, but on the sea wind fumes of brine were blowing in like a light fog, and when I had walked a little way from him, I could hardly see his dark figure in this obscurity. All down the beach I could see the heavy salt air blowing in. Then I turned my back on him, and as I got near to the house, I went swimming again, as I seem to have done after every encounter with Lawrence that summer.

When I got back to the house, I lay down on the terrace. The others came back. I could hear Mother defaming the flower arrangements that had won prizes. None of ours had won anything. Then the house quieted, as it always does at that hour. The children went into the kitchen to get supper and the others went upstairs to bathe. Then I heard Chaddy making cocktails, and the conversation about the flower-show judges was resumed. Then Mother cried, "Tifty! Tifty! Oh, Tifty!"

He stood in the door, looking half dead. He had taken off the bloody bandage and he held it in his hand. "My brother did this," he said. "My brother did it. He hit me with a stone—something—on the beach." His voice broke with self-pity. I thought he was going to cry. No one else spoke. "Where's Ruth?" he cried. "Where's Ruth? Where in hell is Ruth? I want her to start packing. I don't have any more time to waste here. I have important things to do. I have *important* things to do." And he went up the stairs.

They left for the mainland the next morning, taking the six-o'clock boat. Mother got up to say goodbye, but she was the only one, and it is a harsh and an easy scene to imagine—the matriarch and the changeling, looking at each other with a dismay that would seem like the powers of love reversed. I heard the children's voices and the car go down the drive, and I got up and went to the window, and what a morning that was! Jesus, what a morning! The wind was northerly. The air was clear. In the early heat, the roses in the garden smelled like strawberry jam. While I was dressing, I heard the boat whistle, first the warning signal and then the double blast, and I could see the good people on the top deck drinking coffee out of fragile paper cups, and Lawrence at the bow, saying to the sea, "*Thalassa, thalassa,*" while his timid and unhappy children watched the creation from the encirclement of their mother's arms. The buoys would toll mournfully for Lawrence, and while the grace of the light would make it an exertion not to throw out your arms and swear exultantly, Lawrence's eyes would trace the black sea as it fell astern; he would think of the bottom, dark and strange, where full fathom five our father lies.

Oh, what can you do with a man like that? What can you do? How can you dissuade his eye in a crowd from seeking out the cheek with acne, the infirm hand; how can you teach him to respond to the inestimable greatness of the race, the harsh surface beauty of life; how can you put his finger for him on the obdurate truths before which fear and horror are powerless? The sea that morning was iridescent and dark. My wife and my sister were swimming—Diana and Helen—and I saw their uncovered heads, black and gold in the dark water. I saw them come out and I saw that they were naked, unshy, beautiful, and full of grace, and I watched the naked women walk out of the sea.

JULIO CORTÁZAR

(1914–1984)

*J*ulio Cortázar was born in Brussels, where his Argentinian parents were abroad on business. The family returned to Buenos Aires at the end of the war. Cortázar worked as a high-school teacher between 1937 and 1944, when he also wrote his first stories and worked as a translator. He resigned his next post, professor of French literature at the University of Coyo, as a protest against Perón's government. In 1951, dissatisfied with life in Argentina, he travelled to France to study. He lived there the rest of his life, becoming a French citizen in 1981. His first collection of short stories, Bestiary, was published in 1951, and was followed by many others, including End of the Game (1956), Secret Weapons (1958), Cronopios and Famas (1969), All Fires the Fire (1973), and We Love Glenda So Much (1983). His experimental novel Hopscotch (1966) involves the reader in playing the role of co-creator by rearranging the different parts of the novel in a new order. In "On the Short Story and Its Environs," Cortázar offers some advice that can help readers find their way in the often strange world of his fiction: "When I write a story I instinctively try to distance myself by means of a demiurge who will live independently, so the reader will have the impression that what he is reading arises somehow out of himself—with the aid of a deus ex machina, to be sure—through the mediation though never the manifest presence of the demiurge." He goes on to describe the "shapeless mass" that exists when he begins a story, the terror and exultation that accompany the actual writing in which "everything is decided in a place that is foreign to my everyday self." He deprecates the literary merits of these translations from the depths of his psyche, but readers and critics have thought otherwise. His lack of social commitment has troubled some Latin American writers, but his ability to create haunting and powerful fantasy makes such criticism seem rather beside the point.

End of the Game

*L*etitia, Holanda and I used to play by the Argentine Central tracks during the hot weather, hoping that Mama and Aunt Ruth would go up to their siesta so that we could get out past the white gate. After washing the dishes, Mama and Aunt Ruth were always tired, especially when Holanda and I were drying, because it was then that there were arguments, spoons on the floor, secret words that only we understood, and in general, an atmosphere in which the smell of grease, José's yowling, and the dimness of the kitchen would end up in an incredible fight and the subsequent commotion. Holanda specialized in rigging this sort of brawl, for example, letting an already clean glass slip into the pan of dirty water, or casually dropping a remark to the effect that the Loza house had two maids to do all the work. I had other systems: I liked to suggest to Aunt Ruth that she was going to get an allergy rash on her hands if she kept scrubbing the pots instead of doing the cups and plates once in a while, which were exactly what Mama liked to wash, and over which they would confront one another soundlessly in a war of advantage to get the easy item. The heroic expedient, in case the bits of advice and the drawn-out family recollections began to bore us; was to upset some boiling water on the cat's back. Now that's a big lie about a scalded cat, it really is, except that you have to take the reference to cold water literally; because José never backed away from hot water, almost insinuating himself under it, poor animal, when we spilled a half-cup of it somewhere around 220° F., or less, a good deal less, probably, because his hair never fell out. The whole point was to get Troy burning, and in the confusion, crowned by a splendid G-flat from Aunt Ruth and Mama's sprint for the whipstick, Holanda and I would take no time at all to get lost in the long porch, toward the empty rooms off the back, where Letitia would be waiting for us, reading Ponson de Terrail, or some other equally inexplicable book.

Normally, Mama chased us a good part of the way, but her desire to bust in our skulls evaporated soon enough, and finally (we had barred the door and were begging for mercy in emotion-filled and very theatrical voices), she got tired and went off, repeating the same sentence: "Those ruffians'll end up on the street."

Where we ended up was by the Argentine Central tracks, when the house had settled down and was silent, and we saw the cat stretched out under the lemon tree to take its siesta also, a rest buzzing with fragrances and wasps. We'd open the white gate slowly, and when we shut it again with a slam like a blast of wind, it was a freedom which took us by the hands, seized the whole of our bodies and tumbled us out. Then we ran, trying to get the speed to scramble up the low embankment of the right-of-way, and there spread out upon the world, we silently surveyed our kingdom.

Our kingdom was this: a long curve of the tracks ended its bend just opposite the back section of the house. There was just the gravel incline, the crossties, and the double line of track; some dumb sparse grass among the rubble where mica, quartz and feldspar—the components of granite—sparkled like real diamonds in the two o'clock afternoon sun. When we stooped down to touch the rails (not wasting time because it would have been dangerous to spend much time there, not so much from the trains as for fear of being seen from the house), the heat off the stone roadbed flushed our faces, and facing into the wind from the river there was a damp heat against our cheeks and ears. We liked to bend our legs and squat down, rise, squat again, move from one kind of hot zone to the other, watching each other's faces to measure the perspiration—a minute or two later we would be sopping with it. And we were always quiet, looking down the track into the distance, or at the river on the other side, that stretch of coffee-and-cream river.

After this first inspection of the kingdom, we'd scramble down the bank and flop in the meager shadow of the willows next the wall enclosing the house where the white gate was. This was the capital city of the kingdom, the wilderness city and the headquarters of our game. Letitia was the first to start the game; she was the luckiest and the most privileged of the three of us. Letitia didn't have to dry dishes or make the beds, she could laze away the day reading or pasting up pictures, and at night they let her stay up later if she asked to, not counting having a room to herself, special hot broth when she wanted it, and all kinds of other advantages. Little by little she had taken more and more advantage of these privileges, and had been presiding over the game since the summer before, I think really she was presiding over the whole kingdom; in any case she was quicker at saying things, and Holanda and I accepted them without protest, happy almost. It's likely that Mama's long lectures on how we ought to behave toward Letitia had had their effect, or simply that we loved her enough and it didn't bother us that she was boss. A pity that she didn't have the looks for the boss, she was shortest of the three of us and very skinny. Holanda was skinny, and I never weighed over 110, but Letitia was scragglier than we were, and even worse, that kind of skinniness you can see from a distance in the neck and ears. Maybe it was the stiffness of her back that made her look so thin, for instance she could hardly move her head from side to side, she was like a folded-up ironing board, one of those kind they had in the Loza house, with a cover of white material. Like an ironing board with the wide part up, leaning closed against the wall. And she led us.

The best satisfaction was to imagine that someday Mama or Aunt Ruth would find out about the game. If they managed to find out about the game there would be an unbelievable mess. The G-flat and fainting fits, incredible protests of devotion and sacrifice ill-rewarded, and a string of words threatening the more celebrated punishments, closing the bid with a dire prediction of our fates, which consisted of the three of us ending up on the street. This final prediction always left us somewhat perplexed, because to end up in the street always seemed fairly normal to us.

First Letitia had us draw lots. We used to use pebbles hidden in the hand, count to twenty-one, any way at all. If we used the count-to-twenty-one system, we would pretend two or three more girls and include them in the counting to prevent cheating. If one of them came out 21, we dropped her from the group and started drawing again, until one of us won. Then Holanda and I lifted the stone and we got out the ornament-box. Suppose Holanda had won, Letitia and I chose the ornaments. The game took two forms: Statues and Attitudes. Attitudes did not require ornaments but an awful lot of expressiveness, for Envy you could show your teeth, make fists and hold them in a position so as to seem cringing. For Charity the ideal was an angelic face, eyes turned up to the sky, while the hands offered something—a rag, a ball, a branch of willow—to a poor invisible orphan. Shame and Fear were easy to do; Spite and Jealousy required a more conscientious study. The Statues were determined, almost all of them, by the choice of ornaments, and here absolute liberty reigned. So that a statue would come out of it, one had to think carefully of every detail in the costume. It was a rule of the game that the one chosen could not take part in the selection; the two remaining argued out the business at hand and then fitted the ornaments on. The winner had to invent her statue taking into account what they'd dressed her in, and in this way the game was much more complicated and exciting because sometimes there were counterplots, and the victim would find herself rigged out in adornments which were completely hopeless; so it was up to her to be quick then in composing a good statue. Usually when the game called for Attitudes, the winner came up pretty well outfitted, but there were times when the Statues were horrible failures.

Well, the story I'm telling, lord knows when it began, but things changed the day the first note fell from the train. Naturally the Attitudes and Statues were not for our own consumption, we'd have gotten bored immediately. The rules were that the winner had to station herself at the foot of the embankment, leaving the shade of the willow trees, and wait for the train from Tigre that passed at 2:08. At that height above Palermo the trains went by pretty fast and we weren't bashful doing the Statue or the Attitude. We hardly saw the people in the train windows, but with time, we got a bit more expert, and we knew that some of the passengers were expecting to see us. One man with white hair and tortoise-shell glasses used to stick his head out the window and wave at the Statue or the Attitude with a handkerchief. Boys sitting on the steps of the coaches on their way back from school shouted things as the train went by, but some of them remained serious and watching us. In actual fact, the Statue or the Attitude saw nothing at all, because she had to concentrate so hard on holding herself stock-still, but the other two under the willows would analyze in excruciating detail the great success produced, or the audience indifference. It was a Wednesday when the note dropped as the second coach went by. It fell very near Holanda (she did Malicious Gossip that day) and ricocheted toward me. The small piece of paper was tightly folded up and had been shoved through a metal nut. In a man's handwriting, and pretty bad too, it said: "The Statues very pretty. I ride in the third window of the second coach. Ariel B." For all the trouble of stuffing it through the nut and tossing it, it seemed to us a little dry, but it delighted us. We chose lots to see who would keep it, and I won. The next day nobody wanted to play because we all wanted to see what Ariel B. was like, but we were afraid he would misinterpret our interruption, so finally we chose lots and Letitia won. Holanda and I were very happy because Letitia did Statues very well, poor thing. The paralysis wasn't noticeable when she was still, and she was capable of gestures of enormous nobility. With Attitudes she always chose Generosity, Piety, Sacrifice and Renunciation. With Statues she tried for the style of the Venus in the parlor which Aunt Ruth called the Venus de Nilo. For that reason we chose ornaments especially so that Ariel would be very impressed. We hung a piece of green velvet on her like a tunic, and a crown of willow on her hair. As we were wearing short sleeves, the Greek effect was terrific. Letitia practiced a little in the shade, and we decided that we'd show ourselves also and wave at Ariel, discreetly, but very friendly.

Letitia was magnificent, when the train came she didn't budge a finger. Since she couldn't turn her head, she threw it backward, bringing her arms against her body almost as though she were missing them; except for the green tunic, it was like looking at the Venus de Nilo. In the third window we saw a boy with blond curly hair and light eyes, who smiled brightly when he saw that Holanda and I were waving at him. The train was gone in a second, but it was 4:30 and we were still discussing whether he was wearing a dark suit, a red tie, and if he were really nice or a creep. On Thursday I did an Attitude, Dejection, and we got another note which read: "The three of you I like very much. Ariel." Now he stuck his head and one arm out the window and laughed and waved at us. We figured him to be eighteen (we were sure he was no older than sixteen), and we decided that he was coming back every day from some English school, we couldn't stand the idea of any of the regular peanut factories. You could see that Ariel was super.

As it happened, Holanda had the terrific luck to win three days running. She surpassed herself, doing the attitudes Reproach and Robbery, and a very difficult Statue of The Ballerina, balancing on one foot from the time the train hit the curve. The next day I won, and the day after that too; when I was doing Horror, a note from Ariel almost caught me on the nose; at first we didn't understand it: "The prettiest is the laziest." Letitia was the last to understand it; we saw that she blushed and went off by herself, and Holanda and I looked at each other, just a little furious. The first judicial opinion it occurred to us to hand down was that Ariel was an idiot, but we couldn't tell Letitia that, poor angel, with the disadvantage she had to put up with. She said nothing, but it seemed to be understood that the paper was hers, and she kept it. We were sort of quiet going back to the house that day, and didn't get together that night. Letitia was very happy at the supper table, her eyes shining, and Mama looked at Aunt Ruth a couple of times as evidence of her own high spirits. In those days they were trying out a new strengthening treatment for Letitia, and considering how she looked, it was miraculous how well she was feeling.

Before we went to sleep, Holanda and I talked about the business. The note from Ariel didn't bother us so much, thrown from a train going its own way, that's how it is, but it seemed to us that Letitia from her privileged position was taking too much advantage of us. She knew we weren't going to say anything to her, and in a household where there's someone with some physical defect and a lot of pride, everyone pretends to ignore it starting with the one who's sick, or better yet, they pretend they don't know that the other one knows. But you don't have to exaggerate it either, and the way Letitia was acting at the table, or the way she kept the note, was just too much. That night I went back to having nightmares about trains, it was morning and I was walking on enormous railroad beaches covered with rails filled with switches, seeing in the distance the red glows of locomotives approaching, anxiously trying to calculate if the train was going to pass to my left and threatened at the same time by the arrival of an express back of me or—what was even worse—that one of the trains would switch off onto one of the sidings and run directly over me. But I forgot it by morning because Letitia was all full of aches and we had to help her get dressed. It seemed to us that she was a little sorry for the business yesterday and we were very nice to her, telling her that's what happens with walking too much and that maybe it would be better for her to stay in her room reading. She said nothing but came to the table for breakfast, and when Mama asked, she said she was fine and her back hardly hurt at all. She stated it firmly and looked at us.

That afternoon I won, but at that moment, I don't know what came over me, I told Letitia that I'd give her my place, naturally without telling her why. That this guy clearly preferred her and would look at her until his eyes fell out. The game drew to Statues, and we selected simple items so as not to complicate life, and she invented a sort of Chinese Princess, with a shy air, looking at the ground, and the hands placed together as Chinese princesses are wont to do. When the train passed, Holanda was lying on her back under the willows, but I watched and saw that Ariel had eyes only for Letitia. He kept looking at her until the train disappeared around the curve, and Letitia stood there motionless and didn't know that he had just looked at her that way. But when it came to resting under the trees again, we saw that she knew all right, and that she'd have been pleased to keep the costume on all afternoon and all night.

Wednesday we drew between Holanda and me, because Letitia said it was only fair she be left out. Holanda won, darn her luck, but Ariel's letter fell next to me. When I picked it up I had the impulse to give it to Letitia who didn't say a word, but I thought, then, that neither was it a matter of catering to everybody's wishes, and I opened it slowly. Ariel announced that the next day he was going to get off at the nearby station and that he would come by the embankment to chat for a while. It was all terribly written, but the final phrase was handsomely put: "Warmest regards to the three Statues." The signature looked like a scrawl though we remarked on its personality.

While we were taking the ornaments off Holanda, Letitia looked at me once or twice. I'd read them the message and no one had made any comments, which was very upsetting because finally, at last, Ariel was going to come and one had to think about this new development and come to some decision. If they found out about it at the house, or if by accident one of the Loza girls, those envious little runts, came to spy on us, there was going to be one incredible mess. Furthermore, it was extremely unlike us to remain silent over a thing like this; we hardly looked at one another, putting the ornaments away and going back through the white gate to the house.

Aunt Ruth asked Holanda and me to wash the cat, and she took Letitia off for the evening treatment and finally we could get our feelings off our chests. It seemed super that Ariel was going to come, we'd never had a friend like that, our cousin Tito we didn't count, a dumbbell who cut out paper dolls and believed in first communion. We were extremely nervous in our expectation and José, poor angel, got the short end of it. Holanda was the braver of the two and brought up the subject of Letitia. I didn't know what to think, on the one hand it seemed ghastly to me that Ariel should find out, but also it was only fair that things clear themselves up, no one had to out and out put herself on the line for someone else. What I really would have wanted was that Letitia not suffer; she had enough to put up with and now the new treatment and all those things.

That night Mama was amazed to see us so quiet and said what a miracle, and had the cat got our tongues, then looked at Aunt Ruth and both of them thought for sure we'd been raising hell of some kind and were conscience-stricken. Letitia ate very little and said that she hurt and would they let her go to her room to read Rocambole. Though she didn't much want to, Holanda gave her a hand, and I sat down and started some knitting, something I do only when I'm nervous. Twice I thought to go down to Letitia's room, I couldn't figure out what the two of them were doing there alone, but then Holanda came back with a mysterious air of importance and sat next to me not saying a word until Mama and Aunt Ruth cleared the table. "She doesn't want to go tomorrow. She wrote a letter and said that if he asks a lot of questions we should give it to him." Half-opening the pocket of her blouse she showed me the lilac-tinted envelope. Then they called us in to dry the dishes, and that night we fell asleep almost immediately, exhausted by all the high-pitched emotion and from washing José.

The next day it was my turn to do the marketing and I didn't see Letitia all morning, she stayed in her room. Before they called us to lunch I went in for a moment and found her sitting at the window with a pile of pillows and a new Rocambole novel. You could see she felt terrible, but she started to laugh and told me about a bee that couldn't find its way out and about a funny dream she had had. I said it was a pity she wasn't coming out to the willows, but I found it difficult to put it nicely. "If you want, we can explain to Ariel that you feel upset," I suggested, but she said no and shut up like a clam. I insisted for a little while, really, that she should come, and finally got terribly gushy and told her she shouldn't be afraid, giving as an example that true affection knows no barriers and other fat ideas we'd gotten from *The Treasure of Youth*, but it got harder and harder to say anything to her because she was looking out the window and looked as if she were going to cry. Finally I left, saying that Mama needed me. Lunch lasted for days, and Holanda got a slap from Aunt Ruth for having spattered some tomato sauce from the spaghetti on to the tablecloth. I don't even remember doing the dishes, right away we were out under the willows hugging one another, very happy, and not jealous of one another in the slightest. Holanda explained to me everything we had to say about our studies so that Ariel would be impressed, because high school students despised girls who'd only been through grade school and studied just home ec and knew how to do raised needlework. When the train went past at 2:08, Ariel waved his arms enthusiastically, and we waved a welcome to him with our embossed handkerchiefs. Some twenty minutes later we saw him arrive by the embankment; he was taller than we had thought and dressed all in grey.

I don't even remember what we talked about at first; he was somewhat shy in spite of having come and the notes and everything, and said a lot of considerate things. Almost immediately he praised our Statues and Attitudes and asked our names, and why had the third one not come. Holanda explained that Letitia had not been able to come, and he said that that was a pity and that he thought Letitia was an exquisite name. Then he told us stuff about the Industrial High School, it was not the English school, unhappily, and wanted to know if we would show him the ornaments. Holanda lifted the stone and we let him see the things. He seemed to be very interested in them, and at different times he would take one of the ornaments and say, "Letitia wore this one day," or "This was for the Oriental statue," what he meant was the Chinese Princess. We sat in the shade under a willow and he was happy but distracted, and you could see that he was only being polite. Holanda looked at me two or three times when the conversation lapsed into silence, and that made both of us feel awful, made us want to get out of it, or wish that Ariel had never come at all. He asked again if Letitia were ill and Holanda looked at me and I thought she was going to tell him, but instead she answered that Letitia had not been able to come. Ariel drew geometric figures in the dust with a stick and occasionally looked at the white gate and we knew what he was thinking, and because of that Holanda was right to pull out the lilac envelope and hand it up to him, and he stood there surprised with the envelope in his hand; then he blushed while we explained to him that Letitia had sent it to him, and he put the letter in an inside jacket pocket, not wanting to read it in front of us. Almost immediately he said that it had been a great pleasure for him and that he was delighted to have come, but his hand was soft and unpleasant in a way it'd have been better for the interview to end right away, although later we could only think of his grey eyes and the sad way he had of smiling. We also agreed on how he had said goodbye: "Until always," a form we'd never heard at home and which seemed to us so godlike and poetic. We told all this to Letitia who was waiting for us under the lemon tree in the patio, and I would have liked to have asked her what she had said in the letter, but I don't know what, it was because she'd sealed the envelope before giving it to Holanda, so I didn't say anything about that and only told her what Ariel was like and how many times he'd asked for her. This was not at all an easy thing to do because it was a nice thing and a terrible thing at the same time; we noticed that Letitia was feeling very happy and at the same time she was almost crying, and we found ourselves saying that Aunt Ruth wanted us now and we left her looking at the wasps in the lemon tree.

When we were going to sleep that night, Holanda said to me, "The game's finished from tomorrow on, you'll see." But she was wrong though not by much, and the next day Letitia gave us the regular signal when dessert came around. We went out to wash the dishes somewhat astonished, and a bit sore, because that was sheer sauciness on Letitia's part and not the right thing to do. She was waiting for us at the gate, and we almost died of fright when we got to the willows for she brought out of her pocket Mama's pearl collar and all her rings, even Aunt Ruth's big one with the ruby. If the Loza girls were spying on us and saw us with the jewels, sure as anything Mama would learn about it right away and kill us, the nasty little creeps. But Letitia wasn't scared and said if anything happened she was the only one responsible. "I would like you to leave it to me today," she added without looking at us. We got the ornaments out right away, all of a sudden we wanted to be very kind to Letitia and give her all the pleasure, although at the bottom of everything we were still feeling a little spiteful. The game came out Statues, and we chose lovely things that would go well with the jewels, lots of peacock feathers to set in the hair, and a fur that from a distance looked like silver fox, and a pink veil that she put on like a turban. We saw that she was thinking, trying the Statue out, but without moving, and when the train appeared on the curve she placed herself at the foot of the incline with all the jewels sparkling in the sun. She lifted her arms as if she were going to do an Attitude instead of a Statue, her hands pointed at the sky with her head thrown back (the only direction she could, poor thing) and bent her body backwards so far it scared us. To us it seemed terrific, the most regal statue she'd ever done; then we saw Ariel looking at her, hung halfway out the window he looked just at her, turning his head and looking at her without seeing us, until the train carried him out of sight all at once. I don't know why, the two of us started running at the same time to catch Letitia who was standing there, still with her eyes closed and enormous tears all down her face. She pushed us back, not angrily, but we helped her stuff the jewels in her pocket, and she went back to the house alone while we put the ornaments away in their box for the last time. We knew almost what was going to happen, but just the same we went out to the willows the next day, just the two of us, after Aunt Ruth imposed absolute silence so as not to disturb Letitia who hurt and who wanted to sleep. When the train came by, it was no surprise to see the third window empty, and while we were grinning at one another, somewhere between relief and being furious, we imagined Ariel riding on the other side of the coach, not moving in his seat, looking off toward the river with his grey eyes.

BERNARD MALAMUD

(1914–1986)

*B*ernard Malamud was born in Brooklyn, New York, the son of parents who owned a small grocery store. He received a B.A. from City College of New York (1936) and an M.A. in English from Columbia (1942). In 1949, the year his first story was published (in Harper's Bazaar), he left New York for Corvalis, Oregon, where he taught creative writing at Oregon State University for a dozen years. He moved from there to Bennington College in Vermont, where he continued to write the short fiction and novels that made him famous. His early work includes the novels The Natural (1952) and The Assistant (1958) and a collection of short stories, The Magic Barrel (1958), for which he won the National Book Award. Throughout his career, he demonstrated an extraordinary range. A New Life (1961) is a quasi-autobiographical account of the first part of his teaching career; The Fixer (1966), based on an actual historical incident, tells the story of a Jew in Tsarist Russia charged with murdering a Christian boy; The Tenants (1971), set in a gloomy Manhattan wasteland, focuses on the isolation of an aspiring writer; Dubin's Lives (1979) is about a biographer's attempt to deal with aging, boredom, and loneliness; God's Grace (1982) is a powerful dystopian vision in which Malamud muses about man's self-destructive, cruel, and violent tendencies. A volume of his collected stories came out in 1983. Critics have discussed Malamud as a realist, a romantic, a fabulator, a mythic writer, and a Jewish writer. Asked about his obsession with suffering, Malamud said, "I'm against it, but when it occurs why waste the experience?" And his work is perhaps best seen as an extended meditation on the implications of the moral attitudes evoked by this central aspect of human life. His comments on his own short fiction suggest other interests as well:

> I love the pleasures of the short story. One of them is the fast payoff. Whatever happens happens quickly. The writer mounts his personal Pegasus, even if it is an absent-minded nag who never made it to the race track; an ascension occurs and the ride begins. The scenery often surprises, and so do some of the people one meets. Somewhere I've said that a short story packs a self in a few pages predicating a lifetime. The drama is tense, happens fast, and is more often than not outlandish. In a few pages a good story portrays the complexity of a life while producing the surprise and effect of knowledge—not a bad payoff.

The Magic Barrel

Not long ago there lived in uptown New York, in a small, almost meager room, though crowded with books, Leo Finkle, a rabbinical student in the Yeshivah University. Finkle, after six years of study, was to be ordained in June and had been advised by an acquaintance that he might find it easier to win himself a congregation if he were married. Since he had no present prospects of marriage, after two tormented days of turning it over in his mind, he called in Pinye Salzman, a marriage broker whose two-line advertisement he had read in the *Forward*.

The matchmaker appeared one night out of the dark fourth-floor hallway of the graystone rooming house where Finkle lived, grasping a black, strapped portfolio that had been worn thin with use. Salzman, who had been long in the business, was of slight but dignified build, wearing an old hat, and an overcoat too short and tight for him. He smelled frankly of fish, which he loved to eat, and although he was missing a few teeth, his presence was not displeasing, because of an amiable manner curiously contrasted with mournful eyes. His voice, his lips, his wisp of beard, his bony fingers were animated, but give him a moment of repose and his mild blue eyes revealed a depth of sadness, a characteristic that put Leo a little at ease although the situation, for him, was inherently tense.

He at once informed Salzman why he had asked him to come, explaining that his home was in Cleveland, and that but for his parents, who had married comparatively late in life, he was alone in the world. He had for six years devoted himself almost entirely to his studies, as a result of which, understandably, he had found himself without time for a social life and the company of young women. Therefore he thought it the better part of trial and error—of embarrassing fumbling—to call in an experienced person to advise him on these matters. He remarked in passing that the function of the marriage broker was ancient and honorable, highly approved in the Jewish community, because it made practical the necessary without hindering joy. Moreover, his own parents had been brought together by a matchmaker. They had made, if not a financially profitable marriage—since neither had possessed any worldly goods to speak of—at least a successful one in the sense of their everlasting devotion to each other. Salzman listened in embarrassed surprise, sensing a sort of apology. Later, however, he experienced a glow of pride in his work, an emotion that had left him years ago, and he heartily approved of Finkle.

The two went to their business. Leo had led Salzman to the only clear place in the room, a table near a window that overlooked the lamp-lit city. He seated himself at the matchmaker's side but facing him, attempting by an act of will to suppress the unpleasant tickle in his throat. Salzman eagerly unstrapped his portfolio and removed a loose rubber band from a thin packet of much-handled cards. As he flipped through them, a gesture and sound that physically hurt Leo, the student pretended not to see and gazed steadfastly out the window. Although it was still February, winter was on its last legs, signs of which he had for the first time in years begun to notice. He now observed the round white moon, moving high in the sky through a cloud menagerie, and watched with half-open mouth as it penetrated a huge hen, and dropped out of her like an egg laying itself. Salzman, though pretending through eyeglasses he had just slipped on, to be engaged in scanning the writing on the cards, stole occasional glances at the young man's distinguished face, noting with pleasure the long, severe scholar's nose, brown eyes heavy with learning, sensitive yet ascetic lips, and a certain, almost hollow quality of the dark cheeks. He gazed around at shelves upon shelves of books and let out a soft, contented sigh.

When Leo's eyes fell upon the cards, he counted six spread out in Salzman's hand

"So few?" he asked in disappointment.

"You wouldn't believe me how much cards I got in my office," Salzman replied. "The drawers are already filled to the top, so I keep them now in a barrel, but is every girl good for a new rabbi?"

Leo blushed at this, regretting all he had revealed of himself in a curriculum vitae he had sent to Salzman. He had thought it best to acquaint him with his strict standards and specifications, but in having done so, felt he had told the marriage broker more than was absolutely necessary.

He hesitantly inquired, "Do you keep photographs of your clients on file?"

"First comes family, amount of dowry, also what kind promises," Salzman replied, unbuttoning his tight coat and settling himself in the chair. "After comes pictures, rabbi."

"Call me Mr. Finkle. I'm not yet a rabbi."

Salzman said he would, but instead called him doctor, which he changed to rabbi when Leo was not listening too attentively.

Salzman adjusted his horn-rimmed spectacles, gently cleared his throat and read in an eager voice the contents of the top card:

"Sophie P. Twenty four years. Widow one year. No children. Educated high school and two years college. Father promises eight thousand dollars. Has wonderful wholesale business. Also real estate. On the mother's side comes teachers, also one actor. Well known on Second Avenue."

Leo gazed up in surprise. "Did you say a widow?"

"A widow don't mean spoiled, rabbi. She lived with her husband maybe four months. He was a sick boy she made a mistake to marry him."

"Marrying a widow has never entered my mind."

"This is because you have no experience. A widow, especially if she is young and healthy like this girl, is a wonderful person to marry. She will be thankful to you the rest of her life. Believe me, if I was looking now for a bride, I would marry a widow."

Leo reflected, then shook his head.

Salzman hunched his shoulders in an almost imperceptible gesture of disappointment. He placed the card down on the wooden table and began to read another:

"Lily H. High school teacher. Regular. Not a substitute. Has savings and new Dodge car. Lived in Paris one year. Father is successful dentist thirty-five years. Interested in professional man. Well Americanized family. Wonderful opportunity."

"I knew her personally," said Salzman. "I wish you could see this girl. She is a doll. Also very intelligent. All day you could talk to her about books and theyater and what not. She also knows current events."

"I don't believe you mentioned her age?"

"Her age?" Salzman said, raising his brows. "Her age is thirty-two years."

Leo said after a while, "I'm afraid that seems a little too old."

Salzman let out a laugh. "So how old are you, rabbi?"

"Twenty-seven."

"So what is the difference, tell me, between twenty-seven and thirty-two? My own wife is seven years older than me. So what did I suffer?—Nothing. If Rothschild's a daughter wants to marry you, would you say on account her age, no?"

"Yes," Leo said dryly.

Salzman shook off the no in the yes. "Five years don't mean a thing. I give you my word that when you will live with her for one week you will forget her age. What does it mean five years—that she lived more and knows more than somebody who is younger? On this girl, God bless her, years are not wasted. Each one that it comes makes better the bargain."

"What subject does she teach in high school?"

"Languages. If you heard the way she speaks French, you will think it is music. I am in the business twenty-five years, and I recommend her with my whole heart. Believe me, I know what I'm talking, rabbi."

"What's on the next card?" Leo said abruptly.

Salzman reluctantly turned up the third card:

"Ruth K. Nineteen years. Honor student. Father offers thirteen thousand cash to the right bridegroom. He is a medical doctor. Stomach specialist with marvelous practice. Brother in law owns own garment business. Particular people."

Salzman looked as if he had read his trump card.

"Did you say nineteen?" Leo asked with interest.

"On the dot."

"Is she attractive?" He blushed. "Pretty?"

Salzman kissed his finger tips. "A little doll. On this I give you my word. Let me call the father tonight and you will see what means pretty."

But Leo was troubled. "You're sure she's that young?"

"This I am positive. The father will show you the birth certificate."

"Are you positive there isn't something wrong with her?" Leo insisted.

"Who says there is wrong?"

"I don't understand why an American girl her age should go to a marriage broker."

A smile spread over Salzman's face.

"So for the same reason you went, she comes."

Leo flushed. "I am pressed for time."

Salzman, realizing he had been tactless, quickly explained.

"The father came, not her. He wants she should have the best, so he looks around himself. When we will locate the right boy he will introduce him and encourage. This makes a better marriage than if a young girl without experience takes for herself. I don't have to tell you this."

"But don't you think this young girl believes in love?" Leo spoke uneasily.

Salzman was about to guffaw but caught himself and said soberly, "Love comes with the right person, not before."

Leo parted dry lips but did not speak. Noticing that Salzman had snatched a glance at the next card, he cleverly asked, "How is her health?"

"Perfect," Salzman said, breathing with difficulty. "Of course, she is a little lame on her right foot from an auto accident that it happened to her when she was twelve years, but nobody notices on account she is so brilliant and also beautiful."

Leo got up heavily and went to the window. He felt curiously bitter and upbraided himself for having called in the marriage broker. Finally, he shook his head.

"Why not?" Salzman persisted, the pitch of his voice rising.

"Because I detest stomach specialists."

"So what do you care what is his business? After you marry her do you need him? Who says he must come every Friday night in your house?"

Ashamed of the way the talk was going, Leo dismissed Salzman, who went home with heavy, melancholy eyes.

Though he had felt only relief at the marriage broker's departure, Leo was in low spirits the next day. He explained it as arising from Salzman's failure to produce a suitable bride for him. He did not care for his type of clientele. But when Leo found himself hesitating whether to seek out another matchmaker, one more polished than Pinye, he wondered if it could be—his protestations to the contrary, and although he honored his father and mother—that he did not, in essence, care for the matchmaking institution? This thought he quickly put out of mind yet found himself still upset. All day he ran around in the woods—missed an important appointment, forgot to give out his laundry, walked out of a Broadway cafeteria without paying and had to run back with the ticket in his hand; had even not recognized his landlady in the street when she passed with a friend and courteously called out, "A good evening to you, Doctor Finkle." By nightfall, however, he had regained sufficient calm to sink his nose into a book and there found peace from his thoughts.

Almost at once there came a knock on the door. Before Leo could say enter, Salzman, commercial cupid, was standing in the room. His face was gray and meager, his expression hungry, and he looked as if he would expire on his feet. Yet the marriage broker managed, by some trick of the muscles, to display a broad smile.

"So good evening. I am invited?"

Leo nodded, disturbed to see him again, yet unwilling to ask the man to leave.

Beaming still, Salzman laid his portfolio on the table. "Rabbi, I got for you tonight good news."

"I've asked you not to call me rabbi. I'm still a student."

"Your worries are finished. I have for you a first-class bride."

"Leave me in peace concerning this subject." Leo pretended lack of interest.

"The world will dance at your wedding."

"Please, Mr. Salzman, no more."

"But first must come back my strength," Salzman said weakly. He fumbled with the portfolio straps and took out of the leather case an oily paper bag, from which he extracted a hard, seeded roll and a small, smoked white fish. With a quick motion of his hand he stripped the fish out of its skin and began ravenously to chew. "All day in a rush," he muttered.

Leo watched him eat.

"A sliced tomato you have maybe?" Salzman hesitantly inquired.

"No."

The marriage broker shut his eyes and ate. When he had finished he carefully cleaned up the crumbs and rolled up the remains of the fish, in the paper bag. His spectacled eyes roamed the room until he discovered, among some piles of books, a one-burner gas stove. Lifting his hat he humbly asked, "A glass tea you got, rabbi?"

Conscience-stricken, Leo rose and brewed the tea. He served it with a chunk of lemon and two cubes of lump sugar, delighting Salzman.

After he had drunk his tea, Salzman's strength and good spirits were restored.

"So tell me, rabbi," he said amiably, "you considered some more the three clients I mentioned yesterday?"

"There was no need to consider."

"Why not?"

"None of them suits me."

"What then suits you?"

Leo let it pass because he could give only a confused answer.

Without waiting for a reply, Salzman asked, "You remember this girl I talked to you—the high school teacher?"

"Age thirty-two?"

But, surprisingly, Salzman's face lit in a smile. "Age twenty-nine."

Leo shot him a look. "Reduced from thirty-two?"

"A mistake," Salzman avowed. "I talked today with the dentist. He took me to his safety deposit box and showed me the birth certificate. She was twenty-nine years last August. They made her a party in the mountains where she went for her vacation. When her father spoke to me the first time I forgot to write the age and I told you thirty-two, but now I remember this was a different client, a widow."

"The same one you told me about? I thought she was twenty-four?"

"A different. Am I responsible that the world is filled with widows?"

"No, but I'm not interested in them, nor for that matter, in school teachers."

Salzman pulled his clasped hands to his breast. Looking at the ceiling he devoutly exclaimed, "Yiddishe kinder, what can I say to somebody that he is not interested in high school teachers? So what then you are interested?"

Leo flushed but controlled himself.

"In what else will you be interested," Salzman went on, "if you not interested in this fine girl that she speaks four languages and has personally in the bank ten thousand dollars? Also her father guarantees further twelve thousand. Also she has a new car, wonderful clothes, talks on all subjects, and she will give you a first-class home and children. How near do we come in our life to paradise?"

"If she's so wonderful, why wasn't she married ten years ago?"

"Why?" said Salzman with his heavy laugh. "—Why? Because she is *partikiler*. This is why. She wants the *best*."

Leo was silent, amused at how he had entangled himself. But Salzman had aroused his interest in Lily H., and he began seriously to consider calling on her. When the marriage broker observed how intently Leo's mind was at work on the facts he had supplied, he felt certain they would soon come to an agreement.

Late Saturday afternoon, conscious of Salzman, Leo Finkle walked with Lily Hirschorn along Riverside Drive. He walked briskly and erectly, wearing with distinction the black fedora he had that morning taken with trepidation out of the dusty hat box on his closet shelf, and the heavy black Saturday coat he had thoroughly whisked clean. Leo also owned a walking stick, a present from a distant relative, but quickly put temptation aside and did not use it. Lily, petite and not unpretty, had on something signifying the approach of spring. She was au courant, animatedly, with all sorts of subjects, and he weighed her words and found her surprisingly sound—score another for Salzman, whom he uneasily sensed to be some-where around, hiding perhaps high in a tree along the street, flashing the lady signals with a pocket mirror; or perhaps a cloven-hoofed Pan, piping nuptial ditties as he danced his invisible way before them, strewing wild buds on the walk and purple grapes in their path, symbolizing fruit of a union, though there was of course still none.

Lily startled Leo by remarking, "I was thinking of Mr. Salzman, a curious figure, wouldn't you say?"

Not certain what to answer, he nodded.

She bravely went on, blushing, "I for one am grateful for his introduc-ing us. Aren't you?"

He courteously replied, "I am."

"I mean," she said with a little laugh—and it was all in good taste, or at least gave the effect of being not in bad—"do you mind that we came together so?"

He was not displeased with her honesty, recognizing that she meant to set the relationship aright, and understanding that it took a certain amount of experience in life, and courage, to want to do it quite that way. One had to have some sort of past to make that kind of beginning.

He said that he did not mind. Salzman's function was traditional and honorable—valuable for what it might achieve, which, he pointed out, was frequently nothing.

Lily agreed with a sigh. They walked on for a while and she said after a long silence, again with a nervous laugh, "Would you mind if I asked you something a little bit personal? Frankly, I find the subject fascinating." Although Leo shrugged, she went on half embarrassedly, "How was it that you came to your calling? I mean was it a sudden passionate inspiration?"

Leo, after a time, slowly replied, "I was always interested in the Law."

"You saw revealed in it the presence of the Highest?"

He nodded and changed the subject. "I understand that you spent a little time in Paris, Miss Hirschorn?"

"Oh, did Mr. Salzman tell you, Rabbi Finkle?" Leo winced but she went on, "It was ages ago and almost forgotten. I remember I had to return for my sister's wedding."

And Lily would not be put off. "When," she asked in a trembly voice, "did you become enamored of God?"

He stared at her. Then it came to him that she was talking not about Leo Finkle, but of a total stranger, some mystical figure, perhaps even passionate prophet that Salzman had dreamed up for her—no relation to the living or dead. Leo trembled with rage and weakness. The trickster had obviously sold her a bill of goods, just as he had him, who'd expected to become acquainted with a young lady of twenty-nine, only to behold, the moment he laid eyes upon her strained and anxious face, a woman past thirty-five and aging rapidly. Only his self control had kept him this long in her presence.

"I am not," he said gravely, "a talented religious person," and in seeking words to go on, found himself possessed by shame and fear. "I think," he said in a strained manner, "that I came to God not because I loved Him, but because I did not."

This confession he spoke harshly because its unexpectedness shook him.

Lily wilted. Leo saw a profusion of loaves of bread go flying like ducks high over his head, not unlike the winged loaves by which he had counted himself to sleep last night. Mercifully, then, it snowed, which he would not put past Salzman's machinations.

He was infuriated with the marriage broker and swore he would throw him out of the room the minute he reappeared. But Salzman did not come that night, and when Leo's anger had subsided, an unaccountable despair grew in its place. At first he thought this was caused by his disappointment in Lily, but before long it became evident that he had involved himself with Salzman without a true knowledge of his own intent. He gradually realized—with an emptiness that seized him with six hands—that he had called in the broker to find him a bride because he was incapable of doing it himself. This terrifying insight he had derived as a result of his meeting and conversation with Lily Hirschorn. Her probing questions had somehow irritated him into revealing—to himself more than her—the true nature of his relationship to God, and from that it had come upon him, with shocking force, that apart from his parents, he had never loved anyone. Or perhaps it went the other way, that he did not love God so well as he might, because he had not loved man. It seemed to Leo that his whole life stood starkly revealed and he saw himself for the first time as he truly was—unloved and loveless. This bitter but somehow not fully unexpected revelation brought him to a point of panic, controlled only by extraordinary effort. He covered his face with his hands and cried.

The week that followed was the worst of his life. He did not eat and lost weight. His beard darkened and grew ragged. He stopped attending seminars and almost never opened a book. He seriously considered leaving the Yeshivah, although he was deeply troubled at the thought of the loss of all his years of study—saw them like pages torn from a book, strewn over the city—and at the devastating effect of this decision upon his parents. But he had lived without knowledge of himself, and never in the Five Books and all the Commentaries—mea culpa—had the truth been revealed to him. He did not know where to turn, and in all this desolating loneliness there was no *to whom*, although he often thought of Lily but not once could bring himself to go downstairs and make the call. He became touchy and irritable, especially with his landlady, who asked him all manner of personal questions; on the other hand, sensing his own disagreeableness, he waylaid her on the stairs and apologized abjectly, until mortified, she ran from him. Out of this, however, he drew the consolation that he was a Jew and that a Jew suffered. But gradually, as the long and terrible week drew to a close, he regained his composure and some idea of purpose in life: to go on as planned. Although he was imperfect, the ideal was not. As for his quest of a bride, the thought of continuing afflicted him with anxiety and heartburn, yet perhaps with this new knowledge of himself he would be more successful than in the past. Perhaps love would now come to him and a bride to that love. And for this sanctified seeking who needed a Salzman?

The marriage broker, a skeleton with haunted eyes, returned that very night. He looked, withal, the picture of frustrated expectancy—as if he had steadfastly waited the week at Miss Lily Hirschorn's side for a telephone call that never came.

Casually coughing, Salzman came immediately to the point: "So how did you like her?"

Leo's anger rose and he could not refrain from chiding the matchmaker: "Why did you lie to me, Salzman?"

Salzman's pale face went dead white, the world had snowed on him.

"Did you not state that she was twenty-nine?" Leo insisted.

"I give you my word—"

"She was thirty-five, if a day. *At least* thirty-five."

"Of this don't be too sure. Her father told me—"

"Never mind. The worst of it was that you lied to her."

"How did I lie to her, tell me?"

"You told her things about me that weren't true. You made me out to be more, consequently less than I am. She had in mind a totally different person, a sort of semi-mystical Wonder Rabbi."

"All I said, you was a religious man."

"I can imagine."

Salzman sighed. "This is my weakness that I have," he confessed. "My wife says to me I shouldn't be a salesman, but when I have two fine people that they would be wonderful to be married, I am so happy that I talk too much." He smiled wanly. "This is why Salzman is a poor man."

Leo's anger left him. "Well, Salzman, I'm afraid that's all."

The marriage broker fastened hungry eyes on him.

"You don't want any more a bride?"

"I do," said Leo, "But I have decided to seek her in a different way. I am no longer interested in an arranged marriage. To be frank, I now admit the necessity of premarital love. That is, I want to be in love with the one I marry."

"Love?" said Salzman, astounded. After a moment he remarked, "For us, our love is our life, not for the ladies. In the ghetto they—"

"I know, I know," said Leo. "I've thought of it often. Love, I have said to myself, should be a by-product of living and worship rather than its own end. Yet for myself I find it necessary to establish the level of my need and fulfill it."

Salzman shrugged but answered, "Listen, rabbi, if you want love, this I can find for you also. I have such beautiful clients that you will love them the minute your eyes will see them."

Leo smiled unhappily. "I'm afraid you don't understand."

But Salzman hastily unstrapped his portfolio and withdrew a manila packet from it.

"Pictures," he said, quickly laying the envelope on the table.

Leo called after him to take the pictures away, but as if on the wings of the wind, Salzman had disappeared.

March came. Leo had returned to his regular routine. Although he felt not quite himself yet—lacked energy—he was making plans for a more active social life. Of course it would cost something, but he was an expert in cutting corners; and when there were no corners left he would make circles rounder. All the while Salzman's pictures had lain on the table, gathering dust. Occasionally as Leo sat studying, or enjoying a cup of tea, his eyes fell on the manila envelope, but he never opened it.

The days went by and no social life to speak of developed with a member of the opposite sex—it was difficult, given the circumstances of his situation. One morning Leo toiled up the stairs to his room and stared out the window at the city. Although the day was bright his view of it was dark. For some time he watched the people in the street below hurrying along and then turned with a heavy heart to his little room. On the table was the packet. With a sudden relentless gesture he tore it open. For a half-hour he stood by the table in a state of excitement, examining the photographs of the ladies Salzman had included. Finally, with a deep sigh he put them down. There were six, of varying degrees of attractiveness, but look at them long enough and they all became Lily Hirschorn: all past their prime, all starved behind bright smiles, not a true personality in the lot. Life, despite their frantic yoohooings, had passed them by; they were pictures in a brief case that stank of fish. After a while, however, as Leo attempted to return the photographs into the envelope, he found in it another, a snapshot of the type taken by a machine for a quarter. He gazed at it a moment and let out a cry.

Her face deeply moved him. Why, he could at first not say. It gave him the impression of youth—spring flowers, yet age—a sense of having been used to the bone, wasted; this came from the eyes, which were hauntingly familiar, yet absolutely strange. He had a vivid impression that he had met her before, but try as he might he could not place her although he could almost recall her name, as if he had read it in her own handwriting. No, this couldn't be; he would have remembered her. It was not, he affirmed, that she had an extraordinary beauty—no, though her face was attractive enough; it was that *something* about her moved him. Feature for feature, even some of the ladies of the photographs could do better; but she leaped forth to his heart—had *lived*, or wanted to—more than just wanted, perhaps regretted how she had lived—had somehow deeply suffered: it could be seen in the depths of those reluctant eyes, and from the way the light enclosed and shone from her, and within her, opening realms of possibility: this was her own. Her he desired. His head ached and eyes narrowed with the intensity of his gazing, then as if an obscure fog had blown up in the mind, he experienced fear of her and was aware that he had received an impression, somehow, of evil. He shuddered, saying softly, it is thus with us all. Leo brewed some tea in a small pot and sat sipping it without sugar, to calm himself. But before he had finished drinking, again with excitement he examined the face and found it good: good for Leo Finkle. Only such a one could understand him and help him seek whatever he was seeking. She might, perhaps, love him. How she had happened to be among the discards in Salzman's barrel he could never guess, but he knew he must urgently go find her.

Leo rushed downstairs, grabbed up the Bronx telephone book, and searched for Salzman's home address. He was not listed, nor was his office. Neither was he in the Manhattan book. But Leo remembered having written down the address on a slip of paper after he had read Salzman's advertisement in the "personals" column of the *Forward*. He ran up to his room and tore through his papers, without luck. It was exasperating. Just when he needed the matchmaker he was nowhere to be found. Fortunately Leo remembered to look in his wallet. There on a card he found his name written and a Bronx address. No phone number was listed, the reason—Leo now recalled—he had originally communicated with Salzman by letter. He got on his coat, put a hat on over his skull cap and hurried to the subway station. All the way to the far end of the Bronx he sat on the edge of his seat. He was more than once tempted to take out the picture and see if the girl's face was as he remembered it, but he refrained, allowing the snapshot to remain in his inside coat pocket, content to have her so close. When the train pulled into the station he was waiting at the door and bolted out. He quickly located the street Salzman had advertised.

The building he sought was less than a block from the subway, but it was not an office building, nor even a loft, nor a store in which one could rent office space. It was a very old tenement house. Leo found Salzman's name in pencil on a soiled tag under the bell and climbed three dark flights to his apartment. When he knocked, the door was opened by a thin, asthmatic, gray-haired woman, in felt slippers.

"Yes?" she said, expecting nothing. She listened without listening. He could have sworn he had seen her, too, before but knew it was an illusion.

"Salzman—does he live here? Pinye Salzman," he said, "the matchmaker?"

She stared at him a long minute. "Of course."

He felt embarrassed. "Is he in?"

"No." Her mouth, though left open, offered nothing more.

"The matter is urgent. Can you tell me where his office is?"

"In the air." She pointed upward.

"You mean he has no office?" Leo asked.

"In his socks."

He peered into the apartment. It was sunless and dingy, one large room divided by a half-open curtain, beyond which he could see a sagging metal bed. The near side of a room was crowded with rickety chairs, old bureaus, a three-legged table, racks of cooking utensils, and all the apparatus of a kitchen. But there was no sign of Salzman or his magic barrel, probably also a figment of the imagination. An odor of frying fish made Leo weak to the knees.

"Where is he?" he insisted. "I've got to see your husband."

At length she answered, "So who knows where he is? Every time he thinks a new thought he runs to a different place. Go home, he will find you."

"Tell him Leo Finkle."

She gave no sign she had heard.

He walked downstairs, depressed.

But Salzman, breathless, stood waiting at his door.

Leo was astounded and overjoyed. "How did you get here before me?"

"I rushed."

"Come inside."

They entered. Leo fixed tea, and a sardine sandwich for Salzman. As they were drinking he reached behind him for the packet of pictures and handed them to the marriage broker.

Salzman put down his glass and said expectantly, "You found somebody you like?"

"Not among these."

The marriage broker turned away.

"Here is the one I want." Leo held forth the snapshot.

Salzman slipped on his glasses and took the picture into his trembling hand. He turned ghastly and let out a groan.

"What's the matter?" cried Leo.

"Excuse me. Was an accident this picture. She isn't for you."

Salzman frantically shoved the manila packet into his portfolio. He thrust the snapshot into his pocket and fled down the stairs.

Leo, after momentary paralysis, gave chase and cornered the marriage broker in the vestibule. The landlady made hysterical outcries but neither of them listened.

"Give me back the picture, Salzman."

"No." The pain in his eyes was terrible.

"Tell me who she is then."

"This I can't tell you. Excuse me."

He made to depart, but Leo, forgetting himself, seized the matchmaker by his tight coat and shook him frenziedly.

"Please," sighed Salzman. *"Please."*

Leo ashamedly let him go. "Tell me who she is," he begged. "It's very important for me to know."

"She is not for you. She is a wild one—wild, without shame. This is not a bride for a rabbi."

"What do you mean wild?"

"Like an animal. Like a dog. For her to be poor was a sin. This is why to me she is dead now."

"In God's name, what do you mean?"

"Her I can't introduce to you," Salzman cried.

"Why are you so excited?"

"Why, he asks," Salzman said, bursting into tears. "This is my baby, my Stella, she should burn in hell."

Leo hurried up to bed and hid under the covers. Under the covers he thought his life through. Although he soon fell asleep he could not sleep her out of his mind. He woke, beating his breast. Though he prayed to be rid of her, his prayers went unanswered. Through days of torment he endlessly struggled not to love her; fearing success, he escaped it. He then concluded to convert her to goodness, himself to God. The idea alternately nauseated and exalted him.

He perhaps did not know that he had come to a final decision until he encountered Salzman in a Broadway cafeteria. He was sitting alone at a rear table, sucking the bony remains of a fish. The marriage broker appeared haggard, and transparent to the point of vanishing.

Salzman looked up at first without recognizing him. Leo had grown a pointed beard and his eyes were weighted with wisdom.

"Salzman," he said, "love has at last come to my heart."

"Who can love from a picture?" mocked the marriage broker.

"It is not impossible."

"If you can love her, then you can love anybody. Let me show you some new clients that they just sent me their photographs. One is a little doll."

"Just her I want," Leo murmured.

"Don't be a fool, doctor. Don't bother with her."

"Put me in touch with her, Salzman," Leo said humbly. "Perhaps I can be of service."

Salzman had stopped eating and Leo understood with emotion that it was now arranged.

Leaving the cafeteria, he was, however, afflicted by a tormenting suspicion that Salzman had planned it all to happen this way.

Leo was informed by letter that she would meet him on a certain corner, and she was there one spring night, waiting under a street lamp. He appeared, carrying a small bouquet of violets and rosebuds. Stella stood by the lamp post, smoking. She wore white with red shoes, which fitted his expectations, although in a troubled moment he had imagined the dress red, and only the shoes white. She waited uneasily and shyly. From afar he saw that her eyes—clearly her father's—were filled with desperate innocence. He pictured, in her, his own redemption. Violins and lit candles revolved in the sky. Leo ran forward with flowers outthrust.

Around the corner, Salzman, leaning against a wall, chanted prayers for the dead.

CARSON MCCULLERS

(1917–1967)

C arson McCullers was born Lula Carson Smith in Columbus, Georgia, the daughter of a father who was a watchmaker and a mother who was convinced that her first child was destined for greatness. She had rheumatic fever as a teenager, which damaged her heart and was the indirect cause of the crippling strokes she suffered as an adult. McCullers trained to be a concert pianist from an early age, but she abandoned the piano and took up writing, attending creative writing courses at Columbia and New York University. At the age of 23, she published **The Heart Is a Lonely Hunter**, which was a success with both the critics and the public. Stories such as "A Tree. A Rock. A Cloud" and "The Ballad of the Sad Café" won prestigious awards in the early 1940s, and the decade ended with the triumph of **Member of the Wedding** on Broadway and the publication in one volume of her best work, **The Ballad of the Sad Café** (1951). Ill health, alcohol, and a series of complicated relationships with men and women provided the intensity of experience she recreated in her writing. Much of her best short fiction is the product of what Lawrence Graves calls her "early relationship with the properties of the ballad world. Experience heightened far beyond the realm of plausibility is given a valid poetic truth by the propriety of those conventions that make the miraculous seem oddly real. Dreams, superstitions, omens, numbers, musical motifs, all . . . make the inexplicable longings of the characters seem like dark elemental forces in the natural world." In one of the most famous passages from "The Ballad of the Sad Café" (1943), McCullers explains why she finds the dark side of human passion so attractive:

> There are the lover and the beloved, but these two come from different countries. Often the beloved is only a stimulus for all the stored-up love which has lain quiet within the lover for a long time. And somehow every lover knows this. He feels in his soul that his love is a solitary thing. . . . Almost everyone wants to be the lover. And the curt truth is that, in a deep and secret way, the state of being beloved is intolerable to many. The beloved fears and hates the lover, and with the best of reasons. For the lover is forever trying to strip bare his beloved. The lover craves any possible relation with the beloved, even if this experience can cause him only pain.

The evocation of the intense loneliness presupposed by such a view is what makes McCullers's best stories so poignant and so memorable.

A Tree. A Rock. A Cloud

It was raining that morning, and still very dark. When the boy reached the streetcar café he had almost finished his route and he went in for a cup of coffee. The place was an all-night café owned by a bitter and stingy man called Leo. After the raw, empty street the café seemed friendly and bright: along the counter there were a couple of soldiers, three spinners from the cotton mill, and in a corner a man who sat hunched over with his nose and half his face down in a beer mug. The boy wore a helmet such as aviators wear. When he went into the café he unbuckled the chin strap and raised the right flap up over his pink little ear; often as he drank his coffee someone would speak to him in a friendly way. But this morning Leo did not look into his face and none of the men were talking. He paid and was leaving the café when a voice called out to him:

"Son! Hey Son!"

He turned back and the man in the corner was crooking his finger and nodding to him. He had brought his face out of the beer mug and he seemed suddenly very happy. The man was long and pale, with a big nose and faded orange hair.

"Hey Son!"

The boy went toward him. He was an undersized boy of about twelve, with one shoulder drawn higher than the other because of the weight of the paper sack. His face was shallow, freckled, and his eyes were round child eyes.

"Yeah Mister?"

The man laid one hand on the paper boy's shoulders, then grasped the boy's chin and turned his face slowly from one side to the other. The boy shrank back uneasily.

"Say! What's the big idea?"

The boy's voice was shrill; inside the café it was suddenly very quiet.

The man said slowly: "I love you."

All along the counter the men laughed. The boy, who had scowled and sidled away, did not know what to do. He looked over the counter at Leo, and Leo watched him with a weary, brittle jeer. The boy tried to laugh also. But the man was serious and sad.

"I did not mean to tease you, Son," he said. "Sit down and have a beer with me. There is something I have to explain."

Cautiously, out of the corner of his eye, the paper boy questioned the men along the counter to see what he should do. But they had gone back to their beer or their breakfast and did not notice him. Leo put a cup of coffee on the counter and a little jug of cream.

"He is a minor," Leo said.

The paper boy slid himself up onto the stool. His ear beneath the upturned flap of the helmet was very small and red. The man was nodding at him soberly. "It is important," he said. Then he reached in his hip pocket and brought out something which he held up in the palm of his hand for the boy to see.

"Look very carefully," he said.

The boy stared, but there was nothing to look at very carefully. The man held in his big, grimy palm a photograph. It was the face of a woman, but blurred, so that only the hat and dress she was wearing stood out clearly.

"See?" the man asked.

The boy nodded and the man placed another picture in his palm. The woman was standing on a beach in a bathing suit. The suit made her stomach very big, and that was the main thing you noticed.

"Got a good look?" He leaned over closer and finally asked: "You ever seen her before?"

The boy sat motionless, staring slantwise at the man. "Not so I know of."

"Very well." The man blew on the photographs and put them back into his pocket. "That was my wife."

"Dead?" the boy asked.

Slowly the man shook his head. He pursed his lips as though about to whistle and answered in a long-drawn way: "Nuuu—" he said. "I will explain."

The beer on the counter before the man was in a large brown mug. He did not pick it up to drink. Instead he bent down and, putting his face over the rim, he rested there for a moment. Then with both hands he tilted the mug and sipped.

"Some night you'll go to sleep with your big nose in a mug and drown," said Leo. "Prominent transient drowns in beer. That would be a cute death."

The paper boy tried to signal to Leo. While the man was not looking he screwed up his face and worked his mouth to question soundlessly: "Drunk?" But Leo only raised his eyebrows and turned away to put some pink strips of bacon on the grill. The man pushed the mug away from him, straightened himself, and folded his loose crooked hands on the counter. His face was sad as he looked at the paper boy. He did not blink, but from time to time the lids closed down with delicate gravity over his pale green eyes. It was nearing dawn and the boy shifted the weight of the paper sack.

"I am talking about love," the man said. "With me it is a science."

The boy half slid down from the stool. But the man raised his forefinger, and there was something about him that held the boy and would not let him go away.

"Twelve years ago I married the woman in the photograph. She was my wife for one year, nine months, three days, and two nights. I loved her. Yes . . ." He tightened his blurred, rambling voice and said again: "I loved her. I thought also that she loved me. I was a railroad engineer. She had all home comforts and luxuries. It never crept into my brain that she was not satisfied. But do you know what happened?"

"Mgneeow!" said Leo.

The man did not take his eyes from the boy's face. "She left me. I came in one night and the house was empty and she was gone. She left me."

"With a fellow?" the boy asked.

Gently the man placed his palm down on the counter. "Why naturally, Son. A woman does not run off like that alone."

The café was quiet, the soft rain black and endless in the street outside. Leo pressed down the frying bacon with the prongs of his long fork. "So you have been chasing the floozie for eleven years. You frazzled old rascal!"

For the first time the man glanced at Leo. "Please don't be vulgar. Besides, I was not speaking to you." He turned back to the boy and said in a trusting and secretive undertone: "Let's not pay any attention to him, O.K.?"

The paper boy nodded doubtfully.

"It was like this," the man continued. "I am a person who feels many things. All my life one thing after another has impressed me. Moonlight. The leg of a pretty girl. One thing after another. But the point is that when I had enjoyed anything there was a peculiar sensation as though it was laying around loose in me. Nothing seemed to finish itself up or fit in with the other things. Women? I had my portion of them. The same. Afterwards laying around loose in me. I was a man who had never loved."

Very slowly he closed his eyelids, and the gesture was like a curtain drawn at the end of a scene in a play. When he spoke again his voice was excited and the words came fast—the lobes of his large, loose ears seemed to tremble.

"Then I met this woman. I was fifty-one years old and she always said she was thirty. I met her at a filling station and we were married within three days. And do you know what it was like? I just can't tell you. All I had ever felt was gathered together around this woman. Nothing lay around loose in me any more but was finished up by her."

The man stopped suddenly and stroked his long nose. His voice sank down to a steady and reproachful undertone: "I'm not explaining this right. What happened was this. There were these beautiful feelings and loose little pleasures inside me. And this woman was something like an assembly line for my soul. I run these little pieces of myself through her and I come out complete. Now do you follow me?"

"What was her name?" the boy asked.

"Oh," he said. "I called her Dodo. But that is immaterial."

"Did you try to make her come back?"

The man did not seem to hear. "Under the circumstances you can imagine how I felt when she left me."

Leo took the bacon from the grill and folded two strips of it between a bun. He had a gray face, with slitted eyes, and a pinched nose saddled by faint blue shadows. One of the mill workers signaled for more coffee and Leo poured it. He did not give refills on coffee free. The spinner ate breakfast there every morning, but the better Leo knew his customers the stingier he treated them. He nibbled his own bun as though he grudged it to himself.

"And you never got hold of her again?"

The boy did not know what to think of the man, and his child's face was uncertain with mingled curiosity and doubt. He was new on the paper route; it was still strange to him to be out in the town in the black, queer early morning.

"Yes," the man said. "I took a number of steps to get her back. I went around trying to locate her. I went to Tulsa where she had folks. And to Mobile. I went to every town she had ever mentioned to me, and I hunted down every man she had formerly been connected with. Tulsa, Atlanta, Chicago, Cheehaw, Memphis. . . . For the better part of two years I chased around the country trying to lay hold of her."

"But the pair of them had vanished from the face of the earth!" said Leo.

"Don't listen to him," the man said confidentially. "And also just forget those two years. They are not important. What matters is that around the third year a curious thing begun to happen to me."

"What?" the boy asked.

The man leaned down and tilted his mug to take a sip of beer. But as he hovered over the mug his nostrils fluttered slightly; he sniffed the staleness of the beer and did not drink. "Love is a curious thing to begin with. At first I thought only of getting her back. It was kind of mania. But then as time went on I tried to remember her. But do you know what happened?"

"No," the boy said.

"When I laid myself down on a bed and tried to think about her my mind became a blank. I couldn't see her. I would take out her pictures and look. No good. Nothing doing. A blank. Can you imagine it?"

"Say Mac!" Leo called down the counter. "Can you imagine this bozo's mind a blank!"

Slowly, as though fanning away flies, the man waved his hand. His green eyes were concentrated and fixed on the shallow little face of the paper boy.

"But a sudden piece of glass on a sidewalk. Or a nickel tune in a music box. A shadow on a wall at night. And I would remember. It might happen in a street and I would cry or bang my head against a lamppost. You follow me?"

"A piece of glass . . ." the boy said.

"Anything. I would walk around and I had no power of how and when to remember her. You think you can put up a kind of shield. But remembering don't come to a man face forward—it corners around sideways. I was at the mercy of everything I saw and heard. Suddenly instead of me combing the countryside to find her she begun to chase me around in my very soul. *She* chasing *me*, mind you! And in my soul."

The boy asked finally: "What part of the country were you in then?"

"Ooh," the man groaned. "I was sick mortal. It was like smallpox. I confess, Son, that I boozed. I fornicated. I committed any sin that suddenly appealed to me. I am loath to confess it but I will do so. When I recall that period it is all curdled in my mind, it was so terrible."

The man leaned his head down and tapped his forehead on the counter. For a few seconds he stayed bowed over in this position, the back of his stringy neck covered with orange furze, his hands with their long warped fingers held palm to palm in an attitude of prayer. Then the man straightened himself; he was smiling and suddenly his face was bright and tremulous and old.

"It was in the fifth year that it happened," he said. "And with it I started my science."

Leo's mouth jerked with a pale, quick grin. "Well none of we boys are getting any younger," he said. Then with sudden anger he balled up a dishcloth he was holding and threw it down hard on the floor. "You draggle-tailed old Romeo!"

"What happened?" the boy asked.

The old man's voice was high and clear: "Peace," he answered.

"Huh?"

"It is hard to explain scientifically, Son," he said. "I guess the logical explanation is that she and I had fled around from each other for so long that finally we just got tangled up together and lay down and quit. Peace. A queer and beautiful blankness. It was spring in Portland and the rain came every afternoon. All evening I just stayed there on my bed in the dark. And that is how the science come to me."

The windows in the streetcar were pale blue with light. The two soldiers paid for their beers and opened the door—one of the soldiers combed his hair and wiped off his muddy puttees before they went outside. The three mill workers bent silently over their breakfasts. Leo's clock was ticking on the wall.

"It is this. And listen carefully. I meditated on love and reasoned it out. I realized what is wrong with us. Men fall in love for the first time. And what do they fall in love with?"

The boy's soft mouth was partly open and he did not answer.

"A woman," the old man said. "Without science, with nothing to go by, they undertake the most dangerous and sacred experience in God's earth. They fall in love with a woman. Is that correct, Son?"

"Yeah," the boy said faintly.

"They start at the wrong end of love. They begin at the climax. Can you wonder it is so miserable? Do you know how men should love?"

The old man reached over and grasped the boy by the collar of his leather jacket. He gave him a gentle little shake and his green eyes gazed down unblinking and grave.

"Son, do you know how love should be begun?"

The boy sat small and listening and still. Slowly he shook his head. The old man leaned closer and whispered:

"A tree. A rock. A cloud."

It was still raining outside in the street: a mild, gray, endless rain. The mill whistle blew for the six o'clock shift and the three spinners paid and went away. There was no one in the café but Leo, the old man, and the little paper boy.

"The weather was like this in Portland," he said. "At the time my science was begun. I meditated and I started very cautious. I would pick up something from the street and take it home with me. I bought a goldfish and I concentrated on the goldfish and I loved it. I graduated from one thing to another. Day by day I was getting this technique. On the road from Portland to San Diego——"

"Aw shut up!" screamed Leo suddenly. "Shut up! Shut up!"

The old man still held the collar of the boy's jacket; he was trembling and his face was earnest and bright and wild. "For six years now I have gone around by myself and built up my science. And now I am a master. Son. I can love anything. No longer do I have to think about it even. I see a street full of people and a beautiful light comes in me. I watch a bird in the sky. Or I meet a traveler on the road. Everything, Son. And anybody. All stranger and all loved! Do you realize what a science like mine can mean?"

The boy held himself stiffly, his hands curled tight around the counter edge. Finally he asked: "Did you ever really find that lady?"

"What? What say, Son?"

"I mean," the boy asked timidly. "Have you fallen in love with a woman again?"

The old man loosened his grasp on the boy's collar. He turned away and for the first time his green eyes had a vague and scattered look. He lifted the mug from the counter, drank down the yellow beer. His head was shaking slowly from side to side. Then finally he answered. "No,

Son. You see that is the last step in my science. I go cautious. And I am not quite ready yet."

"Well!" said Leo. "Well well well!"

The old man stood in the open doorway. "Remember," he said. Framed there in the gray damp light of the early morning he looked shrunken and seedy and frail. But his smile was bright. "Remember I love you," he said with a last nod. And the door closed quietly behind him.

The boy did not speak for a long time. He pulled down the bangs on his forehead and slid his grimy little forefinger around the rim of his empty cup. Then without looking at Leo he finally asked:

"Was he drunk?"

"No," said Leo shortly.

The boy raised his clear voice higher. "Then was he a dope fiend?"

"No."

The boy looked up at Leo, and his flat little face was desperate, his voice urgent and shrill. "Was he crazy? Do you think he was a lunatic?" The paper boy's voice dropped suddenly with doubt. "Leo? Or not?"

But Leo would not answer him. Leo had run a night café for fourteen years, and he held himself to be a critic of craziness. There were the town characters and also the transients who roamed in from the night. He knew the manias of all of them. But he did not want to satisfy the questions of the waiting child. He tightened his pale face and was silent.

So the boy pulled down the right flap of his helmet and as he turned to leave he made the only comment that seemed safe to him, the only remark that could not be laughed down and despised:

"He sure has done a lot of traveling."

SHIRLEY JACKSON

(1919–1965)

S hirley Jackson was born in San Francisco and attended school in
Burlingame, California. When she was 14, her family moved to
Rochester, New York. She studied English at Syracuse University and
graduated in 1940. All this time she was writing, and The New Yorker
accepted the first of many stories in 1943. Her first novel, The Road
through the Wall, and her most famous short story, "The Lottery,"
were published in 1948. When the story appeared, it instantly created a
sensation. Hundreds of letters from horrified, furious, outraged readers
poured into the magazine's office. To the end of her life, readers asked
Jackson for an explanation of The Lottery, but she disliked talking about
her fiction and reluctantly consented to the story's being described as an
allegory. The story has since been translated into numerous languages
and has been performed as a radio play, a television drama, an opera,
and a ballet. Nothing else she wrote had anything like this impact, and
despite the merits of a number of other stories, as well as The Bird's
Nest (1954) and We Have Always Lived in the Castle (1962), Shirley
Jackson will be remembered as the author of "The Lottery." She told one
friend that the story was based on anti-Semitism, another that all the
characters were drawn from real life, a third that it was based on what
she had learned about folklore at university. A tireless and marvellously
self-disciplined professional and a mother of four, she surprised people
who were expecting a witch or a sinister genius when they met her. But
there was a dark side to her complex personality as well. She once wrote,
"Insecure, uncontrolled, I wrote of neuroses and fear and I think all my
books laid end to end would be one long documentation of anxiety."
When she died of a heart attack at 45, her reputation was secure. Her
short stories are collected in The Magic of Shirley Jackson (1969), for
which volume her husband, the critic Stanley Edgar Hyman, wrote an
illuminating introduction.

The Lottery

T he morning of June 27th was clear and sunny, with the fresh warmth
of a full-summer day; the flowers were blossoming profusely and
the grass was richly green. The people of the village began to gather in
the square, between the post office and the bank, around ten o'clock; in
some towns there were so many people that the lottery took two days
and had to be started on June 26th, but in this village, where there were

only about three hundred people, the whole lottery took less than two hours, so it could begin at ten o'clock in the morning and still be through in time to allow the villagers to get home for noon dinner.

The children assembled first, of course. School was recently over for the summer, and the feeling of liberty sat uneasily on most of them; they tended to gather together quietly for a while before they broke into boisterous play, and their talk was still of the classroom and the teacher, of books and reprimands. Bobby Martin had already stuffed his pockets full of stones, and the other boys soon followed his example, selecting the smoothest and roundest stones; Bobby and Harry Jones and Dickie Delacroix—the villagers pronounced this name "Dellacroy"—eventually made a great pile of stones in one corner of the square and guarded it against the raids of the other boys. The girls stood aside, talking among themselves, looking over their shoulders at the boys, and the very small children rolled in the dust or clung to the hands of their older brothers or sisters.

Soon the men began to gather, surveying their own children, speaking of planting and rain, tractors and taxes. They stood together, away from the pile of stones in the corner, and their jokes were quiet and they smiled rather than laughed. The women, wearing faded house dresses and sweaters, came shortly after their menfolk. They greeted one another and exchanged bits of gossip as they went to join their husbands. Soon the women, standing by their husbands, began to call to their children, and the children came reluctantly, having to be called four or five times. Bobby Martin ducked under his mother's grasping hand and ran, laughing, back to the pile of stones. His father spoke up sharply, and Bobby came quickly and took his place between his father and his oldest brother.

The lottery was conducted—as were the square dances, the teenage club, the Halloween program—by Mr. Summers, who had time and energy to devote to civic activities. He was a round-faced, jovial man and he ran the coal business, and people were sorry for him, because he had no children and his wife was a scold. When he arrived in the square, carrying the black wooden box, there was a murmur of conversation among the villagers, and he waved and called, "Little late today, folks." The postmaster, Mr. Graves, followed him, carrying a three-legged stool, and the stool was put in the center of the square and Mr. Summers set the black box down on it. The villagers kept their distance, leaving a space between themselves and the stool, and when Mr. Summers said, "Some of you fellows want to give me a hand?" there was a hesitation before two men, Mr. Martin and his oldest son, Baxter, came forward to hold the box steady on the stool while Mr. Summers stirred up the papers inside it.

The original paraphernalia for the lottery had been lost long ago, and the black box now resting on the stool had been put into use even before

Old Man Warner, the oldest man in town, was born. Mr. Summers spoke frequently to the villagers about making a new box, but no one liked to upset even as much tradition as was represented by the black box. There was a story that the present box had been made with some pieces of the box that had preceded it, the one that had been constructed when the first people settled down to make a village here. Every year, after the lottery, Mr. Summers began talking again about a new box, but every year the subject was allowed to fade off without anything's being done. The black box grew shabbier each year; by now it was no longer completely black but splintered badly along one side to show the original wood color, and in some places faded or stained.

Mr. Martin and his oldest son, Baxter, held the black box securely on the stool until Mr. Summers had stirred the papers thoroughly with his hand. Because so much of the ritual had been forgotten or discarded, Mr. Summers had been successful in having slips of paper substituted for the chips of wood that had been used for generations. Chips of wood, Mr. Summers had argued, had been all very well when the village was tiny, but now that the population was more than three hundred and likely to keep on growing, it was necessary to use something that would fit more easily into the black box. The night before the lottery, Mr. Summers and Mr. Graves made up the slips of paper and put them in the box, and it was then taken to the safe of Mr. Summers's coal company and locked up until Mr. Summers was ready to take it to the square next morning. The rest of the year, the box was put away, sometimes one place, sometimes another; it had spent one year in Mr. Graves's barn and another year underfoot in the post office, and sometimes it was set on a shelf in the Martin grocery and left there.

There was a great deal of fussing to be done before Mr. Summers declared the lottery open. There were the lists to make up—of heads of families, heads of households in each family, members of each household in each family. There was the proper swearing-in of Mr. Summers by the postmaster, as the official of the lottery; at one time, some people remembered, there had been a recital of some sort, performed by the official of the lottery, a perfunctory, tuneless chant that had been rattled off duly each year; some people believed that the official of the lottery used to stand just so when he said or sang it, others believed that he was supposed to walk among the people, but years and years ago this part of the ritual had been allowed to lapse. There had been, also, a ritual salute, which the official of the lottery had had to use in addressing each person who came up to draw from the box, but this also had changed with time, until now it was felt necessary only for the official to speak to each person approaching. Mr. Summers was very good at all this; in his clean white shirt and blue jeans, with one hand resting carelessly on the black box, he seemed very proper and important as he talked interminably to Mr. Graves and the Martins.

Just as Mr. Summers finally left off talking and turned to the assembled villagers, Mrs. Hutchinson came hurriedly along the path to the square, her sweater thrown over her shoulders, and slid into place in the back of the crowd. "Clean forgot what day it was," she said to Mrs. Delacroix, who stood next to her, and they both laughed softly. "Thought my old man was out back stacking wood," Mrs. Hutchinson went on, "and then I looked out the window and the kids was gone, and then I remembered it was the twenty-seventh and came a-running." She dried her hands on her apron, and Mrs. Delacroix said, "You're in time, though. They're still talking away up there."

Mrs. Hutchinson craned her neck to see through the crowd and found her husband and children standing near the front. She tapped Mrs. Delacroix on the arm as a farewell and began to make her way through the crowd. The people separated good-humoredly to let her through; two or three people said, in voices just loud enough to be heard across the crowd, "Here comes your Missus, Hutchinson," and "Bill, she made it after all." Mrs. Hutchinson reached her husband, and Mr. Summers, who had been waiting, said cheerfully, "Thought we were going to have to get on without you, Tessie." Mrs. Hutchinson said, grinning, "Wouldn't have me leave m'dishes in the sink, now, would you, Joe?" and soft laughter ran through the crowd as the people stirred back into position after Mrs. Hutchinson's arrival.

"Well, now," Mr. Summers said soberly, "guess we better get started, get this over with, so's we can go back to work. Anybody ain't here?"

"Dunbar," several people said. "Dunbar, Dunbar."

Mr. Summers consulted his list. "Clyde Dunbar," he said. "That's right. He's broke his leg, hasn't he? Who's drawing for him?"

"Me, I guess," a woman said, and Mr. Summers turned to look at her. "Wife draws for her husband," Mr. Summers said. "Don't you have a grown boy to do it for you, Janey?" Although Mr. Summers and everyone else in the village knew the answer perfectly well, it was the business of the official of the lottery to ask such questions formally. Mr. Summers waited with an expression of polite interest while Mrs. Dunbar answered.

"Horace's not but sixteen yet," Mrs. Dunbar said regretfully. "Guess I gotta fill in for the old man this year."

"Right," Mr. Summers said. He made a note on the list he was holding. Then he asked, "Watson boy drawing this year?"

A tall boy in the crowd raised his hand. "Here," he said. "I'm drawing for m'mother and me." He blinked his eyes nervously and ducked his head as several voices in the crowd said things like "Good fellow, Jack," and "Glad to see your mother's got a man to do it."

"Well," Mr. Summers said, "guess that's everyone. Old Man Warner make it?"

"Here," a voice said, and Mr. Summers nodded.

A sudden hush fell on the crowd as Mr. Summers cleared his throat and looked at the list. "All ready?" he called. "Now, I'll read the names—heads of families first—and the men come up and take a paper out of the box. Keep the paper folded in your hand without looking at it until everyone has had a turn. Everything clear?"

The people had done it so many times that they only half listened to the directions; most of them were quiet, wetting their lips, not looking around. Then Mr. Summers raised one hand high and said, "Adams." A man disengaged himself from the crowd and came forward. "Hi, Steve," Mr. Summers said, and Mr. Adams said, "Hi, Joe." They grinned at one another humorlessly and nervously. Then Mr. Adams reached into the black box and took out a folded paper. He held it firmly by one corner as he turned and went hastily back to his place in the crowd, where he stood a little apart from his family, not looking down at his hand.

"Allen," Mr. Summers said. "Anderson. . . . Bentham."

"Seems like there's no time at all between lotteries any more," Mrs. Delacroix said to Mrs. Graves in the back row. "Seems like we got through with the last one only last week."

"Time sure goes fast," Mrs. Graves said.

"Clark. . . . Delacroix."

"There goes my old man," Mrs. Delacroix said. She held her breath while her husband went forward.

"Dunbar," Mr. Summers said, and Mrs. Dunbar went steadily to the box while one of the women said, "Go on, Janey," and another said, "There she goes."

"We're next," Mrs. Graves said. She watched while Mr. Graves came around from the side of the box, greeted Mr. Summers gravely, and selected a slip of paper from the box. By now, all through the crowd there were men holding the small folded papers in their large hands, turning them over and over nervously. Mrs. Dunbar and her two sons stood together, Mrs. Dunbar holding the slip of paper.

"Harburt. . . . Hutchinson."

"Get up there, Bill," Mrs. Hutchinson said, and the people near her laughed.

"Jones."

"They do say," Mr. Adams said to Old Man Warner, who stood next to him, "that over in the north village they're talking of giving up the lottery."

Old Man Warner snorted. "Pack of crazy fools," he said. "Listening to the young folks, nothing's good enough for *them*. Next thing you know, they'll be wanting to go back to living in caves, nobody work any more, live *that* way for a while. Used to be a saying about 'Lottery in June, corn be heavy soon.' First thing you know, we'd all be eating stewed chickweed and acorns. There's *always* been a lottery," he added petulantly. "Bad enough to see young Joe Summers up there joking with everybody."

"Some places have already quit lotteries," Mrs. Adams said.

"Nothing but trouble in *that*," Old Man Warner said stoutly. "Pack of young fools."

"Martin." And Bobby Martin watched his father go forward. "Overdyke. . . . Percy."

"I wish they'd hurry," Mrs. Dunbar said to her oldest son. "I wish they'd hurry."

"They're almost through," her son said.

"You get ready to run tell Dad," Mrs. Dunbar said.

Mr. Summers called his own name and then stepped forward precisely and selected a slip from the box. Then he called, "Warner."

"Seventy-seventh year I been in the lottery," Old Man Warner said as he went through the crowd. "Seventy-seventh time."

"Watson." The tall boy came awkwardly through the crowd. Someone said, "Don't be nervous, Jack," and Mr. Summers said, "Take your time, son."

"Zanini."

After that, there was a long pause, a breathless pause, until Mr. Summers, holding his slip of paper in the air, said, "All right, fellows." For a minute, no one moved, and then all the slips of paper were opened. Suddenly, all the women began to speak at once, saying, "Who is it?" "Who's got it?," "Is it the Dunbars?," "Is it the Watsons?" Then the voices began to say, "It's Hutchinson. It's Bill," "Bill Hutchinson's got it."

"Go tell your father," Mrs. Dunbar said to her older son.

People began to look around to see the Hutchinsons. Bill Hutchinson was standing quiet, staring down at the paper in his hand. Suddenly, Tessie Hutchinson shouted to Mr. Summers, "You didn't give him time enough to take any paper he wanted. I saw you. It wasn't fair!"

"Be a good sport, Tessie," Mrs. Delacroix called, and Mrs. Graves said, "All of us took the same chance."

"Shut up, Tessie," Bill Hutchinson said.

"Well, everyone," Mr. Summers said, "that was done pretty fast, and now we've got to be hurrying a little more to get done in time." He consulted his next list. "Bill," he said, "you draw for the Hutchinson family. You got any other households in the Hutchinsons?"

"There's Don and Eva," Mrs. Hutchinson yelled. "Make *them* take their chance!"

"Daughters draw with their husbands' families, Tessie," Mr. Summers said gently. "You know that as well as anyone else."

"It wasn't *fair*," Tessie said.

"I guess not, Joe," Bill Hutchinson said regretfully. "My daughter draws with her husband's family, that's only fair. And I've got no other family except the kids."

"Then, as far as drawing for families is concerned, it's you," Mr. Summers said in explanation, "and as far as drawing for households is concerned, that's you, too. Right?"

"Right," Bill Hutchinson said.

"How many kids, Bill?" Mr. Summers asked formally.

"Three," Bill Hutchinson said. "There's Bill, Jr., and Nancy, and little Dave. And Tessie and me."

"All right, then," Mr. Summers said. "Harry, you got their tickets back?"

Mr. Graves nodded and held up the slips of paper. "Put them in the box, then," Mr. Summers directed. "Take Bill's and put it in."

"I think we ought to start over," Mrs. Hutchinson said, as quietly as she could. "I tell you it wasn't *fair*. You didn't give him time enough to choose. *Every*body saw that."

Mr. Graves had selected the five slips and put them in the box, and he dropped all the papers but those onto the ground, where the breeze caught them and lifted them off.

"Listen, everybody," Mrs. Hutchinson was saying to the people around her.

"Ready, Bill?" Mr. Summers asked, and Bill Hutchinson, with one quick glance around at his wife and children, nodded.

"Remember," Mr. Summers said, "take the slips and keep them folded until each person has taken one. Harry, you help little Dave." Mr. Graves took the hand of the little boy, who came willingly with him up to the box. "Take a paper out of the box, Davy," Mr. Summers said. Davy put his hand into the box and laughed. "Take just *one* paper," Mr. Summers said. "Harry, you hold it for him." Mr. Graves took the child's hand and removed the folded paper from the tight fist and held it while little Dave stood next to him and looked up at him wonderingly.

"Nancy next," Mr. Summers said. Nancy was twelve, and her school friends breathed heavily as she went forward, switching her skirt, and took a slip daintily from the box. "Bill, Jr.," Mr. Summers said, and Billy, his face red and his feet overlarge, nearly knocked the box over as he got a paper out. "Tessie," Mr. Summers said. She hesitated for a minute, looking around defiantly, and then set her lips and went up to the box. She snatched a paper out and held it behind her.

"Bill," Mr. Summers said, and Bill Hutchinson reached into the box and felt around, bringing his hand out at last with the slip of paper in it.

The crowd was quiet. A girl whispered, "I hope it's not Nancy," and the sound of the whisper reached the edges of the crowd.

"It's not the way it used to be," Old Man Warner said clearly. "People ain't the way they used to be."

"All right," Mr. Summers said. "Open the papers. Harry, you open little Dave's."

Mr. Graves opened the slip of paper and there was a general sigh through the crowd as he held it up and everyone could see that it was blank. Nancy and Bill, Jr., opened theirs at the same time, and both beamed and laughed, turning around to the crowd and holding their slips of paper above their heads.

"Tessie," Mr. Summers said. There was a pause, and then Mr. Summers looked at Bill Hutchinson, and Bill unfolded his paper and showed it. It was blank.

"It's Tessie," Mr. Summers said, and his voice was hushed. "Show us her paper, Bill."

Bill Hutchinson went over to his wife and forced the slip of paper out of her hand. It had a black spot on it, the black spot Mr. Summers had made the night before with the heavy pencil in the coal-company office. Bill Hutchinson held it up, and there was a stir in the crowd.

"All right, folks," Mr. Summers said. "Let's finish quickly."

Although the villagers had forgotten the ritual and lost the original black box, they still remembered to use stones. The pile of stones the boys had made earlier was ready; there were stones on the ground with the blowing scraps of paper that had come out of the box. Mrs. Delacroix selected a stone so large she had to pick it up with both hands and turned to Mrs. Dunbar. "Come on," she said. "Hurry up."

Mrs. Dunbar had small stones in both hands, and she said, gasping for breath, "I can't run at all. You'll have to go ahead and I'll catch up with you."

The children had stones already, and someone gave little Davy Hutchinson a few pebbles.

Tessie Hutchinson was in the center of a cleared space by now, and she held her hands out desperately as the villagers moved in on her. "It isn't fair," she said. A stone hit her on the side of the head.

Old Man Warner was saying, "Come on, come on, everyone." Steve Adams was in the front of the crowd of villagers, with Mrs. Graves beside him.

"It isn't fair, it isn't right," Mrs. Hutchinson screamed, and then they were upon her.

DORIS LESSING

(b. 1919)

D oris Lessing was born in Kermanshah, Persia. Her father, an
English bank clerk, lost a leg in the First World War, married
his nurse, and emigrated first to Persia and then to Rhodesia. Lessing
was educated at a convent school and read widely on her own, including
many classic nineteenth-century novels. After two marriages, three children, and two divorces, she left for England in 1949, where a year later
she published her first novel, The Grass Is Singing. Like many British
intellectuals, Lessing sympathized with the Communist Party, but she
abandoned it after the Soviet invasion of Hungary in 1956. Enormously
prolific, Lessing has written novels, short stories, plays, autobiography,
essays, and poetry. Politics, feminism, race relations, writing as ther-
apy—she has played endlessly inventive variations on these themes. A
substantial amount of her writing she publishes unrevised, and she relies
on dreams to help her out when she encounters an obstacle in writing a
book. Her reputation is mixed, her readership large. As Mona Knapp has
observed,

> Lessing's influence and popularity have increased since the
> publication of her first novel. Her works have always provoked
> vehement reactions: she has been scorned as a communist and
> as a traitor to communism; labeled a radical, a feminist, a liberal.
> She has the distinction of being banned from certain bookstore
> shelves as "not decent." In fact, most of her work up to 1974 is
> traditional in style and theme, designed to communicate with
> a large readership through its feet-on-the-ground diagnosis of
> the human situation. The "radicalism" of her realist works lies
> only in their insistence on calling things by their right names.
> The newer books, despite their intergalactic perspective, still
> have as their main subject the exploration of social and psycho-
> logical processes, and are designed to deepen the reader's concept
> of self in relation to the universe.

The Old Chief Mshlanga

They were good, the years of ranging the bush over her father's farm which, like every white farm, was largely unused, broken only occasionally by small patches of cultivation. In between, nothing but trees, the long sparse grass, thorn and cactus and gully, grass and outcrop and thorn. And a jutting piece of rock which had been thrust up from the warm soil of Africa unimaginable eras of time ago, washed into hollows and whorls by sun and wind that had travelled so many thousands of miles of space and bush, would hold the weight of a small girl whose eyes were sightless for anything but a pale willowed river, a pale gleaming castle—a small girl singing: "Out flew the web and floated wide, the mirror cracked from side to side . . ."

Pushing her way through the green aisles of the mealie stalks, the leaves arching like cathedrals veined with sunlight far overhead, with the packed red earth underfoot, a fine lace of red starred witchweed would summon up a black bent figure croaking premonitions: the Northern witch, bred of cold Northern forests, would stand before her among the mealie fields, and it was the mealie fields that faded and fled, leaving her among the gnarled roots of an oak, snow falling thick and soft and white, the woodcutter's fire glowing red welcome through crowding tree trunks.

A white child, opening its eyes curiously on a sun-suffused landscape, a gaunt and violent landscape, might be supposed to accept it as her own, to take the msasa trees and the thorn trees as familiars, to feel her blood running free and responsive to the swing of the seasons.

This child could not see a msasa tree, or the thorn, for what they were. Her books held tales of alien fairies, her rivers ran slow and peaceful, and she knew the shape of the leaves of an ash or an oak, the names of the little creatures that lived in English streams, when the words "the veld" meant strangeness, though she could remember nothing else.

Because of this, for many years, it was the veld that seemed unreal; the sun was a foreign sun, and the wind spoke a strange language.

The black people on the farm were as remote as the trees and the rocks. They were an amorphous black mass, mingling and thinning and massing like tadpoles, faceless, who existed merely to serve, to say "Yes, Baas," take their money and go. They changed season by season, moving from one farm to the next, according to their outlandish needs, which one did not have to understand, coming from perhaps hundreds of miles North or East, passing on after a few months—where? Perhaps even as far away as the fabled gold mines of Johannesburg, where the pay was so much better than the few shillings a month and the double handful of mealie meal twice a day which they earned in that part of Africa.

The child was taught to take them for granted: the servants in the house would come running a hundred yards to pick up a book if she dropped it. She was called "Nkosikaas"—Chieftainess, even by the black children her own age.

Later, when the farm grew too small to hold her curiosity, she carried a gun in the crook of her arm and wandered miles a day, from vlei to vlei, from *kopje* to *kopje*, accompanied by two dogs: the dogs and the gun were an armour against fear. Because of them she never felt fear.

If a native came into sight along the kaffir paths half a mile away, the dogs would flush him up a tree as if he were a bird. If he expostulated (in his uncouth language which was by itself ridiculous) that was cheek. If one was in a good mood, it could be a matter for laughter. Otherwise one passed on, hardly glancing at the angry man in the tree.

On the rare occasions when white children met together they could amuse themselves by hailing a passing native in order to make a buffoon of him; they could set the dogs on him and watch him run; they could tease a small black child as if he were a puppy—save that they would not throw stones and sticks at a dog without a sense of guilt.

Later still, certain questions presented themselves in the child's mind; and because the answers were not easy to accept, they were silenced by an even greater arrogance of manner.

It was even impossible to think of the black people who worked about the house as friends, for if she talked to one of them, her mother would come running anxiously: "Come away; you mustn't talk to natives."

It was this instilled consciousness of danger, of something unpleasant, that made it easy to laugh out loud, crudely, if a servant made a mistake in his English or if he failed to understand an order—there is a certain kind of laughter that is fear, afraid of itself.

One evening, when I was about fourteen, I was walking down the side of a mealie field that had been newly ploughed, so that the great red clods showed fresh and tumbling to the vlei beyond, like a choppy red sea; it was that hushed and listening hour, when the birds send long sad calls from tree to tree, and all the colours of earth and sky and leaf are deep and golden. I had my rifle in the curve of my arm, and the dogs were at my heels.

In front of me, perhaps a couple of hundred yards away, a group of three Africans came into sight around the side of a big antheap. I whistled the dogs close in to my skirts and let the gun swing in my hand, and advanced, waiting for them to move aside, off the path, in respect for my passing. But they came on steadily, and the dogs looked up at me for the command to chase. I was angry. It was "cheek" for a native not to stand off a path, the moment he caught sight of you.

In front walked an old man, stooping his weight on to a stick, his hair grizzled white, a dark red blanket slung over his shoulders like a cloak.

Behind him came two young men, carrying bundles of pots, assegais, hatchets.

The group was not a usual one. They were not natives seeking work. These had an air of dignity, of quietly following their own purpose. It was the dignity that checked my tongue. I walked quietly on, talking softly to the growling dogs, till I was ten paces away. Then the old man stopped, drawing his blanket close.

"Morning, Nkosikaas," he said, using the customary greeting for any time of the day.

"Good morning," I said. "Where are you going?" My voice was a little truculent.

The old man spoke in his own language, then one of the young men stepped forward politely and said in careful English: "My Chief travels to see his brothers beyond the river."

A Chief! I thought, understanding the pride that made the old man stand before me like an equal—more than an equal, for he showed courtesy, and I showed none.

The old man spoke again, wearing dignity like an inherited garment, still standing ten paces off, flanked by his entourage, not looking at me (that would have been rude) but directing his eyes somewhere over my head at the trees.

"You are the little Nkosikaas from the farm of Baas Jordan?"

"That's right," I said.

"Perhaps your father does not remember," said the interpreter for the old man, "but there was an affair with some goats. I remember seeing you when you were . . ." The young man held his hand at knee level and smiled.

We all smiled.

"What is your name?" I asked.

"This is Chief Mshlanga," said the young man.

"I will tell my father that I met you," I said.

The old man said: "My greetings to your father, little Nkosikaas."

"Good morning," I said politely, finding the politeness difficult, from lack of use.

"Morning, little Nkosikaas," said the old man, and stood aside to let me pass.

I went by, my gun hanging awkwardly, the dogs sniffing and growling, cheated of their favourite game of chasing natives like animals.

Not long afterwards I read in an old explorer's book the phrase: "Chief Mshlanga's country." It went like this: "Our destination was Chief Mshlanga's country, to the north of the river; and it was our desire to ask his permission to prospect for gold in his territory."

The phrase "ask his permission" was so extraordinary to a white child, brought up to consider all natives as things to use, that it revived those questions, which could not be suppressed: they fermented slowly in my mind.

On another occasion one of those old prospectors who still move over Africa looking for neglected reefs, with their hammers and tents, and pans for sifting gold from crushed rock, came to the farm and, in talking of the old days, used that phrase again: "This was the Old Chief's country," he said. "It stretched from those mountains over there way back to the river, hundreds of miles of country." That was his name for our district: "The Old Chief's Country"; he did not use our name for it—a new phrase which held no implication of usurped ownership.

As I read more books about the time when this part of Africa was opened up, not much more than fifty years before, I found Old Chief Mshlanga had been a famous man, known to all the explorers and prospectors. But then he had been young; or maybe it was his father or uncle they spoke of—I never found out.

During that year I met him several times in the part of the farm that was traversed by natives moving over the country. I learned that the path up the side of the big red field where the birds sang was the recognized highway for migrants. Perhaps I even haunted it in the hope of meeting him: being greeted by him, the exchange of courtesies, seemed to answer the questions that troubled me.

Soon I carried a gun in a different spirit; I used it for shooting food and not to give me confidence. And now the dogs learned better manners. When I saw a native approaching, we offered and took greetings; and slowly that other landscape in my mind faded, and my feet struck directly on the African soil, and I saw the shapes of tree and hill clearly, and the black people moved back, as it were, out of my life: it was as if I stood aside to watch a slow intimate dance of landscape and men, a very old dance, whose steps I could not learn.

But I thought: this is my heritage, too; I was bred here; it is my country as well as the black man's country; and there is plenty of room for all of us, without elbowing each other off the pavements and roads.

It seemed it was only necessary to let free that respect I felt when I was talking with old Chief Mshlanga, to let both black and white people meet gently, with tolerance for each other's differences: it seemed quite easy.

Then, one day, something new happened. Working in our house as servants were always three natives: cook, houseboy, garden boy. They used to change as the farm natives changed: staying for a few months, then moving on to a new job, or back home to their kraals. They were thought of as "good" or "bad" natives; which meant: how did they behave as servants? Were they lazy, efficient, obedient, or disrespectful? If the family felt good-humoured, the phrase was: "What can you expect from raw black savages?" If we were angry, we said: "These damned niggers, we would be much better off without them."

One day, a white policeman was on his rounds of the district, and he said laughingly: "Did you know you have an important man in your kitchen?"

"What!" exclaimed my mother sharply. "What do you mean?"

"A Chief's son." The policeman seemed amused. "He'll boss the tribe when the old man dies."

"He'd better not put on a Chief's son act with me," said my mother.

When the policeman left, we looked with different eyes at our cook: he was a good worker, but he drank too much at week-ends—that was how we knew him.

He was a tall youth, with very black skin, like black polished metal, his tightly-growing black hair parted white man's fashion at one side, with a metal comb from the store stuck into it; very polite, very distant, very quick to obey an order. Now that it had been pointed out, we said: "Of course, you can see. Blood always tells."

My mother became strict with him now she knew about his birth and prospects. Sometimes, when she lost her temper, she would say: "You aren't the Chief yet, you know." And he would answer her very quietly, his eyes on the ground: "Yes, Nkosikaas."

One afternoon he asked for a whole day off, instead of the customary half-day, to go home next Sunday.

"How can you go home in one day?"

"It will take me half an hour on my bicycle," he explained.

I watched the direction he took; and the next day I went off to look for this kraal; I understood he must be Chief Mshlanga's successor: there was no other kraal near enough our farm.

Beyond our boundaries on that side the country was new to me. I followed unfamiliar paths past *kopjes* that till now had been part of the jagged horizon, hazed with distance. This was Government land, which had never been cultivated by white men; at first I could not understand why it was that it appeared, in merely crossing the boundary, I had entered a completely fresh type of landscape. It was a wide green valley, where a small river sparkled, and vivid water-birds darted over the rushes. The grass was thick and soft to my calves, the trees stood tall and shapely.

I was used to our farm, whose hundreds of acres of harsh eroded soil bore trees that had been cut for the mine furnaces and had grown thin and twisted, where the cattle had dragged the grass flat, leaving innumerable criss-crossing trails that deepened each season into gullies, under the force of the rains.

This country had been left untouched, save for prospectors whose picks had struck a few sparks from the surface of the rocks as they wandered by;

and for migrant natives whose passing had left, perhaps, a charred patch on the trunk of a tree where their evening fire had nestled.

It was very silent: a hot morning with pigeons cooing throatily, the midday shadows lying dense and thick with clear yellow spaces of sunlight between and in all that wide green park-like valley, not a human soul but myself.

I was listening to the quick regular tapping of a woodpecker when slowly a chill feeling seemed to grow up from the small of my back to my shoulders, in a constricting spasm like a shudder, and at the roots of my hair a tingling sensation began and ran down over the surface of my flesh, leaving me goosefleshed and cold, though I was damp with sweat. Fever? I thought; then uneasily, turned to look over my shoulder; and realized suddenly that this was fear. It was extraordinary, even humiliating. It was a new fear. For all the years I had walked by myself over this country I had never known a moment's uneasiness; in the beginning because I had been supported by a gun and the dogs, then because I had learnt an easy friendliness for the Africans I might encounter.

I had read of this feeling, how the bigness and silence of Africa, under the ancient sun, grows dense and takes shape in the mind, till even the birds seem to call menacingly, and a deadly spirit comes out of the trees and the rocks. You move warily, as if your very passing disturbs something old and evil, something dark and big and angry that might suddenly rear and strike from behind. You look at groves of entwined trees, and picture the animals that might be lurking there; you look at the river running slowly, dropping from level to level through the vlei, spreading into pools where at night the bucks come to drink, and the crocodiles rise and drag them by their soft noses into underwater caves. Fear possessed me. I found I was turning round and round, because of that shapeless menace behind me that might reach out and take me; I kept glancing at the files of *kopjes* which, seen from a different angle, seemed to change with every step so that even known landmarks, like a big mountain that had sentinelled my world since I first became conscious of it, showed an unfamiliar sunlit valley among its foothills. I did not know where I was. I was lost. Panic seized me. I found I was spinning round and round, staring anxiously at this tree and that, peering up at the sun which appeared to have moved into an eastern slant, shedding the sad yellow light of sunset. Hours must have passed! I looked at my watch and found that this state of meaningless terror had lasted perhaps ten minutes.

The point was that it was meaningless. I was not ten miles from home: I had only to take my way back along the valley to find myself at the fence; away among the foothills of the *kopjes* gleamed the roof of a neighbour's house, and a couple of hours' walking would reach it. This was the sort of fear that contracts the flesh of a dog at night and sets him howling at the full moon. It had nothing to do with what I thought or felt; and I was more disturbed by the fact that I could become its victim than of the physical sensation itself: I walked steadily on, quietened, in a divided mind, watching my own pricking nerves and apprehensive glances from side to side with a disgusted amusement. Deliberately I set myself to think of this village I was seeking, and what I should do when I entered it—if I could find it, which was doubtful, since I was walking aimlessly and it might be anywhere in the hundreds of thousands of acres of bush that stretched about me. With my mind on that village, I realized that a new sensation was added to the fear: loneliness. Now such a terror of isolation invaded me that I could hardly walk; and if it were not that I came over the crest of a small rise and saw a village below me, I should have turned and gone home. It was a cluster of thatched huts in a clearing among trees. There were neat patches of mealies and pumpkins and millet, and cattle grazed under some trees at a distance. Fowls scratched among the huts, dogs lay sleeping on the grass, and goats friezed a *kopje* that jutted up beyond a tributary of the river lying like an enclosing arm round the village.

As I came close I saw the huts were lovingly decorated with patterns of yellow and red and ochre mud on the walls; and the thatch was tied in place with plaits of straw.

This was not at all like our farm compound, a dirty and neglected place, a temporary home for migrants who had no roots in it.

And now I did not know what to do next. I called a small black boy, who was sitting on a lot playing a stringed gourd, quite naked except for the strings of blue beads round his neck, and said: "Tell the Chief I am here." The child stuck his thumb in his mouth and stared shyly back at me.

For minutes I shifted my feet on the edge of what seemed a deserted village, till at last the child scuttled off, and then some women came. They were draped in bright cloths, with brass glinting in their ears and on their arms. They also stared, silently; then turned to chatter among themselves.

I said again: "Can I see Chief Mshlanga?" I saw they caught the name; they did not understand what I wanted. I did not understand myself.

At last I walked through them and came past the huts and saw a clearing under a big shady tree, where a dozen old men sat cross-legged on the ground, talking. Chief Mshlanga was leaning back against the tree, holding a gourd in his hand, from which he had been drinking. When he saw me, not a muscle of his face moved, and I could see he was not pleased: perhaps he was afflicted with my own shyness, due to being unable to find the right forms of courtesy for the occasion. To meet me, on our own farm, was one thing; but I should not have come here. What had I expected? I could not join them socially: the thing was unheard of.

Bad enough that I, a white girl, should be walking the veld alone as a white man might: and in this part of the bush where only Government officials had the right to move.

Again I stood, smiling foolishly, while behind me stood the groups of brightly-clad, chattering women, their faces alert with curiosity and interest, and in front of me sat the old men, with old lined faces, their eyes guarded, aloof. It was a village of ancients and children and women. Even the two young men who kneeled beside the Chief were not those I had seen with him previously: the young men were all away working on the white men's farms and mines, and the Chief must depend on relatives who were temporarily on holiday for his attendants.

"The small white Nkosikaas is far from home," remarked the old man at last.

"Yes," I agreed, "it is far." I wanted to say: "I have come to pay you a friendly visit, Chief Mshlanga." I could not say it. I might now be feeling an urgent helpless desire to get to know these men and women as people, to be accepted by them as a friend, but the truth was I had set out in a spirit of curiosity: I had wanted to see the village that one day our cook, the reserved and obedient young man who got drunk on Sundays, would one day rule over.

"The child of Nkosi Jordan is welcome," said Chief Mshlanga.

"Thank you," I said, and could think of nothing more to say. There was a silence, while the flies rose and began to buzz around my head; and the wind shook a little in the thick green tree that spread its branches over the old men.

"Good morning," I said at last. "I have to return now to my home."

"Morning, little Nkosikaas," said Chief Mshlanga.

I walked away from the indifferent village, over the rise past the staring amber-eyed goats, down through the tall stately trees into the great rich green valley where the river meandered and the pigeons cooed tales of plenty and the woodpecker tapped softly.

The fear had gone; the loneliness had set into stiff-necked stoicism; there was now a queer hostility in the landscape, a cold, hard, sullen indomitability that walked with me, as strong as a wall, as intangible as smoke; it seemed to say to me: you walk here as a destroyer. I went slowly homewards, with an empty heart: I had learned that if one cannot call a country to heel like a dog, neither can one dismiss the past with a smile in an easy gush of feeling, saying: I could not help it, I am also a victim.

I only saw Chief Mshlanga once again.

One night my father's big red land was trampled down by small sharp hooves, and it was discovered that the culprits were goats from Chief Mshlanga's kraal. This had happened once before, years ago.

My father confiscated all the goats. Then he sent a message to the old Chief that if he wanted them he would have to pay for the damage.

He arrived at our house at the time of sunset one evening, looking very old and bent now, walking stiffly under his regally-draped blanket, leaning on a big stick. My father sat himself down in his big chair below the steps of the house; the old man squatted carefully on the ground before him, flanked by his two young men.

The palaver was long and painful, because of the bad English of the young man who interpreted, and because my father could not speak dialect, but only kitchen kaffir.

From my father's point of view, at least two hundred pounds' worth of damage had been done to the crop. He knew he could not get the money from the old man. He felt he was entitled to keep the goats. As for the old Chief, he kept repeating angrily: "Twenty goats! My people cannot lose twenty goats! We are not rich, like the Nkosi Jordan, to lose twenty goats at once."

My father did not think of himself as rich, but rather as very poor. He spoke quickly and angrily in return, saying that the damage done meant a great deal to him, and that he was entitled to the goats.

At last it grew so heated that the cook, the Chief's son, was called from the kitchen to be interpreter, and now my father spoke fluently in English, and our cook translated rapidly so that the old man could understand how very angry my father was. The young man spoke without emotion, in a mechanical way, his eyes lowered, but showing how he felt his position by a hostile uncomfortable set of the shoulders.

It was now in the late sunset, the sky a welter of colours, the birds singing their last songs, and the cattle, lowing peacefully, moving past us towards their sheds for the night. It was the hour when Africa is most beautiful; and here was this pathetic, ugly scene, doing no one any good.

At last my father stated finally: "I'm not going to argue about it. I am keeping the goats."

The old Chief flashed back in his own language: "That means that my people will go hungry when the dry season comes."

"Go to the police, then," said my father, and looked triumphant.

There was, of course, no more to be said.

The old man sat silent, his head bent, his hands dangling helplessly over his withered knees. Then he rose, the young men helping him, and he stood facing my father. He spoke once again, very stiffly; and turned away and went home to his village.

"What did he say?" asked my father of the young man, who laughed uncomfortably, and would not meet his eyes.

"What did he say?" insisted my father.

Our cook stood straight and silent, his brows knotted together. Then he spoke. "My father says: All this land, this land you call yours, is his land, and belongs to our people."

Having made this statement, he walked off into the bush after his father, and we did not see him again.

Our next cook was a migrant from Nyasaland, with no expectations of greatness.

Next time the policeman came on his rounds he was told this story. He remarked: "That kraal has no right to be there; it should have been moved long ago. I don't know why no one has done anything about it. I'll have a chat with the Native Commissioner next week. I'm going over for tennis on Sunday, anyway."

Some time later we heard that Chief Mshlanga and his people had been moved two hundred miles east, to a proper Native Reserve; the Government land was going to be opened up for white settlement soon.

I went to see the village again, about a year afterwards. There was nothing there. Mounds of red mud, where the huts had been, had long swathes of rotting thatch over them, veined with the red galleries of the white ants. The pumpkin vines rioted everywhere, over the bushes, up the lower branches of trees so that the great golden balls rolled underfoot and dangled overhead: it was a festival of pumpkins. The bushes were crowding up, the new grass sprang vivid green.

The settler lucky enough to be allotted the lush warm valley (if he chose to cultivate this particular section) would find, suddenly, in the middle of a mealie field, the plants were growing fifteen feet tall, the weight of the cobs dragging at the stalks, and wonder what unsuspected vein of richness he had struck.

JACQUES FERRON

(1921–1985)

J acques Ferron was born in Louiseville, Quebec. He graduated in
medicine from the Université Laval and practised for a period in the
rural Gaspé Peninsula that figures largely in so many of his tales. He
later worked as a family doctor in Longueuil. Ferron was always a highly
political figure and an influential social activist in Quebec. He was a
founding member of the Rhinoceros Party, the mock federalist organization whose function is that of national trickster (the party motto: "From
one pond to another"). But it is as the author of over 30 books of
fiction–novels, tales, fables, folk legends–about Quebec's rural and urban
decay that Ferron is now best known both inside Quebec and in English
Canada. He made his reputation with the collection Contes du pays
incertain (1962), which won the Governor General's Award and was
translated by Betty Bednarski as Tales from an Uncertain Country
(1972). His novels include Cotnoir (1962; Dr. Cotnoir, 1973), La nuit
(1965; The Night, 1977), Papa Boss (1966), Le salut de l'Irlande
(1970), and Les roses sauvages (1972; Wild Roses, 1976). But Ferron's only novel in the traditional sense is the historical Le ciel de
Québec (1969), which remains his most complex work. Otherwise Ferron's métier remains a fictional form that plays among the invented
fiction and the folktale, the anecdote and the tale involving historical
figures, represented by collections such as La chaise du Maré Ferrant
(1972), Historiettes (1969), and Gaspé matempa (1980). Whatever
his chosen form, Ferron remained committed to puzzling over what
Stephen Leacock called "the unsolved riddle of social justice," to exposing
the detrimental effects of consumer capitalism, to pondering Quebec's
place in Canada and the place of the individual in Quebec, and to musing
upon his own role as a doctor in contemporary Quebec. The critic Donald
Smith has described this protean writer as a "conteur, a fabulist, a
symbolist, and creator of myths. A literary geographer, historian, botanist, and folklorist of the 'uncertain country,' he, more than any other
Quebec writer, has turned real people and real situations into literary
beings and fictional places."

The Jailer's Son

T he jailer's son was the liveliest boy that ever was. He played chase with himself and always ran away. He even tried hopping and changing feet, but it was never any use; he would still get ahead of himself and come down on the wrong foot, the one that got away. He was forever giving himself the slip like this. And it was just as well. The child he'd have caught up with was an only child, half orphan. The jailer himself trod warily, with measured steps and all the gravity of a hairy, cautious man. He was proud of his son and loved him dearly.

When the son was thirteen his father made him a present of a bear-cub. The cub had been given to him by a hunter from Ferme-Neuve. "Sir," the hunter had said, "I'll never be able to repay you for all the kindness you've shown my poor uncle."

"Your uncle?"

"Yes, old So-and-so. A very special case, requiring very special care." That was what he had said, but who the uncle was, he had not the faintest idea. Clearly though, the fellow's prospects must not be very bright.

The bear-cub was chained to an elm tree which grew by the prison wall. One day, while the jailer's son was playing in the shadow of the wall and the tree, he heard a strange noise, which made him stop still in his tracks, his heart pounding. Perhaps it was the elm tree suffering? Or the cub? The sky, it was true, had been clear all summer; a fierce yellow sun devoured its creation; only the blue of night brought respite to the stricken green. But just at that moment it had begun to rain. The tree received all the water its roots could drink, and the cub, who had been dazed by the heat, perked up and began splashing in the puddles. It rained so hard the grasshoppers turned green again. But still the noise persisted. The child stood motionless, not knowing what to think. His double, sad and lonely, and half orphan, caught up with him.

The jailer, a ponderous man, was proud of the quicksilver in his son, and it disconcerted him to see him stand so still. He asked what was wrong. The child seemed surprised. Wrong? But there was nothing wrong. He was just a little tired from running. "Then rest a while, my boy," said the jailer, only partly reassured. In fact the child had stopped moving in order to listen. Summer ended, and still he had not discovered the cause of the noise. One fall evening, while he was playing outside with the cub, he happened to press his cheek against the prison wall. Then, unmistakably, he heard a low, muffled voice calling for help. Quickly he chalked a circle on the wall by his ear and went inside to bed, still afraid to trust himself, and determined to make absolutely sure, since in this he could rely on no one else.

The next morning he ran back to the wall and pressed his ear against the chalk circle. The voice was still there, low, muffled, monotonous. "Help!" it called. The child cupped his hands to his mouth and shouted into the thick wall: "I can hear you!" But it was no use. The voice did not let up. So he banged on the wall with a stick, a hammer, then a pickaxe. All his efforts were in vain. He realized then that he was only a child. He fell sick, sick with the helplessness of his years, and nearly died. He spent the winter in bed. April brought him back to life.

One afternoon he got up, still shaky, from his bed, and went over to his window. Under the elm tree he could see no sign of the bear-cub. When his father came to see him, he confronted him, his eyes flashing with anger: "Where's the cub!"

"There's no cub any more."

"You've killed him, haven't you!"

The jailer laughed: "I ate him!"

"You ate him!"

"Yes. Hair and hide. I was hungry." Then he added, stroking his son's head, "He's changed, your cub has, just like you. He's a big boy now."

"Where is he?"

"In a hole at the foot of the elm tree. He's spent the winter there, sleeping, just like you."

As the bear seemed in no hurry to come out, it was the boy who went down to the yard. Dazzled, he made his way over the edge of the dark hole, where the bear's chain hung. He bent down and peered inside. The hole was no pit, but a kind of underground tunnel, winding steeply down toward the prison wall, the roots of the elm tree, like wayward arches, criss-crossing to form its vault. And from it there rose up, as from some vent, waves of warm air and a barnyard odour that could not have been produced by a single animal. The jailer's son went back to the house, deep in thought. The next day he decided to pull the chain. He had recovered his strength. The chain was long, but he got to the end of it, got, that is, to the bear's collar, in which there was, however, no bear's neck. Instead, there appeared a shaggy, white head, an ashen brow, the screwed up features of a blind old man, the gaping jaw of a demented convict, a bundle of filthy rags. Instead, it was the uncle of the hunter from Ferme-Neuve who crawled out into the blinding light, staggered to his feet, swayed, and fell moaning to the ground. Help! Help! Help! The boy let go of the chain, slipped into the opening and made his way along under the roots on all fours.

The passage opened onto a small cave, shaped like a cone, the base of which was the prison wall. It was probably in here that the bear had spent the winter. But there was no bear now. On the floor of the cave lay a huge squared stone, a kind of platform. The boy hoisted himself up and found himself peering into a hole, from which the barnyard odour was rising. The cave was perhaps only an anteroom, leading to some vaster and possibly infernal halls. The hole was as wide as the entrance to the tunnel. The boy managed to squeeze through it, and so through the prison wall, landing, surprised but relieved, on top of his bear, who let out a growl. He was exhausted. The bear's growl was answered by titters, shouts and moans. Huddled against the animal, the boy slowly recovered from his exertion, while little by little his eyes adjusted to his new surroundings. He was in a vast underground room, lit feebly by tiny electric bulbs with yellow filaments. Milling about his cellar were forty or so old drunks, apparently all of the same breed as the one he had pulled up on the end of the chain. On the other side of the room there were bars, and behind the bars a guard sat dozing, his head in his hands.

This guard, in his torpor, was not unduly surprised by the appearance of the boy. Already he had accepted the bear as just another hallucination of the crazy old fools in his charge. He did the same now for the boy. Through intermittently open eyes, he watched the new arrival, one more illusion come to challenge the first, saw him shake the bear and the bear reluctantly get to its feet and in a single bound disappear, quite the most natural thing, he thought, for such a bear to do. He also recorded, through one eye or the other, as in a series of camera shots, the gradual disappearance of his patients. This did not dismay him in the least. "Good-riddance!" Before long the room was empty. The guard could rest in peace.

The jailer's son was the last to come up. He unchained the first lunatic, whose cries, now that he could no longer hear the muffled echo of his own voice underground, grew even louder and more shrill. Help! Help! Help! His companions, startled by the soft spring light, thought they had fallen into a trap, and began to shout in terror with him. The boy pushed them all in the direction of the road. They moved off in a long procession, the uncle of the hunter from Ferme-Neuve in the lead, the bear taking up the rear.

Out on the road the highway north sped past on a ribbon of asphalt. The ribbon came to a stop. The motorists, their eyes wide, their mouths agape, dared not blow their horns. The blind procession, like a worm dug up from its decay, lost in the walls of limp and unresisting air, as in a labyrinth, wound back and forth across the road, drawn now to drains, now to cellar windows, unable to find its way. At last, after much twisting and turning, instinct guided it in the right direction. It left the road and moved into the prison drive. By now the shouts had become howls. The police on duty piled sandbags behind the door and aimed their machine guns. Taken by surprise, they thought they were being attacked by the great army of the mad, the blind and the innocent, marching behind the sword of justice. They were determined to fight for their lives, knowing that in defeat there would be no mercy.

Luckily, from his house outside the walls, the jailer had seen every-thing. He appeared in the drive. He did not run, but walked, with short, hurried steps. He shouted to the police inside the fortress: "Don't shoot! They're our lunatics." He finally managed to make himself heard. The huge door swung slowly open and the procession passed through. When the bear was inside, the door was closed. That same day the tunnel was sealed. The bear was never heard of again. As for the jailer's son, he had little choice but to live. But they never did make a decent citizen out of him.

MAVIS GALLANT

(b. 1922)

*M*avis Gallant was born in Montreal. The only child in a troubled family, she was educated in some seventeen different schools in Canada and the United States. She worked for the National Film Board, then as a feature writer for the Montreal Standard in 1944. She left Canada for Europe in 1950, eventually settling in Paris, where she remains Canada's most celebrated expatriate writer. She has published over 100 short stories—her primary form—in the prestigious New Yorker magazine, and she received the Governor General's Award for Home Truths (1981), the collection that contains her Montreal stories and the mini-cycle of autobiographical fictions known collectively as the Linnet Muir stories. "The Ice Wagon Going Down the Street" is from this collection. She is also the author of two novels, Green Water, Green Sky (1959) and A Fairly Good Time (1970), and six other collections of stories, including The Other Paris (1956), The Pegnitz Junction (1973), From the Fifteenth District (1979), and Overhead in a Balloon (1985). In stories distinguished by the sharp clarity of the prose and an understated sense of humour, Gallant often explores the problems of being a stranger in a strange land, including the difficulties faced by Canadian or British protagonists in attempting to participate in a different, usually French or Italian, culture. Often technically dazzling in her handling of multiple points of view, Gallant's deeply humorous stories quietly expose the pathos at the heart of their characters' lives. As the critic George Woodcock has observed, most of Gallant's stories "concern people who have built up a protection from the world, and who in the end have been made to realize how precarious such defences are and how hiding from life has only increased their vulnerability." Her continuing interest in Canadians adrift at home and abroad, and of the lives of those anxious characters at loose ends in various European countries, places Gallant in the first rank of those writers who work mainly in the short story.

The Ice Wagon Going Down the Street

Now that they are out of world affairs and back where they started, Peter Frazier's wife says, "Everybody else did well in the international thing except us."

"You have to be crooked," he tells her.

"Or smart. Pity we weren't."

It is Sunday morning. They sit in the kitchen, drinking their coffee, slowly, remembering the past. They say the names of people as if they were magic. Peter thinks, *Agnes Brusen*, but there are hundreds of other names. As a private married joke, Peter and Sheilah wear the silk dressing gowns they bought in Hong Kong. Each thinks the other a peacock, rather splendid, but they pretend the dressing gowns are silly and worn in fun.

Peter and Sheilah and their two daughters, Sandra and Jennifer, are visiting Peter's unmarried sister, Lucille. They have been Lucille's guests seventeen weeks, ever since they returned to Toronto from the Far East. Their big old steamer trunk blocks a corner of the kitchen, making a problem of the refrigerator door; but even Lucille says the trunk may as well stay where it is, for the present. The Fraziers' future is so unsettled; everything is still in the air.

Lucille has given her bedroom to her two nieces, and sleeps on a camp cot in the hall. The parents have the living-room divan. They have no privileges here; they sleep after Lucille has seen the last television show that interests her. In the hall closet their clothes are crushed by winter overcoats. They know they are being judged for the first time. Sandra and Jennifer are waiting for Sheilah and Peter to decide. They are waiting to learn where these exotic parents will fly to next. What sort of climate will Sheilah consider? What job will Peter consent to accept? When the parents are ready, the children will make a decision of their own. It is just possible that Sandra and Jennifer will choose to stay with their aunt.

The peacock parents are watched by wrens. Lucille and her nieces are much the same—sandy-colored, proudly plain. Neither of the girls has the father's insouciance or the mother's appearance—her height, her carriage, her thick hair, and sky-blue eyes. The children are more cautious than their parents; more Canadian. When they saw their aunt's apartment they had been away from Canada nine years, ever since they were two and four; and Jennifer, the elder, said, "Well, now we're home." Her voice is nasal and flat. Where did she learn that voice? And why should this be home? Peter's answer to anything about his mystifying children is, "It must be in the blood."

On Sunday morning Lucille takes her nieces to church. It seems to be the only condition she imposes on her relations: the children must be decent. The girls go willingly, with their new hats and purses and gloves and coral bracelets and strings of pearls. The parents, ramshackle, sleepy, dim in the brain because it is Sunday, sit down to their coffee and privacy and talk of the past.

"We weren't crooked," says Peter. "We weren't even smart."

Sheilah's head bobs up; she is no drowner. It is wrong to say they have nothing to show for time. Sheilah has the Balenciaga. It is a black afternoon dress, stiff and boned at the waist; long for the fashions of now, but neither Sheilah nor Peter would change a thread. The Balenciaga is their talisman, their treasure; and after they remember it they touch hands and think that the years are not behind them but hazy and marvelous and still to be lived.

The first place they went to was Paris. In the early fifties the pick of the international jobs was there. Peter had inherited the last scrap of money he knew he was ever likely to see, and it was enough to get them over: Sheilah and Peter and the babies and the steamer trunk. To their joy and astonishment they had money in the bank. They said to each other, "It should last a year." Peter was fastidious about the new job; he hadn't come all this distance to accept just anything. In Paris he met Hugh Taylor, who was earning enough smuggling gasoline to keep his wife in Paris and a girl in Rome. That impressed Peter, because he remembered Taylor as a sour scholarship student without the slightest talent for life. Taylor had a job, of course. He hadn't said to himself, I'll go over to Europe and smuggle gasoline. It gave Peter an idea; he saw the shape of things. First you catch your fish. Later, at an international party, he met Johnny Hertzberg, who told him Germany was the place. Hertzberg said that anyone who came out of Germany broke now was too stupid to be here, and deserved to be back home at a desk. Peter nodded, as if he had already thought of that. He began to think about Germany. Paris was fine for a holiday, but it had been picked clean. Yes, Germany. His money was running low. He thought about Germany quite a lot.

That winter was moist and delicate; so fragile that they daren't speak of it now. There seemed to be plenty of everything and plenty of time. They were living the dream of a marriage, the fabric uncut, nothing slashed or spoiled. All winter they spent their money, and went to parties, and talked about Peter's future job. It lasted four months. They spent their money, lived in the future, and were never as happy again.

After four months they were suddenly moved away from Paris, but not to Germany—to Geneva. Peter thinks it was because of the incident at the Trudeau wedding at the Ritz. Paul Trudeau was a French Canadian Peter had known at school and in the Navy. Trudeau had turned into a snob, proud of his career and his Paris connections. He tried to make the difference felt, but Peter thought the difference was only for strangers. At the wedding reception Peter lay down on the floor and said he was dead. He held a white azalea in a brass pot on his chest, and sang, "Oh, hear us when we cry to Thee for those in peril on the sea." Sheilah bent over him and said, "Pete, darling, get up. Pete, listen, every single person who can do something for you is in this room. If you love me, you'll get up."

"I do love you," he said, ready to engage in a serious conversation. "She's so beautiful," he told a second face. "She's nearly as tall as I am. She was a model in London. I met her over in London in the war. I met her there in the war." He lay on his back with the azalea on his chest, explaining their history. A waiter took the brass pot away, and after Peter had been hauled to his feet he knocked the waiter down. Trudeau's bride, who was freshly out of an Ursuline convent, became hysterical; and even though Paul Trudeau and Peter were old acquaintances, Trudeau never spoke to him again. Peter says now that French Canadians always have that bit of spite. He says Trudeau asked the Embassy to interfere. Luckily, back home there were still a few people to whom the name "Frazier" meant something, and it was to these people that Peter appealed. He wrote letters saying that a French-Canadian combine was preventing his getting a decent job, and could anything be done? No one answered directly, but it was clear that what they settled for was exile to Geneva: a season of meditation and remorse, as he explained to Sheilah, and it was managed tactfully, through Lucille. Lucille wrote that a friend of hers, May Fergus, now a secretary in Geneva, had heard about a job. The job was filing pictures in the information service of an international agency in the Palais des Nations. The pay was so-so, but Lucille thought Peter must be getting fed up doing nothing.

Peter often asks his sister now who put her up to it—what important person told her to write that letter suggesting Peter go to Geneva?

"Nobody," says Lucille. "I mean, nobody in the way *you* mean. I really did have this girl friend working there, and I knew you must be running through your money pretty fast in Paris."

"It must have been somebody pretty high up," Peter says. He looks at his sister admiringly, as he has often looked at his wife.

Peter's wife had loved him in Paris. Whatever she wanted in marriage she found that winter, there. In Geneva, where Peter was a file clerk and they lived in a furnished flat, she pretended they were in Paris and life was still the same. Often when the children were at supper, she changed as though she and Peter were dining out. She wore the Balenciaga, and put candles on the card table where she and Peter ate their meal. The neckline of the dress was soiled with make-up. Peter remembers her dabbing on the make-up with a wet sponge. He remembers her in the kitchen, in the soiled Balenciaga, patting on the make-up with a filthy sponge. Behind her, at the kitchen table, Sandra and Jennifer, in buttonless pajamas and bunny slippers, ate their supper of marmalade sandwiches and milk. When the children were asleep, the parents dined solemnly, ritually, Sheilah sitting straight as a queen.

It was a mysterious period of exile, and he had to wait for signs, or signals, to know when he was free to leave. He never saw the job any other way. He forgot he had applied for it. He thought he had been sent to Geneva because of a misdemeanor and had to wait to be released. Nobody pressed him at work. His immediate boss had resigned, and he was alone for months in a room with two desks. He read the *Herald-Tribune*, and tried to discover how things were here—how the others ran their lives on the pay they were officially getting. But it was a closed conspiracy. He was not dealing with adventurers now but civil servants waiting for pension day. No one ever answered his questions. They pretended to think his questions were a form of wit. His only solace in exile was the few happy weekends he had in the late spring and early summer. He had met another old acquaintance, Mike Burleigh. Mike was a serious liberal who had married a serious heiress. The Burleighs had two guest lists. The first was composed of stuffy people they felt obliged to entertain, while the second was made up of their real friends, the friends they wanted. The real friends strove hard to become stuffy and dull and thus achieve the first guest list, but few succeeded. Peter went on the first list straight away. Possibly Mike didn't understand, at the beginning, why Peter was pretending to be a file clerk. Peter had such an air—he might have been sent by a universal inspector to see how things in Geneva were being run.

Every Friday in May and June and part of July, the Fraziers rented a sky-blue Fiat and drove forty miles east of Geneva to the Burleighs' summer house. They brought the children, a suitcase, the children's tattered picture books, and a token bottle of gin. This, in memory, is a period of water and water birds, swans, roses, and singing birds. The children were small and still belonged to them. If they remember too much, their mouths water, their stomachs hurt. Peter says, "It was fine while it lasted." Enough. While it lasted Sheilah and Madge Burleigh were close. They abandoned their husbands and spent long summer afternoons comparing their mothers and praising each other's skin and hair. To Madge, and not to Peter, Sheilah opened her Liverpool childhood with the words "rat poor." Peter heard about it later, from Mike. The women's friendship seemed to Peter a bad beginning. He trusted women but not with each other. It lasted ten weeks. One Sunday, Madge said she needed the two bedrooms the Fraziers usually occupied for a party of sociologists from Pakistan, and that was the end. In November, the Fraziers heard that the summer house had been closed, and that the

Burleighs were in Geneva, in their winter flat; they gave no sign. There was no help for it, and no appeal.

Now Peter began firing letters to anyone who had ever known his late father. He was living in a mild yellow autumn. Why does he remember the streets of the city dark, and the windows everywhere black with rain? He remembers being with Sheilah and the children as if they clung together while just outside their small shelter it rained and rained. The children slept in the bedroom of the flat because the window gave on the street and they could breathe air. Peter and Sheilah had the living-room couch. Their window was not a real window but a square on a well of cement. The flat seemed damp as a cave. Peter remembers steam in the kitchen, pools under the sink, sweat on the pipes. Water streamed on him from the children's clothes, washed and dripping overhead. The trunk, upended in the children's room, was not quite unpacked. Sheilah had not signed her name to this life; she had not given in. Once Peter heard her drop her aitches. "You kids are lucky," she said to the girls. "I never 'ad so much as a sit-down meal. I ate chips out of a paper or I'ad a butty out on the stairs." He never asked her what a butty was. He thinks it means bread and cheese.

The day he heard "You kids are lucky" he understood they were becoming in fact something they had only *appeared* to be until now—the shabby civil servant and his brood. If he had been European he would have ridden to work on a bicycle, in the uniform of his class and condition. He would have worn a tight coat, a turned collar, and a dirty tie. He wondered then if coming here had been a mistake, and if he should not, after all, still be in a place where his name meant something. Surely Peter Frazier should live where "Frazier" counts? In Ontario even now when he says "Frazier" an absent look comes over his hearer's face, as if its owner were consulting an interior guide. What is Frazier? What does it mean? Oil? Power? Politics? Wheat? Real estate? The creditors had the house sealed when Peter's father died. His aunt collapsed with a heart attack in somebody's bachelor apartment, leaving three sons and a widower to surmise they had never known her. Her will was a disappointment. None of that generation left enough. One made it: the granite Presbyterian immigrants from Scotland. Their children, a generation of daunted women and maiden men, held still. Peter's father's crowd spent: they were not afraid of their fathers, and their grandfathers were old. Peter and his sister and his cousins lived on the remains. They were left the rinds of income, of notions, and the memories of ideas rather than ideas intact. If Peter can choose his reincarnation, let him be the oppressed son of a Scottish parson. Let Peter grow up on the cuffs and iron principles. Let him make the fortune! Let him flee the manse! When he was small his patrimony was squandered under his nose. He remembers people dancing in his father's house. He remembers seeing and nearly understanding adultery in a guest room, among a pile of wraps. He thought he had seen a murder; he never told. He remembers licking glasses wherever he found them—on window sills, on stairs, in the pantry. In his room he listened while Lucille read Beatrix Potter. The bad rabbit stole the carrot from the good rabbit without saying please, and downstairs was the noise of the party—the roar of the crouched lion. When his father died he saw the chairs upside down and the bailiff's chalk marks. Then the doors were sealed.

He has often tried to tell Sheilah why he cannot be defeated. He remembers his father saying, "Nothing can touch us," and Peter believed it and still does. It has prevented his taking his troubles too seriously. "Nothing can be as bad as this," he will tell himself. "It is happening to me." Even in Geneva, where his status was file clerk, where he sank and stopped on the level of the men who never emigrated, the men on the bicycles—even there he had a manner of strolling to work as if his office were a pastime, and his real life a secret so splendid he could share it with no one except himself.

In Geneva Peter worked for a woman—a girl. She was a Norwegian from a small town in Saskatchewan. He supposed they had been put together because they were Canadians; but they were as strange to each other as if "Canadian" meant any number of things, or had no real meaning. Soon after Agnes Brusen came to the office she hung her framed university degree on the wall. It was one of the gritty, prideful gestures that stand for push, toil, and family sacrifice. He thought, then, that she must be one of a family of immigrants for whom education is everything. Hugh Taylor had told him that in some families the older children never marry until the youngest have finished school. Sometimes every second child is sacrificed and made to work for the education of the next born. Those who finish college spend years paying back. They are white-hot Protestants, and they live with a load of work and debt and obligation. Peter placed his new colleague on scraps of information. He had never been in the West.

She came to the office on a Monday morning in October. The office was overheated and painted cream. It contained two desks, the filing cabinets, a map of the world as it had been in 1945, and the Charter of the United Nations left behind by Agnes Brusen's predecessor. (She took down the Charter without asking Peter if he minded, with the imprudence of gesture you find in women who wouldn't say boo to a goose; and then she hung her college degree on the nail where the Charter had been.) Three people brought her in—a whole committee. One of them said, "Agnes, this is Pete Frazier. Pete, Agnes Brusen. Pete's Canadian, too, Agnes. He knows all about the office, so ask him anything."

Of course he knew all about the office: he knew the exact spot where the cord of the venetian blind was frayed, obliging one to give an extra tug to the right.

The girl might have been twenty-three: no more. She wore a brown tweed suit with bone buttons, and a new silk scarf and new shoes. She clutched an unscratched brown purse. She seemed dressed in going-away presents. She said, "Oh, I never smoke," with a convulsive movement of her hand, when Peter offered his case. He was courteous, hiding his disappointment. The people he worked with had told him a Scandinavian girl was arriving, and he had expected a stunner. Agnes was a mole: she was small and brown, and round-shouldered as if she had always carried parcels or younger children in her arms. A mole's profile was turned when she said goodbye to her committee. If she had been foreign, ill-favored though she was, he might have flirted a little, just to show that he was friendly; but their being Canadian, and suddenly left together, was a sexual damper. He sat down and lit his own cigarette. She smiled at him, questioningly, he thought, and sat as if she had never seen a chair before. He wondered if his smoking was annoying her. He wondered if she was fidgety about drafts, or allergic to anything, and whether she would want the blind up or down. His social compass was out of order because the others couldn't tell Peter and Agnes apart. There was a world of difference between them, yet it was she who had been brought in to sit at the larger of the two desks.

While he was thinking this she got up and walked around the office, almost on tiptoe, opening the doors of closets and pulling out the filing trays. She looked inside everything except the drawers of Peter's desk. (In any case, Peter's desk was locked. His desk is locked wherever he works. In Geneva he went into Personnel one morning, early, and pinched his application form. He had stated on the form that he had seven years' experience in public relations and could speak French, German, Spanish, and Italian. He has always collected anything important about himself—anything useful. But he can never get on with the final act, which is getting rid of the information. He has kept papers about for years, a constant source of worry.)

"I know this looks funny, Mr. Ferris," said the girl. "I'm not really snooping or anything. I just can't feel easy in a new place unless I know where everything is. In a new place everything seems so hidden."

If she had called him "Ferris" and pretended not to know he was Frazier, it could only be because they had sent her here to spy on him and see if he had repented and was fit for a better place in life. "You'll be all right here," he said. "Nothing's hidden. Most of us haven't got brains enough to have secrets. This is Rainbow Valley." Depressed by the thought that they were having him watched now, he passed his hand over his hair and looked outside to the lawn and the parking lot and the peacocks someone gave the Palais des Nations years ago. The peacocks love no one. They wander about the parked cars looking elderly, bad-tempered, mournful, and lost.

Agnes had settled down again. She folded her silk scarf and placed it just so, with her gloves beside it. She opened her new purse and took out a notebook and a shiny gold pencil. She may have written

> Duster for desk
> Kleenex
> Glass jar for flowers
> Air-Wick because he smokes
> Paper for lining drawers

because the next day she brought each of these articles to work. She also brought a large black Bible, which she unwrapped lovingly and placed on the left-hand corner of her desk. The flower vase—empty—stood in the middle, and the Kleenex made a counterpoise for the Bible on the right.

When he saw the Bible he knew she had not been sent to spy on his work. The conspiracy was deeper. She might have been dispatched by ghosts. He knew everything about her, all in a moment: he saw the ambition, the terror, the dry pride. She was the true heir of the men from Scotland; she was at the start. She had been sent to tell him, "You can begin, but not begin again." She never opened the Bible, but she dusted it as she dusted her desk, her chair, and any surface the cleaning staff had overlooked. And Peter, the first days, watching her timid movements, her insignificant little face, felt, as you feel the approach of a storm, the charge of moral certainty round her, the belief in work, the faith in undertakings, the bread of the Black Sunday. He recognized and tasted all of it; ashes in the mouth.

After five days their working relations were settled. Of course, there was the Bible and all that went with it, but his tongue had never held the taste of ashes long. She was an inferior girl of poor quality. She had nothing in her favor except the degree on the wall. In the real world, he would not have invited her to his house except to mind the children. That was what he said to Sheilah. He said that Agnes was a mole, and a virgin, and that her tics and mannerisms were sending him round the bend. She had an infuriating habit of covering her mouth when she talked. Even at the telephone she put up her hand as if afraid of losing anything, even a word. Her voice was nasal and flat. She had two working costumes, both dull as the wall. One was the brown suit, the other a navy-blue dress with changeable collars. She dressed for no one; she dressed for her desk, her jar of flowers, her Bible, and her box of Kleenex. One day she crossed the space between the two desks and stood over Peter, who was reading a newspaper. She could have spoken to him from her desk, but she may have felt that being on her feet gave her authority. She had plenty of courage, but authority was something else.

"I thought—I mean, they told me you were the person . . ." She got on with it bravely: "If you don't want to do the filing or any work, all right, Mr. Frazier. I'm not saying anything about that. You might have poor health or your personal reasons. But it's got to be done, so if you'll kindly show me about the filing I'll do it. I've worked in Information before, but it was a different office, and every office is different."

"My dear girl," said Peter. He pushed back his chair and looked at her, astonished. "You've been sitting there fretting, worrying. How insensitive of me. How trying for you. Usually I file on the last Wednesday of the month, so you see, you just haven't been around long enough to see a last Wednesday. Not another word, please. And let us not waste another minute." He emptied the heaped baskets of photographs so swiftly, pushing "Iran—Smallpox Control" into "Irish Red Cross" (close enough), that the girl looked frightened, as if she had raised a whirlwind. She said slowly, "If you'll only show me, Mr. Frazier, instead of doing it so fast, I'll gladly look after it, because you might want to be doing other things, and I feel the filing should be done every day." But Peter was too busy to answer, and so she sat down, holding the edge of her desk.

"There," he said, beaming. "All done." His smile, his sunburst, was wasted, for the girl was staring round the room as if she feared she had not inspected everything the first day after all; some drawer, some cupboard, hid a monster. That evening Peter unlocked one of the drawers of his desk and took away the application form he had stolen from Personnel. The girl had not finished her search.

"How could you *not* know?" wailed Sheilah. "You sit looking at her every day. You must talk about *something*. She must have told you."

"She did tell me," said Peter, "and I've just told you."

It was this: Agnes Brusen was on the Burleighs' guest list. How had the Burleighs met her? What did they see in her? Peter could not reply. He knew that Agnes lived in a bed-sitting room with a Swiss family and had her meals with them. She had been in Geneva three months, but no one had ever seen her outside the office. "You *should* know," said Sheilah. "She must have something, more than you can see. Is she pretty? Is she brilliant? What is it?"

"We don't really talk," Peter said. They talked in a way: Peter teased her and she took no notice. Agnes was not a sulker. She had taken her defeat like a sport. She did her work and a good deal of his. She sat behind her Bible, her flowers, and her Kleenex, and answered when Peter spoke. That was how he learned about the Burleighs—just by teasing and being bored. It was a January afternoon. He said, "*Miss Brusen. Talk to me. Tell me everything. Pretend we have perfect rapport. Do you like Geneva?*"

"It's a nice clean town," she said. He can see to this day the red and blue anemones in the glass jar, and her bent head, and her small untended hands.

"Are you learning beautiful French with your Swiss family?"

"They speak English."

"Why don't you take an apartment of your own?" he said. Peter was not usually impertinent. He was bored. "You'd be independent then."

"I am independent," she said. "I earn my living. I don't think it proves anything if you live by yourself. Mrs. Burleigh wants me to live alone, too. She's looking for something for me. It mustn't be dear. I send money home."

Here was the extraordinary thing about Agnes Brusen: she refused the use of Christian names and never spoke to Peter unless he spoke first, but she would tell anything, as if to say, "Don't waste time fishing. Here it is."

He learned all in one minute that she sent her salary home, and that she was a friend of the Burleighs. The first he had expected; the second knocked him flat.

"She's got to come to dinner," Sheilah said. "We should have had her right from the beginning. If only I'd known! But *you* were the one. You said she looked like—oh, I don't even remember. A Norwegian mole."

She came to dinner one Saturday night in January, in her navy-blue dress, to which she had pinned an organdy gardenia. She sat upright on the edge of the sofa. Sheilah had ordered the meal from a restaurant. There was lobster, good wine, and a *pièce-montée* full of kirsch and cream. Agnes refused the lobster; she had never eaten anything from the sea unless it had been sterilized and tinned, and said so. She was afraid of skin poisoning. Someone in her family had skin poisoning after having eaten oysters. She touched her cheeks and neck to show where the poisoning had erupted. She sniffed her wine and put the glass down without tasting it. She could not eat the cake because of the alcohol it contained. She ate an egg, bread and butter, a sliced tomato, and drank a glass of ginger ale. She seemed unaware she was creating disaster and pain. She did not help clear away the dinner plates. She sat, adequately nourished, decently dressed, and waited to learn why she had been invited here—that was the feeling Peter had. He folded the card table on which they had dined, and opened the window to air the room.

"It's not the same cold as Canada, but you feel it more," he said, for something to say.

"Your blood has gotten thin," said Agnes.

Sheilah returned from the kitchen and let herself fall into an armchair. With her eyes closed she held out her hand for a cigarette. She was performing the haughty-lady act that was a family joke. She flung her head back and looked at Agnes through half-closed lids; then she suddenly brought her head forward, widening her eyes.

"Are you skiing madly?" she said.

"Well, in the first place there hasn't been any snow," said Agnes. "So nobody's doing any skiing so far as I know. All I hear is people complaining because there's no snow. Personally, I don't ski. There isn't much skiing in the part of Canada I come from. Besides, my family never had that kind of leisure."

"Heavens," said Sheilah, as if her family had every kind.

I'll bet they had, thought Peter. On the dole.

Sheilah was wasting her act. He had a suspicion that Agnes knew it was an act but did not know it was also a joke. If so, it made Sheilah seem a fool, and he loved Sheilah too much to enjoy it.

"The Burleighs have been wonderful to me," said Agnes. She seemed to have divined why she was here, and decided to give them all the information they wanted, so that she could put on her coat and go home to bed. "They had me out to their place on the lake every weekend until the weather got cold and they moved back to town. They've rented a chalet for the winter, and they want me to come there, too. But I don't know if I will or not. I don't ski, and, oh, I don't know—I don't drink, either, and I don't always see the point. Their friends are too rich and I'm too Canadian."

She had delivered everything Sheilah wanted and more: Agnes was on the first guest list and didn't care. No, Peter corrected; doesn't know. Doesn't care and doesn't know.

"I thought with you Norwegians it was in the blood, skiing. And drinking," Sheilah murmured.

"Drinking, maybe," said Agnes. She covered her mouth and said behind her spread fingers, "In our family we were religious. We didn't drink or smoke. My brother was in Norway in the war. He saw some cousins. Oh," she said, unexpectedly loud, "Harry said it was just terrible. They were so poor. They had flies in their kitchen. They gave him something to eat a fly had been on. They didn't have a real toilet, and they'd been in the same house about two hundred years. We've only recently built our own home, and we have a bathroom and two toilets. I'm from Saskatchewan," she said. "I'm not from any other place."

Surely one winter here had been punishment enough? In the spring they would remember him and free him. He wrote Lucille, who said he was lucky to have a job at all. The Burleighs had sent the Fraziers a second-guest-list Christmas card. It showed a Moslem refugee child weeping outside a tent. They treasured the card and left it standing long after the others had been given the children to cut up. Peter had discovered by now what had gone wrong in the friendship—Sheilah had charged a skirt at a dressmaker to Madge's account. Madge had told her she might, and then changed her mind. Poor Sheilah! She was new to this part of it—to the changing humors of independent friends. Paris was already a year in the past. At Mardi Gras, the Burleighs gave their annual party. They invited everyone, the damned and the dropped, with the prodigality of a child at prayers. The invitation said "in costume," but the Fraziers were too happy to wear a disguise. They might not be recognized. Like many of the guests they expected to meet at the party, they had been disgraced, forgotten, and rehabilitated. They would be anxious to see one another as they were.

On the night of the party, the Fraziers rented a car they had never seen before and drove through the first snowstorm of the year. Peter had not driven since last summer's blissful trips in the Fiat. He could not find the switch for the windshield wiper in his car. He leaned over the wheel. "Can you see on your side?" he asked. "Can I make a left turn here? Does it look like a one-way?"

"I can't imagine why you took a car with a right-hand drive," said Sheilah.

He had trouble finding a place to park; they crawled up and down unknown streets whose curbs were packed with snow-covered cars. When they stood at last on the pavement, safe and sound, Peter said, "This is the first snow."

"I can see that," said Sheilah. "Hurry, darling. My hair."

"It's the first snow."

"You're repeating yourself," she said. "'Please hurry, darling. Think of my poor shoes. My *hair*."

She was born in an ugly city, and so was Peter, but they have this difference: she does not know the importance of the first snow—the first clean thing in a dirty year. He would have told her then that this storm, which was wetting her feet and destroying her hair, was like the first day of the English spring, but she made a frightened gesture, trying to shield her head. The gesture told him he did not understand her beauty.

"Let me," she said. He was fumbling with the key, trying to lock the car. She took the key without impatience and locked the door on the driver's side; and then, to show Peter she treasured him and was not afraid of wasting her life or her beauty, she took his arm and they walked in the snow down a street and around a corner to the apartment house where the Burleighs lived. They were, and are, a united couple. They were afraid of the party, and each of them knew it. When they walk together, holding arms, they give each other whatever each can spare.

Only six people had arrived in costume. Madge Burleigh was disguised as Manet's "Lola de Valence," which everyone mistook for Carmen. Mike was an Impressionist painter, with a straw hat and a glued-on beard. "I am all of them," he said. He would rather have dressed as a dentist, he said, welcoming the Fraziers as if he had parted from them the day before, but Madge wanted him to look as if he had created her. "You know?" he said.

"Perfectly," said Sheilah. Her shoes were stained and the snow had softened her lacquered hair. She was not wasted; she was the most beautiful woman here.

About an hour after their arrival, Peter found himself with no one to talk to. He had told about the Trudeau wedding in Paris and the pot of azaleas, and after he mislaid his audience he began to look round for Sheilah. She was on a window seat, partly concealed by a green velvet curtain. Facing her, so that their profiles were neat and perfect against the night, was a man. Their conversation was private and enclosed, as if they had in minutes covered leagues of time and arrived at the place where everything was implied, understood. Peter began working his way across the room, toward his wife, when he saw Agnes. He was granted the sight of her drowning face. She had dressed with comic intention, obviously with care, and now she was a ragged hobo, half tramp, half clown. Her hair was tucked up under a bowler hat. The six costumed guests who had made the same mistake—the ghost, the gypsy, the Athenian maiden, the geisha, the Martian, and the apache—were delighted to find a seventh; but Agnes was not amused; she was gasping for life. When a waiter passed with a crowded tray, she took a glass without seeing it; then a wave of the party took her away.

Sheilah's new friend was named Simpson. After Simpson said he thought perhaps he'd better circulate, Peter sat down where he had been. "Now look, Sheilah," he began. Their most intimate conversations have taken place at parties. Once at a party she told him she was leaving him; she didn't, of course. Smiling, blue-eyed, she gazed lovingly at Peter and said rapidly, "Pete, shut up and listen. That man. The man you scared away. He's a big wheel in a company out in India or someplace like that. It's gorgeous out there. Pete, the *servants*. And it's warm. It never never snows. He says there's heaps of jobs. You pick them off the trees like . . . orchids. He says it's even easier now than when we owned all those places, because now the poor pets can't run anything and they'll pay *fortunes*. Pete, he says it's warm, it's heaven, and Pete, they pay."

A few minutes later, Peter was alone again and Sheilah part of a closed, laughing group. Holding her elbow was the man from the place where jobs grew like orchids. Peter edged into the group and laughed at a story he hadn't heard. He heard only the last line, which was, "Here comes another tunnel." Looking out from the tight laughing ring, he saw Agnes again, and he thought, I'd be like Agnes if I didn't have Sheilah. Agnes put her glass down on a table and lurched toward the doorway, head forward. Madge Burleigh, who never stopped moving around the room and smiling, was still smiling when she paused and said in Peter's ear, "Go with Agnes, Pete. See that she gets home. People will notice if Mike leaves."

"She probably just wants to walk around the block" said Peter. "She'll be back."

"Oh, stop thinking about yourself, for once, and see that that poor girl gets home," said Madge. "You've still got your Fiat, haven't you?"

He turned away as if he had been pushed. Any command is a release, in a way. He may not want to go in that particular direction, but at least he is going somewhere. And now Sheilah, who had moved inches nearer to hear what Madge and Peter were murmuring, said, "Yes, go, darling," as if he were leaving the gates of Troy.

Peter was to find Agnes and see that she reached home: this he repeated to himself as he stood on the landing, outside the Burleighs' flat, ringing for the elevator. Bored with waiting for it, he ran down the stairs, four flights, and saw that Agnes had stalled the lift by leaving the door open. She was crouched on the floor, propped on her fingertips. Her eyes were closed.

"Agnes," said Peter. "*Miss* Brusen, I mean. That's no way to leave a party. Don't you know you're supposed to curtsey and say thanks? My God, Agnes, anybody going by here just now might have seen you! Come on, be a good girl. Time to go home."

She got up without his help and, moving between invisible crevasses, shut the elevator door. Then she left the building and Peter followed, remembering he was to see that she got home. They walked along the snowy pavement, Peter a few steps behind her. When she turned right for no reason, he turned, too. He had no clear idea where they were going. Perhaps she lived close by. He had forgotten where the hired car was parked, or what it looked like; he could not remember its make or its color. In any case, Sheilah had the key. Agnes walked on steadily, as if she knew their destination, and he thought, Agnes Brusen is drunk in the street in Geneva and dressed like a tramp. He wanted to say, "This is the best thing that ever happened to you, Agnes; it will help you understand how things are for some of the rest of us." But she stopped and turned and, leaning over a low hedge, retched on a frozen lawn. He held her clammy forehead and rested his hand on her arched back, on muscles as tight as a fist. She staightened up and drew a breath but the cold air made her cough. "Don't breathe too deeply," he said. "It's the worst thing you can do. Have you got a handkerchief?" He passed his own handkerchief over her wet weeping face, upturned like the face of one of his little girls. "I'm out without a coat," he said, noticing it. "We're a pair."

"I never drink," said Agnes. "I'm just not used to it." Her voice was sweet and quiet. He had never seen her so peaceful, so composed. He thought she must surely be all right, now, and perhaps he might leave her here. The trust in her tilted face had perplexed him. He wanted to get back to Sheilah and have her explain something. He had forgotten what it was, but Sheilah would know. "Do you live around here?" he said. As he spoke, she let herself fall. He had wiped her face and now she trusted him to pick her up, set her on her feet, take her wherever she ought to be. He pulled her up and she stood, wordless, humble, as he brushed the snow from her tramp's clothes. Snow horizontally crossed the lamplight. The street was silent. Agnes had lost her hat. Snow, which he tasted, melted on her hands. His gesture of licking snow from her hands was formal as a handshake. He tasted snow on her hands and then they walked on.

"I never drink," she said. They stood on the edge of a broad avenue. The wrong turning now could lead them anywhere; it was the changeable avenue at the edge of towns that loses its houses and becomes a highway. She held his arm and spoke in a gentle voice. She said, "In our house we didn't smoke or drink. My mother was ambitious for me, more than for Harry and the others." She said, "I've never been alone before. When I was a kid I would get up in the summer before the others, and I'd see the ice wagon going down the street. I'm alone now. Mrs. Burleigh's found me an apartment. It's only one room. She likes it because it's in the old part of town. I don't like old houses. Old houses are dirty. You don't know who was there before."

"I should have a car somewhere," Peter said. "I'm not sure where we are."

He remembers that on this avenue they climbed into a taxi, but nothing about the drive. Perhaps he fell asleep. He does remember that when he paid the driver Agnes clutched his arm, trying to stop him. She pressed extra coins into the driver's palm. The driver was paid twice.

"I'll tell you one thing about us," said Peter. "We pay everything twice." This was part of a much longer theory concerning North American behavior, and it was not Peter's own. Mike Burleigh had held forth about it on summer afternoons.

Agnes pushed open a door between a stationer's shop and a grocery, and led the way up a narrow inside stair. They climbed one flight, frightening beetles. She had to search every pocket for the latchkey. She was shaking with cold. Her apartment seemed little warmer than the street. Without speaking to Peter she turned on all the lights. She looked inside the kitchen and the bathroom and then got down on her hands and knees and looked under the sofa. The room was neat and belonged to no one.

She left him standing in this unclaimed room—she had forgotten him—and closed a door behind her. He looked for something to do—some useful action he could repeat to Madge. He turned on the electric radiator in the fireplace. Perhaps Agnes wouldn't thank him for it; perhaps she would rather undress in the cold. "I'll be on my way," he called to the bathroom door.

She had taken off the tramp's clothes and put on a dressing gown of orphanage wool. She came out of the bathroom and straight toward him. She pressed her face and rubbed her cheek on his shoulder as if hoping the contact would leave a scar. He saw her back and her profile and his own face in the mirror over the fireplace. He thought, This is how disasters happen. He saw floods of sea water moving with perfect punitive justice over reclaimed land; he saw lava covering vineyards and overtaking dogs and stragglers. A bridge over an abyss snapped in two and the long express train, suddenly V-shaped, floated like snow. He thought amiably of every kind of disaster and thought, This is how they occur.

Her eyes were closed. She said, "I shouldn't be over here. In my family we didn't drink or smoke. My mother wanted a lot from me, more than from Harry and the others." But he knew all that; he had known from the day of the Bible, and because once, at the beginning, she had made him afraid. He was not afraid of her now.

She said, "It's no use staying here, is it?"

"If you mean what I think, no."

"It wouldn't be better anywhere."

She let him see full on her blotched face. He was not expected to do anything. He was not required to pick her up when she fell or wipe her tears. She was poor quality, really—he remembered having thought that once. She left him and went quietly into the bathroom and locked the door. He heard taps running and supposed it was a hot bath. He was pretty certain there would be no more tears. He looked at his watch: Sheilah must be home, now, wondering what had become of him. He descended the beetles' staircase and for forty minutes crossed the city under a windless fall of snow.

The neighbor's child who had stayed with Peter's children was asleep on the living-room sofa. Peter woke her and sent her, sleepwalking, to her own door. He sat down, wet to the bone, thinking, I'll call the Burleighs. In half an hour I'll call the police. He heard a car stop and the engine running and a confusion of two voices laughing and calling goodnight. Presently Sheilah let herself in, rosy-faced, smiling. She carried his trenchcoat over her arm. She said, "How's Agnes?"

"Where were you?" he said. "Whose car was that?"

Sheilah had gone into the children's room. He heard her shutting their window. She returned, undoing her dress, and said, "Was Agnes all right?"

"Agnes is all right. Sheilah, this is about the worst . . ."

She stepped out of the Balenciaga and threw it over a chair. She stopped and looked at him and said, "Poor old Pete, are you in love with Agnes?" And then, as if the answer were of so little importance she hadn't time for it, she locked her arms around him and said, "My love, we're going to Ceylon."

Two days later, when Peter strolled into his office, Agnes was at her desk. She wore the blue dress, with a spotless collar. White and yellow freesias were symmetrically arranged in the glass jar. The room was hot, and the spring snow, glued for a second when it touched the window, blurred the view of parked cars.

"Quite a party," Peter said.

She did not look up. He sighed, sat down, and thought if the snow held he would be skiing at the Burleighs' very soon. Impressed by his kindness to Agnes, Madge had invited the family for the first possible weekend.

Presently Agnes said, "I'll never drink again or go to a house where people are drinking. And I'll never bother anyone the way I bothered you."

"You didn't bother me," he said. "I took you home. You were alone and it was late. It's normal."

"Normal for you, maybe, but I'm used to getting home by myself. Please never tell what happened."

He stared at her. He can still remember the freesias and the Bible and the heat in the room. She looked as if the elements had no power. She felt neither heat nor cold. "Nothing happened," he said.

"I behaved in a silly way. I had no right to. I led you to think I might do something wrong."

"*I* might have tried something," he said gallantly. "But that would be my fault and not yours."

She put her knuckle to her mouth and he could scarcely hear. "It was because of you. I was afraid you might be blamed, or else you'd blame yourself."

"There's no question of any blame," he said. "Nothing happened. We'd both had a lot to drink. Forget about it. Nothing *happened*. You'd remember if it had."

She put down her hand. There was an expression on her face. Now she sees me, he thought. She had never looked at him after the first day. (He has since tried to put a name to the look on her face; but how can he, now, after so many voyages, after Ceylon, and Hong Kong, and Sheilah's nearly leaving him, and all their difficulties—the money owed, the rows with hotel managers, the lost and found steamer trunk, the children throwing up the foreign food?) She sees me now, he thought. What does she see?

She said, "I'm from a big family. I'm not used to being alone. I'm not a suicidal person, but I could have done something after that party, just not to see any more, or think or listen or expect anything. What can I think when I see these people? All my life I heard, educated people don't do this, educated people don't do that. And now I'm here, and you're all educated people, and you're nothing but pigs. You're educated and you drink and do everything wrong and you know what you're doing, and that makes you worse than pigs. My family worked to make me an educated person, but they didn't know you. But what if I didn't see and hear and expect anything any more? It wouldn't change anything. You'd all be still the same. Only *you* might have thought it was your fault. You might have thought you were to blame. It could worry you all your life. It would have been wrong for me to worry you."

He remembered that the rented car was still along a snowy curb somewhere in Geneva. He wondered if Sheilah had the key in her purse and if she remembered where they'd parked.

"I told you about the ice wagon," Agnes said. "I don't remember everything, so you're wrong about remembering. But I remember telling you that. That was the best. It's the best you can hope to have. In a big family, if you want to be alone, you have to get up before the rest of them. You get up early in the morning in the summer and it's you, you, once in your life alone in the universe. You think you know everything that can happen . . . Nothing is ever like that again."

He looked at the smeared window and wondered if this day could end without disaster. In his mind he saw her falling in the snow wearing a tramp's costume, and he saw her coming to him in the orphanage dressing gown. He saw her drowning face at the party. He was afraid for himself. The story was still unfinished. It had to come to a climax, something threatening to him. But there was no climax. They talked that day, and afterward nothing else was said. They went on in the same office for a short time, until Peter left for Ceylon; until somebody read the right letter, passed it on for the right initials, and the Fraziers began the Oriental tour that should have made their fortune. Agnes and Peter were too tired to speak after that morning. They were like a married couple in danger, taking care.

But what were they talking about that day, so quietly, such old friends? They talked about dying, about being ambitious, about being religious, about different kinds of love. What did she see when she looked at him—taking her knuckle slowly away from her mouth, bringing her hand down to the desk, letting it rest there? They were both Canadians, so they had this much together—the knowledge of the little you dare admit. Death, near-death, the best thing, the wrong thing—God knows what they were telling each other. Anyway, nothing happened.

When, on Sunday mornings, Sheilah and Peter talk about those times, they take on the glamor of something still to come. It is then he remembers Agnes Brusen. He never says her name. Sheilah wouldn't remember Agnes. Agnes is the only secret Peter has from his wife, the only puzzle he pieces together without her help. He thinks about families in the West as they were fifteen, twenty years ago—the iron-cold ambition, and every member pushing the next one on. He thinks of his father's parties. When he thinks of his father he imagines him with Sheilah, in a crowd. Actually, Sheilah and Peter's father never met, but they might have liked each other. His father admired good-looking women. Peter wonders what they were doing over there in Geneva—not Sheilah and Peter, *Agnes* and Peter. It is almost as if they had once run away together, silly as children, irresponsible as lovers. Peter and Sheilah are back where they started. While they were out in world affairs picking up microbes and debts, always on the fringe of disaster, the fringe of a fortune, Agnes went on and did—what? They lost each other. He thinks of the ice wagon going down the street. He sees something he has never seen in his life—a Western town that belongs to Agnes. Here is Agnes—small, mole-faced, round-shouldered because she has always carried a younger child. She watches the ice wagon and the trail of ice water in a morning invented for her: hers. He sees the weak prairie trees and the shadows on the sidewalk. Nothing moves except the shadows and the ice wagon and the changing amber of the child's eyes. The child is Peter. He has seen the grain of the cement sidewalk and the grass in the cracks, and the dust, and the dandelions at the edge of the road. He is there. He has taken the morning that belongs to Agnes, he is up before the others, and he knows everything. There is nothing he doesn't know. He could keep the morning, if he wanted to, but what can Peter do with the start of a summer day? Sheilah is here, it is a true Sunday morning, with its dimness and headache and remorse and regrets, and this is life. He says, "We have the Balenciaga." He touches Sheilah's hand. The children have their aunt now, and he and Sheilah have each other. Everything works out, somehow or other. Let Agnes have the start of the day. Let Agnes think it was invented for her. Who wants to be alone in the universe? No, begin at the beginning: Peter lost Agnes. Agnes says to herself somewhere, Peter is lost.

ITALO CALVINO

(1923–1985)

I talo Calvino was born in Havana, where his father was working as an agronomist and his mother as a botanist. The family returned to San Remo, Italy, a town on the Mediterranean coast near the French border, where Calvino was educated. He graduated from the University of Turin in 1947 with a degree in literature, the same year his first novel, The Path to the Nest of Spiders, was published. He joined the Communist Party but gradually became disenchanted and left it after the Soviet invasion of Hungary. In the 1950s, he published three fantasy novels, and important collections of his stories appeared in 1958 and 1963. During the 1960s, he lost all interest in politics and turned exclusively to literature. His other important works include Cosmicomics (1965), If on a Winter's Night a Traveller (1979), and Mr. Palomar (1983). In the last twenty years of his life, Calvino produced the intricate, self-reflexive fiction for which he is best known. In it, for example, he parodies scientific truths, writes a collection of tales in which the tellers use a deck of tarot cards to narrate their stories, and introduces in a novel a protagonist who is reading a novel by Calvino or characters who seek keys to complexities that multiply even as they seem to be resolved. Thus Calvino in his fiction mimics not only the process of reading stories but also that of reading the world, thereby conflating the reader's task and humanity's quest for meaning in an unpredictable cosmos. One of his "imprisoned" characters puts it this way:

> If I succeed in mentally constructing a fortress from which it is impossible to escape, this conceived fortress will either be the same as the real one—and in this case it is certain we shall never escape from here, but at least we will achieve the serenity of one who knows he is here because he could be nowhere else— or it will be a fortress from which escape is even more impossible than from here—and this, then, is a sign that here an opportunity of escape exists: we have only to identify the point where the imagined fortress does not coincide with the real one and then find it.

Crystals

If the substances that made up the terrestrial globe in its incandescent state had had at their disposal a period of time long enough to allow them to grow cold and also sufficient freedom of movement, each of them would have become separated from the others in a single, enormous crystal.

I t could have been different, I know,—*Qfwfq remarked*,—you're telling me: I believed so firmly in that world of crystal that was supposed to come forth that I can't resign myself to living still in this world, amorphous and crumbling and gummy, which has been our lot, instead. I run all the time like everybody else, I take the train each morning (I live in New Jersey) to slip into the cluster of prisms I see emerging beyond the Hudson, with its sharp cusps; I spend my days there, going up and down the horizontal and vertical axes that crisscross that compact solid, or along the obligatory routes that graze its sides and its edges. But I don't fall into the trap: I know they're making me run among smooth transparent walls and between symmetrical angles so I'll believe I'm inside a crystal, so I'll recognize a regular form there, a rotation axis, a constant in the dihedrons, whereas none of all this exists. The contrary exists: glass, those are glass solids that flank the streets, not crystal, it's a paste of haphazard molecules which has invaded and cemented the world, a layer of suddenly chilled lava, stiffened into forms imposed from the outside, whereas inside it's magma just as in the Earth's incandescent days.

I don't pine for them surely, those days: I feel discontented with things as they are, but if, for that reason, you expect me to remember the past with nostalgia, you're mistaken. It was horrible, the Earth without any crust, an eternal incandescent winter, a mineral bog, with black swirls of iron and nickel that dripped down from every crack toward the center of the globe, and jets of mercury that gushed up in high spurts. We made our way through a boiling haze, Vug and I, and we could never manage to touch a solid point. A barrier of liquid rocks that we found before us would suddenly evaporate in our path, disintegrating into an acid cloud; we would rush to pass it, but already we could feel it condensing and striking us like a storm of metallic rain, swelling the thick waves of an aluminum ocean. The substance of things changed around us every minute; the atoms, that is, passed from one state of disorder to another state of disorder and then another still: or rather, practically speaking, everything remained always the same. The only real change would have been the atoms' arranging themselves in some sort of order: this is what Vug and I were looking for, moving in the mixture of the elements without any points of reference, without a before or an after.

Now the situation is different, I admit: I have a wrist watch, I compare the angle of its hands with the angle of all the hands I see; I have an engagement book where the hours of my business appointments are marked down; I have a checkbook on whose stubs I add and subtract numbers. At Penn Station I get off the train, I take the subway, I stand and grasp the strap with one hand to keep my balance while I hold my newspaper up in the other, folded so I can glance over the figures of the stock market quotations: I play the game, in other words, the game of pretending there's an order in the dust, a regularity in the system, or an interpenetration of different systems, incongruous but still measurable, so that every graininess of disorder coincides with the faceting of an order which promptly crumbles.

Before it was worse, of course. The world was a solution of substances where everything was dissolved into everything and the solvent of everything. Vug and I kept on getting lost in its midst, losing our lost places, where we had been lost always, without any idea of what we could have found (or of what could have found us) so as to be lost no more.

We realized it all of a sudden. Vug said: "There!"

She was pointing, in the midst of a lava flow, at something that was taking form. It was a solid with regular, smooth facets and sharp corners; and these facets and corners were slowly expanding, as if at the expense of the surrounding matter, and also the form of the solid was changing, while still maintaining symmetrical proportions . . . And it wasn't only the form that was distinct from all the rest: it was also the way the light entered inside, passing through it and refracted by it. Vug said: "They shine! Lots of them!"

It wasn't the only one, in fact. On the incandescent expanse where once only ephemeral gas bubbles had risen, expelled from the Earth's bowels, cubes now were coming to the surface and octahedrons, prisms, figures so transparent they seemed airy, empty inside, but instead, as we soon saw, they concentrated in themselves an incredible compactness and hardness. The sparkle of this angled blossoming was invading the Earth, and Vug said: "It's spring!" I kissed her.

Now you can understand me: if I love order, it's not—as with so many others—the mark of a character subjected to an inner discipline, a repression of the instincts. In me the idea of an absolutely regular world, symmetrical and methodical, is associated with that first impulse and burgeoning of nature, that amorous tension—what you call eros—while all the rest of your images, those that according to you associate passion with disorder, love with intemperate overflow—river fire whirlpool volcano—for me are memories of nothingness and listlessness and boredom.

It was a mistake on my part, it didn't take me long to understand that. Here we are at the point of arrival: Vug is lost; of the diamond eros only dust remains; the simulated crystal that imprisons me now is base glass. I follow the arrows on the asphalt, I line up at the traffic light, and I start again (today I came into New York by car) when the green comes on (as I do every Wednesday because I take) shifting into first (Dorothy to her psychoanalyst), I try to maintain a steady speed which allows me to pass all the green lights on Second Avenue. This, which you call order, is a threadbare patch over disintegration; I found a parking space but in two hours I'll have to go down again to put another coin in the meter; if I forget they'll tow my car away.

I dreamed of a world of crystal, in those days: I didn't dream it, I saw it, an indestructible frozen springtime of quartz. Polyhedrons grew up, tall as mountains, diaphanous: the shadow of the person beyond pierced through their thickness. "Vug, it's you!" To reach her I flung myself against walls smooth as mirrors; I slipped back; I clutched the edges, wounding myself; I ran along treacherous perimeters, and at every turn there was a different light—diffused, milky, opaque—that the mountain contained.

"Where are you?"

"In the woods!"

The silver crystals were filiform trees, with branches at every right angle. Skeletal fronds of tin and of lead thickened the forest in a geometric vegetation.

In the middle there was Vug, running. "Qfwfq! It's different over there!" she cried. "Gold, green, blue!"

A valley of beryllium opened out, surrounded by ridges of every color, from aquamarine to emerald. I followed Vug with my spirit torn between happiness and fear: happiness at seeing how every substance that made up the world was finding its definitive and solid form, and a still vague fear that this triumph of order in such various fashions might reproduce on another scale the disorder we had barely left behind us. A total crystal I dreamed, a topaz world that would leave out nothing: I was impatient for our Earth to detach itself from the wheel of gas and dust in which all the celestial bodies were whirling, ours should be the first to escape that useless dispersal which is the universe.

Of course, if he chooses, a person can also take it into his head to find an order in the stars, the galaxies, an order in the lighted windows of the empty skyscrapers where between nine and midnight the cleaning women wax the floors of the offices. Rationalize, that's the big task: rationalize if you don't want everything to come apart. Tonight we're dining in town, in a restaurant on the terrace of a twenty-fourth floor. It's a business dinner: there are six of us; there is also Dorothy, and the wife of Dick Bemberg. I eat some oysters, I look at a star that's called (if

I have the right one) Betelgeuse. We make conversation: we husbands talk about production; the ladies, about consumption. Anyway, seeing the firmament is difficult: the lights of Manhattan spread out a halo that becomes mixed with the luminosity of the sky.

The wonder of crystals is the network of atoms that is constantly repeated: this is what Vug wouldn't understand. What she liked—I quickly realized—was to discover in crystals some differences, even minimal ones, irregularities, flaws.

"But what does one atom out of place matter to you, an exfoliation that's a bit crooked," I said, "in a solid that's destined to be enlarged infinitely according to a regular pattern? It's the single crystal we're working toward, the gigantic crystal . . ."

"I like them when there're lots of little ones," she said. To contradict me, surely; but also because it was true that crystals were popping up by the thousands at the same time and were interpenetrating one another, arresting their growth where they came in contact, and they never succeeded in taking over entirely the liquid rock from which they received their form: the world wasn't tending to be composed into an ever-simpler figure but was clotting in a vitreous mass from which prisms and octahedrons and cubes seemed to be struggling to be free, to draw all the matter to themselves . . .

A crater exploded: a cascade of diamonds spread out.

"Look! Aren't they big?" Vug exclaimed.

One every side there were erupting volcanoes: A continent of diamond refracted the sun's light in a mosaic of rainbow chips.

"Didn't you say the smaller they are the more you like them?" I reminded her.

"No! Those enormous ones—I want them!" and she darted off.

"There are still bigger ones," I said, pointing above us. The sparkle was blinding: I could already see a mountain-diamond, a faceted and iridescent chain, a gem-plateau, a Koh-i-noor-Himalaya.

"What can I do with them? I like the ones that can be picked up. I want to have them!" and in Vug there was already the frenzy of possession.

"The diamond will have us, instead. It's the stronger," I said.

I was mistaken, as usual: the diamond was had, not by us. When I walk past Tiffany's, I stop to look at the windows, I contemplate the diamond prisoners, shards of our lost kingdom. They lie in velvet coffins, chained with silver and platinum; with my imagination and my memory I enlarge them, I give them again the gigantic dimensions of fortress, garden, lake, I imagine Vug's pale blue shadow mirrored there. I'm not imagining it: it really is Vug who now advances among the diamonds. I turn: it's the girl looking into the window over my shoulder, from beneath the hair falling across her forehead.

"Vug!" I say. "Our diamonds!"

She laughs.

"Is it really you?" I ask. "What's your name?"

She gives me her telephone number.

We are among slabs of glass: I lived in simulated order, I would like to say to her, I have an office on the East Side, I live in New Jersey, for the weekend Dorothy has invited the Bembergs, against simulated order simulated disorder is impotent, diamond would be necessary, not for us to possess it but for it to possess us, the free diamond in which Vug and I were free . . .

"I'll call you," I say to her, only out of the desire to resume my arguing with her.

In an aluminum crystal, where chance scatters some chrome atoms, the transparency is colored a dark red: so the rubies flowered beneath our footsteps.

"You see?" Vug said. "Aren't they beautiful?"

We couldn't walk through a valley of rubies without starting to quarrel again.

"Yes," I said, "because the regularity of the hexagon . . ."

"Uff!" she said. "Would they be rubies without the intrusion of extraneous atoms? Answer me that!"

I became angry. More beautiful? Or less beautiful? We could go on arguing to infinity, but the only sure fact was that the Earth was moving in the direction of Vug's preferences. Vug's world was in the fissures, the cracks where lava rises, dissolving the rock and mixing the minerals in unpredictable concretions. Seeing her caress walls of granite, I regretted what had been lost in that rock, the exactness of the feldspars, the micas, the quartzes. Vug seemed to take pleasure only in noting how minutely variegated the face of the world appeared. How could we understand each other? For me all that mattered was homogeneous growth, indiscerptibility, achieved serenity; for her, everything had to be separation and mixture, one or the other, or both at once. Even the two of us had to take on an aspect (we still possessed neither form nor future): I imagined a slow uniform expansion, following the crystals' example, until the me-crystal would have interpenetrated and fused with the her-crystal and perhaps together we would have become a unity within the world-crystal; she already seemed to know that the law of living matter would be infinite separating and rejoining. Was it Vug, then, who was right?

It's Monday; I telephone her. It's almost summer already. We spend a day together, on Staten Island, lying on the beach. Vug watches the grains of sand trickle through her fingers.

"All these tiny crystals . . ." she says.

The shattered world that surrounds us is, for her, still the world of the past, the one we expected to be born from the incandescent world. To be sure, the crystals still give the world form, breaking up, being reduced to almost imperceptible fragments rolled by the waves, encrusted with all the elements dissolved in the sea which kneads them together again in steep cliffs, in sandstone reefs, a hundred times dissolved and recomposed, in schists, slates, marbles of glabrous whiteness, simulacra of what they once could have been and now can never be.

And again I am gripped by my stubbornness as I was when it began to be clear that the game was lost, that the Earth's crust was becoming a congeries of disparate forms, and I didn't want to resign myself, and at every irregularity in the porphyry that Vug happily pointed out to me, at every vitrescence that emerged from the basalt, I wanted to persuade myself that these were only apparent flaws, that they were all part of a much vaster regular structure, in which every asymmetry we thought we observed really corresponded to a network of symmetries so complicated we couldn't comprehend it, and I tried to calculate how many billions of sides and dihedral corners this labyrinthine crystal must have, this hypercrystal that included within itself crystals and noncrystals.

Vug has brought a little transistor radio along to the beach with her.

"Everything comes from crystal," I say, "even the music we're hearing." But I know full well that the transistor's crystal is imperfect, flawed, veined with impurities, with rents in the warp of the atoms.

She says: "It's an obsession with you." And it is our old quarrel, continuing. She wants to make me admit that real order carries impurity within itself, destruction.

The boat lands at the Battery, it is evening; in the illuminated network of the skyscraper-prisms I now look only at the dark rips, the gaps. I see Vug home; I go up with her. She lives downtown, she has a photography studio. As I look around I see nothing but perturbations of the order of the atoms; luminescent tubes, TV, the condensing of tiny silver crystals on the photographic plates. I open the icebox, I take out the ice for our whisky. From the transistor comes the sound of a saxophone. The crystal which has succeeded in becoming the world, in making the world transparent to itself, in refracting it into infinite spectral images, is not mine: it is a corroded crystal, stained, mixed. The victory of the crystals (and of Vug) has been the same thing as their defeat (and mine). I'll wait now till the Thelonious Monk record ends, then I'll tell her.

NADINE GORDIMER

(b. 1923)

*N*adine Gordimer was born in Springs, South Africa, a mining town 70 kilometres from Johannesburg. She published her first story at the age of 16 and studied literature at Witwatersrand University. Later her stories appeared in The Yale Review and The New Yorker, and she earned an international reputation with her novels about social and political life in South Africa. Her books include story collections, The Lying Days (1953), Friday's Footprint (1960), A Soldier's Embrace (1980), Something Out There (1984); novels, The Soft Voice of the Serpent (1952), A Guest of Honour (1971), July's People (1981), A Sport of Nature (1987); and essays, The Essential Gesture (1988). She has repudiated apartheid unequivocally: "Whether I like it or not, this has been the crucial experience of my life, as the war was for some people, or membership in the Communist Party for others. I have no religion, no political dogma—only plenty of doubts about everything except my conviction that the colour-bar is wrong and utterly indefensible." But she is not only a political observer in her fiction. She has insisted that her work is based on "a writer's morality" and that "all worthwhile writing . . . always comes from an individual vision, privately pursued." She is as skeptical as Conrad about the white race's mission to bring civilization to black Africa, and she is particularly interested in exploring the liberal's conviction that man acts in his own self-interest, that he can harmonize his desires with those of his fellow citizens, that he can live in harmony with them because he is a rational creature. The commitment to social justice that is the inevitable result of such convictions is subjected in her novels to a withering analysis that exposes the noble futility of the liberal's ideals, and the numbness occasioned by an inability either to realize or abandon them. Yet particularly in her later work, Gordimer suggests that the development of "a true South African culture" is at least a possibility. When that day comes, her ten collections of short stories, nine novels, and diverse essays and reviews will have gone a long way toward defining one essential view of it.

Some Monday for Sure

My sister's husband, Josias, used to work on the railways but then he got this job where they make dynamite for the mines. He was the one who sits out on that little iron seat clamped to the back of the big red truck, with a red flag in his hand. The idea is that if you drive up too near the truck or look as if you're going to crash into it, he waves the flag to warn you off. You've seen those trucks often on the Main Reef Road between Johannesburg and the mining towns—they carry the stuff and have DANGER—EXPLOSIVES painted on them. The man sits there, with an iron chain looped across his little seat to keep him from being thrown into the road, and he clutches his flag like a kid with a balloon. That's how Josias was, too. Of course, if you didn't take any notice of the warning and went on and crashed into the truck, he would be the first to be blown to high heaven and hell, but he always just sits there, this chap, as if he has no idea when he was born or that he might not die in a bed an old man of eighty. As if the dust in his eyes and the racket of the truck are going to last forever.

My sister knew she had a good man but she never said anything about being afraid of this job. She only grumbled in winter, when he was stuck out there in the cold and used to get a cough (she's a nurse), and in summer when it rained all day and she said he would land up with rheumatism, crippled, and then who would give him work? The dynamite people? I don't think it ever came into her head that any day, every day, he could be blown up instead of coming home in the evening. Anyway, you wouldn't have thought so by the way she took it when he told us what it was he was going to have to do.

I was working down at a garage in town, that time, at the petrol pumps, and I was eating before he came in because I was on night shift. Emma had the water ready for him and he had a wash without saying much, as usual, but then he didn't speak when they sat down to eat, either, and when his fingers went into the mealie meal he seemed to forget what it was he was holding and not to be able to shape it into a mouthful. Emma must have thought he felt too dry to eat, because she got up and brought him a jam tin of the beer she had made for Saturday. He drank it and then sat back and looked from her to me, but she said, "Why don't you eat?" and he began to, slowly. She said, "What's the matter with you?" He got up and yawned and yawned, showing those brown chipped teeth that remind me of the big ape at the Johannesburg zoo that I saw once when I went with the school. He went into the other room of the house, where he and Emma slept, and he came back with his pipe. He filled it carefully, the way a poor man does; I saw, as soon as I went to work at the filling station, how the white men fill their pipes, stuffing the tobacco in, picking out any bits they don't like the look of, shoving the tin half-shut back into the glove-box of the car. "I'm going down to Sela's place," said Emma. "I can go with Willie on his way to work if you don't want to come."

"No. Not tonight. You stay here." Josias always speaks like this, the short words of a schoolmaster or a boss-boy, but if you hear the way he says them, you know he is not really ordering you around at all, he is only asking you.

"No, I told her I'm coming," Emma said, in the voice of a woman having her own way in a little thing.

"Tomorrow." Josias began to yawn again, looking at us with wet eyes. "Go to bed," Emma said. "I won't be late."

"No, no, I want to . . ." He blew a sigh. "When he's gone, man—" He moved his pipe at me. "I'll tell you later."

Emma laughed. "What can you tell that Willie can't hear." I've lived with them ever since they were married. Emma always was the one who looked after me, even before, when I was a little kid. It was true that whatever happened to us happened to us together. He looked at me; I suppose he saw that I was a man, now: I was in my blue overalls with *Shell* on the pocket and everything.

He said, "They want me to do something . . . a job with the truck."

Josias used to turn out regularly to political meetings and he took part in a few protests before everything went underground, but he had never been more than one of the crowd. We had Mandela and the rest of the leaders, cut out of the paper, hanging on the wall, but he had never known, personally, any of them. Of course there were his friends Ndhlovu and Seb Masinde who said they had gone underground and who occasionally came late at night for a meal or slept in my bed for a few hours.

"They want to stop the truck on the road—"

"Stop it?" Emma was like somebody stepping into cold dark water; with every word that was said she went deeper. "But how can you do it—when? Where will they do it?" She was wild, as if she must go out and prevent it all happening right then.

I felt that cold water of Emma's rising round the belly because Emma and I often had the same feelings, but I caught also, in Josias's not looking at me, a signal Emma couldn't know. Something in me jumped at it like catching a swinging rope. "They want the stuff inside . . . ?"

Nobody said anything.

I said, "What a lot of big bangs you could make with that, man," and then shut up before Josias needed to tell me to.

"So what're you going to do?" Emma's mouth stayed open after she had spoken, the lips pulled back.

"They'll tell me everything. I just have to give them the best place on the road—that'll be the Free State road, the others're too busy . . . and . . . the time when we pass . . ."

"You'll be dead." Emma's head was shuddering and her whole body shook; I've never seen anybody give up like that. He was dead already, she saw it with her eyes and she was kicking and screaming without knowing how to show it to him. She looked like she wanted to kill Josias herself, for being dead. "That'll be the finish, for sure. He's got a gun, the white man in front, hasn't he, you told me. And the one with him? They'll kill you. You'll go to prison. They'll take you to Pretoria jail and hang you by the rope . . . Yes, he's got the gun, you told me, didn't you—many times you told me—"

"The others've got guns too. How d'you think they can hold us up? They've got guns and they'll come all round him. It's all worked out—"

"The one in front will shoot you, I know it, don't tell me, I know what I say . . ." Emma went up and down and around till I thought she would push the walls down—they wouldn't have needed much pushing, in that house in Alexandra Township—and I was scared of her. I don't mean for what she would do to me if I got in her way, or to Josias, but for what might happen to her: something like taking a fit or screaming that none of us would be able to forget.

I don't think Josias was sure about doing the job before but he wanted to do it now. "No shooting. Nobody will shoot me. Nobody will know that I know anything. Nobody will tell them anything. I'm held up just the same like the others! Same as the white man in front! Who can shoot me? They can shoot me for that?"

"Someone else can go, I don't want it, do you hear? You will stay at home, I will say you are sick . . . You will be killed, they will shoot you . . . Josias, I'm telling you, I don't want . . . I won't . . . ."

I was waiting my chance to speak, all the time, and I felt Josias was waiting to talk to someone who had caught the signal. I said quickly, while she went on and on, "But even on that road there are some cars?"

"Roadblocks," he said, looking at the floor. "They've got the signs, the ones you see when a road's being dug up, and there'll be some men with picks. After the truck goes through they'll block the road so that any other cars turn off on to the old road there by Kalmansdrif. The same thing on the other side, two miles on. There where the farm road goes down to Nek Halt."

"Hell, man! Did you have to pick what part of the road?"

"I know it like this yard. Don't I?"

Emma stood there, between the two of us, while we discussed the whole business. We didn't have to worry about anyone hearing, not only because Emma kept the window wired up in that kitchen, but also because the yard the house was in was a real Alexandra Township one, full of babies yelling and people shouting, night and day, not to mention the transistors playing in the houses all round. Emma was looking at us all the time and out of the corner of my eye I could see her big front going up and down fast in the neck of her dress.

"... so they're going to tie you up as well as the others?"

He drew on his pipe to answer me.

We thought for a moment and then grinned at each other; it was the first time for Josias, that whole evening.

Emma began collecting the dishes under our noses. She dragged the tin bath of hot water from the stove and washed up. "I said I'm taking my day off on Wednesday. I suppose this is going to be next week." Suddenly, yet talking as if carrying on where she let up, she was quite different.

"I don't know."

"Well, I have to know because I suppose I must be at home."

"What must you be at home for?" said Josias.

"If the police come I don't want them talking to *him*," she said, looking at us both without wanting to see us.

"The police—" said Josias, and jerked his head to send them running, while I laughed, to show her.

"And I want to know what I must say."

"What must you say? Why? They can get my statement from me when they find us tied up. In the night I'll be back here myself."

"Oh yes," she said, scraping the mealie meal he hadn't eaten back into the pot. She did everything as usual; she wanted to show us nothing was going to wait because of this big thing, she must wash the dishes and put ash on the fire. "You'll be back, oh yes.—Are you going to sit here all night, Willie?—Oh yes, you'll be back."

And then, I think, for a moment Josias saw himself dead, too; he didn't answer when I took my cap and said, so long, from the door.

I knew it must be a Monday. I notice that women quite often don't remember ordinary things like this, I don't know what they think about— for instance, Emma didn't catch on that it must be Monday, next Monday or the one after, some Monday for sure, because Monday was the day that we knew Josias went with the truck to the Free State mines. It was Friday when he told us and all day Saturday I had a terrible feeling that it was going to be *that* Monday, and it would be all over before I could— what? I didn't know, man. I felt I must at least see where it was going to happen. Sunday I was off work and I took my bicycle and rode into town before there was even anybody in the streets and went to the big station and found that although there wasn't a train on Sundays that would take me all the way, I could get one that would take me about thirty miles. I had to pay to put the bike in the luggage van as well as for my ticket, but I'd got my wages on Friday. I got off at the nearest halt to Kalmansdrif and then I asked people along the road the best way. It was a long ride, more than two hours. I came out on the main road from the sand road just at the turnoff Josias had told me about. It was just like he said: a tin sign KALMANSDRIF pointing down the road I'd come from. And the nice blue tarred road, smooth, straight ahead: was I glad to get on to it! I hadn't taken much notice of the country so far, while I was sweating along, but from then on I woke up and saw everything. I've only got to think about it to see it again now. The veld is flat round about there, it was the end of winter, so the grass was dry. Quite far away and very far apart, there was a hill, and then another, sticking up in the middle of nothing, pink colour, and with its point cut off like the neck of a bottle. Ride and ride, these hills never got any nearer and there were none beside the road. It all looked empty and the sky much bigger than the ground, but there were some people there. It's funny you don't notice them like you do in town. All our people, of course; there were barbed-wire fences, so it must have been white farmers' land, but they've got the water and their houses are far off the road and you can usually see them only by the big dark trees that hide them. Our people had mud houses and there would be three or four in the same place made bare by goats and people's feet. Often the huts were near a kind of crack in the ground, where the little kids played and where, I suppose, in summer, there was water. Even now the women were managing to do washing in some places. I saw children run to the road to jig about and stamp when cars passed, but the men and women took no interest in what was up there. It was funny to think that I was just like them, now, men and women who are always busy inside themselves with jobs, plans, thinking about how to get money or how to talk to someone about something important, instead of like the children, as I used to be only a few years ago, taking in each small thing around them as it happens.

Still, there were people living pretty near the road. What would they do if they saw the dynamite truck held up and a fight going on? (I couldn't think of it, then, in any other way except like I'd seen hold-ups in Westerns, although I've seen plenty of fighting, all my life, among the Location gangs and drunks—I was ashamed not to be able to forget those kid-stuff Westerns at a time like this.) Would they go running away to the white farmer? Would somebody jump on a bike and go for the police? Or if there was no bike, what about a horse? I saw someone riding a horse.

I rode slowly to the next turn-off, the one where a farm road goes down to Nek Halt. There it was, just like Josias said. Here was where the other roadblock would be. But when he spoke about it there was nothing in between! No people, no houses, no flat veld with hills on it! It had been just one of those things grown-ups see worked out in their heads: while all the time, here it was, a real place where people had cooking fires, I could hear a herdboy yelling at a dirty bundle of sheep, a big bird I've never seen in town balanced on the barbed-wire fence right in front of me . . . I got off my bike and it flew away.

I sat a minute on the side of the road. I'd had a cold drink in an Indian shop in the dorp where I'd got off the train, but I was dry again inside my mouth, while plenty of water came out of my skin, I can tell you. I rode back down the road looking for the exact place I would choose if I was Josias. There was a stretch where there was only one kraal with two horses, and that quite a way back from the road. Also there was a dip where the road went over a donga. Old stumps of trees and nothing but cows' business down there; men could hide. I got off again and had a good look around.

But I wondered about the people, up top. I don't know why it was, I wanted to know about those people just as though I was going to have to go and live with them or something. I left the bike down in the donga and crossed the road behind a Cadillac going so fast the air smacked together after it, and I began to trek over the veld to the houses. I know most of our people live like this, in the veld, but I'd never been into houses like that before. I was born in some Location (I don't know which one, I must ask Emma one day) and Emma and I lived in Moroka with our grandmother. Our mother worked in town and she used to come and see us sometimes, but we never saw our father and Emma thinks perhaps we didn't have the same father, because she remembers a man before I was born, and after I was born she didn't see him again. I don't really remember anyone, from when I was a little kid, except Emma. Emma dragging me along so fast my arm almost came off my body, because we had nearly been caught by the Indian while stealing peaches from his lorry: we did that every day.

We lived in one room with our grandmother but it was a tin house with a number and later on there was a streetlight at the corner. These houses I was coming to had a pattern all over them marked into the mud they were built of. There was a mound of dried cows' business, as tall as I was, stacked up in a pattern, too. And then the usual junk our people have, just like in the Location: old tins, broken things collected from white people's rubbish heaps. The fowls ran sideways from my feet and two old men let their talking die away into ahas and ehês as I came up. I greeted them the right way to greet old men and they nodded and went on ehêing and ahaing to show that they had been greeted properly. One of them had very clean ragged trousers tied with string and he sat on the ground, but the other, sitting on a bucket-seat that must have been taken from some scrapyard car, was dressed in a way I've never seen—from the old days, I suppose. He wore a black suit with very wide trousers, laced boots, a stiff white collar and black tie, and on top of it all, a broken old hat. It was Sunday, of course, so I suppose he was all dressed up. I've heard that these people who work for farmers wear sacks most of the time. The old ones didn't ask me what I wanted there. They just peered at me with their eyes gone the colour of soapy water because they were so old. And I didn't know what to say because I hadn't thought what I was going to say, I'd just walked. Then a little kid slipped out of the dark doorway quick as a cockroach. I thought perhaps everyone else was out because it was Sunday but then a voice called from inside the other house, and when the child didn't answer, called again, and a woman came to the doorway.

I said my bicycle had a puncture and could I have some water.

She said something into the house and in a minute a girl, about fifteen she must've been, edged past her carrying a paraffin tin and went off to fetch water. Like all the girls that age, she never looked at you. Her body shook under an ugly old dress and she almost hobbled in her hurry to get away. Her head was tied up in a rag-doek right down to her eyes the way old-fashioned people do, otherwise she would have been quite pretty, like any other girl. When she had gone a little way the kid went pumping after her, panting, yelling, opening his skinny legs wide as scissors over stones and antheaps, and then he caught up with her and you could see that right away she was quite different, I knew how it was, she yelled at him, you heard her laughter as she chased him with the tin, whirled around from out of his clutching hands, struggled with him; they were together like Emma and I used to be when we got away from the old lady, and from the school, and everybody. And Emma was also one of our girls who have the big strong comfortable bodies of mothers even when they're still kids, maybe it comes from always lugging the smaller one round on their backs.

A man came out of the house behind the woman and was friendly. His hair had the dusty look of someone who's been sleeping off drink. In fact, he was still a bit heavy with it.

"You coming from Jo'burg?"

But I wasn't going to be caught out being careless at all, Josias could count on me for that.

"Vereeniging."

He thought there was something funny there—nobody dresses like a Jo'burger, you could always spot us a mile off—but he was too full to follow it up.

He stood stretching his sticky eyelids open and then he fastened on me the way some people will do: "Can't you get me work there where you are?"

"What kind of work?"

He waved a hand describing me. "You got a good work."

" 'Sall right."

"Where you working now?"

"Garden boy."

He tittered, "Look like you work in town," shook his head.

I was surprised to find the woman handing me a tin of beer, and I squatted on the ground to drink it. It's mad to say that a mud house can be pretty, but those patterns made in the mud looked nice. They must have been done with a sharp stone or stick when the mud was smooth and wet, the shapes of things like big leaves and moons filled in with lines that went all one way in this shape, another way in that, so that as you looked at the walls in the sun, some shapes were dark and some were light, and if you moved the light ones went dark and the dark ones got light instead. The girl came back with the heavy tin of water on her head making her neck thick. I washed out the jam tin I'd had the beer in and filled it with water. When I thanked them, the old men stirred and ahaed and ehêed again. The man made as if to walk a bit with me, but I was lucky, he didn't go more than a few yards. "No good," he said. "Every morning, five o'clock, and the pay—very small."

How I would have hated to be him, a man already married and with big children, working all his life in the fields wearing sacks. When you think like this about someone he seems something you could never possibly be, as if it's his fault, and not just the chance of where he happened to be born. At the same time I had a crazy feeling that I wanted to tell him something wonderful, something he'd never dreamed could happen, something he'd fall on his knees and thank me for. I wanted to say, "Soon you'll be the farmer yourself and you'll have shoes like me and your girl will get water from your windmill. Because on Monday, or another Monday, the truck will stop down there and all the stuff will be taken away and they—Josias, me; even you, yes—we'll win forever." But instead all I said was, "Who did that on your house?" He didn't understand and I made a drawing in the air with my hand. "The women," he said, not interested.

Down in the donga I sat a while and then threw away the tin and rode off without looking up again to where the kraal was.

It wasn't that Monday. Emma and Josias go to bed very early and of course they were asleep by the time I got home late on Sunday night— Emma thought I'd been with the boys I used to go around with at weekends. But Josias got up at half past four every morning, then, because it was a long way from the Location to where the dynamite factory was, and although I didn't usually even hear him making the fire in the kitchen which was also where I was sleeping, that morning I was awake the moment he got out of bed next door. When he came into the kitchen I was sitting up in my blankets and I whispered loudly, "I went there yesterday. I saw the turn-off and everything. Down there by the donga, ay? Is that the place?"

He looked at me, a bit dazed. He nodded. Then: "What'd' you mean you went there?"

"I could see that's the only good place. I went up to the houses, too, just to see . . . the people are all right. Not many. When it's not Sunday there may be nobody there but the old man—there were two, I think one was just a visitor. The man and the women will be over in the fields somewhere, and that must be quite far, because you can't see the mealies from the road . . ." I could feel myself being listened to carefully, getting in with him (and if with him, with *them*) while I was talking, and I knew exactly what I was saying, absolutely clearly, just as I would know exactly what I was doing. He began to question me; but like I was an older man or a clever one; he didn't know what to say. He drank his tea while I told him all about it. He was thinking. Just before he left he said, "I shouldn't've told you."

I ran after him, outside, into the yard. It was still dark. I blurted in the same whisper we'd been using, "Not today, is it?" I couldn't see his face properly but I knew he didn't know whether to answer or not. "Not today." I was so happy I couldn't go to sleep again.

In the evening Josias managed to make some excuses to come out with me alone for a bit. He said, "I told them you were a hundred-per-cent. It's just the same as if I know." "Of course, no difference. I just haven't had much of a chance to do anything . . ." I didn't carry on: " . . . because I was too young"; we didn't want to bring Emma into it. And anyway, no one but a real kid is too young any more. Look at the boys who are up for sabotage. I said, "Have they got them all?"

He hunched his shoulders.

"I mean, even the ones for the picks and spades . . .?"

He wouldn't say anything, but I knew I could ask. "Oh, boetie, man, even just to keep a lookout, there on the road . . ."

I know he didn't want to but once they knew I knew, and that I'd been there and everything, they were keen to use me. At least that's what I think. I never went to any meetings or anything where it was planned, and beforehand I only met the two others who were with me at the turn-off in the end, and we were told exactly what we had to do by Seb Masinde. Of course, Josias and I never said a word to Emma. The Monday that we did it was three weeks later and I can tell you, although a lot's happened to me since then, I'll never forget the moment when we flagged the truck through with Josias sitting there on the back in his little seat. Josias! I wanted to laugh and shout there in the veld; I didn't feel scared—what was there to be scared of, he'd been sitting on a load of dynamite every day of his life for years now, so what's the odds. We had one of those tins of fire and a bucket of tar and the ROAD CLOSED signs from the P.W.D. and everything went smooth at our end. It was at the Nek Halt end that the trouble started when one of these A.A. patrol bikes had to come along (Josias says it was something new, they'd never met a patrol on that road that time of day, before) and get suspicious about the block there. In the meantime the truck was stopped all right but someone was shot and Josias tried to get the gun from the white man up in front of the truck and there was a hell of a fight and they had to make a getaway with the stuff in a car and van back through our block, instead of taking over the truck and driving it to a hiding place to offload. More than half the stuff had to be left behind in the truck. Still, they got clean away with what they did get and it was never found by the police. Whenever I read in the papers here that something's been blown up back at home, I wonder if it's still one of our bangs. Two of our people got picked up right away and some more later and the whole thing was all over the papers with speeches by the chief of Special Branch about a master plot and everything. But Josias got away okay. We three chaps at the road block just ran into the veld to where there were bikes hidden. We went to a place we'd been told in Rustenburg district for a week and then we were told to get over to Bechuanaland. It wasn't so bad; we had no money but around Rustenburg it was easy to pinch pawpaws and oranges off the farms . . . Oh, I sent a message to Emma that I was all right; and at that time it didn't seem true that I couldn't go home again.

But in Bechuanaland it was different. We had no money, and you don't find food on trees in that dry place. They said they would send us money; it didn't come. But Josias was there too, and we stuck together; people hid us and we kept going. Planes arrived and took away the big shots and the white refugees but although we were told we'd go too, it never came off. We had no money to pay for ourselves. There were plenty others like us in the beginning. At last we just walked, right up Bechuanaland and through Northern Rhodesia to Mbeya, that's over the border in Tanganyika, where we were headed for. A long walk; took Josias and me months. We met up with a chap who'd been given a bit of money and from there sometimes we went by bus. No one asks questions when you're nobody special and you walk, like all the other African people themselves, or take the buses, that the whites never use; it's only if you've got the money for cars or to arrive at the airports that all these things happen that you read about: getting sent back over the border, refused permits and so on. So we got there, to Tanganyika at last, down to this town of Dar es Salaam where we'd been told we'd be going.

There's a refugee camp here and they give you a shilling or two a day until you get work. But it's out of town, for one thing, and we soon left there and found a room down in the shanty town. There are some nice buildings, of course, in the real town—nothing like Johannesburg or Durban, though—and that used to be the white town, the whites who are left still live there, but the Africans with big jobs in the government and so on live there too. Some of our leaders who are refugees like us live in these houses and have big cars; everyone knows they're important men, here, not like at home where if you're black you're just rubbish for the Locations. The people down where we lived are very poor and it's hard to get work because they haven't got enough work for themselves, but I've got my Standard Seven and I managed to get a small job as a clerk. Josias never found steady work. But that didn't matter so much because the big thing was that Emma was able to come to join us after five months, and she and I earn the money. She's a nurse, you see, and Africanization started in the hospitals and the government was short of nurses. So Emma got the chance to come up with a party of them sent for specially from South Africa and Rhodesia. We were very lucky because it's impossible for people to get their families up here. She came in a plane paid for by the government, and she and the other girls had their photograph taken for the newspaper as they got off at the airport. That day she came we took her to the beach, where everyone can bathe, no restrictions, and for a cool drink in one of the hotels (she'd never been in a hotel before), and we walked up and down the road along the bay where everyone walks and where you can see the ships coming in and going out so near that the men out there wave to you. Whenever we bumped into anyone else from home they would stop and ask her about home, and how everything was. Josias and I couldn't stop grinning to hear us all, in the middle of Dar, talking away in our language about the things we know. That day it was like it had happened already: the time when we are home again and everything is our way.

*   *   *

Well, that's nearly three years ago, since Emma came. Josias has been sent away now and there's only Emma and me. That was always the idea, to send us away for training. Some go to Ethiopia and some go to Algeria and all over the show and by the time they come back there won't be anything Verwoerd's men know in the way of handling guns and so on that they won't know better. That's for a start. I'm supposed to go too, but some of us have been waiting a long time. In the meantime I go to work and I walk about this place in the evenings and I buy myself a glass of beer in a bar when I've got money. Emma and I have still got the flat we had before Josias left and two nurses from the hospital pay us for the other bedroom. Emma still works at the hospital but I don't know how much longer. Most days now since Josias's gone she wants me to walk up to fetch her from the hospital when she comes off duty, and when I get under the trees on the drive I see her staring out looking for me as if I'll never turn up ever again. Every day it's like that. When I come up she smiles and looks like she used to for a minute but by the time we're ten yards on the road she's shaking and shaking her head until the tears come, and saying over and over, "A person can't stand it, a person can't stand it." She said right from the beginning that the hospitals here are not like the hospitals at home, where the nurses have to know their job. She's got a whole ward in her charge and now she says they're worse and worse and she can't trust anyone to do anything for her. And the staff don't like having strangers working with them anyway. She tells me every day like she's telling me for the first time. Of course it's true that some of the people don't like us being here. You know how it is, people haven't got enough jobs to go round, themselves. But I don't take much notice; I'll be sent off one of these days and until then I've got to eat and that's that.

The flat is nice with a real bathroom and we are paying off the table and six chairs she liked so much, but when we walk in, her face is terrible. She keeps saying the place will never be straight. At home there was only a tap in the yard for all the houses but she never said it there. She doesn't sit down for more than a minute without getting up at once again, but you can't get her to go out, even on these evenings when it's so hot you can't breathe. I go down to the market to buy the food now, she says she can't stand it. When I asked why—because at the beginning she used to like the market, where you can pick a live fowl for yourself, quite cheap— she said those little rotten tomatoes they grow here, and dirty people all shouting and she can't understand. She doesn't sleep, half the time, at night, either, and lately she wakes me up. It happened only last night. She was standing there in the dark and she said, "I felt bad." I said, "I'll make you some tea," though what good could tea do. "There must be something the matter with me," she says. "I must go to the doctor tomorrow."

"Is it pains again, or what?"

She shakes her head slowly, over and over, and I know she's going to cry again. "A place where there's no one. I get up and look out the window and it's just like I'm not awake. And every day, every day. I can't ever wake up and be out of it. I always see this town."

Of course it's hard for her. I've picked up Swahili and I can get around all right; I mean I can always talk to anyone if I feel like it, but she hasn't learnt more than *ahsante*—she could've picked it up just as easily, but she *can't*, if you know what I mean. It's just a noise to her, like dogs barking or those black crows in the palm trees. When anyone does come here to see her—someone else from home, usually, or perhaps I bring the Rhodesian who works where I do—she only sits there and whatever anyone talks about she doesn't listen until she can sigh and say, "Heavy, heavy. Yes, for a woman alone. No friends, nobody. For a woman alone, I can tell you."

Last night I said to her, "It would be worse if you were at home, you wouldn't have seen Josias or me for a long time."

But she said, "Yes, it would be bad. Sela and everybody. And the old crowd at the hospital—but just the same, it would be bad. D'you remember how we used to go right into Jo'burg on my Saturday off? The people—ay! Even when you were twelve you used to be scared you'd lose me."

"I wasn't scared, you were the one was scared to get run over sometimes." But in the Location when we stole fruit, and sweets from the shops, Emma could always grab me out of the way of trouble, Emma always saved me. The same Emma. And yet it's not the same. And what could I do for her?

I suppose she wants to be back there now. But still she wouldn't be the same. I don't often get the feeling she knows what I'm thinking about, any more, or that I know what she's thinking, but she said, "You and he go off, you come back or perhaps you don't come back, you know what you must do. But for a woman? What shall I do there in my life? What shall I do here? What time is this for a woman?"

It's hard for her. Emma. She'll say all that often now, I know. She tells me everything so many times. Well, I don't mind it when I fetch her from the hospital and I don't mind going to the market. But straight after we've eaten, now, in the evenings, I let her go through it once and then I'm off. To walk in the streets when it gets a bit cooler in the dark. I don't know why it is, but I'm thinking so bloody hard about getting out there in the streets that I push down my food as fast as I can without her noticing. I'm so keen to get going I feel queer, kind of tight and excited. Just until I can get out and not hear. I wouldn't even mind skipping the meal. In the streets in the evening everyone is out. On the grass along the bay the fat Indians in their white suits with their wives in those fancy coloured clothes. Men and their girls holding hands. Old watchmen like beggars, sleeping in the doorways of the shut shops. Up and down people walk, walk, just sliding one foot after the other because now and then, like somebody lifting a blanket, there's air from the sea. She should come out for a bit of air in the evening, man. It's an old, old place this, they say. Not the buildings, I mean; but the place. They say ships were coming here before even a place like London was a town. She thought the bay was so nice, that first day. The lights from the ships run all over the water and the palms show up a long time even after it gets dark. There's a smell I've smelled ever since we've been here—three years! I don't mean the smells in the shanty town; a special warm night-smell. You can even smell it at three in the morning. I've smelled it when I was standing about with Emma, by the window; it's as hot in the middle of the night here as it is in the middle of the day, at home—funny, when you look at the stars and the dark. Well, I'll be going off soon. It can't be long now. Now that Josias is gone. You've just got to wait your time; they haven't forgotten about you. Dar es Salaam. Dar. Sometimes I walk with another chap from home, he says some things, makes you laugh! He says the old watchmen who sleep in the doorways get their wives to come there with them. Well, I haven't seen it. He says we're definitely going with the next lot. Dar es Salaam. Dar. One day I suppose I'll remember it and tell my wife I stayed three years there, once. I walk and walk, along the bay, past the shops and hotels and the German church and the big bank, and through the mud streets between old shacks and stalls. It's dark there and full of other walking shapes as I wander past light coming from the cracks in the walls, where the people are in their homes.

Norman Levine

(b. 1923)

Norman Levine was born in Ottawa. He served in the Royal Canadian Air Force during the Second World War, joining up at 18, an experience that helped provide the material for his first novel, The Angled Road (1952). He eventually settled in the resort town of St. Ives, Cornwall, which provides the setting for his second novel, From a Seaside Town (1970). For some time before returning to Canada in 1980, Levine was persona non grata in his native country, a consequence of the autobiographical Canada Made Me (1958). This book, which was not published in Canada until 1979, is a depressing account of the dreariness of Canadian life, particularly the underside of that life as Levine experienced it on two cross-country trips through seedy establishments, a sort of "in search of Canada and myself" tour. Although Levine has also published two books of poetry—The Tight-Rope Walker (1950) and I Walk by the Harbour (1976)—it is as a short-story writer that he is celebrated internationally. His short fiction has been widely translated in Europe (by Nobel Prize winner Heinrich Böll in what was then West Germany) and frequently broadcast on radio by the CBC and the BBC. His collections of stories include One-Way Ticket (1961), I Don't Want to Know Anyone Too Well (1971), Selected Stories (1975), Thin Ice (1979), and Champagne Barn (1984), in which "We All Begin in a Little Magazine" appears. As his early novels and stories reveal, Levine was writing in the minimalist style long before it was made more popular by short-story writers such as Raymond Carver. Editor and critic Robert Weaver describes Levine's fictional territory accurately when he remarks: "In his fiction Levine has been preoccupied with the precarious existence of the writer (his Grub Street being a resort town in Cornwall), the abrasions and the loving closeness of marriage and family life, and the need to come to terms with the past."

We All Begin in a Little Magazine

We live in a small coastal town and in the summer, when the place is looking its best, it becomes overcrowded with people who have come away from the cities for their annual holiday by the sea. It is then that we leave and go up to London for our holiday.

My wife usually finds a house by looking through *The Times*. In this way we had the house of a man who built hotels in the poor parts of Africa so that wealthy American Negroes could go back to see where their grandparents came from. Another summer it was an architect's house where just about everything was done by push-button control. A third time, it was in a house whose owner was in the middle of getting a divorce—for non-consummation—and wanted to be out of the country.

This June she saw an ad saying: DOCTOR'S HOUSE AVAILABLE IN LONDON FOR THREE WEEKS. REASONABLE RENT. She phoned the number. And we agreed to take it.

The advertised house was central, near South Kensington tube station, not far from the Gardens. The taxi took us from Paddington—how pale people looked in London on a hot summer's day—and brought us to a wide street, stopping in front of a detached all-white house with acacia trees in the front garden. A bottle of warm milk was on the doorstep. I opened the door with the key and brought our cases inside.

The phone was ringing.

"Hello," I said.

"Is this *ABC*?" a youthful voice asked.

"I'm sorry," I said. "You have the wrong number."

"What is your number?"

"Knightsbridge 4231," I said.

"That *is* the number," the voice said.

"There must be some mistake," I said. "This is a doctor's house."

"Is the doctor there?"

"No," I said. "He's on holiday."

"Can I leave a message for him?"

"Are you ill?"

"No," he said. "Tell him that David White rang. David White of Somerset. He has had my manuscript for over six months now. He said he would let me know over a month ago. I have written him four times."

"I'll tell him," I said.

"If he needs more time," the young man said hesitantly, "I don't mind—"

"OK," I said and hung up.

"I don't know what's going on here," I said to my wife.

But she and the children were busy exploring the rest of the house.

It was a large house and it looked as if it had been lived in. The front room was a children's room with all sorts of games and blackboards and toys and children's books and posters on the walls. There was the sitting-room, the bottom half of the walls were filled with books in shelves. There were more books in the hallway, on the sides of the stairs, and in shelves on every landing. There were three separate baths. A breakfast room where a friendly black cat slept most of the time on top of the oil-fired furnace. And a back garden with a lawn, flowerbeds on the sides, a pond with goldfish, water-lilies, and a copper beech tree at the end.

The phone rang and a shaky voice said.

"May I speak to Doctor Jones?"

"I'm sorry, he's on holiday."

"When will he come back?"

"In three weeks," I said.

"I can't wait that long," the voice said. "I'm going to New York tomorrow."

"Would you," I said, "like to leave a message?"

"I can't hear what you're saying," the voice said. "Can you speak up? I'm a bit deaf and have to wear a hearing aid. The doctors have a cure for this now. If I'd been born two years later I would have been all right."

"I said would you like to leave the doctor a message?"

"I don't think that will do any good," he said. "Could you look in his office and see if he has a poem of mine? It's called 'Goodbye.' If it is in proof, don't bother. I'll wait. But just find out. I am going over to teach creative writing in night school so I can make some money to come back here. The poem will probably be on the floor."

"Hold on," I said.

I went into the office at the top of the house. The floor was cluttered with papers and magazines and manuscripts with letters and envelopes attached. On a wooden table, a large snap file had correspondence. A box had cheques for small amounts. There were also several pound notes, loose change, a sheet of stamps, and two packages of cigarettes. (How trusting, I thought. The doctor doesn't know us—supposing we were crooks?) There was typing paper, large envelopes, a typewriter, a phone, telephone directories, and some galleys hanging on a nail on a wall. A smaller table had an in-and-out tray to do with his medical work, more letters, and copies of the *Lancet*. The neatest part of the room was the area where stacks of unsold copies of *ABC* were on the floor against the far wall.

"I'm sorry," I said on the phone. "I can't see it."

"Oh," he said. He sounded disappointed.

"Well, tell him that Arnold Mest called. M-E-S-T."

"I've got that," I said.

"Goodbye," he said.

"You won't guess," I told my wife. "The doctor edits a little magazine."

"We can't get away from it," she said.

Early next morning the doorbell woke us. It was the postman. He gave me several bundles. There were letters from different parts of England and Europe and air mail ones from Canada, the States, Australia, and South America. There were two review copies of books from publishers. There were other little magazines, and what looked like medical journals, and a few bills.

As I put the envelopes and parcels on the chair in the office and saw the copies of *Horizon* and *New Writing*, the runs of *Encounter, London Magazine*, and a fine collection of contemporary books on the shelves right around the room—it brought back a time twenty years ago when I first came over.

There was still the bomb-damage to be seen, the queues, the ration books, the cigarettes under the counter. And a general seediness in people's clothes. Yet I remember it as one of my happiest times. Perhaps because we were young and full of hope and because we were so innocent of what writing involved. A lot of boys and girls had come to London from different parts. And we would meet in certain pubs, in certain restaurants, Joe Lyons, the French pub, Caves de France, the Mandrake. Then go on somewhere else. I remember going over to see another Canadian, from Montreal, who was writing a novel. He had a studio, by the Chelsea football grounds (we could always tell when a goal was scored). I remember best the cold damp winter days with the fog thick—you could just see the traffic lights—and then going inside and having some hot wine by the open fire and talking about writing, what we were writing, and where we had things out. We used to send our stories, optimistically, to the *name* magazines. But that was like taking a ticket in a lottery. It was the little magazines who published us, who gave encouragement and kept us going.

I remember Miss Waters. She was in her late forties, a pale woman with thinning blonde hair and a docile tabby cat. She edited a little magazine founded by her great-grandfather. She had photographs of Tennyson on the wall, of Yeats and Dylan Thomas. And wooden pigeon-holes, like the sorting room at the post office, with some of the recent back issues. She didn't know when I was coming. But she always greeted me with:

"How nice to see you. Do come in."

She walked ahead, into the dark living-room. Suggested that I take my winter coat off. Then she would bring out a decanter of sherry and fill a glass. Then take out a package of *Passing Clouds*, offer me a cigarette.

I was treated as a writer by this woman when I had very little published. And that did more than anything to keep up morale. And after another sherry, another *Passing Cloud*, and she had asked me what I was working on and seemed very interested in what I said, she told me that her great-grandfather paid Tennyson a thousand pounds for one of his short poems, and two thousand pounds to George Eliot for a short story. (Was she trying to tell me that there was money to be made out of writing?) Then she stood up. And we went into the other room. It was very neat and tidy. Magazines on a table laid out as at a news agent's, books as in a library.

"Is there anything you would like to review?" she asked.

I would pick a novel or two, or a book of short stories.

Then she would say. "And help yourself to four books from that pile."

That pile consisted of books that she didn't want reviewed. She had told me, the first time, to take these books to a bookseller in the Strand who would give me half-price for them, and later sell them to the public libraries. But before I could get the money from him I had to sign my name in what looked like a visiting book. And I saw there, above me, the signature of the leading Sunday and weekly reviewers—they were also selling their review copies for half-price.

And I remember how I would come to her place—with the brown envelopes lying behind the door—broke and depressed. And when I left her, I left feeling buoyed up, cheerful. There would be the few pounds from the review copies. Money enough for a hamburger and a coffee and a small cigar. And there was something to do—the books to review. She always paid in advance.

And before Miss Waters there were others. The press officer at the Norwegian Embassy—he ran a Norwegian little magazine, in English, from London. And another one, from India, also in English. My early stories appeared in both. And when I got a copy of the Indian magazine I saw that my Canadian characters had been turned into Indians. And there was another editor who would ask to borrow your box of matches. Then when you got back to your flat you found he had stuffed a pound note inside the box.

They are all gone—like their magazines.

And something has gone with them.

Those carefree days when you wrote when you felt like it. And slept in when you wanted to. And would be sure of seeing others like yourself at noon in certain places.

Now in the morning, after breakfast, I wait for the mail to come. Then I go upstairs and close the door behind me. And I make myself get on with the novel, the new story, or the article which has been commissioned by a well-paying magazine. I take a break for lunch, then come back up here until four. Once in a while I might take a day off and go on a bus to see what the country is like. I forget that there is so much colour about. Or, for a change, take a train for the day to Plymouth. But otherwise, it is up the stairs to this room. All my energy now goes into work. I light up a small Dutch cigar, and sometimes I talk to myself. I feel reasonably certain now that what I have written will be published. Writing has become my living.

Of course there are still the occasional days when things are going right and the excitement comes back from the work. Not like in those early days when writing and the life we were leading seemed so much to belong together. I had complete faith then in those little magazines.

What I didn't know was that what they bred was infectious. They infected a lot of young people with the notion that to be involved with literature was somehow to be involved with the good life. And by the time you learned differently, it was usually too late.

On Friday I had to be up early. In the morning I was to be interviewed, in a rowing-boat on the Serpentine, for a Canadian television programme on the "Brain-Drain." And later I was to meet my publisher for lunch.

It was very pleasant on the water early in the morning. The sun made patterns. People going to work stopped to watch. While I rowed the interviewer, the cameraman, the sound-recordist, and their equipment— and was asked why wasn't I living in Canada, and why did I write?

I met my publisher in his club. He is an American, from Boston, bald and short. We had a Martini. Then another. Then we went into the dining-room. Smoked salmon followed by duck with wine, then dessert. And ending with brandy and a large Havana cigar.

He asked me what type would I like for the book, could I send him the blurb for the dust-jacket? He told me the number of copies they would print, that one of the Sunday papers wanted to run a couple of extracts before publication. He told me some gossip about other writers, publishers, and agents. And what was I writing now? And which publishing season would he have it for?

I left him after four and caught a taxi back to the house.

"How did it go?" my wife asked.

"OK," I said. "How was the zoo?"

She began to tell me when we heard a noise. It sounded as if it was coming from the front door. We went to look and surprised a man with a key trying to open the door. He was in his late fifties, short and stocky and wearing a shabby raincoat.

"Is the doc in?" he said timidly.

"No," I said. "He's on holiday."

"Oh," he said. "I've come up from Sussex. I always have a bed here when I come up."

He spoke with an educated accent.

"I'm sorry," I said. "But we have the place for three weeks."

"I always have a bed here when I come up."

"There isn't room," I said.

"My name is George Smith," he said. "*ABC* publish me. I'm a poet."

"How do you do," I said. "We'll be gone in ten days. Come in and have a drink."

While I poured him a brandy, I asked what was the name of his last book.

He said he had enough work for a book and had sent the manuscript to—and here he named a well-known publisher.

"But I haven't heard," he said.

"That's a good sign," I said.

"Perhaps they have lost it," he said. "Or they are, like Doc, on holiday."

He brought out a small tin and took some loose tobacco and began to roll his own cigarette and one for me.

"How long," I asked, "have they had it?"

"Nearly five months," he said.

He finished his brandy. I poured him some more.

"I would ring them up and find out," I said. "Or drop them a line."

"Do you think I should?"

"Yes," I said.

I went to the door to see him out. And instead walked him to the bus stop.

The street was full of mountain ash and red berries were lying on the lawns, the sidewalk, and on the road.

"I had a letter from T.S. Eliot," he said. "I kept it all these years. But I sold it last month to Texas for fifty dollars," he said proudly. "My daughter was getting married. And I had to get her a present."

I asked him where he would stay the night.

"I have one or two other places," he said. "I come up about once every six weeks. London is my commercial centre."

I went and bought him a package of cigarettes.

"Thank you," he said.

The red bus came and I watched him get on.

When I got back my wife said.

"Well, do you feel better?"

"No," I said.

It went on like this—right through the time we were there. An assortment of people turned up at the door. There was a young blonde girl— she wanted to lick stamps for literature. There were visiting lecturers and professors from American and Canadian and English universities. There were housewives; one said, over the phone, "I'll do anything to get into print." There were long-distance telephone calls. One rang after midnight and woke us up. "Nothing important," the voice said. "I just wanted to have a talk. We usually do now and then. I've had stories in *ABC*."

There was, it seemed, a whole world that depended on the little magazine.

I tried to be out of the house as much as possible. I went to see my agent. He had a cheque for four hundred dollars, less his commission, waiting for me, for the sale of a story. He took me out for a meal. And we talked about the size of advances, the sort of money paperback publishers were paying these days, the way non-fiction was selling better than fiction. I met other writers in expensive clubs and restaurants. We gossiped about what middle-aged writer was leaving his middle-aged wife to live with a young girl. And what publisher was leaving his firm to form his own house. I was told what magazines were starting—who paid the best.

Then I would come back to the phone ringing, the piles of mail, and people turning up at the door eager to talk about the aesthetics of writing. I didn't mind the young. But it was the men and women who were around my age or older who made me uncomfortable. I didn't like the feeling of superiority I had when I was with them. Or was it guilt? I didn't know.

Meanwhile my wife and kids enjoyed themselves. They went to the Victoria and Albert Museum, the National Gallery, the Tate. And came back with post-card reproductions that they sent to friends. They went to a couple of Proms, to a play, had a day in Richmond Park, Hampton Court, and a boat ride on the Thames.

When the time came to go back—they didn't want to.

But I did.

I had passed through my *ABC* days. And I wanted to get away. Was it because it was a reminder of one's youth? Or of a time which promised more than it turned out to be? I told myself that there was an unreality about it all—that our lives then had no economic base—that it was a time of limbo. But despite knowing these things, I carry it with me. It represents a sort of innocence that has gone.

On the Saturday morning waiting for the taxi to come to take us to Paddington Station, the phone rang. And a young girl's voice wanted to know about her short story.

I said the doctor was away. He would be back later. She ought to ring this evening.

"What time?"

"After nine," I said.

"Have you read the story?" she asked. "What do you think of it?"

"We just rented the house," I said. "We were here for a holiday."

"Oh," she said. "You're not one of us?"

"No," I said.

Then the taxi came. And the driver began to load the cases into the back of the car.

JAMES BALDWIN

(1924–1987)

J ames Baldwin was born and raised in New York's Harlem. He
published stories from an early age in the newspapers of the schools
he attended, but planned on becoming a minister, like his father. At 18,
he renounced the idea and, after graduating from high school, went to
work on the railroad. In 1944 he met Richard Wright, who encouraged
Baldwin to write his first novel and recommended him for the Eugene
Sexton Fellowship. He eventually moved to Paris, where Go Tell It on
the Mountain *was published in 1953. Other prestigious fellowships
and awards enabled him to continue his writing, in which he dealt
courageously with the problems of being black in America. The topicality
of his concerns is evident in the large and impressive body of work that
includes* Notes of a Native Son *(1955),* Tell Me How Long the
Train's Been Gone *(1968),* If Beale Street Could Talk *(1974), and*
The Price of the Ticket *(1985). A volume of his collected stories,*
Going to Meet the Man, *was published in 1965. Therman O'Daniel
summarizes Baldwin as a writer in this way:*

> He is the gifted possessor of that primary element, genuine
> talent. . . . Secondly, he is a very intelligent and deeply percep-
> tive observer of our multifarious contemporary society. . . . In
> the third place, Baldwin is a bold and courageous writer who is
> not afraid to search into the dark corners of our social conscience,
> and to force out into public view many of the hidden, sordid
> skeletons of our society.

*He goes on to praise the clarity and poetic rhythms of Baldwin's style
and concludes that Baldwin's willingness to write for magazines and
newspapers has helped gain him the widest possible audience. Baldwin's
analysis of the anxiety, frustration, and guilt that have accompanied the
failure of the American Dream gives his work a profound and continuing
relevance to the problems that afflict American society and culture.*

Previous Condition

I woke up shaking, alone in my room. I was clammy cold with sweat;
under me the sheet and the mattress were soaked. The sheet was gray
and twisted like a rope. I breathed like I had been running.

I couldn't move for the longest while. I just lay on my back, spread-
eagled, looking up at the ceiling, listening to the sounds of people getting
up in other parts of the house, alarm clocks ringing and water splashing

and doors opening and shutting and feet on the stairs. I could tell when people left for work: the hall doorway downstairs whined and shuffled as it opened and gave a funny kind of double slam as it closed. One thud and then a louder thud and then a little final click. While the door was open I could hear the street sounds too, horses' hoofs and delivery wagons and people in the streets and big trucks and motor cars screaming on the asphalt.

I had been dreaming. At night I dreamt and woke up in the morning trembling, but not remembering the dream, except that in the dream I had been running. I could not remember when the dream—or dreams— had started; it had been long ago. For long periods maybe, I would have no dreams at all. And then they would come back, every night, I would try not to go to bed, I would go to sleep frightened and wake up frightened and have another day to get through with the nightmare at my shoulder. Now I was back from Chicago, busted, living off my friends in a dirty furnished room downtown. The show I had been with had folded in Chicago. It hadn't been much of a part—or much of a show either, to tell the truth. I played a kind of intellectual Uncle Tom, a young college student working for his race. The playwright had wanted to prove he was a liberal, I guess. But, as I say, the show had folded and here I was, back in New York and hating it. I knew that I should be getting another job, making the rounds, pounding the pavement. But I didn't. I couldn't face it. It was summer. I seemed to be fagged out. And every day I hated myself more. Acting's a rough life, even if you're white. I'm not tall and I'm not good looking and I can't sing or dance and I'm not white; so even at the best of times I wasn't in much demand.

The room I lived in was heavy ceilinged, perfectly square, with walls the color of chipped dry blood. Jules Weissman, a Jewboy, had got the room for me. It's a room to sleep in, he said, or maybe to die in but God knows it wasn't meant to live in. Perhaps because the room was so hideous it had a fantastic array of light fixtures: one on the ceiling, one on the left wall, two on the right wall, and a lamp on the table beside my bed. My bed was in front of the window through which nothing ever blew but dust. It was a furnished room and they'd thrown enough stuff in it to furnish three rooms its size. Two easy chairs and a desk, the bed, the table, a straight-backed chair, a bookcase, a cardboard wardrobe; and my books and my suitcase, both unpacked; and my dirty clothes flung in a corner. It was the kind of room that defeated you. It had a fireplace, too, and a heavy marble mantelpiece and a great gray mirror above the mantelpiece. It was hard to see anything in the mirror very clearly— which was perhaps just as well—and it would have been worth your life to have started a fire in the fireplace.

"Well, you won't have to stay here long," Jules told me the night I came. Jules smuggled me in, sort of, after dark, when everyone had gone to bed.

"Christ, I hope not."

"I'll be moving to a big place soon," Jules said. "You can move in with me." He turned all the lights on. "Think it'll be all right for a while?" He sounded apologetic, as though he had designed the room himself.

"Oh, sure. D'you think I'll have any trouble?"

"I don't think so. The rent's paid. She can't put you out."

I didn't say anything to that.

"Sort of stay undercover," Jules said. "You know."

"Roger," I said.

I had been living there for three days, timing it so I left after everyone else had gone, coming back late at night when everyone else was asleep. But I knew it wouldn't work. A couple of tenants had seen me on the stairs, a woman had surprised me coming out of the john. Every morning I waited for the landlady to come banging on the door. I didn't know what would happen. It might be all right. It might not be. But the waiting was getting me.

The sweat on my body was turning cold. Downstairs a radio was tuned in to the Breakfast Symphony. They were playing Beethoven. I sat up and lit a cigarette. "Peter," I said, "don't let them scare you to death. You're a man, too." I listened to Ludwig and I watched the smoke rise to the dirty ceiling. Under Ludwig's drums and horns I listened to hear footsteps on the stairs.

I'd done a lot of traveling in my time. I'd knocked about through St. Louis, Frisco, Seattle, Detroit, New Orleans, worked at just about everything. I'd run away from my old lady when I was about sixteen. She'd never been able to handle me. You'll never be nothin' *but* a bum, she'd say. We lived in an old shack in a town in New Jersey in the nigger part of town, the kind of houses colored people live in all over the U.S. I hated my mother for living there. I hated all the people in my neighborhood. They went to church and they got drunk. They were nice to the white people. When the landlord came around they paid him and took his crap.

The first time I was ever called nigger I was seven years old. It was a little white girl with long black curls. I used to leave the front of my house and go wandering by myself through town. This little girl was playing ball alone and as I passed her the ball rolled out of her hands into the gutter.

I threw it back to her.

"Let's play catch," I said.

But she held the ball and made a face at me.

"My mother don't let me play with niggers," she told me.

I did not know what the word meant. But my skin grew warm. I stuck my tongue out at her.

"I don't care. Keep your old ball." I started down the street.

She screamed after me: "Nigger, nigger, nigger!"

I screamed back: "Your mother was a nigger!"

I asked my mother what a nigger was.

"Who called you that?"

"I heard somebody say it."

"Who?"

"Just somebody."

"Go wash your face," she said. "You dirty as sin. Your supper's on the table."

I went to the bathroom and splashed water on my face and wiped my face and hands on the towel.

"You call that clean?" my mother cried. "Come here, boy!"

She dragged me back to the bathroom and began to soap my face and neck.

"You run around dirty like you do all the time, everybody'll call you a little nigger, you hear?" She rinsed my face and looked at my hands and dried me. "Now, go on and eat your supper."

I didn't say anything. I went to the kitchen and sat down at the table. I remember I wanted to cry. My mother sat down across from me.

"Mama," I said. She looked at me. I started to cry.

She came around to my side of the table and took me in her arms.

"Baby, don't fret. Next time somebody calls you nigger you tell them you'd rather be your color than be lowdown and nasty like some white folks is."

We formed gangs when I was older, my friends and I. We met white boys and their friends on the opposite sides of fences and we threw rocks and tin cans at each other.

I'd come home bleeding. My mother would slap me and scold me and cry.

"Boy, you wanna get killed? You wanna end up like your father?"

My father was a bum and I had never seen him. I was named for him: Peter.

I was always in trouble: truant officers, welfare workers, everybody else in town.

"You ain't never gonna be nothin' *but* a bum," my mother said.

By and by older kids I knew finished school and got jobs and got married and settled down. They were going to settle down and bring more black babies into the world and pay the same rents for the same old shacks and it would go on and on—

When I was sixteen I ran away. I left a note and told Mama not to worry, I'd come back one day and I'd be all right. But when I was twenty-two she died. I came back and put my mother in the ground. Everything was like it had been. Our house had not been painted and the porch floor sagged and there was somebody's raincoat stuffed in the broken window. Another family was moving in.

Their furniture was stacked along the walls and their children were running through the house and laughing and somebody was frying pork chops in the kitchen. The oldest boy was tacking up a mirror.

Last year Ida took me driving in her big car and we passed through a couple of towns upstate. We passed some crumbling houses on the left. The clothes on the line were flying in the wind.

"Are people living there?" asked Ida.

"Just darkies," I said.

Ida passed the car ahead, banging angrily on the horn. "D'you know you're becoming paranoiac, Peter?"

"All right. All right. I know a lot of white people are starving too."

"You're damn right they are. I know a little about poverty myself."

Ida had come from the kind of family called shanty Irish. She was raised in Boston. She's a very beautiful woman who married young and married for money—so now I can afford to support attractive young men, she'd giggle. Her husband was a ballet dancer who was forever on the road. Ida suspected that he went with boys. Not that I give a damn, she said, as long as he leaves me alone. When we met last year she was thirty and I was twenty-five. We had a pretty stormy relationship but we stuck. Whenever I got to town I called her; whenever I was stranded out of town I'd let her know. We never let it get too serious. She went her way and I went mine.

In all this running around I'd learned a few things. Like a prizefighter learns to take a blow or a dancer learns to fall, I'd learned how to get by. I'd learned never to be belligerent with policemen, for instance. No matter who was right, I was certain to be wrong. What might be accepted as just good old American independence in someone else would be insufferable arrogance in me. After the first few times I realized that I had to play smart, to act out the role I was expected to play. I only had one head and it was too easy to get it broken. When I faced a policeman I acted like I didn't know a thing. I let my jaw drop and I let my eyes get big. I didn't give him any smart answers, none of the crap about my rights. I figured out what answers he wanted and I gave them to him. I never let him think he wasn't king. If it was more than routine, if I was picked up on suspicion of robbery or murder in the neighborhood, I looked as humble as I could and kept my mouth shut and prayed. I took a couple of beatings but I stayed out of prison and I stayed off chain gangs. That was also due to luck, Ida pointed out once. "Maybe it would've been better for you if you'd been a little less lucky. Worse things have happened than chain gangs. Some of them have happened to you."

There was something in her voice. "What are you talking about?" I asked.

"Don't lose your temper. I said maybe."

"You mean you think I'm a coward?"

"I didn't say that, Peter."

"But you meant that. Didn't you?"

"No. I didn't mean that. I didn't mean anything. Let's not fight."

There are times and places when a Negro can use his color like a shield. He can trade on the subterranean Anglo-Saxon guilt and get what he wants that way; or some of what he wants. He can trade on his nuisance value, his value as forbidden fruit; he can use it like a knife, he can twist it and get his vengeance that way. I knew these things long before I realized that I knew them and in the beginning I used them, not knowing what I was doing. Then when I began to see it, I felt betrayed. I felt beaten as a person. I had no honest place to stand.

This was the year before I met Ida. I'd been acting in stock companies and little theaters; sometimes fairly good parts. People were nice to me. They told me I had talent. They said it sadly, as though they were thinking, What a pity, he'll never get anywhere. I had got to the point where I resented praise and I resented pity and I wondered what people were thinking when they shook my hand. In New York I met some pretty fine people; easygoing, hard-drinking, flotsam and jetsam; and they liked me; and I wondered if I trusted them; if I was able any longer to trust anybody. Not on top, where all the world could see, but underneath where everybody lives.

Soon I would have to get up. I listened to Ludwig. He shook the little room like the footsteps of a giant marching miles away. On summer evenings (and maybe we would go this summer) Jules and Ida and I would go up to the Stadium and sit beneath the pillars on the cold stone steps. There it seemed to me the sky was far away; and I was not myself, I was high and lifted up. We never talked, the three of us. We sat and watched the blue smoke curl in the air and watched the orange tips of cigarettes. Every once in a while the boys who sold popcorn and soda pop and ice cream climbed the steep steps chattering; and Ida shifted slightly and touched her blue-black hair; and Jules scowled. I sat with my knee up, watching the lighted half-moon below, the black-coated, straining conductor, the faceless men beneath him moving together in a rhythm like the sea. There were pauses in the music for the rushing, calling, halting piano. Everything would stop except the climbing soloist; he would reach a height and everything would join him, the violins first and then the horns; and then the deep blue bass and the flute and the bitter trampling drums; beating, beating and mounting together and stopping with a crash like daybreak. When I first heard the *Messiah* I was alone; my blood bubbled like fire and wine; I cried; like an infant crying for its mother's milk; or a sinner running to meet Jesus.

Now below the music I heard footsteps on the stairs. I put out my cigarette. My heart was beating so hard I thought it would tear my chest apart. Someone knocked on the door.

I thought: Don't answer. Maybe she'll go away.

But the knocking came again, harder this time.

Just a minute, I said. I sat on the edge of the bed and put on my bathrobe. I was trembling like a fool. For Christ's sake, Peter, you've been through this before. What's the worst thing that can happen? You won't have a room. The world's full of rooms.

When I opened the door the landlady stood there, red-and-white-faced and hysterical.

"Who are you? I didn't rent this room to you."

My mouth was dry. I started to say something.

"I can't have no colored people here," she said. "All my tenants are complainin'. Women afraid to come home nights."

"They ain't gotta be afraid of me," I said. I couldn't get my voice up; it rasped and rattled in my throat; and I began to be angry. I wanted to kill her, "My friend rented this room for me," I said.

"Well, I'm sorry, he didn't have no right to do that, I don't have nothin' against you, but you gotta get out."

Her glasses blinked, opaque in the light on the landing. She was frightened to death. She was afraid of me but she was more afraid of losing her tenants. Her face was mottled with rage and fear, her breath came rushed and little bits of spittle gathered at the edges of her mouth; her breath smelled bad, like rotting hamburger on a July day.

"You can't put me out," I said. "This room was rented in my name." I started to close the door, as though the matter was finished: "I live here, see, this is my room, you can't put me out."

"You get outa my house!" she screamed. "I got the right to know who's in my house! This is a white neighborhood, I don't rent to colored people. Why don't you go on uptown, like you belong?"

"I can't stand niggers," I told her. I started to close the door again but she moved and stuck her foot in the way. I wanted to kill her, I watched her stupid, wrinkled frightened white face and I wanted to take a club, a hatchet, and bring it down with all my weight, splitting her skull down the middle where she parted her iron-grey hair.

"Get out of the door," I said. "I want to get dressed."

But I knew that she had won, that I was already on my way. We stared at each other. Neither of us moved. From her came an emanation of fear and fury and something else. You maggot-eaten bitch, I thought.

I said evilly, "You wanna come in and watch me?" Her face didn't change, she didn't take her foot away. My skin prickled, tiny hot needles punctured my flesh. I was aware of my body under the bathrobe; and it was as though I had done something wrong, something monstrous, years ago, which no one had forgotten and for which I would be killed.

"If you don't get out," she said, "I'll get a policeman to put you out."

I grabbed the door to keep from touching her. "All right. All right. You can have the goddamn room. Now get out and let me dress."

She turned away. I slammed the door. I heard her going down the stairs. I threw stuff into my suitcase. I tried to take as long as possible but I cut myself while shaving because I was afraid she would come back upstairs with a policeman.

Jules was making coffee when I walked in.

"Good morning, good morning! What happened to you?"

"No room at the inn," I said. "Pour a cup of coffee for the notorious son of man." I sat down and dropped my suitcase on the floor.

Jules looked at me. "Oh. Well. Coffee coming up."

He got out the coffee cups. I lit a cigarette and sat there. I couldn't think of anything to say. I knew that Jules felt bad and I wanted to tell him that it wasn't his fault.

He pushed coffee in front of me and sugar and cream.

"Cheer up, baby. The world's wide and life—life, she is very long."

"Shut up. I don't want to hear any of your bad philosophy."

"Sorry."

"I mean, let's not talk about the good, the true, and the beautiful."

"All right. But don't sit there holding onto your table manners. Scream if you want to."

"Screaming won't do any good. Besides I'm a big boy now."

I stirred my coffee. "Did you give her a fight?" Jules asked.

I shook my head. "No."

"Why the hell not?"

I shrugged; a little ashamed now. I couldn't have won it. What the hell.

"You might have won it. You might have given her a couple of bad moments."

"Goddamit to hell, I'm sick of it. Can't I get a place to sleep without dragging it through the courts? I'm goddamn tired of battling every Tom, Dick, and Harry for what everybody else takes for granted. I'm tired, man, tired! Have you ever been sick to death of something? Well, I'm sick to death. And I'm scared. I've been fighting so goddamn long I'm not a person any more. I'm not Booker T. Washington. I've got no vision of emancipating anybody. I want to emancipate myself. If this goes on much longer, they'll send me to Bellevue, I'll blow my top, I'll break somebody's head. I'm not worried about that miserable little room. I'm worried about what's happening to me, *to me*, inside. I don't walk the streets, I crawl. I've never been like this before. Now when I go to a strange place I wonder what will happen, will I be accepted, if I'm accepted, can I accept?—"

"Take it easy," Jules said.

"Jules, I'm beaten."

"I don't think you are. Drink your coffee."

"Oh," I cried, "I know you think I'm making it dramatic, that I'm paranoiac and just inventing trouble! Maybe I think so sometimes, how can I tell? You get so used to being hit you find you're always waiting for it. Oh, I know, you're Jewish, you get kicked around, too, but you can walk into a bar and nobody *knows* you're Jewish and if you go looking for a job you'll get a better job than mine! How can I say what it feels like? I don't know. I know everybody's in trouble and nothing is easy, but how can I explain to you what it feels like to be black when I don't understand it and don't want to and spend all my time trying to forget it? I don't want to hate anybody—but now maybe, I can't love anybody either—are we friends? Can we be really friends?"

"We're friends," Jules said, "don't worry about it." He scowled. "If I wasn't Jewish I'd ask you why you don't live in Harlem." I looked at him. He raised his had and smiled—"But I'm Jewish, so I didn't ask you. Ah Peter," he said, "I can't help you—take a walk, get drunk, we're all in this together."

I stood up. "I'll be around later. I'm sorry."

"Don't be sorry. I'll leave my door open. Bunk here for awhile."

"Thanks," I said.

I felt that I was drowning; that hatred had corrupted me like cancer in the bone.

I saw Ida for dinner. We met in a restaurant in the Village, an Italian place in a gloomy cellar with candles on the tables.

It was not a busy night, for which I was grateful. When I came in there were only two other couples on the other side of the room. No one looked at me. I sat down in a corner booth and ordered a Scotch old-fashioned. Ida was late and I had three of them before she came.

She was very fine in black, a high-necked dress with a pearl choker; and her hair was combed page-boy style, falling just below her ears.

"You look real sweet, baby."

"Thank you. It took fifteen extra minutes but I hoped it would be worth it."

"It was worth it. What're you drinking?"

"Oh—what're you drinking?"

"Old-fashioneds."

She sniffed and looked at me. "How many?"

I laughed. "Three."

"Well," she said, "I suppose you had to do something." The waiter came over. We decided on one Manhattan and one lasagna and one spaghetti with clam sauce and another old-fashioned for me.

"Did you have a constructive day, sweetheart? Find a job?"

"Not today," I said. I lit her cigarette. "Metro offered me a fortune to come to the coast and do the lead in *Native Son* but I turned it down. Type casting, you know. It's so difficult to find a decent part."

"Well, if they don't come up with a decent offer soon tell them you'll go back to Selznick. *He'll* find you a part with guts—the very *idea* of offering you *Native Son!* I wouldn't stand for it."

"You ain't gotta tell me. I told them if they didn't find me a decent script in two weeks I was through, that's all."

"Now that's talking, Peter my lad."

The drinks came and we sat in silence for a minute or two. I finished half of my drink at a swallow and played with the toothpicks on the table. I felt Ida watching me.

"Peter, you're going to be awfully drunk."

"Honeychile, the first thing a southern gentleman learns is how to hold his liquor."

"That myth is older than the rock of ages. And anyway you come from Jersey."

I finished my drink and snarled at her: "That's just as good as the South."

Across the table from me I could see that she was readying herself for trouble: her mouth tightened slightly, setting her chin so that the faint cleft showed: "What happened to you today?"

I resented her concern; I resented my need. "Nothing worth talking about," I muttered, "just a mood."

And I tried to smile at her, to wipe away the bitterness.

"Now I know something's the matter. Please tell me."

It sounded trivial as hell: "You know the room Jules found for me? Well, the landlady kicked me out of it today."

"God save the American republic," Ida said. "D'you want to waste some of my husband's money? We can sue her."

"Forget it. I'll end up with lawsuits in every state in the union."

"Still, as a gesture—"

"The devil with the gesture. I'll get by."

The food came. I didn't want to eat. The first mouthful hit my belly like a gong. Ida began cutting up lasagna.

"Peter," she said, "try not to feel so badly. We're all in this together the whole world. Don't let it throw you. What can't be helped you have to learn to live with."

"That's easy for you to say," I told her.

She looked at me quickly and looked away. "I'm not pretending that it's easy to do," she said.

I didn't believe that she could really understand it; and there was nothing I could say. I sat like a child being scolded, looking down at my plate, not eating, not saying anything. I wanted her to stop talking, to stop being intelligent about it, to stop being calm and grown-up about it; good Lord, none of us has ever grown up, we never will.

"It's no better anywhere else," she was saying. "In all of Europe there's famine and disease, in France and England they hate the Jews—nothing's going to change, baby, people are too empty-headed, too empty-hearted—it's always been like that, people always try to destroy what they don't understand—and they hate almost everything because they understand so little—"

I began to sweat in my side of the booth. I wanted to stop her voice. I wanted her to eat and be quiet and leave me alone. I looked around for the waiter so I could order another drink. But he was on the far side of the restaurant, waiting on some people who had just come in; a lot of people had come in since we had been sitting there.

"Peter," Ida said, "Peter please don't look like that.'

I grinned: the painted grin of the professional clown. "Don't worry, baby, I'm all right. I know what I'm going to do. I'm going to go back to my people where I belong and find me a nice, black nigger wench and raise me a flock of babies."

Ida had an old maternal trick; the grin tricked her into using it now. She raised her fork and rapped me with it across the knuckles. "Now, stop that. You're too old for that."

I screamed and stood up screaming and knocked the candle over: "Don't *do* that, you bitch, don't *ever* do that!"

She grabbed the candle and set it up and glared at me. Her face had turned perfectly white: "Sit down! Sit *down!*"

I fell back into my seat. My stomach felt like water. Everyone was looking at us. I turned cold, seeing what they were seeing: a black boy and a white woman, alone together. I knew it would take nothing to have them at my throat.

"I'm sorry," I muttered, "I'm sorry, I'm sorry."

The waiter was at my elbow. "Is everything all right, miss?"

"Yes, quite, thank you." She sounded like a princess dismissing a slave. I didn't look up. The shadow of the waiter moved away from me.

"Baby," Ida said, "forgive me, please forgive me."

I stared at the tablecloth. She put her hand on mine, brightness and blackness.

"Let's go," I said, "I'm terribly sorry."

She motioned for the check. When it came she handed the waiter a ten dollar bill without looking. She picked up her bag.

"Shall we go to a nightclub or a movie or something?"

"No, honey, not tonight." I looked at her. "I'm tired, I think I'll go on over to Jules's place. I'm gonna sleep on his floor for a while. Don't worry about me. I'm all right."

She looked at me steadily. She said: "I'll come see you tomorrow?"

"Yes, baby, please."

The waiter brought the change and she tipped him. We stood up; as we passed the tables (not looking at the people) the ground under me seemed falling, the doorway seemed impossibly far away. All my muscles tensed; I seemed ready to spring; I was waiting for the blow.

I put my hands in my pockets and we walked to the end of the block. The lights were green and red, the lights from the theater across the street exploded blue and yellow, off and on.

"Peter?"

"Yes?"

"I'll see you tomorrow?"

"Yeah. Come by Jules's. I'll wait for you."

"Goodnight, darling."

"Goodnight."

I started to walk away. I felt her eyes on my back. I kicked a bottle-top on the sidewalk.

God save the American republic.

I dropped into the subway and got on an uptown train, not knowing where it was going and not caring. Anonymous, islanded people surrounded me, behind newspapers, behind make-up, fat, fleshy masks and flat eyes. I watched the empty faces. (No one looked at me.) I looked at the ads, unreal women and pink-cheeked men selling cigarettes, candy, shaving cream, nightgowns, chewing gum, movies, sex; sex without organs, drier than sand and more secret than death. The train stopped. A white boy and a white girl got on. She was nice, short, svelte. Nice legs. She was hanging on his arm. He was the football type, blond, ruddy. They were dressed in summer clothes. The wind from the doors blew her print dress. She squealed, holding the dress at the knees and giggled and looked at him. He said something I didn't catch and she looked at me and the smile died. She stood so that she faced him and had her back to me. I looked back at the ads. Then I hated them. I wanted to do something to make them hurt, something that would crack the pink-cheeked mask. The white boy and I did not look at each other again. They got off at the next stop.

I wanted to keep on drinking. I got off in Harlem and went to a rundown bar on Seventh Avenue. My people, my people. Sharpies stood on the corner, waiting. Women in summer dresses pranced by on wavering heels. Click clack. Click clack. There were white mounted policemen in the streets. On every block there was another policeman on foot. I saw a black cop.

God save the American republic.

The juke box was letting loose with "Hamps' Boogie." The place was jumping. I walked over to the man.

"Rye," I said.

I was standing next to somebody's grandmother. "Hello, papa. What you puttin' down?"

"Baby, you can't pick it up," I told her. My rye came and I drank.

"Nigger," she said, "you must think you's somebody."

I didn't answer. She turned away, back to her beer, keeping time to the juke box, her face sullen and heavy and aggrieved. I watched her out of the side of my eye. She had been good looking once, pretty even, before she hit the bottle and started crawling into too many beds. She was flabby now, flesh heaved all over in her thin dress. I wondered what she'd be like in bed; then I realized that I was a little excited by her; I laughed and set my glass down.

"The same," I said. "And a beer chaser."

The juke box was playing something else now, something brassy and commercial which I didn't like. I kept on drinking, listening to the voices of my people, watching the faces of my people. (God pity us, the terrified republic.) Now I was sorry to have angered the woman who still sat next to me, now deep in conversation with another, younger woman. I longed for some opening, some sign, something to make me a part of the life around me. But there was nothing except my color. A white outsider coming in would have seen a young Negro drinking in a Negro bar, perfectly in his element, in his place, as the saying goes. But the people here knew differently, as I did. I didn't seem to have a place.

So I kept on drinking by myself, saying to myself after each drink, Now I'll go. But I was afraid; I didn't want to sleep on Jules's floor; I didn't want to go to sleep. I kept on drinking and listening to the juke box. They were playing Ella Fitzgerald, "Cow-Cow Boogie."

"Let me buy you a drink," I said to the woman.

She looked at me, startled, suspicious, ready to blow her top.

"On the level," I said. I tried to smile. "Both of you."

"I'll take a beer," the young one said.

I was shaking like a baby. I finished my drink.

"Fine," I said. I turned to the bar.

"Baby," said the old one, "what's your story?"

The man put three beers on the counter.

"I got no story, Ma," I said.

FLANNERY O'CONNOR

(1925–1964)

F lannery O'Connor was born in Savannah, Georgia, and moved to Milledgeville, Georgia, when she was 13. She attended the Georgia State College for Women and the Iowa Writer's Workshop. After her first major attack of lupus in 1950, she lived with her mother on their farm in Milledgeville. Her stories won her a wide readership, numerous awards and grants, honorary doctorates, and the respect of her fellow writers. She said in an interview that the crucial influences on her life were "being a Catholic, and a Southerner, and a writer." She contended that belief in Christianity "frees the story teller to observe. It is not a set of rules which fixes what he sees in the world. It affects his writing primarily by guaranteeing his respect for mystery." Her penchant for the grotesque is also in part attributable to her religion. She explained it this way: "The novelist with a Christian conscience will find in modern life distortions which are repugnant to him, and his problem will be to make these appear as distortions to an audience which is used to seeing them as natural; and he may well be forced to take more violent means to get his vision across to this hostile audience." The southern milieu— its preoccupations, types, cadences, rural settings—was a profound influence because it also made its impression on her from an early age, although she contemptuously dismissed the notion that the South could be adequately characterized as the region that had produced a group of writers who dealt in "Gothic monstrosities" and who were preoccupied with "everything deformed." No one can be indifferent to what she called the "wild look" of her fiction, its strange combinations of the violent and the comic, and there are those who object to her morbidity and strangeness; but O'Connor wanted to shock, to raise objections, to wake people up. She is, as Dorothy Walters has argued,

> an absolutist in an age which has embraced relativism on all levels. Thus Flannery O'Connor supports the invisible realm against the world of things, the unseen essence as against the objective manifestation. In this respect, her vision is essentially that of another age, and her work is a persistent attempt to recall those formerly accepted truths to the human consciousness once again.

Revelation

The doctor's waiting room, which was very small, was almost full when the Turpins entered and Mrs. Turpin, who was very large, made it look even smaller by her presence. She stood looming at the head of the magazine table set in the center of it, a living demonstration that the room was inadequate and ridiculous. Her little bright black eyes took in all the patients as she sized up the seating situation. There was one vacant chair and a place on the sofa occupied by a blond child in a dirty blue romper who should have been told to move over and make room for the lady. He was five or six, but Mrs. Turpin saw at once that no one was going to tell him to move over. He was slumped down in the seat, his arms idle at his sides and his eyes idle in his head; his nose ran unchecked.

Mrs. Turpin put a firm hand on Claud's shoulder and said in a voice that included anyone who wanted to listen, "Claud, you sit in that chair there," and gave him a push down into the vacant one. Claud was florid and bald and sturdy, somewhat shorter than Mrs. Turpin, but he sat down as if he were accustomed to doing what she told him to.

Mrs. Turpin remained standing. The only man in the room besides Claud was a lean stringy old fellow with a rusty hand spread out on each knee, whose eyes were closed as if he were asleep or dead or pretending to be so as not to get up and offer her his seat. Her gaze settled agreeably on a well-dressed gray-haired lady whose eyes met hers and whose expression said: if that child belonged to me, he would have some manners and move over—there's plenty of room there for you and him too.

Claud looked up with a sigh and made as if to rise.

"Sit down," Mrs. Turpin said. "You know you're not supposed to stand on that leg. He has an ulcer on his leg," she explained.

Claude lifted his foot onto the magazine table and rolled his trouser leg up to reveal a purple swelling on a plump marble-white calf.

"My!" the pleasant lady said. "How did you do that?"

"A cow kicked him," Mrs. Turpin said.

"Goodness!" said the lady.

Claud rolled his trouser leg down.

"Maybe the little boy would move over," the lady suggested, but the child did not stir.

"Somebody will be leaving in a minute," Mrs. Turpin said. She could not understand why a doctor—with as much money as they made charging five dollars a day to just stick their head in the hospital door and look at you—couldn't afford a decent-sized waiting room. This one was hardly bigger than a garage. The table was cluttered with limp-looking magazines and at one end of it there was a big green glass ash tray full of cigarette butts and cotton wads with little blood spots on them. If she had had anything to do with the running of the place, that would have been emptied every so often. There were no chairs against the wall at the head of the room. It had a rectangular-shaped panel in it that permitted a view of the office where the nurse came and went and the secretary listened to the radio. A plastic fern in a gold pot sat in the opening and trailed its fronds down almost to the floor. The radio was softly playing gospel music.

Just then the inner door opened and a nurse with the highest stack of yellow hair Mrs. Turpin had ever seen put her face in the crack and called for the next patient. The woman sitting beside Claud grasped the two arms of her chair and hoisted herself up; she pulled her dress free from her legs and lumbered through the door where the nurse had disappeared.

Mrs. Turpin eased into the vacant chair, which held her tight as a corset. "I wish I could reduce," she said, and rolled her eyes and gave a comic sigh.

"Oh, *you* aren't fat," the stylish lady said.

"Ooooo I am too," Mrs. Turpin said. "Claud he eats all he wants to and never weighs over one hundred and seventy-five pounds, but me I just look at something good to eat and I gain some weight," and her stomach and shoulders shook with laughter. "You can eat all you want to, can't you, Claud?" she asked, turning to him.

Claud only grinned.

"Well, as long as you have such a good disposition," the stylish lady said, "I don't think it makes a bit of difference what size you are. You just can't beat a good disposition."

Next to her was a fat girl of eighteen or nineteen, scowling into a thick blue book which Mrs. Turpin saw was entitled *Human Development*. The girl raised her head and directed her scowl at Mrs. Turpin as if she did not like her looks. She appeared annoyed that anyone should speak while she tried to read. The poor girl's face was blue with acne and Mrs. Turpin thought how pitiful it was to have a face like that at that age. She gave the girl a friendly smile but the girl only scowled the harder. Mrs. Turpin herself was fat but she had always had good skin, and, though she was forty-seven years old, there was not a wrinkle in her face except around her eyes from laughing too much.

Next to the ugly girl was the child, still in exactly the same position, and next to him was a thin leathery old woman in a cotton print dress. She and Claud had three sacks of chicken feed in their pump house that was in the same print. She had seen from the first that the child belonged with the old woman. She could tell by the way they sat—kind of vacant and white-trashy, as if they would sit there until Doomsday if nobody called and told them to get up. And at right angles but next to the well-dressed pleasant lady was a lank-faced woman who was certainly the child's mother. She had on a yellow sweat shirt and wine-colored slacks, both gritty-looking, and the rims of her lips were stained with snuff. Her dirty yellow hair was tied behind with a little piece of red paper ribbon. Worse than niggers any day, Mrs. Turpin thought.

The gospel hymn playing was, "When I looked up and He looked down," and Mrs. Turpin, who knew it, supplied the last line mentally, "And wona these days I know I'll we-eara crown."

Without appearing to, Mrs. Turpin always noticed people's feet. The well-dressed lady had on red and gray suede shoes to match her dress. Mrs. Turpin had on her good black patent leather pumps. The ugly girl had on Girl Scout shoes and heavy socks. The old woman had on tennis shoes and the white-trashy mother had on what appeared to be bedroom slippers, black straw with gold braid threaded through them—exactly what you would have expected her to have on.

Sometimes at night when she couldn't go to sleep, Mrs. Turpin would occupy herself with the question of who she would have chosen to be if she couldn't have been herself. If Jesus had said to her before he made her, "There's only two places available for you. You can either be a nigger or white-trash," what would she have said? "Please, Jesus, please," she would have said, "just let me wait until there's another place available," and he would have said, "No, you have to go right now and I have only those two places so make up your mind." She would have wiggled and squirmed and begged and pleaded but it would have been no use and finally she would have said, "All right, make me a nigger then—but that don't mean a trashy one." And he would have made her a neat clean respectable Negro woman, herself but black.

Next to the child's mother was a red-headed youngish woman, reading one of the magazines and working a piece of chewing gum, hell for leather, as Claud would say. Mrs. Turpin could not see the woman's feet. She was not white-trash, just common. Sometimes Mrs. Turpin occupied herself at night naming the classes of people. On the bottom of the heap were most colored people, not the kind she would have been if she had been one, but most of them; then next to them—not above, just away from—were the white-trash; then above them were the home-owners, and above them the home-and-land owners, to which she and Claud belonged. Above she and Claud were people with a lot of money and much bigger houses and much more land. But here the complexity of it would begin to bear in on her, for some of the people with a lot of money were common and ought to be below she and Claud and some of the people who had good blood had lost their money and had to rent and then there were colored people who owned their homes and land as well. There was a colored dentist in town who had two red Lincolns and a swimming pool and a farm with registered white-face cattle on it. Usually by the time she had fallen asleep all the classes of people were moiling and roiling around in her head, and she would dream they were all crammed in together in a box car, being ridden off to be put in a gas oven.

"That's a beautiful clock," she said and nodded to her right. It was a big wall clock, the face encased in a brass sunburst.

"Yes, it's very pretty," the stylish lady said agreeably. "And right on the dot too," she added, glancing at her watch.

The ugly girl beside her cast an eye upward at the clock, smirked, then looked directly at Mrs. Turpin and smirked again. Then she returned her eyes to her book. She was obviously the lady's daughter because, although they didn't look anything alike as to disposition, they both had the same shape of face and the same blue eyes. On the lady they sparkled pleasantly but in the girl's seared face they appeared alternately to smolder and to blaze.

What if Jesus had said, "All right, you can be white-trash or a nigger or ugly"!

Mrs. Turpin felt an awful pity for the girl, though she thought it was one thing to be ugly and another to act ugly.

The woman with the snuff-stained lips turned around in her chair and looked up at the clock. Then she turned back and appeared to look a little to the side of Mrs. Turpin. There was a cast in one of her eyes. "You want to know wher you can get you one of themther clocks?" she asked in a loud voice.

"No, I already have a nice clock," Mrs. Turpin said. Once somebody like her got a leg in the conversation, she would be all over it.

"You can get you one with green stamps," the woman said. "That's most likely wher he got hisn. Save you up enough, you can get you most anything. I got me some joo'ry."

Ought to have got you a wash rag and some soap, Mrs. Turpin thought.

"I get contour sheets with mine," the pleasant lady said.

The daughter slammed her book shut. She looked straight in front of her, directly through Mrs. Turpin and on through the yellow curtain and the plate glass window which made the wall behind her. The girl's eyes seemed lit all of a sudden with a peculiar light, an unnatural light like the night road signs give. Mrs. Turpin turned her head to see if there was anything going on outside that she should see, but she could not see anything. Figures passing cast only a pale shadow through the curtain. There was no reason the girl should single her out for her ugly looks.

"Miss Finley," the nurse said, cracking the door. The gum-chewing woman got up and passed in front of her and Claud and went into the office. She had on red high-heeled shoes.

Directly across the table, the ugly girl's eyes were fixed on Mrs. Turpin as if she had some very special reason for disliking her.

"This is wonderful weather, isn't it?" the girl's mother said.

"It's good weather for cotton if you can get the niggers to pick it," Mrs. Turpin said, "but niggers don't want to pick cotton any more. You can't get the white folks to pick it and now you can't get the niggers— because they got to be right up there with the white folks."

"They gonna *try* anyways," the white-trash woman said, leaning forward.

"Do you have one of the cotton-picking machines?" the pleasant lady asked.

"No," Mrs. Turpin said, "they leave half the cotton in the field. We don't have much cotton anyway. If you want to make it farming now, you have to have a little of everything. We got a couple of acres of cotton and a few hogs and chickens and just enough white-face that Claud can look after them himself."

"One thang I don't want," the white-trash woman said, wiping her mouth with the back of her hand. "Hogs. Nasty stinking things, a-gruntin and a-rootin all over the place."

Mrs. Turpin gave her the merest edge of her attention. "Our hogs are not dirty and they don't stink," she said. "They're cleaner than some children I've seen. Their feet never touch the ground. We have a pig-parlor—that's where you raise them on concrete," she explained to the pleasant lady, "and Claud scoots them down with the hose every afternoon and washes off the floor." Cleaner by far than that child right there, she thought. Poor nasty little thing. He had not moved except to put the thumb of his dirty hand into his mouth.

The woman turned her face away from Mrs. Turpin. "I know I wouldn't scoot down no hog with no hose," she said to the wall.

You wouldn't have no hog to scoot down, Mrs. Turpin said to herself.

"A-gruntin and a-rootin and a-groanin," the woman muttered.

"We got a little of everything," Mrs. Turpin said to the pleasant lady. "It's no use in having more than you can handle yourself with help like it is. We found enough niggers to pick our cotton this year but Claud he has to go after them and take them home again in the evening. They can't walk that half a mile. No they can't. I tell you," she said and laughed merrily, "I sure am tired of buttering up niggers, but you got to love em if you want em to work for you. When they come in the morning, I run out and I say, 'Hi yawl this morning?' and when Claud drives them off to the field I just wave to beat the band and they just wave back." And she waved her hand rapidly to illustrate.

"Like you read out of the same book," the lady said, showing she understood perfectly.

"Child, yes," Mrs. Turpin said. "And when they come in from the field, I run out with a bucket of icewater. That's the way it's going to be from now on," she said. "You may as well face it."

"One thang I know," the white-trash woman said. "Two thangs I ain't going to do: love no niggers or scoot down no hog with no hose." And she let out a bark of contempt.

The look that Mrs. Turpin and the pleasant lady exchanged indicated they both understood that you had to *have* certain things before you could *know* certain things. But every time Mrs. Turpin exchanged a look with the lady, she was aware that the ugly girl's peculiar eyes were still on her, and she had trouble bringing her attention back to the conversation.

"When you got something," she said, "you got to look after it." And when you ain't got a thing but breath and britches, she added to herself, you can afford to come to town every morning and just sit on the Court House coping and spit.

A grotesque revolving shadow passed across the curtain behind her and was thrown palely on the opposite wall. Then a bicycle clattered down against the outside of the building. The door opened and a colored boy glided in with a tray from the drugstore. It had two large red and white paper cups on it with tops on them. He was a tall, very black boy in discolored white pants and a green nylon shirt. He was chewing gum slowly, as if to music. He set the tray down in the office opening next to the fern and stuck his head through to look for the secretary. She was not in there. He rested his arms on the ledge and waited, his narrow bottom stuck out, swaying to the left and right. He raised a hand over his head and scratched the base of his skull.

"You see that button there, boy?" Mrs. Turpin said. "You can punch that and she'll come. She's probably in the back somewhere."

"Is thas right?" the boy said agreeably, as if he had never seen the button before. He leaned to the right and put his finger on it. "She sometime out," he said and twisted around to face his audience, his elbows behind him on the counter. The nurse appeared and he twisted back again. She handed him a dollar and he rooted in his pocket and made the change and counted it out to her. She gave him fifteen cents for a tip and he went out with the empty tray. The heavy door swung to slowly and closed at length with the sound of suction. For a moment no one spoke.

"They ought to send all them niggers back to Africa," the white-trash woman said. "That's wher they come from in the first place."

"Oh, I couldn't do without my good colored friends," the pleasant lady said.

"There's a heap of things worse than a nigger," Mrs. Turpin agreed. "It's all kinds of them just like it's all kinds of us."

"Yes, and it takes all kinds to make the world go round," the lady said in her musical voice.

As she said it, the raw-complexioned girl snapped her teeth together. Her lower lip turned downwards and inside out, revealing the pale pink inside of her mouth. After a second it rolled back up. It was the ugliest face Mrs. Turpin had ever seen anyone make and for a moment she was certain that the girl had made it at her. She was looking at her as if she had known and disliked her all her life—all of Mrs. Turpin's life, it seemed too, not just all the girl's life. Why, girl, I don't even know you, Mrs. Turpin said silently.

She forced her attention back to the discussion. "It wouldn't be practical to send them back to Africa," she said. "They wouldn't want to go. They got it too good here."

"Wouldn't be what they wanted—if I had anythang to do with it," the woman said.

"It wouldn't be a way in the world you could get all the niggers back over there," Mrs. Turpin said. "They'd be hiding out and lying down and turning sick on you and wailing and hollering and raring and pitching. It wouldn't be a way in the world to get them over there."

"They got over here," the trashy woman said. "Get back like they got over."

"It wasn't so many of them then," Mrs. Turpin explained.

The woman looked at Mrs. Turpin as if here was an idiot indeed but Mrs. Turpin was not bothered by the look, considering where it came from.

"Nooo," she said, "they're going to stay here where they can go to New York and marry white folks and improve their color. That's what they all want to do, every one of them, improve their color."

"You know what comes of that, don't you?" Claud asked.

"No, Claud, what?" Mrs. Turpin said.

Claud's eyes twinkled. "White-faced niggers," he said with never a smile.

Everybody in the office laughed except the white-trash and the ugly girl. The girl gripped the book in her lap with white fingers. The trashy woman looked around her from face to face as if she thought they were all idiots. The old woman in the feed sack dress continued to gaze expressionless across the floor at the high-top shoes of the man opposite her, the one who had been pretending to be asleep when the Turpins came in. He was laughing heartily, his hands still spread out on his knees. The child had fallen to the side and was lying now almost face down in the old woman's lap.

While they recovered from their laughter, the nasal chorus on the radio kept the room from silence.

"You go to blank blank
And I'll go to mine
But we'll all blank along
To-geth-ther,
And all along the blank

We'll *hep eachother out*
Smile-ling in any kind of
Weath-ther!"

Mrs. Turpin didn't catch every word but she caught enough to agree with the spirit of the song and it turned her thoughts sober. To help anybody out that needed it was her philosophy of life. She never spared herself when she found somebody in need, whether they were white or black, trash or decent. And of all she had to be thankful for, she was most thankful that this was so. If Jesus had said, "You can be high society and have all the money you want and be thin and svelte-like, but you can't be a good woman with it," she would have had to say, "Well don't make me that then. Make me a good woman and it don't matter what else, how fat or how ugly or how poor!" Her heart rose. He had not made her a nigger or white-trash or ugly! He had made her herself and given her a little of everything. Jesus, thank you! she said. Thank you thank you thank you! Whenever she counted her blessings she felt as buoyant as if she weighed one hundred and twenty-five pounds instead of one hundred and eighty.

"What's wrong with your little boy?" the pleasant lady asked the white-trashy woman.

"He has a ulcer," the woman said proudly. "He ain't give me a minute's peace since he was born. Him and her are just alike," she said, nodding at the old woman, who was running her leathery fingers through the child's pale hair. "Look like I can't get nothing down them two but Co'Cola and candy."

That's all you try to get down em, Mrs. Turpin said to herself. Too lazy to light the fire. There was nothing you could tell her about people like them that she didn't know already. And it was not just that they didn't have anything. Because if you gave them everything, in two weeks it would all be broken or filthy or they would have chopped it up for lightwood. She knew all this from her own experience. Help them you must, but help them you couldn't.

All at once the ugly girl turned her lips inside out again. Her eyes fixed like two drills on Mrs. Turpin. This time there was no mistaking that there was something urgent behind them.

Girl, Mrs. Turpin exclaimed silently, I haven't done a thing to you! The girl might be confusing her with somebody else. There was no need to sit by and let herself be intimidated. "You must be in college," she said boldly, looking directly at the girl. "I see you reading a book there."

The girl continued to stare and pointedly did not answer.

Her mother blushed at this rudeness. "The lady asked you a question, Mary Grace," she said under her breath.

"I have ears," Mary Grace said.

The poor mother blushed again. "Mary Grace goes to Wellesley College," she explained. She twisted one of the buttons on her dress. "In Massachusetts," she added with a grimace. "And in the summer she just keeps right on studying. Just reads all the time, a real book worm. She's done real well at Wellesley; she's taking English and Math and History and Psychology and Social Studies," she rattled on, "and I think it's too much. I think she ought to get out and have fun."

The girl looked as if she would like to hurl them all through the plate glass window.

"Way up north," Mrs. Turpin murmured and thought, well, it hasn't done much for her manners.

"I'd almost rather to have him sick," the white-trash woman said, wrenching the attention back to herself. "He's so mean when he ain't. Look like some children just take natural to meanness. It's some gets bad when they get sick but he was the opposite. Took sick and turned good. He don't give me no trouble now. It's me waitin to see the doctor," she said.

If I was going to send anybody back to Africa, Mrs. Turpin thought, it would be your kind, woman. "Yes, indeed," she said aloud, but looking up at the ceiling, "it's a heap of things worse than a nigger." And dirtier than a hog, she added to herself.

"I think people with bad dispositions are more to be pitied than anyone on earth," the pleasant lady said in a voice that was decidedly thin.

"I thank the Lord he has blessed me with a good one," Mrs. Turpin said. "The day has never dawned that I couldn't find something to laugh at."

"Not since she married me anyways," Claud said with a comical straight face.

Everybody laughed except the girl and the white-trash.

Mrs. Turpin's stomach shook. "He's such a caution," she said, "that I can't help but laugh at him."

The girl made a loud ugly noise through her teeth.

Her mother's mouth grew thin and tight. "I think the worst thing in the world," she said, "is an ungrateful person. To have everything and not appreciate it. I know a girl," she said, "who has parents who would give her anything, a little brother who loves her dearly, who is getting a good education, who wears the best clothes, but who can never say a kind word to anyone, who never smiles, who just criticizes and complains all day long."

"Is she too old to paddle?" Claud asked.

The girl's face was almost purple.

"Yes," the lady said, "I'm afraid there's nothing to do but leave her to her folly. Some day she'll wake up and it'll be too late."

"It never hurt anyone to smile," Mrs. Turpin said. "It just makes you feel better all over."

"Of course," the lady said sadly, "but there are just some people you can't tell anything to. They can't take criticism."

"If it's one thing I am," Mrs. Turpin said with feeling, "it's grateful. When I think who all I could have been besides myself and what all I got, a little of everything, and a good disposition besides, I just feel like shouting, 'Thank you, Jesus, for making everything the way it is!' It could have been different!" For one thing, somebody else could have got Claud. At the thought of this, she was flooded with gratitude and a terrible pang of joy ran through her. "Oh thank you, Jesus, Jesus, thank you!" she cried aloud.

The book struck her directly over her left eye. It struck almost at the same instant that she realized the girl was about to hurl it. Before she could utter a sound, the raw face came crashing across the table toward her, howling. The girl's fingers sank like clamps into the soft flesh of her neck. She heard the mother cry out and Claud shout, "Whoa!" There was an instant when she was certain that she was about to be in an earthquake.

All at once her vision narrowed and she saw everything as if it were happening in a small room far away, or as if she were looking at it through the wrong end of a telescope. Claud's face crumpled and fell out of sight. The nurse ran in, then out, then in again. Then the gangling figure of the doctor rushed out of the inner door. Magazines flew this way and that as the table turned over. The girl fell with a thud and Mrs. Turpin's vision suddenly reversed itself and she saw everything large instead of small. The eyes of the white-trashy woman were staring hugely at the floor. There the girl, held down on one side by the nurse and on the other by her mother, was wrenching and turning in their grasp. The doctor was kneeling astride her, trying to hold her arm down. He managed after a second to sink a long needle into it.

Mrs. Turpin felt entirely hollow except for her heart which swung from side to side as if it were agitated in a great empty drum of flesh.

"Somebody that's not busy call for the ambulance," the doctor said in the off-hand voice young doctors adopt for terrible occasions.

Mrs. Turpin could not have moved a finger. The old man who had been sitting next to her skipped nimbly into the office and made the call, for the secretary still seemed to be gone.

"Claud!" Mrs. Turpin called.

He was not in his chair. She knew she must jump up and find him but she felt like some one trying to catch a train in a dream, when everything moves in slow motion and the faster you try to run the slower you go.

"Here I am," a suffocated voice, very unlike Claud's, said.

He was doubled up in the corner on the floor, pale as paper, holding his leg. She wanted to get up and go to him but she could not move. Instead, her gaze was drawn slowly downward to the churning face on the floor, which she could see over the doctor's shoulder.

The girl's eyes stopped rolling and focused on her. They seemed a much lighter blue than before, as if a door that had been tightly closed behind them was now open to admit light and air.

Mrs. Turpin's head cleared and her power of motion returned. She leaned forward until she was looking directly into the fierce brilliant eyes. There was no doubt in her mind that the girl did know her, knew her in some intense and personal way, beyond time and place and condition. "What you got to say to me?" she asked hoarsely and held her breath, waiting, as for a revelation.

The girl raised her head. Her gaze locked with Mrs. Turpin's. "Go back to hell where you came from, you old wart hog," she whispered. Her voice was low but clear. Her eyes burned for a moment as if she saw with pleasure that her message had struck its target.

Mrs. Turpin sank back in her chair.

After a moment the girl's eyes closed and she turned her head wearily to the side.

The doctor rose and handed the nurse the empty syringe. He leaned over and put both hands for a moment on the mother's shoulders, which were shaking. She was sitting on the floor, her lips pressed together, holding Mary Grace's hand in her lap. The girl's fingers were gripped like a baby's around her thumb. "Go on to the hospital," he said, "I'll call and make the arrangements."

"Now let's see that neck," he said in a jovial voice to Mrs. Turpin. He began to inspect her neck with his first two fingers. Two little moon-shaped lines like pink fish bones were indented over her windpipe. There was the beginning of an angry red swelling above her eye. His fingers passed over this also.

"Lea' me be," she said thickly and shook him off. "See about Claud. She kicked him."

"I'll see about him in a minute," he said and felt her pulse. He was a thin gray-haired man, given to pleasantries. "Go home and have yourself a vacation the rest of the day," he said and patted her on the shoulder.

Quit your pattin me, Mrs. Turpin growled to herself.

"And put an ice pack over that eye," he said. Then he went and squatted down beside Claud and looked at his leg. After a moment he pulled him up and Claud limped after him into the office.

Until the ambulance came, the only sounds in the room were the tremulous moans of the girl's mother, who continued to sit on the floor. The white-trash woman did not take her eyes off the girl. Mrs. Turpin looked straight ahead at nothing. Presently the ambulance drew up, a long dark shadow, behind the curtain. The attendants came in and set the stretcher down beside the girl and lifted her expertly onto it and carried her out. The nurse helped the mother gather up her things. The shadow of the ambulance moved silently away and the nurse came back in the office.

"That ther girl is going to be a lunatic, ain't she?" the white-trash woman asked the nurse, but the nurse kept on to the back and never answered her.

"Yes, she's going to be a lunatic," the white-trash woman said to the rest of them.

"Po'critter," the old woman murmured. The child's face was still in her lap. His eyes looked idly out over her knees. He had not moved during the disturbance except to draw one leg up under him.

"I thank Gawd," the white-trash woman said fervently, "I ain't a lunatic."

Claud came limping out and the Turpins went home.

As their pick-up truck turned into their own dirt road and made the crest of the hill, Mrs. Turpin gripped the window ledge and looked out suspiciously. The land sloped gracefully down through a field dotted with lavender weeds and at the start of the rise their small yellow frame house, with its little flower beds spread out around it like a fancy apron, sat primly in its accustomed place between two giant hickory trees. She would not have been startled to see a burnt wound between two blackened chimneys.

Neither of them felt like eating so they put on their house clothes and lowered the shade in the bedroom and lay down, Claud with his leg on a pillow and herself with a damp washcloth over her eye. The instant she was flat on her back, the image of a razor-backed hog with warts on its face and horns coming out behind its ears snorted into her head. She moaned, a low quiet moan.

"I am not," she said tearfully, "a wart hog. From hell." But the denial had no force. The girl's eyes and her words, even the tone of her voice, low but clear, directed only to her, brooked no repudiation. She had been singled out for the message, though there was trash in the room to whom it might justly have been applied. The full force of this fact struck her only now. There was a woman there who was neglecting her own child but she had been overlooked. The message had been given to Ruby Turpin, a respectable, hard-working, church-going woman. The tears dried. Her eyes began to burn instead with wrath.

She rose on her elbow and the washcloth fell into her hand. Claud was lying on his back, snoring. She wanted to tell him what the girl had said. At the same time, she did not wish to put the image of herself as a wart hog from hell into his mind.

"Hey, Claud," she muttered and pushed his shoulder.

Claud opened one pale baby blue eye.

She looked into it warily. He did not think about anything. He just went his way.

"Wha, whasit?" he said and closed the eye again.

"Nothing," she said. "Does your leg pain you?"

"Hurts like hell," Claud said.

"It'll quit terreckly," she said and lay back down. In a moment Claud was snoring again. For the rest of the afternoon they lay there. Claud slept. She scowled at the ceiling. Occasionally she raised her fist and made a small stabbing motion over her chest as if she was defending her innocence to invisible guests who were like the comforters of Job, reasonable-seeming but wrong.

About five-thirty Claud stirred. "Got to go after those niggers," he sighed, not moving.

She was looking straight up as if there were unintelligible handwriting on the ceiling. The proturberance over her eye had turned a greenish-blue. "Listen here," she said.

"What?"

"Kiss me."

Claud leaned over and kissed her loudly on the mouth. He pinched her side and their hands interlocked. Her expression of ferocious concentration did not change. Claud got up, groaning and growling, and limped off. She continued to study the ceiling.

She did not get up until she heard the pick-up truck coming back with the Negroes. Then she rose and thrust her feet in her brown oxfords, which she did not bother to lace, and stumped out onto the back porch and got her red plastic bucket. She emptied a tray of ice cubes into it and filled it half full of water and went out into the back yard. Every afternoon after Claud brought the hands in, one of the boys helped him put out hay and the rest waited in the back of the truck until he was ready to take them home. The truck was parked in the shade under one of the hickory trees.

"Hi yawl this evening?" Mrs. Turpin asked grimly, appearing with the bucket and the dipper. There were three women and a boy in the truck.

"Us doin nicely," the oldest woman said. "Hi you doin?" and her gaze stuck immediately on the dark lump on Mrs. Turpin's forehead. "You done fell down, ain't you?" she asked in a solicitous voice. The old woman was dark and almost toothless. She had on an old felt hat of Claud's set back on her head. The other two women were younger and lighter and they both had new bright green sunhats. One of them had hers on her head; the other had taken hers off and the boy was grinning beneath it.

Mrs. Turpin set the bucket down on the floor of the truck. "Yawl help yourselves," she said. She looked around to make sure Claud had gone. "No, I didn't fall down," she said, folding her arms. "It was something worse than that."

"Ain't nothing bad happen to you!" the old woman said. She said it as if they all knew that Mrs. Turpin was protected in some special way by Divine Providence. "You just had you a little fall."

"We were in town at the doctor's office for where the cow kicked Mr. Turpin," Mrs. Turpin said in a flat tone that indicated they could leave off their foolishness. "And there was this girl there. A big fat girl with her face all broke out. I could look at that girl and tell she was peculiar but I couldn't tell how. And me and her mamma was just talking and going along and all of a sudden WHAM! She throws this big book she was reading at me and . . ."

"Naw!" the old woman cried out.

"And then she jumps over the table and commences to choke me."

"Naw!" they all exclaimed, "naw!"

"Hi come she do that?" the old woman asked. "What ail her?"

Mrs. Turpin only glared in front of her.

"Somethin ail her," the old woman said.

"They carried her off in an ambulance," Mrs. Turpin continued, "but before she went she was rolling on the floor and they were trying to hold her down to give her a shot and she said something to me." She paused. "You know what she said to me?"

"What she say?" they asked.

"She said," Mrs. Turpin began, and stopped, her face very dark and heavy. The sun was getting whiter and whiter, blanching the sky overhead so that the leaves of the hickory tree were black in the face of it. She could not bring forth the words. "Something real ugly," she muttered.

"She sho shouldn't said nothin ugly to you," the old woman said. "You so sweet. You the sweetest lady I know."

"She pretty too," the one with the hat on said.

"And stout," the other one said. "I never knowed no sweeter white lady."

"That's the truth befo' Jesus," the old woman said. "Amen! You des as sweet and pretty as you can be."

Mrs. Turpin knew exactly how much Negro flattery was worth and it added to her rage. "She said," she began again and finished this time with a fierce rush of breath, "that I was an old wart hog from hell."

There was an astounded silence.

"Where she at?" the youngest woman cried in a piercing voice. "Lemme see her. I'll kill her!"

"I'll kill her with you!" the other one cried.

"She b'long in the sylum," the old woman said emphatically. "You the sweetest white lady I know."

"She pretty too," the other two said. "Stout as she can be and sweet. Jesus satisfied with her!"

"Deed he is," the old woman declared.

Idiots! Mrs. Turpin growled to herself. You could never say anything intelligent to a nigger. You could talk at them but not with them. "Yawl ain't drunk your water," she said shortly. "Leave the bucket in the truck when you're finished with it. I got more to do than just stand around and pass the time of day," and she moved off and into the house.

She stood for a moment in the middle of the kitchen. The dark protuberance over her eye looked like a miniature tornado cloud which might any moment sweep across the horizon of her brow. Her lower lip protruded dangerously. She squared her massive shoulders. Then she marched into the front of the house and out the side door and stared down the road to the pig parlor. She had the look of a woman going single-handed, weaponless, into battle.

The sun was a deep yellow now like a harvest moon and was riding westward very fast over the far tree line as if it meant to reach the hogs before she did. The road was rutted and she kicked several good-sized stones out of her path as she strode along. The pig parlor was on a little knoll at the end of a lane that ran off from the side of the barn. It was a square of concrete as large as a small room, with a board fence about four feet high around it. The concrete floor sloped slightly so that the hog wash could drain off into a trench where it was carried to the field for fertilizer. Claud was standing on the outside, on the edge of the concrete, hanging onto the top board, hosing down the floor inside. The hose was connected to the faucet of a water trough nearby.

Mrs. Turpin climbed up beside him and glowered down at the hogs inside. There were seven long-snouted bristly shoats in it—tan with liver-colored spots—and an old sow a few weeks off from farrowing. She was lying on her side grunting. The shoats were running about shaking themselves like idiot children, their little slit pig eyes searching the floor for anything left. She had read that pigs were the most intelligent animal. She doubted it. They were supposed to be smarter than dogs. There had even been a pig astronaut. He had performed his assignment perfectly but died of a heart attack afterwards because they left him in his electric suit, sitting upright throughout his examination when naturally a hog should be on all fours.

A-gruntin and a-rootin and a-groanin.

"Gimme that hose," she said, yanking it away from Claud. "Go on and carry them niggers home and then get off that leg."

"You look like you might have swallowed a mad dog," Claud observed, but he got down and limped off. He paid no attention to her humors.

Until he was out of earshot, Mrs. Turpin stood on the side of the pen, holding the hose and pointing the stream of water at the hind quarters of any shoat that looked as if it might try to lie down. When he had had time to get over the hill, she turned her head slightly and her wrathful eyes scanned the path. He was nowhere in sight. She turned back again and seemed to gather herself up. Her shoulders rose and she drew in her breath.

"What do you send me a message like that for?" she said in a low fierce voice, barely above a whisper but with the force of a shout in its concentrated fury. "How am I a hog and me both? How am I saved and from hell too? Her free fist was knotted and with the other she gripped the hose, blindly pointing the stream of water in and out of the eye of the old sow whose outraged squeal she did not hear.

The pig parlor commanded a view of the back pasture where their twenty beef cows were gathered around the hay-bales Claud and the boy had put out. The freshly cut pasture sloped down to the highway. Across it was their cotton field and beyond that a dark green dusty wood which they owned as well. The sun was behind the wood, very red, looking over the paling of trees like a farmer inspecting his own hogs.

"Why me?" she rumbled. "It's no trash around here, black or white, that I haven't given to. And break my back to the bone every day working. And do for the church."

She appeared to be the right size woman to command the arena before her. "How am I a hog?" she demanded. "Exactly how am I like them?" and she jabbed the stream of water at the shoats. "There was plenty of trash there. It didn't have to be me.

"If you like trash better, go get yourself some trash then," she railed. "You could have made me trash. Or a nigger. If trash is what you wanted why didn't you make me trash?" She shook her fist with the hose in it and a watery snake appeared momentarily in the air. "I could quit working and take it easy and be filthy," she growled. "Lounge about the sidewalks all day drinking root beer. Dip snuff and spit in every puddle and have it all over my face. I could be nasty.

"Or you could have made me a nigger. It's too late for me to be a nigger," she said with deep sarcasm, "but I could act like one. Lay down in the middle of the road and stop traffic. Roll on the ground."

In the deepening light everything was taking on a mysterious hue. The pasture was growing a peculiar glassy green and the streak of highway had turned lavender. She braced herself for a final assault and this time her voice rolled out over the pasture. "Go on," she yelled, "call me a hog! Call me a hog again. From hell. Call me a wart hog from hell. Put that bottom rail on top. There'll still be a top and bottom!"

A garbled echo returned to her.

A final surge of fury shook her and she roared, "Who do you think you are?"

The color of everything, field and crimson sky, burned for a moment with a transparent intensity. The question carried over the pasture and across the highway and the cotton field and returned to her clearly like an answer from beyond the wood.

She opened her mouth but no sound came out of it.

A tiny truck, Claud's, appeared on the highway, heading rapidly out of sight. Its gears scraped thinly. It looked like a child's toy. At any moment a bigger truck might smash into it and scatter Claud's and the niggers' brains all over the road.

Mrs. Turpin stood there, her gaze fixed on the highway, all her muscles rigid, until in five or six minutes the truck reappeared, returning. She waited until it had had time to turn into their own road. Then like a monumental statue coming to life, she bent her head slowly and gazed, as if through the very heart of mystery, down into the pig parlor at the hogs. They had settled all in one corner around the old sow who was grunting softly. A red glow suffused them. They appeared to pant with a secret life.

Until the sun slipped finally behind the tree line, Mrs. Turpin remained there with her gaze bent to them as if she were absorbing some abysmal life-giving knowledge. At last she lifted her head. There was only a purple streak in the sky, cutting through a field of crimson and leading, like an extension of the highway, into the descending dusk. She raised her hands from the side of the pen in a gesture hieratic and profound. A visionary light settled in her eyes. She saw the streak as a vast swinging bridge extending upward from the earth through a field of living fire. Upon it a vast horde of souls were rumbling toward heaven. There were whole companies of white-trash, clean for the first time in their lives, and bands of black niggers in white robes, and battalions of freaks and lunatics shouting and clapping and leaping like frogs. And bringing up the end of the procession was a tribe of people whom she recognized at once as those who, like herself and Claud, had always had a little of every-thing and the God-given wit to use it right. She leaned forward to observe them closer. They were marching behind the others with great dignity, accountable as they had always been for good order and common sense and respectable behavior. They alone were on key. Yet she could see by their shocked and altered faces that even their virtues were being burned away. She lowered her hands and gripped the rail of the hog pen, her eyes small but fixed unblinkingly on what lay ahead. In a moment the vision faded but she remained where she was, immobile.

At length she got down and turned off the faucet and made her slow way on the darkening path to the house. In the woods around her the invisible cricket choruses had struck up, but what she heard were the voices of the souls climbing upward into the starry field and shouting hallelujah.

Margaret Laurence

(1926–1987)

*M*argaret Laurence was born in Neepawa, Manitoba, the small town that inspired the creation of Manawaka, the setting for four of her novels and the short-story cycle A Bird in the House (1970), from which "The Mask of the Bear" is taken and which Laurence described as "semi-autobiographical" fiction. She received an honours English degree from the United College in Winnipeg in 1947. In 1949 she moved with her husband, Jack Laurence, to England, then spent the years 1950–57 in Africa, first in Somaliland (now Somalia) and then in Ghana. After separating from her husband, she returned to England in 1962, and eventually to Canada, where she accepted the position of Chancellor of Trent University. Laurence's writing is often placed in two categories, the African books and the Manawaka books, but it would be a mistake not to recognize that Laurence learned something in Africa that had a profound influence on her view of all people in their persistent struggles for dignity, whether those people be colonized blacks or Canadian women resisting the constraints of a patriarchal society. The African books include the anthology of Somali poetry and prose, A Tree for Poverty (1954), her novel This Side Jordan (1960), the short-story collection The Tomorrow-Tamer (1963), her memoirs of this period, The Prophet's Camel Bell (1963), and her critical study of Nigerian writing in English, Long Drums and Cannons (1968). The celebrated Manawaka novels constitute one of the monumental achievements in Canadian literature, and, along with A Bird in the House, the group includes The Stone Angel (1964), A Jest of God (1966), which won the Governor General's Award, The Fire-Dwellers (1969), and The Diviners (1974), which won her a second Governor General's Award. A Companion of the Order of Canada, Laurence was awarded the Molson Prize in 1975. She is also a popular children's author and an engaging essayist, and shortly before her death she completed a memoir-cum-autobiography that was published posthumously as Dance on the Earth (1989). Laurence's foremost critic, Clara Thomas, has characterized the enduring attraction of the women in Laurence's fiction in this way:

> All of Margaret Laurence's women are strong and strongly maternal. They also feel the imperatives of emotion, of guilt and desire, sexuality and individuality that all women share. And they live, as we do, among the tensions set up between their individual, inner needs and the demands that society imposes on them from the outside. They achieve only the precarious balance that might conceivably issue from their temperaments and their situations. But they do issue as individuals and as members of the human race, with dignity and potential, rights

and responsibilities, which are insistently shown to be equal to men's. Margaret Laurence's great gift to us is that they come indomitably through the pages, with laughter, with bravery, and with reassurance—our ancestors, our sisters, and our friends.

As loved and respected by her fellow women writers for her example in overcoming obstacles to her career as for the writing itself, Laurence has left behind a literary legacy that will be only more appreciated as the years pass.

The Mask of the Bear

I n winter my Grandfather Connor used to wear an enormous coat made out of the pelt of a bear. So shaggy and coarse-furred was this coat, so unevenly coloured in patches ranging from amber to near-black, and so vile-smelling when it had become wet with snow, that it seemed to have belonged when it was alive to some lonely and giant Kodiak crankily roaming a high frozen plateau, or an ancient grizzly scarred with battles in the sinister forests of the north. In actuality, it had been an ordinary brown bear and it had come, sad to say, from no more fabled a place than Galloping Mountain, only a hundred miles from Manawaka. The skin had once been given to my grandfather as payment, in the days when he was blacksmith, before he became a hardware merchant and developed the policy of cash only. He had had it cobbled into a coat by the local shoemaker, and Grandmother Connor had managed to sew in the lining. How long ago that was, no one could say for sure, but my mother, the eldest of his family, said she could not remember a time when he had not worn it. To me, at the age of ten and a half, this meant it must be about a century old. The coat was so heavy that I could not even lift it by myself. I never used to wonder how he could carry that phenomenal weight on himself, or why he would choose to, because it was obvious that although he was old he was still an extraordinarily strong man, built to shoulder weights.

Whenever I went into Simlow's Ladies' Wear with my mother, and made grotesque faces at myself in the long mirror while she tried on dresses, Millie Christopherson who worked there would croon a phrase which made me break into snickering until my mother, who was death on bad manners, tapped anxiously at my shoulders with her slender, nervous hands. *It's you, Mrs. MacLeod*, Millie would say feelingly, *no kidding it's absolutely you*. I appropriated the phrase for my grandfather's winter coat. *It's you*, I would simper nastily at him, although never, of course, aloud.

In my head I sometimes called him "The Great Bear." The name had many associations other than his coat and his surliness. It was the way he would stalk around the Brick House as though it were a cage, on Sundays, impatient for the new week's beginning that would release him into the only freedom he knew, the acts of work. It was the way he would take to the basement whenever a man came to call upon Aunt Edna, which in those days was not often, because—as I had overheard my mother outlining in sighs to my father—most of the single men her age in Manawaka considered that the time she had spent working in Winnipeg had made more difference than it really had, and the situation wasn't helped by her flyaway manner (whatever that might mean). But if ever she was asked out to a movie, and the man was waiting and making stilted weather-chat with Grandmother Connor, Grandfather would prowl through the living room as through seeking a place of rest and not finding it, would stare fixedly without speaking, and would then descend the basement steps to the rocking chair which sat beside the furnace. Above ground, he would not have been found dead sitting in a rocking chair, which he considered a piece of furniture suitable only for the elderly, of whom he was never in his own eyes one. From his cave, however, the angry crunching of the wooden rockers against the cement floor would reverberate throughout the house, a kind of sub-verbal Esperanto, a disapproval which even the most obtuse person could not fail to comprehend.

In some unformulated way, I also associated the secret name with Great Bear Lake, which I had seen only on maps and which I imagined to be a deep vastness of black water, lying somewhere very far beyond our known prairies of tamed fields and barbed-wire fences, somewhere in the regions of jagged rock and eternal ice, where human voices would be drawn into a cold and shadowed stillness without leaving even a trace of warmth.

One Saturday afternoon in January, I was at the rink when my grandfather appeared unexpectedly. He was wearing his formidable coat, and to say he looked out of place among the skaters thronging around the edges of the ice would be putting it mildly. Embarrassed, I whizzed over to him.

"There you are, Vanessa—about time," he said, as though he had been searching for me for hours. "Get your skates off now, and come along. You're to come home with me for supper. You'll be staying the night at our place. Your dad's gone away out to Freehold, and your mother's gone with him. Fine time to pick for it. It's blowing up for a blizzard, if you ask me. They'll not get back for a couple of days, more than likely. Don't see why he don't just tell people to make their own way in to the hospital. Ewen's too easy-going. He'll not get a penny nor a word of thanks for it, you can bet your life on that."

My father and Dr. Cates used to take the country calls in turn. Often when my father went out in the winter, my mother would go with him, in case the old Nash got stuck in the snow and also to talk and thus prevent my father from going to sleep at the wheel, for falling snow has a hypnotic effect.

"What about Roddie?" I asked, for my brother was only a few months old.

"The old lady's keeping care of him," Grandfather Connor replied abruptly.

The old lady meant my Grandmother MacLeod, who was actually a few years younger than Grandfather Connor. He always referred to her in this way, however, as a calculated insult, and here my sympathies were with him for once. He maintained, quite correctly, that she gave herself airs because her husband had been a doctor and now her son was one, and that she looked down on the Connors because they had come from famine Irish (although at least, thank God, Protestant). The two of them seldom met, except at Christmas, and never exchanged more than a few words. If they had ever really clashed, it would have been like a brontosaurus running headlong into a tyrannosaurus.

"Hurry along now," he said, when I had taken off my skates and put on my snow boots. "You've got to learn not to dawdle. You're an awful dawdler, Vanessa."

I did not reply. Instead, when we left the rink I began to take exaggeratedly long strides. But he paid no attention to my attempt to reproach him with my speed. He walked beside me steadily and silently, wrapped in his great fur coat and his authority.

The Brick House was at the other end of town, so while I shuffled through the snow and pulled my navy wool scarf up around my nose against the steel cutting edge of the wind, I thought about the story I was setting down in a five-cent scribbler at nights in my room. I was much occupied by the themes of love and death, although my experience of both had so far been gained principally from the Bible, which I read in the same way as I read Eaton's Catalogue or the collected works of Rudyard Kipling—because I had to read something, and the family's finances in the thirties did not permit the purchase of enough volumes of *Doctor Doolittle* or the *Oz* books to keep me going.

For the love scenes, I gained useful material from The Song of Solomon. *Let him kiss me with the kisses of his mouth, for thy love is better than wine*, or *By night on my bed I sought him whom my soul loveth; I sought him but I found him not.* My interpretation was somewhat vague, and I was not helped to any appreciable extent by the explanatory bits in small print at the beginning of each chapter—*The church's love unto Christ. The church's fight and victory in temptation*, et cetera. These explanations did not puzzle me, though, for I assumed even then that they had simply been put there for the benefit of gentle and unworldly people such as my Grandmother Connor, so that they could read the Holy Writ without becoming upset.

To me, the woman in The Song was some barbaric queen, beautiful and terrible, and I could imagine her, wearing a long robe of leopard skin and one or two heavy gold bracelets, pacing an alabaster courtyard and keening her unrequited love.

The heroine in my story (which took place in ancient Egypt—my ignorance of this era did not trouble me) was very like the woman in The Song of Solomon, except that mine had long wavy auburn hair, and when her beloved left her, the only thing she could bring herself to eat was an avocado, which seemed to me considerably more stylish and exotic than apples in lieu of love. Her young man was a gifted carver, who had been sent out into the desert by the cruel pharaoh (pharaohs were always cruel—of this I was positive) in order to carve a giant sphinx for the royal tomb. Should I have her die while he was away? Or would it be better if he perished out in the desert? Which of them did I like the least? With the characters whom I liked best, things always turned out right in the end. Yet the death scenes had an undeniable appeal, a sombre splendour, with (as it said in Ecclesiastes) the mourners going about the streets and all the daughters of music brought low. Both death and love seemed regrettably far from Manawaka and the snow, and my grandfather stamping his feet on the front porch of the Brick House and telling me to do the same or I'd be tracking the wet in all over the hardwood floor.

The house was too warm, almost stifling. Grandfather burned mainly birch in the furnace, although it cost twice as much as poplar, and now that he had retired from the hardware store, the furnace gave him something to do and so he was forever stoking it. Grandmother Connor was in the dining room, her stout body in its brown rayon dress bending over the canary's cage.

"Hello, pet," she greeted me. "You should have heard Birdie just a minute ago—one of those real long trills. He's been moulting lately, and this is the first time he's sung in weeks."

"Gee," I said enthusiastically, for although I was not fond of canaries, I was extremely fond of my grandmother. "That's swell. Maybe he'll do it again."

"Messy things, them birds," my grandfather commented. "I can never see what you see in a fool thing like that, Agnes."

My grandmother did not attempt to reply to this.

"Would you like a cup of tea, Timothy?" she asked.

"Nearly supper-time, ain't it?"

"Well, not for a little while yet."

"It's away past five," my grandfather said. "What's Edna been doing with herself?"

"She's got the pot-roast in," my grandmother answered, "but it's not done yet."

"You'd think a person could get a meal on time," he said, "considering she's got precious little else to do."

I felt, as so often in the Brick House, that my lungs were in danger of exploding, that the pressure of silence would become too great to be borne. I wanted to point out, as I knew Grandmother Connor would never do, that it wasn't Aunt Edna's fault there were no jobs anywhere these days, and that, as my mother often said of her, she worked her fingers to the bone here so she wouldn't need to feel beholden to him for her keep, and that they would have had to get a hired girl if she hadn't been here, because Grandmother Connor couldn't look after a place this size any more. Also, that the dining-room clock said precisely ten minutes past five, and the evening meal in the Connor house was always at six o'clock on the dot. And—and—a thousand other arguments rose up and nearly choked me. But I did not say anything. I was not that stupid. Instead, I went out to the kitchen.

Aunt Edna was wearing her coral sweater and grey pleated skirt, and thought she looked lovely, even with her apron on. I always thought she looked lovely, though, whatever she was wearing, but if ever I told her so, she would only laugh and say it was lucky she had a cheering section of one.

"Hello, kiddo," she said. "Do you want to sleep in my room tonight, or shall I make up the bed in the spare room?"

"In your room," I said quickly, for this meant she would let me try out her lipstick and use some of her Jergens hand-lotion, and if I could stay awake until she came to bed, we would whisper after the light was out.

"How's *The Pillars of the Nation* coming along?" she asked.

That had been my epic on pioneer life. I had proceeded to the point in the story where the husband, coming back to the cabin one evening, discovered to his surprise that he was going to become a father. The way he ascertained this interesting fact was that he found his wife constructing a birch-bark cradle. Then came the discovery that Grandfather Connor had been a pioneer, and the story had lost its interest for me. If pioneers were like *that*, I had thought, my pen would be better employed elsewhere.

"I quit that one," I replied laconically. "I'm making up another—it's miles better. It's called *The Silver Sphinx*. I'll bet you can't guess what it's about."

"The desert? Buried treasure? Murder mystery?"

I shook my head.

"Love," I said.

"Good Glory," Aunt Edna said, straight-faced. "That sounds fascinating. Where do you get your ideas, Vanessa?"

I could not bring myself to say the Bible. I was afraid she might think this sounded funny.

"Oh here and there," I replied noncommittally. "You know."

She gave me an inquisitive glance, as though she meant to question me further, but just then the telephone rang, and I rushed to answer it, thinking it might be my mother or father phoning from Freehold. But it wasn't. It was a voice I didn't know, a man's.

"Is Edna Connor there?"

"Just a minute, please," I cupped one hand over the mouthpiece fixed on the wall, and the other over the receiver.

"For you," I hissed, grinning at her. "A strange man!"

"Mercy," Aunt Edna said ironically, "these hordes of admirers will be the death of me yet. Probably Todd Jeffries from Burns' Electric about that busted lamp."

Nevertheless, she hurried over. Then, as she listened, her face became startled, and something else which I could not fathom.

"Heavens, where are you?" she cried at last. "At the station *here*? Oh Lord. Why didn't you write to say you were—well, sure I am, but—oh, never mind. No, you wait there. I'll come and meet you. You'd never find the house—"

I had never heard her talk this way before, rattlingly. Finally she hung up. Her face looked like a stranger's, and for some reason this hurt me.

"It's Jimmy Lorimer," she said. "He's at the C.P.R. station. He's coming here. Oh my God, I wish Beth were here."

"Why?" I wished my mother were her, too, but I could not see what difference it made to Aunt Edna. I knew who Jimmy Lorimer was. He was a man Aunt Edna had gone around with when she was in Winnipeg. He had given her the Attar of Roses in an atomiser bottle with a green net-covered bulb—the scent she always sprayed around her room after she had had a cigarette there. Jimmy Lorimer had been invested with a remote glamour in my imagination, but all at once I felt I was going to hate him.

I realised that Aunt Edna was referring to what Grandfather Connor might do or say, and instantly I was ashamed for having felt churlishly disposed towards Jimmy Lorimer. Even if he was a cad, a heel, or a nitwit, I swore I would welcome him. I visualised him as having a flashy appearance, like a riverboat gambler in a movie I had seen once, a check-ered suit, a slender oiled moustache, a diamond tie-pin, a dangerous leer. Never mind. Never mind if he was Lucifer himself.

"I'm glad he's coming," I said staunchly.

Aunt Edna looked at me queerly, her mouth wavering as though she were about to smile. Then, quickly, she bent and hugged me, and I could feel her trembling. At this moment, Grandmother Connor came into the kitchen.

"You all right, pet?" she asked Aunt Edna. "Nothing's the matter, is it?"

"Mother, that was an old friend of mine on the phone just now. Jimmy Lorimer. He's from Winnipeg. He's passing through Manawaka. Is it all right if he comes here for dinner?"

"Well, of course, dear," Grandmother said. "What a lucky thing we're having the pot-roast. There's plenty. Vanessa, pet, you run down to the fruit cellar and bring up a jar of strawberries, will you? Oh, and a small jar of chili sauce. No, maybe the sweet mustard pickle would go better with the pot-roast. What do you think, Edna?"

She spoke as though this were the only important issue in the whole situation. But all the time her eyes were on Aunt Edna's face.

"Edna—" she said, with great effort, "is he—is he a good man, Edna?"

Aunt Edna blinked and looked confused, as though she had been spoken to in some foreign language.

"Yes," she replied.

"You're sure, pet?"

"Yes," Aunt Edna repeated, a little more emphatically than before.

Grandmother Connor nodded, smiled reassuringly, and patted Aunt Edna lightly on the wrist.

"Well, that's fine, dear. I'll just tell Father. Everything will be all right, so don't you worry about a thing."

When Grandmother had gone back to the living room, Aunt Edna began pulling on her black fur-topped overshoes. When she spoke, I didn't know whether it was to me or not.

"I didn't tell her a damn thing," she said in a surprised tone. "I wonder how she knows, or if she really does? *Good*. What a word. I wish I didn't know what she means when she says that. Or else that she knew what I mean when I say it. Glory, I wish Beth were here."

I understood then that she was not speaking to me, and that what she had to say could not be spoken to me. I felt chilled by my childhood, unable to touch her because of the freezing burden of my inexperience. I was about to say something, anything, however mistaken, when my aunt said *Sh*, and we both listened to the talk from the living room.

A friend of Edna's is coming for dinner, Timothy," Grandmother was saying quietly. "A young man from Winnipeg."

A silence. Then, "Winnipeg!" my grandfather exclaimed, making it sound as though Jimmy Lorimer were coming here straight from his harem in Casablanca.

"What's he do?" Grandfather demanded next.

"Edna didn't say."

"I'm not surprised," Grandfather said darkly. "Well, I won't have her running around with that sort of fellow. She's got no more sense than a sparrow."

"She's twenty-eight," Grandmother said, almost apologetically. "Anyway, this is just a friend."

"Friend!" my grandfather said, annihilating the word. Then, not loudly, but with an odd vehemence, "you don't know a blame thing about men, Agnes. You never have."

Even I could think of several well-placed replies that my grandmother might have made, but she did not do so. She did not say anything. I looked at Aunt Edna, and saw that she had closed her eyes the way people do when they have a headache. Then we heard Grandmother's voice, speaking at last, not in her usual placid and unruffled way, but hesitantly.

"Timothy—please. Be nice to him. For my sake."

For my sake. This was so unlike my grandmother that I was stunned. She was not a person who begged you to be kind for her sake, or even for God's sake. If you were kind, in my grandmother's view, it was for its own sake, and the judgement of whether you had done well or not was up to the Almighty. *Judge not, that ye be not judged* —this was her favourite admonition to me when I lost my temper with one of my friends. As a devout Baptist, she believed it was a sin to pray for anything for yourself. You ought to pray only for strength to bear whatever the Lord saw fit to send you, she thought. I was never able to follow this advice, for although I would often feel a sense of uneasiness over the tone of my prayers, I was the kind of person who prayed frantically—"Please, God, please, please *please* let Ross MacVey like me better than Mavis." Grandmother Connor was not self-effacing in her lack of demands either upon God or upon her family. She merely believed that what happened to a person in this life was in Other Hands. Acceptance was at the heart of her. I don't think in her own eyes she ever lived in a state of bondage. To the rest of the family, thrashing furiously and uselessly in various snarled dilemmas, she must often have appeared to live in a state of perpetual grace, but I am certain she didn't think of it that way, either.

Grandfather Connor did not seem to have heard her.

"We won't get our dinner until all hours, I daresay," he said.

But we got our dinner as soon as Aunt Edna had arrived back with Jimmy Lorimer, for she flew immediately out to the kitchen and before we knew it we were all sitting at the big circular table in the dining room.

Jimmy Lorimer was not at all what I had expected. Far from looking like a Mississippi gambler, he looked just like anybody else, any uncle or grown-up cousin, unexceptional in every way. He was neither overwhelmingly handsome nor interestingly ugly. He was okay to look at, but as I said to myself, feeling at the same time a twinge of betrayal towards Aunt Edna, he was nothing to write home about. He wore a brown suit and a green tie. The only thing about him which struck fire was that he had a joking manner similar to Aunt Edna's, but whereas I felt at ease with this quality in her, I could never feel comfortable with the laughter of strangers, being uncertain where an including laughter stopped and taunting began.

"You're from Winnipeg, eh?" Grandfather Connor began. "Well, I guess you fellows don't put much store in a town like Manawaka."

Without waiting for affirmation or denial of this sentiment, he continued in an unbroken line.

"I got no patience with these people who think a small town is just nothing. You take a city, now. You could live in one of them places for twenty years, and you'd not get to know your next-door neighbour. Trouble comes along—who's going to give you a hand? Not a blamed soul."

Grandfather Connor had never in his life lived in a city, so his first-hand knowledge of their ways was, to say the least, limited. As for trouble—the thought of my grandfather asking any soul in Manawaka to give aid and support to him in any way whatsoever was inconceivable. He would have died of starvation, physical or spiritual, rather than put himself in any man's debt by so much as a dime or a word.

"Hey, hold on a minute," Jimmy Lorimer protested. "I never said that about small towns. As a matter of fact, I grew up in one myself. I came from McConnell's Landing. Ever heard of it?"

"I heard of it all right," Grandfather said brusquely, and no one could have told from his tone whether McConnell's Landing was a place of ill-repute or whether he simply felt his knowledge of geography was being doubted. "Why'd you leave, then?"

Jimmy shrugged. "Not much opportunity there. Had to seek my fortune, you know. Can't say I've found it, but I'm still looking."

"Oh, you'll be a tycoon yet, no doubt," Aunt Edna put in.

"You bet your life, kiddo," Jimmy replied. "You wait. Times'll change."

I didn't like to hear him say "kiddo." It was Aunt Edna's word, the one she called me by. It didn't belong to him.

"Mercy, they can't change fast enough for me," Aunt Edna said. "I guess I haven't got your optimism, though."

"Well, I haven't got it, either," he said, laughing, "but keep it under your hat, eh?"

Grandfather Connor had listened to this exchange with some impatience. Now he turned to Jimmy once more.

"What's your line of work?"

"I'm with Reliable Loan Company right now, Mr. Connor, but I don't aim to stay there permanently. I'd like to have my own business. Cars are what I'm really interested in. But it's not so easy to start up these days."

Grandfather Connor's normal opinions on social issues possessed such a high degree of clarity and were so frequently stated that they were well known even to me—all labour unions were composed of thugs and crooks; if people were unemployed it was due to their own laziness; if people were broke it was because they were not thrifty. Now, however, a look of intense and brooding sorrow came into his face, as he became all at once the champion of the poor and oppressed.

"Loan company!" he said. "Them blood-suckers. They wouldn't pay no mind to how hard-up a man might be. Take everything he has, without batting an eye. By the Lord Harry, I never thought the day would come when I'd sit down to a meal alongside one of them fellows."

Aunt Edna's face was rigid.

"Jimmy," she said. "Ignore him."

Grandfather turned on her, and they stared at one another with a kind of inexpressible rage but neither of them spoke. I could not help feeling sorry for Jimmy Lorimer, who mumbled something about his train leaving and began eating hurriedly. Grandfather rose to his feet.

"I've had enough," he said.

"Don't you want your dessert, Timothy?" Grandmother asked, as though it never occurred to her that he could be referring to anything other than the meal. It was only then that I realised that this was the first time she had spoken since we sat down at the table. Grandfather did not reply. He went down to the basement. Predictably, in a moment we could hear the wooden rockers of his chair thudding like retreating thunder. After dinner, Grandmother sat in the living room, but she did not get out the red cardigan she was knitting for me. She sat without doing anything, quite still, her hands folded in her lap.

"I'll let you off the dishes tonight, honey," Aunt Edna said to me. "Jimmy will help with them. You can try out my lipstick, if you like, only for Pete's sake wash it off before you come down again."

I went upstairs, but I did not go to Aunt Edna's room. I went into the back bedroom to one of my listening posts. In the floor there was a round hole which had once been used for a stove-pipe leading up from the kitchen. Now it was covered with a piece of brown-painted tin full of small perforations which had apparently been noticed only by me.

"Where does he get his lines, Edna?" Jimmy was saying. "He's like old-time melodrama."

"Yeh, I know," Aunt Edna sounded annoyed. "But let me say it, eh?"

"Sorry. Honest. Listen, can't you even—"

Scuffling sounds, then my aunt's nervous whisper.

"Not here, Jimmy. Please. You don't understand what they're—"

"I understand, all right. Why in God's name do you stay, Edna? Aren't you ever coming back? That's what I want to know."

"With no job? Don't make me laugh."

"I could help out, at first anyway—"

"Jimmy, don't talk like a lunatic. Do you really think I could?"

"Oh hell, I suppose not. Well, look at it this way. What if I wasn't cut out for the unattached life after all? What if the old leopard actually changed his spots, kiddo? What would you say to that?"

A pause, as though Aunt Edna were mulling over his words.

"That'll be the day," she replied. "I'll believe it when I see it."

"Well, Jesus, lady," he said, "I'm not getting down on my knees. Tell me one thing, though—don't you miss me at all? Don't you miss— everything? C'mon now—don't you? Not even a little bit?"

Another pause. She could not seem to make up her mind how to respond to the teasing quality of his voice.

"Yeh, I lie awake nights," she said at last, sarcastically.

He laughed. "Same old Edna. Want me to tell you something, kiddo? I think you're scared."

"Scared?" she said scornfully. "Me? That'll be the fair and frosty Friday."

Although I spent so much of my life listening to conversations which I was not meant to overhear, all at once I felt, for the first time, sickened by what I was doing. I left my listening post and tiptoed into Aunt Edna's room. I wondered if someday I would be the one who was doing the talking, while another child would be doing the listening. This gave me an unpleasantly eerie feeling. I tried on Aunt Edna's lipstick and rouge, but my heart was not in it.

When I went downstairs again, Jimmy Lorimer was just leaving. Aunt Edna went to her room and closed the door. After a while she came out and asked me if I would mind sleeping in the spare bedroom that night after all, so that was what I did.

I woke in the middle of the night. When I sat up, feeling strange because I was not in my own bed at home, I saw through the window a glancing light on the snow. I got up and peered out, and there were the northern lights whirling across the top of the sky like lightning that never descended to earth. The yard of the Brick House looked huge, a white desert, and the pale gashing streaks of light pointed up the caverns and the hollowed places where the wind had sculptured the snow.

I could not stand being alone another second, so I walked in my bare feet along the hall. From Grandfather's room came the sound of grumbling snores, and from Grandmother's room no sound at all. I stopped beside the door of Aunt Edna's room. It seemed to me that she would not mind if I entered quietly, so as not to disturb her, and crawled in beside her. Maybe she would even waken and say, "It's okay, kiddo—

your dad phoned after you'd gone to sleep—they got back from Freehold all right."

Then I heard her voice, and the held-in way she was crying, and the name she spoke, as though it hurt her to speak it even in a whisper.

Like some terrified poltergeist, I flitted back to the spare room and whipped into bed. I wanted only to forget that I had heard anything, but I knew I would not forget. There arose in my mind, mysteriously, the picture of a barbaric queen, someone who had lived a long time ago. I could not reconcile this image with the known face, nor could I disconnect it. I thought of my aunt, her sturdy laughter, the way she tore into the housework, her hands and feet which she always disparagingly joked about, believing them to be clumsy. I thought of the story in the scribbler at home. I wanted to get home quickly, so I could destroy it.

Whenever Grandmother Connor was ill, she would not see any doctor except my father. She did not believe in surgery, for she thought it was tampering with the Divine Intention, and she was always afraid that Dr. Cates would operate on her without her consent. She trusted my father implicitly, and when he went into the room where she lay propped up on pillows, she would say, "Here's Ewen—now everything will be fine," which both touched and alarmed my father, who said he hoped she wasn't putting her faith in a broken reed.

Late that winter, she became ill again. She did not go into hospital, so my mother, who had been a nurse, moved down to the Brick House to look after her. My brother and I were left in the adamant care of Grandmother MacLeod. Without my mother, our house seemed like a museum, full of dead and meaningless objects, vases and gilt-framed pictures and looming furniture, all of which had to be dusted and catered to for reasons which everyone had forgotten. I was not allowed to see Grandmother Connor, but every day after school I went to the Brick House to see my mother. I always asked impatiently, "When is Grandmother going to be better?" and my mother would reply, "I don't know, dear. Soon, I hope." But she did not sound very certain, and I imagined the leaden weeks going by like this, with her away, and Grandmother MacLeod poking her head into my bedroom doorway each morning and telling me to be sure to make my bed because a slovenly room meant a slovenly heart.

But the weeks did not go by like this. One afternoon when I arrived at the Brick House, Grandfather Connor was standing out on the front porch. I was startled, because he was not wearing his great bear coat. He wore no coat at all, only his dingy serge suit, although the day was fifteen below zero. The blown snow had sifted onto the porch and lay in thin drifts. He stood there by himself, his yellowish-white hair plumed by a wind which he seemed not to notice, his bony and still-handsome face not averted at all from the winter. He looked at me as I plodded up the path and the front steps.

"Vanessa, your grandmother's dead," he said.

Then, as I gazed at him, unable to take in the significance of what he had said, he did a horrifying thing. He gathered me into the relentless grip of his arms. He bent low over me, and sobbed against the cold skin of my face.

I wanted only to get away, to get as far away as possible and never come back. I wanted desperately to see my mother, yet I felt I could not enter the house, not ever again. Then my mother opened the front door and stood there in the doorway, her slight body shivering. Grandfather released me, straightened, became again the carved face I had seen when I approached the house.

"Father," my mother said. "Come into the house. Please."

"In a while, Beth," he replied tonelessly. "Never you mind."

My mother held out her hands to me, and I ran to her. She closed the door and led me into the living room. We both cried, and yet I think I cried mainly because she did, and because I had been shocked by my grandfather. I still could not believe that anyone I cared about could really die.

Aunt Edna came in to the living room. She hesitated, looking at my mother and me. Then she turned and went back to the kitchen, stumblingly. My mother's hands made hovering movements and she half rose from the chesterfield, then she held me closely again.

"It's worse for Edna," she said. "I've got you and Roddie, and your dad."

I did not fully realise yet that Grandmother Connor would never move around this house again, preserving its uncertain peace somehow. Yet all at once I knew how it would be for Aunt Edna, without her, alone in the Brick House with Grandfather Connor. I had not known at all that a death would be like this, not only one's own pain, but the almost unbearable knowledge of that other pain which could not be reached nor lessened.

My mother and I went out to the kitchen, and the three of us sat around the oilcloth-covered table, scarcely talking but needing one another at least to be there. We heard the front door open, and Grandfather Connor came back into the house. He did not come out to the kitchen, though. He went, as though instinctively, to his old cavern. We heard him walking heavily down the basement steps.

"Edna—should we ask him if he wants to come and have some tea?" my mother said. "I hate to see him going like that—there—"

Aunt Edna's face hardened.

"I don't want to see him, Beth," she replied, forcing the words out. "I can't. Not yet. All I'd be able to think of is how he was—with her."

"Oh honey, I know," my mother said. "But you mustn't let yourself dwell on that now."

"The night Jimmy was here," my aunt said distinctly, "she asked Father to be nice, for her sake. For her sake, Beth. For the sake of all the years, if they'd meant anything at all. But he couldn't even do that. Not even that."

Then she put her head down on the table and cried in a way I had never heard any person cry before, as though there were no end to it anywhere.

I was not allowed to attend Grandmother Connor's funeral, and for this I was profoundly grateful, for I had dreaded going. The day of the funeral, I stayed alone in the Brick House, waiting for the family to return. My Uncle Terence, who lived in Toronto, was the only one who had come from a distance. Uncle Will lived in Florida, and Aunt Florence was in England, both too far away. Aunt Edna and my mother were always criticising Uncle Terence and also making excuses for him. He drank more than was good for him—this was one of the numerous fractured bones in the family skeleton which I was not supposed to know about. I was fond of him for the same reason I was fond of Grandfather's horse-trader brother, my Great-Uncle Dan—because he had gaiety and was publicly reckoned to be no good.

I sat in the dining room beside the gilt-boned cage that housed the canary. Yesterday, Aunt Edna, cleaning here, had said, "What on earth are we going to do with the canary? Maybe we can find somebody who would like it."

Grandfather Connor had immediately lit into her. "Edna, your mother liked that bird, so it's staying, do you hear?"

When my mother and Aunt Edna went upstairs to have a cigarette, Aunt Edna had said, "Well, it's dandy that he's so set on the bird now, isn't it? He might have considered that a few years earlier, if you ask me."

"Try to be patient with him," my mother had said. "He's feeling it, too."

"I guess so," Aunt Edna had said in a discouraged voice. "I haven't got Mother's patience, that's all. Not with him, nor with any man."

And I had been reminded then of the item I had seen not long before in the Winnipeg *Free Press*, on the social page, telling of the marriage of James Reilly Lorimer to Somebody-or-other. I had rushed to my mother with the paper in my hand, and she had said, "I know, Vanessa. She knows, too. So let's not bring it up, eh?"

The canary, as usual, was not in a vocal mood, and I sat beside the cage dully, not caring, not even trying to prod the creature into song. I wondered if Grandmother Connor was at this very moment in heaven, that dubious place.

"She believed, Edna," my mother had said defensively. "What right have we to say it isn't so?"

"Oh, I know," Aunt Edna had replied. "But can you take it in, really, Beth?"

"No, not really. But you feel, with someone like her—it would be so awful if it didn't happen, after she'd thought like that for so long."

"She wouldn't know," Aunt Edna had pointed out.

"I guess that's what I can't accept," my mother had said slowly. "I still feel she must be somewhere."

I wanted now to hold my own funeral service for my grandmother, in the presence only of the canary. I went to the bookcase where she kept her Bible, and looked up Ecclesiastes. I intended to read the part about the mourners going about the streets, and the silver cord loosed and the golden bowl broken, and the dust returning to the earth as it was and the spirit unto God who gave it. But I got stuck on the first few lines, because it seemed to me, frighteningly, that they were being spoken in my grandmother's mild voice—*Remember now thy Creator in the days of thy youth, while the evil days come not—*

Then, with a burst of opening doors, the family had returned from the funeral. While they were taking off their coats, I slammed the Bible shut and sneaked it back into the bookcase without anyone's having noticed.

Grandfather Connor walked over to me and placed his hands on my shoulders, and I could do nothing except endure his touch.

"Vanessa—" he said gruffly, and I had at the time no idea how much it cost him to speak at all, "she was an angel. You remember that."

Then he went down to the basement by himself. No one attempted to follow him, or to ask him to come and join the rest of us. Even I, in the confusion of my lack of years, realised that this would have been an impossibility. He was, in some way, untouchable. Whatever his grief was, he did not want us to look at it and we did not want to look at it, either.

Uncle Terence went straight into the kitchen, brought out his pocket flask, and poured a hefty slug of whiskey for himself. He did the same for my mother and father and Aunt Edna.

"Oh Glory," Aunt Edna said with a sigh, "do I ever need this. All the same, I feel we shouldn't, right immediately afterwards. You know— considering how she always felt about it. Supposing Father comes up—"

"It's about time you quit thinking that way, Edna," Uncle Terence said.

Aunt Edna felt in her purse for a cigarette. Uncle Terence reached over and lit it for her. Her hands were unsteady.

"You're telling me," she said.

Uncle Terence gave me a quizzical and yet resigned look, and I knew then that my presence was placing a constraint upon them. When my father said he had to go back to the hospital, I used his departure to slip upstairs to my old post, the deserted stove-pipe hole. I could no longer eavesdrop with a clear conscience, but I justified it now by the fact that I had voluntarily removed myself from the kitchen, knowing they would not have told me to run along, not today.

"An angel," Aunt Edna said bitterly. "Did you hear what he said to Vanessa? It's a pity he never said as much to Mother once or twice, isn't it?"

"She knew how much he thought of her," my mother said.

"Did she?" Aunt Edna said. "I don't believe she ever knew he cared about her at all. I don't think I knew it myself, until I saw how her death hit him."

"That's an awful thing to say!" my mother cried. "Of course she knew, Edna."

"How would she know," Aunt Edna persisted, "if he never let on?"

"How do you know he didn't?" my mother countered. "When they were by themselves."

"I don't know, of course," Aunt Edna said. "But I have my damn shrewd suspicions."

"Did you ever know, Beth," Uncle Terence enquired, pouring himself another drink, "that she almost left him once? That was before you were born, Edna."

"No," my mother said incredulously. "Surely not."

"Yeh. Aunt Mattie told me. Apparently Father carried on for a while with some girl in Winnipeg, and Mother found out about it. She never told him she'd considered leaving him. She only told God and Aunt Mattie. The three of them thrashed it out together, I suppose. Too bad she never told him. It would've been a relief to him, no doubt, to see she wasn't all calm forgiveness."

"How could he?" my mother said in a low voice. "Oh Terence. How could he have done that? To Mother, of all people."

"You know something, Beth?" Uncle Terence said. "I think he honestly believed that about her being some kind of angel. She'd never have thought of herself like that, so I don't suppose it ever would have occurred to her that he did. But I have a notion that he felt all along she was far and away too good for him. Can you feature going to bed with an angel, honey? It doesn't bear thinking about."

"Terence, you're drunk," my mother said sharply. "As usual."

"Maybe so," he admitted. Then he burst out, "I only felt, Beth, that somebody might have said to Vanessa just now, *Look, baby, she was terrific and we thought the world of her, but let's not say angel, eh?* All this angel business gets us into really deep water, you know that?"

"I don't see how you can talk like that, Terence," my mother said, trying not to cry. "Now all of a sudden everything was her fault. I just don't see how you can."

"I'm not saying it was her fault," Uncle Terence said wearily. "That's not what I meant. Give me credit for one or two brains, Beth. I'm only saying it might have been rough for him, as well, that's all. How do any of us know what he's had to carry on his shoulders? Another person's virtues could be an awful weight to tote around. We all loved her. Whoever loved him? Who in hell could? Don't you think he knew that? Maybe he even thought sometimes it was no more than was coming to him."

"Oh—" my mother said bleakly. "That can't be so. That would be— oh, Terence, do you really think he might have thought that way?"

"I don't know any more than you do, Beth. I think he knew quite well that she had something he didn't, but I'd be willing to bet he always imagined it must be righteousness. It wasn't. It was—well, I guess it was tenderness, really. Unfair as you always are about him, Edna, I think you hit the nail on the head about one thing. I don't believe Mother ever realised he might have wanted her tenderness. Why should she? He could never show any of his own. All he could ever come out with was anger. Well, everybody to his own shield in this family. I guess I carry mine in my hip pocket. I don't know what yours is, Beth, but Edna's is more like his than you might think."

"Oh yeh?" Aunt Edna said, her voice suddenly rough. "What is it, then, if I may be so bold as to enquire?"

"Wisecracks, honey," Uncle Terence replied, very gently. "Just wisecracks."

They stopped talking, and all I could hear was my aunt's uneven breathing, with no one saying a word. Then I could hear her blowing her nose.

"Mercy, I must look like the wreck of the Hesperus," she said briskly. "I'll bet I haven't got a speck of powder left on. Never mind. I'll repair the ravages later. What about putting the kettle on, Beth? Maybe I should go down and see if he'll have a cup of tea now."

"Yes," my mother said. "That's a good idea. You do that, Edna."

I heard my aunt's footsteps on the basement stairs as she went down into Grandfather Connor's solitary place.

Many years later, when Manawaka was far away from me, in miles and in time, I saw one day in a museum the Bear Mask of the Haida Indians. It was a weird mask. The features were ugly and yet powerful. The mouth was turned down in an expression of sullen rage. The eyes were empty caverns, revealing nothing. Yet as I looked, they seemed to draw my own eyes towards them, until I imagined I could see somewhere within that darkness a look which I knew, a lurking bewilderment. I remembered then that in the days before it became a museum piece, the mask had concealed a man.

GABRIEL GARCÍA MÁRQUEZ

(b. 1928)

G abriel García Márquez was born in Aracataca, a small town in Colombia that he was to celebrate as Macondo in One Hundred Years of Solitude (1967). He spent his early life with his maternal grandparents, two gifted storytellers who had a profound influence on the young boy, graduated from a Jesuit school in 1946, and entered law school at the National University in Bogota. His early stories, published in local newspapers, reflect a fascination with other realities and reveal a range of experimental techniques he learned from the great modernists. In the midst of a bloody civil war that was to claim the lives of more than 200 000 Colombians, he became a journalist. He worked in Rome as a foreign correspondent, and wrote a novel in Paris, No One Writes to the Colonel (1961). After working for the Cuban news agency under Castro (García Márquez has always had strong socialist sympathies), he went to Mexico, where he published In Evil Hour (1962) and Big Mama's Funeral (1962), a collection of short stories. He lived in Spain for eight years, publishing more short stories and a novel while working as a journalist for a news magazine. Chronicle of a Death Foretold (1981) and Love in the Time of Cholera (1985) have confirmed his reputation as one of the most popular fiction writers not only in Spanish-speaking countries but in the world. García Márquez's "magic realism" has shown writers a new way forward, and no less a figure than John Barth has praised his work as a successful synthesis of "straightforwardness and artifice, realism and magic and myth, political passion and nonpolitical artistry, characterization and caricature, humor and terror," and called him an "exemplary master of the storyteller's art."

Death Constant Beyond Love

S enator Onésimo Sánchez had six months and eleven days to go before his death when he found the woman of his life. He met her in Rosal del Virrey, an illusory village which by night was the furtive wharf for smugglers' ships, and on the other hand, in broad daylight looked like the most useless inlet on the desert, facing a sea that was arid and without direction and so far from everything no one would have suspected that someone capable of changing the destiny of anyone lived there. Even its name was a kind of joke, because the only rose in that village was being worn by Senator Onésimo Sánchez himself on the same afternoon when he met Laura Farina.

It was an unavoidable stop in the electoral campaign he made every four years. The carnival wagons had arrived in the morning. Then came the trucks with the rented Indians who were carried into the towns in order to enlarge the crowds at public ceremonies. A short time before eleven o'clock, along with the music and rockets and jeeps of the retinue, the ministerial automobile, the color of strawberry soda, arrived. Senator Onésimo Sánchez was placid and weatherless inside the air-conditioned car, but as soon as he opened the door he was shaken by a gust of fire and his shirt of pure silk was soaked in a kind of light-colored soup and he felt many years older and more alone than ever. In real life he had just turned forty-two, had been graduated from Göttingen with honors as a metallurgical engineer, and was an avid reader, although without much reward, of badly translated Latin classics. He was married to a radiant German woman who had given him five children and they were all happy in their home, he the happiest of all until they told him, three months before, that he would be dead forever by next Christmas.

While the preparations for the public rally were being completed, the senator managed to have an hour alone in the house they had set aside for him to rest in. Before he lay down he put in a glass of drinking water the rose he had kept alive all across the desert, lunched on the diet cereals that he took with him so as to avoid the repeated portions of fried goat that were waiting for him during the rest of the day, and he took several analgesic pills before the time prescribed so that he would have the remedy ahead of the pain. Then he put the electric fan close to the hammock and stretched out naked for fifteen minutes in the shadow of the rose, making a great effort at mental distraction so as not to think about death while he dozed. Except for the doctors, no one knew that he had been sentenced to a fixed term, for he had decided to endure his secret all alone, with no change in his life, not because of pride but out of shame.

He felt in full control of his will when he appeared in public again at three in the afternoon, rested and clean, wearing a pair of coarse linen slacks and a floral shirt, and with his soul sustained by the anti-pain pills. Nevertheless, the erosion of death was much more pernicious than he had supposed, for as he went up onto the platform he felt a strange disdain for those who were fighting for the good luck to shake his hand, and he didn't feel sorry as he had at other times for the groups of barefoot Indians who could scarcely bear the hot saltpeter coals of the sterile little square. He silenced the applause with a wave of his hand, almost with rage, and he began to speak without gestures, his eyes fixed on the sea, which was sighing with heat. His measured, deep voice had the quality of calm water, but the speech that had been memorized and ground out so many times had not occurred to him in the nature of telling the truth, but, rather, as the opposite of a fatalistic pronouncement by Marcus Aurelius in the fourth book of his *Meditations*.

"We are here for the purpose of defeating nature," he began, against all his convictions. "We will no longer be foundlings in our own country, orphans of God in a realm of thirst and bad climate, exiles in our own land. We will be different people, ladies and gentlemen, we will be a great and happy people."

There was a pattern to his circus. As he spoke his aides threw clusters of paper birds into the air and the artificial creatures took on life, flew about the platform of planks, and went out to sea. At the same time, other men took some prop trees with felt leaves out of the wagons and planted them in the saltpeter soil behind the crowd. They finished by setting up a cardboard façade with make-believe houses of red brick that had glass windows, and with it they covered the miserable real-life shacks.

The senator prolonged his speech with two quotations in Latin in order to give the farce more time. He promised rainmaking machines, portable breeders for table animals, the oils of happiness which would make vegetables grow in the salt-peter and clumps of pansies in the window boxes. When he saw that his fictional world was all set up, he pointed to it. "That's the way it will be for us, ladies and gentlemen," he shouted. "Look! That's the way it will be for us."

The audience turned around. An ocean liner made of painted paper was passing behind the houses and it was taller than the tallest houses in the artificial city. Only the senator himself noticed that since it had been set up and taken down and carried from one place to another the superimposed cardboard town had been eaten away by the terrible climate and that it was almost as poor and dusty as Rosal del Virrey.

For the first time in twelve years, Nelson Farina didn't go to greet the senator. He listened to the speech from his hammock amidst the remains of his siesta, under the cool bower of a house of unplaned boards which he had built with the same pharmacist's hands with which he had drawn and quartered his first wife. He had escaped from Devil's Island and appeared in Rosal del Virrey on a ship loaded with innocent macaws, with a beautiful and blasphemous black woman he had found in Parama- ribo and by whom he had a daughter. The woman died of natural causes a short while later and she didn't suffer the fate of the other, whose pieces had fertilized her own cauliflower patch, but was buried whole and with her Dutch name in the local cemetery. The daughter had inherited her color and her figure along with her father's yellow and astonished eyes, and he had good reason to imagine that he was rearing the most beautiful woman in the world.

Ever since he had met Senator Onésimo Sánchez during his first electoral campaign, Nelson Farina had begged for his help in getting a false identity card which would place him beyond the reach of the law. The senator, in a friendly but firm way, had refused. Nelson Farina never gave up, and for several years, every time he found the chance, he would repeat his request with a different recourse. But this time he stayed in his hammock, condemned to rot alive in that burning den of buccaneers. When he heard the final applause, he lifted his head, and looking over the boards of the fence, he saw the back side of the farce: the props for the buildings, the framework of the trees, the hidden illusionists who were pushing the ocean liner along. He spat without rancor.

"*Merde*," he said. "*C'est le Blacamán de la politique.*"

After the speech, as was customary, the senator took a walk through the streets of the town in the midst of the music and the rockets and was besieged by the townspeople, who told him their troubles. The senator listened to them good-naturedly and he always found some way to console everybody without having to do them any difficult favors. A woman up on the roof of a house with her six youngest children managed to make herself heard over the uproar and the fireworks.

"I'm not asking for much, Senator," she said. "Just a donkey to haul water from Hanged Man's Well."

The senator noticed the six thin children. "What became of your husband?" he asked.

"He went to find his fortune on the island of Aruba," the woman answered good-humoredly, "and what he found was a foreign woman, the kind that put diamonds on their teeth."

The answer brought on a roar of laughter.

"All right," the senator decided, "you'll get your donkey."

A short while later an aide of his brought a good pack donkey to the woman's house and on the rump it had a campaign slogan written in indelible paint so that no one would ever forget that it was a gift from the senator.

Along the short stretch of street he made other, smaller gestures, and he even gave a spoonful of medicine to a sick man who had had his bed brought to the door of his house so he could see him pass. At the last corner, through the boards of the fence, he saw Nelson Farina in his hammock, looking ashen and gloomy, but nonetheless the senator greeted him, with no show of affection.

"Hello, how are you?"

Nelson Farina turned in his hammock and soaked him in the sad amber of his look.

"*Moi, vous savez*," he said.

His daughter came out into the yard when she heard the greeting. She was wearing a cheap, faded Guajiro Indian robe, her head was decorated with colored bows, and her face was painted as protection against the sun, but even in that state of disrepair it was possible to imagine that there had never been another so beautiful in the whole world. The senator was left breathless. "I'll be damned!" he breathed in surprise. "The Lord does the craziest things!"

That night Nelson Farina dressed his daughter up in her best clothes and sent her to the senator. Two guards armed with rifles who were nodding from the heat in the borrowed house ordered her to wait on the only chair in the vestibule.

The senator was in the next room meeting with the important people of Rosal del Virrey, whom he had gathered together in order to sing for them the truths he had left out of his speeches. They looked so much like all the ones he always met in all the towns in the desert that even the senator himself was sick and tired of that perpetual nightly session. His shirt was soaked with sweat and he was trying to dry it on his body with the hot breeze from an electric fan that was buzzing like a horse fly in the heavy heat of the room.

"We, of course, can't eat paper birds," he said. "You and I know that the day there are trees and flowers in this heap of goat dung, the day there are shad instead of worms in the water holes, that day neither you nor I will have anything to do here, do I make myself clear?"

No one answered. While he was speaking, the senator had torn a sheet off the calendar and fashioned a paper butterfly out of it with his hands. He tossed it with no particular aim into the air current coming from the fan and the butterfly flew about the room and then went out through the half-open door. The senator went on speaking with a control aided by the complicity of death.

"Therefore," he said, "I don't have to repeat to you what you already know too well: that my reelection is a better piece of business for you than it is for me, because I'm fed up with stagnant water and Indian sweat, while you people, on the other hand, make your living from it."

Laura Farina saw the paper butterfly come out. Only she saw it because the guards in the vestibule had fallen asleep on the steps, hugging their rifles. After a few turns, the large lithographed butterfly unfolded completely, flattened against the wall, and remained stuck there. Laura Farina tried to pull it off with her nails. One of the guards, who woke up with the applause from the next room, noticed her vain attempt.

"It won't come off," he said sleepily. "It's painted on the wall."

Laura Farina sat down again when the men began to come out of the meeting. The senator stood in the doorway of the room with his hand on the latch, and he only noticed Laura Farina when the vestibule was empty.

"What are you doing here?"

"*C'est de la part de mon père,*" she said.

The senator understood. He scrutinized the sleeping guards, then he scrutinized Laura Farina, whose unusual beauty was even more demanding than his pain, and he resolved then that death had made his decision for him.

"Come in," he told her.

Laura Farina was struck dumb standing in the doorway to the room: thousands of bank notes were floating in the air, flapping like the butterfly. But the senator turned off the fan and the bills were left without air and alighted on the objects in the room.

"You see," he said, smiling, "even shit can fly."

Laura Farina sat down on a schoolboy's stool. Her skin was smooth and firm, with the same color and the same solar density as crude oil, her hair was the mane of a young mare, and her huge eyes were brighter than the light. The senator followed the thread of her look and finally found the rose, which had been tarnished by the saltpeter.

"It's a rose," he said.

"Yes," she said with a trace of perplexity. "I learned what they were in Riohacha."

The senator sat down on an army cot, talking about roses as he unbuttoned his shirt. On the side where he imagined his heart to be inside his chest he had a corsair's tattoo of a heart pierced by an arrow. He threw the soaked shirt to the floor and asked Laura Farina to help him off with his boots.

She knelt down facing the cot. The senator continued to scrutinize her, thoughtfully, and while she was untying the laces he wondered which one of them would end up with the bad luck of that encounter.

"You're just a child," he said.

"Don't you believe it," she said. "I'll be nineteen in April."

The senator became interested.

"What day?"

"The eleventh," she said.

The senator felt better. "We're both Aries," he said. And smiling, he added:

"It's the sign of solitude."

Laura Farina wasn't paying attention because she didn't know what to do with the boots. The senator, for his part, didn't know what to do with Laura Farina, because he wasn't used to sudden love affairs and, besides, he knew that the one at hand had its origins in indignity. Just to have some time to think, he held Laura Farina tightly between his knees, embraced her about the waist, and lay down on his back on the cot. Then he realized that she was naked under her dress, for her body gave off the dark fragrance of an animal of the woods, but her heart was frightened and her skin disturbed by a glacial sweat.

"No one loves us," he sighed.

Laura Farina tried to say something, but there was only enough air for her to breathe. He laid her down beside him to help her, he put out the light and the room was in the shadow of the rose. She abandoned herself to the mercies of her fate. The senator caressed her slowly, seeking her with his hand, barely touching her, but where he expected to find her, he came across something iron that was in the way.

"What have you got there?"

"A padlock," she said.

"What in hell!" the senator said furiously and asked what he knew only too well. "Where's the key?"

Laura Farina gave a breath of relief.

"My papa has it," she answered. "He told me to tell you to send one of your people to get it and to send along with him a written promise that you'll straighten out his situation."

The senator grew tense. "Frog bastard," he murmured indignantly. Then he closed his eyes in order to relax and he met himself in the darkness. *Remember,* he remembered, *that whether it's you or someone else, it won't be long before you'll be dead and it won't be long before your name won't even be left.*

He waited for the shudder to pass.

"Tell me one thing," he asked then. "What have you heard about me?"

"Do you want the honest-to-God truth?"

"The honest-to-God truth."

"Well," Laura Farina ventured, "they say you're worse than the rest because you're different."

The senator didn't get upset. He remained silent for a long time with his eyes closed, and when he opened them again he seemed to have returned from his most hidden instincts.

"Oh, what the hell," he decided. "Tell your son of a bitch of a father that I'll straighten out his situation."

"If you want, I can go get the key myself," Laura Farina said.

The senator held her back.

"Forget about the key," he said, "and sleep awhile with me. It's good to be with someone when you're so alone."

Then she laid his head on her shoulder with her eyes fixed on the rose. The senator held her about the waist, sank his face into woods-animal armpit, and gave in to terror. Six months and eleven days later he would die in that same position, debased and repudiated because of the public scandal with Laura Farina and weeping with rage at dying without her.

(1970)

JOHN BARTH

(b. 1930)

J   *ohn Barth was born and raised in Cambridge, Maryland, a city on
     that state's eastern shore, an area that provides the setting for much
of his fiction. After a brief period at the Juilliard School of Music, he
enrolled in Johns Hopkins University, where he received a B.A. and an
M.A. in creative writing. He has successfully combined a teaching (Penn
State, State University of New York, Johns Hopkins) and a writing
career. His first two novels, written under the influence of existentialist
philosophy,* The Floating Opera *(1956) and* The End of the Road
*(1958), he wrote in a single year at the age of 25. In the novels of the
early 1960s,* The Sot-Weed Factor *(1960) and* Giles Goat-Boy *(1966),
he set out to parody the premises of the novel and related forms. In* Lost
in the Funhouse *(1968), a collection of short stories, and in* Chimera
*(1972), he plays ingeniously with the conventions of storytelling itself.
In* LETTERS *(1979), a spoof of the epistolary novel, he rewrites the
characters from his early work and updates in complex and hilarious
fashion their lives and relations. His more recent fiction,* Sabbatical
(1982) and Tidewater Tales *(1987), suggests that for Barth what he
once called "The Literature of Exhaustion" has given way to "The
Literature of Replenishment." In an article thus entitled, Barth suggests
that a "worthy program for postmodernist fiction" is to synthesize the
antitheses that have characterized twentieth-century writing:*

> *If the modernists, carrying the load of romanticism, taught us
> that linearity, rationality, consciousness, cause and effect, naive
> illusionism, transparent language, innocent anecdote, and
> moral conventions are not the whole story, then from the per-
> spective of these closing decades of our century we may appreci-
> ate that the contraries of these things are not the whole story
> either. Disjunction, simultaneity, irrationalism, anti-illusion-
> ism, self-reflexiveness, medium-as-message, political olympian-
> ism, and moral pluralism approaching moral entropy—these
> are not the whole story either.*

*Barth's fertile intelligence and marvellous technical skill make him a
writer admirably equipped to effect such a synthesis.*

Lost in the Funhouse

F or whom is the funhouse fun? Perhaps for lovers. For Ambrose it is *a place of fear and confusion.* He has come to the seashore with his family for the holiday, *the occasion of their visit is Independence Day, the most important secular holiday of the United States of America.* A single straight underline is the manuscript mark for italic type, *which in turn* is the printed equivalent to oral emphasis of words and phrases as well as the customary type for titles of complete works, not to mention. Italics are also employed, in fiction stories especially, for "outside," intrusive, or artificial voices, such as radio announcements, the texts of telegrams and newspaper articles, et cetera. They should be used *sparingly*. If passages originally in roman type are italicized by someone repeating them, it's customary to acknowledge the fact. *Italics mine.*

Ambrose was "at that awkward age." His voice came out high-pitched as a child's if he let himself get carried away; to be on the safe side, therefore, he moved and spoke with *deliberate calm* and *adult gravity*. Talking soberly of unimportant or irrelevant matters and listening consciously to the sound of your own voice are useful habits for maintaining control in this difficult interval. *Enroute* to Ocean City he sat in the back seat of the family car with his brother Peter, age fifteen, and Magda G——, age fourteen, a pretty girl and exquisite young lady, who lived not far from them on B—— Street in the town of D——, Maryland. Initials, blanks, or both were often substituted for proper names in nineteenth-century fiction to enhance the illusion of reality. It is as if the author felt it necessary to delete the names for reasons of tact or legal liability. Interestingly, as with other aspects of realism, it is an *illusion* that is being enhanced, by purely artificial means. Is it likely, does it violate the principle of verisimilitude, that a thirteen-year-old boy could make such a sophisticated observation? A girl of fourteen is *the psychological coeval* of a boy of fifteen or sixteen; a thirteen-year-old boy, therefore, even one precocious in some other respects, might be three years *her emotional junior.*

Thrice a year—on Memorial, Independence, and Labor Days—the family visits Ocean City for the afternoon and evening. When Ambrose and Peter's father was their age, the excursion was made by train, as mentioned in the novel *The 42nd Parallel* by John Dos Passos. Many families from the same neighborhood used to travel together, with dependent relatives and often with Negro servants; schoolfuls of children swarmed through the railway cars; everyone shared everyone else's Maryland fried chicken, Virginia ham, deviled eggs, potato salad, beaten biscuits, iced tea. Nowadays (that is, in 19—, the year of our story) the journey is made by automobile—more comfortably and quickly though without the extra fun though without the *camaraderie* of a general excursion. It's all part of the deterioration of American life, their father declares; Uncle Karl supposes that when the boys take *their* families to Ocean City for the holidays they'll fly in Autogiros. Their mother, sitting in the middle of the front seat like Magda in the second, only with her arms on the seat-back behind the men's shoulders, wouldn't want the good old days back again, the steaming trains and stuffy long dresses; on the other hand she can do without Autogiros, too, if she has to become a grandmother to fly in them.

Description of physical appearance and mannerisms is one of several standard methods of characterization used by writers of fiction. It is also important to "keep the senses operating"; when a detail from one of the five senses, say visual, is "crossed" with a detail from another, say auditory, the reader's imagination is oriented to the scene, perhaps unconsciously. This procedure may be compared to the way surveyors and navigators determine their positions by two or more compass bearings, a process known as triangulation. The brown hair on Ambrose's mother's forearms gleamed in the sun like. Though right-handed, she took her left arm from the seat-back to press the dashboard cigar lighter for Uncle Karl. When the glass bead in its handle glowed red, the lighter was ready for use. The smell of Uncle Karl's cigar smoke reminded one of. The fragrance of the ocean came strong to the picnic ground where they always stopped for lunch, two miles inland from Ocean City. Having to pause for a full hour almost within sound of the breakers was difficult for Peter and Ambrose when they were younger; even at their present age it was not easy to keep their anticipation, *stimulated by the briny spume*, from turning into short temper. The Irish author James Joyce, in his unusual novel entitled *Ulysses*, now available in this country, uses the adjectives *snot-green* and *scrotum-tightening* to describe the sea. Visual; auditory; tactile; olfactory; gustatory. Peter and Ambrose's father, while steering their black 1936 LaSalle sedan with one hand, could with the other remove the first cigarette from a white pack of Lucky Strikes and, more remarkably, light it with a match forefingered from its book and thumbed against the flint paper without being detached. The matchbook cover merely advertised U. S. War Bonds and Stamps. A fine metaphor, simile, or other figure of speech, in addition to its obvious "first-order" relevance to the thing it describes, will be seen upon reflection to have a second order of significance: it may be drawn from the *milieu* of the action, for example, or be particularly appropriate to the sensibility of the narrator, even hinting to the reader things of which the narrator is unaware; or it may cast further and subtler lights upon the things it describes, sometimes ironically qualifying the more evident sense of the comparison.

To say that Ambrose's and Peter's mother was *pretty* is to accomplish nothing; the reader may acknowledge the proposition, but his imagination is not engaged. Besides, Magda was also pretty, yet in an altogether different way. Although she lived on B—— Street she had very good manners and did better than average in school. Her figure was very well developed for her age. Her right hand lay casually on the plush upholstery of the seat, very near Ambrose's left leg, on which his own hand rested. The space between their legs, between her right and his left leg, was out of the line of sight of anyone sitting on the other side of Magda, as well as anyone glancing into the rear-view mirror. Uncle Karl's face resembled Peter's—rather, vice versa. Both had dark hair and eyes, short husky statures, deep voices. Magda's left hand was probably in a similar position on her left side. The boy's father is difficult to describe; no particular feature of his appearance or manner stood out. He wore glasses and was principal of a T—— County grade school. Uncle Karl was a masonry contractor.

Although Peter must have known as well as Ambrose that the latter, because of his position in the car, would be the first to see the electrical towers of the power plant at V——, the halfway point of their trip, he leaned forward and slightly toward the center of the car and pretended to be looking for them through the flat pinewoods and tuckahoe creeks along the highway. For as long as the boys could remember "looking for the Towers" had been a feature of the first half of their excursions to Ocean City, "looking for the standpipe" of the second. Though the game was childish, their mother preserved the tradition of rewarding the first to see the Towers with a candy-bar or piece of fruit. She insisted now that Magda play the game; the prize she said, was "something hard to get nowadays." Ambrose decided not to join in; he sat far back in his seat. Magda, like Peter, leaned forward. Two sets of straps were discernible through the shoulders of her sun dress; the inside right one, a brassiere-strap, was fastened or shortened with a small safety pin. The right armpit of her dress, presumably the left as well, was damp with perspiration. The simple strategy for being first to espy the Towers, which Ambrose had understood by the age of four, was to sit on the right-hand side of the car. Whoever sat there, however, had also to put up with the worst of the sun, and so Ambrose, without mentioning the matter, chose sometimes the one and sometimes the other. Not impossibly Peter had never caught on to the trick, or thought that his brother hadn't simply because Ambrose on occasion preferred shade to a Baby Ruth or tangerine.

The shade-sun situation didn't apply to the front seat, owing to the windshield; if anything the driver got more sun, since the person on the passenger side not only was shaded below by the door and dashboard but might swing down his sunvisor all the way too.

"Is that them?" Magda asked. Ambrose's mother teased the boys for letting Magda win, insinuating that "somebody [had] a girlfriend." Peter and Ambrose's father reached a long thin arm across their mother to butt his cigarette in the dashboard ashtray, under the lighter. The prize this time for seeing the Towers first was a banana. Their mother bestowed it after chiding their father for wasting a half-smoked cigarette when everything was so scarce. Magda, to take the prize, moved her hand from so near Ambrose's that he could have touched it as though accidentally. She offered to share the prize, things like that were so hard to find; but everyone insisted it was hers alone. Ambrose's mother sang an iambic trimeter couplet from a popular song, femininely rhymed:

> "What's good is in the Army;
> What's left will never harm me."

Uncle Karl tapped his cigar ash out the ventilator window; some particles were sucked by the slipstream back into the car through the rear window on the passenger side. Magda demonstrated her ability to hold a banana in one hand and peel it with her teeth. She still sat forward; Ambrose pushed his glasses back onto the bridge of his nose with his left hand, which he then negligently let fall to the seat cushion immediately behind her. He even permitted the single hair, gold, on the second joint of his thumb to brush the fabric of her skirt. Should she have sat back at that instant, his hand would have been caught under her.

Plush upholstery prickles uncomfortably through gabardine slacks in the July sun. The function of the *beginning* of a story is to introduce the principal characters, establish their initial relationships, set the scene for the main action, expose the background of the situation if necessary, plant motifs and foreshadowings where appropriate, and initiate the first complication or whatever of the "rising action." Actually, if one imagines a story called "The Funhouse," or "Lost in the Funhouse," the details of the drive to Ocean City don't seem especially relevant. The *beginning* should recount the events between Ambrose's first sight of the funhouse early in the afternoon and his entering it with Magda and Peter in the evening. The *middle* would narrate all relevant events from the time he goes in to the time he loses his way; middles have the double and contradictory function of delaying the climax while at the same time preparing the reader for it and fetching him to it: Then the *ending* would tell what Ambrose does while he's lost, how he finally finds his way out, and what everybody makes of the experience. So far there's been no real dialogue, very little sensory detail, and nothing in the way of a *theme*. And a long time has gone by already without anything happening; it makes a person wonder. We haven't even reached Ocean City yet: we will never get out of the funhouse.

The more closely an author identifies with the narrator, literally or metaphorically, the less advisable it is, as a rule, to use the first-person narrative viewpoint. Once three years previously the young people *afore-mentioned* played Niggers and Masters in the backyard; when it was Ambrose's turn to be Master and theirs to be Niggers Peter had to go serve his evening papers; Ambrose was afraid to punish Magda alone, but she led him to the whitewashed Torture Chamber between the wood-shed and the privy in the Slaves Quarters; there she knelt sweating among bamboo rakes and dusty Mason jars, pleadingly embraced his knees, and while bees droned in the lattice as if on an ordinary summer afternoon, purchased clemency at a surprising price set by herself. Doubt-less she remembered nothing of this event; Ambrose on the other hand seemed unable to forget the least detail of his life. He even recalled how, standing beside himself with awed impersonality in the reeky heat, he'd stared the while at an empty cigar box in which Uncle Karl kept stone-cutting chisels: beneath the words *El Producto* a laureled, loose-toga'd lady regarded the sea from a marble bench; beside her, forgotten or not yet turned to, was a five-stringed lyre. Her chin reposed on the back of her right hand; her left depended negligently from the bench arm. The lower half of the scene and lady was peeled away; the words EXAMINED BY ____ were inked there into the wood. Nowadays cigar boxes are made of pasteboard. Ambrose wondered what Magda would have done, Ambrose wondered what Magda would do when she sat back on his hand as he resolved she should. Be angry. Make a teasing joke of it. Give no sign at all. For a long time she leaned forward, playing cow-poker with Peter against Uncle Karl and Mother and watching for the first sign of Ocean City. At nearly the same instant, picnic ground and Ocean City standpipe hove into view; an Amoco filling station on their side of the road cost Mother and Uncle Karl fifty cows and the game; Magda bounced back, clapping her right hand on Mother's right arm; Ambrose moved clear "in the nick of time."

At this rate our hero, at this rate our protagonist will remain in the funhouse forever. Narrative ordinarily consists of alternating dramatiza-tion and summarization. One symptom of nervous tension, paradoxically, is repeated and violent yawning; neither Peter nor Magda nor Uncle Karl nor Mother reacted in this manner. Although they were no longer small children, Peter and Ambrose were each given a dollar to spend on board-walk amusements in addition to what money of their own they'd brought along. Magda too, though she protested she had ample spending money. The boys' mother made a little scene out of distributing the bills; she pretended that her sons and Magda were small children and cautioned them not to spend the sum too quickly or in one place. Magda promised with a merry laugh and, having both hands free, took the bill with her left. Peter laughed also and pledged in a falsetto to be a good boy. His imitation of a child was not clever. The boys' father was tall and thin, balding, fair-complexioned. Assertions of that sort are not effective; the reader may acknowledge the proposition, but. We should be much farther along than we are; something has gone wrong; not much of this preliminary rambling seems relevant. Yet everyone begins in the same place; how is it that most go along without difficulty but a few lose their way?

"Stay out from under the boardwalk," Uncle Karl growled from the side of his mouth. The boys' mother pushed his shoulder *in mock annoyance*. They were all standing before Fat May the Laughing Lady who advertised the funhouse. Larger than life, Fat May mechanically shook, rocked on her heels, slapped her thighs, while recorded laughter— uproarious, female—came amplified from a hidden loudspeaker. It chuckled, wheezed, wept; tried in vain to catch its breath; tittered, groaned, exploded raucous and anew. You couldn't hear it without laughing yourself, no matter how you felt. Father came back from talking to a Coast-Guardsman on duty and reported that the surf was spoiled with crude oil from tankers recently torpedoed offshore. Lumps of it, difficult to remove, made tarry tidelines on the beach and stuck on swimmers. Many bathed in the surf nevertheless and came out speckled; others paid to use a municipal pool and only sunbathed on the beach. We would do the latter. We would do the latter. We would do the latter.

Under the boardwalk, matchbook covers, grainy other things. What is the story's theme? Ambrose is ill. He perspires in the dark passages; candied applies-on-a-stick, delicious-looking, disappointing to eat. Funhouses need men's and ladies' rooms at intervals. Others perhaps have also vomited in corners and corridors; may even have had bowel movements liable to be stepped in in the dark. The word *fuck* suggests suction and/or and/or flatulence. Mother and Father; grandmothers and grandfathers on both sides; great-grandmothers and great-grandfathers on four sides, et cetera. Count a generation as thirty years: in approximately the year when Lord Baltimore was granted charter to the province of Maryland by Charles I, five hundred twelve women—English, Welsh, Bavarian, Swiss—of every class and character, received into themselves the penises the intromittent organs of five hundred twelve men, ditto, in every circumstance and posture, to conceive the five hundred twelve ancestors of the two hundred fifty-six ancestors of the et cetera et cetera et cetera et cetera et cetera et cetera et cetera of the author, of the narrator, of this story, *Lost in the Funhouse*. In alleyways, ditches, canopy beds, pinewoods, bridal suites, ship's cabins, coach-and-fours, coaches-and-four, sultry toolsheds; on the cold sand under boardwalks, littered with *El Producto* cigar butts, treasured with Lucky Strike cigarette stubs, Coca-Cola caps, gritty turds, cardboard lollipop sticks, matchbook covers warning that A Slip of the Lip Can Sink a Ship. The shluppish whisper, continuous as seawash round the globe, tidelike falls and rises with the circuit of dawn and dusk.

Magda's teeth. She *was* left-handed. Perspiration. They've gone all the way, through, Magda and Peter, they've been waiting for hours with Mother and Uncle Karl while Father searches for his lost son; they draw french-fried potatoes from a paper cup and shake their heads. They've named the children they'll one day have and bring to Ocean City on holidays. Can spermatozoa properly be thought of as male animalcules when there are no female spermatozoa? They grope through hot, dark windings, past Love's Tunnel's fearsome obstacles. Some perhaps lose their way.

Peter suggested then and there that they do the funhouse; he had been through it before, so had Magda, Ambrose hadn't and suggested, his voice cracking on account of Fat May's laughter, that they swim first. All were chuckling, couldn't help it; Ambrose's father, Ambrose's and Peter's father came up grinning like a lunatic with two boxes of syrup-coated popcorn, one for Mother, one for Magda; the men were to help themselves. Ambrose walked on Magda's right; being by nature left-handed, she carried the box in her left hand. Up front the situation was reversed.

"What are you limping for?" Magda inquired of Ambrose. He supposed in a husky tone that his foot had gone to sleep in the car. Her teeth flashed. "Pins and needles?" It was the honeysuckle on the lattice of the former privy that drew the bees. Imagine being stung there. How long is this going to take?

The adults decided to forego the pool; but Uncle Karl insisted they change into swimsuits and do the beach. "He wants to watch the pretty girls," Peter teased, and ducked behind Magda from Uncle Karl's pretended wrath. "You've got all the pretty girls you need right here," Magda declared, and Mother said: "Now that's the gospel truth." Magda scolded Peter, who reached over her shoulder to sneak some popcorn. "Your brother and father aren't getting any." Uncle Karl wondered if they were going to have fireworks that night, what with the shortages. It wasn't the shortages, Mr. M ____ replied; Ocean City had fireworks from pre-war. But it was too risky on account of the enemy submarines, some people thought.

"Don't seem like Fourth of July without fireworks," said Uncle Karl. The inverted tag in dialogue writing is still considered permissible with proper names or epithets, but sounds old-fashioned with personal pronouns. "We'll have 'em again soon enough," predicted the boys' father. Their mother declared she could do without fireworks: they reminded her too much of the real thing. Their father said all the more reason to shoot off a few now and again. Uncle Karl asked *rhetorically* who needed reminding, just look at people's hair and skin.

"The oil, yes," said Mrs. M ____.

Ambrose had a pain in his stomach and so didn't swim but enjoyed watching the others. He and his father burned red easily. Magda's figure was exceedingly well developed for her age. She too declined to swim, and got mad, and became angry when Peter attempted to drag her into the pool. She always swam, he insisted; what did she mean not swim? Why did a person come to Ocean City?

"Maybe I want to lay here with Ambrose," Magda teased.

Nobody likes a pedant.

"Aha," said Mother. Peter grabbed Magda by one ankle and ordered Ambrose to grab the other. She squealed and rolled over on the beach blanket. Ambrose pretended to help hold her back. Her tan was darker than even Mother's and Peter's. "Help out, Uncle Karl!" Peter cried. Uncle Karl went to seize the other ankle. Inside the top of her swimsuit, however, you could see the line where the sunburn ended and, when she hunched her shoulders and squealed again, one nipple's auburn edge. Mother made them behave themselves. "*You* should certainly know," she said to Uncle Karl. Archly. "That when a lady says she doesn't feel like swimming, a gentleman doesn't ask questions." Uncle Karl said excuse *him*; Mother winked at Magda; Ambrose blushed; stupid Peter kept saying "Phooey on *feel like!*" and tugging at Magda's ankle; then even he got the point, and cannon-balled with a holler into the pool.

"I swear," Magda said, in mock *in feigned* exasperation.

The diving would make a suitable literary symbol. To go off the high board you had to wait in a line along the poolside and up the ladder. Fellows tickled girls and goosed one another and shouted to the ones on the top to hurry up, or razzed them for bellyfloppers. Once on the springboard some took a great while posing or clowning or deciding on a dive or getting up their nerve; others ran right off. Especially among the younger fellows the idea was to strike the funniest pose or do the craziest stunt as you fell; a thing that got harder to do as you kept on and kept on. But whether you hollered *Geronimo!* or *Sieg heil!*, held your nose or "rode a bicycle," pretended to be shot or did a perfect jackknife or changed your mind halfway down and ended up with nothing, it was over in two seconds, after all that wait. Spring, pose, splash. Spring, neat-o, splash. Spring, awe fooey, splash.

The grown-ups had gone on; Ambrose wanted to converse with Magda; she was remarkably well developed for her age; it was said that that came from rubbing with a turkish towel, and there were other theories. Ambrose could think of nothing to say except how good a diver Peter was, who was showing off for her benefit. You could pretty well tell by looking at their bathing suits and arm muscles how far along the different fellows were. Ambrose was glad he hadn't gone in swimming, the cold water shrank you up so. Magda pretended to be uninterested in the diving; she probably weighed as much as he did. If you knew your way around in the funhouse like your own bedroom, you could wait until a girl came along and then slip away without ever getting caught, even if her boyfriend was right with her. She'd think *he* did it! It would be better to be the boyfriend, and act outraged, and tear the funhouse apart.

Not act; *be*.

"He's a master diver," Ambrose said. In feigned admiration. "You really have to slave away at it to get that good." What would it matter anyhow if he asked her right out whether she remembered, even teased her with it as Peter would have?

There's no point in going farther; this isn't getting anybody anywhere; they haven't even come to the funhouse yet. Ambrose is off the track, in some new or old part of the place that's not supposed to be used; he strayed into it by some one-in-a-million chance, like the time the roller coaster car left the tracks in the nineteen-teens against all the laws of physics and sailed over the boardwalk in the dark. And they can't locate him because they don't know where to look. Even the designer and operator have forgotten this other part, that winds around on itself like a whelk shell. That winds around the right part like the snakes on Mercury's caduceus. Some people, perhaps, don't "hit their stride" until their twenties, when the growing-up business is over and women appreciate other things besides wisecracks and teasing and strutting. Peter didn't have one-tenth the imagination *he* had, not one-tenth. Peter did this naming-their-children thing as a joke, making up names like Aloysius and Murgatroyd, but Ambrose knew *exactly* how it would feel to be married and have children of your own, and be a loving husband and father, and go comfortably to work in the mornings and to bed with your wife at night, and wake up with her there. With a breeze coming through the sash and birds and mockingbirds singing in the Chinese-cigar trees. His eyes watered, there aren't enough ways to say that. He would be quite famous in his line of work. Whether Magda was his wife or not, one evening when he was wise-lined and gray at the temples he'd smile gravely, at a fashionable dinner party, and remind her of his youthful passion. The time they went with his family to Ocean City; the *erotic fantasies* he used to have about her. How long ago it seemed, and childish! Yet tender, too, *n'est-ce pas?* Would she have imagined that the world-famous whatever remembered how many strings were on the lyre on the bench beside the girl on the label of the cigar box he'd stared at in the toolshed at age ten while she, age eleven. Even then he had felt *wise beyond his years*; he'd stroked her hair and said in his deepest voice and correctest English, as to a dear child: "I shall never forget this moment."

But though he had breathed heavily, groaned as if ecstatic, what he'd really felt throughout was an odd detachment, as though some one else were Master. Strive as he might to be transported, he heard his mind take notes upon the scene: *This is what they call passion. I am experiencing it.* Many of the digger machines were out of order in the penny arcades and could not be repaired or replaced for the duration. Moreover the prizes, made now in USA, were less interesting than formerly, pasteboard items for the most part, and some of the machines wouldn't work on white pennies. The gypsy fortune-teller machine might have provided a foreshadowing of the climax of this story if Ambrose had operated it. It was even dilapidateder than most: the silver coating was worn off the brown metal handles, the glass windows around the dummy were cracked and taped, her kerchiefs and silks long-faded. If a man lived by himself, he could take a department-store mannequin with flexible joints and modify her in certain ways. *However*: by the time he was that old he'd have a real woman. There was a machine that stamped your name around a white-metal coin with a star in the middle: A ____. His son would be the second, and when the lad reached thirteen or so he would put a strong arm around his shoulder and tell him calmly: "It is perfectly normal. We have all been through it. It will not last forever." Nobody knew how to be what they were right. He'd smoke a pipe, teach his son how to fish and softcrab, assure him he needn't worry about himself. Magda would certainly give, Magda would certainly yield a great deal of milk, although guilty of occasional solecisms. It don't taste so bad. Suppose the lights came on now!

The day wore on. You think you're yourself, but there are other persons in you. Ambrose gets hard when Ambrose doesn't want to, *and obversely*. Ambrose watches them disagree; Ambrose watches him watch. In the funhouse mirror-room you can't see yourself go on forever, because no matter how you stand, your head gets in the way. Even if you had a glass periscope, the image of your eye would cover up the thing you really wanted to see. The police will come; there'll be a story in the papers. That must be where it happened. Unless he can find a surprise exit, an unofficial backdoor or escape hatch opening on an alley, say, and then stroll up to the family in front of the funhouse and ask where everybody's been; *he's* been out of the place for ages. That's just where it happened, in that last lighted room: Peter and Magda found the right exit; he found one that you weren't supposed to find and strayed off into the works somewhere. In a perfect funhouse you'd be able to go only one way, like the divers off the highboard; getting lost would be impossible; the doors and halls would work like minnow traps or the valves in veins.

On account of German U-boats, Ocean City was "browned out": streetlights were shaded on the seaward side; shop-windows and board-walk amusement places were kept dim, not to silhouette tankers and Liberty-ships for torpedoing. In a short story about Ocean City, Maryland, during World War II, the author could make use of the image of sailors on leave in the penny arcades and shooting galleries, sighting through the crosshairs of toy machine guns at swastika'd subs, while out in the black Atlantic a U-boat skipper squints through his periscope at real ships outlined by the glow of penny arcades. After dinner the family strolled back to the amusement end of the boardwalk. The boys' father had burnt red as always and was masked with Noxema, a minstrel in reverse. The grown-ups stood at the end of the boardwalk where the Hurricane of '33 had cut an inlet from the ocean to Assawoman Bay.

"Pronounced with a long *o*," Uncle Karl reminded Magda with a wink. His shirt sleeves were rolled up; Mother punched his brown biceps with the arrowed heart on it and said his mind was naughty. Fat May's laugh came suddenly from the funhouse, as if she'd just got the joke; the family laughed too at the coincidence. Ambrose went under the board-walk to search for out-of-town matchbook covers with the aid of his pocket flashlight; he looked out from the edge of the North American continent and wondered how far their laughter carried over the water. Spies in rubber rafts; survivors in lifeboats. If the joke had been beyond his understanding, he could have said: *"The laughter was over his head."* And let the reader see the serious wordplay on second reading.

He turned the flashlight on and then off at once even before the woman whooped. He sprang away, heart athud, dropping the light. What had the man grunted? Perspiration drenched and chilled him by the time he scrambled up to the family. "See anything?" his father asked. His voice wouldn't come; he shrugged and violently brushed sand from his pants legs.

"Let's ride the old flying horses!" Magda cried. I'll never be an author. It's been forever already, everybody's gone home, Ocean City's deserted, the ghost-crabs are tickling across the beach and down the littered cold streets. And the empty halls of clapboard hotels and abandoned fun-houses. A tidal wave; an enemy air raid; a monster-crab swelling like an island from the sea. *The inhabitants fled in terror.* Magda clung to his trouser leg; he alone knew the maze's secret. "He gave his life that we might live," said Uncle Karl with a scowl of pain, as he. The fellow's hands had been tattooed; the woman's legs, the woman's fat white legs had. *An astonishing coincidence.* He yearned to tell Peter. He wanted to throw up for excitement. They hadn't even chased him. He wished he were dead.

One possible ending would be to have Ambrose come across another lost person in the dark. They'd match their wits together against the funhouse, struggle like Ulysses past obstacle after obstacle, help and encourage each other. Or a girl. By the time they found the exit they'd be closest friends, sweethearts if it were a girl; they'd know each other's inmost souls, be bound together *by the cement of shared adventure;* then they'd emerge into the light and it would turn out that his friend was a Negro. A blind girl. President Roosevelt's son. Ambrose's former archenemy.

Shortly after the mirror room he'd groped along a musty corridor, his heart already misgiving him at the absence of phosphorescent arrows and other signs. He's found a crack of light—not a door, it turned out, but a seam between the plyboard wall panels—and squinting up to it, espied a small old man, *in appearance not unlike* the photographs at home of Ambrose's late grandfather, nodding upon a stool beneath a bare, speckled bulb. A crude panel of toggle- and knife-switches hung beside the open fuse box near his head; elsewhere in the little room were wooden levers and ropes belayed to boat cleats. At the time, Ambrose wasn't lost enough to rap or call; later he couldn't find that crack. Now it seemed to him that he'd possibly dozed off for a few minutes somewhere along the way; certainly he was exhausted from the afternoon's sunshine and the evening's problems; he couldn't be sure he hadn't dreamed part or all of the sight. Had an old black wall fan droned like bees and shimmied two flypaper streamers? Had the funhouse operator—gentle, somewhat sad and tired-appearing, in expression not unlike the photographs at home of Ambrose's late Uncle Konrad—murmured in his sleep? Is there really such a person as Ambrose, or is he a figment of the author's imagination? Was it Assawoman Bay or Sinepuxent? Are there other errors of fact in this fiction? Was there another sound besides the little slap slap of thigh on ham, like water sucking at the chine-boards of a skiff?

When you're lost, the smartest thing to do is stay put till you're found, hollering if necessary. But to holler guarantees humiliation as well as rescue; keeping silent permits some saving of face—you can act surprised at the fuss when your rescuers find you and swear you weren't lost, if they do. What's more you might find your own way yet, *however belatedly*.

"Don't tell me your foot's still asleep!" Magda exclaimed as the three young people walked from the inlet to the area set aside for ferris wheels, carrousels, and other carnival rides, they having decided in favor of the vast and ancient merry-go-round instead of the funhouse. What a sentence, everything was wrong from the outset. People don't know what to make of him, he doesn't know what to make of himself, he's only thirteen, *athletically and socially inept*, not astonishingly bright, but there are antennae; he has . . . some sort of receivers in his head; things speak to him, he understands more than he should, the world winks at him through its objects, grabs grinning at his coat. Everybody else is in on some secret he doesn't know; they've forgotten to tell him. Through simple *procrastination* his mother put off his baptism until this year. Everyone else had it done as a baby; he'd assumed the same of himself, as had his mother, so she claimed, until it was time for him to join Grace Methodist-Protestant and the oversight came out. He was mortified, but pitched sleepless through his private catechizing, intimidated by the ancient mysteries, a thirteen year old would never say that, resolved to experience conversion like St. Augustine. When the water touched his brow and Adam's sin left him, he contrived by a strain like defecation to bring tears into his eyes—but felt nothing. There was some simple, radical difference about him; he hoped it was genius, feared it was madness, devoted himself to amiability and inconspicuousness. Alone on the sea-wall near his house he was seized by the terrifying transports he'd thought to find in toolshed, in Communion-cup. The grass was alive! The town, the river, himself, were not imaginary; time roared in his ears like wind; the world was *going on*! This part ought to be dramatized. The Irish author James Joyce once wrote. Ambrose M ——— is going to scream.

There is no *texture of rendered sensory detail*, for one thing. The faded distorting mirrors beside Fat May; the impossibility of choosing a mount when one had but a single ride on the great carrousel; the *vertigo attendant on his recognition* that Ocean City was worn out, the place of fathers and grandfathers, straw-boatered men and parasoled ladies survived by their amusements. Money spent, the three paused at Peter's insistence beside Fat May to watch the girls get their skirts blown up. The object was to tease Magda, who said: "I swear, Peter M ——, you've got a one-track mind! Amby and me aren't *interested* in such things." In the tumbling-barrel, too, just inside the Devil's-mouth entrance to the funhouse, the girls were upended and their boyfriends and others could see up their dresses if they cared to. Which was the whole point, Ambrose realized. Of the entire funhouse! If you looked around, you noticed that almost all the people on the boardwalk were paired off into couples except the small children; in a way, that was the whole point of Ocean City! If you had X-ray eyes and could see everything going on at that instant under the boardwalk and in all the hotel rooms and cars and alleyways, you'd realize that all that normally *showed*, like restaurants and dance halls and clothing and test-your-strength machines, was merely preparation and intermission. Fat May screamed.

Because he watched the goings-on from the corner of his eye, it was Ambrose who spied the half-dollar on the boardwalk near the tumbling-barrel. Losers weepers. The first time he'd heard some people moving through a corridor not far away, just after he'd lost sight of the crack of light, he'd decided not to call to them, for fear they'd guess he was scared and poke fun; it sounded like roughnecks; he'd hoped they'd come by and he could follow in the dark without their knowing. Another time he'd heard just one person, unless he imagined it, bumping along as if on the other side of the plywood; perhaps Peter coming back for him, or Father, or Magda lost too. Or the owner and operator of the funhouse. He'd called out once, as though merrily: "Anybody know where the heck we are?" But the query was too stiff, his voice cracked, when the sounds stopped he was terrified: maybe it was a queer who waited for fellows to get lost, or a longhaired filthy monster that lived in some cranny of the funhouse. He stood rigid for hours it seemed like, scarcely respiring. His future was shockingly clear, in outline. He tried holding his breath to the point of unconsciousness. There ought to be a button you could push to end your life absolutely without pain; disappear in a flick, like turning out a light. He would push it instantly! He despised Uncle Karl. But he despised his father too, for not being what he was supposed to be. Perhaps his father hated *his* father, and so on, and his son would hate him, and so on. Instantly!

Naturally he didn't have nerve enough to ask Magda to go through the funhouse with him. With incredible nerve and to everyone's surprise he invited Magda, quietly and politely, to go through the funhouse with him. "I warn you, I've never been through it before," he added, *laughing easily*; "but I reckon we can manage somehow. The important thing to remember, after all, is that it's meant to be a *fun*house; that is, a place of amusement. If people really got lost or injured or too badly frightened in it, the owner'd go out of business. There'd even be lawsuits. No character in a work of fiction can make a speech this long without interruption or acknowledgment from the other characters."

Mother teased Uncle Karl: "Three's a crowd, I always heard." But actually Ambrose was relieved that Peter now had a quarter too. Nothing was what it looked like. Every instant, under the surface of the Atlantic Ocean, millions of living animals devoured one another. Pilots were falling in flames over Europe; women were being forcibly raped in the South Pacific. His father should have taken him aside and said: "There is a simple secret to getting through the funhouse, as simple as being first to see the Towers. Here it is. Peter does not know it; neither does your Uncle Karl. You and I are different. Not surprisingly, you've often wished you weren't. Don't think I haven't noticed how unhappy your childhood has been! But you'll understand, when I tell you, why it had to be kept secret until now. And you won't regret not being like your brother and your uncle. *On the contrary!*" If you knew all the stories behind all the people on the boardwalk, you'd see that *nothing* was what it looked like. Husbands and wives often hated each other; parents didn't necessarily love their children; et cetera. A child took things for granted because he had nothing to compare his life to and everybody acted as if things were as they should be. Therefore each saw himself as the hero of the story, when the truth might turn out to be that he's the villain, or the coward. And there wasn't one thing you could do about it!

Hunchbacks, fat ladies, fools—that no one chose what he was was unbearable. In the movies he'd meet a beautiful young girl in the funhouse; they'd have hairs-breadth escapes from real dangers; he'd do and say the right things; she also; in the end they'd be lovers; their dialogue lines would match up; he'd be perfectly at ease; she'd not only like him well enough, she'd think he was *marvelous*; she'd lie awake thinking about *him*, instead of vice versa—the way *his* face looked in different lights and how he stood and exactly what he'd said—and yet that would be only one small episode in his wonderful life, among many many others. Not a *turning point* at all. What had happened in the toolshed was nothing. He hated, he loathed his parents! One reason for not writing a lost-in-the-funhouse story is that either everybody's felt what Ambrose feels, in which case it goes without saying, or else no normal person feels such things, in which case Ambrose is a freak. "Is anything more tiresome, in fiction, than the problems of sensitive adolescents?" And it's all too long and rambling, as if the author. For all a person knows the first time through, the end could be just around the corner; perhaps, *not impossibly* it's been within reach any number of times. On the other hand he may be scarcely past the start, with everything yet to get through, an intolerable idea.

Fill in: His father's raised eyebrows when he announced his decision to do the funhouse with Magda. Ambrose understands now, but didn't then, that his father was wondering whether he knew what the funhouse was *for*—especially since he didn't object, as he should have, when Peter decided to come along too. The ticket-woman, witchlike, mortifying him when inadvertently he gave her his name-coin instead of the half-dollar, then unkindly calling Magda's attention to the birthmark on his temple: "Watch out for him, girlie, he's a marked man!" She wasn't even cruel, he understood, only vulgar and insensitive. Somewhere in the world there was a young woman with such splendid understanding that she'd see him entire, like a poem or story, and find his words so valuable after all that when he confessed his apprehensions she would explain why they were in fact the very things that made him precious to her . . . and to Western Civilization! There was no such girl, the simple truth being. Violent yawns as they approached the mouth. Whispered advice from an old-timer on a bench near the barrel: "Go crabwise and ye'll get an eyeful without upsetting!" Composure vanished at the first pitch: Peter hollered joyously, Magda tumbled, shrieked, clutched her skirt; Ambrose scrambled crabwise, tight-lipped with terror, was soon out, watched his dropped name-coin slide among the couples. Shamefaced he saw that to get through expeditiously was not the point; Peter feigned assistance in order to trip Magda up, shouted "I see Christmas!" when her legs went flying. The old man, his latest betrayer, cackled approval. A dim hall then of black-thread cobwebs and recorded gibber: he took Magda's elbow to steady her against revolving discs set in the slanted floor to throw your feet out from under, and explained to her in a calm, deep voice his theory that each phase of the funhouse was triggered either automatically, by a series of photoelectric devices, or else manually by operators stationed at peepholes. But he lost his voice thrice as the discs unbalanced him; Magda was anyhow squealing; but at one point she clutched him about the waist to keep from falling, and her right cheek pressed for a moment against his belt-buckle. Heroically he drew her up, it was his chance to clutch her close as if for support and say: "I love you." He even put an arm lightly about the small of her back before a sailor-and-girl pitched into them from behind, sorely treading his left big toe and knocking Magda asprawl with them. The sailor's girl was a string-haired hussy with a loud laugh and light blue drawers; Ambrose realized that he wouldn't have said "I love you" anyhow, and was smitten with self-contempt. How much better it would be to be that common sailor! A wiry little Seaman 3rd, the fellow squeezed a girl to each side and stumbled hilarious into the mirror room, closer to Magda in thirty seconds than Ambrose had got in thirteen years. She giggled at something the fellow said to Peter; she drew her hair from her eyes with a movement so womanly it struck Ambrose's heart; Peter's smacking her backside then seemed particularly coarse. But Magda made a pleased indignant face and cried, "All right for *you*, mister!" and pursued Peter into the maze without a backward glance. The sailor followed after, leisurely, drawing his girl against his hip; Ambrose understood not only that they were all so relieved to be rid of his burdensome company that they didn't even notice his absence, but that he himself shared their relief. Stepping from the treacherous passage at last into the mirror-maze, he saw once again, more clearly than ever, how readily he deceived himself into supposing he was a person. He even foresaw, wincing at his dreadful self-knowledge, that he would repeat the deception, at ever-rarer intervals, all his wretched life, so fearful were the alternatives. Fame, madness, suicide; perhaps all three. It's not believable that so young a boy could articulate that reflection, and in fiction the merely true must always yield to the plausible. Moreover, the symbolism is in places heavy-footed. Yet Ambrose M ____ understood, as few adults do, that the famous loneliness of the great was no popular myth but a general truth—furthermore, that it was as much cause as effect.

All the preceding except the last few sentences is exposition that should've been done earlier or interspersed with the present action instead of lumped together. No reader would put up with so much with such *prolixity*. It's interesting that Ambrose's father, though presumably an intelligent man (as indicated by his role as grade-school principal), neither encouraged nor discouraged his sons at all in any way—as if he either didn't care about them or cared all right but didn't know how to act. If this fact should contribute to one of them's becoming a celebrated but wretchedly unhappy scientist, was it a good thing or not? He too might someday face the question; it would be useful to know whether it had tortured his father for years, for example, or never once crossed his mind.

In the maze two important things happened. First, our hero found a name-coin someone else had lost or discarded: *AMBROSE*, suggestive of the famous lightship and of his late grandfather's favorite dessert, which his mother used to prepare on special occasions out of coconut, oranges, grapes, and what else. Second, as he wondered at the endless replication of his image in the mirrors, second, as he *lost himself in the reflection* that the necessity for an observer makes perfect observation impossible, better make him eighteen at least, yet that would render other things unlikely, he heard Peter and Magda chuckling somewhere together in the maze. "Here!" "No, here!" they shouted to each other; Peter said, "Where's Amby?" Magda murmured. "Amb?" Peter called. In a pleased, friendly voice. He didn't reply. The truth was, his brother was a *happy-go-lucky youngster* who'd've been better off with a regular brother of his own, but who seldom complained of his lot and was generally cordial. Ambrose's throat ached; there aren't enough different ways to say that. He stood quietly while the two young people giggled and thumped through the glittering maze, hurrah'd their discovery of its exit, cried out in joyful alarm at what next beset them. Then he set his mouth and followed after, as he supposed, took a wrong turn, strayed into the pass *wherein he lingers yet.*

The action of conventional dramatic narrative may be represented by a diagram called Freitag's Triangle:

$$\begin{array}{ccc} & B & \\ A & & C \end{array}$$

or more accurately by a variant of that diagram:

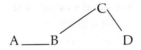

in which *AB* represents the exposition, *B* the introduction of conflict, *BC* the "rising action," complication, or development of the conflict, *C* the climax, or turn of the action, *CD* the dénouement, or resolution of the conflict. While there is no reason to regard this pattern as an absolute necessity, like many other conventions it became conventional because great numbers of people over many years learned by trial and error that it was effective; one ought not to forsake it, therefore, unless one wishes to forsake as well the effect of drama or has clear cause to feel that deliberate violation of the "normal" pattern can better can better effect that effect. This can't go on much longer; it can go on forever. He died telling stories to himself in the dark; years later, when that vast unsuspected area of the funhouse came to light, the first expedition found his skeleton in one of its labyrinthine corridors and mistook it for part of the entertainment. He died of starvation telling himself stories in the dark; but unbeknownst unbeknownst to him, an assistant operator of the funhouse, happening to overhear him, crouched just behind the plyboard partition and wrote down his every word. The operator's daughter, an exquisite young woman with a figure unusually well developed for her age, crouched just behind the partition and transcribed his every word. Though she had never laid eyes on him, she recognized that here was one of Western Culture's truly great imaginations, the eloquence of whose suffering would be an inspiration to unnumbered. And her heart was torn between her love for the misfortunate young man (yes, she loved him, though she had never laid though she knew him only—but how well!—through his words, and the deep, calm voice in which he spoke them) between her love et cetera and her womanly intuition that only in suffering and isolation could he give voice et cetera. Lone dark dying. Quietly she kissed the rough plyboard, and a tear fell upon the page. Where she had written in shorthand *Where she had written in shorthand* Where she had written in shorthand *Where she* et cetera. A long time ago we should have passed the apex of Freitag's Triangle and made brief work of the *dénouement;* the plot doesn't rise by meaningful steps but winds upon itself, digresses, retreats, hesitates, sighs, collapses, expires. The climax of the story must be its protagonist's discovery of a way to get through the funhouse. But he had found none, may have ceased to search.

What relevance does the war have to the story? Should there be fireworks outside or not?

Ambrose wandered, languished, dozed. Now and then he fell into his habit of rehearsing to himself the unadventurous story of his life, narrated from the third-person point of view, from his earliest memory parenthesis of maple leaves stirring in the summer breath of tidewater Maryland end of parenthesis to the present moment. Its principal events, on this telling, would appear to have been *A, B, C,* and *D.*

He imagined himself years hence, successful, married, at ease in the world, the trials of his adolescence far behind him. He has come to the seashore with his family for the holiday: how Ocean City has changed! But at one seldom at one ill-frequented end of the boardwalk a few derelict amusements survive from times gone by: the great carrousel from the turn of the century, with its monstrous griffins and mechanical concert band; the roller coaster rumored since 1916 to have been condemned; the mechanical shooting gallery in which only the image of our enemies changed. His own son laughs with Fat May and wants to know what a funhouse is; Ambrose hugs the sturdy lad close and smiles around his pipestem at his wife.

The family's going home. Mother sits between Father and Uncle Karl, who teases him good-naturedly who chuckles over the fact that the comrade with whom he'd fought his way shoulder to shoulder through the funhouse had turned out to be a blind Negro girl—to their mutual discomfort, as they'd opened their souls. But such are the walls of custom, which even. Whose arm is where? How must it feel. He dreams of a funhouse vaster by far than any yet constructed; but by then they may be out of fashion, like steamboats and excursion trains. Already quaint and seedy: the draperied ladies on the frieze of the carrousel are his father's father's mooncheeked dreams; if he thinks of it more he will vomit his apple-on-a-stick.

He wonders: will he become a regular person? Something has gone wrong; his vaccination didn't take; at the Boy-Scout initiation campfire he only pretended to be deeply moved, as he pretends to this hour that it is not so bad after all in the funhouse, and that he has a little limp. How long will it last? He envisions a truly astonishing funhouse, incredibly complex yet utterly controlled from a great central switchboard like the console of a pipe organ. Nobody had enough imagination. He could design such a place himself, wiring and all, and he's only thirteen years old. He would be its operator: panel lights would show what was up in every cranny of its cunning of its multifarious vastness; a switch-flick would ease this fellow's way, complicate that's, to balance things out; if anyone seemed lost or frightened, all the operator had to do was.

He wishes he had never entered the funhouse. But he has. Then he wishes he were dead. But he's not. Therefore he will construct funhouses for others and be their secret operator—though he would rather be among the lovers for whom funhouses are designed.

DONALD BARTHELME

(1931–1989)

*D*onald Barthelme was born in Philadelphia, the son of an architect who became a professor of architectural design at the University of Houston. Stimulated by the intellectual environment his father moved in, Barthelme decided at a very early age to become a writer. He studied journalism at university and worked for the Houston Post, mostly writing reviews. He founded a literary journal, then became director of the Contemporary Arts Museum in Houston at the age of 30. He published his first story in The New Yorker two years later and became a semipermanent contributor to its fiction columns. The recipient of numerous literary awards, he taught creative writing courses at many American universities. He published three novels, Snow White (1967), The Dead Father (1975), and Paradise (1987), and eight collections of short stories, of which the best known are Come Back, Dr. Caligari (1964), Unspeakable Practices, Unnatural Acts (1968), and Sixty Stories (1981). Barthelme's fiction challenges readers with a randomness that is born of the postmodern writer's attempt to find new forms for fiction. He mixes styles, tones, fictional devices, and formulas. His work is often parodic or satiric but the general sense of play militates against the reader's taking anything too seriously. As Charles Molesworth suggests: "In a society committed to change and upward mobility the only recourse for writers is to create some form of romance, even if it is based on failed desires, with only junk as the signs of reality. Barthelme's double-mindedness suggests that there are only desires and fantasies, and they are never to be satisfied."

Captain Blood

W hen Captain Blood goes to sea, he locks the doors and windows of his house on Cow Island personally. One never knows what sort of person might chance by, while one is away.

When Captain Blood, at sea, paces the deck, he usually paces the foredeck rather than the afterdeck—a matter of personal preference. He keeps marmalade and a spider monkey in his cabin, and four perukes on stands.

When Captain Blood, at sea, discovers that he is pursued by the Dutch Admiral Van Tromp, he considers throwing the women overboard. So that they will drift, like so many giant lotuses in their green, lavender, purple, and blue gowns, across Van Tromp's path, and he will have to stop and pick them up. Blood will have the women fitted with life jackets under their dresses. They will hardly be in much danger at all. But what about the jaws of sea turtles? No, the women cannot be thrown overboard. Vile, vile! What an idiotic idea! What could he have been thinking of? Of the patterns they would have made floating on the surface of the water, in the moonlight, a cerise gown, a silver gown . . .

Captain Blood presents a façade of steely imperturbability.

He is poring over his charts, promising everyone that things will get better. There has not been one bit of booty in the last eight months. Should he try another course? Another ocean? The men have been quite decent about the situation. Nothing has been said. Still, it's nerve-wracking.

When Captain Blood retires for the night (leaving orders that he be called instantly if something comes up) he reads, usually. Or smokes, thinking calmly of last things.

His hideous reputation should not, strictly speaking, be painted in the horrible colors customarily employed. Many a man walks the streets of Panama City, or Port Royal, or San Lorenzo, alive and well, who would have been stuck through the gizzard with a rapier, or smashed in the brain with a boarding pike, had it not been for Blood's swift, cheerful intervention. Of course, there are times when severe measures are unavoidable. At these times he does not flinch, but takes appropriate action with admirable steadiness. There are no two ways about it: when one looses a seventy-four-gun broadside against the fragile hull of another vessel, one gets carnage.

Blood at dawn, a solitary figure pacing the foredeck.

No other sail in sight. He reaches into the pocket of his blue velvet jacket trimmed with silver lace. His hand closes over three round, white objects: mothballs. In disgust, he throws them over the side. One *makes* one's luck, he thinks. Reaching into another pocket, he withdraws a folded parchment tied with ribbon. Unwrapping the little packet, he finds that it is a memo that he wrote to himself ten months earlier. *"Dolphin,* Captain Darbraunce, 120 tons, cargo silver, paprika, bananas, sailing Mar. 10 Havana. *Be there!"* Chuckling, Blood goes off to seek his mate, Oglethorpe—that laughing blond giant of a man.

Who will be aboard this vessel which is now within cannon-shot? wonders Captain Blood. Rich people, I hope, with pretty gold and silver things aplenty.

"Short John, where is Mr. Oglethorpe?"

"I am not Short John, sir. I am John-of-Orkney."

"Sorry, John. Has Mr. Oglethorpe carried out my instructions?"

"Yes, sir. He is forward, crouching over the bombard, lit cheroot in hand, ready to fire."

"Well, fire then."

"Fire."

BAM!

"The other captain doesn't understand what is happening to him!"

"He's not heaving to!"

"He's ignoring us!"

"The dolt!"

"Fire again!"

BAM!

"That did it!"

"He's turning into the wind!"

"He's dropped anchor!"

"He's lowering sail!"

"Very well, Mr. Oglethorpe. You may prepare to board."

"Very well, Peter."

"And Jeremy—"

"Yes, Peter?"

"I know we've had rather a thin time of it these last few months."

"Well it hasn't been so bad, Peter. A little slow, perhaps—"

"Well, before we board, I'd like you to convey to the men my appreciation for their patience. Patience and, I may say, tact."

"We knew you'd turn up something, Peter."

"Just tell them for me, will you?"

Always a wonderful moment, thinks Captain Blood. Preparing to
board. Pistol in one hand, naked cutlass in the other. Dropping lightly to
the deck of the engrappled vessel, backed by one's grinning, leering,
disorderly, rapacious crew who are nevertheless under the strictest buccaneer discipline. There to confront the little band of fear-crazed victims
shrinking from the entirely possible carnage. Among them, several beautiful women, but one really spectacular beautiful woman who stands a bit
apart from her sisters, clutching a machete with which she intends, against
all reason, to—

When Captain Blood celebrates the acquisition of a rich prize, he goes
down to the galley himself and cooks *tallarínes a la catalána* (noodles, spare
ribs, almonds, pine nuts) for all hands. The name of the captured vessel
is entered in a little book along with the names of all the others he has
captured in a long career. Here are some of them: the *Oxford*, the *Luis*,
the *Fortune*, the *Lambe*, the *Jamaica Merchant*, the *Betty*, the *Prosperous*, the
Endeavor, the *Falcon*, the *Bonadventure*, the *Constant Thomas*, the *Marquesa*,
the *Señora del Carmen*, the *Recovery*, the *María Gloriosa*, the *Virgin Queen*,
the *Esmeralda*, the *Havana*, the *San Felipe*, the *Steadfast* . . .

The true buccaneer is not persuaded that God is not on his side, too—
especially if, as is often the case, he turned pirate after some monstrously
unjust thing was done to him, such as being press-ganged into one or
another of the Royal Navies when he was merely innocently having a

drink at a waterfront tavern, or having been confined to the stinking dungeons of the Inquisition just for making some idle, thoughtless, light remark. Therefore, Blood feels himself to be devout *in his own way*, and has endowed candles burning in churches in most of the great cities of the New World. Although not under his own name.

Captain Blood roams ceaselessly, making daring raids. The average raid yields something like 20,000 pieces-of-eight, which is apportioned fairly among the crew, with wounded men getting more according to the gravity of their wounds. A cut ear is worth two pieces, a *cut-off* ear worth ten to twelve. The scale of payments for injuries is posted in the forecastle.

When he is on land, Blood is confused and troubled by the life of cities, where every passing stranger may, for no reason, assault him, if the stranger so chooses. And indeed, the stranger's mere presence, multiplied many times over, is a kind of assault. Merely having to *take into account* all these hurrying others is a blistering occupation. This does not happen on a ship, or on a sea.

An amusing incident: Captain Blood has overhauled a naval vessel, has caused her to drop anchor (on this particular voyage he is sailing with three other ships under his command and a total enlistment of nearly one thousand men), and is now interviewing the arrested captain in his cabin full of marmalade jars and new perukes.

"And what may your name be, sir? If I may ask?"

"Jones, sir."

"What kind of a name is that? English, I take it?"

"No, it's American, sir."

"American? What is an American?"

"America is a new nation among the nations of the world."

"I've not heard of it. Where is it?"

"North of here, north and west. It's a very small nation, at present, and has only been a nation for about two years."

"But the name of your ship is French."

"Yes it is. It is named in honor of Benjamin Franklin, one of our American heroes."

"*Bon Homme Richard?* What has that to do with Benjamin or Franklin?"

"Well it's an allusion to an almanac Dr. Franklin published called—"

"You weary me, sir. You are captured, American or no, so tell me— do you surrender, with all your men, fittings, cargo, and whatever?"

"Sir, I have not yet begun to fight."

"Captain, this is madness. We have you completely surrounded. Furthermore there is a great hole in your hull below the waterline where our warning shot, which was slightly miscalculated, bashed in your timbers. You are taking water at a fearsome rate. And still you wish to fight?"

"It is the pluck of us Americans, sir. We are just that way. Our tiny nation has to be pluckier than most if it is to survive among the bigger, older nations of the world."

"Well, bless my soul, Jones, you are the damnedest goatsucker I ever did see. Stab me if I am not tempted to let you go scot-free, just because of your amazing pluck."

"No sir, I insist on fighting. As founder of the American naval tradition, I must set a good example."

"Jones, return to your vessel and be off."

"No, sir, I will fight to the last shred of canvas, for the honor of America."

"Jones, even in America, wherever it is, you must have encountered the word 'ninny.' "

"Oh. I see. Well then. I think we'll be weighing anchor, Captain, with your permission."

"Choose your occasions, Captain. And God be with you."

Blood, at dawn, a solitary figure pacing the foredeck. The world of piracy is wide, and at the same time, narrow. One can be gallant all day long, and still end up with a spider monkey for a wife. And what does his mother think of him?

The favorite dance of Captain Blood is the grave and haunting Catalonian *sardana*, in which the participants join hands facing each other to form a ring which gradually becomes larger, then smaller, then larger again. It is danced without smiling, for the most part. He frequently dances this with his men, in the middle of the ocean, after lunch, to the music of a single silver trumpet.

ALICE MUNRO

(b. 1931)

A lice Munro was born in Wingham, Ontario. She studied English for two years at the University of Western Ontario before moving first to Vancouver and then to Victoria, British Columbia, where she ran a bookstore with her husband. She currently lives on a farm near Clinton, Ontario. Her first collection of short stories, Dance of the Happy Shades *(1968), won the Governor General's Award. She has followed this with a book every few years, comprised mostly of stories first published in* The New Yorker: Something I've Been Meaning to Tell You *(1974);* Who Do You Think You Are? *(1978), which also won the Governor General's Award and was runner-up for Britain's most prestigious literary award, the Booker Prize;* The Moons of Jupiter *(1982);* The Progress of Love *(1986), which was among a handful of best books of the year selected by the* New York Times; *and* Friend of My Youth *(1990). The title of her one novel,* Lives of Girls and Women *(1971), summarizes the enduring subject of her short stories. In them she describes in photographic detail the appearance of both the characters and their environment and explores the deeper emotional lives of women of all ages. In an interview with novelist Graeme Gibson, she described her fascination with surfaces this way: "I'm not a writer who is very concerned with ideas. I'm very, very excited by what you might call the surface of life. . . . It seems to me very important to be able to get at the exact tone or texture of how things are." Munro's stories evoke worlds (most often the world of small-town southwestern Ontario) that are at once familiar and estranging in the ways they can suddenly tilt characters and readers, and sometimes even the narrator herself, into radically different perspectives on the events that touch their lives.*

Who Do You Think You Are?

T here were some things Rose and her brother Brian could safely talk about, without running aground on principles or statements of position, and one of them was Milton Homer. They both remembered that when they had measles and there was a quarantine notice put up on the door — this was long ago, before their father died and before Brian went to school — Milton Homer came along the street and read it. They heard him coming over the bridge and as usual he was complaining loudly. His progress through town was not silent unless his mouth was full of candy; otherwise he would be yelling at dogs and bullying the trees and telephone poles, mulling over old grievances.

"And I did not and I did not and I did not!" he yelled, and hit the bridge railing.

Rose and Brian pulled back the quilt that was hung over the window to keep the light out, so they would not go blind.

"Milton Homer," said Brian appreciatively.

Milton Homer then saw the notice on the door. He turned and mounted the steps and read it. He could read. He would go along the main street reading all the signs out loud.

Rose and Brian remembered this and they agreed that it was the side door, where Flo later stuck on the glassed-in porch; before that there was only a slanting wooden platform, and they remembered Milton Homer standing on it. If the quarantine notice was there and not on the front door, which led into Flo's store, then the store must have been open; that seemed odd, and could only be explained by Flo's having bullied the Health Officer. Rose couldn't remember; she could only remember Milton Homer on the platform with his big head on one side and his fist raised to knock.

"Measles, huh?" said Milton Homer. He didn't knock after all; he stuck his head close to the door and shouted, "Can't scare me!" Then he turned around but did not leave the yard. He walked over to the swing, sat down, took hold of the ropes and began moodily, then with mounting and ferocious glee, to give himself a ride.

"Milton Homer's on the swing, Milton Homer's on the swing!" Rose shouted. She had run from the window to the stairwell.

Flo came from wherever she was to look out the side window.

"He won't hurt it," said Flo surprisingly. Rose had thought she would chase him with the broom. Afterwards she wondered: could Flo have been frightened? Not likely. It would be a matter of Milton Homer's privileges.

"I can't sit on the seat after Milton Homer's sat on it!"

"You! You go on back to bed."

Rose went back into the dark smelly measles room and began to tell Brian a story she thought he wouldn't like.

"When you were a baby, Milton Homer came and picked you up."

"He did not."

"He came and held you and asked what your name was. I remember."

Brian went out to the stairwell.

"Did Milton Homer come and pick me up and ask what my name was? Did he? When I was a baby?"

"You tell Rose he did the same for her."

Rose knew that was likely, though she hadn't been going to mention it. She didn't really know if she remembered Milton Homer holding Brian, or had been told about it. Whenever there was a new baby in a house, in that recent past when babies were still being born at home, Milton Homer came as soon as possible and asked to see the baby, then asked its name, and delivered a set speech. The speech was to the effect that if the baby lived, it was to be hoped it would lead a Christian life, and if it died, it was to be hoped it would go straight to Heaven. The same idea as baptism, but Milton did not call on the Father or the Son or do any business with water. He did all this on his own authority. He seemed to be overcome by a stammer he did not have at other times, or else he stammered on purpose in order to give his pronouncements more weight. He opened his mouth wide and rocked back and forth, taking up each phrase with a deep grunt.

"And *if* the Baby — *if* the Baby — *if* the Baby — *lives* —"

Rose would do this years later, in her brother's living room, rocking back and forth, chanting, each *if* coming out like an explosion, leading up to the major explosion of *lives*.

"He will live a — good life — and he will — and he will — *not* sin. He will lead a *good life* — a *good life* — and he will *not sin*. He will *not sin!*"

"And if the baby — if the baby — if the baby — *dies* —"

"Now that's enough. That's enough, Rose," said Brian, but he laughed. He could put up with Rose's theatrics when they were about Hanratty.

"How can you remember?" said Brian's wife Phoebe, hoping to stop Rose before she went on too long and roused Brian's impatience. "Did you see him do it? That often?"

"Oh no," said Rose, with some surprise. "I didn't see him do it. What I saw was Ralph Gillespie *doing* Milton Homer. He was a boy in school. Ralph."

Milton Homer's other public function, as Rose and Brian remembered it, was to march in parades. There used to be plenty of parades in Hanratty. The Orange Walk, on the Twelfth of July; the High School Cadet Parade, in May; the schoolchildren's Empire Day Parade, the Legion's Church Parade, the Santa Claus Parade, the Lions Club Old-Timers' Parade. One of the most derogatory things that could be said about anyone in Hanratty was that he or she was fond of parading around, but almost every soul in town — in the town proper, not West Hanratty, that goes without saying — would get a chance to march in public in some organized and approved affair. The only thing was that you must never look as if you were enjoying it; you had to give the impression of being called forth out of preferred obscurity, ready to do your duty and gravely preoccupied with whatever notions the parade celebrated.

The Orange Walk was the most splendid of all the parades. King Billy at the head of it rode a horse as near pure white as could be found, and the Black Knights at the rear, the noblest rank of Orangemen — usually thin, and poor, and proud and fanatical old farmers — rode dark horses and wore the ancient father-to-son top hats and swallow-tail coats. The banners were all gorgeous silks and embroideries, blue and gold, orange and white, scenes of Protestant triumph, lilies and open bibles, mottoes of godliness and honor and flaming bigotry. The ladies came beneath their sunshades, Orangemen's wives and daughters all wearing white for purity. Then the bands, the fifes and drums, and gifted step-dancers performing on a clean hay-wagon as a movable stage.

Also, there came Milton Homer. He could show up anywhere in the parade and he varied his place in it from time to time, stepping out behind King Billy or the Black Knights or the step-dancers or the shy orange-sashed children who carried the banners. Behind the Black Knights he would pull a dour face, and hold his head as if a top hat was riding on it; behind the ladies he wiggled his hips and diddled an imaginary sunshade. He was a mimic of ferocious gifts and terrible energy. He could take the step-dancers' tidy show and turn it into an idiot's prance, and still keep the beat.

The Orange Walk was his best opportunity, in parades, but he was conspicuous in all of them. Head in the air, arms whipping out, snootily in step, he marched behind the commanding officer of the Legion. On Empire Day he provided himself with a Red Ensign and a Union Jack, and kept them going like whirligigs above his head. In the Santa Claus parade he snatched candy meant for children; he did not do it for a joke.

You would think that somebody in authority in Hanratty would have put an end to this. Milton Homer's contribution to any parade was wholly negative; designed, if Milton Homer could have designed anything, just to make the parade look foolish. Why didn't the organizers and the paraders make an effort to keep him out? They must have decided that was easier said than done. Milton lived with his two old-maid aunts, his parents being dead, and nobody would have liked to ask the two old ladies to keep him home. It must have seemed as if they had enough on their hands already. How could they keep him in, once he had heard the band? They would have to lock him up, tie him down. And nobody wanted to haul him out and drag him away once things began. His protests would have ruined everything. There wasn't any doubt that he would protest. He had a strong, deep voice and he was a strong man, though not very tall. He was about the size of Napoleon. He had kicked through gates and fences when people tried to shut him out of their yards. Once he had smashed a child's wagon on the sidewalk, simply because it was in his way. Letting him participate must have seemed the best choice, under the circumstances.

Not that it was done as the best of bad choices. Nobody looked askance at Milton in a parade; everybody was used to him. Even the

Commanding Officer would let himself be mocked, and the Black Knights with their old black grievances took no notice. People just said, "Oh, there's Milton," from the sidewalk. There wasn't much laughing at him, though strangers in town, city relatives invited to watch the parade, might point him out and laugh themselves silly, thinking he was there officially and for purposes of comic relief, like the clowns who were actually young businessmen, unsuccessfully turning cartwheels.

"Who is that?" the visitors said, and were answered with nonchalance and a particularly obscure sort of pride.

"That's just Milton Homer. It wouldn't be a parade without Milton Homer."

"The village idiot," said Phoebe, trying to comprehend these things, with her inexhaustible unappreciated politeness, and both Rose and Brian said that they had never heard him described that way. They had never thought of Hanratty as a village. A village was a cluster of picturesque houses around a steepled church on a Christmas card. Villagers were the costumed chorus in the high school operetta. If it was necessary to describe Milton Homer to an outsider, people would say that he was "not all there." Rose had wondered, even at that time, what was the part that wasn't there? She still wondered. Brains, would be the easiest answer. Milton Homer must surely have had a low I.Q. Yes; but so did plenty of people, in Hanratty and out of it, and they did not distinguish themselves as he did. He could read without difficulty, as shown in the case of the quarantine sign; he knew how to count his change, as evidenced in many stories about how people had tried to cheat him. What was missing was a sense of precaution, Rose thought now. Social inhibition, though there was no such name for it at that time. Whatever it is that ordinary people lose when they are drunk, Milton Homer never had, or might have chosen not to have — and this is what interests Rose — at some point early in life. Even his expressions, his everyday looks, were those that drunks wear in theatrical extremity — goggling, leering, drooping looks that seemed boldly calculated, and at the same time helpless, involuntary; is such a thing possible?

The two ladies Milton Homer lived with were his mother's sisters. They were twins; their names were Hattie and Mattie Milton, and they were usually called Miss Hattie and Miss Mattie, perhaps to detract from any silly sound their names might have had otherwise. Milton had been named after his mother's family. That was a common practice, and there was probably no thought of linking together the names of two great poets. That coincidence was never mentioned and was perhaps not noticed. Rose did not notice it until one day in high school when the boy who sat behind her tapped her on the shoulder and showed her what he had written in his English book. He had stroked out the word *Chapman's* in the title of a poem and inked in the word *Milton*, so that the title now read: *On First Looking into Milton Homer.*

Any mention of Milton Homer was a joke, but this changed title was also a joke because it referred, rather weakly, to Milton Homer's more scandalous behavior. The story was that when he got behind somebody in a line-up at the Post Office or a movie theater, he would open his coat and present himself, then lunge and commence rubbing. Though of course he wouldn't get that far; the object of his passion would have ducked out of his way. Boys were said to dare each other to get him into position, and stay close ahead of him until the very last moment, then jump aside and reveal him in dire importunity.

It was in honor of this story — whether it was true or not, had happened once, under provocation, or kept happening all the time — that ladies crossed the street when they saw Milton coming, that children were warned to stay clear of him. *Just don't let him monkey around* was what Flo said. He was allowed into houses on those ritual occasions when there was a new baby — with hospital births getting commoner, those occasions diminished — but at other times the doors were locked against him. He would come and knock, and kick the door panels, and go away. But he was let have his way in yards, because he didn't take things, and could do so much damage if offended.

Of course, it was another story altogether when he appeared with one of his aunts. At those times he was hangdog-looking, well-behaved; his powers and his passions, whatever they were, all banked and hidden. He would be eating candy the aunt had bought him, out of a paper bag. He offered it when told to, though nobody but the most greedy person alive would touch what might have been touched by Milton Homer's fingers or blessed by his spittle. The aunts saw that he got his hair cut; they did their best to keep him presentable. They washed and ironed and mended his clothes, sent him out in his raincoat and rubbers, or knitted cap and muffler, as the weather indicated. Did they know how he conducted himself when out of their sight? They must have heard, and if they heard they must have suffered, being people of pride and Methodist morals. It was their grandfather who had started the flax mill in Hanratty and compelled all his employees to spend their Saturday nights at a Bible Class he himself conducted. The Homers, too, were decent people. Some of the Homers were supposed to be in favor of putting Milton away but the Milton ladies wouldn't do it. Nobody suggested they refused out of tender-heartedness.

"They won't put him in the Asylum, they're too proud."

Miss Hattie Milton taught at the high school. She had been teaching there longer than all the other teachers combined and was more important than the Principal. She taught English — the alteration in the poem was the more daring and satisfying because it occurred under her nose — and the thing she was famous for was keeping order. She did this without apparent effort, through the force of her large-bosomed, talcumed, spectacled, innocent and powerful presence, and her refusal to see that there was any difference between teen-agers (she did not use the word) and students in Grade Four. She assigned a lot of memory work. One day she wrote a long poem on the board and said that everyone was to copy it out, then learn it off by heart, and the next day recite it. This was when Rose was in her third or fourth year at high school and she did not believe these instructions were to be taken literally. She learned poetry with ease; it seemed reasonable to her to skip the first step. She read the poem and learned it, verse by verse, then said it over a couple of times in her head. While she was doing this Miss Hattie asked her why she wasn't copying.

Rose replied that she knew the poem already, though she was not perfectly sure that this was true.

"Do you really?" said Miss Hattie. "Stand up and face the back of the room."

Rose did so, trembling for her boast.

"Now recite the poem to the class."

Rose's confidence was not mistaken. She recited without a hitch. What did she expect to follow? Astonishment, and compliments, and unaccustomed respect?

"Well, you may know the poem," Miss Hattie said, "but that is no excuse for not doing what you were told. Sit down and write it in your book. I want you to write every line three times. If you don't get finished you can stay after four."

Rose did have to stay after four, of course, raging and writing while Miss Hattie got out her crocheting. When Rose took the copy to her desk Miss Hattie said mildly enough but with finality, "You can't go thinking you are better than other people just because you can learn poems. Who do you think you are?"

This was not the first time in her life Rose had been asked who she thought she was; in fact the question had often struck her like a monotonous gong and she paid no attention to it. But she understood, afterwards, that Miss Hattie was not a sadistic teacher; she had refrained from saying what she now said in front of the class. And she was not vindictive; she was not taking revenge because she had not believed Rose and had been proved wrong. The lesson she was trying to teach here was more important to her than any poem, and one she truly believed Rose needed. It seemed that many other people believed she needed it, too.

The whole class was invited, at the end of the senior year, to a lantern slide show at the Miltons' house. The lantern slides were of China, where Miss Mattie, the stay-at-home twin, had been a missionary in her youth. Miss Mattie was very shy, and she stayed in the background, working the slides, while Miss Hattie commented. The lantern slides showed a yellow country, much as expected. Yellow hills and sky, yellow people, rickshaws, parasols, all dry and papery-looking, fragile, unlikely, with black zigzags where the paint had cracked, on the temples, the roads and faces. At this very time, the one and only time Rose sat in the Miltons' parlor, Mao was in power in China and the Korean War was underway, but Miss Hattie made no concessions to history, any more than she made concessions to the fact that the members of her audience were eighteen and nineteen years old.

"The Chinese are heathens," Miss Hattie said. "That is why they have beggars."

There was a beggar, kneeling in the street, arms outstretched to a rich lady in a rickshaw, who was not paying attention to him.

"They do eat things we wouldn't touch, " Miss Hattie said. Some Chinese were pictured poking sticks into bowls. "But they eat a better diet when they become Christians. The first generation of Christians is an inch and a half taller."

Christians of the first generation were standing in a row with their mouths open, possibly singing. They wore black and white clothes.

After the slides, plates of sandwiches, cookies, tarts were served. All were home-made and very good. A punch of grape juice and ginger-ale was poured into paper cups. Milton sat in a corner in his thick tweed suit, a white shirt and a tie, on which punch and crumbs had already been spilled.

"Some day it will just blow up in their faces," Flo had said darkly, meaning Milton. Could that be the reason people came, year after year, to see the lantern slides and drink the punch that all the jokes were about? To see Milton with his jowls and stomach swollen as if with bad intentions, ready to blow? All he did was stuff himself at an unbelievable rate. It seemed as if he downed date squares, hermits, Nanaimo bars and fruit drops, butter tarts and brownies, whole, the way a snake will swallow frogs. Milton was similarly distended.

Methodists were people whose power in Hanratty was passing, but slowly. The days of the compulsory Bible Class were over. Perhaps the Miltons didn't know that. Perhaps they knew it but put a heroic face on their decline. They behaved as if the requirements of piety hadn't changed and as if its connection with prosperity was unaltered. Their brick house, with its overstuffed comfort, their coats with collars of snug dull fur, seemed proclaimed as a Methodist house, Methodist clothing, inelegant on purpose, heavy, satisfactory. Everything about them seemed to say that they had applied themselves to the world's work for God's sake, and God had not let them down. For God's sake the hall floor shone with wax around the runner, the lines were drawn perfectly with a straight pen in the account book, the begonias flourished, the money went into the bank.

But mistakes were made, nowadays. The mistake the Milton ladies made was in drawing up a petition to be sent to the Canadian Broadcasting Corporation, asking for the removal from the air of the programs that interfered with church-going on Sunday nights: Edgar Bergen and Charlie McCarthy; Jack Benny; Fred Allen. They got the minister to speak about their petition in church — this was in the United Church, where Methodists had been outnumbered by Presbyterians and Congregationalists, and it was not a scene Rose witnessed, but had described to her by Flo — and afterwards they waited, Miss Hattie and Miss Mattie, one on each side of the outgoing stream, intending to deflect people and make them sign the petition, which was set up on a little table in the church vestibule. Behind the table Milton Homer was sitting. He had to be there; they never let him get out of going to church on Sunday. They had given him a job to keep him busy; he was to be in charge of the fountain pens, making sure they were full and handing them to signers.

That was the obvious part of the mistake. Milton had got the idea of drawing whiskers on himself, and had done so, without the help of a mirror. Whiskers curled out over his big sad cheeks, up towards his bloodshot foreboding eyes. He had put the pen in his mouth, too, so that ink had blotched his lips. In short, he had made himself so comical a sight that the petition which nobody really wanted could be treated as a comedy, too, and the power of the Milton sisters, the flax-mill Methodists, could be seen as a leftover dribble. People smiled and slid past; nothing could be done. Of course the Milton ladies didn't scold Milton or put on any show for the public, they just bundled him up with their petition and took him home.

"That was the end of them thinking they could run things," Flo said. It was hard to tell, as always, what particular defeat — was it that of religion or pretension? — she was so glad to see.

The boy who showed Rose the poem in Miss Hattie's own English class in Hanratty high school was Ralph Gillespie, the same boy who specialized in Milton Homer imitations. As Rose remembered it, he hadn't started on the imitations at the time he showed her the poem. They came later, during the last few months he was in school. In most classes he sat ahead of Rose or behind her, due to the alphabetical closeness of their names. Beyond this alphabetical closeness they did have something like a family similarity, not in looks but in habits or tendencies. Instead of embarrassing them, as it would have done if they had really been brother and sister, this drew them together in helpful conspiracy. Both of them lost or mislaid, or never adequately provided themselves with, all the pencils, rulers, erasers, pen-nibs, ruled paper, graph paper, the compass, dividers, protractor, necessary for a successful school life; both of them were sloppy with ink, subject to spilling and blotting mishaps; both of them were negligent about doing homework but panicky about not having done it. So they did their best to help each other out, sharing whatever supplies they had, begging from their more provident neighbors, finding someone's homework to copy. They developed the comradeship of captives, of soldiers who have no heart for the campaign, wishing only to survive and avoid action.

That wasn't quite all. Their shoes and boots became well acquainted, scuffling and pushing in friendly and private encounter, sometimes resting together a moment in tentative encouragement; this mutual kindness particularly helped them through those moments when people were being selected to do mathematics problems on the blackboard.

Once Ralph came in after noon hour with his hair full of snow. He leaned back and shook the snow over Rose's desk, saying, "Do you have those dandruff blues?"

"No. Mine's white."

This seemed to Rose a moment of some intimacy, with its physical frankness, its remembered childhood joke. Another day at noon hour, before the bell rang, she came into the classroom and found him, in a ring of onlookers, doing his Milton Homer imitation. She was surprised and worried; surprised because his shyness in class had always equalled hers and had been one of the things that united them; worried that he might not be able to bring it off, might not make them laugh. But he was very good; his large, pale, good-natured face took on the lumpy desperation of Milton's; his eyes goggled and his jowls shook and his words came out in a hoarse hypnotized singsong. He was so successful that Rose was amazed, and so was everybody else. From that time on Ralph began to do imitations; he had several, but Milton Homer was his trademark. Rose never quite got over a comradely sort of apprehension on his behalf. She had another feeling as well, not envy but a shaky sort of longing. She wanted to do the same. Not Milton Homer; she did not want to do Milton Homer. She wanted to fill up in that magical, releasing way, transform herself; she wanted the courage and the power.

Not long after he started publicly developing these talents he had, Ralph Gillespie dropped out of school. Rose missed his feet and his breathing and his finger tapping her shoulder. She met him sometimes on the street but he did not seem to be quite the same person. They never stopped to talk, just said hello and hurried past. They had been close and conspiring for years, it seemed, maintaining their spurious domesticity, but they had never talked outside of school, never gone beyond the most formal recognition of each other, and it seemed they could not, now. Rose never asked him why he had dropped out; she did not even know if he had found a job. They knew each other's necks and shoulders, heads and feet, but were not able to confront each other as full-length presences.

After a while Rose didn't see him on the street any more. She heard that he had joined the Navy. He must have been just waiting till he was old enough to do that. He had joined the Navy and gone to Halifax. The war was over, it was only the peacetime Navy. Just the same it was odd to think of Ralph Gillespie, in uniform, on the deck of a destroyer, maybe firing off guns. Rose was just beginning to understand that the boys she knew, however incompetent they might seem, were going to turn into men, and be allowed to do things that you would think required a lot more talent and authority than they could have.

There was a time, after she gave up the store and before her arthritis became too crippling, during which Flo went out to Bingo games and sometimes played cards with her neighbors at the Legion Hall. When Rose was home on a visit conversation was difficult, so she would ask Flo about the people she saw at the Legion. She would ask for news of her own contemporaries, Horse Nicholson, Runt Chesterton, whom she could not really imagine as grown men; did Flo ever see them?

"There's one I see and he's around there all the time. Ralph Gillespie."

Rose said that she had thought Ralph Gillespie was in the Navy.

"He was too but he's back home now. He was in an accident."

"What kind of accident?"

"I don't know. It was in the Navy. He was in a Navy hospital three solid years. They had to rebuild him from scratch. He's all right now except he walks with a limp, he sort of drags the one leg."

"That's too bad."

"Well, yes. That's what I say. I don't hold any grudge against him but there's some up there at the Legion that do."

"Hold a grudge?"

"Because of the pension," said Flo, surprised and rather contemptuous of Rose for not taking into account so basic a fact of life, and so natural an attitude, in Hanratty. "They think, well, he's set for life. I say he must've suffered for it. Some people say he gets a lot but I don't believe it. He doesn't need much, he's all on his own. One thing, if he suffers pain he don't let on. Like me. I don't let on. Weep and you weep alone. He's a good darts player. He'll play anything that's going. And he can imitate people to the life."

"Does he still do Milton Homer? He used to do Milton Homer at school."

"He does him. Milton Homer. He's comical at that. He does some others too."

"Is Milton Homer still alive? Is he still marching in parades?"

"Sure he's still alive. He's quietened down a lot, though. He's out there at the County Home and you can see him on a sunny day down by the highway keeping an eye on the traffic and licking up an ice cream cone. Both the old ladies is dead."

"So he isn't in the parades any more?"

"There isn't the parades to be in. Parades have fallen off a lot. All the Orangemen are dying out and you wouldn't get the turnout, anyway, people'd rather stay home and watch their T.V."

On later visits Rose found that Flo had turned against the Legion.

"I don't want to be one of those old crackpots," she said.

"What old crackpots?"

"Sit around up there telling the same stupid yarns and drinking beer. They make me sick."

This was very much in Flo's usual pattern. People, places, amusements, went abruptly in and out of favor. The turnabouts had become more drastic and frequent with age.

"Don't you like any of them any more? Is Ralph Gillespie still going there?"

"He still is. He likes it so well he tried to get himself a job there. He tried to get the part-time bar job. Some people say he got turned down because he already has got the pension but I think it was because of the way he carries on."

"How? Does he get drunk?"

"You couldn't tell if he was, he carries on just the same, imitating, and half the time he's imitating somebody that the newer people that's come to town, they don't know even who the person was, they just think it's Ralph being idiotic."

"Like Milton Homer?"

"That's right. How do they know it's supposed to be Milton Homer and what was Milton Homer like? They don't know. Ralph don't know when to stop. He Milton Homer'd himself right out of a job."

After Rose had taken Flo to the County Home — she had not seen Milton Homer there, though she had seen other people she had long believed dead — and was staying to clean up the house and get it ready for sale, she herself was taken to the Legion by Flo's neighbors, who thought she must be lonely on a Saturday night. She did not know how to refuse, so she found herself sitting at a long table in the basement of the hall, where the bar was, just at the time the last sunlight was coming across the fields of beans and corn, across the gravel parking lot and through the high windows, staining the plywood walls. All around the walls were photographs, with names lettered by hand and taped to the frames. Rose got up to have a look at them. The Hundred and Sixth, just before embarkation, 1915. Various heroes of that war, whose names were carried on by sons and nephews, but whose existence had not been known to her before. When she came back to the table a card game had started. She wondered if it had been a disruptive thing to do, getting up to look at the pictures. Probably nobody ever looked at them; they were not for looking at; they were just there, like the plywood on the walls. Visitors, outsiders, are always looking at things, always taking an interest, asking who was this, when was that, trying to liven up the conversation. They put too much in; they want too much out. Also, it could have looked as if she was parading around the room, asking for attention.

A woman sat down and introduced herself. She was the wife of one of the men playing cards. "I've seen you on television," she said. Rose was always a bit apologetic when somebody said this; that is, she had to control what she recognized in herself as an absurd impulse to apologize. Here in Hanratty the impulse was stronger than usual. She was aware of having done things that must seem high-handed. She remembered her days as a television interviewer, her beguiling confidence and charm; here as nowhere else they must understand how that was a sham. Her acting was another matter. The things she was ashamed of were not what they must think she was ashamed of; not a flopping bare breast, but a failure she couldn't seize upon or explain.

This woman who was talking to her did not belong to Hanratty. She said she had come from Sarnia when she was married, fifteen years ago.

"I still find it hard to get used to. Frankly I do. After the city. You look better in person than you do in that series."

"I should hope so," said Rose, and told about how they made her up. People were interested in things like that and Rose was more comfortable, once the conversation got on the technical details.

"Well, here's old Ralph," the woman said. She moved over, making room for a thin, gray-haired man holding a mug of beer. This was Ralph Gillespie. If Rose had met him on the street she would not have recognized him, he would have been a stranger to her, but after she had looked at him for a moment he seemed quite unchanged to her, unchanged from himself at seventeen or fifteen, his gray hair which had been light brown still falling over his forehead, his face still pale and calm and rather large for his body, the same diffident, watchful, withholding look. But his body was thinner and his shoulders seemed to have shrunk together. He wore a short-sleeved sweater with a little collar and three ornamental buttons; it was light-blue with beige and yellow stripes. This sweater seemed to Rose to speak of aging jauntiness, a kind of petrified adolescence. She noticed that his arms were old and skinny and that his hands shook so badly that he used both of them to raise the glass of beer to his mouth.

"You're not staying around here long, are you?" said the woman who had come from Sarnia.

Rose said that she was going to Toronto tomorrow, Sunday, night.

"You must have a busy life," the woman said, with a large sigh, and honest envy that in itself would have declared out-of-town origins.

Rose was thinking that on Monday at noon she was to meet a man for lunch and to go to bed. This man was Tom Shepherd, whom she had known for a long time. At one time he had been in love with her, he had written love letters to her. The last time she had been with him, in Toronto, when they were sitting up in bed afterwards drinking gin and tonic — they always drank a good deal when they were together — Rose suddenly thought, or knew, that there was somebody now, some woman he was in love with and was courting from a distance, probably writing letters to, and that there must have been another woman he was robustly bedding, at the time he was writing letters to her. Also, and all the time, there was his wife. Rose wanted to ask him about this; the necessity, the difficulties, the satisfactions. Her interest was friendly and uncritical but she knew, she had just enough sense to know, that the question would not do.

The conversation in the Legion had turned on lottery tickets, Bingo games, winnings. The men playing cards — Flo's neighbor among them — were talking about a man who was supposed to have won ten thousand dollars, and never publicized the fact, because he had gone bankrupt a few years before and owed so many people money.

One of them said that if he had declared himself bankrupt, he didn't owe the money any more.

"Maybe he didn't owe it then," another said. "But he owed it now. The reason is, he's got it now."

This opinion was generally favored.

Rose and Ralph Gillespie looked at each other. There was the same silent joke, the same conspiracy, comfort; the same, the same.

"I hear you're quite a mimic," Rose said.

That was wrong; she shouldn't have said anything. He laughed and shook his head.

"Oh, come on. I hear you do a sensational Milton Homer."

"I don't know about that."

"Is he still around?"

"Far as I know he's out at the County Home."

"Remember Miss Hattie and Miss Mattie? They had the lantern slide show at their house."

"Sure."

"My mental picture of China is still pretty well based on those slides."

Rose went on talking like this, though she wished she could stop. She was talking in what elsewhere might have been considered an amusing, confidential, recognizably and meaninglessly flirtatious style. She did not get much response from Ralph Gillespie, though he seemed attentive, even welcoming. All the time she talked, she was wondering what he wanted her to say. He did want something. But he would not make any move to get it. Her first impression of him, as boyishly shy and ingratiating, had to change. That was his surface. Underneath he was self-sufficient, resigned to living in bafflement, perhaps proud. She wished that he would speak to her from that level, and she thought he wished it, too, but they were prevented.

But when Rose remembered this unsatisfactory conversation she seemed to recall a wave of kindness, of sympathy and forgiveness, though certainly no words of that kind had been spoken. That peculiar shame which she carried around with her seemed to have been eased. The thing she was ashamed of, in acting, was that she might have been paying attention to the wrong things, reporting antics, when there was always something further, a tone, a depth, a light, that she couldn't get and wouldn't get. And it wasn't just about acting she suspected this. Everything she had done could sometimes be seen as a mistake. She had never felt this more strongly than when she was talking to Ralph Gillespie, but when she thought about him afterwards her mistakes appeared unimportant. She was enough a child of her time to wonder if what she felt about him was simply sexual warmth, sexual curiosity; she did not think it was. There seemed to be feelings which could only be spoken of in translation; perhaps they could only be acted on in translation; not speaking of them and not acting on them is the right course to take because translation is dubious. Dangerous, as well.

For these reasons Rose did not explain anything further about Ralph Gillespie to Brian and Phoebe when she recalled Milton Homer's ceremony with babies or his expression of diabolical happiness on the swing. She did not even mention that he was dead. She knew he was dead because she still had a subscription to the Hanratty paper. Flo had given Rose a seven-year subscription on the last Christmas when she felt obliged to give Christmas presents; characteristically, Flo said that the paper was just for people to get their names in and hadn't anything in it worth reading. Usually Rose turned the pages quickly and put the paper in the firebox. But she did see the story about Ralph which was on the front page.

FORMER NAVY MAN DIES

Mr. Ralph Gillespie, Naval Petty Officer, retired, sustained fatal head injuries at the Legion Hall on Saturday night last. No other person was implicated in the fall and unfortunately several hours passed before Mr. Gillespie's body was discovered. It is thought that he mistook the basement door for the exit door and lost his balance, which was precarious due to an old injury suffered in his naval career which left him partly disabled.

The paper went on to give the names of Ralph's parents, who were apparently still alive, and of his married sister. The Legion was taking charge of the funeral services.

Rose didn't tell this to anybody, glad that there was one thing at least she wouldn't spoil by telling, though she knew it was lack of material as much as honorable restraint that kept her quiet. What could she say about herself and Ralph Gillespie, except that she felt his life, close, closer than the lives of men she'd loved, one slot over from her own?

Friend of My Youth

With thanks To R.J.T.

I used to dream about my mother, and though the details in the dream varied, the surprise in it was always the same. The dream stopped, I suppose because it was too transparent in its hopefulness, too easy in its forgiveness.

In the dream I would be the age I really was, living the life I was really living, and I would discover that my mother was still alive. (The fact is, she died when I was in my early twenties and she in her early fifties.) Sometimes I would find myself in our old kitchen, where my mother would be rolling out piecrust on the table, or washing the dishes in the battered cream-colored dishpan with the red rim. But other times I would run into her on the street, in places where I would never have expected to see her. She might be walking through a handsome hotel lobby, or lining up in an airport. She would be looking quite well—not exactly youthful, nor entirely untouched by the paralyzing disease that held her in its grip for a decade or more before her death, but so much better than I remembered that I would be astonished. Oh, I just have this little tremor in my arm, she would say, and a little stiffness up this side of my face. It is a nuisance but I get around.

I recovered then what in waking life I had lost—my mother's liveliness of face and voice before her throat muscles stiffened and a woeful, impersonal mask fastened itself over her features. How could I have forgotten this, I would think in the dream—the casual humor she had, not ironic but merry, the lightness and impatience and confidence? I would say that I was sorry I hadn't been to see her in such a long time—meaning not that I felt guilty but that I was sorry I had kept a bugbear in my mind, instead of this reality—and the strangest, kindest thing of all to me was her matter-of-fact reply.

Oh, well, she said, better late than never. I was sure I'd see you someday.

When my mother was a young woman with a soft, mischievous face and shiny, opaque silk stockings on her plump legs (I have seen a photograph of her, with her pupils), she went to teach at a one-room school, called Grieves School, in the Ottawa Valley. The school was on a corner of the farm that belonged to the Grieves family—a very good farm for that country. Well-drained fields with none of the Precambrian rock shoulder-ing through the soil, a little willow-edged river running alongside, a sugar bush, log barns, and a large, unornamented house whose wooden walls had never been painted but had been left to weather. And when wood weathers in the Ottawa Valley, my mother said, I do not know why this is, but it never turns gray, it turns black. There must be something in the air, she said. She often spoke of the Ottawa Valley, which was her home— she had grown up about twenty miles away from Grieves School—in a dogmatic, mystified way, emphasizing things about it that distinguished it from any other place on earth. Houses turn black, maple syrup has a taste no maple syrup produced elsewhere can equal, bears amble within sight of farmhouses. Of course I was disappointed when I finally got to see this place. It was not a valley at all, if by that you mean a cleft between hills; it was a mixture of flat fields and low rocks and heavy bush and little lakes—a scrambled, disarranged sort of country with no easy har-mony about it, not yielding readily to any description.

The log barns and unpainted house, common enough on poor farms, were not in the Grieveses' case a sign of poverty but of policy. They had the money but they did not spend it. That was what people told my mother. The Grieveses worked hard and they were far from ignorant, but they were very backward. They didn't have a car or electricity or a telephone or a tractor. Some people thought this was because they were Cameronians—they were the only people in the school district who were of that religion—but in fact their church (which they themselves always called the Reformed Presbyterian) did not forbid engines or electricity or any inventions of that sort, just card playing, dancing, movies, and, on Sundays, any activity at all that was not religious or unavoidable.

My mother could not say who the Cameronians were or why they were called that. Some freak religion from Scotland, she said from the perch of her obedient and lighthearted Anglicanism. The teacher always boarded with the Grieveses, and my mother was a little daunted at the thought of going to live in that black board house with its paralytic Sundays and coal-oil lamps and primitive notions. But she was engaged by that time, she wanted to work on her trousseau instead of running around the country having a good time, and she figured she could get home one Sunday out of three. (On Sundays at the Grieveses' house, you could light a fire for heat but not for cooking, you could not even boil the kettle to make tea, and you were not supposed to write a letter or swat a fly. But it turned out that my mother was exempt from these rules. "No, no," said Flora Grieves, laughing at her. "That doesn't mean you. You must just go on as you're used to doing." And after a while my mother had made friends with Flora to such an extent that she wasn't even going home on the Sundays when she'd planned to.)

Flora and Ellie Grieves were the two sisters left of the family. Ellie was married, to a man called Robert Deal, who lived there and worked the farm but had not changed its name to Deal's in anyone's mind. By the way people spoke, my mother expected the Grieves sisters and Robert Deal to be middle-aged at least, but Ellie, the younger sister, was only about thirty, and Flora seven or eight years older. Robert Deal might be in between.

The house was divided in an unexpected way. The married couple didn't live with Flora. At the time of their marriage, she had given them the parlor and the dining room, the front bedrooms and staircase, the winter kitchen. There was no need to decide about the bathroom, because there wasn't one. Flora had the summer kitchen, with its open rafters and uncovered brick walls, the old pantry made into a narrow dining room and sitting room, and the two back bedrooms, one of which was my mother's. The teacher was housed with Flora, in the poorer part of the house. But my mother didn't mind. She immediately preferred Flora, and Flora's cheerfulness, to the silence and sickroom atmosphere of the front rooms. In Flora's domain it was not even true that all amusements were forbidden. She had a crokinole board—she taught my mother how to play.

The division had been made, or course, in the expectation that Robert and Ellie would have a family, and that they would need the room. This hadn't happened. They had been married for more than a dozen years and there had not been a live child. Time and again Ellie had been pregnant, but two babies had been stillborn, and the rest she had miscarried. During my mother's first year, Ellie seemed to be staying in bed more and more of the time, and my mother thought that she must be pregnant again, but there was no mention of it. Such people would not mention it. You could not tell from the look of Ellie, when she got up and walked around, because she showed a stretched and ruined though slack-chested shape. She carried a sickbed odor, and she fretted in a childish way about everything. Flora took care of her and did all the work. She washed the clothes and tidied up the rooms and cooked the meals served in both sides of the house, as well as helping Robert with the milking and separating. She was up before daylight and never seemed to tire. During the first spring my mother was there, a great housecleaning was embarked upon, during which Flora climbed the ladders herself and carried down the storm windows, washed and stacked them away, carried all the furniture out of one room after another so that she could scrub the woodwork and varnish the floors. She washed every dish and glass that was sitting in the cupboards supposedly clean already. She scalded every pot and spoon. Such need and energy possessed her that she could hardly sleep—my mother would wake up to the sound of stovepipes being taken down, or the broom, draped in a dish towel, whacking at the smoky cobwebs. Through the washed uncurtained windows came a torrent of unmerciful light. The cleanliness was devastating. My mother slept now on sheets that had been bleached and starched and that gave her a rash. Sick Ellie complained daily of the smell of varnish and cleansing powders. Flora's hands were raw. But her disposition remained topnotch. Her kerchief and apron and Robert's baggy overalls that she donned for the climbing jobs gave her the air of a comedian—supportive, unpredictable.

My mother called her a whirling dervish.

"You're a regular whirling dervish, Flora," she said, and Flora halted. She wanted to know what was meant. My mother went ahead and explained, though she was a little afraid lest piety should be offended. (Not piety exactly—you could not call it that. Religious strictness.) Of course it wasn't. There was not a trace of nastiness or smug vigilance in Flora's observance of her religion. She had no fear of heathens—she had always lived in the midst of them. She liked the idea of being a dervish, and went to tell her sister.

"Do you know what the teacher says I am?"

Flora and Ellie were both dark-haired, dark-eyed women, tall and narrow-shouldered and long-legged. Ellie was a wreck, of course, but Flora was still superbly straight and graceful. She could look like a queen, my mother said—even riding into town in that cart they had. For church they used a buggy or a cutter, but when they went to town they often had to transport sacks of wool—they kept a few sheep—or of produce, to sell, and they had to bring provisions home. The trip of few miles was not made often. Robert rode in front, to drive the horse—Flora could drive a horse perfectly well, but it must always be the man who drove. Flora would be standing behind holding on to the sacks. She rode to town and back standing up, keeping an easy balance, wearing her black hat. Almost ridiculous but not quite. A gypsy queen, my mother thought she looked like, with her black hair and her skin that always looked slightly tanned, and her lithe and bold serenity. Of course she lacked the gold bangles and the bright clothes. My mother envied her her slenderness, and her cheekbones.

Returning in the fall for her second year, my mother learned what was the matter with Ellie.

"My sister has a growth," Flora said. Nobody then spoke of cancer.

My mother had heard that before. People suspected it. My mother knew many people in the district by that time. She had made particular friends with a young woman who worked in the post office; this woman was going to be one of my mother's bridesmaids. The story of Flora and Ellie and Robert had been told—or all that people knew of it—in various versions. My mother did not feel that she was listening to gossip, because she was always on the alert for any disparaging remarks about Flora— she would not put up with that. But indeed nobody offered any. Everybody said that Flora had behaved like a saint. Even when she went to extremes, as in dividing up the house—that was like a saint.

Robert came to work at Grieveses' some months before the girls' father died. They knew him already, from church. (Oh, that church, my mother said, having attended it once, out of curiosity—that drear building miles on the other side of town, no organ or piano and plain glass in the windows and a doddery old minister with his hours-long sermon, a man hitting a tuning fork for the singing.) Robert had come out from Scotland and was on his way west. He had stopped with relatives or people he knew, members of the scanty congregation. To earn some money, probably, he came to Grieveses'. Soon he and Flora were engaged. They could not got to dances or to card parties like other couples, but they went for long walks. The chaperone—unofficially—was Ellie. Ellie was then a wild tease, a long-haired, impudent, childish girl full of lolloping energy. She would run up hills and smite the mullein stalks with a stick, shouting and prancing and pretending to be a warrior on horseback. That, or the horse itself. This when she was fifteen, sixteen years old. Nobody but Flora could control her, and generally Flora just laughed at her, being too used to her to wonder if she was quite right in the head. They were wonderfully fond of each other. Ellie, with her long skinny body, her long pale face, was like a copy of Flora—the kind of copy you often see in families, in which because of some carelessness or exaggeration of features or coloring, the handsomeness of one person passes into the plainness—or almost plainness—of the other. But Ellie had no jealousy about this. She loved to comb out Flora's hair and pin it up. They had great times, washing each other's hair. Ellie would press her face into Flora's throat, like a colt nuzzling its mother. So when Robert laid claim to Flora, or Flora to him—nobody knew how it was—Ellie had to be included. She didn't show any spite toward Robert, but she pursued and waylaid them on their walks; she sprung on them out of the bushes or sneaked up behind them so softly that she could blow on their necks. People saw her do it. And they heard of her jokes. She had always been terrible for jokes and sometimes it had got her into trouble with her father, but Flora had protected her. Now she put thistles in Robert's bed. She set his place at the table with the knife and fork the wrong way around. She switched the milk pails to give him the one with the hole in it. For Flora's sake, maybe, Robert humored her.

The father had made Flora and Robert set the wedding day a year ahead, and after he died they did not move it any closer. Robert went on living in the house. Nobody knew how to speak to Flora about this being scandalous or looking scandalous. Flora would just ask why. Instead of putting the wedding ahead, she put it back—from next spring to early fall, so that there should be a full year between it and her father's death. A year from wedding to funeral—that seemed proper to her. She trusted fully in Robert's patience and in her own purity.

So she might. But in the winter a commotion started. There was Ellie, vomiting, weeping, running off and hiding in the haymow, howling when they found her and pulled her out, jumping to the barn floor, running around in circles, rolling in the snow. Ellie was deranged. Flora had to call the doctor. She told him that her sister's periods had stopped—could the backup of blood be driving her wild? Robert had had to catch her and tie her up, and together he and Flora had put her to bed. She would not take food, just whipped her head from side to side, howling. It looked as if she would die speechless. But somehow the truth came out. Not from the doctor, who could not get close enough to examine her, with all her thrashing about. Probably, Robert confessed. Flora finally got wind of the truth, through all her high-mindedness. Now there had to be a wedding, though not the one that had been planned.

No cake, no new clothes, no wedding trip, no congratulations. Just a shameful hurry-up visit to the manse. Some people, seeing the names in the paper, thought the editor must have got the sisters mixed up. They thought it must be Flora. A hurry-up wedding for Flora! But no—it was Flora who pressed Robert's suit—it must have been—and got Ellie out of bed and washed her and made her presentable. It would have been Flora who picked one geranium from the window plant and pinned it to her sister's dress. And Ellie hadn't torn it out. Ellie was meek now, no longer flailing or crying. She let Flora fix her up, she let herself be married, she was never wild from that day on.

Flora had the house divided. She herself helped Robert build the necessary partitions. The baby was carried full term—nobody even pretended that it was early—but it was born dead after a long, tearing labor. Perhaps Ellie had damaged it when she jumped from the barn beam and rolled in the snow and beat on herself. Even if she hadn't done that, people would have expected something to go wrong, with that child or maybe one that came later. God dealt out punishment for hurry-up marriages—not just Presbyterians but almost everybody else believed that. God rewarded lust with dead babies, idiots, harelips and withered limbs and clubfeet.

In this case the punishment continued. Ellie had one miscarriage after another, then another still birth and more miscarriages. She was constantly pregnant, and the pregnancies were full of vomiting fits that lasted for days, headaches, cramps, dizzy spells. The miscarriages were as agonizing as full-term births. Ellie could not do her own work. She walked around holding on to chairs. Her numb silence passed off, and she became a complainer. If anybody came to visit, she would talk about the peculiarities of her headaches or describe her latest fainting fit, or even—in front of men, in front of unmarried girls or children—go into bloody detail about what Flora called her "disappointments." When people changed the subject or dragged the children away, she turned sullen. She demanded new medicine, reviled the doctor, nagged Flora. She accused Flora of washing the dishes with a great clang and clatter, out of spite, of pulling her—Ellie's—hair when she combed it out, of stingily substituting water-and-molasses for her real medicine. No matter what she said, Flora soothed her. Everybody who came into the house had some story of that kind to tell. Flora said, "Where's my little girl, then? Where's my Ellie? This isn't my Ellie, this is some crosspatch got in here in place of her!"

In the winter evenings after she came in from helping Robert with the barn chores, Flora would wash and change her clothes and go next door to read Ellie to sleep. My mother might invite herself along, taking whatever sewing she was doing, on some item of her trousseau. Ellie's bed was set up in the big dining room, where there was a gas lamp over the table. My mother sat on one side of the table, sewing, and Flora sat on the other side, reading aloud. Sometimes Ellie said, "I can't hear you." Or if Flora paused for a little rest Ellie said, "I'm not asleep yet."

What did Flora read? Stories about Scottish life—not classics. Stories about urchins and comic grandmothers. The only title my mother could remember was *Wee Macgregor*. She could not follow the stories very well, or laugh when Flora laughed and Ellie gave a whimper, because so much was in Scots dialect or read with that thick accent. She was surprised that Flora could do it—it wasn't the way Flora ordinarily talked, at all.

(But wouldn't it be the way Robert talked? Perhaps that is why my mother never reports anything that Robert said, never has him contributing to the scene. He must have been there, he must have been sitting there in the room. They would only heat the main room of the house. I see him black-haired, heavy-shouldered, with the strength of a plow horse, and the same kind of sombre, shackled beauty.)

Then Flora would say, "That's all of that for tonight," She would pick up another book, an old book written by some preacher of their faith. There was in it such stuff as my mother had never heard. What stuff? She couldn't say. All the stuff that was in their monstrous old religion. That put Ellie to sleep, or made her pretend she was asleep, after a couple of pages.

All that configuration of the elect and the damned, my mother must have meant—all the arguments about the illusion and necessity of free will. Doom and slippery redemption. The torturing, defeating, but for some minds irresistible pileup of interlocking and contradictory notions. My mother could resist it. Her faith was easy, her spirits at that time robust. Ideas were not what she was curious about, ever.

But what sort of thing was that, she asked (silently), to read to a dying woman? This was the nearest she got to criticizing Flora.

The answer—that it was the only thing, if you believed it—never seemed to have occurred to her.

By spring a nurse had arrived. That was the way things were done then. People died at home, and a nurse came in to manage it.

The nurse's name was Audrey Atkinson. She was a stout woman with corsets as stiff as barrel hoops, marcelled hair the color of brass candlesticks, a mouth shaped by lipstick beyond its own stingy outlines. She drove a car into the yard—her own car, a dark-green coupé, shiny and smart. News of Audrey Atkinson and her car spread quickly. Questions were asked. Where did she get the money? Had some rich fool altered his will on her behalf? Had she exercised influence? Or simply helped herself to a stash of bills under the mattress? How was she to be trusted?

Hers was the first car ever to sit in the Grieveses' yard overnight.

Audrey Atkinson said that she had never been called out to tend a case in so primitive a house. It was beyond her, she said, how people could live in such a way.

"It's not that they're poor, even," she said to my mother. "It isn't, is it? That I could understand. Or it's not even their religion. So what is it? They do not care!"

She tried at first to cozy up to my mother, as if they would be natural allies in this benighted place. She spoke as if they were around the same age—both stylish, intelligent women who liked a good time and had modern ideas. She offered to teach my mother to drive the car. She offered her cigarettes. My mother was more tempted by the idea of learning to drive than she was by the cigarettes. But she said no, she would wait for her husband to teach her. Audrey Atkinson raised her pinkish-orange eyebrows at my mother behind Flora's back, and my mother was furious. She disliked the nurse far more than Flora did.

"I knew what she was like and Flora didn't," my mother said. She meant that she caught a whiff of a cheap life, maybe even of drinking establishments and unsavory men, of hard bargains, which Flora was too unworldly to notice.

Flora started into the great housecleaning again. She had the curtains spread out on stretchers, she beat the rugs on the line, she leapt up on the stepladder to attack the dust on the molding. But she was impeded all the time by Nurse Atkinson's complaining.

"I wondered if we could have a little less of the running and clattering?" said Nurse Atkinson with offensive politeness. "I only ask for my patient's sake." She always spoke of Ellie as "my patient" and pretended that she was the only one to protect her and compel respect. But she was not so respectful of Ellie herself. "Allee-oop," she would say, dragging the poor creature up on her pillows. And she told Ellie she was not going to stand for fretting and whimpering. "You don't do yourself any good that way," she said. "And you certainly don't make me come any quicker. What you just as well might do is learn to control yourself." She exclaimed at Ellie's bedsores in a scolding way, as if they were a further disgrace of the house. She demanded lotions, ointments, expensive soap—most of them, no doubt, to protect her own skin, which she claimed suffered from the hard water. (How could it be hard, my mother asked her—sticking up for the household when nobody else would—how could it be hard when it came straight from the rain barrel?)

Nurse Atkinson wanted cream, too—she said that they should hold some back, not to sell it all to the creamery. She wanted to make nourishing soups and puddings for her patient. She did make puddings, and jellies, from packaged mixes such as had never before entered this house. My mother was convinced that she ate them all herself.

Flora still read to Ellie, but now it was only short bits from the Bible. When she finished and stood up, Ellie tried to cling to her. Ellie wept, sometimes she made ridiculous complaints. She said there was a horned cow outside, trying to get into the room and kill her.

"They often get some kind of idea like that," Nurse Atkinson said. "You mustn't give in to her or she won't let you go day or night. That's what they're like, they only think about themselves. Now, when I'm here alone with her, she behaves herself quite nice. I don't have any trouble at all. But after you been in here I have trouble all over again because she sees you and she gets upset. You don't want to make my job harder for me, do you? I mean, you brought me here to take charge, didn't you?"

"Ellie, now, Ellie dear, I must go," said Flora, and to the nurse she said, "I understand. I do understand that you have to be in charge and I admire you, I admire you for your work. In your work you have to have so much patience and kindness."

My mother wondered at this—was Flora really so blinded, or did she hope by this undeserved praise to exhort Nurse Atkinson to the patience and kindness that she didn't have? Nurse Atkinson was too thick-skinned and self-approving for any trick like that to work.

"It is a hard job, all right, and not many can do it," she said. "It's not like those nurses in the hospital, where they got everything laid out for them." She had not time for more conversation—she was trying to bring in "Make-Believe Ballroom" on her battery radio.

My mother was busy with the final exams and the June exercises at the school. She was getting ready for her wedding in July. Friends came in cars and whisked her off to the dressmaker's, to parties, to choose the invitations and order the cake. The lilacs came out, the evenings lengthened, the birds were back and nesting, my mother bloomed in everybody's attention, about to set out on the deliciously solemn adventure of marriage. Her dress was to be appliquéd with silk roses, her veil held by a cap of seed pearls. She belonged to the first generation of young women who saved their money and paid for their own weddings—far fancier than their parents could have afforded.

On her last evening, the friend from the post office came to drive her away, with her clothes and her books and the things she had made for her trousseau and the gifts her pupils and others had given her. There was great fuss and laughter about getting everything loaded into the car. Flora came out and helped. This getting married is even more of a nuisance than I thought, said Flora, laughing. She gave my mother a dresser scarf, which she had crocheted in secret. Nurse Atkinson could not be shut out of an important occasion—she presented a spray bottle of cologne. Flora stood on the slope at the side of the house to wave goodbye. She had been invited to the wedding, but of course she had said she could not come, she could not "go out" at such a time. The last my mother ever saw of her was this solitary, energetically waving figure in her house cleaning apron and bandanna, on the green slope by the black-walled house, in the evening light.

"Well, maybe now she'll get what she should've got the first time round," the friend from the post office said. "Maybe now they'll be able to get married. Is she too old to start a family? How old is she, anyway?"

My mother thought that this was a crude way of talking about Flora and replied that she didn't know. But she had to admit to herself that she had been thinking the very same thing.

When she was married and settled in her own home, three hundred miles away, my mother got a letter from Flora. Ellie was dead. She had died firm in her faith, Flora said, and grateful for her release. Nurse Atkinson was staying on for a little while, until it was time for her to go off to her next case. This was late in the summer.

News of what happened next did not come from Flora. When she wrote at Christmas, she seemed to take for granted that information would have gone ahead of her.

"You have in all probability heard," wrote Flora, "that Robert and Nurse Atkinson have been married. They are living on here, in Robert's part of the house. They are fixing it up to suit themselves. It is very impolite of me to call her Nurse Atkinson, as I see I have done. I ought to have called her Audrey."

Of course the post-office friend had written, and so had others. It was a great shock and scandal and a matter that excited the district—the wedding as secret and surprising as Robert's first one had been (though surely not for the same reason), Nurse Atkinson permanently installed in the community, Flora losing out for the second time. Nobody had been aware of any courtship, and they asked how the woman could have enticed him. Did she promise children, lying about her age?

The surprises were not to stop with the wedding. The bride got down to business immediately with the "fixing up" that Flora mentioned. In came the electricity and then the telephone. Now Nurse Atkinson—she would always be called Nurse Atkinson—was heard on the party line lambasting painters and paperhangers and delivery services. She was having everything done over. She was buying an electric stove and putting in a bathroom, and who knew where the money was coming from? Was it all hers, got in her deathbed dealings, in shady bequests? Was it Robert's, was he claiming his share? Ellie's share, left to him and Nurse Atkinson to enjoy themselves with, the shameless pair?

All these improvements took place on one side of the house only. Flora's side remained just as it was. No electric lights there, no fresh wallpaper or new venetian blinds. When the house was painted on the outside—cream with dark-green trim—Flora's side was left bare. This strange open statement was greeted at first with pity and disapproval, then with less sympathy, as a sign of Flora's stubbornness and eccentricity (she could have bought her own paint and made it look decent), and finally as a joke. People drove out of their way to see it.

There was always a dance given in the schoolhouse for a newly married couple. A cash collection—called "a purse of money"—was presented to them. Nurse Atkinson sent out word that she would not mind seeing this custom followed, even though it happened that the family she had married into was opposed to dancing. Some people thought it would be a disgrace to gratify her, a slap in the face to Flora. Others were too curious to hold back. They wanted to see how the newlyweds would behave. Would Robert dance? What sort of outfit would the bride show up in? They delayed a while, but finally the dance was held, and my mother got her report.

The bride wore the dress she had worn at her wedding, or so she said. But who would wear such a dress for a wedding at the manse? More than likely it was bought specially for her appearance at the dance. Pure-white satin with a sweetheart neckline, idiotically youthful. The groom was got up in a new dark-blue suit, and she had stuck a flower in his buttonhole. They were a sight. Her hair was freshly done to blind the eye with brassy reflections, and her face looked as if it would come off on a man's jacket, should she lay it against his shoulder in the dancing. Of course she did dance. She danced with every man present except the groom, who sat scrunched into one of the school desks along the wall. She danced with every man present—they all claimed they had to do it, it was the custom—and then she dragged Robert out to receive the money and to thank everybody for their best wishes. To the ladies in the cloakroom she even hinted that she was feeling unwell, for the usual newlywed reason. Nobody believed her, and indeed nothing ever came of this hope, if she really had it. Some of the women thought that she was lying to them out of malice, insulting them, making them out to be so credulous. But nobody challenged her, nobody was rude to her— maybe because it was plain that she could summon a rudeness of her own to knock anybody flat.

Flora was not present at the dance.

"My sister-in-law is not a dancer," said Nurse Atkinson. "She is stuck in the olden times." She invited them to laugh at Flora, whom she always called her sister-in-law, though she had no right to do so.

My mother wrote a letter to Flora after hearing about all these things. Being removed from the scene, and perhaps in a flurry of importance due to her own newly married state, she may have lost sight of the kind of person she was writing to. She offered sympathy and showed outrage, and said blunt disparaging things about the woman who had—as my mother saw it—dealt Flora such a blow. Back came a letter from Flora saying that she did not know where my mother had been getting her information, but that it seemed she had misunderstood, or listened to malicious people, or jumped to unjustified conclusions. What happened in Flora's family was nobody else's business, and certainly nobody needed to feel sorry for her or angry on her behalf. Flora said that she was happy and satisfied in her life, as she always had been, and she did not interfere with what others did or wanted, because such things did not concern her. She wished my mother all happiness in her marriage and hoped that she would soon be too busy with her own responsibilities to worry about the lives of people that she used to know.

This well-written letter cut my mother, as she said, to the quick. She and Flora stopped corresponding. My mother did become busy with her own life and finally a prisoner in it.

But she thought about Flora. In later years, when she sometimes talked about the things she might have been, or done, she would say, "If I could have been a writer—I do think I could have been; I could have been a writer—then I would have written the story of Flora's life. And do you know what I would have called it? 'The Maiden Lady.'"

The Maiden Lady. She said these words in a solemn and sentimental tone of voice that I had no use for. I knew, or thought I knew, exactly the value she found in them. The stateliness and mystery. The hint of derision turning to reverence. I was fifteen or sixteen years old by that time, and I believed that I could see into my mother's mind. I could see what she would do with Flora, what she had already done. She would make her into a noble figure, one who accepts defection, treachery, who forgives and stands aside, not once but twice. Never a moment of complaint. Flora goes about her cheerful labors, she cleans the house and shovels out the cow byre, she removes some bloody mess from her sister's bed, and when at last the future seems to open up for her—Ellie will die and Robert will beg forgiveness and Flora will silence him with the proud gift of herself— it is time for Audrey Atkinson to drive into the yard and shut Flora out again, more inexplicably and thoroughly the second time than the first. She must endure the painting of the house, the electric lights, all the prosperous activity next door. "Make-Believe Ballroom," "Amos 'n' Andy." No more Scottish comedies or ancient sermons. She must see them drive off to the dance—her old lover and that coldhearted, stupid, by no means beautiful woman in the white satin wedding dress. She is mocked. (And of course she has made over the farm to Ellie and Robert, of course he has inherited it, and now everything belongs to Audrey Atkinson.) The wicked flourish. But it is all right. It is all right—the elect are veiled in patience and humility and lighted by a certainty that events cannot disturb.

That was what I believed my mother would make of things. In her own plight her notions had turned mystical, and there was sometimes a hush, a solemn thrill in her voice that grated on me, alerted me to what seemed a personal danger. I felt a great fog of platitudes and pieties lurking, an incontestable crippled-mother power, which could capture and choke me. There would be no end to it. I had to keep myself sharp-tongued and cynical, arguing and deflating. Eventually I gave up even that recognition and opposed her in silence.

This is a fancy way of saying that I was no comfort and poor company to her when she had almost nowhere else to turn.

I had my own ideas about Flora's story. I didn't think that I could have written a novel but that I would write one. I would take a different tack. I saw through my mother's story and put in what she left out. My Flora would be as black as hers was white. Rejoicing in the bad turns done to her and in her own forgiveness, spying on the shambles of her sister's life. A Presbyterian witch, reading out of her poisonous book. It takes a rival ruthlessness, the comparatively innocent brutality of the thick-skinned nurse, to drive her back, to flourish in her shade. But she is driven back; the power of sex and ordinary greed drive her back and shut her up in her own part of the house with the coal-oil lamps. She shrinks, she caves in, her bones harden and her joints thicken, and—oh, this is it, this is it, I see the bare beauty of the ending I will contrive!—she becomes crippled herself, with arthritis, hardly able to move. Now Audrey

Atkinson comes into her full power—she demands the whole house. She wants those partitions knocked out that Robert put up with Flora's help when he married Ellie. She will provide Flora with a room, she will take care of her. (Audrey Atkinson does not wish to be seen as a monster, and perhaps she really isn't one.) So one day Robert carries Flora—for the first and last time he carries her in his arms—to the room that his wife Audrey had prepared for her. And once Flora is settled in her well-lit, well-heated corner Audrey Atkinson undertakes to clean out the newly vacated rooms, Flora's rooms. She carries a heap of old books out into the yard. It's spring again, housecleaning time, the season when Flora herself performed such feats, and now the pale face of Flora appears behind the new net curtains. She has dragged herself from her corner, she sees the light-blue sky with its high skidding clouds over the watery fields, the contending crows, the flooded creeks, the reddening tree branches. She sees the smoke rise out of the incinerator in the yard, where her books are burning. Those smelly old books, as Audrey has called them. Words and pages, the ominous dark spines. The elect, the damned, the slim hopes, the mighty torments—up in smoke. There was the ending.

To me the really mysterious person in the story, as my mother told it, was Robert. He never has a word to say. He gets engaged to Flora. He is walking beside her along the river when Ellie leaps out at them. He finds Ellie's thistles in his bed. He does the carpentry made necessary by his and Ellie's marriage. He listens or does not listen while Flora reads. Finally he sits scrunched up in the school desk while his flashy bride dances by with all the men.

So much for his public acts and appearances. But he was the one who started everything, in secret. He *did it to* Ellie. He did it to that skinny wild girl at a time when he was engaged to her sister, and he did it to her again and again when she was nothing but a poor botched body, a failed childbearer, lying in bed.

He must have done it to Audrey Atkinson, too, but with less disastrous results.

Those words, *did it to*—the words my mother, no more than Flora, would never bring herself to speak—were simply exciting to me. I didn't feel any decent revulsion or reasonable indignation. I refused the warning. Not even the fate of Ellie could put me off. Not when I thought of that first encounter—the desperation of it, the ripping and striving. I used to sneak longing looks at men in those days. I admired their wrists and their necks and any bit of their chests a loose button let show, and even their ears and their feet in shoes. I expected nothing reasonable of them, only to be engulfed by their passion. I had similar thoughts about Robert.

What made Flora evil in my story was just what made her admirable in my mother's—her turning away from sex. I fought against everything my mother wanted to tell me on this subject; I despised even the drop in her voice, the gloomy caution, with which she approached it. My mother had grown up in a time and in a place where sex was a dark undertaking for women. She knew that you could die of it. So she honored the decency, the prudery, the frigidity, that might protect you. And I grew up in horror of that very protection, the dainty tyranny that seemed to me to extend to all areas of life, to enforce tea parties and white gloves and all other sorts of tinkling inanities. I favored bad words and a breakthrough, I teased myself with the thought of a man's recklessness and domination. The odd thing is that my mother's ideas were in line with some progressive notions of her times, and mine echoed the notions that were favored in my time. This in spite of the fact that we both believed ourselves independent, and lived in backwaters that did not register such changes. It's as if tendencies that seem most deeply rooted in our minds, most private and singular, have come in as spores on the prevailing wind, looking for any likely place to land, any welcome.

Not long before she died, but when I was still at home, my mother got a letter from the real Flora. It came from that town near the farm, the town that Flora used to ride to, with Robert, in the cart, holding on the sacks of wool or potatoes.

Flora wrote that she was no longer living on the farm.

"Robert and Audrey are still there," she wrote. "Robert has some trouble with his back but otherwise he is very well. Audrey has poor circulation and is often short of breath. The doctor says she must lose weight but none of the diets seem to work. The farm has been doing very well. They are out of sheep entirely and into dairy cattle. As you may have heard, the chief thing nowadays is to get your milk quota from the government and then you are set. The old stable is all fixed up with milking machines and the latest modern equipment, it is quite a marvel. When I go out there to visit I hardly know where I am."

She went on to say that she had been living in town for some years now, and that she had a job clerking in a store. She must have said what kind of a store this was, but I cannot now remember. She said nothing, of course, about what had led her to this decision—whether she had in fact been put off her own farm, or had sold out her share, apparently not to much advantage. She stressed the fact of her friendliness with Robert and Audrey. She said her health was good.

"I hear that you have not been so lucky in that way," she wrote. "I ran into Cleta Barnes who used to be Cleta Stapleton at the post office out at home, and she told me that there is some problem with your muscles and she said your speech is affected too. This is sad to hear but they can do such wonderful things nowadays so I am hoping that the doctors may be able to help you."

An unsettling letter, leaving so many things out. Nothing in it about

God's will or His role in our afflictions. No mention of whether Flora still went to that church. I don't think my mother ever answered. Her fine legible handwriting, her schoolteacher's writing, had deteriorated, and she had difficulty holding a pen. She was always beginning letters and not finishing them. I would find them lying around the house. *My dearest Mary,* they began. *My darling Ruth, My dear little Joanne (though I realize you are not little anymore), My dear old friend Cleta, My lovely Margaret.* These women were friends from her teaching days, her Normal School days, and from high school. A few were former pupils. I have friends all over the country, she would say defiantly. I have dear, dear friends.

I remember seeing one letter that started out: *Friend of my Youth.* I don't know whom it was to. They were all friends of her youth. I don't recall one that began with *My dear and most admired Flora.* I would always look at them, try to read the salutation and the few sentences she had written, and because I could not bear to feel sadness I would feel an impatience with the flowery language, the direct appeal for love and pity. She would get more of that, I thought (more from myself, I meant), if she could manage to withdraw with dignity, instead of reaching out all the time to cast her stricken shadow.

I had lost interest in Flora by then. I was always thinking of stories, and by this time I probably had a new one on my mind.

But I have thought of her since. I have wondered what kind of a store. A hardware store or a five-and-ten, where she has to wear a coverall, or a drugstore, where she is uniformed like a nurse, or a Ladies' Wear, where she is expected to be genteelly fashionable? She might have had to learn about food blenders or chain saws, negligees, cosmetics, even condoms. She would have to work all day under electric lights, and operate a cash register. Would she get a permanent, paint her nails, put on lipstick? She must have found a place to live—a little apartment with a kitchenette, overlooking the main street, or a room in a boarding house. How could she go on being a Cameronian? How could she get to that out-of-the-way church unless she managed to buy a car and learned to drive it? And if she did that she might drive not only to church but to other places. She might go on holidays. She might rent a cottage on a lake for a week, learn to swim, visit a city. She might eat meals in a restaurant, possibly in a restaurant where drinks were served. She might make friends with women who were divorced.

She might meet a man. A friend's widowed brother, perhaps. A man who did not know that she was a Cameronian or what Cameronians were. Who knew nothing of her story. A man who had never heard about the partial painting of the house or the two betrayals, or that it took all her dignity and innocence to keep her from being a joke. He might want to take her dancing, and she would have to explain that she could not go. He would be surprised but not put off—all that Cameronian business might seem quaint to him, almost charming. So it would to everybody. She was brought up in some weird religion, people would say. She lived a long time out on some godforsaken farm. She is a little bit strange but really quite nice. Nice-looking, too. Especially since she went and got her hair done.

I might go into a store and find her.

No, no. She would be dead a long time now.

But suppose I had gone into a store—perhaps a department store. I see a place with the brisk atmosphere, the straightforward displays, the old-fashioned modern look of the fifties. Suppose a tall, handsome woman, nicely turned out, had come to wait on me, and I had known, somehow, in spite of the sprayed and puffed hair and the pink or coral lips and fingernails—I had known that this was Flora. I would have wanted to tell her that I knew, I knew her story, though we had never met. I imagine myself trying to tell her. (This is a dream now, I understand it as a dream.) I imagine her listening, with a pleasant composure. But she shakes her head. She smiles at me, and in her smile there is a degree of mockery, a faint, self-assured malice. Weariness, as well. She is not surprised that I am telling her this, but she is weary of it, of me and my idea of her, my information, my notion that I can know anything about her.

Of course it's my mother I'm thinking of, my mother as she was in those dreams, saying, It's nothing, just this little tremor; saying with such astonishing lighthearted forgiveness, Oh, I knew you'd come someday. My mother surprising me, and doing it almost indifferently. Her mask, her fate, and most of her affliction taken away. How relieved I was, and happy. But I now recall that I was disconcerted as well. I would have to say that I felt slightly cheated. Yes. Offended, tricked, cheated, by this welcome turnaround, this reprieve. My mother moving rather carelessly out of her old prison, showing options and powers I never dreamed she had, changes more than herself. She changes the bitter lump of love I have carried all this time into a phantom—something useless and uncalled for, like a phantom pregnancy.

The Cameronians, I have discovered, are or were an uncompromising remnant of the Covenanters—those Scots who in the seventeenth century bound themselves, with God, to resist prayer books, bishops, any taint of popery or interference by the King. Their name comes from Richard Cameron, an outlawed, or "field," preacher, soon cut down. The Cameronians—for a long time they have preferred to be called the Reformed Presbyterians—went into battle singing the seventy-fourth and the seventy-eighth Psalms. They hacked the haughty Bishop of St. Andrews to death on the highway and rode their horses over his body. One of their ministers, in a mood of firm rejoicing at his own hanging, excommunicated all the other preachers in the world.

MORDECAI RICHLER

(b. 1931)

M ordecai Richler was born in Montreal. He attended Sir George Williams College (now Concordia) for a few terms, but dropped out and travelled to Spain and Paris, where as part of a second wave of expatriate writers and artists in the early 1950s he haunted the cafés of the famous Left Bank. In 1954 he moved to England and began buying time to write his novels with work as a scriptwriter and journalist. He won the Screenwriters Guild of America Award for the screenplay of his 1959 novel The Apprenticeship of Duddy Kravitz. In 1972 Richler returned to live in Montreal, but long before that time he had been returning in his fiction, frequently portraying the experience of growing up in Montreal's poorer Jewish neighbourhoods. Thanks to Duddy Kravitz, the autobiographical short stories of The Street (1961), and the extensive flashbacks in such novels as St. Urbain's Horseman (1971)—which won the Governor General's Award—Joshua Then and Now (1980), and Solomon Gursky Was Here (1989), the environs of Montreal's St. Urbain Street have become a Canadian literary landmark. In an essay entitled "Why I Write," Richler explained his inspiration this way: "No matter how long I continue to live abroad, I do feel forever rooted in Montreal's St. Urbain Street. That was my time, my place, and I have elected myself to get it right." His fiction is deeply humanistic and scathingly satiric at times, with his favourite targets being the inanities of mass culture, any form of hypocrisy, Canadian nationalism— or any brand of special pleading from any group. W.H. New offers an insightful generalization of the relation between Richler, his moral fiction, and his satiric target, which is contemporary society: "Exploring his guilt and his innocence takes Richler into an analysis of complex moral dilemmas. They become, in the process, a guide to the burdens contemporary people carry and to the potential for happiness which their innate and unassailable weakness still allows them." In addition to being Canada's finest comic novelist—one of the English-speaking world's finest, in fact—Richler is a refreshingly unconventional children's author and the wittily perceptive essayist of such collections as Hunting Tigers Under Glass (1968), which won the Governor General's Award, Shovelling Trouble (1972), The Great Comic Book Heroes (1978), Home Sweet Home: My Canadian Album (1984), and Broadsides (1990). His other novels include The Incomparable Atuk (1963) and Cocksure (1968), the second of which also won the Governor General's Award.

Mervyn Kaplansky, Wordsmith

Mervyn Kaplansky stepped out of the rain on a dreary Saturday afternoon in August to inquire about our back bedroom.

"It's twelve dollars a week," my father said, "payable in advance."

Mervyn set down forty-eight dollars on the table. Astonished, my father retreated a step. "What's the rush-rush? Look around first. Maybe you won't like it here."

"You believe in electricity?"

There were no lights on in the house. "We're not the kind to skimp," my father said. "But we're orthodox here. Today is *shabus*."

"No, no, no. Between people."

"What are you? A wise-guy."

"I do. And as soon as I came in here I felt the right vibrations. Hi, kid." Mervyn grinned breezily at me, but the hand he mussed my hair with was shaking. "I'm going to love it here."

My father watched, disconcerted but too intimidated to protest, as Mervyn sat down on the bed, bouncing a little to try the mattress. "Go get your mother right away," he said to me.

Fortunately, she had just entered the room. I didn't want to miss anything.

"Meet your new roomer," Mervyn said, jumping up.

"Hold your horses." My father hooked his thumbs in his suspenders. "What do you do for a living?" he asked.

"I'm a writer."

"With what firm?"

"No, no, no. For myself. I'm a creative artist."

My father could see at once that my mother was enraptured and so, reconciled to yet another defeat, he said, "Haven't you any . . . things?"

"When Oscar Wilde entered the United States and they asked him if he had anything to declare, he said, 'Only my genius.' "

My father made a sour face.

"My things are at the station," Mervyn said, swallowing hard. "May I bring them over?"

"Bring."

Mervyn returned an hour or so later with his trunk, several suitcases, and an assortment of oddities that included a piece of driftwood, a wine bottle that had been made into a lamp base, a collection of pebbles, a twelve-inch-high replica of Rodin's *The Thinker*, a bull-fight poster, a Karsh portrait of G.B.S., innumerable notebooks, a ball-point pen with a built-in flashlight, and a framed cheque for fourteen dollars and eighty-five cents from the *Family Herald & Weekly Star*.

"Feel free to borrow any of our books," my mother said.

"Well, thanks. But I try not to read too much now that I'm a wordsmith myself. I'm afraid of being influenced, you see."

Mervyn was a short, fat boy with curly black hair, warm wet eyes, and an engaging smile. I could see his underwear through the triangles of tension that ran from button to button down his shirt. The last button had probably burst off. It was gone. Mervyn, I figured, must have been at least twenty-three years old, but he looked much younger.

"Where did you say you were from?" my father asked.

"I didn't."

Thumbs hooked in his suspenders, rocking on his heels, my father waited.

"Toronto," Mervyn said bitterly. "Toronto the Good. My father's a big time insurance agent and my brothers are in ladies' wear. They're in the rat-race. All of them."

"You'll find that in this house," my mother said, "we are not materialists."

Mervyn slept in—or, as he put it, stocked the unconscious—until noon every day. He typed through the afternoon and then, depleted, slept some more, and usually typed again deep into the night. He was the first writer I had ever met and I worshipped him. So did my mother.

"Have you ever noticed his hands," she said, and I thought she was going to lecture me about his chewed-up fingernails, but what she said was, "They're artist's hands. Your grandfather had hands like that." If a neighbour dropped in for tea, my mother would whisper, "We'll have to speak quietly," and, indicating the tap-tap of the typewriter from the back bedroom, she'd add, "in there, Mervyn is creating." My mother prepared special dishes for Mervyn. Soup, she felt, was especially nourishing. Fish was the best brain food. She discouraged chocolates and nuts because of Mervyn's complexion, but she brought him coffee at all hours, and if a day passed with no sound coming from the back room my mother would be extremely upset. Eventually, she'd knock softly on Mervyn's door. "Anything I can get you?" she'd ask.

"It's no use. It just isn't coming today. I go through periods like that, you know."

Mervyn was writing a novel, his first, and it was about the struggles of our people in a hostile society. The novel's title was, to begin with, a secret between Mervyn and my mother. Occasionally, he read excerpts to her. She made only one correction. "I wouldn't say 'whore'," she said. "It isn't nice, is it? Say 'lady of easy virtue.' " The two of them began to go in for literary discussions. "Shakespeare," my mother would say, "Shakespeare knew everything." And Mervyn, nodding, would reply, "But he stole all his plots. He was a plagiarist." My mother told Mervyn about her father, the rabbi, and the books he had written in Yiddish. "At his funeral," she told him, "they had to have six motorcycle policemen to control the crowds." More than once my father came home from work to find the two of them still seated at the kitchen table, and his supper wasn't ready or he had to eat a cold plate. Flushing, stammering apologies, Mervyn would flee to his room. He was, I think, the only man who was ever afraid of my father, and this my father found very heady stuff. He spoke gruffly, even profanely in Mervyn's presence, and called him Moitle behind his back. But, when you come down to it, all my father had against Mervyn was the fact that my mother no longer baked potato kugel. (Starch was bad for Mervyn.) My father began to spend more of his time playing cards at Tansky's Cigar & Soda, and when Mervyn fell behind with the rent, he threatened to take action.

"But you can't trouble him now," my mother said, "when he's in the middle of his novel. He works so hard. He's a genius maybe."

"He's peanuts, or what's he doing here?"

I used to fetch Mervyn cigarettes and headache tablets from the drugstore round the corner. On some days when it wasn't coming, the two of us would play casino and Mervyn, at his breezy best, used to wisecrack a lot. "What would you say," he said, "if I told you I aim to out-Emile Zola?" Once he let me read one of his stories, *Was The Champ A Chump?*, that had been printed in magazines in Australia and South Africa. I told him that I wanted to be a writer too. "Kid," he said, "a word from the wise. Never become a wordsmith. Digging ditches would be easier."

From the day of his arrival Mervyn had always worked hard, but what with his money running low he was now so determined to get his novel done, that he seldom went out any more. Not even for a stroll. My mother felt this was bad for his digestion. So she arranged a date with Molly Rosen. Molly, who lived only three doors down the street, was the best looker on St. Urbain, and my mother noticed that for weeks now Mervyn always happened to be standing by the window when it was time for Molly to pass on the way home from work. "Now you go out," my mother said, "and enjoy. You're still a youngster. The novel can wait for a day."

"But what does Molly want with me?"

"She's crazy to meet you. For weeks now she's been asking questions."

Mervyn complained that he lacked a clean shirt, he pleaded a headache, but my mother said, "Don't be afraid she won't eat you." All at once Mervyn's tone changed. He tilted his head cockily. "Don't wait up for me," he said.

Mervyn came home early. "What happened?" I asked.

"I got bored."

"*With* Molly?"

"Molly's an insect. Sex is highly over-estimated, you know. It also saps an artist's creative energies."

But when my mother came home from her Talmud Torah meeting and discovered that Mervyn had come home so early she felt that she had been personally affronted. Mrs. Rosen was summoned to tea.

"It's a Saturday night," she said, "she puts on her best dress, and that cheapskate where does he take her? To sit on the mountain. Do you know that she turned down three other boys, including Ready-To-Wear's *only* son, because you made such a *gedille?*"

"With dumb-bells like Ready-to-Wear she can have dates any night of the week. Mervyn's a creative artist."

"On a Saturday night to take a beautiful young thing to sit on the mountain. From those benches you can get piles."

"Don't be disgusting."

"She's got on her dancing shoes and you know what's for him a date? To watch the people go by. He likes to make up stories about them he says. You mean it breaks his heart to part with a dollar."

"To bring up your daughter to be a gold-digger. For shame."

"All right. I wasn't going to blab, but if that's how you feel—modern men and women, he told her, experiment *before* marriage. And right there on the bench he tried dirty filthy things with her. He . . ."

"Don't draw me no pictures. If I know your Molly he didn't have to try so hard."

"How dare you! She went out with him it was a favour for the marble cake recipe. The dirty piker he asked her to marry him he hasn't even got a job. She laughed in his face."

Mervyn denied that he had tried any funny stuff with Molly—he had too much respect for womankind, he said—but after my father heard that he had come home so early he no longer teased Mervyn when he stood by the window to watch Molly pass. He even resisted making wisecracks when Molly's kid brother returned Mervyn's thick letters unopened. Once, he tried to console Mervyn. "With a towel over the face," he said gruffly, "one's the same as another."

Mervyn's cheeks reddened. He coughed. And my father turned away, disgusted.

"Make no mistake," Mervyn said with a sudden jaunty smile. "You're talking to a boy who's been around. We pen-pushers are notorious lechers."

Mervyn soon fell behind with the rent again and my father began to complain.

"You can't trouble him now," my mother said. "He's in agony. It isn't coming today."

"Yeah, sure. The trouble is there's something coming to me."

"Yesterday he read me a chapter from his book. It's so beautiful you could die." My mother told him that F.J. Kugelman, the Montreal correspondent of *The Jewish Daily Forward*, had looked at the book. "He says Mervyn is a very deep writer."

"Kugelman's for the birds. If Mervyn's such a big writer, let him make me out a cheque for the rent. That's my kind of reading, you know."

"Give him one week more. Something will come through for him, I'm sure."

My father waited another week, counting off the days. "E-Day minus three today," he'd say. "Anything come through for the genius?" Nothing, not one lousy dime, came through for Mervyn. In fact he had secretly borrowed from my mother for the postage to send his novel to a publisher in New York. "E-Day minus one today," my father said. And then, irritated because he had yet to be asked what the E stood for, he added, "E for Eviction."

On Friday my mother prepared an enormous potato kugel. But when my father came home, elated, the first thing he said was, "Where's Mervyn?"

"Can't you wait until after supper, even?"

Mervyn stepped softly into the kitchen. "You want me?" he asked.

My father slapped a magazine down on the table. *Liberty*. He opened it at a short story titled *A Doll For The Deacon*. "Mel Kane, Jr.," he said, "isn't that your literary handle?"

"His *nom-de-plume*," my mother said.

"Then the story is yours." My father clapped Mervyn on the back. "Why didn't you tell me you were a writer? I thought you were a . . . well, a fruitcup. You know what I mean. A long-hair."

"Let me see that," my mother said.

Absently, my father handed her the magazine. "You mean to say," he said, "you made all that up out of your own head?"

Mervyn nodded. He grinned. But he could see that my mother was displeased.

"It's a top-notch story," my father said. Smiling, he turned to my mother. "All the time I thought he was a sponger. A poet. He's a writer. Can you beat that?" He laughed, delighted. "Excuse me," he said, and he went to wash his hands.

"Here's your story, Mervyn," my mother said. "I'd rather not read it."

Mervyn lowered his head.

"But you don't understand, Maw. Mervyn has to do that sort of stuff. For the money. He's got to eat too, you know."

My mother reflected briefly. "A little tip, then," she said to Mervyn. "Better he doesn't know why . . . well, you understand."

"Sure I do."

At supper my father said, "Hey, what's your novel called, Mr. Kane?"

"The DIRTY JEWS."

"*Are you crazy?*"

"It's an ironic title," my mother said.

"Wow! It sure is."

"I want to throw the lie back in their ugly faces," Mervyn said.

"Yeah. Yeah, sure." My father invited Mervyn to Tansky's to meet the boys. "In one night there," he said, "you can pick up enough material for a book."

"I don't think Mervyn is interested."

Mervyn, I could see, looked dejected. But he didn't dare antagonize my mother. Remembering something he had once told me, I said, "To a creative writer every experience is welcome."

"Yes, that's true," my mother said. "I hadn't thought of it like that."

So my father, Mervyn and I set off together. My father showed *Liberty* to all of Tansky's regulars. While Mervyn lit one cigarette off another, coughed, smiled foolishly and coughed again, my father introduced him as the up-and-coming writer.

"If he's such a big writer what's he doing on St. Urbain Street?"

My father explained that Mervyn had just finished his first novel. "When that comes out," he said, "this boy will be batting in the major leagues."

The regulars looked Mervyn up and down. His suit was shiny.

"You must understand," Mervyn said, "that, at the best of times, it's difficult for an artist to earn a living. Society is naturally hostile to us."

"So what's so special? I'm a plumber. Society isn't hostile to me, but I've got the same problem. Listen here, it's hard for anybody to earn a living."

"You don't get it," Mervyn said, retreating a step. "*I'm* in rebellion against society."

Tansky moved away, disgusted. "Gorki, there was a writer. This boy. . . ."

Molly's father thrust himself into the group surrounding Mervyn. "You wrote a novel," he asked, "it's true?"

"It's with a big publisher in New York right now," my father said.

"You should remember," Takifman said menacingly, "only to write good things about the Jews."

Shapiro winked at Mervyn. The regulars smiled, some shyly, others hopeful, believing. Mervyn looked back at them solemnly. "It is my profound hope," he said, "that in the years to come our people will have every reason to be proud of me."

Segal stood Mervyn for a Pepsi and a sandwich. "Six months from now," he said, "I'll be saying I knew you when. . . ."

Mervyn whirled around on his counter stool. "I'm going to out-Emile Zola," he said. He shook with laughter.

"Do you think there's going to be another war?" Perlman asked.

"Oh, lay off," my father said. "Give the man air. No wisdom outside of office hours, eh, Mervyn?"

Mervyn slapped his knees and laughed some more. Molly's father pulled him aside. "You wrote this story," he said, holding up *Liberty*, "and don't lie because I'll find you out."

"Yeah," Mervyn said, "I'm the grub-streeter who knocked that one off. But it's my novel that I really care about."

"You know who I am? I'm Molly's father. Rosen. Put it there, Mervyn. There's nothing to worry. You leave everything to me."

My mother was still awake when we got home. Alone at the kitchen table. "You were certainly gone a long time," she said to Mervyn.

"Nobody forced him to stay."

"He's too polite," my mother said, slipping her tooled leather bookmark between the pages of *Wuthering Heights*. "He wouldn't tell you when he was bored by such common types."

"Hey," my father said, remembering. "Hey, Mervyn. Can you beat that Takifman for a character?"

Mervyn started to smile, but my mother sighed and he looked away. "It's time I hit the hay," he said.

"Well," my father pulled down his suspenders. "If anyone wants to use the library let him speak now or forever hold his peace."

"*Please, Sam.* You only say things like that to disgust me. I know that."

My father went into Mervyn's room. He smiled a little. Mervyn waited, puzzled. My father rubbed his forehead. He pulled his ear. "Well, I'm not a fool. You should know that. Life does things to you, but . . ."

"It certainly does, Mr. Hersh."

"You won't end up a zero like me. So I'm glad for you. Well, good night."

But my father did not go to bed immediately. Instead, he got out his collection of pipes, neglected all these years, and sat down at the kitchen table to clean and restore them. And, starting the next morning, he began to search out and clip items in the newspapers, human interest stories with a twist, that might be exploited by Mervyn. When he came home from work—early, he had not stopped off at Tansky's—my father did not demand his supper right off but, instead, went directly to Mervyn's room. I could hear the two men talking in low voices. Finally, my mother had to disturb them. Molly was on the phone.

"Mr. Kaplansky. Mervyn. Would you like to take me out on Friday night? I'm free."

Mervyn didn't answer.

"We could watch the people go by. Anything you say, Mervyn."

"Did your father put you up to this?"

"What's the diff? You wanted to go out with me. Well, on Friday, I'm free."

"I'm sorry. I can't do it."

"Don't you like me any more?"

"I sure do. And the attraction is more than merely sexual. But if we go out together it will have to be because you so desire it."

"Mervyn, if you don't take me out on Friday he won't let me out to the dance Saturday night with Solly. Please, Mervyn."

"Sorry. But I must answer in the negative."

Mervyn told my mother about the telephone conversation, and immediately she said, "You did right." But a few days later, she became tremendously concerned about Mervyn. He no longer slept in each morning. Instead, he was the first one up in the house, to wait by the window for the postman. After he had passed, however, Mervyn did not settle down to work. He'd wander sluggishly about the house or go out for a walk. Usually, Mervyn ended up at Tansky's. My father would be waiting there.

"You know," Sugarman said, "many amusing things have happened to me in my life. It would make *some* book."

The men wanted to know Mervyn's opinion of Sholem Asch, the red menace, and ungrateful children. They teased him about my father. "To hear him tell it you're a guaranteed genius."

"Well," Mervyn said, winking, blowing on his fingernails and rubbing them against his jacket lapel, "Who knows?"

But Molly's father said, "I read in the *Gazette* this morning where Hemingway was paid a hundred thousand dollars to make a movie from *one* story. A complete book must be worth at least five short stories. Wouldn't you say?"

And Mervyn, coughing, clearing his throat, didn't answer, but walked off quickly. His shirt collar, too highly starched, cut into the back of his hairless, reddening neck. When I caught up with him, he told me, "No wonder so many artists have been driven to suicide. Nobody understands us. We're not in the rat-race."

Molly came by at seven-thirty on Friday night.

"Is there something I can do for you?" my mother asked.

"I'm here to see Mr. Kaplansky. I believe he rents a room here."

"Better to rent out a room than give fourteen ounces to the pound."

"If you are referring to my father's establishment then I'm sorry he can't give credit to everybody."

"We pay cash everywhere. Knock wood."

"I'm sure. Now, may I see Mr. Kaplansky, *if you don't mind*?"

"He's still dining. But I'll inquire."

Molly didn't wait. She pushed past my mother into the kitchen. Her eyes were a little puffy. It looked to me like she had been crying. "Hi," she said. Molly wore her soft black hair in an upsweep. Her mouth was painted very red.

"Siddown," my father said. "Make yourself homely." Nobody laughed. "It's a joke," he said.

"Are you ready, Mervyn?"

Mervyn fiddled with his fork. "I've got work to do tonight," he said.

"I'll put up a pot of coffee for you right away."

Smiling thinly, Molly pulled back her coat, took a deep breath, and sat down. She had to perch on the edge of the chair either because of her skirt or that it hurt her to sit. "About the novel," she said, smiling at Mervyn, "congrats."

"But it hasn't even been accepted by a publisher yet."

"It's good, isn't it?"

"Of course it's good," my mother said.

"Then what's there to worry? Come on," Molly said, rising. "Let's skidaddle."

We all went to the window to watch them go down the street together.

"Look at her how she's grabbing his arm," my mother said. "Isn't it disgusting?"

"You lost by a T.K.O.," my father said.

"*Thanks,*"my mother said, and she left the room.

My father blew on his fingers. "Whew," he said. We continued to watch by the window. "I'll bet you she sharpens them on a grindstone every morning to get them so pointy, and he's such a shortie he wouldn't even have to bend over to . . ." My father sat down, lit his pipe, and opened *Liberty* at Mervyn's story. "You know, Mervyn's not *that* special a guy. Maybe it's not as hard as it seems to write a story."

"Digging ditches would be easier," I said.

My father took me to Tansky's for a coke. Drumming his fingers on the counter, he answered questions about Mervyn. "Well, it has to do with this thing . . . The Muse. On some days, with the Muse, he works better. But on other days . . ." My father addressed the regulars with a daring touch of condescension; I had never seen him so assured before. "Well, that depends. But he says Hollywood is very corrupt."

Mervyn came home shortly after midnight.

"I want to give you a word of advice," my mother said. "That girl comes from very common people. You can do better, you know."

My father cracked his knuckles. He didn't look at Mervyn.

"You've got your future career to think of. You must choose a mate who won't be an embarrassment in the better circles."

"Or still better stay a bachelor," my father said.

"Nothing more dreadful can happen to a person," my mother said, "than to marry somebody who doesn't share his interests."

"Play the field a little," my father said, drawing on his pipe.

My mother looked into my father's face and laughed. My father's voice fell to a whisper. "You get married too young," he said, "and you live to regret it."

My mother laughed again. Her eyes were wet.

"I'm not the kind to stand by idly," Mervyn said, "while you insult Miss Rosen's good name."

My father, my mother, looked at Mervyn as if surprised by his presence. Mervyn retreated, startled. *"I mean that,"* he said.

"Just who do you think you're talking to?" my mother said. She looked sharply at my father.

"Hey, there," my father said.

"I hope," my mother said, "success isn't giving you a swelled head."

"Success won't change me. I'm steadfast. But you are intruding into my personal affairs. Good night."

My father seemed both dismayed and a little pleased that someone had spoken up to my mother.

"And just what's ailing you?" my mother asked.

"Me? Nothing."

"If you could only see yourself. At your age. A pipe."

"According to the *Digest* it's safer than cigarettes."

"You know absolutely nothing about people. Mervyn would never be rude to me. It's only his artistic temperament coming out."

My father waited until my mother had gone to bed and then he slipped into Mervyn's room. "Hi." He sat down on the edge of Mervyn's bed. "Tell me to mind my own business if you want me to, but . . . well, have you had bad news from New York? The publisher?"

"I'm still waiting to hear from New York."

"Sure," my father said, jumping up. "Sorry. Good night." But he paused briefly at the door. "I've gone out on a limb for you. Please don't let me down."

Molly's father phoned the next morning. "You had a good time Mervyn?"

"Yeah. Yeah, sure."

"Atta boy. That girl she's crazy about you. Like they say she's walking on air."

Molly, they said, had told the other girls in the office at Susy's Smart-Wear that she would probably soon be leaving for, as she put it, tropical climes. Gitel Shanlinsky saw her shopping for beach wear on Park Avenue—in November, this—and the rumour was that Mervyn had already accepted a Hollywood offer for his book, a guaranteed best-seller. A couple of days later a package came for Mervyn. It was his novel. There was a printed form enclosed with it. The publishers felt the book was not for them.

"Tough luck," my father said.

"It's nothing," Mervyn said breezily. "Some of the best wordsmiths going have had their novels turned down six-seven times before a publisher take it. Besides, this outfit wasn't for me in the first place. It's a homosexual company. They only print the pretty-pretty prose boys." Mervyn laughed, he slapped his knees. "I'll send the book off to another publisher today."

My mother made Mervyn his favorite dishes for dinner. "You have real talent," she said to him, "and everything will come to you." Afterwards, Molly came by. Mervyn came home very late this time, but my mother waited up for him all the same.

"I'm invited to eat at the Rosens on Saturday night. Isn't that nice?"

"But I ordered something special from the butcher for us here."

"I'm sorry. I didn't know."

"So now you know. Please yourself, Mervyn. Oh, it's alright. I changed your bed. But you could have told me, you know."

Mervyn locked his hands together to quiet them. "Tell you what, for Christ's sake? There's nothing to tell."

"It's alright, *boyele*," my mother said. "Accidents happen."

Once more my father slipped into Mervyn's room. "It's O.K.," he said, "don't worry about Saturday night. Play around. Work the kinks out. But don't put anything in writing. You might live to regret it."

"I happen to think Molly is a remarkable girl."

"Me too. I'm not as old as you think."

"No, no, no. You don't understand."

My father showed Mervyn some clippings he had saved for him. One news story told of two brothers who had discovered each other by accident after twenty-five years, another was all about a funny day at court. He also gave Mervyn an announcement for the annual Y.M.H.A. *Beacon* short story contest. "I've got an idea for you," he said. "Listen, Mervyn, in the movies . . . well, when Humphrey Bogart, for instance, lights up a Chesterfield or asks for a coke you think he doesn't get a nice little envelope from the companies concerned? Sure he does. Well, your problem seems to be money. So why couldn't you do the same thing in books? Like if your hero has to fly somewhere, for instance, why use an unnamed airline? Couldn't he go TWA because it's the safest, the best, and maybe he picks up a cutie-pie on board? Or if your central character is . . . well, a lush, couldn't he always insist on Seagram's because it's the greatest? Get the idea? I could write, say, TWA, Pepsi, Seagram's and Adam's Hats and find out just how much a book plug is worth to them, and you . . . well, what do you think?"

"I could never do that in a book of mine, that's what I think. It would reflect on my integrity. People would begin to talk, see."

But people had already begun to talk. Molly's kid brother told me Mervyn had made a hit at dinner. His father, he said, had told Mervyn he felt, along with the moderns, that in-laws should not live with young couples, not always, but the climate in Montreal was a real killer for his wife, and if it so happened that he ever had a son-in-law in, let's say,

California . . . well, it would be nice to visit . . . and Mervyn agreed that families should be close-knit. Not all the talk was favourable, however. The boys on the street were hostile to Mervyn. An outsider, a Torontonian, they felt, was threatening to carry off our Molly.

"There they go," the boys would say as Molly and Mervyn walked hand-in-hand past the pool room, "Beauty and the Beast."

"All these years they've been looking, and looking, and looking, and there he is, the missing link."

Mervyn was openly taunted on the street.

"Hey, big writer. Lard-ass. How many periods in a bottle of ink?"

"Shakespeare, come here. How did you get to look like that, or were you paid for the accident?"

But Mervyn assured me that he wasn't troubled by the boys. "The masses," he said, "have always been hostile to the artist. They've driven plenty of our number to self-slaughter, you know. But I can see through them."

His novel was turned down again.

"It doesn't matter," Mervyn said. "There are better publishers."

"But wouldn't they be experts there," my father asked. "I mean maybe . . ."

"Look at this, will you? This time they sent me a personal letter! You know who this is from? It's from one of the greatest editors in all of America."

"Maybe so," my father said uneasily, "but he doesn't want your book."

"He admires my energy and enthusiasm, doesn't he?"

Once more Mervyn mailed off his novel, but this time he did not resume his watch by the window. Mervyn was no longer the same. I don't mean that his face had broken out worse than ever—it had, it's true, only that was probably because he was eating too many starchy foods again—but suddenly he seemed indifferent to his novel's fate. I gave birth, he said, sent my baby out into the world, and now he's on his own. Another factor was that Mervyn had become, as he put it, pregnant once more (he looks it too, one of Tansky's regulars told me): that is to say, he was at work on a new book. My mother interpreted this as a very good sign and she did her utmost to encourage Mervyn. Though she continued to change his sheets just about every other night, she never complained about it. Why, she even pretended this was normal procedure in our house. But Mervyn seemed perpetually irritated and he avoided the type of literary discussion that had formerly given my mother such deep pleasure. Every night now he went out with Molly and there were times when he did not return until four or five in the morning.

And now, curiously enough, it was my father who waited up for Mervyn, or stole out of bed to join him in the kitchen. He would make coffee and take down his prized bottle of apricot brandy. More than once

I was wakened by his laughter. My father told Mervyn stories of his father's house, his boyhood, and the hard times that came after. He told Mervyn how his mother-in-law had been bedridden in our house for seven years, and with pride implicit in his every word—a pride that would have amazed and maybe even flattered my mother—he told Mervyn how my mother had tended to the old lady better than any nurse with umpteen diplomas. "To see her now," I heard my father say, "is like night and day. Before the time of the old lady's stroke she was no sour-puss. Well, that's life." He told Mervyn about the first time he had seen my mother, and how she had written him letters with poems by Shelley, Keats and Byron in them, when all the time he had lived only two streets away. But another time I heard my father say, "When I was a young man, you know, there were days on end when I never went to bed. I was so excited. I used to go out and walk the streets better than snooze. I thought if I slept maybe I'd miss something. Now isn't that crazy?" Mervyn muttered a reply. Usually, he seemed weary and self-absorbed. But my father was irrepressible. Listening to him, his tender tone with Mervyn and the surprise of his laughter, I felt that I had reason to be envious. My father had never talked like that to me or my sister. But I was so astonished to discover this side of my father, it was all so unexpected, that I soon forgot my jealousy.

One night I heard Mervyn tell my father, "Maybe the novel I sent out is no good. Maybe it's just something I had to work out of my system."

"Are you crazy it's no good? I told everyone you were a big writer."

"It's the apricot brandy talking," Mervyn said breezily. "I was only kidding you."

But Mervyn had his problems. I heard from Molly's kid brother that Mr. Rosen had told him he was ready to retire. "Not that I want to be a burden to anybody," he had said. Molly had begun to take all the movie magazines available at Tansky's. "So that when I meet the stars face to face," she had told Gitel, "I shouldn't put my foot in it, and embarrass Merv."

Mervyn began to pick at his food, and it was not uncommon for him to leap up from the table and rush to the bathroom, holding his hand to his mouth. I discovered for the first time that my mother had bought a rubber sheet for Mervyn's bed. If Mervyn had to pass Tansky's, he no longer stopped to shoot the breeze. Instead, he would hurry past, his head lowered. Once, Segal stopped him. "What's a matter," he said, "you too good for us now?"

Tansky's regulars began to work on my father.

"All of a sudden, your genius there, he's such a B.T.O.," Sugarman said, "that he has no time for us here."

"Let's face it," my father said. "You're zeros. we all are. But my friend Mervyn . . ."

"Don't tell me, Sam. He's full of beans. Baked beans."

My father stopped going to Tansky's altogether. He took to playing solitaire at home.

"What are you doing here?" my mother asked.

"Can't I stay home one night? It's my house too, you know."

"I want the truth, Sam."

"Aw, those guys. You think those cockroaches know what an artist's struggle is?" He hesitated, watching my mother closely. "By them it must be that Mervyn isn't good enough. He's no writer."

"You know," my mother said, "He owes us seven weeks' rent now."

"The first day Mervyn came here," my father said, his eyes half-shut as he held a match to his pipe, "he said there was a kind of electricity between us. Well, I'm not going to let him down over a few bucks."

But something was bothering Mervyn. For that night and the next he did not go out with Molly. He went to the window to watch her pass again and then retreated to his room to do the crossword puzzles.

"Feel like a casino?" I asked.

"I love that girl," Mervyn said. "I adore her."

"I thought everything was O.K., but. I thought you were making time."

"No, no, no. I want to marry her. I told Molly that I'd settle down and get a job if she'd have me."

"Are you crazy? A job? With your talent?"

"That's what she said."

"Aw, let's play casino. It'll take your mind off things."

"She doesn't understand. Nobody does. For me to take a job is not like some ordinary guy taking a job. I'm always studying my own reactions. I want to know how a shipper feels from the inside."

"You mean you'd take a job *as a shipper*?"

"But it's not like I'd really be a shipper. It would look like that from the outside, but I'd really be studying my co-workers all the time. I'm an artist, you know."

"Stop worrying, Mervyn. Tomorrow there'll be a letter begging you for your book."

But the next day nothing came. A week passed. Ten days.

"That's a very good sign," Mervyn said. "It means they are considering my book very carefully."

It got so we all waited around for the postman. Mervyn was aware that my father did not go to Tansky's any more and that my mother's friends had begun to tease her. Except for his endless phone calls to Molly he hardly ever came out of his room. The phone calls were futile. Molly wouldn't speak to him.

One evening my father returned from work, his face flushed. "Son-of-a-bitch," he said, "that Rosen he's a cockroach. You know what he's saying? He wouldn't have in his family a faker or a swindler. He said you were not a writer, Mervyn, but garbage." My father started to laugh. "But I trapped him for a liar. You know what he said? That you were going to take a job as a shipper. Boy, did I ever tell him."

"What did you say?" my mother asked.

"I told him good. Don't you worry. When I lose my temper, you know. . . ."

"Maybe it wouldn't be such a bad idea for Mervyn to take a job. Better than go into debt he could—"

"You shouldn't have bragged about me to your friends so much," Mervyn said to my mother. "I didn't ask it."

"*I'm* a braggart? You take that back. You owe me an apology, I think. After all, *you're* the one who said you were such a big writer."

"My talent is unquestioned. I have stacks of letters from important people and—"

"I'm waiting for an apology, Sam?"

"I have to be fair. I've seen some of the letters, so that's true. But that's not to say Emily Post would approve of Mervyn calling you a—"

"My husband was right the first time. When he said you were a sponger, Mervyn."

"Don't worry," Mervyn said, turning to my father. "You'll get your rent back no matter what. Good night."

I can't swear to it. I may have imagined it. But when I got up to go to the toilet late that night it seemed to me that I heard Mervyn sobbing in his room. Anyway, the next morning the postman rang the bell and Mervyn came back with a package and a letter.

"Not again," my father said.

"No. This happens to be a letter from the most important publisher in the United States. They are going to pay me two thousand five hundred dollars for my book in advance against royalties."

"Hey. Lemme see that."

"Don't you trust me?"

"Of course we do." My mother hugged Mervyn. "All the time I knew you had it in you."

"This calls for a celebration," my father said, going to get the apricot brandy.

My mother went to phone Mrs. Fisher. "Oh, Ida, I just called to say I'll be able to bake for the bazaar after all. No, nothing new here. Oh, I almost forgot. Remember Mervyn you were saying he was nothing but a little twerp? Well, he just got a fantastic offer for his book from a publisher in New York. No, I'm only allowed to say it runs into four figures. Excited? That one. I'm not even sure he'll accept."

My father grabbed the phone to call Tansky's.

"One minute. Hold it. Couldn't we keep quiet about this, and have a private sort of celebration?"

My father got through to the store. "Hello, Sugarman? Everybody come over here. Drinks on the house. Why, of Korsakov. No, wise-guy. She certainly isn't. At her age? It's Mervyn. He's considering a five thousand dollar offer just to sign a contract for his book."

The phone rang an instant after my father had hung up.

"Well, hello Mrs. Rosen," my mother said. "Well, thank you. I'll give him the message. No, no, why should I have anything against you we've been neighbours for years. No. Certainly not. It wasn't *me* you called a piker. Your Molly didn't laugh in my face."

Unnoticed, Mervyn sat down on the sofa. He held his head in his hands.

"There's the doorbell," my father said.

"I think I'll lie down for a minute. Excuse me."

By the time Mervyn came out of his room again many of Tansky's regulars had arrived. "If it had been up to me," my father said, "none of you would be here. But Mervyn's not the type to hold grudges."

Molly's father elbowed his way through the group surrounding Mervyn. "I want you to know," he said, "that I'm proud of you today. There's nobody I'd rather have for a son-in-law."

"You're sort of hurrying things. Aren't you?"

"What? Didn't you propose to her a hundred times she wouldn't have you? And now I'm standing here to tell you alright and you're beginning with the shaking in the pants. This I don't like."

Everybody turned to stare. There was some good natured laughter.

"You wrote her such letters they still bring a blush to my face—"

"But they came back unopened."

Molly's father shrugged and Mervyn's face turned grey as a pencil eraser.

"But you listen here," Rosen said. "For Molly, if you don't mind, it isn't necessary for me to go begging."

"Here she is," somebody said.

The regulars moved in closer.

"Hi," Molly smelled richly of Lily of the Valley. You could see the outlines of her bra through her sweater (both were in Midnight Black, from Susy's Smart-Wear). Her tartan skirt was held together by an enormous gold-plated safety pin. "Hi, doll." She rushed up to Mervyn and kissed him. "Maw just told me." Molly turned to the others, her smile radiant. "Mr. Kaplansky has asked for my hand in matrimony. We are engaged."

"Congratulations!" Rosen clapped Mervyn on the back. "The very best to you both."

There were whoops of approval all around.

"When it comes to choosing a bedroom set you can't go wrong with my son-in-law Lou."

"I hope," Takifman said sternly, "yours will be a kosher home."

"Some of the biggest crooks in town only eat kosher and I don't mind saying that straight to your face, Takifman."

"He's right, you know. And these days the most important thing with young couples is that they should be sexually compatible."

Mervyn, surrounded by the men, looked over their heads for Molly. He spotted her trapped in another circle in the far corner of the room. Molly was eating a banana. She smiled at Mervyn, she winked.

"Don't they make a lovely couple?"

"Twenty years ago they said the same thing about us. Does that answer your question?"

Mervyn was drinking heavily. He looked sick.

"Hey," my father said, his glass spilling over, "tell me, Segal, what goes in hard and stiff and comes out soft and wet?"

"Oh, for Christ's sake," I said. "Chewing gum. It's as old as the hills."

"You watch out," my father said. "You're asking for it."

"You know," Miller said. "I could do with something to eat."

My mother moved silently and tight-lipped among the guests collecting glasses just as soon as they were put down.

"I'll tell you what," Rosen said in a booming voice, "let's all go over to my place for a decent feed and some schnapps."

Our living room emptied more quickly than it had filled.

"Where's your mother?" my father asked, puzzled.

I told him she was in the kitchen and we went to get her. "Come on," my father said, "let's go to the Rosens."

"And who, may I ask, will clean up the mess you and your friends made here?"

"It won't run away."

"You have no pride."

"Oh, please. Don't start. Not today."

"Drunkard."

"Ray Milland, that's me. Hey, what's that coming out of the wall? A bat."

"That poor innocent boy is being railroaded into a marriage he doesn't want and you just stand there."

"Couldn't you enjoy yourself *just once*?"

"You didn't see his face how scared he was? I thought he'd faint."

"Who ever got married he didn't need a little push? Why, I remember when I was a young man—"

"You go, Sam. Do me a favour. Go to the Rosen's."

My father sent me out of the room.

"I'm not," he began, "well, I'm not always happy with you. Not day in and day out. I'm telling you straight."

"When I needed you to speak up for me you couldn't. Today courage comes in bottles. Do me a favour, Sam. Go."

"I wasn't going to go and leave you alone. I was going to stay. But if that's how you feel. . . ."

My father returned to the living room to get his jacket. I jumped up.

"Where are *you* going?" he asked.

"To the party."

"You stay here with your mother you have no consideration."

"God damn it."

"You heard me." But my father paused for a moment at the door. Thumbs hooked in his suspenders, rocking to and fro on his heels, he raised his head so high his chin jutted out incongruously. "I wasn't always your father. I was a young man once."

"So?"

"Did you know," he said, one eye half-shut, "that LIVE spelled backwards is EVIL?"

I woke at three in the morning when I heard a chair crash in the living room; somebody fell, and this was followed by the sound of sobbing. It was Mervyn. Dizzy, wretched and bewildered. He sat on the floor with a glass in his hand. When he saw me coming he raised his glass. "The wordsmith's bottled enemy," he said, grinning.

"When you getting married?"

He laughed. I laughed too.

"I'm not getting married."

"Wha'?"

"Sh."

"But I thought you were crazy about Molly?"

"I was. I am no longer." Mervyn rose, he tottered over to the window.

"Have you ever looked up at the stars," he said, "and felt how small and unimportant we are?"

It hadn't occurred to me before.

"Nothing really matters. In terms of eternity our lives are shorter than a cigarette puff. Hey," he said. "Hey!" He took out his pen with the built-in flashlight and wrote something in his notebook. "For a writer," he said, "everything is grist to the mill. Nothing is humiliating."

"But what about Molly?"

"She's an insect. I told you the first time. All she wanted was my kudos. My fame . . . If you're really going to become a wordsmith remember one thing. The world is full of ridicule while you struggle. But once you've made it the glamour girls will come crawling."

He had begun to cry again. "Want me to sit with you for a while," I said.

"No. Go to bed. leave me alone."

The next morning at breakfast my parents weren't talking. My mother's eyes were red and swollen and my father was in a forbidding mood. A telegram came for Mervyn.

"It's from New York," he said. "They want me right away. There's an offer for my book from Hollywood and they need me."

"You don't say?"

Mervyn thrust the telegram at my father. "Here," he said. "You read it."

"Take it easy. All I said was . . ." But my father read the telegram all the same. "Son-of-a-bitch," he said. "Hollywood."

We helped Mervyn pack.

"Shall I get Molly?" my father asked.

"No. I'll only be gone for a few days. I want to surprise her."

We all went to the window to wave. Just before he got into the taxi Mervyn looked up at us, he looked for a long while, but he didn't wave, and of course we never saw him again. A few days later a bill came for the telegram. It had been sent from our house. "I'm not surprised," my mother said.

My mother blamed the Rosens for Mervyn's flight, while they held us responsible for what they called their daughter's disgrace. My father put his pipes aside again and naturally he took a terrible ribbing at Tansky's. About a month later five dollar bills began to arrive from Toronto. They came sporadically until Mervyn had paid up all his back rent. But he never answered any of my father's letters.

Robert Coover

(b. 1932)

*R*obert Coover was born in Charles City, Iowa. He graduated from Indiana University in 1953 and joined the U.S. Navy. His reputation as a writer of short fiction began to develop with the publication of Pricksongs & Descants in 1969; the stories in this volume and the novels such as The Universal Baseball Association, Inc., J. Henry Waugh, Prop. (1968) and The Public Burning (1977) have made him one of the most prominent postmodernist writers in America. He has lectured at a number of American universities and has made interesting comments on contemporary fiction in numerous interviews. He described his own task as a writer this way:

> The role of the author, the fiction maker, the mythologizer, is to be the creative spark in the process of renewal; he is the one who tears apart the old story, speaks the unspeakable, makes the ground shake, then shuffles the bits back together into a new story. Partly anarchical, in other words, partly creative—or re-creative. The organizers of society—the politicians, chiefs, bureaucrats—will go ahead and rebuild the thing from time to time, but that's not what the storytellers are doing. . . . I enjoy the fun of stirring things up, breaking the rules, punching holes in the structures so as to see through the mysteries—even if only to rediscover what it was you liked about society when it was still all of a piece. The artist's role, then, is priestly in a way; he's there, at his best, as a voice of disturbance.

The mixture of healthy iconoclasm, questionable taste, inspired wit, corny jokes, complex irony, and crude satire that results is calculated to disorient the reader, revivify dead conventions, and reveal the myths that inform our culture for what they are.

The Brother

right there right there in the middle of the damn field he says he wants to put that thing together him and his buggy ideas and so me I says "how the hell you gonna get it down to the water?" but he just focuses me out sweepin the blue his eyes rollin like they do when he gets het on some new lunatic notion and he says not to worry none about that just would I help him for God's sake and because he don't know how he can get it done in time otherwise and though you'd have to be loonier than him to say yes I says I will of course I always would crazy as my brother is I've done little else since I was born and my wife she says "I can't figure it out I can't see why you always have to be babying that old fool he ain't never done nothin for you God knows and you got enough to do here fields need plowin it's a bad enough year already my God and now that red-eyed brother of yours wingin around like a damn cloud and not knowin what in the world he's doin buildin a damn boat in the country my God what next? you're a damn fool I tell you" but packs me some sandwiches just the same and some sandwiches for my brother Lord knows *his* wife don't have no truck with him no more says he can go starve for all she cares she's fed up ever since the time he made her sit out on a hillside for three whole days rain and everything because he said she'd see God and she didn't see nothin and in fact she like to die from hunger nothin but berries and his boys too they ain't so bright neither but at least they come to help him out with his damn boat so it ain't just the two of us thank God for *that* and it ain't no goddamn fishin boat he wants to put up neither in fact it's the biggest damn thing I ever heard of and for weeks *weeks* I'm tellin you we ain't doin nothin but cuttin down pine trees and haulin them out to his field which is really pretty high up a hill and my God *that's* work lemme tell you and my wife she sighs and says I am really crazy *r-e-a-l-l-y* crazy and her four months with a child and tryin to do my work and hers too and still when I come home from haulin timbers around all day she's got enough left to rub my shoulders and the small of my back and fix a hot meal her long black hair pulled to a knot behind her head and hangin marvelously down her back her eyes gentle but very tired my God and I says to my brother I says "look I got a lotta work to do buddy you'll have to finish this idiot thing yourself I wanna help you and all I can you know that but" and he looks off and he says "it don't matter none your work" and I says "the hell it don't how you think me and my wife we're gonna eat I mean where do you think this food comes from you been puttin away man? you can't eat this goddamn boat out here ready to rot in that bastard sun" and he just sighs long and says "no it just don't matter" and he sits him down on a rock kinda tired like and stares off and looks like he might even for God's sake cry and so I go back to bringin wood up to him and he's already started on the keel and frame God knows how *he* ever found out to build a damn boat lost in *his* fog where he is Lord he was twenty when I was born and the first thing I remember was havin to lead him around so he didn't get kicked by a damn mule him who couldn't never do nothin in a normal way just a huge oversize fuzzyface boy so anyway I take to gettin up a few hours earlier ever day to do my farmin my wife apt to lose the baby if she should keep pullin around like she was doin then I go to work on the boat until sundown and on and on the days hot and dry and my wife keepin good food in me or else I'd of dropped sure and no matter what I say to try and get out of it my brother he says "you come and help now the rest don't matter" and we just keep hammerin away and my God the damn thing is big enough for a hundred people and at least I think at *least* it's a place to live and not too bad at that at least it's good for somethin but my wife she just sighs and says no good will come of it and runs her hands through my hair but she don't ask me to stop helpin no more because she knows it won't do no good and she's kinda turned into herself now these days and gettin herself all ready and still we keep workin on that damn thing that damn boat and the days pass and my brother he says we gotta work harder we ain't got much time and from time to time he gets a coupla neighbors to come over and give a hand them sucked in by the size and the novelty of the thing makin jokes some but they don't stay around more than a day or two and they go away shakin their heads and swearin under their breath and disgusted they got weasled into the thing in the first place and me I only get about half my place planted and see to my stock as much as I can my wife she takes more care of them than I can but at least we won't starve we say if we just get some rain and finally we get the damn thing done all finished by God and we cover it in and out with pitch and put a kinda fancy roof on it and I come home on that last day and I ain't never goin back ain't *never* gonna let him talk me into nothin again and I'm all smellin of tar and my wife she cries and cries and I says to her not to worry no more I'll be home all the time and me I'm cryin a little too though she don't notice just thinkin how she's had it so lonely and hard and all and for one whole day I just sleep the whole damn day and the rest of the week I work around the farm and one day I get an idea and I go over to my brother's place and get some pieces of wood left over and whaddaya know? they are all livin on that damn boat there in the middle of nowhere him and his boys and some women and my brother's wife she's there too but she's madder than hell and carpin at him to get outa that damn boat and come home and he says she's got just one more day and then he's gonna drug her on the boat but he don't say it like a threat or nothin more like a fact a plain fact tomorrow he's gonna drug her on the boat well I ain't one to get mixed up in domestic quarrels God knows so I grab up the wood and beat it back to my farm and that evenin I make a little cradle a kinda fancy one with little animal figures cut in it and polished down and after supper I give it to my wife as a surprise and she cries and cries and holds me tight and says don't never go away again and stay close by her and all and I feel so damn good and warm about it all and glad the boat thing is over and we get out a little wine and we decide the baby's name is gonna be either Nathaniel or Anna and so we drink an extra cup to Nathaniel's health and we laugh and we sigh and drink one to Anna and my wife she gently fingers the little animal figures and says they're beautiful and really they ain't I ain't much good at that sorta thing but I know what she means and then she says "where did you get the wood?" and I says "it's left over from the boat" and she don't say nothin for a moment and then she says "you been over there again today?" and I says "yes just to get the wood" and she says "what's he doin now he's got the boat done?" and I says "funny thing they're all living in the damn thing all except the old lady she's over there hollerin at him how he's gettin senile and where does he think he's sailin to and how if he ain't afraid of runnin into a octypuss on the way he oughta get back home and him sayin she's a nut there ain't no water and her sayin that's what *she's* been tellin *him* for six months" and my wife she laughs and it's the happiest laugh I've heard from her in half a year and I laugh and we both have another cup of wine and my wife she says "so he's just livin on that big thing all by hisself?" and I says "no he's got his boys on there and some young women who are maybe wives of the boys or somethin I don't know I ain't never seen them before and all kindsa damn animals and birds and things I ain't never seen the likes" and my wife she says "animals? what animals?" and I says "oh all kinds I don't know a whole damn menagerie all clutterin and stinkin up the boat *God* what a mess" and my wife laughs again and she's a little silly with the wine and she says "I bet he ain't got no pigs" and "oh yes I seen them" I says and we laugh thinking about pigs rootin around in that big tub and she says "I bet he ain't got no jackdaws" and I says "yes I seen a couple of them too or mostly I heard them you couldn't hardly hear nothin else" and we laugh again thinking about them crows and his old lady and the pigs and all and my wife she says "*I* know what he ain't got I bet he ain't got no lice" and we both laugh like crazy and when I can I says "oh yes he does less he's took a bath" and we both laugh till we're cryin and we finish off the wine and my wife says "look now I *know* what he ain't got he ain't got no termites" and I says "you're right I don't recollect no termites maybe we oughta make him a present" and my wife she holds me close quiet all of a sudden and says "he's really movin Nathaniel's really movin" and she puts my hand down on her round belly and the little fella is kickin up a terrific storm and I says kinda anxious "does it hurt? do you think that—?" and "no" she says "it's good" she says and so I says with my hand on her belly "here's to you Nathaniel" and we drain what's left in the bottom of our cups and the next day we wake up in each other's arms and it's rainin and *thank God* we say and since it's rainin real good we stay inside and do things around the place and we're happy because the rain has come just in time and in the evenin things smell green and fresh and delicious and it's still rainin a little but not too hard so I decide to take a walk and I wander over by my brother's place thinking I'll ask him if he'd like to take on some pet termites to go with his collection and there by God is his wife on the boat and I don't know if he drug her on or if she just finally come by herself but she ain't sayin nothin which is damn unusual and the boys they ain't sayin nothin neither and my brother he ain't sayin nothin they're just all standin up there on top and gazin off and I holler up at them "nice rain ain't it?" and my brother he looks down at me standin there in the rain and still he don't say nothin but he raises his hand kinda funny like and then puts it back on the rail and I decide not to say nothin about the termites and it's startin to rain a little harder again so I turn away and go back home and I tell my wife about what happened and my wife she just laughs and says "they're *all* crazy he's finally got them *all* crazy" and she's cooked me up a special pastry with fresh meat and so we forget about them but by God the next day the rain's still comin down harder than ever and water's beginnin to stand around in places and after a week of rain I can see the crops is pretty well ruined and I'm havin trouble keepin my stock fed and my wife she's cryin and talkin abut our bad luck that we might as well of built a damn boat as plant all them crops and still we don't figure things out I mean it just don't come to our minds not even when the rain keeps spillin down like a ocean dumped upsidedown and now water is beginnin to stand around in big pools really big ones and water up to the ankles around the house and leakin in and pretty soon the whole damn house is gettin fulla water and I keep sayin maybe we oughta go use my brother's boat till this blows over but my wife she says "never" and then she starts in cryin again so finally I says to her I says "we can't be so proud I'll go ask him" and so I set out in the storm and I can hardly see where I'm going and I slip up to my neck in places and finally I get to where the boat is and I holler up and my brother he comes out and he looks down at where I am and he don't say nothin that bastard he just looks at me and I shout up at him I says "hey is it all right for me and my wife to come over until this thing blows over?" and still he don't say a damn word he just raises his hand in that same sillyass way and I holler "hey you stupid sonuvabitch I'm soakin wet goddamn it and my house is fulla water and my wife she's about to have a kid and she's apt to get sick all wet and cold to the bone and all I'm askin you—" and right then right while I'm still talkin he turns around and he goes back in the boat and I can't hardly believe it me his brother but he don't come back out and I push up under the boat and I beat on it with my fists and scream at him and call him ever name I can think up and I shout for his boys and for his wife and for anybody inside and nobody comes out "GOD*damn* YOU" I cry out at the top of my lungs and half sobbin and sick and then feelin too beat out to do anythin more I turn around and head back for home but the rain is thunderin down like mad now and in places I gotta swim and I can't make it no further and I recollect a hill nearby and I head for it and when I get to it I climb up on top of it and it feels good to be on land again even if it is soggy and greasy and I vomit and retch there awhile and move further up and the next thing I know I'm wakin up the rain still in my face and the water halfway up the hill toward me and I look out and I can see my brother's boat is floatin and I wave at it but I don't see nobody wave back and then I quick look out towards my own place and all I can see is the top of it and of a sudden I'm scared scared about my wife and I go tearin for the house swimmin most all the way and cryin and shoutin and the rain still comin down like crazy and so now well now I'm back here on the hill again what little there is left of it and I'm figurin maybe I got a day left if the rain keeps comin and it don't show no signs of stoppin and I can't see my brother's boat no more gone just water how *how* did he know? that bastard and yet I gotta hand it to him it's not hard to see who's crazy around here I can't see my house no more I just left my wife inside where I found her I couldn't hardly stand to look at her the way she was

ELIZABETH MCGRATH

(b. 1932)

E lizabeth McGrath was born in St. John's, Newfoundland, and
raised in St. Mary's, Harbour Grace, St. John's, and Montreal.
After she returned to St. John's to live in 1979, McGrath wrote "Fog-
bound in Avalon" as a response to a way of life that was, in her words,
"at once familiar and alien, and in which voices and faces and landscapes
were invested with an almost overwhelmingly beautiful dreamlike qual-
ity. To be 'fogbound' is to be prevented from moving from a place because
the fog prevents being able to see where to go or how to get there." The
"Avalon" of the title refers both to the Avalon Peninsula, the most
densely settled area of Newfoundland and site of the earliest colonies,
and to the Avalon of Arthurian romance.

Fogbound in Avalon

N either Laurel nor I will ever be certifiable, I imagine, though,
having put in, between us, going on a hundred years in this world,
we have inevitably had a brush or two with the darker side of things. So
this will not be a story of alienation. And to put your mind at rest, right
from the beginning, we have never been in love with each other, in spite
of having been reared in the most repressive of girls' schools from the
ages of five to eighteen.

Laurel and I, middle-aged, neurotic, still thin, still suffering, still fascinated by the world and ourselves in it, are friends. We were born in this
rock, Newfoundland, and are fixed in the cracks of it, through and beyond
the sparse topsoil, in a way that makes us neither want to nor be able to
free ourselves, ever. Laurel, except for holidays in Europe and the Caribbean and occasional forays into New York, has been here all her life. I,
Anne-Marie, onetime academic—Presentation Convent, Collège Sophie-
Barat, Memorial, Oxford—am another kettle of fish.

For about twenty years we circled each other, meeting once a year
when I came back from wherever I had been, tentative, polite, mildly
admiring of each other, gradually spilling a bean here and a bean there
until so many beans had been spilled that there was no going back from
it. And we found ourselves, not unhappily, in that giggling communion
characteristic of the passionate friendships of thirteen and a half. What
we don't know about each other now you could put in your eye. What
is more, what she and I don't know about the others on this rock isn't
worth knowing. When we put our heads together, and we frequently do,

we can pool enough of everyone's tatty little secrets to blackmail all the professions, including the oldest, the civil service, the clergy, and every House of Assembly back to 1855.

Just about everybody here is related by blood, marriage, or sheer tomfoolery to everybody else, and we all know our cousins to the third and fourth degree. At the rate we reproduce, emigrate, wander the world, and keep in touch, there is no secret service that can approach us. What may be called ESP elsewhere can be nailed down here by genealogy, and we are all expert. Yesterday morning Laurel was telling me that when they were five she and her twin brother took the diapers off the minister's daughter to get a look at what was so carefully concealed. In the afternoon I called her and said, "Hey, remember Daphne Green?" "Remember her?" said Laurel. "She's the one Leonard and I took the diapers off. What in God's name made you ask about her?" "I've been hearing little baby voices all day," I said, "whispering to me, '*Daphne Green, Daphne Green.*'"

The truth is, I'd been warming a bench at Canada Manpower most of the afternoon with one of the other rock-born overeducated, bilingual unemployed and Daphne's name came up, the way names do, because I'd asked who his wife was. All you need in this town to get a reputation for extraordinary powers is a large acquaintance, a few elementary research skills, and coincidence. Laurel, of course, being a thoroughgoing romantic, wants to believe in the spookies and so she does. I don't, but I like to cater to her. My own reluctant rationalism is one of the things that keep me from going mad, but I do break out from time to time.

Fern, Laurel's husband—surgeon, reliable backbencher, utterly devoted to her (christened, unfortunately, Ferdinand, because his mother was a great reader of the lesser works of Lord Beaconsfield)—is the only one of us who can pass muster as a healthy, well-integrated, well-adjusted dealer with life. If he weren't there to remind us unremittingly of health, sanity, hard work, and the old-fashioned values of the Church of England in Canada, I don't know where we'd be. He and Laurel have lived amid her storms and his calms for twenty years, and their daughters, both at college on the mainland, are beautiful and bright and loving and a credit to them. Actually, all our children are pretty good.

Though the men on this island are great talkers—never shutting up, as the rest of the country has cause to know—they don't talk much about themselves to women. If they do talk to each other of how they feel, they certainly don't let on about it. As a charter member of the Status of Women Council I should, I suppose, hack away at that, but I don't and won't. I am concerned with what people do. What they think in the inner recesses of their own beings is their own damned business. Unless they are moved to tell me, I will never know, and it is better not to ask. It wasn't very long ago that my children's father, Con O'Neill, told me what was in his head, at my request. It took him four and a half days, at the end of which

I prevailed upon him to buy me four plane tickets from Vancouver to St. John's. I then resigned from the only really good job I have ever had and launched myself back to the rock, the Public Service Commission, Canada Manpower, the vagaries of Memorial University, and a dilapidated three-story frame dwelling fifty yards from where I had been born forty-two years before.

*   *   *

Not five hours out of Vancouver, coincidence and further disaster over-took me in the person of Hugh Forbes, run into at Halifax Airport as I shepherded three dazed and baffled kids off one flight and onto another. Hugh, asking loudly, "Jesus, Annie, what have you got there, a traveling circus?" Hugh, whom I hadn't seen since the winter I was twenty-one, changed almost beyond recall but merging into himself, Cape Shore voice and all, as we talked on the two-seat side of the DC-9 and the kids slept, across the aisle, on the three-seat side.

I had braced myself for what had appeared to be only the first of many awkward but insignificant encounters with my past. After the usual stylized exchanges, I realized I had miscalculated.

"Going home on holiday, Annie?" asked Hugh.

"Not exactly," I said.

The feeling of being at a disadvantage with Hugh was familiar. Even the setting was eerily appropriate—Hugh and I, side by side in some vehicle, each wondering who would be the first to break the silence. I plunged in. "As a matter of fact, I am right this moment *leaving* home. I'm a bit punchy, so don't expect me to make too much sense."

"Annie, I don't remember your ever making too much sense. But I think I get the message. You blew it."

Lack of directness had never been one of Hugh's failings. I must have looked stricken, for he was immediately contrite and slightly embarrassed.

"Annie, I'm sorry. I didn't mean to be quite so blunt."

"It's all right," I said, making a face at him. "I find it reassuring that you haven't changed all that much."

He still looked embarrassed.

"Perhaps I'd better go sit somewhere else." He started to unbuckle his seat belt. "You'd probably rather not be bothered with me right now."

"Hugh, no," I said. "I'd like to talk. Please."

I looked at him. He seemed solid and friendly and, in spite of being annoyed with himself for his blunder, amused and curious. So I gave him fifteen minutes of the story of my life.

He listened without interrupting. As I talked, I watched his hands rebuckling the seat belt, unbuttoning his jacket, adjusting the tray, reaching for coffee from the stewardess, scratching his head, using a handkerchief, twisting his ring. Guilt and nostalgia flooded over me.

"Your hands," I said, "your arms, they're all right!"

He turned his palms upward, flexed his fingers, stretched his arms. "Yes," he said. "Good enough."

"How did you do it?"

"On hate, mostly."

There was a long silence. Nineteen fifty-nine had been the year of the last St. John's polio epidemic. Hugh, home from McGill, engineer's iron ring on his finger, job offer in his pocket, had found himself one August morning, after a weekend of pain and fever, flat on his back in the Fever Hospital with both arms immovable.

"September," he said quietly, looking at me with a face devoid of expression. "All September I spent two hours a day watching my girl Annie making a public spectacle of herself on bloody television. I told myself that I was going to get my hands and arms back, if only to wring your neck. I hated and Ma prayed. It worked like a charm. By Christmas I was going to dances. My arms were in slings, but the fingers were good. By spring I had the slings off. After eighteen months I was able to work. After two years I was ready to pick a fight with Con O'Neill and break his jaw. After that I packed my bags and lit out for Ontario, all cured."

"None of it had anything to do with Con," I said.

"As I perceived it, it had a great deal to do with Con. And apart from everything else I was disgusted with your whole carry on."

"I was afraid of you," I said. "You scared me to death. All I could see was you beating around while I minded youngsters and forgot how to read and write."

"It wouldn't have been like that."

"Don't tell me," I said. "Anyway, what about my neck?"

"What?" He was momentarily puzzled.

"Do you want to wring it?"

"Hell, no, girl. I never wring ladies' necks when they're down and out. I kiss them instead. Better for everybody."

He leaned across and kissed me. The tears stung in my eyes.

"Oh my God, Annie, you're not still at that!"

"I always get tears in my eyes when in the grip of strong feeling," I said in my lecture-room voice.

He looked at me in amazed disbelief, then looked again and exploded into laughter. I could feel the hot blush climbing to my hairline.

"Dear Lord above! Every time I'd put my arm around you, you'd start to bawl. I thought you were afraid for your virtue. Well, I'm damned."

I blinked, sniffed, and smiled at him. "Well, now you know," I said. "Better late than never."

Hugh smiled back. "Thanks, Annie."

Sweetest Mother, I thought, I love him. "Hugh," I said quietly, "I think we scuttled the ship."

"Yes," he said. "We sure as hell did."

He turned to look out the window, then adjusted his seat to the horizontal and closed his eyes.

"My son Gerald," he said. "My wife Clare."

Again there was silence. He readjusted his seat to the vertical and turned back to face me. "Gerald died one night when he was six months old. Crib death, they called it; no explanation, no one's guilt, they said. Still, Clare took to the bottle and after three years of it I took to the girls. And there we are. But we're still married and we're going to stay married. Make no mistake."

I said nothing. Hugh's forthrightness had left me stunned.

"One thing more, Annie. If you and I are going to be friends, you will never refer to any of it again. But I want you to keep it in mind."

He pointed a thumb across the aisle at the sleeping children. "What about them? Were you good at it?"

"Yes," I said, clutching at a subject I could at least talk about. "Like falling off a log. It's in the blood."

He looked at me speculatively. "I should have stuffed you full of babies and stuck you down with Mom on Cape St. Mary's. She'd have learned you the five sorrowful mysteries all right."

"I learned," I said.

"I don't know. Seems to me you could still use some toughening up."

He took my hand, called the stewardess, ordered a bottle of champagne, and told her we had just got engaged.

"Forbes," she said, "if you get engaged on my flight one more time, I will personally drown you in champagne."

The landing was the worst I have ever had, even in Torbay fog. Passengers I recognized as old hands showed in the rigid set of their shoulders what I myself felt—too much airspeed, the runway overshot, and a violent touchdown with too many rebounds off the tarmac. I was trying to remember if the runway ended at a cliff, a hill, or the woods, when we came to a shuddering stop. There was absolute quiet and then the captain's voice: "Ladies and gentlemen, as you may have noticed, we have just landed at St. John's."

A ripple of laughter ran through the aircraft and an audible communal sigh of relief. Hugh stood up, collected his briefcase and raincoat, and touched my shoulder with his free hand. "That time, Annie, it almost ended happily ever after." He smiled bleakly. "I'll call you."

I watched him as he headed up the aisle, and then I busied myself with the children. My sister Catherine met me in the crowded terminal. We went to Mother's, put the still groggy children to bed, took care of half a bottle of Captain Morgan, and turned in ourselves. The next morning I was going to have to turf my tenants out of my house on St. Columb's Street and start job hunting.

*   *   *

What happens when you bolt after sixteen years, four universities, three kids, the whole of Eng. Lit. read together, Paris, Florence, London, Oxford, Toronto, Lisbon, Washington, Vancouver, and hundreds of friends held in common? What I did was stash my books in Vancouver and go back home. I went because I wanted to do nothing else. I didn't want to face another city, another group of strangers. My ears hungered for the accents of the island. I wanted the smells and sights and sounds of St. John's Harbor, my father's grave, my mother's tenacious grip on life, old people I had known when they were young, middle-aged people I had known when they were children. I wanted my house on St. Columb's Street, groceries from Belbin's, gas from Fred and Eric Adams, vitamins from Stowe's Pharmacy, understanding from Laurel and Fern, and the children of my friends for my children. I wanted to terrify myself climbing up Barter's Hill in the sleet, to drive to Corner Brook and back in a night and a day, seeing if I could still evade the Mounties and not kill myself, to lie on the grass listening to the blessed silence in St. Mary's, and to breathe on the embers of old friendships and see if the flames would light my way out of the dark.

In spite of the encounter with Hugh, I was in good shape when I arrived. "Am I not the very picture of the wronged wife?" I said to Fern, and he laughed and hugged me and we all had a drink to celebrate. Five months later I had lost twenty-five pounds I could ill afford losing, my temper was unreliable, and I was still unemployed, but my children were happy and my house was looking less like a slum.

St. Columb's Street used to be solidly middle-class, occupied by people associated with the ships and stores of the port. My own house once belonged to a ship's chandler. Some of the others were built by captains and shipowners who lived here because of the incomparable view of the town and the harbor—every ship that comes and goes can be seen from my kitchen window. Now many of the bigger houses have become "multiple-family dwellings," the pretty, decrepit terraces are occupied by the poor, and some foreign entrepreneur has put up a yellow brick apartment house directly opposite me. The roadway is potholed, the sidewalks crumbling and cracked. Rough-looking teen-agers skylark and catcall outside the corner stores, speaking a dialect that suggests a lengthy inheritance of infected adenoids and bad teeth.

But at the top of the street is the hospital where I was born; farther down is St. Columb's Church, which my grandmother's grandfather helped build; and beside it is St. Columb's Convent, which houses an elderly nun who taught me to read and write and made me, over six years, memorize the whole of Butler's *Catechism* and MacLaren and Campbell's *Grammar*. These are the things I think about on the days when I struggle with the idea that I do not really belong here. And, try as I may, I cannot see myself old, with my grandchildren visiting, in this house on St. Columb's Street. It makes me unbearably, unutterably, sad. The Heritage Foundation is interested in us now and determined to improve us. I am afraid I may have to move, along with the other poor, since I cannot afford to be improved any further. Sooner or later someone with the money to repair the roof flashings and the rotting window frames and the exterior paint and the leaking laundry room will make me an offer and I will have to accept it.

The house—my house for the moment—is a narrow, plain three-story with bow windows and a peaked roof. It must have been intended for a large family with no servants, for the kitchen is the biggest room and there is only one bathroom and no back stairs. Built the year that I was born, it just misses being good, even of its kind. I suppose the ship's chandler ran out of money, too. The house has that look. The exterior walls and the floors are sound and strong and draftproof; the fireplaces are pleasant thirties neoclassical; the doors are paneled and the windows big and generously framed. But the walls are surfaced with painted or papered fiberboard instead of plaster, and the wainscoting and the additions made over the years are ill-conceived and cheap, running to plywood and wood-grained Arborite and acoustic tile.

How I acquired the house at all is an earnest of the emotional myopia with which I am afflicted. My marriage to Con had gone through one of its intermittent crises following a move from Toronto to Vancouver. Con suggested that since we hadn't much capital, certainly not enough to buy a house in expensive Vancouver, it would be sensible to invest in a house in an older part of St. John's, live in it for a summer, and then rent it. Our children would then have a base of operations, a home that would exist in their minds wherever they happened to be in actuality. To me the proposal made perfect sense. I had never seen myself as an emigrant, merely a traveler. The idea of a home on the island appealed to me and I liked the implicit promise that we would eventually all return. When the break came, the house was there, with boxes of old toys and baby clothes in the attic, discarded prams and pushchairs in the cellar, clothes hooks with the children's names on them in the bathroom, and odds and ends of furniture from my own childhood home in the bedrooms and living room.

By then responsibility for the house, for keeping it insured and tenanted, had gradually devolved on me. I was mildly mystified but not displeased. I saw the process as being one with the independence I was gaining as the children grew older and I settled, once again, into a full-time job at the university. The years during which I had been, uncomfortably and resentfully, a financial dependent faded away and I assumed, along with the house on St. Columb's Street, responsibility for paying for almost everything to do with myself and the children, except keeping the Vancouver roof over our heads. Food, clothing, dentistry, toys, Christmas, birthdays came out of my income from my job. We had been setting the stage for years. When the curtain went up, I said my lines and made my moves. We all did, even the children. "We knew it was a matter of time," my daughter said. "We just didn't know when. We thought it wouldn't be so soon." Nor did I.

*   *   *

My first morning in St. John's, Laurel met me at Mother's and came with me to look at the house. All my tenants had been university students, so I assumed that not much housekeeping had been done. They had rented rooms to one another in a complex set of permutations that I had never tried to keep track of as long as they paid the rent punctually. Time and the salt air had worked their will on the exterior paint of the house, but it had been fairly shabby to begin with. When I opened the door, Laurel went rigid with shock. An effluvium of Victorian dimensions assaulted us. The hall was crammed with old boots and dust-laden cartons of empty beer bottles. The windows were opaque with dirt, and where the panes had been broken, one either side of the door, pieces of plastic had been stretched over them and secured with bits of rough lath nailed into the moldings. The walls and floors had not been washed since I had left. The carpets were stained and felted with dog hair. Filthy and half furnished, without curtains or pictures, with its paint scabby, its wallpaper peeling, and its plastic tile discolored, the house was tawdry. "You cannot propose to live in this," Laurel said flatly. But I could and I did.

The children, when I moved them in, wept over their shattered fantasies. I attacked what I could with bucket and mop, Glass Wax and cloth, crowbar and paintbrush. The children, after their initial distress, channeled their energies and their disappointment into working with me. They took apart the broken fences and cut them into kindling. They lugged out sheets of wallboard and plywood and eight-foot two-by-fours as my crowbar did its work. They carried mattresses and bedsteads down from the attic and up from the cellar. I had not realized how strong ten- and twelve-year-olds can be when they have a job they want to do. When a semblance of normality had been achieved, they just quit and concentrated once again on their private concerns—school, games, hobbies, squabbling, television, and eating.

They were puzzled by my evident lack of pleasure in just being alive, in having a house to live in and enough to eat and wear and them to love me. I overheard one saying, "Why is she unhappy?" and another answering, "Life gave her a raw deal." I felt ashamed of not being happier and tried to smile more, but they asked me why I had that funny look on my face. I opted for the truth, which they found odd but uninteresting.

The process of recovering the house was alternately uplifting and depressing. "I refuse to lie here and watch you seesaw," said my mother, but she did it nonetheless. When I had got one room fit for human habitation I persuaded her to stop for lunch on her way back from a visit to her doctor. "This is perfectly respectable," she said, on looking around my sitting room. "I fail to see what you are making such a fuss about." At that point, I found myself wanting not even to think about another tin of paint. I let the brushes dry and the children revert to their usual slovenly practices. I began, in spite of myself, to think of what it was going to mean to be on my own with no one to bitch at, no one to protect the kids from my habitual anxieties, no one to lean on, no one to sleep with, and, above all, no one to tell me, perhaps for the rest of my life, that I was essential to his breathing and being. Hugh? It was two months before Hugh turned up.

I was hammering palings into the front fence when a Land-Rover stopped at the curb and Hugh got out. I wanted to put my arms around him, but he had a very don't-touch-me look about him, so I just said it was good to see him and held on to my hammer for security. He said that he had just swung by to see how I was getting on and that I should write or call if there was anything he could do to help. I replied dryly that there were more accessible sources of help than his sweet self but that I would be glad to see him any time he got tired of doing whatever it was he did. He gave me his card, said he'd be back to share a dinner the following weekend, got into his Land-Rover, saluted, and drove off. I looked at the card and put it in my pocket. It had a Toronto address, and I thought how for seven years we had probably lived no more than fifteen blocks from each other in Don Mills.

I threw down the hammer and went into the house to make tea. I drank it too fast, burned my tongue, and fired the mug viciously against the fireplace, smashing it and splattering tea over the newly scrubbed hearthrug. The mug had had a motto painted on the side. Later, I fitted the bits together, and read, "A house is made of bricks and stone but a home is made of love alone." I put the pieces on the hearth and bashed them to powder with the poker.

Hugh then appeared out of nowhere every two or three weeks, only to disappear into nowhere again. It seemed he did something with fish and oil and airplanes for the federal government. That made for a connection with Fern and Laurel. Sometimes he arrived on my doorstep monumentally plastered, mirthful and bawdy, two quintals and a fathom of black-hearted, cod-fed bayman. Sometimes, rarely, he was sober and subtle, all civil servant and about as friendly as a cobra. I would hear his acquired Toronto accent overpowering the dental *t*'s and fog-soft vowels of the Cape Shore, and it served to remind me of what I would have preferred to forget.

I didn't ask questions of Hugh. He was there or he wasn't. He was sober or he wasn't. He loved me or he didn't. When he was drunk, I told him how beautiful he was and how I adored him. When he was sober, we talked politics and oil and mutual friends; I was careful not to show temper, and we tacitly avoided discussing how we felt. Either way, I was put into a state of elevation that sometimes lasted for days. The rest of my life the cats could have. But what was there to do? Making things happen was not my line. I watched, I listened, I cared. Nothing else was possible for me. I was through with moral imperatives: I care, therefore I am. I think, therefore I will make mistakes.

Though jobless, I was neither idle nor solitary. There was, if anything, too much to do, too many obligations, hordes of visiting children, and endless chores. I was ruthless about protecting my privacy, however, and my three hours of peace after the children were in bed and before midnight had overtaken me. I did not, except on very rare occasions, turn on television or stereo or take to drink. Except for smoking, I tried to do myself as little physical or spiritual harm as possible. Sometimes I even went to mass at St. Columb's, just in case. But I did, all the same, spend many days and nights in domestic squalor and intellectual tedium. I would go as much as six or eight weeks without balancing my checkbook, reading nothing but old copies of the *Atlantic* and the *Saturday Review*, washing the children's clothes in the bathwater and hanging them to dry on the bannister rails because I couldn't be bothered calling the repairman to fix the washer and dryer. I was sick to death of being bullied by ambition, concepts of efficiency, the demands of an academic conscience, fear at being out of work or even my own convenience.

Laurel held Hugh responsible for my otherwise unaccountable behavior. I was a veteran of unrequited love, though, and surely familiar with its symptoms. I diagnosed, rather, some unease of the soul. Muddled and grubby, I read third-rate fiction and fourth-rate biography, thought fifth-rate thoughts, and felt sixth-rate emotions. And I was not at home on St. Columb's Street. I was instead, like a bird on a bush, waiting for whatever would happen next so that I would know what to do.

I talked a lot to Laurel. We were on the phone for at least thirty minutes a day. She visited me only rarely, for both the house and the neighborhood were in a world she did not care to inhabit and they made her uneasy. More frequently I visited her, early in the morning after I left the children off at school. I entered her world more easily than she did mine. We would sit in her ordered living room (oh, the relief of it!), me in jeans and sweater, with untidy hair, she combed and brushed and tidily made up but in an ugly green fuzzy dressing gown, hands shaking from insomnia and cigarettes and not following the diet required by her mild diabetes. We would ask each other if we were, as people told us, eccentric or simply made as hares. We considered our acquaintances and determined that by and large they were even more appalling than ourselves, apart from the few saints who were out of our league and therefore irrelevant to the discussion. We concluded that we did not want to be other than who we were. What we were was another question. We spent a scandalous amount of time talking it out. I talked about my past, my emotions, unemployment, the current state of my house, my mind, or my bank account. She talked about her depression, the causes of which had never emerged. I talked about my rages, the causes of which had been only too evident. We compared childhoods, holiday trips, attitudes, fantasies. I suggested that she got depressed because of hunger, perversity, boredom, and the indulgence of an excess of sensibility. She suggested that my malaise could be cured by Hugh. I told her that it was just as likely to be cured by the Atlantic Loto, the Riding of Placentia-St. Mary's, or the Henrietta Harvey Professorship. Even as I said it, I thought it was probably not true. But if I had lived my life as Hugh said I should have done, I should now be like Laurel and be hankering after the kind of life I had had and botched.

Laurel knows that everyone assumes that she is lazy and self-indulgent and ought to have a job to do. But I am aware of how scared she is and how her mind and energy are drained by fear, so that she stays in bed for days and weeks at a time. Her concern for Fern makes her come awake long enough to straighten the house and get the meals, and she always seems to deal with any emergencies, including the most trivial social ones. Her usual waking time, though, is between three and eight in the morning, when she reads, makes notes, writes letters and poems in her head that never see the light of day, thinks of killing herself, and tries to stop the shakes by force of will. Her will power is irresistible, and sooner or later anyone who has much to do with her will be made to dance to her tune. Though she has had virtually every psychogenic symptom known to medicine, she succeeds always in looking as healthy as a chestnut in blossom.

Once Laurel actually did swallow sleeping pills and then, in her wayward fashion, followed them with a tin of anchovies and was sick all over the kitchen. She cleaned up while Fern continued to sleep the sleep of the just. As she tells it, he had one of his rare fits of furious exasperation when she refused to get up and prepare his breakfast. There is no questioning that in Laurel's life the farcical element continually intrudes.

All the same, her headlong emotionalism may be one of the things that make Laurel a superb political wife. She and Fern attract a variegated tribe of friends, because he is true blue and she is beautiful and amusing and enormously sympathetic. Some of her enthusiasms have led to dinner parties that could bring the government down, and Fern has learned to keep a covert eye on their guest list. Because Laurel takes everyone at face value, she is the repository of a multitude of confidences, which frequently inspire her to quixotic action. One Saturday, early on, she dropped in at my house without calling first and encountered Hugh. Hugh will inflict his adventures on anyone he can pin down, but even when well oiled he tends to keep himself to himself. Laurel got more out of him in ten minutes than I had done in as many weeks.

After she had left, he turned to me indignantly and said, "Why do I tell Laurel all that stuff? I must be cracked."

"People do," I said, and shrugged. "They spend five minutes with her or get her when they've dialed a wrong number and she has their life stories, just like that."

"I suppose she knows enough of both of us now to write the book."

"No," I said. "But she has eyes in her head. And she loves me. She may try to help things along. I can't stop her, you know."

He made a particularly vulgar comment.

*　　　*　　　*

When Laurel gets upset and concerned about someone, she has the gall of a robber's horse. Last February, I had an especially trying couple of weeks, with frozen water pipes, an ill-functioning furnace, kids home from school with the flu, and three job interviews at which I had been told I was overqualified. I was tense and miserable and jumpy. I had been expecting Hugh and looking forward to seeing him, but he hadn't turned up. Laurel called to say that she and Fern had met Hugh at a government function the previous night and that he had been in great form. One of the crosses I was having to bear was being unable to prevent Laurel from reporting on Hugh's whereabouts. I heard her out and then I ventilated for an hour and used some fairly extravagant language, including a reference to slitting my wrists Roman style so that I wouldn't leave too much mess behind.

That evening Hugh was at my door. I had temporarily dismissed him from my mind and had been attempting to concentrate on sick, crotchety children and on the dirt and snow and oil handprints left by furnace men and plumbers. I needed a bath and was red-eyed and sleepless from nights of keeping coal fires going in the bedroom grates and was in no mood for dealing with Hugh's usual attitude of detached amusement at my ridiculous plight.

"Come in," I said. "If you can get in." A gust of icy wind accompanied him—and more snow. "Don't bother taking off your boots. The mess is past the point where I even care about it."

"You're all right, though?" he asked, looking at me warily.

"Sure," I said. "Dandy." I jammed my coal-blackened hands into the pockets of my jeans and leaned against the newel post.

"You look done in," he said.

"Beat to a rag. Want some coffee?"

"No thanks. I just took a notion to stop by. I've got a meeting to get back to. You're sure you're all right?"

"Perfectly fine." I tried what I hoped was a cheerful grin. "I'm cold, I'm tired, I'm unemployed, and the house is falling down. Don't expect Pollyanna in this climate."

"Kids O.K.?"

"Sick as pigs," I said. "And crooked as sin."

"Anything I can do? You've only to ask."

"I know," I said, "I know. But there isn't anything, truly. I just need some sleep and a change in the weather."

"Don't overdo it, Annie." He put his hand under my chin and made me look at him. "Anything on your mind? You're sure you're all right?"

This sort of solicitude was unheard of from Hugh, who would normally only inquire about my state of being if he found me with my head under my arm like the ghost of Anne Boleyn. I had a sudden shattering glimmer of understanding.

"Have you seen Fern lately?" I hazarded.

"Not this trip," he replied blandly. "Too busy." He looked at his watch. "I'd better get back. Take care, Annie."

"Sure," I said. "Pray for a thaw."

As soon as I'd closed the door on Hugh, I called Laurel.

"What did you tell him, Laurel?" I said. "That I was about to hang myself in my garters because he done me wrong?"

"An-nie, you puz-zle me," she said in her most nervous and distinct Bishop Spencer College accents.

"And you are a damned liar," I said.

"You know I ne-ver tell an untruth, An-nie."

"Laurel," I said, "I can tell when you're lying within five syllables. I'll see you in the morning if I don't die of shame first." I hung up.

After another night of sleeplessness, half a bottle of Irish whiskey, and a packet of lethal American cigarettes from our all-night pizza parlor, I went to Laurel's to tell her to get off my case. It wasn't easy. In twenty years we had never had a serious difference. With the help of a couple of pints of Strongbow, I managed to enlighten her on the enormity of what she had done. By lunchtime, when Fern got home, I was wandering the house barefoot, hugging the cider mug and humming a dirty song that I'd learned from Hugh when I was a freshman. Fern patted me on the head, said it must be great to have nothing to do, and went back to the hospital to see someone whose legs were in traction. Laurel took her telling-off better than I dealt it out, and promised never to interfere again.

Then she asked me how my life was going and how I thought it would all work out. I turned the question back to her, and she said she should never have thrown up the pills. I said that perhaps she and Hugh would be killed in a car crash when they wickedly, and in heedless contravention of all the ground rules of friendship, slipped off to Clarenville for a weekend, leaving me and Fern, given a decent interval of mourning, to console each other. Her eyes widened and she laughed with delight.

"An-nie, you are naugh-ty," she said. "How per-fect!" And I knew I had not been all that far from the truth.

"It won't work," I said. "It's a horrible cliché."

"No, no," she said, and laughed again. "I can't wait to tell Fern."

What actually did occur was one night in early spring, having read myself into a stupor, fully clothed in my bed, along with dirty ashtrays, my accounts and calculator, carbons of job applications, the phone, an alarm clock, unanswered letters, unsent Christmas cards, *The Oxford Book of Oxford*, unread, *The Pauper's Cook Book*, and an illustrated essay on the paintings of Edvard Munch, I fell asleep smoking a cigarette and woke at dawn to find that I had burned a hole through two carbons, a book bill from Blackwell's, and my only pair of sheets.

For some minutes I stared at the burn without moving, then I headed for the bathroom. My hands were shaking and my eyes were large and dark and frightened. My impulse was to wrap myself in a blanket, crawl back into bed, and go to sleep—deeply, deeply to sleep—when one of the children knocked at the door and asked the time. I snapped to attention, cleaned out the sink, called the others, and went downstairs. I made an unusually big breakfast and insisted that it be eaten. After I had taken the children to school, I returned home, washed the dishes, then gathered up all the loose papers I could find—the year's small collection of books and the 1669 Donne I had brought in my pocket from Vancouver. I put them in the ashcan, and carried it out to the sidewalk. I washed my hair, had a bath, and dressed in a silk shirt and a suit. I called my mother's cleaning woman and arranged for three days of her time. As I left the house again, the phone rang, and while I stood in the doorway, not answering it, I saw that the ashmen had been and gone. I got into the car and drove slowly down St. Columb's Street.

The fog was coming in through the Narrows, but the sun was still shining and the town and the harbor were brilliant with color and beautiful beyond the reaches of fantasy. My throat hurt and I could hardly see. I thought about my grandmother's grandfather leaning out over the

unfinished walls of St. Columb's, watching the arrival of the White
Fleet. I thought about Sister Columba in her convent and about the day
I was born in the hospital at the top of the street. I thought about
Hugh and Laurel and Fern and the Heritage Foundation. My heart was
breaking, for I knew inescapably that I had already, once again, set
out on my travels.

EDNA O'BRIEN

(b. 1932)

E *dna O'Brien was born in County Clare in the west of Ireland. She was educated in the Irish system of convents and National Schools before moving to London in 1960. There she achieved immediate success with the publication of the novel* The Country Girls *(1960); the novel created something of a sensation because O'Brien had the courage to write about Irish women's sexual lives with a frankness and power unheard of at the time. She followed her first novel with* The Lonely Girl *(1962) and* Girls in Their Married Bliss *(1963), and together the three novels form the trilogy that confirmed O'Brien's stature among contemporary novelists. She has continued to be a prolific writer of stories and novels, among which are* August Is a Wicked Month *(1964),* A Pagan Place *(1971),* Night *(1972),* Johnny I Hardly Knew You *(1977),* Casualties of Peace *(1966),* The High Road *(1988),* Mrs. Reinhardt and Other Stories *(1978),* A Scandalous Woman and Other Stories *(1972), and the story collection* Lantern Slides *(1990). A regular contributor of short stories to the prestigious* New Yorker *magazine, O'Brien has earned a wide readership and the praise of fellow writers, one of whom, Philip Roth, has said this about a volume of her selected stories: "The sensibility is on two levels and shuttles back and forth, combining the innocence of childhood with the scars of maturity. It is what gives these stories their wounded vigor. The words themselves are chiseled. The welter of emotion is rendered so sparsely that the effect is merciless, like an autopsy." Like many twentieth-century writers, O'Brien is an exile. In a memoir-cum–travel book,* Mother Ireland *(1976), she reflects on the profound influence her native land has had on her life and her fiction:*

> *Ireland for me is moments of its history, and its geography, a few people who embody its strange quality, the features of a face, a holler, a line from a Synge play, the whiff of night air, but Ireland insubstantial like the goddesses poets dream of, who lead them down into strange circles. I live out of Ireland because something in me warns me that I might stop if I lived there, that I might cease to feel what it has meant to have such a heritage, might grow placid when in fact I want yet again and for indefinable reasons to trace that same route, that trenchant childhood route, in the hope of finding some clue that will, or would, or could, make possible the leap that would restore one to one's original place and state of consciousness, to the radical innocence of the moment just before birth.*

My Mother's Mother

I loved my mother, yet I was glad when the time came to go to her mother's house each summer. It was a little house in the mountains and it commanded a fine view of the valley and the great lake below. From the front door, glimpsed through a pair of very old binoculars, one could see the entire Shannon Lake studded with various islands. On a summer's day this was a thrill. I would be put standing on a kitchen chair, while someone held the binoculars, and sometimes I marveled though I could not see at all, as the lenses had not been focused properly. The sunshine made everything better, and though we were not down by the lake, we imagined dipping our feet in it, or seeing people in boats fishing and then stopping to have a picnic. We imagined lake water lapping.

I felt safer in that house. It was different from our house, not so imposing, a cottage really, with no indoor water and no water closet. We went for buckets of water to the well, a different well each summer. These were a source of miracle to me, these deep cold wells, sunk into the ground, in a kitchen garden, or a paddock, or even a long distance away, wells that had been divined since I was last there. There was always a tin scoop nearby so that one could fill the bucket to the very brim. Then of course the full bucket was an occasion of trepidation, because one was supposed not to spill. One often brought the bucket to the very threshold of the kitchen and then out of excitement or clumsiness some water would get splashed onto the concrete floor and there would be admonishments, but it was not like the admonishments in our own house, it was not calamitous.

My grandfather was old and thin and hoary when I first saw him. His skin was the color of a clay pipe. After the market day he would come home in the pony and trap drunk, and then as soon as he stepped out of the trap he would stagger and fall into a drain or whatever. Then he would roar for help, and his grandson, who was in his twenties, would pick him up, or rather, drag him along the ground and through the house and up the stairs to his feather bed, where he moaned and groaned. The bedroom was above the kitchen, and in the night we would be below, around the fire, eating warm soda bread and drinking cocoa. There was nothing like it. The fresh bread would only be an hour out of the pot and cut in thick pieces and dolloped with butter and greengage jam. The greengage jam was a present from the postmistress, who gave it in return for the grazing of a bullock. She gave marmalade at a different time of year and a barmbrack at Halloween. He moaned upstairs, but no one was frightened of him, not even his own wife, who chewed and chewed and said, "Bad cess to them that give him the drink." She meant the publicans.

She was a minute woman with a minute face and her thin hair was pinned up tightly. Her little face, though old, was like a bud, and when she was young she had been beautiful. There was a photo of her to prove it.

Sitting with them at night I thought that maybe I would not go home at all. Maybe I would never again lie in bed next to my mother, the two of us shivering with expectancy and with terror. Maybe I would forsake my mother.

"Maybe you'll stay here," my aunt said, as if she had guessed my thoughts.

"I couldn't do that," I said, not knowing why I declined, because indeed the place had definite advantages. I stayed up as late as they did. I ate soda bread and jam to my heart's content, I rambled around the fields all day, admiring sally trees, elder bushes, and the fluttering flowers, I played "shop" or I played teaching in the little dark plantation, and no one interfered or told me to stop doing it. The plantation was where I played secrets, and always I knew the grownups were within shouting distance, if a stranger or a tinker should surprise me there. It was pitch dark and full of young fir trees. The ground was a carpet of bronzed fallen fir needles. I used to kneel on them for punishment, after the playing.

Then when that ritual was done I went into the flower garden, which being full of begonias and lupins was a mass of bright brilliant colors. Each area had its own color, as my aunt planned it that way. I can see them now, those bright reds, like nail varnish, and those yellows like the gauze of a summer dress and those pale blues like old people's eyes, with the bees and the wasps luxuriating in each petal, or each little bell, or each flute, and feel the warmth of the place, and the drone of the bees, and see again tea towels and gray flannelette drawers that were spread out on the hedge to dry. The sun garden, they called it. My aunt got the seeds and just sprinkled them around, causing marvelous blooms to spring up. They even had tulips, whereas at home we had only a diseased rambling rose on a silvered arch and two clumps of devil's pokers. Our garden was sad and windy, the wind had made holes and indentations in the hedges, and the dogs had made further holes where they slept and burrowed. Our house was larger, and there was better linoleum on the floor, there were brass rods on the stairs, and there was a flush lavatory, but it did not have the same cheeriness and it was imbued with doom.

Still, I knew that I would not stay in my grandmother's forever. I knew it for certain when I got into bed and then desperately missed my mother, and missed the little whispering we did, and the chocolate we ate, and I missed the smell of our kind of bedclothes. Theirs were gray flannel, which tickled the skin, as did the loose feathers, and their pointed ends kept irking one. There was a gaudy red quilt that I thought would come to life and turn into a sinister Santa Claus. Except that they had told me that there was no Santa Claus. My aunt told me that, she insisted.

There was my aunt and her two sons, Donal and Joe, and my grand-mother and grandfather. My aunt and Joe would tease me each night, say that there was no Santa Claus, until I got up and stamped the floor, and in contradicting them welled up with tears, and then at last, when I was on the point of breaking down, they would say that there was. Then one night they went too far. They said that my mother was not my real mother. My real mother, they said, was in Australia and I was adopted. I could not be told that word. I began to hit the wall and screech, and the more they insisted, the more obstreperous I became. My aunt went into the parlor in search of a box of snaps to find a photo of my real mother and came out triumphant at having found it. She showed me a woman in knickerbockers with a big floppy hat. I could have thrown it in the fire so violent was I. They watched for each new moment of panic and furious disbelief, and then they got the wind up when they saw I was getting out of control. I began to shake like the weather conductor on the chapel chimney and my teeth chattered, and before long I was just this shaking creature, unable to let out any sound, and seeing the room's contents swim away from me, I felt their alarm almost as I felt my own. My aunt took hold of my wrist to feel my pulse, and my grandmother held a spoonful of tonic to my lips, but I spilled it. It was called Parishes Food and was the color of cooked beetroot. My eyes were haywire. My aunt put a big towel around me and sat me on her knee, and as the terror lessened, my tears began to flow and I cried so much that they thought I would choke because of the tears going back down the throat. They said I must never tell anyone and I must never tell my mother.

"She is my mother," I said, and they said, "Yes, darling," but I knew that they were appalled at what had happened.

That night I fell out of bed twice, and my aunt had to put chairs next to it to keep me in. She slept in the same room, and often I used to hear her crying for her dead husband and begging to be reunited with him in heaven. She used to talk to him and say, "Is that you, Michael, is that you?" I often heard her arms striking against the headboard, or heavy movements when she got up to relieve herself. In the daytime we used the fields, but at night we did not go out for fear of ghosts. There was a gutter in the back kitchen that served as a channel, and twice a week she put disinfectant in it. The crux in the daytime was finding a private place and not being found or spied on by anyone. It entailed much walking and then much hesitating so as not to be seen.

The morning after the fright, they pampered me, scrambled me an egg, and sprinkled nutmeg over it. Then along with that my aunt announced a surprise. Our workman had sent word by the mail-car that he was coming to see me on Sunday and the postman had delivered the message. Oh, what a glut of happiness. Our workman was called Carnero and I loved him too. I loved his rotting teeth and his curly hair and his strong hands and his big stomach, which people referred to as his "corporation." He was nicknamed Carnero after a boxer. I knew that when he came he would have bars of chocolate, and maybe a letter or a silk hanky from my mother, and that he would lift me up in his arms and swing me around and say "Sugarbush." How many hours were there until Sunday, I asked.

Yet that day, which was Friday, did not pass without event. We had a visitor—a man. I will never know why but my grandfather called him Tim, whereas his real name was Pat, but my grandfather was not to be told that. Tim, it seems, had died and my grandfather was not to know, because if any of the locals died, it brought his own death to his mind and he dreaded death as strenuously as did all the others. Death was some weird journey that you made alone and unbefriended, once you had embarked on it. When my aunt's husband had died, in fact had been shot by the Black and Tans, my aunt had to conceal the death from her own parents, so irrational were they about the subject. She had to stay up at home the evening her husband's remains were brought to the chapel, and when the chapel bell rang out intermittently, as it does for a death, and they asked who it was, again and again, my poor aunt had to conceal her own grief, be silent about her own tragedy, and pretend that she did not know. Next day she went to the funeral on the excuse that it was some forester whom her husband knew. Her husband was supposed to be transferred to a barracks a long way off, and meanwhile she was going to live with her parents and bring her infant sons until her husband found accommodation. She invented a name for the district where her husband was supposed to be, it was in the North of Ireland, and she invented letters that she had received from him, and the news of the Troubles up there. Eventually, I expect, she told them, and I expect they collapsed and broke down. In fact, the man who brought these imaginary letters would have been Tim, since he had been the postman, and it was of his death my grandfather must not be told. So there in the porch, in a worn suit, was a man called Pat answering to the name of Tim, and the news that a Tim would have, such as how were his family and what crops had he put in and what cattle fairs had he been to. I thought that it was peculiar that he could answer for another, but I expect that everyone's life story was identical.

Sunday after Mass I was down by the little green gate skipping and waiting for Carnero. As often happens, the visitor arrives just when we look away. The cuckoo called, and though I knew I would not see her, I looked in a tree where there was a ravaged bird's nest, and at that moment heard Carnero's whistle. I ran down the road, and at once he hefted me up onto the crossbar of his bicycle.

"Oh, Carnero," I cried. There was both joy and sadness in our reunion. He had brought me a bag of tinned sweets, and the most glamorous present—as we got off the bicycle near the little gate he put it on me. It was a toy watch—a most beautiful red, and each bit of the bracelet was the shape and color of a raspberry. It had hands, and though they did not move, that did not matter. One could pull the bracelet part by its elastic thread and cause it to snap in or out. The hands were black and curved like an eyelash. He would not say where he had got it. I had only one craving, to stay down there by the gate with him and admire the watch and talk about home. I could not talk to him in front of them because a child was not supposed to talk or have any wants. He was puffing from having cycled uphill and began to open his tie, and taking it off, he said, "This bloody thing." I wondered who he had put it on for. He was in his Sunday suit and had a fishing feather in his hat.

"Oh, Carnero, turn the bike around and bring me home with you."

Such were my unuttered and unutterable hopes. Later my grandfather teased me and said was it in his backside I saw Carnero's looks, and I said no, in every particle of him.

That night as we were saying the Rosary my grandfather let out a shout, slouched forward, knocking the wooden chair and hitting himself on the rungs of it, then falling on the cement floor. He died delirious. He died calling on his Maker. It was ghastly. Joe was out and only my grandmother and aunt were there to assist. They picked him up. His skin was purple, the exact color of the iron tonic, and his eyes rolled so that they were seeing every bit of the room, from the ceiling, to the whitewashed wall, to the cement floor, to the settle bed, to the cans of milk, seeing and bulging. He writhed like an animal and then let out a most beseeching howl, and that was it. At that moment my aunt remembered I was there and told me to go into the parlor and wait. It was worse in there, pitch dark, and I in a place where I did not know my footing or my way around. I'd only been in there once, to fetch a teapot and a sugar tongs when Tim came. Had it been in our own house I would have known what to cling to, the back of a chair, the tassel of a blind, the girth of a plaster statue, but in there I held on to nothing and thought how the thing he dreaded had come to pass and now he was finding out those dire things that all his life his mind had shirked from.

"May he rest in peace, may the souls of the faithful departed rest in peace."

It was that for two days, along with litanies and mourners smoking clay pipes, plates being passed around and glasses filled. My mother and father were there, among the mourners. I was praised for growing, as if it were something I myself had caused to happen. My mother looked older in black, and I wished she had worn a georgette scarf, something to give her a bit of brightness around the throat. She did not like when I said that, and sent me off to say the Confiteor and three Hail Marys. Her eyes were dry. She did not love her own father. Neither did I. Her sister and she would go down into the far room and discuss whether to bring out another bottle of whiskey or another porter cake, or whether it was time to offer the jelly. They were reluctant, the reason being that some provisions had to be held over for the next day, when the special mourners would come up after the funeral. Whereas that night half the parish was there. My grandfather was laid out upstairs in a brown habit. He had stubble on his chin and looked like a frosted plank lying there, gray-white and inanimate. As soon as they had paid their respects, the people hurried down to the kitchen and the parlor, for the eats and the chat. No one wanted to be with the dead man, not even his wife, who had gone a bit funny and was asking my aunt annoying questions about the food and the fire, and how many priests were going to serve at the High Mass.

"Leave that to us," my mother would say, and then my grandmother would retell the world what a palace my mother's house was, and how it was the nicest house in the countryside, and my mother would say "Shhhh," as if she were being disgraced. My father said, "Well, missy," to me twice, and a strange man gave me sixpence. It was a very thin, worn sixpence and I thought it would disappear. I called him Father, out of reverence, because he looked like a priest, but he was in fact a boatman.

The funeral was on an island on the Shannon. Most of the people stayed on the quay, but we, the family, piled into two rowboats and followed the boat that carried the coffin. It was a jolty ride, with big waves coming in over us and our feet getting drenched. The island itself was full of cows. The sudden arrivals made them bawl and race about, and I thought it was quite improper to see that happening while the remains were being lowered and buried. It was totally desolate, and though my aunt sniffled a bit, and my grandmother let out ejaculations, there was no real grief, and that was the saddest thing.

Next day they burned his working clothes and threw his muddy boots on the manure heap. Then my aunt sewed black diamonds of cloth on her clothes, on my grandmother's, and on Joe's. She wrote a long letter to her son in England, and enclosed black diamonds of cloth for him to stitch onto his effects. He worked in Liverpool in a motorcar factory. Whenever they said Liverpool, I thought of a whole mound of bloodied liver, but then I would look down at my watch and be happy again and pretend to tell the time. The house was gloomy. I went off with Joe, who was mowing hay, and sat with him on the mowing machine and fell slightly in love. Indoors was worst, what with my grandmother sighing and recalling old times, such as when her husband tried to kill her with a carving knife, and then she would snivel and miss him and say, "The poor old creature, he wasn't prepared . . ."

Out in the fields Joe fondled my knee and asked was I ticklish. He had a lovely long face and a beautiful whistle. He was probably about twenty-four, but he seemed old, especially because of a slouchy hat and because of a pair of trousers that were several times too big for him. When the mare passed water he nudged me and said, "Want lemonade?" and when she broke wind he made disgraceful plopping sounds with his lips. He and I ate lunch on the headland and lolled for a bit. We had bread and butter, milk from a flask, and some ginger cake that was left over from the funeral. It had gone damp. He sang, "You'll be lonely, little sweetheart, in the spring," and smiled a lot at me, and I felt very privileged. I knew that all he would do was tickle my knees, and the backs of my knees, because at heart he was shy and not like some of the local men who would want to throw you to the ground and press themselves over you so that you would have to ask God for protection. When he lifted me onto the machine, he said that we would bring out a nice little cushion on the morrow so that I would have a soft seat. But on the morrow it rained and he went off to the sawmill to get shelving, and my aunt moaned about the hay getting wet and perhaps getting ruined and possibly there being no fodder for cattle next winter.

That day I got into dire disaster. I was out in the fields playing, talking, and enjoying the rainbows in the puddles, when all of a sudden I decided to run helter-skelter toward the house in case they were cross with me. Coming through a stile that led to the yard, I decided to do a big jump and landed head over heels in the manure heap. I fell so heavily onto it that every bit of clothing got wet and smeared. It was a very massive manure heap, and very squelchy. Each day the cow house was cleaned out and the contents shoveled there, and each week the straw and old nesting from the hen house were dumped there, and so was the pigs' bedding. So it was not like falling into a sack of hay. It was not dry and clean. It was a foul spot I fell into, and as soon as I waded out, I decided it was wise to undress. The pleated skirt was ruined and so was my blouse and my navy cardigan. Damp had gone through to my bodice, and the smell was dreadful. I was trying to wash it off under an outside tap, using a fist of grass as a cloth, when my aunt came out and exclaimed, "Jesus, Mary, and Joseph, glory to the great God today and tonight, but what have you done to yourself!" I was afraid to tell that I fell, so I said I was doing washing and she said in the name of God what washing, and then she saw the ruin on the garments. She picked up the skirt and said why on earth had she let me wear it that day, and wasn't it the demon that came with me the day I arrived with my attaché case. I was still trying to wash and not answer this barrage of questions, all beginning with the word "why." As if I knew why! She got a rag and some pumice stone, plus a can of water, and stripped to the skin, I was washed and reprimanded. Then my clothes were put to soak in the can, all except for the skirt, which had to be brought in to dry, and then cleaned with a clothes brush. Mercifully my grandmother was not told.

My aunt forgave me two nights later when she was in the dairy churning and singing. I asked if I could turn the churn handle for a jiff. It was changing from liquid to solid and the handle was becoming stiff. I tried with all my might, but I was not strong enough.

"You will, when you're big," she said, and sang to me. She sang "Far Away in Australia" and then asked what I would like to do when I grew up. I said I would like to marry Carnero, and she laughed and said what a lovely thing it was to be young and carefree. She let me look into the churn to see the mound of yellow butter that had formed. There were drops of water all over its surface, it was like some big bulk that had bathed but had not dried off. She got two sets of wooden pats, and together we began to fashion the butter into dainty shapes. She was quicker at it than I. She made little round balls of butter with prickly surfaces, then she said wouldn't it be lovely if the curate came up for tea. He was a new curate and had rimless spectacles.

The next day she went to the town to sell the butter and I was left to mind the house along with my grandmother. My aunt had promised to bring back a shop cake, and said that, depending on the price, it would be either a sponge cake or an Oxford Lunch, which was a type of fruit cake wrapped in beautiful dun silverish paper. My grandmother donned a big straw hat with a chin strap and looked very distracted. She kept thinking that there was a car or a cart coming into the back yard and had me looking out windows on the alert. Then she got a flush and I had to conduct her into the plantation and sit on the bench next to her, and we were scarcely there when three huge fellows walked in and we knew at once that they were tinkers. The fear is indescribable. I knew that tinkers took one off in their cart, hid one under shawls, and did dire things to one. I knew that they beat their wives and children, got drunk, had fights among themselves, and spent many a night cooling off in the barracks. I jumped up as they came through the gate. My grandmother's mouth fell wide open with shock. One of them carried a shears and the other had a weighing pan in his hand. They asked if we had any sheep's wool and we both said no, no sheep, only cattle. They had evil eyes and gamey looks. There was no knowing what they would do to us. Then they asked if we had any feathers for pillows or mattresses. She was so crazed with fear that she said yes and led the way to the house. As we walked along, I expected a strong hand to be clamped on my shoulder. They were dreadfully silent. Only one had spoken and he had a shocking accent, what my mother would call "a gurrier's." She sent me upstairs to get the two bags of feathers out of the wardrobe, and I knew that she stayed below so that they would not steal a cake or bread or crockery or any other things. She was agreeing on a price when I came down, or rather, requesting a price. The talking member said it was a barter job. We would get a lace cloth in return. She asked how big this cloth was, and he said very big, while his companion put his hand into the bag of feathers to make sure that there was not anything else in there, that we were not trying to fob them off with grass or sawdust or something. She asked where was the cloth. They laughed. They said it was down in the caravan, at the crossroads, ma'am. She knew then she was being cheated, but she tried to stand her ground. She grabbed one end of the bag and said, "You'll not have these."

"D'you think we're mugs?" one of them said, and gestured to the others to pick up the two bags, which they did. Then they looked at us as if they might mutilate us, and I prayed to St. Jude and St. Anthony to keep us from harm. Before going, they insisted on being given new milk. They drank in great slugs.

"Are you afraid of me?" one of the men said to her.

He was the tallest of the three and his shirt was open. I could see the hair on his chest, and he had a very funny look in his eyes as if he was not thinking, as if thinking was beyond him. His eyes had a thickness in them. For some reason he reminded me of meat.

"Why should I be afraid of you," she said, and I was so proud of her I would have clapped, but for the tight shave we were in.

She blessed herself several times when they'd gone and decided that what we did had been the practical thing to do, and in fact our only recourse. But when my aunt came back and began an intensive cross-examination, the main contention was how they learned in the first place that there were feathers in the house. My aunt reasoned that they could not have known unless they had been told, they were not fortune-tellers. Each time I was asked, I would seal my lips, as I did not want to betray my grandmother. Each time she was asked, she described them in detail, the holes in their clothes, the safety pins instead of buttons, their villainous looks, and then she mentioned the child, me, and hinted about the things they might have done and was it not the blessing of God that we had got rid of them peaceably! My aunt's son joked about the lace cloth for weeks. He used to affect to admire it, by picking up one end of the black oilcloth on the table and saying, "Is it Brussels lace or is it Carrickmacross?"

Sunday came and my mother was expected to visit. My aunt had washed me the night before in an aluminum pan. I had to sit in it, and was terrified lest my cousin should peep in. He was in the back kitchen shaving and whistling. It was a question of a "Saturday splash for Sunday's dash." My aunt poured a can of water over my head and down my back. It was scalding hot. Then she poured rainwater over me and by contrast it was freezing. She was not a thorough washer like my mother, but all the time she kept saying that I would be like a new pin.

My mother was not expected until the afternoon. We had washed up the dinner things and given the dogs the potato skins and milk when I started in earnest to look out for her. I went to the gate where I had waited for Carnero, and seeing no sign of her, I sauntered off down the road. I was at the crossroads when I realized how dangerous it was, as I was approaching the spot where the tinkers said their caravan was pitched. So it was back at full speed. The fuchsia was out and so were the elderberries. The fuchsia was like dangling earrings and the riper elderberries were in maroon smudges on the road. I waited in hiding, the better to surprise her. She never came. It was five, and then half past five, and then it was six. I would go back to the kitchen and lift the clock that was face down on the dresser, and then hurry out to my watch post. By seven it was certain that she would not come, although I still held out hope. They hated to see me sniffle, and even hated more when I refused a slice of cake. I could not bear to eat. Might she still come? They said there was no point in my being so spoiled. I was imprisoned at the kitchen table in front of this slice of seed cake. In my mind I lifted the gate hasp a thousand times and saw my mother pass by the kitchen window, as fleeting as a ghost; and by the time we all knelt down to say the Rosary, my imagination had run amuck. I conceived of the worst things, such as she had died, or that my father had killed her, or that she had met a man and eloped. All three were unbearable. In bed I sobbed and chewed on the blanket so as not to be heard, and between tears and with my aunt enjoining me to dry up, I hatched a plan.

On the morrow there was no word or no letter, so I decided to run away. I packed a little satchel with bread, my comb, and, daftly, a spare pair of ankle socks. I told my aunt that I was going on a picnic and affected to be very happy by humming and doing little reels. It was a dry day and the dust rose in whirls under my feet. The dogs followed and I had immense trouble getting them to go back. There were no tinkers' caravans at the crossroads and because of that I was jubilant. I walked and then ran, and then I would have to slow down, and always when I slowed down, I looked back in case someone was following me. While I was running I felt I could elude them, but there was no eluding the loose stones and the bits of rock that were wedged into the dirt road. Twice I tripped. If, coming toward me, I saw two people together, I then felt safe, but if I saw one person it boded ill, as that one person could be mad, or drunk, or likely to accost. On three occasions I had to climb into a field and hide until that one ominous person went by. Fortunately, it was a quiet road, as not many souls lived in that region.

When I came off the dirt road onto the main road, I felt safer, and very soon a man came by in a pony and trap and offered me a lift. He looked a harmless enough person, in a frieze coat and a cloth cap. When I stepped into the trap I was surprised to find two hens clucking and agitating under a seat.

"Would you be one of the Linihans?" he asked, referring to my grandmother's family.

I said no and gave an assumed name. He plied me with questions. To get the most out of me, he even got the pony to slow down, so as to lengthen the journey. We dawdled. The seat of black leather was held down with black buttons. He had a tartan rug over him. He spread it out over us both. Quickly I edged out from under it, complaining about fleas and midges, neither of which there were. It was a desperately lonely road with only a house here and there, a graveyard, and sometimes an orchard. The apples looked tempting on the trees. To see each ripening apple was to see a miracle. He asked if I believed in ghosts and told me that he had seen the riderless horse on the moors.

"If you're a Minnogue," he said, "you should be getting out here," and he pulled on the reins.

I had called myself a Minnogue because I knew a girl of that name who lived with her mother and was separated from her father. I would like to have been her.

"I'm not," I said, and tried to be as innocent as possible. I then had to say who I was, and ask if he would drop me in the village.

"I'm passing your gate," he said, and I was terrified that I would have to ask him up, as my mother dreaded strangers, even dreaded visitors, since these diversions usually gave my father the inclination to drink, and once he drank he was on a drinking bout that would last for weeks, and that was notorious. Therefore I had to conjure up another lie. It was that my parents were both staying with my grandmother and that I had been dispatched home to get a change of clothing for us all. He grumbled at not coming up to our house, but I jumped out of the trap and said we would ask him to a card party for sure, in December.

There was no one at home. The door was locked and the big key in its customary place under the pantry window. The kitchen bore signs of my mother having gone out in a hurry, as the dishes were on the table, and on the table, too, were her powder puff, a near-empty powder box, and a holder of papier-mâché in which her toiletries were kept. Had she gone to the city? My heart was wild with envy. Why had she gone without me? I called upstairs, and then hearing no reply, I went up with a mind that was buzzing with fear, rage, suspicion, and envy. The beds were made. The rooms seemed vast and awesome compared with the little crammed rooms of my grandmother's. I heard someone in the kitchen and hurried down with renewed palpitations. It was my mother. She had been to the shop and got some chocolate. It was rationed because of its being wartime, but she used to coax the shopkeeper to give her some. He was a bachelor. He liked her. Maybe that was why she had put powder on.

"Who brought you home, my lady?" she said stiffly.

She hadn't come on Sunday. I blurted that out. She said did anyone ever hear such nonsense. She said did I not know that I was to stay there until the end of August till school began. She was even more irate when she heard that I had run away. What would they now be thinking but that I was in a bog hole or something. She said had I no consideration and how in heaven's name was she going to get word to them, an SOS.

"Where's my father?" I asked.

"Saving hay," she said.

I gathered the cups off the table so as to make myself useful in her eyes. Seeing the state of my canvas shoes and the marks on the ankle socks, she asked had I come through a river or what. All I wanted to know was why she had not come on Sunday as promised. The bicycle got punctured, she said, and then asked did I think that with bunions, corns, and welts she could walk six miles after doing a day's work. All I thought was that the homecoming was not nearly as tender as I hoped it would be, and there was no embrace and no reunion. She filled the kettle and I laid clean cups. I tried to be civil, to contain the pique and misery that was welling up in me. I told her how many trams of hay they had made in her mother's house, and she said it was a sight more than we had done. She hauled some scones from a colander in the cupboard and told me I had better eat. She did not heat them on the top of the oven, and that meant she was still vexed. I knew that before nightfall she would melt, but where is the use of a thing that comes too late?

I sat at the far end of the table watching the lines on her brow, watching the puckering, as she wrote a letter to my aunt explaining that I had come home. I would have to give it to the mail-car man the following morning and ask the postman to deliver it by hand. She said, God only knows what commotion there would be all that day and into the night looking for me. The ink in her pen gave out, and I held the near-empty ink bottle sideways while she refilled it.

"Go back to your place," she said, and I went back to the far end of the table like someone glued to her post. I thought of fields around my grandmother's house and the various smooth stones that I had put on the windowsill, I thought of the sun garden, of the night my grandfather had died and my vigil in the cold parlor. I thought of many things. Sitting there, I wanted both to be in our house and to be back in my grandmother's missing my mother. It was as if I could taste my pain better away from her, the excruciating pain that told me how much I loved her. I thought how much I needed to be without her so that I could think of her, dwell on her, and fashion her into the perfect person that she clearly was not. I resolved that for certain I would grow up and one day go away. It was a sweet thought, and it was packed with punishment.

John Updike

(b. 1932)

J ohn Updike was born in Reading, Pennsylvania, and grew up in
Shillington, where his father taught high school and his mother was
a writer. He graduated from Harvard summa cum laude *in 1954 and
went to the Ruskin School of Fine Art in Oxford. Returning to America,
Updike became a regular contributor to* New Yorker *as author of some
of "The Talk of the Town" columns. In 1957, to absent himself from the
distractions of the literary scene in New York and the city's hectic pace,
he and his family took up residence in Ipswich, Massachusetts, where he
proceeded to write novels and short stories that were to earn him a
reputation as one of America's best writers:* Rabbit, Run *(1960),* The
Centaur *(1963),* Couples *(1968),* Bech: A Book *(1970),* Rabbit Redux
(1971), and A Month of Sundays *(1975). "To transcribe middleness
with all its goals, bumps and anonymities, in its fullness of satisfaction
and mystery" is how Updike himself describes his project in his fiction.
In such recent works as* The Witches of Eastwick *(1984),* Roger's
Version *(1986), and* S. *(1988), he has experimented with a more satiric
view of contemporary society, its fascination with the occult, with technology, and with various forms of "liberation." In a foreword to* Olinger
Stories *(1964), Updike responds to critics who complain that although
his fiction meticulously records the American experience, it seems lacking
in overall significance: "The point, to me, is plain, and is the point, more
or less, of all these Olinger stories. We are rewarded unexpectedly.
The muddled and inconsequent surface of things now and then parts to
yield us a gift." The rewards of reading Updike involve the pleasure
elicited by his astonishing technical virtuosity and the feelings occasioned
by the encounters with such moments, when life yields up its provisional
sense and its radiance.*

A & P

I n walks these three girls in nothing but bathing suits. I'm in the third
checkout slot, with my back to the door, so I don't see them until
they're over by the bread. The one that caught my eye first was the one
in the plaid green two-piece. She was a chunky kid, with a good tan and
a sweet broad soft-looking can with those two crescents of white just
under it, where the sun never seems to hit, at the top of the backs of her
legs. I stood there with my hand on a box of HiHo crackers trying to
remember if I rang it up or not. I ring it up again and the customer starts

giving me hell. She's one of these cash-register-watchers, a witch about fifty with rouge on her cheekbones and no eyebrows, and I know it made her day to trip me up. She's been watching cash registers for fifty years and probably never seen a mistake before.

By the time I got her feathers smoothed and her goodies into a bag—she gives me a little snort in passing, if she'd been born at the right time they would have burned her over in Salem—by the time I get her on her way the girls had circled around the bread and were coming back, without a pushcart, back my way along the counters, in the aisle between the checkouts and the Special bins. They didn't even have shoes on. There was this chunky one, with the two-piece—it was bright green and the seams on the bra were still sharp and her belly was still pretty pale so I guessed she just got it (the suit)—there was this one, with one of those chubby berry-faces, the lips all bunched together under her nose, this one, and a tall one, with black hair that hadn't quite frizzed right, and one of these sunburns right across under the eyes, and a chin that was too long—you know, the kind of girl other girls think is very "striking" and "attractive" but never quite makes it, as they very well know, which is why they like her so much—and then the third one, that wasn't quite so tall. She was the queen. She kind of led them, the other two peeking around and making their shoulders round. She didn't look around, not this queen, she just walked straight on slowly, on these long white prima-donna legs. She came down a little hard on her heels, as if she didn't walk in her bare feet that much, putting down her heels and then letting the weight move along to her toes as if she was testing the floor with every step, putting a little deliberate extra action into it. You never know for sure how girls' minds work (do you really think it's a mind in there or just a little buzz like a bee in a glass jar?) but you got the idea she had talked the other two into coming in here with her, and now she was showing them how to do it, walk slow and hold yourself straight.

She had on a kind of dirty-pink—beige maybe, I don't know—bathing suit with a little nubble all over it and, what got me, the straps were down. They were off her shoulders looped loose around the cool tops of her arms, and I guess as a result the suit had slipped a little on her, so all around the top of the cloth there was this shining rim. If it hadn't been there you wouldn't have known there could have been anything whiter than those shoulders. With the straps pushed off, there was nothing between the top of the suit and the top of her head except just *her*, this clean bare plane of the top of her chest down from the shoulder bones like a dented sheet of metal tilted in the light. I mean, it was more than pretty.

She had sort of oaky hair that the sun and salt had bleached, done up in a bun that was unravelling, and a kind of prim face. Walking into the A & P with your straps down, I suppose it's the only kind of face you *can* have. She held her head so high her neck, coming up out of those white shoulders, looked kind of stretched, but I didn't mind. The longer her neck was, the more of her there was.

She must have felt in the corner of her eye me and over my shoulder Stokesie in the second slot watching, but she didn't tip. Not this queen. She kept her eyes moving across the racks, and stopped, and turned so slow it made my stomach rub the inside of my apron, and buzzed to the other two, who kind of huddled against her for relief, and then they all three of them went up the cat-and-dog-food-breakfast-cereal-macaroni-rice-raisins-seasonings-spreads-spaghetti-soft-drinks-crackers-and-cookies aisle. From the third slot I look straight up this aisle to the meat counter, and I watched them all the way. The fat one with the tan sort of fumbled with the cookies, but on second thought she put the package back. The sheep pushing their carts down the aisle—the girls were walking against the usual traffic (not that we have one-way signs or anything)—were pretty hilarious. You could see them, when Queenie's white shoulders dawned on them, kind of jerk, or hop, or hiccup, but their eyes snapped back to their own baskets and on they pushed. I bet you could set off dynamite in an A & P and the people would by and large keep reaching and checking oatmeal off their lists and muttering "Let me see, there was a third thing, began with A, asparagus, no, ah, yes, applesauce!" or whatever it is they do mutter. But there was no doubt, this jiggled them. A few houseslaves in pin curlers even looked around after pushing their carts past to make sure what they had seen was correct.

You know, it's one thing to have a girl in a bathing suit down on the beach, where what with the glare nobody can look at each other much anyway, and another thing in the cool of the A & P, under the fluorescent lights, against all those stacked packages, with her feet paddling along naked over our checkerboard green-and-cream rubber-tile floor.

"Oh Daddy," Stokesie said beside me. "I feel so faint."

"Darling," I said. "Hold me tight." Stokesie's married, with two babies chalked up on his fuselage already, but as far as I can tell that's the only difference. He's twenty-two, and I was nineteen this April.

"Is it done?" he asks, the responsible married man finding his voice. I forgot to say he thinks he's going to be manager some sunny day, maybe in 1990 when it's called the Great Alexandrov and Petrooshki Tea Company or something.

What he meant was, our town is five miles from a beach, with a big summer colony out on the Point, but we're right in the middle of town, and the women generally put on a shirt or shorts or something before they get out of the car into the street. And anyway these are usually women with six children and varicose veins mapping their legs and nobody, including them, could care less. As I say, we're right in the middle of town, and if you stand at our front doors you can see two banks and

Why does his family say it's the sad part of the story.

the Congregational church and the newspaper store and three real-estate offices and about twenty-seven old freeloaders tearing up Central Street because the sewer broke again. It's not as if we're on the Cape; we're north of Boston and there's people in this town haven't seen the ocean for twenty years.

The girls had reached the meat counter and were asking McMahon something. He pointed, they pointed, and they shuffled out of sight behind a pyramid of Diet Delight peaches. All that was left for us to see was old McMahon patting his mouth and looking after them sizing up their joints. Poor kids, I began to feel sorry for them, they couldn't help it.

Now here comes the sad part of the story, at least my family says it's sad, but I don't think it's so sad myself. The store's pretty empty, it being Thursday afternoon, so there was nothing much to do except lean on the register and wait for the girls to show up again. The whole store was like a pinball machine and I didn't know which tunnel they'd come out of. After a while they come around out of the far aisle, around the light bulbs, records at discount of the Caribbean Six or Tony Martin Sings or some such gunk you wonder they waste the wax on, sixpacks of candy bars, and plastic toys done up in cellophane that fall apart when a kid looks at them anyway. Around they come, Queenie still leading the way, and holding a little gray jar in her hand. Slots Three through Seven are unmanned and I could see her wondering between Stokes and me, but Stokesie with his usual luck draws an old party in baggy gray pants who stumbles up with four giant cans of pineapple juice (what do these bums *do* with all that pineapple juice? I've often asked myself) so the girls come to me. Queenie puts down the jar and I take it into my fingers icy cold. Kingfish Fancy Herring Snacks in Pure Sour Cream: 49¢. Now her hands are empty, not a ring or a bracelet, bare as God made them, and I wonder where the money's coming from. Still with that prim look she lifts a folded dollar bill out of the hollow at the center of her nubbled pink top. The jar went heavy in my hand. Really, I thought that was so cute.

Then everybody's luck begins to run out. Lengel comes in from haggling with a truck full of cabbages on the lot and is about to scuttle into that door marked MANAGER behind which he hides all day when the girls touch his eye. Lengel's pretty dreary, teaches Sunday school and the rest, but he doesn't miss that much. He comes over and says, "Girls, this isn't the beach."

Queenie blushes, though maybe it's just a brush of sunburn I was noticing for the first time, now that she was so close. "My mother asked me to pick up a jar of herring snacks." Her voice kind of startled me, the way voices do when you see the people first, coming out so flat and dumb yet kind of tony, too, the way it ticked over "pick up" and "snacks." All of a sudden I slid right down her voice into her living room. Her father

Why does Lengel read the way he does? What is the real source of conflict bet. the two parties?

and the other men were standing around in ice-cream coats and bow ties and the women were in sandals picking up herring snacks on toothpicks off a big glass plate and they were all holding drinks the color of water with olives and sprigs of mint in them. When my parents have somebody over they get lemonade and if it's a real racy affair Schlitz in tall glasses with "They'll Do It Every Time" cartoons stencilled on.

"That's all right," Lengel said. "But this isn't the beach." His repeating this struck me as funny, as if it had just occurred to him, and he had been thinking all these years the A & P was a great big dune and he was the head lifeguard. He didn't like my smiling—as I say he doesn't miss much—but he concentrates on giving the girls that sad Sunday-school-superintendent stare.

Queenie's blush is no sunburn now, and the plump one in plaid, that I liked better from the back—a really sweet can—pipes up. "We weren't doing any shopping. We just came in for the one thing."

"That makes no difference," Lengel tells her, and I could see from the way his eyes went that he hadn't noticed she was wearing a two-piece before. "We want you decently dressed when you come in here."

"We *are* decent," Queenie says suddenly, her lower lip pushing, getting sore now that she remembers her place, a place from which the crowd that runs the A & P must look pretty crummy. Fancy Herring Snacks flashed in her very blue eyes.

"Girls, I don't want to argue with you. After this come in here with your shoulders covered. It's our policy." He turns his back. That's policy for you. Policy is what the kingpins want. What the others want is juvenile delinquency.

All this while, the customers had been showing up with their carts but, you know, sheep, seeing a scene, they had all bunched up on Stokesie, who shook open a paper bag as gently as peeling a peach, not wanting to miss a word. I could feel in the silence everybody getting nervous, most of all Lengel, who asks me, "Sammy, have you rung up their purchase?"

I thought and said "No" but it wasn't about that I was thinking. I go through the punches, 4, 9, GROC, TOT—it's more complicated than you think, and after you do it often enough, it begins to make a little song, that you hear words to, in my case "Hello (*bing*) there, you (*gung*) happy *pee*-pul (*splat*)!"—the *splat* being the drawer flying out. I uncrease the bill, tenderly as you may imagine, it just having come from between the two smoothest scoops of vanilla I had ever known were there, and pass a half and a penny into her narrow pink palm, and nestle the herrings in a bag and twist its neck and hand it over, all the time thinking.

The girls, and who'd blame them, are in a hurry to get out, so I say "I quit" to Lengel quick enough for them to hear, hoping they'll stop and watch me, their unsuspected hero. They keep right on going, into the electric eye; the door flies open and they flicker across the lot to their car,

[handwritten top margin: Why does he look for "my girls"? Why will this hurt his parents; his life? What are his options?]

Queenie and Plaid and Big Tall Goony-Goony (not that as raw material she was so bad), leaving me with Lengel and a kink in his eyebrow.

"Did you say something, Sammy?"

"I said I quit."

"I thought you did."

"You didn't have to embarrass them."

"It was they who were embarrassing us."

I started to say something that came out "Fiddle-de-doo." It's a saying of my grandmother's, and I know she would have been pleased.

"I don't think you know what you're saying," Lengel said.

"I know you don't," I said. "But I do." I pull the bow at the back of my apron and start shrugging it off my shoulders. A couple of customers that had been heading for my slot begin to knock against each other, like scared pigs in a chute.

Lengel sighs and begins to look very patient and old and gray. He's been a friend of my parents for years. "Sammy, you don't want to do this to your Mom and Dad," he tells me. It's true, I don't. But it seems to me that once you begin a gesture it's fatal not to go through with it. I fold the apron, "Sammy" stitched in red on the pocket, and put it on the counter, and drop the bow tie on top of it. The bow tie is theirs, if you've ever wondered. "You'll feel this for the rest of your life," Lengel says, and I know that's true, too, but remembering how he made that pretty girl blush makes me so scrunchy inside I punch the No Sale tab and the machine whirs "pee-pul" and the drawer splats out. One advantage to this scene taking place in summer, I can follow this up with a clean exit, there's no fumbling around getting your coat and galoshes, I just saunter into the electric eye in my white shirt that my mother ironed the night before, and the door heaves itself open, and outside the sunshine is skating around on the asphalt.

[handwritten left margin: outside as contrast]

I look around for my girls, but they're gone, of course. There wasn't anybody but some young married screaming with her children about some candy they didn't get by the door of a powder-blue Falcon station wagon. Looking back in the big windows, over the bags of peat moss and aluminum lawn furniture stacked on the pavement, I could see Lengel in my place in the slot, checking the sheep through. His face was dark gray and his back stiff, as if he'd just had an injection of iron, and my stomach kind of fell as I felt how hard the world was going to be to me hereafter. *[handwritten: Why does he feel this way?]*

[handwritten bottom margin questions:]
① How is the store described: note items in store. *[handwritten right margin: what is the org. of King's 5 & Dime; mrg snacks]*
② What is the tone of the description.
③ What do the girls represent in the author's mind (esp. in context of the store).
④ What is the role of Stokesi & Lengel?
⑤ What kind of town is this?

The Happiest I've Been

[handwritten: Olinger, Penn.]

Neil Hovey came for me wearing a good suit. He parked his father's blue Chrysler on the dirt ramp by our barn and got out and stood by the open car door in a double-breasted tan gabardine suit, his hands in his pockets and his hair combed with water, squinting up at a lightning rod an old hurricane had knocked crooked.

We were driving to Chicago, so I had dressed in worn-out slacks and an outgrown corduroy shirt. But Neil was the friend I had always been most relaxed with, so I wasn't very disturbed. My parents and I walked out from the house, across the low stretch of lawn that was mostly mud after the thaw that had come on Christmas Day, and my grandmother, though I had kissed her good-bye inside the house, came out onto the porch, stooped and rather angry-looking, her head haloed by wild old woman's white hair and the hand more severely afflicted by arthritis waggling at her breast in a worried way. It was growing dark and my grandfather had gone to bed. "Nev-er trust the man who wears the red necktie and parts his hair in the middle," had been his final advice to me.

We had expected Neil since middle afternoon. Nineteen almost twenty, I was a college sophomore home on vacation; that fall I had met in a fine arts course a girl I had fallen in love with, and she had invited me to the New Year's party her parents always gave and to stay at her house a few nights. She lived in Chicago and so did Neil now, though he had gone to our high school. His father did something—sell steel was my impression, a huge man opening a briefcase and saying "The I-beams are very good this year"—that required him to be always on the move, so that at about thirteen Neil had been boarded with Mrs. Hovey's parents, the Lancasters. They had lived in Olinger since the town was incorporated. Indeed, old Jesse Lancaster, whose sick larynx whistled when he breathed to us boys his shocking and uproarious thoughts on the girls that walked past his porch all day long, had twice been burgess. Meanwhile Neil's father got a stationary job, but he let Neil stay to graduate; after the night he graduated, Neil drove throughout the next day to join his parents. From Chicago to this part of Pennsylvania was seventeen hours. In the twenty months he had been gone Neil had come east fairly often; he loved driving and Olinger was the one thing he had that was close to a childhood home. In Chicago he was working in a garage and getting his teeth straightened by the Army so they could draft him. Korea was on. He had to go back, and I wanted to go, so it was a happy arrangement. "You're all dressed up," I accused him immediately.

"I've been saying good-bye." The knot of his necktie was loose and the corners of his mouth were rubbed with pink. Years later my mother recalled how that evening his breath stank so strongly of beer she was frightened to let me go with him. "*Your* grandfather always thought *his* grandfather was a very dubious character," she said then.

My father and Neil put my suitcases into the trunk; they contained all the clothes I had brought, for the girl and I were going to go back to college on the train together, and I would not see my home again until spring.

"Well, good-bye, boys," my mother said. "I think you're both very brave." In regard to me she meant the girl as much as the roads.

"Don't you worry, Mrs. Nordholm," Neil told her quickly. "He'll be safer than in his bed. I bet he sleeps from here to Indiana." He looked at me with an irritating imitation of her own fond gaze. When they shook hands good-bye it was an equality established on the base of my helplessness. His being so slick startled me, but then you can have a friend for years and never see how he operates with adults.

I embraced my mother and over her shoulder with the camera of my head tried to take a snapshot I could keep of the house, the woods behind it and the sunset behind them, the bench beneath the walnut tree where my grandfather cut apples into skinless bits and fed them to himself, and the ruts in the soft lawn the bakery truck had made that morning.

We started down the half-mile of dirt road to the highway that, one way, went through Olinger to the city of Alton and, the other way, led through farmland to the Turnpike. It was luxurious, after the stress of farewell, to two-finger a cigarette out of the pack in my shirt pocket. My family knew I smoked but I didn't do it in front of them; we were all too sensitive to bear the awkwardness. I lit mine and held the match for Hovey. It was a relaxed friendship. We were about the same height and had the same degree of athletic incompetence and the same curious lack of whatever force it was that aroused loyalty and compliance in beautiful girls. There was his bad teeth and my skin allergy; these were being remedied now, when they mattered less. But it seemed to me the most important thing—about both our friendship and our failures to become, for all the love we felt for women, actual lovers—was that he and I lived with grandparents. This improved both our backward and forward vistas; we knew about the bedside commodes and midnight coughing fits that awaited most men, and we had a sense of childhoods before 1900, when the farmer ruled the land and America faced west. We had gained a humane dimension that made us gentle and humorous among peers but diffident at dances and hesitant in cars. Girls hate boys' doubts: they amount to insults. Gentleness is for married women to appreciate. (This is my thinking then.) A girl who has received out of nowhere a gift worth all Africa's ivory and Asia's gold wants more than just humanity to bestow it on.

Coming onto the highway, Neil turned right toward Olinger instead of left toward the Turnpike. My reaction was to twist and assure myself through the rear window that, though a pink triangle of sandstone stared through the bare treetops, nobody at my house could possibly see.

When he was again in third gear, Neil asked, "Are you in a hurry?"

"No. Not especially."

"Schuman's having his New Year's party two days early so we can go. I thought we'd go for a couple hours and miss the Friday night stuff on the Pike." His mouth moved and closed carefully over the dull, silver, painful braces.

"Sure," I said. "I don't care." In everything that followed there was this sensation of my being picked up and carried.

It was four miles from the farm to Olinger; we entered by Buchanan Road, driving past the tall white brick house I had lived in until I was fifteen. My grandfather had bought it before I was born and his stocks became bad, which had happened in the same year. The new owners had strung colored bulbs all along the front door frame and the edges of the porch roof. Downtown the cardboard Santa Claus still nodded in the drug store window but the loudspeaker on the undertaker's lawn had stopped broadcasting carols. It was quite dark now, so the arches of red and green lights above Grand Avenue seemed miracles of lift; in daylight you saw the bulbs were just hung from a straight cable by cords of different lengths. Larry Schuman lived on the other side of town, the newer side. Lights ran all the way up the front edges of his house and across the rain gutter. The next-door neighbor had a plywood reindeer-and-sleigh floodlit on his front lawn and a snowman of papier-mâché leaning tipsily (his eyes were x's) against the corner of his house. No real snow had fallen yet that winter. The air this evening, though, hinted that harder weather was coming.

The Schumans' living room felt warm. In one corner a blue spruce drenched with tinsel reached to the ceiling; around its pot surged a drift of wrapping paper and ribbon and boxes, a few still containing presents, gloves and diaries and other small properties that hadn't yet been absorbed into the mainstream of affluence. The ornamental balls were big as baseballs and all either crimson or indigo; the tree was so well-dressed I felt self-conscious in the same room with it, without a coat or tie and wearing an old green shirt too short in the sleeves. Everyone else was dressed for a party. Then Mr. Schuman stamped in comfortingly, crushing us all into one underneath his welcome, Neil and I and the three other boys who had showed up so far. He was dressed to go out on the town, in a vanilla topcoat and silvery silk muffler, smoking a cigar with the band still on. You could see in Mr. Schuman where Larry got the red hair and white eyelashes and the self-confidence, but what in the son was smirking and pushy was in the father shrewd and masterful. What the one used to make you nervous the other used to put you at ease. While Mr. was jollying us, Zoe Loessner, Larry's probable fiancée and the only other girl at the party so far, was talking nicely to Mrs., nodding with her entire neck and fingering her Kresge pearls and blowing cigarette smoke through the corners of her mouth, to keep it away from the middle-aged woman's face. Each time Zoe spat out a plume, the shelf of honey overhanging her temple bobbed. Mrs. Schuman beamed serenely above her mink coat and rhinestone pocketbook. It was odd to see her dressed in the trappings of the prosperity that usually supported her good nature invisibly, like a firm mattress under a bright homely quilt. Everybody loved her. She was a prime product of the county, a Pennsylvania Dutch woman with sons, who loved feeding her sons and who imagined that the entire world, like her life, was going well. I never saw her not smile, except at her husband. At last she moved him into the outdoors. He turned at the threshold and did a trick with his knees and called in to us, "Be good and if you can't be good, be careful."

With them out of the way, the next item was getting liquor. It was a familiar business. Did anybody have a forged driver's license? If not, who would dare to forge theirs? Larry could provide India ink. Then again, Larry's older brother Dale might be home and would go if it didn't take too much time. However, on weekends he often went straight from work to his fiancée's apartment and stayed until Sunday. If worse came to worse, Larry knew an illegal place in Alton, but they really soaked you. The problem was solved strangely. More people were arriving all the time and one of them, Cookie Behn, who had been held back one year and hence was deposited in our grade, announced that last November he had become in honest fact twenty-one. I at least gave Cookie my share of the money feeling a little queasy, vice had become so handy.

The party was the party I had been going to all my life, beginning with Ann Mahlon's first Hallowe'en party, that I attended as a hot, lumbering, breathless, and blind Donald Duck. My mother had made the costume, and the eyes kept slipping, and were further apart than my eyes, so that even when the clouds of gauze parted, it was to reveal the frustrating depthless world seen with one eye. Ann, who because her mother loved her so much as a child had remained somewhat childish, and I and another boy and girl who were not involved in any romantic crisis went down into Schuman's basement to play circular ping-pong. Armed with paddles, we stood each at a side of the table and when the ball was stroked ran around it counter-clockwise, slapping the ball and screaming. To run better the girls took of their heels and ruined their stockings on the cement floor. Their faces and arms and shoulder sections became flushed, and when a girl lunged forward toward the net the stiff neckline of her semi-formal dress dropped away and the white arcs of her brassiere could be glimpsed cupping fat, and when she reached high her shaved armpit gleamed like a bit of chicken skin. An earring of Ann's flew off and the two connected rhinestones skidded to lie near the wall, among the Schuman's power mower and badminton poles and empty bronze motor-oil cans twice punctured by triangles. All these images were immediately lost in the whirl of our running; we were dizzy before we stopped. Ann leaned on me getting back into her shoes.

When we pushed it open the door leading down into the cellar banged against the newel post of the carpeted stairs going to the second floor; a third of the way up these, a couple sat discussing. The girl, Jacky Iselin, cried without emotion—the tears and nothing else, like water flowing over wood. Some people were in the kitchen mixing drinks and making noise. In the living room others danced to records: 78s then, stiff discs stacked in a ponderous leaning cylinder on the spindle of the Schumans' console. Every three minutes with a click and a crash another dropped and the mood abruptly changed. One moment it would be "Stay As Sweet As You Are": Clarence Lang with the absolute expression of an idiot standing and rocking monotonously with June Kaufmann's boneless sad brown hand trapped in his and their faces, staring in the same direction, pasted together like the facets of an idol. The music stopped; when they parted, a big squarish dark patch stained the cheek of each. Then the next moment it would be Goodman's "Loch Lomond" or "Cherokee" and nobody but Margaret Lento wanted to jitterbug. Mad, she danced by herself, swinging her head recklessly and snapping her backside; a corner of her skirt flipped a Christmas ball onto the rug, where it collapsed into a hundred convex reflectors. Female shoes were scattered in innocent pairs about the room. Some were flats, resting under the sofa shyly toed in; others were high heels lying cockeyed, the spike of one thrust into its mate. Sitting alone and ignored in a great armchair, I experienced within a warm keen dishevelment, as if there were real tears in my eyes. Had things been less unchanged they would have seemed less tragic. But the girls who had stepped out of these shoes were with few exceptions the ones who had attended my life's party. The alterations were so small: a haircut, an engagement ring, a franker plumpness. While they wheeled above me I sometimes caught from their faces an unfamiliar glint, off of a hardness I did not remember, as if beneath their skins these girls were growing more dense. The brutality added to the features of the boys I knew seemed a more willed effect, more desired and so less grievous. Considering that there was a war, surprisingly many were present, 4-F or at college or simply waiting to be called. Shortly before midnight the door rattled and there, under the porchlight, looking forlorn and chilled in their brief athletic jackets, stood three members of the class ahead of ours who in the old days always tried to crash Schuman's parties. At Olinger High they had been sports stars, and they still stood with that well-coördinated looseness, a look of dangling from strings. The three of them had enrolled together at Melanchthon, a small Lutheran college on the edge of Alton, and in this season played on the Melanchthon basket-ball team. That is, two did; the third hadn't been good enough. Schuman, out of cowardice more than mercy, let them in, and they hid without hesitation in the basement and didn't bother us, having brought their own bottle.

There was one novel awkwardness. Darryl Bechtel had married Emmy Johnson and the couple came. Darryl had worked in his father's greenhouse and was considered dull; it was Emmy that we knew. At first no one danced with her, and Darryl didn't know how, but then Schuman, perhaps as host, dared. Others followed, but Schuman had her in his arms most often, and at midnight, when we were pretending the new year began, he kissed her; a wave of kissing swept the room now, and everyone struggled to kiss Emmy. Even I did. There was something about her being married that made it extraordinary. Her cheeks in flame, she kept glancing around for rescue, but Darryl, embarrassed to see his wife dance, had gone into old Schuman's den, where Neil sat brooding, sunk in mysterious sorrow.

When the kissing subsided and Darryl emerged, I went in to see Neil. He was holding his face in his hands and tapping his foot to a record playing on Mr. Schuman's private phonograph: Krupa's "Dark Eyes." The arrangement was droning and circular and Neil had kept the record going for hours. He loved saxophones; I guess all of us children of that Depression vintage did. I asked him, "Do you think the traffic on the Turnpike had died down by now?"

He took down the tall glass off the cabinet beside him and took a convincing swallow. His face from the side seemed lean and somewhat blue. "Maybe," he said, staring at the ice cubes submerged in the ochre liquid. "The girl in Chicago's expecting you?"

"Well, yeah, but we can call and let her know, once *we* know."

"You think she'll spoil?"

"How do you mean?"

"I mean, won't you be seeing her all the time after we get there? Aren't you going to marry her?"

"I have no idea. I might."

"Well then: you'll have the rest of Kingdom Come to see her." He looked directly at me, and it was plain in the blur of his eyes that he was sick-drunk. "The trouble with you guys that have all the luck," he said slowly, "is that you don't give a fuck about us that don't have any." Such melodramatic rudeness coming from Neil surprised me, as had his blarney with my mother hours before. In trying to evade his wounded stare, I discovered there was another person in the room: a girl sitting with her shoes on, reading *Holiday*. Though she held the magazine in front of her face I knew from her clothes and her unfamiliar legs that she was the girl friend Margaret Lento had brought. Margaret didn't come from Olinger but from Riverside, a section of Alton, not a suburb. She had met Larry Schuman at a summer job in a restaurant and for the rest of high school they had more or less gone together. Since then, though, it had dawned on Mr. and Mrs. Schuman that even in a democracy distinctions exist, probably welcome news to Larry. In the cruellest and most stretched-out way he could manage he had been breaking off with her throughout the year now nearly ended. I had been surprised to find her at this party. Obviously she had felt shaky about attending and had brought the friend as the only kind of protection she could afford. The other girl was acting just like a hired guard.

There being no answer to Neil, I went into the living room, where Margaret, insanely drunk, was throwing herself around as if wanting to break a bone. Somewhat in time to the music she would run a few steps, then snap her body like a whip, her chin striking her chest and her hands flying backward, fingers fanned, as her shoulders pitched forward. In her state her body was childishly plastic; unharmed, she would bounce back from this jolt and begin to clap and kick and hum. Schuman stayed away from her. Margaret was small, not more than 5'3", with the smallness ripeness comes to early. She had bleached a section of her black hair platinum, cropped her head all over, and trained the stubble into short hyacinthine curls like those on antique statues of boys. Her face seemed quite coarse from the front, so her profile was classical unexpectedly. She might have been Portia. When she was not putting on her savage pointless dance she was in the bathroom being sick. The pity and the vulgarity of her exhibition made everyone who was sober uncomfortable; our common guilt in witnessing this girl's rites brought us so close together in that room that it seemed never, not in all time, could we be parted. I myself was perfectly sober. I had the impression then that people only drank to stop being unhappy and I nearly always felt at least fairly happy.

Luckily, Margaret was in a sick phase around one o'clock, when the elder Schumans came home. They looked in at us briefly. It was a pleasant joke to see in their smiles that, however corrupt and unwinking we felt, to them we looked young and sleepy: Larry's friends. Things quieted after they went up the stairs. In half an hour people began coming out of the kitchen balancing cups of coffee. By two o'clock four girls stood in aprons at Mrs. Schuman's sink, and others were padding back and forth carrying glasses and ashtrays. Another blameless racket pierced the clatter in the kitchen. Out on the cold grass the three Melanchthon athletes had set up the badminton net and in the faint glow given off by the house were playing. The bird, ascending and descending through uneven bars of light, glimmered like a firefly. Now that the party was dying Neil's apathy seemed deliberately exasperating, even vindictive. For at least another hour he persisted in hearing "Dark Eyes" over and over again, holding his head and tapping his foot. The entire scene in the den had developed a fixity that was uncanny; the girl remained in the chair and read magazines, *Holiday* and *Esquire*, one after another. In the meantime, cars came and went and raced their motors out front; Schuman took Ann Mahlon off and didn't come back; and the athletes carried the neighbor's artificial snowman into the center of the street and disappeared. Somehow in the arrangements shuffled together at the end, Neil had contracted to drive Margaret and the other girl home. Margaret convalesced in the downstairs bathroom for most of that hour. I unlocked a little glass bookcase ornamenting a desk in the dark dining room and removed a volume of Thackeray's Works. It turned out to be Volume II of *Henry Esmond*. I began it, rather than break another book out of the set, which had been squeezed in there so long the bindings had sort of inter-penetrated.

Henry was going off to war again when Neil appeared in the archway and said, "O.K., Norseman. Let's go to Chicago." "Norseman" was a variant of my name he used only when feeling special affection.

We turned off all the lamps and left the hall bulb burning against Larry's return. Margaret Lento seemed chastened. Neil gave her his arm and led her into the back seat of his father's car; I stood aside to let the other girl get in with her, but Neil indicated that I should. I supposed he realized this left only the mute den-girl to go up front with him. She sat well over on her side, was all I noticed. Neil backed into the street and with unusual care steered past the snowman. Our headlights made vivid the fact that the snowman's back was a hollow right-angled gash; he had been built up against the corner of a house.

From Olinger, Riverside was diagonally across Alton. The city was sleeping as we drove through it. Most of the stoplights were blinking green. Among cities Alton had a bad reputation; its graft and gambling and easy juries and bawdy houses were supposedly notorious throughout the Middle Atlantic states. But to me it always presented an innocent face; row after row of houses built of a local dusty-red brick the shade of flowerpots, each house fortified with a tiny, intimate, balustraded porch, and nothing but the wealth of movie houses and beer signs along its main street to suggest that its citizens loved pleasure more than the run of mankind. Indeed, as we moved at moderate speed down these hushed streets bordered with parked cars, a limestone church bulking at every corner and the hooded street lamps keeping watch from above, Alton seemed less the ultimate center of an urban region than itself a suburb of some vast mythical metropolis, like Pandemonium or Paradise. I was conscious of evergreen wreaths on door after door and of fanlights of stained glass in which the house number was embedded. I was also conscious that every block was one block further from the Turnpike.

M's house

Riverside, fitted into the bends of the Schuylkill, was not so regularly laid out. Margaret's house was one of a short row, composition-shingled, which we approached from the rear, down a tiny cement alley speckled with drains. The porches were a few inches higher than the alley. Margaret asked us if we wanted to come in for a cup of coffee, since we were going to Chicago; Neil accepted by getting out of the car and slamming his door. The noise filled the alley, alarming me. I wondered at the easy social life that evidently existed among my friends at three-thirty in the morning. Margaret did, however, lead us in stealthily, and she turned on only the kitchen switch. The kitchen was divided from the living room by a large sofa, which faced into littered gloom where distant light from beyond the alley spilled over the window sill and across the spines of a radiator. In one corner the glass of a television set showed; the screen would seem absurdly small now, but then it seemed disproportionately elegant. The shabbiness everywhere would not have struck me so definitely if I hadn't just come from Schuman's place. Neil and the other girl sat on the sofa; Margaret held a match to a gas burner and, as the blue flame licked an old kettle, doled instant coffee into four flowered cups.

Some man who had once lived in this house had built by the kitchen's one window a breakfast nook, nothing more than a booth, a table between two high-backed benches. I sat in it and read all the words I could see: "Salt," "Pepper," "Have Some LUMPS," "December," "Mohn's Milk Inc— A Very Merry Christmas and Joyous New Year—Mohn's Milk is *Safe Milk*—'Mommy, Make It Mohn's!,'" "Matches," "Hotpoint," "PRESS," Magee Stove FEDERAL & FURNACE Corp.," "God Is In This House," "Ave Maria Gratia Plena," "SHREDDED WHEAT Benefits Exciting New Pattern KUNGSHOLM." After serving the two on the sofa, Margaret came to me with coffee and sat down opposite me in the booth. Fatigue had raised two blue welts beneath her eyes.

"Well," I asked her, "did you have a good time?"

She smiled and glanced down and made the small sound "Ch," vestigal of "Jesus." With absent-minded delicacy she stirred her coffee, lifting and replacing the spoon without a ripple.

"Rather odd at the end," I said, "not even the host there."

"He took Ann Mahlon home."

"I know." I was surprised that she knew, having been sick in the bathroom for that hour.

"You sound jealous," she added.

"Who does? I do? I don't."

"You like her, John, don't you?" Her using my first name and the quality of the question did not, although discounting parties we had just met, seem forward, considering the hour and that she had brought me coffee. There is very little further to go with a girl who has brought you coffee.

"Oh, I like everybody," I told her, "and the longer I've known them the more I like them, because the more they're me. The only people I like better are ones I've just met. Now Ann Mahlon I've known since kindergarten. Every day her mother used to bring her to the edge of the schoolyard for months after all the other mothers had stopped." I wanted to cut a figure in Margaret's eyes, but they were too dark. Stoically she had gotten on top of her weariness, but it was growing bigger under her.

"Did you like her then?"

"I felt sorry for her being embarrassed by her mother." *(ann Mahlon)*

She asked me, "What was Larry like when he was little?"

"Oh, bright. Kind of mean."

"Was he mean?"

"I'd say so. Yes. In some grade or other he and I began to play chess together. I always won until secretly he took lessons from a man his parents knew and read strategy books."

Margaret laughed, genuinely pleased. "Then did he win?"

"Once. After that I really tried, and after *that* he decided chess was kid stuff. Besides, I was used up. He'd have these runs on people where you'd be down at his house every afternoon, then in a couple of months he'd get a new pet and that'd be that."

"He's funny," she said. "He has a kind of cold mind. He decides on what he wants, then he does what he has to do, you know, and nothing anybody says can change him."

"He does tend to get what he wants," I admitted guardedly, realizing that to her this meant her. Poor bruised little girl, in her mind he was all the time cleaving with rare cunning through his parents' objections straight to her.

My coffee was nearly gone, so I glanced toward the sofa in the other room. Neil and the girl had sunk out of sight behind its back. Before this it had honestly not occurred to me that they had a relationship, but now that I saw, it seemed plausible and, at this time of night, good news, though it meant we would not be going to Chicago yet.

So I talked to Margaret about Larry, and she responded, showing really quite an acute sense of him. To me, considering so seriously the personality of a childhood friend, as if overnight he had become a factor in the world, seemed disproportionate; I couldn't deeply believe that even in her world he mattered much. Larry Schuman, in little more than a year, had become nothing to me. The important thing, rather than the subject, was the conversation itself, the quick agreements, the slow nods, the weave of different memories; it was like one of those Panama baskets shaped underwater around a worthless stone.

She offered me more coffee. When she returned with it, she sat down, not opposite, but beside me, lifting me to such a pitch of gratitude and affection the only way I could think to express it was by *not* kissing her, as if a kiss were another piece of abuse women suffered. She said, "Cold. Cheap bastard turns the thermostat down to sixty," meaning her father. She drew my arm around her shoulders and folded my hand around her bare forearm, to warm it. The back of my thumb fitted against the curve of one breast. Her head went into the hollow where my arm and chest joined; she was terribly small, measured against your own body. Perhaps she weighed a hundred pounds. Her lids lowered and I kissed her two beautiful eyebrows and then the spaces of skin between the rough curls, some black and some bleached, that fringed her forehead. Other than this I tried to keep as still as a bed would be. It *had* grown cold. A shiver starting on the side away from her would twitch my shoulders when I tried to repress it; she would frown and unconsciously draw my arm tighter. No one had switched the kitchen light off. On Margaret's foreshortened upper lip there seemed to be two pencil marks; the length of wrist my badly fitting sleeve exposed looked pale and naked against the spiralling down of the smaller arm held beneath it.

Outside on the street the house faced there was no motion. Only once did a car go by: around five o'clock, with twin mufflers, the radio on and a boy yelling. Neil and the girl murmured together incessantly; some of what they said I could overhear.

"No. Which?" she asked.

"I don't care."

"Wouldn't you want a boy?"

"I'd be happy whatever I got."

"I know, but which would you *rather* have? Don't men want boys?"

"I don't care. You."

Somewhat later, Mohn's truck passed on the other side of the street. The milkman, well-bundled, sat behind headlights in a warm orange volume the size of a phone booth, steering one-handed and smoking a cigar that set on the edge of the dashboard when, his wire carrier vibrant, he ran out of the truck with bottles. His passing led Neil to decide the time had come. Margaret woke up frightened of her father; we hissed our farewells and thanks to her quickly. Neil dropped the other girl off at her house a few blocks away; he knew where it was. Sometime during that night I must have seen this girl's face, but I have no memory of it. She is always behind a magazine or in the dark or with her back turned. Neil married her years later, I know, but after we arrived in Chicago I never saw him again either.

Red dawn light touched the clouds above the black slate roof as, with a few other cars, we drove through Alton. The moon-sized clock of a beer billboard said ten after six. Olinger was deathly still. The air brightened as we moved along the highway; the glowing of my home hung above the woods as we rounded the long curve by the Mennonite dairy. With a .22 I could have had a pane of my parents' bedroom window, and they were dreaming I was in Indiana. My grandfather would be up, stamping around in the kitchen for my grandmother to make him breakfast, or outside, walking to see if any ice had formed on the brook. For an instant I genuinely feared he might hail me from the peak of the barn roof. Then trees interceded and we were safe in a landscape where no one cared.

At the entrance to the Turnpike Neil did a strange thing, stopped the car and had me take the wheel. He had never trusted me to drive his father's car before; he had believed my not knowing where the crankshaft and fuel pump were handicapped my competence to steer. But now he was quite complacent. He hunched under an old mackinaw and leaned his head against the metal of the window frame and soon was asleep. We crossed the Susquehanna on a long smooth bridge below Harrisburg, then began climbing toward the Alleghenies. In the mountains there was snow, a dry dusting like sand, that waved back and forth on the road surface. Further along there had been a fresh fall that night, about two inches, and the plows had not yet cleared all the lanes. I was passing a Sunoco truck on a high curve when without warning the scraped section gave out and I realized I might skid into the fence if not over the edge. The radio was singing "Carpets of clover, I'll lay right at your feet," and the speedometer said 85. Nothing happened; the car stayed firm in the snow and Neil slept through the danger, his face turned skyward and his breath struggling in his nose. It was the first time I heard a contemporary of mine snore.

When we came into tunnel country the flicker and hollow amplification stirred Neil awake. He sat up, the mackinaw dropping to his lap, and lit a cigarette. A second after the scratch of his match occurred the moment of which each following moment was a slight diminution, as we made the long irregular descent toward Pittsburgh. There were many reasons for my feeling so happy. We were on our way. I had seen a dawn. This far, Neil could appreciate, I had brought us safely. Ahead, a girl waited who, if I asked, would marry me, but first there was a vast trip: many hours and towns interceded between me and that encounter. There was the quality of the 10 A.M. sunlight as it existed in the air ahead of the windshield, filtered by the thin overcast, blessing irresponsibility—you felt you could slice forever through such a cool pure element—and springing, by implying how high these hills had become, a widespreading pride: Pennsylvania, your state—as if you had made your life. And there was knowing that twice since midnight a person had trusted me enough to fall asleep beside me.

PHILIP ROTH

(b. 1933)

P hilip Roth was born and educated in Newark, New Jersey. He describes himself as "a good, responsible, well-behaved boy, controlled (rather willingly) by the social regulations of the self-conscious and orderly lower-middle-class neighborhood where I had been raised, and mildly constrained still by the taboos that had filtered down to me, in attenuated form, from the religious orthodoxy of my immigrant grandparents." He studied English at Bucknell University and took his M.A. at the University of Chicago. After a brief stint in the army, he turned to writing and teaching (at Iowa, Princeton, Pennsylvania) and has successfully combined these careers ever since. He won the National Book Award for Goodbye, Columbus *(1959).* Portnoy's Complaint *(1969) was an instant bestseller and permanently established Roth's reputation. His other books include* When She Was Good *(1967),* Our Gang *(1971),* The Great American Novel *(1973),* Zuckerman Unbound *(1985),* The Counterlife *(1986),* Deception *(1990), and* The Facts, *an autobiography published in 1988. The critic Hermione Lee has described Roth's materials as "psychoanalysis, alienation, erotic fixations, pornography, urban violence, strains on the family, divorce, . . . alarm at the implications of Zionism for twentieth-century Jewish history, dismay at the ineffectuality of liberalism, and national political guilt and disillusion," and she identifies his fictional strategies as "anecdotal realism, surrealism, pastiche, confessionals, case-histories, psychic fantasies . . . [and] coolly objectified autobiographies." The two lists combine to give some sense of the multifaceted quality of Roth's achievement. The zany humour, revealing subjectivity, and compassionate engagement with life in his own time have made Roth one of America's most respected writers.*

The Conversion of the Jews

"You're a real one for opening your mouth in the first place," Itzie said. "What do you open your mouth all the time for?"

"I didn't bring it up, Itz, I didn't," Ozzie said.

"What do you care about Jesus Christ for anyway?"

"I didn't bring up Jesus Christ. He did. I didn't even know what he was talking about. Jesus is historical, he kept saying. Jesus is historical." Ozzie mimicked the monumental voice of Rabbi Binder.

"Jesus was a person that lived like you and me," Ozzie continued. "That's what Binder said—"

"Yeah? . . . So what! What do I give two cents whether he lived or not. And what do you gotta open your mouth!" Itzie Lieberman favored closed-mouthedness, especially when it came to Ozzie Freedman's questions. Mrs. Freedman had to see Rabbi Binder twice before about Ozzie's questions and this Wednesday at four-thirty would be the third time. Itzie preferred to keep *his* mother in the kitchen; he settled for behind-the-back subtleties such as gestures, faces, snarls and other less delicate barnyard noises.

"He was a real person, Jesus, but he wasn't like God, and we don't believe he is God." Slowly, Ozzie was explaining Rabbi Binder's position to Itzie, who had been absent from Hebrew School the previous afternoon.

"The Catholics," Itzie said helpfully, "they believe in Jesus Christ, that he's God." Itzie Lieberman used "the Catholics" in its broadest sense—to include the Protestants.

Ozzie received Itzie's remark with a tiny head bob, as though it were a footnote, and went on. "His mother was Mary, and his father probably was Joseph," Ozzie said. "But the New Testament says his real father was God."

"His *real* father?"

"Yeah," Ozzie said, "that's the big thing, his father's supposed to be God."

"Bull."

"That's what Rabbi Binder says, that it's impossible—"

"Sure it's impossible. That stuff's all bull. To have a baby you gotta get laid," Itzie theologized. "Mary hadda get laid."

"That's what Binder says: 'The only way a woman can have a baby is to have intercourse with a man.' "

"He said *that*, Ozz?" For a moment it appeared that Itzie had put the theological question aside. "He said that, intercourse?" A little curled smile shaped itself in the lower half of Itzie's face like a pink mustache. "What you guys do, Ozz, you laugh or something?"

"I raised my hand."

"Yeah? Whatja say?"

"That's when I asked the question."

Itzie's face lit up. "Whatja ask about—intercourse?"

"No, I asked the question about God, how if He could create the heaven and earth in six days—the light especially, that's what always gets me, that He could make the light. Making fish and animals, that's pretty good—"

"That's damn good." Itzie's appreciation was honest but unimaginative: it was as though God had just pitched a one-hitter.

"But making light . . . I mean when you think about it, it's really something," Ozzie said. "Anyway, I asked Binder if He could make all that in six days, and He could *pick* the six days He wanted right out of nowhere, why couldn't He let a woman have a baby without having intercourse."

"You said intercourse, Ozz, to Binder?"

"Yeah."

"Right in class?"

"Yeah."

Itzie smacked the side of his head.

"I mean, no kidding around," Ozzie said, "that'd really be nothing. After all that other stuff, that'd practically be nothing."

Itzie considered a moment. "What'd Binder say?"

"He started all over again explaining how Jesus was historical and how he lived like you and me but he wasn't God. So I said I understood that. What I wanted to know was different."

"What Ozzie wanted to know was always different. The first time he had wanted to know how Rabbi Binder could call the Jews "The Chosen People" if the Declaration of Independence claimed all men to be created equal. Rabbi Binder tried to distinguish for him between political equality and spiritual legitimacy, but what Ozzie wanted to know, he insisted vehemently, was different. That was the first time his mother had to come.

Then there was the plane crash. Fifty-eight people had been killed in a plane crash at La Guardia. In studying a casualty list in the newspaper his mother had discovered among the list of those dead eight Jewish names (his grandmother had nine but she counted Miller as a Jewish name); because of the eight she said the plane crash was "a tragedy." During free-discussion time on Wednesday Ozzie had brought to Rabbi Binder's attention this matter of "some of his relations" always picking out the Jewish names. Rabbi Binder had begun to explain cultural unity and some other things when Ozzie stood up at his seat and said that what he wanted to know was different. Rabbi Binder insisted that he sit down and it was then that Ozzie shouted that he wished all fifty-eight were Jews. That was the second time his mother came.

"And he kept explaining about Jesus being historical, and so I kept asking him. No kidding, Itz, he was trying to make me look stupid."

"So what he finally do?"

"Finally he starts screaming that I was deliberately simple-minded and a wise guy, and that my mother had to come, and this was the last time. And that I'd never get bar-mitzvahed if he could help it. Then, Itz, then he starts talking in that voice like a statue, real slow and deep, and he says that I better think over what I said about the Lord. He told me to go to his office and think it over." Ozzie leaned his body towards Itzie. "Itz, I thought it over for a solid hour, and now I'm convinced God could do it."

Ozzie had planned to confess his latest transgression to his mother as soon as she came home from work. But it was a Friday night in November and already dark, and when Mrs. Freedman came through the door she tossed off her coat, kissed Ozzie quickly on the face, and went to the kitchen table to light the three yellow candles, two for the Sabbath and one for Ozzie's father.

When his mother lit the candles she would move her two arms slowly towards her, dragging them through the air, as though persuading people whose minds were half made up. And her eyes would get glassy with tears. Even when his father was alive Ozzie remembered that her eyes had gotten glassy, so it didn't have anything to do with his dying. It had something to do with lighting the candles.

As she touched the flaming match to the unlit wick of a Sabbath candle, the phone rang, and Ozzie, standing only a foot from it, plucked it off the receiver and held it muffled to his chest. When his mother lit candles Ozzie felt there should be no noise; even breathing, if you could manage it, should be softened. Ozzie pressed the phone to his breast and watched his mother dragging whatever she was dragging, and he felt his own eyes get glassy. His mother was a round, tired, gray-haired penguin of a woman whose gray skin had begun to feel the tug of gravity and the weight of her own history. Even when she was dressed up she didn't look like a chosen person. But when she lit candles she looked like something better; like a woman who knew momentarily that God could do anything.

After a few mysterious minutes she was finished. Ozzie hung up the phone and walked to the kitchen table where she was beginning to lay the two places for the four-course Sabbath meal. He told her that she would have to see Rabbi Binder next Wednesday at four-thirty, and then he told her why. For the first time in their life together she hit Ozzie across the face with her hand.

All through the chopped liver and chicken soup part of the dinner Ozzie cried; he didn't have any appetite for the rest.

On the Wednesday, in the largest of the three basement classrooms of the synagogue, Rabbi Marvin Binder, a tall, handsome, broad-shouldered man of thirty with thick strong-fibered black hair, removed his watch from his pocket and saw that it was four o'clock. At the rear of the room Yakov Blotnik, the seventy-one-year-old custodian, slowly polished the large window, mumbling to himself, unaware that it was four o'clock or six o'clock, Monday or Wednesday. To most of the students Yakov Blotnik's mumbling, along with his brown curly beard, scythe nose, and two heel-trailing black cats, made of him an object of wonder, a foreigner, a relic, towards whom they were alternately fearful and disrespectful. To Ozzie the mumbling had always seemed a monotonous, curious prayer;

what made it curious was that old Blotnik had been mumbling so steadily for so many years, Ozzie suspected he had memorized the prayers and forgotten all about God.

"It is now free-discussion time," Rabbi Binder said. "Feel free to talk about any Jewish matter at all—religion, family, politics, sports—"

There was silence. It was a gusty, clouded November afternoon and it did not seem as though there ever was or could be a thing called baseball. So nobody this week said a word about that hero from the past, Hank Greenberg—which limited free discussion considerably.

And the soul-battering Ozzie Freedman had just received from Rabbi Binder had imposed its limitation. When it was Ozzie's turn to read aloud from the Hebrew book the rabbi had asked him petulantly why he didn't read more rapidly. He was showing no progress. Ozzie said he could read faster but that if he did he was sure not to understand what he was reading. Nevertheless, at the rabbi's repeated suggestion Ozzie tried, and showed a great talent, but in the midst of a long passage he stopped short and said he didn't understand a word he was reading, and started in again at a drag-footed pace. Then came the soul-battering.

Consequently when free-discussion time rolled around none of the students felt too free. The rabbi's invitation was answered only by the mumbling of feeble old Blotnik.

"Isn't there anything at all you would like to discuss?" Rabbi Binder asked again, looking at his watch. "No questions or comments?"

There was a small grumble from the third row. The rabbi requested that Ozzie rise and give the rest of the class the advantage of his thought.

Ozzie rose. "I forget it now," he said, and sat down in his place.

Rabbi Binder advanced a seat towards Ozzie and poised himself on the edge of the desk. It was Itzie's desk and the rabbi's frame only a dagger's-length away from his face snapped him to sitting attention.

"Stand up again, Oscar," Rabbi Binder said calmly, "and try to assemble your thoughts."

Ozzie stood up. All his classmates turned in their seats and watched as he gave an unconvincing scratch to his forehead.

"I can't assemble any," he announced, and plunked himself down.

"Stand up!" Rabbi Binder advanced from Itzie's desk to the one directly in front of Ozzie; when the rabbinical back was turned Itzie gave it five-fingers off the tip of his nose, causing a small titter in the room. Rabbi Binder was too absorbed in squelching Ozzie's nonsense once and for all to bother with titters. "Stand up, Oscar. What's your question about?"

Ozzie pulled a word out of the air. It was the handiest word. "Religion."

"Oh, now you remember?"

"Yes."

"What is it?"

Trapped, Ozzie blurted the first thing that came to him. "Why can't He make anything he wants to make!"

As Rabbi Binder prepared an answer, a final answer, Itzie, ten feet behind him, raised one finger on his left hand, gestured it meaningfully towards the rabbi's back, and brought the house down.

Binder twisted quickly to see what had happened and in the midst of the commotion Ozzie shouted into the rabbi's back what he couldn't have shouted to his face. It was a loud, toneless sound that had the timbre of something stored inside for about six days.

"You don't know! You don't know anything about God!"

The rabbi spun back towards Ozzie. "What?"

"You don't know—you don't—"

"Apologize, Oscar, apologize!" It was a threat.

"You don't—"

Rabbi Binder's hand flicked out at Ozzie's cheek. Perhaps it had only been meant to clamp the boy's mouth shut, but Ozzie ducked and the palm caught him squarely on the nose.

The blood came in a short, red spurt on to Ozzie's shirt front.

The next moment was all confusion. Ozzie screamed, "You bastard, you bastard!" and broke for the classroom door. Rabbi Binder lurched a step backwards, as though his own blood had started flowing violently in the opposite direction, then gave a clumsy lurch forward and bolted out the door after Ozzie. The class followed after the rabbi's huge blue-suited back, and before old Blotnik could turn from his window, the room was empty and everyone was headed full speed up the three flights leading to the roof.

If one should compare the light of day to the life of man: sunrise to birth; sunset—the dropping down over the edge—to death; then as Ozzie Freedman wiggled through the trapdoor of the synagogue roof, his feet kicking backwards bronco-style at Rabbi Binder's outstretched arms—at that moment the day was fifty years old. As a rule, fifty or fifty-five reflects accurately the age of late afternoons in November, for it is in that month, during those hours, that one's awareness of light seems no longer a matter of seeing, but of hearing: light begins clicking away. In fact, as Ozzie locked shut the trapdoor in the rabbi's face, the sharp click of the bolt into the lock might momentarily have been mistaken for the sound of the heavier gray that had just throbbed through the sky.

With all his weight Ozzie kneeled on the locked door; any instant he was certain that Rabbi Binder's shoulder would fling it open, splintering the wood into shrapnel and catapulting his body into the sky. But the door did not move and below him he heard only the rumble of feet, first loud then dim, like thunder rolling away.

A question shot through his brain. "Can this be *me*?" For a thirteen-year-old who had just labeled his religious leader a bastard, twice, it was not an improper question. Louder and louder the question came to him—"Is it me? Is it me?"—until he discovered himself no longer kneeling, but racing crazily towards the edge of the roof, his eyes crying, his throat screaming, and his arms flying everywhichway as though not his own.

"Is it me? Is it me ME ME ME ME! It has to be me—but is it!"

It is the question a thief must ask himself the night he jimmies open his first window, and it is said to be the question with which bridegrooms quiz themselves before the altar.

In the few wild seconds it took Ozzie's body to propel him to the edge of the roof, his self-examination began to grow fuzzy. Gazing down at the street, he became confused as to the problem beneath the question: was it, is-it-me-who-called-Binder-a-bastard? or, is-it-me-prancing-around-on-the-roof? However, the scene below settled all, for there is an instant in any action when whether it is you or somebody else is academic. The thief crams the money in his pockets and scoots out the window. The bridegroom signs the hotel register for two. And the boy on the roof finds a streetful of people gaping at him, necks stretched backwards, faces up, as though he were the ceiling of the Hayden Planetarium. Suddenly you know it's you.

"Oscar! Oscar Freedman!" A voice rose from the center of the crowd, a voice that, could it have been seen, would have looked like the writing on scroll. "Oscar Freedman, get down from there. Immediately!" Rabbi Binder was pointing one arm stiffly up at him; and at the end of that arm, one finger aimed menacingly. It was the attitude of a dictator, but one— the eyes confessed all—whose personal valet had spit neatly in his face.

Ozzie didn't answer. Only for a blink's length did he look towards Rabbi Binder. Instead his eyes began to fit together the world beneath him, to sort out people from places, friends from enemies, participants from spectators. In little jagged starlike clusters his friends stood around Rabbi Binder, who was still pointing. The topmost point on a star compounded not of angels but of five adolescent boys was Itzie. What a world it was, with those stars below, Rabbi Binder below . . . Ozzie, who a moment earlier hadn't been able to control his own body, started to feel the meaning of the word control: he felt Peace and he felt Power.

"Oscar Freedman, I'll give you three to come down."

Few dictators give their subjects three to do anything; but, as always, Rabbi Binder only looked dictatorial.

"Are you ready, Oscar?"

Ozzie nodded his head yes, although he had no intention in the world—the lower one or the celestial one he'd just entered—of coming down even if Rabbi Binder should give him a million.

"All right then," said Rabbi Binder. He ran a hand through his black

Samson hair as though it were the gesture prescribed for uttering the first digit. Then, with his other hand cutting a circle out of the small piece of sky around him, he spoke. "One!"

There was no thunder. On the contrary, at that moment, as though "one" was the cue for which he had been waiting, the world's least thunderous person appeared on the synagogue steps. He did not so much come out of the synagogue door as lean out, onto the darkening air. He clutched at the doorknob with one hand and looked up at the roof.

"Oy!"

Yakov Blotnik's old mind hobbled slowly, as if on crutches, and though he couldn't decide precisely what the boy was doing on the roof, he knew it wasn't good—that is, it wasn't-good-for-the-Jews. For Yakov Blotnik life had fractionated itself simply: things were either good-for-the-Jews or no-good-for-the-Jews.

He smacked his free hand to his in-sucked cheek, gently. "Oy, Gut!" And then quickly as he was able, he jacked down his head and surveyed the street. There was Rabbi Binder (like a man at an auction with only three dollars in his pocket, he had just delivered a shaky "Two!"); there were the students, and that was all. So far it-wasn't-so-bad-for-the-Jews. But the boy had to come down immediately, before anybody saw. The problem: how to get the boy off the roof?

Anybody who has ever had a cat on the roof knows how to get him down. You call the fire department. Or first you call the operator and you ask her for the fire department. And the next thing there is great jamming of brakes and clanging of bells and shouting of instructions. And then the cat is off the roof. You do the same thing to get a boy off the roof.

That is, you do the same thing if you are Yakov Blotnik and you once had a cat on the roof.

When the engines, all four of them, arrived, Rabbi Binder had four times given Ozzie the count of three. The big hook-and-ladder swung around the corner and one of the firemen leaped from it, plunging headlong towards the yellow fire hydrant in front of the synagogue. With a huge wrench he began to unscrew the top nozzle. Rabbi Binder raced over to him and pulled at his shoulder.

"There's no fire . . ."

The fireman mumbled back over his shoulder and, heatedly, continued working at the nozzle.

"But there's no fire, there's no fire . . ." Binder shouted. When the fireman mumbled again, the rabbi grasped his face with both his hands and pointed it up at the roof.

To Ozzie it looked as though Rabbi Binder was trying to tug the fireman's head out of his body, like a cork from a bottle. He had to giggle at the picture they made: it was a family portrait—rabbi in black skullcap, fireman in red fire hat, and the little yellow hydrant squatting beside like a kid brother, bareheaded. From the edge of the roof Ozzie waved at the portrait, a one-handed, flapping, mocking wave; in doing it his right foot slipped from under him. Rabbi Binder covered his eyes with his hands.

Firemen work fast. Before Ozzie had even regained his balance, a big, round, yellowed net was being held on the synagogue lawn. The firemen who held it looked up at Ozzie with stern, feelingless faces.

One of the firemen turned his head towards Rabbi Binder. "What, is the kid nuts or something?"

Rabbi Binder unpeeled his hands from his eyes, slowly, painfully, as if they were tape. Then he checked: nothing on the sidewalk, no dents in the net.

"Is he gonna jump, or what?" the fireman shouted.

In a voice not at all like a statue, Rabbi Binder finally answered, "Yes, yes, I think so . . . He's been threatening to . . ."

Threatening to? Why, the reason he was on the roof, Ozzie remembered, was to get away: he hadn't even thought about jumping. He had just run to get away, and the truth was that he hadn't really headed for the roof as much as he'd been chased there.

"What's his name, the kid?"

"Freedman," Rabbi Binder answered. "Oscar Freedman."

The fireman looked up at Ozzie. "What is it with you, Oscar? You gonna jump, or what?"

Ozzie did not answer. Frankly, the question had just arisen.

"Look, Oscar, if you're gonna jump, jump—and if you're not gonna jump, don't jump. But don't waste our time, willya?"

Ozzie looked at the fireman and then at Rabbi Binder. He wanted to see Rabbi Binder cover his eyes one more time.

"I'm going to jump."

And then he scampered around the edge of the roof to the corner, where there was no net below, and he flapped his arms at his sides, swishing the air and smacking his palms to his trousers on the downbeat. He began screaming like some kind of engine, "Wheeeee . . . wheeeeee," and leaning way out over the edge with the upper half of his body. The firemen whipped around to cover the ground with the net. Rabbi Binder mumbled a few words to Somebody and covered his eyes. Everything happened quickly, jerkily, as in a silent movie. The crowd, which had arrived with the fire engines, gave out a long, Fourth-of-July fireworks oooh-aahhh. In the excitement no one had paid the crowd much heed, except, of course, Yakov Blotnik, who swung from the door now counting heads. "Fier und tsvansik . . . finf und tsvantsik . . . Oy, Gut!" It wasn't like this with the cat.

Rabbi Binder peeked through his fingers, checked the sidewalk and net. Empty. But there was Ozzie racing to the other corner. The firemen raced with him but were unable to keep up. Whenever Ozzie wanted to he might jump and splatter himself upon the sidewalk, and by the time the firemen scooted to the spot all they could do with their net would be to cover the mess.

"Wheeeee . . .wheeeeee . . ."

"Hey, Oscar," the winded fireman yelled, "What the hell is this, a game or something?"

"Wheeeee . . .wheeeee . . ."

"Hey, Oscar—"

But he was off now to the other corner, flapping his wings fiercely. Rabbi Binder couldn't take it any longer—the fire engines from nowhere, the screaming suicidal boy, the net. He fell to his knees, exhausted, and with his hands curled together in front of his chest like a little dome, he pleaded, "Oscar, stop it, Oscar. Don't jump, Oscar. Please come down . . . Please don't jump."

And further back in the crowd a single voice, a single young voice, shouted a lone word to the boy on the roof.

"Jump!"

It was Itzie. Ozzie momentarily stopped flapping.

"Go ahead, Ozz—jump!" Itzie broke off his point of the star and courageously, with the inspiration not of a wise-guy but of a disciple, stood alone. "Jump, Ozz, jump!"

Still on his knees, his hands still curled, Rabbi Binder twisted his body back. He looked at Itzie, then, agonizingly, back to Ozzie.

"OSCAR, DON'T JUMP! PLEASE, DON'T JUMP . . . please, please . . ."

"Jump!" This time it wasn't Itzie but another point of the star. By the time Mrs. Freedman arrived to keep her four-thirty appointment with Rabbi Binder, the whole little upside down heaven was shouting and pleading for Ozzie to jump, and Rabbi Binder no longer was pleading with him not to jump, but was crying into the dome of his hands.

Understandably Mrs. Freedman couldn't figure out what her son was doing on the roof. So she asked.

"Ozzie, my Ozzie, what are you doing? My Ozzie, what is it?"

Ozzie stopped wheeeeeing and slowed his arms down to a cruising flap, the kind birds use in soft winds, but he did not answer. He stood against the low, clouded, darkening sky—light clicked down swiftly now, as on a small gear—flapping softly and gazing down at the small bundle of a woman who was his mother.

"What are you doing, Ozzie?" She turned towards the kneeling Rabbi Binder and rushed so close that only a paper-thickness of dusk lay between her stomach and his shoulders.

"What is my baby doing?"

Rabbi Binder gaped up at her but he too was mute. All that moved was the dome of his hands; it shook back and forth like a weak pulse.

"Rabbi, get him down! He'll kill himself. Get him down, my only baby . . ."

"I can't," Rabbi Binder said, "I can't . . ." and he turned his handsome head towards the crowd of boys behind him. "It's them. Listen to them."

And for the first time Mrs. Freedman saw the crowd of boys, and she heard what they were yelling.

"He's doing it for them. He won't listen to me. It's them." Rabbi Binder spoke like one in a trance.

"For them?"

"Yes."

"Why for them?"

"They want him to . . ."

Mrs. Freedman raised her two arms upward as though she were conducting the sky. "For them he's doing it!" And then in a gesture older than pyramids, older than prophets and floods, her arms came slapping down to her sides. "A martyr I have. Look!" She tilted her head to the roof. Ozzie was still flapping softly. "My martyr."

"Oscar, come down, *please*," Rabbi Binder groaned.

In a startling even voice Mrs. Freedman called to the boy on the roof. "Ozzie, come down, Ozzie. Don't be a martyr, my baby."

As though it were a litany, Rabbi Binder repeated her words. "Don't be a martyr, my baby. Don't be a martyr."

"Gawhead, Ozz—*be* a Martin!" It was Itzie. "Be a Martin, be a Martin," and all the voices joined in singing for Martindom, whatever *it* was. "Be a Martin, be a Martin . . ."

Somehow when you're on a roof the darker it gets the less you can hear. All Ozzie knew was that two groups wanted two new things: his friends were spirited and musical about what they wanted; his mother and the rabbi were eventoned, chanting, about what they didn't want. The rabbi's voice was without tears now and so was his mother's.

The big net stared up at Ozzie like a sightless eye. The big, clouded sky pushed down. From beneath it looked like a gray corrugated board. Suddenly, looking up into that unsympathetic sky, Ozzie realized all the strangeness of what these people, his friends, were asking: they wanted him to jump, to kill himself; they were singing about it now—it made them happy. And there was an even greater strangeness: Rabbi Binder was on his knees, trembling. If there was a question to be asked now it was not "Is it me?" but rather "Is it us? . . . Is it us?"

Being on the roof, it turned out, was a serious thing. If he jumped would the singing become dancing? Would it? What would jumping stop? Yearningly, Ozzie wished he could rip open the sky, plunge his hands through, and pull out the sun; and on the sun, like a coin, would be stamped JUMP or DON'T JUMP.

Ozzie's knees rocked and sagged a little under him as though they were setting him for a dive. His arms tightened, stiffened, froze, from shoulders to fingernails. He felt as if each part of his body were going to vote as to whether he should kill himself or not—and each part as though it were independent of *him*.

The light took an unexpected click down and the new darkness, like a gag, hushed the friends singing for this and the mother and rabbi chanting for that.

Ozzie stopped counting votes, and in a curiously high voice, like one who wasn't prepared for speech, he spoke.

"Mamma?"

"Yes, Oscar."

"Mamma, get down on your knees, like Rabbi Binder."

"Oscar—"

"Get down on your knees," he said, "or I'll jump."

Ozzie heard a whimper, then a quick rustling, and when he looked down where his mother had stood he saw the top of a head and beneath that a circle of dress. She was kneeling beside Rabbi Binder.

He spoke again. "Everybody kneel." There was the sound of everybody kneeling.

Ozzie looked around. With one hand he pointed towards the synagogue entrance. "Make *him* kneel."

There was a noise, not of kneeling, but of body-and-cloth stretching. Ozzie could hear Rabbi Binder saying in a gruff whisper, " . . . or he'll *kill* himself," and when next he looked there was Yakov Blotnik off the doorknob and for the first time in his life upon his knees in the Gentile posture of prayer.

As for the firemen—it is not as difficult as one might imagine to hold a net taut while you are kneeling.

Ozzie looked around again; and then he called to Rabbi Binder.

"Rabbi?"

"Yes, Oscar."

"Rabbi Binder, do you believe in God?"

"Yes."

"Do you believe God can do Anything?" Ozzie leaned his head out into the darkness. "Anything?"

"Oscar, I think—"

"Tell me you believe God can do Anything."

There was a second's hesitation. Then: "God can do Anything."

"Tell me you believe God can make a child without intercourse."

"He can."

"Tell me!"

"God," Rabbi Binder admitted, "can make a child without intercourse."

"Mamma, you tell me."

"God can make a child without intercourse," his mother said.

"Make *him* tell me." There was no doubt who *him* was.

In a few moments Ozzie heard an old comical voice say something to the increasing darkness about God.

Next, Ozzie made everybody say it. And then he made them all say they believed in Jesus Christ—first one at a time, then all together.

When the catechizing was through it was the beginning of evening. From the street it sounded as if the boy on the roof might have sighed.

"Ozzie?" A woman's voice dared to speak. "You'll come down now?"

There was no answer, but the woman waited, and when a voice finally did speak it was thin and crying, and exhausted as that of an old man who has just finished pulling the bells.

"Mamma, don't you see—you shouldn't hit me. He shouldn't hit me. You shouldn't hit me about God, Mamma. You should never hit anybody about God—"

"Ozzie, please come down now."

"Promise me, promise me you'll never hit anybody about God."

He had asked only his mother, but for some reason everyone kneeling in the street promised he would never hit anybody about God.

Once again there was silence.

"I can come down now, Mamma," the boy on the roof finally said. He turned his head both ways as though checking the traffic lights. "Now I can come down . . ."

And he did, right into the center of the yellow net that glowed in the evening's edge like an overgrown halo.

AUSTIN C. CLARKE

(b. 1934)

*A*ustin C. Clarke *was born in Barbados. He was educated there, eventually becoming a teacher, before moving to Canada in 1955 and continuing his education at Trinity College, University of Toronto. Clarke's career is as distinguished by his numerous political and civil service appointments in both his native country and Canada as it is by his novels and stories about Barbadians at home and in Toronto. He has been an adviser to the Prime Minister of Barbados, cultural attaché at the Embassy of Barbados in Washington, general manager of the Caribbean Broadcasting Corporation, multiculturalism adviser to the leader of the Ontario Progressive Conservative Party, and vice-chairman of the Ontario Film Review Board. The recipient of numerous awards and fellowships, he has also been Visiting Professor and writer-in-residence at many universities, including Yale, Brandeis, Williams College, Duke, University of Texas, and the University of Western Ontario. Clarke's social conscience is expressed in the compassionate and humorous stories he writes about the difficulties that his countrymen—both Canadian and West Indian—have in dealing with life in the "new Canada," a Canada no longer dominated exclusively by the descendants of white Europeans. His first two works of fiction are set in Barbados, the novel* The Survivors of the Crossing *(1964) and the short-story collection* Amongst Thistles and Thorns *(1965). These two works depict a Barbados that offers very little scope to the talents, ambitions, and dreams of its citizenry. The ambitious Barbadian must look elsewhere for satisfaction, and many look to Canada, specifically to Toronto. Clarke's next three novels constitute a trilogy dealing with the lives of Caribbean immigrants in Toronto:* The Meeting Point *(1967),* Storm of Fortune *(1973), and* The Bigger Light *(1975). As much as Mordecai Richler's* The Apprenticeship of Duddy Kravitz *(1959) repudiated Hugh MacLennan's fictional vision of a middle-class Canada centred in Montreal, Clarke's trilogy exposed the hidden racism and smug hypocrisy of Morley Callaghan's Toronto, unsettling any complacent notions readers harboured about "Toronto the good." His other books include the story collection* When He Was Free and Young and He Used To Wear Silks *(1971) and the novel* The Prime Minister *(1977). Clarke has also published two volumes of an autobiography that is fascinating for its presentation of the ways in which today's individuals and nations are shaped by the international community of nations,* Growing Up Stupid Under the Union Jack *(1980) and* Colonial Innocency *(1982).*

When He Was Free and Young and He Used To Wear Silks

I n the lavishness of the soft lights, indications of detouring life that took out of his mind the concentration of things left to do still, as a man, before he could be an artist, lights that put into his mind instead a certain crawling intention which the fingers of his brain stretched towards one always single table embraced by a man and a wife who looked like his woman, her loyalty bending over the number of beers he poured against the side of her bottle he had forgotten to count, in those struggling days when the atmosphere was soft and silk and just as treacherous, in those days in the *Pilot Tavern* the spring and the summer and the fall were mixed into one chattering ambition of wanting to have meaning, a better object of meaning and of craving, better meaning that a beer bought on the credit of friendships and love by the tense young oppressed men and women who said they were oppressed and tense because they were artists and not because they were incapable, or burdened by the harsh sociology of no talent, segregated around smooth black square tables from the rest of the walking men and walking women outside the light of our *Pilot* of the Snows; and had not opened nor shut their minds to the meaning of their other lives; legs of artless girls touching this man's in a hide-and-seek under the colourblind tables burdened by conversation and aspirations and promises of cheques and hopes and bedding and beer and bottles; in those days when he first saw her, and the only conversation she could invent was "haii!" because she was put on a pedestal by husbandry, and would beg his pardon without disclosing her eyes of red and shots and blots and blood-shot liquor; the success of his mind and the woman's mind in his legs burnt like the parts of the chicken he ate, he was free and young and he was wearing the silks of indecision and near-failure. But he mustn't forget the curry: for the curry was invented by people and Blessings, Indians; or perhaps they were the intractable Chinese, the curry was the saviour of his mind and indigestion just as the woman guarded for no reason in the safe soft velvet of her unbelieving husband's love, guarding her in her turns as they sat opposite each other in the different callings of paint and metals and skin and negatives and thirst during all those dark days in the *Pilot*, the curry was the saviour of a madness which erupted in his mouth with the after-taste of the bought beer and the swirling bowels after the beer and after the curry; she was like the lavishness in the light except that the colour surrounding her in the darkened room hid everything, every thought in his mind just as the wholesome curry in the parts of chicken hid the unwholesome social class which it could not always distinguish from the bones any suitable dog in shaggy-haired and shaggy-sexed Rosedale would eat, and if the dog in Rosedale and the dog in him did eat them, the dog might make them, like this woman sitting with her drinking man, into an exotic meal packaged through some sense of beer and the sense of time and place, and looking at it in one imaginative sense, turn it into something called *soul food*: now, there are many commercial and irrelevant soul food kitchens these days in night-time Toronto, and any man could, if he had no soul and silks on the body of his thoughts, if his soul were occupied and imprisoned only with thoughts of *her* sitting there badly in the wrong light of skin, he could make a fortune of thoughts and sell them like dog meat and badly licenced food to all the becauseful people who wore jeans and heavy-weave expensive sweaters walking time into eternity in dirty clothes and rags because they were the "beautiful people" as someone called their ugliness, like *her* of soon-time piloted to a tavern, married to a man who did not deserve the understanding of her; these the becauseful people, people who didn't have to do this because they didn't want to think about that, because they were people living in the brighter light of the soft darkness which they all liked because they were artists and people, the becauseful people like her, liked her and likened her to a white horse not because of the length of her legs nor the grey in her mind, but because in the lavishness of the wholesome light of the *Pilot* she looked as secure and was silent as the fingers of the tumbling avoirdupoids of the man who made mud-pies in the piles of quarters and dollars mixmasterminding them in the cash register. It is so dark sometimes in the *Pilot* that if you wear dark glasses, which all the artists wore on their minds, you may stumble up the single step beside the fat man sitting on a humptydumpling stool and where she always sat on her pedestal of distance and protection chastised in pickled beer, and you may not know whether it is afternoon on Yonge Street outside, for time now has no boundaries, only the dimensions of her breasts which her husband keeps in the palm of his flickering eyeballs; it is so dark in the early afternoon that with your dark glasses on, you might be in Boston walking the climb in the street climbing like a hill to where the black and coloured people live; or you might be here in Toronto walking where the coloured people and the kneegrows say they "live" but where they squat, here where E. P. Taylor says he does not live but where his influence strangles some resident life and breeds racehorses of the people, where Garfield Weston lives in a mad biscuit box crumbling in broken crackers; in the lavishness of the night thrown from your dark glasses, you might stumble upon a pair of legs and not know the colour of time, or what shape it is, or where you are, or who you are: he thinks he should haul his arse out of this bar of madness and mad dreams, drinking himself into an erection stiff to the touch of ghosts in her legs and the legs of the tables. He had seen her, "this young tall thing," walking to the bar through winter in boots and rain in blue jeans and sandals, insisting without words in the fierce determination of her poverty and dedication to nothing she could prove or do that this was her personal calvary to the cross of being Canada's best poetic-photographer, unknown in the meaning of her life beyond the tavern, unknown like the word she would use, "budgerigar," having years ago thrown out Layton, Cohen, Birney and Purdy in the dishwater of her weatherbeaten browbeaten body and heavy sweaters; he could see her mostly among women stuck to their chairs by the chewing-gum beer, free women freed by their men for an afternoon while art imprisoned the men with beer, wallpaper along the talking walls like flowers, their own flower long faded into the dust of the artificial potato chips they all ate in the nitty of their gloom because it was like the grit for their reality, their "dinner" an unknown reality like her word, "budgerigar," in the despised bourgeois vocabulary and apartment-lairs of their lives; and in this garden of grass growing in their beds he had hand-picked her out five years ago, this one wallflowering woman who wore large hats in the summerstreet, and cream sweaters in winter. She always sat beside the man who sat as if he was her husband; tall in her thighs with the walk of a man, this white horse woman with the body of a bull; and the eye of her disposition through the bottom of the beer bottle warned him that the "gentlest touch of his desire might be fatal to the harmony" of the two ordered beers which they drank like siamese twins in the double-bed of their marriage. He, the watchman-man, was harnessed by island upbringing and fear in the lavishness of the dim light, ravishing her ravishing beauty with his eyes they could not see, eyes they saw only once and spoke to once when they saw him entering or leaving; for five years. For five years of not knowing whether the sun would sink in the space between her breasts, or whether butter ever dried in the warmth of that melting space, he watched her like a timekeeper. Once he saw her leaving her husband's side and he followed her spinster's canter all the way in his mind down the railing guard of parallel eyes honouring her backside sitting on the spinning stools where the working class reigned and into the bathroom, past two wash basins and the machine that saved pregnancies and populations with a quarter, on to the toilet bowl, under the dress she had plucked her hand and had pulled up her dress and did not soil her seat or sit on it because it was in the *Pilot*, and he smiled when she reappeared with fresh garlic on her lipstick mouth; and he looked at the edges of her powder, and he looked into the lascivious dimness and saw her and smiled and she smiled but the smile belonged to the mud-piling man at the cash register or to another table where they were talking about the Isaacs Gallery and the Artists Jazz Bann where Dennis Burton's garter belts were exhibited in stiff canvas and wore houndstooth suits and the thick heavy honey of colours and materials thicker than words. He had walked around her life in circles and bottle rings of desire and of lust and she was always there, the centre of dreams frizzled on a pillow soaked with the tears of drinking; he followed her like a detective in the wishes of his dreams, and from his inspection of a future together got a headache over them and over her, and over the meanings of these dreams. *Mickey* and *Cosmospilitane* and other dream books did not ease the riders of the head in his pain, and nothing could unhinge his desperation from the wishful slumber of those unconscious nights of double broken vision. And then, like a cherry falling under the tree because the sun had failed it, after long thoughts and wishes of waiting she fell into his path, and he almost crushed her. He remembered the long afternoons waiting for the indelible rings of the melting bottles to ripen, waiting for the departure of shoppers who lived above the Rosedale subway station to stop shopping in the Pickering Farms market so he could shop and not have to listen to the loud-talking friendly butcher in the fluorescent meat department, and whisper loud under the sun-tanned arms of the meaty houswives and commonlaw-wives, "One pound of pigs feet, chicken necks and bones—for soup," and hear the unfeeling bitch, "Er-er! Who's next?" behind the counter dressed like a surgeon with blood on his chest, saying, "You're really taking care of that dog, ain't you, sir?" Godblindyou, dog! godblindyou, butcher! this meat is for the dog in front of you; and he remembered her now, single, on this summer-street under the large hat as she was five years ago under the drinking mural under the picture of hotdogs and fried eggs that some heartless hungry painter drew on the wall where she sat beneath when she was in the *Pilot*. He fell into the arms of her greeting like an apple to the core and he looked down into her dress and saw nothing not even one small justification for the long unbitten imprisonment of his mouth and his ambition, thinking of the nutseller selling his nuts next door. She was away now from the *Pilot*. And he did not even know her name: not for five years, he never was introduced to her name: "Hurley or Weeks . . . Weeks or Hurley . . ." either one would do? "they are both mine, and I use either one any time," but Weeks is her maiden time; although she was no longer a maiden, though single and with no husband for weeks and months now. There was no large gold ring on the finger of her personal self-regard, which she said ended mutual on a visit of her once-accompanying husband warming radically, like forgotten beer, into her haphazard lover; there was no bitterness in the eyes of her separation because she missed only the cooking which he would do every evening, when she said she was too tired, or couldn't be bothered to cook, which was every evening, when he would do the cooking in her kitchen and leave her afterwards like the dishes, panting from thirst and a thorough cleaning, so her eyes said on this summer afternoon, hungry in the frying pan of their doublebed bedroom, where he kept the materials of his stockings, feet and trade, his love of meddling with medals and metals and sculpture, and where she kept a large over-grown blow-up of her brother's success in the cowboys and movies in the West, shooting the horses over the head of the never-setting bedpost, her brother with a gun in his hand, a gun loaded at the ready to be fired at the nearest rivalry of badmen and bad women, a gun which he gave her, a gun which remained nevertheless loaded, hung-up, cocked and frustrated and constipated from no practice or trigger-happiness; and this she talked about; she did not stay in one place, she said she was rambling, not along the streets because she did not like to walk, but that she was rambling and that she had to be alone in the constitutional of her thoughts, from one bar to the next bar; she admitted she might have a problem, but it was not this problem which changed her husband's heart into a dying lover drifting apart at the semen in the widening sea of her jammed ambition: "I do not know what I want to do, I know what I don't want to do, and that is stay married, but I don't really know what I really want to do"; she bore her wandering in her hair, loose and landing on her broad shoulders like the rumps of two cowboy horses; and her dress was short, short enough for the eyes to roam about in and follow her over all her landscape at a canter—that's how she was put away; she was put away as if she could be put to pasture for work and for love and for bearing responsibility: "I know I don't want to have a child. What am I going to *do* with a child? I know I can have children and I know I can have a child. I want a child, but not now, because a child *needs* love . . . and and and I I I haven't any left right now for . . ." He looked at her and wandered and wondered why she couldn't give a child a chance, a chance of love, with all the pasture in her body, all her body, with all her breasts, with all her milk bottled in brassieres that had no bones stitched in them, with all her thighs that spilled over her dress-hem, "A-hem!", but perhaps she was really talking about another kind of love and another need for love, which was not the same as the need for love her lover-husband needed from her when she was a child in his arms late at night, and was crying with him in the double-minded cradle of his sculptures. *Haii! Austin!* He looked into her eyes and made a wish that her body under his eye would not be completely bloodless as her hands sometimes seemed five years ago when she was fresh from the basement washroom, and the Snow on the women walking out of the cold corner of Yonge and Bloor in the arctic months; that her body would not reveal the theft he had in mind to put it through, the theft her husband had put it through; that she would not be like Desdemona and wax, but that she would be a queen from the entrails of Africa and Nefrititi, plucked out in olive black-ness luscious to the core of her imagined seed, like the Marian from the alligator troughs of Georgia. He dreamed a long dream standing there on the street with summer before her, and he killed the colour of her body because it needed too much Eno's before it could go down; and he wrapped her in a coffin stained in wood in blood, and made her again to look like Marian from way across the bad lands of enroped and ruptured Georgia, *Haii, Austin!*: he was back in those good old days, good because they had no responsibility for paying the good deeds artists incurred in debts and made them bad, bad debts and artists on the segregation of walls and memories, he was here and he was there in Georgia in the double ghost of a second, for artists were bad for debts and for business in those young days when he was free and the only silk was his ambition; he remembered her in those days, and on this summer afternoon already obliterated in the history of the past, nights in the crowded *Pilot Tavern*, searching the faces of the girls and women for one face that would have had a meaning like Marian's, and he could not find one head with truth written in its clenched curled black-peppers of hair, one mask with the intelligent face of Nefrititi the history of Africa from Africa, not from the store on Yonge Street, "Africa Modern" selling blackness cheap to whites, written brazenly upon its ivory; a mask, a mask from that land not unlike Georgia, he had watched for one face like a timekeeper keeping a watch that had no end of time in it, and he had to paint the faces black, blacken them as he had blackened the red clay sculpture a woman did of him once, like an Indian in his blood, and had made it something approaching the man he wanted to be, something like the man Amiri Baraka talked about becoming in the later years of his new muslim wisdom; he remembered the sweet-smelling Georgia woman in those soft nights when the bulbs were silk as moths among the books overhead like a heavy chastisement to be intelligent, like a too-self-conscious intention; with the sherry which she drank in proper southern quantities, like bourbon warm to the blood, and her fingers were long and pointed and expressive, impressing upon his back, once, her once beautiful intent, as they writhed in pain with glory and some victory, after she lay like a submarine in a water pyre of soft soapy suds, white flowers of *Calgon* upon her black vegetation, going and coming, he remembered her in the shiny cheap stockings proclaiming her true colour of mind and pocket and spirit and background and intention: *a black student*; a black woman, black and shining in that velvet of time and black skin, a black woman, black and powerful down to her black marrow; there was something in the ring of her laughter, perhaps in the gurgle of her bourbon, in the *ding-ing* of her voice when she laughed in two accents, northern and southern, something that said she was true-and-through beautiful, and because she was black, and because she was beautiful, she was beautiful; she could withstand any ravages of history, of storms, of stories that wailed in the rope-knotted night of Georgia; she could stand on a pedestal under any tree which no village smithy in white Georgia would dare to stand up to: a man who had no burning conviction could not put his arms as high as her waist, for she had seen certain sheets of a whiteness which were wrapped around a black man's testicles in a bestial passion-play, and she had seen, in her mother's memories, this play as it showed the germ of someone's bed linen made into sheets that were worn as masks of superiority testing a presumption that some men would always walk on all-fours like a southern lizard; *haii, austin!* this woman standing on the summerstreet in the silk of time stopped without desire; and that woman lying in the rich water with her smell whom he remembered best holding down her head in love, in some shame, looking into a book of tears because his words were spoken harder than the text of any African philosophy. He remembered that woman and not this woman, well: Marian, his; ploughing the fields of poverty and a commitment in her barefoot days, dress tangled amongst the tango of weeds, sticking in the crease of her strength silken from perspiration, and her dreams cloggy as the soil, and in her after-days in the northern rich-poor city, her long-fingered hands again dipping into the soil of soiled sociology Jewished out of some context, maintained backyards, maintained yardbird poverty, backward in instruction the smell of soil the soiled smell of the land in which she was born, the smell of poverty, a new kind of perfume to freshen her northern ideas, a new kind of perfume truer than the fragrance of an underarm of ploughing, more telling than the tale in the perspiration of her body, in the fields, in the sociology, in the kitchen, in the bed, in the summer subway sweaty and safe with policemen and black slum dwellers from Dorchester, in the heat, in the bus stations, in the bathtub in Boston; a perfume of sweet sweat that clothed her body with a blessing of pearls, like a birthwrap of wet velvet skin: "Honnn-neee!" the word she always used; honey was the only taste to use; honey was the only word she used always; for it was a turbulence of love and time from the lowered eyelids from the vomiting guts up to the tip of the touch of her skin. She was a woman; she was a woman without woe; she was to be his woman, she should be here in the summerstreet; now in the summer street, he watches this alter-native of that woman, he understands that the transparency of this dress, tucked above her knees by the hand of fashion, is really nothing but the vagueness of this doll; he sees now that this transparency is the woman, like the negatives she meddled in, for five years' time, like the film on a pond's surface, like white powder, like a glass of water with Eno's in it, like a glass of water in the sun, the water clear and unpolluted, the water the top soil of the sediments at the sentimental bottom; he wanted to mix this water with that water in the bathtub in Boston, the water and the mud into some heart, into that thick between-the-toes soul of the Georgia woman; he wanted to break the glass that contained that water for the *Calgon* bath and the sherry and the bathwater; break the vessel, spill and despoil, spill and expel this wateringdown of the drink of his long thirst; stir it up and mix the sentiments in the foundation with the upper crust of the water, shake it to the foundation of its scream and yell and turn it to the thickness of chocolate rich in the cup, thick and rich and hot and swimming with pools of fat, so he could drink, so he would have to put his hand into the black avalanche of feeling and emotion and sediment, deep and gurgling as the tenor in her laughter, down the tuningfork of her throat resounding with love and make her say a word, speak a thought, be some witness to the blood in her love. This was his Marian in the vision in the summerstreet. This was Marian. And the five-year stranger, estranged from her husband's love in a transparency, in the costume of a lover, this woman who used to sit upon the pin of his desires, now on this summerstreet where he thought he saw her, she is nothing more vivacious than a feather worn in her broad-grinned hat: not like the scarf *she* wore with conchshells and liberty-scars and paisley marked into it with water; this negative of Marian passed like the cloud above the roof of the *Park Plaza* where one afternoon she sat drinking water, when he was playing he was playing golf in the new democratic diminutive green of the eighteenth floor bar; and a cloud passed overhead like the loss of lust of a now dead moment, with the woman; and when the sun was bright again, when the sun was like the sun in Georgia, fierce and full, when the sun was a purpose and passion, when the sun was as bright as the sweat it wrung from the barrels of a black woman's breasts, the laughing beautiful Marian was there, not in his mind only but larger, dispossessing the summerstreet in the buxom jeans of her hips, red accusing blouse belafonted down the ladylike tip of the gorge of sustenance between her breasts, and around her neck around her throat, a yellow handkerchief and a chain of a star and a moon in some quarter of her sensual religion. He saw her with passion and with greed, he saw her clearer than the truth-serum syrup of a dream, than the germ of love, true as the guinness in the egg and the Marian was his stout, this woman. He remembered all this standing in the summerstreet: when before she climbed the steps to her hospital, she held his hands like a wife going in to die upon a cot, and drew him just a suggestion of new life closer to the relationship and her breasts, and with the sweet saliva of her lips she said in the touch of that kiss, "Take care of yourself." He was young and free again, to live or to travel imprisoned in a memory of freed love, chained to her body and her laughter by the spinal cord of anxious longdistance, reminders said before and after, by the long engineering of a drive from Yale to Brandeis to Seaver Street to Brandeis dull in the winter Zion of brains, dull in the autumn three hours in miles hoping that the travel won't end like an underground railroad at the door of this nega-tive woman, but continue even through letters and quarrels and long miles down the short street up the long stairs in the marble of her memory, clenched in her absent embrace but rejoicing with his fingers in the velvet feeling of her silken black natural hair . . .

Rudy Wiebe

(b. 1934)

*R*udy Wiebe *was born on the farm near Fairholme, Saskatchewan, to which his parents had immigrated from the Soviet Union in 1930. He received his B.A. in 1956 and an M.A. in creative writing from the University of Alberta in 1960. He has been an English professor at that university since 1967. Wiebe's Mennonite heritage figures centrally in his early novel* Peace Shall Destroy Many *(1962) and in the short-story cycle* The Blue Mountains of China *(1970).* First and Vital Candle *(1966) was the first of Wiebe's books to display his interest in exploring, and to some extent championing, the lives of native peoples relegated to the fringes of white society (Inuit and northern Indians). Subsequently, the history of the Prairies and their aboriginal inhabitants and heroes in the 1870s comes to occupy Wiebe's fictional concerns in such novels as* The Temptations of Big Bear *(1973),* The Scorched-Wood People *(1977), and* The Mad Trapper *(1980). W.J. Keith has written that Wiebe's heroes "must be worthy of their position, though they are never tiresome prototypes of impeccable virtue. However much he may sympathize with Big Bear and Louis Riel, [Wiebe] knows that their personalities can be interpreted less positively, and his invented characters . . . must all come to terms with their imperfections." His most recent novel,* My Lovely Enemy *(1983), is something of a departure for Wiebe in that it deals with the relation between human and divine love in a contemporary setting. Wiebe is also the author of three collections of short stories:* Where Is the Voice Coming From? *(1974),* Alberta/A Celebration *(1979), and* The Angel of the Tar Sands and Other Stories *(1982). He has edited numerous short-story anthologies and written a play,* As Far as the Eye Can See *(1977). As the story that follows shows, Wiebe is something of a rarity in being both a highly moral writer and, in his later fiction especially, an experimenter in fictional forms and techniques. Interested in exploring the generic territory between history and fiction, he often employs a number of voices to tell the story and utilizes documentary evidence to craft a fiction that might better be described as polyphonic meta-history—that is, as a multiple-perspective account of how we come to know what we know about our collective past.*

Where Is the Voice Coming From?

T he problem is to make the story.

One difficulty of this making has been excellently stated by Teilhard de Chardin: "We are continually inclined to isolate ourselves from the things and events which surround us . . . as though we were spectators, not elements, in what goes on." Arnold Toynbee does venture, "For all that we know, Reality is the undifferentiated unity of the mystical experience," but that need not here be considered. This story ended long ago; it is one of finite acts, of orders, of elemental feelings and reactions, of obvious legal restrictions and requirements.

Presumably all the parts of the story are themselves available. The difficulty is that they are, as always, available only in bits and pieces. Though the acts themselves seem quite clear, some written reports of the acts contradict each other. As if these acts were, at one time, too well known; as if the original nodule of each particular fact had from somewhere received non-factual accretions; or even more, as if, since the basic facts were so clear perhaps there were a larger number of facts than any one reporter, or several, or even any report had ever attempted to record. About facts that are still simply told by this mouth to that ear, of course, even less can be expected.

An affair seventy-five years old should acquire some of the shiny transparency of an old man's skin. It should.

Sometimes it would seem that it would be enough—perhaps more than enough—to hear the names only. The grandfather One Arrow; the mother Spotted Calf; the father Sounding Sky; the wife (wives rather, but only one of them seems to have had a name, though their fathers are Napaise, Kapahoo, Old Dust, The Rump)—the one wife named, of all things, Pale Face; the cousin Going-Up-To-Sky; the brother-in-law (again, of all things) Dublin. The names of the police sound very much alike; they all begin with Constable or Corporal or Sergeant, but here and there an Inspector, then a Superintendent and eventually all the resonance of an Assistant Commissioner echoes down. More. Herself: Victoria, by the Grace of God etc., etc., QUEEN, Defender of the Faith etc., etc.; and witness 'Our Right Trusty and Right Well-Beloved Cousin and Councillor the Right Honorable Sir John Campbell Hamilton-Gordon, Earl of Aberdeen; Viscount Formartine, Baron Haddo, Methlic, Tarves and Kellie, in the Peerage of Scotland; Viscount Gordon of Aberdeen, County of Aberdeen, in the Peerage of the United Kingdom; Baronet of Nova Scotia, Knight Grand Cross of Our Most Distinguished Order of Saint Michael and Saint George etc., Governor General of Canada.' And of course himself: in the award proclamation named 'Jean-Baptiste' but otherwise known only as Almighty Voice.

But hearing cannot be enough; not even hearing all the thunder of A Proclamation: "Now Hear Ye that a reward of FIVE HUNDRED DOLLARS will be paid to any person or persons who will give such information as will lead . . . this Twentieth day of April, in the year of Our Lord one thousand eight hundred and ninety-six, and the Fifty-ninth year of Our Reign . . ." etc. and etc.

Such hearing cannot be enough. The first item to be seen is the piece of white bone. It is almost triangular, slightly convex—concave actually as it is positioned at this moment with its corners slightly raised—graduating from perhaps a strong eighth to a weak quarter of an inch in thickness, its scattered pore structure varying between larger and smaller on its perhaps polished, certainly shiny surface. Precision is difficult since the glass showcase is at least thirteen inches deep and therefore an eye cannot be brought as close as the minute inspection of such a small, though certainly quite adequate, sample of skull would normally require. Also, because of the position it cannot be determined whether the several hairs, well over a foot long, are still in some manner attached or not.

The seven-pounder cannon can be seen standing almost shyly between the showcase and the interior wall. Officially it is known as a gun, not a cannon, and clearly its bore is not large enough to admit a large man's fist. Even if it can be believed that this gun was used in the 1885 Rebellion and that on the evening of Saturday, May 29, 1897 (while the nine-pounder, now unidentified, was in the process of arriving with the police on the special train from Regina), seven shells (all that were available in Prince Albert at that time) from it were sent shrieking into the poplar bluff as night fell, clearly such shelling could not and would not disembowel the whole earth. Its carriage is now nicely lacquered, the perhaps oak spokes of its petite wheels (little higher than a knee) have been recently scraped, puttied and varnished; the brilliant burnish of its brass breeching testifies with what meticulous care charmen and women have used nationally-advertised cleaners and restorers.

Though it can also be seen, even a careless glance reveals that the same concern has not been expended on the one (of two).44-calibre 1866 model Winchesters apparently found at the last in the pit with Almighty Voice. It also is preserved in a glass case; the number 1536735 is still, though barely, distinguishable on the brass cartridge section just below the brass saddle ring. However, perhaps because the case was imperfectly sealed at one time (though well enough sealed not to warrant disturbance now), or because of simple neglect, the rifle is obviously spotted here and there with blotches of rust and the brass itself reveals discolourations almost like mildew. The rifle bore, the three long strands of hair themselves, actually bristle with clots of dust. It may be that this museum cannot afford to be as concerned as the other; conversely, the disfiguration may be something inherent in the items themselves.

The small building which was the police guardroom at Duck Lake, Saskatchewan Territory, in 1895 may also be seen. It had subsequently been moved from its original place and used to house small animals, chickens perhaps, or pigs—such as a woman might be expected to have under her responsibility. It is, of course, now perfectly empty, and clean so that the public may enter with no more discomfort than a bend under the doorway and a heavy encounter with disinfectant. The door-jamb has obviously been replaced; the bar network at one window is, however, said to be original; smooth still, very smooth. The logs inside have been smeared again and again with whitewash, perhaps paint, to an insistent point of identity-defying characterlessness. Within the small rectangular box of these logs not a sound can be heard from the streets of the, probably dead, town.

> *Hey Injun you'll get hung for stealing that steer*
> *Hey Injun for killing that government cow you'll get three*
> *weeks on the woodpile Hey Injun*

The place named Kinistino seems to have disappeared from the map but the Minnechinass Hills have not. Whether they have ever been on a map is doubtful but they will, of course, not disappear from the landscape as long as the grass grows and the rivers run. Contrary to general report and belief, the Canadian prairies are rarely, if ever, flat and the Minnechinass (spelled five different ways and translated sometimes as "The Outside Hill," sometimes as "Beautiful Bare Hills") are dissimilar from any other of the numberless hills that everywhere block out the prairie horizon. They are not bare; poplars lie tattered along their tops, almost black against the straw-pale grass and sharp green against the grey soil of the plowing laid in half-mile rectangular blocks upon their western slopes. Poles holding various wires stick out of the fields, back down the bend of the valley; what was once a farmhouse is weathering into the cultivated earth. The poplar bluff where Almighty Voice made his stand has, of course, disappeared.

The policemen he shot and killed (not the ones he wounded, of course) are easily located. Six miles east, thirty-nine miles north in Prince Albert, the English Cemetery. Sergeant Colin Campbell Colebrook, North West Mounted Police Registration Number 605, lies presumably under a gravestone there. His name is seventeenth in a very long "list of non-commissioned officers and men who have died in the service since the inception of the force." The date is October 29, 1895, and the cause of death is anonymous: "Shot by escaping Indian prisoner near Prince Albert." At the foot of this grave are two others: Constable John R. Kerr, No. 3040, and Corporal C. H. S. Hockin, No. 3106. Their cause of death on May 28, 1897 is even more anonymous, but the place is relatively precise: "Shot by Indians at Min-etch-inass Hills, Prince Albert District."

The gravestone, if he has one, of the fourth man Almighty Voice killed is more difficult to locate. Mr. Ernest Grundy, postmaster at Duck Lake in 1897, apparently shut his window the afternoon of Friday, May 28, armed himself, rode east twenty miles, participated in the second charge into the bluff at about 6.30 PM, and on the third sweep of that charge was shot dead at the edge of the pit. It would seem that he thereby contributed substantially not only to the Indians' bullet supply, but his clothing warmed them as well.

The burial place of Dublin and Going-Up-To-Sky is unknown, as is the grave of Almighty Voice. It is said that a Metis named Henry Smith lifted the latter's body from the pit in the bluff and gave it to Spotted Calf. The place of burial is not, of course, of ultimate significance. A gravestone is always less evidence than a triangular piece of skull, provided it is large enough.

Whatever further evidence there is to be gathered may rest on pictures. There are, presumably, almost numberless pictures of the policemen in the case, but the only one with direct bearing is one of Sergeant Colebrook who apparently insisted on advancing to complete an arrest after being warned three times that if he took another step he would be shot. The picture must have been taken before he joined the force; it reveals him as a large-eared young man, hair brush-cut and ascot tie, his eyelids slightly drooping, almost hooded under thick brows. Unfortunately a picure of Constable R. C. Dickson, into whose charge Almighty Voice was apparently committed in that guardroom and who after Cole-brook's death was convicted of negligence, sentenced to two month's hard labour and discharged, doesn't seem to be available.

There are no pictures to be found of either Dublin (killed early by rifle fire) or Going-Up-To-Sky (killed in the pit), the two teenage boys who gave their ultimate fealty to Almighty Voice. There is, however, one said to be of Almighty Voice, Junior. He may have been born to Pale Face during the year, two hundred and twenty-one days that his father was a fugitive. In the picture he is kneeling before what could be a tent, he wears striped denim overalls and displays twin babies whose sex cannot be determined from the double-laced dark bonnets they wear. In the supposed picture of Spotted Calf and Sounding Sky, Sounding Sky stands slightly before his wife; he wears a white shirt and a striped blanket folded over his left shoulder in such a manner that the arm in which he cradles a long rifle cannot be seen. His head is thrown back; the rim of his hat appears as a black half-moon above eyes that are pressed shut in, as it were, profound concentration; above a mouth clenched thin in a downward curve. Spotted Calf wears a long dress, a sweater that could also be a man's dress coat, and a large fringed and embroidered shawl which would appear distinctly Doukhobour in origin if the scroll patterns on it were more irregular. Her head is small and turned slightly toward her husband so as to reveal her right ear. There is what can only be called a quizzical expression on her crumpled face; it may be she does not understand what is happening and that she would have asked a question, perhaps of her husband, perhaps of the photographers, perhaps even of anyone, anywhere in the world if such questioning were possible for an Indian lady.

There is one final picture. That is one of Almighty Voice himself. At least it purports to be of Almighty Voice himself. In the Royal Canadian Mounted Police Museum on the Barracks Grounds just off Dewdney Avenue in Regina, Saskatchewan, it lies in the same showcase, as a matter of fact immediately beside, that triangular piece of skull. Both are unequivocally labelled, and it must be assumed that a police force with a worldwide reputation would not label *such* evidence incorrectly. But here emerges an ultimate problem in making the story.

There are two official descriptions of Almighty Voice. The first reads: "Height about five feet, ten inches, slight build, rather good looking, a sharp hooked nose with a remarkably flat point. Has a bullet scar on the left side of his face about 1½ inches long running from near corner of mouth towards ear. The scar cannot be noticed when his face is painted but otherwise is plain. Skin fair for an Indian." The second description is on the Award Proclamation: "About twenty-two years old, five feet ten inches in height, weight about eleven stone, slightly erect, neat small feet and hands; complexion inclined to be fair, wavy dark hair to shoulders, large dark eyes, broad forehead, sharp features and parrot nose with flat tip, scar on left cheek running from mouth towards ear, feminine appearance."

So run the descriptions that were, presumably, to identify a well-known fugitive in so precise a manner that an informant could collect five hundred dollars—a considerable sum when a police constable earned between one and two dollars a day. The nexus of the problem appears when these supposedly official descriptions are compared with the supposedly official picture. The man in the picture is standing on a small rug. The fingers of his left hand touch a curved Victorian settee, behind him a photographer's backdrop of scrolled patterns merges into vaguely paradisiacal trees and perhaps a sky. The moccasins he wears make it impossible to deduce whether his feet are "neat small." He may be five feet, ten inches tall, may weigh eleven stone, he certainly is "rather good looking" and, though it is a frontal view, it may be that the point of his long and flaring nose could be called "remarkably flat." The photograph is slightly over-illuminated and so the unpainted complexion could be said to be "inclined to be fair"; however, nothing can be seen of a scar, the hair is not wavy and shoulder-length but hangs almost to the waist in two thick straight braids worked through with beads, fur, ribbons and cords. The right hand that holds the corner of the blanket-like coat in position is large and, even in the high illumination, heavily veined. The neck is concealed under coiled beads and the forehead seems more low than "broad."

Perhaps, somehow, these picture details could be reconciled with the official description if the face as a whole were not so devastating.

On a cloth-backed sheet two feet by two and one-half feet in size, under the Great Seal of the Lion and the Unicorn, dignified by the names of the Deputy of the Minister of Justice, the Secretary of State, the Queen herself and all the heaped detail of her "Right Trusty and Right Well-Beloved Cousin," this description concludes: "feminine appearance." But the picture: any face of history, any believed face that the world acknowledges as *man*—Socrates, Jesus, Attila, Genghis Khan, Mahatma Gandhi, Joseph Stalin—no believed face is more *man* than this face. The mouth, the nose, the clenched brows, the eyes—the eyes are large, yes, and dark, but even in this watered-down reproduction of unending reproductions of that original, a steady look into those eyes cannot be endured. It is a face like an axe.

It is now evident that the de Chardin statement quoted at the beginning has relevance only as it proves itself inadequate to explain what has happened. At the same time, the inadequacy of Aristotle's much more famous statement becomes evident: "The true difference [between the historian and the poet] is that one relates what *has* happened, the other what *may* happen." These statements cannot explain the storyteller's activity since, despite the most rigid application of impersonal investigation, the elements of the story have now run me aground. If ever I could, I can no longer pretend to objective, omnipotent disinterestedness. I am no longer *spectator* of what *has* happened or what *may* happen: I am become *element* in what is happening at this very moment.

For it is, of course, I myself who cannot endure the shadows on that paper which are those eyes. It is I who stand beside this broken veranda post where two corner shingles have been torn away, where barbed wire tangles the dead weeds on the edge of this field. The bluff that sheltered Almighty Voice and his two friends has not disappeared from the slope of the Minnechinass, no more than the sound of Constable Dickson's voice in that guardhouse is silent. The sound of his speaking is there even if it has never been recorded in an official report:

> *Hey Injun you'll get*
> *hung*

> *for stealing that steer*
> *Hey Injun for killing that government*
> *cow you'll get three*
> *weeks on the woodpile Hey Injun*

The unknown contradictory words about an unprovable act that move a boy to defiance, an implacable Cree warrior long after the three-hundred-and-fifty-year war is ended, a war already lost the day the Cree watch Cartier hoist his gun ashore at Hochelaga and they begin the long retreat west; these words of incomprehension, of threatened incomprehensible law are there to be heard just as the unmoving tableau of the three-day siege is there to be seen on the slopes of the Minnechinass. Sounding Sky is somewhere not there, under arrest, but Spotted Calf stands on a shoulder of the Hills a little to the left, her arms upraised to the setting sun. Her mouth is open. A horse rears, riderless, above the scrub willow at the edge of the bluff, smoke puffs, screams tangle in rifle barrage, there are wounds, somewhere. The bluff is so green this spring, it will not burn and the ragged line of seven police and two civilians is staggering through, faces twisted in rage, terror, and rifles sputter. Nothing moves. There is no sound of frogs in the night; twenty-seven policemen and five civilians stand in a cordon at thirty-yard intervals and a body also lies in the shelter of a gully. Only a voice rises from the bluff:

> *We have fought well*
> *You have died like braves*
> *I have worked hard and am hungry*
> *Give me food*

but nothing moves. The bluff lies, a bright green island on the grassy slope surrounded by men hunched forward rigid over their long rifles, men clumped out of rifle-range, thirty-five men dressed as for fall hunting on a sharp spring day, a small gun positioned on a ridge above. A crow is falling out of the sky into the bluff, its feathers sprayed as by an explosion. The first gun and the second gun are in position, the beginning and end of the bristling surround of thirty-five Prince Albert Volunteers, thirteen civilians and fifty-six policemen in position relative to the bluff and relative to the unnumbered whites astride their horses, standing up in their carts, staring and pointing across the valley, in position relative to the bluff and the unnumbered Indians squatting silent along the higher ridges of the Hills, motionless mounds, faceless against the Sunday morning sunlight edging between and over them down along the tree tips, down into the shadows of the bluff. Nothing moves. Beside the second gun the red-coated officer has flung a handful of grass into the motionless air, almost to the rim of the red sun.

And there is a voice. It is an incredible voice that rises from among the young poplars ripped of their spring bark, from among the dead somewhere lying there, out of the arm-deep pit shorter than a man; a voice rises over the exploding smoke and thunder of guns that reel back in their positions, worked over, serviced by the grimed motionless men in bright coats and glinting buttons, a voice so high and clear, so unbelievably high and strong in its unending wordless cry.

The voice of "Gitchie-Manitou Wayo"—interpreted as "voice of the Great Spirit"—that is, The Almighty Voice. His death chant no less incredible in its beauty than in its incomprehensible happiness.

I say "wordless cry" because that is the way it sounds to me. I could be more accurate if I had a reliable interpreter who would make a reliable interpretation. For I do not, of course, understand the Cree myself.

CAROL SHIELDS

(b. 1935)

*C*arol Shields was born in Oak Park, Illinois, and moved to Canada *in 1957 with her husband, Donald Hugh Shields, with whom she had five children. She was educated at Hanover College (B.A. 1957) and the University of Ottawa (M.A. 1975). She wrote her master's thesis on the nineteenth-century pioneer-writer Susanna Moodie, a study that was eventually published as* Susanna Moodie: Voice and Vision *(1982). She lives in Winnipeg and teaches at the University of Manitoba. Best known as the author of such award-winning novels as* Small Ceremonies *(1976),* The Box Garden *(1977),* Happenstance *(1980),* A Fairly Conventional Woman *(1982), and* Swann: A Mystery *(1988), Shields has also published books of poetry,* Others *(1972) and* Intersect *(1974); an award-winning play,* Women Waiting *(1983); and two volumes of short stories,* Various Miracles *(1985) and* The Orange Fish *(1989). Her fiction is distinguished by its evocation of a lovingly observed domestic world, especially by the lyrical, or quietly epiphanic moments when that "ordinary" world comes into contact with the extraordinary. The story that follows is representative in depicting the involuntary, apparently accidental processes at work when these two worlds—the ordinary and the mysterious—move toward interpenetration.*

Sailors Lost at Sea

*O*ne afternoon, out of curiosity or else boredom, Hélène wandered into an abandoned church. A moment later she found herself locked inside.

This was in France, in Brittany, and Hélène was a girl of fourteen who had been walking home from the village school to the house where she and her mother were temporarily living. Why she had stopped and touched the handle of the church door, she didn't know. She had been told, several times, that the little church was kept tightly locked, but today the door had opened easily at her touch. This was puzzling, though not daunting, and she had entered bravely, holding her head high. She had recently, since arriving in France, come to understand the profit that could be had from paying attention to good posture, how she could, by a minor adjustment of her shoulders or a lifting of her chin, turn herself into someone who had certain entitlements.

She and her mother were from Canada and, despite her Manitoba accent—which she knew seemed quaint, even comic to French ears, funnier even than Québécois—she was regarded with envy and awe by the girls in the village school in St. Quay. That she was from a place called Winnipeg, the girls found exotic. "Weenie-pegg," they said, with a giggling way of hanging on to the final "g." Her mother said this was because St. Quay was an out-of-the-way sort of place.

This was true. It was a fact that only two girls in her level had ever been to Paris, which was just five hours away by train, and a surprising number of them had never been even as far as Rennes. Also impressive to these girls was the fact that Hélène's mother was a poet, a real poet, who had published three books. *Trois livres? Vraiment?* Their eyes had opened wide at this and they weren't giggling any longer. ("That's one thing about the French," Hélène's mother told her, "they respect writers.") The girls at l'école Jeanne d'Arc were forever asking Hélène how her mother was getting on with her poetry. *"Ta mère, elle travaille bien?"* Their own mothers were the wives of fishermen or shopkeepers. Hélène had been presented to some of these mothers in the village streets; thick-ankled, round-faced women wearing old woolen coats and carrying groceries in bags made of plastic net.

Hélène and her mother had never intended to spend the whole year in St. Quay. They had planned to travel, to drift like migrants along the edges of the country. (*La France* has the shape of a hexagon, Hélène has been taught in the village school; this fact is repeated often, as though it carries mystical significance.) Instead of traveling, they had attached themselves like barnacles—this was how Hélène's mother put it—to this quiet spot on the channel coast, and Hélène had enrolled in the local school. There was a very good reason for this, her mother suprised her by saying. "The only way to get the feel of the country is to become a part of it." Of course, as Hélène now knew, and as her mother would soon discover, it was not possible at all for them to become part of the community. Everywhere they went, to the boulangerie, to the post office, everywhere, there was a rustle and a whisper that went before them, announcing, just behind the weak smiles of welcome, "Ah, les Canadiennes!" It made Hélène feel weak; she always was having to compose herself, to imagine how she must look from the outside.

In St. Quay there were a number of old churches, though the largest, a church dating from the thirteenth century, had been torn down ten years earlier. It had been replaced with a brown brick building which was square and ugly like a factory, and distressingly empty, distressing, that is, to the local priest, a Father Dominic. He was an old man with creased yellow skin and a stiff manner, but he was the only friend Hélène's mother had so far found in St. Quay.

"Alas," said Father Dominic, rubbing his long chin, "Brittany was once the most religious corner of France, and now it has become, over-

night"— he made a zigzag in the air to signify lightning—"*secularized.*"
He said this in his loud, lonely voice, speaking as though there could be
no reversal.

"The church," he said, "had lost out to television and motorbikes and
modernism in general, and it had all happened in a flash."

Well, this was not quite the truth, Hélène's mother explained later.
The truth was that during the French Revolution Brittany had been filled
with ranting anticlerical mobs who tore the statues out of church niches
and removed stone chunks (heads chiefly or the fingers of upraised
hands) from the roadside calvaries that dotted the Côte du Nord. *Quel
dommage*, Hélène's mother said in sly imitation of Father Dominic, her
only friend.

The particular church where Hélène found herself imprisoned on a
Thursday afternoon was one of these small, desecrated churches, statue-
less and plain, its heavy doors shorn clean of carving and its windows
replaced by dull opalescent glass. The church was officially closed. She
knew that; it had been closed for many years.

Father Dominic had explained to them that it was no longer served
by a priest. Nowadays there was but a single mass celebrated here each
year—it was he who had the privilege of serving—and that was on a
certain spring day set aside by tradition to honor sailors who had been
lost at sea. On that particular Sunday in early April, the doors would be
thrown open and people would enter carrying armloads of spring flowers; after that, a procession would wind over the rocks and down to the
beach itself.

When Hélène's mother heard Father Dominic talking about this festival, her eyes had softened with feeling and she had nodded as though
she, too, had had occasion to pay tribute to lost seamen—which, of course,
coming from Winnipeg, she had not.

"That will be something to see," she said to Hélène, and wrote the
name of the festival in her notebook. At that moment, seeing her mother
writing down the details of the fête and imagining the blond sunniness
of this festive day, Hélène truly understood that they would be staying
here the entire year, that their drifting, which she had loved, all ten days
of it, was not to be resumed.

The old church stood just outside the village on the rue des Chiens,
the same street where they had found a house to rent. "We've installed
ourselves in a cheap stone house on Dog Street." Hélène's mother had
written this in a cheerful letter to a friend back home, as though having
an inelegant address gave them an unconquerable ascendancy over the
difficulties the little stone house presented. There it stood, surrounded
by drenched shrubbery, a dragging lace of rain falling from the corners
of the steep roof. The landlord, a scowling, silent widower with three
teeth in his head, lived in the basement, and his presence cast a spell of

restraint over them so that they tiptoed about the house, *his* house, in bedroom slippers and spoke to each other in hushed formal voices, more like a pair of elderly sisters than a mother and daughter. The bathroom stank despite the minty blue deoderizer Hélène had bought and attached to the wall, and the kitchen was damp and without cupboards. The two armchairs in the living room were covered with ancient, oily tapestry cloth, badly frayed. In the morning her mother made coffee, carried it to one of these repellent chairs, and sat down with her notebooks. There she spent her time, scarcely getting up and looking out at the sea all day. Hélène knew without asking that the poems were not coming easily.

By good fortune the Canadian government had seen fit to award her mother a sum of money so that she could come to France for a year in order to write poetry. She had long desired—and this was explained at great length in the application—to touch the soil where her ancestral roots lay. (But these roots, she now admitted to Hélène in one of their long whispered talks, were more deeply buried than she had thought. Her forebears had gone to Canada a long time ago, first to Quebec, then making their way to Manitoba.) And she was not entirely certain which region of France they had come from, though it was generally believed to have been either Brittany or Normandy. Now she was here, breathing French air, eating French bread, drinking bitter black coffee and taking weekend walks on the wild wetted path that went along the coast, but what really was the use of this? What had she expected? For the so-called roots to rise up and embrace her?

It seemed to Hélène that her mother had childish notions about the magic of places. A field of oats was a field of oats. The blackberries they'd found along the coast path had the same beaded precision as those at home. Her mother had a way of making too much of things, always seeing secondary meanings, things that weren't really there, and her eyes watered embarrassingly when she spoke of these deeper meanings. It was infantile, the way she went on and on about the *fond* of human experience. What was the *fond* but carrying home the groceries, trying to keep warm in the drafty stone house, walking down the dark road in the morning to school where the other girls waited for her, admiring her warm wool sweaters and asking her how her mother, the poet, was doing.

Recently Hélène's mother, as if to make up for the lack of poems, had latched with fevered intensity on to particles of local lore, prising them out of Michelin guides and storing them up in notebooks—not the same notebooks the poems went into, but pale green spiral-bound books with squared-off pages, notebooks (meant for young school children) that she bought in the village at the Maison de la Presse. In one of these notebooks, she had recorded:

There are two legends surrounding the founding of St. Quay,

stories that contain similar elements but that occupy different sides of a coin. In the "good" story, a fourth-century Irish saint called St. Quay arrives in a stone boat to bring Christianity to the wild Breton coast. A bird flies ahead to tell the villagers of his imminent arrival, and the women (why just women?) joyfully run to the shore to greet him, bringing with them armloads of flowers and calling "St. Quay, St. Quay," guiding the boat to safety with their cries.

In the second version, the "bad" version, the same bird arrives to say that a stranger is approaching in a stone boat. The women (women again!) of the village are suspicious and hostile, and they run to the shore with rough stalks of gorse in their hands which they brandish ferociously, all the time crying, "*Quay, quay,*" which means in old Gaelic, "Away, away."

Her mother asked Hélène one day which version she preferred, but before Hélène could decide, she herself had said, "I think the second version must be true." Then she qualified. "Not true, of course, not in a real sense, but containing the elements, the *fond* of truth."

"Why?" Hélène had asked. She saw the shine on her mother's face and felt an obligation to keep it there. "Why not the first version?"

"It's a matter of perspective," her mother said. "It's just where I am now. In my life, I mean. I can believe certain things but not others."

Because of the way she had said this, and the way she had squeezed her eyes shut, Hélène knew her mother was thinking about Roger, the man in Winnipeg she was in love with. She had been in love before, several times. Love, or something like it, was always happening to her.

But now something had happened to Hélène; she was locked inside a church, chosen somehow, the way characters in stories are chosen. The thought gave her a wavelet of happiness. And a flash of guilty heat. She should not have entered the door; it should not have been unlocked and she should not be standing here—but she was. And what could she do about it—nothing. The feeling of powerlessness made her calm and almost sleepy. She looked about in the darkness for a place to sit down. There was nothing, no pews, no chairs, only the stone floor.

She tried the door again. The handle was heavy and made of some dull metal that filled her hand. She set her school bag on the floor and tried turning the handle and pushing on the door at the same time, leaning her shoulder into the wood. Then she pulled the door toward her, rattled it sharply and pushed it out again.

"Open," she said out loud, and heard a partial echo float to the roof. It contained, surprisingly, the half-bright tone of triumph.

"I'm fourteen years old and locked in a French church." These words slid out like a text she had been asked to read aloud. Calm sounds surrounded by their own well of calm; this was a fact. It was no more and no less than what had happened.

Perhaps there was another door. She began to look around. The window, high up along the length of the church, let in soft arches of webbed light, but the light was fading fast. It was almost five o'clock and would be dark she knew, in half an hour. Her mother would be waiting at home, the kitchen light on already, something started for supper.

High overhead was a dense, gray collision of dark beams and stone arches, and the arches were joined in such a way that curving shadows were formed, each of them like the quarter slice out of a circle. Hélène had made such curves with her pencil and compass under the direction of Sister Ste. Adolphe at the village school, and had been rewarded with a dainty-toothed smile and a low murmur, "*Très, très bon.*" Sister Ste. Adolphe gave her extra pencils, showed her every favor, favors that, instead of exciting envy among the girls, stirred their approval. Hélène was a foreigner and deserved privileges. It was unjust.

It occurred to Hélène that there must be a reason for the church to be open. Perhaps there was a workman about or perhaps Father Dominic himself had come to see that the church was safe and undisturbed during its long sleep between festivals.

"Hello," she called out. "*Bonjour.* Is there anyone here?" She stood still, pulling her coat more closely around her and waiting for an answer.

While she waited, she imagined two versions of her death. She would be discovered in the spring when the doors were flung open for the festival. The crowds, rushing in with armloads of flowers, would discover what was left of her, a small skeleton, odorless, as neat on the floor as a heap of stacked kindling, and the school bag nearby with its books and pencils and notebooks would provide the necessary identification.

Or some miracle of transcendence might occur. This was a church, after all, and close by was the sea. She might be lifted aloft and found with long strands of seaweed in her hair; her skin would be bleached and preserved so that it gleamed with the lustre of certain kinds of shells, and her lips, caked with salt, would be parted to suggest a simple attitude of prayerfulness. (She and her mother, in their ten days of wandering, had visited the grave of an imbecile, a poor witless man who had lived as a hermit in the fourteenth century. It was said, a short time after his death and burial, that a villager had noticed a golden lily growing from the hermit's grave, and when the body was exhumed it was discovered that the bulb of the plant was located in his throat, a testimonial to his true worth and a rebuke to those who had ignored him in his life.)

It occurred to Hélène that her mother would blame herself and not France. Lately, she was always saying, "One thing about France, the coffee has real flavor." Or, "At least the French aren't sentimental about animals," or "You can say one thing for France, things are expensive but quality is high." It seemed her mother was compelled to justify this place where she had deliberately settled down to being lonely and uncomfortable and unhappy.

It had all been a mistake, and now her mother, though she didn't say it, longed for home and for Roger. "A man friend" is what she called Roger, saying this phrase with special emphasis as though it was an old joke with a low wattage of energy left in it. Roger loved her and wanted to marry her. They had known each other for two years. His first wife left him. "He's very bitter," Hélène's mother said, "and for someone like Roger, this can be a terrible blow, a great humiliation."

He was a chef at the Convention Center in downtown Winnipeg. When he was a young man, he was taken into the kitchens of the Ritz Carleton in Montreal where he learned sauces and pastries and salads. He learned to make sculptures out of butter or lard or ice or sugar, and even—for it was an arduous apprenticeship, he tells Hélène—how to fold linen table napkins in twenty classic folds. Would she like a demonstration? She had said yes, despising herself, and Roger had instantly obliged, but he could remember only thirteen of the twenty ways. Now, at the Convention Center, he seldom does any cooking himself, but supervises the kitchen from a little office where he spends his time answering the phone and keeping track of grocery orders.

On Saturday nights he used to come to the apartment in St. Vital where Hélène and her mother lived, and there in the tiny kitchen he made them veal in cream or croquettes or a dish of steamed fish, pickerel with white mushrooms and pieces of green onion.

"Tell me what you like best," he'd say to Hélène, "and next week I'll try it out on you."

Of course, he often stayed the night. He was astonishingly neat, never leaving so much as a toothbrush in the bathroom. On Sunday mornings he made them poached eggs on toast—ducks in their nests he calls them. He had a trick with the eggs, lifting them from the simmering water with a spatula, then flipping them onto a clean, cotton tea towel, patting them dry, and then sliding them onto buttered triangles of toast—all this without breaking the yolks. He learned to do this at the Ritz Carleton when he was a young man. "It would not have been acceptable," he said, "to serve an egg that was *wet*." He does it all very quickly and lightly, moving like a character in a speeded-up movie. The first time he did it for Hélène—she was only twelve at the time—she had clapped her hands, and now he's made it into a ceremony, one of several that has unsettled the household.

"Come here, little duckie," he says, flashing his spatula. "Turn yourself over like a good little duck for Hélène." Hélène, when he said this, found it hard to look at her mother, who laughed loudly at this showmanship, her mouth wide and crooked.

Later, after Roger had left, there were a few minutes of tender questioning between them. Hélène's mother, settling down on the plumped cushions, talked slowly, evenly, taking, it would seem, full measure of the delicate temperamental balance of girls in their early adolescence. About the disruption to the household, she was apologetic, saying, "This is only temporary." And, saying with her eyes, "This is not how I planned things." ("Shhh," she said to Roger when he became too merry, when he was about to tell another joke or another story about his apprenticeship.) "How do you like Roger?" her mother asked her. Then, instead of waiting for an answer, her mother began to talk about Roger's ex-wife, how vicious she had been, how she left him for another man.

"I hope I'm not barging in," Roger said, if he dropped by in the middle of the week. He was always bringing presents, not just food, but jewelry, once an alarm clock, once a coat for her mother and a silk blouse for herself. ("I don't know what girls like," he'd said abjectly on this occasion. "I can take it back.")

This is what made Hélène numb. She couldn't say a word in reply, and her silence ignited a savage shame. What was the matter? The matter was that they were waiting for her. They were waiting for her to make up her mind, just as the girls in the schoolyard with their *cartables* and their regulation blouses wait for her to arrive in the dark mornings and bring some improbable substance into the cement schoolyard. "Tell us about Weenie-pegg. Tell us about the snow."

It was growing very cold inside the church, but then even the churches they had visited in September had been cold. Hélène and her mother had carried cardigans. "You can never tell about the weather here," her mother had said, puzzled. This was a point scored against France, a plus for Manitoba where you at least knew what to expect.

And soon it would be dark. Frail moons of light pressed like mouths on the floor, though the walls themselves were darkly invisible. Hélène reached out and rubbed her hand along the rough surface. This was— she began to figure—this was a fourteenth-century church; twenty centuries take away fourteen—that left six; that meant this church was 600 years old, walls that were planted by the side of a road called rue des Chiens in a village called St. Quay, which was hidden away in the hexagon that was France. And her body would not be found until spring.

O Mother of God, she said to herself, and rubbed at her hair. O Mother of Jesus.

She tried the door again, putting her ear to the wood to see if she could sound out the inner hardware. There was only a thickish sound of metal butting against wood and the severed resistance of moving parts. She was going to perish. Perish. At fourteen. The thought struck her that her mother would never get over this. She would go back home and tell Roger she couldn't marry him. She would stop writing poems about landscapes that were "jawbone simple and picked clean by wind" and about the "glacé moon pinned like a brooch in the west." She would sink into the *fond* and her mouth would sag open—this was not how she had planned things. And whose fault was it?

By now the church was entirely dark, but at the far end the altar gleamed dully. It seemed a wonder to Hélène that she could summon interest in this faint light. What was it? There was no gold or ornamentation, only a wooden railing that had been polished or worn by use, and the last pale light lay trapped there on the smooth surface like a pool of summer water.

O Mother of God, she breathed, thinking of Sister Ste. Adolphe, her tiny teeth.

She ran her hand along its edge. There was something else at one end. Altar candles. The light didn't reach this far, but her hand felt them in the darkness, a branched candle holder, rising toward the center. She counted the tall candles with her fingers. Up they went like little stairs, one, two, three, four, five, six and then down again on the other side.

There might be matches, she thought, and fumbled at the base of the candle holder. Then she remembered she had some in her school bag. Her mother had asked her to stop at the *tobagie* for cigarettes and matches. (At home in St. Vital they had refused to sell cigarettes to minors, but here in France no one blinked an eye; a point for France.)

She felt her way back to where she left the bag, rummaged for the matches, and then moved back along the wall to the candles. She managed to light them all, using only three matches, counting under her breath. The stillness of the flames seemed of her own creation, and a feeling of virtue struck her, a ridiculous steamroller. She thought how she would never again in her life be able to take virtue seriously.

Astonishing how much light twelve candles gave off. The stone church shrank in the light so that it seemed not a church at all, but a cheerful meeting room where any minute people might burst through the door and call out her name.

And, of course, that was what would happen, she realized. The lit-up church would attract someone's notice. It was a black night and rain was falling hard on the roof, but nevertheless someone—and soon—would pass by and see the light from the church. An immediate investigation would be in order. Father Dominic would be summoned at once.

This might take several minutes; he would have to find his overshoes, his umbrella, not to mention the key to the church. Then there would be the mixed confusion of embracing and scolding. How could you? Why on earth? Thank God in all his mercy.

Until then, there was a width of time she would enter and inhabit. There was nothing else she could do; it was laughable. All she had to do was stand here warming her hands in the heat of the twelve candles—how beautiful they were really!—and wait for rescue to come.

Will she be rescued.

What is the significance of the title, Sailors Lost at Sea?

Helena's mother states that her response to the St. Quay story is "a matter of perspective." It's just "... " 9170.

Discuss How does this statement underlies the story in total. Use specific examples Focus your answer

AUDREY THOMAS

(b. 1935)

*A*udrey Thomas was born in Binghamton, New York, and came to Canada (Vancouver) in 1959. She was educated at Smith College, Massachusetts, St. Andrew's University in Scotland, and the University of British Columbia (M.A. 1963). Like Margaret Laurence, she lived for a period in Ghana, and she too was profoundly influenced by that experience, which she has explored a number of times in her fiction. Thomas made her reputation as a writer of experimental fiction, but in recent years her writing has become more conventional stylistically and, consequently, more accessible to a wider readership. In her fiction, women living on the fringes of white middle-class society struggle to divest themselves of guilt over past mistakes or to fashion more meaningful lives in counterpoint to the repressive societies in which they live. That may sound bleak, and in Thomas's fiction the prospect is often not promising; but any account of her work must also deal with the rich humour and wit with which she explores her fictional territory. Her first book of stories was **Ten Green Bottles** (1967), and her first novel, **Mrs. Blood** (1970). She has also published two companion novellas in one volume, **Munchmeyer** and **Prospero on the Island** (1971). Other novels include **Songs My Mother Taught Me** (1973), **Blown Figures** (1974), and **Latakia** (1979); her other collections of stories are **Ladies and Escorts** (1977), from which "Initram" is taken (whose title is a mirror image—a favourite technique of Thomas's), **Real Mothers** (1981), **Goodbye, Harold, Good Luck** (1988), and **The Wild Blue Yonder** (1990).

Initram

For Bob Amussen

W riters are terrible liars. There are nicer names for it, of course, but liars will do. They will take a small incident and blow it up, like a balloon—puff puff— and the out-of-work man who comes to ask if he can cut the grass ends up in their story as an out-of-control grey-faced, desperate creature who hurls himself through the garden gate and by his sheer presence wrecks a carefully arranged afternoon between a married woman and her impending lover.

The truth is I was reading the manuscript of an old friend. The truth is I thought the man hadn't gone but was lurking in the back lane just beyond the blackberry bushes.

The truth is I only thought I saw him there—flashes of a red-plaid shirt beyond the green. (Writers also lie to themselves.)

The truth is that when the police came and I was asked to describe this man I was overcome with shame and embarrassment to suddenly notice him, half a block away, moving a neighbour's lawn mower up and down in regular and practiced stripes.

The truth is I still insisted (to myself, after the grinning policeman had gone) that the man had been sinister, menacing, unpleasant. And of course he is, in my story.

But what do writers do with the big events in life—births and broken hearts and deaths—the great archetypal situations that need no real enhancement or "touching up"? Surely they simply *tell* these, acting as mediums through which the great truths filter. Not at all—or not usually or maybe sometimes when they happen to other people.

That is why I decided to call Lydia when my marriage broke up. I was living on an island—felt I needed a wider audience, an audience that would understand and accept my exaggerations for what they were. It had to be a fellow writer, preferably a woman. I called her up long-distance. One of her daughters answered and said she wasn't there could I leave my number? I put the phone down, already planning the ferry-trip, the excitement of the telling of my terrible news. Lydia was perfect. Yes. I couldn't wait for her to call me back.

I didn't, in fact, know her very well. I had done a review of her first published book and then later, when I went to visit her city, had on a sudden whim called from a phone booth and identified myself. She had told me to come right over. I had my husband and three kids with me. That seemed too much of an imposition on anyone we didn't know so I took the littlest and he agreed to take the others to the Wax Museum. We drove up a very classy road, with huge houses—some were really what we used to call mansions—on either side. I began to get cold feet.

I had visions of a patrician face and perfect fingernails—drinking tea from her grandmother's bone china cups. We would talk about Proust and Virginia Woolf with a few casual remarks about *Nightwood* and the diaries of Anaïs Nin.

As we drove up to the front door of a big, imposing, mock-tudor residence I thought of "Our Gal Sunday," a soap-opera I had loved when I was a kid. It always began with a question as to whether a beautiful young girl from a small mining town in the West could find happiness as the wife of England's most wealthy and titled lord, Lord Henry Brinthrop.

It was her stories, you see. They were about life on the Prairies—

about farms and poverty (both spiritual and material) and, very often, a young girl's struggle against those things. Yet here was this house, on this road and a statue in the garden.

"Wait for me," I said to my husband. "If a butler or maid answers, I'm not going in."

But Lydia answered—in black slacks and an old black sweater and no shoes. She gave me a hug and I went in with my littlest child and didn't look back.

Through the hall in to the sitting room, then the dining room (an impression of a piano and lots of books, of a big antique dining table covered with clutter generally, now that I think back on it. Somewhere upstairs a small child was screaming), through another narrow hall and into a big kitchen. She asked if my little girl wanted some orange juice. She wouldn't answer, so I answered for her as mothers do on such occasions.

"Yes, please."

When Lydia opened the refrigerator door a great pile of things fell out on the kitchen floor. Frozen pizzas, a dish of left-over mashed potatoes, the bottle of juice, something unidentifiable in a glass jar. We looked at each other and began to laugh.

"The house," I said. "I was terrified."

"I *hate* this house," she said. "I hate it."

Then talked and talked while our two little girls (we each had three, extraordinary!, we each had the same dinner set bought on special at the Hudson's Bay Company years before—"Cherry Thieves," it was called— she used one of the saucers for an ash tray) played something or other upstairs.

She was older than I was (but not much) and incredibly beautiful, with dark, curly chaotic hair and the kind of white skin that gives off the radiance a candle does when it has burnt down at the core and the sides are still intact. Her book had brought her fame (if not fortune), but she was having trouble with her second one, a novel.

She hated the house and couldn't keep it up. Her husband was a professor—he loved it. It was miserably cold in the winter—sometimes the furnace stopped all together. What did I think of Doris Lessing, of Joyce Carol Oates, of *The Edible Woman*? Her daughter had made a scene in the supermarket and called her a "fucking bitch." Did that kind of thing happen to me? Her neighbour was a perfect housewife, perfect. She was always sending over cakes and preserves. One day she took one of her neighbour's cheese cakes and stamped all over it with her bare feet, she said. An aging Canadian writer (male) had told her drunkenly, "Well, I might read ya but I'd never fuck ya." Did I think it was all right to send a kid to day care when she was only three?

And even while I was talking with her, marvelling at her, helping her mop up the floor, I kept wondering why she didn't write about all this, why she had stopped at twenty, years ago, and written nothing about her marriage or this house or her child who had been still-born and how the doctor (male) and her husband couldn't understand why it took her so long to get over it. I wondered about her husband, but he was off somewhere practising with a chamber-music group. He liked old instruments, old houses, things with a patina of history and culture. His family accepted her now that she'd won awards.

I only saw her a few times after that—we lived in different cities and there was a boat ride between us. But we wrote (occasionally); she had large, round handwriting, like a child's.

Her novel was not going well—it kept turning itself into stories—she was going to Ireland with her husband for a holiday. How was I? Not literary letters: we were both too busy, too involved in our own affairs. Just little notes, like little squeezes or hugs which said, "Sister, I am here."

We read once, at a Women's Week, or rather I read, with two others while Lydia sat on the blue-carpeted floor with a Spanish cape over her head and let somebody else read for her. She and I were both scared and had gotten drunk before we went—by not reading I felt she had somehow let me down. We four ladies all had dinner together and talked about what it was like to be woman and writer and egged each other on to new witticisms and maybe a few new insights, but I did not feel close to Lydia that evening. I was still sore about the way she'd plonked herself down on the carpet and pulled her shawl over her head and let somebody else read for her. It was very clever, I thought to myself, and very dramatic. For there was Lydia's story, unrolling out of the mouth of another woman (whose story it was not) and there was the author herself sitting like an abandoned doll, on the floor beside the reader. The audience loved it and sent out sympathetic vibrations to her. I thought it was a con. And almost said to her, "Lydia, I think that was a very clever con," but didn't because I realized that maybe I wished I had thought of it first and why not store it away for some future date—it was a nice piece of dramatic business.

And once we had lunch in her city—at a medieval place—where we swept in in our capes (I had a cape too by then) and ate and drank our way through a rainy West Coast afternoon. I wasn't staying overnight so I still hadn't met her husband. Her novel was out and she was winning awards. I was a little jealous. My books came out and vanished into the well of oblivion. She just went up and up and up. "I've been writing for twenty years," she said, "don't forget that. Two books in twenty years."

She had used to pretend she was making the sitting room curtains when her neighbours invited her over for coffee. She always worked in a basement room. Now her secret was well and truly out.

"How does your husband feel about it all?"

"Oh, I never write about *him*," she said. She lit a cigarette. "He's probably my biggest fan."

Now I waited for her to call me back. My husband (correction, my ex-husband) was coming over to be with his children. I had a whole day and a night off. Whether I wanted it or not I had to leave this place. And I wanted to, I really wanted to. What was the point in hanging around while he was here, crying over spilt milk, locking empty, horseless barn doors, trying to pick up nine stitches, or mopping up all the water under the goddamn bridge. I baked bread and cleaned the cabin and got supper for the kids and still she hadn't called. My ex-husband called, however, and said in his new strained, estranged voice, was it all set for tomorrow, and I said sure but began to feel really sorry for myself because there was really no place I wanted to go except this one place, Lydia's, and I'd got it into my head that if I couldn't go there I couldn't go anywhere and would have to end up going back to the city I had left behind and getting a room in some cheap hotel down near Hastings street, and drink myself into oblivion with cheap red wine. Or going back and forth all day on the ferry, ending up at midnight on one of the neighbouring islands, getting a room at the inn. A stranger in a brown wool cape. Going into the public room and ordering a drink. Did they have a public room? Would there be local characters sitting around and playing darts—a handsome stranger whose sailing boat was tied up because of the storm? There was not even a small-craft warning out, but never mind—the weather was almost as fickle as friendship—it was not inconceivable that a sailboat-disabling storm could blow up by tomorrow night—

"I'll always care what happens to you," he said.

We were teasing wool on the floor in front of the pot-belly stove, the three of us—the youngest child was asleep. There was only the oil lamp on and the CBC was broadcasting a documentary about Casals. "The quality of a man's life is as important as the quality of his art," the old man said. Our hands were soft and oily from the lanolin in the wool. We touched each other's faces with our new, soft, hands. Yes. I thought, yes. And maybe I'll be all right after all. The fleece had been bought by my husband's lover, my ex-best friend. It was from New Zealand, the finest wool in the world. I paid for it, the wool. I had left a cheque on the table the last time I was in town. On the phone my husband mentioned it wasn't enough, she'd mistaken the price or the price had been incorrectly quoted. But it was all right, he'd make up the difference.

"I bet you will," I said.

I was seeing everything symbolically. Lydia phoned and I said, "Just a minute. I have to light a candle." The room with the phone in it was in darkness. I stuck the candle in the window and picked up the phone again with my soft lanolin-soaked hands.

"Hello," I said, "Can I come and visit you tomorrow and stay overnight?" Her voice sounded a bit funny, but that could be the line, which was notoriously bad.

"Sure," she said, "of course. But I'll be out until suppertime. Can you find something to do until suppertime?"

"Can I come a little before? I want to talk to you."

"Come around four," she said. She sounded as though she had a cold.

"I'll bring a bottle," I said.

"Fine."

I had to be away on the first ferry—what would I do all day? I rubbed lanolin into my face. Sheep shed their old coats and went on living. Snakes too. I could hear Casals' child laughing in the background. Someone had lent us a spinner and it stood in the corner of the front room. Not a fairytale spinner which would turn straw into gold. Very solid and unromantic—an Indian spinner without even the big wheel. Nothing for a Sleeping Beauty to prick her finger on—It worked like an old treadle sewing machine but I didn't have the hang of it yet—my wool always broke. Whirr Whirr. There was something nice about just pressing down on the treadle.

I took the candle into the kitchen and wrapped my bread in clean tea towels. I put out a jar of blackberry jam and two poems folded underneath the jar. That would have to do.

When I got to Lydia's house she was frying chicken in the kitchen. Same black slacks and old black sweater. Same bare feet and clutter. There were two enormous frying pans full of chicken wings both hissing and spitting away and Lydia had a long two-prong kitchen fork in her hand.

I took off my cape and sat down, unwrapping the bottle.

"Good," she said, "pour us a glass." Her voice didn't sound as though she had a cold any more, it sounded harsh and a little loud, as though she were talking to someone slightly deaf. She was jabbing the chicken wings as though they were sausages in need of pricking. She couldn't leave those chicken wings alone, and after my second glass I began.

"Listen," I said, "I've got something I want to tell you."

"I've got something I want to tell you too," she said, and then, rather absent-mindedly, "Did you only buy one bottle?"

"Sorry. But have some more, it doesn't matter."

"It's all right," she said, "we'll drink the dinner wine. Tony will just have to bring some more."

I was anxious to begin. I wanted to make it funny and witty and brave—to get rid of the pain or to immortalize it and fix it—which? I

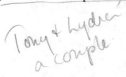

Tony & Lydia
a couple

don't know, I never know. I took another drink of my sherry and wished she'd stop poking at those chicken wings.

"I don't actually live here any more," she said, waving the long-handled fork. "I only come back to cook the dinners."

"You what??"

Turning all the chicken wings over one more time, she lowered the heat under the pans and came to sit down next to me. She kept her fork with her, however, and laid it on the tablecloth, where it left a greasy two-pronged stain.

"I've left him," she said, "the bastard." Her voice was very harsh, very tough. I felt she'd put something over on me, just as I'd felt the day of the reading when she sat on the floor and pulled her cape over her head.

"I wish you'd told me over the phone."

"I couldn't. It's too complicated. Besides, I come back here every day in any case."

It was both moving and bizarre. He had been supposed to move out, she had even found him an apartment only a few minutes away. But at the last minute he panicked, said he couldn't live in an apartment, talked about his piano, his collection of old instruments, the upheaval. He suggested she move out instead.

"But what about the children?"

"That's the trouble, of course. I have to pick Ellen up from school—he can't do it, of course, and so I just stay on and make the dinners. The other two are all right. It's only the little one who still needs to be looked after."

"But that's crazy."

"Is it? What would you do?"

I admitted that I didn't know.

"But how can you all eat together—how can you stand it?"

"I can't," she admitted, "but he won't move out, and finding a house big enough for me and the girls is going to take time." She got up and rummaged in the pantry. Came back with a bottle of wine.

"I think we'd better start on this," she said. I undid the cork while she got up to turn the chicken wings.

"He brought her right to the house," she said. "When I was on that reading tour. Brought her right here and the children were here too."

The name of the wine was *Sangre de Toro*. bull's blood

"At least she wasn't your best friend," I said.

"I knew her, I knew her, she's one of his students. I used to think she was mousey. I encouraged her to do something with herself. Ha. And I think the lady next door too," she said.

"The one who bakes cakes?"

"That's the one. The perfect mother."

"Maybe you're just being paranoid."

"Maybe."

We began the *Sangre de Toro.*

"What's your big news?" she said.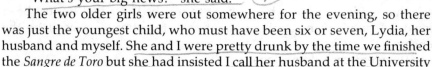

The two older girls were out somewhere for the evening, so there was just the youngest child, who must have been six or seven, Lydia, her husband and myself. She and I were pretty drunk by the time we finished the *Sangre de Toro* but she had insisted I call her husband at the University and ask him to bring home another bottle.

"Tell him specifically what you want," she yelled at me from the kitchen. "Otherwise he'll bring home Calona Red."

I told him. Now he sat opposite me with two huge plates of chicken wings between us. I didn't want to look at his baffled eyes, his embarrassed smile.

"He still wears a white handkerchief in his breast pocket," she had said. "Irons them himself."

The vegetable was frozen peas and there was bread on the table because Lydia had forgotten all about the potatoes. The child was raucous and unpleasant. I wondered what happened when she woke up in the night with a bad dream and whether he went in to her or whether her teen-age sisters did. I wondered if she had been the one to tell about the student. Kids will do things like that and not always out of innocence.

Lydia ate one chicken wing after another. We were all going out as soon as the dishes were done and the baby-sitter came. My real self didn't want to go, but my drunken self thought What the hell? It's better than staying here with these three miserable people.

While Tony was doing the dishes, Lydia hauled me upstairs, pulled me up after her like an older sister a younger, or a mother a reluctant child. I understood the fierce energy of her anger. It was like someone who is hurt during an exciting game. While the excitement is there the pain is simply not felt. She hurled me into their bedroom.

"Look," she said.

I don't know what I expected to see. Stained sheets piled up in a corner or the student stark naked and manacled to the bed or what. But everything seemed all right. No shattered mirrors or blood-stained bedspreads, just an ordinary pleasant-looking bedroom.

"I don't see."

"Look." She was pointing to the walk-in closet. "I've left all my shoes here except one pair. Crazy, isn't it? I just can't seem to take my shoes away."

"Maybe you don't really want to go."

"Oh no, I want to go. I have to go. Or he does. One of us anyway. It isn't just the girl."

"It never is."

On his side of the closet the tweed jackets and neatly pressed trousers were hung with military precision. On her side there were only empty hangers and a large heap of shoes piled any which way. Was that significant, the order/disorder? Was it an attempt to break through this orderly self that made him bring his student to this bed? Or had he just been lonely? I didn't want to think about that, for after all, wasn't he the enemy?

We went back downstairs.

The baby-sitter came and we went out. Lydia had put on a filthy white crocheted wool poncho. Tony objected mildly. "Are you going out in that? It's dirty."

"That's tough," Lydia said.

They were playing to me, an audience of one. Maybe that's why we were going out—to gain a larger audience. I panicked—what if I had too much to drink and began to cry? Lydia looked witchy and wicked with her uncombed hair and dirty poncho—I felt she was quite capable of doing something terrible to her husband—mocking him or humiliating him in some way and I was to be her accomplice. He had a heavy projector in his hand.

"We had arranged to show some slides," he said, "before we knew you were coming."

"Slides of our European trip," Lydia said. "One of Tony's colleagues is going this summer—he wanted to see them."

I thought it was strange they didn't invite him over here, but maybe Lydia had refused to actually entertain. I found the whole thing strange—sitting between them in the car, following them up the steps to their friend's house, saying hello and taking off my cape, patting my face to keep the smile in place, the way some women pat their hair before they go into a room. Our host was shy and pale and had a club foot—there didn't seem to be any hostess. But there were two other people in the sitting room, a tall, lean man in a bright blue shirt, string tie and cowboy boots and a plump woman in a black creepy dress, black pointy fifties shoes, and a rhinestone brooch. Both the man and the woman had nice faces, expectant faces, as though they expected that whoever walked through the next door was bound to be cheerful and interesting and good. Innocent faces, almost the faces of small children. We were introduced and asked what we would like to drink and Tony began to set up the projector.

Lydia was talking to Tony's colleague in her strange new brassy tough-gal voice, flirting with him, making him smile. "Does he know?" I wondered. He had introduced her as Tony's wife. I sat down next to the man in the blue shirt.

"What do you do?" I asked.

"I'm a bee-keeper," he said.

"You might say he's a bee-baron," said his brother. I could see they were brothers in their smiles and something to do with their ears, a strange extra little fold where the ear joined the head. Other than that they didn't really look alike, the one small and dark and with the pallor of the academic, the other tall and fair and with what we call a "weathered" skin.

"A swarm of bees in May," said Lydia, "is worth a load of hay. I remember hearing farmers say that when I was a kid. I grew up on a farm," she said and flashed a smile at the bee-keeper's wife.

"Do you like it," I asked, "keeping bees?" I had thought of buying one or two hives for the island. I already had hens and a fleece for spinning and would have my nine bean rows in the spring. Lydia had laughed when I told her my real dream was to have a little farm.

"Ha. Only city people yearn to live on a farm. I hated it."

"Why?"

"I'm not even sure why any more. The constant work—the catastrophes—the exhaustion—the women always in the kitchen—something always being butchered beheaded or skinned or pickled or preserved."

"Maybe it doesn't have to be that way."

"It has to be that way. If you really live off the land you live off the land. Nothing can be put off or wasted or ignored. I always felt the kitchen smelled of blood or sugar or vinegar or manure or all of these. I felt I went to school stinking of all of it."

"Those are good smells. Honest smells. I worked in an asylum once—I got that smell on me. I used carbolic soap and tried to get it off."

She shook her head and changed the subject, only adding, "They weren't good smells when I was going to school."

Had she been teased, then? Had the boys pulled chicken feathers out of her dark curly hair—had her dresses been too long—were her hands all wrinkled from washwater? I realized how little I actually knew about her except through her stories. I guess this conversation took place before her novel came out.

Tony asked in his apologetic manner if we were ready to see the slides. Lydia and the bee-keeper's wife were sitting in easy chairs on the other side of the room, where the screen had been set up so they had to move. Lydia came and sat cross-legged on the floor by my feet. The bee-keeper and I were on the couch and we shoved over to make room for the bee-keeper's wife. Tony was next to me, behind the projector, and his friend was next to him on a kitchen chair. He got up and, after offering us another drink (only Lydia and I accepted), turned out all the lights.

I don't remember much about the slide show. Tony projected and Lydia commented. Ireland, England, Scotland, Wales and then across the Channel into France and down through Spain. They were all "views"—that is to say they told me nothing about the two people who had taken that trip. Alone. Without the children. Was that when they first suspected they had nothing to say to one another. Had they set off with high hopes and become more and more disenchanted? What had finally driven that orderly controlled man to introduce the student into his bedroom? Not secretly but openly, "In front of the children." From where I was sitting I could see that his hands shook every time he put in another slide.

"You've got that one in backwards," Lydia said. We all came to attention and studied the screen—it was a bull fight scene and looked perfectly all right to me.

"I don't think—" Tony began.

"Look for yourself. Look at it. Can't you see it's back to front?"

"I sure don't see anything funny," said the bee-keeper.

" 'Initram'," Lydia said in her bold brassy voice. "Look at the advertisements and tell me what kind of a drink is Initram."

"Oh," he said. "Sorry."

"Ha."

His hands shook a little more as he carefully pried out the offending slide and turned it around.

"There," he said. "Is that better?"

"Oh God," said Lydia. "You've done it again." And sure enough he had. There was "Initram" being advertised again.

"I'd like another drink," said Lydia. "Initram on the rocks."

Tony switched the projector off and for a minute we were in a complete tension-filled darkness before his friend had enough presence of mind to reach up and switch on the lights.

"That's all, folks," he said, trying to sound like Woody Woodpecker, trying to be funny.

"Don't you want to show the rest of the slides?" Lydia said.

"No, I think that's enough."

"Well, tell us about bees, then" she said, turning around and facing the sofa, backing away a little bit so she could gaze up at the bee-keeper, her pretty head cocked on one side.

"What do you want to know?" he said, smiling. But uncomfortable, too, for he was not so dumb or naive that he didn't see what she was doing to her husband.

"Oh. Everything. Everything." She waved her hand. "Their mating habits for instance. Do they really only mate once? The queens, I mean."

"No, they can mate more than once, maybe two, three times. But usually only once. It's funny," he said, "when you stop to think of it. From a human point of view the drone that wins is the loser really."

"I don't follow you," I said. I really know nothing about bees. Whereas I had a funny feeling about Lydia. Would a kid who had a grandfather who kept bees—? or maybe she never did have such a grandfather. Maybe her grandfather just said that whenever he saw a swarm—the way my father used to say, "Red sky at night, sailor's delight" when he'd never been near the ocean.

"Fun, frolic and death," he said, "fun, frolic and death. Those drones are the laziest devils you'd like to see. Waited on hand and foot by their sisters—don't have to do nothing except eat and lie around and take the occasional look-see outside. Then one day the queen just zooms up into the blue with hundreds of those drones dashin' after her. A fantastic sight—fantastic."

"And the race is to the swift," said Lydia, taking a long sip of her drink as though it were some strange nectar, then parting her lips and looking up at the bee-keeper with her bold new look.

"The strongest and swiftest catches her," he said. "Sometimes she even zooms back towards 'em, because she wants to be caught, you know. That's all part of it."

"She wants to be caught," repeated Lydia. "She has to be caught."

She took another long sip of her drink. The bee-keeper's wife just sat back against the cushions and smiled.

"She has to be caught—it's her nature."

"So she is caught."

"And then?"

"And then he clasps her to him, face to face—there's a little explosion as all his male organs pop out and they fly together like that face to face while he fertilizes her."

"Then he dies?" I asked.

"Then he dies. You see, they fall to the ground together, outside the home hive of the queen, and when she tries to pull away, he's stuck so fast to her she pulls most of his abdomen away."

"Ab-do-men," said Lydia, lightly mocking him. But not in the way she said "Initram."

"My brother probably knows more about bees than any man in North America," said the man with the club foot. "He could write a book about them."

"It's my job," he said simply.

"Oh don't," cried Lydia. "Don't ever write a book about them."

She gave a mock shudder. "I wonder what it feels like," she said. "To fly out like that after the darkness of the hive into the blue sky and the green trees and to feel the sunshine on her back. To know that her destiny is about to be fulfilled." Then she turned towards the bee-keeper's wife. "And you. Is it your life too? Bees?"

She nodded her head, serene in her black dress and rhinestones. She had a strong Southern accent.

"It's my life too."

Then the bee-keeper did a beautiful thing. He just reached over and put his lean brown hand over hers.

"We try to study the bees," he said. "We try to do what they do."

"Fun, frolic and death?" said Lydia, flirting, slyly mocking.

"No," he said, but not angrily. He didn't swat at her any more than he might swat at a bee who flew a little too close to his ear.

"They are true communists—the bees. No one works for any profit to himself. Everything is done only for the good of the colony. If we could live like that—"

"Ah, yes, Utopia." Lydia sighed. "Perhaps if we all ate more honey?" She was mocking him again, circling back. She smiled at the three men in the room. All she needed was a yellow sweater.

"Who knows? That's where our word honeymoon comes from, you know—the old belief in the magical powers of honey. Germany I think it was, or Austria. The newly married couple would drink mead for a month after the wedding."

"What was it supposed to do for them?"

"Now *that* I'm not sure of. Make 'em happy and industrious, I guess."

"Is it true," said Lydia, "that the queen can sting over and over—that she doesn't die when she stings? I read that somewhere, I think. Tony, do you remember reading that somewhere or somebody telling us that the queen could sting over and over?"

"I don't remember."

"Well, it's true, isn't it?" She appealed to the bee-keeper.

"It's true. She has to defend herself. It's her nature."

"There, you see Tony? I was right. It's her nature."

"There is usually only one queen," said the bee-keeper. "She kills off all the others."

"Why not?" Lydia said. "It's natural."

Then we were all leaving—I can't remember who stood up first. We said good-bye to the bee-keeper and his wife. I wrote down the name of a supply house where I could get supers and bee suits. I wrote down the names of two books. He (the bee-keeper) went out to his van and came back with a little jar of honey for each of us. Alfalfa honey, clear and thick and golden.

"Jim Ritchie and Sons," it said, "Abbotsford, B. C." and "Unpasteurized" underneath. "Mary Beth designed the labels," he said proudly.

I slept downstairs in a little parlour with a fireplace. They had coal and started a fire for me. Made up the Hide-A-Bed and went off upstairs together. I lay in the darkness under Lydia's grandmother's Star of Bethlehem quilt and smelled the smell of the coal fire and was back fourteen years under a quilt in a big double-bed in Scotland. On my honeymoon. The maid had come in with a stone hot-water bottle but we were already warm from drinking a strange mixture in the public bar—something called Athol Bross—and now that I thought of it, I seemed to remember that it was made of porridge and honey. Or maybe I just had honey on the brain.

What had happened to us? What had happened to us all? I began to cry while Lydia made noisy love upstairs. I heard her—she wanted me to hear her. It was the last line in the last paragraph of the story she'd been writing all evening. I wondered if she'd come down the next morning with Tony's abdomen irrevocably stuck to her front.

We don't see each other very much any more. She lives in a distant city. But once a year we meet, at the Writers Union annual general meeting, and compare children and lovers and ideas for stories, usually in that order. We flirt, we get drunk, we congratulate ourselves that somehow miraculously we have survived another year, that we each have money and a room of one's own and are writing fiction. This year I told her (lying) that I was thinking of writing a story about her.

"I'm calling it 'Chicken Wings'," I said.

"Chicken Wings?"

"The night I came to see you, and you and Tony had just split up."

"And you wanted to tell me about your break-up."

"*Sangre de Toro*," I said. We began to laugh.

"Do you remember the bee-keeper and his wife?"

"Of course, they're in the story."

"Fun, frolic and death—Oh God."

We laughed until we cried.

"What name d'you want?" I said. "You can choose your own name."

"Lydia," she said. "I always wanted to be called Lydia."

"All right," I said. "You can be Lydia."

"But I don't like your title," she said. "I think you'll have to change it."

ALISTAIR MACLEOD

(b. 1936)

A listair MacLeod was born in North Battleford, Saskatchewan. However, it is Cape Breton, Nova Scotia, where he lived as a teenager on the family farm, that MacLeod has staked out as his fictional territory. He was educated at St. Francis Xavier University near the east coast of Nova Scotia, the University of New Brunswick, and Notre Dame (Ph.D. 1968). He has been a teacher all of his working life, first at the University of Indiana and then at the University of Windsor, where he is the fiction editor of The University of Windsor Review. *A slow and painstaking writer of short stories, MacLeod's two collections are* The Lost Salt Gift of Blood *(1976) and* As Birds Bring Forth the Sun *(1988). "Island," a story yet to appear in a collection, was first published in* Ontario Review. *It displays MacLeod's talents to fine effect: the particular and haunting evocation of the Maritime region, the mythic impulse of many of the more recent stories especially, the elegiac tone, and the ability to convey an impression of a whole life in a short story.*

Island

A ll day the rain fell upon the island and she waited. Sometimes it slanted against her window with a pinging sound which meant it was close to hail, and then it was visible as tiny pellets for a moment on the pane before the pellets vanished and rolled quietly down the glass, each drop leaving its own delicate trickle. At other times it fell straight down, hardly touching the window at all, but still there beyond the glass, like a delicate, beaded curtain at the entrance to another room.

She poked the fire within the stove, turning the half-burned lengths of wood so that they would burn more evenly. Some of the wood lengths were old fence posts or timbers which had been hauled from the shore before being cut into sizes which would fit the stove. Some of them contained ancient nails which were bent and twisted deep into the wood's core. When the fire was very hot, they glowed to a cherry red, reminiscent of a blacksmith's shop or, perhaps, their earliest casting. They would glow in the intense heat while the wood was consumed around them and, in the morning, they would be shaken down with the ashes, black and twisted but still there in the grayness of the ashpan. On days when the fire burned with less intensity because the wood was damp or the drafts poor, they remained a rusted brown while the damp wood sputtered and hissed reluctantly before releasing them from the coffins in which they were confined. Today was such a day.

She went to the window and looked out once more. Beneath the table the three black and white dogs followed her with their eyes but made no other movement. They had been outside several times during the day and the wetness of their coats gave off the odor of damp woolen garments which have been hung to dry. When they came in, they shook themselves vigorously beside the stove, causing further sputtering and hissing, as the water droplets fell against the heated steel.

Through the window and the beaded sheets of rain she could see the gray shape of *tir mòr*, the mainland, more than two miles away. Because of her failing sight and the nature of the weather she was not sure if she could really see it. But she had seen it in all weathers and over so many decades that the image of it was clearly in her mind, and whether she actually saw it or remembered it, now, seemed to make no difference.

The mainland was itself but another large island although most people did not think of it in that way. It was, as many said, larger than the province of Prince Edward Island and even some European countries and it had paved roads and cars and now even shopping centers and a fairly large population.

On rainy or foggy evenings such as this, it was always hard to see and to understand the mainland but when the sun shone it was clearly visible with its white houses and red or gray barns, and with the green lawns and fields surrounding the houses while the rolling mountains of dark green spruce rose behind them. At night the individual houses, and the communities they formed, seemed to be magnified because of the lights. In the daytime if you looked at a certain spot you might see only one house and, perhaps, a barn, but at night there might be several lights shining from the different windows of the house, and perhaps a light at the barn and other lights shining from hydro poles in the yard, or in the driveway or along the road. And there were the moving lights caused by the headlights of the travelling cars. It all seemed more glamorous at night, perhaps because of what you could not see, and conversely a bit more disappointing in the day.

She had been born on the island at a time so long ago that there was now nobody living who could remember it. The event no longer lived in anybody's mind nor was it recorded with accuracy anywhere on paper. She had been born a month prematurely at the beginning of the spring breakup when crossing from the island to the mainland was impossible.

At other times her mother had tried to reach the mainland before her children were born. Sometimes she would cross almost a month before the expected delivery because the weather and the water in all seasons, except summer, could never be depended upon. She had planned to do so this time as well but the ice that covered the channel during the winter months began to decay earlier than usual. It would not bear the weight of a horse and sleigh or even a person on foot and there were visible channels of open water running like eager rivers across what seemed like the gray-white landscape of the rotting ice. It was too late for foot travel and too early for a boat because there was not, as yet, enough open water. And then too she was born a month earlier than expected. All of this she was, of course, told much later. She was also told that when the winter began her parents did not realize that her mother was pregnant. Her father was sixty at the time and her mother close to fifty and they were already grandparents. They had not had any children for five years and had thought their child-bearing years were past and the usual signs were no longer there or at least not recognized until later in the season. So her birth, as her father said, was "unexpected" in more ways than one.

She was the first person ever born on the island as far as anybody knew.

Later she was brought across to the mainland to be christened. And still later when the clergyman was sending his baptismal records to the provincial capital he included hers along with those of the children who had been born on the mainland. And perhaps to simplify matters he recorded her birthplace as being the same as that of the other children and of her brothers and sisters or if he did not intend to simplify perhaps he had merely forgotten. He also had the birthdate wrong and it was thought that perhaps he had forgotten to ask the parents or had forgotten what they had told him and by the time he was ready to send in his records they had already gone back to the island and he could not contact them. So he seemed to have counted back a number of days before the christening and selected his own date. Her middle name was wrong too. Her parents had called her Agnes but he had somehow copied it down as Angus. Again perhaps he had forgotten or was preoccupied and he was a very old man at the time, as evidenced by his shaky, spidery handwriting. And, it was pointed out, his own middle name was Angus. She did not know any of this until years later when she sent for her official birth certificate in anticipation of her own marriage. Everyone was surprised that a single document could contain so many errors and by that time the old clergyman had died.

Although hers was thought to be the only birth to have occurred on the island there had been a number of deaths. One of them was that of her own grandfather who died one November from a "pain in the side" after pulling up his boat for the winter—thinking there would be no further need for a boat until the spring. He was only forty when it happened, the death occurring only two weeks after his birthday. His widow and children did not know what to do as there was no adequate radio communication and they were not strong enough to get the boat he had so recently hauled up, back into the water. They waited for two days hoping the sullen gray waves would subside, stretching his body out on the kitchen table and covering it with white sheets—afraid to put too much fire in the kitchen stove lest it might hasten the body's decay.

On the third day they launched a small skiff and tried to row across to the mainland. They did not know if they would be strong enough to make it so they gathered large numbers of dried cattails and reeds from one of the island's marshes and placed them in a metal washtub and doused them with the oil used for the lamp at the lighthouse. They placed the tub in the prow of the skiff and when they rowed out beyond the shape of the island they set the contents of the tub on fire hoping that it might act as a signal and a sign. On the mainland someone saw the rising funnel of gray-black smoke and the shooting flames at its base and then the skiff moving erratically—rowed by the desperate hands of the woman and her children. Most of the mainland boats had already been pulled up for the winter but one was launched and the men went out to what looked like a burning boat and tossed a line to it and towed it in to the wharf after first taking off the woman and her children and comforting them and listening to their story. Later the men went out to the island and brought the man's body over to the mainland so that although he died on the island, he was not buried there. And still later that evening someone went over to light the lamp in the lighthouse so that it might send out its flashing warning to possible travellers on the nighttime sea. Even in the face of her husband's death, the woman, as well as her family, harbored fears that they might lose the job if the Government realized the lightkeeper was dead. They had already purchased their supplies for the winter and there was no other place to go so late in the season, so they decided to say nothing until the spring and returned to the island after the funeral accompanied by the woman's brother.

The original family had gone to the island because of death or rather to aid in death's reduction. The lighthouse was established in the previous century because of the danger the island represented to ships travelling in darkness or in uncertain weather. It was thought that the light would warn sea travellers of the danger of the island or, conversely, that it might represent hope to those already at the sea's mercy and who yearned so much to reach its rocky shore. Before the establishment of the light there had been a number of wrecks which might or might not have been avoided had there been a light. What was known with certainty was that survivors had landed on the island only to die from exposure and starvation because no one knew that they were there. Their skeletons being found, accidently by fishermen in the spring—huddled under trees or outcrops of rock in the positions of their deaths. Some still had the remains of their arms around one another. Some still with tattered, flapping clothes covering their bones although the flesh between the clothing and the bones was no longer there.

When the family first went they were told that their job was to keep the light and to offer salvation to any of those who might come ashore. The Government erected buildings for them which were better than those of their relatives on the mainland and helped them with the purchase of livestock and original supplies. To some it seemed they had a good job— a Government job. In answer to the question of the isolation, they told themselves they would get used to it. They told themselves they were already used to it, coming as they did from a people in the far north of Scotland who had for generations been used to the sea and the sleet and the wind and the rocky outcrops at the edge of their part of Europe. Used to the long nights when no one spoke and to the isolation of islands. Used to seeing their men going to work for the Hudson's Bay Company and the North West Company and not expecting them back for years. Used to seeing their men going to the vast ocean-like tracts of prairie in places like Montana and Wyoming to work as sheepherders. Spending months that sometimes stretched into years, talking only to dogs or to themselves or to imaginary people who blended into ghosts. Startled by the response to their own voices when they appeared, strange and unexpectedly, at the camp or at the store or at the rural trading post. In demand as sheepherders, because it was believed, and because they had been told, that they did not mind the isolation. "Of course I spoke to ghosts," a man was supposed to have said once upon his returning. "Wouldn't you if there was no one else to speak to?"

In the early days on the island, there was no adequate radio communication and if they were in trouble and unable to get across they would light fires on the shore in the hope that such signs would be visible on the mainland. In the hope that they who had gone to the island as part of the business of salvation, might they themselves be saved. And when the Great War was declared, it was said, they did not know of it for weeks, coming ashore to be told the news by their relatives, coming ashore to a world which would be forever changed.

Gradually, with the passage of the years, the family's name as well as their identity became entwined with that of the island. So that although the island had an official name on the marine and nautical charts it became known generally as MacPhedran's Island while they themselves became known less as MacPhedrans than as people "of the island." Being identified as "John the Island," "James the Island," "Mary of the Island," "Theresa of the Island." As if in giving their name to the island they had received its own lonely designation in return.

All of this was already history by the time she was born and she had no choice in any of it. Not choosing, for herself, to be born on the island (although the records said she was not) and not choosing the rather surprised individuals who became her parents after they had already become the grandparents of others. For by the time she was born the intertwined history of her family and the island was already far advanced. And when she was later told the story of the man who died from the pain in his side, it seemed very far away to her although it was not for her father who had been one of the children in the skiff, rowing with small desperate freezing hands at the bidding of his mother. By the time of her early memories, the Government had already built a wharf at the island which was superior to any on the mainland. The wharf was built "to service" the lighthouse but it also attracted mainland fishermen who were drawn to its superior facilities. Especially during the lobster season months of May and June, men came to live in the shacks and shanties they erected along the shore. Leaving their shanties at four in the morning and returning in the early afternoon to sell their catches to the buyers who came in their big boats from far away. And returning to their mainland homes on Saturday and coming back again on Sunday, late in the afternoon or in the early evening, their weekly supplies of bread and provisions in burlap bags lying at the bottom of their boats. Sometimes lying in the bottoms of the boats there were also yearling calves with trussed feet and eyes bulging with fear who were brought to the island for summer pasturage and would be taken off half-wild in the cold, gray months of fall. Later in the summer the energetic, stifled rams would be brought in the same way, to spend monastic, frustrated months in all-male company before returning to the mainland and the fall fury of the breeding season.

He came to the island the summer she was seventeen. Came before the rams or the young cattle or the buyers' boats. Came at the end of April when there were still white cakes of ice floating in the ocean and when the family's dogs still ran down to the wharf to bark at the approaching boats and to snarl at the men who got out of them. In the time before such boats and men became familiar sights and sounds and odors. Yet even as the boat came into the wharf the dogs seemed to make less fuss than was usual and whatever he said quietened them and caused them to be still. She saw all this from the window of the kitchen. She was drying the dishes for her mother at the time and she wrapped the damp dish towel around her hand as if it were a bandage and then she as quickly unwrapped it again. As he bent to loop the boat's rope to the wharf, his cap fell off and she saw the redness of his hair. It seemed to flash and reflect in the April sun like the sudden and different energy of spring. She and most of her people were dark-haired and had dark eyes as well.

He had come, she learned, to fish for the season with one of the regular men from the mainland. He was the nephew of the man's wife and came from a place located over the mountain. From a distance of some twenty-five miles which was a long distance at the time. He had come early to make preparations for the season. To work on the shanty and repair the winter's damages, to repair the man's lobster traps and to make a few new ones. He told them all of this in the evening when he came up to the lighthouse to borrow oil for his lamp. He brought them bits and scraps of news from the mainland as well although they did not have that many people in common. He spoke in both Gaelic and English although his accent was different from theirs. He seemed about twenty years of age and his eyes were very blue.

They looked at one another often. They were the youngest people in the room.

In the early madness of the lobster season they did not speak to one another although they saw each other almost every day. The men were often up at three in the morning brewing their tea by the flickering lamps, casting their large shadows eerily upon the shanties' walls as they moved about in the semi-darkness. At night they sometimes fell asleep by eight. Sometimes still sitting on their chairs, their heads tilting suddenly forward or backward and their mouths dropping open. She worked with her mother, planting the garden and the potatoes. Sometimes in the evening she would walk down by the shanties but not very often. Not because her parents openly disapproved but because she felt uncomfortable walking so close to so many men. Sometimes they nodded and smiled as all of them knew her name and who she was and some of them were her distant relatives. But at other times she felt uneasy, hearing only bits of the comments and remarks exchanged among them as they stood in their doorways or sat on their homemade chairs or overturned lobster crates. The remarks seemed mainly for themselves, to demonstrate their wit and masculinity to each other. As if they were young schoolboys instead of being mostly beyond middle age. Sometimes they reminded her of the late summer rams, playful and friendly and generally grazing contentedly in *achadh nan caoraich*, the field of the sheep, although sometimes given to spontaneous rages against those who would trespass into their territory or sometimes unleashing their suppressed fury against one another. Rearing and smashing against one another until their skulls thundered and reverberated like the growling icebergs of spring and their pent-up semen ejaculated in spurting jets, leaving them stunned and weak in the knees.

She and her mother were the only women on the island.

One evening she walked to the back of the island, down to the far shore which did not face the mainland but only the open sea. There was a small cove there which was known as *bagh na long bhriseadh*, bay of the shipwreck, because there were timbers found there in the long ago time before the lighthouse was established. She sat on *creig a bhoird*, the table rock which was called so because of its shape, and looked out across the seeming infinity of the sea. And then he was standing beside her. He made no sound in coming and the dog which had accompanied her gave no signal of his approach.

"Oh," she said, on realizing him so unexpectedly close. She stood up quickly.

"Do you come here often?" he said.

"No," she said. "Well yes, sometimes."

The ocean stretched out flat and far before them.

"Were you born here?" he asked.

"Yes," she said. "I guess so."

"Do you stay here all the time? Even in the winter?"

"Yes," she said, "most of the time."

She was defensive, like most of her family, on the subject of the island. Knowing that they were often regarded as slightly eccentric because of how and where they lived. Always anticipating questions about the island's loneliness.

"Some people are lonely no matter where they are," he said, as if he were reading her mind.

"Oh," she said. She had never heard anyone say anything quite like that before.

"Would you like to live somewhere else?" he asked.

"I don't know," she said. "Maybe."

"I have to go now," he said. "I'll see you later. I'll come back."

And then he was gone. As suddenly as he had come. Seeming to vanish behind the table rock and the water's edge. She waited for a while, sitting down once more upon the rock to compose herself and then walking up the island's rise towards the lighthouse. Later when she looked down from the kitchen window towards the shanties, she could see him hammering lathes onto a broken lobster trap and readying the bait buckets for the morning. His cap was pushed back upon his head and the evening sun caught the golden highlights of his burnished hair. He looked up once and her hand tightened the cloth she was holding. Her mother asked her if she would like some tea.

It was into the next week before she again walked down by the shanties. He was sitting on a lobster crate splicing rope. As she went by she thought she heard him say *Àite na cruinneachadh*. She quickened her step as she felt her color rise, hoping or perhaps imagining that he had said "the meeting place." She went there immediately, down to the bay of shipwrecks and the table rock and waited. She faced out to the sea and sat in such a way that she could not see him *not* coming if that was the way it was supposed to be. The dog sat at her feet and neither of them moved when he came to stand beside them.

"I told you I'd come back," he said.

"Oh," she said. "Oh yes. You did."

In the weeks that followed they went more frequently to the meeting place. Standing and later sitting on the table rock and looking out across the vastness of the sea. Talking more and sometimes laughing and, in retrospect, she could not remember when he asked her to marry him but only that she had burst into tears when she said "Oh yes" and they joined their hands on the flatness of the table rock which was still warm from the retained heat of the descending sun. "Oh yes," she had said. "Oh yes. Oh yes."

He planned to work in a sawmill, he said, after the lobster season was done; and then in the fall or early winter, after the snows began to fall and the ground became frozen, he would go to work in the winter woods of Maine. He would return to fish with the same man the next spring and then in the summer they would marry. They would go then, he said, "to live somewhere else."

"Oh yes," she said. "Oh yes, we will."

It was in the late fall, on the night following a day of cold and slanting rain that she was awakened by the dog pulling at the blankets that lay so heavily upon her bed. She sat up, even as she shivered and pulled the blankets about her shoulders, and tried to adjust her eyes to the darkness of the room. The rain slanted against the window with a pinging sound which meant that it was close to hail and even in the darkness she could see the near-white pellets visible for a moment before they vanished on the pane. The eyes of the dog seemed to glow in the dark and she felt the cold wetness of its nose when she extended her hand beyond the boundary of the bed. She could smell the wetness of its coat and when she moved her hand across its head and down its neck the water filmed upon her palm. She got up then, throwing on what clothes she could find in the darkness of the room, and followed the clacking nails of the dog as it moved down the hallway and past the door behind which her parents snored, sometimes snoring regularly and at other times with fitful catches in their sound. She went down through the kitchen and through the tiny puddles caused by the rain slanting through the opened door. Outside it was wet and windy although nothing like a gale and she followed the dog down the darkened path. And then in the revolving cycle of the high lighthouse light the pale beam shone in a straight but moving path. In a single white instant she saw the dark shape of the boat bobbing at the wharf and his straight but dripping form by the corner of the shanties.

The creaky door of the summer shanty yielded easily to his familiar shoulder. Inside it was slightly musty although the wind persisted through some of the unsealed cracks. Their eyes adjusted to the gloom and the few sticks of basic furniture that still remained. The primitive mattresses had been stored away to protect them from mice and the dampness of the sea. They held one another in their urgency and lay upon the floor fumbling with the encumbrances of their clothes. She felt the wet burden of his garments almost heavy upon her although the length of his body seemed light within them.

"Oh," she said, digging her fingers into the dampness of his neck, "when we are married we can do this all the time."

At the moment of explosion their breaths bonded into a single gasp that bordered on a cry.

She thought of this later as she passed the closed door of her parents' room. Thought of how her breath and his had become one and contrasted it with the irregular individual snoring which came from beyond her parents' door. She could not imagine them ever being young.

The same wonder was there the next morning as she watched her father in his undershirt preparing the fire and later going to polish the thick glass of the lighthouse lamp. She watched her mother washing the dishes and then reaching for her knitting needles and the always present ball of yarn.

She went outside and walked down towards the shanties. The door was pulled tight and she had a hard time getting it to move. Inside it all seemed different, probably, she thought, because of the daylight. She looked at the gray boards of the floor thinking she might see the outline of their bodies or even a spot of dampness but there was nothing. She went outside and walked to the wharf, to the spot where the dark boat was moored, but again there was no sign. He had "borrowed" the boat of the man he had fished with and had to have it back before dawn.

The wind was rising as the temperature was dropping. The hail-like rain had given way to stinging snow and the ground was beginning to freeze. She touched her body to see if it had been a dream.

As the winter began she was alive with the prospect of marriage. She sent for her birth certificate without ever revealing why and helped her mother with the knitting. As the winter deepened she looked at the calendar more often.

When the ice began to rot and break in the spring she looked out the window more frequently. It seemed like a later spring than usual although her father said there was nothing unusual about it. One day the channel would be clear of ice but the next day it would again be solid. The wind shifted and blew from inconsistent directions. On the mainland they could see, or imagined they could see, men moving about and readying their gear for the opening of the season. Because of the ice they were still afraid to launch their boats into the water. They all looked very small and far away.

When the first boats finally came the dogs ran down to the wharf barking and snarling and her father went down also, calling to the dogs and welcoming the men and telling them not to be afraid. She looked out the window but did not see him in the boats or on the wharf nor moving about the familiar shanties. But neither did she see the mainland man he fished with nor his boat.

When her father came in he was filled with news and carried some fresh supplies and a bundle of newspapers and a bag of mail.

In the midst of all the newness it was a long time before he mentioned the mainland fisherman's name and added, almost as an afterthought, "That young man who fished with him last year was killed in the woods this winter. Went to Maine and was killed on a skidway. He's looking for another man right now."

When her father spoke he was already looking at a marine catalogue and had put on his glasses. He raised his eyes above the rims of his spectacles as he lowered the catalogue and looked towards them. "You remember him," he said without emotion, "the young fellow with the red hair."

"Oh poor fellow," said her mother. "God have mercy on his soul."

"Oh," was all she could say. Her hands tightened so whitely on the metal knitting needles that the point of one pierced and penetrated the ball of her thumb.

"Your hand is bleeding," said her mother. "What happened? You'll have to be more careful or you'll get blood on your knitting and everything will be ruined. What happened?" she asked again. "You'll have to be more careful."

"Nothing," she said, rising quickly and going to the door. "Nothing at all. Yes I'll have to be more careful."

She went outside and looked down towards the shanties where the newly arrived men were busy preparing for the new spring season. The banter of their voices seemed to float on the current of the wind. Sometimes she could hear their actual words but at other times they were lost and unknown. She could not believe the magnitude and suddenness of change. Could not believe the content of the news nor the method of its arrival. Could not believe that news of such outstanding impact could arrive in such a casual manner and mean so little to all of those around her.

She looked down at her bloodied hand. "Why didn't he write?" she asked herself and considered going back in to recheck the contents of the mailbag. But then she thought that both of them were beyond letters and that in the instant of his death it was already too late for that. She did not even know if he could read or write. She had never thought to ask. It had not seemed important at the time. The blood was beginning to darken and dry upon her palm and between her fingers. Suddenly last winter, although it was barely over, seemed like a long, long time ago. She pressed her hand against her stomach and turned her face away from the mainland and the sea.

When it became obvious that she was expecting a child there was great wonder as to how it came to be. She herself was rather surprised that no one had ever seen them together. It was true that she had always walked "over" or "across" the island while he had walked "around": seeming to emerge suddenly and unexpectedly out of the sea by the table rock of their meeting place. Still the island was small and, especially during the fishing season, there was little opportunity for privacy. Perhaps, she thought, they had been more successful, in some ways, than they planned. It was as if he had been invisible to everyone but herself. She was struck by this and tried to relive over and over again their last damp meeting in the dark. Only the single instant of his dark silhouette in the lighthouse beam was recallable to vision. All the rest of it had been touching in the dark. She remembered the lightness of his body in his dark, wet clothes but it was a memory of feeling rather than of sight. She had never seen him with all his clothes off. Had never slept with him in a bed. She had no photograph to emphasize reality. It was as if in vanishing from her future he had also vanished from her past. It was almost as if he had been a ghost, and as she advanced in her pregnancy she found the idea strangely attractive.

"No," she kept saying to the pressure of their questions. "I don't know. I can't say. No, I can't tell you what he looked like."

She wavered only twice. The first time was a week before her delivery at a time when the approximate date of the conception was more than obvious. They were all on the mainland and the late August heat shimmered in layers above the clear deep water. The shape of the island loomed gray and blue and green across the channel and she who had wished to leave it now wished she might return. They were at her aunt's house and she would remain there until her baby would be born. She and her aunt had never liked each other and it bothered her now to be dependent upon her. Before her parents left to return to the island they came into her room accompanied by the aunt who turned to her father and said, "Well go ahead. Tell her what people are saying."

She was shocked to see the pained embarrassment on his face as he twisted his cloth cap and looked out the window in the direction of the island.

"It is just the way we live," he said. "Some say there was no other man."

She remembered the erratic snoring coming from her parents' room and how she could not imagine that they ever had been young.

"Oh," she said. "I'm sorry."

"Is that all you have to say for yourself?" said her aunt.

She wavered a moment. "Yes," she said. "That's all. That's all I have to say."

After the birth of her daughter, with the jet black hair, she received a visit from the clergyman. He was an old man although not as old as she imagined the one who had confused her own birth records, it seemed to her, so very long ago.

At that time it was in the power of clergymen to refuse to christen children unless they knew the identities of both parents. In cases such as hers the identities could be kept as confidential.

"Well," he said. "Can you tell me who the father is?"

"No," she said. "I can't say."

He looked at her as if he had heard it all before. And as if it were an aspect of his job he did not greatly like. He looked at her daughter and back at her. "We wouldn't want innocent people to burn in hell because of the willfulness of others," he said.

She was startled and frightened and looked towards the window.

"Tell me," he said quietly. "Is it your father?"

She thought for a flash of her own unexpected birth and of how her father was surprised again although the situation was so very much different.

"No," she said firmly. "It isn't him."

He seemed vastly relieved. "Good," he said. "I didn't think he would ever do anything like that. I will stop the rumors."

He moved towards the door as if one answer were all answers but then he hesitated with his hand upon the knob. "Tell me then," he said, "one more thing. Do I know him? Is he from around here?"

"No," she said, gaining confidence from seeing his hand upon the knob. "He isn't from around here at all."

That fall she stayed on the mainland until quite late into the season. It seemed as if her daughter were constantly sick and each time the journey was planned a new variation of illness appeared to stifle the departure. Out on the island her parents seemed to grow old all at once or maybe it was just that she saw them in a different light. Of course they had always seemed old to her and she had often thought of having grandparents for parents. But now they seemed for the first time to be almost afraid of the island and the coming of winter. Never since the first year of their marriage had they been there without a child. When her father fell from the ladder leading up to the lighthouse lamp it was almost as if the fall and the resulting broken arm had been expected.

Ever since her grandfather's death from a "pain in the side," the Government had more or less left them alone. It was as if the officials had been embarrassed by the widow's reluctance to tell them of her husband's death and by her fear that she might lose, in addition to her husband, the only income the family possessed. It was as if the officials had understood that "some MacPhedran" would always be on the island that bore the name and that no further questions ever would be asked. The checks always arrived and the light always shone.

But when her father fell it brought a deeper seriousness. He could neither climb to the light nor navigate the boat across the channel, nor manage, quite, to look after the house and buildings and the animals. It seemed best that they should all try to stay on the mainland for the winter.

Her brother came home from Halifax, reluctantly, and manned the light deep into fall. He was a single man who worked on construction crews and who drank quite heavily at times and was given to moods of deep depression. He was uneasy about the island although he understood it and was regarded as "an excellent man in a boat." At the beginning of the winter he said to his father who stood in the departing boat, "I don't want to stay here. I don't want to stay here at all."

"Oh," said his father, "you'll get used to it," which was what they had always said to one another.

But it seemed he did not get used to it. Deep in the blizzards of February one of the island dogs crossed on the ice to the mainland and came to a familiar door. It was impossible to see or move for three days because of the severe temperatures and the force of the wind-driven snow. Impossible for a man to stand upright in the wind or, as they said, for one "to see the palm of his hand in front of his face." When the storm abated four men started across the vast white landscape of the ice. They could feel parts of their exposed faces freezing and the exhaled moisture of their breath froze upon their eyebrows and they could see their eyelashes drooping heavily with ice. As they neared the island's wharf they could see that it was almost buried under gigantic pans of ice. Some of the pans had been pushed so far up on the shore that they almost tilted against the doors of the summer shanties. There was no smoke from the chimney of the house. The dogs came down snarling and circling at first, but the one who had crossed to the mainland had returned and had a calming effect upon the others. The door of the house was open and the stove was cold. The water in the crockery teapot had frozen causing the teapot itself to split into two delicate halves. There was nobody in any of the rooms and no answer to their calls. Outside, the barn doors were open and swinging in the wind. The animals were all dead, still tied and frozen in their stalls. The frozen flesh of some of them had been gnawed on by the dogs.

It seemed his coat and cap and winter mitts were missing but that was all. A loaded rifle and a shotgun were hanging in the porch. The men started a fire in the stove and made themselves something to eat from the store of winter provisions. Later they went outside again. Some walked across the island and some walked around it. They found no tracks other than their own. They looked at the dogs for a signal or a sign. They even spoke to them and asked them questions but they received nothing in return. He had vanished like his tracks beneath the winter snow.

The men remained for the night and the next day crossed back to the mainland. They told what they had found and not found. The sun shone and although it was a weak February sun it was stronger that it had been a week earlier. It melted the ice upon the window panes and someone pointed out that the days were getting longer and that the winter was more than half way over.

Under the circumstances they decided to go back but to leave the baby behind.

"There seems almost no reason to go back now," said her father, looking through the melting ice on the windows. His broken arm had healed although he knew it would never be the same.

She was often to think of why she went back although at the time there seemed little conscious thought surrounding the decision. While her parents were willing to leave the island to the care of their son they were not willing to abandon it to others. They had found life on the mainland not as attractive as it sometimes seemed when viewed from across the water. They also seemed bothered by complicated shafts of guilt concerning their lost son and their headstrong daughter and while these shafts might persist on the island there would be no people to emphasize and expose them. She, herself, as the child of their advanced years seemed suddenly willing to consider herself old also and to identify with the past now that her future seemed to point in that direction.

She went back with almost a bitter gladness. Glad to leave her carping aunt and her mainland family behind although worried about leaving her sickly daughter in their care. Still, she knew they were right to say that the winter island was no place for a sick child and she felt also that if she did not go her parents could not manage.

"Who will climb up to the light?" asked her father simply. They viewed her youth as their immediate salvation and thought of her as their child rather than as someone else's mother.

It seemed a long time since the red-haired man had asked her to marry him and to share his life in the magical region of "somewhere else." In her persistent refusal to identify him she had pushed him so far back into the recesses of her mind that he seemed even more ghostly than before. She thought sometimes of his body in the dark and of his silhouette by the sea. She was struck by the mystery of his age—if he had an age she thought it had suddenly "stopped" and he had become part of a kind of timelessness—unlike the visible deterioration she witnessed in her father.

In the winter cold of February they returned with a certain sense of relief, each harboring individual reasons. Because of her youth she did most of the work, dressing in her father's heavy, shapeless clothes and following easily the rituals and routines that had become part of her since childhood. More and more her parents remained close to the stove, talking in Gaelic and sometimes playing cards or merely looking at the fire or out the frosted windows.

When March came in with its howling blizzards it seemed that they had been betrayed by the fickle promise of the February sun and although her father's will was strong his aging body seemed also to contribute to a pattern of betrayal. He was close to eighty and it seemed that each day there was another function which his body refused to perform. It was as if it had suddenly grown tired and was in the process of forgetting.

One day when there was a lull in the storms some of their relatives crossed the ice with a horse and sleigh. They were shocked at the condition and appearance of her father, seeing him changed "suddenly" after an absence of weeks while those who were with him had seen him change but gradually. They insisted that he return with them while the weather was good and the ice still strong. Reluctantly he agreed on the condition that his wife go with him.

After years of isolated permanence he was aware of all the questionable movement.

"Sometimes life is like that," he said to his daughter as he sat bundled in the sleigh at the moment before departure. "It goes on and on at a certain level and then there comes a year when everything changes."

Suddenly a gust of wind passed between them, whipping their faces with fine, sharp granules of snow. And suddenly she knew in that instant that she would never ever see him again. She wanted to tell him, to thank him or perhaps confess now that their time was vanishing between them. The secret of her own loneliness came down upon her and she reached towards his bundled body and his face which was muffled in scarves except for his eyes which were filled with water converting to ice.

"It was," she said, "the red-haired man."

"Oh yes," he said but she did not know with what degree of comprehension he said it. And then the sleigh moved off with its runners squeaking on the winter snow.

Although she was prepared for the death of her father she had not anticipated the loss of her mother who died ten days behind her husband. There was no physical explanation for her death and it seemed not unlike that of certain animals who pine away without their mates or who are unwilling or unable to adjust to new surroundings. As wild birds die in captivity or those who have been caged die from the shock of unexpected freedom or the loss of familiar boundaries.

Because of the spring breakup she was unable to attend either of their funerals and on the respective days she looked across the high gray waves and the grotesque icebergs that rolled between. From the edge of the island she saw the long funeral processions following the horse-drawn coffins along the muddy roads to the graveyard by the mainland church. She turned her face into the wind and climbed up towards the light.

That spring and summer she continued to tend the light although she had little to do with the mainland fishermen and never walked down by the shanties. She began to sign the requisition slips for government supplies with the name "A. MacPhedran" because her initial and that of her father were the same. After a while the checks came in the name of "A. MacPhedran" and she had no trouble cashing any of them. No one came to question the keeper of the light, and the sex of A. MacPhedran seemed ambiguously unimportant. After all, she told herself, wryly, her official birth certificate stated that her given name was Angus.

When the fall came she decided to remain on the island for the winter. Some of her relatives approved because they wanted "some MacPhedran" to remain on the island and they cited her youth and the fact that she was "used to it" as part of their reasoning. They were interested in "maintaining tradition" as long as they were not the ones to maintain that specific part of it. Others disapproved and towards them she was, secretly, most defiant. Her aunt and her aunt's family had grown attached to her daughter, had "gotten used to her" as they said and regarded the child as their own. When she visited them she experienced a certain fearful hostility on their part, as if they feared that she might snatch the child and flee while they were busy in another room.

Most of her relatives, however, either willingly or unwillingly, agreed to help her with the island, by assisting her with supplies, by doing some of the heavier autumn work or even by visiting occasionally. She settled into the life with a sort of willful determination tempered by the fact that she was still waiting for something to happen and to bring about the change.

Two years later on a hot summer afternoon, she was in the lighthouse tower when she saw the boat approaching. She had been restless all day and had walked the length and width of the island twice. She had gone to its edge as if testing the boundaries, somewhat as a restless animal might explore the limitations of its cage. She had walked out into the cold salt water feeling it move gradually up and through and under the legs of her father's coveralls which had become, for her, a sort of uniform. She walked farther out feeling the water rise as she felt the rocks turning beneath her feet. She looked downward and saw her coveralled limbs distorted in the green water, shot through by the summer sun. They seemed not to be a part of her but to have become disembodied and convoluted and to be almost floating away from her at a horizontal level. When she closed her eyes she could feel them intensely but when she looked at them they did not appear the way they felt. The dogs lay on the shore, just above the water line, and watched her. They were panting in the summer heat and drops of water fell from the extended redness of their tongues.

She returned to the shore, still dripping, and walked among the shanties. The lobster fishermen had departed at the end of the season leaving very little of themselves behind. She walked among the deserted buildings looking at the few discarded objects, sometimes touching and turning them with her toes: a worn woolen sock, a length of spliced and twisted rope, a rusted knife with a broken blade, tobacco packages with bleached and faded lettering, a rubber boot with a hole in it. It was as if she were walking through the masculine remnants of an abandoned and vanished civilization. She went back to the house to put on dry coveralls and to hang the wet ones on the outside clothesline. As she left to climb to the lighthouse she looked over her shoulder and was startled by the sight of the vertical coveralls. Their dangling legs rasped together with the gentlest of frictions and the moisture had changed their color up to the waist. Droplets dripped from them onto the summer grass which was visibly distorted by their own moving shadow.

There were four men in the approaching boat and she realized that they were mackerel fishing and did not have the island in mind as a specific destination. The boat zigzagged back and forth across the stillness of the blue-green water stopping frequently while the men tossed their weighted lines overboard. They jerked their lines up and down rhythmically hoping to attract the fish by the movement of the lures. Sometimes they dipped their hands into pails or tubs of *gruth*, dried cottage cheese, and flung the white handfuls onto the surface of the water, waiting and hoping for the unseen fish to strike. She turned her head and looked towards the back of the island. From her high vantage point she could see, or thought she could see, pods or schools of mackerel breaking the surface, beyond the meeting place and the table rock, and beyond the bay of the shipwreck. They seemed like moving, floating islands, changing the clear, flat surface into agitated areas that resembled boiling water.

She hurried down from the lighthouse and shouted and gestured to the men in the boat. They were still far offshore and, perhaps, saw her before they heard her but were still unable to comprehend her message. They directed the boat towards the island. As they approached she realized that the movement of her arm, which was intended as a pointing gesture to the back of the island, was also a beckoning gesture, as they might understand it.

When they were within earshot she shouted to them, "The mackerel. At the back of the island. Go around."

They stopped the boat and leaned forward trying to catch the meaning of her words. One of the younger men, probably the one with the best hearing, understood her first and relayed the message to the others.

"Behind the island?" shouted the oldest man, cupping his hands to his mouth.

"Yes," she shouted back. "By the bay of the shipwreck."

She almost added, "By the meeting place" before realizing that the phrase would be meaningless to them.

"Thank you," shouted the oldest man. He took off his cap and tipped it to her and she could see the whiteness of his hair. "Thank you," he repeated. "We'll go around."

They changed the course of the boat and began to go around the island.

She rushed up to the house and changed out of her coveralls and put on a summer dress which she found in the back of a closet. She walked across the island accompanied by the dogs and went down to the meeting place where she sat on the table rock and waited. The rock was hot from the heat of the day's sun and burned her thighs and the backs of her legs. She could see the floating islands of frenzied mackerel beyond the mouth of the bay. They were deep into their spawning season and she hoped they would still be there when the men in the boat arrived.

"They seem to be taking an awfully long time," she said to no one in particular. And then she saw the prow of the boat rounding the island's end.

She stood up and pointed to the boiling, bubbling mackerel but they had already seen them and even as they waved back they were in the process of readying all their available lines. The boat glided silently towards the fish and by the time the first one struck it was almost completely stilled. The mackerel seemed to surround the boat, changing the water to black by their own density. Their snapping mouths fastened on anything thrown their way and when the men jerked up their lines there were sometimes two or three fish on a single hook. Sometimes they broke the surface as if they would jump into the boat and sometimes their bodies were so densely packed that they became "snagged" as the hooks went into their bellies or their eyes or their backs or their tails. The scent of their own blood spreading within the water spurred them to an even greater frenzy and they fell upon the mutilated fellows, snapping the still living flesh from the moving bones. The men moved in their own frenzy as if to keep pace. Hooks snagged in their thumbs and the singing, sizzling lines burned through the calluses on their hands. The fish filled the bottom of the boat and began to rise in a blue-green, flopping, snapping mass to the level of the men's knees. And then, suddenly, they were gone. The hooks brought back nothing but clear drops of water or shreds of mutilated seaweed. There was no indication of them anywhere either on the surface of the sea or beneath. It was as if they had never been, apart from the heaving weight which caused the boat to ride so low within the water. The men wiped the sweat from their foreheads with swollen hands, sometimes leaving other streaks behind. Some of the streaks contained a mixture of fishblood and their own.

The men looked towards the shore and saw her rise from the table rock and come towards them until she reached the water's edge. They guided the boat across the glass-like sea until its prow grounded heavily on the gravelly shore. They tossed the painter rope to her and she caught it with willing hands.

All afternoon they lay on the table rock. At first they seemed driven by the frenzy of all that had happened and not happened to them. By all the heat and the loneliness and the waiting and all the varied events that had conspired to create their day. The clothes of the men were sprinkled with blackening clots of blood and the golden spawn of the female fish and the milky white semen of the male. She had never seen fully aroused men before, having known only one man at one time, and having experienced in that damp darkness more of feeling than of sight.

She was to remember, for the rest of her life, the oldest man with the white hair. How he took off his cap and then pulled his heavy navy-blue jersey over his shoulders and folded it neatly and placed it on the rock beside her. She was to remember the whiteness of his skin and arms compared with the bronzed redness of his face and neck and that of his bleeding and swollen hands. As if, without clothes, his upper body was still clothed in a costume made of two different materials. The whiteness of his skin and the whiteness of his hair were the same color but totally different as well. After he had folded his jersey he placed his cap neatly upon it. It was as if he were doing it out of long habit and was preparing to lie down with his wife. She almost expected him to brush his teeth.

After the first frenzy they were quieter, lying stretched beneath the sun. Sometimes one of the younger men got up and skipped flat stones across the surface of the sea. The dogs lay above the waterline panting and watching everything. She was later to think how often she had watched them in the fury of their own mating. And how she had seen their surplus young placed in burlap bags, weighted down with rocks, and tossed over the boat's side into the sea.

The sun began to decline and the tide began to fall, the water receding from the heavy boat which was in danger of becoming beached. The men got up and adjusted their clothes. Some walked some distance away to urinate. They came back and all four of them put their shoulders to the prow and prepared to push the boat back into the water.

"One, two, three, heave!" they said, moving in concentrated unison on the last syllable. Their bodies were stretched out almost horizontally as they pushed, the toes of their rubber boots scrabbling in the loose beach gravel. The boat began to move, grudgingly at first, and then more rapidly as the water took its weight. The men scrambled over the prow and over the sides. Most of them were wet up to their waists. They seized their oars to push the boat further out so there would be room to turn it around and face it towards home.

She watched them leave, standing on the shore. As the boat moved out, she noticed her undergarment crumpled and discarded by the edge of the table rock. The boat moved farther out and farther away and the men waved to her. She felt her arm rising in a similar gesture, almost without her willing it. The man with the white hair tipped his cap. She knew in one of those intuitive flashes that they would never be back. As the boat rounded the island's end, she scrunched up her undergarment and threw it into the sea. She began to walk up towards the lighthouse. She touched her body. It was sticky with blood and fishspawn and human seed. "It will have to happen this time," she thought, "because there was so much of it and it went on so long." Comparing the afternoon to her one previous brief encounter in the dark.

When she reached the lighthouse she heard the cries of the scavenging gulls. She looked in the direction of the sound and saw the boat cutting a "v" in the placid water on its way to the mainland. The men were bent double grasping their fishforks and throwing the dead mackerel back into the sea. The gulls swooped and screamed in a whitened noisy cloud.

Two years later she was in a mainland store ordering supplies to take back to the island. Usually she made arrangements with one of her relatives to take the supplies from the store to the water's edge and then ferry them across to the island but on this day she could not find the particular young man. One of the items was a bag of flour. As she stood paying her bill and looking out the door in some agitation, she saw, out of the corner of her eye, the white-haired man in the navy-blue jersey.

"This is too heavy for you," he said. "Let me help," and he bent down and picked up the hundred pound flour sack and threw it easily onto his shoulder. When it landed some of the flour puffed out, sprinkling his blue jersey and his cap and his hair with its fine white powder. She remembered the whiteness of his body beneath the blue jersey and the frenzied afternoon beneath the summer sun. As they were going out the door they met her young relative.

"Here, I'll take that," he said, relieving the man of the bag of flour.

"Thank you," she said to the man.

"My pleasure," he said and tipped his cap towards her. The flour dust fell from his cap onto the floor between them.

"He is a real nice fellow," said her young relative as they moved towards the shore. "But of course you don't know him the way we do."

"No," she said. "Of course I don't." She looked across the channel to the stillness of the island. Her expected child had never arrived.

The years of the next decade passed by in a blur of monotonous sameness. She realized that she was becoming more careless of her appearance and that such carelessness was regarded as further evidence of eccentricity. She came ashore less frequently preferring to try to understand the world through radio. She found her teen-age daughter to be foreign and aloof and embarrassed by her presence. Her aunt's family harbored doubts about their decision to rear the girl and, one day, when she was visiting, suggested that she might want to live on the island with her "real mother." The girl laughed and walked into another room.

Gradually during the next years things changed even more, but so quietly that, in retrospect, she could not link the specific events to the specific years. Many of them had to do with changes on the mainland. The Government built a splendid new wharf and the spring fishermen no longer came to inhabit the shanties which began to fall into disrepair, their doors banging in the wind and the shingles flying from their roofs. Sometimes she looked at the initials carved by the absent men on the shanties' walls but his, as she knew, would never be among them.

Community pastures were established, with regular attendants, and the bound young cattle and the lusty rams no longer came to the summer pasturage. The sweeping headlights of cars became a regular feature of her night vision, mirroring in a myriad manner the beam from her solitary lighthouse. One night after a quarrel with her aunt's family, her daughter left in such a car, and vanished into the mystery of Toronto. She did not know of it until weeks later when she came ashore for the purchase of supplies.

The wharf at the island began to deteriorate and the visitors came less often. She found herself often dealing with members of a newer generation. Many of them were sulky and contributed to the maintaining of island tradition with the utmost reluctance and only because of the badgering of their parents.

Yet the light still shone and the various missives to and from "A. MacPhedran" continued to travel through the mails. The nature of such missives also changed, however gradually. When the first generation of her family went to the island it had been close to the age of sail when captains were at the mercies of the winds. In her own time she had seen the coming of the larger ships and the increasing sophistication of their technology. There had not been a wreck upon the island in all her time of habitation and no freezing, ice-caked travellers had ever knocked upon her midnight door. The "emergency chest" and its store of supplies remained unopened from one inspection to the next.

One summer she realized with a shock that her child-bearing years were over and that that part of her life was past.

Mainland boat operators began to offer "trips around the island," taking tourists on circumnavigational voyages. Very often because of time limitations they did not land but merely circled or anchored briefly offshore. When the boats approached the dogs barked, bringing her to her door or sometimes to the water's edge. At first she was not aware of the image she presented to the tourists with their binoculars or their cameras. Nor was she aware of how she was described by the operators of the boats. Standing at the edge of the sea in her dishevelled men's clothing and surrounded by her snarling dogs, she later realized, she had passed into folklore. She had, without realizing it, become "the mad woman of the island."

It was on a hot summer's day, some years later when, in answer to the barking of the dogs, she looked out the window and saw the big boat approaching. The men wore tan-colored uniforms and the Canadian flag flew from the mast. They tied the boat to the remnants of the wharf and began to climb towards the house as she called off the dogs. The decision had been made, they told her quietly, while sitting in the kitchen, to close the lighthouse officially. The light would still shine but it would be maintained by "modern technology." It would operate automatically and be serviced by supply boats which would come at certain times of the year or, in emergency, they added, by helicopter. It would, however, be maintained in its present state for approximately a year and a half. After that, they said, she would have "to live somewhere else." They got up to leave and thanked her for her decades of fine service.

After they had gone she walked the length and width of the island. She repeated all the place names, many of them in Gaelic, and marvelled that the places would remain but the names would vanish. "Who would know?" she wondered that this spot had once been called *achadh nan caoraich*, or that another was called *creig a bhoird*. And who she thought, with a catch in her heart, would ever know of *Àite na cruinneachadh* and of what had transpired there. She looked across the landscape repeating the phrases of the place-names as if they were those of children about to be abandoned without knowledge of their names. She felt like whispering their names to them so they would not forget.

She realized with a type of shock that in spite of generations of being people "of the island" they had never really owned it in any legal sense. There was nothing physical of it that was, in strict reality, formally theirs.

That autumn and winter her rituals seemed without meaning. There was no need of so many supplies because the future was shorter and she approached each winter task with the knowledge that it would be her last. She approached spring with a longing born of confused emotions. She who had wanted to leave and wanted to return and wanted to stay felt the approaching ache of those who leave the familiar behind. She felt, perhaps, as those who leave bad places or bad situations or bad marriages behind them. As those who must look over their shoulders one last time and who say quietly to themselves, "Oh I have given a lot of my life to this, such as it was, and such was I. And no matter where I go I will never be the same."

That April as the ice broke, for her the final time, she was drying the dishes and looking through the window. Because of her failing eyesight she did not see the boat until it was almost at the remains of the wharf and the dogs did not make their usual sound. She saw the man bending to loop the boat's rope to the wharf and as he did so his cap fell off and she saw the redness of his hair. It seemed to flash and reflect in the April sun like the sudden and different energy of spring. She wrapped the damp dish towel around her hand as if it were a bandage and then she as quickly unwrapped it again.

He started up the path towards the house and the dogs ran happily beside him. She stood in the doorway uncertainly. As he approached she realized that he was talking to the dogs and his accent was slightly unfamiliar. He seemed about twenty years of age and his eyes were very blue. He had an earring in his ear.

"Hello," he said, extending his hand. "I don't know if you recognize me."

It had been so long and so much had happened that she did not know what to say. Her hand tightened on the cloth she was still holding. She stepped aside to let him enter the house and watched as he sat on a chair.

"Do you stay here all the time?" he asked, looking around the kitchen, "even in the winter?"

"Yes," she said. "Most of the time."

"Were you born here?"

"Yes," she said. "I guess so."

"It must be lonely," he said, "but I guess some people are lonely no matter where they are."

She looked at him as if he were a ghost.

"Would you like to live somewhere else?" he asked.

"I don't know," she said. "Maybe."

He raised his hand and touched the earring as if to make certain it was still there. His glance travelled about the kitchen, seeming to rest lightly on each of the familiar objects. She realized that the kitchen had hardly changed since that other April visit so long ago. She could not think of what to say.

"Would you like some tea?" she asked after a moment of awkward silence.

"No thank you," he said. "I'm pressed for time right now but perhaps we'll have it later."

She nodded although she was not certain of his meaning. The dogs lay under the table, now and then thumping the floor with their tails. Through the window she could see the white gulls hanging over the ocean which was still dotted with cakes of floating ice.

He looked at her carefully, as if remembering, and he smiled. Neither of them seemed to know just what to say.

"Well," he said getting up suddenly. "I have to go now. I'll see you later. I'll come back."

"Wait," she said rising as quickly, "please don't go," and she almost added the word "again."

"I'll be back," he said, "in the fall. And then I will take you with me. We will go and live somewhere else."

"Yes," she said and then added almost as an afterthought, "Where have you been?"

"In Toronto," he said. "I was born there. They told me on the mainland that you are my grandmother."

She looked at him as if he were a genetic wonder which indeed he seemed to be.

"Oh," she said.

"I have to go now," he repeated, "but I'll see you later. I'll come back."

"Oh yes," she said, "Oh yes we will."

And then he was gone. She sat transfixed not daring to move. Part of her felt that she should rush and call him back and another fearful part told her she should not know what she might see. Finally she went to the window. Halfway across to the mainland there was a single man in a boat but she could make no clear identification. She did not say anything to anyone about the visit. She could think of no way she could tactfully introduce it. After years of secrecy it seemed a dangerous time to bring up the subject of the red-haired man. Perhaps, again, no one else had seen him? She did not wish to add further evidence to her designation as "the mad woman of the island." She scanned the faces of her relatives carefully but could find nothing. Perhaps he had visited them, she thought, and they had told him not to come. Perhaps they considered themselves in the business of not disturbing the disturbed.

Now as the October rain fell she added yet another stick to the fire. She was no longer bothered by the declining stock of wood because she would not need it for the winter. The rain fell turning more to the consistency of hail and she knew this by its sound as well as by her sight. She looked away from the door as she had so many years ago, the first time at the table rock. Deliberately not looking in the direction of his possible coming so that she could not see him *not* coming if that was the way it was supposed to be. She waited, listening to the regular pattern of the rain, and wondered if she were on the verge of sleep. Suddenly the door blew open and the hail-like rain skittered across the floor. The wet dogs moved from beneath the table and she heard them rather than saw. Perhaps she could mop the wet floor she thought but then she remembered that they planned to tear the house down anyway and its cleanliness seemed like a minor virtue. The water rippled across the floor in rolling little wind-driven waves. The dog came in, its nails clacking across the floor even as little spurts of water rose from beneath its padded paws. It came and lay its head upon her lap. She got up not daring to believe. Outside it was wet and windy and she followed the dog down the darkened path. And then in the revolving cycle of the high lighthouse light she saw in a single white instant the dark shape of the boat bobbing at the wharf and his straight but dripping form by the corner of the shanties.

They moved towards each other.

"Oh," she said, digging her fingers into the dampness of his neck.

"I told you I'd come back," he said.

"Oh," she said. "Oh yes. You did."

She ran her fingers over his face in the darkness and when the light revolved again she saw the blueness of his eyes and his red hair darkened by the dripping water. He was not wearing any earring.

"How old are you?" she asked, embarrassed by the girlish triviality of the question which had bothered her all these years.

"Twenty-one," he said. "I thought I told you."

He took her hands and walked backwards while facing her, down to the darkness of the bobbing boat and the rolling sea.

"Come," he said. "Come with me. It is time we went to live somewhere else."

"Oh yes," she said. "Oh yes we will."

She dug her nails into the palms of his hands as he guided her over the spume-drenched rocks.

"This boat," he said, "has to be back before dawn."

The wind was rising as the temperature was dropping. The hail-like rain had given way to stinging snow and the ground they left behind was beginning to freeze.

A dog barked once. And when the light revolved, its solitary beam found no MacPhedrans on the island or the sea.

JACK HODGINS

(b. 1938)

J ack Hodgins was born in British Columbia's Comox Valley. He grew
up on Vancouver Island, and the north part of the island, with its
*array of extended and eccentric families, has provided the setting for
much of his fiction. Even when his island characters travel within Canada
or to foreign countries such as Ireland, they do so encased in the insular
security and oddity of their place of origin—like some species of West
Coast turtle, they carry their homes with them. Hodgins studied creative
writing with Earle Birney at the University of British Columbia, where
he was active in the student writing community as editor of a number
of school anthologies, receiving his B.Ed. in 1961. He has held a number
of writer-in-residence appointments, including an extended stay at the
University of Ottawa, and is now a professor of creative writing at the
University of Victoria. Anecdotes, legends and fables, and tall tales form
the staple of Hodgins's fiction, works that attest again and again to the
re-creative power of the human spirit and imagination. His novels
include* The Invention of the World *(1977),* The Resurrection of
Joseph Bourne *(1980), which won the Governor General's Award,* The
Honorary Patron *(1987), and* Innocent Cities *(1990); his short-story
collections are* Spit Delaney's Island *(1976) and* The Barclay Family
Theatre *(1981), from which "The Concert Stages of Europe" is taken.
Critic David Jeffrey has described Hodgins's idiosyncratic fictional universe as follows:*

> *The island world of Jack Hodgins is a fallen world, but it is not
> a Calvinist prison or a Jansenist labyrinth. Neither is it a
> Platonist or a millenarian utopia. Instead, it appears as a macro-
> cosm of the questing heart, surrounded by a curious body,
> wondering about its elusive soul. Hodgins' prospect is thus like
> the imagination of some of his characters, usually hovering
> about the "dividing line," trying to learn how to look both ways
> and see reality as a continuum. His realism is neither locked
> into the determinism of mundane order nor fixed upon a distant
> star. It is, consistent with the traditions of pastoral comedy and
> Christian romance, and the new realism of our time, striving
> for a kind of incarnational imagination in which we are able to
> see our reality in both its possible and actual aspects at once.*

The Concert Stages of Europe

N ow I know Cornelia Horncastle would say I'm blaming the wrong person. I know that. I know too that she would say thirty years is a long time to hold a grudge, and that if I needed someone to blame for the fact that I made a fool of myself in front of the whole district and ruined my life in the process, then I ought to look around for the person who gave me my high-flown ideas in the first place. But she would be wrong; because there is no doubt I'd have led a different sort of life if it weren't for her, if it weren't for that piano keyboard her parents presented her with on her eleventh birthday. And everything—everything would have been different if that piano keyboard hadn't been the kind made out of stiff paper that you unfolded and laid out across the kitchen table in order to do your practising.

I don't suppose there would have been all that much harm in her having the silly thing, if only my mother hadn't got wind of it. What a fantastic idea, she said. You could learn to play without even making a sound! You could practise your scales without having to hear that awful racket when you hit a wrong note! A genius must have thought of it, she said. Certainly someone who'd read his Keats: *Heard melodies are sweet, but those unheard are sweeter.* "And don't laugh," she said, "because Cornelia Horncastle is learning to play the piano and her mother doesn't even have to miss an episode of *Ma Perkins* while she does it."

That girl, people had told her, would be giving concerts in Europe some day, command performances before royalty, and her parents hadn't even had to fork out the price of a piano. It was obvious proof, if you needed it, that a person didn't have to be rich to get somewhere in this world.

In fact, Cornelia's parents hadn't needed to put out even the small amount that paper keyboard would have cost. A piano teacher named Mrs. Humphries had moved onto the old Dendoff place and, discovering that almost no one in the district owned a piano, gave the keyboard to the Horncastles along with a year's free lessons. It was her idea, apparently, that when everyone heard how quickly Cornelia was learning they'd be lining up to send her their children for lessons. She wanted to make the point that having no piano needn't stop anyone from becoming a pianist. No doubt she had a vision of paper keyboards in every house in Waterville, of children everywhere thumping their scales out on the kitchen table without offending anyone's ears, of a whole generation turning silently into Paderewskis without ever having played a note.

They would, I suppose, have to play a real piano when they went to her house for lessons once a week, but I was never able to find out for myself, because all that talk of Cornelia's marvellous career on the concert stages of Europe did not prompt my parents to buy one of those fake keyboards or sign me up for lessons with Mrs. Humphries. My mother was born a Barclay, which meant she had a few ideas of her own, and Cornelia's glorious future prompted her to go one better. We would buy a *real* piano, she announced. And I would be sent to a teacher we could trust, not to that newcomer. If those concert stages of Europe were ever going to hear the talent of someone from the stump ranches of Waterville, it wouldn't be Cornelia Horncastle, it would be Barclay Desmond. Me.

My father nearly choked on his coffee. "But Clay's a boy!"

"So what?" my mother said. *All* those famous players used to be boys. What did he think Chopin was? Or Tchaikovsky?

My father was so embarrassed that his throat began to turn a dark pink. Some things were too unnatural even to think about.

But eventually she won him over. "Think how terrible you'd feel," she said, "if he ended up in the bush, like you. If Mozart's father had worked for the Comox Logging Company and thought piano-playing was for sissies, where would the world be today?"

My father had no answer to that. He'd known since before his marriage that though my mother would put up with being married to a logger, expecting every day to be made a widow, she wouldn't tolerate for one minute the notion that a child of hers would follow him up into those hills. The children of Lenora Barclay would enter the professions.

She was right, he had to agree; working in the woods was the last thing in the world he wanted for his sons. He'd rather they take up ditch-digging or begging than have to work for that miserable logging company, or take their orders from a son-of-a-bitch like Tiny Beechman, or get their skulls cracked open like Stanley Kirck. It was a rotten way to make a living, and if he'd only had a decent education he could have made something of himself.

Of course, I knew he was saying all this just for my mother's benefit. He didn't really believe it for a minute. My father loved his work. I could tell by the way he was always talking about Ab Jennings and Shorty Cresswell, the men he worked with. I could tell by the excitement that mounted in him every year as the time grew near for the annual festival of loggers' sports where he usually won the bucking contest. It was obvious, I thought, that the man really wanted nothing more in this world than that one of his sons should follow in his footsteps. And much as I disliked the idea, I was sure that I was the one he'd set his hopes on. Kenny was good in school. Laurel was a girl. I was the obvious choice. I even decided that what he'd pegged me for was high-rigger. I was going to be one of those men who risked their necks climbing hundreds of feet up the bare lonely spar tree to hang the rigging from the top. Of course I would fall and kill myself the first time I tried it, I knew that, but there was no way I could convey my hesitation to my father since he would never openly admit that this was really his goal for me.

And playing the piano on the concert stages of Europe was every bit as unattractive. "Why not Kenny?" I said, when the piano had arrived, by barge, from Vancouver.

"He's too busy already with his school work," my mother said. Kenny was hoping for a scholarship, which meant he got out of just about everything unpleasant.

"What about Laurel?"

"With her short fat fingers?"

In the meantime, she said, though she was no piano-player herself (a great sigh here for what might have been), she had no trouble at all identifying which of those ivory keys was the all-important Middle C and would show it to me, to memorize, so that I wouldn't look like a total know-nothing when I showed up tomorrow for my first lesson. She'd had one piano lesson herself as a girl, she told me, and had learned all about Mister Middle C, but she'd never had a second lesson because her time was needed by her father, outside, helping with the chores. Seven daughters altogether, no sons, and she was the one who was the most often expected to fill the role of a boy. The rest of them had found the time to learn chords and chromatic scales and all those magic things she'd heard them practising while she was scrubbing out the dairy and cutting the runners off strawberry plants. They'd all become regular show-offs in one way or another, learning other instruments as well, putting on their own concerts and playing in dance bands and earning a reputation all over the district as entertaining livewires—The Barclay Sisters. And no one ever guessed that all the while she was dreaming about herself at that keyboard, tinkling away, playing beautiful music before huge audiences in elegant theatres.

"Then it isn't me that should be taking lessons," I said. "It's you."

"Don't be silly." But she walked to the new piano and pressed down one key, a black one, and looked as if I'd tempted her there for a minute. "It's too late now," she said. And then she sealed my fate: "But I just know that you're going to be a great pianist."

When my mother "just knew" something, that was as good as guaranteeing it already completed. It was her way of controlling the future and, incidentally, the rest of us. By "just knowing" things, she went through life commanding the future to fit into certain patterns she desired while we scurried around making sure that it worked out that way so she'd never have to be disappointed. She'd had one great disappointment as a girl—we were never quite sure what it was, since it was only alluded to in whispers with far-off looks—and it was important that it never happened again. I was trapped.

People were always asking what you were going to be when you grew up. As if your wishes counted. In the first six years of my life the country had convinced me it wanted me to grow up and get killed fighting Germans and Japanese. I'd seen the coils of barbed wire along the beach and knew they were there just to slow down the enemy while I went looking for my gun. The teachers at school obviously wanted me to grow up and become a teacher just like them, because as far as I could see nothing they ever taught me could be of any use or interest to a single adult in the world except someone getting paid to teach it to someone else. My mother was counting on my becoming a pianist with a swallow-tail coat and standing ovations. And my father, despite all his noises to the contrary, badly wanted me to climb into the crummy every morning with him and ride out those gravelly roads into mountains and risk my life destroying forests.

I did not want to be a logger. I did not want to be a teacher. I did not want to be a soldier. And I certainly did not want to be a pianist. If anyone had ever asked me what I did want to be when I grew up, in a way that meant they expected the truth, I'd have said quite simply that what I wanted was to be a Finn.

Our new neighbours, the Korhonens, were Finns. And being a Finn, I'd been told, meant something very specific. A Finn would give you the shirt off his back, a Finn was as honest as the day is long, a Finn could drink anybody under the table and beat up half a dozen Germans and Irishmen without trying, a Finn was not afraid of work, a Finn kept a house so clean you could eat off the floors. I knew all these things before ever meeting our neighbours, but as soon as I had met them I was able to add a couple more generalizations of my own to the catalogue: Finnish girls were blonde and beautiful and flirtatious, and Finnish boys were strong, brave, and incredibly intelligent. These conclusions were reached immediately after meeting Lilja Korhonen, whose turned-up nose and blue eyes fascinated me from the beginning, and Larry Korhonen, who was already a teenager and told me for starters that he was actually Superman, having learned to fly after long hours of practice off their barn roof. Mr. and Mrs. Korhonen, of course, fitted exactly all the things my parents had told me about Finns in general. And so I decided my ambition in life was to be just like them.

I walked over to their house every Saturday afternoon and pretended to read their coloured funnies. I got in on the weekly steam-bath with Larry and his father in the sauna down by the barn. Mr. Korhonen, a patient man whose eyes sparkled at my eager attempts, taught me to count to ten—*yksi, kaksi, kolme, nelja, viisi, kuusi, seitseman, kahdeksan, yhdek-san, kymmenen*. I helped Mrs. Korhonen scrub her linoleum floors and put down newspapers so no one could walk on them, then I gorged myself on cinnamon cookies and *kala loota* and coffee sucked through a sugar cube. If there was something to be caught from just being around them,

I wanted to catch it. And since being a Finn seemed to be a full-time occupation, I didn't have much patience with my parents, who behaved as if there were other things you had to prepare yourself for.

The first piano teacher they sent me to was Aunt Jessie, who lived in a narrow, cramped house up a gravel road that led to the mountains. She'd learned to play as a girl in Toronto, but she had no pretensions about being a real teacher, she was only doing this as a favour to my parents so they wouldn't have to send me to that Mrs. Humphries, an outsider. But one of the problems was that Aunt Jessie—who was no aunt of mine at all, simply one of those family friends who somehow get saddled with an honorary family title—was exceptionally beautiful. She was so attractive, in fact, that even at the age of ten I had difficulty keeping my eyes or my mind on the lessons. She exuded a dreamy sort of delicate femininity; her soft, intimate voice made the hair on the back of my neck stand on end. Besides that, her own playing was so much more pleasant to listen to than my own stumbling clangs and clunks that she would often begin to show me how to do something and become so carried away with the sound of her own music that she just kept right on playing through the rest of my half-hour. It was a simple matter to persuade her to dismiss me early every week so that I'd have a little time to play in the creek that ran past the back of her house, poling a home-made raft up and down the length of her property while her daughters paid me nickels and candies for a ride. At the end of a year my parents suspected I wasn't progressing as fast as I should. They found out why on the day I fell in the creek and nearly drowned, had to be revived by a distraught Aunt Jessie, and was driven home soaked and shivering in the back seat of her old Hudson.

Mr. Korhonen and my father were huddled over the taken-apart cream separator on the verandah when Aunt Jessie brought me up to the door. My father, when he saw me, had that peculiar look on his face that was halfway between amusement and concern, but Mr. Korhonen laughed openly. "That boy lookit like a drowny rat."

I felt like a drowned rat too, but I joined his laughter. I was sure this would be the end of my piano career, and could hardly wait to see my mother roll her eyes to the ceiling, throw out her arms, and say, "I give up."

She did nothing of the sort. She tightened her lips and told Aunt Jessie how disappointed she was. "No wonder the boy still stumbles around on that keyboard like a blindfolded rabbit; he's not going to learn the piano while he's out risking his life on the *river!*"

When I came downstairs in dry clothes Aunt Jessie had gone, no doubt wishing she'd left me to drown in the creek, and my parents and the Korhonens were all in the kitchen drinking coffee. The Korhonens sat at either side of the table, smoking hand-rolled cigarettes and squinting at me through the smoke. Mrs. Korhonen could blow beautiful white streams down her nostrils. They'd left their gumboots on the piece of newspaper just inside the door, of course, and wore the same kind of grey work-socks on their feet that my father always wore on his. My father was leaning against the wall with both arms folded across his chest inside his wide elastic braces, as he sometimes did, swishing his mug gently as if he were trying to bring something up from the bottom. My mother, however, was unable to alight anywhere. She slammed wood down into the firebox of the stove, she rattled dishes in the sink water, she slammed cupboard doors, she went around the room with the coffee pot, refilling mugs, and all the while she sang the song of her betrayal, cursing her own stupidity for sending me to a friend instead of to a professional teacher, and suddenly in a flash of inspiration dumping all the blame on my father: "If you hadn't made me feel it was somehow pointless I wouldn't have felt guilty about spending more money!"

From behind the drifting shreds of smoke Mr. Korhonen grinned at me. Sucked laughter between his teeth. "Yust teenk, boy, looks like-it you're saved!"

Mrs. Korhonen stabbed out her cigarette in an ashtray, picked a piece of tobacco off her tongue, and composed her face into the most serious and ladylike expression she could muster. "Yeh! Better he learn to drive the tractor." And swung me a conspirator's grin.

"Not on your life," my mother said. Driving a machine may have been a good enough ambition for some people, she believed, but the Barclays had been in this country for four generations and she knew there were a few things higher. "What we'll do is send him to a real teacher. Mrs. Greensborough."

Mrs. Greensborough was well known for putting on a public recital in town once a year, climaxing the program with her own rendition of Grieg's Piano Concerto—so beautiful that all went home, it was said, with tears in their eyes. The problem with Mrs. Greensborough had nothing to do with her teaching. She was, as far as I could see, an excellent piano teacher. And besides, there was something rather exciting about playing on her piano, which was surrounded and nearly buried by a thousand tropical plants and dozens of cages full of squawking birds. Every week's lesson was rather like putting on a concert in the midst of the Amazon jungle. There was even a monkey that swung through the branches and sat on the top of the piano with the metronome between its paws. And Mrs. Greensborough was at the same time warm and demanding, complimentary and hard to please—though given a little, like Aunt Jessie, to taking off on long passages of her own playing, as if she'd forgotten I was there.

It took a good hour's hard bicycling on uphill gravel roads before I could present myself for the lesson—past a dairy farm, a pig farm, a turkey farm, a dump, and a good long stretch of bush—then more wash-board road through heavy timber where driveways disappeared into the trees and one dog after another lay in wait for its weekly battle with my right foot. Two spaniels, one Irish setter, and a bulldog. But it wasn't a spaniel or a setter or even a bulldog that met me on the driveway of the Greensboroughs' chicken farm, it was a huge German shepherd that came barking down the slope the second I had got the gate shut, and stuck its nose into my crotch. And kept it there, growling menacingly, the whole time it took me to back him up to the door of the house. There was no doubt in my mind that I would come home from piano lesson one Satur-day minus a few parts. Once I had got to the house, I tried to get inside quickly and shut the door in his face, leaving him out there in the din of cackling hens; but he always got his nose between the door and the jamb, growled horribly and pushed himself inside so that he could lie on the floor at my feet and watch me hungrily the whole time I sat at the kitchen table waiting for Ginny Stamp to finish off her lesson and get out of there. By the time my turn came around my nerves were too frayed for me to get much benefit out of the lesson.

Still, somehow I learned. That Mrs. Greensborough was a marvellous teacher, my mother said. The woman really knew her stuff. And I was such a fast-learning student that it took less than two years for my mother to begin thinking it was time the world heard from me.

"Richy Ryder," she said, "is coming to town."

"What?"

"Richy Ryder, CJMT. *The Talent Show.*"

I'd heard the program. Every Saturday night Richy Ryder was in a different town somewhere in the province, hosting his one-hour talent contest from the stage of a local theatre and giving away free trips to Hawaii.

Something rolled over in my stomach.

"And here's the application form right here," she said, whipping two sheets of paper out of her purse to slap down on the table.

"No thank you," I said. If she thought I was going in it, she was crazy.

"Don't be silly. What harm is there in trying?" My mother always answered objections with great cheerfulness, as if they were hardly worth considering.

"I'll make a fool of myself."

"You play beautifully," she said. "It's amazing how far you've come in only two years. And besides, even if you don't win, the experience would be good for you."

"You have to go door-to-door ahead of time, begging for pledges, for money."

"Not begging," she said. She plunged her hands into the sink, peeling carrots so fast I couldn't see the blade of the vegetable peeler. "Just giving people a chance to vote for you. A dollar a vote." The carrot dropped, skinned naked, another one was picked up. She looked out the window now toward the barn and, still smiling, delivered the argument that never failed. "I just know you'd win if you went in, I can feel it in my bones."

"Not this time!" I shouted, nearly turning myself inside out with the terror. "Not this time. I just can't do it."

Yet somehow I found myself riding my bicycle up and down all the roads around Waterville, knocking at people's doors, explaining the contest, and asking for their money and their votes. I don't know why I did it. Perhaps I was doing it for the same reason I was tripping over everything, knocking things off tables, slamming my shoulder into door-jambs; I just couldn't help it, everything had gone out of control. I'd wakened one morning that year and found myself six feet two inches tall and as narrow as a fence stake. My feet were so far away they seemed to have nothing to do with me. My hands flopped around on the ends of those lanky arms like fish, something alive. My legs had grown so fast the bones in my knees parted and I had to wear elastic bandages to keep from falling apart. When I turned a corner on my bicycle, one knee would bump the handlebar, throwing me into the ditch. I was the same person as before, apparently, saddled with this new body I didn't know what to do with. Everything had gone out of control. I seemed to have nothing to do with the direction of my own life. It was perfectly logical that I should end up playing the piano on the radio, selling myself to the countryside for a chance to fly off to Hawaii and lie on the sand under the whispering palms.

There were actually two prizes offered. The all-expense, ten-day trip to Hawaii would go to the person who brought in the most votes for himself, a dollar a vote. But lest someone accuse the radio station of getting its values confused, there was also a prize for the person judged by a panel of experts to have the most talent. This prize, which was donated by Nelson's Hardware, was a leatherette footstool.

"It's not the prize that's important," people told me. "It's the chance to be heard by all those people."

I preferred not to think of all those people. It seemed to me that if I were cut out to be a concert pianist it would be my teacher and not my parents encouraging me in this thing. Mrs. Greensborough, once she'd forked over her two dollars for two votes, said nothing at all. No doubt she was hoping I'd keep her name out of it.

But it had taken no imagination on my part to figure out that if I were to win the only prize worth trying for, the important thing was not to spend long hours at the keyboard, practising, but to get out on the road hammering at doors, on the telephone calling relatives, down at the General Store approaching strangers who stopped for gas. Daily piano practice shrank to one or two quick run-throughs of "The Robin's Return", school homework shrank to nothing at all, and home chores just got ignored. My brother and sister filled in for me, once in a while, so the chickens wouldn't starve to death and the woodbox would never be entirely empty, but they did it gracelessly. It was amazing, they said, how much time a great pianist had to spend out on the road, meeting his public. Becoming famous, they said, was more work than it was worth.

And becoming famous, I discovered, was what people assumed I was after. "You'll go places," they told me. "You'll put this place on the old map." I was a perfect combination of my father's down-to-earth get-up-and-go and my mother's finer sensitivity, they said. How wonderful to see a young person with such high ambition!

"I always knew this old place wouldn't be good enough to hold you," my grandmother said as she fished out a five-dollar bill from her purse. But my mother's sisters, who appeared from all parts of the old farmhouse in order to contribute a single collective vote, had some reservations to express. Eleanor, the youngest, said she doubted I'd be able to carry it off, I'd probably freeze when I was faced with a microphone, I'd forget what a piano was for. Christina announced she was betting I'd faint, or have to run out to the bathroom right in the middle of my piece. And Mabel, red-headed Mabel who'd played accordion once in an amateur show, said she remembered a boy who made such a fool of himself in one of these things that he went home and blew off his head. "Don't be so morbid," my grandmother said. "The boy probably had no talent. Clay here is destined for higher things."

From behind her my grandfather winked. He seldom had a chance to contribute more than that to a conversation. He waited until we were alone to stuff a five-dollar bill in my pocket and squeeze my arm.

I preferred my grandmother's opinion of me to the aunts'. I began to feed people lies so they'd think that about me—that I was destined for dizzying heights. I wanted to be a great pianist, I said, and if I won that trip to Hawaii I'd trade it in for the money so that I could go off and study at the Toronto Conservatory. I'd heard of the Toronto Conservatory only because it was printed in big black letters on the front cover of all those yellow books of finger exercises I was expected to practise.

I don't know why people gave me their money. Pity, perhaps. Maybe it was impossible to say no to a six-foot-two-inch thirteen-year-old who trips over his own bike in front of your house, falls up your bottom step, blushes red with embarrassment when you open the door, and tells you he wants your money for a talent contest so he can become a Great Artist. At any rate, by the day of the contest I'd collected enough money to put me in the third spot. I would have to rely on pledges from the studio audience and phone-in pledges from the radio audience to rocket me up to first place. The person in second place when I walked into that theatre to take my seat down front with the rest of the contestants was Cornelia Horncastle.

I don't know how she managed it so secretly. I don't know where she found the people to give her money, living in the same community as I did, unless all those people who gave me their dollar bills when I knocked on their doors had just given her two the day before. Maybe she'd gone into town, canvassing street after street, something my parents wouldn't let me do on the grounds that town people already had enough strangers banging on their doors every day. Once I'd got outside the vague boundaries of Waterville I was to approach only friends or relatives or people who worked in the woods with my dad, or stores that had— as my mother put it—done a good business out of us over the years. Cornelia Horncastle, in order to get herself secretly into that second place, must have gone wild in town. Either that or discovered a rich relative.

She sat at the other end of the front row of contestants, frowning over the sheets of music in her hands. A short nod and a quick smile were all she gave me. Like the other contestants, I was kept busy licking my dry lips, rubbing my sweaty palms together, wondering if I should whip out to the bathroom one last time, and rubbernecking to get a look at people as they filled up the theatre behind us. Mrs. Greensborough, wearing dark glasses and a big floppy hat, was jammed into the far corner at the rear, studying her program. Mr. and Mrs. Korhonen and Lilja came partway down the aisle and found seats near the middle. Mr. Korhonen winked at me. Larry, who was not quite the hero he had once been, despite the fact that he'd recently beat up one of the teachers and set fire to the bus shelter, came in with my brother Kenny—both of them looking uncomfortable—and slid into a back seat. My parents came all the way down front, so they could look back up the slope and pick out the seats they wanted. My mother smiled as she always did in public, as if she expected the most delightful surprise at any moment. They took seats near the front. Laurel was with them, reading a book.

My mother's sisters—with husbands, boyfriends, a few of my cousins—filled up the entire middle section of the back row. Eleanor, who was just a few years older than myself, crossed her eyes and stuck out her tongue when she saw that I'd turned to look. Mabel pulled in her chin and held up her hands, which she caused to tremble and shake. Time to be nervous, she was suggesting, in case I forgot. Bella, Christina, Gladdy, Frieda—all sat puffed up like members of a royal family, or the owners of this theatre, looking down over the crowd as if they believed every one of these people had come here expressly to watch their nephew and for no other reason. "Look, it's the Barclay girls," I heard someone behind me say. And someone else: "Oh, *them*." The owner of the first voice giggled. "It's a wonder they aren't all entered in this thing, you know how they like to perform." A snort. "They *are* performing, just watch them." I could tell by the muffled "Shhh" and the rustling of clothing that one of them was nudging the other and pointing at me, at the back of my neck. "One of them's son." When I turned again, Eleanor stood up in the aisle by her seat, did a few steps of a tap dance, and quickly sat down. In case I was tempted to take myself seriously.

When my mother caught my eye, she mouthed a silent message: stop gawking at the audience, I was letting people see how unusual all this was to me, instead of taking it in my stride like a born performer. She indicated with her head that I should notice the stage.

As if I hadn't already absorbed every detail. It was exactly as she must have hoped. A great black concert grand with the lid lifted sat out near the front of the stage, against a painted backdrop of palm trees along a sandy beach, and—in great scrawled letters—the words "Richy Ryder's CJMT Talent Festival". A long blackboard leaned against one end of the proscenium arch, with all the contestants' names on it and the rank order of each. Someone named Brenda Roper was in first place. On the opposite side of the stage, a microphone seemed to have grown up out of a heap of pineapples. I felt sick.

Eventually Richy Ryder came out of whatever backstage room he'd been hiding in and passed down the row of contestants, identifying us and telling us to get up onto the stage when our turns came without breaking our necks on those steps. "You won't be nervous, when you get up there," he said. "I'll make you feel at ease." He was looking off somewhere else as he said it, and I could see his jaw muscles straining to hold back a yawn. And he wasn't fooling me with his "you won't be nervous" either, because I knew without a doubt that the minute I got up on that stage I would throw up all over the piano.

Under the spotlight, Richy Ryder acted like a different person. He did not look the least bit like yawning while he told the audience the best way of holding their hands to get the most out of applause, cautioned them against whistling or yelling obscenities, painted a glorious picture of the life ahead for the talented winner of this contest, complimented the audience on the number of happy, shiny faces he could see out there in the seats, and told them how lucky they were to have this opportunity of showing off the fine young talent of the valley to all the rest of the province. I slid down in my seat, sure that I would rather die than go through with this thing.

The first contestant was a fourteen-year-old girl dressed up like a gypsy, singing something in a foreign language. According to the blackboard she was way down in ninth place, so I didn't pay much attention until her voice cracked open in the middle of a high note and she clutched at her throat with both hands, a look of incredulous surprise on her face. She stopped right there, face a brilliant red, and after giving the audience a quick curtsey hurried off the stage. A great beginning, I thought. If people were going to fall to pieces like that through the whole show no one would even notice my upchucking on the Heintzman. I had a vision of myself dry-heaving the whole way through "The Robin's Return".

Number two stepped up to the microphone and answered all of Richy Ryder's questions as if they were some kind of test he had to pass in order to be allowed to perform. Yes sir, his name was Roger Casey, he said with a face drawn long and narrow with seriousness, and in case that wasn't enough he added that his father was born in Digby, Nova Scotia, and his mother was born Esther Romaine in a little house just a couple blocks up the street from the theatre, close to the Native Sons' Hall, and had gone to school with the mayor though she'd dropped out of Grade Eight to get a job at the Safeway cutting meat. And yes sir, he was going to play the saxophone because he'd taken lessons for four years from Mr. D.P. Rowbottom on Seventh Street though he'd actually started out on the trumpet until he decided he didn't like it all that much. He came right out to the edge of the stage, toes sticking over, leaned back like a rooster about to crow, and blasted out "Softly As in a Morning Sunrise" so loud and hard that I thought his bulging eyes would pop right out of his head and his straining lungs would blast holes through that red-and-white shirt. Everyone moved forward, tense and straining, waiting for something terrible to happen—for him to fall off the stage or explode or go sailing off into the air from the force of his own fantastic intensity—but he stopped suddenly and everyone fell back exhausted and sweaty to clap for him.

The third contestant was less reassuring. A kid with talent. A smart-aleck ten-year-old with red hair, who told the audience he was going into show business when he grew up, started out playing "Swanee River" on his banjo, switched in the middle of a bar to a mouth organ, tap-danced across the stage to play a few bars on the piano, and finished off on a trombone he'd had stashed away behind the palm tree. He bowed, grinned, flung himself around the stage as if he'd spent his whole life on it, and looked as if he'd do his whole act again quite happily if the audience wanted him to. By the time the tremendous applause had died down my jaw was aching from the way I'd been grinding my teeth the whole time he was up there. The audience would not have gone quite so wild over him, I thought, if he hadn't been wearing a hearing aid and a leg brace.

Then it was my turn. A strange calm fell over me when my name was called, the kind of calm that I imagine comes over a person about to be executed when his mind finally buckles under the horror it has been faced with, something too terrible to believe in. I wondered for a moment if I had died. But no, my body at least hadn't died, for it transported me unbidden across the front of the audience, up the staircase (with only a slight stumble on the second step, hardly noticeable), and across the great wide stage of the theatre to stand facing Richy Ryder's enormous expanse of white smiling teeth, beside the microphone.

"And you are Barclay Philip Desmond," he said.

"Yes," I said.

And again "yes", because I realized that not only had my voice come out as thin and high as the squeal of a dry buzz-saw, but the microphone was at least a foot too low. I had to bend my knees to speak into it.

"You don't live in town, do you?" he said. He had no intention of adjusting that microphone. "You come from a place called . . . Waterville. A logging and farming settlement?"

"Yes," I said.

And again "yes" because while he was speaking my legs had straightened up, I'd returned to my full height and had to duck again for the microphone.

He was speaking to me but his eyes, I could see, were busy keeping all that audience gathered together, while his voice and his mind were obviously concentrated on the thousands of invisible people who were crouched inside that microphone, listening, the thousands of people who—I imagined now—were pulled up close to their sets all over the province, wondering if I was actually a pair of twins or if my high voice had some peculiar way of echoing itself, a few tones lower.

"Does living in the country like that mean you have to milk the cows every morning before you go to school?"

"Yes."

And again "yes".

I could see Mrs. Greensborough cowering in the back corner. I promise not to mention you, I thought. And the Korhonens, grinning. I had clearly passed over into another world they couldn't believe in.

"If you've got a lot of farm chores to do, when do you find the time to practise the piano?"

He had me this time. A "yes" wouldn't be good enough. "Right after school," I said, and ducked to repeat. "Right after school. As soon as I get home. For an hour."

"And I just bet," he said, throwing the audience an enormous wink, "that like every other red-blooded country kid you hate every minute of it. You'd rather be outside playing baseball."

The audience laughed. I could see my mother straining forward; she still had the all-purpose waiting-for-the-surprise smile on her lips but her eyes were frowning at the master of ceremonies. She did not approve of the comment. And behind that face she was no doubt thinking to herself "I just know he's going to win" over and over so hard that she was getting pains in the back of her neck. Beside her, my father had a tight grin on his face. He was chuckling to himself, and sliding a look around the room to see how the others were taking this.

Up at the back, most of my aunts—and their husbands, their boy-friends—had tilted their chins down to their chests, offering me only the tops of their heads. Eleanor, however, had both hands behind her neck. She was laughing harder than anyone else.

Apparently I was not expected to respond to the last comment, for he had another question as soon as the laughter had died. "How old are you, son?"

"Thirteen."

For once I remembered to duck the first time.

"Thirteen. Does your wife like the idea of your going on the radio like this?"

Again the audience laughed. My face burned. I felt tears in my eyes. I had no control over my face. I tried to laugh like everyone else but realized I probably looked like an idiot. Instead, I frowned and looked embarrassed and kicked at one shoe with the toe of the other.

"Just a joke," he said, "just a joke." The jerk knew he'd gone too far. "And now seriously, one last question before I turn you loose on those ivories over there."

My heart had started to thump so noisily I could hardly hear him. My hands, I realized, had gone numb. There was no feeling at all in my fingers. How was I ever going to play the piano?

"What are you going to be when you grow up?"

The thumping stopped. A strange, cold silence settled over the world. I was going to die right in front of all those people. What I was going to be was a corpse, dead of humiliation, killed in a trap I hadn't seen being set. What must have been only a few seconds crawled by while something crashed around in my head, trying to get out. I sensed the audience, hoping for some help from them. My mother had settled back in her seat and for the first time that surprise-me smile had gone. Rather, she looked confident, sure of what I was about to say.

And suddenly, I was aware of familiar faces all over that theatre. Neighbours. Friends of the family. My aunts. People who had heard me answer that question at their doors, people who thought they knew what I wanted.

There was nothing left of Mrs. Greensborough but the top of her big hat. My father, too, was looking down at the floor between his feet. I saw myself falling from that spar tree, high in the mountains.

"Going to be?" I said, turning so fast that I bumped the microphone with my hand, which turned out after all not to be numb.

I ducked.

"Nothing," I said. "I don't know. Maybe . . . maybe nothing at all."

I don't know who it was that snorted when I screwed up the stool, sat down, and stood up to screw it down again. I don't know how well I played, I wasn't listening. I don't know how loud the audience clapped, I was in a hurry to get back to my seat. I don't know what the other contestants did, I wasn't paying any attention, except when Cornelia Horncastle got up on the stage, told the whole world she was going to be a professional pianist, and sat down to rattle off Rachmaninoff's Rhapsody on a Theme of Paganini as if she'd been playing for fifty years. As far as I know it may have been the first time she'd ever heard herself play it. She had a faint look of surprise on her face the whole time, as if she couldn't quite get over the way the keys went down when you touched them.

As soon as Cornelia came down off the stage, smiling modestly, and got back into her seat, Richy Ryder announced a fifteen-minute intermission while the talent judges made their decision and the studio audience went out into the lobby to pledge their money and their votes. Now that the talent had been displayed, people could spend their money according to what they'd heard rather than according to who happened to come knocking on their door. Most of the contestants got up to stretch their legs but I figured I'd stood up once too often that night and stayed in my seat. The lower exit was not far away; I contemplated using it; I could hitch-hike home and be in bed before any of the others got out of there.

I was stopped, though, by my father, who sat down in the seat next to mine and put a greasy carton of popcorn in my lap.

"Well," he said, "that's that."

His neck was flushed. This must have been a terrible evening for him. He had a carton of popcorn himself and tipped it up to gather a huge mouthful. I had never before in my life, I realized, seen my father eat popcorn. It must have been worse for him than I thought.

Not one of the aunts was anywhere in sight. I could see my mother standing in the far aisle, talking to Mrs. Korhonen. Still smiling. She would never let herself fall apart in public, no matter what happened. My insides ached with the knowledge of what it must have been like right then to be her. I felt as if I had just betrayed her in front of the whole world. Betrayed everyone.

"Let's go home," I said.

"Not yet. Wait a while. Might as well see this thing to the end."

True, I thought. Wring every last drop of torture out of it.

He looked hard at me a moment, as if he were trying to guess what was going on in my head. And he did, he did, he always knew. "My old man wanted me to be a doctor," he said. "My mother wanted me to be a florist. She liked flowers. She thought if I was a florist I'd be able to send her a bouquet every week. But what does any of that matter now?"

Being part of a family was too complicated. And right then I decided I'd be a loner. No family for me. Nobody whose hearts could be broken every time I opened my mouth. Nobody *expecting* anything of me. Nobody to get me all tangled up in knots trying to guess who means what and what is it that's really going on inside anyone else. No temptations to presume I knew what someone else was thinking or feeling or hoping for.

When the lights had flickered and dimmed, and people had gone back to their seats, a young man with a beard came out onto the stage and changed the numbers behind the contestants' names. I'd dropped to fifth place, and Cornelia Horncastle had moved up to first. She had also, Richy Ryder announced, been awarded the judges' footstool for talent. The winner of the holiday in sunny Hawaii would not be announced until the next week, he said, when the radio audience had enough time to mail in their votes.

"And that," my mother said when she came down the aisle with her coat on, "is the end of a long and tiring day." I could find no disappointment showing in her eyes, or in the set of her mouth. Just relief. The same kind of relief that I felt myself. "You did a good job," she said, "and thank goodness it's over."

As soon as we got in the house I shut myself in the bedroom and announced I was never coming out. Lying on my bed, I tried to read my comic books but my mind passed from face to face all through the community, imagining everyone having a good laugh at the way my puffed-up ambition had got its reward. My face burned. Relatives, the aunts, would be ashamed of me. Eleanor would never let me forget. Mabel would remind me of the boy who'd done the only honourable thing, blown off his head. Why wasn't I doing the same? I lay awake the whole night, torturing myself with these thoughts. But when morning came and the hunger pains tempted me out of the bedroom as far as the breakfast table, I decided the whole wretched experience had brought one benefit with it: freedom from ambition. I wouldn't worry any more about becoming a pianist for my mother. Nor would I worry any more about becoming a high-rigger for my father. I was free at last to concentrate on pursuing the only goal that ever really mattered to me: becoming a Finn.

Of course I failed at that too. But then neither did Cornelia Horncastle become a great pianist on the concert stages of Europe. In fact, I understand that once she got back from her holiday on the beaches of Hawaii she announced to her parents that she was never going to touch a piano again as long as she lived, ivory, or cardboard, or any other kind. She had already, she said, accomplished all she'd ever wanted from it. And as far as I know, she's kept her word to this day.

ERIC MCCORMACK

(b. 1938)

E *ric McCormack was born in Scotland and came to Canada in 1966.*
He received his Ph.D. from the University of Manitoba, having
written his dissertation on the seventeenth-century writer Robert Bur-
ton's Anatomy of Melancholy. *Since 1970 he has taught English at*
the University of St. Jerome's College in Waterloo, Ontario. The short
stories in his first book, Inspecting the Vaults *(1987), created some-*
thing of a sensation with their bold inventiveness, graphic descriptions,
and highly polished writing. It is fair to say that nothing quite like this
had been seen before in Canadian fiction. In the catalogic detail, fabulous
elements, surrealism, metafictional concerns, and arch humour of stories
such as "Eckhardt at a Window" can be traced the influence of such
writers as Burton, Nathaniel Hawthorne, Jorge Luis Borges, and Franz
Kafka. He has also published a novel, The Paradise Motel *(1989), and*
is working on another. McCormack describes his writing as dabbling
in the marginal, slightly alien areas of everyday experience. . . .
The need to write about them is probably like the need to drink
whisky, or to take drugs, or to do all three at the same time.
And the reasons for the need are as complex. The writer may be
in love, or in love with words. He may be in despair at the state
of the world, or at his own state. Or he may be, in a roundabout
way, just celebrating, having a great time.

Eckhardt at a Window

T he dusty wooden frame of the window holds nine double-glazed
panes of glass, three levels of three panes on top of each other. If
Inspector Eckhardt stands on tiptoe on the threadbare carpet, the top
panes are at his eye level. The middle row is comfortably situated for him,
for he is a man of medium height. He has to stoop slightly, however, his
chin on the sill, to look through the bottom row. If he stands a few feet
away, the window is all one greater window, the panes look symmetrical,
crystalline, even identical. But from close up, at nose distance, which he
prefers, each pane is individual, unique, each discloses new worlds to
Inspector Eckhardt's eye. A bevel in the double glass here, a warp there,
reveal the reflections of twin, overlapping grotesque faces in two grotesque rooms, Chinese boxes that do not quite fit. As for what he sees on
the outside—a warp in the pane, a bubble, a bevel, invent a city he can

scarcely recognize of monstrous trees and nightmare houses reshaping themselves constantly as he moves his grey head, a landscape of plastic writhing forever in an inferno.

Inspector Eckhardt is thinking about the deaths, one year ago, of a woman and a man. He remembers the tall, beautiful, fair-haired woman he first met on that dull, November day, in this northern city. She was shivering, wearing a thin dress under a short coat. Her face was oval, a noticeable nose, green, green eyes. The lower lids were convex, half-eclipsing those two green worlds.

Inspector Eckhardt, a widower without children, a meditative man, liked the look of her right away, her voice, an innocence about her. She was long-legged, long-striding in spite of her grief—she had come to the old police station to report a death. In her deep, surprising voice, she wanted to tell him about the ludicrous accident that had happened less than an hour before. Her strange eyelids could not stop the tears from spilling out.

She was apologetic, but not about her grief. She was sorry for this: that in her confusion, she hadn't paid much attention to the location of the house where the accident had happened. It had no telephone, so she ran outside, along the street till she found a taxi, and asked for the nearest police station. And now, where was the house with the dead body? She was sure of one thing only: it was on a tree-lined street, maybe a mile or two away.

The Inspector smiled at her insistence on this fact. He did not tell her that the entire district for miles around the station was full of tree-lined streets, that it was a forest masquerading as a city. People who had lived here a long time knew their way around, knew how to see the differences between one street of trees and another. His new men often lost their way the first few times out.

Darkness was sinking in as she talked, sitting in the wooden chair in front of his desk. Through the window behind her, Inspector Eckhardt could see those very streets beginning to fade into night. It was a cold November darkness, and the lamps would hardly illumine those streets, making it useless to go looking for the house. She didn't know, in fact she said she'd never known, even the number of the house, or the name of the street. He told her, as kindly as he could, that it didn't matter much. Her friend, being dead, would be content to wait till the morning.

She shuddered. Yet she wanted to talk, and he wanted to listen to her, to watch the movement of those strange eyes, as much because of the pleasure it gave him as to help her ease herself of her burden of sorrow. He told her a formal statement could wait till the morning, but that he'd like to hear all about her friend. She should just relax and say whatever came to mind.

"A little spout of blood." She used that phrase several times. She said this little spout of blood, just a drop or two, used to spurt from her friend's forehead right between his eyebrows at least once a day. Surely that would be remarkable in anyone. The blood would trickle down his face, and he'd wipe it with a Kleenex, nervously, a horse flicking at flies. She wasn't long up from the country, and had been sitting in a bar, when he picked her up a month ago. She liked the look of him, and said nothing even when she first saw the blood spout. It used to frighten her, and it would fill him with a devastating sadness. But she said nothing.

She found out, eventually, why the blood made him so sad. One day they were sitting, talking. He was stroking, as usual, the crystal of his digital watch as he talked, intent on the nervous transformations of the little figures under the glass. He looked up and stared into her eyes. He was afraid, he said, that the blood that spouted out of his forehead wasn't his own. It was the blood of all the people he'd killed gushing back out of him.

Killings. He saw how shocked she was, and so he began telling her about them.

When he used to kill, he said, he felt as though he was watching someone else do it, a creature who looked like him, but who was on the other side of a two-way mirror. Years ago, when he was a child, he used to think it must be some other child who looked like him burying cats alive or setting them alight with gasoline, watching them try to leap out of their pain, living Catherine wheels. Then, years later, surely that was some other young boy who just happened to look like him, pushing another lonely boy into a disused canal, standing there, fascinated by the muddy gurgles, and the eventual brown calm. Or shoulder-charging an old man, light as a feather, down the dark stairwell of an apartment building and watching him crumple silently at the bottom, a broken butterfly with blood at the mouth. And even now, he could hardly admit that this killer was no one else but himself, this brown-bearded man who killed for hire and showed no pity for any of those he destroyed with his gun, his knife, his car, by fire, by water, or by other necessary means.

But one night as he was getting ready for bed, the blood gushed, for the first time, out of his head. He was undressing in front of the mirror, trying to comprehend the man on the other side of the glass, when it erupted. He quickly wiped it away, already fearful, and saw that there was no sign of a cut, not even a burst pimple, only the smooth forehead of a killer.

It wasn't long after, one night in a bar, that he met her, and they became lovers, he loving someone, and that, too, for the first time in his life.

He told her he felt he was divided once more into separate parts by meeting her. She'd somehow built a transparent wall around him, so that now his past life was someone else's, an unloved man he hardly knew.

He wanted to dedicate himself now to loving, the way he had before to killing. He wondered if love could cancel out, somehow, all of the deaths. So he began taking her to the places where he'd done his murders over the years, and they made love standing up in alleys and hallways, lying down in city parks and seedy basements, in daytime and in the night. Always, in spite of everything, the blood came.

Then, just that day, they went to a house in a tree-lined street. He'd phoned her early in the afternoon, and they'd taken a taxi to the house.

They went straight upstairs, she hardly noticing the creaky stairs, the faded prints in their cracked frames on the walls, to a dusty room with some shabby chairs and a rusted wall-mirror. In the middle of the bare floor stood a metal-framed coffee table with a glass top.

They made love in front of the mirror. She watched his hands move under her clothing in the reflection: the image of the two lovers in the mirror before her, and the feel of his hands on her flesh doubled her pleasure.

After the love-making, he'd sent her downstairs to the kitchen to make coffee. She was standing by the stove when she heard a crash upstairs. She called up to him from the hall to ask if anything was wrong. She thought he called back that it was okay, so she went into the kitchen again.

After a few minutes, a drip fell past her head onto the chipped white stove, a reddish splotch. And another. For a moment she didn't understand. She looked up at the ceiling where a reddish-brown drip was gathering. She knew then what it was.

Terrified, she ran out of the kitchen and up the stairs, her feet hollow on the worn linoleum, hardly noticing the faded prints of hunting scenes behind broken glass. She reached the landing and looked through the open living-room door.

The bearded man is spread-eagled across the frame of a low coffee table whose glass top has collapsed. He himself is impaled upon a sliver of green glass about eighteen inches long. It has pierced his back, travelling on through his body inside the left shoulder-blade, driven by his weight, slicing through his heart like a butcher's knife.

The point of the glass protrudes through his chest without tearing his green silk shirt, but far enough to make an obscene bosom. His eyes are open and he looks surprised. In the middle of his forehead, a little ruby of wet blood is forming.

She runs to him, sobbing. He is quite, quite dead.

He must have sat right down on the glass-topped table, making it cave in, explode at the weight of him. It was meant to take a vase of flowers, or a glossy picture book, never a man's weight. He must have fallen backward into the empty frame, crucifying himself, skewered by a long sliver wedged against the floor, his body making new lips to suck in the glass.

Inspector Eckhardt felt sorry for her. Her green eyes were full of tears, this tall, fair-haired woman, occasionally touching his arm as she talked. She still couldn't believe what had happened. For so long she too had been alone, sad. Then she met the bearded man and her life was full of meaning, love became a barricade against an unbearable past. And now the barrier had been demolished.

She looked tired now. The Inspector nodded in sympathy. He didn't even know her name, but that could wait. Nor did she call the bearded man any name at all. Always it was "he," with a little emphasis. Inspector Eckhardt wondered if she even knew the man's name, but he didn't ask. He'd enjoyed listening to her, and he could get all the details from her tomorrow morning.

He told her she could go home now and come back in the morning early to make a statement and help them find the house. Again, her strange green eyes filled. She said she'd no place to go, she'd given up her apartment just that day, so that she could move in with the bearded man.

Inspector Eckhardt looked at her, liking the looks of her, tall and warm. He liked the way she would reach out across the desk and touch his arm quite unselfconsciously, trusting him.

It was no problem, he said. She could stay in the station's little night-shift room. He'd ask the duty sergeant to get her a cup of coffee and a sandwich. She should try to sleep, even though it was early, because next morning she'd have to help them find the house with the body of her dead lover.

After she left with the sergeant, the Inspector sat for a while, thinking about her, and the strange accident she'd come to report. He thought, too, about his own mood of contentment, that he'd be seeing her again in the morning. He couldn't help feeling that in some way he wasn't yet sure of, this was a remarkable day for him.

Inspector Eckhardt did indeed see her very early the next morning. The fair-haired woman must have slipped out of the station during the night, and when he saw her in the early morning, there was a great change in her condition.

Dawn is just breaking, a frosty November dawn in the city. The sky is a heavy sheet of opaque glass with fissures prised apart by wedges of sunlight.

On a piece of waste ground stands a huddle of men, their breath silently trumpeting in front of them. A car pulls up on the nearby street, the engine throbbing, and a grey-haired, older man in a heavy winter coat picks his way through the sparkling weeds toward the men.

"Over here, Inspector Eckhardt."

The Inspector nods to the men, and leans forwards to look at the shape lying on the iron ground. He can see that it is the frozen body of a long-legged young woman in a skimpy dress, her clothes, her fair hair sculpted in hoar-frost, a sparkling Christmas bundle. She is sprawled on her back. Her eyes are the eyes of a statue, completely whitened in the frost of this November morning.

Inspector Eckhardt also sees, glittering in the occasional sunshine, the long splinter of frosted glass protruding from her belly, a lethal banner which she grips in her two frozen hands.

Inspector Eckhardt was too shocked by this death, too saddened by the thought that he'd never see the woman again. He knew he must work, and work, and work. The investigation of her death wasn't in his hands; it was his job to find the body of the bearded man, and he'd waste no time that day in getting on with it.

He and his team knocked on door after door, peered through dozens of dusty windows, examined every house that seemed unoccupied in those tree-lined streets. In vain. Some of Inspector Eckhardt's men wondered out loud whether, perhaps, her story was just a bit far-fetched. Late in the afternoon, he himself began to probe the fringes of that possibility: that there was no body, that she had made up an insane lie.

Then, just before dusk, news came in that the body had been found.

The house is on one of those tree-lined streets in the maze of tree-lined streets surrounding the station. The streets are mirror images of each other. Only a bump on the road here, an oddity in architecture there makes the difference to those who know.

The grey-haired man steps out of the cruiser and walks up the pathway of a small, run-down house. The door opens, and staleness makes a brief raid on the sharp, colder outside air. He notes the creaky stairs, the faded prints on the wall, the worn linoleum. On the dim landing, he glimpses three rooms: a bathroom with a chipped sink, an empty bedroom with a cracked mirror on the wall. Then the living-room, with another smell, one he knows only too well.

"Right in here, Inspector Eckhardt."

Through the parasitic fuss of photographers and detectives, the Inspector sees, by the light of a bare ceiling bulb, the dead man, crucified on a rectangular metal frame, broken glass all around him, his eyes wide open. His face is bearded, a thin brown beard on a thin face, his hairline receding. It is the face of a young man who has never been young. His cheeks are lined with experience and sadness.

But two things are ominously wrong. No gush of blood stains the dead forehead, one of the last things she had told him. The bearded man's brow is smooth and unmarked. But more disturbing still, he has not been pierced through his back. Instead, Inspector Eckhardt can see, as can all the others, the broad end of a long sliver of glass protruding sickly from between his legs, an obscene phallus coated in blood and excrement.

That was all a year ago, a year in which no resolution to the mystery of the deaths had appeared. Inspector Eckhardt had made sure the investigation of the fair-haired woman's death was pursued without slacking. But no witness could be found, no motive appeared. Her past was a blank, no one claimed her or identified her. The investigators dealt with her death as a murder, but they did concede that it was just possible she might have stabbed herself with the shard of glass—a very unpleasant way to commit suicide.

As for the bearded man impaled on the glass, nothing could be discovered about him except that he had just recently paid a year's rent on the old house on the tree-lined street.

Inspector Eckhardt remembered how she said they'd always make love on the scene of former killings. So, day after day he wearied his eyes with the dust and faded type of old files. He even began having nightmares about seedy crimes camouflaged by the trees of those streets. But he could find no record of a killing in that house. It belonged to an old couple who had retired and migrated to the South.

Soon the entire case of the fair-haired woman and the bearded man was interred, in its turn, in a filing cabinet. Inspector Eckhardt's superiors told him plainly that the two deaths, no matter how strange, of an apprentice hooker and a presumed lover-cum-hired-killer were of minor importance in the general scheme of things.

But Inspector Eckhardt did not forget, could not forget. For him, he didn't quite know why, the case was of major importance in his "general scheme of things." He'd stand for hours looking out of his window, a juggler with too many rubber balls, trying just once to put it all together. He was beginning to consider that his career up to that point had been a time of innocence, a novitiate. He felt that he too had walked right through a mirror, and everything was changed.

The case, he had to admit to himself, delighted him as much as it puzzled him with its possibilities, its enigmas. Yes, she was dead. But now he was high priest of his own private religion, and must create a theology around the mysteries. Part of his ritual was to meditate daily upon the fair-haired woman, at times his goddess, at times a demon. Why had the description she'd given of the death of the bearded man been so accurate yet so wrong? How could the dead man have answered her call from the kitchen? Why had she left the police station during the night? What had made her go to the waste ground to die?

Daily, he invents ingenious resolutions to the mystery. For example, he theorizes, keeping the details sketchy, that it could be a murder-suicide. The essence is this: the fair-haired woman must murder the bearded man by somehow (this is one of the very vague parts) forcing him to sit on the fragment of glass in the old house, then she must slip away to the waste ground to stab herself in the stomach.

Or, in another version, it is the bearded man who must be the murderer. He must go to the waste ground to meet the fair-haired woman, stab her in the stomach with the piece of glass, then return to that musty house and sit down, quite deliberately, on the sliver of glass.

Naturally, in this second version of the murder-suicide theory, the order of the deaths is reversed. But then, neither first nor second version accounts for her visit to the police-station, nor for her determination to tell her story. Yet the Inspector finds something satisfying in both versions, maybe the suggestion of a doomed, perverted love, maybe the symbolism of the glass. Or maybe, it's just the enigma of which of the two is the murderer, which the suicide.

Inspector Eckhardt is also gently nursing a double-murder theory. It goes like this: someone wants to kill the fair-haired woman and the bearded man, perhaps to avenge one of his paid killings—the motive is unclear. The murderer somehow forces the bearded man to sit on the sliver of glass (again, the Inspector is unhappy with this part), somehow terrifies the fair-haired woman into lying convincingly to the police (slightly less difficult for the Inspector to imagine), and then into leaving the station in the middle of the night for the waste ground, to meet her own murderer (tricky, this part too, the Inspector admits).

Sometimes the Inspector even proposes two separate murderers, one for the bearded man, one for the girl, perhaps acting in collusion, perhaps not, although the use of the glass is so unusual it suggests a conspiracy. The flexibility of the two-murderer theory, however, is its main appeal; the permutations of which-killer-kills-whom-and-why are expanded marvellously by this simple ploy.

Inspector Eckhardt likes all variations of the double-murder theory for another reason. They exonerate the fair-haired woman, making her perhaps the tragic victim of her love for a felon. Besides, the slaying of the bearded man, an admitted assassin, is reassuring for the Inspector: justice, no matter how rough, still prowls the streets of the city.

But one thing always bothers him. Why, he constantly asks himself, did the fair-haired woman come to the station and lie? That, he still finds hardest of all to take.

For a year, Inspector Eckhardt speculated and speculated, enjoyed speculating, standing there by his window. He never lost patience at the incompleteness of his theories, for he felt confident that, in time, the whorls, the distortions, the bumps would disappear, and the clear, inevitable truth would stand forth.

Then, just that morning, almost a year to the day after the deaths, he was obliged to look at the whole matter differently. Not a mile from the station, a crew of hydro-company men had been making routine inspections of the lines. They had been checking out an old house when they found something grisly.

The grey-haired man, stocky in his winter coat, swings his legs out of the cruiser. He walks along the path to the door of the house where some men in hard hats stand smoking and talking. It's a small house, paint peeling from the clapboard. This house would be hard to distinguish from most of the others in the tree-lined street.

He pushes open the creaky door, ducking past a brief ambush by the stale air, and walks along the hallway to the staircase—he can hear the sound of voices upstairs. He climbs the creaking staircase with its worn linoleum, his shoes echoing. He notes the faded prints on the walls. He stops on the landing, where the smell is even mustier. In a room with an open door, a few men are scuttling around, maggots in uniform.

"Come in, Inspector Eckhardt," one of them says, without turning. And he sees what occupies their attention.

The fully-clothed body of a man lies on its back in the metal frame of a glass-topped coffee-table surrounded by broken glass. The body has lain there a long time. The Inspector can see that the face and the exposed parts of the flesh have turned a mottled blue. The cheeks have partly decomposed, exposing the bone. The eyes have dried up to raisins. The clothing and the floor beneath the skeletal frame of the table are heavily stained by the leakage of body fluids.

The cause of death is very clear: the body has been pierced through the back by a long sliver of glass, wedged against the floor. The glass has penetrated so deeply that the point, a deadly nipple, sticks out of the chest through the material of what was once a light green shirt.

Lying on the button band of the shirt, a rag of brown hair has peeled away from the chin. A scalp of long brown hair hangs from the back of the lolling head like a trophy. The ends of the fingers have decomposed, exposing bone, but on the mottled blue left wrist, a digital watch dangles. The angular numbers are still prowling agitatedly under their glass cover.

Inspector Eckhardt, back in his office in the station, stands by his window, late in the afternoon. He is thinking of the fair-haired girl, the bearded men, and the possibility of faceless, shadowy avengers. In the window panes, he fancies he sees them, playing a variety of parts, here stabbing themselves, there stabbing each other, or each being stabbed by all the others in a frenzy of glass.

The Inspector sighs. The darkness outside is deepening, and soon he will see with cockroach eyes the multiple images of himself reflected more distinctly in the window. Vaguely, through the double glaze, the nightscape of the city will emerge on this November afternoon, creating itself in light, the beginnings of a miraculous painting-by-numbers.

Inspector Eckhardt, standing by his window, is not discontented with the way things have worked out. He knows now that he has no wish ever to solve his mystery (he feels sure that it *is* his, meant for him alone), only to contemplate it, to delight in its complexities.

He walks slowly back to his desk marvelling again at the discovery of the second bearded man's body. Behind him, nine, or is it eighteen, other misshapen Inspector Eckhardts slide, hobble, somersault back to their separate desks. They sit down in unison. After a moment's pause, as on a signal given, all of them, with the most convoluted motions, reach for pencils, find them with an impossible accuracy, and begin to write.

JOYCE CAROL OATES

(b. 1938)

*J*oyce Carol Oates was born in Lockport, New York, and educated at Syracuse and the University of Wisconsin. After teaching at the University of Detroit and the University of Windsor, she moved to Princeton, where she continues to teach in the Creative Writing Program. She has published some twenty novels and fifteen collections of short stories, four volumes of poetry, and books of distinguished literary criticism. Her astonishing productivity has earned her a reputation as one of the most important American writers in the 1970s and 1980s. Puzzled attempts to categorize her protean imagination and wry comments about the desirability of creative contraception still figure in much of what is written about her. Of her own fiction she has remarked: "My method has always been to combine the 'naturalistic' world with the 'symbolic' method of expression, so that I am always—or usually—writing about real people in a real society, but the means of expression may be naturalistic, realistic, surreal, or parodic. In this way I have, to my own satisfaction at least, solved the old problem—should one be faithful to the 'real' world, or to one's imagination?" One reason she is so interested in the breakdown of fiction's conventional boundaries is her belief that the "ego-consciousness" of Western culture, a legacy of the Renaissance, is itself breaking down: "Far from being locked inside our own skins, inside the 'dungeons' of ourselves, we are now able to recognize that our minds belong, quite naturally, to a collective 'mind,' a mind in which we share everything that is mental, most obviously language itself, and that the old boundary of the skin is no boundary at all but a membrane connecting the inner and outer experiences of existence." The characters in her fiction often find themselves groping in the direction of the sense of oneness that Oates's didactic mysticism points toward.

Dying

"**C**ome closer, sit here on the edge of the bed. Or are you afraid of me?"

"Why should I be afraid of you?"

"You might catch my disease."

"You don't have any disease."

She saw that he was irritated, in spite of his smile. It was too warm in this room again, everything crowded and musty; as usual he had not opened the window. Each time she came to visit him she felt herself more tediously familiar with the furniture of his life, now narrowed strangely to this room in a half-empty old apartment building with a TV-Radio repair shop on the first floor. Things lay where she had seen them last: a pile of old newspapers, books from the city library, dirty trousers collapsed on the floor. The man himself, sitting propped up in bed, watched her distaste with a kind of malicious triumph, as if he were proud of residing over this particular kingdom.

"Well," she said, setting down the bag she carried, "how much do you weigh today?"

"I didn't bother weighing myself."

She sat at the little kitchen table, only a few yards from his bed. As she crossed her legs she could not help but glance down at them, and this annoyed her; she said coldly, "What's wrong with you now? As soon as I came in you were irritated."

"That isn't true—"

"It's true."

He scratched at his bare chest. She could hear his fingernails against his skin and smiled at the familiarity of the sound. "So I suppose you won't be coming any more," he said.

"Please, not that again."

They were silent. She could hear the sound of machines from somewhere, not far away. These sounds and even the sight of his room pleased her, as if she were coming home to something, and now their routine disagreement seemed to fit in precisely with what she had expected. He made a sound of impatience. His hair was tousled, yet she could see clearly that he would be bald soon; that sandy boyish hair was a disguise that had never fooled her. They had met years ago at college, both of them dissociated from the larger social world of the university by their having the wrong clothes, the wrong mannerisms, the wrong nervous intensity. To her he seemed to have changed little. To him, she guessed, she was more attractive than she had been; surely her blond hair wound in thick braids about her head and her expensive clothes must draw all the light of this shabby room to her. "Here, look what I brought you today," she said suddenly. "Why should we always fight?"

"Is that all for me?"

"Of course, everything." She sat with her back arched as if she were a princess, elegantly conscious of sitting this way as he watched her, and began to take things out of the bag. "Some wonderful fresh fruit; look at these colors. Look at this apple, isn't it beautiful? No, seriously. Do you want an apple now?"

"I don't like the skins on apples. The noise they make—"

"How preposterous," she said, laughing.

"I can't help it."

"But how can you be so weak?"

"Are you going to start that again?"

"No, no, look at these bananas—but they're not ripe. I bought you some eggs, here. And some oranges, do you want an orange?"

"I don't care."

"Well, do you want it or not?"

"Oranges make a mess."

"Do you want me to peel it for you?"

He shrugged his shoulders. She watched him through her lowered lashes, as if trying to reconcile this man with the man she had once known, whose shoulders and arms had been broad—not muscular, exactly, but solid—while in this man hints of bone had begun to assert themselves fragilely beneath his flesh. "I'll put these things away and peel one for you," she said. She looked around; he said, "You can use that newspaper there." She nodded and put the paper on the table. Peeling the orange with her short chipped nails, she smiled at him as if she were performing an intimate gesture, parodying some intimate gesture. "Of course I'm coming to see you again," she said. "Why do you always ask that? Of course I'm coming. I like to take that bus, I even like to walk past that damn construction area. Those men in the white helmets—"

"What are they doing for so long?"

"I told you, widening the street. Putting an overpass in too."

"What about the men in the helmets?"

"The sun glares off the helmets, the men work with their shirts off, they're very tanned—"

"Not like me."

"When it's sunny, like today, everything is hot and gleaming. On overcast days it's something else again, another scene. All the light drains out and everything is sluggish, even the machines seem slower."

"How have you been this week?"

"Oh, fine. Wonderful. And you?"

"The same."

"You didn't get out, I suppose."

"No."

"I'm glad you're so pleased with yourself."

"What do you mean by that?"

"You promised you'd get out somewhere, go downtown or to the park, any goddamn thing. Now you tell me you stayed here."

"I wasn't up to it."

"You'll never be up to it, then."

"Look, for a bag of fruit I don't have to put up with this. I'm not your husband."

She frowned; then she laughed. Her laughter surprised her, for she knew it was not the right response to his eager, sullen tone. "No," she said. If she were to look at him, she knew, he would be staring at her with his big angry eyes, grown larger now that his face was thin, trying to involve her in some mysterious hurt. But this was familiar. Always he led her to talk about her husband, angrily and wistfully, as if trying to trap her in a lie.

"What do you mean by that 'no'? Is the idea so absurd?"

"Certainly not."

"You do mean it."

"Here's the orange, it smells wonderful. Do you want a plate or something? I'd better get you one." Dishes were piled in the sink, some still dabbed with food. She took a saucer and rinsed it and brought it to him. "I suppose I could wash those dishes for you, but I don't want to. I can't stand to do dishes."

"Okay, thanks," he said. He put the saucer on his thigh and picked up the orange carefully. "Why don't you sit here? On the edge, there's room."

She sat on the edge of the bed. "My feet ache, I wore these shoes without stockings. It's so hot, even for July. Can I ask you why this window is never open?"

"Noise from outside."

"But you open it at night?"

"Yeah." He was eating a section of the orange, self-consciously. She saw him glance at her crossed legs. "Your shoes got dirty."

"All that dust out there, yes."

"Do you wear high heels like that to attract attention?"

"Whose attention?"

"I don't know, anyone's. Is that why women wear them?"

"I don't know."

"How stupid!"

"Yes, stupid. Why don't you get out of bed?"

He ate the orange angrily. Now a spurt of juice appeared on his chin. "Why don't you come in here with me?" he said.

She smiled and looked vaguely away—at a calendar on the wall with half its numbers X'd out. "You don't really want that," she said.

"Look, I'm sick as hell of your telling me you know what I want. You know me better than I know myself, crap like that. Maybe you talk to your husband like that, but—"

"I never talk to him like that."

"Then to your friends."

"No, only to you." She paused. "You're my only friend."

He laughed. Then an unpleasant mottled flush appeared on his face. She was fascinated at his embarrassment, which came and went for reasons she could never understand. It was true, she thought, watching him eat, that he was her only friend; only to him could she talk, he existed for her as a face and a voice, a presence, a spirit, as no one else existed. Yet it was her husband she loved. Her love for her husband was so secure that it could be neglected and returned to, forgotten, and nothing would ever happen to it. Now this strange man, lying in his rumpled bed and supposing himself sick, was so moved by her having said that he was her friend that he could not for a moment even look at her. He ate the orange, slowly and deliberately, sullenly, as if it were a duty he did to please her. "Yes, my only friend," she said, touching his shoulder. At his look of irritation she withdrew her hand. "You were my only friend at college, too. Later on, when I didn't see you much any more, I still thought about you. That was what upset me—I always thought about you, you were always there. I didn't always want you so close to me, do you understand? You created something in me that stayed alive. . . . And just last year I thought that you couldn't be dead, nothing could have happened to you or I would have known it. And then our meeting like that, by magic. . . ."

"Magic, hell. Accident."

"By accident . . ."

"Did you ever tell your husband about me?"

"I told him about every man I had been involved with."

"What do you mean, involved with?"

"Made love with."

He stared down at the saucer. She felt his muscles tense as if he were stiffening himself against a blow. "We didn't make love," he said.

"Yes."

"We didn't, no, for Christ's sake. You say that now—you've imagined that now—to keep us apart. We never did."

"We did, yes. I remember."

"Look, this is ridiculous, every time we argue about it! We never made love, you never let me touch you, you were never any closer than this and you know it. What the hell are you trying to pull?"

"You've forgotten it, that's all."

"I've forgotten nothing!"

"Why are you so angry?"

"Because you're lying—it's a trick to keep us apart now, when you know how I feel about you—"

She lowered her gaze. When he talked like this she felt a peculiar comfortable lassitude overtake her, as if he were safely set upon a speech already written and memorized, something she might have helped write herself. "No, honey," she said, taking the saucer from him, "that's not true. I don't involve myself with other men now. I'm not interested. You don't seem to understand about my marriage; you have the idea that marriage is—"

"You've never admitted the truth about your marriage."

She set the saucer on the bureau. There were a number of bottles there, a stained spoon, an ash tray. "What's this?" she said. She picked up a small blue bottle filled with capsules. "Is this new?"

"No. Herzog's tranquilizers. He said nothing was wrong with me, just to keep calm. No anxiety."

"Well?"

"The fat old bastard! Seven dollars for those things."

She set the bottle down and forgot about it. "Well, let's not argue; I don't want to waste time that way. Why do you always want to talk about my marriage when it only upsets you? It has nothing to do with you, nothing at all. I shouldn't have told you about him that time, but I thought you'd be pleased to know what my life is like now. After all, when we knew each other I wasn't very happy. Would you like me to be that way now?"

"Yes."

"But that's a—" She stared. Before her gaze little bluish lines seemed to appear beneath his eyes and at the sides of his nose, near his nostrils. "That's selfish," she said.

"So what? Who isn't selfish?"

"How am I selfish?"

"You talk to me about him, to make me miserable. You lie. You lie to me and you won't—you won't—"

"But I said it wasn't going to be that way, the first time I came. I love you as a friend. Don't you know how important that is, what it means to me? What does a lover mean beside a friend? Doesn't that mean anything to you?"

"Christ, you really believe that." He drew his hand across his eyes; she could hear the slight elastic sound of his eyeballs being rubbed. "I hate that, stop it," she said, pulling at his wrist. "That noise—"

"Huh?"

"Oh, nothing."

"What noise?"

"Oh, nothing, it's silly. Nothing."

He stared at her, saw she was embarrassed about something. After a moment he said, "Doing any painting?"

"No."

"Anything wrong?"

"Of course not."

"Well, I just asked."

"I'm not angry, I'm sorry. I haven't been working but I think I have an idea. For two weeks or so . . ."

"You never did a portrait of your husband, did you?"

"No, I'm past that stage. Anyway, I wouldn't call it that, I never did portraits. That thing of you wasn't a portrait."

"Did you really see me that way?"

"Oh, I don't know."

"You never talk about your painting, why is that?"

"I don't know anything about it, I suppose."

"How old are you now?"

She laughed. "Why do you ask? You know I'm thirty-four."

"You're still young, then."

"Why do you say that, that way? You're the same age."

"Well, the success you've had with it, without trying, and you're so healthy—" Nervously she caressed his wrist, avoiding his sticky fingers. She could feel waves of hatred in the stuffy air between them. "If that magazine had carried that story of you last year, how do you know what might have happened?"

"I never expected them to run the story."

"So you were crowded out, but look how close it was, that stupid news magazine with the artsy-craftsy color section! Just like that. Some half-wit takes a liking to a painting and there you go, easy as that."

"It hasn't been easy, I wouldn't say that."

"For Christ's sake don't tell me that. You've never worried about it, not once. You don't give a damn about it."

"But it isn't my life, I'm not like you—"

"Not your life!" He drew away from her. Now he did look ill: perhaps he was not imagining everything after all. His lips were dry and loose and contemptuous. "Of course it isn't your life. You're married. You're in love. You've got money. You've even got a friend you can show off to, that you visit surreptitiously."

"What a foolish word—"

"Surreptitiously? What else should I say?"

"Nothing."

"You've got everything, why should you worry about your work? Your career? You worry about nothing. You sleep at night. You have no headaches, no fears, no moments of darkness when you know absolutely that everyone is going to die and that you—you can't escape it."

"But you're not going to die. Don't torture yourself with it."

"I wasn't talking about myself, what makes you think that!"

"You never talk about anything but yourself."

"And look at my work, all scattered around here, those goddamn papers on the floor there . . ."

"Oh, have you been working?"

He grinned contemptuously. "What do you think?"

"But you said last week you had an idea."

"No good."

"But if you started to write, something might happen. It used to be that way, didn't it? I still remember one of your stories, the one that was dedicated to me—About that German woman who worked for the family—"

"Forget it."

"But I liked that story."

"I didn't. So forget it."

"What was wrong with it?"

He had begun to breathe heavily. His eyes narrowed as if resisting pain. "I should think you'd play some music, at least," she said softly. "Should I put something on?" He seemed not to hear her at first; was he truly in pain, did he imagine it or did he pretend? "No, thanks, no," he said rigidly. "Don't you like the records I bought? Is something wrong with them? That fifth symphony is supposed to be a perfect cutting—" "No, forget it," he said. "Are you all right?" she said. He nodded impatiently. "But you don't want any music on?" she said. "Not while you're here." "But in the background—to blot out that noise—" "I don't put music on to blot out noise!" he said shrilly. He closed his eyes. She touched his chest and was surprised at how cool and damp his skin was. "That goddamn orange," he muttered.

"Do you want a pill? Anything?"

"No."

She bowed her head and caressed his chest vaguely. While she waited for his pain to pass she looked down at the floor—unfinished boards painted an ugly brown. Something had been spilled near the bed. "I'm going to exhibit some things in Chicago, by the way," she said. "In September. *He's* going to go down with me and help."

He pushed her hand away. "I'm all right."

"Are you going to see the doctor this week, then?"

"I suppose so."

"But how have you been, worse?"

"I weigh a hundred fifty-six."

"Oh."

"So that crap you made me eat, that goddamn nutritious cereal, didn't work. Matter of fact it made me throw up."

"Maybe if you went out sometime—went for a walk—"

"Out here?"

"You could move closer to the city. Near a park, why not? How did you ever find this apartment; it isn't in the city or in the country, there isn't anything here but vacant lots and buildings half torn down and that factory, or whatever it is, down that way—What a stupid place! It's inconvenient for me, too, since I don't drive—"

"Inconvenient for you!"

"Well, I mean—"

"I thought you liked to take that bus. Liked to walk by the men working out there so they can watch you. In your high heels."

"What's wrong with you?"

"Nothing."

"If I took a taxi out here next time, would you come back with me? We could go to that doctor near my house; I told you about him. I think your doctor at the clinic is too busy."

"Near your house? I couldn't afford it."

"Don't be silly."

"What? On that check they send me? How could I afford it?"

"I mean, don't be silly, I'd pay for it myself. Of course I'd pay for it. I always said that examination they gave you wasn't complete—"

"Your husband would pay for it."

"I have my own money."

"And his money too, you have his money! I saw his ads in the paper, real estate in a commercial area, will build to suit tenant— I was proud to see it."

"Don't talk about him, please. Be sensible, be nice. We've got to do something about your health. You keep losing weight, we've got to do something about it. Why don't you look around at me?"

"What do you want from me anyway? Why do you keep coming here?"

His face was brittle with anguish. She knew in that instant that she had never been apart from him during all those years, but that they had been regarding each other with this same inexplicable anguish, always, confusing other faces with the one face they desired, confusing other voices with that single unique voice neither of them could quite reject. She was humiliated by her bondage to this whining, helpless man.

"Why do you keep coming here?" he said.

She stood. She turned away. "I don't know."

"You never know anything!"

"Leave me alone. I'm going now."

"What time is it?"

"I'm going."

"Is it time for the bus?"

"You exhaust me, for God's sake—"

"But don't go yet, I mean it isn't time for the bus, is it? What time is it?"

His desperation shamed her. She stared over at the sink. "I know, I'll do your dishes for you," she said.

"No, the hell with them—"

"It's dirty this way, you'll make yourself sick," she said. "Don't you ever want to get well?" She inhaled slowly, feeling tears about to come into her eyes. She waited. Nothing happened, no tears. "Don't you ever want to get well?" she repeated, as if this remark were a cue that would inspire her to sorrow.

He had heard her coming on the stairs and opened the door for her. "Well, hello," she said. "How good you look! What's happened?"

"Oh, the weather change after the heat wave, I guess," he said. He was leaning back against the sink, smiling. Behind him the grimy window faced nothing—she could not tell if it looked out upon another anonymous building or upon the gray sky. "Come on in, sit down. Sorry about last time."

"Last time?"

He glanced at her. She was still smiling, pleased at his being out of bed and dressed, but now she saw that she had said something wrong. "Oh, yes, last time," she said. She recalled their argument vaguely—he had refused to come with her to a doctor. "Then I know what," she said, not sitting in the chair he had offered her, "let's go out for a walk. Not that way, where they're working, but up this other way. . . ."

He hesitated. She saw that his hair had been dampened and combed recently, that it looked thin. For a moment he was about to agree; then, as if terrified by something, he turned away slightly. "Maybe later on."

"Please, a nice walk. You said yourself the weather is nice. Come on."

"No." He went past her and sat on the edge of the bed. His movements were cautious, even rigid, as if he were in some kind of danger. She sat in the chair and felt the atmosphere of the room go heavy with failure. "So," he said, "how's your work been going?"

"I've started a painting." She saw that he was barefoot. His long, bony white toes cringed as she spoke. "I've been working on it for three days."

"Yeah, how is it? Anything like the last one?"

"I guess not." Watching his toes, she heard her voice go thick with embarrassment. "Men working on a road, a lot of white, in fact everything's white or black or gray. No colors. The weeds alongside the road have been whitened by dust . . . they look like bones of something, skeletons. . . ."

He smiled sourly. "Not putting this place in, are you?"

"Well, no. I don't want any buildings."

"Why not? This is a picturesque dump and you like picturesque things. Television antennae on the roof. Quaint things."

"What do you mean, quaint?"

"You like quaint things, don't you? Men working, with white helmets. What happened to their suntans? Transfixed weeds, transfigured weeds—"

"Just what do you mean, quaint? What do you mean?"

He was still smiling but she knew he was nervous, ready to back down. "Forget it," he said. "I'm doing some work too."

Her heart was beating rapidly. For a moment she did not hear what he had said. Then she said, "Oh, that's nice. Really. Are you going to let me read it?"

"Maybe, when it's done."

"What is it?"

"A story."

"Oh, a story," she said. The flatness of her voice startled her. "But how are you? How do you feel?"

"The same."

"I'm so glad to hear you're working. . . ." She glanced over at the kitchen table, which was cluttered with dishes and newspapers, as if seeking out evidence of his work. "A story, did you say? About what?"

"A man and a woman."

"A love story?"

"Yes."

"You'll let me read it when it's finished?"

"Sure."

"I always liked what you wrote. In college . . . I thought you were the most intelligent man I ever met."

"Now you know better, huh?"

"I didn't mean that."

"You think I've changed some?"

"No. But we've all changed. . . ."

"Some of us for the better."

"We've grown older. Grown into adults. Surely there's nothing wrong with that."

"What are you suggesting?"

"I don't understand you."

"Are you suggesting I haven't grown up?"

"I didn't say that, my God. How touchy you are! As far as I'm concerned you were always grown up. You had no childhood." And now she could see that he was not well, really, that she had imagined when she first came in that his being up, his smiling so confidently, had meant much more than it did. "How much did you say you weigh?"

"A little less."

"But how much?"

"A hundred forty something. I don't know."

She winced. Her hand came up before her in a gesture of pity, or defense, as if she supposed he expected some movement from her. "Please tell me what you're doing for yourself."

"I'm resting. Thinking."

"Be serious, will you? This is important."

"How can anything about me be important?"

"It's important to me!"

"But why to you? Who are you?" He stood up, excited. Then he sat down and lay back on the bed, laughing. "My God, if you could explain that to me. Why you bother with me."

"Because you're my friend," she said contemptuously.

"I'm your friend," he said. "But why? Why? If this is the last time you come, everything should be settled between us. Right now you're thinking—"

"You don't know what I'm thinking."

"You're wishing you hadn't come. A sick man isn't a man at all."

"But what has that got to do with it?"

He swung his legs around off the bed. "What has what got to do with it?"

"What you said—"

"What? What?"

"Oh, I don't know. You're giving me a headache. And I wish you'd open that window, noise or no noise, it smells in here—"

"A sick man isn't a man, huh? That's what you think?"

"I never said that!"

"You don't let me be a man!"

"Look, please, if you're—" She made a gesture of rising that was insincere; he did not respond. They were silent for a while. "So you lost more weight," she said. She looked over at his little calendar, something from a service station, on which the new month was being X'd out. For some reason this pleased her, as if it were a landmark.

"Yes. And you, you're looking very good."

"With these lines under my eyes?"

"What? Let's see. I don't see anything."

"You never notice anything. I was up until four last night, drawing weeds. Don't laugh. Then I couldn't sleep when I did go to bed." As she spoke, a wave of excitement rose in her that she had to hide from him. His narrow glittering eyes were hostile.

"You're looking very good just the same. Very healthy."

Her excitement was transformed suddenly into a sensation of dismay. She put her hands to her eyes in a melodramatic gesture. "Why do you hate me so," she said.

"What?"

"You hate me, I can feel it. You hate me. There's something inside me that was born when I met you—when a woman meets any man, it happens—and this thing, this creature that becomes me when I'm with you, you're killing it, you hate it and want to destroy it—"

"That's not true," he said quietly.

"You want me to come to bed with you so you can kill it. We're fighting each other, I bring you love and we're antagonists; what's wrong with us? The other time it wasn't like that. We were close to each other and it was beautiful—" He said nothing. She went on, in spite, "But of course you don't believe that ever happened. You've forgotten it, like all men."

He made a gesture that indicated nothing. He looked confused and ill. A hand might have been pressing against his chest, pushing him back down on the soiled pillow that was propped up against the headboard. He took a package of cigarettes out of his pocket, as if for something to do.

"Anyway," she said, "you should open that window."

"I open it at night."

"You're so remote here; my God, this is the end of the world. That window is all you have, and you keep it closed. How can you live like this?"

"He lit a cigarette. "You're very generous, then, to come here in spite of everything. To come here and let me admire you. See what I can't have."

"Do you think that's why I come here?" she said sharply.

"How do I know? Why you began, or why you're stopping—"

"Why I began? When I saw you downtown that day I couldn't have walked away. Are you serious? Don't you know what you mean to me? You looked so sick—I guess I thought you were drunk— There was never any question about my coming to see you."

"Is that true?"

"Yes."

"And about stopping?"

"Why do you always bring that up?"

"Because I'm afraid."

She got up slowly. In spite of his watching her, she stretched her arms and stifled a yawn. "I'm still sleepy. I got up at seven this morning. . . . Now you, you say you're afraid, afraid of what? How strange you are—" She came to sit by him on the edge of the bed. He was pleased at this; she saw the cunning rigidity of his face relax. "Afraid of what?"

"The usual."

"But what nonsense—something you can't even explain—" She watched him closely, as if jealous of something. He took hold of her arm and caressed it without affection. She smiled sharply. "Tell me what you're afraid of."

"I'm not sure."

"Not that thing that bothered you once before, I hope. That awful accident—"

"Oh, that. The woman by the bus? No, not that, but I still dream about it sometimes. No. Something else. Earlier than that, years ago. . . . But hell, I don't want to talk about it."

"I want to talk about it. I want to know."

"Do you? I was working at the hospital then, I told you about that. I was twenty-seven— Where were you at twenty-seven?"

"Married."

"To him?"

"I've only been married once."

"At the hospital, then. . . ." But he said, with a harsh burst of laughter, "Hell, I'm crazy, what's the difference? Do you think I don't know absolutely every truth about myself, even how I look to you?"

"That's not possible."

"Do you suppose your mind is so impregnable? I can see everything—everything. And if I say I'm crazy, do you think I don't prefer this to something else? Huh?"

His fingers had become hard against her arm. She seized his hand and brought it to her lips. "Don't hurt me," she said.

"Don't hurt you! You come to watch me suffer and you're afraid of getting hurt yourself!"

"Do you think I come to watch you suffer?"

"Why else? Why? You could let me lie in bed and rot, what the hell does it matter? It occurs to me now that you won't let me alone until I'm dead, dead and stinking. Then you'll go back home and wash your hands."

"Please don't talk like that—"

He jerked his hand away. "And I didn't do any writing either. A lot of crap; I was lying. I did nothing."

"I know."

"I wish I could tell you what I thought when I heard you coming up the stairs. I feel I'm learning a new language, that this is a prison and I have to talk in code. You have a key that lets you in and out and you're a spy they've sent in here, and I have to talk to you, I can't help it, I lie here and wait for you and think, What if she doesn't come! What if she's left me! And then when you leave I feel worse, I wish you had never come. And you're a spy, you want to get that secret from me and show it to them, paint it up, transfigure it so that it becomes symmetrical and quaint—ending up in five colors, reproduced in that news magazine! Do you think I don't know you? Everything about you? You might be a character in something I've written, that's how well I know you! A woman, a devouring woman—"

"If that's so, then you wanted me that way. If you created me, you created me that way."

He smiled bitterly at this. "To hell with that psychological crap! And you want me to go for a walk—as if I can go for a walk! As if I can walk down those stairs! And so sympathetic with suffering—other people's. So appreciative of suffering. So sweet, solicitous. And all you ask in return is that I love you. And if I did tell you what I dreamt about, could you understand it? No. Could you feel it? Only as a picture. You'd get a vision, a sight, the picture of what happened, but you wouldn't know what I know. You weren't there. People like you never happen to be there."

"Tell me about it."

"And then what?"

"What do you mean?"

"What will you do for me?"

She half-closed her eyes as if seriously thinking. Then she said, "What I've always done for you."

He turned away with a grunt. His hatred for her made him shudder; she watched with fascination the convulsive jerking of his hand. "So I'm your jailer now," she whispered.

"I didn't say that."

"I'm a spy, then. That your jailers have sent."

"Hell, I know I'm crazy, that was just talk. No one cares about me except you. Forget it." He shivered. She was frightened, physically frightened, by the shift in his expression: His anger had been overwhelmed by a look of passive terror. "But what's wrong with you?" she wanted to cry. "What is it? What do you know that I don't know? Why are you dying?" But she said nothing. She held his hand and pressed it against her throat and would not let him pull it away.

She believed she heard something, it must have been him telling her to come in. So she opened the door. He lay in bed, evidently just waking, his eyes narrowed and vague as if out of focus. A stale, sharp odor was in the room. Immediately she began to breathe shallowly, as if in the presence of danger. "Did I wake you?" she said. She had brought him a bag of groceries and some magazines; she put the things down slowly on the cluttered table. A coffee cup was nearly overturned—still half filled with coffee, with a cigarette butt floating in it. "Are you all right?" He raised himself on his elbow. The sheet fell away to show his pale, bluish chest. He stared at her and began to smile. She faced his smile with fear, for it seemed to her ghastly, its very eagerness terrifying. "You didn't forget I was coming, did you?" she said coquettishly. But the lilt of the remark was ludicrous in this musty room and she felt her cheeks burn with shame. He did not notice. "Come in, sit down," he said. "I guess I was asleep." She came to him and stood nervously by the bed as he sat up and tried to smooth his hair down. She wanted to pull the sheet up about him, to protect him. "God, what a taste in my mouth," he said, making a face. "Could you get me some water or something?"

She brought him a glass of water. He drank it eagerly. The side of his face was crisscrossed with reddened wrinkles from the pillow. She took the glass from him when he finished. "I was lying here thinking about you, I wasn't asleep," he said, touching her arm. "I was thinking how I loved you. And if you didn't come this time . . . If I thought it was the wrong day or something. . . ." Then in mid-sentence his tone changed; she could see him swallow and then struggle not to show something—

anxiety, malice. He tugged at her wrist. "Come down here with me. Just this one time, will you? It isn't too hot in here. I can brush this off the bed—crumbs or something, what is it?" He began brushing something off angrily. "I've been thinking about you ever since you left last time. And a whole week in between—that goddamn exhibit you had to go to— Of course you had to go to it. Come on here."

She laughed nervously and tried to pull away. "I brought you some magazines—"

"Look, goddamn you, you—" But he stopped. He grated his teeth. "You don't know how I've been waiting for you," he said softly.

"Please, let go. What's wrong with you?"

"With me?"

"I come in here and see how you've let yourself go—see what you've done to yourself— There's nothing wrong with you, don't you know that? Nothing! You're weak, whining, and now you want—"

"What?"

She turned away from him. She was overcome with disgust and shame and could not look at him. "How can you think I'm like that, that I would want to make love with a dying man!" she said.

And, as soon as this was said, the tension between them dissolved; even the foul air of the room seemed to weaken. She looked over her shoulder at him. He was sitting up, the wrinkled sheet fallen down to his stomach, his body hunched and skeletal and contemplative. So that is what he looks like, she thought sharply, and could not remember if he had really changed or if she had never seen him before. After a moment he glanced up and smiled shakily. "Magazines, huh?" he said. "What kind?"

She brought them to him. She sat on the edge of the bed. He looked at the glossy covers, smiling, and leafed through the pages perfunctorily. "And how have you been this week?" she said. She saw that his vague familiar smile did not change, that he had not heard, and she had to repeat her question.

RAYMOND CARVER

(1939–1988)

R aymond Carver was born in Clatskanie, Oregon, and educated at Humboldt State College and the University of Iowa. He married after finishing high school and worked as a janitor, farm worker, and delivery boy to support his family. He published his first story while attending Humboldt State College, from which he graduated in 1963. His work eventually appeared in The New Yorker, Esquire, Antaeus, The Atlantic Monthly, Triquarterly, The Paris Review, Harper's, New England Review, Western Humanities Review, and other well-known journals. He taught writing at the University of California (Santa Cruz and Berkeley), the University of Iowa, the University of Texas, and Syracuse University. His collections of short stories include Put Yourself in My Shoes (1974), Will You Please Be Quiet, Please? (1976), What We Talk About When We Talk About Love (1981), and Cathedral (1984). He also published a number of volumes of poetry and won numerous fellowships that enabled him to pursue his career. He claimed that the work involved in bringing up two children made him choose the short-story form because it was impossible for him to find the time necessary for writing novels. Like John Updike, he writes about the "middle" life, the trials and delights of ordinary people. He deplored the imitative and superficial nature of a great deal of experimental writing, and insisted that it was possible "to write about commonplace things and objects using commonplace but precise language, and to endow those things—a chair, a window curtain, a fork, a stove, a woman's earring—with immense, even startling power. It is possible to write a line of seemingly innocuous dialogue and have it send a chill along the reader's spine." In his best fiction, Carver follows these basic aesthetic principles to illuminate the strangeness, the violence, the tenderness, the poignancy that characterize human life.

Menudo

I can't sleep, but when I'm sure my wife Vicky is asleep, I get up and look through our bedroom window, across the street, at Oliver and Amanda's house. Oliver has been gone for three days, but his wife Amanda is awake. She can't sleep either. It's four in the morning, and there's not a sound outside—no wind, no cars, no moon even—just Oliver and Amanda's place with the lights on, leaves heaped up under the front windows.

A couple of days ago, when I couldn't sit still, I raked our yard—
Vicky's and mine. I gathered all the leaves into bags, tied off the tops,
and put the bags alongside the curb. I had an urge then to cross the street
and rake over there, but I didn't follow through. It's my fault things are
the way they are across the street.

I've only slept a few hours since Oliver left. Vicky saw me moping
around the house, looking anxious, and decided to put two and two
together. She's on her side of the bed now, scrunched on to about ten
inches of mattress. She got into bed and tried to position herself so she
wouldn't accidentally roll into me while she slept. She hasn't moved since
she lay down, sobbed, and then dropped into sleep. She's exhausted. I'm
exhausted too.

I've taken nearly all of Vicky's pills, but I still can't sleep. I'm keyed
up. But maybe if I keep looking I'll catch a glimpse of Amanda moving
around inside her house, or else find her peering from behind a curtain,
trying to see what she can see over here.

What if I do see her? So what? What then?

Vicky says I'm crazy. She said worse things too last night. But who
could blame her? I told her—I had to—but I didn't tell her it was Amanda.
When Amanda's name came up, I insisted it wasn't her. Vicky suspects,
but I wouldn't name names. I wouldn't say who, even though she kept
pressing and then hit me a few times in the head.

"What's it matter *who?*" I said. "You've never met the woman," I lied.
"You don't know her." That's when she started hitting me.

I feel *wired*. That's what my painter friend Alfredo used to call it when
he talked about friends of his coming down off something. *Wired*. I'm
wired.

This thing is nuts. I know it is, but I can't stop thinking about Amanda.
Things are so bad just now I even find myself thinking about my first
wife, Molly. I loved Molly, I thought, more than my own life.

I keep picturing Amanda in her pink nightgown, the one I like on
her so much, along with her pink slippers. And I feel certain she's in the
big leather chair right now, under the brass reading lamp. She's smoking
cigarettes, one after the other. There are two ashtrays close at hand, and
they're both full. To the left of her chair, next to the lamp, there's an end
table stacked with magazines—the usual magazines that nice people read.
We're nice people, all of us, to a point. Right this minute, Amanda is, I
imagine, paging through a magazine, stopping every so often to look at
an illustration or a cartoon.

Two days ago, in the afternoon, Amanda said to me, "I can't read
books any more. Who has the time?" It was the day after Oliver had left,
and we were in this little café in the industrial part of the city. "Who can
concentrate anymore?" she said, stirring her coffee. "Who reads? Do you
read?" (I shook my head.) "Somebody must read, I guess. You see all these

books around in store windows, and there are those clubs. Somebody's reading," she said. "Who? I don't know anybody who reads."

That's what she said, apropos of nothing—that is, we weren't talking about books, we were talking about our *lives*. Books had nothing to do with it.

"What did Oliver say when you told him?"

Then it struck me that what we were saying—the tense, watchful expressions we wore—belonged to the people on afternoon TV programs that I'd never done more than switch on and then off.

Amanda looked down and shook her head, as if she couldn't bear to remember.

"You didn't admit who it was you were involved with, did you?"

She shook her head again.

"You're sure of that?" I waited until she looked up from her coffee.

"I didn't mention any names, if that's what you mean."

"Did he say where he was going, or how long he'd be away?" I said, wishing I didn't have to hear myself. This was my neighbor I was talking about. Oliver Porter. A man I'd helped drive out of his home.

"He didn't say where. A hotel. He said I should make my arrangements and be gone—*be gone*, he said. It was like biblical the way he said it—out of his house, out of his *life*, in a week's time. I guess he's coming back then. So we have to decide something real important, real soon, honey. You and I have to make up our minds pretty damn quick."

It was her turn to look at me now, and I know she was looking for a sign of life-long commitment. "A week," I said. I looked at my coffee, which had gotten cold. A lot had happened in a little while, and we were trying to take it in. I don't know what long-term things, if any, we'd thought about those months as we moved from flirtation to love, and then afternoon assignations. In any case, we were in a serious fix now. Very serious. We'd never expected—not in a hundred years—to be hiding out in a café, in the middle of the afternoon, trying to decide matters like this.

I raised my eyes, and Amanda began stirring her coffee. She kept stirring it. I touched her hand, and the spoon dropped out of her fingers. She picked it up and began stirring again. We could have been anybody drinking coffee at a table under fluorescent lights in a run-down café. Anybody, just about. I took Amanda's hand and held it, and it seemed to make a difference.

Vicky's still sleeping on her side when I go downstairs. I plan to heat some milk and drink that. I used to drink whiskey when I couldn't sleep, but I gave it up. Now it's strictly hot milk. In the whiskey days I'd wake up with this tremendous thirst in the middle of the night. But, back then, I was always looking ahead: I kept a bottle of water in the fridge, for instance. I'd be dehydrated, sweating from head to toe when I woke, but I'd wander out to the kitchen and could count on finding that bottle of cold water in the fridge. I'd drink it, all of it, down the hatch, an entire quart of water. Once in a while I'd use a glass, but not often. Suddenly I'd be drunk all over again and weaving around the kitchen. I can't begin to account for it—sober one minute, drunk the next.

The drinking was part of my destiny—according to Molly, anyway. She put a lot of stock in destiny.

I feel wild from lack of sleep. I'd give anything, just about, to be able to go to sleep, and sleep the sleep of an honest man.

Why do we have to sleep anyway? And why do we tend to sleep less during some crises and more during others? For instance, that time my dad had his stroke. He woke up after a coma—seven days and nights in a hospital bed—and calmly said "Hello" to the people in his room. Then his eyes picked me out. "Hello, son," he said. Five minutes later, he died. Just like that—he died. But, during that whole crisis, I never took my clothes off and didn't go to bed. I may have catnapped in a waiting-room chair from time to time, but I never went to bed and *slept*.

And then a year or so ago I found out Vicky was seeing somebody else. Instead of confronting *her*, I went to bed when I heard about it, and stayed there. I didn't get up for days, a week maybe—I don't know. I mean, I got up to go to the bathroom, or else to the kitchen to make a sandwich. I even went out to the living room in my pajamas, in the afternoon, and tried to read the papers. But I'd fall asleep sitting up. Then I'd stir, open my eyes and go back to bed and sleep some more. I couldn't get enough sleep.

It passed. We weathered it. Vicky quit her boyfriend, or he quit her, I never found out. I just know she went away from me for a while, and then she came back. But I have the feeling we're not going to weather this business. This thing is different. Oliver has given Amanda that ultimatum.

Still, isn't it possible that Oliver himself is awake at this moment and writing a letter to Amanda, urging reconciliation? Even now he might be scribbling away, trying to persuade her that what she's doing to him and their daughter Beth is foolish, disastrous, and finally a tragic thing for the three of them.

No, that's insane. I know Oliver. He's relentless, unforgiving. He could slam a croquet ball into the next block—and has. He isn't going to write any such letter. He gave her an ultimatum, right?—and that's that. A week. Four days now. Or is it three? Oliver may be awake, but if he is, he's sitting in a chair in his hotel room with a glass of iced vodka in his hand, his feet on the bed, TV turned on low. He's dressed, except for his shoes. He's not wearing shoes—that's the only concession he makes. That and the fact he's loosened his tie.

Oliver is relentless.

I heat the milk, spoon the skin from the surface and pour it up. Then I turn off the kitchen light and take the cup into the living room and sit on the sofa, where I can look across the street at the lighted windows. But I can hardly sit still. I keep fidgeting, crossing one leg and then the other. I feel like I could throw off sparks, or break a window—maybe rearrange all the furniture.

The things that go through your mind when you can't sleep! Earlier, thinking about Molly, for a moment I couldn't even remember what she *looked* like, for Christ's sake, yet we were together for years, more or less continuously, since we were kids. Molly, who said she'd love me forever. The only thing left was the memory of her sitting and weeping at the kitchen table, her shoulders bent forward, and her hands covering her face. *Forever*, she said. But it hadn't worked out that way. Finally, she said, it didn't matter, it was of no real concern to her, if she and I lived together the rest of our lives or not. Our love existed on a "higher plane." That's what she said to Vicky over the phone that time, after Vicky and I had set up housekeeping together. Molly called, got hold of Vicky, and said, "You have your relationship with him, but I'll always have mine. His destiny and mine are linked."

My first wife, Molly, she talked like that. "Our destinies are linked." She didn't talk like that in the beginning. It was only later, after so much had happened, that she started using words like "cosmic" and "empowerment" and so forth. But our destinies are *not* linked—not now, anyway, if they ever were. I don't even know where she is now, not for certain.

I think I could put my finger on the exact time, the real turning point, when it came undone for Molly. It was after I started seeing Vicky, and Molly found out. They called me up one day from the high school where Molly taught and said, "Please. Your wife is doing handsprings in front of the school. You'd better get down here." It was after I took her home that I began hearing about "higher power" and "going with the flow"— stuff of that sort. Our destiny had been "revised." And if I'd been hesitating before, well, I left her then as fast as I could—this woman I'd known all my life, the one who'd been my best friend for years, my intimate, my confidante. I bailed out on her. For one thing, I was scared. *Scared.*

This girl I'd started out with in life, this sweet thing, this gentle soul, she wound up going to fortune-tellers, palm readers, *crystal ball gazers*, looking for answers, trying to figure out what she should do with her life. She quit her job, drew out her teacher's retirement money, and thereafter never made a decision without consulting the *I Ching*. She began wearing strange clothes—clothes with permanent wrinkles and a lot of burgundy and orange. She even got involved with a group that sat around, I'm not kidding, trying to levitate.

When Molly and I were growing up together, she was a part of me and, sure, I was a part of her, too. We loved each other. It *was* our destiny. I believed in it then myself. But now I don't know what to believe in. I'm not complaining, simply stating a fact. I'm down to nothing. And I have to go on like this. No destiny. Just the next thing meaning whatever you think it does. Compulsion and error, just like everybody else.

Amanda? I'd like to believe in her, bless her heart. But she was looking for somebody when she met me. That's the way with people when they get restless: they start up something, knowing that's going to change things for good.

I'd like to go out in the front yard and shout something. "None of this is worth it!" That's what I'd like people to hear.

"Destiny," Molly said. For all I know she's still talking about it.

All the lights are off over there now, except for that light in the kitchen. I could try calling Amanda on the phone. I could do that and see how far it gets me! What if Vicky heard me dialing or talking on the phone and came downstairs? What if she lifted the receiver upstairs and listened? Besides, there's always the chance Beth might pick up the phone. I don't want to talk to any kids this morning. I don't want to talk to anybody. Actually, I'd talk to Molly, if I could, but I can't any longer—she's some-body else now. She isn't *Molly* anymore. But—what can I say?—I'm somebody else, too.

I wish I could be like everybody else in this neighborhood—your basic, normal, unaccomplished person—and go up to my bedroom, and lie down, and sleep. It's going to be a big day today, and I'd like to be ready for it. I wish I could sleep and wake up and find everything in my life different. Not necessarily just the big things, like this thing with Amanda or the past with Molly. But things clearly within my power.

Take the situation with my mother: I used to send money every month. But then I started sending her the same amount in twice-yearly sums. I gave her money on her birthday, and I gave her money at Christ-mas. I thought: I won't have to worry about forgetting her birthday, and I won't have to worry about sending her a Christmas present. I won't have to worry, period. It went like clockwork for a long time.

Then last year she asked me—it was in between money times, it was in March, or maybe April—for a radio. A radio, she said, would make a difference to her.

What she wanted was a little clock radio. She could put it in her kitchen and have it out there to listen to while she was fixing something to eat in the evening. And she'd have the clock to look at too, so she'd know when something was supposed to come out of the oven, or how long it was until one of her programs started.

A little clock radio.

She hinted around at first. She said, "I'd sure like to have a radio. But

I can't afford one. I guess I'll have to wait for my birthday. That little radio I had, it fell and broke. I miss a radio." *I miss a radio.* That's what she said when we talked on the phone, or else she'd bring it up when she'd write.

Finally—what'd I say? I said to her over the phone that I couldn't afford any radios. I said it in a letter too, so she'd be sure and understand. *I can't afford any radios*, is what I wrote. I can't do anymore, I said, than I'm doing. Those were my very words.

But it wasn't true! I could have done more. I just said I couldn't. I could have afforded to buy a radio for her. What would it have cost me? Thirty-five dollars? Forty dollars or less, including tax. I could have sent her a radio through the mail. I could have had somebody in the store do it, if I didn't want to go to the trouble myself. Or else I could have sent her a forty-dollar check along with a note saying, *This money is for your radio, mother*.

I could have handled it in any case. Forty dollars—are you kidding? But I didn't. I wouldn't part with it. It seemed there was a principle involved. That's what I told myself anyway—there's a *principle* involved here.

Ha.

Then what happened? She died. She *died*. She was walking home from the grocery store, back to her apartment, carrying her sack of groceries, and she fell into somebody's bushes and died.

I took a flight out there to make the arrangements. She was still at the coroner's, and they had her purse and her groceries behind the desk in the office. I didn't bother to look in the purse they handed me. But what she had from the grocery store was a jar of Metamucil, two grapefruits, a carton of cottage cheese, a quart of buttermilk, some potatoes and onions, and a package of ground meat that was beginning to change color.

Boy! I cried when I saw those things. I couldn't stop. I didn't think I'd ever quit crying. The woman who worked at the desk was embarrassed and brought me a glass of water. They gave me a bag for my mother's groceries and another bag for her personal effects—her purse and her dentures. Later, I put the dentures in my coat pocket and drove them down in a rental car and gave them to somebody at the funeral home.

The light in Amanda's kitchen is still on. It's a bright light that spills out on to all those leaves. Maybe she's like I am, and she's scared. Maybe she left that light burning as a night-light. Or maybe she's still awake and is at the kitchen table, under the light, writing me a letter. Amanda is writing me a letter, and somehow she'll get it into my hands later on when the real day starts.

Come to think of it, I've never had a letter from her since we've known each other. All the time we've been involved—six months, eight months—and I've never once seen a scrap of her handwriting. I don't even know if she's *literate* that way.

I think she is. Sure, she is. She talks about books, doesn't she? It doesn't matter of course. Well, a little, I suppose. I love her in any case, right?

But I've never written anything to her, either. We always talked on the phone or else face to face.

Molly, she was the letter writer. She used to write me even after we weren't living together. Vicky would bring her letters in from the box and leave them on the kitchen table without a word. Finally the letters dwindled away, became more and more infrequent and bizarre. When she did write, the letters gave me a chill. They were full of talk about "auras" and "signs." Occasionally she reported a voice that was telling her something she ought to do or some place she should go. And once she told me that no matter what happened, we were still "on the same frequency." She always knew exactly what I felt, she said. She "beamed in on me," she said, from time to time. Reading those letters of hers, the hair on the back of my neck would tingle. She also had a new word for destiny: *Karma.* "I'm following out my karma," she wrote. "Your karma has taken a bad turn."

I'd like to go to sleep, but what's the point? People will be getting up soon. Vicky's alarm will go off before much longer. I wish I could go upstairs and get back in bed with my wife, tell her I'm sorry, there's been a mistake, let's forget all this—then go to sleep and wake up with her in my arms. But I've forfeited that right. I'm outside all that now, and I can't get back inside! But say I did that. Say I went upstairs and slid into bed with Vicky as I'd like to do. She might wake up and say, *You bastard. Don't you dare touch me, son of a bitch.*

What's she talking about, anyway? I wouldn't touch her. Not in that way, I wouldn't.

After I left Molly, after I'd pulled out on her, about two months after, then Molly really did it. She had her real collapse then, the one that'd been coming on. Her sister saw to it that she got the care she needed. What am I saying? *They put her away.* They had to, they said. They put my wife away. By then I was living with Vicky, and trying not to drink whiskey. I couldn't do anything for Molly. I mean, she was there, I was here, and I couldn't have gotten her out of that place if I'd wanted to. But the fact is, I didn't want to. She was in there, they said, because she *needed* to be in there. Nobody said anything about destiny. Things had gone beyond that.

And I didn't even go visit her—not once! At the time, I didn't think I could stand seeing her in there. But, Christ, what was I? A fair-weather friend? We'd been through plenty. But what on earth would I have said to her? *I'm sorry about all this, honey.* I could have said that, I guess. I intended to write, but I didn't. Not a word. Anyway, when you get right down to it, what could I have said in a letter? *How are they treating you, baby? I'm sorry you're where you are, but don't give up. Remember all the good times? Remember when we were happy together? Hey, I'm sorry they've done this to you. I'm sorry it turned out this way. I'm sorry everything is just garbage now.* I'm sorry, Molly.

I didn't write. I think I was trying to forget about her, to pretend she didn't exist. Molly who?

I left my wife and took somebody else's: Vicky. Now I think maybe I've lost Vicky, too. But Vicky won't be going away to any summer camp for the mentally disabled. She's a hard case. She left her former husband, Joe Kraft, and didn't bat an eye; I don't think she ever lost a night's sleep over it.

Vicky Kraft-Hughes. Amanda Porter. This is where my destiny has brought me? To this street in this neighborhood, messing up the lives of these women?

Amanda's kitchen light went off when I wasn't looking. The room that was there is gone now, like the others. Only the porch light is still burning. Amanda must have forgotten it, I guess. Hey, Amanda.

Once, when Molly was away in that place and I wasn't in my right mind—let's face it, I was crazy too—one night I was at my friend Alfredo's house, a bunch of us drinking and listening to records. I didn't care any longer what happened to me. Everything, I thought, that could happen had happened. I felt unbalanced. I felt lost. Anyway, there I was at Alfredo's. His paintings of tropical birds and animals hung on every wall in his house, and there were paintings standing around in the rooms, leaning against things—table-legs, say, or his brick-and-board bookcase, as well as being stacked on his back porch. The kitchen served as his studio, and I was sitting at the kitchen table with a drink in front of me. An easel stood off to one side in front of the window that overlooked the alley, and there were crumpled tubes of paint, a palette, and some brushes lying at one end of the table. Alfredo was making himself a drink at the counter a few feet away. I loved the shabby economy of that little room. The stereo music that came from the living room was turned up, filling the house with so much sound the kitchen windows rattled in their frames. Suddenly I began to shake. First my hands began to shake, and then my arms and shoulders, too. My teeth started to chatter. I couldn't hold the glass.

"What's going on, man?" Alfredo said, when he turned and saw the state I was in. "Hey, what is it? What's going on with you?"

I couldn't tell him. What could I say? I thought I was having some kind of an attack. I managed to raise my shoulders and let them drop.

Then Alfredo came over, took a chair and sat down beside me at the kitchen table. He put his big painter's hand on my shoulder. I went on shaking. He could feel me shaking.

"What's wrong with you, man? I'm real sorry about everything, man. I know it's real hard right now." Then he said he was going to fix *menudo* for me. He said it would be good for what ailed me. "Help your nerves, man," he said. "Calm you right down." He had all the ingredients for *menudo*, he said, and he'd been wanting to make some anyway.

"You listen to me. Listen to what I say, man. I'm your family now," Alfredo said.

It was two in the morning, we were drunk, there were these other drunk people in the house and the stereo was going full blast. But Alfredo went to his fridge and opened it and took some stuff out. He closed the fridge door and looked in his freezer compartment. He found something in a package. Then he looked around in his cupboards. He took a big pan from the cabinet under the sink, and he was ready.

Tripe. He started with tripe and about a gallon of water. Then he chopped onions and added them to the water, which had started to boil. He put *chorizo* sausage in the pot. After that, he dropped peppercorns into the boiling water and sprinkled in some chili powder. Then came the olive oil. He opened a big can of tomato sauce and poured that in. He added cloves of garlic, some slices of white bread, salt, and lemon juice. He opened another can—it was hominy—and poured that in the pot, too. He put it all in, and then he turned the heat down and put a lid on the pot.

I watched him. I sat there shaking while Alfredo stood at the stove making *menudo*, talking—I didn't have any idea what he was saying— and, from time to time, he'd shake his head, or else start whistling to himself. Now and then people drifted into the kitchen for beer. But all the while Alfredo went on very seriously looking after his *menudo*. He could have been home, in Morelia, making *menudo* for his family on New Year's day.

People hung around in the kitchen for a while, joking, but Alfredo didn't joke back when they kidded him about cooking *menudo* in the middle of the night. Pretty soon they left us alone. Finally, while Alfredo stood at the stove with a spoon in his hand, watching me, I got up slowly from the table. I walked out of the kitchen into the bathroom, and then opened another door off the bathroom to the spare room—where I lay down on the bed and fell asleep. When I woke it was mid-afternoon. The *menudo* was gone. The pot was in the sink, soaking. Those other people must have eaten it! They must have eaten it and grown calm. Everyone was gone, and the house was quiet.

I never saw Alfredo more than once or twice afterward. After that night, our lives took us in separate directions. And those other people who were there—who knows where they went? I'll probably die without ever tasting *menudo*. But who can say?

Is this what it all comes down to then? A middle-aged man involved with his neighbor's wife, linked to an angry ultimatum? What kind of destiny is that? A week, Oliver said. Three or four days now.

A car passes outside with its lights on. The sky is turning gray, and I hear some birds starting up. I decide I can't wait any longer. I can't just sit here, doing nothing—that's all there is to it. I can't keep waiting. I've waited and waited and where's it gotten me? Vicky's alarm will go off soon, Beth will get up and dress for school, Amanda will wake up, too. The entire neighborhood.

On the back porch I find some old jeans and a sweatshirt, and I change out of my pajamas. Then I put on my white canvas shoes—"wino" shoes, Alfredo would have called them. Alfredo, where are you?

I go outside to the garage and find the rake and some lawn bags. By the time I get around to the front of the house with the rake, ready to begin, I feel I don't have a choice in the matter any longer. It's light out—light enough at any rate for what I have to do. And then, without thinking about it any more, I start to rake. I rake our yard, every inch of it. It's important it be done right, too. I set the rake right down into the turf and pull hard. It must feel to the grass like it does whenever someone gives your hair a hard jerk. Now and then a car passes in the street and slows, but I don't look up from my work. I know what the people in the cars must be thinking, but they're dead wrong—they don't know the half of it. How could they? I'm happy, raking.

I finish our yard and put the bag out next to the curb. Then I begin next door on the Baxters' yard. In a few minutes Mrs. Baxter comes out on her porch, wearing her bathrobe. I don't acknowledge her. I'm not embarrassed, and I don't want to appear unfriendly. I just want to keep on with what I'm doing.

She doesn't say anything for a while, and then she says, "Good morning, Mr. Hughes. How are you this morning?"

I stop what I'm doing and run my arm across my forehead. "I'll be through in a little while," I say. "I hope you don't mind."

"We don't mind," Mrs. Baxter says. "Go right ahead, I guess." I see Mr. Baxter standing in the doorway behind her. He's already dressed for work in his slacks and sports coat and tie. But he doesn't venture on to the porch. Then Mrs. Baxter turns and looks at Mr. Baxter, who shrugs.

It's okay, I've finished here anyway. There are other yards, more important yards for that matter. I kneel, and, taking a grip low down on the rake handle, I pull the last of the leaves into my bag and tie off the top. Then, I can't help it, I just stay there, kneeling on the grass with the rake in my hand. When I look up, I see the Baxters come down the porch steps together and move slowly toward me through the wet, sweet-smelling grass. They stop a few feet away and look at me closely.

"There now," I hear Mrs. Baxter say. She's still in her robe and slippers. It's nippy out; she holds her robe at the throat. "You did a real fine job for us, yes, you did."

I don't say anything. I don't even say, "You're welcome."

They stand in front of me a while longer, and none of us says anything more. It's as if we've come to an agreement on something. In a minute, they turn around and go back to their house. High over my head, in the branches of the old maple—the place where these leaves come from—birds call out to each other. At least I think they're calling to each other.

Suddenly a car door slams. Mr. Baxter is in his car in the drive with the window rolled down. Mrs. Baxter says something to him from the front porch which causes Mr. Baxter to nod slowly and turn his head in my direction. He sees me kneeling there with the rake, and a look crosses his face. He frowns. In his better moments, Mr. Baxter is a decent, ordinary guy—a guy you wouldn't mistake for anyone special. But he *is* special. In my book, he is. For one thing he has a full night's sleep behind him, and he's just embraced his wife before leaving for work. But even before he goes, he's already expected home a set number of hours later. True, in the grander scheme of things, his return will be an event of small moment—but an event nonetheless.

Baxter starts his car and races the engine. Then he backs effortlessly out of the drive, brakes, and changes gears. As he passes on the street, he slows and looks briefly in my direction. He lifts his hand off the steering wheel. It could be a salute or a sign of dismissal. It's a sign, in any case. And then he looks away toward the city. I get up and raise my hand, too—not a wave, exactly, but close to it. Some other cars drive past. One of the drivers must think he knows me because he gives his horn a friendly little tap. I look both ways and then cross the street.

MARGARET ATWOOD

(b. 1939)

*M*argaret Atwood was born in Ottawa and educated at the University of Toronto (B.A. 1961) and Harvard University (M.A. 1962). As poet, novelist, short-story writer, essayist, and activist in such organizations as PEN International, she has gained an international reputation of high standing, earning a worldwide readership equalled by few Canadian writers. And she has accomplished this without sacrificing literary integrity to win popular acclaim. Atwood established her reputation as a poet in the mid-1960s with The Circle Game (1966), which won the Governor General's Award. At this time she was also instrumental in promoting the new literary publishing houses, such as House of Anansi, that were part of the nationalist resurgence of Canadian culture in that decade. Subsequently she made a mark in academic critical circles with her thematic guide to the study of Canadian literature, Survival (1970). Other books of poetry include The Journals of Susanna Moodie (1970), a "documentary poem" that has become a mainstay in Canadian literature courses, Power Politics (1973), and recently her Selected Poems II (1988). Musing on Atwood's place in the Canadian psyche, one reviewer of her poetry wrote, "Atwood has arrived: she is the mirror which, tilted at various angles, shows us all the different faces of ourselves, including our doubts about the absolute value of things Canadian. She enables us to be self-effacing at the expense of someone else." Although it often seems that Atwood came to fiction later in her career, she had already demonstrated her considerable abilities in the genre in the late 1960s with the comic novel The Edible Woman (1969). Her other novels include Surfacing (1972), Lady Oracle (1976), The Handmaid's Tale (1985), and Cat's Eye (1988). In total, she has published some ten books of poetry, seven novels, two books of criticism and essays, and three books of short stories—in all of them displaying an eye for the telling and often estranging detail, an intellect that can't help but express itself wittily, and the dedicated craftsman's way with a polished sentence. She is also the editor of The New Oxford Book of Canadian Verse in English (1982) and Canadian Short Stories (1985). Her own short stories have been collected in Dancing Girls (1977), Murder in the Dark (1983), and Bluebeard's Egg (1983). Although she is better known as a novelist and poet, it could be argued that Atwood's gifts are shown to best advantage in the short story. There, her poetic skills—concision, aphoristic wit, and a sharp eye for the powerful image—combine with her novelistic—compelling narrative and laconic dialogue—to create stories of remarkable, often startling impact.

The Grave of the Famous Poet

T here are a couple of false alarms before we actually get there, towns
we pass through that might be it but aren't, uninformative stores
and houses edging the road, no signs. Even when we've arrived we aren't
sure; we peer out, looking for a name, an advertisement. The bus pauses.

"This has to be it," I say. I have the map.

"Better ask the driver," he says, not believing me.

"Have I ever been wrong?" I say, but I ask the driver anyway. I'm
right again and we get off.

We're in a constricted street of grey flat-fronted houses, their white
lace curtains pulled closed, walls rising cliff-straight and lawnless from
the narrow sidewalk. There are no other people; at least it isn't a tourist
trap. I have to eat, we've been travelling all morning, but he wants to find
a hotel first, he always needs a home base. Right in front of us there's a
building labelled HOTEL. We hesitate outside it, patting down our hair,
trying to look acceptable. When he finally grits up the steps with our
suitcase the doors are locked. Maybe it's a pub.

Hoping there may be a place further along, we walk down the hill,
following the long stone wall, crossing the road when the sidewalk disap-
pears at the corners. Cars pass us, driving fast as though on their way to
somewhere else.

At the bottom of the hill near the beach there's a smattering of shops
and a scarred, listing inn. Radio music and hilarious voices from inside.

"It seems local," I say, pleased.

"What does 'Inn' mean here?" he asks, but I don't know. He goes in
to see; then he comes out, dispirited. I'm too tired to think up solutions;
I'm scarcely noticing the castle on the hill behind us, the sea.

"No wonder he drank," he says.

"I'll ask," I say, aggrieved: it was his idea, he should do the finding.
I try the general store. It's full of people, women mostly, with scarves on
their heads and shopping baskets. They say there is no hotel; one woman
says her mother has some rooms free though, and she gives me directions
while the others gaze pityingly, I'm so obviously a tourist.

The house, when we find it, is eighteenth century and enormous, a
summer residence when the town was fashionable. It offers Bed and
Breakfast on a modest sign. We're glad to have something spelled out for
us. The door is open, we go into the hall, and the woman emerges from
the parlour as though startled; she has a forties bobby-soxer hairdo with
curious frontal lobes, only it's grey. She's friendly to us, almost sprightly,
and yes, she has a room for us. I ask, in a lowered voice, if she can tell us
where the grave is.

"You can almost see it right from the window," she says, smiling—she knew we would ask that—and offers to lend us a book with a map in it of the points of interest, his house and all. She gets the book, scampers up the wide maroon-carpeted staircase to show us our room. It's vast, chill, high-ceilinged, with floral wallpaper and white-painted woodwork; instead of curtains the windows have inside shutters. There are three beds and numerous dressers and cupboards, crowded into the room as though in storage, a chunky bureau blocking the once-palatial fireplace. We say it will be fine.

"The grave is just up the hill, that way," she says, pointing through the window. We can see the tip of a church. "I'm sure you'll enjoy it."

I change into jeans and boots while he opens and closes the drawers on all the pieces of furniture, searching for ambushes or reading matter. He discovers nothing and we set out.

We ignore the church—he once said it was unremarkable—and head for the graveyard. It must rain a lot: ivy invades everything, and the graveyard is lush with uncut grass, succulent and light green. Feet have beaten animal-trail paths among the tombstones. The graves themselves are neatly tended, most of them have the grass clipped and fresh flowers in the tea-strainer-shaped flower holders. There are three old ladies in the graveyard now, sheaves of flowers in their arms, gladioli, chrysanthemums; they are moving among the graves, picking out the old flowers and distributing the new ones impartially, like stewardesses. They take us for granted, neither approaching nor avoiding us: we are strangers and as such part of this landscape.

We find the right grave easily enough; as the book says, it's the only one with a wooden cross instead of a stone. The cross has been recently painted and the grave is planted with a miniature formal-garden arrangement of moss roses and red begonias; the sweet alyssum intended for a border hasn't quite worked. I wonder who planned it, surely it wouldn't have been her. The old ladies have been here and have left a vase, yellowish glassware of the kind once found in cereal boxes, with orange dahlias and spikes of an unknown pink flower. We've brought nothing and have no ceremonies to perform; we muse for an acceptable length of time, then retreat to the scrollworked bench up the hill and sit in the sun, listening to the cows in the field across the road and the murmur of the ladies as they stoop and potter below us, their print dresses fluttering in the easy wind.

"It's not such a bad place," I say.

"But dull," he answers.

We have whatever it was we came for, the rest of the day is our own. After a while we leave the graveyard and stroll back down the main street, holding hands absentmindedly, looking in the windows of the few shops: an overpriced antique store, a handicrafts place with pottery and

Welsh weaving, a nondescript store that sells everything, including girlie joke magazines and copies of his books. In the window, half-hidden among souvenir cups, maps and faded pennants, is a framed photograph of his face, three-quarters profile. We buy a couple of ice-cream bars; they are ancient and soapy.

We reach the bottom of the winding hill and decide to walk along to his house, which we can see, an indistinct white square separated from us by half a mile of rough beach. It's his house all right, it was marked on the map. At first we have no trouble; there's a wide uneven pathway, broken asphalt, the remains or perhaps the beginning of a road. Above us at the edge of the steep, leaf-covered cliff, what is left of the castle totters down, slowly, one stone a year. For him, turrets are irresistible. He finds a scrabbly trail, a children's entrance up sheer mud.

He goes up sideways, crabwise, digging footholds with the sides of his boots. "Come on!" he shouts down. I'm hesitant but I follow. At the top he reaches his hand to me, but, perpendicular and with the earth beside me, afraid of losing my balance, I avoid it and scramble the last few feet, holding on to roots. In wet weather it would be impossible.

He's ahead, eager to explore. The tunnel through the undergrowth leads to a gap in the castle wall; I follow his sounds, rustlings, the soft thud of his feet. We're in the skeleton of a garden, the beds marked by brick borders now grass-infested, a few rose bushes still attempting to keep order in spite of the aphids, nothing else paying any attention. I bend over a rose, ivory hearted, browning at the edges; I feel like a usurper. He's already out of sight again, hidden by an archway.

I catch up to him in the main courtyard. Everything is crumbling, stairways, ramparts, battlements; so much has fallen it's hard for us to get our bearings, translate this rubbish back into its earlier clear plan.

"That must have been the fireplace," I say, "and that's the main gate. We must have come round from the back." For some reason we speak in whispers; he tosses a fragment of stone and I tell him to be careful.

We go up the remnants of a stairway into the keep. It's almost totally dark; the floors are earth-covered. People must come here though, there's an old sack, an unidentifiable piece of clothing. We don't stay long inside: I'm afraid of getting lost, though it's not likely, and I would rather be able to see him. I don't like the thought of finding his hand suddenly on me unannounced. Besides, I don't trust the castle; I expect it to thunder down on us at the first loud laugh or false step. But we make it outside safely.

We pass beneath the gateway, its Norman curve still intact. Outside is another, larger courtyard, enclosed by the wall we have seen from outside and broken through; it has trees, recent trees not more than a hundred years old, dark-foliaged as etchings. Someone must come here to cut the grass: it's short, hair-textured. He lies down on it and draws me down beside him and we rest on our elbows, surveying. From the front the castle is more complete; you can see how it could once have been lived in by real people.

He lies down, closing his eyes, raising his hand to shade them from the sun. He's pale and I realize he must be tired too. I've been thinking of my own lack of energy as something he has caused and must therefore be immune from.

"I'd like to have a castle like that," he says. When he admires something he wants to own it. For an instant I pretend that he does have the castle, he's always been here, he has a coffin hidden in the crypt, if I'm not careful I'll be trapped and have to stay with him forever. If I'd had more sleep last night I'd be able to frighten myself this way but as it is I give up and lean back on the grass beside him, looking up at the trees as their branches move in the wind, every leaf sharpened to a glass-clear edge by my exhaustion.

I turn my head to watch him. In the last few days he's become not more familiar to me as he should have but more alien. Close up, he's a strange terrain, pores and hairs; but he isn't nearer, he's further away, like the moon when you've finally landed on it. I move back from him so I can see him better, he misinterprets, thinking I'm trying to get up, and stretches himself over me to prevent me. He kisses me, teeth digging into my lower lip; when it hurts too much I pull away. We lie side by side, both suffering from unrequited love.

This is an interval, a truce; it can't last, we both know it, there have been too many differences, of opinion we called it but it was more than that, the things that mean safety for him mean danger for me. We've talked too much or not enough: for what we have to say to each other there's no language, we've tried them all. I think of the old science-fiction movies, the creature from another galaxy finally encountered after so many years of signals and ordeals only to be destroyed because he can't make himself understood. Actually it's less a truce than a rest, those silent black-and-white comedians hitting each other until they fall down, then getting up after a pause to begin again. We love each other, that's true whatever it means, but we aren't good at it; for some it's a talent, for others only an addiction. I wonder if they ever came here while he was still alive.

Right now though there's neither love nor anger, no resentment, it's a suspension, of fear even, like waiting for the dentist. But I don't want him to die. I feel nothing but I concentrate, somebody's version of God, I will him to exist, right now on the vacant lawn of this castle whose name we don't know in this foreign town we're in only because dead people are more real to him than living ones. Despite the mistakes I want everything to stay the way it is; I want to hold it.

He sits up: he's heard voices. Two little girls, baskets over their arms as though for a picnic or a game, have come into the grounds and are walking towards the castle. They stare at us curiously and decide we are harmless. "Let's play in the tower," one calls and they run and disappear among the walls. For them the castle is ordinary as a backyard.

He gets up, brushing off bits of grass. We haven't visited the house yet but we still have time. We find our break in the wall, our pathway, and slide back down to sealevel. The sun has moved, the green closes behind us.

The house is further than it looked from the village. The semi-road gives out and we pick our way along the stoney beach. The tide is out; the huge bay stretches as far as we can see, a solid mud-flat except for the thin silty river that cuts along beside us. The dry part narrows and vanishes, we are stranded below the tide line, clambering over slippery masses of purplish-brown rock or squelching through the mud, thick as clotted cream. All around us is an odd percolating sound: it's the mud, drying in the sun. There are gulls too, and wind bending the unhealthy-coloured rushes by the bank.

"How the hell did he get back and forth?" he says. "Think of doing this drunk on a dark night."

"There must be a road further up," I say.

We reach the house at last. Like everything else here it has a wall; this one is to keep out the waves at high tide. The house itself is on stilts, jammed up against the cliff, painted stone with a spindly-railed two-decker porch. It hasn't been lived in for many years: one window is broken and the railings are beginning to go. The yard is weed-grown, but maybe it always was. I sit on the wall, dangling my legs, while he pokes around, examining the windows, the outhouse (which is open), the shed once used perhaps for a boat. I don't want to see any of it. Graves are safely covered and the castle so derelict it has the status of a tree or a stone, but the house is too recent, it is still partly living. If I looked in the window there would be a table with dishes not yet cleared away, or a fresh cigarette or a coat just taken off. Or maybe a broken plate: they used to have fights, apparently. She never comes back and I can see why. He wouldn't leave her alone.

He's testing the railing on the second-storey porch; he's going to pull himself up by it.

"Don't do that," I say wearily.

"Why not?" he says. "I want to see the other side."

"Because you'll fall and I don't want to have to scrape you off the rocks."

"Don't be like that," he says.

How did she manage? I turn my head away, I don't want to watch. It will be such an effort, the police, I'll have to explain what I was doing here, why he was climbing and fell. He should be more considerate. But for once he thinks better of it.

There is another road, we discover it eventually, along the beach and up an asphalt walk beside a neat inhabited cottage. Did they see us coming, are they wondering who we are? The road above is paved, it has a railing and a sign with the poet's name on it, wired to the fence.

"I'd like to steal that," he says.

We pause to view the house from above. There's an old lady in a garden-party hat and gloves, explaining things to an elderly couple. "He always kept to himself, he did," she is saying. "No one here ever got to know him really." She goes on to detail the prices that have been offered for the house: America wanted to buy it and ship it across the ocean, she says, but the town wouldn't let them.

We start back towards our room. Halfway along we sit down on a bench to scrape the mud from our boots; it clings like melted marshmallow. I lean back; I'm not sure I can make it to the house, whatever reserves my body has been drawing on are almost gone. My hearing is blurred and it's hard to breathe.

He bends over to kiss me. I don't want him to, I'm not calm now, I'm irritated, my skin prickles, I think of case histories, devoted wives who turn kleptomaniac two days a month, the mother who threw her baby out into the snow, it was in *Reader's Digest*, she had a hormone disturbance, love is all chemical. I want it to be over, this long abrasive competition for the role of victim; it used to matter that it should finish right, with grace, but not now. One of us should just get up from the bench, shake hands and leave, I don't care who is last, it would sidestep the recriminations, the totalling up of scores, the reclaiming of possessions, your key, my book. But it won't be that way, we'll have to work through it, boring and foreordained though it is. What keeps me is a passive curiosity, it's like an Elizabethan tragedy or a horror movie, I know which ones will be killed but not how. I take his hand and stroke the back of it gently, the fine hairs rasping my fingertips like sandpaper.

We'd been planning to change and have dinner, it's almost six, but back in the room I have only strength enough to pull off my boots. Then with my clothes still on I crawl into the enormous, creaking bed, cold as porridge and hammock-saggy. I float for an instant in the open sky on the backs of my eyelids, free fall, until sleep rushes up to meet me like the earth.

I wake up suddenly in total darkness. I remember where I am. He's beside me but he seems to be lying outside the blankets, furled in the bedspread. I get stealthily out of the bed, grope to the window and open one of the wooden shutters. It's almost as dark outside, there are no streetlights, but by straining I can read my watch; two o'clock. I've had my eight hours and my body thinks it's time for breakfast. I notice I still have my clothes on, take them off and get back in bed, but my stomach won't let me sleep.

I hesitate, then decide it won't do him any harm and turn on the bedside lamp. On the dresser there's a crumpled paper bag; inside it is a Welsh cake, a soft white biscuit with currants in it. I bought it yesterday near the train station, asking in bakeries crammed with English buns and French pastries, running through the streets in a crazed search for local colour that almost made us late for the bus. Actually I bought two of them. I ate mine yesterday, this one is his, but I don't care; I take it out of the bag and devour it whole.

In the mirror I'm oddly swollen, as though I've been drowned, my eyes are purple-circled, my hair stands out from my head like a second-hand doll's, there's a diagonal scar-like mark across my cheek where I've been sleeping on my face. This is what it does to you. I estimate the weeks, months, it will take me to recuperate. Fresh air, good food and plenty of sun.

We have so little time and he just lies there, rolled up like a rug, not even twitching. I think of waking him, I want to make love, I want all there is because there's not much left. I start to think what he will do after I'm over and I can't stand that, maybe I should kill him, that's a novel idea, how melodramatic; nevertheless I look around the room for a blunt instrument; there's nothing but the bedside lamp, a grotesque woodland nymph with metal tits and a lightbulb coming out of her head. I could never kill anyone with that. Instead I brush my teeth, wondering if he'll ever know how close he came to being murdered, resolving anyway never to plant flowers for him, never to come back, and slide in among the chilly furrows and craters of the bed. I intend to watch the sun rise but I fall asleep by accident and miss it.

Breakfast, when the time for it finally comes, is shabby, decorous, with mended linens and plentiful but dinted silver. We have it in an ornate, dilapidated room whose grandiose mantelpiece now supports only china spaniels and tinted family photos. We're brushed and combed, thoroughly dressed; we speak in subdued voices.

The food is the usual: tea and toast, fried eggs and bacon and the inevitable grilled tomato. It's served by a different woman, grey-haired also but with a corrugated perm and red lipstick. We unfold our map and plan the route back; it's Sunday and there won't be a bus to the nearest railway town till after one, we may have trouble getting out.

He doesn't like fried eggs and he's been given two of them. I eat one for him and tell him to hack the other one up so it will look nibbled at least, it's only polite. He is grateful to me, he knows I'm taking care of him, he puts his hand for a moment over mine, the one not holding the fork. We tell each other our dreams; his of men with armbands, later of me in a cage made of frail slat-like bones, mine of escaping in winter through a field.

I eat his grilled tomato as an afterthought and we leave.

Upstairs in our room we pack; or rather I pack, he lies on the bed.

"What're we going to do till the bus comes?" he says. Being up so early unsettles him.

"Go for a walk," I say.

"We went for a walk yesterday," he says.

I turn around and he's holding out his arms, he wants me to come and lie down beside him. I do and he gives me a perfunctory initial kiss and starts to undo my buttons. He's using only his left hand, the right one is underneath me. He's having trouble. I stand up and take off, reluctantly, the clothes I've so recently put on. It's time for sex; he missed out on it last night.

He reaches up and hauls me in among the tangled sheets. I tense; he throws himself on me with the utilitarian urgency of a man running to catch a train, but it's more than that, it's different, he's biting down on my mouth, this time he'll get blood if it kills him. I pull him into me, wanting him to be with me, but for the first time I feel it's just flesh, a body, a beautiful machine, an animated corpse, he isn't in it any more, I want him so much and he isn't here. The bedsprings mourn beneath us.

"Sorry about that," he says.

"It's all right."

"No, shit, I really am sorry. I don't like it when that happens."

"It's all right," I say. I smooth his back, distancing him: he's back by the deserted house, back lying on the grass, back in the graveyard, standing in the sun looking down, thinking of his own death.

"We better get up," I say, "she might want to make up the room."

We're waiting for the bus. They lied to me in the general store, there is a hotel, I can see it now, it's just around the corner. We've had our quarrel, argument, fight, the one we were counting on. It was a routine one, a small one comparatively, its only importance the fact that it was the last. It carries the weight of all the other, larger things we said we forgave each other for but didn't. If there were separate buses we'd take them. As it is we wait together, standing a little apart.

We have over half an hour. "Let's go down to the beach," I say. "We can see the bus from there; it has to go the other way first." I cross the road and he follows me at a distance.

There's a wall; I climb it and sit down. The top is scattered with sharp flakes of broken stone, flint possibly, and bleached thumbnail-sized cockleshells, I know what they are because I saw them in the museum two days ago, and the occasional piece of broken glass. He leans against the wall near me, chewing on a cigarette. We say what we have to say in even, conversational voices, discussing how we'll get back, the available trains. I wasn't expecting it so soon.

After a while he looks at his watch, then walks away from me towards the sea, his boots crunching on the shells and pebbles. At the edge of the reed bank by the river he stops, back to me, one leg slightly bent. He holds his elbows, wrapped in his clothes as though in a cape, the storm breaks, his cape billows, thick leather boots sprout up his legs, a sword springs to attention in his hand. He throws his head back, courage, he'll meet them alone. Flash of lightning. Onward.

I wish I could do it so quickly. I sit calmed, frozen, not yet sure whether I've survived, the words we have hurled at each other lying spread in fragments around me, solidified. It's the pause during the end of the world; how does one behave? The man who said he'd continue to tend his garden, does that make sense to me? It would if it were only a small ending, my own. But we aren't more doomed than anything else, it's dead already, at any moment the bay will vaporize, the hills across will lift into the air, the space between will scroll itself up and vanish; in the graveyard the graves will open to show the dry puffball skulls, his wooden cross will flare like a match, his house collapse into itself, cardboard and lumber, no more language. He will stand revealed, history scaling away from him, the versions of him I made up and applied, stripped down to what he really is for a last instant before he flames up and goes out. Surely we should be holding each other, absolving, repenting, saying goodbye to each other, to everything because we will never find it again.

Above us the gulls wheel and ride, crying like drowning puppies or disconsolate angels. They have black rims around their eyes; they're a new kind, I've never seen any like that before. The tide is going out; the fresh wet mud gleams in the sun, miles of it, a level field of pure glass, pure gold. He stands outlined against it; a dark shape, faceless, light catching the edges of his hair.

I turn aside and look down at my hands. They are covered with greyish dust: I've been digging among the shells, gathering them together. I arrange them in a border, a square, each white shell overlapping the next. Inside I plant the flints, upright in tidy rows, like teeth, like flowers.

PATRICK O'FLAHERTY

(b. 1939)

P atrick O'Flaherty was born at Conception Bay, Newfoundland. He earned a B.A. (1959) and an M.A. (1960) from Memorial University, and received his Ph.D. from the University of London in 1963. He taught for two years at the University of Manitoba, but since 1965 he has been a professor in the Department of English at Memorial University. He has worked as a journalist and is currently a freelance broadcaster for CBC radio, commenting on matters of regional interest. Active in provincial politics, he has twice stood as a candidate for the Liberal Party. O'Flaherty has written books of literary criticism—The Rock Observed: Studies in the Literature of Newfoundland (1979)—edited a number of anthologies, and published books of short stories—Summer of the Greater Yellowlegs (1979) and A Small Place in the Sun (1989)—and the novel Priest of God (1990). His fiction is characterized by its realistic evocation of a maritime way of life and by the whimsical and poignant witness it bears to the resilience of the human spirit under harsh conditions.

A Small Place in the Sun

T hat there were deep differences between his family and some of their neighbours became clear to Jimmy Byrne about ten o'clock one night in the late summer of his eighth year, when Ken Slade came by for a visit. Mr. Slade lived only a quarter of a mile away, but he was a man who kept to himself, and his wife Fanny was delicate. It was strange for anyone to come in the house at such a late hour, let alone him. "I allowed this mornin' there was goin't' be trouble," Granny Byrne said when she heard the latch lift on the porch door. The old black horse named Dandy had come right up to the kitchen window just after daylight and looked in. That meant the worst kind of luck. It might even be a death in the house. "Now look what we got," she said. "A stranger."

"Oh, Christ, Ma, it's only Ken," Jimmy's father said when he saw who it was. He got up from the settle where he'd been napping and spent a few minutes talking to the visitor about the fishery. "Hauled twelve fleets of lines this morning and got twenty-five codfish," he said. "My dear man, this place is finished. I got around forty, forty-five quintals out in the store, that's all. Never seen the like of it. No herring worth a damn, either. And the few salmon I got in the spring I had to sell to Art Champion for fifteen cents a pound. She's gone bottom up, head over heels."

"That's Long Beach for you," his wife Molly said as she lifted a damper on the kitchen stove and poked the fire. It was already starting to get cold in the evenings. She gave him a look. "Told you, didn't I?" He made no answer, but only rubbed his eyes.

Then he said to one and all: "Down on your knees." This too was strange, for the rosary, taken up vigorously in May month, had been given up for the summer. But now the sorrowful mysteries were dutifully intoned, though not without murmurs from the five children, who were getting used to playing Chinese checkers and listening to the radio before their mother sent them off to bed. By the Carrying of the Cross, Colin, who was nine and should have known better, had been slapped by Granny Byrne for kneeling on the cat's tail; and even Alphonsus, going on twelve, had to have his ear pulled for pinching his sister Elizabeth and making her squeal. The Hail Holy Queen came none too soon, and Jimmy, not having stirred from his place on the kitchen floor because experience had taught him it was best to leave your knees in one spot, turned to look at the clock on the mantelpiece. Would he miss the start of the Cisco Kid? was what he was thinking. He was surprised by what he saw. In the straight-backed chair by the washstand sat Mr. Slade, head bowed, hands buried deep in the pockets of his overalls. Not only was he sitting up, but he wasn't even saying "poor banished children of Eve" or sending up sighs with the rest of them. No holy rosary for him.

His mother later explained to Jimmy what Mr. Slade was, and when he looked around the church next Sunday, sure enough, he could see that the Slade children, Harold and Gwendolyn, weren't present. Nor were Winston Reynolds and George Dale, two more chums. Well, not chums exactly, in the way that Will Joe Hogan was a chum. Jimmy didn't throw rocks at the birds or at the bottles on the telegraph poles with them, or go in the woods in their company to catch trout or pick berries. If he had gone to school with them—and he now knew why he didn't— it might have been different. But when he went to the sandy beach in Northern Bay, a mile up the shore, on Sunday afternoons to swim in the fresh-water pool or lie around under the hot sun, he would see them and talk to them. Sometimes, they would all walk back together from the sands. They were all right, especially Gwendolyn, who said she was getting a sun tan. "I'd sun tan her if I owned her," Molly said. He liked going up to Northern Bay, because that was where his mother came from and he had uncles and cousins there.

In the fall his father gave up fishing early and went to Halifax to work on the docks. His letters home were filled with adventures. Once a woman with blonde hair came up to him on Barrington Street and caught hold of him. He had a job to get clear of her, he wrote. When he had trouble sleeping, he got pills from a German doctor. A German doctor in Halifax, and the war only just over! He stayed in his boarding house most nights because he heard what had happened in Halifax on V-E Day; the streets weren't safe. Through what his family gathered was some kind of masterful stroke, he had managed to get in the union when others couldn't and, being thought of as Irish, was well liked. He could go down to Boston if he wanted to and work on the docks. He was half tempted to move his whole family to the States. There was more money to be made there than in Canada. "I'm liable to send down for you any old day," he wrote. "All you have to have is an Irish name, and you got it made with the union. You're in like Flynn. They look after you." Molly, who had once been a teacher, explained what a union was. The house was full of grand talk.

Early in the spring their cow got sick with milk fever, and Alphonsus found her lying shivering on the cold stable floor. All efforts to get her on her feet were in vain. The new calf had to be fed with a bottle and kept in the porch of the house until the cow got better. *If* she got better. Ebe Tucker from Burnt Point, three miles down the shore, was sent for. He said the only way to save her was to pump her up. It was a new way to treat milk fever. It had worked on two of his cows, and he couldn't see why it wouldn't work on one from Long Beach. "Cows are all the same, not like people," he said. He wanted an answer straightaway; was he to do it or wasn't he? He was a busy man. Granny Byrne shook her head. "Pump!" she snorted. "What next, what next!"

But Molly said "Go ahead," and while skeptical neighbours who had, with Granny, advised other treatments looked on, Mr. Tucker got a pump from his truck and pumped air into the cow's udder through each of her tits. Jimmy watched from a distance with Gwendolyn. "Tit is not a nice word," she said. A day later the cow was up on her legs eating hay and the calf was back in the stable. Jimmy and Colin made sure that her pen was swept out every day and the calf had a good place to lie down. They gave Dandy's pen a good cleaning, too, because it had been neglected during the cow's sickness. After shovelling the manure out from under him, they cleaned off his legs and sides with the horse comb.

Then something even worse happened. Their sister Lucy got sick with diarrhea and vomiting, and started to lose weight. The doctor came down twice from Western Bay, far up the shore, to look at her, but couldn't do anything to help. Molly, afraid that Lucy was going to die, sent a wire to Halifax from the post office in Northern Bay, and back their father came in May, bringing bottles of cod liver oil and B-1 tonic, a bag of oranges, miraculous medals, and renewed devotion to the rosary. "Down on your knees," he said an hour after he landed in the house. Later in the night, Jimmy woke up to hear his parents saying the sorrowful mysteries again in their bedroom. Sure enough, Lucy started getting better right away and was soon out of bed and playing in the kitchen. All hands were now wearing medals around their necks, even the cow and calf. They needed looking after too, his father said.

He brought something else with him from Halifax: a money belt filled with banknotes. Not trusting banks, he had kept all his savings under the mattress in his boarding house, and the evening after he came back he counted it on the kitchen table in front of his family: $1,700. As a fisherman, he was used to living on credit. Now he had money. He fingered it, stacked the bills on top of each other. What would he do with it all? Fishing had brought him only hard work and misery. He didn't want to start that again. If he did, he'd lose the little bit of hair he had left on his head after Halifax. "A shop!" said Molly. "Let's start a little shop up on the road. There's no place to buy a pound of sugar in Long Beach. We're halfway between the big dealers. Ron Woodfine and Will Johnson might deal with us. And we'd get a bit of money from the children going back and forth to school. The only thing we have in this hole is the school."

She forgot the church, which was in Long Beach too. Jimmy noticed that she didn't mention Ken Slade. Wouldn't he deal with them? He lived no further away than the Johnsons and Woodfines.

This was something, a Byrne owning a shop! His father fell back on the settle with his hands clasped behind his head, sized up the money, looked out through the window towards the salt water, and burst out laughing. He laughed a lot. Then he turned serious. "I'll have to ask somebody about this," he said. "Not the priest," said Molly. Granny Byrne jumped out of the rocking chair and went to the stove, where somebody had left the cover off the teapot. "More trouble and torment," she said.

The next day was Saturday. His father took Jimmy with him and walked down to see Marmaduke Tucker, the merchant who owned Thomas Tucker and Sons Limited. Jimmy hadn't been down as far as Burnt Point before, but he knew that was the place they had the parade every July, led by the man on the white horse. His father was dressed up in his new blue serge suit of clothes and quiff hat. He had a bit of style about him since his trip to Halifax. Everyone said so.

It was a long walk on the dusty road, and Jimmy was tired when they got to the shop. A big car was in front of the door, and a crowd of men and boys looked at them as they went in. What a shop it was! Jimmy could see shelf upon shelf of tins, boxes, bottles, dishes, pans, dry goods, everything. The really special thing, he knew from his mother, was in dry goods, but he wasn't in a rush and the whole shop was fun to look at. Besides, it was nice to put things off. He watched the clerks at work, serving the customers. When you wanted a piece of line to tie up a parcel, all you had to do was reach up and pull some down from a reel about ten feet above the counter. It was easy to break the line by hooking it around your thumb and hauling. There was one shelf with nothing on it but tinned spaghetti, his favourite meal. A big ham and an even bigger cheese lay on the counter, but someone would be sure to notice if you tried to cut a piece off with a pocketknife. He hadn't brought his pocket-knife with him, and anyway, it would be wrong. But Will Joe Hogan would have a piece if he was here. A delicious smell of apples made his mouth water. He could see the apples in a box, the ones on top nice and shiny, and the ones in the next tier wrapped in pieces of paper.

After twenty minutes or so Duke Tucker appeared, spoke to his father, took the quiff and put it on his own head, and led them off towards a room at the back. "You wait in the shop, sonny," the merchant said. "We'll only be in the office a half-hour." The door closed, and Jimmy couldn't see what they were doing, because the little window in the door was too high. He soon got tired of standing and decided to sit down on a box, but a man serving customers shouted from inside the counter, "Hey, get your ass off that, that's sweet biscuits." If his father was out here, he wouldn't be yelled at like that, he thought. But he got up and walked over to the front door, since it wasn't time yet for the special treat. It soon would be. A boy about his own size looked in at him and stuck out his tongue. At first Jimmy didn't recognize him because the glass in the door was dirty, but then he saw it was Harold Slade. Harold stuck out his tongue again and made a fist at him. Then he grabbed his crotch and pulled it up and down as if he were trying to tear it loose, all the while shaking his fist with the free hand. Other boys stood around on the steps, pointing inside and laughing, grabbing their crotches too. "See any horses?" one of them yelled at him. What did that mean? Should he go out and ask? It was a mystery.

Something happened to him then. He felt that he was inside the door and would never get through it. He was shut in, cut off. As he stared out, he could feel the medal hanging around his neck and was glad it was inside his shirt where nobody would notice it. "See any horses?" a laughing boy screamed. Jimmy looked down the road through the big window in front of the shop and saw, not horses, but Gwendolyn playing hop-scotch with three girls. She was jumping up and down and clapping her hands. When her dress bounced up, he could see her naked legs above her stockings. He thought she must have cousins down here.

Recovering himself, he at last went over to dry goods and looked at the toys in the glass case. He had already decided what he wanted to be when he grew up. No fishing boat for him, his father said; if Alphonsus took up doctoring, he might go into teaching. That was a good racket, too. His mother ruled out Christian brothers or priests. But he had his own secret hopes. Now he feasted his eyes on the glittering six-shooters, and dreamed of fleeing bandits, sunlit canyons, beautiful senoritas rescued from danger, and white stallions.

He was still there, nose to the glass, an hour later when the two men came out of the office, talking loudly about Canada and the baby bonus. "Long Beach'll have no worries when the baby bonus comes," Mr. Tucker said, "you can mark that down." They were both red in the face, and Jimmy hadn't seen his father grin this way before. "What's your name, sonny?" Mr. Tucker said to him and, on getting the reply "James Byrne, sir," called out to the man who had ordered him off the biscuit box, "Harry, give old Jim here a candy." Harry came over and gave him a peppermint knob, which he put in his breeches' pocket. "So I'll be talking to you later, Paddy," Mr. Tucker said as they went out through the door. But his father had to go back to the office to get the quiff. Then they went out again.

There was nobody outside now because it had started to rain. The wind was up too; they leaned into it and started back up the shore. At a couple of places on the walk, his father had to go into the woods by the side of the road. Jimmy thought he could smell B-1 tonic off him. He knew his mother would be mad with them because they got their shoes so dirty. But Jimmy wasn't mad. Although he was a big boy, before they got to Long Beach he reached out and took his father's hand. For the first time he noticed how rough and hard it was. He held on tight until they got home.

SANDRA BIRDSELL

(b. 1942)

S *andra Birdsell was born in rural Manitoba. After publishing stories in such literary magazines as* Grain, Capilano Review, NeWest Review, *and* Prairie Fire, *and winning the National Magazine Award and the Gerald Lampert Award, she made her reputation with the short-story collection* Night Travellers *(1982), a story cycle set in rural Manitoba. Her second collection,* Ladies of the House *(1984), confirmed her standing as a new voice in Canadian short fiction, one that had set itself the task of expressing the often eccentric lives of the inhabitants of the fictional town of Agassiz. Birdsell has also written filmscripts for the National Film Board and plays for Winnipeg theatres. She has served a number of terms as a writer-in-residence, including an extended appointment at the University of St. Jerome's College in Waterloo, Ontario, and was named one of Canada's most promising writers of fiction. Her first novel,* The Missing Child *(1989), is again set in Agassiz, though this book marks a significant development in Birdsell's style. More in the tradition of fabulation than the earlier stories, it is in the mode of fiction that unapologetically merges impossible happenings with believable events. This new fictional venture has also been greeted with critical and popular success, winning the W.H. Smith Books in Canada First Novel Award.*

The Bride Doll

"A pretty wedding was solemnized," Virginia Colpitts read. "Pink and white peonies and blue delphinium in white baskets were placed on the altar and satin bows designated pews reserved for the guests."

Virginia and I lay out on a blanket in her back yard. We had always lived on the same street. First she had lived at the top of the street in an unpainted, unsteady house which had not survived the last flooding of the river, and then at the bottom of the street, in a bright new bungalow.

We lay in the shadow of a red barn, seeking shelter from the hot dry wind, and read accounts of weddings, placing ourselves inside the church as honoured guests. I was smitten by the descriptions of veils, seed pearls and lily-point sleeves. I imagined satin to be as iridescent as moths' wings, shiny and silvery. I gleaned notices of weddings from the columns in the *Agassiz Herald* and then on Saturdays, Virginia and I waited outside to catch a glimpse of the newly married couple as they came from the church, looking over-starched with self-consciousness. Where once the couple had been as close as Siamese twins, they stood apart, awkward in their new state. I imagined doves fluttering above their heads.

Even though I had been taught not to pray for tangible things as that was a mark of selfishness (a waste of God's valuable time when one considered the numberless starving children), I prayed fervently for a bride doll.

"Why do you want one?" my mother asked.

"Because," was all I could say as I lay in the gutted bedroom where wall boards had been pulled loose and moist wood shavings tumbled free in order to dry. Wet shavings would swell and cause a fire, my father said.

Instead of praying for bride dolls, it was better to confess sins, my mother said, and then to try to make right the wrongs we did. And what about the crusts of bread I'd hidden behind furniture because I didn't want to eat them? I was told to think of those poor starving children and so that night I crawled beneath the bed and fished a crust of bread out from a corner and I ate it. Stinging pain sent me into my parents' room where, to their horror, my mouth lit up with the phosphorus glow of rat poison.

When I imagine myself as I was then, I see a slightly chubby person with legs as stocky as tree trunks, standing solidly in the middle of a tangled, confused yard. About me, in the ruined furniture and rotting lumber, is the reminder of chaos, an event which had turned our lives topsy turvey. But I can't remember the actual flooding of the river, I can only recall the immediate years after it, being warned not to touch any of the debris, to wash my hands thoroughly before meals, of things like diphtheria and having one's jaw locked shut. But the worst was the tearing down and re-building of our house.

When I look at photographs from around that time, I am usually wearing a white dress. The thick lenses of my glasses are heavy and they slide down my nose as I frown to keep them in place while I am forever peering out through the heavy blonde bangs of my over-grown butch cut. A shoemaker's children need shoes, my mother said, a butcher's, meat. And we were always in need of a hair cut. In most group photographs, I am either turned right around or looking off at something to the side of me. I was a sheet of jelly then, a hectograph, the old copier teachers used to prepare our work. They wrote on the gelatin with an indelible pencil (it was poison, we were warned not to chew on it). As the year progressed, the faint ghosts of past tests, the damp outlines of art work, criss-crossed, becoming a road map of the whole year.

Virginia never tanned or was affected by the sun in any way but my legs and face grew prickly and red in the hot wind. While we lay out there on the blanket, I wished I could climb above it, up where the vapour trails of jet planes arched into the sun, away from the shining of the electric saw and the hollow thud of a hammer echoing in the trees in the park as across a field, Mr. Pankratz finished building his new house.

Pankratz, the packrat, we'd named him because he'd built the house almost entirely from scrap. He'd paid little for the land because it bordered the edge of town and would be on the wrong side of the dike once it was in place. My father had branded him a "plain damned fool," but I didn't think he was that harmless. I walked in wide circles around the man to escape his clammy, pale hands which were forever reaching to pat my arm or the top of my head. In spring, my father said, water would back up from the river into the first and then the second park, flow across the road and completely surround Mr. Pankratz's house. So the man had built it up, had hauled in fill to raise the foundation as high as the level of the last flood. As a result, the house looked down over the whole town, the park, the bridge which spanned the Red River and the highway climbing to meet St. Mary's Road as it wound past Horseshoe Lake.

When Mr. Pankratz came to build our kitchen cupboards, my mother asked him why he had chosen to live there. "It must be terrible for mosquitoes," she said. And the park was a strange place in spring with oak trees standing in water, reflected back over and over. Once the water subsided, the ground remained soft and overnight, flesh-white toadstools, spongy and tall, sprung up from dampness. Virginia and I played down there. We told no one. The park floor was littered with flood-contaminated stock from the drugstore and off-limits. We played wedding. We collected toadstools and laid them out on wild rhubarb leaves for the wedding feast. Do you take this man as your lawful wedded husband? I asked. Do you take this woman to be your awful wife? Virginia would say, laughing, spoiling the ceremony. To her it was a game, the same as playing Dale Evans and Roy Rogers.

Mr. Pankratz removed his painter's cap and ran his hand across his smooth bald head when my mother asked him why he chose to build his house on the outskirts of town. He took his pencil out from behind his ear, squinted and said, "The town is for families. What would an old bachelor like me want in town?"

He's worse than an old woman, my mother complained because Mr. Pankratz liked to tell stories while he built the cupboards. He liked his new house, he told us. Know what he liked about it the most? My brothers and sisters and I were sitting on the floor around galvanized wash tubs, washing mud from my mother's canning sealers. I could see my mother's shoulders bunch with irritation. "I wouldn't know," she said.

"The indoor toilet," he said and set aside the board he was about to cut, freeing his hands to illustrate some point in the story with a bunched fist or a sweeping motion. He had been thinking that morning when he got up, what a good thing it was that he no longer needed to worry about digging another pit for the outhouse. The indoor toilet in his new house was the best thing. When he'd lived on the farm, of all the chores, he'd hated moving the outhouse most. When the lime had been dumped into the pit too often the ground all around the outhouse became spongy. He was afraid that someday he would step off the narrow plank and sink up to his knees. Then it would be up to him to dig another hole, move the outhouse onto it and fill in the other.

"The job came to me, everytime," he complained. "I always did all the dirty work. Take David for instance," Mr. Pankratz said in a wounded voice to remind us of his sacrifice, how he had taken his sister's boy so she could be free to marry and move away to British Columbia and not have to live with the tragedy of David, who had stopped growing the day they discovered him up-ended in a water-filled rain barrel. "My sister has written only twice this year," he whined. "And I don't think she will even come to the wedding."

Throughout all the hammering and the sporadic whine of the electric saw, David sat on a chair outside, leaning against the house, blond head bent over his lap as he chipped and coaxed oddly shaped animals from blocks of wood his uncle had discarded. All the while, he smiled at something we couldn't see. When he walked, he seemed to feel his way along, as though he travelled through a dream.

"The bride chose a waltz-length dress, featuring a cumberbund and a lace bolero," Virginia read from the *Agassiz Herald*. What was waltz length? I wondered as I watched David's intense carving and Mr. Pankratz's struggle with a sheet of chalk board. Drywall, it is called now, but we called it chalk board because when it crumbled we salvaged pieces to draw our hopscotch on the sidewalks. Mr. Pankratz's house was new, but looked old. The roof had come from many roofs, the windows from the old school. And the style of it was like all the other old houses in Agassiz, like the one I lived in, a tall, two-storey house, windows arranged unimaginatively, two up and two down.

"You are welcome to come to the wedding of Lena Harms to David Pankratz, July 12, at 2 pm," the note read. There was no posting an announcement in the *Agassiz Herald* for this wedding. The announcement came in the form of a note delivered by a small child, which we were instructed to pass on from door to door. When my mother finished laughing, she let me read it. "Feel free to invite a friend. Come and bring your own refreshments," it said. The wording of the note had been the bride's mother's idea, Mr. Pankratz explained, his weathered cheeks flaring red. "She says in Paraguay, at a wedding, the whole village comes. For this reason, I thought it best we hold the affair at my place."

I had been inside the Harmses' house with Virginia when she went to collect for the newspaper and I agreed. The family had come from Paraguay the previous year. There had been gossip about the father and the family having been sent from the Mennonite colony because of something he'd done. They lived in a bricksiding cottage which had been badly flooded. You can't trust bricksiding, my father said. It doesn't let moisture escape and a house can look perfectly sound from the outside but be rotten to the core. The Harmses' house had three rooms for fourteen people. Along the walls, boxes filled with clothing were stacked one on top of another. The women of the town had collected the clothing when the family had disembarked at the train station in the dead of winter wearing only thin muslin. Each day, the children pulled what they would wear from the boxes. All around us in the cramped kitchen were children. They sat on the table, squatted on the floor, babies lay on a cot beside the stove, all dark-eyed, dark-skinned. One swung down from the top of the door and stared at us with lively eyes, eyes like the eldest, Lena's, the colour of black walnut. Dirty faces peered in at us through the window. When we'd come into the yard, we'd noticed a gas-powered washing machine standing idle and Lena bending over a pile of clothing on the ground. A kettle boiled on a hot plate.

No understand, no understand, the woman said in broken English. She pushed her feet into a pair of man's plaid slippers and took the kettle from the hot plate. We followed her outside with most of the children. Lena stood beside the washing machine on one foot, scratching at the back of her leg with the other. She was taller than her mother, slender, a strong nose, not the fleshy little ball of a nose that her mother possessed. For two days she'd sat behind me in school in a desk that was too small for her so that she had to turn sideways in it and her tanned, sandalled foot bobbed up and down in the centre of the aisle. Turn around, the teacher warned me when I couldn't stop staring. Lena's heavy black braids trailed down from her shoulders and lay against her full breasts. At recess, the boys turned rope for her so she could jump and they could watch her breasts bouncing beneath the paisley print dress. But she never knew. She skipped and laughed and you could tell she thought she was one of us.

Despite all the children, the jumble of clothing, I remember that the house was clean and the woman herself radiated the pleasant odour of oranges. Virginia and I explained why we had come. The woman and girl spoke to each other in Spanish. The mother frowned. No money, she explained. No money for anything. Not for gasoline. My husband, he take for his car, she said, ducking her head in a shy manner. She shouted to the children in Spanish and they came running with a pail. Gasoline, gasoline, they cried in high musical voices as they went from door to door.

But if the wording of the wedding letter had been the mother's idea, the marriage itself had been Mr. Pankratz's. He'd been walking down in the second park on the west side of the bridge where the trees were dense and it was cooler, he said. He'd looked up and saw David and the girl walking along the bridge. Why did she come every evening to lean on his fence and call for David? he wondered and had followed them, he told my mother, because he worried about David getting lost. And as he saw how she held David's hand, and how willingly he followed, the idea had come streaking down and "hit me like a bolt of lightning. Too soon oldt, too late schmart," he said. "I'm not getting any younger," he told my mother. "David needs someone to watch out for him."

"But is she able?" my mother asked. She shook her hands free of soap suds, slipped her wedding band back on and sat down for once, to listen. I wondered what her wedding dress had looked like. When I asked, she put me off, saying that it was not a regular dress, but pretty, and had buttons at the shoulder. There was no photograph of my parents' wedding in the album, although all her relatives were there in their matrimonial finery. There was only one photograph of them together and it was a surprising picture. My mother sat on my father's knee, bare legs exposed and on her feet, tiny pointed-toed shoes with bows. Her hair was longer than I ever remember her wearing it. She had swept it up behind one ear and the other side swung forward, a dark wedge against her white skin. A dark-haired Marlene Dietrich. She raised a glass to the person behind the camera. My father rested his chin on her shoulder and laughed. What was the occasion? I wondered. She didn't remember. A party of some sort. It was before, she searched for the words, before, she said. Before the flooding of the river? No, no, long before that. It was before I became a better person, she said without explaining.

"The mother says that in Paraguay they teach girls in school all things a woman should know," Mr. Pankratz said.

"Be that as it may," my mother said. "There's more to it than cooking and cleaning. She looks so young. She doesn't look any older than thirteen or fourteen."

"Sixteen," Mr. Pankratz said. The air was thick with sawdust and the warm smell of wood. A two-by-four thundered to the floor. "It's a good bargain for the girl to get her out of that place," Mr. Pankratz said. "And the mother sees it as well. It'll be one less mouth for her to feed."

My mother sighed. "Well, they will make a nice couple," she said. "Lena is a good-looking girl."

"He only wants someone to wash his dirty socks," she said when Mr. Pankratz had gone.

Virginia folded the newspaper and held it against her chest. The sun transformed dry patches on her arms into silvery scales. Virginia and I were best friends. She had Psoriasis and I, the coke-bottle eye glasses. "Dolores uses Kotex now," Virginia said. She scratched at her arms and blinked in the sunlight. Her eyes were always red-rimmed and sore-looking.

I didn't want to know what Kotex was but she took me inside the house which smelled sharply of aging varnish and cough medicine, a smell I thought came with their old house, but the odour had followed them here. Charlie Colpitts would walk a mile to get out of work, people said of Virginia's father and I associated the smell of the house with sloth. Mrs. Colpitts was a nurse at the hospital. She had scooped babies up from between legs, washed backs and bottoms and poked into bed pans and so people knew enough to leave the Colpittses alone. Mrs. Colpitts, Verna, was a short, sharp-featured woman with hair as stiff and unmanageable as Virginia's and Dolores's. She was the possessor of special knowledge. When I told her what my mother had said about Mr. Pankratz wanting someone to wash his socks, her face snapped to attention. His socks worsht, she said. Huh. As long as that's all he wants.

Virginia and I stood in Dolores's closet, examining a Kotex pad. "She puts it between her legs," Virginia explained. I resisted the explanation. I did not want to envision anything blotted or stained beneath satin skirts. "No, no," Virginia said. "They plan for that. They count the days so it won't happen."

The day of the wedding my mother sent me to Mr. Pankratz's house with a batch of buns. The sun had risen above the horizon which, beyond the shock of twisted oak trees in the park, was the stark horizontal line of St. Mary's Road. Above Horseshoe Lake, a veil of mist would be lifting and in the shallow ditches, ivory clouds of yarrow bobbed in a green sea. The bittersweet scent of a prickly rose bush growing thickly among the rusting shell of a car made my throat ache. As I walked, I remembered the same road muddy and slick after the flood and the sudden sound of rushing water stopping me dead. There, inches before my feet, the road fell away into a large hole. I stood mesmerized, watching with horror the yellow water roaring and tumbling beneath the road, carrying rocks and debris along with it. A temporary underground stream, my father explained but it didn't diminish the feeling I had of a world surging beneath my feet and I about to be swallowed and swept along underground with it.

I pictured my destination. I imagined that Mr. Pankratz had knocked lightly on the groom's door as he passed into the kitchen and heard the immediate, anxious reply of the bedsprings and then footsteps as David followed him into the kitchen. It was one of the "dirty jobs" Mr. Pankratz had explained to my mother, teaching David not to arise in the morning until he knocked. One winter David had wandered away from the house in his night clothes and suffered frost bite. I imagined the two men bent in silence over their breakfast plates, eating quickly, almost furtively, but as I entered the yard, I heard voices and came upon them behind the house on their hands and knees, weeding the garden.

"Already, visitors," Mr. Pankratz greeted me, scrambling to his feet.

The glint of metal in the seat of his pants caught my eye. Once Mr. Pankratz had been crawling across a roof and split the seam in his trousers and he had used a length of stove-pipe wire to hold it together. Wired for sound, people joked. Old Pankratz doesn't want to miss a thing. Would the bride be required to mend his pants? From the park came the sudden scolding of a squirrel. Startled upright by the sound, David listened, a weed still clenched in his fist.

"Look who's here," Mr. Pankratz said to David, touching him to draw his attention. "Look what she brought." But David never looked at any of us directly. He seemed to be in another place, the place where his animal carvings took shape. From a fir tree at the back of the yard came the coo of a mourning dove. The sound was right for that time of day while the air was still cool and the dew had not yet been burned off by the sun. The sound was like gently moving air, like my mother's sigh.

I wondered what the bride was doing at that very moment. Mr. Pankratz had given the mother money to buy a dress, he'd said, so she would look half-decent. Was she awaking, stretching and yawning and seeing the dress, did her heart beat faster?

"Tell your Momma, thank you," Mr. Pankratz said. As he took the buns from me, his cool hands brushed against mine and I stepped back quickly, feeling in my mind his sticky touch on my arm. "Hurry, hurry," he said sharply to David as he carried the still-warm buns into the house. "They aren't going to be able to make their bachelor jokes about my garden today."

From across the field came the sound of Virginia's india rubber ball smacking against the cement and calling me to play.

The sun was hot and high in the sky, casting short, sharp shadows in the dirt of the yard when Virginia, Mrs. Colpitts and I crossed the field to the wedding. Mrs. Colpitts had allowed us to paint our nails for the occasion and I admired the poppy-red splashes on my hands. My mother, several of my sisters and brothers, and a few other women were already there. My father would not close down his barber shop to come. The only time he had ever closed his shop was when my oldest sister insisted on getting married on a Saturday, and then it was only for half a day. Mr. Pankratz and David had changed from their work clothes into white shirts and black pants. They sat on a makeshift bench, leaning against the house, waiting. And then, as though people had agreed to arrive at the same time, a line of cars travelled down the dirt road, slowly and almost silently. The brittle call of a crow down in the park grated at our silent expectancy. People came walking, carrying dishes and pans of food. Mr. Pankratz nodded his greeting to each one. The women, with quiet efficiency, began setting the food out on the table which Mr. Pankratz had made of plyboard and sawhorses. We strolled about the yard waiting for the arrival of the bride. Mr. Pankratz mopped his ruddy face and squinted at us from behind his handkerchief. Sit sill, my mother cautioned. I sat on a chair and thought the people were like chickens, the way they glanced at David from the sides of their faces, advancing towards him so far, as though they might peck him on the leg, and then veering away quickly at the last moment. The way they craned their necks to peer down the road to see if the bride was coming. David whittled at a piece of wood, seeming not to notice any of us.

And then suddenly, everyone fell silent. Even the smallest ones paused in their restless games to see what was happening. My throat began to tighten. The crow flapped up from the trees in the park, laughing loudly as two smaller birds cried and darted about its head. At the top of the road, we could hear a flutter of sound, a light tinny clamour and then, growing louder, it became the voices of children singing. We all stood up. Down the road they came, the entire Harms family, barefoot children jumping around Lena in circles singing, "She's a bride, she's a bride. Lena is a bride." The older ones carried smaller ones on their hips. The parents each carried a bundle. Closer and closer they came, dancing and laughing and shouting in Spanish. My dress stuck to my back. My heart twisted at the sight of the bride and the pink flowers in her arms. Everyone stood motionless, staring, as single file, the family crossed the plank that spanned the ditch. David pulled at Mr. Pankratz's arm and smiled suddenly. "Lena," he said. "It's Lena."

"What the hell," Mr. Pankratz swore softly. "She didn't buy the girl a dress."

On Lena's blue-black head, attached with many pins, was an ivory lace curtain. Her dress appeared to be a bedsheet gathered at the waist with a man's necktie. The flowers were plastic and coated with dust. People moved aside to let the family pass through into the yard, carrying with them the smell of dust and heat and oranges. The mother stood before the groom, foxtail fur wound tightly about her neck. Above it, perspiration beaded her wide mottled face.

"I bring her to you," she said and dropped the bundle at his feet.

Mr. Pankratz stepped forward, his white hands on Lena's dark skin as he drew her towards him and led her over to David's side.

The father stood before them, grinning and nodding his approval. His dark hair, slicked straight back, shone with oil. "How you say. Good luck?" He looked to see if anyone appreciated his humour.

Lena's bold smile revealed large, straight teeth. She turned and spoke to two girls behind her who scrambled about arranging the curtain veil until it fanned out across the grass like a frayed fish tail.

I heard a sharp intake of breath. "Pity the poor thing." I thought I heard my mother's voice.

"Well, he's a better person than I to take the both of them on," a man said.

About me, I saw the evidence of laughter withheld in the flickering of muscles around mouths. Tears welled and spurted behind my glasses. "She's beautiful," I heard myself say. "The bride is beautiful."

Mr. Pankratz cleared his throat noisily. The women began to nod. "Yes of course, isn't she lovely?" someone said quickly.

"More than that. Every bride is lovely, but Truda is right, she is beautiful," my mother said as I ran from the yard crying.

"Well missy, what was that scene all about?" my mother asked. She removed her hat and set it down on top of the china cupboard. The cupboard stood in the centre of the dining room instead of its usual place against the wall beside the chimney. The linoleum had been ripped up from the floor, revealing the rippled floorboards beneath. Light filtering through the curtains made the air seem granular and grey. I imagined I could see molecules dancing in front of me. My mother had gone visiting after the wedding. As she set her hat down, a splash of gold sunlight rested on her cheek.

"A curtain," my mother said, not waiting for my reply. "Imagine. I think it was one of the things I sent over there." The floor boards groaned suddenly beneath our feet. A crack zigzagged up the wall behind her head. She frowned uneasily. My father had come home and gone into the basement to work. For weeks he'd been jacking the house up in an attempt to level the floors. Easy does it, he said. And little by little, the warped, twisted house was being straightened. The house groaned and china plates shivered in the cabinet. A chunk of plaster broke loose from the ceiling and scattered on the floor. "Oh Lord," my mother said. I was about to turn from the sight of it when my mother's hands flew up in front of her face. She shrieked. The china cupboard wobbled forward, dishes sliding together. Her shriek rose above the sound of shattering china as the cupboard crashed to the floor.

My father came running and stood in the doorway, red-faced and panting. "Is everything all right?" he asked.

My mother folded up and crumpled to her knees. "Is everything all right?" she cried. "Look, look at what you've done," she said and raising her hands to the cracked walls, the crumbling ceiling, she began to cry.

My father stepped forward and then flung the crowbar he'd been carrying across the room. "It was an accident, for God's sake, Mika," he said. "It's only dishes. I thought it was something serious."

My mother's voice cracked. "But it was all I had," she said. "It was all I had left."

My brothers and sisters stood gaping. I left the house. My mother's cries were as birds' wings churning the air about my head as I ran down the road. Breathless and chilled, I leaned against the red barn, my back warmed by heat trapped in the weathered boards. I waited until the china scraps were gathered and scattered into the garden and the cabinet thrown on top of the heap of rubble in the back of the yard. I waited beside the red barn until I saw them later on, before my sister came calling and searching for me. The wedding couple walked among the trees in the park in their wedding clothes, two pale ghosts moving among the purple shadows, a flutter of silver and white. The following day, in the heat of high noon, they stood beside the road, waist-deep in the bobbing yarrow, holding hands, and smiled at me. Another evening, I saw them out by Horseshoe Lake while thunder rolled over the cattails and the air hung thick with the scent of a storm. And one night as I watched from a window in my tall narrow house, the groom held the bride's veil high as they walked up and down the streets of town and no one laughed. Below them in the flood-littered park, for a fractured second, among the toadstools a lady slipper glowed, singly and silent.

EDNA ALFORD

(b. 1947)

E dna Alford was born in Turtleford, Saskatchewan. Active in the
provincial literary scene, she was a founding editor of the magazine
Dandelion. *She has published numerous stories in such leading literary*
magazines as Prism International, The Fiddlehead, *and* Journal of
Canadian Fiction, *and had others broadcast on* CBC *radio. Her first*
collection of short stories, A Sleep Full of Dreams *(1981), is a story*
cycle set in a senior citizens' home in Alberta, and it immediately
established Alford as a writer of range, compassion, and considerable
skill. The following story, "The Bid," is taken from her second collection
of stories, The Garden of Eloise Loon *(1986), a second book that*
already shows marked development in technique, a broadening of fictional
concerns, and confirmation that Alford is indeed a writer who will help
chart the future of Canadian fiction.

The Bid

C assie left the work unfinished on her desk. She could not remember
making a conscious decision to leave. She couldn't remember selecting a destination, had no previous plan of which she was aware. Nevertheless, she was on her way home. Not to her apartment on 25th Street,
but home. North.

The campus was unearthly quiet in full term. This is the only difference so far, she thought. A stillness in the air. Not unlike the ordinary
stillness in the fall but not the same somehow. She pulled out onto College
Drive at the Memorial Gates, registered a numb, synthetic calm.

She had taken nothing with her. She had been researching certain
linguistic transformations, changes in usage. St. Mary of Bethlehem Hospital in London to Bedlam, for example. Stages of transition. Initial com-
pression related to convenience—Bethlehem. To Beth'lem. Then a
colloquial modification, a conversion primarily due to dialect. Bedlam.
Not a bad example of inversion, either, she had reflected before she left
her office, before the news had come.

Over the bridge. No bottleneck. The others must not have had time
to collect themselves, or perhaps they were merely staying where they
were. The river metallic in its bed, the banks a riot of fall, the leaves like
twirling yellow coins, the swoop of gulls.

On her left, the Bessborough Hotel, the prairie castle; even the fairytales she remembered hearing as a child had to go some to surpass the

pink and white turrets of the Bessborough rising out of the early April river mist, pink and grey, she on the Broadway Bridge on the number four bus, her mouth a small round yawn. Over the arches of the bridge carefully concrete drawn on the map of a comfortable farm roughly a million square miles around. Her childhood wrapped in a hazy high blue dome. She had never known hunger, had never seen a gun.

On Hallowe'en she carried a collection box for UNICEF and, after an evening under the streetlights, a controlled dark interrupted at regular intervals with a beacon on the corner of every block, she had turned in her copper coins, fancied she had cured the children blind and halt and hungry, covered with sores and scars, come from other lands, their hands outstretched as she had seen them on a poster one clear morning in her school. Which was new. And brightly lit with many windows which in winter gave out on the snow. The school had a goldfish pool near the entrance to the girls' cloakroom and a wishing well where you could stop and look at the beautiful fish when you came in from the cold. Often she would stop there before moving on to her home room. She stood and watched the goldfish swimming around and thought about wishes, about "The Fisherman and the Goldfish" and other fairytales she had heard or read from far off lands.

Pushkin. A. Pushkin was the man who wrote that one, her teacher said. Remarkable how a little detail like that will stay with you, she thought now, smiling, for nineteen years later, half a world away, she had seen it again. "The Fisherman and the Goldfish." A. Pushkin. In the largest bookstore in Leningrad. On an educational tour.

She had been there with a group of teachers from the prairie. In the days when Russia had opened up again, relaxed a little. Salvage and restoration everywhere. Even in Moscow. The magnificent golden turrets of the churches within the Kremlin Wall, right off Red Square. Their preservation had taken her by surprise. The icons of Rubeloff, the eyes of Christ burning among the columns of lapis lazuli and malachite, hovering over archways above the wooden doors, under the domes of fresh gold leaf which shone like a cluster of suns beneath the high blue frost, just as before. The previous year she had taken the West Coast tour, Disneyland, Monterey, Big Sur, San Francisco. And three years before that, the Oriental tour. Impossible now to believe she had actually been there, stood in each place. Remarked to herself the marvellous circumference of the earth, the expanding dimensions of the corporeal universe.

How had she come to be thinking like this again when she swore she wouldn't dwell on what she could not change. She would concentrate only on the immediate goal, imagined herself walk in through her mother's door and stand before the fragile cabinet, spend whatever time was left peering through pearly glass inspecting the porcelain set of Snow White and the Seven Dwarves, the two-headed Stavanger troll and all the other bric-a-brac. The elves. One new, in a red hat, holding a lady bug. Cassie had brought it back from the Black Forest. The leprachaun from County Down. The Honolulu girl whose grass skirt swept the china cupboard glass, appeared to lightly dust the oak floor of her shelf. And beside the dancing girl, two old farmers made of straw stuffed into minature denim overalls; one stood, one sat on a small, three-legged stool made of wood. Now she knew. Turning right at the bottom of the bridge, she knew exactly why all of this had come unbidden back. The Bessborough. The Bessborough backward through the fairy tales, fast forward to St. Basil's and Red Square.

By the time she had passed the old Sion on Idlewyld Drive, she knew she would be too warm driving in her coat. This morning she had worn the cocoa suede with the mink trim. She pulled over to the curb and took it off, folded it over her arm and placed it carefully on the back seat which was black, warm from the sun. She wiped her brow, brushed her brown bangs away from her eyes. She returned to the front of the car, got in and pulled away again, passed the turn-off to the Master Bakery (ordinarily she would have stopped there and picked up bagels for her mother). The thought of the bakery reminded her she should be hungry by now. She had had no lunch. But she wasn't hungry. Under the circumstances, how could she be.

She caught up with the traffic at last, bumper to bumper out on the highway, and so hot in the car, stuffy, but if she opened the vents, she would get all the exhaust. She rolled her window halfway down. There was still frost on some of the fields although the sun had melted most of it off. Almost all the crops in swath, the harvest late this fall. These fields may as well be the whole world, she thought. And then she was struck by an odd and inappropriate thought. She was pleased that she could now see well, especially now. The blue bell sky bright, the right colour, the clear consistency of childhood skies.

Late last spring she had had something go wrong with her eyes. A kind of inversion of vision. Everything dark appeared to her as light, and all the places common to the light presented darker than a swallowed star. She had been utterly terrified throughout that time. Almost three weeks. The Coutts-Hallmark image of a butterfly on her calendar had metamorphosed into a sinister creature not unlike a leech. Or a medieval winged beast. Everything awry. A print of "The Potato Harvesters" hanging in the foyer of the library became a pack of ghosts reaping god knows what deadly fruit; the winged caps of the stooping women were all she could see, their dark bodies lost for a time like priests in the dark and umber fields which before her very eyes turned blizzard white. Over which hung the now black wings of reaping things. A configuration of the mind as much as sight, finally. There had even been a time toward the end when she wished she couldn't see at all.

But now especially, she was grateful for her sight, relieved she was able to see well. She knew all the towns on this line. She'd been over the road so many times before. Their order a personal litany—Dalmaney, Langham, Borden, Radisson, Fielding, Maymont, Ruddell—At Langham she read the sign. "Repent: Acts 3—" something or other, the print too fine to read at this speed. "Of what?" she asked out loud, "Precisely what?" she almost yelled at the blue Ford in front of her, furious. On the sign there was a rudimentary picture of a clock like a cardboard clock on a kindergarten wall used to teach children to tell the time the old way, where there was a past, a present and a future, all together, time one round, comprehensible whole. These days there were children who couldn't even read such a clock, Cassie realized. Everything was digital now; there was only now. Five to twelve, the old clock read, stopped, but Cassie was gone, halfway between Lanham and the next town.

The words were coming numb, undone. The poet was right. The fancy could not cheat so well. San Francisco and St. Basil's. How long, she wondered, how long did she have. How long would it take? The words were coming numb, undone. And the flying off into fantasy would not work this time. The content gone.

Why she would give a damn about the yellow river hills now was a mystery to her. But she did. She still did. She wanted to see clearly, now more than ever. A steady eye. She resolved she would no longer lie, even to herself. And yet she had to confess that part of her wanted to lie. Wanted to imagine a loophole, the eye of the needle, slip through and leave all the others behind.

Which was how it had been for a while now with words, she thought, the living lie. Because it was human and merciful to hide, to long for an imaginary place where the story was done, where you could protect everyone and everything within the spine of a book, confine the evil, give wings to the words of the good. Where magic was with the world again and time was one. Where fantastic creatures walked among us. Elves and trolls and dragons and the lot. And prophets talked. But what would they say now, Cassie wondered. What was there left to say. *I told you so* echoing all down through the tunnel of conscious time. *I told you so. I told you so.* Hell bent for Rangnarok. Their time finally come. What little satisfaction there must be in that, whatever version. For there were, as Cassie knew, many versions and many subscribers to each.

She had not been alone. At first. Those left on the faculty floor had been numb as well. Many did not feel the need for any empirical confirmation, intuitive powers being what they are. For a department whose very existence depended on words, there were precious few uttered and fewer yet were actually heard, she was sure, because of the shock. Articulation dumb and for a certain time there seemed to her to be a high sweet hum in the air, of wings, and in that space of sound, everything around her went on as usual. Someone asked if there was any mail, for instance. Victor placed a paper on Loreen's desk to be taken to the steno pool for typing. It was to be ready for Monday, he said, when he would be delivering "The Word," as he called it, to a group of businessmen on convention. Over his shoulder, Cassie read the title page on the desk. "Linguistics and Commerce." Ironic now, but at the time it had seemed perfectly relevant.

Loreen took the paper and walked toward the door. Cassie assumed she planned to take the paper over to the steno pool, but she did not. She dropped it on the floor. Then she took her coat from the rack and left, never looked back or said goodbye. By that time doors were opening all along the hall, 324, 328, 326; one after another the scholars emerged, up to and including the department head. "I am going home," Victor said. And Cassie left her work undone, lying on her desk.

Langham, Borden, Radisson; Fielding, Maymont, Ruddell. A rosary of towns. And like rosary beads, the towns were similar, one to another. The names of towns. Unlikely litany, her chant. But probably as effective as any other just now. The alphabet would surely do as well, she thought.

They had been given to understand they wouldn't have much time. But if there was one thing Cassie had always known it was that Trestle, Saskatchewan was not likely to be the target of a first strike. This used to be a joke around home. So Cassie figured she might have a couple of hours; if she were lucky, maybe a whole day; if things moved in the manner described in the projections given with various alterations over the years, depending on the oil fields and the proximity of the base. For they had been at this business of projections for a very long time now. Cassie was familiar with the pattern. She had made herself familiar with the pattern, in spite of herself.

Nevertheless, her foot was to the floor. But she did not appear to be gaining on the blue Ford ahead of her. Around the curl of the lip of the hill and down toward the old Borden Bridge, three arches of concrete drawn over the river calm and winding quietly, small brown eddies swirling in the warm, familiar sun. Red willows and the dry grasses on the bank. The berry bushes not yet picked full clean by birds, the canners taken all they mean to do by now. Do down, do down. This was the season of preserves. The sealers whirled. The sealer rings, the rubber rings, everything began to spin. The words were coming numb, undone, just as her sight had come undone before.

Denholm, Brada, North Battleford. Normally Cassie would have stopped here for gas. From the outskirts, North Battleford, too, looked the same as it always had, maybe a winter Sunday afternoon sort of silence. She passed the familiar sign which still amused her. CEMETERY in bold letters on a diamond-shaped sign. A thick black arrow pointing straight up. Why not. In a world where one million three hundred thousand dollars a minute had been spent on building bombs while in the same minute thirty or more children died of starvation or disease, anything was possible. Anything, she thought. Why not. What an obscenity to pretend we even tried. It was true. The fancy could not finally cheat so well. Her prophetic sign seemed pathetic to her now. The cemetery in the sky.

She turned right at Territorial Drive which circled the heart of the city and headed North. As she left the city limits, she remembered having heard a doctor speak one evening in the composite high school here. He was from Saskatoon and she had been on her way through one weekend, on her way to Trestle. He had told them that even if they could fight a limited nuclear war, as civil defence departments would have liked them to think, Saskatchewan would essentially be devastated by radiation from attacks on missile bases in North Dakota and Montana. Not that they'd ever heard of Saskatchewan. Not that it mattered now. Cassie had met many people in other parts of her own country who had never heard of North Battleford. Then again, there were many places in the county she had been unfamiliar with as well. This had been, after all, the second largest country in the world.

But the good doctor had his point. There really were an astonishing number of people who had thought they were safe up here. Even intelligent people who had paid little more than lip service to the whole matter while there may have been time to do something about it.

"Nausea, vomiting, and diarrhea would occur within a few hours of exposure," he had said. "These symptoms would disappear during the honeymoon period. Then hair would start to fall out and bruises would appear from spontaneous bleeding." No. She had told herself a thousand times before. No. There was no point to this anymore. She would make this an inviolable vow. She would stop thinking about it altogether. She would stop. "An individual will start to die within two to three weeks. Usually not quickly, but slowly by bleeding and from the infections that start to take hold." No. "The very young, the unborn—" No. "and the very old will be especially susceptible." As usual, Cassie thought, and then *NO*. The sweats had taken hold. This time she wished the words would come undone. Scramble. Delete. Erase. Whatever would remove them from her head.

She had promised herself before that she would not think about this or speak about what she had come to know over the years, even to herself. This was a machination of the mind, the memory, the words. As if she were under interrogation in a small dark room beneath a funnel of bright light, listening to her disembodied voice played back to her at an intolerable speed, measured, slow. If only there were a way of erasing the fact that she had known, they had known. For they had known. For some reason this was the part that bothered her the most. If only they had not known; possibly that would have been forgiveable. But to know and still proceed. A trick of her black track mind again. No.

The light was beginning to fade. There was no mistake. She would rather go blind than to say, but it faded into grey hills like ash near Jackfish Lake, just over the first rise but before the descent into Cochin. Just over the rise and then the falling away into all the smaller, countless hills; cattle on a thousand hills, and the image of the promised land gone still and blind behind her eyes.

She began to wish it were completely dark. Anything to extinguish the gold, the ghastly light. The whole country lacquered in it by the time she hit the Cochin Hill, habitually diminished speed as she moved down into the town, toward the shrine.

She was tempted to stop at the shrine. She braked and pulled into the driveway of the church, the gravel rumbling under the wheels of the car. She was intruding, making too much noise. A shroud of silence surrounded the shrine. She parked and got out of the car, started toward the clump of figures huddled around a small white plaster shell beside the lake. The Lady, like an expectorate pearl, remained kneeling, inert, before the plaster cast of the Deity within, all lacquered in an underwater light, grey and yellow. Right now She seemed to Cassie more like La Belle Dame Sans Merci than the Holy Mother of Bethlehem. And when Cassie drew closer, close enough to see the faces of the huddled frightened few, she knew she could not stay with them.

There were old women wearing work moccasins and rubbers, young men with long dark braids wearing high school hockeyjackets with crests sewn on the back, the shoulders, the sides. There were men in peaked caps and wide-brimmed straw hats. Young men clutching small girls, their braids secured with red and yellow and turquoise loops of small glass beads.

Cassie had once seen the world champion hoop dancer on the Reservation near Trestle. At the Pow Wow. He had danced the creation. In the final movement of the dance, the imaginary whole fell apart and all the hoops, so cleverly constructed in the shape of a sphere around the body of the dancing man, had dropped to the dancer's feet and the little wire world had disappeared in the tall grass. The people at the shrine were from another Reservation nearby, Cassie thought. It must seem like the second coming of the end of the world to them. They have already seen something similar before. From within. Of this she was sure. But she could not stay. She was intruding, once again. And she knew she could not pray, not now, even with them. She turned away and watched the sun trace the last of the passing day with a grim impersonation of the light.

When she was back on the highway, she resolved she would not think at all, nor would she observe. At least not until she got to the next town. Not until the fall of the actual night. By then it would at least be dark. The twilight was intolerable, the in-between time.

But it didn't work. No sooner had she made the resolution than she began to think: we have all been through this awful day so many times before, in our heads; the dress rehearsals in the press, the poets and the novelists, the old myths: the rather tardy invocations of the high priests of the new myth. Laboratories, shrines. What difference had it really made, in retrospect.

At one point, they saw fit to inform the general population of the onset of the long winter after the event which no one was supposed to mention specifically. The Southern Hemisphere would not be exempt, they said, because of the dimming of the sun, the cold, the coming catastrophic cold. Well then, Cassie had thought at the time, in this part of the world (and in Russia too, she supposed) there is nothing we know better than the cold. And little which commands as much respect. Fire and ice. By a man named Frost, if you please. How do the poets know. At any rate, she thought, ice was not imaginary here, not fragmented myth, although it was sometimes full of light. The day of the triple dog sun, for example. Providing the sun hit the ice crystals in just such a fashion as to fill them full of light. This was true. But with the dimming of the sun, Cassie supposed the ice would be blacker than the clichéd ace of spades. So much for hemispheres. And for her resolutions.

Actually, toward the end, Cassie's family had finally made a resolution of its own because their gatherings had become so grim. Surrounded as they had been with good food, homemade wine, abundant and beautiful children, each other (this must have been the promised land or the closest thing to it, Cassie thought now when she looked back, although she would not have postulated such an arrogant premise at the time), their after-dinner conversations repeatedly engaged, in one form or another, the unspeakable event.

It got so they almost dreaded seeing one another, because of their conversations at such gatherings. They had to set limits. No one was to say anything about *the event* ever again, no matter how many wood lilies bloomed or patches of lady slippers found (and wouldn't it be a shame). The images had, over the years of apprehension, worn thin, become trite, but not the pain. Ironically, that remained intact the whole time. No matter how many fish caught, no matter how many bushels to the acre, no matter how many pounds of blueberries put down for the winter. The event was to remain literally unspeakable.

Not that they actually did anything to prevent it. That was the worst of it. What could they do? They knew people who sent letters to the government and marched against the deployment of various weapons along the way and things like that. But for some reason, they had done nothing at all. Hardly anybody had, when Cassie stopped to think about it now. Hardly anybody all over the world. But for a few brave souls. There was sometimes a price to pay, after all. Greenham Common, Cold Bay and the like. These were women, mostly mothers.

But before the family ban, Cassie remembered, they'd had convoluted, lengthy discussions. Most of the time Cassie talked to her brother, Soren, who was a man of science. He held no hope for the species but he was of comfort, ironically, to those who had lost the faith, or any faith. Which by that time was most of them. He especially seemed vulnerable to the talk about the end of the world. Cassie thought it might have been because he was so very close to his children. He had one boy and one girl. But Soren could be persuaded to talk about field physics on occasion as well, and he was far more familiar with the concept of infinity, for example, than were many of the others. During those days, he, of all people, had been their greatest source of something which resembled metaphysical hope; though he protested, he protested in vain. For it had been he who had reunited them with the plausibility of eternity and the presence of wonder and all that would remain when they were gone. Soren. Soren had all the wood for his house milled in this town, Cassie thought, as she approached the sprinkle of light on the horizon.

She passed the mill on her right, just before the grain elevators. A sign along the highway said "North to Meadow Lake"; she planned to take the turn after the water tower, the narrow road north, home. But the light from the dim sun setting through the red haze frightened her again although all the way from Cochin she had done well, thought mainly of her mother's cabinet and of the pale, intricate pattern on the Hardanger runner and of the elves. At last count, her mother had forty-three elves. Cassie had contributed many of them herself. Souvenirs of her travels. But the last few miles, the burnt haze of late light through the thickening brush had begun to look like red teeth, the stand of trees a sulfur mouth. So she pulled off the highway into the town and parked in front of the auction mart on the corner of the main street. It was directly opposite the Co-op Store and down from the Post Office. There were many cars and half-ton trucks parked on the main street and on the highway down past the cafe and the motel, all the way down to the burned-out gas station at the far end of town.

The auction was in progress. The side door of the mart was open and a shallow light leaned toward the street. She rolled her window all the way down. She could hear the auctioneer from the car; his voice was like gravel but his words were clear. She opened the car door, got out and rolled the window up.

For a while she stood leaning against the open door, her arms folded across her breast, resting. She discovered she was stiff and the muscles at the back of her neck were rigid. She massaged them slowly with her left hand. What time was it? Anybody's guess, she thought. Her watch had stopped. The auction mart was long and grey, clapboard, a false front facing the grocery store, but this side was long and unadorned. It could have been a barn. She slammed the car door and started walking toward the lighted entrance to the auction mart.

She slipped in through the light and made her way to one of the benches at the back. She sat down near a young woman. The auctioneer's right-hand man wore a red peaked cap and had a long soft face. He held up a sack of onions and a number, 34. The auction was only beginning. The auctioneer was doing food. Cassie had stopped here several times before on her way home and she was familiar with the routine. The food came up on the block first. Bagged carrots and beets and crates of apples and oranges were stacked beside cases of juice and Kleenex and paper towels along three walls of a raised platform lit by two lightbulbs swinging shadows slowly forth and back, back and forth. A woman sat at a plywood table on the platform keeping track with lists of consigned goods lying before her, lined up in the correct order.

The auctioneer was a jovial man, tall and heavy set but not fat. He had a full red beard and a moustache and an enormous bush of wiry red hair which puffed out from under a black cowboy hat. He wore a black silk western shirt with pearl buttons, a red rose embroidered on either shoulder. When he turned and bent toward the onions, Cassie saw he had three roses on his back.

"I want to tell you folks something," he said. "There are three important things a good auctioneer has got to remember, and this is fact. Number one: get good before you get fast. Number two: stay clear so people can understand you. And number three: there is nothing, I repeat, folks, *nothing* in the world which cannot be sold by auction. Which really means there's nothing can't be bought. World champion auctioneer told me that." And then he began to chant, "Whatamibid whatamibid. Onions. Ten pound sacks. Five to the man in the straw hat. Ten to the Blue Boy Cafe. Five to the lady in pink at the back. Five to the back. Ten more sacks. We've got to move ten more sacks. Whatamibid whatamibid—"

Dazed, Cassie looked around the room. The sound of the man's voice ricocheted everywhere. Her ears rung. A chant for ninety-eight bales of hay, a case of ketchup, a crate of eggs, seventy-five bushels of seed grain, forty gallons of antifreeze and two black calves which bawled outside the double doors to the left of the platform. There were long tables set end to end the length of both walls. A buffet of clocks and burnished copper oil derricks, knick-knacks of all description, monkeypod salad bowls, velvet paintings, garden tools and spice racks. Butter churns. Depression glass.

The auctioneer hoisted a crate of grapes. He tilted the crate and held it out to the crowd. The grapes were large and dark purple. They were in a California crate. "Whatamibid whatamibid," he bellowed into the microphone. His left black boot caught the cord and he slid a little, staggered back and laughed out loud. "No bid? No bid. They're all yours. Compliments of the house." He laughed again and reached into the crate, grabbed a bunch of grapes and threw them hard. A small brown boy in the front row caught them and ran toward his mother who was standing near the coffee urn at the back with the rest of her people, a dark knot from where Cassie sat.

Everywhere arms in the crowd, waving, reaching out, and the grapes flew from the auctioneer's hands till the crate was empty and the right-hand man passed him a box full of boots and shoes.

"You, Lou" said the auctioneer, pointing to a man in green overalls standing by the wall halfway down the room. "You need these shoes. I know you do. I know that for a fact because I sold you a box of shoes last spring and there wasn't a thing in that box a man could wear, no soles or tongues or laces in a single pair. How about it, Lou? Whatamibid whatamibid. You're too late, Lou," he finally said, sadly. "I got a bid over here. Whatabuy. Lou, my friend," he said, gesturing to him, "another golden opportunity has just passed you by, flew out these double doors over here on my right. Time waits for no one, my friend. Not time. Not my old man time. Don't matter where you live. In Livelong or in gay Paree—(Lou here is from Livelong, folks)—it's all the same to me. In the end." He turned and bent, heaved his black buttocks into the air and undulated twice. Then he was gone. The crowd roared.

Cassie couldn't believe her eyes. The bulbs on the platform swung from side to side. The door through which she had entered slammed shut with the wind and and the lights died. But the voice began to rise. "Whatamibid whatamibid—"

An enormous postcard appeared before them, floodlit the full height and almost the whole length of the platform. First the mailing side, the back. "Leningrad, Pisskariovskoye Memorial Cemetery, Statue of Motherland, 1960, Sculptors: V. Isayeva, R. Taurit; Architects: E. Levninson, A. Valyev." Then it flipped over in a flash of light and on the front was a photograph of a statue, a woman carved of stone holding what looked like a net in her outstretched arms. She was elevated on a marble base. A knot of random men and women stood at the base, the backs of their heads to the camera so you couldn't make out a face. But Cassie recognized the stone woman and in her mind she surveyed the half million mounded in mass graves surrounding the monument. Civilians from the siege of Leningrad. Singing floated from the back of the auction mart. A female voice. High and slow and operatic. A dirge. And now Cassie remembered the music too, the chill April afternoon. And the guide who refused to answer whether or not it was true: that the female-male ratio in Russia after the Second World War had been seven to one. (Although you would never have known it from the Presidium, Cassie thought. There were no women in the Presidium. Not one.) They must have thought few people knew. Give us back our sons, implored the stone.

"Whatamibid whatamibid. From the USSR. Complete with birthing rope, the Ring of Glory and of hope," the auctioneer chanted. "This is a motherhood issue, folks. You bet your sweet life. Whatamibid, whatamibid. SOLD!"

The young woman beside Cassie had raised her hand. She turned toward Cassie now and frowned. Her hair was clean and long and blonde. Her face was wet, lit with reflected light. She fondled a tattered quilt in her lap. Apparently she had brought it with her to the auction mart. It hadn't come up on the block. It was made up of patches from the great coats, uniforms from World War One, grey and blue and brown. Canadian coats come home. Four numbers were stitched on a corner square, 1931. It had taken someone all those years to put it together, thought Cassie. Or maybe there wasn't a need until then. Depression. Anything to keep the family going, keep the family warm.

The room grew cold. Then filled with sparks and smoke. "Are you ready folks," the auctioneer began, "from China. Whatamibid for the Harbin Ice Lantern Show. Direct. The genuine article. We got to move this *now*, folks. Everything's got to go." The voice of the crowd exploded in one startled OH. Cassie's and the young woman's among them. Ohh. An arc of ice and coloured light appeared on the platform. A rainbow. And above it an arc of multicoloured fireworks against a dark sky, red and green and purple and yellow and blue. "This ain't chinoiserie, ladies and gents. This is the real thing. Whatamibid whatamibid whatamibid— SOLD! To the owner of the Blue Boy Cafe. I guess that's only right folks, whatdaya say?" The people roared.

Cassie herself placed no bid throughout the auction, although I was aware the whole time that the author wished she would. I don't know which I would say was more difficult, all said and done. Working for Chicken Littles like Cass' creator or for one of their counterparts who have been running around whispering, "The sky is not falling in; the sky is not falling in. I believe you, brother." Neither of them makes the least bit of sense from my point of view. Not that my perspective interferes. The assignments appear to be indiscriminate and right now I am here with Cass and this loony auctioneer.

The fact is I, too, harbour soft spots for the Honeyman Dunes on the Oregon Coast and for Tofino and the new Roy Thompson Hall, Vigeland and Mount Hoodna; the Grand Canyon and Madison Square Gardens and, for old times' sake, the wild and steamy two-room suite in that deliciously seedy hotel in the Bahamas. Nonetheless, there are certain things on which I will not bid, regardless of creative pressure, regardless of the apocalyptic vision of yet one more writer. And, although the plaintive quilt may function as a fine image in some ways, I suspect it will emerge that most women have had it up to here with the quiet, fatalistic weeping over the systematic mutilation of human beings, their literal handiwork thus far.

So, for the first time, I refused to deliver the lines assigned—what were supposed to be my last words in this case. For one thing, nothing is so plentiful these days as apocalyptic visions. They are a dime a dozen. The cliché of our time. Nothing easier to imagine (on a superficial level, at any rate) than the logical progression, the obvious end, the earned increment of ten thousand years.

My decision remained firm. Even so, I was sorely tempted twice. In the assignment of this role. In the voice of the character, Cass. It was all I could do to refrain from bidding when the Hermitage came up on the block. I have had many Russian assignments in the past, some in the Winter Palace itself and, over the centuries, I have watched the collection amass from Catherine onward. Lately I have taken a particular fancy to the large canvasses of Matisse, especially "The Dancing Women" series, these because I have recently been in demand for roles which focused on the liberation of the female spirit. I have also recently been stoned to death because I was wearing perfume in the former land of the former Peacock Throne. Before World War Two, the Russians crated the most valuable works in the Hermitage collection and hid them in the Ural Mountains.

The last temptation came when the whole room started to spin and Cassie found herself peering out over the rim of a large Blue Willow teacup in Disneyland. Tinkerbell was just beginning her ascent over the castle in Fantasyland trailing stardust from her toes which not only took Cassie back to the Bessborough in the fall and the banks of the river of her home town and ahead to the Palace of Congresses in the Russian spring, high in the cold air, the sparkled gown of the Prima Ballerina of the Bolshoi Ballet dancing "Don Quixote" before a sell-out crowd, but also forward again to her mother's home near Trestle and to her china cabinet filled with fairies and with matadors, Snow White and the Seven Dwarves.

It also took me back to the Pacific Rim off the West Coast of Canada and another story I am to be involved with later on. I am to be a man who walks along the sand at night trailing bits of light behind him. A phenomenon called bioluminescence in which light is produced by the aggravation of an organism called phytoplankton found both in the sea and in the sand. The working title is "The Totem of a Modern Man."

Yet I was never as tempted to bid as when the man said "Whatamibid, whatamibid, whatamibid for Disneyland?" Cassie often travelled in other lands and she always brought back something for the kids.

ANN BEATTIE

(b. 1947)

A nn Beattie was born in Washington, D.C. She was educated at
American University (B.A. 1969) and the University of Connecticut (M.A. 1972), but has said that she became a writer because she was
bored with graduate work in English. Her first story was published in
1972, and since then she has published in most of the important American
journals. Collections of her stories include Distortions (1976), Secrets
and Surprises (1979), and Where You'll Find Me, and Other Stories
(1986). She has also published four novels, Chilly Scenes of Winter
(1976), Falling in Place (1980), Love Always (1985), and Picturing
Will (1989). She has taught English at the University of Virginia and
at Harvard, and has won a number of distinguished awards, including an
honorary Doctor of Humane Letters degree from American University.
Because so much of her work focuses on characters who were profoundly
affected by the sixties' experience, critics often discuss Beattie as a spokes-
person for that decade. She resists this label, though she has admitted
that she does write about "a rather small, neurotic, overmonied, in some
ways overprivileged and unhappy group of people." Her minimalist
prose has also made her part of a group of neo-realist American writers
that includes Raymond Carver and Bobbie Ann Mason. John Updike
describes the most striking characteristic of her work, its leisurely pace,
this way:

> Her details—which include the lyrics of the songs her characters
> overhear on the radio and the recipes of the rather junky food
> they eat—calmly accrue; her dialogue trails down the pages
> with an uncanny fidelity to the low-level heartbreaks behind the
> banal; her resolutely unmetaphorical style builds around us a
> maze of familiar truths that nevertheless has something airy,
> eerie, and in the end lovely about it. Her America is like the
> America one pieces together from the National Enquirers that
> her characters read—a land of pathetic monstrosities, of pain
> clothed in clichés, of extraterrestrial trivia. Things happen "out
> there," and their vibes haunt the dreary "here" we inhabit.

Shifting

The woman's name was Natalie, and the man's name was Larry. They had been childhood sweethearts; he had first kissed her at an ice-skating party when they were ten. She had been unlacing her skates and had not expected the kiss. He had not expected to do it, either—he had some notion of getting his face out of the wind that was blowing across the iced-over lake, and he found himself ducking his head toward her. Kissing her seemed the natural thing to do. When they graduated from high school he was named "class clown" in the yearbook, but Natalie didn't think of him as being particularly funny. He spent more time than she thought he needed to studying chemistry, and he never laughed when she joked. She really did not think of him as funny. They went to the same college, in their hometown, but he left after a year to go to a larger, more impressive university. She took the train to be with him on weekends, or he took the train to see her. When he graduated, his parents gave him a car. If they had given it to him when he was still in college, it would have made things much easier. They waited to give it to him until graduation day, forcing him into attending the graduation exercises. He thought his parents were wonderful people, and Natalie liked them in a way, too, but she resented their perfect timing, their careful smiles. They were afraid that he would marry her. Eventually, he did. He had gone on to graduate school after college, and he set a date six months ahead for their wedding so that it would take place after his first-semester final exams. That way he could devote his time to studying for the chemistry exams.

When she married him, he had had the car for eight months. It still smelled like a brand-new car. There was never any clutter in the car. Even the ice scraper was kept in the glove compartment. There was not even a sweater or a lost glove in the back seat. He vacuumed the car every weekend, after washing it at the car wash. On Friday nights, on their way to some cheap restaurant and a dollar movie, he would stop at the car wash, and she would get out so he could vacuum all over the inside of the car. She would lean against the metal wall of the car wash and watch him clean it.

It was expected that she would not become pregnant. She did not. It had also been expected that she would keep their apartment clean, and keep out of the way as much as possible in such close quarters while he was studying. The apartment was messy, though, and when he was studying late at night she would interrupt him and try to talk him into going to sleep. He gave a chemistry-class lecture once a week, and she would often tell him that overpreparing was as bad as underpreparing.

She did not know if she believed this, but it was a favorite line of hers. Sometimes he listened to her.

On Tuesdays, when he gave the lecture, she would drop him off at school and then drive to a supermarket to do the week's shopping. Usually she did not make a list before she went shopping, but when she got to the parking lot she would take a tablet out of her purse and write a few items on it, sitting in the car in the cold. Even having a few things written down would stop her from wandering aimlessly in the store and buying things that she would never use. Before this, she had bought several pans and cans of food that she had not used, or that she could have done without. She felt better when she had a list.

She would drop him at school again on Wednesdays, when he had two seminars that together took up all the afternoon. Sometimes she would drive out of town then, to the suburbs, and shop there if any shopping needed to be done. Otherwise, she would go to the art museum, which was not far away but hard to get to by bus. There was one piece of sculpture in there that she wanted very much to touch, but the guard was always nearby. She came so often that in time the guard began to nod hello. She wondered if she could ever persuade the man to turn his head for a few seconds—only that long—so she could stroke the sculpture. Of course she would never dare ask. After wandering through the museum and looking at least twice at the sculpture, she would go to the gift shop and buy a few postcards and then sit on one of the museum benches, padded with black vinyl, with a Calder mobile hanging overhead, and write notes to friends. (She never wrote letters.) She would tuck the postcards in her purse and mail them when she left the museum. But before she left, she often had coffee in the restaurant: she saw mothers and children struggling there, and women dressed in fancy clothes talking with their faces close together, as quietly as lovers.

On Thursdays he took the car. After his class he would drive to visit his parents and his friend Andy, who had been wounded in Vietnam. About once a month she would go with him, but she had to feel up to it. Being with Andy embarrassed her. She had told him not to go to Vietnam—told him that he could prove his patriotism in some other way—and finally, after she and Larry had made a visit together and she had seen Andy in the motorized bed in his parents' house, Larry had agreed that she need not go again. Andy had apologized to her. It embarrassed her that this man, who had been blown sky-high by a land mine and had lost a leg and lost the full use of his arms, would smile up at her ironically and say, "You were right." She also felt as though he wanted to hear what she would say now, and that now he would listen. Now she had nothing to say. Andy would pull himself up, relying on his right arm, which was the stronger, gripping the rails at the side of the bed, and sometimes he would take her hand. His arms were still weak, but the doctors said he would regain complete use of his right arm with time. She had to make an effort not to squeeze his hand when he held hers because she found herself wanting to squeeze energy back into him. She had a morbid curiosity about what it felt like to be blown from the ground—to go up, and to come crashing down. During their visit Larry put on the class-clown act for Andy, telling funny stories and laughing uproariously.

Once or twice Larry had talked Andy into getting in his wheelchair and had loaded him into the car and taken him to a bar. Larry called her once, late, pretty drunk, to say that he would not be home that night— that he would sleep at his parents' house. "My God," she said. "Are you going to drive Andy home when you're drunk?" "What the hell else can happen to him?" he said.

Larry's parents blamed her for Larry's not being happy. His mother could only be pleasant with her for a short while, and then she would veil her criticisms by putting them as questions. "I know that one thing that helps enormously is good nutrition," his mother said. "He works so hard that he probably needs quite a few vitamins as well, don't you think?" Larry's father was the sort of man who found hobbies in order to avoid his wife. His hobbies were building model boats, repairing clocks, and photography. He took pictures of himself building the boats and fixing the clocks, and gave the pictures, in cardboard frames, to Natalie and Larry for Christmas and birthday presents. Larry's mother was very anxious to stay on close terms with her son, and she knew that Natalie did not like her very much. Once she had visited them during the week, and Natalie, not knowing what to do with her, had taken her to the museum. She had pointed out the sculpture, and his mother had glanced at it and then ignored it. Natalie hated her for her bad taste. She had bad taste in the sweaters she gave Larry, too, but he wore them. They made him look collegiate. That whole world made her sick.

When Natalie's uncle died and left her his 1965 Volvo, they immediately decided to sell it and use the money for a vacation. They put an ad in the paper, and there were several callers. There were some calls on Tuesday, when Larry was in class, and Natalie found herself putting the people off. She told one woman that the car had too much mileage on it, and mentioned body rust, which it did not have; she told another caller, who was very persistent, that the car was already sold. When Larry returned from school she explained that the phone was off the hook because so many people were calling about the car and she had decided not to sell it after all. They could take a little money from their savings account and go on the trip if he wanted. But she did not want to sell the car. "It's not an automatic shift," he said. "You don't know how to drive it." She told him that she could learn. "It will cost money to insure it," he said, "and it's old and probably not even dependable." She wanted to keep the car. "I know," he said, "but it doesn't make sense. When we have more money, you can have a car. You can have a newer, better car."

The next day she went out to the car, which was parked in the driveway of an old lady next door. Her name was Mrs. Larsen and she no longer drove a car, and she told Natalie she could park their second car there. Natalie opened the car door and got behind the wheel and put her hands on it. The wheel was covered with a flaky yellow-and-black plastic cover. She eased it off. A few pieces of foam rubber stuck to the wheel. She picked them off. Underneath the cover, the wheel was a dull red. She ran her fingers around and around the circle of the wheel. Her cousin Burt had delivered the car—a young opportunist, sixteen years old, who said he would drive it the hundred miles from his house to theirs for twenty dollars and a bus ticket home. She had not even invited him to stay for dinner, and Larry had driven him to the bus station. She wondered if it was Burt's cigarette in the ashtray or her dead uncle's. She could not even remember if her uncle smoked. She was surprised that he had left her his car. The car was much more comfortable than Larry's, and it had a nice smell inside. It smelled a little the way a field smells after a spring rain. She rubbed the side of her head back and forth against the window and then got out of the car and went in to see Mrs. Larsen. The night before, she had suddenly thought of the boy who brought the old lady the evening newspaper every night; he looked old enough to drive, and he would probably know how to shift. Mrs. Larsen agreed with her—she was sure that he could teach her. "Of course, everything has its price," the old lady said.

"I know that. I meant to offer him money," Natalie said, and was surprised, listening to her voice, that she sounded old too.

She took an inventory and made a list of things in their apartment. Larry had met an insurance man one evening while playing basketball at the gym who told him that they should have a list of their possessions, in case of theft. "What's worth anything?" she said when he told her. It was their first argument in almost a year—the first time in a year, anyway, that their voices were raised. He told her that several of the pieces of furniture his grandparents gave them when they got married were antiques, and the man at the gym said that if they weren't going to get them appraised every year, at least they should take snapshots of them and keep the pictures in a safe-deposit box. Larry told her to photograph the pie safe (which she used to store linen), the piano with an inlaid mother-of-pearl decoration of the music rack (neither of them knew how to play), and the table with hand-carved wooden handles and a marble top. He bought her an Instamatic camera at the drugstore, with film and flash bulbs. "Why can't you do it?" she said, and an argument began. He said that she had no respect for his profession and no understanding of the amount of study that went into getting a master's degree in chemistry.

That night he went out to meet two friends at the gym, to shoot baskets. She put the little flashcube into the top of the camera, dropped in the film and closed the back. She went first to the piano. She leaned forward so that she was close enough to see the inlay clearly, but she found that when she was that close the whole piano wouldn't fit into the picture. She decided to take two pictures. Then she photographed the pie safe, with one door open, showing the towels and sheets stacked inside. She did not have a reason for opening the door, except that she remembered a *Perry Mason* show in which detectives photographed everything with the doors hanging open. She photographed the table, lifting the lamp off it first. There were still eight pictures left. She went to the mirror in their bedroom and held the camera above her head, pointing down at an angle, and photographed her image in the mirror. She took off her slacks and sat on the floor and leaned back, aiming the camera down at her legs. Then she stood up and took a picture of her feet, leaning over and aiming down. She put on her favorite record: Stevie Wonder singing "For Once in My Life." She found herself wondering what it would be like to be blind, to have to feel things to see them. She thought about the piece of sculpture in the museum—the two elongated mounds, intertwined, the smooth gray stone as shiny as sea pebbles. She photographed the kitchen, bathroom, bedroom and living room. There was one picture left. She put her left hand on her thigh, palm up, and with some difficulty—with the camera nestled into her neck like a violin— snapped a picture of it with her right hand. The next day would be her first driving lesson.

He came to her door at noon, as he had said he would. He had on a long maroon scarf, which made his deep-blue eyes very striking. She had only seen him from her window when he carried the paper in to the old lady. He was a little nervous. She hoped that it was just the anxiety of any teen-ager confronting an adult. She needed to have him like her. She did not learn about mechanical things easily (Larry had told her that he would have invested in a "real" camera, except that he did not have the time to teach her about it), so she wanted him to be patient. He sat on the footstool in her living room, still in coat and scarf, and told her how a stick shift operated. He moved his hand through the air. The motion he made reminded her of the salute spacemen gave to earthlings in a science-fiction picture she had recently watched on late-night television. She nodded. "How much—" she began, but he interrupted and said, "You can decide what it was worth when you've learned." She was surprised and wondered if he meant to charge a great deal. Would it be her fault and would she have to pay him if he named his price when the lessons were over? But he had an honest face. Perhaps he was just embarrassed to talk about money.

He drove for a few blocks, making her watch his hand on the stick shift. "Feel how the car is going?" he said. "Now you shift." He shifted. The car jumped a little, hummed, moved into gear. It was an old car and didn't shift too easily, he said. She had been sitting forward, so that when he shifted she rocked back hard against the seat—harder than she needed to. Almost unconsciously, she wanted to show him what a good teacher he was. When her turn came to drive, the car stalled. "Take it easy," he said. "Ease up on the clutch. Don't just raise your foot off of it like that." She tried it again. "That's it," he said. She looked at him when the car was in third. He sat in the seat, looking out the window. Snow was expected. It was Thursday. Although Larry was going to visit his parents and would not be back until late Friday afternoon, she decided she would wait until Tuesday for her next lesson. If he came home early, he would find out that she was taking lessons, and she didn't want him to know. She asked the boy, whose name was Michael, whether he thought she would forget all he had taught her in the time between lessons. "You'll remember," he said.

When they returned to the old lady's driveway, the car stalled going up the incline. She had trouble shifting. The boy put his hand over hers and kicked the heel of his hand forward. "You'll have to treat this car a little roughly, I'm afraid," he said. That afternoon, after he left, she made spaghetti sauce, chopping little pieces of pepper and onion and mushroom. When the sauce had cooked down, she called Mrs. Larsen and said that she would bring over dinner. She usually ate with the old lady once a week. The old lady often added a pinch of cinnamon to her food, saying that it brought out the flavor better than salt, and that since she was losing her sense of smell, food had to be strongly flavored for her to taste it. Once she had sprinkled cinnamon on a knockwurst. This time, as they ate, Natalie asked the old lady how much she paid the boy to bring the paper.

"I give him a dollar a week," the old lady said.

"Did he set the price, or did you?"

"He set the price. He told me he wouldn't take much because he has to walk this street to get to his apartment anyway."

"He taught me a lot about the car today," Natalie said.

"He's very handsome, isn't he?" the old lady said.

She asked Larry, "How were your parents?"

"Fine," he said. "But I spent almost all the time with Andy. It's almost his birthday, and he's depressed. We went to see Mose Allison."

"I think it stinks that hardly anyone else ever visits Andy," she said.

"He doesn't make it easy. He tells you everything that's on his mind, and there's no way you can pretend that his troubles don't amount to much. You just have to sit there and nod."

She remembered that Andy's room looked like a gymnasium. There were handgrips and weights scattered on the floor. There was even a psychedelic pink hula hoop that he was to put inside his elbow and then move his arm in circles wide enough to make the hoop spin. He couldn't do it. He would lie in bed with the hoop in back of his neck, and holding the sides, lift his neck off the pillow. His arms were barely strong enough to do that, really, but he could raise his neck with no trouble, so he just pretended that his arms pulling the loop were raising it. His parents thought that it was a special exercise that he had mastered.

"What did you do today?" Larry said now.

"I made spaghetti," she said. She had made it the day before, but she thought that since he was mysterious about the time he spent away from her ("in the lab" and "at the gym" became interchangeable), she did not owe him a straight answer. That day she had dropped off the film and then she had sat at the drugstore counter to have a cup of coffee. She bought some cigarettes, though she had not smoked since high school. She smoked one mentholated cigarette and then threw the pack away in a garbage container outside the drugstore. Her mouth still felt cool inside.

He asked if she had planned anything for the weekend.

"No," she said.

"Let's do something you'd like to do. I'm a little ahead of myself in the lab right now."

That night they ate spaghetti and made plans, and the next day they went for a ride in the country, to a factory where wooden toys were made. In the showroom he made a bear marionette shake and twist. She examined a small rocking horse, rhythmically pushing her finger up and down on the back rung of the rocker to make it rock. When they left they took with them a catalogue of toys they could order. She knew that they would never look at the catalogue again. On their way to the museum he stopped to wash the car. Because it was the weekend there were quite a few cars lined up waiting to go in. They were behind a blue Cadillac that seemed to inch forward of its own accord, without a driver. When the Cadillac moved into the washing area, a tiny man hopped out. He stood on tiptoe to reach the coin box to start the washing machine. She doubted if he was five feet tall.

"Look at the poor son of a bitch," he said.

The little man was washing his car.

"If Andy could get out more," Larry said. "If he could get rid of that feeling he has that he's the only freak . . . . I wonder if it wouldn't do him good to come spend a week with us."

"Are you going to take him in the wheelchair to the lab with you?" she said. "I'm not taking care of Andy all day."

His face changed. "Just for a week was all I meant," he said.

"I'm not doing it," she said. She was thinking of the boy, and of the car. She had almost learned how to drive the car.

"Maybe in the warm weather," she said. "When we could go to the park or something."

He said nothing. The little man was rinsing his car. She sat inside when their turn came. She thought that Larry had no right to ask her to take care of Andy. Water flew out of the hose and battered the car. She thought of Andy, in the woods at night, stepping on the land mine, being blown into the air. She wondered if it threw him in an arc, so he ended up somewhere away from where he had been walking, or if it just blasted him straight up, if he went up the way an umbrella opens. Andy had been a wonderful ice skater. They all envied him his long sweeping turns, with his legs somehow neatly together and his body at the perfect angle. She never saw him have an accident on the ice. Never once. She had known Andy, and they had skated at Parker's pond, for eight years before he was drafted.

The night before, as she and Larry were finishing dinner, he had asked her if she intended to vote for Nixon or McGovern in the election. "McGovern," she said. How could he not have known that? She knew then that they were farther apart than she had thought. She hoped that on Election Day she could drive herself to the polls—not go with him and not walk. She planned not to ask the old lady if she wanted to come along because that would be one vote she could keep Nixon from getting.

At the museum she hesitated by the sculpture but did not point it out to him. He didn't look at it. He gazed to the side, above it, at a Francis Bacon painting. He could have shifted his eyes just a little and seen the sculpture, and her, standing and staring.

After three more lessons she could drive the car. The last two times, which were later in the afternoon than her first lesson, they stopped at the drug store to get the old lady's paper, to save him from having to make the same trip back on foot. When he came out of the drugstore with the paper, after the final lesson, she asked him if he'd like to have a beer to celebrate.

"Sure," he said.

They walked down the street to a bar that was filled with college students. She wondered if Larry ever came to this bar. He had never said that he did.

She and Michael talked. She asked why he wasn't in high school. He told her that he had quit. He was living with his brother, and his brother was teaching him carpentry, which he had been interested in all along. On his napkin he drew a picture of the cabinets and bookshelves he and his brother had spent the last week constructing and installing in the house of two wealthy old sisters. He drummed the side of his thumb against the edge of the table in time with the music. They each drank beer, from heavy glass mugs.

"Mrs. Larsen said your husband was in school," the boy said. "What's he studying?"

She looked up, surprised. Michael had never mentioned her husband to her before. "Chemistry," she said.

"I liked chemistry pretty well," he said. "Some of it."

"My husband doesn't know you've been giving me lessons. I'm just going to tell him that I can drive the stick shift, and surprise him."

"Yeah?" the boy said. "What will he think about that?"

"I don't know," she said. "I don't think he'll like it."

"Why?" the boy said.

His question made her remember that he was sixteen. What she had said would never have provoked another question from an adult. The adult would have nodded or said, "I know."

She shrugged. The boy took a long drink of beer. "I thought it was funny that he didn't teach you himself, when Mrs. Larsen told me you were married," he said.

They had discussed her. She wondered why Mrs. Larsen wouldn't have told her that, because the night she ate dinner with her she had talked to Mrs. Larsen about what an extraordinarily patient teacher Michael was. Had Mrs. Larsen told him that Natalie talked about him?

On the way back to the car she remembered the photographs and went back to the drugstore and picked up the prints. As she took money out of her wallet she remembered that today was the day she would have to pay him. She looked around at him, at the front of the store, where he was flipping through magazines. He was tall and he was wearing a very old black jacket. One end of his long thick maroon scarf was hanging down his back.

"What did you take pictures of?" he said when they were back in the car.

"Furniture. My husband wanted pictures of our furniture, in case it was stolen."

"Why?" he said.

"They say if you have proof that you had valuable things, the insurance company won't hassle you about reimbursing you."

"You have a lot of valuable stuff?" he said.

"My husband thinks so," she said.

A block from the driveway she said, "What do I owe you?"

"Four dollars," he said.

"That's nowhere near enough," she said and looked over at him. He had opened the envelope with the pictures in it while she was driving. He was staring at the picture of her legs. "What's this?" he said.

She turned into the driveway and shut off the engine. She looked at the picture. She could not think what to tell him it was. Her hands and heart felt heavy.

"Wow," the boy said. He laughed. "Never mind. Sorry. I'm not looking at any more of them."

He put the pack of pictures back in the envelope and dropped it on the seat between them.

She tried to think what to say, of some way she could turn the pictures into a joke. She wanted to get out of the car and run. She wanted to stay, not to give him the money, so he would sit there with her. She reached into her purse and took out her wallet and removed four one-dollar bills.

"How many years have you been married?" he asked.

"One," she said. She held the money out to him. He said "Thank you" and leaned across the seat and put his right arm over her shoulder and kissed her. She felt his scarf bunched up against their cheeks. She was amazed at how warm his lips were in the cold car.

He moved his head away and said, "I didn't think you'd mind if I did that." She shook her head no. He unlocked the door and got out.

"I could drive you to your brother's apartment," she said. Her voice sounded hollow. She was extremely embarrassed, but she couldn't let him go.

He got back in the car. "You could drive me and come in for a drink," he said. "My brother's working."

When she got back to the car two hours later she saw a white parking ticket clamped under the windshield wiper, flapping in the wind. When she opened the car door and sank into the seat, she saw that he had left the money, neatly folded, on the floor mat on his side of the car. She did not pick up the money. In a while she started the car. She stalled it twice on the way home. When she had pulled into the driveway she looked at the money for a long time, then left it lying there. She left the car unlocked, hoping the money would be stolen. If it disappeared, she could tell herself that she had paid him. Otherwise she would not know how to deal with the situation.

When she got into the apartment, the phone rang. "I'm at the gym to play basketball," Larry said. "Be home in an hour."

"I was at the drugstore," she said. "See you then."

She examined the pictures. She sat on the sofa and laid them out, the twelve of them, in three rows on the cushion next to her. The picture of the piano was between the picture of her feet and the picture of herself that she had shot by aiming into the mirror. She picked up the four pictures of their furniture and put them on the table. She picked up the others and examined them closely. She began to understand why she had them. She had photographed parts of her body, fragments of it, to study the pieces. She had probably done it because she thought so much about Andy's body and the piece that was gone—the leg, below the knee, on his left side. She had had two bourbon-and-waters at the boy's apartment, and drinking always depressed her. She felt very depressed looking at the pictures, so she put them down and went into the bedroom. She undressed. She looked at her body—whole, not a bad figure—in the mirror. It was an automatic reaction with her to close the curtains when she was naked, so she turned quickly and went to the window and did that. She went back to the mirror; the room was darker now and her body looked better. She ran her hands down her sides, wondering if the feel of her skin was anything like the way the sculpture would feel. She was sure that the sculpture would be smoother—her hands would move more quickly down the slopes of it than she wanted—that it would be cool, and that somehow she could feel the grayness of it. Those things seemed preferable to her hands lingering on her body, the imperfection of her skin, the overheated apartment. If she were the piece of sculpture and if she could feel, she would like her sense of isolation.

This was in 1972, in Philadelphia.

KATHERINE GOVIER

(b. 1948)

K atherine Govier was born in Edmonton, Alberta. She studied at the University of Alberta (B.A. 1970) and York University (M.A. 1972). A winner of numerous awards for her work as a free-lance journalist, she lived in Washington and London, England. She taught at Leeds University before settling in Toronto, where she has been visiting lecturer at various postsecondary institutions, including a stint teaching creative writing at the University of Toronto. She has established a reputation as a writer of short stories and novels dealing with the lives of the quietly desperate, upwardly mobile urban middle classes of Toronto's Annex district, though she has also used Calgary as a setting in her novels. Her stories, collected in Fables of Brunswick Avenue *(1985) and* Before and After *(1989), have been widely anthologized, and her novels include* Random Descent *(1979),* Going Through the Motions *(1981), and* Between Men *(1987). In a 1987 interview, she mused on her interest in exploring the depths of her characters' lives: "I'm a frustrated historian. It's like a travel bug. I think the past is very much in everything we do, because I see it as a layer beneath the surface. I find it impossible to look at a person right now and think that's all there is and not start searching back through the detritus to find out what went before."*

The Immaculate Conception Photography Gallery

S andro named the little photography shop on St Clair Avenue West, between Lord's Shoes and Bargain Jimmie's, after the parish church in the village where he was born. He had hankered after wider horizons, the rippled brown prairies, the hard-edged mountains. But when he got to Toronto he met necessity in the form of a wife and babies and, never having seen a western sunset, he settled down in Little Italy. He photographed brides in their fat lacquered curls and imported lace, and their quick babies in christening gowns brought over from home. Blown up to near life-size on cardboard cutouts, their pictures filled the windows of his little shop.

Sandro had been there ten years already when he first really saw his sign, and the window. He stood still in front of it and looked. A particularly buxom bride with a lace bodice and cap sleeves cut in little scallops shimmered in a haze of concupiscence under the sign reading Immaculate Conception Photography Gallery. Sandro was not like his neighbours any more, he was modern, a Canadian. He no longer went to church. As he stared, one of the street drunks shuffled into place beside him. Sandro knew them all, they came into the shop in winter. (No-one ought to have to stay outside in that cold, Sandro believed.) But he especially knew Becker. Becker was a smart man; he used to be a philosopher at a university.

"Immaculate Conception," said Sandro to Becker. "What do you think?"

Becker lifted his eyes to the window. He made a squeezing gesture at the breasts. "I never could buy that story," he said.

Sandro laughed, but he didn't change the sign that year or the next and he got to be forty-five and then fifty and it didn't seem worth it. The Immaculate Conception Photography Gallery had a reputation. Business came in from as far as Rosedale and North Toronto, because Sandro was a magician with a camera. He also had skills with brushes and lights and paint, he reshot his negatives, he lined them with silver, he had tricks even new graduates of photography school couldn't (or wouldn't) copy.

Sandro was not proud of his tricks. They began in a gradual way, fixing stray hairs and taking wrinkles out of dresses. Then he met with a situation that would have started a feud in the old country. During a very large and very expensive wedding party Tony the bridegroom seduced Alicia the bridesmaid in the basketball storage room under the floor of the parish hall. Six months later Tony confessed, hoping perhaps to be released from his vows. But the parents judged it was too late to dissolve the union: Diora was used, she was no longer a virgin, there was the child coming. Tony was reprimanded, Diora consoled, the mothers became enemies, the newlyweds made up. Only Alicia remained to be dealt with. The offence became hers.

In Italy, community ostracism would have been the punishment of choice. But this was Canada, and if no-one acknowledged Alicia on the street, if no-one visited her mother, who was heavy on her feet and could not get out and sat on the sofa protesting her daughter's innocence, if no-one invited her father out behind to drink home-made wine, Alicia didn't care. She went off to her job behind the till in a drugstore with her chin thrust out much as before. The in-laws perceived that the young woman could not be subdued by the old methods and, this being the case, it was better she not exist at all.

That was why Diora's mother turned up at Sandro's counter with the wedding photos. The pain Alicia had caused! she began. It was Diora's mother's very own miserable wages saved these eighteen years that had paid for these photographs! She wept. The money was spent, but the joy was spoiled. When she and Diora's father looked at the row of faces flanking bride and groom there she was — Alicia, the whore! She wiped her tears and made her pitch.

"You can solve our problem, Sandro. I will get you a new cake, we will all come to the parish hall. You will take the photographs again. Of course," she added, "we can't pay you again."

Sandro smiled, it was so preposterous. "Even if I could afford to do all that work for nothing, I hate to say it, but Diora's out to here."

"Don't argue with me."

"I wouldn't be so bold," said Sandro. "But I will not take the photographs over."

The woman slapped the photographs where they lay on the counter. "You will! I don't care how you do it!"

Sandro went to the back and put his negatives on the light box. He brought out his magic solution and his razor blades and his brushes. He circled Alicia's head and shoulders in the first row and went to work. He felt a little badly, watching the bright circle of her face fade and swim, darken down to nothing. But how easily she vanished! He filled in the white spot with a bit of velvet curtain trimmed from the side.

"I'm like a plastic surgeon," he told his wife. "Take that patch of skin from the inner thigh and put it over the scar on the face. Then sand the edges. Isn't that what they do? Only it isn't a face I'm fixing, it's a memory."

His wife stood on two flat feet beside the sink. She shook the carrot she was peeling. "I don't care about Alicia," she said, "but Diora's mother is making a mistake. She is starting them off with a lie in their marriage. And why is she doing it? For her pride! I don't like this, Sandro."

"You're missing the point," said Sandro. The next day he had another look at his work. Alicia's shoulders and the bodice of her dress were still there, in front of the chest of the uncle of the bride. Removing them would leave a hole in Uncle. Sandro had nothing to fill the hole, no spare male torsos in black tie. He considered putting a head on top, but whose head? There was no such thing as a free face. A stranger would be questioned, a friend would have an alibi. Perhaps Diora's mother would not notice the black velvet space, as where a tooth had been knocked out, between the smiling faces.

Indeed she didn't, but kissed his hand fervently and thanked him with tears in her eyes. "Twenty-five thousand that wedding cost me. Twenty-five thousand to get this photograph, and you have rescued it."

"Surely you got dinner and a dance too?" said Sandro.

"The wedding was one day. This is forever," said Diora's mother. "I won't do that again," said Sandro, putting the cloth over his head and looking into his camera lens to do a passport photo. In the community the doctored photograph had been examined and re-examined. Alicia's detractors enjoyed the headless shoulders as evidence of a violent punishment.

"No, I won't do that again at all," said Sandro to himself, turning aside compliments with a shake of his head. But there was another wedding. After the *provolone e melone*, the veal piccata, the many-tiered cake topped with swans, the father of the bride drew Sandro aside and asked for a set of prints with the groom's parents removed.

"My God, why?" said Sandro.

"He's a bastard. A bad man."

"Shouldn't have let her marry his son, then," said Sandro, pulling a cigarette out of the pack in his pocket. These conversations made him nervous.

The father's weathered face was dark, his dinner jacket did not button around his chest. He moaned and ground his lower teeth against his uppers. "You know how they are, these girls in Canada. I am ashamed to say it, but I couldn't stop her."

Sandro said nothing.

"Look, I sat here all night long, said nothing, did nothing. I don't wanna look at him for the next twenty years."

Sandro drew in a long tube of smoke.

 "I paid a nice bundle for this night. I wanna remember it nice-like."

The smoke made Sandro nauseated. He dropped his cigarette and ground it into the floor with his toe, damning his own weakness. "What am I going to do with the table?"

The father put out a hand like a tool, narrowed his eyes, and began to saw, where the other man sat.

"And leave it dangling, no legs?"

"So make new legs."

"I'm a photographer, not a carpenter," said Sandro. "I don't make table legs."

"Where you get legs is your problem," said the father. "I'm doing well here. I've got ten guys working for me. You look like you could use some new equipment."

 And what harm was it after all, it was only a photograph, said Sandro to himself. Then too there was the technical challenge. Waiting till they all got up to get their *bonboniere*, he took a shot of the head table empty. Working neatly with his scalpel, he cut the table from this second negative, removed the in-laws and their chairs from the first one, stuck the empty table-end onto the table in the first picture, blended over the join neatly, and printed it. Presto! Only one set of in-laws.

"I don't mind telling you, it gives me a sick feeling," said Sandro to his wife. "I was there. I saw them. We had a conversation. They smiled at me. Now — " he shrugged. "An empty table. lucky I don't go to church any more."

"Let the man who paid good money to have you do it confess, not you," she said. "A photograph is a photograph."

"And that's what I thought, too," said Sandro.

The next morning Sandro went to the Donut House, got himself a takeout coffee, and stood on the street beside the window.

"Why do people care about photographs so much?" he said to Becker. Becker had newspaper stuffed in the soles of his shoes. He had on a pair of stained brown pants tied up at the waist with a paisley necktie. His bottle was clutched in a paper bag gathered around the neck.

"You can put them on your mantel," said Becker. " They don't talk back."

"Don't people prefer life?" said Sandro.

"People prefer things," said Becker.

"Don't they want their memories to be true?"

"Another thing. Are we here just to get our photograph taken? Do we have a higher purpose?"

Becker pulled one of the newspapers out of his shoe. There were Brian and Mila Mulroney having a gloaty kiss. They were smeared by muddy water and depressed by the joint in the ball of Becker's foot.

"I mean real people," said Sandro. "Have we not loyalty to the natural?"

"These are existential questions, Sandro," said Becker. "Too many more of them and you'll be out here on the street with the rest of us."

Sandro drained the coffee from his cup, pitched it in the bin painted Keep Toronto Clean, and went back into his gallery. The existential questions nagged. But he did go out and get the motor drive for the camera. In the next few months he eradicated a pregnancy from a wedding photo, added a daughter-in-law who complained of being left out of the Christmas shots, and made a groom taller. Working in the darkroom, he was hit by vertigo. He was on a slide, beginning a descent. He wanted to know what the bottom felt like.

It was after a year of such operations that a man from the Beaches came in with a tiny black-and-white photo of a long-lost brother. He wanted it coloured and fitted into a family shot around a picnic table on Centre Island.

"Is this some kind of joke?" said Sandro. It was the only discretion he practised now; he wanted to talk about it before he did it.

"No, I'm going to send it to my mother. She thinks Christopher wrote us all off."

"Did he?" said Sandro.

"Better she should not know."

Sandro neglected to ask if Christopher was fat or thin. He ended up taking a medium-sized pair of shoulders from his own cousin and propping them up behind a bush, with Christopher on top. Afterwards, Sandro lay sleepless in his bed. Suppose that in the next few months Christopher should turn up dead, say murdered. Then Mother would produce the photograph stamped Immaculate Conception Photography Gallery, 1816 St Clair Avenue West. Sandro would be implicated. The police might come.

"Adding is worse than taking away," he said to his wife.

"You say yes to do it, then you do it. You think it's wrong, you say no."

"Let me try this on you, Becker," said Sandro the next morning. "To take a person out is only half a lie. It proves nothing except that he was not in that shot. To add a person is a whole lie: it proves that he was there, when he was not."

"You haven't proven a thing. You're just fooling around with celluloid. Have you got a buck?" said Becker.

"It is better to be a murderer than a creator. I am playing God, outplaying God at his own game." He was smarter than Becker now. He knew it was the photographs that lasted, not people. In the end the proof was in the proof. Though he hadn't prayed in thirty years, Sandro began to pray. It was like riding a bicycle: he got the hang of it again instantly. "Make me strong," he prayed, "strong enough to resist the new equipment that I might buy, strong enough to resist the temptation to expand the gallery, to buy a house in the suburbs. Make me say no to people who want alterations."

But Sandro's prayers were not answered. When people offered him money to dissolve an errant relative, he said yes. He said yes out of curiosity. He said yes out of a desire to test his skills. He said yes out of greed. He said yes out of compassion. "What is the cost after all of a little happiness?" he said. "Perhaps God doesn't count photographs. After all, they're not one of a kind."

Sandro began to be haunted, in slow moments behind the counter in the Immaculate Conception, by the faces of those whose presence he had tampered with. He kept a file —Alicia the lusty bridesmaid, Antonia and Marco, the undesired in-laws. Their heads, their shoes, and their hands, removed from the scene with surgical precision, he saved for the moment when, God willing, a forgiving relative would ask him to replace them. But the day did not come. Sandro was not happy.

"Becker," he said, for he had a habit now of buying Becker a coffee first thing in the morning and standing out if it was warm, or in if it was cold, for a chat. "Becker, let's say it's a good service I'm doing. It makes people happy, even if it tells lies."

"Sandro," said Becker, who enjoyed his coffee, "these photographs, doctored by request of the subjects, reflect back the life they wish to have.

The unpleasant bits are removed, the wishes are added. If you didn't do it, someone else would. Memory would. It's a service."

"It's also money," said Sandro. He found Becker too eager to make excuses now. He liked him better before.

"You're Tintoretto, painting in his patron, softening his greedy profile, lifting the chin of his fat wife. It pays for the part that's true art."

"Which part is that?" said Sandro, but Becker didn't answer. He was still standing there when Diora came in. She'd matured, she'd gained weight, and her twins, now six years old, were handsome and strong. Sandro's heart flew up in his breast. Perhaps she had made friends with Alicia, perhaps Diora had come to have her bridesmaid reinstated.

"The long nightmare is over," said Diora. "I've left him."

The boys were running from shelf to shelf lifting up the photographs with their glass frames and putting them down again. Sandro watched them with one eye. He knew what she was going to say.

"I want you to take him out of those pictures," she said.

"You'd look very foolish as a bride with no groom," he said severely.

"No, no, not those," she said. "I mean the kids' birthday shots."

They had been particularly fine, those shots, taken only two weeks ago, Tony tall and dark, Diora and the children radiant and blond.

"Be reasonable, Diora," he said. "I never liked him myself. But he balances the portrait. Besides, he was there."

"He was not there!" cried Diora. Her sons went on turning all the pictures to face the walls. "He was never there. He was running around, in his heart he was not with me. I was alone with my children."

"I'll take another one," said Sandro. "Of you and the boys. Whenever you like. This one stays like it is."

"We won't pay."

"But Diora," said Sandro, "everyone knows he's their father."

"They have no father," said Diora flatly.

"It's Immaculate Conception," said Becker gleefully.

But Diora did not hear. "It's our photograph, and we want him out. You do your job. The rest of it's none of your business." She put one hand on the back of the head of each of her twins and marched them out the door.

Sandro leaned on his counter idly flipping the pages of a wedding album. He had a vision of a great decorated room, with a cake on the table. Everyone had had his way, the husband had removed the wife, the wife the husband, the bridesmaid her parents, and so forth. There was no-one there.

"We make up our lives out of the people around us," he said to Becker. "When they don't live up to standard, we can't just wipe them out."

"Don't ask me," said Becker. "I just lit out for the streets. Couldn't live up to a damn thing." Then he too went out the door.

"Lucky bugger," said Sandro.

Alone, he went to his darkroom. He opened his drawer of bits and pieces. His disappeared ones, the inconvenient people. His body parts, his halves of torsos, tips of shiny black shoes. Each face, each item of clothing punctured him a little. He looked at his negatives stored in drawers. They were scarred, pathetic things. I haven't the stomach for it, not any more, thought Sandro. As he walked home, St Clair Avenue seemed very fine. The best part was, he thought, there were no relationships. Neither this leaning drunk nor that window-shopper was so connected to any other as to endanger his, or her, existence. The tolerance of indifference, said Sandro to himself, and tried to remember it to tell Becker.

But Sandro felt ill at ease in his own home, by its very definition a dangerous and unreliable setting. His wife was stirring something, with her lips tight together. His children, almost grown up now, bred secrets as they looked at television. He himself only posed in the doorway, looking for hidden seams and the faint hairlines of an airbrush.

That night he stood exhausted by his bed. His wife lay on her side with one round shoulder above the sheet. Behind her on the wall was the photo he'd taken of their village before he left Italy. He ought to reshoot it, take out that gas station and clean up the square a little. His pillow had an indentation, as if a head had been erased. He slept in a chair.

In the morning he went down to the shop. He got his best camera and set up a tripod on the sidewalk directly across the street. He took several shots in the solid bright morning light. He locked the door and placed the CLOSED sign in the window. In the darkroom he developed the film, floating the negatives in the pungent fluid until the row of shop fronts came through clearly, the flat brick faces, the curving concrete trim, the two balls on the crowns. Deftly he dissolved each brick of his store, the window, and the sign. Deftly he reattached each brick of the store to the west side to the bricks of the store to the east.

I have been many things in my life, thought Sandro, a presser of shutters, a confessor, a false prophet. Now I am a bricklayer, and a good one. He taped the negatives together and developed them. He touched up the join and then photographed it again. He developed this second negative and it was perfect. Number 1812, Lord's Shoes, joined directly to 1820 Bargain Jimmie's: the Immaculate Conception Photography Gallery at 1816 no longer existed. Working quickly, because he wanted to finish before the day was over, he blew it up to two feet by three feet. He cleared out his window display of brides and babies and stood up this new photograph — one of the finest he'd ever taken, he thought. Then he took a couple of cameras and a bag with a tripod and some lenses. He turned out the light, pulling the door shut behind him, and began to walk west.

IAN MCEWAN

(b. 1948)

*I*an McEwan was born in Oxford, England, where he currently lives *with his wife and four children. His first book of stories,* First Love, Last Rites *(1975), won the Somerset Maugham Award for the best work of fiction published in the preceding year. In it he displays the skill and boldness of imagination that have marked his fictional world as one where the improbable and the impossible happen without apology, in a manner suggesting the influence of the traditional fable and the American tall tale. His second book of stories is titled* In Between the Sheets *(1979), and his novels include* The Cement Garden *(1978),* The Comfort of Strangers *(1981), and* The Child in Time *(1987). His most recent novel,* The Innocent *(1990), is set in Berlin after the Second World War and deals with the personal and public trials and intrigues of the Cold War period. McEwan has written a libretto for an oratorio by Michael Berkeley,* Or Shall We Die, *and has also supported his writing of fiction with work for television and the movies, collecting some of his plays for television in* The Imitation Game and Other Plays *(1982). Of the similarities between writing short stories and writing for television, he has observed:*

> As a short story writer I was attracted by its [TV's] scale, its intimacy. The possibilities and limitations presented by the thirty, fifty, or even seventy-five minute television play seemed very close in some ways to those presented by the short story: the need for highly selective detail and for the rapid establishment of people and situation, the possibility of chasing one or two ideas to logical, or even illogical, conclusion, the dangers of becoming merely anecdotal.

First Love, Last Rites

From the beginning of summer until it seemed pointless, we lifted the thin mattress on to the heavy oak table and made love in front of the large open window. We always had a breeze blowing into the room and smells of the quayside four floors down. I was drawn into fantasies against my will, fantasies of the creature, and afterwards when we lay on our backs on the huge table, in those deep silences I heard it faintly running and clawing. It was new to me, all this, and I worried, I tried to talk to Sissel about it for reassurance. She had nothing to say, she did not make abstractions or discuss situations, she lived inside them. We watched the seagulls wheeling about in our square of sky and wondered if they had been watching us up there, that was the kind of thing we talked about, mildly entertaining hypotheses of the present moment. Sissel did things as they came to her, stirred her coffee, made love, listened to her records, looked out the window. She did not say things like I'm happy, or confused, or I want to make love, or I don't, or I'm tired of the fights in my family, she had no language to split herself in two, so I suffered alone what seemed like crimes in my head while we fucked, and afterwards listened alone to it scrabbling in the silence. Then one afternoon Sissel woke from a doze, raised her head from the mattress and said, "What's that scratching noise behind the wall?"

My friends were far away in London, they sent me anguished and reflective letters, what would they do now? Who were they, and what was the point of it all? They were my age, seventeen and eighteen, but I pretended not to understand them. I sent back postcards, find a big table and an open window, I told them. I was happy and it seemed easy, I was making eel traps, it was so easy to have a purpose. The summer went on and I no longer heard from them. Only Adrian came to see us, he was Sissel's ten-year-old brother and he came to escape the misery of his disintegrating home, the quick reversals of his mother's moods, the endless competitive piano playing of his sisters, the occasional bitter visits of his father. Adrian and Sissel's parents after twenty-seven years of marriage and six children hated each other with sour resignation, they could no longer bear to live in the same house. The father moved out to a hostel a few streets away to be near his children. He was a businessman who was out of work and looked like Gregory Peck, he was an optimist and had a hundred schemes to make money in an interesting way. I used to meet him in the pub. He did not want to talk about his redundancy or his marriage, he did not mind me living in a room over the quayside with his daughter. Instead he told me about his time in the Korean war, and when he was an international salesman, and of the legal fraudery of his friends who were now at the top and knighted, and then one day of the eels in the River Ouse, how the river bed swarmed with eels, how there was money to be made catching them and taking them live to London. I told him how I had eighty pounds in the bank, and the next morning we bought netting, twine, wire hoops and an old cistern tank to keep eels in. I spent the next two months making eel traps.

On fine days I took my net, hoops and twine outside and worked on the quay, sitting on a bollard. An eel trap is cylinder-shaped, sealed at one end, and at the other is a long tapering funnel entrance. It lies on the river bed, the eels swim in to eat the bait and in their blindness cannot find their way out. The fishermen were friendly and amused. There's eels down there, they said, and you'll catch a few but you won't make no living on it. The tide'll lose your nets fast as you make them. We're using iron weights, I told them, and they shrugged in a good-natured way and showed me a better way to lash the net to the hoops, they believed it was my right to try it for myself. When the fishermen were out in their boats and I did not feel like working I sat about and watched the tidal water slip across the mud, I felt no urgency about the eel traps but I was certain we would be rich.

I tried to interest Sissel in the eel adventure, I told her about the rowing-boat someone was lending to us for the summer, but she had nothing to say. So instead we lifted the mattress on to the table and lay down with our clothes on. Then she began to talk. We pressed our palms together, she made a careful examination of the size and shape of our hands and gave a running commentary. Exactly the same size, your fingers are thicker, you've got this extra bit here. She measured my eyelashes with the end of her thumb and wished hers were as long, she told me about the dog she had when she was small, it had long white eyelashes. She looked at the sunburn on my nose and talked about that, which of her brothers and sisters went red in the sun, who went brown, what her youngest sister said once. We slowly undressed. She kicked off her plimsolls and talked about her foot rot. I listened with my eyes closed, I could smell mud and seaweed and dust through the open window. Wittering on, she called it, this kind of talk. Then once I was inside her I was moved, I was inside my fantasy, there could be no separation now of my mushrooming sensations from my knowledge that we could make a creature grow in Sissel's belly. I had no wish to be a father, that was not in it at all. It was eggs, sperms, chromosomes, feathers, gills, claws, inches from my cock's end the unstoppable chemistry of a creature growing out of a dark red slime, my fantasy was of being helpless before the age and strength of this process and the thought alone could make me come before I wanted. When I told Sissel she laughed. Oh, Gawd, she said. To me Sissel was right inside the process, she *was* the process and the power of its fascination grew. She was meant to be on the pill and every month she forgot it at least two or three times. Without discussion we came to that arrangement that I was to come outside her, but it rarely worked. As we were swept down the long slopes to our orgasms, in those last desperate seconds I struggled to find my way out but I was caught like an eel in my fantasy of the creature in the dark, waiting, hungry, and I fed it great white gobs. In those careless fractions of a second I abandoned my life to feeding the creature, whatever it was, in or out of the womb, to fucking only Sissel, to feeding more creatures, my whole life given over to this in a moment's weakness. I watched out for Sissel's periods, everything about women was new to me and I could take nothing for granted. We made love in Sissel's copious, effortless periods, got good and sticky and brown with the blood and I thought we were the creatures now in the slime, we were inside fed by gobs of cloud coming through the window, by gases drawn from the mudflats by the sun. I worried about my fantasies, I knew I could not come without them. I asked Sissel what she thought about and she giggled. Not feathers and gills, anyway. What *do* you think about, then? Nothing much, nothing really. I pressed my question and she withdrew into silence.

I knew it was my own creature I heard scrabbling, and when Sissel heard it one afternoon and began to worry, I realized her fantasies were involved too, it was a sound which grew out of our lovemaking. We heard it when we were finished and lying quite still on our backs, when we were empty and clear, perfectly quiet. It was the impression of small claws scratching blindly against a wall, such a distant sound it needed two people to hear it. We thought it came from one part of the wall. When I knelt down and put my ear to the skirting-board it stopped, I sensed it on the other side of the wall, frozen in its action, waiting in the dark. As the weeks passed we heard it at other times in the day, and now and then at night. I wanted to ask Adrian what he thought it was. Listen, there it is, Adrian, shut up a moment, what do you think that noise is, Adrian? He strained impatiently to hear what we could hear but he would not be still long enough. There's nothing there, he shouted. Nothing, nothing, nothing. He became very excited, jumped on his sister's back, yelling and yodelling. He did not want whatever it was to be heard, he did not want to be left out. I pulled him off Sissel's back and we rolled about on the bed. Listen again, I said, pinning him down, there it was again. He struggled free and ran out of the room shouting his two-tone police-car siren. We listened to it fade down the stairs and when I could hear him no more I said, Perhaps Adrian is really afraid of mice. Rats, you mean, said his sister, and put her hands between my legs.

By mid-July we were not so happy in our room, there was a growing dishevelment and unease, and it did not seem possible to discuss it with Sissel. Adrian was coming to us every day now because it was the summer holidays and he could not bear to be at home. We would hear him four floors down, shouting and stamping on the stairs on his way up to us. He came in noisily, doing handstands and showing off to us. Frequently he jumped on Sissel's back to impress me, he was anxious, he was worried we might not find him good company and send him way, send him back home. He was worried too because he could no longer understand his sister. At one time she was always ready for a fight, and she was a good fighter, I heard him boast that to his friends, he was proud of her. Now changes had come over his sister, she pushed him off sulkily, she wanted to be left alone to do nothing, she wanted to listen to records. She was angry when he got his shoes on her skirt, and she had breasts now like his mother, she talked to him now like his mother. Get down off there, Adrian. Please, Adrian, please, not now, later. He could not quite believe it all the same, it was a mood of his sister's, a phase, and he went on taunting and attacking her hopefully, he badly wanted things to stay as they were before his father left home. When he locked his forearms round Sissel's neck and pulled her backwards on to the bed his eyes were on me for encouragement, he thought the real bond was between us, the two men against the girl. He did not see there was no encouragement, he wanted it so badly. Sissel never sent Adrian away, she understood why he was here, but it was hard for her. One long afternoon of torment she left the room almost crying with frustration. Adrian turned to me and raised his eyebrows in mock horror. I tried to talk to him then but he was already making his yodelling sound and squaring up for a fight with me. Nor did Sissel have anything to say to me about her brother, she never made general remarks about people because she never made general remarks. Sometimes when we heard Adrian on his way up the stairs she glanced across at me and seemed to betray herself by a slight pursing of her beautiful lips.

There was only one way to persuade Adrian to leave us in peace. He could not bear to see us touch, it pained him, it genuinely disgusted him. When he saw one of us move across the room to the other he pleaded with us silently, he ran between us, pretending playfulness, wanted to decoy us into another game. He imitated us frantically in a desperate last attempt to show us how fatuous we appeared. Then he could stand it no more, he ran out of the room machine-gunning German soldiers and young lovers on the stairs.

But Sissel and I were touching less and less now, in our quiet ways we could not bring ourselves to it. It was not that we were in decline, not that we did not delight in each other, but that our opportunities were faded. It was the room itself. It was no longer four floors up and detached, there was no breeze through the window, only a mushy heat rising off the quayside and dead jellyfish and clouds of flies, fiery grey flies who found our armpits and bit fiercely, houseflies who hung in clouds over our food. Our hair was too long and dank and hung in our eyes. The food we bought melted and tasted like the river. We no longer lifted the mattress on to the table, the coolest place now was the floor and the floor was covered with greasy sand which would not go away. Sissel grew tired of her records, and her foot rot spread from one foot to the other and added to the smell. Our room stank. We did not talk about leaving because we did not talk about anything. Every night now we were woken by the scrabbling behind the wall, louder now and more insistent. When we made love it listened to us behind the wall. We made love less and our rubbish gathered around us, milk bottles we could not bring ourselves to carry away, grey sweating cheese, butter wrappers, yogurt cartons, overripe salami. And among it all Adrian cart-wheeling, yodelling, machine-gunning and attacking Sissel. I tried to write poems about my fantasies, about the creature, but I could see no way in and I wrote nothing down, not even a first line. Instead I took long walks along the river dyke into the Norfolk hinterland of dull beet fields, telegraph poles, uniform grey skies. I had two more eel nets to make, I was forcing myself to sit down to them each day. But in my heart I was sick of them, I could not really believe that eels would ever go inside them and I wondered if I wanted them to, if it was not better that the eels should remain undisturbed in the cool mud at the bottom of the river. But I went on with it because Sissel's father was ready to begin, because I had to expiate all the money and hours I had spent so far, because the idea had its own tired, fragile momentum now and I could no more stop it than carry the milk bottles from our room.

Then Sissel found a job and it made me see we were different from no one, they all had rooms, houses, jobs, careers, that's what they all did, they had cleaner rooms, better jobs, we were anywhere's striving couple. It was one of the windowless factories across the river where they canned vegetables and fruit. For ten hours a day she was to sit in the roar of machines by a moving conveyor belt, talk to no one and pick out the rotten carrots before they were canned. At the end of her first day Sissel came home in a pink-and-white nylon raincoat and pink cap. I said, Why don't you take it off? Sissel shrugged. It was all the same to her, sitting around in the room, sitting around in a factory where they relayed Radio One through speakers strung along the steel girders, where four hundred women half listened, half dreamed, while their hands spun backwards and forwards like powered shuttles. On Sissel's second day I took the ferry across the river and waited for her at the factory gates. A few women stepped through a small tin door in a great windowless wall and a wailing siren sounded all across the factory complex. Other small doors opened and they streamed out, converging on the gates, scores of women in pink-and-white nylon coats and pink caps. I stood on a low wall and tried to see Sissel, it was suddenly very important. I thought that if I could not pick her out from this rustling stream of pink nylon then she was lost, we were both lost and our time was worthless. As it approached the factory gates the main body was moving fast. Some were half running in the splayed, hopeless way that women have been taught to run, the others walked as fast as they could. I found out later they were hurrying home to cook suppers for their families, to make an early start on the housework. Latecomers on the next shift tried to push their way through in the opposite direction. I could not see Sissel and I felt on the edge of panic, I shouted her name and my words were trampled underfoot. Two older women who stopped by the wall to light cigarettes grinned up at me. Sizzle yerself. I walked home by the long way, over the bridge, and decided not to tell Sissel I had been to wait for her because I would have to explain my panic and I did not know how. She was sitting on the bed when I came in, she was still wearing her nylon coat. The cap was on the floor. Why don't you take that thing off? I said. She said, Was that you outside the factory? I nodded. Why didn't you speak to me if you saw me standing there? Sissel turned and lay face downwards on the bed. Her coat was stained and smelled of machine oil and earth. I dunno, she said into the pillow, I didn't think. I didn't think of anything after my shift. Her words had a deadening finality, I glanced around our room and fell silent.

Two days later, on Saturday afternoon, I bought pounds of rubbery cows' lungs sodden with blood (lights, they were called) for bait. That same afternoon we filled the traps and rowed out into mid-channel at low tide to lay them on the river bed. Each of the seven traps was marked by a buoy. Four o'clock Sunday morning Sissel's father called for me and we set out in his van to where we kept the borrowed boat. We were rowing out now to find the marker buoys and pull the traps in, it was the testing time, would there be eels in the nets, would it be profitable to make more nets, catch more eels and drive them once a week to Billings-gate market, would we be rich? It was a dull windy morning, I felt no anticipation, only tiredness and a continuous erection. I half dozed in the warmth of the van's heater. I had spent many hours of the night awake listening to the scrabbling noises behind the wall. Once I got out of bed and banged the skirting-board with a spoon. There was a pause, then the digging continued. It seemed certain now that it was digging its way into the room. While Sissel's father rowed I watched over the side for markers. It was not as easy as I thought to find them, they did not show up white against the water but as dark low silhouettes. It was twenty minutes before we found the first. As we pulled it up I was amazed at how soon the clean white rope from the chandlers had become like all other rope near the river, brown and hung about with fine strands of green weed. The net too was old-looking and alien, I could not believe that one of us had made it. Inside were two crabs and a large eel. He untied the closed end of the trap, let the two crabs drop into the water and put the eel in the plastic bucket we had brought with us. We put fresh lights in the trap and dropped it over the side. It took another fifteen minutes to find the next trap and that one had nothing inside. We rowed up and down the channel for half an hour after that without finding another trap, and by this time the tide was coming up and covering the markers. It was then that I took the oars and made for the shore.

We went back to the hostel where Sissel's father was staying and he cooked breakfast. We did not want to discuss the lost traps, we pretended to ourselves and to each other that we would find them when we went out at the next low tide. But we knew they were lost, swept up or downstream by the powerful tides, and I knew I could never make another eel trap in my life. I knew also that my partner was taking Adrian with him on a short holiday, they were leaving that afternoon. They were going to visit military airfields, and hoped to end up at the Imperial War Museum. We ate eggs, bacon and mushrooms and drank coffee. Sissel's father told me of an idea he had, a simple but lucrative idea. Shrimps cost very little on the quayside here and they were very expensive in Brussels. We could drive two vanloads across there each week, he was optimistic in his relaxed, friendly way and for a moment I was sure his scheme would work. I drank the last of my coffee. Well, I said, I suppose that needs some thinking about. I picked up the bucket with the eel in, Sissel and I could eat that one. My partner told me as we shook hands that the surest way of killing an eel was to cover it with salt. I wished him a good holiday and we parted, still maintaining the silent pretence that one of us would be rowing out at the next low tide to search for the traps.

After a week at the factory I did not expect Sissel to be awake when I got home, but she was sitting up in bed, pale and clasping her knees. She was staring into one corner of the room. It's in here, she said. It's behind those books on the floor. I sat down on the bed and took off my wet shoes and socks. The mouse? You mean you heard the mouse? Sissel spoke quietly. It's a rat. I saw it run across the room, and it's a rat. I went over to the books and kicked them, and instantly it was out, I heard its claws on the floorboards and then I saw it run along the wall, the size of a small dog it seemed to me then, a rat, a squat, powerful grey rat dragging its belly along the floor. It ran the whole length of the wall and crept behind a chest of drawers. We've got to get it out of here, Sissel wailed, in a voice which was strange to me. I nodded, but I could not move for the moment or speak, it was so big, the rat, and it had been with us all summer, scrabbling at the wall in the deep, clear silences after our fucking, and in our sleep, it was our familiar. I was terrified, more afraid than Sissel, I was certain the rat knew us as well as we knew it, it was aware of us in the room now just as we were aware of it behind the chest of drawers. Sissel was about to speak again when we heard a noise outside on the stairs, a familiar stamping, machine-gunning noise. I was relieved to hear it. Adrian came in the way he usually did, he kicked the door and leaped in, crouching low, a machine-gun ready at his hip. He sprayed us with raw noises from the back of his throat, we crossed our lips with our fingers and tried to hush him. You're dead, both of you, he said, and got ready for a cartwheel across the room. Sissel shushed him again, she tried to wave him towards the bed. Why sshh? What's wrong with you? We pointed to the chest of drawers. It's a rat, we told him. He was down on his knees at once, peering. A rat? he gasped. Fantastic, it's a big one, look at it. Fantastic. What are you going to do? Let's catch it. I crossed the room quickly and picked up a poker from the fireplace, I could lose my fear in Adrian's excitement, pretend it was just a fat rat in our room, an adventure to catch it. From the bed Sissel wailed again. What are you going to do with that? For a moment I felt my grip loosen on the poker, it was not just a rat, it was not an adventure, we both knew that. Meanwhile Adrian danced his dance, Yes, that, use that. Adrian helped me carry the books across the room, we built a wall right round the chest of drawers with only one gap in the middle where the rat could get through. Sissel went on asking, What are you doing? What are you going to do with that? but she did not dare leave the bed. We had finished the wall and I was giving Adrian a coat hanger to drive the rat out with when Sissel jumped across the room and tried to snatch the poker from my hand. Give me that, she cried, and hung on to my lifted arm. At that moment the rat ran out through the gap in the books, it ran straight at us and I thought I saw its teeth bared and ready. We scattered, Adrian jumped on the table, Sissel and I were back on the bed. Now we all had time to see the rat as it paused in the centre of the room and then ran forward again, we had time to see how powerful and fat and fast it was, how its whole body quivered, how its tail slid behind it like an attendant parasite. It knows us, I thought, it wants us. I could not bring myself to look at Sissel. As I stood up on the bed, raised the poker and aimed it, she screamed. I threw it as hard as I could, it struck the floor point first several inches from the rat's narrow head. It turned instantly and ran back between the gap in the books. We heard the scratch of its claws on the floor as it settled itself behind the chest of drawers to wait.

I unwound the wire coat-hanger, straightened it and doubled it over and gave it to Adrian. He was quieter now, slightly more fearful. His sister sat on the bed with her knees drawn up again. I stood several feet from the gap in the books with the poker held tight in both hands. I glanced down and saw my pale bare feet and saw a ghost rat's teeth bared and tearing nail from flesh. I called out, Wait, I want to get my shoes. But it was too late, Adrian was jabbing the wire behind the chest of drawers and now I dared not move. I crouched a little lower over the poker, like a batsman. Adrian climbed on to the chest and thrust the wire right down into the corner. He was in the middle of shouting something to me, I did not hear what it was. The frenzied rat was running through the gap, it was running at my feet to take its revenge. Like the ghost rat its teeth were bared. With both hands I swung the poker down, caught it clean and whole smack under its belly, and it lifted clear off the ground, sailed across the room, borne up by Sissel's long scream through her hand in her mouth, it dashed against the wall and I thought in an instant, It must have broken its back. It dropped to the ground, legs in the air, split from end to end like a ripe fruit. Sissel did not take her hand from her mouth, Adrian did not move from the chest, I did not shift my weight from where I had struck, and no one breathed out. A faint smell crept across the room, musty and intimate, like the smell of Sissel's monthly blood. Then Adrian farted and giggled from his held-back fear, his human smell mingled with the wide-open rat smell. I stood over the rat and prodded it gently with the poker. It rolled on its side, and from the mighty gash which ran its belly's length there obtruded and slid partially free from the lower abdomen a translucent purple bag, and inside five pale crouching shapes, their knees drawn up around their chins. As the bag touched the floor I saw a movement, the leg of one unborn rat quivered as if in hope, but the mother was hopelessly dead and there was no more for it.

Sissel knelt by the rat, Adrian and I stood behind her like guards, it was as if she had some special right, kneeling there with her long red skirt spilling round her. She parted the gash in the mother rat with her forefinger and thumb, pushed the bag back inside and closed the blood-spiked fur over it. She remained kneeling a little while and we still stood behind her. Then she cleared some dishes from the sink to wash her hands. We all wanted to get outside now, so Sissel wrapped the rat in newspaper and we carried it downstairs. Sissel lifted the lid of the dustbin and I placed it carefully inside. Then I remembered something, I told the other two to wait for me and I ran back up the stairs. It was the eel I came back for, it lay quite still in its few inches of water and for a moment I thought that it too was dead till I saw it stir when I picked up the bucket. The wind had dropped now and the cloud was breaking up, we walked to the quay in alternate light and shade. The tide was coming in fast. We walked down the stone steps to the water's edge and there I tipped the eel back in the river and we watched him flick out of sight, a flash of white underside in the brown water. Adrian said goodbye to us, and I thought he was going to hug his sister. He hesitated and then ran off, calling out something over his shoulder. We shouted after him to have a good holiday. On the way back Sissel and I stopped to look at the factories on the other side of the river. She told me she was going to give up her job there.

We lifted the mattress on to the table and lay down in front of the open window, face to face, they way we did at the beginning of summer. We had a light breeze blowing in, a distant smoky smell of autumn, and I felt calm, very clear. Sissel said, This afternoon let's clean the room up and then go for a long walk, a walk along the river dyke. I pressed the flat of my palm against her warm belly and said, Yes.

JANE URQUHART

(b. 1949)

J ane Urquhart was born in Geraldton, Ontario, and lives with her
husband, the artist Tony Urquhart, and their daughter, Emily Jane,
*in the town of Wellesley, Ontario, near Waterloo. She was educated at
the University of Guelph, where she earned a B.A. in English and art
history (1976). She is the author of three books of poetry,* False Shuffles
(1981), I Am Walking in the Garden of His Imaginary Palace
(1982), and The Little Flowers of Madame de Montespan *(1984),
the short-story collection* Storm Glass *(1989), and the highly acclaimed
novels* The Whirlpool *(1988) and* Changing Heaven *(1990). She
became a writer of short fiction because of the "desire to explain, if only
to myself, a landscape, an era, a human being, an event, about which I
had little knowledge and to which I had but limited access." The Whirl-*
pool *and* Changing Heaven *are distinguished by an accuracy of detail
and imagery that contribute to a convincing re-creation of a nineteenth-
century milieu. "The Death of Robert Browning" illustrates her skill in
creating such a setting and her empathetic imagination.*

The Death of Robert Browning

I n December of 1889, as he was returning by gondola from the general
vicinity of the Palazzo Manzoni, it occurred to Robert Browning that
he was more than likely going to die soon. This revelation had nothing
to do with either his advanced years or the state of his health. He was
seventy-seven, a reasonably advanced age, but his physical condition was
described by most of his acquaintances as vigorous and robust. He took
a cold bath each morning and every afternoon insisted on a three-mile
walk during which he performed small errands from a list his sister had
made earlier in the day. He drank moderately and ate well. His mind was
as quick and alert as ever.

Nevertheless, he knew he was going to die. He also had to admit that
the idea had been with him for some time—two or three months at
least. He was not a man to ignore symbols, especially when they carried
personal messages. Now he had to acknowledge that the symbols were
in the air as surely as winter. Perhaps, he speculated, a man carried the
seeds of his death with him always, somewhere buried in his brain, like
the face of a woman he is going to love. He leaned to one side, looked
into the deep waters of the canal, and saw his own face reflected there. As

broad and distinguished and cheerful as ever, health shining vigorously, robustly from his eyes—even in such a dark mirror.

Empty Gothic and Renaissance palaces floated on either side of him like soiled pink dreams. Like sunsets with dirty faces, he mused, and then, pleased with the phrase, he reached into his jacket for his notebook, ink pot and pen. He had trouble recording the words, however, as the chill in the air had numbed his hands. Even the ink seemed affected by the cold, not flowing as smoothly as usual. He wrote slowly and deliberately, making sure to add the exact time and the location. Then he closed the book and returned it with the pen and pot to his pocket, where he curled and uncurled his right hand for some minutes until he felt the circulation return to normal. The celebrated Venetian dampness was much worse in winter, and Browning began to look forward to the fire at his son's palazzo where they would be beginning to serve afternoon tea, perhaps, for his benefit, laced with rum.

A sudden wind scalloped the surface of the canal. Browning instinctively looked upwards. Some blue patches edged by ragged white clouds, behind them wisps of grey and then the solid dark strip of a storm front moving slowly up on the horizon. Such a disordered sky in this season. No solid, predictable blocks of weather with definite beginnings, definite endings. Every change in the atmosphere seemed an emotional response to something that had gone before. The light, too, harsh and metallic, not at all like the golden Venice of summer. There was something broken about all of it, torn. The sky, for instance, was like a damaged canvas. Pleased again by his own metaphorical thoughts, Browning considered reaching for the notebook. But the cold forced him to reject the idea before it had fully formed in his mind.

Instead, his thoughts moved lazily back to the place they had been when the notion of death so rudely interrupted them; back to the building he had just visited. Palazzo Manzoni. *Bello, bello* Palazzo Manzoni! The colourful marble medallions rolled across Browning's inner eye, detached from their home on the Renaissance façade, and he began, at once, to reconstruct for the thousandth time the imaginary windows and balconies he had planned for the building's restoration. In his daydreams the old poet had walked over the palace's swollen marble floors and slept beneath its frescoed ceilings, lit fires underneath its sculptured mantels and entertained guests by the light of its chandeliers. Surrounded by a small crowd of admirers he had read poetry aloud in the evenings, his voice echoing through the halls. *No R.B. tonight*, he had said to them, winking, *Let's have some real poetry*. Then, moving modestly into the palace's impressive library, he had selected a volume of Dante or Donne.

But they had all discouraged him and it had never come to pass. Some of them said that the façade was seriously cracked and the foundations were far from sound. Others told him that the absentee owner would never part with it for anything resembling a fair price. Eventually, friends and family wore him down with their disapproval and, on their advice, he abandoned his daydream though he still made an effort to visit it, despite the fact that it was now damaged and empty and the glass in its windows was broken.

It was the same kind of frustration and melancholy that he associated with his night dreams of Asolo, the little hill town he had first seen (and then only at a distance), when he was twenty-six years old. Since that time, and for no rational reason, it had appeared over and over in the poet's dreams as a destination on the horizon, one that, due to a variety of circumstances, he was never able to reach. Either his companions in the dream would persuade him to take an alternate route, or the road would be impassable, or he would awaken just as the town gate came into view, frustrated and out of sorts. "I've had my old Asolo dream again," he would tell his sister at breakfast, "and it has no doubt ruined my work for the whole day."

Then, just last summer, he had spent several months there at the home of a friend. The house was charming and the view of the valley delighted him. But, although he never once broke the well-established order that ruled the days of his life, a sense of unreality clouded his perceptions. He was visiting the memory of a dream with a major and important difference. He had reached the previously elusive hill town with practically no effort. Everything had proceeded according to plan. Thinking about this, under the December sky in Venice, Browning realized that he had known since then that it was only going to be a matter of time.

The gondola bumped against the steps of his son's palazzo.

Robert Browning climbed onto the terrace, paid the gondolier, and walked briskly inside.

Lying on the magnificent carved bed in his room, trying unsuccessfully to surrender himself to his regular pre-dinner nap, Robert Browning examined his knowledge like a stolen jewel he had coveted for years; turning it first this way, then that, imagining the reactions of his friends, what his future biographers would have to say about it all. He was pleased that he had prudently written his death poem at Asolo in direct response to having received a copy of Tennyson's "Crossing the Bar" in the mail. How he detested that poem! What *could* Alfred have been thinking of when he wrote it? He had to admit, none the less, that to suggest that mourners restrain their sorrow, as Tennyson had, guarantees the flood-gates of female tears will eventually burst open. His poem had, therefore, included similar sentiments, but without, he hoped, such obvious senti-mentality. It was the final poem of his last manuscript which was now, mercifully, at the printers.

Something for the biographers and for the weeping maidens; those who had wept so copiously for his dear departed, though soon to be reinstated wife. Surely it was not too much to ask that they might shed a few tears for him as well, even if it was a more ordinary death, following, he winced to have to add, a fairly conventional life.

How had it all happened? He had placed himself in the centre of some of the world's most exotic scenery and had then lived his life there with the regularity of a copy clerk. A time for everything, everything in its time. Even when hunting for lizards in Asolo, an occupation he considered slightly exotic, he found he could predict the moment of their appearance; as if they knew he was searching for them and assembled their modest population at the sound of his footsteps. Even so, he was able to flush out only six or seven from a hedge of considerable length and these were, more often than not, of the same type. Once he thought he had seen a particularly strange lizard, large and lumpy, but it had turned out to be merely two of the ordinary sort, copulating.

Copulation. What sad dirge-like associations the word dredged up from the poet's unconscious. All those Italians; those minstrels, dukes, princes, artists, and questionable monks whose voices had droned through Browning's pen over the years. Why had they all been so end-lessly obsessed with the subject? He could never understand or control it. And even now, one of them had appeared in full period costume in his imagination. A duke, no doubt, by the look of the yards of velvet which covered his person. He was reading a letter that was causing him a great deal of pain. Was it a letter from his mistress? A draught of poison waited on an intricately tooled small table to his left. Perhaps a pistol or a dagger as well, but in this light Browning could not quite tell. The man paced, paused, looked wistfully out the window as if waiting for someone he knew would never, ever appear. Very, very soon now he would begin to speak, to tell his story. His right hand passed nervously across his eyes. He turned to look directly at Robert Browning who, as always, was beginning to feel somewhat embarrassed. Then the duke began:

> At last to leave these darkening moments
> These rooms, these halls where once
> We stirred love's poisoned potions
> The deepest of all slumbers,
> After this astounds the mummers
> I cannot express the smile that circled
> Round and round the week
> This room and all our days when morning
> Entered, soft, across her cheek.
> She was my medallion, my caged dove,
> A trinket, a coin I carried warm,

> *Against the skin inside my glove*
> *My favourite artwork was a kind of jail*
> *Our portrait permanent, imprinted by the moon*
> *Upon the ancient face of the canal.*

The man began to fade. Browning, who had not invited him into the room in the first place, was already bored. He therefore dismissed the crimson costume, the table, the potion housed in its delicate goblet of fine Venetian glass and began, quite inexplicably, to think about Percy Bysshe Shelley; about his life, and under the circumstances, more importantly, about his death.

Dinner over, sister, son and daughter-in-law and friend all chatted with and later read to, Browning returned to his room with Shelley's death hovering around him like an annoying, directionless wind. He doubted, as he put on his nightgown, that Shelley had *ever* worn one, particularly in those dramatic days preceding his early demise. In his night-cap he felt as ridiculous as a humorous political drawing for *Punch* magazine. And, as he lumbered into bed alone, he remembered that Shelley would have had Mary beside him and possibly Clare as well, their minds buzzing with nameless Gothic terrors. For a desperate moment or two Browning tried to conjure a Gothic terror but discovered, to his great disappoint-ment, that the vague shape taking form in his mind was only his dreary Italian duke coming, predictably, once again into focus.

Outside the ever calm waters of the canal licked the edge of the terrace in a rhythmic, sleep-inducing manner; a restful sound guaranteeing peace of mind. Browning knew, however, that during Shelley's last days at Lerici, giant waves had crashed into the ground floor of Casa Magni, prefiguring the young poet's violent death and causing his sleep to be riddled with wonderful nightmares. Therefore, the very lack of activity on the part of the water below irritated the old man. He began to pad around the room in his bare feet, oblivious of the cold marble floor and the dying embers in the fireplace. He peered through the windows into the night, hoping that he, like Shelley, might at least see his double there, or possibly Elizabeth's ghost beckoning to him from the centre of the canal. He cursed softly as the night gazed back at him, serene and cold and entirely lacking in events—mysterious or otherwise.

He returned to the bed and knelt by its edge in order to say his evening prayers. But he was completely unable to concentrate. Shelley's last days were trapped in his brain like fish in a tank. He saw him surrounded by the sublime scenery of the Ligurian coast, searching the horizon for the boat that was to be his coffin. Then he saw him clinging desperately to the mast of that boat while lightning tore the sky in half and the ocean spilled across the hull. Finally, he saw Shelley's horrifying corpse rolling on the shoreline, practically unidentifiable except for the copy of Keats' poems housed in his breast pocket. *Next to his heart*, Byron had commented, just before he got to work on the funeral pyre.

Browning abandoned God for the moment and climbed beneath the blankets.

"I might at least have a nightmare," he said petulantly to himself. Then he fell into a deep and dreamless sleep.

Browning awakened the next morning with an itchy feeling in his throat and lines from Shelley's *Prometheus Unbound* dancing in his head.

"Oh, God," he groaned inwardly, "now this. And I don't even *like* Shelley's poetry any more. Now I suppose I'm going to be plagued with it, day in, day out, until the instant of my imminent death."

How he wished he had never, ever, been fond of Shelley's poems. Then, in his youth, he might have had the common sense *not* to read them compulsively to the point of total recall. But how could he have known in those early days that even though he would later come to reject both Shelley's life and work as being too impossibly self-absorbed and emotional, some far corner of his brain would still retain every syllable the young man had committed to paper. He had memorized his life's work. Shortly after Browning's memory recited *The crawling glaciers pierce me with spears / Of their moon freezing crystals, the bright chains / Eat with their burning cold into my bones,* he began to cough, a spasm that lasted until his sister knocked discreetly on the door to announce that, since he had not appeared downstairs, his breakfast was waiting on a tray in the hall.

While he was drinking his tea, the poem "Ozymandias" repeated itself four times in his mind except that, to his great annoyance, he found that he could not remember the last three lines and kept ending with *Look on my works, ye Mighty, and despair.* He knew for certain that there were three more lines, but he was damned if he could recall even one of them. He thought of asking his sister but soon realized that, since she was familiar with his views on Shelley, he would be forced to answer a series of embarrassing questions about why he was thinking about the poem at all. Finally, he decided that *Look on my works, ye Mighty, and despair* was a much more fitting ending to the poem and attributed his lack of recall to the supposition that the last three lines were either unsuitable or completely unimportant. That settled, he wolfed down his roll, donned his hat and coat, and departed for the streets in hopes that something, anything, might happen.

Even years later, Browning's sister and son could still be counted upon to spend a full evening discussing what he might have done that day. The possibilities were endless. He might have gone off hunting for a suitable setting for a new poem, or for the physical characteristics of a duke by examining handsome northern Italian workmen. He might have gone, again, to visit his beloved Palazzo Manzoni, to gaze wistfully at its marble medallions. He might have gone to visit a Venetian builder, to discuss plans for the beautiful tower he had talked about building at Asolo, or out to Murano to watch men mould their delicate bubbles of glass. His sister was convinced that he had gone to the Church of S.S. Giovanni e Paolo to gaze at his favourite equestrian statue. His pious son, on the other hand, liked to believe that his father had spent the day in one of the few English churches in Venice, praying for the redemption of his soul. But all of their speculations assumed a sense of purpose on the poet's part, that he had left the house with a definite destination in mind, because as long as they could remember, he had never acted without a predetermined plan.

Without a plan, Robert Browning faced the Grand Canal with very little knowledge of what, in fact, he was going to do. He looked to the left, and then to the right, and then, waving aside an expectant gondolier, he turned abruptly and entered the thick of the city behind him. There he wandered aimlessly through a labyrinth of narrow streets, noting details; *putti* wafting stone garlands over windows, door knockers in the shape of gargoyles' heads, painted windows that fooled the eye, items that two weeks earlier would have delighted him but now seemed used and lifeless. Statues appeared to leak and ooze damp soot, window-glass was fogged with moisture, steps that led him over canals were slippery, covered with an unhealthy slime. He became peculiarly aware of smells he had previously ignored in favour of the more pleasant sensations the city had to offer. But now even the small roof gardens seemed to grow as if in stagnant water, winter chrysanthemums emitting a putrid odour, which spoke less of blossom than decay. With a kind of slow horror, Browning realized that he was seeing his beloved city through Shelley's eyes and immediately his inner voice began again: *Sepulchres where human forms / Like pollution nourished worms / To the corpse of greatness cling / Murdered and now mouldering.*

He quickened his steps, hoping that if he concentrated on physical activity his mind would not subject him to the complete version of Shelley's "Lines Written Among the Euganean Hills." But he was not to be spared. The poem had been one of his favourites in his youth and, as a result, his mind was now capable of reciting to him, word by word, with appropriate emotional inflections, followed by a particularly moving rendition of "Julian and Maddalo" accompanied by mental pictures of Shelley and Byron galloping along the beach at the Lido.

When at last the recitation ceased, Browning had walked as far as possible and now found himself at the edge of the Fondamente Nuove with only the wide flat expanse of the Laguna Morta in front of him.

He surveyed his surroundings and began, almost unconsciously, and certainly against his will, to search for the islanded madhouse that Shelley had described in "Julian and Maddalo": *A building on an island; such a one / As age to age might add, for uses vile / A windowless, deformed and dreary pile.* Then he remembered, again against his will, that it was on the other side, near the Lido. Instead, his eyes came to rest on the cemetery island of San Michele whose neat white mausoleums and tidy cypresses looked fresher, less sepulchral than any portion of the city he had passed through. Although he had never been there, he could tell, even from this distance, that its paths would be raked and its marble scrubbed in a way that the rest of Venice never was. Like a disease that cannot cross the water, the rot and mould of the city had never reached the cemetery's shore.

It pleased Browning, now, to think of the island's clean-boned inhabitants sleeping in their white-washed houses. Then, his mood abruptly changing, he thought with disgust of Shelley, of his bloated corpse upon the sands, how his flesh had been saturated by water, then burned away by fire, and how his heart had refused to burn, as if it had not been made of flesh at all.

Browning felt the congestion in his chest take hold, making his breathing shallow and laboured, and he turned back into the city, attempting to determine the direction of his son's palazzo. Pausing now and then to catch his breath, he made his way slowly through the streets that make up the Fondamente Nuove, an area with which he was completely unfamiliar. This was Venice at its most squalid. What little elegance had originally existed in this section had now faded so dramatically that it had all but disappeared. Scrawny children screamed and giggled on every narrow walkway and tattered washing hung from most windows. In doorways, sullen elderly widows stared insolently and with increasing hostility at this obvious foreigner who had invaded their territory. A dull panic began to overcome him as he realized he was lost. The disease meanwhile had weakened his legs, and he stumbled awkwardly under the communal gaze of these women who were like black angels marking his path. Eager to be rid of their judgemental stares, he turned into an alley, smaller than the last, and found to his relief that it was deserted and graced with a small fountain and a stone bench.

The alley, of course, was blind, went nowhere, but it was peaceful and Browning was in need of rest. He leaned back against the stone wall and closed his eyes. The fountain murmured *Bysshe, Bysshe, Bysshe* until the sound finally became soothing to Browning and he dozed, on and off, while fragments of Shelley's poetry moved in and out of his consciousness.

Then, waking suddenly from one of these moments of semi-slumber, he began to feel again that he was being watched. He searched the upper windows and the doorways around him for old women and found none. Instinctively, he looked at an archway which was just a fraction to the left of his line of vision. There, staring directly into his own, was the face of Percy Bysshe Shelley, as young and sad and powerful as Browning had ever known it would be. The visage gained flesh and expression for a glorious thirty seconds before returning to the marble that it really was. With a sickening and familiar sense of loss, Browning recognized the carving of Dionysus, or Pan, or Adonis, that often graced the tops of Venetian doorways. The sick old man walked toward it and, reaching up, placed his fingers on the soiled cheek. "Suntreader," he mumbled, then he moved out of the alley, past the black, disapproving women, into the streets towards a sizeable canal. There, bent over his walking stick, coughing spasmodically, he was able to hail a gondola.

All the way back across the city he murmured, "Where have you been, where have you been, where did you go?"

Robert Browning lay dying in his son's Venetian palazzo. Half of his face was shaded by a large velvet curtain which was gathered by his shoulder, the other half lay exposed to the weak winter light. His sister, son, and daughter-in-law stood at the foot of the bed nervously awaiting words or signs from the old man. They spoke to each other silently by means of glances or gestures, hoping they would not miss any kind of signal from his body, mountain-like under the white bedclothes. But for hours now nothing had happened. Browning's large chest moved up and down in a slow and rhythmic fashion, not unlike an artificially manipulated bellows. He appeared to be unconscious.

But Browning was not unconscious. Rather, he had used the last remnants of his free will to make a final decision. There were to be no last words. How inadequate his words seemed now compared to Shelley's experience, how silly this monotonous bedridden death. He did not intend to further add to the absurdity by pontificating. He now knew that he had said too much. At this very moment, in London, a volume of superfluous words was coming off the press. All this chatter filling up the space of Shelley's more important silence. He now knew that when Shelley had spoken it was by choice and not by habit, that the young man's words had been a response and not a fabrication.

He opened his eyes a crack and found himself staring at the ceiling. The fresco there moved and changed and finally evolved into Shelley's iconography—an eagle struggling with a serpent. *Suntreader*. The clouds, the white foam of the clouds, like water, the feathers of the great wings becoming lost in this. *Half angel, half bird*. And the blue of the sky, opening now, erasing the ceiling, limitless so that the bird's wing seemed to vaporize. *A moulted feather, an eagle feather*. Such untravelled distance in which light arrived and disappeared leaving behind something that was not darkness. *His radiant form becoming less radiant*. Leaving its own natural absence with the strength and the suck of a vacuum. No alternate atmosphere to fill the place abandoned. *Suntreader*.

And now Browning understood. It was Shelley's absence he had carried with him all these years until it had passed beyond his understanding. *Soft star*. Shelley's emotions so absent from the old poet's life, his work, leaving him unanswered, speaking through the mouths of others, until he had to turn away from Shelley altogether in anger and disgust. The drowned spirit had outdistanced him wherever he sought it. *Lone and sunny idleness of heaven*. The anger, the disgust, the evaporation. *Suntreader, soft star*. The formless form he never possessed and was never possessed by.

Too weak for anger now, Robert Browning closed his eyes and relaxed his fists, allowing Shelley's corpse to enter the place in his imagination where once there had been only absence. It floated through the sea of Browning's mind, its muscles soft under the constant pressure of the ocean. Limp and drifting, the drowned man looked as supple as a mermaid, arms swaying in the current, hair and clothing tossed as if in a slow, slow wind. His body was losing colour, turning from pastel to opaque, the open eyes staring, pale, as if frozen by an image of the moon. Joints unlocked by moisture, limbs swung easy on their threads of tendon, the spine undulating and relaxed. The absolute grace of his death, that life caught there moving in the arms of the sea. Responding, always responding to the elements.

Now the drowned poet began to move into a kind of Atlantis consisting of Browning's dream architecture; the unobtainable and the unconstructed. In complete silence the young man swam through the rooms of the Palazzo Manzoni, slipping up and down the staircase, gliding down halls, in and out of fireplaces. He appeared briefly in mirrors. He drifted past balconies to the tower Browning had thought of building at Asolo. He wavered for a few minutes near its crenellated peak before moving in a slow spiral down along its edges to its base.

Browning had just enough time to wish for the drama and the luxury of a death by water. Then his fading attention was caught by the rhythmic bump of a moored gondola against the terrace below. The boat was waiting, he knew, to take his body to the cemetery at San Michele when the afternoon had passed. Shelley had said somewhere that a gondola was a butterfly of which the coffin was a chrysalis.

Suntreader. Still beyond his grasp. The eagle on the ceiling lost in unfocused fog. *A moulted feather, an eagle feather, well I forget the rest*. The drowned man's body separated into parts and moved slowly out of Browning's mind. The old poet contented himself with the thought of one last journey by water. The coffin boat, the chrysalis. Across the Laguna Morta to San Michele. All that cool white marble in exchange for the shifting sands of Lerici.

GUY VANDERHAEGHE

(b. 1951)

G *uy Vanderhaeghe was born in Esterhazy, Saskatchewan. He was educated at the University of Saskatchewan, from which he received a B.A. (1972) and an M.A. in history (1975), and at the University of Regina (B.Ed. 1978). He earned wide acclaim and a Governor General's Award for his first collection of stories,* Man Descending *(1982). His first novel,* My Present Age *(1984), continues the story of Ed, the "descending man" of the collection's title story. Vanderhaeghe's weak-willed heroes are the products of an age in which moral anaemia and a detached ironic attitude to contemporary society results in a lack of commitment to life itself. Ultimately, the characters who possess this sort of vision, which is lack of vision, must turn the wry jaundiced eye upon themselves. Another book of stories,* The Trouble with Heroes *(1983), and the novel* Homesick *(1989) have confirmed Vanderhaeghe's status as one of Canada's finest younger writers of fiction.*

Man Descending

I t is six-thirty; my wife returns home from work. I am shaving when I hear her key scratching at the lock. I keep the door of our apartment locked at all times. The building has been burgled twice since we moved in and I don't like surprises. My caution annoys my wife; she sees it as proof of a reluctance to approach life with the open-armed camaraderie she expected in a spouse. I can tell that this bit of faithlessness on my part has made her unhappy. Her heels click down our uncarpeted hallway with a lively resonance. So I lock the door of the bathroom to forestall her.

I do this because the state of the bathroom (and my state) will only make her unhappier. I note that my dead cigarette butt has left a liverish stain of nicotine on the edge of the sink and that it has deposited droppings of ash in the basin. The glass of Scotch standing on the toilet tank is not empty. I have been oiling myself all afternoon in expectation of the New Year's party that I would rather not attend. Since Scotch is regarded as a fine social lubricant, I have attempted, to the best of my ability, to get lubricated. Somehow I feel it hasn't worked.

My wife is rattling the door now, "Ed, are you in there?"

"None other," I reply, furiously slicing great swaths in the lather on my cheeks.

"Goddamn it, Ed," Victoria says angrily. "I asked you. I asked you *please* to be done in there before I get home. I have to get ready for the party. I told Helen we'd be there by eight."

"I didn't realize it was so late," I explain lamely. I can imagine the stance she has assumed on the other side of the door. My wife is a social worker and has to deal with people like me every day. Irresponsible people. By now she has crossed her arms across her breasts and inclined her head with its shining helmet of dark hair ever so slightly to one side. Her mouth has puckered like a drawstring purse, and she has planted her legs defiantly and solidly apart, signifying that she will not be moved.

"Ed, how long are you going to be in there?"

I know that tone of voice. Words can never mask its meaning. It is always interrogative, and it always implies that my grievous faults of character could be remedied. *So why don't I make the effort?*

"Five minutes," I call cheerfully.

Victoria goes away. Her heels are brisk on the hardwood.

My thoughts turn to the party and then naturally to civil servants, since almost all of Victoria's friends are people with whom she works. Civil servants inevitably lead me to think of mandarins, and then Asiatics in general. I settle on Mongols and being to carefully carve the lather off my face, intent on leaving myself with a shaving-cream Fu Manchu. I do quite a handsome job. I slit my eyes.

"Mirror, mirror on the wall," I whisper. "Who's the fiercest of them all?"

From the back of my throat I produce a sepulchral tone of reply. "You Genghis Ed, Terror of the World! You who raise cenotaphs of skulls! You who banquet off the backs of your enemies!" I imagine myself sweeping out of Central Asia on a shaggy pony, hard-bitten from years in the saddle, turning almond eyes to fabulous cities that lie pliant under my pitiless gaze.

Victoria is back at the bathroom door. "Ed!"

"Yes, dear?" I answer meekly.

"Ed, explain something to me," she demands.

"Anything, lollipop," I reply. This assures her that I have been alerted to danger. It is now a fair fight and she does not have to labour under the feeling that she has sprung upon her quarry from ambush.

"Don't get sarcastic. It's not called for."

I drain my glass of Scotch, rinse it under the tap, and stick a toothbrush in it, rendering it innocuous. The butt is flicked into the toilet, and the nicotine stain scrubbed out with my thumb. "I apologize," I say, hunting madly in the medicine cabinet for mouthwash to disguise my alcoholic breath.

"Ed, you have nothing to do all day. Absolutely nothing. Why couldn't you be done in there before I got home?"

I rinse my mouth. Then I spot my full, white Fu Manchu and begin scraping. "Well, dear, it's like this," I say. "You know how I sweat. And I do get nervous about these little affairs. So I cut the time a little fine. I admit that. But one doesn't want to appear at these affairs too damp. I like to think that my deodorant's power is peaking at my entrance. I'm sure you see—"

"Shut up and get out of there," Victoria says tiredly.

A last cursory inspection of the bathroom and I spring open the door and present my wife with my best I'm-a-harmless-idiot-don't-hit-me smile. Since I've been unemployed I practise my smiles in the mirror whenever time hangs heavy on my hands. I have one for every occasion. This particular one is a faithful reproduction. Art imitating Life. The other day, while out talking a walk, I saw a large black Labrador taking a crap on somebody's doorstep. We established instant rapport. He grinned hugely at me while his body trembled with exertion. His smile was a perfect blend of physical relief, mischievousness, and apology for his indiscretion. A perfectly suitable smile for my present situation.

"Squeaky, pretty-pink clean," I announce to my wife.

"Being married to an adolescent is a bore," Victoria says, pushing past me into the bathroom. "Make me a drink. I need it."

I hurry to comply and return in time to see my wife lowering her delightful bottom into a tub of scalding hot, soapy water and ascending wreaths of steam. She lies back and her breasts flatten; she toys with the tap with delicate ivory toes.

"Christ," she murmurs, stunned by the heat.

I sit down on the toilet seat and fondle my drink, rotating the transparent cylinder and its amber contents in my hand. Then I abruptly hand Victoria her glass and as an opening gambit ask, "How's Howard?"

My wife does not flinch, but only sighs luxuriantly, steeping herself in the rich heat. I interpret this as hardness of heart. I read in her face the lineaments of a practised and practising adulteress. For some time now I've suspected that Howard, a grave and unctuously dignified psychologist who works for the provincial Department of Social Services, is her lover. My wife has taken to working late and several times when I have phoned her office, disguising my voice and playing the irate beneficiary of the government's largesse, Howard has answered. When we meet socially, Howard treats me with the barely concealed contempt that is due an unsuspecting cuckold.

"Howard? Oh, he's fine," Victoria answers blandly, sipping at her drink. Her body seems to elongate under the water, and for a moment I feel justified in describing her as statuesque.

"I like Howard," I say. "We should have him over for dinner some evening."

My wife laughs. "Howard doesn't like you," she says.

"Oh?" I feign surprise. "Why?"

"You know why. Because you're always pestering him to diagnose you. He's not stupid, you know. He knows you're laughing up your sleeve at him. You're transparent, Ed. When you don't like someone you belittle their work. I've seen you do it a thousand times."

"I refuse," I say, "to respond to innuendo."

This conversation troubles my wife. She begins to splash around in the tub. She cannot go too far in her defence of Howard.

"He's not a bad sort," she says. "A little stuffy, I grant you, but sometimes stuffiness is preferable to complete irresponsibility. You, on the other hand, seem to have the greatest contempt for anyone whose behaviour even remotely approaches sanity."

I know my wife is now angling the conversation toward the question of employment. There are two avenues open for examination. She may concentrate on the past, studded as it is with a series of unmitigated disasters, or on the future. On the whole I feel the past is safer ground, at least from my point of view. She knows that I lied about why I was fired from my last job, and six months later still hasn't got the truth out of me.

Actually, I was shown the door because of "habitual uncooperativeness." I was employed in an adult extension program. For the life of me I couldn't master the terminology, and this created a rather unfavourable impression. All that talk about "terminal learners," "life skills," etc., completely unnerved me. Whenever I was sure I understood what a word meant, someone decided it had become charged with nasty connotations and invented a new "value-free term." The place was a goddamn madhouse and I acted accordingly.

I have to admit, though, that there was one thing I liked about the job. That was answering the phone whenever the office was deserted, which it frequently was since everyone was always running out into the community "identifying needs." I greeted every caller with a breezy "College of Knowledge. Mr. Know-It-All here!" Rather juvenile, I admit, but very satisfying. And I was rather sorry I got the boot before I got to meet a real, live, flesh-and-blood terminal learner. Evidently there were thousands of them out in the community and they were a bad thing. At one meeting in which we were trying to decide what should be done about them, I suggested, using a bit of Pentagon jargon I had picked up on the late-night news, that if we ever laid hands on any of them or their ilk, we should have them "terminated with extreme prejudice."

"By the way," my wife asks nonchalantly, "were you out looking today?"

"Harry Wells called," I lie. "He thinks he might have something for me in a couple of months."

My wife stirs uneasily in the tub and creates little swells that radiate from her body like a disquieting aura.

"That's funny," she says tartly. "I called Harry today about finding work for you. He didn't foresee anything in the future."

"He must have meant the immediate future."

"He didn't mention talking to you."

"That's funny."

Victoria suddenly stands up. Venus rising from the bath. Captive water sluices between her breasts, slides down her thighs.

"Damn it, Ed! When are you going to begin to tell the truth? I'm sick of all this." She fumbles blindly for a towel as her eyes pin me. "Just remember," she adds, "behave yourself tonight. Lay off my friends."

I am rendered speechless by her fiery beauty, by this many-times-thwarted love that twists and turns in search of a worthy object. Meekly, I promise.

I drive to the party, my headlights rending the veil of thickly falling, shimmering snow. The city crews have not yet removed the Christmas decorations; strings of lights garland the street lamps, and rosy Santa Clauses salute with good cheer our wintry silence. My wife's stubborn profile makes her disappointment in me palpable. She does not understand that I am a man descending. I can't blame her because it took me years to realize that fact myself.

Revelation comes in so many guises. A couple of years ago I was paging through one of those gossipy newspapers that fill the news racks at supermarkets. They are designed to shock and titillate, but occasionally they run a factual space-filler. One of these was certainly designed to assure mothers that precocious children were no blessing, and since most women are the mothers of very ordinary children, it was a bit of comfort among gloomy predictions about San Francisco toppling into the sea or Martians making off with tots from parked baby carriages.

It seems that in eighteenth-century Germany there was an infant prodigy. At nine months he was constructing intelligible sentences; at a year and a half he was reading the Bible; at three he was teaching himself Greek and Latin. At four he was dead, likely crushed to death by expectations that he was destined to bear headier and more manifold fruits in the future.

This little news item terrified me. I admit it. It was not because this child's brief passage was in any way extraordinary. On the contrary, it was because it followed such a familiar pattern, a pattern I hadn't until then realized existed. Well, that's not entirely true. I had sensed the pattern, I knew it was there, but I hadn't really *felt* it.

His life, like very other life, could be graphed: an ascent that rises to a peak, pauses at a particular node, and then descends. Only the gradient changes in any particular case; this child's was steeper than most, his descent swifter. We all ripen. We are all bound by the same ineluctable law, the same mathematical certainty.

I was twenty-five then; I could put this out of my mind. I am thirty now, still young I admit, but I sense my feet are on the down slope. I know now that I have begun the inevitable descent, the leisurely glissade which will finally topple me at the bottom of my own graph. A man descending is propelled by inertia; the only initiative left him is whether or not he decides to enjoy the passing scene.

Now, my wife is a hopeful woman. She looks forward to the future, but the same impulse that makes me lock our apartment door keeps me in fear of it. So we proceed in tandem, her shoulders tugging expectantly forward, my heels digging in, resisting. Victoria thinks I have ability; she expects me, like some arid desert plant that shows no promise, to suddenly blossom before her wondering eyes. She believes I can choose to be what she expects. I am intent only on maintaining my balance.

Helen and Everett's house is a blaze of light, their windows sturdy squares of brightness. I park the car. My wife evidently decides we shall make our entry as a couple, atoms resolutely linked. She takes my arm. Our host and hostess greet us at the door. Helen and Victoria kiss, and Everett, who distrusts me, clasps my hand manfully and forgivingly, in a holiday mood. We are led into the living-room. I'm surprised that it is already full. There are people everywhere, sitting and drinking, even a few reclining on the carpet. I know almost no one. The unfamiliar faces swim unsteadily for a moment, and I begin to realize that I am quite drunk. Most of the people are young, and, like my wife, public servants.

I spot Howard in a corner, propped against the wall. He sports a thick, rich beard. Physically he is totally unlike me, tall and thin. For this reason I cannot imagine Victoria in his arms. My powers of invention are stretched to the breaking-point by the attempt to believe that she might be unfaithful to my body type. I think of myself as bearish and cuddly. Sex with Howard, I surmise, would be athletic and vigorous.

Someone, I don't know who, proffers a glass and I take it. This is a mistake. It is Everett's party punch, a hot cider pungent with cloves. However, I dutifully drink it. Victoria leaves my side and I am free to hunt for some more acceptable libation. I find a bottle of Scotch in the kitchen and pour myself a stiff shot, which I sample. Appreciating its honest taste (it is obviously liquor; I hate intoxicants that disguise their purpose with palatability), I carry it back to the living-room.

A very pretty, matronly young woman sidles up to me. She is one of those kind people who move through parties like wraiths, intent on making late arrivals comfortable. We talk desultorily about the party, agreeing it is wonderful and expressing admiration for our host and hostess. The young woman, who is called Ann, admits to being a lawyer. I admit to being a naval architect. She asks me what I am doing on the prairies if I am a naval architect. This is a difficult question. I know nothing about naval architects and cannot even guess what they might be doing on the prairies.

"Perspectives," I say darkly.

She looks at me curiously and then dips away, heading for an errant husband. Several minutes later I am sure they are talking about me, so I duck back to the kitchen and pour myself another Scotch.

Helen finds me in her kitchen. She is hunting for olives.

"Ed," she asks, "have you seen a jar of olives?" She shows me how big with her hands. Someone has turned on the stereo and I sense a slight vibration in the floor, which means people are dancing in the living-room.

"No," I reply. "I can't see anything. I'm loaded," I confess.

Helen looks at me doubtfully. Helen and Everett don't really approve of drinking—that's why they discourage consumption by serving hot cider at parties. She smiles weakly and gives up olives in favour of employment. "How's the job search?" she asks politely while she rummages in the fridge.

"Nothing yet."

"Everett and I have our ears cocked," she says. "If we hear of anything you'll be the first to know." Then she hurries out of the kitchen carrying a jar of gherkins.

"Hey, you silly bitch," I yell, "those aren't olives, those are *gherkins!*"

I wander unsteadily back to the living-room. Someone has put a waltz on the stereo and my wife and Howard are revolving slowly and serenely in the limited available space. I notice that he has insinuated his leg between my wife's thighs. I take a good belt and appraise them. They make a handsome couple. I salute them with my glass but they do not see, and so my world-weary and cavalier gesture is lost on them.

A man and a woman at my left shoulder are talking about Chile and Chilean refugees. It seems that she is in charge of some and is having problems with them. They're divided by old political enmities; they won't learn English; one of them insists on driving without a valid operator's licence. Their voices, earnest and shrill, blend and separate, separate and blend. I watch my wife, skilfully led, glide and turn, turn and glide. Howard's face floats above her head, an impassive mask of content.

The wall clock above the sofa tells me it is only ten o'clock. One year is separated from the next by two hours. However, they pass quickly because I have the great good fortune to get involved in a political argument. I know nothing about politics, but then neither do any of the people I am arguing with. I've always found that a really lively argument depends on the ignorance of the combatants. The more ignorant the disputants, the more heated the debate. This one warms nicely. In no time several people have denounced me as a neo-fascist. Their lack of objectivity pleases me no end. I stand beaming and swaying on my feet. Occasionally I retreat to the kitchen to fill my glass and they follow, hurling statistics and analogies at my back.

It is only at twelve o'clock that I realize the extent of the animosity I have created by this performance. One woman genuinely hates me. She refuses a friendly New Year's buss. I plead that politics should not stand in the way of fraternity.

"You must have learned all this stupid, egotistical individualism from Ayn Rand," she blurts out.

"Who?"

"The writer. Ayn Rand."

"I thought you were referring to the corporation," I say.

She calls me an ass-hole and marches away. Even in my drunken stupor I perceive that her unfriendly judgement is shared by all people within hearing distance. I find myself talking loudly and violently, attempting to justify myself. Helen is wending her way across the living-room toward me. She takes me by the elbow.

"Ed," she says, "you look a little the worse for wear. I have some coffee in the kitchen."

Obediently I allow myself to be led away. Helen pours me a cup of coffee and sits me down in the breakfast nook. I am genuinely contrite and embarrassed.

"Look, Helen," I say, "I apologize. I had too much to drink. I'd better go. Will you tell Victoria I'm ready to leave?"

"Victoria went out to get some ice," she says uneasily.

"How the hell can she get ice? She doesn't drive."

"She went with Howard."

"Oh . . . okay. I'll wait."

Helen leaves me alone to ponder my sins. But I don't dwell on my sins; I dwell on Victoria's and Howard's. I feel my head, searching for the nascent bumps of cuckoldry. It is an unpleasant joke. Finally I get up, fortify myself with another drink, find my coat and boots, and go outside to wait for the young lovers. Snow is still falling in an unsettling blur. The New Year greets us with a storm.

I do not have long to wait. A car creeps cautiously up the street, its headlights gleaming. It stops at the far curb. I hear car doors slamming and then laughter. Howard and Victoria run lightly across the road. He seems to be chasing her, at least that is the impression I receive from her high-pitched squeals of delight. They start up the walk before they notice me. I stand, or imagine I stand, perfectly immobile and menacing.

"Hi, Howie," I say. "How's tricks?"

"Ed," Howard says, pausing. He sends me a curt nod.

"We went for ice," Victoria explains. She holds up the bag for proof.

"Is that right, Howie?" I ask, turning my attention to the homebreaker. I am uncertain whether I am creating this scene merely to discomfort Howard, whom I don't like, or because I am jealous. Perhaps a bit of both.

"The name is Howard, Ed."

"The name is Edward, Howard."

Howard coughs and shuffles his feet. He is smiling faintly. "Well, Ed," he says, "what's the problem?"

"The problem, Howie, is my wife. The problem is cuckoldry. Likewise the incredible amount of hostility I feel toward you this minute. Now, you're the psychologist, Howie, what's the answer to my hostility?"

Howard shrugs. The smile which appears frozen on his face is wrenched askew with anger.

"No answer? Well, here's my prescription. I'm sure I'd feel much better if I bopped your beanie, Bozo," I say. Then I begin to do something very stupid. In this kind of weather I'm taking off my coat.

"Stop this," Victoria says. "Ed, stop it right now!"

Under this threat of violence Howard puffs himself up. He seems to expand in the night; he becomes protective and paternal. Even his voice deepens; it plumbs the lower registers. "I'll take care of this, Victoria," he says gruffly.

"Quit acting like children," she storms. "Stop it!"

Poor Victoria. Two wilful men, rutting stags in the stilly night.

Somehow my right arm seems to have got tangled in my coat sleeve. Since I'm drunk, my attempt to extricate myself occupies all my attention. Suddenly the left side of my face goes numb and I find myself flat on my back. Howie towers over me.

"You son of a bitch," I mumble, "*that* is not cricket." I try to kick him in the family jewels from where I lie. I am unsuccessful.

Howard is suddenly the perfect gentleman. He graciously allows me to get to my feet. Then he ungraciously knocks me down again. This time the force of his blow spins me around and I make a one-point landing on my nose. Howie is proving more than I bargained for. At this point I find myself wishing I had a pipe wrench in my pocket.

"Had enough?" Howie asks. The rooster crowing on the dunghill.

I hear Victoria. "Of course he's had enough. What's the matter with you? He's drunk. Do you want to kill him?"

"The thought had entered my mind."

"Just you let me get my arm loose, you son of a bitch," I say, "we'll see who kills who." I *have* had enough, but of course I can't admit it.

"Be my guest."

Somehow I tear off my coat. Howard is standing waiting, bouncing up on his toes, weaving his head. I feel slightly dizzy trying to focus on his frenetic motion. "Come on," Howard urges me. "Come on."

I lower my head and charge at his midriff. A punch on the back of the neck pops my tongue out of my mouth like a released spring. I pitch head first into the snow. A knee digs into my back, pinning me, and punches begin to rain down on the back of my head. The best I can hope for in a moment of lucidity is that Howard will break a hand on my skull.

My wife saves me. I hear her screaming and, resourceful girl that she is, she hauls Howard off my back by the hair. He curses her; she shouts; they argue. I lie on the snow and pant.

I hear the front door open, and I see my host silhouetted in the door-frame.

"Jesus Christ," Everett yells, "what's going on out here?"

I roll on my back in time to see Howard beating a retreat to his car. My tigress has put him on the run. He is definitely piqued. The car roars into life and swerves into the street. I get to my feet and yell insults at his tail-lights.

"Victoria, is that you?" Everett asks uncertainly.

She sobs a yes.

"Come on in. You're upset."

She shakes her had no.

"Do you want to talk to Helen?"

"No."

Everett goes back into the house nonplussed. It strikes me what a remarkable couple we are.

"Thank you," I say, trying to shake the snow off my sweater. "In five years of marriage you've never done anything nicer. I appreciate it."

"Shut up."

"Have you seen my coat?" I begin to stumble around searching for my traitorous garment.

"Here." She helps me into it. I check my pockets. "I suspect I've lost the car keys," I say.

"I'm not surprised." Victoria has calmed down and is drying her eyes on her coat sleeves. "A good thing too, you're too drunk to drive. We'll walk to Albert Street. They run buses late on New Year's Eve for drunks like you."

I fall into step with her. I'm shivering with cold but I know better than to complain. I light a cigarette and wince when the smoke sears a cut on the side of my mouth. I gingerly test a loosened tooth with my tongue.

"You were very brave," I say. I am so touched by her act of loyalty I take her hand. She does not refuse it.

"It doesn't mean anything."

"It seems to me you made some kind of decision back there."

"A perfect stranger might have done the same."

I allow that this is true.

"I don't regret anything," Victoria says. "I don't regret what happened between Howard and me; I don't regret helping you."

"Tibetan women often have two husbands," I say.

"What is that supposed to mean?" she asks, stopping under a street-light.

"I won't interfere any more."

"I don't think you understand," she says, resuming walking. We enter a deserted street, silent and white. No cars have passed here in hours, the snow is untracked.

"It's New Year's Eve," I say hopefully, "a night for resolutions."

"You can't change, Ed." Her loss of faith in me shocks me. I recover my balance. "I could," I maintain. "I feel ready now. I think I've learned something. Honestly."

"Ed," she says, shaking her head.

"I resolve," I say solemnly, "to find a job."

"Ed, no."

"I resolve to tell the truth."

Victoria actually reaches up and attempts to stifle my words with her mittened hands. I struggle. I realize that, unaccountably, I am crying. "I resolve to treat you differently," I manage to say. But as I say it, I know that I am not capable of any of this. I am a man descending and I should not make promises that I cannot keep, not to her—of all people.

"Ed," she says firmly, "I think that's enough. There's no point any more."

She is right. We walk on silently. Injuries so old could likely not be healed. Not by me. The snow seems to fall faster and faster.

Tatyana Tolstaya

(b. 1951)

*T atyana Tolstaya the great-grandniece of Leo Tolstoy and grand-
daughter of Alexey Tolstoy, was born in Leningrad. She graduated
from Leningrad University in 1974. She has published short stories in
such Soviet literary journals as Neva, Novy Mir, and Oktyabr. Her
first collection of stories came out in the Soviet Union in 1987, appearing
two years later in English translation as On the Golden Porch. The
blend of fantasy and reality, the stylistic experimentation, the shifting
points of view quickly established her as an important writer in the era
of glasnost. As Henry Gifford has argued, "Her stories must be read
with close attention to their economy, the inner coherences that bring
out their meaning, and to the oblique but searching light they cast on
the daily pressures and restrictions of Soviet life." Tolstaya was writer-
in-residence at the University of Richmond, Virginia, in 1988, and has
subsequently become something of a media personality in the United
States for her comments on contemporary issues affecting Soviet women.*

Peters

E ven as a child, Peters had flat feet and a woman's broad belly. His
late grandmother, who loved him as he was, taught him good
manners—chew every little bit thoroughly, tuck your napkin under your
chin, and be quiet when adults are talking. So his grandmother's friends
all liked him. When she took him visiting with her, he could safely be
allowed to touch an expensive book with illustrations—he wouldn't tear
it—and at the table he never pulled the fringe from the tablecloth or
crumbled his cookies—a wonderful boy. They liked the way he entered,
too, tugging down his jacket in a dignified manner, adjusting his bow tie
or lace jabot, as yellowed as his grandmother's cheeks; and clicking the
heels of his flat feet, he would introduce himself to the old ladies using
the old Russian "s" (a contraction for "sir") at the end of his name.
"Peters!" He noticed that amused and touched them.

"Ah, Petya, child! So you call him *Peter*, do you?"

"Yes . . . well . . . we're studying German now," his grandmother
would say casually. And reflected in dull mirrors, Peters walked in measured tread down the hallway, past old trunks, past old smells, into rooms
where rag dolls sat in corners, where green cheese dreamt under a green
cover on the table and homemade cookies gave off a vanilla aroma. While

the hostess put out the small silver spoons, corroded on one side, Peters wandered around the room, examining the dolls on the chest, the portrait of the severe, offended old man with a mustache like a long spoke, the vignettes on the wallpaper, or approached the window and looked through the thickets of aloe out into the sunny cold air where blue pigeons flew and rosy-cheeked children sledded down tracked hills. He wasn't allowed to go outside.

The stupid nickname Peters stuck the rest of his life.

Peters's mother, Grandmother's daughter, ran off to warmer climes with a scoundrel, his father spent time with loose women and took no interest in his son. Listening to the grownups' conversation, Peters pictured the scoundrel as a Negro under a banana palm and Father's women as light blue and airy, floating around untethered like spring clouds; but, well brought up by his grandmother, he said nothing. Besides a grandmother, he also had a grandfather who used to lie quietly in the corner in an armchair, saying nothing and watching Peters with shining glassy eyes, then they laid him out on the dining room table, kept him there for two days and then took him away. They had rice porridge that day.

Grandmother promised Peters that if he behaved, he would live marvelously when he grew up. Peters said nothing. In the evenings, in bed with his fuzzy bunny, he described his future life to it—how he would go out whenever he felt like it, play with all the kids, how Mama and the scoundrel would come visit and bring him sweet fruits, how father's loose women would float around with him, as if in a dream. The bunny believed him.

His grandmother gave Peters slapdash German lessons. They played the very old game, Black Peter, drawing cards from each other's hand and matching up pairs—goose and gander, rooster and hen, dogs with haughty faces. Only the cat, Black Peter, had no pair, he was always alone—grim and withdrawn—and whoever got stuck with Black Peter at the end of the game lost and just sat there like a fool.

They also had color postcards with captions: Wiesbaden, Karlsruhe; there were transparent inserts without feathers but with a window: if you look into the window, you see someone distant, tiny, on horseback. They also sang "O Tannenbaum, O Tannenbaum!" All that was German lessons.

When Peters turned six, his grandmother took him to a New Year's party. The children had been checked out: not infectious. Peters walked as fast as he could in the snow, his grandmother barely kept up. His throat was snugly wrapped in a white scarf, his eyes shone in the dark like a cat's. He was in a hurry to make friends. The marvelous life was beginning. The big hot apartment smelled of pine, toys and stars sparkled, other people's mothers bustled with pies and soft pretzels, quick, agile children squealed and raced around. Peters stopped in the middle of the room and waited for them to make friends. "Catch us, tubby!" they shouted. Peters ran blindly and then stopped. They smashed into him, he fell and stood up, like a weighted doll. Hard adult hands moved him toward the wall. He stood there until tea was served.

At tea all the children behaved badly except Peters. He ate his portion, wiped his mouth, and awaited events, but there were no events. Only one girl, as black as a beetle, asked him if he had any warts and showed him hers.

Peters immediately fell in love with the girl with the warts and dogged her every step. He asked her to sit on the couch with him and that no one else come near her. But he couldn't wiggle his ears or roll his tongue into a tube, which she requested, and she quickly grew bored and abandoned him. Then he didn't know what to do. Then he wanted to spin in place and shout loudly, and he spun and shouted, and then his grandmother was dragging him home through blue snow banks saying indignantly that she simply didn't recognize him, that he was all sweaty and that they would no longer visit children. And in fact, they were never there again.

Until he was fifteen, Peters held his grandmother's hand when they walked on the street. First she supported him and then vice versa. At home they played dominoes and solitaire. Peters used a jigsaw. He wasn't a good student. Before dying, his grandmother got Peters into a library school and willed him to protect his throat and wash his hands thoroughly.

The day she was buried the ice broke on the Neva River.

In the library where Peters worked, the women were not attractive. And he liked attractive women. But what could he offer such a woman, if he ever met one? A pink belly and tiny eyes? If only he were a brilliant conversationalist, if only he knew German well; but no, all he remembered from his childhood was Karlsruhe. But in his imagination he has an affair with a gorgeous woman. While she does this and that, he reads Schiller out loud to her. In the original. Or Hölderlin. She doesn't understand a word, naturally, nor could she, but that's not important; what's important is how he reads—with inspiration, with a musical ripple in his voice. . . . Holding the book close to his nearsighted eyes . . . No, no, of course he'll get contact lenses. Though they say they pinch. So, here he is reading. "Drop the book," she says. Kisses, tears, and the dawn, the dawn . . . And the contacts pinch. He'll blink and squint and poke his fingers in his eyes. . . . She'll wait a bit and then say, "Just peel those damned bits of glass off, good lord!" And get up and slam the door.

No. This is better. A sweet, quiet blonde. Her head on his shoulder. He is reading Hölderlin out loud. Maybe Schiller. Dark forests, mermaids . . . He's reading and reading, his mouth is dried out. She'll yawn and say, "Good lord, how long am I supposed to listen to this stuff?"

No, that wouldn't do, either.

What if he left out the German? Without the German, it could go something like this: a knockout woman, like a leopard. And he's like a tiger. Have to have ostrich feathers, a lithe silhouette on the couch. . . . (Have it slipcovered.) The silhouette, then. The cushions fall to the floor. And the dawn, the dawn . . . Maybe I'll even marry her. Why not? Peters looked at his reflection in the mirror, the fat nose, the eyes rolling with passion, the soft flat feet. And so what? He looked a bit like a polar bear, women ought to like that and be pleasantly frightened. Peters blew at himself in the mirror to cool off. But neither friendships nor affairs happened.

Peters tried going to dances, stumbling about, panting, and stepping on young ladies' feet: he would approach a group of laughing and chatting people, clasp his hands behind his back, tilt his head to one side, and listen to the conversation. It was getting dark, August was blowing cool air from the stiff bushes, sprinkling the red dust of the last rays over the black foliage and the park's paths; lights went on in the stalls and kiosks selling wine and meat, and Peters went past severely, holding on to his wallet, but unable to resist the wave of hunger that engulfed him, bought a half dozen pastries, went off to the side, and in the gathered darkness hurriedly consumed them from the glinting metal plate. When he came out of the darkness, blinking, licking his lips, with white cream on his chin, and mustered his courage, he approached people and introduced himself—blindly, headlong, seeing nothing out of fear, clicking the heels of his flat feet—and women recoiled and men intended to punch him, but took a closer look and changed their minds.

No one wanted to play with him.

At home Peters beat egg yolks and sugar for his throat, washed and dried the glass, then set his slippers neatly on the bedside rug, got into bed, stretching his arms out on top of the covers, and lay motionless, staring into the twilit, pulsating ceiling until sleep came for him.

Sleep came, invited him into its loopholes and corridors, made dates on secret stairways, locked the doors and rebuilt familiar houses, frightening him with trunks and women and bubonic plagues and black diamonds, quickly led him along dark passages, and pushed him into a stuffy room where a man sat at a table twiddling his thumbs, shaggy and laughing mockingly, knowledgeable in many nasty things.

Peters thrashed in his sheets, begged forgiveness, and forgiven this time, once again plunged to the bottom until morning, confused in the reflections of the crooked mirrors of the magic theater.

When a new person appeared in the library, dark and perfumed, in a berry-colored dress, Peters grew agitated. He went to the barber and had his colorless hair cut, then swept his apartment an extra time, and switched the chest of drawers and armchair around. Not that he expected Faina to come over right away; but just in case, Peters had to be ready.

At work there was a New Year's party, and Peters bustled about, cutting out snowflakes the size of saucers and pasting them on the library windows, hanging pink crepe paper, getting tangled in foil icicles, the small Christmas tree lights were reflected in his rolling eyes, it smelled of pine and garlic, and dry snow came through the open window. He thought: if she has, say, a fiancé, I could come over to him, quietly take him by the hand and ask in a regular, man-to-man way: leave Faina, leave her for me, what's it to you, you can find someone else for yourself, you know how to do it. But I don't, my mother ran off with a scoundrel, my father's floating in the sky with blue women, Grandmother ate Grandfather with the rice porridge, ate my childhood, my only childhood, and girls with warts don't want to sit on the couch with me. Come on, give me something, huh?

The burning candles stood, chest-high in translucent apple light, a promise of goodness and peace, the pink-yellow flame nodded its head, champagne fizzed, Faina sang to guitar accompaniment, Dostoevsky's picture on the wall averted its eyes; then they told fortunes, opening Pushkin at random. Peters got: "Adele, love my reed." They laughed at him and asked him to introduce them to Adele; they forgot about it, talking on their own, and he sat quietly in the corner, crunching on cake, figuring out how he would see Faina home. As the party broke up, he ran after her to the coat room, held her fur coat in outstretched arms, watched her change shoes, putting her foot in colored stocking into the cozy fur-lined boot, wrapping a white scarf around her head, and hoisting her bag on her shoulder—everything excited him. She slammed the door, and he saw only her—she waved a mitten, jumped into the trolley, and vanished in the white blizzard. But even that was like a promise.

Triumphant bells rang in his ears, and his eye saw what had previously been invisible. All roads led to Faina, all winds trumpeted her glory, shouted out her dark name, whirled over the steep slate roofs, over towers and spires, snaked in snowy strands and threw themselves at her feet, and the whole city, all the islands and the water and embankments, statues and gardens, bridges and fences, wrought-iron roses and horses, everything blended into a circle, weaving a rattling winter wreath for his beloved.

He could never manage to be alone with her and he sought her out on the street, but she always whizzed past him like the wind, a ball, a snowball thrown by a strong arm. And her friend who looked in at the library in the evenings was horrible, impossible, like a toothache—an outgoing journalist, all creaking leather, long-legged, long-haired, full of international jokes about a Russian, a German, and a Pole measuring the fatness of their women and the Russian winning. The journalist wrote an article in the paper, where he lied and said that "it is always very crowded at the stands with books on beet raising" and that "visitors call librarian Faina A. the pilot of the sea of books." Faina laughed, happy to be in the newspaper, Peters suffered in silence. He kept mustering his strength to at last take her by the hand, lead her to his house, and after a session of passion discuss their future life together.

Toward the end of winter on a damp, tubercular evening Peters was drying his hands in the men's room under the hot blast of air and eavesdropping on Faina talking on the telephone in the corridor. The dryer shuddered and shut up, and in the ensuing silence the beloved voice laughed: "No, we have nothing but women on our staff. Who? . . . Him? . . . That's not a man; he's a wimp. An endocrinological sissy."

Adele, love my reed. Inside, Peters felt as if he had been run over by a trolley. He looked around at the pathetic yellowed tile, the old mirror, swollen from inside with silver sores, the faucet leaking rust—life had selected the right place for the final humiliation. He wound the scarf around his throat carefully, so as not to catch cold in his glands, wended his way home, felt for his slippers, went to the window, out of which he planned to fall, and pulled the blind. The window was thoroughly taped for the winter and he didn't want to waste his work. Then he turned on the oven, placed his head on the rack with cold bread crumbs, and waited. Who would eat rice porridge in his memory? Then Peters remembered that there hadn't been any gas all day, they were doing repairs, grew furious, with trembling finger dialed the dispatcher and screamed horribly and incoherently about the outrageous service, got into his grandfather's chair and sat there till morning.

In the morning, large snowflakes fell slowly. Peters looked at the snow, at the chastened sky, at the new snow banks, and quietly rejoiced that he would have no more youth.

But a new spring came, through the connecting courtyards, the snows died, a cloying smell of decay came from the soil, blue ripples ran over puddles, and Leningrad's cherry trees once again showered white on the matchbox sailboats and newspaper ships—and did it matter at all where you start a new voyage, in a ditch or an ocean, when spring calls and the wind is the same everywhere? And marvelous were the new galoshes Peters bought—their insides laid with the flesh of flowering fuchsia, the taut rubber shining like patent leather, promising to mark his earthly paths with a chain of waffle ovals no matter where he went in search of happiness. And without hurrying, hands behind his back, he strolled along the stone streets, peering deeply into yellow archways, sniffling the air of canals and rivers; and the evening and Saturday women gave him long looks that boded no good, thinking: here's a sickie, we don't need him.

But he didn't need them, either; but Valentina caught his eyes, small and sinfully young—she was buying spring postcards on the sunny embankment, and the fortunate wind, gusting, built, changed, and rebuilt hairdos on her black, short-cropped head. Peters dogged Valentina's steps, afraid to come too close, afraid of failure. Athletic young men ran up to the beauty, grabbed her, laughing, and she went off with them, bouncing, and Peters saw violets—dark, purple—bought and presented, heard them call her by name—it tore away and flew with the wind, the laughing people turned the corner, and Peters was left with nothing— dumpy, white, unloved. And what could he have said to her—to her, so young, so bevioleted? Come up on his flabby legs and offer his flabby hand: "Peter-s . . ." (What a strange name . . ." "My grandmother . . ." "Why did your grandmother . . ." "A little German . . ." "You know German?" "No, but Grandmother . . .")

Ah, if only he had learned German then! Oh then, probably . . . Then, of course . . . Such a difficult language, it hisses, clicks, and moves around in the mouth, O Tannenbaum, probably no one even knows it. . . . But Peters will go and learn it and astonish the beauty. . . .

Looking over his shoulder for the police, he posted notices on street lamps: "German Lessons Wanted." They hung all through the summer, fading, moving their pseudopods. Peters visited his native lampposts, touching up the letters washed away by rain, gluing the torn corners, and in late fall he was called, and it was like a miracle—from the sea of humanity two floated up, responding to his quiet, faint call, slanted purple on white. Hey, did you call? I did, I did! He rejected the persistent and deep-voiced one, who dissolved once more into oblivion, while he thoroughly questioned the tinny lady, Elizaveta Frantsevna from Vasiliyevsky Island: how to get there, where exactly, and how much, and was there a dog, for he was afraid of dogs.

Everything was settled, Elizaveta Frantsevna expected him in the evening, and Peters went to his favorite corner to wait for Valentina—he had been watching and he knew she would come by as usual, waving her gym bag, at twenty to four, and would hop into the big red building, and would work out on the beam amid others like her, swift and young. She would pass, not suspecting that Peters existed, that he had a great plan, that life was marvelous. He decided that the best way would be to buy a bouquet, a big yellow bouquet, and silently, that was important, silently but with a bow hand it to Valentina on the familiar corner. "What's this? Ah!"—and so on.

The wind was blowing, swirling, and it was pouring when he came out on the embankment. Through the veil of rain the red barrier of the damp fortress showed murkily, its lead spire murkily raised its index finger. It had been pouring since last night, and they had laid in a generous supply of water up there. The Swedes, when they left these rotten shores, forgot to take away the sky, and now they probably gloated on their neat little peninsula—they had clear, blue frost, black firs and white rabbits, while Peters was coughing here amid the granite and mildew.

In the fall, Peters took great pleasure in hating his home town, and the city repaid him in kind: it spat icy streams from pounding roof tops, filling his eyes with opaque, dark flows, shoved especially damp and deep puddles under his feet, slapped the cheeks of his nearsighted face, his felt hat, and his tummy with lashes of rain. The slimy buildings that bumped into Peters were purposely covered with tiny white mushrooms and a mossy toxic velvet, and the wind, which had come from big high-wayman roads, tumbled around his soggy feet in deathly tubercular figure eights.

He took his post with the bouquet, and October poured from the skies, and his galoshes were like bathtubs, and the newspaper wrapped three times around the expensive yellow flowers fell apart into shreds, the time came and went and Valentina did not come and would not come but he stood there chilled through to his underwear, to his white hairless body sprinkled with tender red birthmarks.

The clock struck four. Peters shoved his bouquet in a garbage can. Why wait? He understood it was stupid and too late to learn German, that the lovely Valentina, brought up among athletic and vernal youths, would merely laugh and step over him, lumpy and broadwaisted; not for him were fiery passions and light steps, fast dances and leaps on the beam, or casually bought damp April violets, or the sunny wind from the gray waters of the Neva, or laughter and youth; that all attempts were futile, that he should have married his own grandmother and quietly melted away in the warm room to the ticking of the clock, eating sugar buns and planting his old stuffed rabbit in front of his plate for coziness and amusement.

He was hungry, and he went to the first friendly light he saw, bought some soup, and sat down next to two beauties eating patties with onions and blowing away the foggy skin on their cooling pinkish cocoa.

The girls were chattering about love, of course, and Peters heard the story of a certain Irochka, who had been working a long time on a comrade from fraternal Yemen, or maybe Kuwait, in hopes that he would marry her. Irochka had heard that there in the sandy steppes of the Arabian land, oil was as plentiful as berries, every decent man was a millionaire and flew in his own jet with a gold toilet seat. It was that seat that drove Irochka crazy, for she grew up in the Yaroslavl region, where the conveniences were three walls without the fourth with a view of the pea field; all in all, it was like Ilya Repin's painting *Space*. But the Arab was in no hurry to wed, and when Irochka put it to him straight, he replied in the vein of, "Oh, yeah, your mother wears army boots. So long, sucker!" and so on, and tossed Irochka out with her pathetic belongings. The girls paid no attention to Peters, and he listened and felt sorry for the unknown Irochka and pictured the pea-covered expanses of Yaroslavl, trimmed around the horizon with dark, wolf-filled forests, melting in the blissful silence under the blue shimmer of the northern sun, or the dry, grim squeak of millions of sand grains, the taut push of a desert hurricane, the brown light through the deep murk, forgotten white palaces filmed with mortal dust or enchanted by long-dead sorcerers.

The girls moved to the story of the complicated relationship of Olya and Valery, of Anyuta's heartlessness, and Peters, drinking his broth, listened openly, entering someone else's story invisibly, he came in close contact with someone's secrets, he was standing at the door with bated breath, he felt, smelled, and saw, as if in a magical movie, and it was all unbearably accessible—just reach out—flickering faces, tears in injured eyes, explosions of smiles, sunlight in hair, cascading pink and green sparks, dust motes in the ray and the heat of warmed parquet floors, creaking nearby, in that strange, happy, and lively life.

"We're done, let's go!" one beauty commanded the other, and spreading their transparent umbrellas, like signs of another, higher existence, they floated out into the rain and rose into the skies, into the blue beyond the clouds, hidden from his eyes.

Peters selected a rough piece of cardboard from the plastic glass serving as napkin holder and wiped his mouth. Life roared by, bypassing him, and hurried on, like a swift-flowing river goes around a heavy mound of rocks.

The cleaning woman whirled like a sand storm among the tables, flipped her rag in Peters's face, and deftly picked up twenty dirty dishes and disappeared in the yeasty air.

"It's not my fault," Peters said to someone. "It's not my fault at all. I want to participate. But they won't take me. No one wants to play with me. Why? But I'll try harder, I'll win!"

He went out—under icy splashes, under the cold, lashing water. I'll win. Win. I'll clench my teeth and push on through. And I will learn that damned language. There, on Vasiliyevsky Island, in the dampest of Leningrad's damp, Elizaveta Frantsevna is waiting, swimming like a seal or mermaid, mumbling easily in the dark German tongue. He would come and they would chatter together. O Tannenbaum! O, I repeat, Tannenbaum! How does it go after that? I'll find out when I get there.

Oh, well, farewell Valentina and her quick sister, ahead lies only an old German woman—he braced himself. . . . Peters imagined his path, his looplike track in the wet city, and failure, running on his tail, sniffing the waffle prints of his shoes, and the old woman at the end of his path, and in order to confuse fate he hailed a taxi and sailed through the rain— steam rose from his feet, the driver was grim, and he wanted to get out right away. *Tacka-tacka-tacka-tacka*, ticked away his money.

"Stop here."

A doorman guarded the entrance to a gilded place—a door into a subcellar, and beyond it muffled music blared, and lamps shone in the windows like long tubes of acid syrup. Young men—all pretenders for Valentina's hand, farewell Valentina—huddled in front of the door, teeth chattering in the whirlwinds of rain, there was no room in the restaurant, but the doorman, deceived by Peters's solid appearance, let him in, and Peters passed through and two others slipped in by his side. A good place. Peters took off his hat and raincoat in a dignified manner, promised a tip with his eyes, stepped into the noisy room, and trumpeted his arrival in his handkerchief. A fine place. He ordered a pink cocktail, a pagoda pastry, drank, ate, drank some more and relaxed. A very, very fine place. And at his elbow appeared a moth-girl, from out of thin air, from the colored cigarette smoke; her red, green dress—the colored lights blinked—blossomed on her like an orchid, and her eyelashes blinked like wings, and bracelets jangled on her thin arms, and she was completely loyal to Peters to her dying breath. He signaled for more pink alcohol, afraid to speak, to scare off the girl, the marvelous Peri, the flying flower, and they sat in silence, as amazed by each other as would be a goat and an angel upon meeting.

He waved his hand—and they gave even more and some meat.

"Ahem," said Peters, praying to heaven not to recall its messenger right away. "As a child I had a stuffed bunny—a friend in fact and I promised him so much. And now I'm off to my German lesson, ahem."

"I like stuffed bunnies, they're really cute," the Peri noted coldly.

Peters was surprised by the angel's stupidity—a stuffed bunny couldn't be cute, he was either a friend or a nonentity, a sack of sawdust.

"And we also played cards and I always got the cat," Peters recalled.

"Cats are really cute, too," the girl replied through her teeth, like a familiar lesson, looking over the crowd.

"No! Why do you say that?" Peters countered, getting upset. "That's not the point. I'm not talking about that, I'm talking about life, it keeps teasing you, showing and taking away, showing and taking away. You know, it's like a shop window, it shines and it's locked, and you can't take anything. And, I ask, why not?"

"You're really cute, too," the indifferent girl insisted, not listening. "You dropped something."

When he finally got up from the table, the angel had risen to heaven, and with it, Peters's wallet and money. Got it. Well. So be it. Peters sat with his leftovers, as immobile as a suitcase, sobering up, imagining how he would have to explain, ask—the scorn and mockery of the coat check—fish for damp rubles in the swampy pockets of his raincoat, shaking out change that slipped fishlike into the lining. . . . The music machine stomped and beat the drums, announcing someone's coming passion. The cocktail evaporated through his ears. *Cuc-koo!* There.

What are you, life? A silent theater of Chinese shadows, a chain of dreams, a charlatan's store? Or a gift of unrequited love—that's all that is intended for me? What about happiness? What is happiness? Ingrate, you're alive, you weep love strive fall and that's not enough? What? . . . Not enough? Oh, is that so? There isn't anything else.

"I'm waiting! I'm waiting!" shouted Elizaveta Frantsevna, a quick, curly-haired lady, throwing back latches and bolts, letting in the robbed Peters, dark, dangerous, full of misery up to his throat, to his top tight button.

"This way. Let's start right away. Sit down on the couch. First lotto, then tea. All right? Quickly take a card. Who has a goat? I have a goat? Who has a guinea hen?"

I'm going to kill her, decided Peters. Elizaveta Frantsevna, look away, I'm going to kill you. You, and my late grandmother, and the girl with warts, and Valentina, and the fake angel, and all those others—all of them who promised and tricked me, seduced and abandoned me; I'll kill them in the name of all fat and wheezy, tongue-tied and awkward men, in the name of all of those locked in the dark closet, all those not invited to the party, get ready, Elizaveta Frantsevna, I'm going to smother you with that embroidered pillow. And no one will ever know.

"Frantsevna!" someone shouted and pounded on the door. "Give me three rubles, I'll wash the hallway for you."

The urge passed, Peters put aside the pillow. He wanted to sleep. The old woman rustled her money, Peters looked down at the "Domestic Animals" card.

"What are you thinking about? Who has a cat?"

"I have a cat," Peters said. "Who else has one?" And he sidled out, crushing the cardboard cat in his fist. The hell with life. Sleep, sleep, fall asleep and don't wake up.

Spring came and spring went and came again, and spread out blue flowers in the meadows and waved her hand and called through his sleep, "Peters! Peters!" but he slept soundly and heard nothing.

Summer rustled, wandered free in gardens, sitting on benches, swinging bare feet in the dust, calling Peters out on the warm street, the hot sidewalks; whispered, sparkling in the shimmer of linden trees, in the flutter of poplars; called, didn't get an answer, and left, dragging its hem, into the light part of the horizon.

Life got on tiptoe and peered into the window in surprise: why was Peters asleep, why wasn't he coming out to play its cruel games?

But Peters slept and slept and lived in his dream: neatly wiping his mouth, he ate vegetables and drank dairy products; he shaved his dull face—around his shut mouth and under his sleeping eyes—and once, accidentally, in passing, he married a cold, hard woman with big feet, with a dull name. The woman regarded people severely, knowing that people were crooks, that you couldn't trust anyone; her basket held dry bread.

She took Peters with her everywhere, holding his hand tight, the way his grandmother once did, on Sundays they went to the zoological museum, into the resonant, polite halls—to look at still, woolen mice or the white bones of a whale; on weekdays they went out to stores, bought dead yellow macaroni, old people's brown soap, and watched heavy vegetable oil pour through the narrow funnel, as thick as depression, endless and viscous, like the sands of the Arabian desert.

"Tell me," the woman asked severely, "are the chickens chilled? Give me that one." And "that one" is placed in the old shopping bag, and sleeping Peters carried home the cold young chicken, who had known neither love nor freedom, nor green grass nor the merry round eye of a girlfriend. And at home, under the watchful eye of the hard woman, Peters himself had to open up the chest of the chilled creature with knife and axe and tear out the slippery purplish heart, the red roses of the lungs, and the blue breathing stalk, in order to wipe out the memory in the ages of the one who was born and hoped, moved his young wings and dreamed of a green royal tail, of pearl grains, of the golden dawn over the waking world.

The summers and winters slipped by and melted, dissolving and fading, harvests of rainbows hung over distant houses, young greedy blizzards marauded from the northern forests, moving time forward, and the day came when the woman with big feet abandoned Peters, quietly shutting the door and leaving to buy soap and stir pots for another. Then Peters carefully opened his eyes and woke up.

The clock was ticking, fruit compote floated in a glass pitcher, and his slippers had grown cold overnight. Peters felt himself, counted his fingers and hairs. Regret flickered and passed. His body still remembered the quiet of past years, the heavy sleep of the calendar, but in the depths of his spiritual flesh something long forgotten, young and trusting, was stirring, sitting up, shaking itself and smiling.

Old Peters pushed the window frame—the blue glass rang, a thousand yellow birds flew up, and the naked golden spring cried, laughing: catch me, catch me! New children played in the puddles with their buckets. And wanting nothing, regretting nothing, Peters smiled gratefully at life—running past, indifferent, ungrateful, treacherous, mocking, meaningless, alien—marvelous, marvelous, marvelous.

Glossary of Critical Terms

ALLEGORY A story in which the characters and their actions are equated with general truths about human conduct. The characters in an allegory often represent abstract concepts, such as faith, innocence, or evil. See SYMBOL.

ALLUSION A reference to a famous historical, fictional, or mythological person, place, or event outside the story. Allusions enrich a story by suggesting similarities to comparable circumstances in another time or place.

ANTAGONIST The character (or force) that is in direct conflict with the protagonist. An antagonist may be another person, the physical or social environment, or some aspect of the protagonist's own personality. See PROTAGONIST.

ANTICLIMAX A ludicrous or trivial incident that occurs instead of an event of significance. Sometimes the anticlimax appears in the middle of the story as an intentional digression. More often it takes place after the story has reached its climax. See CLIMAX.

ARCHETYPE An image, plot pattern, or character type that recurs frequently in myth, religion, folklore, or literature. According to the psychologist Carl Jung, archetypal experiences such as birth and death form part of the "collective unconscious" that the mind inherits from its racial or cultural past.

AUTHORIAL STATEMENT An interpretation of the events in a story stated directly by the author or indirectly by one of the characters. See THEME.

CHARACTER A person in the story. Most stories contain one or more major characters and several minor characters.

> **DYNAMIC CHARACTER** A person who undergoes significant development or change during the story.

> **FLAT CHARACTER** A person with little depth or complexity, who may be described in one or two phrases.

> **ROUND CHARACTER** A person with a fully developed, complex (even contradictory) personality, who defies simple analysis or description.

> **STATIC CHARACTER** A person who remains essentially unchanged throughout the story.

CHARACTERIZATION The methods by which writers create, reveal, or develop their characters. Writers can focus on the *external reality* of their characters by describing their appearance, actions, or manner of speech. They can also portray the *inner reality* of their characters by revealing their thoughts and feelings.

CLIMAX The moment in the story when the major action reaches its turning point. The climax (also called the *crisis*) marks the end of the story's development and propels it toward its conclusion. See ANTICLIMAX.

COMPLICATION That part of the plot where the various conflicts that have been introduced in the exposition are developed in greater detail before they reach the climax.

CONFLICT The struggle that grows out of the collision of various forces within a story. Although such conflicts may be many, often clashing with one another on several levels, they usually occur in three patterns: (1) the conflict between one person and another, (2) the conflict between a person and that person's physical or social environment, (3) the conflict between a person and some aspect of his or her personality. See ANTAGONIST; PROTAGONIST.

CONNOTATION The suggested or implied meaning of a word, as contrasted with its literal meaning or *denotation*. These additional associations may be personal (the result of individual experience) or universal (the product of the collective human experience). See DENOTATION.

CRISIS See CLIMAX.

CRITICAL ANALYSIS The systematic division of a work of literature (in this case a short story) into its various parts (or elements) in order to achieve a better understanding of the whole.

DENOTATION The literal dictionary definition of a word, apart from any emotional or intellectual association or *connotation* it may evoke. See CONNOTATION.

DÉNOUEMENT A French word meaning the untangling of a knot. As applied to fiction, the term refers to the conclusion of a story where the various conflicts (knots) are resolved (untangled). The dénouement may add a surprising twist to the story, but it does not usually add new information. See RESOLUTION.

DIALOGUE The direct speech of characters in a story, punctuated by quotation marks. Dialogue can be used to introduce or explain the conflict in a plot, to represent the qualities of various characters, or to reveal the point of view of the central character or narrator.

DRAMATIC IRONY See IRONY.

DYNAMIC CHARACTER See CHARACTER.

EPISODE A brief period of action, often complete in itself, that forms part of a larger narrative. A story may contain several related episodes that advance the plot toward the single scene or episode that marks the climax.

EXPOSITION The part of the story, near the beginning, that introduces ("exposes") the elements of setting, character, and conflict that exist prior to the major action of the story.

FABLE A brief narrative devised to illustrate a moral lesson. The chief characters in a fable are often animals who talk and act like human beings. The plots of many fables come from folklore or superstition and focus on unusual or supernatural events.

FLASHBACK An interruption in the flow of a story to introduce an earlier scene or episode. Various devices ranging from simple recollection to dream sequences can be used to present information from the past that helps explain or comments on the present situation in the narrative.

FLAT CHARACTER See CHARACTER.

FOIL A character who enhances and clarifies the features of the protagonist by providing a direct and distinctive contrast to the major character.

FORESHADOWING The introduction of clues early in the story to suggest or anticipate significant events that will develop later.

IMAGERY The use of words or figures of speech to create a mental picture. Imagery exploits all five senses to produce a single powerful impression or to create a cluster of impressions that convey a dominant mood.

IRONY A term that suggests some sort of discrepancy between appearance and reality. Although irony is a broad term that can be applied to events both trivial and tragic, it depends on the ability of the reader to recognize contradictions and incongruities. Irony usually takes three forms:

1. **VERBAL IRONY** is speech in which what is said is directly opposite to what is meant. Verbal irony differs from sarcasm in that the tone of the speaker is lighter, even though the effect produced may be just as devastating.

2. **DRAMATIC IRONY** is a circumstance in which characters reveal their inability to understand their own situation. Dramatic irony is most effective when characters make fateful choices based on information the reader realizes is incorrect.

3. **SITUATIONAL IRONY** is a situation that demonstrates an incongruity between what the reader expects or presumes to be appropriate and what actually occurs.

METAFICTION A fiction about the making of fiction itself, wherein the author's subject is the process of writing and its various aspects.

METAPHOR A figure of speech in which an imaginative comparison is made between two dissimilar things without the use of the words *like* or *as*.

MOTIVATION The character traits, environmental forces, desires, and goals that alone or in combination explain a character's pattern of behaviour.

NARRATOR The person who tells the story. The narrator may be a character who is directly or indirectly involved in the action, or a detached observer who wants to explain what happened. See also POINT OF VIEW.

OBJECTIVE POINT OF VIEW See POINT OF VIEW.

OMNISCIENT POINT OF VIEW See POINT OF VIEW.

PACE The speed with which events are narrated. Some stories can be told quickly, with details omitted, time compressed, and events summarized. Others must be told slowly, with all details included, time extended, and events dramatized as scenes. The pace of a story will vary according to the nature of the events being recounted and their importance to the plot.

PARABLE A short narrative offered as an answer to a difficult moral question or to illustrate a moral truth. See FABLE.

PARADOX A rhetorical device making an assertion which on one level appears to be a contradiction but which on another level may be actually true.

PARODY A composition that imitates the distinctive features of a serious piece of writing for comic or satiric purposes. See SATIRE.

PLOT The essential structure of a story arranged according to a coherent sequence of events. The plot is usually divided into three major parts: (1) the EXPOSITION, where the existing conflicts are established; (2) the COMPLICATION, where new conflicts are introduced or old conflicts are increased in intensity until they reach a CLIMAX or CRISIS; and (3) the DÉNOUEMENT, where the conflicts are resolved.

POINT OF VIEW The vantage point or perspective from which the story is told. Point of view refers to both position (the narrator's proximity to the action in time and space) and person (the narrator's character and attitude). See also NARRATOR. There are four basic points of view:

1. **THIRD-PERSON OMNISCIENT** The narrator, usually assumed to be the author, tells the story. He or she can move at will through time, across space, and into the mind of each character to tell us anything we need to know to understand the story.

2. **THIRD-PERSON LIMITED OMNISCIENT** Although the author is still the narrator, he or she gives up total omniscience and limits the point of view to the experience and perception of one character in the story. Instead of knowing everything, the reader knows only what this one character knows or is able to learn.

3. **FIRST-PERSON** The author selects one of the characters in the narrative to tell the story. This character may be involved in the action or may view it from the position of an observer. This character may tell about events as they are happening or many years after they have taken place.

4. **OBJECTIVE** The author presents the external action of the story as if it were being filmed by a movie camera. The story is presented without any attempt to comment on or interpret the characters' private thoughts or feelings. All that the reader knows about the events must be inferred from the characters' public words and deeds.

PROTAGONIST The character who is engaged in the central conflict of the story, sometimes called the hero or heroine. See ANTAGONIST; CHARACTER; CONFLICT; FOIL.

REFLEXIVE FICTION Fiction in which the reader is reminded directly or indirectly that the story is artifice, the creation of a writer who is consciously shaping all the narrative elements, not reporting facts. The effect is to draw the reader into a consideration of the creative process as well as that which is created; it is an increasingly common approach in modern writing, especially in experimental fiction. See VERISIMILITUDE.

RESOLUTION The events that occur after the climax and bring the conflicts in the story to an appropriate conclusion. See DÉNOUEMENT; PLOT.

REVERSAL A sudden change or turnabout in the fortunes of the protagonist.

ROUND CHARACTER See CHARACTER.

SATIRE A work of literature that ridicules vice or folly in ideas, institutions, or individuals. Although a satiric work treats its subject with varying degrees of amusement and scorn, its ultimate purpose is to bring about improvement by calling attention— either directly or indirectly—to higher standards of human behaviour. See PARODY.

SETTING The time, place, and social reality within which a story takes place. In a limited sense, setting refers to the physical landscape; in a broader sense, setting refers to the cultural landscape—the assumptions, rituals, and shared beliefs that shape the characters and their world.

STATIC CHARACTER See CHARACTER.

STEREOTYPE An oversimplified character who recurs so frequently in literary works that his or her behaviour has become predictable.

STYLE A writer's distinctive manner of expression. Among the many features that characterize a writer's style are diction, sentence structure, and strategies for selecting, analyzing, and interpreting experience. See TONE; VOICE.

SYMBOL A person, act, or thing that has both literal significance and additional abstract meanings. Unlike an allegory, where such things are equated with one or two abstract ideas, a symbol usually refers to several complex ideas that may radiate contradictory or ambiguous meanings. See ALLEGORY.

THEME The central or unifying idea about human experience that grows out of all the other elements in the story. Occasionally the theme may be stated directly by the author or indirectly by one of the characters. More often the theme must be derived from an attempt to understand the complex interaction of forces within the narrative.

TONE The author's attitude toward the situations and characters in the story. By combining a variety of verbal strategies—diction, sentence structure, imagery, symbolism—authors create a tone that establishes the mood, atmosphere, or emotional colouring of a story. See STYLE; VOICE.

VERISIMILITUDE The attempt to make fictional elements seem lifelike and real rather than creations of the writer. Until very recently, most fiction aimed at a sense of verisimilitude. See REFLEXIVE FICTION.

VOICE The personality of the author or narrator that is revealed through a distinctive and habitual mode of expression. See STYLE; TONE.

Index of Authors and Stories

A & P 1117
Across the Bridge 751
Admiring the Scenery 710
ALFORD, EDNA 1298
Ancient Lineage 746
ANDERSON, SHERWOOD 455
Antigone 798
Araby 477
ATWOOD, MARGARET 1271

BABEL, ISAAC 631
Babette's Feast 565
Babylon Revisited 641
BALDWIN, JAMES 948
BARTH, JOHN 1005
BARTHELME, DONALD 1025
Bartleby the Scrivener 122
BEATTIE, ANN 1311
The Bid 1298
BIRDSELL, SANDRA 1287
The Birthmark 42
The Boarding House 481
BORGES, JORGE LUIS 694
BOWEN, ELIZABETH 703
The Bride Doll 1287
The Brother 1082

CALLAGHAN, MORLEY 745
CALVINO, ITALO 918
Captain Blood 1025
CARVER, RAYMOND 1259
CHEEVER, JOHN 822
CHEKHOV, ANTON 322
CHOPIN, KATE 245
The Chrysanthemums 718
CLARKE, AUSTIN C. 1148
The Concert Stages of Europe 1217
CONRAD, JOSEPH 251
The Conversion of the Jews 1135
COOVER, ROBERT 1082
CORTÁZAR, JULIO 841
CRANE, STEPHEN 434
Crystals 919

The Daughters of the Late Colonel 592
DE BALZAC, HONORÉ 15
DE MAUPASSANT, GUY 238
Death Constant Beyond Love 998
Death in the Woods 456
The Death of Iván Ilých 153
The Death of Robert Browning 1342
The Demon Lover 703
DINESEN, ISAK 564
Dry September 660
DUNCAN, SARA JEANNETTE 367
Dying 1243

Eckhardt at a Window 1233
End of the Game 841

The Fall of the House of Usher 72
FAULKNER, WILLIAM 659
FERRON, JACQUES 893
First Confession 737
First Love, Last Rites 1332
FITZGERALD, F. SCOTT 641
Fogbound in Avalon 1088
FORSTER, E.M. 466
Friend of My Youth 1045

GALLANT, MAVIS 892
GARCÍA MÁRQUEZ, GABRIEL 998
The Garden of Forking Paths 695
GOGOL, NIKOLAY 100
Goodbye, My Brother 823
GORDIMER, NADINE 925
GOVIER, KATHERINE 1323
The Grave of the Famous Poet 1272
GREENE, GRAHAM 751
Guests of the Nation 727

HAWTHORNE, NATHANIEL 41
Heart of Darkness 252
HEMINGWAY, ERNEST 670
HODGINS, JACK 1216
Hoodoo Valley 789
The Horse Dealer's Daughter 534

The Hostelry of Mr. Smith 418

The Ice Wagon
  Going Down the Street 899
The Immaculate Conception
  Photography Gallery 1323
In the Hollow 335
Initram 1176
Island 1190

JACKSON, SHIRLEY 874
The Jailer's Son 894
JAMES, HENRY 210
JOYCE, JAMES 476
The Jolly Corner 210

KAFKA, FRANZ 494
Kew Gardens 488

A Lady with a Dog 322
LAURENCE, MARGARET 980
LAWRENCE, D.H. 533
LEACOCK, STEPHEN 417
LESSING, DORIS 882
LEVINE, NORMAN 940
Ligeia 87
The Little Milliner 409
Lost in the Funhouse 1006
The Lottery 874

MCCORMACK, ERIC 1233
MCCULLERS, CARSON 866
MCEWAN, IAN 1332
MCGRATH, ELIZABETH 1088
MACLEOD, ALISTAIR 1190
The Magic Barrel 852
MALAMUD, BERNARD 851
Man Descending 1352
MANSFIELD, KATHERINE 591
The Mask of the Bear 981
MELVILLE, HERMAN 121
Menudo 1259
Mervyn Kaplansky, Wordsmith
  1063
The Metamorphosis 494
A Mother in India 368
MUNRO, ALICE 1030
My Kinsman, Major Molineux 55

My Mother's Mother 1104

NABOKOV, VLADIMIR 677
No Place for You, My Love 806
The Nose 101
The Notorious Jumping
  Frog of Calaveras County 205

OATES, JOYCE CAROL 1243
O'BRIEN, EDNA 1103
O'CONNOR, FLANNERY 961
O'CONNOR, FRANK 727
Odour of Chrysanthemums 547
O'FAOLÁIN, SEÁN 709
O'FLAHERTY, PATRICK 1281
The Old Chief Mshlanga 883
One's a Heifer 775
The Open Boat 435

Peters 1363
POE, EDGAR ALLAN 71
PORTER, KATHERINE ANNE 619
Previous Condition 948

The Return 239
Revelation 962
RICHLER, MORDECAI 1062
The Road from Colonus 467
Roman Fever 397
ROSS, SINCLAIR 775
ROTH, PHILIP 1135
ROY, GABRIELLE 788

Sailors Lost at Sea 1166
Sarrasine 15
SCOTT, DUNCAN CAMPBELL 408
SHIELDS, CAROL 1166
Shifting 1312
SINGER, ISAAC BASHEVIS 760
A Small Place in the Sun 1281
Soldier's Home 671
Some Monday for Sure 926
The Spinoza of Market Street 760
Spring in Fialta 678
STEINBECK, JOHN 717
The Story of My Dovecot 632
The Storm 246

That Tree 619
The Happiest I've Been 1123
THOMAS, AUDREY 1176
The Three Hermits 198
TOLSTAYA, TATYANA 1363
TOLSTOY, LEO 152
A Tree. A Rock. A Cloud 867
TWAIN, MARK 204

UPDIKE, JOHN 1117
URQUHART, JANE 1342

VANDERHAEGHE, GUY 1352
A Visit to the Frontier 609

WATSON, SHEILA 797
We All Begin in a Little Magazine
    940
WELTY, EUDORA 805
WHARTON, EDITH 397
When He Was Free and Young
    and He Used to Wear Silks 1149
Where Is the Voice Coming From?
    1158
Who Do You Think You Are? 1030
WIEBE, RUDY 1157
WILSON, ETHEL 609
WOOLF, VIRGINIA 487